P.L. Simmonds

Dictionary of Trade Products

SALZWASSER
VERLAG

P.L. Simmonds

Dictionary of Trade Products

Reprint of the original, first published in 1859.

1st Edition 2022 | ISBN: 978-3-37512-679-7

Verlag (Publisher): Salzwasser Verlag GmbH, Zeilweg 44, 60439 Frankfurt, Deutschland
Vertretungsberechtigt (Authorized to represent): E. Roepke, Zeilweg 44, 60439 Frankfurt, Deutschland
Druck (Print): Books on Demand GmbH, In de Tarpen 42, 22848 Norderstedt, Deutschland

DICTIONARY

OF

TRADE PRODUCTS,

COMMERCIAL, MANUFACTURING, AND TECHNICAL TERMS:

WITH A DEFINITION OF THE

MONEYS, WEIGHTS, AND MEASURES,

OF ALL COUNTRIES,

REDUCED TO THE BRITISH STANDARD.

BY

P. L. SIMMONDS, F.R.G.S., F.S.S.

AUTHOR OF "THE COMMERCIAL PRODUCTS OF THE VEGETABLE KINGDOM," AND OF "THE DESCRIPTIVE CATALOGUES OF ANIMAL PRODUCTS IN THE SOUTH KENSINGTON MUSEUM," ETC., ETC.

LONDON:
G. ROUTLEDGE & CO., FARRINGDON STREET;
AND 18, BEEKMAN STREET, NEW YORK.
1858.

TO

DR. LYON PLAYFAIR, C.B., F.R.S.,

PRESIDENT OF THE CHEMICAL SOCIETY, ETC., ETC., ETC.,

WHO,

FROM HIS LONG-CONTINUED AND SUCCESSFUL LABOURS IN THE CAUSE

OF

Science, Arts, Manufactures, and Commerce,

WILL READILY APPRECIATE ITS EXTENDED RANGE AND

GENERAL UTILITY,

THIS LITTLE WORK IS DEDICATED,

BY HIS FAITHFUL AND OBLIGED SERVANT,

THE AUTHOR.

PREFACE.

THE present is especially a practical, commercial, and industrial age: newspapers, lecturers, popular authors, all lend their efforts towards the diffusion of sound and useful knowledge among the masses; and the commercial and industrial element has become the leading feature of instruction. The reason of this is obvious, if we but glance at the amazing strides of British Commerce, the wide range of Products and Manufactures in which we are interested, the constant and rapid inter-communication carried on with Foreign countries, and the progress of settlement in our Colonies. The Trade and Commerce of all Nations are now daily brought before us prominently through the press; new Products are continually introduced, new Trades are established, and the Raw Materials of Commerce now imported, are so numerous, and so widely different from what they were a quarter of a century ago, that it is difficult for those who are not specially engaged in a particular trade, to keep pace with the general information necessary to be acquired.

We have scientific dictionaries in abundance, purely technological, or devoted to one or other of the arts and sciences. We have popular and useful commercial and nautical dictionaries, and cyclopædias—works, entering elaborately into the discussion of the laws, history, and regulations of trade, the geography of countries, &c.—but we have hitherto had no popular and concise work of reference on Trades and Trade Products, which might be conveniently consulted for the simple explanation of some strange term, some undefined raw material, or some new manufacture. At the time of the Great Exhibition of 1851, it was found impossible even to make out a list of trades, although the attempt was made.

As the city editor of a daily paper, and contributing largely to many class journals, I especially found the want of a work of easy reference, defining the moneys, weights, and measures of the foreign countries with which we are engaged in trade. On the arrival of any foreign mail, extracts are made from the journals and prices-current thus received, in which such words as arrobas, piculs, maunds, garces, contos, milreis, &c. are mentioned; or products are named and quoted, probably under their local or native designations, of which the majority of readers know nothing, but to which they can now readily turn for a definition. Any one who glances through the various foreign tariffs will be especially struck with the number of articles which are perfectly unintelligible by the names in which they appear, and yet a word or two of explanation would suffice to point them out clearly and intelligibly. The attention which India has lately attracted, and the abstracts from letters and Eastern journals led also to the continual recurrence of names and terms which were not understood by the ordinary reading public, and an explanation of which appeared to be exceedingly necessary.

Commencing with a limited list of definitions for my own use as a journalist, I was gradually led to extend it, and have been induced to include in the work many foreign names for trades and products, which it appeared desirable to define, and to render accessible to those who had not various foreign dictionaries at hand.

The scope and objects of the work are specially stated on the title-page; and I trust it will be found useful to many classes young and old, and supply a want as yet unfilled by the bulky and expensive books previously published; for of the 22,000 words and upwards given, the greater proportion could not be found in any other work of reference. It is especially a dictionary of substances or articles manufactured, imported, bought, sold, or dealt in, at home or abroad, and of the makers or dealers in these.

It professes to define only the ordinary and popular names—English or foreign; and consequently an article must be sought for under its common designation. If an animal or vegetable product, its scientific name is given, and as much general information relating thereto as the limited space at command, in order to secure a cheap and portable volume, would allow. The statistics have been brought down, in all cases, to the latest period; and this feature alone will be found exceedingly valuable, for the ordinary purposes of ready consultation, by saving much time and trouble in referring to bulky Parliamentary papers and numerous trade reports.

I may state, without fear of contradiction, that few persons have possessed such peculiar facilities for the completion of a work of this kind. From my extended connection with periodical literature, and receiving regularly, for a long period, nearly all the brokers' circulars, the principal foreign and colonial journals, and prices-current, I have become familiarized with the products, terms, and customs of different countries.

As one of the editors of the *Farmer's Encyclopedia*, and a regular contributor to the *Mark-lane Express*, the *Farmer's Magazine*, and the Edinburgh *Journal of Agriculture*—as a writer for many years past in the *Shipping and Mercantile Gazette*, the *Engineer*, the *Mining Journal*, the *Civil Engineer's Journal*, the *Building News*, the *Journal of the Society of Arts*, the *Pharmaceutical Journal*, and other class publications, I have necessarily become acquainted with the technicalities, the subjects, and the products brought under discussion; and there is scarcely a trade article named which has not come under my notice, from specimens in my own private collection, or in the South Kensington Museum, at which I am engaged. The information and materials thus derived from so many original sources, have been carefully weighed, compared, and tested.

A work like this, however, can never be complete. With the extending range and wants of Commerce, new articles are brought in, new trades arise, new technical terms are introduced in the arts and manufactures, with which it is scarcely possible to keep pace, unless by an annual edition. Yet the groundwork has been here laid for a more extensive and comprehensive work, should it be considered desirable; and those readers into whose hands this little volume passes, will, at least, have the advantage of much useful information in a small compass, which has only been acquired by very extensive research, and years of assiduous plodding over volumes and journals and trade circulars in all languages.

During the progress of the work, I have experienced the advantage of a careful second revision of the proof sheets by Dr. P. A. Nuttall, an experienced lexicographer; and amongst numerous other friends to whom I am indebted for much valuable information, are Dr. Lyon Playfair, F.R.S.; Mr. Hyde Clarke, the author of a new and comprehensive dictionary of the English language; Mr. P. Le Neve Foster, Secretary of the Society of Arts; Mr. Daniel Hanbury; Messrs. Adam Spielmann and Co., foreign bankers and bullion merchants; and Messrs. Spon, of Bucklersbury. Nor, must I omit to mention my especial indebtedness to Mr. John Christie, the well-informed Reader in the office of Messrs. M'Corquodale and Co., who has, from time to time, suggested many additions, modifications, and corrections, and bestowed the most careful revision on the work, while passing through the press, so as to contribute in every respect to its accuracy and completeness.

Notwithstanding all the attention and care, however, which have been given to the work by myself and friends, I can scarcely expect that a dictionary of so novel a character, and embracing so wide a range of subjects, can be wholly free from error. I shall therefore be glad to be favoured with any suggestions or corrections for adoption in future editions.

P. L. SIMMONDS.

8, Winchester Street, Pimlico,
February, 1858.

A DICTIONARY

OF

TRADES, TRADE PRODUCTS, COMMERCIAL, MANUFACTURING, AND OTHER TECHNICAL TERMS: MONEY, WEIGHTS AND MEASURES, &c.

A.

A 1, an affix to a vessel's name at Lloyd's, the letter denoting the first class character of the hull for build and sea worthiness; the figure 1 that she is well-found in rigging, gear, &c.; the figure 2 would imply that she was insufficiently found.

Aal, an Indian name for the root of the *Morinda citrifolia*, a dyeing substance.

Aam, a Dutch liquid measure, in German written Ahme, sometimes Aime and Aum, corresponding to the English tierce, and ranging from 29 to 39 gallons.

Ab, the Hindustanee name for water.

Aba, a woollen stuff made in Turkey.

Abab, the government proportion or share, of revenue accounts in the East Indies.

Abaca, a name in the Philippines for what is termed Manilla hemp, which is the fibre obtained from *Musa textilis*, a variety of the plantain.

Abacus, a counting machine for performing arithmetical calculations.

Abad, an Eastern term for a cultivated tract of country, or settled village.

Abades, the Spanish name for the cantharides, or blistering flies.

Abaesum, an oxide of iron formerly used in medicine.

Abaiser, a name for ivory black, or animal charcoal.

Abamurus, a buttress or support to a wall.

Abandonment, in navigation, the leaving a ship as dangerous or unseaworthy; a relinquishment of vessel and cargo to establish a claim on the underwriters.

Abas, a Persian silver coin worth about 10d., occasionally called Abbajeer; also an Eastern weight for pearls equal to 2⅛ grains troy.

Abassi, a Persian coin. *See* Abushee.

Abatement, a discount allowed for prompt payment, damage, overcharge, or other reasons.

Abattoir, the French name for a slaughter-house.

Abbajeer. *See* Abas.

Abbas, coarse woollens worn by the majority of the people in Turkey.

Abbs, a term in the wool-trade for the yarn of a weaver's warp.

Abda, land in the East, which is held rent free.

Abee, a woven stuff of wool and cotton made in Aleppo.

Abeer, an Indian incense.

Abelmoschus, the musk seed of the Hindoos, the *Hibiscus Abelmoschus*, used by the Arabs to flavour coffee.

Abermoordeep, the Persian name for sponge.

Abgangs-Rechnung, in German commerce the amount of tare allowed on goods.

Abhir, in India one engaged in pastoral occupations, as herding cattle and tending sheep.

Abhul, an Indian name for the common juniper berries.

Abi, or **Abistani**, in the East, land artificially watered.

Abir-Ubeer, a yellowish red powder, with which the natives in the East stain their flesh and clothes.

Abkar, a maker or retailer of spirituous drinks in India.

Abkari, revenues in the East Indies derived from various duties or licences on spirits, opium, and from gaming-houses, &c.

Ablette, a French name for the bleak fish (*Leuciscus alburnus*); from a solution of the bright silvery scales of this fish and the dace, artificial pearls are made.

Abnoos, an Eastern name for ebony wood.

Abordage, the French term for a collision between ships at sea.

Abra, a Polish silver coin about the value of a shilling; also a Spanish mining term for a fissure in a mountain, or a cavity in the rock or lode.

Abrac, **Abraka**, names for talc, of which in India there are several kinds obtained from Bengal, Behar, Ghatti, &c.

Abraum, a red ochre used to darken new mahogany.

Abronzado, the Spanish name for sulphuret of copper.

ABROTANUM, a name given by Pliny to the southernwood, a species of Artemisia, *Ad. abrotanum*; hence its specific name.

ABSINTH, or wormwood, is the produce of *Artemisia absinthium*, which is much used in medicine for its bitter properties.

ABSTRICHMESSER, a German butcher's knife.

ABSTERGENTS, lotions and other cleansing medicines.

ABUCCO, a Burmese weight which is less than half-a-pound avoirdupois, viz., 2060 grains.

ABUQUELP, another name for the griselo, an Egyptian coin, worth 90 aspers, or about 7s.

ABUSHEE, a money of Persia and Arabia, worth about 1s. 8d.

ABUSIVA, an undefined money of account, employed in minor trading operations in Genoa.

ABYSSINIAN TEA, the dried leaves of the *Catha edulis*, used by the Arabs.

ACACIA, the Mimosa tribe of trees, which furnish to commerce various gums, extracts, and barks for tanning.

ACADEMY, in popular phraseology a school: thus there are educational academies, dancing academies, &c.

ACAJOU, the French name for mahogany.

ACAJOU-NUT, a German name for the cashew-nut.

ACAYOIBA, a Spanish name for mahogany.

ACCEPTANCE, in commercial transactions agreeing to the price or terms proposed; the acknowledgment of a debt, equivalent to a promise to pay; the debtor's name written on a bill of exchange, usually with the word accepted.

ACCOMMODATION-BILL, a fictitious bill of exchange, drawn and accepted to raise money on, and not bona-fide given in payment of a debt.

ACCOMMODATION-LADDER, a set of suspensory steps fixed at the side of a large ship when lying high out of the water, to facilitate ascending from or descending to boats.

ACCON, a small French flat-bottomed boat.

ACCORDION, a small keyed wind instrument played by the hand.

ACCORDION NOTES, printed music for the accordion, which is largely imported from the continent into London.

ACCOUCHEUR, a man midwife.

ACCOUNTANT, a professional or official calculator, skilled in posting and balancing the books of tradesmen or joint-stock associations.

ACCOUNTANT-GENERAL, a comptroller of accounts; superior public officers of the Crown, having charge of the finances of the Navy, &c.

ACCOUNT-BOOK, a ruled book for entering details of receipts and expenditure.

ACCOUNT-BOOK MAKER, a stationer who makes account-books, such as ledgers, journals, day-books, &c.

ACCOUNT-CURRENT, a plain statement of account, or of the particulars rendered to a party, showing his transactions with another.

ACCOUNT DAY, a half monthly settling day on the Stock Exchange, when differences are adjusted between stockbrokers.

ACCOUNT-SALE, a statement of particulars or details rendered by a merchant to his consignor, of the disposition of a parcel of goods.

ACCOUTREMENTS, the military dress, fittings, and equipage of a soldier.

ACCUMULATOR, an India-rubber spring, either simple or compound; which accumulates lifting force and can be applied to many useful purposes in ships, machines, work-shops, &c.

ACEITE, the Spanish name for oil; also for a resin which exudes from the fir-trees.

ACEMITE, grits; a pottage made of parched half-ground wheat in Spain.

ACENE, an ancient Greek measure of length; the Olympic acene being equal to 3½ English yards.

ACERO, the Spanish name for steel.

ACETABULUM, an ancient Roman dry and liquid measure, the former = 0·00191 bushel, the latter to 0·0178 gallon.

ACETATES, crystallisable salts, formed by the combination of any salifiable base with acetic acid; thus there are acetates of copper, of lead, of potash, &c., which bear other names in commerce, as verdigris, sugar of lead, &c.

ACETIC ACID, or pyroligneous acid; a concentrated vinegar obtained by distillation from wood.

ACETIFIER, an apparatus for acidifying fermented liquors.

ACETOMETER, a species of hydrometer, for testing the strength of acids.

ACETONE, a name for pyro-acetic spirit.

ACH, an Indian name for the *Morinda tinctoria*, a dye.

ACHANA, an ancient Greek grain measure, equal to rather more than 1¼ English bushel.

ACHAR, the Malay name for pickles.

ACHARI, skilled artisans, mechanics, smiths, &c., in the East; masters or teachers of the arts.

ACHAT, the French name for a purchase.

ACHCHA, a name in parts of India for a printer, or pressman, and for the mould or press for taking impressions.

ACHETEUR, the French name for a purchaser.

ACHIAR, the young shoots of the bamboo pickled, imported into Holland from the Eastern Archipelago.

ACHIDAIYAN, the Tamil name for a barber.

ACHIRA, a plant with a large esculent root, a species of *Canna* which yields a quantity of starch, superior to the ordinary arrow root, or *Maranta arundinacea*.

ACHITA, in the East a cartload of ten bharas, or about 2 tons.

ACHOTE, an American name for the seeds of the arnotto plant, *Bixa orellana*.

ACHURA, the Bengalee name for rice-straw.

ACHRO, an Indian drug.

ACHROMATIC GLASSES, object lenses which collect light without producing coloured images.

ACHTEL, in Germany, the eighth part of a weight or measure; also a grain measure equal to 1·49 imperial bushel; in Austria and Holland it is occasionally known as achteling.

Achtendeel, an old dry measure of Holland, about 8 gallons; the name was also applied to the old schepel or bushel of the Dutch towns.

Achterli, a dry measure in Switzerland, the eighth part of a maess, and equal to rather more than three English pints.

Achu-kavali, a grant or allowance given in India to one who watches growing crops.

Acicular, needle-shaped, a Cornish mining term for slender, straight crystals.

Acidimeter, an instrument for testing the strength of acids.

Acidimetry, the process for measuring the strength of acids.

Acids, chemical preparations of a sharp and sour taste, of which the number is very large, but those of commercial importance will be found in their alphabetical order. It may be here stated, however, that the termination of the prefix denotes the strength of the acid, *ic* being applied to the stronger acids and *ous* to those of a weaker kind.

Acidulous Waters, mineral waters which contain free acids in solution.

Acier, the French name for steel; in France 1000 kilogrammes of steel go to the ton of freight.

Acino, the twentieth part of the Neapolitan trapeso, which is the thirtieth part of their ounce, and equal to 0·687 English grains.

Acitometry, the chemical process of ascertaining the quantity of acid in a sample by weight.

Acker, a German superficial measure of variable proportions in different states, ranging from half an English acre to rather more than two acres.

Ackie, an African monetary term, the equivalent of 1600 cowry shells, and worth about 4s. 2d. English. *See* Akie.

Acknowledgment, a receipt, an admission.

Ackroot, or **Akroot**, the Indian name for walnuts.

Acori, **Acorus**, an African blue coral.

Acorn, the seed or fruit of the oak, frequently used for food.

Acorn Cups, a large article of import for the use of tanners. *See* Valonia.

Acorn Oil, an oil expressed from the seed of the oak.

Acorus Calamus, the aromatic root of the sweet flag, imported as a drug, and also in repute in the bazaars in India.

Acotars, pieces of wood filled in between the flooring timber under the kelson in French ships.

Acoumeter, an instrument for measuring the extent of hearing power.

Acow, a name in some of the Pacific Islands for wood.

Acquittance, a release, a written discharge or receipt in full for money due.

Acre, an English land measure of 4840 square yards.

Acrospire, a name given by the maltster to the sprout or plumule of barley when germinating.

Acrusite, a crystal of carbonate of lead coated black.

Actinometer, an instrument for measuring the intensity of the rays of the sun.

Action, a suit of law; also the name for shares in French and other Continental companies, hence the owner is styled the actionnaire—equivalent to our term shareholder.

Actor, a player; one who takes a part.

Actuary, a skilled calculator, an officer of an insurance company.

Actus, an ancient Roman superficial measure applied to a slip of ground, 120 Roman feet long by four broad = 38·65 yards.

Acullico, the Spanish name for a ball of coca leaves, &c., prepared for mastication.

Acumbre. *See* Azumbre.

Ada, the Hindoo and Bengalee name for ginger.

Adada, the Indian name for a bark canoe made in Demerara. *See* Wood-skin.

Adahari, the Hindoo name for an unbroken steer.

Adamantine Spar, a brown species of corundum. *See* Corundum.

Adam's Needle, a name for the dagger-plant (*Yucca aloifolia et gloriosa*), useful for its fibre.

Adarme, or **Arienzo**, the sixteenth part of the Spanish ounce, agreeing very nearly with the English drachm, although only half a Spanish drachm.

Adas-manis, the Malay name for aniseed.

Adat, the Bengalee name for a wholesale store or monopoly warehouse.

Adda, a measure in India, equal to 8½ pints; also a station where people assemble for business or pleasure. In some places it is applied to a salt-heap.

Addaca, a name for betel-nut in Travancore.

Addana, an Indian measure equal to half a pint.

Adda-sunka, a duty collected in India from those who sell sheep.

Adde, an Indian name in some localities for rent or wages.

Addendum, something added to.

Addi, a Bengalee money-changer.

Adelantadillo, red wine, made of the first ripe grapes in Spain.

Ademador, the Spanish name for a carpenter, or workman employed in lining the sides of mines with planks.

Adenanthera, the seeds of the pods of a leguminous tree, weighing almost uniformly four grains, which are frequently employed by jewellers in the east as weights; so are those of *Abrus precatorius*.

Adenos, the Spanish name for a kind of cotton.

Adeps, a concrete oily matter contained in the cells of the adipose tissue; the fat about the loins and kidneys of animals.

Adhaca, an ancient Hindoo measure of capacity, equivalent to 7½ English pints.

Adhak, an Indian dry measure, the 16th part of a khari; of variable capacity; for grain ranging from 5lbs. to 7lbs. 11oz. avoirdupois. It is also called a marcal.

Adheli, an Indian term for half, as half a rupee.

Adhelo, a name for the half pice, a petty Indian copper coin less than a farthing.

Adhesive Plaster, a preparation for holding the edges of wounds together.

Adhesive Slate, a yellow or gray mass found in the gypsum beds of Paris.

Adhi, or **Adi**, a Bengalee dry measure equal to two maunds, 156 to 164 lbs.; also the Tamil short foot, equal to about 10¼ inches.

Adholy. *See* **Adowly**.

Adike, a Karnatic name for the betel-nut.

Adikol, an Indian measuring-rod.

Adhilah, an imaginary money of Malwa, the half of a pice, or less than a farthing.

Adinole, a fusible horn-stone, or compact feldspar.

Adipose, fat in general, the fat of the kidneys.

Adit, a horizontal shaft or sough for draining or ventilating a mine.

Adjali, an undefined oil obtained in the East Indies.

Adjournment, the postponement of a meeting; putting off till another time.

Adjudication, a legal decision or sentence.

Adjutage, the tube through which a fountain is played.

Adjutant, **Adjutant-general**, officers who have charge of the discipline of an army.

Adl, an eastern term for a stamp or impression.

Adler-stein, the German name for eagle-stone.

Administrator, a person empowered by the Ecclesiastical Court to manage the estate of a deceased individual.

Admiral, the leading or directing ship in a fleet of merchantmen; also a superior officer of the Royal Navy.

Admiralty Court, a supreme marine tribunal which holds jurisdiction over causes arising on the high seas and coasts.

Admiralty Droits, pieces of wreck and other articles without owner, found at sea, claimed by the Admiralty.

Adobado, the Spanish name for pickled pork.

Adobes, unburnt bricks made of straw, earth, and dung dried in the sun.

Adowly, **Adholy**, an Indian dry measure, which varies both as a weight and measure in different localities; as a weight it ranges from 4 to 5½ lbs. avoirdupois.

Adpao, **Adpowe**, a weight in the Bombay presidency, the half of the pao seer, and equal to 1723 grains; in Bangalore and Mysore it is 1849 grains.

Adrak, the vernacular name in Bengal and many parts of the East for ginger, which is sold either rough or scraped.

Adrian the Spanish name for corn.

Adriatic Oak, the *Quercus cerris*.

Adruck. *See* **Adrak**.

Adseer, *or* **Ashwa**, the half of a seer in Bombay, and equal to nearly one pound avoirdupois.

Adu, *or* **Attu**, an Indian name for goats and sheep.

Aducar, a coarse kind of silk stuff formerly used in Spain.

Adularia, a name for the moon stone; a transparent gem used for ornaments.

Adul Oil, a medicinal oil obtained in Travancore, and shown at the Great Exhibition in 1851; the botanical name of the plant producing it is not yet given.

Adulteration, the injuring or debasing by foreign and spurious admixtures. In commerce there are several kinds of adulteration: conventional, to suit the taste and demands of the public; fraudulent, for deceptive and gainful purposes; and accidental or unintentional adulteration, arising from carelessness in the preparation of the staple or commodity at the place of growth or shipment.

Ad-valorem, according to the value, an assessment by the Customs for duty.

Advance, a sum of money paid on account of goods, or before receiving the work to be done, &c.

Advance-notes, authorized drafts on the owner or agent of a vessel, executed by the master, generally for one month's wages, given to the seamen on their signing the articles of agreement.

Adventure, an enterprise or doubtful speculation of any kind, commercial or financial.

Adventurer, in mining phraseology, a shareholder in working a mine; in commerce a speculator, or one who undertakes a risk.

Advertisement, a business announcement in a public journal or periodical.

Advice, due notice given in respect of any monetary or commercial transaction; notice of a bill drawn.

Ady, the name of the Malabar foot, equal to about 10¼ English inches.

Adze, a sharp edged tool for shaping timber; an axe with an arched edge, and its blade athwart the handle.

Aem, a local mode of spelling the Aum.

Aemgen, a liquid measure of Prussia, equal to 6¼ imperial gallons.

Aerated Waters, soda water, lemonade, and other waters artificially impregnated with carbonic acid.

Aerating Machine, a syphon and apparatus for making soda water and other gaseous drinks.

Aerator, a blower or contrivance for fumigating wheat, and other corn, to bleach it and destroy fungi and insects.

Aerometer, an instrument for ascertaining the mean bulk of gases.

Aeronaut, a traveller in the air, one who ascends in or manages a balloon.

Aerophane, a kind of light gauze, or imitation crape.

Aerugo, a name for carbonate of copper.

Aetite, a name for eagle-stone, formerly used in medicine.

Afeem, a vernacular name in some parts of India for opium.

Affa, a weight on the Guinea coast of Africa, equal to an English ounce.

Affiche, the French name for a posting bill.

Affidavit, a declaration in writing made on oath before a magistrate or some competent officer.

Affinage, a refining of metals.

Affirmation, a declaration made in courts of law by those who object to taking oaths.

Affreteur, in French, one who charters or freights vessels.

Afim, a Hindustanee name for opium.

Aflatoon, the Arabic name for gum bdellium.

African Hemp, one of the names of the fibre obtained from the leaves of the *Sanseviera zeylanica*.

African Oak or **Teak**, a valuable wood for some purposes of ship-building, obtained from the *Oldfieldia Africana*.

Afsunteen, a vernacular name among the Arabs for absinth.

Aft, Abaft, a nautical term, denoting towards or near the stern; hence we have after-part, after-body, after-timbers, &c.

Aftab-gir, a large portable sun-shade or flat parasol used in the East.

Aftermath, the second crop of grass.

Agabanee, cotton embroidered with silk made in Aleppo.

Agaiti, a plant cultivated for its oil in Eastern Africa, believed to be the *Didynamia gymnosperma*.

Agalla, a Spanish name for the nut gall.

Agallochum Wood, a celebrated wood of the ancients, the lign aloes, calambak, or eagle-wood of Eastern commerce; the best is supposed to be obtained from *Aquilaria Malaccensis*, while the *Aloexylum agallochum* of Loureiro and the *Excæcaria agallocha*, also furnish other kinds of aloe wood. It is used medicinally, and also for inlaying cabinet work.

Agaphite, a mineralogical term for turquoise.

Agar, an Eastern name for a salt-pit; also an orchard or plantation of palms.

Agar-Agar, a sea-weed forming a large article of commerce in the Eastern seas, being used for making jellies, and for stiffening purposes.

Agaric, a generic name for many fungi, including the *Polyporus igniarius*, growing on the larch, oak, &c., and used for dyeing, and in medicine as a styptic.

Agarikoon, the name in the Indian bazaars for the agaric fungus.

Agastera, a liquid measure in some of the Ionian Islands, equal to about 2 pints.

Agate, a silicious stone, chiefly composed of quartz variegated with colouring matter, as in the Scotch pebble.

Agave, a genus of plants producing fibre, and furnishing an intoxicating beverage, known in Mexico as pulque.

Agayadi, a small rice nursery for transplantations.

Agenda, a list or memorandum-book of business to be done.

Agent, one who represents a principal, or buys and sells for another; in large cities there are many special agents for particular localities or separate trades, as East Indian, colonial, Australian, and American agents—news-agents, advertising-agents, passenger-agents, custom-house-agents, &c.; the manager of an estate in Ireland.

Agent de Change, the French name for a stockbroker.

Ager, a Roman acre of land, a field.

Aghani, the grain harvest in India, which is reaped during the cold season of November and December.

Agi, Aji, a name for the Guinea or red Indian dwarf bird-pepper, a species of capsicum, grown in Peru; also a sort of sauce made of it in America.

Agilla Wood, the name in Siam for the aloe-wood.

Agio, a term on the Continent for the premium or percentage allowed between two sorts of money, one being of a superior mintage value to the other, or between paper and specie.

Agiotador, the Spanish name for a bill-broker.

Agiotage, stock-jobbing, speculation on the rise or fall of the public funds.

Agioteur, the French name for a stock-jobber.

Agiraque, a weight on the Guinea coast of Africa equal to sixty-two grains.

Agistment, taking in cattle to pasture.

Agito, the fourth part of a vis, a weight used in Pegu, and equal to 5937½ grains; it is sometimes called a giro.

Agnel, an ancient French coin worth less than 1s.

Agnesite, a name for carbonate of bismuth.

Agound, in Bengal the flowering shoot or upper part of the sugar cane.

Agrees, certain special advocates, employed in pleading before the tribunals of commerce in some of the large cities of France.

Agrès, the French name for the rigging and tackle of a ship.

Agriaz, the Spanish name for cinnamon.

Agricultural Agent, one who attends to the business of farmers, receiving and executing orders for purchases and sales.

Agricultural Chemist, one skilled in the chemistry of agricultural products, and who makes it a business to analyze and report upon soils, manures, the component parts of plants, &c.

Agricultural Implements, various mechanical implements and tools for tillage, &c., as ploughs, harrows, horse-hoes, thrashing-machines, &c., made for home use and export.

Agriculturist, a farmer or husbandman.

Agropila, a Spanish name for the German bezoar.

Agtendeel. *See* **Achtendeel**.

Aguajaque, the Spanish name for a kind of gum ammoniac.

Aguamiel, Hydromel, a name given to the sap of the American aloe, as it flows from the leaves, which has the flavour of honey-water.

Aguanafa, orange-flower water made in Spain.

Aguardiente, a name for alcohol, principally applied to brandy in Spain.

Aguarras, the Spanish name for spirits of turpentine.

Aguila, the Spanish term for a gold coin—the American eagle, worth nearly £2, 2s.

Agustite, a scientific term for the emerald.

Ahak, in India slaked lime.

Ahan, an Eastern name for iron.

Ahar, in Bengal a small pit; also a channel for irrigation.

Ahi, a name in the Pacific Islands for sandal-wood.

Ahila Wood, a name for the aloe-wood.

Ahku, an Eastern name for the sugar-cane.

Ahm. *See* **Aum**.

Ahmedi, an old Indian gold coin of five pagodas, value £2 5s.

Aigrette, a pointed tuft of feathers.

AIN, a large French fishing-hook.

AIPI, a Brazilian edible root, from which a beverage is also extracted.

AIR-BED, an Indian-rubber or other air proof case or mattress inflated with air for the use of invalids.

AIR-BLADDER, the floating organ of many fishes. See ISINGLASS and FISHMAW.

AIR-CANE, usually an atmospheric gun fitted in a walking-stick.

AIR-CUSHION, an inflated seat for railway carriages, chairs, &c.

AIR-FUNNEL, a cavity formed in the openings of the timbers of a ship to admit the free passage of air.

AIR-GUN, a pneumatic machine, whose propelling force is condensed air.

AIRISH MOW, a contrivance for the preservation of corn in rainy seasons.

AIR-PIPES, tubes of iron or wood for ventilating a mine.

AIR-PUMP, a pneumatic machine for producing a vacuum; part of a steam-engine which draws off the water from the condenser.

AIR-VALVE, the safety valve fixed at the top of the boiler of a steam-engine.

AJI. See AGI.

AJINA, in India a tiger's or antelope's skin dressed for a seat.

AJIR, AJURA, a slave or hired servant in India.

AJMOD, the Hindoo name for a species of Apium, *Apium involucratum*.

AJONJOLI, an oily purging grain, in Central America; the small seeds closely resemble the teel seed of India, *Sesame orientalis*.

AJOUAN, AJOWAN, one of the vernacular names in India for the *Ptychotis Ajowan* of Roxburgh, a useful umbelliferous plant. The fruits have an aromatic smell and warm pungent taste, and are used medicinally.

AK, one of the Hindoo names of the mudar, *Calotropis gigantea*, a large shrub, the roots and milky juice of which have medicinal properties.

AKARAKARA, the vernacular name in India for the pellitory root (*Anthemis pyrethrum*), which is esteemed as a masticatory, and for its excitant properties; also written Akurkuka.

AKE, an abbreviation of Ackie or Akey, the monetary standard of the Gold coast of Africa. As a weight for gold dust it is considered to be equal to 20 grains. See ACKIE.

AKEEK, an Indian name for carnelian.

AKENA, an ancient Greek superficial measure equal to 0·0023 acre.

AKHA, water-bags or panniers carried by a horse or bullock in the East.

AKKI, husked rice for boiling in India.

AKRA, a twining grass, the vetch (*Vicia sativa*), used in India for fodder.

AKROT, ACKROOT, an Indian name for walnuts.

AKSHATA, coloured grains of rice, presented by way of compliment to guests in India.

AKU, the Eastern name for a leaf, as of the betel, &c.

AKUND, a Sanscrit name for the mudar, *Calotropis* (or *Asclepias*) *gigantea*. See AK.

AL, or AAL. See AWL.

ALABANDINE, a name for sulphuret of manganese.

ALABASTER, a species of granular gypsum, or massive sulphate of lime, semi-transparent and resembling marble, used for statuary and ornamental purposes, of which we import several hundred tons. Also the name of an ancient liquid measure, containing 9 oz. of oil, or 10 of wine.

ALAGA, a species of Spanish yellow wheat.

ALAGAI, a kind of silk with a little cotton interwoven, imported into Turkey from the Black-Sea ports.

ALAM, the Hindoo name for sticks or supports for climbing plants.

ALAMODE—fashionable; the name of a thin glossy black silk, formerly made, used chiefly for women's hoods and men's scarfs.

ALAMODE BEEF, a thick gravy soup or bouilli made from shins of beef.

ALARIJES, a large sort of grapes in the Peninsula.

ALARUM, an alarm-bell or warning applied to watches, timepieces, bells, &c.

ALASANDI, the Karnatic name for a common pulse in the East, the *Dolichos catjang*.

ALATA, one who measures land and grain in Mysore.

ALAVI, a ryot's lease or agreement in India.

ALAWA, the Indian name for a fire-place.

ALB, another name for a Turkish asper.

ALBA, in low Latin, a lighthouse or sea beacon; a white surplice of muslin worn under the vestment, used by Catholic priests.

ALBAAJREE, another name for the abas, a Persian silver coin worth about 10d.

ALBANGKA, the Malay name for a crowbar.

ALBANIL, the Spanish name for a mason or bricklayer.

ALBARICOQUERO, the Spanish name for the apricot (*Armeniaca vulgaris*).

ALBARIJO, a variety of Spanish wheat.

ALBARIUM, a pure white lime or stucco, obtained from burnt marble.

ALBATA, a name for British plate, also called German silver.

ALBATOZA, a small Spanish covered boat.

ALBATRE, the French name for alabaster.

ALBENTOLA, a slight net made of very thin twine, for catching small fish.

ALBERT CHAIN, a short gold chain for attaching to a watch in the waistcoat pocket from the buttonhole.

ALBERT COAL, a beautiful carbonaceous product from New Brunswick, which is referred to both coal and asphaltum.

ALBERTUS, or ALBERT'S DOLLAR, a Dutch silver coin, and money of account in Russia, worth 4s.

ALBICORE, a large sea-fish (*Auxis Sloanei*), much resembling the tunny.

ALBITE, a variety of felspar.

ALBORGA, a kind of sandal made of matweed.

ALBORNOZ, a sort of coarse Spanish woollen cloth; a cloak.

ALBUM, a Danish superficial measure of 0·0563 acre; also a book kept for the writings and inscriptions of friends.

ALBUMEN, a constituent of the animal and vegetable fluids and solids, which enters into commerce in a dried state; chiefly the albumen of the egg and of blood. The principal use of albumen is in photography, and in the print manufactories at Manchester and in other districts.

ALBUM-GRÆCUM, a name given to the white fæces of dogs, collected in kennels, consisting chiefly of bone earth, which is used by tanners for one or two commercial purposes.

ALBUMINOUS, consisting of albumen.

ALBUS, a petty silver German coin, the Hessian albus being worth about one-fifth of a penny, and the imperial albus of some of the other states about one penny.

ALCALDE, ALCADE, a Spanish judge; a parish officer, a governor, and jailer.

ALCANDIA, the Spanish name for millet.

ALCANFOR, the Spanish name for camphor.

ALCAPARRA, the Peninsular name for the caper bush, *Capparis Spinosa*.

ALCARAHUETA, the Spanish name for the caraway seed.

ALCARRAZAS, the Spanish name for porous unglazed earthenware coolers.

ALCAVALA, a customs duty levied on foreign goods at the Spanish ports.

ALCHEMY, the art of transmuting metals.

ALCHORNEA, a Jamaica tree, to which has been ascribed the alcornorco bark.

ALCOHOL, a term frequently given to spirituous liquors, but properly applied only to highly rectified spirits of wine; also the Spanish name for antimony, and galena or sulphuret of lead.

ALCOHOLOMETER, an instrument for ascertaining the strength of spirits.

ALCOHOLOMETRY, the process for ascertaining the quantity of alcohol in a fluid.

ALCORAN, in the East, a high slender tower or minaret.

ALCORNOQUE, the Spanish name for the cork-tree, *Quercus suber*.

ALCORNOCO BARK, a bitter and astringent medicinal bark derived in Venezuela from the *Bowdichia virgiliodes* of Kunth.

ALCORQUE, clogs or soles made of cork wood.

ALCORZA, in Spain, a paste of sugar and starch for sweetmeats.

ALCPEEN, a manufacture of silk and cotton, imported at the Danubian ports.

ALDER, the wood of the *Betula alnus*, much used by turners, and also valuable for pumps, pipes, &c. The bark can be used for tanning.

ALDERMAN, a civil magistrate of a corporate city.

ALE, a fermented liquor, made by infusing malted barley and hops in water. The mercantile varieties of ale are very numerous, comprising old ale, mild ale, bitter or pale ale, Burton ale, Stogumber ale, Scotch ale, &c.

ALE, ALAI, the name for a sugar-mill or cane-press, in some parts of the East Indies.

ALEATORY SALE, a contingent sale, the completion of which depends upon the passing of some uncertain event or events.

ALE CONNER, a legal officer appointed to inspect measures used by publicans.

ALEE, ALI, a Hindustanee land measure of four bisis, or 19,200 square yards.

ALEGAR, sour ale or beer used for dyeing and other manufacturing purposes.

ALE HOOF, a common name for the ground ivy (*Glechoma hederacea*), owing to its use for preserving ale before the bitter property of hops was known.

ALEJIJAS, a Spanish name for soup made of barley.

ALEMBIC, a vessel used in distillation; the head of a retort or still.

ALEN, ALN, a Danish long measure of 24⅝ inches; in Iceland it is rather less.

ALENCON LACE, a kind of French lace, with a six-sided mesh of two threads, made with pure hand-spun linen thread; it is the richest, finest, strongest, and most expensive of the French laces, and second only to Brussels lace.

ALEUROMETER, an instrument for determining the quantity of gluten in flour.

ALEWIFE, a name in the British North American colonies for a fish of the herring family (*Alosa tyrannus*).

ALEXANDRIAN LAUREL, the *Ruscus racemosus*, from which an oil is obtained.

ALFENCHA, a name in Portugal for the legumes or pods of the carob-tree (*Ceratonia siliqua*), used as food.

ALFENIQUE, a sugar paste in Spain flavoured with oil of sweet almonds.

ALFILETE, dough made with coarse flour of wheat.

ALFOLI, the Spanish term for a granary, and a depository of salt.

ALFONSIGO, the Spanish name for the pistacio nut.

ALFORFON, a name for buck-wheat in Spain.

ALGÆ, a general name for sea-weeds.

ALGAROTH POWDER, an oxychloride of antimony, used in the preparation of tartar-emetic.

ALGAROVILLA, the agglutinated seeds and husks of the legumes of *Prosopis pallida*, occasionally imported in mass from Chile. It contains a good deal of tannin.

ALGARROBO, the Spanish name for the carob-tree (*Ceratonia siliqua*); the legumes contain a large proportion of saccharine, and are consumed to a considerable extent in Spain, Portugal, Crete, &c.

ALGATRANE, a kind of pitch.

ALGODON, the Spanish name for cotton wool, or pods; Algodonal being a cotton-plantation, and Algodonero, the cotton-plant.

ALGORIN, a place in the oil-mills in Spain, for receiving the olives for expressing.

ALHOCIGO, another name for the pistacio-tree.

ALHONDIGA, the Spanish name for a public granary or corn market.

ALIAKOO, an Indian tree, the *Memecylon tinctorium*, the leaves of which are used for dyeing yellow.

ALIAS, a false name.

ALIEN, a foreigner, or person not naturalized, not a denizen or subject of the state, and therefore incapable of inheriting land, or acquiring or succeeding to property.

ALIJAR, a Spanish term for separating the wool of cotton from the seed.

ALIMENT, any substance which may be used as food.

ALIZAINE, a fine red volatile colouring matter, in the form of crystals, found in madder, and which yields the Turkey-red dye.

ALIZARI, a name in Tripoli for madder.

ALJEZON, the Spanish name for gypsum.

ALK, a resinous gum of Northern Africa, which flows from the *Pistacia terebinthus*, also called Lek.

ALKALIES, saline bases, of which the principal entering into commerce are AMMONIA, POTASH, and SODA.

ALKALIMETER, a graduated glass tube divided into one hundred parts for measuring and determining the quantity and strength of free alkali in the potash and alkali of commerce, first invented by M. Descroizelles; much more simple instruments, such as Dr. Ure's and Mr. Griffin's, are now in general use.

ALKALUK, a striped shawl material of Cashmere wool, worn by the nobles of Lucknow in the cold season in India.

ALKANET, the commercial name for the root of *Anchusa tinctoria*, a species of bugloss, from the South of Europe and the Levant, which imparts an elegant red colour to oils, and is used for staining wood.

ALKERMES, a confection of kermes berries (*Quercus coccifera?*) used in Tuscany, also imported in the liquid state.

ALKOOL, a black dye used by females in eastern countries to tinge their eyelids. *See* HENNA.

ALLEGE, the French term for a tender or lighter for a ship.

ALLIGATOR PEAR, a vulgar name for the Avocado pear, the succulent fruit of *Persea gratissima*.

ALLIGAZANT, a kind of black rosewood.

ALLMICULEE, an old Turkish silver coin worth 3s.

ALLODIAL TENURE, a free tenure of land among our ancestors, by which the tenant had no quit-rent to pay.

ALLOTMENT NOTE, an order for periodical payment of a portion of a seaman's wages to some second party.

ALLOTTEE, one to whom an allotment is made, as in the case of the holder of an allotment note of newly issued shares in a joint-stock company, &c.

ALLOY, in coinage a mixture of baser metal added to gold or silver; there are other alloys also in trade manufactures, consisting of the fusion of metals, such as bronze, brass, and printing-type.

ALLSPICE, the popular name for the dried berries of *Eugenia pimenta* of Decandolle, used as a spice in cookery.

ALLU, an Indian name for a handful of grain or merchandise, taken as a cess or payment.

ALLUBODAN, a common building wood of Ceylon, obtained from the *Calyptranthes Jambolana*.

ALLUVIUM, the earthy deposits left by rivers.

ALMACEN, the Spanish name for a warehouse or store-room.

ALMACENAGE, housage or warehouse rent.

ALMACIGA, one of the Spanish names for mastic.

ALMADRABA, a general name in the Peninsula for the tunny fishery.

ALMADY, a bark canoe, or fishing vessel of Africa; a larger boat, bearing the same name, is common in Southern India.

ALMAGRA, a purplish red ochre, formerly used in medicine and as a pigment.

ALMANAC, a book or sheet containing a calendar for the year, with other useful details for reference.

ALMANCEBE, a Spanish fishing-boat.

ALMANDINE, a name for the carbuncle or precious garnet of mineralogy.

ALMARA, the Hindoo name for a cabinet or wardrobe, probably derived from the Portuguese ulmaria.

ALMARRAES, combing instruments in the Spanish colonies by which the cotton wool is separated from the seed.

ALMAS, the Arabic name for the diamond.

ALMATRERO, a fisherman in the Peninsular ports who fishes with nets for shad.

ALMAZARA, an oil-mill in Spain.

ALMECHA, the Spanish name for shell, and for some shell-fish.

ALMENDRO, **ALMENDRON**, woods of Central America, the produce of varieties of the almond-tree.

ALMENE, an Indian weight of about 2lbs., formerly used for weighing saffron.

ALMIBAR, the Spanish name for syrup, and for succades or fruits preserved in sugar.

ALMIDON, the Spanish name for feculas or starches.

ALMIRAH, an Indian name for a wardrobe or clothes' press. *See* ALMARA.

ALMIZCLE, the Spanish term for musk.

ALMOCRATE, the Spanish name for sal-ammoniac.

ALMOJABA, smoked tunny fish.

ALMOJABANA, a kind of omelet or cake made in Spain, of cheese and flour, or of butter, eggs, and sugar.

ALMONA, the Spanish term for the shad fishery, also for a soap manufactory.

ALMOND, COUNTRY, a name in the East for a kind of myrobalan, the fruit of *Terminalia catappa*, used for tanning and dyeing.

ALMOND, JAVA, a name in the east for *Canarium commune*.

ALMOND-OIL is obtained both from the bitter and sweet almonds, but the former are chiefly turned to account for that purpose; on the Continent, sweet almond oil is largely used for its medicinal properties.

ALMONDS, the fruit of some varieties of Amygdalus, which enter largely into commerce, and are ranged under two great classes, the sweet and the bitter.

ALMUD, a variable measure for liquids and grain in the Peninsula, ranging for liquids from 8½ to 5½ English gallons; for grain from 8½ to 11 pints.

ALMUDADA, in Spain, a piece of ground which takes half a fanega of grain to sow it; the fanega weighs about half a hundred-weight. *See* FANEGA.

ALMUDI, a Spanish dry measure containing six cahices or bushels. [pints.

ALMUT, a grain measure of Majorca, of

Aln, the Swedish ell, or aune of two feet; equal to 23½ inches.

Alnage, a toll or due paid for measuring cloth.

Alnager, a continental term for an ell-measure.

Alo, a name in the Pacific islands for hogs' lard.

Aloes, a drastic drug of large consumption, obtained from the inspissated juice of the leaves of several varieties of the aloe plant in Asia, Africa, and the West Indies; the drug is, however, usually classed under four commercial denominations, Socotrine, Barbados, Cape, and Hepatic.

Aloe-wood. *See* Agallochum Wood.

Aloja, the Spanish name for metheglin, a common sweet beverage.

Aloo, the Persian name for prunes.

Alosa, the generic name for the shad fish. *See* Shad.

Alosna, the Spanish name for wormwood.

Alpaca, the wool of the llama, or goat of Peru and Chile; also a fabric made from a mixture of the silky goat's hair with the harder fibre of sheep's wool.

Alpamisqua, a kind of honey made in some of the districts of the river Plate by a very small bee.

Alpargata, a light kind of sandal or shoe, made of rushes (*Macrochlia tenacissima*), worn by the Valencian peasantry.

Alphabet, a set of letters or types; the index to a ledger.

Alpiste, the Spanish name for canary seed.

Alquiere, a Portuguese wine measure, of 2¾ to 3¾ gallons, but varying considerably in different parts of Portugal and Brazil.

Alquifoux, **Aquifoux**, a continental name for an ore of lead, used in glazing pottery.

Alquitira, a Spanish name for gum tragacanth.

Alrota, in Spain a very coarse sort of tow.

Alsi, an Indian name for flax.

Alta, an Indian name for cotton steeped in lac dye.

Altimeter, a quadrant or instrument for taking altitudes, or measuring heights geometrically.

Altin, a Russian money equal to three copecks, worth about threepence and 3-5ths of a penny sterling.

Altmichlik, a small silver Turkish coin of the value of 2½d.

Altometer, a name for the theodolite, an instrument for measuring heights and distances.

Alto-relievo, sculptured works in high relief.

Alubo, a Ceylonese name for the wood of the *Calyptranthes jambolana*, used for common house buildings.

Aluchi, a resin obtained from Madagascar, believed to be the produce of *Wintera aromatica*.

Aludel, a name in Ceylon for the wood of the *Artocarpus pubescens*, used for boats and buildings; also an earthen vessel without a bottom, used in chemical operations.

Alum, an efflorescence found in aluminous rocks and lava, used in medicine, and in various manufactures of leather, paper, dyeing, &c.

Alum, Factitious, a powerful astringent salt in crystals, a bisulphate of alumina and potash, used in medicine and dyeing; of which many thousand tons are annually manufactured.

Alumina, a kind of earth, which consists of pure clay or argil; in its crystalline form it is the base of corundum, emery, and other hard polishing substances used in the arts; combinations of it yield fuller's earth, pipeclay, ochres, &c.; a dye for calico-printers is procured from it, and it enters into the manufacture of porcelain.

Aluminium, a new metal, on which much experimental research has recently been expended in France, by M. Deville, at the chemical works at Javel.

Alum Meal, the granular alum which occurs in the manufacture of salt.

Alum Slate, a bituminous slate of a dark colour.

Alum Stone, a crystalline rock from which alum was formerly made.

Alunite, a hard variety of alum stone, which in Hungary is used for millstones.

Alva, a conserve of quinces, forming an article of commerce in the East.

Alva-marina, a commercial name for certain dried sea-weeds used for stuffing beds, &c.

Alverja, the Spanish name for the common vetch or tare.

Amada, a vernacular name in Bengal for the root of *Curcuma amada*, also known as mango ginger.

Amadou, a species of fungus, *Polyporus igniarius*, which, after having been beaten with a mallet, and dipped in a solution of saltpetre, forms the spunk or German tinder of commerce; it is also used as a styptic, and made into razor strops.

Amadum, a vernacular name in some parts of India for the castor-oil plant, *Ricinus communis*.

Amalaca, the Sanscrit name for the Emblic myrobalan, or fruit of the *Emblica officinalis*.

Amaldar, an Indian revenue or tax collector.

Amalgagar, the Hindoo name for a government revenue officer.

Amalgam, a mixture of metals, as of quicksilver with gold or silver, zinc, sulphur, &c. An amalgam of tin and mercury forms the coating of glass for mirrors.

Amalgamation, the process of extracting gold and silver from their ores by means of quicksilver or mercury.

Aman, an Indian name for the winter crop of rice; a blue cotton cloth from the Levant.

Amanbluce, a kind of calico made in France.

Amande, the French name for almond; *amandes cassées* being shelled almonds, and *amandes en coques*, unshelled.

Amanji, **Amji**, compulsory service exacted from the natives in the East.

Amateur, an unprofessional actor, or inexperienced workman.

Ama-tsja, the Japanese name for the dried leaves of *Hydrangea Thunbergii*, figuratively meaning the tea of heaven.

Amazon Stone, a variety of feldspar of a beautiful apple-green colour.

AMBALO, an article of merchandise in the Netherlands' Indian trade; the fruit of an undefined tree, believed to cure the ear-ache.
AMBAR, a common name in many of the Indian dialects for a store or heap of anything, as a granary.
AMBARAI, in India a grove of mango-trees.
AMBAREE, a vernacular name for the fibre of the brown Indian hemp (*Hibiscus cannabinus*).
AMBASHTA, a Sanscrit name for the three-leaved sorrel (*Oxalis corniculata*).
AMBASSADOR, a delegate, but in ordinary acceptation the representative of his sovereign in a foreign country, and thence enjoying, with his staff, special immunities and privileges.
AMBER, a valuable fossil resin used in the arts, in pharmacy, and for articles of personal decoration.
AMBERGRIS, an odoriferous substance obtained from the sperm whale (*Physeter macrocephalus*), valued as a perfume and as a stimulant aromatic. In the East it is used in cookery.
AMBLI, an Indian name for the tamarind.
AMBOOSEE, an Indian name for dried mangoes.
AMBOYNA-WOOD, a beautiful mottled and curled wood, obtained from the *Pterospermum Indicum*, a tree of India.
AMBRA, a mode of spelling amber in some of the Continental states; also, in Saxon times, a measure of salt.
AMBREINE, a peculiar fragrant fatty substance contained in ambergris, soluble in alcohol, to which its use as a perfume is owing.
AMBRETTE, a kind of French pear.
AMBULANCE, a travelling medical carriage for transporting invalids or wounded persons.
AMBULANTS, uncertificated brokers in Holland.
AMELCORN, a name given to corn used for starch.
AMELEON, the French name for weak cider.
AMENEKA, the Singhalese name for the seed of the castor-oil plant (*Ricinus communis*).
AMERICAN-ALOE, the *Agave Americana* or *Mexicana*, from which the intoxicating liquor named pulque is made.
AMERICAN-DOLLAR, a silver coin in large circulation in various countries, of the intrinsic value of about 4s. 2d., but in many localities at a high premium. *See* DOLLAR.
AMERICAN-LEATHER, a kind of varnished or enamelled cloth, prepared in imitation of leather for covering chairs, sofas, &c.
AMERICAN-POLISH, an impalpable powder of silver, made from a calcedonic rock in Vermont, and used for the same purposes as emery.
AMERICAN-VERMILION, an incorrect name given to a red pigment, which consists principally of subchromate of lead.
AMERSFOORT, a kind of tobacco used for cigars and snuff.
AMETHYST, a precious stone, a species of quartz, of a purple or violet colour.
AMFUK, a name given locally to the cloth made in India from the reticulated bark of *Celtis orientalis*.
AMIANTHUS, one of the names for asbestos.
AMIDINE, the soluble part of starch.
AMIDONNIER, a starch-maker in France.
AMIDULINE, a modified starch.
AMINEUR, a French salt meter.
AMINCIAS, thin sheepskins prepared for the lining of hats in Spain.
AMLA, the Bengalee name for the fruit of the *Emblica officinalis*, used in tanning and dyeing.
AMLIKA, one of the Sanscrit names for the three-leaved sorrel (*Oxalis corniculata*).
AMMA, MAS, a weight in the Sunda islands, the 16th part of the tael or Eastern ounce, rather more than 69 grains.
AMMAH, an ancient Hebrew measure of length, equal to about half a yard.
AMMAS, a weight for gold and silver in Madras, equal to 36¼ grains.
AMMIOLITE, a mineral from Chile in red powder, which appears to be an antimonite of quicksilver.
AMMOMUM, a dry measure of Ceylon, containing 8 parahs — rather more than 5¼ bushels.
AMMONIA, a volatile alkali, a compound of azote and hydrogen; several combinations of it enter into commerce, as liquid or caustic ammonia, spirits of hartshorn, and sulphate of ammonia from the liquor of gas-works.
AMMONIACUM, a fetid gum-resin, having properties similar to asafœtida, obtained from *Dorema ammoniacum*.
AMMONITES, spiral fossil shells, collected for cabinets, &c.
AMMUNITION, a general term in commerce for certain military stores, such as powder, shot, shells, &c., required for large and small arms.
AMOLA, a liquid measure of Genoa, equal to about a quarter of a gallon.
AMONTILLADO, a dry kind of sherry of a light colour, much used to reduce the colour of other sherries when too high.
AMOMUM, a land measure in Ceylon equal to about two acres and two roods. [AJOUAN.
AMOOS, the Arab name for lovage. *See*
AMORGIS. *See* ARCHIL. [fund.
AMORTIZATION, the redemption by a sinking
AMPELITA, the Spanish name for cannel coal.
AMPELITE, a generic name given to slates.
AMPHIBIOUS, living in or frequenting land and water.
AMPHIGENE SPAR. *See* LAPIS LAZULI.
AMPHIOEN, a name in some parts of the Eastern archipelago for opium.
AMPHITHEATRE, a building of a circular form, arranged for large audiences.
AMPHORA, an ancient Roman liquid measure of about 6¾ gallons. *See* ANFORA.
AMPHOREUS, an old Greek measure for liquids equal to 10¼ gallons.
AMPUTATION, the act of cutting off a limb.
AMRA, a name in Bengal for the fruit of the mango (*Mangifera Indica*).
AMT, a land division in Norway.
AMULET, articles of various kinds sold as imaginary charms to ward off evil from the wearer.

AMILSARAT, an Indian name for crystallized sulphur.

AMURCA, a name in Sardinia and Italy for the cake or grounds of the olive remaining after the oil is expressed; used as manure, and for cattle food.

AMURCOUS, full of dregs or lees.

AMYLACEOUS, resembling or appertaining to starch.

AMYLATE, a compound of starch with a base.

AMYLINE, AMYLUM, the fecula or crystallized starch of wheat.

ANA, an Indian name for the sixteenth part of any thing, as the link of a measuring chain; the 16th of the gonta, a land measure, or 7½ square yards.

ANABASSES, a coarse blanketing formerly made in France for bartering on the African coast.

ANACOSTA, a sort of woollen diaper for the Spanish market, made in Holland.

ANALYSIS, a close examination.

ANALYST, one who analyzes articles; an examiner.

ANAR, an Indian name for the pomegranate.

ANAPAIMA, a tree of great size which abounds in the rocky districts of British Guiana, and possesses a close-grained wood.

ANASTATIC PRINTING, a mode of copying engravings and printed matter by saturating the print or drawing with an acid; it is then transferred on a plate.

ANASTRE. *See* ARRASTRE.

ANATOMIST, one who dissects and examines animal bodies.

ANATTO, one of the modes of spelling the dye-stuff Annotto.

ANAYAN, the Malay name for a herdsman or shepherd.

ANBAUER, the German name for a cultivator or planter.

ANCHARA, an Indian term for the estimate of a crop.

ANCHETA, in Spain a shipment on private adventure of goods to India.

ANCHOIS, the French mode of spelling anchovies.

ANCHORAGE, a roadstead or suitable holding-ground where ships can cast anchor.

ANCHORAGE DUES, charges payable in certain ports to the Crown for anchoring.

ANCHORS, wrought iron holdfasts for ships, which range in weight from a quarter of a ton to five tons, according to the size of the vessel to be held or secured by them. A vessel of twenty tons burden requires an anchor of a cwt., and so on in proportion; the largest ships have as many as seven anchors, which bear different names as sheet, bower, stream, kedge, &c. There are about six commercial varieties of anchors, many thousands of tons weight of which are annually exported.

ANCHOR-SMITH, one engaged in the forging of ships' anchors.

ANCHOR-STOCK, the cross bar of wood or iron at the upper end of the shank.

ANCHOVY, a small and delicate pickled fish of commerce, the *Engraulis encrasicolus*; belonging to the *Clupinæ* or herrings, and chiefly obtained in the Mediterranean. It may be readily distinguished from the sprat and other kindred species by the anal fin being remarkably short.

ANCHOVY PEAR, the succulent fruit of the *Persea gratissima*, an esteemed edible butyraceous fruit of the tropics.

ANDALUSITE, a crystal from the Tyrol, also found in California.

ANDARAC, an Indian name for red orpiment.

ANDERSON, a name in Northern India for the *Ptycholis involucrata*, used as a substitute for parsley.

ANDERE, a name in Ceylon for the wood of the *Acacia Arabica*.

ANDESINE. *See* FELDSPAR.

ANDIRONS. *See* AWNDIERNS.

ANEMOMETER, an instrument for determining the velocity or force of the wind, erected in insurance offices, exchanges, and observatories, &c.; the most common forms are those of Dr. Whewell and Mr. Osler.

ANEMOSCOPE, a weather vane and register to indicate the changes of the wind and weather.

ANFORA, a Venetian liquid measure containing about 114 imperial gallons. Also an ancient Roman and Greek measure; sometimes written Amphora.

ANGA, in India, a pace or stride of three feet.

ANGADI, an oriental name for a moveable stall or booth.

ANGADIA, a trustworthy person employed in some parts of India to convey valuables concealed about his person.

ANGAN, an enclosed area or court yard in India.

ANGARILLAS, the Spanish name for large wicker baskets or panniers for horses.

ANGARIPOLA, a kind of coarse linen in Spain.

ANGEL, an ancient gold coin of England, of 80 grains, worth, according to fineness, from 8s. to 10s.

ANGELET, or half angel, a common coin in the reigns of the Tudors, valued then at forty pence.

ANGELICA, the candied green stems of the *Archangelica officinalis*, which enter into commerce as an aromatic condiment.

ANGELOT, a sort of cheese.

ANGEL-WATER, a name for eau de Portugal.

ANGLE, a small measure of length in Bangalore, represented by three grains of rice, equal to about one inch.

ANGLE-BARS, pieces of iron for forming the edges of iron gates, bridges, and ships, or to be riveted to the corners of iron boilers, tanks, &c., to connect the side plates.

ANGLER, a fisherman, usually applied to one who fishes only for pleasure instead of business.

ANGLESITE, a sulphate of lead, produced by the decomposition of GALENA, which sometimes contains silver.

ANGOLA, a light and fashionable cloth, made from the Angora goat's wool, which is also made into plush, and from its repelling heat is used for paletots, cloaks, and overcoats. *See* ANGORA-WOOL.

ANGOLA-WEED, the name of a lichen, *Ramolina furfuracea*, from which ARCHIL and CUDBEAR are made.

ANGOON, the Malay name for grapes.

ANGORA-WOOL, the long white hair of the Angora goat (*Capra Angorensis*), which is highly prized in manufactures, having a silky appearance, which fits it for lace, shawls, braids, and other decorative purposes.

Angostura-bark, an aromatic bitter bark, obtained in South America from the *Galipea cusparia*, or *officinalis*; a false Angostura bark, of dangerous properties, is peeled from the *Strychnos nux vomica* in India.

Angrai-bark, an undefined bark mentioned in the tariff of exports from Siam.

Angster, a small money of account in Switzerland, 240 going to the florin of 1s. 8d.

Angula, a Singhalese long measure, equal to seven grains of paddy or rice, and about 2¼ inches; the carpenter's angula being equal to the space between the second and third joint of the forefinger; also a division of the Indian cubit, varying in different localities from ¾ to 1 inch.

Anicut, an Indian term for a weir or dam across a river; an embanked channel for irrigation.

Anileria, the Spanish name for an indigo manufactory.

Animal Charcoal, principally carbonized bone, used by sugar-refiners and by ironmakers in blistering steel; when obtained cheap, it forms a valuable fertilizer for land.

Animal Fat. The chief animal fats of commerce are tallow and lard, but horse grease, bear's grease, and blubber, are other articles of trade.

Animal Jelly. *See* Gelatin.

Animal Manures, hair, blood, bones, fish, and other substances, bought or collected by farmers, and used to fertilize land.

Animi, a fossil African resin of great value in commerce, some of which is believed to be obtained from the *Hymenæa courbaril* of South America.

Aniseed, the fruit of *Pimpinella anisum*, very generally used as a condiment in the East, and in Europe for essential oil, for flavouring in medicine, &c.; star anise, the capsule and seeds of *Illicium anisatum*, constitutes an important article of commerce in the Eastern bazaars, and is imported into this country.

Anisette, a cordial made from aniseed.

Anjan, a fodder grass in the north-west provinces of India.

Anjana, the Hindustanee name for a common kind of rice.

Anjr, in India cotton prepared or cleaned, ready to be spun.

Anjil, an Arab name for the marshmallow.

Ankara, an Indian name for discount.

Anker, a small cask or runlet containing 8½ gallons, which in this country is now obsolete. The anker is still, however, a common liquid measure in many of the Continental states, varying from 7½ to 9½ gallons.

Ankerite, a mineral highly prized as an iron-ore, and as a flux for smelting.

Ank-kar, a money changer, or assayer in the East, also one who marks or stamps.

Anklet, a band for the leg, made of silver, gold, cane, or glass, worn by the Indian women. *See* Bangles.

Ankoose, an elephant-driver's weapon, having a spear head and hook.

Anna, an Eastern name for rice boiled for food. An Indian coin worth 1½d.; also a salt measure in the East, weighing 2¼ tons.

Annealing, a process of tempering or seasoning glass and metals, by graduating the heat to which they are subjected.

Annotto, a dye-stuff prepared from the red pulp of the seeds of the *Bixa orellana*, which enters into commerce under two forms, flag and roll.

Annuity, a sum paid or received annually, or after a yearly rate; a portion of the English government stocks or funds, divided into long or terminable, and irredeemable or perpetual annuities.

Annul, to cancel or render void, as an agreement, proposition, or entry.

Annunciator, a kind of bell telegraph used in North America.

Anola, a name in India for the myrobalan-tree, one of the Terminalia; the fruits of the *Emblica officinalis* are used as a tanning substance.

Anorthite, a variety of feldspar.

Anou, a name in Sumatra for the coarse black bristly ejoo or gomutu fibre obtained from the *Arenga saccharifera* palm, the *Saguerus rumphii* of some authors.

Ant, the native name in some parts of India for a credit account.

Antacids, medicines used to correct acidity in the stomach; alkalies are those chiefly used; but crabs'-eyes, calcareous concretions of the cray-fish, cuttle bones, &c., are sometimes vended for the purpose.

Antal, a wine measure used in the Tokay district of Hungary, about 116 imperial gallons.

Ante, the Spanish name for a dressed buck or buffalo skin.

Anthal. *See* Antal.

Anthracite, a valuable kind of stone coal, for steam fuel, obtained in Wales, and largely in Pennsylvania and other parts of America, being there used for other purposes; it is also called blind or glance coal.

Anthrakometer, an instrument for measuring the carbonic acid in the air.

Antiar, a poison obtained in Java from the acrid juice of the upas tree, *Antiaris toxicaria*.

Antipato, the Spanish name for black coral.

Anti-friction Grease, a composition for lubricating machinery and wheels.

Antigropelos, spatterdashes, long riding or walking boots for wet weather.

Anti-macassar, an open worked napkin or loose fancy covering, to preserve a chair or couch.

Antimeter, an optical instrument for measuring angles with precision.

Antimonial-wine, a preparation of tartar-emetic.

Antimonite, the grey ore or sulphuret of antimony, which is largely used for commercial purposes.

Antimony, a mineral substance which enters into commerce, in the form of regulus or ore, crystals, powder, &c.; the ore is imported to a considerable extent now from Borneo.

Antimony-yellow, a preparation of antimony, of a durable colour, used in enamel and porcelain painting.

Antiquarian, a large kind of drawing paper, measuring 56 by 38 inches.

Antique-bronze, an alloy of copper and tin, used for statuary, casts, &c.

Antiseptic, any substance which prevents decomposition, as glycerine, charcoal, chloride of lime, &c.

Antispasmodics, tonics and stimulant remedies, used in certain debilitated states of the nervous system; from the animal kingdom, musk, hyraceum, castoreum, civet, ambergris, &c., are supposed to have properties of this kind; in the vegetable kingdom, asafœtida, galbanum, ammoniacum, myrrh, &c., are employed.

Antlers, the branched horns of a stag. *See* Horns.

Ants'-brood, Ants'-eggs, an article of import in some of the northern countries, probably for making formic acid; dissolved in water they serve the purpose of vinegar in Norway.

Antwerp-blue, a colour rather lighter in tint than Prussian blue.

Antwerp-brown, a painter's colour made from asphaltum ground in drying oil.

Anvil, a heavy block of iron with a smooth surface, used by smiths, farriers, and other workers in metals; anvils range in weight from 28 lb. to 6 cwt.; several hundred tons are made yearly in South Staffordshire, and they are exported to some extent.

Anzeige, the German term for an announcement or advertisement.

Apartado, a smelting-house in the Spanish colonies where gold is separated from silver.

Apatite, a fibrous and compact translucent mineral, a compound of phosphate of lime with fluoride of calcium; the beds of phosphate in Estremadura and in Norway, have been largely drawn upon for apatite, for the use of agriculturists as a manure.

Apfelmost, Apfelwein, the German name for cider.

Aphtee, a name for the windgall in Austria.

Apiary, a beehive.

Apilada, the Spanish name for dry and peeled chestnuts.

Apios, a South American name for the *Arracacha esculenta*, an edible root largely cultivated for culinary purposes, uniting the flavour of the potato and the parsnip.

Aplome, a mineral of a deep orange colour.

Apostaleos, in Spain, planks from five to seven inches thick.

Apothecaries' Company, one of the city companies of London, incorporated in 1606, whose hall is situated in Water Lane, Blackfriars, where genuine medicines are vended to the public; they have by charter the power of examining and licensing dispensers of medicines in town and country.

Apothecaries-weight, the weight by which drugs are dispensed, differing only in its subdivisions from the common troy weight. *See* Avoirdupois and Troy Weight.

Apothecary, a compounder and dispenser of medicines.

Appalachian Tea, a name given in North America to the leaves of *Viburnum cassinoides*, and of *Prinos glaber*, which are occasionally used as substitutes for the tea of China.

Appalto, a Turkish licence to sell articles, or an exclusive right to any particular revenue or branch of trade.

Apparatus, a term usually applied to a complete set of chemical vessels or instruments for experiments.

Apparel, in the official returns of exports numberless small articles of dress are grouped under this name; but in trade the term is usually applied to slops and negro clothing. Haberdashery, millinery, ready-made clothing, and other items of export, come under this general classification, although treated of under other heads.

Apparitor, a public officer in a law court in France.

Appasam, a name in the northern Circars, India, for a water channel.

Apples, a well-known fruit, the numerous varieties of which are obtained by grafting on the *Pyrus malus*; apples form an important article of commerce in most temperate countries, both in their green and dried state, and for the cider made from them.

Appliqué Lace, a name given to lace when the patterns have been cut out and sewn on a foundation of net; by this means the same patterns may be transferred from a veil to a scarf or lappet, and they will wear out several foundations.

Appointe, the French name for a cabin or state passenger in a ship.

Appraiser, a sworn licensed valuer to estimate and fix the value of goods.

Apprentice, a lad under age bound by indenture to serve another, at sea or in trade, for a term of years.

Apricot, the fruit of the *Armeniaca vulgaris*, not a common fruit in England, but bearing more plentifully in warmer climates; oil of the finest kind is made in India by expression from the kernels; the wood of the apricot-tree is used by the French for turning.

Apron, a platform raised at the entrance of a dock, the sill of a window, a lady's or workman's covering for the person; the Apron of a Ship, is a false or inner stem above the foremost part of the keel.

Aquafortis, the common name for a valuable chemical acid, known as dilute nitric acid; when more concentrated, it is called spirits of nitre.

Aquamarine or Beryl, a gem named from its resemblance to the colour of the sea; it is found in shades of green, blue, and pale yellow.

Aquatint, a kind of engraving or etching on copper, obtained by the combined action of dilute acid and powdered resin.

Aqua-vitæ, an old name for alcohol, still occasionally used for whisky, gin, and other home-manufactured spirits.

Aqua-vivarium, a glass globe or tank for keeping aquatic plants and marine animals alive, usually ornamented with rock-work and shells.

Aqueduct, a raised channel for water carried over a valley, or a conduit or tunnel through the earth.

Aquila, an ecclesiastical reading-desk in the form of an eagle with extended wings.

Aquirabaegu, an undefined gum obtained in the States of the Argentine confederation.

Ara, the Hindoo name for a saw; also the Malay name for a river.

Araba, an Indian and Turkish cart.

Arabian-bedstead, a modern half tester, with carved foot-board, pillars, &c.

Arabic, an extensively used gum of commerce, obtained in Africa and the East from various species of acacia; Arabic is the type of true gum, being readily soluble in water.

Arabine, the mucilage of gum Arabic and gum Senegal; it is also contained in linseed.

Arachis Oil, a fine limpid oil expressed from the seeds of the *Arachis hypogæa*, generally known in commerce as nut oil.

Arad, an Indian name for flour.

Araki, the Arabic name for alcohol or brandy.

Aragonite, a snow-white columnar crystal.

Aragu, crude stick-lac taken from the tree.

Arale, the Karnatic name for cotton.

Araloo, the Singhalese name for the Chebulic myrobalan. *See* Myrobalons.

Arançada, Arranzada, a superficial measure of Spain used for vineyard purposes, and generally estimated at 48,400 square feet.

Arang, a Malay name for charcoal.

Arangoes, large East Indian beads made of cornelians, which are much in request on the coast of Africa.

Arapende, an ancient Spanish measure of 120 square feet.

Arar, a name in Northern Africa for the *Thuya articulata*, a valuable wood of which the Mohammedan mosques are built; it also furnishes gum sandarac.

Arastre. *See* Arrastre.

Arat, a wholesome warehouse in India.

Arata, a name in some parts of Portugal for the *arroba*.

Arbaccio, a coarse woollen cloth made in Sardinia from the wool of the Nuoro sheep, an inferior breed.

Arbalest, a cross-bow.

Arbitration, a mode of settling differences in mercantile affairs, by reference for adjudication to one or more impartial but well-informed parties.

Arbitrator, a judge; one chosen to decide differences between disputants.

Arbol-a-brea, a resin of a greenish-gray colour, obtained from the *Canarium album* in the Philippines.

Arboon, an Arabic term for earnest-money.

Arbor, a term used by watchmakers and others for an axis or spindle.

Arcade, an arched avenue or enclosure, with shops or stalls.

Arcanson, a French name for common dark rosin or colophony.

Arch, in the mining districts, a piece of ground left unworked near a shaft.

Archeen, a Russian linear measure equal to 28 inches.

Archery Bows, yew, lancewood, or other bows used for archery.

Archil, a violet red paste prepared from various lichens, such as *Roccella tinctoria* and *fuciformis*. The most esteemed comes from the Canaries and the Cape de Verde islands; it is extensively used for dyeing silks and woollens, but, although it imparts a beautiful colour, it lacks permanence; other products are called persis and cudbear. *See* Orchilla.

Archimedean Screw, a hydrostatic screw named after its inventor, now applied for propelling vessels by steam through the water; also a drill or boring screw.

Architect, a designer of buildings, one who plans or superintends the erection of works.

Architrave, in building the principal beam which rests on a column; also the entablature or wave moulding in a cornice.

Archive, a record; a chamber for preserving records.

Archivolt, in building a curve formed by the upper sides of the *voussoirs* or arch stones.

Arcilla, the Spanish name for clay.

Arcot-Rupee. *See* Rupee.

Arctic, any thing relating to the northern regions.

Ardasas, Ardasses, the coarsest sort of Persian silk; Ardasinas being the finest kind.

Ardawa, the Indian name for ground pulse given to horses, or a mixture of chick-pease and barley.

Ardeb, an Egyptian corn measure containing 7½ to 9½ English bushels, but it varies considerably, in some parts of Africa being only one-third of a bushel.

Ardeel, a quantity more than eight bushels.

Ardent Spirits, alcoholic liquors.

Ardep. *See* Ardeb.

Ardesia, the Italian name for roofing slates.

Ardite, an ancient Spanish coin.

Ardoise, the French name for slate.

Ardrika, or **Ardrukum**, a Hindoo name for ginger.

Are, the unity of surface in French measures; a square of ten metres on a side, equivalent to 1076 English feet.

Area, the superficial contents.

Areca Nut. *See* Betel Nut.

Arejouits, a Spanish name for dried peaches.

Arel, a kind of large cribble used to sift corn.

Arena, the Spanish name for sand; *arenilla* being fine sand or fine ore.

Arendi, an Indian name for the castor-oil plant.

Areometer, an instrument for measuring the density or gravity of fluids. *See* Hydrometer.

Argali, the wild aboriginal sheep which inhabit the high mountains of central Asia.

Argana, the Spanish name for a crane or machine for raising stones and heavy weights.

Argand Lamp, a burner or lamp in common use, with a circular wick to admit a double current of air.

Argel, or **Arghel**, the leaf of the *Cynanchum arghel*, which is much used abroad for adulterating Alexandrian senna.

Argent, the French name for silver metal or coined money. [silver.

Argentiferous, containing, or yielding

Argentine, white metal coated with silver.

Argentite, sulphuret of silver.

Argol, an acidulous concrete salt, the crust or sediment of wine vats and casks, which when purified is denominated cream of tartar; it is white or red, according to the wine of which it is the deposit, and largely used in medicine and the arts; also a Tartar name for the dried excrements of animals moulded into cakes and sold as fuel.

Argoudan, a kind of raw cotton.

Arguajaque, a Spanish name for gum ammoniacum.

Argus Pheasant, a rare bird (*Argus giganteus*), whose beautiful plumage is highly valued in the East; the large wing feathers, nearly three feet long, marked with eyes, are used for tiaras for the head, and the smaller ones for plumes.

Arhar, the Hindoo name of the *Dolichos catjan*, a common pulse of India.

Arhat, an Indian revolving wheel for raising water.

Ari, an Indian name for a bunch or handful of rice, corn, or other grain.

Arienzo, a Spanish weight the same as the adarme, about one drachm, or 60 grains; also an old coin of Castile.

Arindi, an Indian agent or broker.

Aripo, the Singhalese name for expressed gingelly seed.

Arisch, **Arich**, a measure of length in Persia, equal to 38¼ English inches.

Aristolochia. See **Serpentary Root**.

Arjaka, the Sanscrit name for a species of basil, *Ocymum sanctum*, sacred to Vishnu.

Arjuna, a Sanscrit name for the fruit of the *Terminalia alata*.

Arka, a Sanscrit name for the mudar, *Calotropis or Asclepias gigantea*.

Arlet, the name for cumin seed in some parts of India.

Arlienanse, a sort of Spanish linen.

Arlota, the Spanish name for tow of flax or hemp.

Armadillo, the armour plates of this animal form an article of export from Siam, the flesh is eaten in South America.

Armateur, the French name for a shipowner, or one who fits out a ship for a voyage.

Armature, a French term for the various iron holdfasts used by carpenters.

Armenian Bole, a soft earth of a red colour, found in some parts of the Continent, and also in India, where it forms an article of the materia medica, and is employed in native painting and gilding, and for red lead.

Arming Press, a tool used by bookbinders.

Armorer, a gunsmith, one who has the charge in a vessel of war, or armory, of the offensive and defensive weapons.

Armor, defensive weapons and clothing.

Armozeen, **Armozine**, a thick plain silk, generally black, used for clerical robes and funeral purposes.

Armpad, a protective pad used by tailors.

Arms, a term applied to offensive and defensive weapons: arms and ammunition form considerable articles of commerce, particularly in times of war. [Russia.

Arnaout, a kind of hard wheat grown in

Arnotto. See **Annotto**.

Arobe. See **Arroba**.

Arola, a sweet Indian grass, the ripe seeds of which are sometimes used as food by the poor natives.

Aromatic Confection, a medicine for diarrhœa, composed of chalk and aromatics.

Aromatic Vinegar, acetic acid flavoured with aromatics.

Aroona, a name in Bengal for **Munjeet**.

Aroospa, a name in Chittagong, India, for the fibre obtained from the *Callicarpa cana*.

Arpent, the French acre or land measure, which varies, but will average about 1¼ or 1·20 of an English acre.

Arpentærio, the Spanish name for a scavenger.

Arquebuse, an old-fashioned kind of heavy hand gun.

Arrack, a common Indian name for ardent spirits distilled from rice, palm juice, &c.; but in our commerce it is applied chiefly to the toddy or spirit obtained from palms in the East.

Arrage, in the northern mining districts of England a sharp point or corner.

Arranzada. See **Arancada**.

Arrastre, the Spanish name for a crushing mill to pulverize, grind, and reduce ores.

Arrate, the Spanish pound, nearly the same as the English. [7084 grains.

Arratel, the Portuguese pound, containing

Arrel, a Spanish weight of four pounds.

Arremene, a name in Ceylon for the wood of the *Sumatra cassia*, used for furniture and house building.

Arrest, incarceration, a deprivation of liberty by imprisonment, which may either be for debt, contempt of court, or for misdemeanour, &c.

Arrhes, earnest-money given in France.

Arriero, the Spanish name for a muleteer.

Arrimage, **Arrumage**, the French name for the arrangement or stowage of a ship's cargo in the hold.

Arroba, a Spanish and Portuguese measure of weight and capacity, in general use throughout those parts of America formerly belonging to Spain, and in Manilla and the East; equal to 25¼ lbs. English. According to the Spanish standard weight, it should be 25·36 lbs. As a liquid measure for wine, it is equal to 3·54, and for oil to 2·78 imperial gallons.

Arrope, sherry boiled down to a syrup, and used as a colouring liquid for other wines.

Arrove, another name for the arroba.

Arrow-root, a commercial name for the powder or starch obtained from the roots of various plants, as the *Cassava*, *Maranta arundinacea*, &c.

Arroz, the Spanish name for rice.

Arruse, a Brazilian name for the arroba.

Arsa, one of the names for koumis, a spirituous liquor made by the Kalmucks from mare's milk.

Arschin. *See* Archeen.

Arsenal, a naval or military storehouse for materials of war.

Arseniate, the union of a base, as of copper, potash, &c., to arsenic acid.

Arsenic, a prepared metal, which, in its sublimated form, is a deadly poison; it is used in medicine and the arts.

Arsenical iron, silver-white pyrites, worked as an ore of arsenic, and furnishing the white oxide of commerce and realgar.

Arsenicite, *arseniate of lime.*

Arsenic-weight, the Dutch apothecaries' weight, the pound of which is equal to ⅞ of a pound avoirdupois, and, like it, subdivided into 16 ounces.

Arsenious-acid. *See* Arsenic.

Arsenite, the oxide of arsenic, a very poisonous substance. *See* Arsenic.

Arsolah, an Eastern grain measure, rather more than half a pint.

Arson, incendiarism, the felonious act of wilfully setting fire to property.

Artaba, a Persian measure of capacity used for grain, from 10 to 14½ gallons; as an Arab weight it is 145½ pounds.

Artesian-well, a well sunk to a great depth by boring, to reach the spring and ensure a continuous supply of pure water, or to sink surface refuse.

Arthal, a drug in the East India markets.

Artichokes, a common vegetable, the *Cynara*, cultivated for its head; the tubers of another plant, the Jerusalem artichoke, *Helianthus tuberosus*, occasionally form an article of commerce dry or in oil.

Arties, pieces of timber used in the Madras Presidency for building.

Artificial-eye Maker, one who makes imitation eyes for the human subject, or for stuffed specimens of natural history.

Artificial Flowers, a considerable commerce is carried on in flowers made of linen, feathers, shells, &c., from the Continent, South America, and other quarters; at the Customs artificial flowers are entered by the foot.

Artificial-manures, fertilizers of various kinds, organic and inorganic, prepared for the use of agriculturists.

Artillery, a military name for heavy ordnance and their appurtenances.

Artist, a word very generally applied to skilled workmen, but more properly restricted to painters or sculptors and those who take likenesses.

Artole, the Indian name for the weight of half a rupee, or 90 troy grains.

Aru, a cloth measure used in Dantzic, rather more than half an English ell.

Aruga, the Sanscrit name for rice.

Arur. *See* Arrack.

Arundi, a Hindoo name for the castor-oil plant.

Arzeneibereiter, the German name for an apothecary.

Arzeneiwaaren, the German name for drugs or medicinal preparations.

Arzo, a name for the almond-tree in Morocco.

As, the ancient Roman pound, not quite equal to three-quarters of a pound avoirdupois; also the principal Roman copper coin. In several of the Continental states the As ranges as a weight from ⅞ to nearly one English grain.

Asafœtida, a fetid resinous gum, the produce of *Ferula asafœtida*, which in this country is of importance in medicine, and an extensive article of commerce in the East, where it is used as a seasoning for food.

Asar, a gold coin of some of the countries bordering on the Persian Gulf, equal to *about 6s. 8d. sterling.*

Asarabacca, a name for the *Asarum Europæum*, the leaves and roots of which are emetic, and used in farriery. The powdered leaves form the basis of most cephalic snuffs. [Asarabacca.

Asaroon, a name for the dried plant of the

Asbestos, a fibrous incombustible mineral, which is coming into use for various chemical and manufacturing purposes; it is also called amianthus.

Asbolane, an earthy black cobalt used in the manufacture of smalt.

Ash, a useful British wood, obtained from several species of *Fraxinus*, which is much used by the shipwright and cabinet-maker, and for various implements of husbandry.

Ashblick, a chemical production of copper and lime water.

Ashbox, the box beneath the furnace; also a house receptacle for cinders.

Ashes, the saline and earthy particles of burnt substances; the principal commercial ashes are bone ash, potash, and pearlash, for medicine and manufacturers, and coal ashes for manure. [the quarry.

Ashlar, a rough unsmoothed stone from

Ash-pit, the place where the cinders fall under a furnace.

Ashrabat, an Arabic name for spirituous or fermented liquors, forbidden by the Mahommedan laws.

Ashrafi, **Ashrufi**, an Indian coin, the gold mohur, worth 16 rupees, or about 32s.

Ashur, the Arab name for the mudar, or *Asclepias gigantea*, a valuable Indian shrub.

Asiya, the Hindoo name for a water or other mill, and a millstone.

Asnee, **Anee**, an old French grain measure of from 5 to 7 Winchester bushels; also a liquid measure equal to 18 gallons.

Aspalath, a name given to the Rhodes wood (*Convolvulacea*), and to *Aquilaria Malaccensis.* *See* Agallochum Wood.

Asparagus, a well-known culinary vegetable, cultivated for its young shoots.

Asparez, an ancient Armenian itinerary measure of two kinds, the greater 0·19 mile, and the lesser 0·134 mile.

Asper, a petty Turkish money of account, the third part of a para, of very uncertain value, in some places equal to about ¼d.

Asphalte, a composition of bitumen, pitch, and gravel, used for forming pavements, and as a waterpoof cement for bridges roofs, &c.

Asphaltum, a mineral pitch or bitumen obtained from the Levant, America, and the West Indies; formerly used for embalming, now chiefly employed by artists for a black coating or varnish.

Aspic, a savoury meat jelly.

Assal, the name in Syria and Egypt for the honey of the bee.

Assam, a Malay name for the tamarind.

Assamee, an Indian name for the ryot or cultivator.

Assam tea, a valuable kind of tea raised and manufactured by the Assam company in the upper Assam district of India.

Assaroo, an Indian term for plants sown during the rainy season.

Assay, a chemical analysis for determining the fineness of bullion or gold.

Assay balance, a very accurate balance used by assayers.

Assayer, one who tests metals and ores, to ascertain their purity or commercial value.

Assembly-room, a place for public gatherings, concerts, balls, &c.

Assessed taxes, certain taxes levied from time to time by the State, on dogs, carriages, houses, &c.

Asses' skins, the skins of a well-known beast of burden, which, when prepared, were formerly used for pocket-tablets, and various other purposes; asses' milk was at one time in repute for consumptive people.

Assessor, one whose duty it is to assess the value of property for local or public taxation; usually called a surveyor.

Assets, the funds and property of a trader; real and personal estate, debts due, &c.

Assette, French, a slater's hammer.

Assignat, an obsolete species of national French paper-money, nominally of the value of 100 francs, issued to a large extent during the great French revolution of 1789.

Assignee, an official manager appointed to administer an insolvent's estate; trade assignees are appointed by the creditors.

Assignment, an absolute transfer of property; the making over of freight, bill of lading, &c.

Assignor, one who assigns or makes over his interest in property to another.

Assistant, a servant or clerk; one employed, to aid or help another in his trade, business, or employment.

Assizement, a legalized inspection of weights and measures, and of the quality of commodities, &c.

Assize of bread, a legal tariff of bread, regulating its weight and price.

Ass-load, the pack load for an ass; the average weight of which in South America is 170 lbs.

Association, a union of persons for some common object; a joint-stock company.

Assogue, a kind of Spanish ship.

Assortment, a selection or variety of goods, samples, &c.

Assurance, a money arrangement between parties, by which security against contingent loss is guaranteed to the assurer or his heirs. *See* **Insurance**.

Assured, the party who is secured from loss by a policy effected in an insurance office.

Assya, a name in Russia for succades or fruits stewed in syrup.

Asta, the name of a bast obtained in the East Indies, also called Patoo.

Astah, a cloth measure of eighteen inches used in Penang.

Asteria, a species of star sapphire, exhibiting six milk-white rays, radiating from the centre of an hexagonal prism.

Astragal, in building, &c., a semicircular projection or small round moulding.

Astringent, a binding medicine.

Astrolabe, an astronomical instrument for taking the altitude of the stars at sea.

Astromara, a concave representation of the heavens.

Astronomer, one who studies or describes the celestial bodies.

Astruck, the Indian name for gum ammoniacum.

Asul, a name, in India, for the *Tamarix ferax*, a tree on which nut-galls are formed. [84lbs.

Asumbra, a liquid measure in Paraguay, of

Aswattha, a common Indian name for the pepul tree, the *Ficus religiosa*.

Asyke, Alsike, a species of clover seed imported into Scotland from the Continent.

Atabal, a Moorish kettle-drum or tabor.

Atal, an Indian cattle pound.

Atap, the leaves of a stemless plant, the *Nipa fruticans*, which are largely used for thatching in the East.

Atarimeter, a philosophical instrument used in a fixed observatory.

Atasee. *See* **Atees**.

Atoom, an old petty coin of Turkey worth but two-thirds of a farthing.

Atees, the vernacular name in India for linseed. [silk.

Atelas, a Malay name for embroidered

Atelier, a French workshop, sculptor's studio, or building dock.

Atlas, a large kind of paper 34 by 26 inches; rich Indian embroidered satin; also a collection of maps in one volume.

Atmagupta, the Sanscrit name for cowitch, the fine hairs covering the pods of *Mucuna pruriens*, which are used as a vermifuge, and also in cases of cholera.

Atmometer, an evaporometer, or instrument to measure vaporous exhalations.

Atmospheric railway, a railway over which carriages are propelled by the power of air in iron tubes; but which in practice is not found to answer.

Atoll, a coral lagoon island or insular reef.

Atomo, a minute measure of length in Italy, the thousandth part of the braccio which is 30½ inches.

Atropia, a formidable alkali obtained from the deadly nightshade.

Attachment, a summary criminal process; also a judicial impounding by a creditor of the money or personal property of his debtor in the hands of a third party, which is authorized in London, Bristol, and some other places.

Attak, a nominal money of 200 cash, in the island of Lombok, which is equal to one Java rupee or 2s.

ATTAKME, a Singhalese superficial measure of 500 bandern-bambas, and equal to 4500 feet.

ATTAREEN, the Arabic name for a chemist and druggist.

ATTAR OF ROSES, the essential oil of roses, a very costly fragrant perfume.

ATTENDANT, a follower or assistant.

ATTERAH-MAUND, a weight used at Bussorah equal to 28 lbs.

ATTESTATION, the legal act of witnessing a deed by affixing one's signature thereto.

ATTIC, a room in the uppermost story of a house.

ATTIFET, French, a woman's head-dress.

ATTIRE, articles of clothing or dress.

ATTISE, French, fagots of fire-wood.

ATTISEUR, French, a stoker.

ATTLE, a mining term for rubbish, or stone, containing little or no ore.

ATTORNEY, a representative or deputy, one holding a power or authority to act for another. The name in the West Indies for the general supervisor or manager of plantations; a solicitor or law agent employed to prosecute or defend a claim or suit in a court of law.

ATTU, an Indian name for goats and sheep.

AUBAN, French, a licence or permit to deal.

AUBERGE, an inn, a house for the lodging and entertainment of travellers.

AUBERGISTE, an innkeeper, a landlord.

AUD. *See* ASUL.

AUBUSSON CARPET, a carpet made in the style of the Louises of France.

AUCTION, a public competitive sale by a licensed vender.

AUCTIONEER, a vender; one who manages a public sale and disposes of goods to the highest bidder.

AUDIENCE, an official or legal interview.

AUDIENCIA, in Spanish, a court of law.

AUDIT, a regular examination of books, vouchers, or accounts by one or more qualified parties.

AUDITOR, one who inspects or examines and certifies accounts; a judge.

AUFGEDINGE, the money premium received with an apprentice in Germany.

AUGAGE, a Persian land measure; the distance one can walk in an hour, usually estimated at 4½ miles.

AUGELOT, French, a skimmer used by salt-boilers.

AUGER, a wimble or boring tool.

AUGUST, a gold coin of Saxony, more frequently known as a pistole, worth from 16s. 1d. to 16s. 4d.

AULOS, another name for the ancient Greek stadium, a measure of length, nearly 197 yards.

AUM, a German liquid measure varying in size in different localities, but answering to about one-seventh of the English tun.

AUNAGE, a measuring by the ell.

AUNCEL, the old name for weighing by the steelyard; abolished by various statutes.

AUNE, the French cloth ell; the old aune of Paris is equal to 46 and 4-5ths English inches; the aune usuelle, 47¼ inches.

AURANTIA WINE, a wine made in India and England from the Chinese orange, *Citrus aurantium*.

AUREO, an ancient Spanish gold coin, also a weight of four scruples.

AUREUS, a former Greek weight of twenty drachms; also a gold coin equal to a crown sterling.

AURIFEROUS, containing or yielding gold.

AURIST, an ear-doctor, one who attends to the cure of disorders of the ears.

AURUNG, an Indian name for the place where goods are manufactured.

AUTHOR, a literary writer.

AUTOCHRONOGRAPH, a machine for the instantaneous marking or printing of time.

AUTOGRAPH, a person's own handwriting, an original manuscript.

AUTOGRAPHIC PRESS, a portable printing-machine for taking copies from a lithographic stone.

AUTOMATON, a self-moving machine, a name given to any cleverly contrived mechanism which performs the actions of animals.

AUTOPHON, a barrel-organ, the tunes of which are produced by means of perforated sheets of mill-board.

AUTUNITE, a beautiful yellowish-green mineral found in granite, also called uranite.

AUZITE, a dark mineral, a constituent of volcanic rocks.

AVA, a long measure in Cadiz, the 16th part of the vara—rather more than two inches; also a name given to the intoxicating long-pepper, the *Macropiper methysticum* in the Pacific islands.

AVADAVAT, a small cage bird with prettily marked plumage, kept by the natives of India, and commonly sold in the bazaars.

AVAL, the signing of a draft, note or bill of exchange, a French declaration of responsibility or guarantee for its payment.

AVALAKKI, a Karnatic name for rice beaten or bruised for food.

AVANCAGE, a French coach-stand.

AVANTURINE, a yellow or reddish-brown mineral freckled with gold spots, used in jewellery; of which there are artificial kinds made.

AVATI, an Indian name for a goldsmith's stamp.

AVELLANA, the Spanish name for the filbert, the fruit of the *Corylus avellana;* avellanar being a plantation of hazels or nut-trees.

AVENAGE, a tithe on oats; oats paid to a landlord instead of rent.

AVENS-ROOT, the root of *Geum urbanum*, which possessing astringent and aromatic properties has been used in medicine, and is also said to impart a pleasant clove-like flavour to wine and beer.

AVENUE, a shady walk or drive between rows of trees.

AVER, a provincial name for a draught or working animal.

AVERAGE, a balance struck, a fair sample; in the corn trade, the official price at which grain is fixed; in marine insurance, the equitable adjustment of the proportion of loss which is sustained by insurers; a general or gross contribution made by different parties towards a loss sustained by some for the benefit of all, as in making good any damage sustained by a ship, in throwing cargo overboard, in a storm, &c. It may be special or particular, and customary or petty average, as expressed in the bill of lading.

AVERAGE-STATER, AVERAGE-TAKER, an officer in a marine insurance office, who computes averages.

AVERRUNCATOR, an instrument for pruning young trees.

AVIADOR, the Spanish name for one who advances money to work a mine, or to carry on mining operations.

AVIARY, an enclosure for keeping and rearing birds, made of wire-netting or wooden frame-work.

AVIGNON-BERRIES, the small yellow dyeing berries of commerce, the produce of the buckthorn, *Rhamnus infectorius*.

AVIRON, the French name for an oar or scull.

AVIS, French, an advertisement.

AVOCADO PEAR, the pulpy fruit of *Persea gratissima*, highly esteemed as a vegetable in the tropics; oil has been made from it.

AVOCAT, a French barrister, or counsellor at-law.

AVOINE, the name for oats in France.

AVOIRDUPOIS, the ponderous commercial weight of England. The avoirdupois pound of 16 oz. contains 7000 grains, and the troy pound of 12 oz., 5760 grains. The avoirdupois pound is to the pound troy as 175 to 144.

AVOS, a monetary division of the Java rupee, 100 going to the rupee of two shillings.

AVOUE, a French attorney or solicitor.

AWA, an Indian potter's kiln or furnace.

AWAK, the Hindoo name for insurance, or for a speculative advance made on a shipment of goods.

AWARD, the decision given by an arbitrator; the amount of salvage or other sum granted by a competent court.

AWL, a shoemaker's and saddler's piercing tool.

AWL-TREE, the *Morinda citrifolia*, or Indian mulberry, the roots of which are used for dyeing.

AWNDIERNS, usually spelt andirons; dogs, rests, or supports of iron for logs of wood, on a fire hearth.

AWNING, a canvas canopy or covering fixed to keep off the sun in boats or ships.

AWTY, a preparation of food among the natives of the Pacific Islands.

AXAYACAT, a Spanish name for the eggs of a species of fly deposited on rush mats, and sold as a caviare in Mexico.

AXE, a sharp-edged cutting instrument used by carpenters, &c.

AXE-STONE, a name for jade, a species of serpentine, of which the Pacific islanders make hatchets.

AXINITE, a mineral susceptible of a high polish, but scarcely brilliant enough for an ornamental stone.

AXLE, AXLE-TREE, the bar which supports the wheels of carriages, usually made of iron.

AXMINSTER CARPET, an imitation Turkey carpet, noted for its thick and soft pile; the worsted being thrown entirely to the surface, instead of appearing on both sides. These carpets are woven in one piece.

AXONGE, French, hog's lard.

AYACUT, the reputed measurement of land in India when ready for cultivation.

AYAH, a lady's maid or nurse in India.

AYAM, the Malay name for fowls.

AYMINATE, a superficial measure used in Perpignan, equal to nearly 1½ English acre.

AYNET, French, a skewer.

AYUSTONE. *See* SNAKESTONE.

AYVAZ, a scullion who attends at meals in Turkey, usually an Armenian.

AZABARA, the Spanish name for the common aloe, from the leaves of which fibre is made.

AZABRA, a small Spanish coasting vessel.

AZAFRAN, the Spanish name for saffron.

AZARIA, a kind of coral. [Spain.

AZARJA, an instrument for winding silk in

AZBE, a black silk Turkish head-dress.

AZEN, a subdivision of the Netherlands troy engel, 32 azens making one engel, and 20 engels one English ounce.

AZIMUTH, a nautical instrument for finding the sun's magnetical azimuth.

AZOGUE, the Spanish name for quicksilver; also a market-place.

AZUA, a beverage made of Indian corn.

AZULEJO, the Spanish name for Dutch glazed tiles painted blue.

AZUMBRE, a liquid measure in Spain, the eighth part of the arroba, ranging in different localities from 3½ to 5 pints.

AZURE, a pale but clear and brilliant blue colour; a name for ultramarine, formerly made from lapis lazuli, but now artificially compounded.

AZURE SPAR, a variety of lazulite or blue spar.

AZURITE, blue carbonate of copper, a valuable ore found in various localities at home and abroad.

AZYME, French, unleavened bread.

B

BAARD, a kind of transport-ship.

BAAT, a money of Siam. *See* BAT.

BAAZAS, a sort of guitar.

BABBACHIRE, an Indian cook, often written Bawurchee.

BABEURRE, French, buttermilk.

BABI, the Malay name for a pig.

BABOO, a title of respect given to a merchant, head-clerk, or superior person in India.

BABOOL, BABULA, the Indian name for the *Acacia Arabica*, which furnishes a useful common gum, of properties similar but inferior to that of the *Acacia vera*.

The bark is a powerful astringent, and the rind of the fruit is used by calico printers for dyeing brown.

BABOUCHE, a Turkish slipper.

BABY-JUMPER, a suspensory hoop or framework with elastic cords, sometimes fitted to a frock or dress, to place a young child in to keep it on its legs.

BAC, the French name for a ferry-boat; a large tub.

BACALIAU, BACCALLAO, the French and Spanish names for stockfish, salted ling or cod.

BACASSAS, a kind of French lighter.

BACCILE. *See* BACILE.

BACHANG, a Malay name for the horse-mango; a coarse variety of the fruit.

BACHE, the French name for a wherry, and for the tilt of a cart.

BACHEL, a corn measure in the Morea, the third part of the staro, and equal to about 6¼ gallons.

BACHOTEUR, a French boatman, one who plies a wherry.

BACHOU, the name for a bucket or pail in France.

BACILE, a dry measure in the Ionian islands, about 1⅜ imperial bushel; also a land measure there of ⅛ of an English acre, generally called a misura.

BACINO, a dry measure in Corsica, the twelfth part of a stajo, and equal to 2⅝ imperial gallons.

BACK, a large vat or cask used in breweries and distilleries to hold beer, spirits, or water, of from 300 to 500 gallons' capacity. They have been made so large as to hold 1200 barrels. In many breweries a back is simply a very large flat tub used to cool wort.

BACK AND VAT MAKER, a cooper who makes large flat tubs and casks.

BACKGAMMON-BOARD, a board or table with two divisions or folding leaves to hold the men, dice and boxes, used for playing the game of backgammon on certain black and white spaces called points. It is generally made to imitate the exterior of a bound book.

BACKING, in bookbinding, preparing the back of a book by gluing &c., for receiving the cover or case.

BACK-RAG, a Dutch wine.

BACK RENT, rent paid by a farmer after harvest time.

BACKS, the thickest and stoutest tanned hides, used chiefly for sole leathers.

BACKSHEE, BACKSHEESH, an eastern term for a gratuity, fee, or present.

BACKWARDATION, a stock-exchange term for an allowance made for carrying over stock, shares, &c., to the next account-day, instead of settling or delivering at once.

BACK-WASHED, a manufacturer's term for wool cleansed from the oil after combing.

BACK-WATER, a stream of water employed to scour out harbours, and prevent the accumulation of sand or shingle; also a nautical term for reversing the forward motion of a boat.

BACK-WOODSMAN, a settler in the uncleared districts of North America.

BACON, the cured and smoked flesh of the hog, forming a large article of commerce. Ireland and the United States are the countries where the trade in bacon is most largely carried on. Sometimes, when intended for home use, bacon is simply salted and dried green instead of smoked.

BACON-DRIER, one who cures pork, and smokes it for bacon.

BADANA, the Spanish name for a dressed sheep's skin.

BADDAM, a species of bitter almond imported into some parts of India from Persia, and used as money, the general value being about 60 baddams per pic, and worth about one farthing. The baddam is sometimes called badan.

BADDERLOCKS, a common name for the *Alaria esculenta*, a nutritious sea-weed sometimes used as food.

BADEN RUBBERS, coarse rough towels and gloves, used for drying the skin after bathing.

BADERNE, a kind of cable or rope on the continent.

BADGER, a carnivorous quadruped (*Meles vulgaris*) whose hair is made into shaving brushes and brushes for painters; the skin dressed with the hair on is sometimes used for trunks, and the hide makes good pistol furniture. In several countries the flesh of the animal cured as hams or bacon is esteemed a delicacy; a ticket porter, one entitled to wear a badge; a licensed carrier; one who buys corn or victuals for itinerating sale.

BADIAGA, a small sponge.

BADIAN, an Indian name for star-anise (*Illicium anisatum*). The aromatic capsules constitute an important article of commerce in the East, and are sold in all the native bazaars; they are also imported into this country.

BADIGEON, the French name for whitewash, gypsum, or plaster of Paris; also a composition of saw-dust and glue, used by joiners to fill up chinks in wood; a colouring substance or thick mortar for hiding defects in stone work.

BADLA, an Indian name for gold and silver thread.

BADSTUB, a commercial term in Russia for the refuse of the rakitzer flax.

BADULAM, a name in Ceylon for the *Ardisia humilis*, a small shrub, the fruit of which is used medicinally.

BAEE, a garden in Assam where the cultivation of tea is carried on.

BAEL, BEL, a name for the Indian quince-tree (*Ægle Marmelos*). The preserved fruit imported from the East, is valued as a medicine for its mild sub-astringent properties.

BAETAS, a plain unchecked woollen stuff, manufactured in Spain and Portugal.

BAFT, a blue or white cotton used in the African trade. Baftas are also a kind of Indian cotton piece goods.

BAG, a canvas sack or enclosed wrapper intended to contain grain or any other description of dry merchandise. There is no certain defined quantity that a bag shall commercially hold, the weight necessarily varying with the contents, which range from 1½ to 2½ cwt. *See* BALE, and SACK.

BAGA, the Spanish name for a little head of flax with its seed.

BAGATELLE-BOARD, a cloth-covered board pierced with nine holes, for playing a game, with a set of ivory balls.

BAGATTINO, a small copper coin of Venice; the half of a soldi, about one farthing.

BAGAZO, the marc or refuse of grapes, sugar-canes, &c., after they have been pressed.

BAGEDIA, in Spain a pound of twelve ounces.

BAGGAGE, the wearing apparel and personal effects of a passenger, contra-distinguished from merchandise; heavy travelling luggage—hence baggage-waggons and baggage-trains are for the conveyance of weighty goods.

BAGGAGE-WAREHOUSE, a special department of the Customs at the docks, where baggage may be left, or is taken to be examined and cleared.

BAGGING, a coarse kind of stuff made of hemp, old ropes, &c., for covering bales of cotton or other merchandise. In the United States about 80,000 bales of Indian bagging are required yearly to wrap the cotton crop in for shipment. *See* GUNNY BAGS.

BAGNIO, a bathing-house, a brothel.

BAGPIPE, a musical instrument peculiar to Scotland, consisting of a leathern bag, with three pipes, blown by the mouth and inflated by compression of the arm.

BAGRE, a delicious fish of the American seas and rivers.

BAGUALES, a Spanish name for wild horses in South America.

BAHAMAS SPONGE, a coarse kind of sponge fished up about the Bahamas islands, used for common purposes. *See* SPONGE.

BAHAR, a heavy eastern measure of weight, varying considerably in different localities the range being from 223 to 625 lbs. *See* CANDY.

BAHJEERIE, the Singhalese name for the Italian species of millet.

BAHU, a land measure in Java, equal to 7½ acres, also called a Boru.

BAHUT, a leather trunk made in France.

BAIES, the French name for berries.

BAIGNEUR, French, a bath keeper.

BAIL, one who stands bondsman or security for the appearance of another in a court of law under certain penalties.

BAILA, the Spanish name for sea-trout.

BAILIE, the magistrate of a Scotch burgh.

BAILIFF, a sheriff's officer, to whom is deputed the duty of arrest for debt; also a superior farm servant, the understeward of a manor.

BAILIWICK, the district or boundary within which a bailiff or his deputy exercises jurisdiction.

BAILLE, an old coal measure used in Rochelle, the 80th part of a muid, and equal to rather more than two bushels.

BAILLEUR-DE-FONDS, a French money lender.

BAILLIQUE, the French name for ostrich feathers.

BAILMENT, a legal term for goods delivered in trust to be taken care of.

BAILS, hoops to support a tilt hammer.

BAIOCCO, a Venetian money. *See* BAJOCCO.

BAIR, the Indian name for the egg plum, the fruit of *Ziryphus jujuba*, which are highly esteemed by the natives in India, not only when green and ripe, but also when dried and preserved in various ways.

BAIT, food for a horse, hence the term "livery and bait stables;" a lure placed on a hook to entice fish. The mackerel fisher cuts a shining strip of the skin from one of the fish to bait his hook. Capelin and squids are used as bait in the cod fishery. White-bait is a small esteemed fish, the *Clupea alba*, caught in the Thames.

BAIT-MILL, a machine used by the American fishermen for cutting mackerel or salted herrings into small pieces for bait. It consists of an oblong wooden box, standing on one end, containing a roller armed with knives, which is turned by a crank on the outside.

BAIZE, a coarse kind of flannel, an open woollen fabric with a long nap, chiefly used as a covering or wrapping material.

BAIZE-MANUFACTURER, a maker of coarse woollen or of painted canvas, &c.

BAIZE-PAINTER, a decorator, one who figures and ornaments canvas and baize for table covers and other purposes.

BAJA, the Malay name for steel.

BAJAH, the name for a plough, also for manure in the East.

BAJJA, the Hindustani name for a band of music.

BAJOCA, the Spanish name for green kidney beans.

BAJOCCO, a base copper coin of five quatrins, current in the Papal States; worth about three farthings. It is frequently written bayoque.

BAJOCHELLO, BAJOCCELL, a base silver coin at Rome of two to four bajocchi.

BAJOGLER, a name for the ducat in Persia.

BAJOW-LAUT, a name in the East for men who prowl about the shores and islets of the Eastern Archipelago, and are called sea gipsies.

BAJREE, an Indian name for the spiked millet, the grain of *Penicillaria spicata*, a common food of the poorer class of natives, which yields a sweet palatable flour, and is excellent for fattening poultry.

BAKEHOUSE, a place with an oven, where baking is conducted for the convenience of the public.

BAKER, a bread-maker, one who takes in joints and other food for baking.

BAKERS' PEEL-MAKER, a workman who makes the long wooden slides on which loaves are placed to be put in or removed from the oven.

BAKING-PAN, an earthenware or tinned dish used for baking.

BAKKUL, the fibrous bark of the roots of certain trees which is used in Malwa and other parts of India as a cheap substitute for string and cord.

BAKUL, the Malay name for a basket.

BAL, a name in Cornwall for a mine.

BALACHONG, a preparation in the Eastern seas, consisting of small fish with prawns and shrimps, first fermented and then dried. This article gives rise to a considerable traffic, as no vegetable food is deemed palatable without it, and its use extends to every country from China to Bengal.

BALAGAR, in Spain, long straw or hay preserved as winter fodder.

BALAGUERO, a hay-rick or pile of straw stored for fodder in Spain.

BALANCE, a well-known instrument for weighing commodities, of which there are many kinds, as the beam and scales, the steelyard, the weighing machine, &c.; but the term is chiefly applied to a very accurate scale used for chemical analysis, and for the precious metals. The term is also applied to the difference between a debtor and creditor account.

BALANCE-BOOK, a book in which the adjusted accounts of debtors and creditors have been posted from the ledger.

BALANCE-GATE, a species of flood-gate used in Holland.

BALANCE, HYDROSTATIC, an instrument for determining the specific gravity of bodies.

BALANCE OF TRADE, the difference in the money value of the produce or manufactures received and exported. If we receive more than we transmit, we have to make up the balance in specie shipments, which tells adversely against the trade interests of the country.

BALANCE-SHEET, a statement of a trader's position or pecuniary affairs, showing the balances of property and debts, profits and losses.

BALANCE-WHEEL, part of a watch or chronometer.

BALANCIA, the Spanish name for the water melon, and for a kind of white grape.

BALANCING BOOKS, in commercial parlance the closing or adjusting of each personal or general account in the ledger, and clearing up a trader's or banker's books.

BALANDRAN, a loose surtout worn by Spanish priests; also a large coarse cloak used in France.

BALANDRE, a small kind of sea vessel.

BALANZA, a Spanish fishing net.

BALANZON, a copper pan used by silversmiths in Spain.

BALAOU, the Spanish name for a kind of sprat.

BALAS RUBY, a lapidary's term for the rose-red varieties of spinel.

BALASSE, the French name for what in England is termed a paillasse, a mattress stuffed with straw, moss, or chaff.

BALAZEE, a sort of cotton.

BALCONY, a projecting walk on the first floor of a house; a raised gallery in a room, &c.

BALDACHIN, BALDAQUIN, the fringed canopy covering a Roman Catholic altar; a French name for a tent-bed.

BALDE, an oil measure of Lisbon, the tenth part of a pipe; also a dry or coal measure equal to 12·70 bushels.

BALDES, BALDRES, the Spanish term for a piece of dressed skin.

BALE, a package of merchandise of variable dimensions; the most extensive articles of commerce received in bales being cotton and wool. *Bales of Cotton* vary in weight from year to year in different localities. In 1856, the weight of the bales of cotton, of all descriptions imported, averaged 407 lbs. per package. In 1853 those from America averaged 475 lbs., from the East Indies 383, Brazil, 180. The following was the average weight and measure per bale of the different kinds of cotton received at Liverpool in 1856:—

	Average Weight.	Cubic Measure.
Mobile	404 lbs.	33 feet
New Orleans	454 "	32 "
Upland	390 "	22 "
Sea Island	333 "	35 "
East Indian	383 "	16 "
Egyptian	245 "	27 "
West Indian	212 "	25 "
Brazilian	182 "	17 "

Of *Bales of Wool*, the average weights of Australian range from 2 to 3 cwt.; East Indian and German from 3 to 4 cwt.; Russian 3½ to 4 cwt.; Spanish and Portuguese 1 to 2 cwt.; South American 4½ to 8 cwt.; Goat's wool 1½ to 2 cwt.; Peruvian 56 to 84 lbs.

BALE, a sea term for dipping out water from a boat.

BALEEN. *See* WHALEBONE.

BALEINIER, the French name for a whaler.

BALEINON, a young whale.

BALE LASHINGS, packing cordage usually sold in lengths of 17 fathoms.

BALERANG, the Malay name for sulphur.

BALESTON, a name on the French coasts for the sprit of a lug-sail.

BALIK, a Tartar name for fish, and especially mullet, on the Black-Sea coasts. The red mullet is called khan-balik.

BALIKI, a name for the back pieces of the sturgeon which are salted and smoked in Russia for home use and for export.

BALINE, a kind of coarse canvas for packing.

BALING PAPER, an American name for stout wrapping or packing paper for parcels.

BALISE, BALIZE, a timber frame raised as a landmark, a buoy, or sea-beacon.

BALISIER, the name for an Indian cane on the continent.

BALK, a technical name in the timber trade for logs of squared timber which vary in length from 20 to 90 feet, and from 8 to 30 inches in square.

BALKERS, a name on the fishing coasts of Cornwall, &c., for those who, standing on an elevated point, signalize to the boatmen with the cast-nets the direction the shoals of fish are taking.

BALL, a shot; a round plaything; a printer's inking pad; a signal hoisted on a flag-staff, sometimes in connection with a flag.

BALLAD-SINGER, an itinerant vocalist.

BALLAM, a canoe hollowed out of timber in which men wash out the pearls from the oysters in Ceylon.

BALLAST, shingle, water, stone, pigs of iron, or any heavy material placed in the hold of a ship to steady it in the water. A ship which leaves a port without a cargo is said to be "in ballast." *See* KENTLEDGE.

Ballastage, a toll or charge for taking ballast in a harbour.

Ballast-engine, a steam engine for dredging up shingle in a river, or drawing gravel or earth on a railway.

Ballast-heaver, a ballast porter or river carrier.

Ballasting, a term for gravel, stone, clay, or other material applied to the covering of roads generally, but to the metalling or bottoming of railways in particular.

Ballast-lighter, a barge for conveying ballast on a river, &c.

Ballast-train Guard, a railway official in charge of a train of loaded trucks.

Ballatoons, large heavy luggage boats in Russia, used in the transport of timber from Astracan to Moscow.

Ball-cartridge, the charge for a musket or gun packed in paper or canvas and having a ball at the end, in contradistinction to one containing only powder, termed a blank cartridge.

Ball-cock, a tap with an air ball to shut off the supply when the receiver is full.

Ballet-girl, an opera figure dancer, one who takes part in the ballet at a theatre.

Balliage, a city due paid to the corporation of London on foreign goods.

Ballin, a French provincial term for a package.

Balling Furnace, an oven in which iron is heated to a welding heat.

Ballistic Pendulum, a mechanical contrivance for ascertaining the strength of gunpowder, by computing the velocity of a cannon ball, which is made to strike a revolving or swinging beam.

Ball Leathers, the outer skin-covering of the pads nailed to the ball stocks used by printers for inking type.

Ballon, a very long boat, brigantine-rigged, in Siam, shaped out of a single trunk; also a package of various goods, thus a ballon of paper is 14 reams, of glass 12½ bundles.

Ballone, in Italy, a large bale.

Balloon, a machine made of silk, inflated with coal gas for aërostation.

Ballot, a term in Sweden for ten reams of paper, and in the silk and other trades for a small bale or pack.

Ballot-box, a secret voting box, in which small balls or cards are dropped.

Ballotes, baskets for holding grapes, used during the vintage in France.

Balm, a hardy perennial, the *Melissa officinalis*; at one time invested with extraordinary medicinal virtues, but now only employed as an infusion in preparing an exhilarating drink, or in giving flavor to a weak factitious wine.

Balm of Gilead, the common name in some parts of North America for a species of poplar, the *Populus balsamifera*; also an aromatic resin, or balsam, obtained in the East.

Balon. *See* Balloon.

Balonea, a name for the oak of the South of Europe and Grecian Archipelago, large quantities of the acorn cups of which are shipped to England for tanners' use. *See* Valonea.

Balot, a small bundle or package.

Balsa, a raft or fishing float of skins used principally on the Pacific coasts of South America.

Balsam Apple, the fruit of the *Momordica balsamina*, used medicinally.

Balsam Fir, the *Abies balsamea*, a North American tree from which the Canadian balsam is obtained.

Balsams, semi-fluid, aromatic oleo-resins, of which several enter largely into commerce.

Balsam Weed, an American name for the *Gnaphalium polycephalum*, which possesses some medicinal properties, and has lately been used for the manufacture of paper.

Baltic Oak, the wood of the *Quercus pedunculata*, imported chiefly for ship-building.

Balister, a rail, part of a balustrade. *See* Banister.

Balustrade, the name for balusters or rails fixed under the coping of the parapet of a bridge or balcony, &c.

Baly, a commercial weight in Sumatra equal to 81 lbs. 6 oz. avoirdupois, divided into 10 gantons or 60 catties; also a dry or grain measure in several of the other islands of the Eastern Archipelago, ranging from 1 to 1¼ bushel.

Balzarine, a light mixed material of worsted and cotton, for ladies' dresses.

Bamba, a Singhalese measure, equal to the length of the extended arms from the tips of the fingers, or about six feet.

Bambagello, a Spanish paint.

Bambagino, Italian for calico.

Bamboo, a variable dry measure in Eastern countries, ordinarily about five English pints. An Indian maund of rice of 75 lbs. contains 21 bamboos; in the Moluccas, the bamboo of rice, however, weighs only 1 lb. 10 oz. avoirdupois. As a measure of length the ancient Hindoo bamboo of Akbar was about fourteen yards; in Burmah it is rather more, namely, 14½ yards.

Bamboo-chungah. *See* Chungah.

Bamboo Pandanus, a name for the Agave in the Bengal presidency.

Bamboos, the tall siliceous hollow grasses or canes of the *Bambusa* genus, which are very serviceable for a variety of commercial purposes in the East and West Indies. They are turned to almost every use, for posts and buildings, ladders, masts, water-pipes, pitchers, drinking-cups, or cooking utensils. When split they are made into mats and sails; but there is scarcely a domestic article in China and Asia in which the bamboo is not a whole or component part from the cradle to the coffin.

Bamier, a culinary vegetable in Egypt.

Bammia, a name on the west coast of Africa for a species of *Hibiscus*; for the uses of which *see* Ochro.

Ban, the Spanish name for a kind of fine muslin.

Banana, the fruit of *Musa sapientum*, which when ripe is generally of a sweeter and more luscious character than the plantain. It is an article of large consumption in all tropical countries, either raw, roasted, or fried.

BANASTA, in Spain, a large basket made of twigs or laths.

BANCAL, an Indian weight of about seventeen drachms avoirdupois; also the Spanish name for a thrown or twisted carpet.

BANCALERO, in Spain a carpet manufacturer.

BANCA-TIN, a valuable kind of tin, equal to English refined, obtained in the Eastern Archipelago, originally from the island of Banca exclusively; but much is now procured in Malacca, and sent to Singapore for shipment.

BANCHI, the Malay name for a carpenter's axe.

BANCO, a word used in many States on the Continent as a prefix to paper money, and also for sums inscribed in the books of the bank opposite the names of those who have deposited money or specie there. Banco is worth on an average 23 per cent. more than ordinary currency; but the premium necessarily varies with the nature of the security.

BAND, a tie; a waist-girdle; an ornament; a body of musicians; a weight used on some parts of the coast of Western Africa for weighing gold dust, and equal to about two ounces troy. The word is used in Riga to denote the number of twenty, or half a schock.

BANDAGE, a ligature; a linen roll or other support or protection for the limbs, sold by chemists and instrument makers.

BANDAL, BANDLE, a linear or cloth measure used in the southern and western parts of Ireland, which is rather more than half a yard.

BANDALA, a kind of fibre made in Manila from the hard strong outer layers of the abaca or *Musa textilis*. It is employed in the fabrication of cordage, and furnishes the well-known Manila white rope.

BANDANA, a silk or cotton handkerchief, originally dyed of a bright uniform colour, but with figures or patterns subsequently produced by chemically discharging the colour.

BANDANA-PRINTER, a manufacturer of bandana handkerchiefs.

BANDBOX, a thin box of slight wood papered.

BANDBOX-MAKER, one who manufactures slight boxes for milliners, and others, &c.

BANDEAU, a fillet, wreath, or veil; a lady's ornament for the head.

BANDER, the vintage season in France.

BANDEGE, the French name for a round metal tea-tray or waiter; in Spanish it is bandeja.

BANDERA-BAMBA, a Singhalese long measure of about nine feet, estimated by the height a man can reach above his head with his hand.

BANDHERA, the Nepaulese name for a species of large wild sheep, *Ovis Ammonoides*, found on the Himmalayas.

BANDICOOT, a marsupial animal (*Perameles nasuta*) which bears a great resemblance to a large overgrown rat, and is an equal depredator upon farm-yards and granaries in India. Its flesh is eaten in Australia.

BANDIES, a clumsy description of gig or buggy, used in the Madras presidency.

BANDIKAI, a name in the Madras presidency for the *Hibiscus esculentus*, the okhro of the West Indies, the fruit of which is an esteemed esculent vegetable, and the fibre makes a tough cordage.

BANDITORE, a common crier in Italy.

BANDLE. *See* BANDAL.

BANDMASTER, the leader of a military band.

BANDOLIER, a wooden cartridge-box, or case carried to hold the charges of powder.

BANDOLINE, a kind of stick pomatum, or gummy fixature for keeping the hair smooth.

BANDORE, an ancient stringed instrument resembling a lute.

BANDSMAN, a musician, one who plays in a band.

BANDSTRING TWIST, small lashing done up in papers of about two dozen knots each. The knot is by established practice 32 yards.

BANDUJO, a large Spanish sausage.

BANDY, a bullock cart in the East.

BANGHY, a bamboo pole carried over the shoulder by an Indian porter, for slinging baskets or boxes on.

BANGHY-WALLAH, an Indian porter, who carries the baggage of a dawk or palankin traveller; he is usually the bearer of two light boxes, swung on a pole borne over the shoulder.

BANGLES, anklets and bracelets made of shell, glass, gold, &c., which are often richly ornamented with precious stones, and are much used in India. *See* CHANKS

BANGRA, a species of hempen cloth made in Nepaul from the fibre of a gigantic stinging nettle; being hard and stiff it is not suited for cordage and nets.

BANISTER, the handrail of a staircase, a corruption of baluster.

BANISTER-BRUSH, a domestic sweeping brush for the stairs.

BANJERCE, a kind of perfumed oil in the East Indies.

BANJO, a negro's stringed instrument.

BANK-BOOK, the book given out from a bank to a depositor, to contain a debtor and creditor statement of his account.

BANK CLERK, an assistant officer employed in a banking-house.

BANK DIRECTOR, a shareholder appointed one of a committee of management to conduct the affairs of a bank.

BANKER, a dealer in money; one who is entrusted with the care of the funds of others; also the name for a vessel employed on the Newfoundland banks in cod fishing. Those fitted out from Nova Scotia are of from 20 to 50 tons; those from the American ports and Newfoundland are larger.

BANK-FISHERY, the cod fishery on the Banks of Newfoundland.

BANK-HOURS, the time within which money is paid or received at a banking-house, usually between ten and four.

BANK-NOTE, a promissory note for money to be paid on demand by a Banking company. In England bank notes under £5 are not allowed to be issued; but in Scotland £1 notes are still circulated, and in many of the West India colonies dollar notes are issued, while even smaller notes are circulated on the Continent. The aggregate amount of bank-notes in circulation in the United Kingdom, at one time, ranges from £32,000,000 to £42,000,000, more than *half* of which are those issued by the Bank of England, and this great establishment issues nine classes of notes ranging from £5 up to £1000. About 30,000 notes are printed every day at the Bank, and 9,000,000 issued per annum, representing nearly £300,000,000 of money. The notes are never re-issued from the Bank of England, but are cancelled as fast as they are presented for payment.

BANK-PORTER, a messenger employed in a banking-house.

BANK POST, a large kind of letter-paper, ranging in weight from 5½ to 10 lbs. the ream.

BANK-POST-BILL, an order or cheque given by a banker for money deposited with him, forming a safe and convenient mode of transmitting money from one part of the kingdom to another, or for persons travelling on the Continent.

BANK-PROPRIETOR, the holder of shares or stock in a bank.

BANKRUPT, a trader who is unable to meet his pecuniary engagements, or to pay his creditors their claims in full.

BANKRUPTCY-COMMISSIONER, an official appointed to investigate and adjudicate upon the affairs of bankrupt traders.

BANKRUPTCY COURT, the official place where bankrupts are examined, and their assets collected and distributed.

BANKS, establishments for lodging money, and for the convenient transaction of monetary operations. They are of two classes, private and joint-stock. A private bank has not more than six partners; a joint-stock may have many hundreds. The capital of one is fluctuating, of the other permanent. The joint-stock bank's affairs are governed by a board of directors meeting periodically; those of the private bank by its partners. The condition and prosperity of the private bank are less known than those of the joint-stock bank, whose dividends are publicly announced, and the market price of its shares, which are transferable, affords a fair indication of the character it holds, and the security it offers for investment. In 1855 there were 1100 banks in the United Kingdom, of which 580 were joint-stock banks. In London there were in the same year fifty-nine private banks, and twenty-three joint-stock-banks. Banks is also a local name for a large pottery manufactory.

BANK-STOCK, the paid-up capital of any bank, but chiefly applied to the corporate stock of the Bank of England, a marketable security, maintaining a high premium. The stock of other joint-stock-banks is usually divided into shares.

BANNE, the French name for a tilt or awning spread over a boat.

BANNER, a standard or emblematic device carried by hand.

BANNETTE, a French commercial term for a certain number of hides.

BANNOCK, the Scotch name for a cake of oat or other meal baked upon a girdle over the fire.

BANQUEROUTIER, the French term for a bankrupt or insolvent trader.

BANQUETTE in road-making a raised footway or protecting mound of earth at the side of a sloping bank.

BANQUIER, the name applied on the Continent to a merchant, banker, or one who deals in bills of exchange, &c.

BANQUOIS, a name in the Mauritius for the *Pandanus vacua* or screw pine, the leaves of which are much used for making sacks for holding coffee, sugar, and grain.

BANS, BANSH, an Indian name for the bamboo.

BANSE, a large square basket used in France.

BANS-KEORA, one of the names in the Bengal presidency for the Agave, which is also known as the Bamboo pandanus.

BANTAM, a small kind of fowl.

BANTAM-WORK, gaudily varnished japanned work.

BANTA, a local name for black ebony in British Guiana.

BANYAN, a name for the *Ficus Indica*; also a Hindoo merchant or trader, a confidential cashier and broker for a mercantile firm.

BAR, in navigation, an obstruction at the entrance of a harbour or river. Sometimes in bar-harbours vessels have to wait for the rise of the tide before they can enter or quit the port; the place in an inn or steamer railed off by a counter, where liquors, &c. are vended to customers; hence the attendants are called bar-man and bar-maid, &c.; a bolt or protection for a door or shutter; an arbitrary commercial *term* and monetary standard of value on the West coast of Africa, forming a capricious medium of exchange. Certain goods are said to be equal to a bar in different localities; but the trade value of the bar varies from about half a dollar, in Sierra Leone, to 3d. in Old Calabar. Bar is also a French name for the millier, equal to 9 tons, 16 cwt., 3 qrs. 12 lbs.

BARACHIERE, Italian, a sutler.

BARADURA, in Spanish, the stranding of a vessel.

BARAL, an ancient liquid measure used in some parts of France, ranging from 5½ to 11¼ gallons, according to the locality and fluid measured.

BARANGAY, an Indian vessel propelled by oars.

BARAQUE, the name for a small shop in France.

BARAROOPA, a class of men in India who, from their dexterity in disguising themselves, are employed as spies.

BARAUMER (Hindustani), a cloak.

BARB, an Arab horse; part of a fish-hook.

BARBACUE, BARBECUE, a paved or cemented platform, on which the coffee beans or berries are exposed to the sun to dry for a week or ten days, and taken in or covered over at night.

BARBADOS-TAR, a species of petroleum or bituminous oil, obtained in Barbados, which possesses some medicinal properties, as an external and internal application.

Barba Hispanica, a name for the horse-hair-like fibres obtained about the Mississippi, from an epiphyte, *Tillandsia usneoides*, which, under the commercial name of Spanish moss, is largely used in America for stuffing cushions, mattresses, &c. *See* Moss.

Barber, one who shaves the beard and cuts and trims hair, from the Latin *barba*, a beard or tuft of hair.

Barbers' Company, one of the livery companies of London, whose common hall is in Monkwell-street. The barbers and surgeons were incorporated by the statute of 32 Henry VIII., cap. 42, whereby it was enacted that no barber should keep a shop within London unless free of the company.

Barbone, a silver coin used in Lucca, containing 12 soldi, and of the value of about 4*d*.

Barbotine, an East Indian vegetable product, the chief constituents of which are wax, gum, and bitter extract; also a name for worm-seed. *See* Worm-seed.

Barca, a Portuguese two-masted vessel.

Barcaza, a large Spanish barge, or ferry-boat.

Barcel, a kind of gun used on board some French ships.

Barcella, an incense censer; a kind of wine. *See* Barchilla.

Barcigo, in Spain, dry bass or strips of bark for making mats, ropes, &c.

Barchent, the German name for fustian.

Barchet, a term used in Germany for a piece of stuff of 22 to 24 ells. The barchet is the 45th part of the fardel.

Barchilla, a corn measure of Spain, ranging from 2½ to 4½ gallons. It is the twelfth of a Cahiz. *See* Cahiz.

Barcon, a Mediterranean luggage boat.

Bar-copper, copper of a high percentage, but unrefined.

Bardaquexa, the Spanish name for the agnus castus seed.

Barde, the French name for a long saddle for a mule, bardelle being a quilted or canvas saddle for breaking young colts.

Bardeau, the French name for a shingle or sort of wooden tiling.

Bardella, Italian, a pack-saddle.

Bardeur, a hodman, a mason's day labourer in France, one who carries a hand-barrow.

Bardiglio, Bardella, a deep blue Sicilian [marble.

Barege, a thin material used for ladies' dresses, commonly made of cotton and wool, but the best are chiefly of silk.

Bare-pump, a suction pump for drawing liquors from a cask.

Bargain, an acknowledged agreement or verbal contract, a sale or purchase.

Bargain-men, labourers who perform piece-work in the collieries at an agreed or contract price.

Barge, a flat-bottomed boat, of which there are several kinds; they are mostly used on navigable rivers, for transferring coal, sand, grain, &c., from ships to wharves, or from one quay to another; a double-banked row-boat used by commanding officers of the navy.

Barge-board, a facing to conceal laths, [tiles, &c.

Barge-builder, one who constructs strong shallow river boats.

Bargeman, a river boatman employed in poling or guiding a barge.

Barge-master, the leading boatman or owner of a barge.

Barile, Barrile, a Sicilian and Italian cask as a liquid measure, varying, in different localities, from about 7 to 16 imperial gallons. In Malta the wine barrile is equal to 9¼ imperial gallons; in the oil barrile there is half a gallon less. At Ancona the barrile is 11·340; at Corsica, 34·985 gallons; at Cerigo for oil, 14·0298; at Florence, 10·038, and for wine, 12·0422; at Genoa, 19·096 for wine, and 17·083 for oil. At Leghorn, 12·041 for wine, and 11 gallons for spirits; at Naples the barile is 11·573; at Palermo, 9·436; at Rome, 12·412 for wine, and 15·183 for oil. In Sardinia the barile contains 8·870 galls. The barile of salt, in Cephalonia, usually weighs 63·244 lbs., and of fish in Leghorn, 74·850 lbs. In Trieste the Austrian barile is 14¾ imperial gallons.

Barilet, a little cask.

Barilla, an alkali of commerce obtained by the combustion of sea-weeds. British barilla is the crude soda-ash left from common salt in the carbonate of soda manufactories; a Spanish name for copper-ore in dust.

Barillo, an inferior sort of Spanish silk.

Bar-iron, iron shaped into bars, and fitted for all sorts of iron work. Railway bars form a large article of home consumption and export.

Barium, a silver-white metal, the base of the earth barytes.

Bark, Barque, a square sterned ship with three masts, without a mizen topsail.

Barkary, a house for keeping bark in at a tan-yard.

Bark-bed, a layer of spent bark used in a stove or hothouse for forcing plants.

Bark-canoe, a light Indian skiff shaped from the bark of a tree. *See* Wood-skin.

Barkers, touters employed at mock auctions to induce purchasers to enter the sale-room; a provincial term in Devonshire for a rubber or whet-stone.

Barking, a technical name for coloring or tanning sails, nets, cordage, &c.; also for stripping trees of their bark for the use of tanners.

Barking Irons, instruments used to peel the bark from trees.

Bark-mill, a mill for crushing bark for tanners' and dyers' use.

Barks, the outer covering of trees, many of which enter largely into commerce for various economical and manufacturing purposes. Some are used by tanners and dyers, others for their medicinal properties, and many for their fibre.

Bark-stove, a hothouse containing a bed of tan or bark for forcing plants.

Barilettajo, Italian, a cooper.

Barley, a common grain, the genus *Hordeum*, of which there are many cultivated varieties used for human food, for cattle-feeding, and especially for malting. Barley is valuable for culinary purposes, especially for thickening broths, soups, and puddings, after it has undergone the process of pearling. This is done by machinery, which removes the husk for pot, and a portion of the outside or the kernel for pearl, barley; leaving the remainder smooth and round like shot. The average yield of barley is about 40 bushels to the acre, and the weight 50 lbs. per bushel.

BARLEY-AVELER, BARLEY-AWNER, BARLEY-HUMMELER, various names for machines for taking off the haums, awns, or avels from barley, leaving the kernels clean and the sample perfect. It consists of parallel iron plates fixed to a frame, and is sometimes used by a labourer on the barn-floor to separate the awns of barley from the grain.

BARLEY-CHUMPER, a rolling machine for breaking the beard from the grain.

BARLEYCORN, the ancient rude unit of English long measure—the third part of an inch; three grains of wheat plucked from the middle of the ear, laid end to end, being considered equal to an inch.

BARLEY MEAL, the flour of barley, which, in the northern parts of the kingdom, is used extensively in making bread; in other districts, for feeding domestic cattle and poultry.

BARLEY-MILL, a mill for preparing barley for various domestic uses.

BARLEY-MOW, a rick or stack of barley in the straw.

BARLEY, PEARLED. *See* BARLEY.

BARLEY SUGAR, a sweetmeat consisting of sugar boiled until it becomes brittle, and run into lumps or sticks. It was at one time boiled with a decoction of barley; whence the name.

BARLEY-WATER, a mucilaginous drink for invalids made by boiling pearled barley.

BARM, a common name for yeast, the creamy froth of beer.

BAR-MAID, a female attendant at a tavern, beer shop, or spirit store.

BARMASTER, BARGHMASTER, a comptroller of mines.

BARMILLIANS, an old trade-name for a kind of fustian, exported in pieces of about thirty yards.

BARMOTE, BAR-MOOT, BARGHMOTE, a court held occasionally to carry out certain inspections and privileges connected with mines. Thus a barmote may be called "for the soke and wapentake of Wirkworth, &c.," old words signifying the district and hundred, &c., over which the privilege extends. To these motes or meetings there belong a barmaster and a deputy-barmaster.

BARN, a farm building used for a storehouse or granary.

BARNACLES, a twitching instrument used by farriers, &c., to hold horses by the nose that are troublesome; a name given to the cirripedes (*Balanus*) which are often found adhering to logs of wood in sea water, and to ships' bottoms. Some large kinds as *B. psittacus*, form a common and highly esteemed food on the Chilian coasts of South America. Another small mollusc, which bores into timber in salt water, is the sea worm, *Teredo navalis*.

BARN-BAY, the threshing-floor of a barn.

BARN-GALLON, a double gallon of milk.

BARNIZ, the resin of the juniper-tree; a common Spanish name for varnish in general, and for paint and printing-ink.

BAROCCIAJO, (Italian) a carter.

BAROGRAPH, a French instrument for registering barometrical variations.

BAROLITE, a carbonate of barytes.

BAROMETER, a pneumatic instrument for measuring the weight of the atmosphere or, of its pressure on the surface of the globe, and thus indicating the state of the weather.

BAROMETER-MAKER, a meteorological instrument maker.

BARONY, an ancient Saxon land measure, which, according to Dugdale, contained 40 hides of land, equivalent to 4840 acres.

BAROO, an Indian name for roots.

BAROONEE, a large cloak with sleeves, worn by the Turks and Persians, to protect the person from rain.

BAROSCOPE, an instrument for testing the weight of the atmosphere.

BAROTIER, a carter or driver of a vehicle in France

BAROTTI, a weight in the Molucca islands of 11 lb. 15 oz. avoirdupois; a grape basket used in France.

BAROUCHE, an uncovered pleasure carriage.

BARQUE, a three-masted vessel, which differs from one ship-rigged in carrying no square sails on her mizen-mast.

BARQUEROLLE, the name in France for a fleet of small boats without masts.

BARQUILLO, a Spanish cock-boat; also a candle mould, and a measure. *See* BARCHILLA.

BARRA, the Spanish term for a share in a mine.

BARRAGAN, a coarse camlet of wool or mixed material.

BARRACARA, a name in Demerara for the *Erythrina Corallodendron*, a hard, close, and even-grained wood. The red seeds are used for ornamental purposes.

BARRACK, a building for lodging soldiers or workmen.

BARRACK-MASTER, the resident superintending officer of a barrack.

BARRACOON, a slave warehouse or enclosed fort on the west coast of Africa.

BARRACOUTA, a broad fleshy fish of the tropics (*Sphyræna barracuda*); the sea pike.

BARRAGE, BARREGE, a linen interwoven with worsted flowers in Normandy.

BARRAGE, turnpike money; a passage toll paid in France.

BARRAL, the Spanish name for a large bottle capable of holding an arroba or four gallons.

BARRAS, BARROS, a cloth measure of Spain and Portugal, ranging from 72 to 94½ Paris ells. Barras is also a kind of resin or gum met with in French commerce.

BARRATRY, any intentional act, on the part of mariners, for defrauding the owner or insurer of a ship, such as feloniously making away with property, or purposely injuring the cargo or vessel.

BARRATTEES, a kind of plain silk.

Barrel, a cask forming a measure of capacity for sundry dry goods and liquids, &c.; a barrel of flour being 196 lbs. avoirdupois; of potatoes, about 200 lbs.; of soap about 256 lbs.; of butter, 224 lbs.; of gunpowder, 1 cwt.; of candles, 120 lbs.; of anchovies, 16 to 30 lbs.; of pilchards, 41½ imperial gallons; of herrings, 26⅔ ditto. A barrel of tin for export weighs from 2 to 4 cwt., or about the 6th of a ton. The beer barrel is 36 gallons, or 2 kilderkins. In Ireland the barrel of culm is 24 cwt., of wheat, pease, beans, and rye, 20 stone, each 14 lbs. The barrel of barley, bere, or rape-seed, 16 stone; the barrel of oats generally 14 stone, and of malt, 12 stone. The barrel for liquids in the United States, is 31·5 wine gallons; the barrel for corn, 5 Winchester bushels; for salted provisions, 31·9 gallons. The barrel of fish in Maryland weighs 220 lbs.; of wine, 320 lbs. The barrel of Malaga raisins weighs 50·6 lbs; the barrel of honey in the Havana contains 6 gallons.

Barrel *of a pump*, the hollow cylinder in which the piston moves.

Barrel *of a wheel*, the cylindrical axle round which the rope travels.

Barrel-bulk, in shipping phraseology, a measure of capacity for freight, equal to 5 cubic feet; 8 barrels bulk, or 40 cubic feet making one ton of measurement.

Barrel-drain. *See* Culvert.

Barrel-organ, a hand-organ, much used by itinerant musicians, and playing popular tunes.

Barrenero, a Spanish mining name for a boy who attends with boring tools.

Barretero, one who works with a pick or crow-bar in the Spanish mines.

Barrilejo, the Spanish name for a runlet.

Barrillet, the small cylinder of a watch, about which the spring is coiled; the funnel of a sucking pump.

Barriquaut, the French name for a small keg or barrel.

Barrique, a large cask or hogshead employed for liquids, of variable capacity, ranging according to the commodity, in different countries, from 40 to 83 gallons.

Barrister, a counsellor at law, a pleader at the bar.

Barrow, a castrated hog; a tray or light carriage of several kinds, there being hand-barrows for two persons, wheel-barrows, load-barrows for wheeling sacks and porters' barrows or trucks. *See* Wheel-barrow.

Barrow-maker, a manufacturer of hand and wheel barrows.

Bar-shoe, a particular kind of horse shoe, made to protect the tender frog of a horse from injury.

Bar-shot, cannon balls connected by a bar.

Bar-silver, fine silver melted into bars or ingots.

Barsowite, a massive snow-white mineral, resembling scapolite, which with borax fuses into a transparent glass.

Bartavelle, a large red partridge met with in France.

Barter, an exchange of commodities; a rude mode of trade which, since the general diffusion of coined money, and the precious metals, is almost obsolete, except in a few still uncivilized countries.

Baru, a name for the candy, a measure of 20 maunds in Mangalore, which varies from 571 to 580½ lbs.

Baruay, a name for the Bahar, a ponderous weight equal to 482½ lbs. avoirdupois. Some authorities, however, estimate it at from 485½ to 500 lbs.; the latter being the Madras baruay. *See* Candy.

Barus Camphor. In Sumatra the best camphor is obtained in a district called Barus, and hence all good camphor bears that distinguishing local name.

Baruth, an oriental measure for pepper, equal to about half a hundred-weight.

Barutine, a silk manufactured in Persia.

Bar-wood, a red dye-wood, the produce of *Baphia nitida*, imported from Angola and Gaboon in Western Africa.

Baryd, an itinerary measure in Mocha of four farsak or twelve miles.

Barytes, a heavy spar or sulphate, the white varieties of which are ground and made into paint. The nitrates are used for producing a green flame; nearly all the salts are virulent poisons.

Barytone, **Baritone**, a kind of bass viol.

Bas, the French name for hose or stockings.

Basalt, a black and very hard stone used for the assaying of gold and silver.

Basand, a name for tanned sheep-skin in France, used for book-binding.

Basanite, a flinty slate of variable shades of colour, used on the Rhine for building and millstones; when grayish-black, it is called Lydian stone.

Basarago, a small Indian coin.

Bascule Bridge, a kind of lifting bridge.

Basement, the lower part or foundation story of a building; a cellar or room on the ground-floor.

Bases, in chemistry, bodies which, united with acids, form salts; they are organic and inorganic.

Bashee, a money of Persia, worth about 16d. sterling.

Basil, the *Ocymum basilicum*, a favourite pot-herb among French cooks, being used, from its aromatic odour and pungency, to give a further zest to highly seasoned dishes, and for flavouring soups and salads; an aromatic ethereal oil is obtained from the root. Tanned sheep's skin; also the angle at which a cutting tool is ground.

Basilicon, Yellow, an ointment composed of resin, wax, and olive-oil.

Basin, a bowl, of various size and material for containing fluids; a wet dock, or harbour-inclosure for ships; the French name for dimity, a white cotton stuff mostly striped; a powder for cleansing the hair in India, made with ground orange-peel and pea-meal.

Basket, a vessel made of twigs, osiers, or rushes, and used for the stowage or conveyance of merchandise, tools, &c. In the East, all sort of basket-work is made of split cane; baskets are also made of the date palm. In Burmah and Arracan, the basket is the common dry measure for rice, and it weighs from 55½ to 58¼ lbs., according to the season and quality of the rice. In Arracan, 100 bushels, of 12 sens each, are equal to 30 Bengal maunds. The Teng, or large Burmese basket, contains about 2 bushels.

Basket-carriage, a small pony chaise made of basket-work.

Basket-hilt, a protection or cover for the hand on a weapon.

Basket-maker, a weaver of basket rods and rushes into utensils for various economic purposes.

Basket-maker's Company, one of the livery companies of the metropolis.

Basket-rods, bundles of osiers not exceeding 3 feet in circumference. The merchant is at liberty to girth the bundles as close or hard as he can.

Basking Shark, the *Squalus maximus*. From the liver of this species of shark, which is very large, much oil is obtained; a large fish will yield eight barrels.

Basotti, Bassotti, the Italian name for a mess of macaroni.

Bassa-gum. *See* Bassora-gum.

Bass, Bast, a thin strand of bark or rush, used by gardeners for binding or covering plants; also a kind of matting made from the lime or linden tree in Russia, of which millions are used annually for baking and packing purposes, &c. A full-sized Russian bast-mat weighs about five pounds when new and quite dry, is seven feet long and four feet broad, and is made with the rougher and worst strands worked crossways, and the thinner and long strands, lengthways in the mats.

Bassa, a liquid measure of Verona, nearly equal to an imperial gallon.

Basse, a salt-water fish of North America, the *Labrax lineatus*, one to three feet long, having stripes or black bands running the whole length of the fish. The little white basse (*L. pallidus*), a river fish, is best known by its popular name of white perch.

Basset, a name in some of the mining districts for an outcrop of coal or mineral at the surface; an incline upwards; in France a terrier.

Bassette, a small bass viol.

Bassia Butter, a name given to the solid oil from *Bassia butyracea*, sometimes called Galam butter. Another species, *B. latifolia*, furnishes the Mohwa oil of Bengal, and the Shea butter is obtained from *B. Parkii* in Africa.

Bassinet, a child's cradle usually without rockers; in France a small basin or pan.

Bassinoire, a French warming-pan.

Bass Mats, thin layers of bark, used chiefly by gardeners, and for packing furniture, &c. *See* Bass.

Bassoolah, an Indian form of adze for preparing turnery woods.

Bassoon, a musical wind instrument, a bass oboe made of several tubes of wood bound together, whence its name.

Bassora-gum, the produce of several species of acacia in Asia.

Bass-viol, a well-known stringed instrument, larger than the common violin, bringing out the lowest or deepest sound in an instrumental concert.

Bass-wood, a name given to the American lime or linden tree, *Tilia Americana*. The wood is soft, easily worked and is used for the panels of carriage bodies, seats of chairs and the fans of fanning mills. In severe winters, the farmers fell a tree to feed cattle on the twigs and buds, which are glutinous and nutritious.

Bast, rope, cord, and matting made from the bass or linden tree; also a name for the bark or tough fibres of the flax and hemp plants. *See* Bass.

Bastaio, Bastiere, the Italian name for a saddler.

Bastardella, in Italy a copper pan.

Bastard-indigo, a name given in India to *Tephrosia tinctoria*.

Bastards, a product of the manufacture of loaf-sugar.

Bastard-stucco, the last coat of stucco given in plastering, containing a little hair.

Baste, a name in Flanders for Chinese silk.

Basterne, a kind of brougham or carriage for general use, a wheel-carriage drawn by oxen.

Basting, the act of moistening joints roasting at the fire, with butter or gravy.

Basting-ladle, a tin spoon or ladle for basting meat.

Basto, an Italian pack-saddle.

Bastude, a kind of French fishing-net.

Bat, a name for the tical of silver in the East, weighing 236 grains; a club or striking instrument; a builder's term for a broken piece of brick.

Batan, the Spanish name for a fulling-mill.

Batarde, the largest sail of a galley on the French coast.

Batardelle, a square sterned row-galley.

Batatas, a colonial name for the sweet potato (*Batatas edulis*), the camote of the Spanish colonies—which is largely grown in most tropical countries for its tubers.

Batch, the quantity of bread baked at one time.

Batch, Batze, a small base coin, formerly current in Switzerland, and some parts of Germany, worth about three halfpence. *See* Batzen.

Bateau, a long and narrow boat of light draught.

Bateau-a-vapeur, the French name for a steam-boat.

Batel, a Spanish fishing-boat; in Ceylon a lighter.

Batelage, a waterman's fare; batelier being a waterman in French.

Bateleiro, a Portuguese lighterman or waterman.

Batelet, a small French boat.

Bat-fowling, a method of catching birds at night by torches and nets.

Bath, a receptacle for washing the body in, either fixed or portable, and usually made of metal or stone. Also an ancient Hebrew liquid measure equal to 10½ gallons.

Bath-brick, a preparation of calcareous earth, used in cleaning knives, and for polishing purposes.

Bath-can, a tin vessel for holding water in a room.

Bath-chair, a small hand-carriage, with a hood, for invalids.

BATH-CHAPS, the cheeks or face of the hog, cured and smoked.

BATHING MACHINE, a portable shed or room on wheels placed upon the sea-beach for the convenience of bathers.

BATH-KEEPER, the owner of private hot or cold baths, or of a marine bathing establishment.

BATH METAL, an alloy of copper and zinc, in the proportion of nearly equal quantities.

BATH POST, a kind of letter paper.

BATHS, public establishments inland or on the coast appropriated for bathing; there are warm and cold baths, vapor, medicated and swimming baths.

BATH STONE, a volatile limestone used in building, of a soft and absorbent character, which deteriorates greatly by exposure, and is not therefore a durable material.

BATH-TOWELS, a rough and coarse kind of towels of cotton, with a plush or looped linen nap or surface on both sides, used for drying the body.

BATIER, in France a maker and vender of pack-saddles.

BATISSEUR, a person engaged in building operations in France.

BATISTE, the French name for cambric or lawn, the finest kind of linen, named after Batiste, who first made it at Cambray.

BATMAN, an oriental weight; in Bokhara equal to 291 lbs. In Turkey, the great batman is about 157½ lbs.; the lesser only a fourth of the greater. At Aleppo and Smyrna the batman weighs but 17 lbs.; in Persia 6½ and 10½ lbs. respectively. *See* MAUND.

BATS. *See* CRICKET-BAT-MAKER.

BAT'S DUNG, the excrementitious deposit of bats, forming a large article of commerce in the Eastern seas, where it is collected from caves, and used as a valuable fertilizer.

BATSWING BURNER, a particular kind of gas-burner.

BATT, a hat-maker's term for a portion of the skin or bowed materials for a hat.

BATTA, an Indian term for a per-centage, premium, or allowance.

BATTAGE, the operation of threshing corn in France.

BATTEL, a cylindrical dry measure of capacity in the Philippine islands, 18½ inches high and the same in diameter; also a weight there of forty pounds.

BATTEN, in weaving, an instrument for striking the weft home; in building, &c., a piece of pine scantling not exceeding seven inches in breadth, about two and a-half inches thick, and six or more feet in length.

BATTENED-DOWN, a sea term for having the hatches on deck securely closed to prevent danger from shipping seas.

BATTEN-ENDS, pieces of wood less than six feet long.

BATTER, to injure; to bulge out; a building term for the face of a leaning wall; a smooth paste of eggs, flour, and milk.

BATTERING PLUMB-RULE, an instrument for levelling sloping work, in which the sides are specially cut to the necessary batter or incline, instead of being truly parallel to the central line over which the plummet hangs.

BATTER LEVEL. *See* CLINOMETER.

BATTERY, a park of artillery, usually about six guns; also applied to mounted pieces of ordnance in a ship or fort; a combination of glass jars or plates of metal, &c. for electrical purposes.

BATTILANO, an Italian carder of wool.

BATTILORO, a gold beater in Italy.

BATTING, a technical name for beating, opening, and cleaning cotton wool.

BATTING-STAFF, a French laundress's stick for beating linen to cleanse it in water.

BATTLEDORE, a rack; a child's plaything for keeping up a shuttlecock; an implement for striking a tennis-ball.

BATTLEDORE-BARLEY, a name given to the two-rowed sprat barley (*Hordeum disticho-zeocriton*), and the six-rowed sprat (*H. hexasticho-zeocriton*); the first is much esteemed in Germany where it is termed rice-barley. *See* BERE, and BIGG.

BATTORY, a Continental name for a foreign factory.

BATTY, a dry measure in some parts of the Eastern archipelago: used for rice in Mysore, and equal to 120 lbs.

BATU, the Malay name for stone, batu klikir being gravel; batu laut, rock; batu pasir, granite; batu bata, bricks; batu rubin, slabs; batu-marmar, marble.

BATZEN, an alloyed petty silver money of Germany and Switzerland, now obsolete, worth from 1d. to 1½d; there were pieces of 2½, 3, 5, and 10½ batzen.

BATZENDIOLE, a measure of capacity for grain used in some parts of Switzerland, the 16th part of a mass, and equal to 1¼ English pint.

BAU, a Dutch land measure of 500 square yards used in Java; also a superficial measure of Oldenburg, equal to a little more than the third of an acre.

BAUBLE, a gew-gaw, a trifle.

BAUDET, French, a donkey.

BAUDRUCHE, the French name for gold-beaters' skin.

BAUGDORE, a strong cotton halter for holding a horse, used by grooms in India.

BAUGE, a drugget made in France with thread spun upon thick and coarse wool; common mortar of clay and straw.

BAUGEE, a dry measure used in some parts of Bengal for the sale of *grain*; a baugee of paddy weighs about 8 lbs. avoirdupois, and of cleaned rice about 9½ lbs.

BAULK, a long beam of timber. *See* BAWLK.

BAUM (German), a name in North America for the wood marten (*Mustela martis*); its glossy fur is in great request for manufacturing into various articles of ladies' dress; hence the skins form an extensive article of commerce.

BAUSCH, BUSCHT, a German term in the paper trade for 181 sheets of paper.

BAUWERCHEE, an Indian cook.

BAVARY, the name of a peculiar-shaped cloak.

BAVINS, fagots or bundles of brush-wood for fuel.

BAWBEE, a name in Scotland and some of the northern counties for the half-penny.

BAWCHEE SEED, an oil seed, the produce of *Psoralia corylifolia* recently imported in small quantities from India.

BAWLA, matting for thatch made of the leaves of the coco-nut palm in the Pacific islands.

BAWLK, in building, a tye-beam; the squared trunk of a tree.

BAWLO, a name in the Pacific islands for the capsicum.

BAWSIN, leather made from sheep's skin.

BAWURCHEE, an Indian superior cook employed in large establishments. *See* BABBACHEE.

BAY, a horse of a bright-red brown, inclining to a chestnut colour; a curved extension of the sea.

BAYAL, a fine kind of cotton.

BAY BERRIES, the aromatic fruit of *Laurus nobilis*, chiefly imported from the Mediterranean; an American name for the wax myrtle (*Myrica cerifera*); from the vegetable wax attached to the berries candles are made.

BAYETAS, coarse common baize made in Spain.

BAY LEAVES, the leaves of the sweet bay, *Laurus nobilis*, which, having an aromatic stimulant taste, are frequently used in cookery and by confectioners to flavour creams.

BAYNDIR, a name in some parts of the east for the ochro (*Hibiscus esculentus*); of the stalk fibre and paper pulp is made, and the fruit is used as an esculent.

BAYONET, a pointed spear, an offensive weapon made to fix on the barrel of a musket.

BAYOQUE, a copper coin of Rome. *See* BAJOCCO.

BAYOU, a name in North America for a small creek.

BAY RUSH, a plant common in the Bahamas, which furnishes much farina, that can be made into bread.

BAY-SALT, salt made in the salinas or natural ponds by evaporation from sea-water exposed to the sun.

BAY-WINDOW, a curved window projecting outwards, erroneously termed a bow window.

BAY-WOOD, a cheap substitute for mahogany imported from the State of Honduras, and used for desks, shop-counters, coach panels, &c.

BAZAAR, BAZAR, the name for a general market in the East, a collection of various shops or stalls; at home chiefly applied to a fancy repository.

BAZAAR-MAUND, an Indian commercial weight of 82 lbs. 2 oz. and 2 drachms.

BAZAAR-WEIGHT, a commercial distinction applied chiefly to the Indian maund and seer in the Eastern ports, in contradistinction to the factory weight. The factory maund contains 2 qrs. 18 lb. 10⅔ oz.; the bazaar maund, 2 qrs. 26 lb. 3 oz.

BAZARUCHO, a piece of base coin formerly current in Goa for about five French deniers.

BDELLIUM, a gum-resin of which two sorts are described, one Indian, resembling myrrh, produced by *Balsamodendron Mukul*, Hooker; the other African, yielded by *Heudelotia Africana*, Guil. et Perot.

BEACH, the ocean strand or sea coast.

BEACON, a signal, a buoy, or light for the guidance of mariners.

BEAD AND QUIRK, a bead stuck on the edge of a piece of stuff.

BEADING, a moulding; also an artificial property given to spirits, of beading on the surface, or hanging in pearly drops on the sides of the glass containing it.

BEADLE, the messenger of a livery company or wardmote, an officer of a public court, a petty officer of a Scotch church, &c.

BEADLEMER, a kind of seal sought for its oil and skin. *See* BEDLAMER.

BEAD-PLANE, a moulding plane of semi-cylindrical contour. *See* PLANE.

BEAD-PROOF, the standard strength among distillers for alcoholic liquors, when tested by the glass bubbles or hollow beads used as floats, but which are now giving way to more accurate meters. *See* ALCOHOLOMETER.

BEADS, ornaments for the person, which form a large article of commerce in Eastern countries and Africa; they are of glass, coral, amber, carnelian, and other substances, and range from seed beads to a very large size. The home manufacture exceeds in value £20,000 to £30,000 a-year.

BEAD-STRINGER, one who makes a business of threading beads.

BEAGLE, a small hound or hunting dog.

BEAK, a weight used in Mocha for gold and silver, equal to one and a half ounce troy.

BEAKER, a jug with a spout.

BEAK-IRONS, instruments for working sheet metal; the pointed part of an anvil.

BEAM, a large piece of timber used as a support for flooring in a house, or for the decks of a ship, &c. The beam of a balance is the horizontal bar or support of iron or other metal, from the ends of which the scales are suspended.

BEAM AND SCALES, a balance or mechanical contrivance for weighing the precious metals, merchandise, &c.

BEAM AND SCALE MAKER, a manufacturer of weights and scales, balances, &c.

BEAM COMPASSES, an extending instrument for drawing circles or axes of very large radius.

BEAMS, horizontal girders of iron or wood, used to support weights, or bind walls together.

BEAN-COD, a small Portuguese river fishing and pilot boat.

BEAN-MEAL, the flour of beans, which is used for fattening hogs and cattle, and in some counties is still mixed surreptitiously with the flour of wheat for making bread.

BEAN-MILL, a mill for splitting pulse for horse feed; also for crushing and grinding beans into flour, worked by steam power.

BEANS, a well-known pulse (*Vicia faba*) of which there are one or two varieties cultivated for culinary purposes in gardens, and a more extensive scale in fields, for horse provender, and cattle feeding. Besides those grown here we import large quantities from the Continent. The kidney-bean is the *Phaseolus vulgaris*. In Central America and Brazil pulse forms a large article of food.

BEAN-SOWING MACHINE, a drill for planting beans in rows.

BEAR. There are several species of this quadruped; the most important, however, are the brown and black bears, *Ursus Arctos et Americanus*, and the Polar bear, *Ursus maritimus*. The bear is an object of commercial utility for menageries and zoological collections, and also for its skin and grease. The flesh of the black bear is extremely delicate, the hams in particular being much esteemed. The white bear is eaten by the Esquimaux and the Danes of Greenland, and, when young and cooked after the manner of a beefsteak, is by no means to be despised, although rather insipid; a stock-exchange term for a jobber or dealer who has an interest in depressing prices, wishing to buy back stock or shares at lower rates than are current; also an iron instrument or roller.

BEAR'S GREASE, an unguent used for promoting the growth of the hair.

BEAR SKINS, the skins of the black bear and the Polar or white bear of North America, as well as those of the brown and grey beard, are much prized for army clothing and accoutrements, and also for hearth rugs and sleigh coverings. The skins of the white bear, after being well cleaned of flesh, are towed overboard and then packed in tight casks filled with brine. Calmucks made of wool are called bear skins.

BEAST, a name usually given to any large quadruped, wild or domesticated.

BEATERS, the striking parts of thrashing or other machines or mills.

BEAUFET, a sideboard.

BEAVER, a kind of broad-cloth; a small rodent (the *Castor fiber*), familiar to commerce, furnishing fur which is made into muffs, tippets, cuffs, hats, and other articles of apparel, and a peculiar odoriferous secretion termed castoreum. The flesh of the beaver is eaten by the Indians and Canadian voyageurs.

BEAVER-CLOTHS, a species of felted woollens made in America.

BEAVER CUTTER, a preparer of beaver skins; one who unhairs them, and fits them for use as furs.

BEAVERTEEN, a kind of fustian made of coarse twilled cotton, which is shorn after dyeing.

BEBEERINE, an alkaloid obtained from the bark of the greenheart-tree of Demerara, and used like quinine as a febrifuge and tonic. *See* GREENHEART.

BEC[illegible], a large Spanish boat; also a kind of French grapes.

BECCAFICO, the *Sylvia hortensis*, a bird highly prized by the Italians and Maltese on account of the delicacy of its flesh in autumn, when it feeds on figs, berries, &c.

BECERRILLO, BECERRO, Spanish names for a calf skin tanned and dressed.

BECHE-DE-MER, a French name for the tripang or sea-slug, a species of Holothuria, much esteemed as a culinary delicacy by the Chinese.

BECHER, a dry measure in Switzerland and Germany, about 0·06 Winchester bushel.

BECHERLEIN, a Swiss liquid measure equal to 0·035 wine gallon, but of variable dimensions in different countries.

BECHET, a kind of camel.

BECK, a tank in a dye-house.

BECKET, a sea term for a piece of rope.

BECSKA, a liquid measure in Poland of about 26½ wine gallons.

BED, a couch for sleeping on.

BEDAGOSA, a name in Brazil for the seeds of the *Cassia occidentalis*, which are frequently roasted and used as a substitute for coffee.

BEDANA, BEDANNAH, Indian names for quince seed.

BED AND MATTRESS MAKER, one who prepares these articles for upholsterers and private families.

BED-CHAMBER, a sleeping room.

BED-CLOTHES, the blankets, sheets, and quilts spread upon a bed.

BEDDING, the furniture and appurtenances for a sleeping couch; in mining parlance a layer of ore placed on the brake sieve.

BEDDING PLANTS, young plants from a nursery, fit to be transplanted into beds.

BED-FEATHER MANUFACTURER, a cleanser and preparer of goose or poultry feathers for filling beds.

BED-HANGINGS, the valance and curtains for a bed.

BED-LACE-MAKER, a manufacturer of lashings and bindings for bed sackings.

BEDLAMER, a sealer's name for a year old hood seal, *Stemmatopus cristatus*.

BEDOOR, a weight in Malacca, used chiefly for tin, rather less than 2⅔ lbs.

BED-PILLAR-CARVER, a workman whose business it is to make ornamental cornerposts for bedsteads.

BEDPOST, the tall upright columns or corner supports of a bed frame, which carry the tester or canopy.

BED-QUILT, a covering for a bed. *See* COUNTERPANE.

BED-ROOM, a chamber appropriated to beds; the retiring room for rest.

BED-SACKING, the canvas material stretched on the framework of a bedstead, for supporting the beds and bedclothes, &c.

BED-SACKING MAKER, a manufacturer of coarse canvas for bedstead frames.

BED-SCREW, a screw to hold parts of a bedstead together; a common name for a hand-wrench to turn the screws.

BED-SCREW MAKER, a manufacturer of screws and wrenches for beds.

BED-SPREAD, the American name for a coverlet or counterpane.

BEDSTEAD, a framework of wood or metal, to support a bed. Bedsteads bear various names, according to shape and size, and are largely manufactured for home use. Iron and brass ones are also shipped.

BED-STEPS, an article of furniture for a sleeping room, to aid in ascending to a lofty bed.

BED-TICKING, a stout material of cotton or linen, for making bed-cases to hold feathers, flocks, chaff, &c.

BEDWARMER, a brass covered pan with a handle, to hold fire for warming the sheets of a bed in cold weather.

BEECH-MAST, the seed or fruit of *Fagus sylvaticus*, a valuable native forest tree; swine are fed on them; roasted they form a tolerable substitute for coffee, and before the use of corn they were like acorns, the food of uncivilized men; dried and ground into meal, they make a wholesome bread.

BEECH-OIL, an oil obtained from beech mast or nuts in France, by pressure; a bushel of mast will produce about a gallon of oil. In some parts of the Continent it is used instead of butter for culinary purposes.

BEEF, the flesh of oxen or cows, fit for food, which is either used fresh or cured. Salted beef of commerce is classed into common, mess, and family beef; beef is also dried or jerked, and spiced and smoked.

BEEFSTEAK, a slice of beef.

BEEFSTEAK-PUDDING, beefsteaks boiled in a casing of dough.

BEEF-WOOD, an Australian red-coloured wood, obtained from *Stenocarpus salignus*; it is sometimes called the swamp oak.

BEEGAH, BIGGA, a variable Indian land measure in different districts, but which may be roughly taken at about one third of the English acre. The Calcutta beegah is 0·33 acre; the Malwa beegah ranges from 0·45 to 0·58 acre; the Surat beegah 0·60, while the common ryoty beegah in Bengal contains only 1600 square yards.

BEE-HIVE, a straw basket, glass case, or other enclosure set apart for bees to carry on their industrial operations in.

BEE-HIVE MANUFACTURER, a maker of hives, for the housing and preservation of the honey-bee.

BEER, a popular fermented beverage made from malt and hops, an article of large consumption in England and Germany.

BEER, BLACK. *See* SPRUCE.

BEER-ENGINE, an hydraulic machine for drawing beer or other liquors out of a cask in a cellar or vault.

BEER-ENGINE-MAKER, a manufacturer of machines for drawing beer by a force-pump from casks.

BEER-SHOP, an alehouse or small public-house licensed to retail beer.

BEER-TAP, a wooden or metal tap for drawing beer from a cask.

BEERTIA, an Indian name for the Italian millet (*Setaria Italica*).

BEESEE, a land measure in the hill part of Kumaon, India, of 4800 square yards, or as much land as can be sown with a maund of grain.

BEES-WAX, the wax-comb after the honey is removed, which is used for making candles, sealing-wax, polishing furniture, &c. We import quantities from India, Africa, and other parts of the world. Two kinds occur in commerce, the yellow and the white or bleached.

BEETAX, an instrument for paring turf.

BEETLE, a heavy wooden hammer or mallet for driving piles, palisades, &c.: when used by paviors it is called a rammer.

BEETLE'S WINGS, the elytra or wing-cases of some brilliant coloured beetles, which are made into garlands and ornaments, and used to decorate muslin, scarfs, and ball-dresses.

BEET-ROOT, a root largely cultivated for culinary and commercial purposes, of which there are eight or nine varieties.

BEET-ROOT-SUGAR, a sugar of commerce largely manufactured on the Continent. The root which produces the largest quantity of saccharine is the Silesian beet (*Beta alba*), after which follow the yellow (*B. major*), the red (*B. Romana*), and the common or field beet (*B. sylvestris*).

BEEVES, a common name in America for oxen or slaughter cattle; the term is sometimes used by graziers in this country.

BEFFTA, the Arabic name for calico.

BEGASS, an American name for the stalk of the sugar-cane after the juice has been expressed, which is used for fuel and manure. In the West Indies it is called megass and trash.

BEGGAR, a mendicant; an itinerant pauper.

BEGGUD, the Indian name for tinfoil, usually shipped in packages of 2000 leaves (100 corges).

BEGTI, another name for the Cockup an Indian fish, the *Lates nobilis*.

BEGUAN, a bezoar found in the Iguana lizard.

BEIGE, a French coarse cloth.

BEJUCO, a Spanish name for the lianes, or twining parasitical canes which ascend the forest trees of South America.

BEKA, an ancient Hebrew weight equal to 0·016 lb.

BELANDRE, BYLANDER, a small French coasting vessel with two masts.

BELAWINA, BHELAWAN, an Indian name for the marking nut.

BELAYING-PIN, a pin on board ship, to which a rope is made fast, by a few turns, and easily loosened.

BELFRY, a clock tower.

BELGAUM WALNUT, an Indian name for the nut of the *Aleurites triloba*.

BELLAMAN, an Indian name for the marking nut.

BELL-CORAL, a child's ornament and plaything with bells attached to jingle.

BELL-FOUNDER, one who casts bells.

BELL-HANGER, one whose business it is to fix house-bells and their connecting-wires.

BELLMAN, a public crier in small towns.

BELL-METAL, an alloyed metal usually in the proportion of three-fourths copper and one fourth of tin, but for cymbals and gongs the proportions are four-fifths copper and one-fifth tin.

BELLON, a large cider-tub used in France.

BELLOWS-MAKER, one who makes bellows or instruments for increasing the activity and heat of a fire for domestic or manufacturing purposes.

Bell-pepper, a species of capsicum.

Bell-rope, a fancy cord frequently attached to a bell in rooms, but now much superseded by cranks and pulleys.

Bell-rope-maker, a manufacturer of bell pulls and cords.

Bells, sonorous instruments of various sizes, constructed of hollow metal, for calling attention in a house or shop, or for ringing chimes and striking the hours and quarters, &c., or in churches and public buildings. Small bells are cast in sand, large bells in loam. There are a great variety of bells made for belfry-towers, for church-clocks, for ships, for bell-buoys, for houses, &c.

Bell-wether, a sheep with a bell attached to his neck, which leads the flock.

Belly-band, a strap, part of the gear for a horse; a child's wrapper or support for the stomach.

Belmont-wax and Sperm, a commercial name for a very superior class of candles, produced by a large joint-stock company in London, the seat of whose principal manufactory is at the Belmont Works, Vauxhall.

Belontourka, a variety of Russian wheat.

Beloo, in the Pacific Islands, drinking-cups made from the leaf of the plantain.

Belotes, a name in Spain and Italy for the edible seeds of *Quercus gramuntia* and *Castagnara*.

Belt, a leather strap or sling; an article of dress of various materials; thus there are sword-belts, shoulder-belts, waist-belts, cross-belts, ladies' belts, and children's belts, &c.; a border of trees in park lands.

Beltigay, a name for coarse rice in some parts of Southern India.

Belvidere, a terrace on the top of a house; an elevated pavilion from whence there is a fine prospect.

Bench, a seat, a carpenter's work-table.

Bend, a name in the leather trade for a butt or rounded crop cut in two. A mode of fastening a rope of which there are several kinds, as the short bend, fisherman's bend, &c. *See* Hitch, and Knot.

Benda, a West African weight, equivalent to 2¼ ounces avoirdupois; or by some authorities computed at 0·141 pound, and the benda nifa at 0·07 pound. On the coast of Guinea the benda weighs 989¼ grains.

Bendiky, the two-dollar piece, a coin current in Morocco, nominally worth 27 ounces, each ounce being in value nearly fourpence.

Benecarlo, a kind of wine shipped in hogsheads to the West Indies.

Benelli, a woollen cap made in Tuscany, and worn by the Turks.

Bengals, a thin slight stuff made of silk and hair for women's apparel; imitations of striped muslins formerly made at Paisley.

Benitier, a holy-water pot or vessel, sometimes a large shell, used in Catholic countries.

Benjamin, another name for gum benzoin. *See* Benzoin.

Ben-nuts, a commercial name for the winged seeds contained in the leguminous pods of *Moringa pterygosperma*, the horse-radish tree of the West Indies.

Benny, Bennie, a name for the grain of the *Sesamum Indicum*, at Sierra Leone, and in some parts of the West Indies.

Ben, Oil of, a fine colourless limpid oil obtained from the seeds of the *Moringa pterygosperma*, much valued by watchmakers and perfumers, for its sweetness and fluidity.

Ben-teak, a name for an inferior kind of teak, also for the wood of *Lagerstrœmia microcarpa*, used in India for buildings and common carts, bandy shafts, and spokes of wheels; it is a close-grained wood like the cherry.

Bent-timber Manufacturer, a shaper of timber by steam and pressure.

Benzine, another name for Benzole, a hydrocarbonic oil, which has been found a very useful abstergent of grease.

Benzoin, Benjamin, an odoriferous gum-resin, obtained in Siam, and the Eastern Archipelago, from *Styrax Benzoin*, and used in perfumery and incense. It is of a yellowish gold colour with occasionally white almond-like masses in it; there are, however, two or three varieties which enter into commerce.

Benzole, an oil obtained from coal-naphtha, of great solvent powers, which is used by manufacturers of India-rubber and gutta-percha, by chemists for making oil of bitter almonds, in the preparation of varnishes, for cleaning soiled kid gloves, and other purposes.

Berberine, a bitter crystalline powder obtained from the root of *Berberis vulgaris*, used as a substitute for quinine, and for colouring cottons and silks.

Berche, the French name for a small brass cannon.

Bercheroot, the Russian pound, forty of which make a Russian pood.

Bercovett, Bercowitz. *See* Berquett.

Bere, one of the kinds of six-rowed barley, grown in Scotland and other northern climates, valued for its hardy properties; it is sometimes called bigg, and is used for the distillation of whisky.

Berengena, the Spanish name for the egg-plant (*Solanum*), an esculent vegetable.

Beretti, an Eastern name for the Tunis red caps.

Bergamot, an essential oil obtained by distillation from *Mentha citrata*, and also from the rind of a fragrant species of citron; large quantities of this essence are imported.

Bergolo, a kind of basket used in Italy.

Bergot, a bow-net used in France to fish in the rivers.

Berlin, a kind of chariot.

Berlinga, the Spanish name for round timber of six inches in diameter.

Berlin Gloves, thread or cotton gloves for summer wear.

Berlin Warehouse, a fancy repository for ladies' wares; a shop where worsteds, crewels, knitting-needles, patterns, &c., are sold.

Berlin Wool, various kinds of dyed worsted yarns, used by ladies for knitting and tapestry work.

Berlin-work, a species of embroidery in coloured worsteds.

Bermillians, linen or fustian formerly exported in pieces not exceeding 30 yards in length.

Bernardiere, a variety of pear in France.

Berneta, the Arabic name for a hat.

Berquet, Bercovett, a Russian weight of ten poods or rather more than 361·2 pounds English, by which hemp and other gross goods are weighed.

Berri, an itinerary measure of Turkey, equal to 1826 English yards.

Berriarah, an Indian shepherd, frequently employed by families in the up-country stations to supply them with meat.

Berries, the seeds of plants, many of which enter into commerce, as bay-berries, juniper-berries, &c; French and Persian berries are the small dried fruit of *Rhamnus infectorius* used for dyeing, also called yellow berries.

Berry Wax, a green vegetable wax obtained from the seeds of the candle-berry myrtle, *Myrica cerifera*, in the Cape colony and America, which is well suited for the manufacture of candles.

Bersimlichi, a kind of Greek silk used for sewing and embroidery.

Beryl, a precious stone of a deep brown carnelian, and sometimes of a yellow and red colour.

Beshan, a name in Arabia for the *Protium gileadense*, a tree which produces the balsam of Mecca; it is also called Balessan.

Beshmet, grapes made into a consistence resembling honey, a staple product of some of the mountainous districts of Asia minor. The production in the district of Alexandreita is 250,000lbs. a year; it forms a great article of food among the natives of the country.

Besi, a variety of pear grown in France.

Beslic, a petty Turkish money equal to 1½ pence; also a silver coin worth about 3s. 3d.

Besom, a broom.

Beson, a liquid measure of Augsburg, equal to about 2½ English gallons; 96 besons make one fuder.

Besugo, the Spanish name for the bream, a fish; besuguete being the red bream.

Bet, a wager, a name in several parts of India for species of *Calamus* which are used for all the ordinary purposes of cane.

Betaorceine, a blue substance obtained from the orchilla weed, or archil of commerce.

Betel Leaf, the leaf of the *Piper betel*, an ingredient of the betel masticatory, known as Pan in the East, where it forms nearly as extensive an article of commerce as tobacco in the West. There are several species of this scandent plant, which flourishes best in the islands of the Indian archipelago, furnishing leaves fit for use the second year, and continuing to yield them for more than thirty.

Betel Nut, the small hard inner seeds or fruit of *Areca catechu*, about the size of a nutmeg, which are largely used as a masticatory throughout Eastern countries. In the Bombay market three kinds are met with; white from Shevurdhan, which are three times the value of those from other countries; red—which are half the value of the best white; and nuts in the husk sold by the thousand. The crushed nut is generally used with the leaf of the betel pepper and chunam or shell-lime. About 4,000 tons of these nuts are shipped annually from Ceylon to different quarters. *See* Pan.

Bethile, the French name for a thick sort of muslin made in India.

Beton, a kind of concrete or hydraulic cement, rendered more compact by being mixed with gravel, pebbles, &c., which is used in submarine works as a foundation for masonry. It is also called grubbstone mortar.

Betterave, the French name for the red beet.

Betuline, a colourless resin or camphor extracted from birch bark.

Beuna, a gold-coloured Spanish wine.

Beurre, the French name for butter.

Beut, the Spanish name for a kind of sea-fish.

Bevel, to shape or smooth away to an angle; a carpenter's tool to strike angles with.

Bevelling, a term applied to any deviation from a square or right angle.

Bevel Plumb-rule, a surveyor's instrument for adjusting the face of the slopes in embankments.

Bevel-wheel, a wheel with teeth at an angle.

Beverage, a common name for any kind of drink.

Beyche Seed, a name in Siam for *Strychnos nux vomica*.

Beyupura, a large kind of fish on the coasts of Spain.

Bezan, white or striped cotton cloth.

Bezestan, a public market in Turkey.

Bezoar, a morbid concretion found in the stomachs of some animals, and possessing many fanciful medicinal properties.

Bhaaral, a species of wild sheep found in the Nepaulese territories; the *Ovis Ammon*.

Bhabbur, a name in the Himalayas for the silky leaves of the cotton grass, *Eriophorum cannabinum* of Royle. It is largely used for cordage, and cables for suspension-bridges are made of it. From the silky substance clothing the seeds, wicks of candles and paper are made, and it is used to stuff pillows.

Bhallaparasa, an Indian battle axe.

Bhang, the Indian name for an intoxicating drug obtained in the East from the *Cannabis sativa* or hemp plant.

Bharra, a Malayan measure of capacity of about 3½ piculs, or 466 lbs.

Bhat, Bhaut, boiled rice, which is much used by Europeans, and also forms the staple food of the bulk of the natives in the East.

Bhaur, a Surat weight of 900 lbs. *See* Bahar.

Bhaut. *See* Bhat.

Bheesty, properly Bihishtee, an Indian water-carrier, who fills a sheepskin bucket or bag from the nearest water, reservoir or river, and supplies domestic establishments.

Bhela, or **Bhelawan**, one of the Indian names for the marking nut. [riage.

Bhily, the Indian name for a native car-

Bhoe Mong, or **Moong Phullee**, an Indian name for the ground-nut *Arachis hypogæa*.

Bhoku Leaves. *See* **Buchu-Leaves**.

Bhorah, a Bengalee name for the mangrove.

Bhorenda, an Indian name for the castor-oil plant.

Bhurral, a local name for the wild sheep of the Himalayas.

Bhyangee, a name for sheep's wool, obtained in Little Thibet.

Bia, a Siamese name for the cowry shell, a money of account in minor transactions.

Biasse, a French name for coarse raw silk imported from the Levant; in Spanish, Biasa.

Biawak, the Malay name for the iguana.

Bib, an European species of cod—the *Gadus luscus*, highly esteemed; an infant's clothes' preserver worn on the breast.

Biberhobil, the German name for castoreum. [Testaments.

Bible, a book containing the Old and New

Bica, a sea-fish of the Spanish coasts.

Bicarbonate of Soda. *See* **Soda, Carbonate of**.

Bicheree, an old land measure of France, 8 acres, 31 perches; as a superficial measure in Lyons, it was 1547 square yards.

Bichet, **Bichot**, a grain measure of about 2 bushels, formerly used in France, and still employed in some parts of Switzerland. It was of a most variable character, ranging from 3½ up to 55 gallons.

Bichetti, a kind of French fishing-net.

Bichieraio, an Italian glass-blower.

Bichoor, in India, a dagger with more than one blade.

Bichromate of Potash, a beautiful crystalline salt in large prisms, of a brilliant red color, used in dyeing and calico printing, obtained from chromate of iron, and which is the source of the chrome pigments. Mixed with sulphuric acid, it is a powerful oxidizing agent for bleaching oils and fats.

Bickern. *See* **Beak-iron**.

Biconcia, a liquid measure of Venice, the fourth part of the amphora, and equal to 28¼ gallons.

Bicongius, an ancient Roman liquid measure, equal to nearly 1½ imperial gallon.

Bid, an offer made, a price tendered for an article at an auction.

Biday, a local Eastern name for the Indian black-wood.

Biddery Ware, articles made in India of a metallurgical compound, which are greatly admired for the elegance of their form, as well as for the gracefulness of the patterns with which their surface is engraved. The alloy appears to consist of sixteen parts of copper, four of lead, and two of tin, to which a large proportion of spelter is added. It is inlaid with silver or gold, and polished.

Bidet, a small horse; a close stool.

Bientenant, a landholder in France.

Biffin, a dried and pressed apple.

Bifurcated, divided into two prongs or forks, as in a piece of timber; a river which separates into two branches, &c.

Bigarade, a French name for the Seville or bitter orange.

Bigarreau, a name for the white-heart cherry, derived from the French.

Bigg, a cereal grass which has six rows of seeds on the spike, hence termed *Hordeum hexastichum*, sometimes used for malting. It is also known under the name of bere.

Biggah, a land measure of India. *See* **Beegah**.

Biggin, a small wooden can; also a metal receiver for making coffee.

Bighera, a name for thread lace in Italy.

Bight, the slack part of a rope.

Bihai, the *Heliconia humilis* of Caraccas, believed to be the wild stock-plant of the cultivated varieties of plantain.

Bihul, a name in the Himalayas for the bark of the *Grewia oppositifolia*, used for making ropes.

Bijou, a gem, a small jewel.

Bijouterie, small articles of vertu, jewellery, trinkets, toys, &c.

Bijoutier, a French jeweller; a goldsmith.

Bilan, the French name for an account-book; a balance-sheet of debtor and creditor.

Bilander, **Bylander**, a small coasting vessel with two masts, resembling a hoy.

Bilboes, a common name for sliding shackles of iron for the feet, fastened to long bars, to confine persons as in wooden stocks. They are used in slavers, and in vessels of war.

Bilge, the swell or protuberant part of a cask; the projecting parts of a ship's bottom, or floor on each side of the keel.

Bilge Pump, a pump on ship-board for clearing a vessel of water that has settled in the hold.

Bill, an account rendered; an acceptance; a term among letter-founders for a fount of type.

Bill-book, a book in which entry is made of the particulars of bills and notes, in favour or against a person or firm.

Bill-broker, one who deals in discounts.

Billet, a small clump of fire-wood; also the French name for a ticket or note, &c.

Billeting, quartering troops on an innkeeper, or the inhabitants of a town or village, for lodging and accommodation, at the charge of the government.

Bill-head, a printed form with name, address, or business, used for making out accounts.

Bill-hook, the colonial name for a small curved hand-chopper, or reaper, for cutting sugar-canes, brushwood, &c. in the West Indies.

Billiard Balls, red and white globes of ivory with which the game of billiards is played.

Billiard Cloths, green woollen broad cloth, manufactured to cover a billiard table, which are piece dyed, and seventy-two to eighty-one inches wide.

BILLIARD-CUE, the rod or stick with which the billiard balls are struck.

BILLIARD-MARKER, an attendant at a billiard table, who marks the strokes and score of the game for the players.

BILLIARD TABLE, a table usually made of slate covered with cloth, having padded cushions and netted bags at the corners, and used for playing the game of billiards, with ivory balls and a cue or mace.

BILLIARD TABLE-MAKER, a manufacturer of tables for playing the game of billiards.

BILLINGSGATE, the great fish-market of London, situate on the river just below London Bridge.

BILL OF ENTRY, a note of the particulars of goods entered at the Custom House.

BILL OF EXCHANGE, an order in writing, on a duly stamped form addressed by one person to another, to pay a certain sum on demand, or at a time specified, to a third person or to his order. If payable to order, it must be transferred by indorsement and delivery. Foreign bills are those drawn in one country and payable in another. Inland bills are those drawn and made payable in the same country. In 1856 it was calculated that the average amount represented by the bills of exchange, inland and foreign, in circulation at one time in this country, was not less than £200,000,000 sterling.

BILL OF HEALTH, an official document required in some countries to be produced by the master of a vessel coming from a port suspected to be unhealthy, and certifying as to the condition of the passengers and the crew; it is either a clean bill of health, or a foul bill.

BILL OF LADING, a certified document or invoice from the master of the ship, acknowledging the receipt on board for transport, of certain goods to be delivered up to the consignee or producer of the bill of lading, on payment of freight and charges due.

BILL OF PARCELS, the account of goods sold by one merchant to another, or to a whole-sale-dealer, given to the purchaser, containing a specification of the quantities, prices, date, and other particulars.

BILL OF SALE, a registered transfer of goods to a person for some consideration, empowering him to dispose of them upon non-fulfilment of certain conditions.

BILL OF SIGHT, a temporary form of entry at the Customs, permitting goods to be provisionally landed for examination.

BILL OF SUFFERANCE, a coasting licence to trade from port to port, without paying customs duty, the dutiable goods being loaded and landed at sufferance wharves.

BILLON, the French name for gold or silver, which has been coined below the standard value, alloyed with copper.

BILLOT, a term applied to bullion before it is coined.

BILL-POSTER, BILL-STICKER, an itinerant employed to paste placards or announcements on boardings and walls.

BILLS PAYABLE, a title given to notes, bills and other paper claims outstanding against an individual or firm.

BILLS RECEIVABLE, the unpaid notes, bills &c. claimable by an individual or firm.

BILLY-BOY, a hoy or river barge, a peculiar kind of coasting craft.

BILSTON-GRINDSTONE, a variety of sandstone obtained from Staffordshire.

BILSAH, a fine kind of tobacco, grown in the province of Malwa, India.

BILTONGUE, a name for sun-dried meat in the Cape colony.

BILUDU, a Malay name for velvet.

BIMARS, the Spanish name for a kind of Brazil wood.

BIMBELOTERIE, a French term for toys and playthings in various materials, children's hand-carriages, &c.

BIMBELOTIER, a French toy-man, a vendor of children's playthings and small fancy wares.

BIMBI, a small grain grown at the Maldives.

BIN, a box or locker fitted to the side of a stable, store-room and ship, &c. for holding provender, goods, &c.; an enclosure for bottles in a wine cellar.

BINARD, a large French cart in which the four wheels are of equal size.

BIND, in the fish trade, a term applied to 250 eels or ten strikes, each containing a quarter of a hundred.

BINDOOS, a name in India for pieces of timber used in building.

BINGSTEAD, a place near to smelting works, where all the dressed ore is deposited.

BINH, an Annam weight of nearly sixty-nine pounds.

BINNACLE, the case in which the mariner's compass is secured on board ship, within sight of the helmsman or man at the wheel.

BINNACLE COMPASS, a box compass kept on deck for the helmsman to steer by.

BINOCLE, a dioptrical telescope.

BIOLCA, a land measure of Italy of very variable dimensions; in Bologna, equal to 19,600 square feet; in Ferrara to 40,000; in Modena to 10,368 feet.

BIQUET, the vulgar name in France for a money scale for weighing gold.

BIRAMBI, the fruit of a shrub, the *Averrhoa Bilimbi* from Berbice, which makes an excellent pickle and a delicious preserve.

BIRCH, a well-known tree, of which there are many species. The *Betula alba*, or Norway birch, furnishes an inferior timber used for common articles of furniture and in ship-building. Black birch is valuable for floorings and keelsons, and parts of ships which are constantly under water. Birch wood is used for many economical purposes, as for herring barrels and butter-tubs, cattle-yokes, turnery-ware, &c. The bark is made into canoes in North America, and the leaves are used for tea in Finland.

BIRCH AND HEATH BROOM-MAKER, a broom manufacturer.

BIRCH-BROOMS, common sweeping brooms made from the young shoots or twigs of the birch tree, and from heath.

BIRCH-WINE, a medicinal drink made from the sap of the birch-tree, which is said to possess antiscorbutic and diuretic properties.

Bird-and-beast Stuffer, one who mounts and sets up dead birds and other animals for cabinets or cases.

Bird-cage, a portable frame-work or enclosure for birds.

Bird-cage Maker, a workman who makes brass-wire, wicker-work, wood, and other cages for birds.

Bird-call, a kind of whistle.

Bird-fancier, a dealer in cage-birds, pigeons, &c.

Birding-piece, a long fowling-piece for shooting wild fowl.

Bird-lime, a glutinous viscid substance, prepared in various ways, but chiefly extracted from the bark of the holly, the mistletoe, and the distaff thistle, used for entangling birds.

Bird-pepper, the small capsicum or fruit of the shrubs, *C. frutescens and minimum*, from which cayenne is chiefly made.

Bird-seed, canary, hemp, millet, and other small seeds used for feeding cage birds.

Bird's-eye, a fine kind of tobacco partly made from the stalks of the leaves of certain species of *Nicotiana;* artificial glass eyes for stuffed birds are extensively sold.

Bird's-eye Crape, a thin material made for the East Indian markets.

Bird's-eye Diaper, a kind of towelling.

Bird's-eye Maple, an esteemed variegated cabinet wood, arising from an accidental form in the arrangement of the fibre of the rock or sugar maple (*Acer saccharinum*) of America. Curled maple consists of undulations in the same wood.

Bird-skins. Many skins of foreign birds, with bright plumage are imported to be stuffed as ornaments or illustrations of natural history in Museums; and some, as of the swan, grebe, &c., are used for trimmings, and lining garments.

Bird's-mouth Quoin, a building term.

Birds' Nests, the nests of a species of swallow, *Hirundo esculenta*, which form a large article of commerce in the Eastern seas, being highly prized by the Chinese for their muco-albuminous properties. The nest is formed from sea-weed, jelly-fish and other glutinous substances. About 16,000 tons are said to be imported annually into Canton.

Birds of Paradise, the skins and plumage of several elegant birds, *Paradisea apoda*, and other species, imported from islands of the Eastern seas, which realize a high price. In preparing them for the market the bird is disembowelled, smoked, and deprived of its legs.

Birds, Singing, many descriptions of cage birds are imported, including canaries, parrots, &c. Birds are also brought to this country as specimens of natural history, either alive or stuffed.

Bireme, a doubled-banked rowing galley.

Birling, a small sea-vessel.

Birmingham Warehouse, a shop where iron hardware goods, and the various articles of Birmingham manufacture are sold.

Birotine, a kind of silk from the Levant.

Birouza, a name for the turquoise.

Birt, a kind of turbot.

Birth, Berth, a nautical term applied to the position in which a ship is moored or anchored, as a port birth, good birth, wide birth, &c. Also a small sleeping crib or cabin built up against the ship's side.

Bisa, a Burmese coin worth about 1s. 8d. sterling.

Bisaccia, a corn measure in Sicily; the fourth part of the salma, and equal to 1·885 bushel.

Bisage, a French term for cloth, linen, &c., which has been twice dyed.

Biscacha, a small rodent animal of South America, the *Lagostomus trichodactylus* or *Callomys bizcacha*, whose flesh is used for food, and the skins are imported into England for the fur.

Biscaien, a kind of musket; also a shot weighing one pound.

Biscot, part of a waggon in the Cape colony.

Biscotin, a French sweet cake or confection.

Biscuit, an unglazed white porcelain ware made to imitate marble; also baked flour cakes of different kinds. There are many fancy biscuits sold by pastry cooks, such as captains', arrow-root, rice, abernethy and wine biscuits, &c. Crackers are a small, American-made biscuit. Ships' biscuits are coarser and harder baked, and are mostly made of pollard, or an inferior kind of flour; but there are some whiter varieties for cabin use, and a kind also called pilot biscuits.

Biscuit-baker, a maker of fancy or ship biscuit.

Biscuit-stamp, a metal shape or pricker for cutting dough and marking biscuits.

Biseigle, a French shoemaker's measure or rule.

Bisella, the Arabic name for pease.

Bisette, a narrow French lace.

Biseur, the name for a dyer in France.

Bishop, a drink of wine, oranges, and sugar.

Bist, a gigantic tree of British Guiana, the wood of which is exceedingly durable, and used by the Indians in constructing their corials and canoes.

Bisk, a gravy soup made by boiling several kinds of meat together.

Bismer, a Danish name for the steelyard.

Bismer-pound, the weight usually attached to the steel-yard in Norway and Denmark, and weighing about 12½ lbs. avoirdupois.

Bismuth, a reddish-white metal, occurring in brilliant plates, obtained chiefly in Saxony, and used as an alloy in type-metal and pewter. It is sometimes called by workmen tin-glass.

Bismuth Ochre, an oxide of bismuth found in Saxony, Bohemia, and Siberia.

Bison, the American buffalo (*Bos Americanus*).

Bispon, the Spanish name for a roll of oil-cloth.

Bisquain, a French name for a sheep's skin with the wool on.

Bisquine, a kind of French vessel.

Bissowa, a land measure in Ghazepore, East Indies; the 20th part of a beegah, the beegah there being 2755½ square yards, British.

Bistoquet, a kind of large billiard mace used in France.

Bistort, the *Polygona bistorta*, a powerful astringent and tonic.

Bistoury, a surgeon's incision knife, of which there are various forms.

Bistre, a pigment made of the soot of wood, water, and gum.

Biswa, the 20th part of the biggah, a land measure which varies greatly in India. *See* Beegah.

Bit. Bitt, an alloyed kind of silver coin, formerly circulating to some extent in the West Indies, and valued at about 5d. sterling. It is properly the Spanish real of provincial plate, equal to two reals vellon. The term bit is also applied to the small circular piece frequently cut out of the centre of the dollar coin. The bit, as a money of account in Madeira, is 100 reas. A carpenter's boring instrument which fits into a stock or handle; the iron mouth-piece of a bridle, of which there are several kinds, as snaffles, curbs, &c.; two uprights supporting the windlass on each side of a ship's bowsprit are called bitts.

Bit and Auger Maker, an operative in the hardware districts, who prepares these tools for carpenters.

Bitch, a she-dog.

Bitlaban, an Indian name for black salt, a specific in high repute in the East.

Bit-maker, one who makes iron bits or mouth-pieces for horse-bridles.

Bitnoben. *See* Black Salt.

Bitord, the French name for a small kind of rope or cordage.

Bitter Ale, a clear strong ale, chiefly brewed at Burton-upon-Trent for export and home use.

Bitter Almond. *See* Almond.

Bittern, the residual liquor after the separation of the salt from the water of a brine-spring, from which bromine is made. Also a composition of *Cocculus Indicus*, quassia, liquorice, tobacco, and sulphate of iron, said to be used by brewers in adulterating beer.

Bitter Oak, the Adriatic oak, *Quercus Cerris*, of which there are several varieties, which bear the valonia or acorn cups used in tanning.

Bitters, a stomachic drink for promoting digestion and improving the appetite, consisting of spirits in which wormwood, gentian, or some other bitter herb has been steeped.

Bitter Salt, Epsom salts, the sulphate of magnesia.

Bitter-sweet, a common name for the *Solanum Dulcamara*, a wild hedge plant, which is a dangerous narcotic, but used medicinally with advantage; also a variety of apple.

Bitterwood, a common name for the *Xylopia glabra*, a tree of the West Indies, all the parts of which are aromatic and intensely bitter.

Bitumen, a solidified earth-oil, or naphtha, which constitutes the inflammable principle of coal. *See* Asphaltum.

Bituminous Coal. *See* Coal.

Bizantine, an old Turkish gold coin worth £15.

Bizcacha. *See* Biscacha.

Bizcochada, in Spanish a soup made of biscuits.

Black, a money of Riga equal to about two French deniers or pennies; the darkest of colours used in painting.

Black Ash, the wood of *Fraxinus sambucifolia*.

Black-ball, a blacking composition used for polishing shoes.

Black-band, a name for iron-stone, which contains coal.

Black beer, a common name for Dantzic spruce.

Blackberry, the fruit of the bramble (*Rubus fruticosus*) collected for pies and puddings, &c.

Black Birch, (*Betula lenta*,) a tree of North America. *See* Birch.

Black-borderer, a person employed in painting the edges and borders of writing-paper, envelopes, &c., with a margin of black, for the use of persons in mourning.

Black Bully-wood, a hard wood of a greenish colour, the produce of *Achras Sapota*, imported for ship-building purposes. *See* Bully Tree.

Black Cane, a name for the *Bambusa nigra*.

Black Cattle, a collective name for the larger description of domestic animals, horses, bulls, oxen, cows, &c.

Black Chalk, a grayish or bluish black slaty substance, also a preparation of ivory black and fine clay, used in crayon drawing.

Black-cherry, a name in the United States for the wood of *Cerasus serotina*.

Blackcock, a kind of grouse, the *Tetrao tetrix*.

Black Currant, the fruit of *Ribes nigrum*, which is held in estimation for puddings and pies, for making wine and jam, and for lozenges for sore throats.

Black Draught, a popular purgative medicine, composed of epsom salts, senna, liquorice, and aromatics.

Black-ebony, a well-known hard heavy wood, susceptible of a high polish, obtained from various species of *Diospyros*.

Black-flux, a preparation of cream of tartar ignited in a close crucible; a carbonate of potash and charcoal.

Black-Ginger, a variety of *Zingiber*, which produces larger and more numerous rhizomes than the ordinary species.

Black Greenheart. *See* Greenheart.

Blackheart, a useful wood of Demerara, adapted for house frames, and for making furniture. It will square from 6 to 7 inches, from 20 to 30 feet long.

Blackheart Ebony, a hard and ponderous wood, the produce of *Brya Ebenus* of Jamaica, susceptible of a very high polish.

Black-heart Fiddlewood, a Jamaica wood occasionally imported into this country.

Blacking, a polishing paste or liquid, the chief ingredients of which are powdered bone black, sperm or linseed oil, molasses, sour beer or vinegar, oil of vitriol and copperas. Many thousands of tons of blacking are annually made in England.

Blacking Manufacturer, a maker of liquid blacking, or polishing-pastes for leather.

Black Ink. *See* Ink.

Black Jack, a mining name for zinc blende or sulphuret of zinc; a drinking cup of tin or leather; caramel or burnt sugar, which is used to colour spirits, vinegar, coffee, &c.; a trade name for adulterated butter.

Black Japan, a varnishing material made with tar and alcohol, or with lamp-black and resins.

Black-lead, a polishing material for iron stoves, &c. *See* Graphite and Plumbago.

Black-lead Maker, one who refines and prepares plumbago for various uses.

Black-lead-pencil Maker, a manufacturer of pencils for drawing, marking, &c.

Black-Letter, the Gothic type or Old English alphabet.

Black Oak, the *Quercus tinctoria*, a tree of North America.

Black Paint, the darkest pigment used. In oil colours there are ivory blacks, blue blacks, and lamp blacks; in water colors we have also Indian ink.

Black Pepper, the dried unripe drupes of *Piper nigrum*. *See* Pepper.

Black Plates, a commercial name for thin sheets of iron not coated with tin.

Black Pudding, a kind of sausage, made of sheep and pigs' blood, groats, suet, &c., enclosed in the dried intestines of swine and boiled. Many thousands of tons of these are made annually in Great Britain.

Blackrowgrams, an iron-stone.

Black-reviver Maker, a manufacturer of a chemical preparation, for restoring the brilliancy of black dyed articles.

Blacks, a name for ink used in copper-plate printing, prepared from the charred husks of the grape and residue of the winepress.

Black-salt, a chemical product in high repute as a specific among the natives of India. It is nothing more than muriate of soda, fused with a species of myrobalan, whereby it acquires some of the qualities of the fruit, and a portion of iron. It also passes under the names of bitlaban, or bit-noben.

Blacksmith, a worker in iron; one engaged in beating and shaping malleable iron.

Blacksmith's Company, one of the livery companies of the city of London. Having no common hall, the company transacts its business at Guildhall.

Black Spruce, (*Abies nigra*,) a tree of North America. The wood furnishes the spruce deals of commerce, which constitute one of the largest and most valuable exports of the British North American colonies. It is distinguished for strength, lightness, and elasticity, and furnishes as fine yards and top-masts as any in the world. From the young branches the essence of spruce is obtained. *See* Spruce.

Black Strap, a name for bad liquor; vile port wine.

Black Tea. The principal varieties of black tea made in China, are Bohea, Campoi, Caper, Congou, Pekoe, and Souchong. *See* Tea.

Black-thorn, a name for the *Prunus spinosa*, bearing the sloe.

Black Tin, tin ore, beaten into a black and fine powder for smelting.

Black Wad, an ore of manganese used as a dryer for painters' colours.

Black Walnut, the *Juglans nigra*, a tree of America.

Blackwash, a lotion of calomel and lime-water.

Blackwell Hall Factors, agents in London for woollen manufacturers in the country; they are so called from Blackwell Hall, formerly in Basinghall street, which is the metropolitan seat of the wool and woollen trades.

Blackwood, a valuable furniture wood obtained in Malabar, the best being from the *Dalbergia latifolia*. It is locally called rose-wood. The blackwood of New South Wales, also known as light wood, is the *Acacia melanoxylon*.

Bladder-dealer, a cleanser and vender of the bladders and intestines of animals, for the use of sausage makers; and for holding blood-puddings, polonies, &c.

Bladders, the urinary vessels of oxen, pigs, calves, and sheep, which are chemically prepared for holding lard and other purposes. Quantities of bladder are imported from North America and the Continent, packed in salt, or pickle.

Blade, the flat cutting part of a sword or knife.

Blade-forger, a workman employed in the spring-knife cutlery trade for forging metal blades at the anvil.

Blades, a commercial name for the four large shell plates on the sides, and the five large ones from the middle of the carapace of the sea-turtle; these yield the best tortoise-shell.

Blaffert, a small coin at Cologne.

Blamuse, a money of account in some parts of Germany, the eighth part of a rixdollar and worth about fourpence.

Blanca, a petty money of account in Malaga, 68 making one real vellon, which is 2½d.

Blanchimeter, an instrument for measuring the bleaching powers of chloride of lime and potash.

Blanching, the process of whitening any thing, such as removing the skin of almonds; covering iron plates with a solution of tin; annealing, boiling, and cleansing coined money to give it lustre and brilliancy, &c.

Blanchisseuse, a French laundress.

Blanc-manger, a shaped opaque jelly made of milk and isinglass, or gelatine, boiled, and flavoured with sugar and spice, &c.

Blandurillo, a fine soft pomatum made in Spain.

Blank, a division of the English troy grain, formerly used by moneyers; a metal shape for a key-hole; a number in a lottery which has drawn no prize; an unwritten paper or form; an unmarked counter; a rough unfashioned piece of metal cut out for making a spoon, or fork.

Blank Cartridge, an enclosed charge of powder for a gun, without any ball or shot, usually fired for warnings or salutes, and in exercising troops.

Blank Credit, an authorized permission given to draw on an individual or firm to a certain amount.

Blank Cutting-machines; machines for cutting the blanks for keys; for shaping or punching blanks for buttons, &c.

Blankeel, Blanquillo, a small coin and money of account in some parts of Africa, on the Mediterranean shores. The ounce, worth about 4d., is divided into four blankeels, and the blankeel again subdivided into 20 or 24 fluce.

Blankets, soft loosely woven woollen stuff pieces used for bed-coverings or wrappers. Besides those vended at home, five or six million yards are annually shipped to various countries. They are chiefly made at Dewsbury, Heckmondwike, and Wakefield.

Blanquette, a delicate sort of white wine, a large variety of pear; the French name for kelp.

Blaque, a French tobacco pouch.

Blare, a Swiss coin worth about one penny.

Blast, air introduced into a furnace artificially.

Blast-Furnace, an enclosed fire-place where an extra degree of heat is generated by a powerful forge-bellows.

Blasting, a speedy process for removing or detaching heavy masses of stone, earth, &c., by exploding charges of gunpowder.

Blasting Powder, a coarse kind of powder for mining and quarrying purposes.

Blast-Pipe, the tube in a locomotive, which carries off the waste steam, and produces a greater draught for the fire.

Blast-Regulator, a cylinder of iron for holding and conveying air to a blast furnace.

Blaze, a white spot on the forehead or face of a horse.

Blé, the French name for grain, but chiefly applied to wheat.

Bleacher, one who whitens linens, &c., by chemical agency, or by exposure to the atmosphere.

Bleaching, the chemical process of removing the colour of cloth or vegetable substances.

Bleaching Powder, chloride of lime, made by exposing slaked lime to the action of chlorine, which is used for bleaching linens, calicoes, and paper materials: many thousand tons of it are made annually in the kingdom.

Blende, native sulphuret of zinc, the Black Jack of miners, of little value owing to the difficulty of extracting the metal from the ore. Purple or antimony blende is the mineral kermes.

Blesbok, in the Cape colony an antelope with a white face.

Blei, the German name for lead, bleyglotte being litharge, and bleyweess white lead.

Blight, damage or failure to a growing crop.

Blind, a sun screen or shade for a window fitted within or without, and made of different kinds. A common inside window-blind is a plain hanging of union holland or linen; a wire blind is a short transparent frame of woven wire, gauze, or perforated zinc, painted, which is either plain, or lettered and figured. Outside window blinds are known as Spanish, Florentine, Venetian, and shutter. Inside blinds, Venetian, dwarf, spring patent, or common roller. There are also spring-blinds for shop-fronts and sky-lights, and iron rolling blinds for shop-windows.

Blind Coal. *See* Anthracite.

Blinkers, square pieces of leather fastened to the head-stall of a horse to make him look before him instead of aside.

Blistering Fly. *See* Cantharides.

Blistering Plaster, a preparation of powdered cantharides upon adhesive plaster, to raise a blister on the skin.

Blister Steel, wrought iron which has blisters on the surface, owing to the evolution of gas from the interior of the bar.

Bloater, a commercial name for a slightly cured and smoked herring; bloaters are made into a paste for a breakfast relish.

Blocco, Italian, paper and hair used in paying the seams in a ship's bottom.

Block, a solid mass, a square stone placed diagonally on railway tracks, as a support for the rails; in colonial parlance a piece of land; the wooden mould on which hats are formed; a shaped piece of wood containing a sheave traversing on a spindle for passing ropes through. Blocks are of two kinds, made or morticed; the latter consisting of a single block, the former of several pieces. Block is also an interruption or stoppage of vehicular traffic on a thoroughfare. In stereotype printing a wood block, or cut, is an engraved piece of box wood from which impressions can be taken.

Blockade, the official closing of a port or coast during war, by guarding and watching it with vessels of war to prevent commercial intercourse. Due notice is always legally given by proclamation to the mercantile world of the commencement and raising of a blockade.

Block-Machine, a complicated system of machinery for making the blocks and sheaves required for pulleys for naval purposes and shore use. The block machinery in Portsmouth dockyard is the most effective and perfect of its kind.

Block-maker, one who makes blocks for pulleys, &c.

Block Tin, tin cast into blocks or ingots; tin ore which has been treated with copper and sulphuric acid, and is ready for smelting. Metal reduced from the tin stone or ore is less pure than that made from stream or grain tin. A block of tin weighs about the sixth of a ton.

Blonde, a choice kind of silk lace, used by ladies.

Blood, the fluid which circulates in the heart and blood-vessels of animals, which is used for many commercial purposes: it is stirred and run into casks for the use of sugar refiners; it is made into animal charcoal; coagulated, it is sold to calico-printers for dyeing Turkey red, and is chemically prepared for printers' use. In some of the agricultural districts it is employed as a fertilizer of land. Albumen is made from blood. *See* Albumen and Black Pudding.

Blood-drier, a preparer of blood for the use of sugar refiners and other manufacturers.

Bloodhound, the sleuth dog, a variety of the canine species, used for tracking individuals by the acuteness of its scent.

Blood-juice, the sap of a tree of Norfolk Island, which makes an indelible marking ink, and is said to be used as a dye for calicoes, &c.

Blood Pudding. *See* Black Pudding.

Blood-root, a popular name for the fleshy rhizomes of *Sanguinaria Canadensis*, which furnishes an alkaloid, considered to be an acrid emetic, with stimulant and narcotic powers; also for the root of *Geum Canadense*, which has some reputation as a mild tonic.

Blood-stone, a dark-green stone with red spots, much used for signet-rings; a kind of chalcedony; also the name for a species of hard hematite used as a burnisher, in several trades.

Bloom, a name given to the yellowish fawn-coloured deposit from the tanning liquor on the surface of the leather, and penetrating to a slight depth; a technical term in the iron districts for a mass of metal taken out of the furnace to be hammered.

Bloomery, the furnace from which a mass of iron is brought, to be subjected to the forge hammer.

Bloom Raisins, a fine quality of sun-dried grapes.

Blotting-book, Blotting-case, a book or pad with sheets of unsized paper for drying the ink on newly written documents.

Blotting Paper, unsized paper used for drying inked manuscripts. It is either white or colored, and some is specially prepared for chemical purposes: Swedish filtering paper is more free from impurity than any other.

Blouse, a sort of linen smock-frock or outer garment, worn by workmen.

Blousse, the French name for short wool.

Blower, a smelter of tin; a plate of tin or iron, affixed to the front of a chimney to increase the draught, and prevent its smoking; a fan used on board American river steam-boats, to increase the current of air, and stimulate the combustion of the anthracite coal which is burnt.

Blowing-machine Maker, a manufacturer of forge and other large bellows' apparatus.

Blow-pipe, an important instrument, in the shape of a hollow tube, used by chemists, and many workers in metals, to increase the heat of a flame, and concentrate it on a particular point. Large blow-pipes are blown by a bellows instead of the mouth.

Blow-pipe Maker, a manufacturer of blow-pipes for chemical and other purposes.

Blow-tubes, in the glass manufacture, hollow iron rods, five to six feet long, with which the workmen gather up the fluid metal from the pots, to blow and form it into the desired shape.

Blubber, the cellular membrane in which the oil or fat of the whale is encased, this name is also given to the thick fat casing of other sea-animals, before it is boiled to extract the train oil.

Blucher, a kind of strong leather half boot worn by men and boys.

Blue Asbestos, a hydrosilicate of iron, in delicate fibres, of an indigo blue color.

Blue-backs, a name for the North American herring, *Clupea elongata;* a variety of the money cowry.

Blue Cloth, an Indian cotton fabric shipped from Madras.

Blue Copper, an ore of copper, of an indigo blue colour.

Blue Gum-wood, a fine lofty tree of Australia, the *Eucalyptus piperita*, which is chiefly used for shipbuilding purposes.

Blue-ink. *See* Ink.

Blue-john, a miner's name for fluor-spar, an esteemed variety of Derbyshire marble, which is worked up into vases and other ornaments.

Blue Lead. *See* Galena.

Blue Light, a kind of firework or night-signal which throws out a vivid light visible at a great distance.

Blue Paints; of these some of the recognised commercial varieties are celestial, Prussian, common verditer, refiners' verditer, and indigo.

Blue-peter, a square flag with a white centre and blue border, usually hoisted at the mast-head of a ship to announce her intended departure for sea.

Blue Pill, a preparation of mercury with confection of roses, liquorice root in powder, and other substances; a common medicine.

Blue Polishing-stone, a dark slate imported in small lengths for workers in silver, metal, &c., to polish off their work.

Blue-stone, a common name for sulphate of copper and vitriol.

Blue-vitriol, the sulphate of copper, which is used medicinally and to burn off proud flesh, for dyeing and electrotyping.

Bluhar, the Malay name for brush-wood.

Bluholtz, a German name for logwood, the Nicaragua dyewood.

Blunderbuss, a short gun with a large bore.

Blunk, a Scotch name for heavy cotton cloth.

Bluteau, the French name for a bolter or sieve.

Boa, a fur or woollen comforter for the neck, worn by ladies.

Boar, a male pig.

Board, a term in carpentry for all timber sawn into a less thickness than nine inches; when above that thickness it is called plank. The term is also applied to a managing committee or body of directors.

Boarder, a pensioner; one who is maintained at fixed rate.

Boarding-clerk, the servant of a custom-house agent or shipping firm, whose duty it is to communicate with vessels on their arrival in port.

Boarding-house, a private hotel or lodging-house where meals are supplied at agreed rates.

Boarding-pike, an offensive weapon used on board ship.

Boarding-school, an educational establishment where children are taught and boarded at fixed rates.

Board of Trade, the Lords Commissioners of the Privy Council of Trade.

Board-wages, a money allowance given to hired servants in lieu of their customary meals, in order that they may provide food for themselves.

Boat, a small open or decked vessel, usually propelled by oars. There are numerous kinds of boats, the construction and names of which differ, according to the service required of them: they will be found described in their alphabetical order

Boat-builder, a person who designs or assists in the making of boats, wherries, skiffs, and galleys, of various kinds.

Boat-hook, a pole with a hook, used by boatmen.

Boatman, a river seaman or waterman engaged in ferrying in harbours, &c.

Boat-plug, the stopple in a boat's bottom by which the water shipped is let out when required.

Boatswain, a warrant officer in a vessel of war; in a merchant ship a subordinate officer having charge of the sails and ropes and other gear.

Boatswain's mate, the assistant or deputy of a boatswain—in a man-of-war this functionary has to administer corporal punishment.

Boatswain's Yeoman, the man who issues boatswain's stores in a man-of-war.

Bob, a small leather-buff wheel used in Birmingham for polishing the bowls of spoons, &c.; a mining name for the beam of an engine.

Bobbin, a package or hank of Russian flax, made up according to quality in 6, 9 or 12 heads; a wooden pin to wind thread on; thin cord used by sempstresses; the brass reel or winder of a lace machine, with a narrow hollow surface for receiving the thread.

Bobbin-net, a machine-made lace.

Bobbin-net Machine, a very complicated piece of machinery for making lace net.

Bobelin, a kind of shoe made in France.

Bobineuse, one engaged in winding silk in France.

Boboi, a preparation of food in the Pacific Islands.

Bobstays, the rope which confines the bowsprit of a ship to the stem.

Bocaran, a fine sort of Spanish buckram.

Bocasine, a kind of calamanco or woollen stuff.

Boccale, a liquid measure of Italy equal to about 2 *English* quarts, but varying in different places from 1½ to 3¾ pints.

Bocking, a course woollen; also a red-herring.

Bocoy, the name for a cask in Cuba, containing 36 wine gallons. As a package for coffee, sugar, &c. the bocoy varies. The coffee cask is either great or small, the bocoy grande containing 40 arrobas, and the bocoy pequino, 28. The sugar cask holds from 50 to 54 arrobas, and the cask for molasses, 110 gallons.

Boda, (Hindustani,) a buffalo.

Bodega, a wine vault in Spain.

Bodegage, warehouse rent.

Bodian, a sea-fish caught on the Spanish coasts.

Bodice, the upper part of a lady's dress.

Bodkin, a printer's tool for picking letters out of a column or page in correcting; a sharp-pointed steel instrument for piercing holes, used by book-binders and others; a large-eyed blunt-pointed threading needle used by tailors, sempstresses, staymakers, and others.

Bodle, a small coin; a Scotch penny.

Bodocal, a kind of Spanish black grapes.

Body, thickness; a printer's term for the size of the shank of type.

Body-coat, a gentleman's swallow-tailed dress-coat.

Body-maker, a workman who makes the bodies of carriages.

Body-varnish, a thick and quick drying copal varnish used for carriages and other objects requiring to be polished.

Boerboon, the Hottentot name for the legumes of a species of *Schotea*, which are eaten when young.

Boesse, a French chisel.

Bogassieries, a name in the Danubian provinces for trimming, hosiery, and other small goods.

Bogeta, the Spanish name for a kind of herring.

Boghead Charcoal, the refuse of the Torbanehill mineral after the gas is extracted, which is used by gardeners and others as an absorbent of gaseous matters and offensive odours.

Bog-iron Ore, a peroxide of iron.

Bohar, an Arab weight about the tenth part of a ton.

Bohea, a kind of black tea.

Bohmen, a money of account in Prague equal to three kreutzers, or about one penny.

Boiard, a hand barrow for fish used in France.

Boiled Oil, a drying oil made by boiling a small quantity of litharge in linseed oil, till it is dissolved.

Boiler, a pot or caldron; a cast or wrought iron tank or vessel to hold water for generating into steam. Boilers are of various shapes, globular, cylindrical, waggon-shaped, or rectangular and tubular; sometimes for chemical and other purposes they are wrought of copper. Also a cooking vessel or culinary sauce-pan.

Boiler-maker, a manufacturer of iron boilers for steam engines.

Boiler Plates, flat sheets of iron used for making boilers, tanks, bridges, vessels, &c.

Boiling-house, the building on a sugar plantation allotted to the preparation of the cane juice into sugar.

Bois, the French name for wood, *bois de brûler* is fire wood; *bois de construction* building timber, *bois de teinture* dye-wood.

Boischene, a name in St. Domingo for the wood of *Bignonia longissima*, applied to ship-building purposes.

Boisseau, the old French bushel or decalitre, which, by the new measures of France, is 12½ litres, equal to 763 English cubic inches, or rather more than a third of an imperial bushel. As a superficial measure, the boisseau was equal to 0·04 acre, but it varied in different localities, and also according to the grain measured.

Boisselee, an agrarian measure formerly used in France, varying from 6050 square feet of Paris, to 9375 feet.

Boisselier, the French name for a turner in wood.

Boisson, a liquid measure in the old metrical system of France, the eighth part of a French pint, the pint being nearly equal to an English quart; a common draught wine made from the marc or husks of grapes, by throwing water upon them and pressing them afresh.

Boissons, the general French term for drinkables, as wine, spirits, beer, &c.

Boka, a leathern bag or bucket for drawing water in the East.

Bokhara Clover, a name given to the *Melilotus arborea;* a fodder plant which grows so freely as to yield five or six cuttings of green herbage in a season. It also furnishes a strong fibre.

Bokkena, the name for a corn-bag in some parts of India.

Bola, a Bengalese name for the fibre of *Hibiscus tiliaceus*, closely allied to the Mahoe tree of the West Indies.

Bolas, stone or iron balls attached to the ends of a twisted leather cord, used by the Gauchos and Patagonians for catching cattle and horses by entangling their legs.

Bolauk, a nasal trinket worn by the native women of India.

Bolaxinhas, small cakes shipped from Portugal to the river Gambia and other parts of Western Africa.

Bolchen, the German name for codfish.

Bole, a hydrated silicate of alumina; a friable argillaceous earth, which forms a paste when moistened with water. The red or Armenian bole is used as a tooth-powder, and for giving a colour to sprats when pickled as anchovies, or potted as paste for a breakfast relish. Powdered bole is used as an absorbent application sprinkled over ulcers. In time of scarcity this and other unctuous earths have been used in some countries as a mechanical substitute for food.

Boleah, a small covered boat used on the Ganges.

Bolection, a builder's term for a fancy [moulding.

Boleta, a Spanish name for cigarettes, or cut tobacco rolled in small pieces of paper.

Boley-oil, an undefined East Indian oil.

Bolide, a native ore of iron.

Boll, a measure for corn in Scotland, prior to the introduction of the imperial system of weights and measures. In the flour measures at present in use the boll or half sack is considered equal to 140 lbs avoirdupois, and is divided into 10 stones or pecks. The boll of pease and beans weighs 280 lb.; of oats 264 lb.; of barley about 320 lbs.; of oatmeal 140 lbs.

Bollard, a large post to secure hawsers to.

Bollico, a small loaf or cake made in Spain of flour, sugar, milk, and eggs.

Bolls, the pericarp seed-vessels of flax, which have to be crushed in the process of preparing the fibre.

Bologna Stone, a ponderous spar and a phosphorescent variety of sulphate of barytes.

Bologna Sausage, a polony made of bacon, veal, and pork fat.

Bolognini, a copper coin of Italy, from 80 to 100 going to the scudo or dollar, according to the locality. It is also called a soldi. *See* Bajocchio.

Bolsa, in Spanish a piece of money; also the exchange or place of business for money-changers and dealers.

Bolster, a long pillow or cushion stuffed with flocks, hair, or feathers, &c. a tool for punching holes, and making bolts.

Bolt, a compact parcel or roll of canvas containing about 40 yards, 24 inches in width, or 28 ells, and weighing about 28lbs.; a bolt of silk is a long narrow roll; a fastening, an iron or brass bar for securing a door.

Bolt and Screw Maker, a manufacturer of these articles in the hardware districts.

Bolt-boat, a strongly built boat, fitted to encounter rough and stormy seas.

Bolt-cutter, a shaper of bolts.

Bolter, the machinery of a flour-mill, set in motion for separating the flour from the bran.

Bolting-cloths, wire, hair, and other sieves of different degrees of fineness, used by millers for dressing or sifting flour and meal.

Bolt-rope, a rope sewed to the edges of sails to strengthen them and prevent their splitting.

Bomb, a cast-iron projectile or combustible shell; a mortar vessel.

Bombarde, the French name for a bomb vessel or gun-boat; a Maltese boat.

Bombay Candy. *See* Candy.

Bombay Duck, a name in India for the Bummalo fish when exported in a dried state; large quantities are also consumed fresh.

Bombay-maund. *See* Maund.

Bombay Shells, a name in India for the *Cassis rufa* imported at Bombay in large quantities from Zanzibar, and re-shipped to England, and to France for cutting cameos.

Bombazet, a woollen material of various colors, woven, plain, or twilled.

Bombazine, a dress material for ladies, made of silk and worsted, the warp being of the former, the weft of the latter. It was formerly largely made at Norwich, but has now gone out of fashion.

Bombic Acid, a chemical product obtained by distilling silk with sulphuric acid.

Bomb-ketch, a small vessel strengthened with large beams, for carrying mortars to throw shells in bombarding a town or fort.

Bon, the French name for a debenture, bill, or bond.

Bonanza, the Spanish name for a dividend.

Bonbonniere, a French sweetmeat box.

Bonbons, sugar plums or small confections.

Bond, an engagement in which a party's legal responsibility is involved with pecuniary security; an executed deed given for a debt.

Bonded Store-keeper, the owner of a warehouse, or store, where exciseable articles, or goods subject to customs duty, are permitted to be kept in bond.

BONDED WAREHOUSE, a storehouse where goods liable to customs duty may be lodged in bond without payment of the duty until they are removed or cleared.

BON DE TRESOR, a French Treasury bond, or government security bearing a varying rate of interest.

BONDON, the French name for a bung or stopple.

BONDONNIERE, a French cooper's tool for boring.

BOND-SERVANT, a slave, or one bound to the service of another.

BONDSMAN, one who is bound or gives security for the faithful performance of any contract or money payments, due from another. See BAIL.

BONDUC-NUT-OIL, an East Indian oil, obtained from the seed of *Guilandia Bonduc*.

BONE-ASH, calcined bones reduced to a powder, used for burnt hartshorn, for sugar refining, and for making cupels.

BONE-BLACK, a name for animal charcoal, the carbonaceous substance which remains after the calcination of bones in close vessels.

BONE BOILER AND CRUSHER, one who receives and prepares bones for various purposes, for manufacturers' and agriculturists' use.

BONE-DUST, ground bones used for manure.

BONE-EARTH, the phosphate of lime, or residue of bones which have been calcined.

BONE-GRUBBER, an itinerant who collects bones from the gutters and ash-heaps, &c., for sale.

BONES, the solid supports forming the skeleton or framework of the bodies of animals, which enter largely into commerce for manufacturing purposes, being employed by cutlers, turners, &c.; for manure and for making animal charcoal, also for gelatine, for the size used by dyers and finishers of fustians, velveteens, &c.

BONE-WASTE, the dust or refuse of bones, after the gelatine has been extracted by the bone boilers, extensively used for manure.

BONOKAL. See BUNGAL.

BON-GROS, a local name in Prussia for a money of account worth about 1½d., the 24th part of a rixdollar or thaler.

BONHAM, the name for a small pig in Ireland.

BONIGAR, a kind of round white fig grown in Spain.

BONITO, the name of a fish, the *Thymnus pelamis*, the sun-dried flesh of which is a staple commodity in the Maldives. When properly cured it is as hard as horn, and is cut for export into pieces of a few ounces' weight.

BONNET, a lady's covering for the head. Bonnets are made of different materials, according to season and fashion, as silk, straw, lace, crape, &c.

BONNET-BLOCK MAKER, a turner who makes wooden shapes for straw-bonnets to be pressed on.

BONNET-BOX, a kind of paper or thin wooden band-box.

BONNET-CLEANER, a person who carries on the trade of bleaching and renovating bonnets.

BONNET-MAKER, a maker of ladies' bonnets either a modiste or milliner, or a straw-bonnet maker.

BONNET-PEPPER, a species of capsicum.

BONNET-PRESSER, one who irons and shapes straw bonnets.

BONNET-SHAPE MAKER, a manufacturer of willow squares, or of net and other foundations for ladies' bonnets.

BONNET-WIRE MAKER, a worker in wire, who prepares shapes and trimmings for ladies' bonnets.

BONNIER, a Dutch and Flemish land measure, of very variable extent, ranging from 81 to 137⅔ French ares.

BONNY VIS, BUENO VISTA, the name in Barbados and other parts of the West Indies for varieties of *Lablab*, a kind of pulse.

BONTEN, a narrow woollen stuff.

BOOAGA, a name in some of the Pacific islands for swine.

BOOBOOT, a weight in the Sunda Isles of 5 catties; the twentieth part of a picul, or 6⅔lb. avoirdupois. See BAMBOO.

BOOK, a bound collection of printed leaves or sheets, or of blank or ruled paper.

BOOK AND CARD-EDGE GILDER AND MARBLER, a workman who ornaments and finishes off the edges of books, &c.

BOOKBINDER, one who attends to the binding of books in cloth or leather, stitching the sheets, covering and lettering &c.

BOOK-BINDER'S CLOTH-MAKER, one who prepares coloured stamped linens for binding.

BOOK-BINDER'S MATERIAL DEALER, a tradesman who keeps a supply of the tools, fittings, and essentials for the business of book-binding.

BOOK-BINDER'S PLOUGH-KNIFE MAKER, a manufacturer of the shaving plane or cutting tools for trimming or ploughing the edges of the leaves of books, paper, &c.

BOOK-BINDER'S-PRESS MAKER, a carpenter who prepares presses for the use of the book-binder.

BOOK-BINDER'S TOOL-CUTTER AND ENGRAVER, a manufacturer of metal tools for ornamenting book-covers.

BOOK-CASE, an article of furniture for a library or sitting-room, generally glazed to preserve the books from dust.

BOOK-DEBT, a charge for goods supplied, or work and labor done, entered in the ledger of a tradesman, or professional man.

BOOK-EDGE LOCK AND CLASP-MAKER, a mechanic who prepares locks and fastenings for private ledgers, pocket-books, &c.

BOOKING-OFFICE, a place where passengers or parcels are booked for sea or land transit.

BOOK-KEEPER, an accountant, or one who has charge of the books in a bank or business establishment.

BOOK-MARKER, a place-marker of ivory bone, ribbon, &c., left in a book by readers.

BOOK MUSLIN, a plain and clear fabric woven for working in the tambour; a thin kind of muslin, of which there are several kinds, made, for dresses, curtains, &c., as sacchorillo, tarlatan, leno, &c.

Book-post, the facility offered for forwarding printed matter and unstamped publications by the mails in the United Kingdom and to the Colonies at certain low rates.

Books, in a general sense, printed volumes, which furnish extensive employment both in their manufacture, and sale. Besides the home circulation, a great many are exported, and many foreign books are also brought into the kingdom for sale and to order.

Bookseller, a dealer in books, who frequently combines the business of publisher and stationer. There are many class-booksellers who confine their business to one particular branch of literature as law, medicine, divinity, &c.

Book-stall, an exposed stand for books at a shop-window or railway station, &c.

Book-trade, the business of printing and publishing books, a most important branch of London trade, which employs a large capital and a numerous class of venders, wholesale and retail, termed booksellers, who dispose of new and second-hand books.

Book-work, a printer's term for the composition or setting of type for the pages of books.

Boole, the local name for a spotted shell in the Pacific islands.

Boolgarka, a name for varieties of black and blue-eared spring wheat grown around the sea of Azof.

Booloo, a name for gum, pitch, or any other adhesive substance in the Pacific islands; also for the husk of the coco-nut.

Boom, a projecting spar in a ship run out amidships or fore and aft, as a jib-boom on the bowsprit, studding-sail boom to the yards, &c.

Boomerang, a peculiar shaped native Australian missile which recoils when thrown; a steam screw-propeller fitted on the same principle.

Boon, a name for the shove or central wood-like part of the flax stem.

Boope, the Spanish name for a species of whale.

Booraha, a pure gum obtained in the East from *Bombax malabaricum*.

Booree, a name in Sindh for the pollen of a species of Typha, which, like that of Lycopodium, is inflammable.

Boorans, a name in India for the wood of the *Rhododendron arboreum*.

Bourjooke, Borjooke, a name given to glass beads of various colours, which are used as small money in Abyssinia.

Boorka, a Circassian felted cloth.

Boornous, a woollen cloak with capuchin and without sleeves, worn by the Arabs.

Boosa, an Indian name for chaff or chopped straw for cattle provender.

Boossat, the Arabic name for a rug or carpet.

Bootka, the Arabic name for a bungalow or rest house.

Boot, the French name for a Baltic sloop; a wine measure of Antwerp consisting of 132 stoops or about 88 gallons; the space under the box-seat of a coach, where small parcels are put.

Boot-back, the hinder leather of long boots, which is often imported from the Continent ready shaped for making up.

Boot-blocker, a division of the boot and shoe trade.

Boot-blocking-machine, a contrivance for stretching leather for men's boots.

Boot-closer, one who sews together the upper leather of boots.

Boot-counter Maker, a workman who fits the stiff padding and leather at the lower part of the boot-back.

Boot-crimper, an operative who crinkles patent leather for boots and shoes on a kind of last.

Bootee, a white spotted Dacca muslin.

Boot-gram, a common Indian name for the seeds of *Cicer arietinum*.

Booth, a large canvas tent, or pavilion.

Boot-hooks, holdfasts for drawing long boots on the feet.

Boot-jack, a contrivance for taking off long boots by a pressure at the heel.

Boot-lace, a cord or tie of silk, leather or other material for fastening boots.

Boot-lace-maker, a preparer of cords and laces for boots.

Boot-last. *See* **Boot-tree.**

Boot-peg-maker, a workman who prepares wooden or metal pegs for the shoe trade.

Boot-rack, a stand to hang boots and shoes on.

Boots, leather coverings or protections for the feet; a common name for the under porter, messenger, or shoe-black at an inn.

Boot-top-maker, one who makes tops for hunting-boots and livery servants.

Boot-topping, the process of scraping a vessel's bottom to clear it from accumulated weed, &c., and daubing it with tallow, or some other mixture.

Boot-tree, an instrument for stretching the leg of a boot.

Boot-tree-maker, a manufacturer of stretcher-blocks or shapes for boots.

Booza, the Arabic name for beer.

Bopau, a small canoe in the Pacific islands, hollowed from the trunk of a tree.

Boquet, a kind of shovel used in France.

Boquin, a coarse sort of Spanish baize.

Bora, the Hindoo name for the *Dolichos Cajan*, a common pulse, also called Burbutee; a sack used in India for holding rice.

Boracic acid, a scaly saline substance, found native in the lagoons of Tuscany and in some minerals; which is chiefly used to combine with soda for the purpose of forming borax. It consists of the element Boron united with oxygen.

Borax, the biborate of soda. This salt is largely imported from India under the name of tincal, and after purification forms the refined borax of commerce. It is chiefly used as a flux for metals, and a constituent of the glazes for porcelain.

Borbi or, Burbi, a copper coin in Egypt; also a money of account in Tunis; the eighth part of a medino, 40 medini making one piastre.

Bordadillo, a Spanish name for double-flowered taffety.

Borderreau, the French name for an account.
Borderie, a small dairy or farm in France.
Bordigue, a French trawl for taking fish.
Bore, the hollow cavity or calibre of a piece of ordnance; the inside of the barrel of small arms; a tidal wave or great rush of the sea at the entrance of rivers, or in bays and harbours.
Borecole, a winter cabbage.
Borell, a timber measure on the Malabar coast, the 12th part of a covid, or 1½ inch when the timber is sawed, but *only* ⅞ of an inch when the timber is *unsawn*. *See* Bourel.
Borer, a workman employed in well-sinking.
Borilla, a rich copper ore in dust.
Boring, an operation for obtaining water, or for ascertaining the composition of a soil.
Boring-machine, the apparatus used in seeking for water in the soil; a cutting or edged tool for smoothing the internal surface of cast-iron cylinders; also a kind of drill for making small apertures.
Boron, the base of boracic acid.
Borjooke. *See* Boorjooke.
Borona, a sort of grain grown in Spain.
Boronia, a Spanish dish made of apples, pumpkins, and green capsicums.
Borracha, the Portuguese name for Indian rubber.
Bourel, **Borell**, a name for the Malabar inch; the kole of 24 borrels answers to about 20 English inches; in Travancore the borrel is nearly 1¼ English inch.
Borro, a duty laid on sheep in Spain.
Borsenhalle, a continental exchange hall or meeting-place for merchants.
Borsten, the German name for bristles.
Boscage, the food obtained by swine and cattle in forests, such as acorns, beech-mast, pig-nuts, &c.
Bosh, stuff; a trade name for mixed or adulterated butter.
Boshah, a kind of silk handkerchief made in Turkey.
Boss, a master weaver in the United States, who takes in work at his own house from a manufacturer, and employs others to execute it.
Bosse, a liquid measure of Switzerland, equal to 201·18 English gallons.
Botany Bay Oak, a local name for several species of *Casuarina* growing in New South Wales, the wood of which is ornamental, and well adapted for inlaying and marquetry. It is of a light yellowish brown colour often marked with short red veins.
Botany Bay Gum, a name for the *gum acroides* of the druggists, a yellowish red resin yielded by *Xanthorrhœa hastilis*, and *arborea* in Australia.
Botargo, the spawn of the mullet cured, which is of a deep reddish brown; the best comes from Tunis.
Botcher, a rough or unskilled workman, a bungler.
Botelho, a small river and coasting sloop used in the Persian Gulf.
Botschka, the butt or pipe of Russia, a liquid measure containing 40 vedros, and equal to rather more than 108¼ imperial gallons.
Botta, a very variable liquid measure in the Italian States, in some towns only 106 wine gallons; in others as much as 246 gallons.
Bottajo, the Italian name for a cooper.
Botte, the French name for a boot; a truss or bundle.
Bott-hammer, a wooden block with a long bent helve or handle, and having channels or flutings under its face used to beat flax.
Bottle, an earthenware or glass vessel of various sizes for holding liquors.
Bottle-boots, strong leather cases for holding bottles in the process of corking, &c.
Bottle-glass, the commonest kind of green glass.
Bottle-gourd, the fruit of the *Lagenaria vulgaris*. The hard and tough rind, cleared of the pulp and seeds, is used like the calabash for ready-made bowls and vessels for holding water.
Bottle-jack, a mechanical clock-work contrivance for roasting, the machinery of which being wound up, keeps the suspended joint revolving before the fire.
Bottle-labels, suspensory name plates for wine or spirit bottles.
Bottle-manufacturer, a glass-blower who makes bottles.
Bottle-merchant, a wholesale dealer in glass bottles.
Bottle-mould-maker, one who manufactures iron moulds in which bottles are blown to a regular size and shape.
Bottle-rack, a wooden frame with open shelves to place bottles on to drain.
Bottle-screw. *See* Cork-screw.
Bottle-stand, a liquor frame; a cruet-stand; a wooden rest for draining bottles after they have been washed.
Bottling-pliers, a kind of pincers for fastening wire over the corks and necks of bottles.
Bottoming. *See* Ballasting.
Bottomry-bond, a mortgage or pledge of a ship as security for the repayment of money advanced to the master or owner, for the purpose of enabling him to prosecute his voyage. If the ship be lost the lender loses the whole of his money. *See* Hypothecation.
Bottu, an Indian name for the husk or chaff of grain, also the 64th part of the coin formerly known as the pagoda.
Boucaner, a French term for drying and smoking meat, fish, &c.
Boucassin, the French name for bunting.
Boucaut, the French name for a large cask or hogshead.
Bouchardé (French), a sculptor's chisel.
Bouches-à-feu, the French name for cannon or artillery; guns of all kinds.
Bouchin, a French term for the extreme breadth of a ship.
Bouchon, the French term for a stopple or cork; a low public house.
Boudinier, the French name for a maker of sausages, black puddings, &c.
Boueur, a dustman or scavenger in France.

Bougie, a surgical instrument; the French name for a wax candle.

Bougie and Catheter-maker, a manufacturer of surgical instruments for delicate operations on the urethra, &c.

Bouilli, a French name for boiled meat, generally beef.

Boulanger, a baker in France, one who makes or sells bread.

Boulders, a species of rounded flint stones collected on the Sussex shores, in the first instance for ballast and transport to the northern ports, when they are forwarded to the Potteries.

Bouli, a Siamese teapot.

Boulicue, the French name for a large earthenware vessel used at sea.

Bouncing-bet, a common name in America for the soap-wort, (*Saponaria officinalis*), which by some is considered superior as an alterative to sarsaparilla.

Bounty, a bonus or premium given by some countries on the importation or exportation of certain commodities, in order to encourage and promote special trades and avocations. France grants a bounty to her fishermen. Also an advance or sum granted to recruits for the army.

Bounty Emigrant, one who receives a passage wholly or partially paid out of the colonial land funds.

Bounty Land Warrants, warrants of the United States Government, entitling the holders to selections of land in various western states and territories of the Union.

Bouquet, (French), a nosegay or a bunch of flowers; an agreeable flavor or perfume. The bouquet of wine is the pleasant aroma and etheric flavor of choice wine.

Bouquet-holder, a lady's ornamental metal hand-support for flowers.

Bourbine, a copper coin and money of account in Tunis; the twelfth part of an asper.

Bourdin, a variety of peach grown in [France.

Bourdon, a French printing term for an "out," or omission from the copy.

Bourgeois, an intermediate-sized type between brevier and long primer, 102 lines occupying about a foot; a French citizen or burgess; a landlord.

Bourrelier, the French name for a collar or harness maker.

Bourse, a name given in France, and some other parts of the Continent, to the money-market or Stock-Exchange, where the merchants and *agents de change* meet for monetary transactions.

Bouse, a term for lead ore in some of its stages of mechanical preparation.

Boussole, a French marine compass.

Boutargue, caviar or pickled fish spawn. *See* Botargo.

Bouteillage, a tax on wine in France.

Boutiquier, a French shopkeeper; a tradesman.

Boutre, another name for the dow, an Arabian coasting vessel.

Bouw, an Eastern land measure of 500 square roods. *See* Bahu.

Bovello, a Persian coin of twelve abushees, about fifteen shillings.

Bovey-coal, fossil wood, impregnated with bitumen or petroleum and containing pyrites and alum.

Bow, a bent piece of wood used for archery, made of lancewood or yew; also a small stick furnished with hair for playing the violin, &c.; the sharp or rounded front part of a vessel.

Bower Anchor, a working anchor, one to which the cable is bent; the most effective or reliable anchor of a ship.

Bowie Knife, a large sharp knife often used as a dagger or offensive weapon in the United States.

Bowline, a particular rope in a ship.

Bowline-knot, a kind of fastening which forms a loop on a rope that will not slip.

Bowls, smooth round heavy wooden balls, used for playing on a bowling-green.

Bow-pen, a metallic ruling pen.

Bowstring Hemp, a name given by Dr. Roxburgh to the strong silky fibres of the *Sanseveira zeylanica*, a liliaceous plant, because the natives of the East make their best bowstrings of it.

Bowstring-maker, one who makes hatters' bowstrings, strings for archery bows, &c.

Bowyer, a maker of archery bows.

Bowyers' Company, one of the livery companies of the city of London.

Box, a receptacle of any kind, large or small, made of various materials, wood, paper, tin, iron, mill-board, &c. Thus there are tea-chests, trunks, packing-cases, deed boxes, snuff-boxes, pill-boxes, lucifer-match boxes, &c.; a division of a printer's letter case.

Box-coat, a thick over-coat for driving, sometimes with heavy capes to carry off the rain.

Box-iron, a laundress's smoothing iron, containing a heater in a case, differing in this respect from a flat-iron which is itself heated.

Box-keeper, an attendant at a theatre or other place of public amusement.

Box-wood, a pale yellow fine-grained wood; exceedingly valuable to the turner—chiefly obtained from the *Buxus balearica*—of which about 7000 tons are annually brought from the Mediterranean ports. It is used for wood engraving, mathematical and musical instruments, &c. The box-wood of India is the *Buxus emarginata*. A good deal of box-wood is grown in this country. The American box-wood is the *Cornus florida*.

Boya, a Spanish mining term for a rich lode.

Boyam, a native Australian name for the bulbous roots of certain orchids, esteemed for the viscid mucilage they contain.

Boye, an Indian aromatic wood.

Boyer, a smack; a Flemish vessel.

Boyn, a cheese-vat.

Bozza, a liquid measure of Italy. In the Ionian Isles 80 bozze make a wine barrel of 18 English gallons.

Bozzolo, in Italy a certain quantity of corn or meal claimed by the miller for grinding.

BRAACK, a Russian establishment for officially inspecting and certifying the quality and denomination of flax and some other staple exports. Braack of some goods implies the second quality or refuse.

BRAACKERS, official inspectors selected by the Russian and foreign merchants from amongst merchants who have left the trade, whose duty it is to examine and report upon the quality of goods to be shipped.

BRABANT ELL, a measure of length used in the Prussian States about ¾ of an English yard. The common German ell is only 21½ inches.

BRACA, a name for the fathom in Portugal; the land braca is about 2·30 yards, but the marine braca is only 1·80 English yards.

BRACCIO, the Italian name for the ell, a variable cloth measure of Austria and the Papal States ranging from 21 to 27 imperial inches.

BRACE, an iron holdfast or tie, a carpenter's tool for drilling and boring; a rope attached to the yard of a ship for moving it; a name in some of the mining districts for the mouth of a shaft.

BRACE AND BELT-MAKER, a manufacturer of these articles.

BRACELET, a lady's ornament; an armlet of ornamented shell, metal, beads, &c. The manufacture and sale of decorative ornaments for ladies forms an important item of jewellers' trade.

BRACES, articles of male attire worn across the shoulders to suspend the trousers.

BRACHE, a cloth measure in Switzerland, which varies in length in different cantons.

BRACHYTYPE, a variety of calcareous spar.

BRACKET, a small fancy shelf or support projecting from a wall.

BRADOON, BRIDOON, a kind of bit for horses; the snaffle and rein of a military bridle.

BRADS, small short nails with a very slight head.

BRAHMIN'S BEADS, a name given in India to the spherical corrugated seeds of species of *Elæocarpus*, which are used by the Brahmin priests; they are also made into necklaces, *bracelets*, &c., which are much admired, and fetch a high price when capped with silver.

BRAID, a sort of plaited, twisted, or woven trimming used to ornament garments.

BRAID-COMB, a lady's back-comb for the hair.

BRAID-MAKER, a manufacturer of trimmings.

BRAILS, ropes attached to the foot or lower corner of ships' sails for hauling them up to the yards to facilitate furling them.

BRAIRD, a Scottish term for the vigorous growth of young plants.

BRAISE, a name for small coal or charcoal in France.

BRAKE, a drag applied to the wheels of carriages to check their velocity; also a machine fitted with wooden swords or teeth for dressing flax; the handle of a ship's pump.

BRAKESMAN, a servant in a railway carriage who applies the wooden brake to the rim of the wheels by a hand lever to check the speed.

BRAMAH-LOCK, a peculiar lock, constructed by the ingenious locksmith whose name it bears.

BRAMAH-PRESS, a hydrostatic press.

BRAN, the refuse of the exterior husk of wheat in grinding, which, besides its nutritious properties, has some commercial value in tanning, in calico-printing, for filling dolls, cushions, &c.

BRANGADA, the Spanish name for a drag-net.

BRANCH, the metal piece screwed on to the end of the hose of a fire engine, carrying the jet at its termination.

BRAND, properly an indelible mark made with a hot iron on a cask or case, but also applied to the distinguishing marks on cattle and sheep. Some kinds of goods as Scotch herrings, American flour, salt provisions, &c., bear an official brand as a test of their good quality, after having been supervised and examined. The government brand for naval stores is the broad arrow. Articles of foreign manufacture bearing the private brands or trade-marks of British manufacturers, are not allowed to be imported here.

BRANDING-IRON, BRANDER, the metal hand tool with which casks and cattle, &c., are branded.

BRAND-MARKS, distinguishing letters or characters burnt on the coats of domestic animals, logs of timber, &c. to claim and identify them.

BRANDY, a distillation from light-coloured wines and the skins of grapes, manufactured chiefly in the South of Europe; the trade in this spirit being very large. Cognac is the purest, oldest, and palest brandy. British brandy is a cheaper compound of rectified spirits.

BRANDY PAWNEE, a diluted alcoholic beverage in India; brandy and water.

BRANK, a provincial name for buckwheat.

BRAGRDITE, a red silver ore.

BRAS, the Malay name for rice.

BRASADA, a Spanish land measure, equal to 72·33 English inches.

BRASIER, a pan for holding live coals; a stew-pan, a camp-kettle.

BRASS, an alloy of zinc and copper, in the proportion of about one part of zinc to four of copper. It is used for watch work, kitchen utensils, &c.

BRASSAGE, a sum levied to pay the expenses of coinage.

BRASSE, a short ell used at Basle, equal to 21·41 English inches. The French brasse is 0·88 English fathom.

BRASSES, sepulchral engravings on brass, set into church pavements, &c.

BRASSEUR, the French name for a brewer.

BRASS-FINISHER, a workman who perfects and polishes articles made of brass.

BRASS-FOUNDER, a maker of brass.

BRASSIN, the name for a brewer's copper in France.

BRASS-PLATE MAKER, a manufacturer of door plates, &c., of brass.

Brass-rule, lengths of thin metal used by printers for cutting into sizes to separate advertisements and newspaper columns; also for page rules and table work in book printing, &c.

Brass-rule Cutter, a preparer of column and other metal rules, for the use of printers.

Brass Turner, a shaper and moulder of brass.

Brass Wire, copper drawn into lengths of various thicknesses, extensively used in pin-making, and also for bird cages and other purposes.

Brattice, a partition in a coal mine or under-ground work.

Brattishing, open carved work.

Brawl, an Indian cloth.

Brawn, the flesh of the hog, boned, rolled or collared, boiled, and sold fresh or pickled.

Brayer, a printer's wooden rubber, for spreading or diffusing ink on the block, now superseded by the inking roller.

Braza, a long measure in Spain, of nearly six English feet, also called Toesa. The square braza is two varas, and 200 square brazas make a fanegada.

Brazier, one who works in brass and tin, &c.

Brazilletto, the colonial name of a small tree, the *Cæsalpinia Brasiliensis*, the wood of which is much used for ornamental cabinet work, and is peculiarly adapted for carriage-wheel spokes. It was formerly used as a dye, but *C. echinata* has superseded it.

Brazilian Pebbles, lenses for spectacles, ground from pure, transparent, colourless quartz, or rock-crystal.

Brazilian Tea, a tea-substitute sold in Austria, prepared from the leaves of *Stachytarpheta mutabilis*. Another substitute in Brazil, is the *Lantana pseudothea*.

Brazil Nuts, the well-known edible seeds obtained from the capsules of the *Bertholletia excelsa*.

Brazil-wood, a dye-wood obtained from the *Cæsalpinia echinata*, imported chiefly from Pernambuco and Costa Rica. It yields rose, red, or yellow color, according to the mordant used; but it is very fugitive, and now not largely used.

Brazing, the operation of hard soldering brass and other metals by means of the blow-pipe.

Brazzeto, a measure of length in Tessino, somewhat less than half a yard: =0·434 yard.

Bread, food made of flour or ground corn baked; largely manufactured and consumed in loaves, in all civilised countries. The meal used, however, differs; in some it is chiefly wheaten flour, in others, rye, barley, or an admixture of meal.

Bread-basket, a metal or papier mâché tray, for holding bread at table.

Bread-corn, grain grown for bread, in contradistinction to cereal crops raised for cattle and horse food, and for malting.

Bread-fruit, the fruit of the *Artocarpus incisa*, which is an admirable esculent, either roasted or boiled.

Bread-knife, an ornamented knife for slicing bread.

Bread-meal, the name given to a kind of earth which in the northern parts of Sweden and Finland, is mixed with bread, and consumed in hundreds of cart-loads every year.

Bread Nut, a name in Jamaica for the fruit of the *Brosimum Alicastrum*. When boiled with salt meat or fish, they have frequently been the support of the negroes and poorer class of white persons in times of scarcity.

Bread-platter, a fancy wooden trencher for cutting bread on.

Bread-room, the store-room of a ship, where biscuit for the voyage is kept.

Bread-stuffs, an American commercial term for grain and meal; the produce of food plants which enter into commerce.

Bread-tray, a wooden or metal tray for holding loaves at table.

Bread-trencher. *See* Bread-platter.

Breadth, transverse width, contradistinguished from length.

Break, Brake, a drag put on the wheel of a coach or railway carriage to check its speed; the fly-wheel of a carriage or machine. Also the sudden rise or termination in the decks of some vessels; a substantial frame-work carriage, for breaking in young horses to harness.

Breaker, a small ship's or boat's cask for holding water.

Breakfast cups, china or earthenware cups larger than the ordinary-sized tea-cups.

Breakfast-set, the china or earthenware pieces suited for a breakfast service.

Breakfast-tray, a large metal or papier mâché tray for the breakfast ware.

Breaking Bulk, the act of commencing to discharge a cargo.

Bream, the *Abramis Brama*, a fresh water fish of the carp family, which is much eaten in the Black Sea. The sea-bream is a species of *Pargus*.

Breaming, the act of graving or cleansing the bottom of a vessel by burning.

Breane, a crystalline extract from Elemi resin.

Breast-plate, a piece of metal armour.

Breast-summer, a lintel beam, supporting the superincumbent outer wall.

Breast-wheel, an hydraulic motor which receives the water on the float-boards below the level of the axis.

Brebiage, a tax on sheep in France.

Breeches, men's garments for the lower part of the body.

Breeching, the hinder part of the harness of a horse; the tackling of a cannon.

Breeze, the small dust-coal of the mines, used to some extent for making coke and artificial fuel; also ashes and cinders used in brick burning.

Brefock, (German,) the square sail of a sloop or schooner.

Breihan, Itch Dutch ale.

Brelandinier, a petty, itinerant trader or huckster in France.

Breluche, a French drugget or floor-cloth, a mixture of thread and worsted.

BREMEN-GREEN, a pigment. *See* VERDITER.

BRENT, a provincial measure for milk in the West of England, equal to twelve gallons.

BRENTA, an Italian liquid measure of varying capacity, but in Milan equal to 15¾ imperial gallons; also used in Berge as a dry measure for plaster, containing 1½ Winchester bushel.

BREQUET-CHAIN, a gold watch-guard or chain for a gentleman's waistcoat pocket.

BRESICATE, a name in France for a kind of baize.

BRESSUMMER, the name of a kind of girder.

BRETTICES, wooden planks to support strata of earth, &c., falling.

BREVET, a short declaration of a patent-right; a royal privilege.

BREVIER, an intermediate-sized type between bourgeois and minion; 112½ lines would be contained in a foot.

BREWER, one who prepares ale and beer from malt and hops.

BREWERS' COMPANY, one of the livery companies of London, whose hall is in Addle-street, Wood-street.

BREWERS' GRAINS, the refuse malt of a brewery, used for feeding milch cows and swine.

BRIAGA, in Spain, a rope made of bass or straw.

BRICK-AXE, a workman's tool for cutting the soffits of bricks.

BRICK-BAT, a piece of a brick.

BRICKBAT-CHEESE, a Wiltshire cheese made of new milk and cream, so named from the shape of the square pieces into which it is formed.

BRICK-CLAY, a peculiar kind of earth suited for making bricks.

BRICK-DUST, powdered Bath brick, used for polishing knives and metals.

BRICKLAYER, a mason who builds with bricks.

BRICKLAYERS' COMPANY, one of the livery companies of the City of London, which has no hall of its own.

BRICKLAYING, the business of joining and cementing bricks and walling, tiling and paving.

BRICKMAKING MACHINE, a machine worked by hand or steam for moulding bricks.

BRICK-NOGGING, brick-work built up between timber framing.

BRICKS, a common building material of burnt clay, sand, and ashes, of which there are many sorts and qualities known among the trade, as malms, stocks, place-bricks, fire-bricks, pickings, paviors, seconds, Suffolk white, compass, concave, Dutch clinkers, &c. *See* CUTTERS and PLACE BRICKS.

BRICK-TEA, a kind of adulterated tea sold in many parts of Asia formed of the refuse tea-leaves and sweepings of granaries, damped and pressed into a mould, generally with bullock's blood. The coarsest is sewed up in sheep-skin; the friable masses being packed in paper. The Tartars and Thibetans make a soup of it with milk, butter and salt.

BRICK-YARD, a piece of ground where bricks are moulded and burned.

BRIDE-CAKE, an ornamented pound-cake made for a wedding breakfast, &c.

BRIDGE, a stone erection, a wooden, iron, or other platform thrown over a river, harbour, or valley to facilitate communication. There are many kinds of bridges.

BRIDGE-WARDEN, one who has the supervision or care of a bridge.

BRIDLE, a curb or leather head-piece with guiding reins and a bit for horses.

BRIDLE-CUTTER, a shaper of leather into strips for bridles.

BRIDLE-MAKER, one who makes and repairs bridles; generally the business of a saddler.

BRIDOON. *See* BRADOON.

BRIEF, a lawyer's abridged case or note of instructions.

BRIG, a vessel carrying square sails on her two masts.

BRIGANTINE, an hermaphrodite brig carrying small square sails aloft at the main.

BRIGHTENING, a process in the Manchester districts of rendering the colour of prints more brilliant by boiling in soda, &c.

BRIGNOLES, another name for Provence prunes; a kind of French plum.

BRILL, a large flat fish resembling a turbot.

BRILLIANT, a cut diamond.

BRIM, the edge; the Spanish name for canvas, or any coarse and strong linen cloth.

BRIMSTONE, a name for sulphur. *See* SULPHUR.

BRINE, dissolved salt which has been used for curing meat or pickling.

BRINE-PIT, a reservoir for brine-pickle, or water holding salt.

BRINGAL, a name for the egg plant in the East Indies.

BRINJAREE, Indian carriers, who transport goods on bullocks.

BRINS, a French name for coloured threads used in tapestry; the radiating sticks of a fan, which may be from 12 to 24 in number, and about four inches long. The two outermost, which are wider and stronger, are called panaches.

BRIQUETIER, the French name for a brick-maker.

BRISKET, a piece of meat cut from the chest of an animal.

BRISOIR, a brake for flax used in France.

BRISTLES, the strong glossy hairs on the back of the hog, used by brushmakers, saddlers, shoemakers, and others. Those from the wild boars of Russia are most esteemed.

BRISTOL BOARD, a stiff card-board.

BRISTOL DIAMONDS, a name given to fine specimens of quartz or rock crystal cut and polished.

BRISTOL-STONE, a kind of quartz or rock-crystal found at Clifton, used for vases, urns, mirrors, &c.

BRISTOL WATER, a mineral water.

BRITANNIA METAL, an alloy of tin in variable proportions with about 10 per cent of antimony and very small quantities of zinc and copper.

BRITANNIA WARE, articles made of block tin with a little copper added to give hardness to the metal.

BRITISH BRANDY, a common kind of brandy; a rectified and flavoured corn-spirit highly coloured, and made in London.

British Gum, roasted starch, a stiffening substance made for the calico printers from potatoes, wheat, or sago; also called dextrine.

British Plate, imitation silver or white metal. *See* Albata and Argentine.

British Wines, raisin, gooseberry, and other home-made wines.

Britt, a very small kind of herring (*Clupea minima*), which sometimes appears in incredible numbers on the American coasts, serving as food for other fish.

Britzska, a travelling carriage or chariot.

Broach, a tool or fitting for an Argand gas burner.

Broad-brim, a particular kind of man's hat like those worn by members of the Society of Friends.

Broad-cast, seed loosely scattered by handfuls, instead of being closely sown or drilled.

Broad-cloth, a fine kind of woollen for men's garments, exceeding twenty-nine inches wide; all of less width are known as narrow cloths.

Broad-leaf, a name in Jamaica for the *Terminalia latifolia*, the wood of which is used for boards, scantling, shingles, and staves. It is sometimes called the almond-tree from the shape of its fruit.

Broad-gauge, the wide distance between the lines of rails on a railway line; contradistinguished from the narrow gauge.

Broadside, a printer's term for a full printed page of any sized sheet; also the full length or side of a ship.

Broad-pennant, a square piece of bunting carried at the mast-head of a commodore's vessel.

Broad-sword, a sabre or short double edged weapon.

Brocade, a rich stout silk; a common name for any kind of stuff wrought and enriched with raised flowers, &c.; also a cloth of gold and silk, which in eastern countries bears the name of kinkbobs.

Brocanteur, the French name for a broker.

Brocatelle, the French name for linsey-woolsey; a variegated kind of marble artificially made from fragments of other marbles; a silk material for drapery, linings for carriages, &c.

Broccoli, a well-known culinary vegetable; a kind of cabbage.

Brocket, a red deer two years old.

Broderkin, German for embroidery.

Broderers Company, the embroiderers, one of the livery companies of the city of London, but which has no hall.

Brogans, rough-made shoes used in the North American States chiefly by slaves, and similar to those worn by the miners of South Staffordshire.

Brogues, the shoes of the Irish peasantry; also a name for breeches.

Brojobasser, an armed watchman in India.

Broken-backed, a term applied to a vessel which is hogged or loosened so as to droop at each end.

Broker, an intermediate business agent between buyer and seller in the purchase or disposal of goods, shares, &c.; a dealer on the stock-exchange commissioned to buy or sell stocks and shares, which he does through the intervention of a jobber; also a licensed corporate agent in London who transacts the business of merchants, buying and selling produce, &c. for others, but restricted from trading on his own account.

Brokerage, the percentage, commission, or consideration paid to a broker for buying or selling, and for making advances, &c.

Broker's Note, a bought or sold note; a voucher delivered by a broker to his principal, giving particulars of the sale or purchase, price, &c.

Broker's Shop, a warehouse for old goods, second-hand furniture, &c.

Broma, a chocolate preparation from the cocoa seeds or beans.

Bromine, a chemical product from sea-water and ocean springs, which is used in medicine for the same purposes as iodine, and also to some extent in photography. It bleaches as well as chlorine, but is poisonous to animal life.

Bronce-sulphuret, sulphuret of copper.

Bronco, the Italian name for the conger-eel.

Bronze, an alloy of copper in the proportion of 70 or 80 per cent., with 20 to 30 per cent. of zinc, and small quantities of tin or lead; used for castings, &c. The proportion of the metals varies.

Bronze-powder, a metallic powder resembling gold-dust. The principal uses of bronze colours are for japanning and bronzing tin and iron goods, statues, gas-fittings, papier mâché work, printing, ornamental painting, and such like purposes. *See* Leaf Metal.

Bronzist, one who casts bronzes, or lacquers metal, plaster figures, &c.

Brood-boon, a Dutch name in the Cape colony for the *Encephalartos Caffer*, a species of *Zamia*, the pith of which is prepared and baked into cakes as food.

Brood-mare, a mare kept for breeding from.

Broom, a name for the *Genista*; a decoction of the tops and seeds is used in medicine as a diuretic in dropsies.

Broom-corn, the *Sorghum dora*, which is cultivated for its stalk to make brooms; the grain of the panicles forms excellent food for poultry. In many of the United States of America it is extensively grown,—the annual produce of the plant, in the State of New York, is valued at one million sterling.

Broom Handles, slight wooden sticks prepared to fix in broom-heads.

Broom-maker. *See* Brush-maker.

Brooms, besoms or sweeping brushes. In the East they are made of coco-nut and date palm leaves; in America of broom-corn; in Great Britain of sedge, birch, twigs, the common heath or broom, &c.

Broom Seed. The seeds of *Spartium scoparium*, have been roasted and used as a substitute for coffee.

Brosemeal Brock, a name in Scotland for the refuse obtained in making pease-meal, which is used in feeding stock.

Broth, a thin meat soup.

Brougham, a kind of carriage for general use, which is either single or double, for two or four persons.

BROWN BESS, a name occasionally given to a musket with a brown barrel.
BROWN COAL, the German name for a species of lignite.
BROWN EBONY. *See* WAMARA.
BROWN HEMP, a name in Bombay for the fibre of *Hibiscus cannabinus*.
BROWN HOLLAND, an unbleached linen, used for various articles of clothing and upholstery.
BROWNING, a varnishing surface given to metals, as gun barrels, &c., by chloride of antimony.
BROWN OCHRE, a peroxide of iron.
BROWN PAINTS, in oil colours we have the following commercial varieties: English, Turkey, and burnt umbers, T. (I). Sienna, and burnt Sienna, Vandyke, purple, washed and Spanish browns.
BROWN SPAR, a crystallized form of carbonate of iron.
BROWN SUGAR, common dark Muscovado sugar.
BROWSE, a species of slag which requires reburning.
BRUCIATA, an Italian name for roasted chestnuts.
BRUCINE, an alkali extracted from the bark of the *Strychnos nux vomica* and other species.
BRUISER, a concave grinding tool used in making specula for telescopes.
BRUISING-MACHINES, crushing machines for breaking or grinding pulse, oats, maize, &c., for cattle.
BRUJULA, the Spanish name for the mariner's compass.
BRUMANDUNDOO, a Tamil and Telugu name for a limpid oil obtained from the round corrugated seeds of the prickly poppy (*Argemone Mexicana*). In Madura they are called Coorookoo Veray.
BRUNO, in Spain a term for the finest kind of bees-wax.
BRUNETA, a kind of coarse black Spanish cloth.
BRUNSWICK GREEN, a pigment of various shades of colour, according to the sulphates added.
BRUSH, a daubing or cleansing instrument, of which there are endless varieties, for clothes, the hair, sweeping, painting, and white-washing, &c.; small close underwood or thicket, sometimes called scrub in Australia; a sportsman's name for the tail of a fox.
BRUSH-APPLE, one of the native woods of New South Wales, the produce of *Achras Australis*.
BRUSH-CHERRY, one of the native woods of Australia, the produce of *Trochocarpa laurina*, a very handsome shrub.
BRUSH-MAKER, one who makes and sells brushes and brooms of various materials.
BRUSH-WEIR, a weir formed of stakes, driven at regular intervals, and interwoven with twigs, for catching fish in shallow bays, coves, rivers, &c.
BRUSH-WHEEL, a circular revolving brush used by the turner or lapidary for polishing, &c.
BRUSSELS-CARPETING, a superior kind of carpeting which has a basis composed of a warp and woof of strong linen thread; in the warp there is added to every two threads of linen, ten threads of woollen of different colours; the use of the linen is to bind the worsted together, and it is not visible on the upper surface. The woollen threads are from time to time drawn up in loops to form the figures: each row passes over a wire, which is withdrawn without cutting the yarn.
BRUSSELS-LACE, the most expensive and esteemed kind of lace made. "Brussels point" has the network made by the pillow and bobbins and a pattern of sprigs worked with the needle. "Brussels ground" has a six-sided mesh, formed by twisting four flaxen threads to a perpendicular line of mesh. "Brussels wire ground" is of silk; the meshes are partly straight and partly arched, and the pattern is worked separately by the needle.
BRUSSELS-SPROUTS, small delicate cabbage sprouts, used as a pot herb.
BRUTIA, a kind of silk.
BRYONIA-OIL, an oil used for burning in lamps in some parts of India where the fruit abounds. It is extracted by boiling in water, and is procurable commercially only in very small quantities.
BUAH, a Malay name for fruit.
BUAH-PALA, the Malay name for nutmegs.
BUAYA, a Malay name for the alligator and crocodile.
BUBBLES, small glass beads or hollow floating globes for testing the strength of spirits.
BUCELLAS, a light French wine.
BUCENTORO, the state galley or gondola formerly used by the Doge of Venice.
BUCHERON, the French name for a woodcutter, one who fells timber, cleaves firewood, &c.
BUCHU-LEAVES, a medicinal product obtained from some species of *Barosma* indigenous to the Cape colony, which have an aromatic smell, and are esteemed in pharmacy for their diuretic properties.
BUCK, a male rabbit, also applied to deer, and in some parts of the United States to a ram.
BUCKBEAN, a name for the marsh trefoil (*Trifolium paludosum*) which has some medicinal properties, being tonic and cathartic. It is said to cure the rot in sheep.
BUCKET, a lifting pail or vessel for holding water, of wood, leather, metal, gutta percha or other material.
BUCKING, the process of cleaning or bleaching linen and cotton goods in an alkaline lye.
BUCKINGHAM-LACE, a common description of lace resembling Alençon-lace.
BUCKING-HAMMER, an instrument for crushing ores fine for sampling.
BUCKING-IRON, a tool with which copper ore is pulverized.
BUCKLE-CHAPE, the part by which the buckle is affixed to the band.
BUCKLE-MAKER, one who makes buckles.
BUCKLERS, blocks of wood made to fit in the hawser holes of a ship.

Buckles, links of metal or other substance used to fasten harness, belts or parts of dress together. They are used as fastenings for shoes, knee-bands, stocks, ladies' waist-belts, &c. Buckles, as shoe and knee ornaments, have gone out of fashion of late years.

Buck-mast. *See* Beech-mast.

Buck, or **Bock-pot**, an earthenware pot made by the Indians of a peculiar description of clay found on the banks of the rivers in various parts of British Guiana, used for making the mess called pepperpot.

Buckram, strong stiffened linen cloth.

Buckramanni-peppers, a local name for capsicums in Demerara.

Buck-shot, the seeds of species of Canna which are used by the Indians of Guiana for shot. From the rhizoma of this plant is obtained the *Tous-les-mois* starch of commerce.

Buck-skin, a name often given to the tawed skins of the kid and goat, sheep, lamb, and deer, and sometimes calf-skins. Buckskin gloves ought to be made of the white tanned skins of the common deer. Buckskin leather is used for boots and shoes, breeches, saddle-seating, braces, polishing leathers, &c. A kind of cloth, also called doeskin.

Buck-thorn, the *Rhamnus catharticus*. A syrup is made from the berries which is used in cases of dropsy and worms. The juice stains paper green.

Buckum-wood. *See* Sappan-wood.

Buck Wax, a colonial name for the inspissated juice of the mani, or candle-wood tree, a species of *Amyris* or *Icica*, used by the Indians for preserving their nets and cordage, and for the same purposes as pitch. It is also called kannan.

Buckwheat, a species of *Polygonum*, cultivated for the farinaceous albumen of its seeds, which form a delicious human food, and are given to cattle, poultry, and swine. Buckwheat is grown in many countries as a fodder-plant, cut green, and converted into hay. *P. fagopyrum* is the species chiefly grown in Europe and America; *P. emarginatum*, in Asia.

Buck Yam, the *Dioscorea triphylla*, which is a native of Java and the Eastern Archipelago, and is also grown in the West Indies for its tubers.

Bucosidad, the Spanish term for tonnage or capacity of a ship.

Buddam, an Indian name for almonds; a nominal and very minute weight for pearls in Bombay; the sixteenth part of the docra, and not reducible to English weight; another mode of spelling the baddam, a nominal money of some parts of the East. *See* Chow.

Buddle, in mining, a box for washing ore in.

Buddling, Puddling, the process of separating the ores from their earthy alloy, by means of an inclined hatch or cistern.

Bude-light, a powerful concentrated light from many burners, each of which has an [illegible] circle or cylinder.

Bud[illegible]rook, an obsolete money of account on the Malabar coast.

Buff, a light drab colour; an oiled leather for polishing.

Buff and Glazer Maker, a Sheffield workman who prepares glazers of roughed leather for polishing knives.

Buffer, a striking block with elastic springs attached to a railway carriage, for deadening the concussion received from the engine.

Buffet, a kind of open cupboard or sideboard, on which plate and glass are kept for ready use, or for show.

Buff Leather, strong oil-leather prepared for sword-belts, army accoutrements, and manufacturing purposes, from the skins of the ox, buffalo, elk, &c.

Buff-sticks, pieces of wood with strips of buff leather fastened on, sometimes used for polishing.

Bufi, the Spanish name for a kind of watered camlet.

Bugalet, a sort of small French coasting vessel.

Bugalla, the Spanish name for nut-galls.

Buggalow, a crazy ill-built decked vessel, used in the coasting trade of the Peninsula of India, with one mast and a latteen sail.

Buggarah, a small Arab vessel used in navigating the Persian Gulf.

Buggasins, an old trade name for calicoes.

Buggy, a sporting dog-cart; in India the name is applied to a kind of gig; also a slide-top or phaeton carriage used in America.

Bugis, a prahu or boat of the Eastern seas, which trades between Singapore, Celebes, and other islands of the Archipelago.

Bugle, a wind instrument; also a kind of glass bead formed into pipes, and broken into various lengths, which are chiefly made in the Levant and Austria.

Bugle and Bead Maker, a manufacturer of glass and other decorative ornaments for the person.

Buhl-cutter, a fancy carver or perforator of wood, &c.

Buhl-work. *See* Marquetry.

Builder, one who superintends and carries out building operations from the plans of an architect.

Builders' Measurement, a distinction in the admeasurement of mercantile tonnage; builders' measurement being nearly double the legal registered tonnage of a ship.

Building, an edifice, a raised superstructure.

Building Slip, the inclined plane in a dock or builder's yard, on which a ship is constructed upon piles of blocks.

Building Society, a joint-stock benefit society, regulated by the act 6 and 7 Wm. IV., cap. 3, and of which there are now several thousand established in the United Kingdom and the colonies. They comprise two classes of persons, borrowers and investers. Ostensibly these societies are established to facilitate the acquisition of landed property and houses, by small periodical payments.

Building-stance, a Scotch term for a piece of building ground.

BUITRON, a Spanish fish-pot made of osiers; also a furnace for smelting silver ore.
BUJRAU, a round-bottomed barge without a keel, containing two or three cabins, used on the Ganges.
BUKE MUSLIN, a plain clear kind of muslin, woven for working in the tambour, and used for ladies' dresses. It is generally called "book" muslin.
BUKKUM-WOOD, a name in Scinde for the *Cæsalpina Sapan*, a dye-wood.
BUKSHEE, the Hindustani name for a paymaster from "Bukshish;" money paid or presented.
BULAN, the Malay term for month.
BULIONG, a Malayan axe.
BULK, dimensions; the cargo of a ship when stowed.
BULK-HEADS, the divisions or partitions which separate one part of a ship from another.
BULL, a Stock-exchange term for a jobber who has an interest in the rise of the market, and wishes to sell at a higher price than he bought at; the male of the ox tribe; a sailor's term for a small keg, holding one or two gallons.
BULLACE, a wild plum.
BULLAH, a measure of weight for grain in Mysore and Bangalore equal to 4½ lbs. In Coimbatore, as a dry measure, it is 181¼ cubic inches; in Daraporan, 216 cubic inches.
BULLET, a small round leaden ball for a gun or pistol.
BULLET-MOULD, a mould for casting leaden balls for guns, &c.
BULLION, the commercial name for uncoined gold and silver, which is imported in large quantities into the country duty free. See GOLD and SILVER.
BULLOCK, a gelded bull.
BULLOCK DRAY, a cart or waggon, &c. drawn by oxen.
BULLOCK DRIVER, one in charge of cattle, either at large or yoked.
BULLOCK'S HEART, an Indian name for a fruit tree, the *Anona reticulata*.
BULLOCK-YOKE, a wooden neck-yoke or collar for draught cattle.
BULLOOT, a name in India for the acorns of *Quercus incana*, which are sold in the bazaars as a medicine.
BULL'S EYE, a policeman's lantern; a small thick piece of glass let into the deck of a ship to admit light to a cabin; a ship's block, a wooden thimble without a sheave, having a hole through the centre and a groove round it; the centre of a target.
BULLY TREE, a fine species of *Mimusops* which is abundant in Demerara and Berbice, and is employed for house frames, posts, floors, &c., and the upper portion of the trunk and branches for making shingles, wheel-spokes, palings, &c. It squares from 20 to 30 inches, and may be obtained from 20 to 30 feet long. See also BLACK BULLY WOOD.
BULRUSHES, the leaves of a marshy plant (*Typha*) which are employed in many parts of Europe for making mats and winter coverings for plants as well as for chair bottoms. They are imported in bundles of about 34 inches in circumference, 63 bundles making a load.
BULTOW, a mode of fishing practised on the Bank fisheries, by stringing a number of hooks on one line, which is hauled into the boat from time to time heavily laden with cod fish.
BULWARKS, the top sides of a vessel, the wood-work of a ship above the upper deck.
BUMBOAT, a boat which supplies provisions to a ship in harbour or in a roadstead.
BUMMALO, BUMMELOW, BUMMOLAH, a small glutinous transparent fish about the size of a smelt, caught in the Indian seas. When dried they are much eaten by Europeans and Hindoos, and are facetiously termed Bombay ducks.
BUMMAREES, a speculative class of dealers in fish at Billingsgate, who buy largely of the salesmen and sell in smaller quantities to the fishmongers.
BUN, BOON, a name in Hindustan for coffee-berries before they are ground.
BUNCAL, BUNKAL, a goldsmith's weight in some parts of the East. At Singapore it is considered equal to the weight of two Spanish dollars or 835 to 836 grains troy. In Penang it is two or three grains less.
BUNCHIS, the Malay name for beans and many kinds of legumes.
BUND, in India an embankment against inundation; a conventional Indian term for different months and seasons.
BUNDER, the Hindustani name for a port or harbour. a Dutch superficial measure, about 2½ acres.
BUNDER-BOAT, a strong, well-built boat, employed to land passengers from vessels on the pier at Bombay.
BUNDLE, a package; two reams of printing paper.
BUNDAY, the name for a small package in Cambay and other parts of India.
BUNG, a large cork or wooden stopple for a cask; also the Persian name for hemp, *Cannabis sativa*.
BUNGALOW, an Indian dwelling-house of a single floor, which is either thatched or tiled. Those inhabited by Europeans are generally built of very large sun-dried bricks.
BUNGAPALA, the Malay name for mace, the arillus of the nutmeg.
BUNGLER, a botcher, a bad workman.
BUNNEAH, a kind of itinerant chandler in India; a camp follower.
BUNS, small sweet cakes sold by pastry-cooks and bakers, of which there are many varieties, such as Chelsea buns, Bath buns, plum buns, butter buns, &c.
BUNT, the middle of a ship's sail.
BUNTING, a thin open-made kind of worsted stuff goods, used chiefly for flags.
BUNTING AND SAY MANUFACTURER, a maker of serge and thin worsted fabrics for flags, &c.
BUNTONS, strong bawks of timber used in the coal districts.
BUOY, a floating mark or sea-beacon, usually made of copper but sometimes of cork, wood, &c., anchored over some danger, or placed at certain spots to mark the channel. Buoys are also fastened to moorings for vessels to make fast to in harbour, or to warp by, and to indicate the position of the anchor of a ship.

Buprestis, of ancient writers is the golden fly (*sundmuki*) of the Indian bazaars.

Bur, the rough head of the burdock, &c., a general name for any kind of grass seed which attaches itself to the sheep's fleece; "burry" wool requires more labour to clean it for manufacturing purposes.

Burates, a thin woollen stuff imported into Venezuela for veils.

Burba, an African money of undefined value.

Bur-bark, a fibre obtained from the *Triumfetta semitriloba*, a common weed in the West Indies.

Burber, a petty copper coin of Suez, the twelfth part of a medine.

Burbo, a money of account at Tunis, twelve burboes making the asper, and fifty-two aspers the piastre.

Burbutter. *See* Bora.

Burchio, the Italian name for a wherry or lighter.

Burdett, a cotton stuff.

Burdock, the *Arctium Lappa*; a decoction of the plant is used medicinally as an aperient, diuretic and sudorific.

Bureau, a chest of drawers, or escrutoire; also a public post-office.

Burgage, a tenure by which town lands are held in some Continental cities at a yearly ground-rent.

Burgee, a kind of small coal, suited for burning in the furnaces of engines; a three-cornered flag or distinguishing pennant used by cutters, yachts, and merchant vessels.

Burgher, a burgess or free citizen of a Dutch town.

Burgomaster, the mayor or chief magistrate of a Dutch city or Flemish town.

Burgundy, a light French wine.

Burgundy Pitch, a resin obtained from the spruce-fir.

Burhey, the Hindoo name for a carpenter.

Burin, an engraver's tool.

Burkek, a Malay name for the snipe.

Burlers, women employed in the clothing districts in picking out with tweezers all irregular knots, threads, hairs, dirt, &c., from the web of the fabric.

Burlesque, a humorous travestied or paraphrased piece at a theatre.

Burmookee, a scented oil or attar in the East Indies.

Burner, the mouth-piece for a lamp or gas-pipe. Of gas burners there are many kinds, such as lantern burners with jets, fan, star, bats'-wing, fish-tail, imitation candle, &c.

Burnet, a pasture grass.

Burning Fluid. *See* Camphine.

Burning-glass, a small glass lens or mirror for concentrating the sun's rays to a focus.

Burnisher, a bookbinder's tool, mounted with agate, blood-stone, or steel, for smoothing; it is also used by watchmakers.

Burnous, a cloak, or Arab wrapping for the head.

Burnt Sugar, caramel used for darkening the colour of liquors.

Burro, in Spanish, a whim or windlass.

Burr-oak, the *Quercus macrocarpa*, a useful and ornamental tree of North America; the wood is tough and close-grained, and more durable than the white oak.

Burroo, an Indian name for country quills or pens, and for those brought to Bombay from Muscat; they are sold by the hundred.

Burrow, the mining name for a heap of rubbish; a rabbit's hole or covert in a warren.

Burr-stones, rough hard white stones which are imported for millers' grinding-stones.

Burslochan, a vernacular name in India for tabasheer, the siliceous secretion found in the joints of the bamboo, and used medicinally.

Burthen, the weight or measure that a sea-going vessel will convey or contain. *See* Tonnage.

Burton, a tackle composed of two or more blocks with a hook in the bight of one of the running parts.

Burton Ale, an ale of great strength brewed at Burton-upon-Trent.

Burujo, a Spanish name for the marc or dregs of prepared olives or from grapes.

Bus, a common abbreviation for omnibus, a street carriage.

Buscones, miners who work on tribute or part proceeds; those who search or prospect for ores.

Bush, a piece of metal let into the centre of the sheave of a block to strengthen it.

Bushel, the principal measure for corn and dry commodities in England and her dependencies. It is the eighth of the quarter, and should weigh 80 lbs. avoirdupois of water.

Bush Syrup, a name in the Cape colony for a saccharine liquid obtained from the flowers of the *Protea mellifera*, and which is administered medicinally for diseases of the chest.

Bush-tea, the leaflets of a species of *Cyclopia*, probably *C. latifolia*, native of the Cape of Good Hope, supposed to possess expectorant and restorative properties: a few bags of this drug have been imported into London.

Busi, the Malay name for iron, busi brani being a magnet.

Busk-maker, a maker of flat whalebone, steel or wooden supports for the corsets or stays of females.

Busses, the Dutch name for large decked fishing luggers.

Bussola, in Italy a compass.

Bussolo, a small corn measure in Florence, equal to 0·335 pint.

Bussorah Gum, an Indian gum found in irregular white or yellow semi-transparent fragments, never very large. It makes a peculiar noise when chewed, and swells in water, but does not mix with it completely.

Bussu a Brazilian name for a palm, the *Manicaria saccifera* of Gaertner, which is applied to many useful purposes; the large leaves for thatch, and the spathe for making durable cloth and ready-made bags.

Bust, a half length statue, the representation of a person above the stomach.

Bustle, a lady's dress-pad.

Busuck, a small weight used in Borneo for gold and precious stones, the eighth part of a mace, and equal to 4·80 troy grains.

Butarookh, a name in India for the dried roe of fishes which forms an article of the Eastern Materia Medica. The dried roe of a kind of shad of enormous size, constitutes an article of commerce in the *Eastern* archipelago. *See* Balachong and Caviar.

Butcher, a slaughterer of beasts and vender of flesh meat; in Scotland he is called a flesher.

Butchers' Company, one of the livery companies of London, whose hall is situate in Eastcheap.

Butchers' Tray, a long wooden tray with small projecting handles for carrying meat in, usually borne on the shoulder.

Butch-root, an Indian name for the root of the *Zingiber Zerumbet*, which is used with other ingredients to keep off the attacks of the white ant from sugar canes, &c.

Butea Kino, a ruby-coloured astringent gum-resin obtained in India from the Dhak-tree (*Butea frondosa*) which affords a powerful and permanent dye.

Butler, a family servant who is entrusted with the charge of wines, &c.

Butler's Tray, a wooden tray for conveying articles to a dining-room.

Butron, a snare-net in Spain for catching birds.

Butsha, an Arabian money equal to twenty-five commassees.

Butt, the end of a plank; a large cask of any kind. The beer-butt usually contains three barrels or 108 imperial gallons, and the wine-butt the same, although it formerly contained 130 of the old wine gallons; in the leather trade a rounded crop or full hide.

Butte, a German dry measure for coal, lime, &c. ranking from 3½ to 4½ bushels.

Butter, a common name for all animal and vegetable solid oils and fats, but popularly applied to that from the milk of the cow, used for food. The home production of butter is very considerable; but we also import large quantities from the United States, the Continent, and Ireland. Fresh butter is sold in printed pats, or one pound rolls—salted butter in bulk.

Butter Cooler, a porous earthenware or glass vessel, to place butter in water during hot weather.

Butter Crock, an earthenware panning or jar for keeping salted butter, and bringing it to market; when filled it weighs about half a cwt.

Butter Knife, a blunt edged ornamental knife for a butter dish.

Butterman, a dealer in butter.

Butter-Nut, a species of walnut, the produce of *Juglans cinerea*, imported from North America. The kernels of the hard oblong nuts are very oily; the Indians formerly pounded and boiled them, and separating the oily substance which floated on the surface, mixed it with their food; hence the name. The wood is used for furniture, for wainscoting, fitting up libraries, the arches and ceilings of churches, and the panels of coaches and carriages. Sugar is made from the sap of the tree.

Butter of Cacao, a concrete oil of most agreeable flavor, obtained by pressure from the seeds or chocolate beans of *Theobroma Cacao*, and on which the nutritive properties of chocolate or cocoa depends; 100 parts of the seed yield 86 parts of oil.

Butter of Canara, a white solid oil obtained from the fruit of the *Vateria Indica*, by boiling; also called piney tallow. It makes excellent candles.

Butter-print, a fancy turned wooden mould, for giving an ornamental appearance to butter pats.

Butter-print Cutter, a turner who makes butter prints.

Butter Salesman, a wholesale vender of butter.

Butt Hinges, large hinges for doors.

Buttima, a name sometimes given to the batman in Persia.

Butt Load, a provincial name for six seams of wheat, which would be four quarters.

Buttock of Beef, a rump of beef.

Button Factor, a Scotch dealer in buttons.

Button-hole, a loop or hole in a garment, to admit a button.

Button-hook, a curved metal loop for fastening the buttons on boots, breeches, or gaiters, &c.

Button-maker, a die-sinker and moulder; a cutter or shaper of buttons used for various purposes.

Buttons, projecting knobs to fasten boots, articles of dress, &c. They are made of various substances; metal, pearl, shell, horn, bone, wood, glass, silk, porcelain, &c.

Button-wood, a name for the timber of the *Conocarpus erectus*. In North America this name is also given to the wood of *Platanus occidentalis*.

Butty, a miner who raises coal or ore by contract, at a stated price per ton.

Buttraceous having the qualities of or resembling butter

Buvande, the French term for thin or bad small wine, used as swipes is with us for small or weak beer.

Buveau, the French name for a bevel or square rule.

Buvetier, a publican or tavern keeper in France.

Buyer, a purchaser.

Buying and Selling, sale or exchange; the transmission of property from one person to another, in consideration of some price or recompence in value. If the transfer is for money it is a sale.

Buyo, a name in the Philippines for a roll of betel, the prepared masticatory for the day's use, which is carried in little boxes or bags, and handed about as a pinch of snuff or a pipe is in other countries. A fresh buyo or roll is put in the mouth every hour. *See* Betel.

Buytron, the Spanish name for a smelting furnace for ores.

Byapar, Byohar, in Hindustani, business affairs, a trade or calling; also a loan, hence byohara is a creditor or lender.

Bylander, a French coasting vessel, so named from its seldom or never losing sight of land.

By-laws, regulations of any kind, enacted, adopted, and agreed upon for the better governance of certain trades, corporations, or joint-stock associations. In some instances these have to be legally registered or published in order to be binding, as in the case of Friendly societies, insurance offices, railway companies, &c.

Bylee, a common native cart used in the interior of India.

Byner, a name in Canara for the *Caryota urens*, from which jaggery or coarse sugar, toddy, and other products are obtained.

Byre, a name in the north of Scotland for a cow-house or barn for storing turnips, &c.

Byre-trough, a hollow feeding tray in a cow-house.

Bysabole, an Indian name for coarse myrrh, a fragrant gum-resin.

Byssus, a viscid silky fibre produced by the wing-shell mollusc (*Pinna angusta*) in the Mediterranean and West Indies, &c. The filaments are extremely fine and strong, and often reach 3 feet in length. The colour, which is a reddish brown, never fades. Stockings, gloves, and other articles have been woven of it, but more as a curiosity than for use.

Byzant, or Byzantine, a Turkish gold coin of the value of £15 sterling.

C.

C, a Roman numeral, representing one hundred; CC, two hundred.

Caa, an Indian name for the leaves of the Paraguay tea-plant, a species of holly.

Ca-aapia, a Portuguese name for the emetic root of the *Dorstenia brasiliensis*, which is chewed by the natives of Brazil.

Caapiba, a Brazilian name for the Pareira brava root of South America, the product of *Cissampelos Pareira*, the wild vine or velvet-leaf, which is employed as a tonic and diuretic.

Cab, an ancient Hebrew dry measure of 1¾ to 2 pints; also a liquid measure; a popular and generally adopted abbreviation for cabriolet, a street carriage, which is either light on two wheels, with the driver perched on an elevated seat behind, and called a Hansom cab; or a heavier four-wheeled vehicle with the driver seated in front, adapted for carrying more than two persons.

Cabacalli, a wood of British Guiana impregnated with a bitter principle which defends it against worms; it lasts well under water, and is much used for planking colonial craft, but requires to be fastened with copper nails. It will square 12 to 16 inches, or even more, from 40 to 45 feet long.

Cabacinha, the Portuguese name for the cucurbitaceous fruit of the *Luffa purgans* of Martius, used medicinally as a drastic purgative in Brazil.

Cabal, a luscious beverage or rich raisin wine made in Portugal.

Cabal-rupate, Cabaluste, the Spanish name for a kind of saddle.

Caballaria, an ancient tenure of land.

Caballeria, Cavalleria, a Spanish superficial measure equal to about 32 English acres, or as much as may be sown with 60 fanegadas of grain. It is usually 1000 paces long, by 600 paces broad. *See* Fanegada.

Caballine, any thing belonging to a horse; hence coarse aloes, used in veterinary medicine, are called caballine aloes.

Caban, Cavan, an eastern measure of capacity. In the Philippines the caban of rice weighs 133 lbs. avoird., and of cocoa 83½ lbs. In Ternate, however, the caban of rice will weigh but 100½ lbs. avoirdupois; also a French cloak with a hood.

Cabaner (French), to overturn a boat keel upwards.

Cabanil, a herd or keeper of mules and asses employed in carrying corn in Spain.

Cabaret, a French tavern, or tippling and smoking house.

Cabaretier, an alehouse or tavern-keeper in France.

Cabarre, a small French flat-bottomed vessel.

Cabas, Cabat, a frail basket made of rushes; a drum, or small package of figs.

Cabaza, a large Spanish cloak.

Cabbage, a well-known pot-herb, of which there are many cultivated culinary varieties, used in a boiled state, salted, or pickled. (*See* Saur Kraut.) Cabbages are grown extensively for feeding cattle. Also a name for cloth purloined by tailors from the materials furnished to make into garments.

Cabbage-lettuce, a species of lettuce with leaves forming a low full head like the cabbage.

Cabbage-net, a small net made of twine to hold vegetables in a pot.

Cabbage-oil. *See* Colza-oil.

Cabbage-palm, the *Oreodoxa oleracea*, one of the loftiest of all palms; the brittle flakes or young shoots form an esteemed esculent in the West Indies.

Cabbling, a process in iron making, which consists in breaking up the flat masses of iron into pieces, to be again heated in a furnace, and wrought or hammered into bar iron.

Cabda, an Arab name for the palm, a measure which is equal to 3·15 inches.

Cabeça (literally a head), a nominal money of account for small purchases on some parts of the West coast of Africa, represented by cowry shells. Four large or eight small cabeças go to the ounce an imaginary coin, worth twelve thousand cowries. *See* Cowries.

CABEÇA, CABESSE, the Portuguese name for the finest kinds of silk received from India.

CABESTRILLO, a Spanish neck chain, of gold or silver.

CAB-FARE, the amount paid or demanded for the hire of a cab.

CABIDO, CAVIDO, other names for the covado, a measure of length in Portugal.

CABILLAUD, a French name for cod-fish.

CABIN, an apartment or sleeping berth in a ship; a small hut or rudely constructed cottage.

CABIN-BOY, an attendant in the captain's cabin of a merchant ship.

CABINET, a small closet or room; a set of drawers; the French name for an office.

CABINET-BRASS-FOUNDER, a workman who prepares articles for cabinet workers.

CABINET-CARVER, a wood worker in the cabinet trade.

CABINET-DE-LECTEUR, a French reading-room.

CABINET-FURNITURE, articles of furniture suited for small rooms.

CABINET-INLAYER, an artisan who veneers or variegates cabinet work with inserted materials; a workman who ornaments articles of furniture by inlaying.

CABINET-LEAD-LINER, a workman who lines boxes, cases, and articles with lead.

CABINET-MAKER, a manufacturer or repairer of wooden articles of furniture and upholstery for rooms, such as chairs, tables, couches, &c.

CABINET-PIANO, a neat compact piano, occupying little space.

CABINET-PICTURE, a small-sized picture.

CABINET-WOODS, ornamental woods suited to the purposes of the cabinet-maker.

CABIN-FURNITURE, light, compact, and folding articles, for the convenience of a passenger at sea, and occupying little space. See CAMP-FURNITURE.

CABIN PASSENGER, a voyager at sea who has the best accommodation the ship affords; in contradistinction to the steerage and intermediate passengers.

CABINS, apartments or rooms in ships, apportioned to the officers and passengers; in vessels of war, the seamen usually sleep in hammocks.

CABLE, a strong rope or chain for anchoring a ship, &c.: vessels under 150 tons are bound to have at least 150 fathoms of chain cable; those of 250 to 350 tons, 200 fathoms; 700 tons and upwards, 300 fathoms; a length of cable generally consists of about fifteen fathoms. When hempen cables are used, one-sixth more in length is required. Cables are of various sizes, from one to eighteen inches in circumference. A rope cable is always composed of three strands, every strand of three ropes, and every rope of three twists; the twist is, however, made of more or less threads, according as the cable is to be thicker or thinner. A rope two inches in circumference, and 120 fathoms long, is generally found to weigh nearly one cwt.

CABLE-LAID, any thing twisted after the manner of a cable: thus there are cable-pattern gold chains, &c.

CABLE'S LENGTH, a maritime measurement, ordinarily signifying 120 fathoms, or 240 yards; but the usual length of a ship's cable is only about seventy-five fathoms.

CABLET, a small cable.

CABLE-TIER, the space on the orlop deck or in the hold of a ship, where the cables are stowed.

CABLE-TOW, a small stream cable.

CABMAN, the driver of a cab.

CABO (Spanish), a cape; cordage or thread.

CABOB, an oriental dish.

CABOCHE, a French name for hob-nails.

CABOCHON, the French name for a precious stone, polished, but not cut.

CABOOLEAT, an agreement entered into by the Zemindars with the Indian government to farm and manage the land revenue.

CABOOSE, a house on deck where the cooking is done; a ship's fire-hearth, or stove, fitted with boilers, ovens, &c., for cooking meals for those on board. It is generally termed a galley.

CABOT, a dry measure in general use in Jersey, 19 of which are computed equal to one imperial quarter of wheat, and 11 to a quarter of barley. The potato cabot is considered to weigh 40 Jersey pounds, 13 local pounds being equal to 14 English. The cabot of apples averages 38 lbs. For other commodities, the cabot differs according to the specific gravity of the article introduced. The French name for the millet.

CABOTAGE (French), CABOTTAGGIO (Italian); names for the coasting-trade. Petit cabotage is a coasting voyage carried on in small vessels below 70 tons, between ports not far distant from each other; grand cabotage, coasting voyages to distant ports of Europe.

CABOTIER, a French coasting vessel.

CAB-OWNER, a cab proprietor; the master of a cab.

CABRERO, a Spanish goat-herd.

CABRINO, a goat-skin.

CABRIOLE, a French easy chair, formerly in use, named after the inventor.

CABRIOLET, a carriage on two or four wheels. See CAB.

CABRIOLET-PHAETON, a private carriage for general use.

CABRITILLA (Spanish), a tanned or dressed lamb or sheep-skin.

CABRON, the French name for a kid-skin.

CABROUET, a sort of cart used in sugar plantations.

CAB-STAND, an appointed place where cabs wait to be hired.

CABURNS, small lashings for binding a cable.

CACAO, the seeds of the *Theobroma Cacao*, commonly known in their prepared forms as Cocoa and Chocolate. See those heads.

CACAO-BUTTER, a yellowish solid fat, obtained by expression from the nuts or kernels of the *Theobroma Cacao*.

CACHALOT, the sperm whale (*Physeter macrocephalus*), which furnishes oil and spermaceti; and hence the fishing for it is an object of commercial importance.

CACHARADO, a kind of Spanish linen.

CACHE, a deposit of provisions made in the arctic regions by the natives or travellers; secured either by burying in the ground, or by erecting a cairn of stones over it to protect it from the foxes and bears.

CACHIBOU-RESIN, a resin obtained from the *Bursera gummifera* in the West Indies.

CACHICAN, the overseer of a farm in Spain.

CACHOLONG, a kind of chalcedony, a yellowish form of quartz.

CACHORRENAS, a kind of soap made in Spain.

CACHOMBO, the hard cocoa wood of a palm.

CACHUNDE, a paste flavoured with musk and other aromatics in Spain. A Chinese stimulant, considered efficacious in nervous complaints.

CACOMITE, a species of *Tigridia*, from the bulbs of which a good farina is extracted in Mexico.

CACOON, a name for the seeds of *Entada gigalobium*, which are used for making purses, scent-bottles, &c.

CACTINE, a name given to the red colouring matter obtained from the fruit of some species of *Cacti* and *Opuntia*.

CACTUS, a common name for many of the *Opuntia* family; an interesting genus of plants, most of which are curious and handsome but of little use except as fences in the tropics. *Opuntia cochinillifera* is, however, of importance, as on it are reared the cochineal insects. The fruit is not much esteemed as an edible, but it is used for feeding pigs in many quarters, and has lately been turned to some account in producing alcohol.

CAD, the conductor or attendant of an omnibus; a hanger-on about coach-yards and railway stations.

CADARP, a liquid measure of some parts of Spain, equal to 3·627 pints.

CADARZO, a name in Spain for coarse silk, which cannot be spun with a wheel.

CADASTRE, the French and Peninsular name for a terrier, or official survey and valuation of real property; a register in which are inscribed the names and particulars of all the landed property of the country, and the owners thereof, with a valuation of their incomes.

CADDIS, CADDAS, an old name for ribbons of a peculiar make; which were usually imported in pieces of thirty-six yards; a kind of tape lint for dressing a wound.

CADDY, an ancient measure for wine; also a small tea chest or box for table use.

CADE, a keg or small barrel; also a variable fish measure; 500 herrings or 1000 sprats make a cade.

CADEE, another name for the canne or covid of *Morocco*, a long measure of twenty-one inches.

CADENAS, the French name for a padlock.

CADENE, a kind of common carpet formerly imported from the Levant.

CADE-OIL, an empyreumatic oil obtained by distillation in a retort, from the wood of *Juniperus Oxycedrus*. It is much used in France in veterinary medicine.

CADERNO, the name for a small quantity of paper in Portugal, usually five or six sheets.

CADGER, a beggar; a huckster, or dealer in dairy produce.

CADIS, a French name for a kind of coarse serge.

CADJAN, an Indian name for the leaves of the palmyra or fan palm, used for writing on with an iron style; also for matting.

CADJARA, a silk horse-cloth or trapping used in Russia.

CADMIA, the crust deposited in furnaces in which zinc ore is sublimed, containing from ten to twenty per cent of cadmium.

CADMIUM, a beautiful white metal, harder than tin, and very ductile and malleable, which frequently occurs in zinc ores.

CADMIUM YELLOW, the commercial name for the sulphide of cadmium, an artist's paint, the finest and most permanent of all the yellow pigments in use.

CADO, a corn measure of Santa Maura, one of the Ionian islands, containing about 1¼ bushel; but, according to some authorities, it reaches to 3¾ bushels.

CADRAN, a French name for a dial-plate.

CADY, a street porter in Edinburgh.

CAEN STONE, a fine white stone from Normandy, much used for Gothic structures.

CAFA, plait made in the Pacific islands from coco-nut coir; a cotton stuff in Spain.

CAFE (French), the bean or berry of coffee; also a coffee-house.

CAFETIER (French), the keeper of a coffee-house; a vessel for holding the beverage.

CAFFEINE, the active nitrogenous principle giving the flavour to coffee, and which is similar to theine in tea.

CAFFIR CORN, a variety of *Sorghum* cultivated in parts of Southern Africa for its seed.

CAFFISE, CAFFISO, a measure of capacity for grain and liquids in the Mediterranean ports. In Messina and Trieste the Caffiso for fluids is 2½ gallons, in Malta 4½. For grain the Caffiso ranges from 1 to 2 quarters.

CAFILAH, CAFFILA, the Persian name for an official or government caravan; a company of travellers or merchants.

CAFTAN, a thick quilted cloak or robe of wool or silk used in Arabia and Turkey; it is generally white with pale flowers and is sometimes lined with fur.

CAG, a small barrel or cask. *See* KEG.

CAGARRACHE, one who washes the olives in an oil-mill in Spain.

CAGE, a basket or enclosed frame for ascending and descending coal mines; a prison for birds. *Cage of a Whim*, is a mining name for the barrel on which the rope is wound up.

CAGLIARESO, a petty copper coin of Sardinia.

CAGMAG, an opprobrious term applied to bad meat or poultry.

CAHAN, a nominal Indian currency, equivalent to 6d. or the fourth part of a rupee.

CAHIER, a term employed in the paper trade on the Continent, signifying a parcel of 5 or 6 sheets, the fourth or fifth of a quire.

CAHIZ (plural CAHICES), a variable dry measure in Spain. The standard cahiz of 12 fanegas used in Cadiz and other places is rather more than 18 imperial bushels, and in Valencia 100 cahices are equal to 70¼ quarters. In some provincial districts of Spain the cahiz is only 5 to 5½ bushels.

...uperficial measure of Spain, ... six fanegadas, and equal ...ght perches. What is generally ...ood by a cahizada, is the ...d that can be sown with a ...

...local name for a superior ...n the Tonga islands.

...NE, a plume-like palm, the ...phunx of Martius, native of ...bearing nuts, which grow in ...ke a bunch of grapes; an oil ...d from them by expression equal ...om the coco-nut.

... nominal money of Arracan and ... calculated in cowry shells, and ...o 6d. sterling.

... the Brazilian name for the American ...m, *Elais melanococca*; and of its very ...k leaves ropes are made. The oil is ...cally used in Brazil, but not much exported.

CAICO (Italian), a small skiff, a jolly boat.

CAILCEDRA, a bark, obtained from the *Khaya Senegalensis*, and which yields a bitter principle. The bark is much used by the negroes of the Gambia (in infusion and decoction), in the treatment of the violent fevers of that country.

CAIMAN, CAYMAN, a South American name for the crocodile.

CAIMEHS, the Turkish name for the paper currency of the Sultan, 120 piastres in Caimehs being only equal to about 117 specie.

CAIQUE, a light bark used on the Bosphorus.

CAIRN, an erection of stones, of Celtic origin, for monumental or religious uses; but still applied to a heap raised for signal or memorial purposes.

CAIRNGORM, a variety of rock-crystal used by the Scotch to ornament their accoutrements, and of which seals, necklaces, and other trinkets are made.

CAISSON, a water-tight box for facilitating the commencement of the foundations of piers, bridges, &c.

CAJEPUT, an essential oil of a green colour, obtained by distillation from the leaves and twigs of the *Melaleuca Leucadendron*, a native of the East. It is a powerful antispasmodic, stimulant, and sudorific.

CAJON, CAXON, the Spanish name for a chest. In the South American mining districts it is applied to a weight of 50 quintals of mineral; but in some of the western republics of South America it is two montons or 64 quintals.

CAKE, a kneaded or solid mass of any kind, as a cake of copper, of Indian ink, of pastry or baked dough, &c.

CAKE-BREAKER, a crushing and cutting implement for breaking up oil-cake for the feeding of stock, and pressing rape-cake for manure.

CAKE-MOULD, a confectioner's metal pattern for baking fancy pastry in.

CAKE, OIL. *See* OIL-CAKE.

CAKE-TOASTER, a toasting fork.

CAL, a Cornish mining name for wolfram; a kind of iron ...; the Spanish name for lime; Caleros being lime burners.

CALABASHES, a name in Tunis for the Ottoman red-caps; also the fruit of the *Crescentia cujete*, which when young are pickled. The hard rind or covering, when the pulp has been taken out, is made into all kinds of domestic utensils by the negroes — cups and saucers, baskets and bowls, pepper and salt dishes, &c., which take the place of crockery, and are not so easily broken or destroyed. Many will stand the fire for cooking as well as an iron pot.

CALABASSI, a red fez or military cap made in Tunis, and largely shipped to the Levant for Turkish use.

CALABAZATE, in Spain, pumpkins preserved in sugar, or steeped in honey.

CALAFATARE (Italian), to caulk a ship or stop her leaks.

CALAITE, a name for the turquoise.

CALAMANCO, a glossy woollen stuff, chequered in the warp, either ribbed or plain, formerly manufactured in the Netherlands, now made in Bradford.

CALAMANDER WOOD, a valuable furniture wood of Ceylon.

CALAMBAK. *See* AGALLOCHUM WOOD.

CALAMBOUR, a kind of eagle or aloes wood, sometimes used for inlaying and cabinet work.

CALAMINE, a carbonate of zinc.

CALAMUS OIL, an oil obtained from the root of the sweet flag, *Acorus Calamus*.

CALANCA (Italian), printed cotton.

CALAVANCE, a name for several kinds of pulse, including the *Dolichos Barbadensis* and *sinensis*.

CALCAR, a calcining furnace in a glass-works.

CALCAREOUS CEMENT, an artificial water cement for building.

CALCAREOUS EARTH, a gritty soil which contains a large percentage of lime.

CALCAREOUS SPAR, a carbonate of lime.

CALCAVELLA, a high-flavoured Lisbon white wine.

CALCEDONY. *See* CHALCEDONY.

CALCINATION, the reduction of substances to cinders or ash.

CALCINER, a name given to the burning house, or place where minerals, &c. are pulverized by heat.

CALCIUM, the metallic base of lime, a silver-white metal obtained by the same method as barium. Fluoride of calcium is the Derbyshire or fluor spar.

CALCO, a weight in the Ionian islands, of twenty-four troy grains, twenty calcisi making one troy ounce.

CALCQUIN. *See* CALKING.

CALCULATING MACHINE, an instrument with toothed wheels, each turning freely on its own centre for automaton calculation. The schwan-pan of the Chinese, and the Roman abacus, are also species of counting machines for facilitating calculations.

CALCULATOR, one who reckons or estimates matters of figures or detail.

CALDERAIO (Italian), CALDERERO (Spanish), a brazier or tinker.

CALDRON, a large iron boiler or pot.

CALECHE, CALASH, a lady's hood; also a small hooded carriage running on low wheels.

CALENCART, a kind of calico imported into Hayti.

CALENDAR, an almanac.

CALENDER, a machine for smoothing or hot-pressing fabrics between rollers, to give them a glossy or wavy appearance.

CALENDERER, a smoother and presser of fabrics; one engaged in scouring and hot-pressing cloth.

CALESIN, a one-horse chaise in Spain.

CALF, prepared leather for book-binding, &c.: the young of a cow, usually so termed until it is past six months old, when it becomes a yearling. Calves generally become fat enough for veal in eight or nine weeks.

CALF-PEN, an out-house or enclosure where calves are kept.

CALF'S-FOOT JELLY. See CALVES'-FOOT JELLY.

CALF-SKINS, the hide of the calf which, when tanned, forms the material for one of the most valuable kinds of leather, and is used by accoutrement-makers and boot-makers; calf-skins are also converted into vellum.

CALLATOUR, an Indian red wood.

CALIBRE (French), a word now generally adopted to express the bore of a piece of ordnance.

CALIBRE COMPASSES. See CALLIPERS.

CALICHE, a name for nitrate of soda found in Peru.

CALICO, a general term for any plain white cloth made from cotton, but which receives peculiar distinctive names as it improves in quality and strength, and according to the purposes for which it is used. In the United States the term is restricted by popular usage to prints. Dyed calicoes are used for book-binding. There are super calicoes, shirting calicoes, unbleached calicoes, &c.

CALICO AND SILK PRINTER, a workman who imprints coloured figures on silks and cottons, by cylindrical machinery, but the term is usually applied to the master-manufacturers or owners of print-works.

CALICO-GLAZER, one who smooths or hot-presses calicoes. See CALENDERER.

CALICO-PRINTER'S BLOCK-CUTTER, a maker of blocks for the use of calico-printers.

CALICO-PRINTING, the process of impressing figured patterns upon cotton by coloured substances.

CALIDAD, the best kind of Cuba tobacco.

CALIFORNIA-GOLD. The gold discoveries in California were made in 1848; and the total produce of the mines was estimated, on good authority, up to the close of 1855, to have amounted to upwards of £80,000,000 sterling. The California gold received at the United States' mints to the close of 1854, was to the amount of £54,000,000; whilst about £6,000,000 was circulating locally in coin, or held in bullion, and used in manufactures, &c. The officially registered shipments of gold from California, in the five years 1851-55, were to the value of nearly £47,000,000; but much was shipped unregistered.

CALIGA, a kind of leather half-boots worn by the Roman soldiers.

CALIN, an alloy of lead and tin, used by the Chinese for tea canisters and other articles.

CALIPER. See CALLIPERS.

CALIS, the Spanish name for ...

CALISAYA-BARK, a valuable ... obtained from *Cinchona* ... Bolivian tree, which is ric... loid.

CALISHERAS, insulated depo... nitrate of soda in Peru.

CALISTHENIC INSTRUMENT-MA... facturer of chest expanders, ...

CALK, a name for lime.

CALKING, the process of tracing ... or hard pencil, through a p... has been rubbed with coloured c... back; or copying a drawing ... with chalk. See CAULKING.

CALKINS, CAWKINS, the prominent or ... extremities of the horse's shoe, for... and turned downwards to prevent s...

CALL, a visit; the demand for payme... an instalment due on shares; a speculati... on the Stock Exchange.

CALLA, a commercial term used on some parts of the coast of Africa, indicating exchange or barter in goods, in contradistinction to *Calla-biera*, which means cash or currency.

CALLEMANDRA, a kind of Spanish woollen stuff.

CALLIGRAPHY, the art of fine penmanship.

CALLIPASH, the upper part of the turtle.

CALLIPEE, the under part of the turtle.

CALLIPERS, instruments used in gauging; large compasses to measure a diameter.

CALLIPEVA, an esteemed river mullet of the West Indian seas (*Mugil lisa*), seldom extending further than the embouchures of streams or into the ponds and marshes. Its scales are useful for making ornaments, and its roe forms an excellent caviare.

CALLOU (Spanish), a wine or fermented liquor extracted from palms.

CALMUCKS, a sort of hair-cloth.

CALOMEL, a mild preparation of mercury, the dichloride, used as an alterative or purgative.

CALORIMETER, an instrument to indicate the heat given out by bodies in cooling or passing from one temperature to another, which is ascertained by the quantity of ice it will melt.

CALOTYPE, an improved method of taking photographs on paper, invented by Mr. Talbot.

CALOTYPE-PAPER, photogenic paper chemically prepared for the calotype process.

CALOW, the Polish inch. The old Polish calow was 0·977 English inch; the new calow, since 1819, is equal to 0·94 inch. In Cracow, however, the calow runs to 1·17 inch.

CALPIZQUE, a rent collector in Spain.

CALQUING. See CALKING.

CALUMBA. See COLOMBO-ROOT.

CALVES'-FOOT JELLY, a nutritious jelly made by boiling the feet of calves, and flavouring the extract.

CALVIA (plural CALVIE), a grain measure of Venetian Lombardy, 2·636 gallons.

CALX, an obsolete name for metallic oxides.

CALZADO (Spanish), a shoe or sandal of any kind.

CALZETTAIO (Italian), a hosier.

CALZOLAIO (Italian), a shoemaker.

CAM, a substitute for the crank movement in weaving.

CAMACO, an Ionian long measure equal to 5¼ imperial yards.

CAMAIL (French), a domino; a capuchin or short cloak sometimes made of fur.

CAMANONCA, a kind of Spanish stuff formerly used for linings.

CAMARA, a store-house for grain; a wood obtained in Essequibo from *Dipteryx odorata*; it is hard, tough, and durable in an eminent degree, and it is said that a portion of its timber, one inch square and of a given length, bears 100lbs more weight than any other timber in Guiana of the same dimensions. It is therefore well adapted for shafts, mill-wheels, or cogs. It will square 18 or 20 inches from 40 to 50 feet long.

CAMARAGE, rent paid for a granary.

CAMAROES, a Portuguese name for large shrimps or prawns.

CAMASPEE, a money of account at Mocha on the Red Sea, the 60th part of a dollar.

CAMATA, the commercial name for half-grown acorns dried, which are imported for tanning; Camatina are incipient acorns used for the same purpose.

CAMBAY STONE, a kind of carnelian obtained in the East Indies.

CAMBER, a repairing wet dock or inlet from a harbour.

CAMBER-BEAM, an arched beam used in platforms.

CAMBER-SLIP, an instrument for drawing arches.

CAMBETTA, a provincial dry measure of France equal to 2¼ pints, sometimes called Gambetta.

CAMBIADOR, a banker or money-changer in Spain.

CAMBIALE (Italian), a bill of exchange.

CAMBIO (Spanish), barter, the giving or taking bills of exchange; a rise or fall in the course of exchange.

CAMBIST, a banker; one well versed in exchanges and foreign moneys; a trafficker in bills. Also applied to a book descriptive of moneys, weights and measures of various countries. The two best known British works on this subject are Kelly's Cambist, and Tate's Cambist; the former of these however is now obsolete in its definitions.

CAMBIUNTE, a kind of Spanish camlet.

CAMBLET. See CAMLET.

CAMBOO, an Indian native name for the grain of *Holcus spicatus*, the *Penicillaria spicata* of Willdenow. See COUSCOUS.

CAMBRAYON, a Spanish name for coarse cambric.

CAMBREL, an iron with hooks to hang meat on.

CAMBRIC, a cotton fabric in imitation of fine linen; its varieties are glazed, white, and coloured for linings; twilled, figured, striped, and corded. Cotton cambrics are either white or printed for dresses, or used as French cambrics. The former are made chiefly in Lancashire, the latter in Glasgow. Scotch cambric is an imitation cambric made from fine hard twisted cotton.

CAMBRIC MUSLIN, a very fine and thin linen fabric, an imitation of cambric, and used for the same purposes.

CAME, a name in some parts of India for the half rupee or 1s.

CAMEL, a contrivance for lifting ships over a bar or shoal that obstructs the navigation of a river; also the well-known beast of burden (*Camelus Bactrianus*) with two humps. The milk of the camel is excellent and supplies butter and cheese. The flesh is hard and unsavoury, and little esteemed even by the Tartars. They use the hump cut into slices, which dissolved in tea serves the purpose of butter. The hide furnishes the Arab with sandals and belts, and the dung is an important article of fuel in arid countries.

CAMELEER, a driver or attendant on camels.

CAMEL-HAIR PENCIL, a small brush used by painters in water-colours made of badgers' hair, camels' hair, or other suitable material.

CAMELLIA, a genus of beautiful evergreen shrubs; the seeds of the *Camellia oleifera*, a native of China, yield an excellent table oil. The large, splendid, rose-like flowers of several species of camellia are much prized in the metropolis, being cultivated in private hot-houses, and sold by florists.

CAMEL-LOAD, the load a camel will carry. The Bactrian camel can carry a burden of six cwt.; but the usual load for a camel, on a short journey, is from 400 to 500 lbs.; on longer journeys about 100 lbs. less. Their pace being about two miles and a half per hour, they are the measurers of distance in the East, the mile there being equal to two and a half English miles, and called an hour, from the time the camel takes in traversing it.

CAMELOT. See CAMLET.

CAMELS'-HAIR, is much longer than sheep's wool, and often as fine as silk. There are three kinds, red, white, and grey. The hair on a camel would weigh about 10 lbs.

CAMELS' HAIR PENCIL MAKER, a manufacturer of small hair paint-brushes used in water-colour painting.

CAMELS' HAY, a name given to some of the fragrant grasses of the *Andropogon* family.

CAMEO-CUTTER, an engraver of cameos, one who cuts and embosses stones, shells, &c.

CAMEOS, gems worked in *relievo*; small bas-reliefs cut on various substances, as stone, shell, lava, ivory, &c. They are frequently cut on certain conch shells or strombs, the substance of which consists of two distinct layers of different colours, textures and hardness. The black conch offers the most decided contrast of colour in the layers. Shell cameos are now very common, and some display a great deal of taste in the design, cutting, and adaptation of the various layers of the helmet, and other shells to the required tint.

CAMERA OBSCURA, literally a dark chamber, or an optical apparatus in the shape of a box, for collecting light, and exhibiting external objects in their natural colours on a white surface.

CAMES, rods of cast lead used by glaziers in framing church windows and other quarrels of glass.

CAMFERING, taking off an angle or edge of timber.

CAMICIOTTO (Italian), a linen petticoat.

CAMICO, a measure of length in the Ionian islands, consisting of 5½ yards.

CAMIONNAGE (French), cartage or dray hire.

CAMISA, an inner linen garment worn in Spain.

CAMISON, a blouse or outer frock worn by workmen in Spain.

CAMLET, a stuff made originally of goats' hair, now frequently of hair and silk, or wool and thread.

CAMOMILE, CHAMOMILE; the flowers of *Anthemis nobilis*, in Europe are employed medicinally as a cheap tonic carminative anodyne; when taken in large doses, however, they prove powerfully emetic. Another species, *A. Pyrethrum* furnishes the pellitory root.

CAMOSCIO (Italian), tanned leather.

CAMOTES, a Spanish name for the sweet potato.

CAMP, the ground on which an army pitches its tents.

CAMPANINO, a variety of Spanish marble.

CAMPEACHY WOOD, a hard red dye-wood from the *Hæmatoxylon campechianum*, better known as logwood.

CAMP-BED, a folding iron bedstead, with tester laths, for field use.

CAMP-EQUIPAGE MAKER, a maker of portable articles of light materials adapted for easy transport. *See* CAMP-FURNITURE.

CAMP-FOLLOWERS, the attendants on an army.

CAMP-FURNITURE, articles of cabinet work made compact, light, and portable, so as to be easily folded and transported; such as camp-stools, camp-bedsteads, tables, &c.

CAMPHINE, a popular name for essential resinous oils, such as the purified oil or distilled spirits of turpentine. When intended for a burning fluid, it is mixed with alcohol in various proportions.

CAMPHINE LAMP, a lamp made with proper precautions for burning camphine, having a reservoir generally of glass, placed between the supporting pillar and the burner, to hold the spirit and the cotton wick dips into it.

CAMPHOR, a concrete acrid drug, of a highly penetrating smell, obtained from trees indigenous to Japan, and the Eastern archipelago. The China or Japan camphor-tree is the *Laurus camphora* of Linnæus, the *Camphora officinarum* of Nees. The camphor-tree of Sumatra and Borneo, is the *Dryobalanops camphora*.

CAMPHOR JULEP, a name in America for camphor water.

CAMPHOR WATER, a solution of camphor used as a vehicle for the administration of fever medicines.

CAMPHOR-WOOD-OIL, an oil obtained in the East from *Dryobalanops camphora*, which is largely used at Singapore instead of turpentine.

CAMPIONE (Italian), a journal, ledger, or shopkeeper's book.

CAMP-KETTLE, an iron pot for the use of soldiers and colonists.

CAMPO, an Italian superficial measure, varying in different localities from 0·688 acre to 1·285 acre.

CAMPOI, a kind of tea.

CAMPSOR, a money-changer.

CAMP-STOOL, a light portable folding stool.

CAMBOTO (Italian), a cabin boy.

CAMWOOD, a red dyeing wood, the produce of *Baphia nitida* imported from the West coast of Africa.

CAN, a tin vessel for milk or beer, for holding flax and for other purposes; a liquid measure of Siam equal to 4·19 pints; also an abbreviated name for the candareen, a Chinese weight and measure.

CANA, a name in some of the Pacific islands for sponge; a long and superficial measure used in Italy and some parts of France, which is of very variable dimensions. The maximum is 117·68 inches the builders' measure in Florence, the minimum 61·10 inches in Barcelona. *See* CANNE.

CANABALLA, a kind of Spanish fishing-boat.

CANADA, CANADO, a liquid measure of Spain and Portugal; also occasionally used in Ceylon. In Lisbon the canada is equal to nearly 2¼ pints; in Brazil it is more than five times the dimensions of the Lisbon canada, being equal to 12¼ pints. In Ceylon the canada passes for 2·66 English pints. The Spanish canada is much larger, being equal to 8·68 gallons.

CANADA-BALSAM, an oleo-resin, obtained from the American silver-fir, *Abies balsamifera*. It is used for medicinal and manufacturing purposes, and makes a fine transparent varnish for water-colour drawings, which does not become darker with time.

CANADA-RICE, a wild species of rice, the *Zizania aquatica*, growing in all the shallow streams and swamps of N. West America. It is exceedingly prolific of farinaceous seeds, which afford a very good meal. The plant seems designed by nature to become the indigenous bread-corn of the newly settled regions; for its seeds contribute essentially to the support of the wandering tribes of Indians, and feed immense flocks of wild fowl.

CANADA-SUGAR, dark sugar made from the sap of the sugar-maple tree, *Acer saccharinum*.

CANADIAN CURRENCY. The pounds, shillings, and pence in the British North American colonies, commonly called Halifax currency, are in value ten per cent below the same coins in sterling money; hence £100 sterling is equivalent to £110 currency. The pound sterling passes under the Act Aug. 2, 1854, for £1 : 4 : 6 currency.

CANADIAN TIMBER. A large trade is carried on with the ports of the river St. Lawrence for timber obtained from the Ottawa district and other parts of Lower Canada. In 1854 the squared timber exported from Quebec amounted to [illegible]16,000 feet, besides 3,476,491 standard of deals, lathwood, staves, masts, spars, railway sleepers, and other manufactures of wood: 160 Liverpool vessels were engaged in the trade.

CANADIAN YELLOW-ROOT, the *Hydrastis Canadensis*, which furnishes a valuable bitter and a useful yellow dye.

CANAHR, a name in the Pacific for the mullet fish.

CANAKIN, a small can.

CANAL, an artificial navigable water channel formed for the passage of boats or vessels with cargo.

CANAL-BOAT, a flat-bottomed barge or boat of light draught adapted for navigating canals.

CANAL-BOAT WEIGHING MACHINE, a patent lock poising-machine for weighing canal boats and their cargoes.

CANAL-LIFT, an hydro-pneumatic elevator for raising boats from one level to another.

CANAL-LOCK, a stop-gate or sluice to the chamber of a canal, for passing boats through, from a higher to a lower level of the channel, or *vice versa*.

CANAMO, the Spanish name for hemp.

CANAN. *See* CAN.

CANAPUCCIA (Italian), hemp-seed.

CANARY, a wine made in the Canary islands, also known as sack.

CANARY BIRD, a well-known song bird, the *Carduelis canaria*, which is largely bred here, and also imported from Germany, where the rearing of these birds is extensively carried on.

CANARY MOSS, a lichen used for dyeing, the *Parmelia perlata*.

CANARY SEED, the seeds of *Phalaris canariensis*, a native grass of Britain, which are given to birds, and of which as much as 500 tons are annually sold for that purpose.

CANARY STONE, a beautiful yellow species of carnelian, rather rare, and named from the resemblance of its colour to the plumage of a canary bird.

CANARY WOOD, a name given to the wood of the *Laurus Indica*, a native of Madeira, and *Laurus Canariensis*, a native of the Canaries.

CANASTER, C'NASTER, a kind of American tobacco, which derives its name from a particular kind of rush basket, in which it was formerly imported.

CAN-BUOY, a large floating buoy.

CANCHA, an ore found in Chile.

CAND, a name in the Cornish mining districts, for fluor spar.

CANDACA, a dry measure used in the Mysore district of India, equal to 3¼ bushels.

CANDAGON, a grain measure of Bangalore. *See* CANDY.

CANDARA, a frame of laths for sifting earth or sand, used in Spain.

CANDAREEN, a Chinese weight, the 100th part of a tael, and containing ten le or cash. In accounts the money value of the candareen ranges from ten to fourteen copper cash, but as a weight, whether for silver or any other article, the le or cash continues to be the same integral part of a candareen. The candareen may be estimated at 5¾ grains, although in some quarters of the East it weighs 5·38 grains.

CANDEAL, a kind of Spanish wheat.

CANDEE, a measure of length in Cochin China, equal to 19·12 inches English.

CANDELABRUM, an ornamental metal stand with branches for holding lights.

CANDEROS, an Indian resin of a pellucid white, which, being susceptible of a good polish, has been turned into small ornaments and toys.

CANDIDATE, an aspirant or suitor for a public office or business post.

CANDIED, dried with sugar.

CANDIED-PEEL, preserved lemon or citron peel, used for pastry and confectionery.

CANDIL, a weight in Sumatra of about 433½ lbs. *See* CANDY.

CANDIOTA, the name for a barrel or keg in Spain; a large earthen jar.

CANDITEERS, wooden frames or fagots to protect workmen.

CANDLEBERRY MYRTLE, a name given to the *Myrica cerifera*; from the berries a beautiful green wax is obtained in America and the Cape colony, which has been found useful for candles.

CANDLE-BOX, a receptacle for candles usually nailed to the wall of a kitchen, &c.

CANDLE-ENDS, pieces of candle partially burnt, which are often disposed of by those who object to seeing short candles.

CANDLE-MAKER, a tallow-chandler; one who makes candles of one or more kinds.

CANDLE-MOULD FRAME, a frame or case to hold the shapes or moulds into which the heated tallow or wax is run.

CANDLE-MOULD-MAKER, an artisan who makes the pewter metal moulds or shapes used by candle-makers.

CANDLENUT, a trade name given to the nuts of *Aleurites triloba*, imported into London.

CANDLES, wicks covered with solidified oil or fat, for giving light. There are many varieties, dips and moulds being chiefly tallow, while hard and composition candles are made of spermaceti, stearine, paraffine, wax, or palm oil.

CANDLESTICK, the receiver or holder for a candle, which is made either of metal, glass, or earthenware; and of two shapes, tall or erect, or short with a flat bottom.

CANDLE-WICK, a twisted length of cotton, round which the oil or fat is poured and solidifies.

CANDROY, CONDRAY, a Spanish fishing-boat; a machine used in cotton-printing.

CANDY, an eastern dry measure of capacity and weight, which varies in different places. In Madras and Colombo it is equal to 500 lbs. avoirdupois; in Bombay and Mangalore to 560 lbs. The Calicut candy is 610 lbs. For wool, coir, spices, and some other staples, in Bombay the candy is 588 lbs. The Malabar candy is 603½ lbs. The Surat candy, for many articles of merchandise, is 588 lbs.; for others 784 lbs.; and for some few 821½ lbs.; the Mysore candy is equal to 560 lbs.; also a long measure of Malabar, equal to one cubic kole, or 28¼ English inches.

CANDY-SUGAR, crystallized sugar formed upon strings by repeated boiling and clarifying, and suffered to crystallize slowly; it is sold white, brown, or pink.

CANE, a walking stick; a long measure in Italy and France. *See* CANNA.

CANE-CHAIR, a chair with a platted cane seat or bottom, or one framed with bamboo or other cane.

CANE-HOLE, a trench dug in the cane-fields, for planting cuttings of the sugar-cane in.

CANE-JUICE, the juice of the sugar-cane, expressed between the rollers of a mill, or by hydraulic pressure.

CANE-MILL, a set of rollers for crushing the sugar-cane, which are either horizontal or vertical, and set in motion by steam, water, wind, or cattle power.

CANELLA-ALBA, the commercial and botanical name of the wild cinnamon, a cheap, aromatic bark which occurs in dry buff pieces, thin cylinders, or large thick fragments. It is chiefly obtained from the Bahamas.

CANELON, the Spanish name for a kind of bastard cinnamon or canella, grown in Bogota; also a name for sweetmeats.

CANE-PIECE, a field or plot of land planted with sugar-canes.

CANE-PLANER, a splitter and smoother of canes for cane-work.

CANES, the common commercial name for many important grasses, embracing especially the varieties of the sugar-cane, bamboos, rattans, and Spanish canes. The stems of several small palms are also called canes. Under the name of reed canes, the culm or stem of a grass often forty feet long is largely imported from New Orleans, for the purpose of making weavers' shuttles, &c. The several canes will be found described under their common special names.

CANE SPLITTER, a preparer of canes for platting or basket-work; the instrument with which he works.

CANESTRA (Italian), a basket.

CANE-SUGAR, the juice obtained from the saccharine of the sugar-cane, reduced to a concrete state.

CANE-TOP-CUTTER, a machine for cutting the upper part or sprouting shoots of the sugar-cane for cattle.

CANE-TRASH, the dead or withered leaves stripped from the stalk to enable the sugar-cane to ripen; also the stalk after the juice has been expressed, used for fuel and manure, sometimes called megass.

CANETTE, a Belgian liquid measure averaging one quart.

CANE-WORKER, a maker of articles in rattans, Spanish and other canes; a basket-maker.

CANGAN, KANGAN, a piece of coarse Chinese cloth, thinly woven, 19 inches broad, and 6 yards long, which has a fixed currency value.

CANGANY, a class of natives employed by the Ceylon coffee planters to hire coolies from the Indian continent.

CANGE, Spanish for exchange.

CAN-HOOKS, flat hooks fastened to ropes for hoisting barrels or light casks.

CANICA, a species of wild cinnamon growing in Cuba.

CANISTER, a small box or case usually of metal, for holding groceries, &c.

CANISTER-MAKER, a maker of tin cases, for holding groceries and other articles.

CANISTER-SHOT, small shot packed in a metal cartridge for charging a piece of ordnance.

CANNA (Italian). CANNE (French). CANA (Spanish), a linear and superficial measure in some parts of France, Spain, and the Italian States. It varies in length according to the use to which it is applied; in Barcelona it is 21 inches, in Marseilles 79½. The surveyors' canna in Italy is about 3½ yards, for cloth and silk rather more than 2¼ yards. It is also a Dutch liquid measure in the Cape colony, 388 cannes making a leaguer.

CANNA, the plant which furnishes the starch of commerce known as *Tous-les-mois*.

CANNABINE, a narcotic gum-resin obtained from *Cannabis sativa*.

CANNAMELE (Italian), sugar cane.

CANNATA, CANNATE, a liquid measure o. Greece equal to 2·82 pints.

CANNE. *See* CANNA.

CANNEL-COAL, a hard coal which does not soil the fingers. Being very solid it is often turned into trinkets and other ornaments in imitation of jet.

CANNELLE, the French name for cinnamon.

CANNEQUIN, a kind of white cotton, formerly made in India, in pieces of about 8 ells, chiefly for sale on the West coast of Africa.

CANNON, a piece of ordnance of iron or brass for discharging balls, made of many sizes according to the service required of it.

CANNON-BALL, CANNON-SHOT, a cast-iron ball to be thrown from cannon.

CANNON-LOCK, a contrivance to place over the touch-hole of a piece of ordnance to explode the charge.

CANNON-LOCK-MAKER, a manufacturer of pulley triggers for firing pieces of ordnance.

CANNON-METAL, a brass alloy for casting ordnance from, containing 91 per cent of copper and 9 parts of tin.

CANOE, a rudely formed boat, shaped out of the trunk of a tree by cutting or burning; also a skin or bark boat used by uncivilized natives. *See* WOODSKIN.

CANOE-BIRCH, a North American tree, the *Betula papyracea*, from the bark of which the Indians manufacture their celebrated bark canoes. The wood is of a fine glossy grain, susceptible of a good finish, but lacks durability and strength, and therefore is but little used in the manufacturing arts.

CANON, the largest sized printing-type with a specific name.

CANON-BIT, that part of the iron which is in the horse's mouth.

CANONGOE, CANOONGO, a registrar of land-revenue in India; one versed in the customs, tenure, produce, and rental of the district.

CANOPY, a covering over head, the decoration crowning a pulpit, chair, throne, bed, &c.

CANOTTA (Italian), a small boat.

CANT, any thing standing awry, timbers out of the perpendicular, or not fixed square.

CANTALOON, a species of woollen stuff.

Cantar, an abbreviation for the cantaro.

Cantara, Cantaro, a liquid measure of Spain ranging from 2½ to 4 gallons; 100 however may be taken as equal to 358 imperial gallons. The name is also sometimes given to the alqueire or pot of Portugal. As a commercial weight in the Levant the cantaro is synonymous to the quintal of Europe, being employed in the sale of ponderous commodities; but it varies considerably in different localities. In Syria the ordinary cantaro amounts to 502¾lbs.; in Sardinia to 93¾ lbs.; and in Cairo to 95lbs; while at Rome it is but 74¾lbs. The Maltese cantaro of 100 rottoli is 175lbs. avoirdupois; in Smyrna it is 127¾lbs.

Cantarello, the name of the quintal in Sardinia, equal to 89¼ lbs. avoirdupois; the cantarello of Cagliari is, however, heavier, weighing 93¾ lbs. *See* Cantara.

Canteen, a tap or public house for the sale of spirituous liquors. In England the term is usually restricted to a tap in barracks or military quarters, but in the Cape and other Colonies it is of more general application. Also a tin case for holding food, &c., carried by soldiers and others on the march.

Canteen-maker, a tinman, one who makes portable drinking vessels.

Canter, in horsemanship, a hand gallop.

Canterbury, a small ornamental music-stand, with two or three hollow topped partitions, framed in light slips of mahogany for holding music books.

Canterbury Crane, a pivot crane.

Canterellk, the Italian name for the Cantharides, or Spanish blistering-flies.

Canteroy, a weight for gold and silver used in Bangalore, equal to 5·87 grains.

Cantharides, the commercial name for various blistering beetles, often termed Spanish flies; but which are also imported from China, Russia, Sicily, and Germany. The large genus *Mylabris* furnishes many insects possessing strong vesicatory powers.

Cantharidine, a crystalline principle obtained from *Lytta vesicatoria*, *gigas*, *violacea*, and other species of the Spanish blistering fly, powdered and steeped in an alcoholic tincture.

Cantiere (Italian), a dockyard.

Cantilever, Cantalever, an iron, wooden, or other projecting support in a wall, on which the eaves or cornice rests.

Cantilla, gold and silver bullion fringe.

Cantinière, a vivandière or female sutler to a French regiment.

Cant-moulding, a moulding with a bevelled surface, used on the capitals of columns.

Cantucciaio, an Italian pastry-cook or biscuit maker.

Canvas, a strong kind of flaxen fabric, used for ship sails, awnings, tents, &c., manufactured in Ireland and Scotland. No. 1. is the coarsest and strongest kind. There are some other more open kinds of canvas made for tapestry and buckram.

Canvas-back, a wild duck, the *Fuligula valisneria*, met with in some of the American rivers, which is highly esteemed by epicures for the delicacy of its flesh, and realizes a high price for the table.

Canvas-loom, a frame for making canvas in.

Canvasser, one who solicits votes, or seeks support for any person, project, or publication.

Caoutchouc, an elastic gum, the India-rubber of commerce; the inspissated milky juice or sap obtained from the *Siphonia elastica*, and several of the fig tribe in India and South America. Owing to its impenetrability to moisture, its flexibility, elasticity, and cheapness, and the ease with which it may be cut or spun into various forms and fabrics, caoutchouc is an article of the highest importance in several arts and manufactures.

Caoutchouc Manufacturer, a maker of goods in India-rubber or elastic gum.

Cap, a cover for the head. Caps for ladies are made of lace, net, or some such light material; widows' caps are in a set and particular style; those for men are of cloth, fur, leather, and fancy materials, &c. In ship-building, a cap is a thick, strong block of wood fastened to the head of a lower mast, through which the upper mast slides. A percussion-cap is a metal capsule for the nipple of a gun, containing detonating powder, to explode the charge in the barrel; cap is a cutler's term for a ring of metal surrounding a wooden wheel or lap, and it is also applied to a stratum overlying the useful beds of Portland stone.

Capa, a term in Cuba for good tobacco, the best or outside leaves being suited for the wrappers of cigars.

Capacity, the power of containing, the extent of room or space in a vessel or cask.

Cape, a wine made in the Cape colony, of which there are two kinds, white and red; a lady's article of dress; that part of a garment which covers the shoulders, as the cape of a cloak, coat, and the shoulder-trimmings of a dress.

Cape Aloes, an inspissated juice obtained chiefly from *Aloe spicata* and *Commelini*, species of aloe growing wild in the Cape colony. The odour is stronger and more disagreeable than that of the product made in Barbados and Socotra.

Capecha, Capicha, a corn measure in Persia, twenty-five capechas making one artaba, equal to 1·86 Winchester bushel.

Capelin, a small migratory fish of the North American seas, from four to seven inches long, not unlike the smelt. It is a very delicate fish, but serves chiefly for bait for cod to the Newfoundland fisherman; and is imported into this country dried, to be eaten as a relish.

Capellone, a silver coin of Modena, of six soldi and eight denari.

Capel-master, a director of music.

Capercailzie, a Scotch name for the wood grouse, *Tetrao urogallus*, which is now rarely met with in Britain, although common in the northern countries of Europe.

Capers, the flower-buds of various species of *Capparis*, grown in the South of Europe, which form a well-known pickle.

CAPER-SCHIFF (German), a privateer.

CAPER-TEA, a black tea, a superior kind of souchy with a knotty curled leaf; so named from its fanciful resemblance to the caper. That sold here is usually scented with chloranthus, jasmine, or other flowers.

CAPE-WEED, a commercial name for a dye lichen, the *Rocella tinctoria*, imported from the Cape de Verd islands.

CAPH, an ancient Jewish liquid measure, the cadaa of the Arabians, which was equal to nearly 2¼ pints.

CAPIAS, a writ or judgment for arrest on execution.

CAPICHA. *See* CAPECHA.

CAPIDGI, a Turkish porter or door-keeper, sometimes applied to chamberlains and superior officers.

CAPILLAIRE, a syrup made from maiden-hair in North America; also the common name for any simple syrup flavoured with orange-flower water.

CAPILLAIRE AND WINE AND SPIRIT COLOURING-MAKER, a cordial maker, one who prepares caramel, &c.

CAPIN, the eighth part of a bahar, an Eastern measure, about 60 lbs. avoirdupois.

CAPITAL, the amount of money or property subscribed or employed in a joint-stock association; the money assets invested in business by a trading firm or individual; the net worth of a party; a large letter or type in printing.

CAPITALIST, a man of large property, one who has a considerable sum invested in the funds or in stock in trade.

CAPITALIZE, to convert into capital or shares.

CAPITATION, a poll tax, or imposition upon each person.

CAPITOZZA (Italian), the pollard oak.

CAPIVI. *See* COPAIVA.

CAP-MANUFACTURER, a wholesale maker of caps.

CAPOC, a fine short-stapled cotton wool, used in India for stuffing cushions and lining palanquins, &c.

CAPON, a young cock gelded to fatten for the table.

CAPOOR KITCHELY, KAPOOR KUCHREE, an aromatic drug of the Indian markets, the rhizoma of *Hedychium spicatum*.

CAPOTE, a long cloak for females; a great-coat with a hood worn by males on the Continent and by soldiers on guard.

CAPPADINE, a sort of silk flock or waste obtained from the cocoon after the silk has been reeled off and used for shag.

CAP-PAPER, a coarse kind of brown paper used for making bags.

CAP-PEAK, the front part of a man's cap, the shade over the eyes, that part which is ordinarily taken hold of to remove it from the head.

CAP-PEAK MAKER, a workman who makes glazed-leather fronts or peaks for caps, and cockades, &c.

CAPPELLAJO (Italian), a hatter.

CAPPING, ridge or roll metal, galvanized iron, &c. for roofing.

CAPRIFICATION, an artificial process of early ripening figs, by depositing insects, which puncture the fruit.

CAPSA, a cylindrical box for clothes, or books, &c.

CAP-SPRING MAKER, a maker of metal springs fitting to the head for ladies' caps, for flowers, wreaths, &c.

CAPSICUM, a genus of plants producing pungent capsules of various shapes, which are very generally used as seasonings and condiments. The pods of *C. annuum* and *C. baccatum* pounded, furnish the cayenne-pepper of commerce.

CAPSTAN, a cylinder or truncated cone of wood placed vertically in the deck of a vessel, moved by levers or hand-bars; chiefly used for weighing anchors, hoisting yards, sails, &c. or any purpose in a man-of-war, where great purchase is required. A windlass is a sort of horizontal capstan in the fore part of the ship.

CAPSTAN-BARS, the wooden levers put in the capstan holes in order to move it, and to wind up the cable on.

CAPSULE, a small gummy envelope for nauseous medicines; the metallic seal or cover for closing a bottle. The capsules or seed-vessels of many plants enter into commerce, as poppy-heads, capsicums, cardamoms, &c.

CAPTAIN, the superintendent of a mine, the chief officer in command of a vessel, a military officer.

CAPTAIN-DRESSER, an overlooker of those who dress ores.

CAPTION, the arrest of a person under a judicial process; a name in the United States for the heading to a paragraph.

CAPUCHIN, a cloak with a hood worn by females on the Continent.

CARACOLE, a spiral staircase.

CARACOLY, an alloyed metal of gold, silver, and copper, of which rings and trinkets are made, intended for shipment to quarters where the natives are not able to test the intrinsic value of the material.

CARACTER, a Spanish apothecary's weight equal to three grains.

CARAFE, a glass water decanter for the table.

CARAFFA (Italian), a flagon or bottle; also a Neapolitan liquid measure equal 0·192 gallon, and a weight for oil in Tripoli, about 8¾ lbs.

CARAFON (French), a small decanter; a half pint.

CARAGE, a measure for lime of 64 bushels.

CARAGI, a name in the Turkish dominions for import and export duties.

CARA-GROUCH, the old Turkish medium of exchange, or par dollar, equal to five sololas or 120 aspers, about 7s.

CARAILA, CARAVELLA, Indian names for the small, black, aromatic seeds of *Cleome pentaphylla*, which are used medicinally by the natives in decoction as a stimulant.

CARARACA, a Tamil name for the chebulic myrobalan (*Terminalia chebula*), used medicinally in India.

CARAMEL, a black soluble powder obtained by burning sugar, which is used to colour wines and other liquids.

CARAMOOLOO, an Indian name for a black pulse.

CARANA-PALM, a name in South America for the *Mauritia carana*, the triangular leaves of which are used for thatching.

CARANA-RESIN, a resin obtained in the West Indies and Central America, from *Bursera gummrifera*, and used in materia medica.

CARANTANO, an Austrian money, equal to a halfpenny.

CARAP OIL, CRAB OIL, an oil obtained in South America from the seed of the *Carapa guianensis* of Aublet.

CARAPACE, the shell of the sea-turtle. *See* TORTOISE-SHELL.

CARARA, a weight in Leghorn of 110½ lbs.

CARAT, a jeweller's weight; 156 carats make one troy ounce. It is also used for precious stones, for diamonds being equal to 3 1-6th troy grains, and for pearls 3½ grains. The term is used to express the fineness of gold; the carat being the 24th part of the old French marc or half pound. Pure gold is said to be 24 carats fine, and every proportion of alloy detracts so many carats therefrom. The standard for the current coin of the realm is 22 carats fine, for watch cases, &c. 18 carats fine, and so on. A coin of Mocha the 7th part of the commassee.

CARATELLO, the Italian name for a keg for liquor.

CARATO, a small Italian weight, the tenth part of a ferlino, and equal to about three grains; 16 ferlinos making the ounce of the Bologna pound.

CARATOE, KURATO, a name in the West Indies for the American aloe (*Agave Americana*).

CARAVAN, a troop of travellers by land, who band together on a journey to assist and protect each other; the name in St. Petersburg for a number of large vessels or barks which bring down hemp; a travelling show carriage frequenting fairs, &c.

CARAVAN-JOURNEY, a mode of computing distance in some parts of Africa and Asia, by the day's journey of the camel; usually about 30 miles.

CARAVANSERAI, a rest-house or reception-inn for travellers, in some parts of the East.

CARAVELAO, a Portuguese vessel used in the Azores.

CARAVELLE, a fishing boat used on the French coasts.

CARAVERU, a name given by the Indians of Guiana to a red pigment obtained from the *Bignonia Chica*, with which they stain their skin. The colouring matter is used as a dye in the United States, and for artistical purposes would rival madder.

CARAWAY, a hardy British biennial umbelliferous plant (*Carum carui*), which produces the aromatic seeds used by confectioners, in pharmacy as a carminative, and for making an essential oil. The roots of the plant are very agreeable, and are eaten in the north of Europe.

CARAWAY CAKE, CARAWAY COMFIT, confections into which caraway seeds enter.

CARBINE, a small short-barrelled gun, carried by mounted troopers.

CARBOLIC ACID, a tar creasote, which possesses extraordinary antiseptic properties, and has been used to preserve bodies for dissection, and the skins of animals intended to be stuffed. A valuable dye-stuff is still made from it, called carboazotic acid, which gives magnificent straw-coloured yellows on silk and woollen fabrics.

CARBON, a commercial name for wood charcoal; the soot and smoke of lamps, gas, and other substances of vegetable origin, is carbon almost pure. Carbon has many uses; it forms the base of a durable ink; of crayons; of the filtering substances, such as charcoal, bone, and ivory black. It is a valuable fertilizer, and deodorizer, and one of the best fuels for reducing metals.

CARBONADE, a cutlet or steak; animal substances sliced and seasoned, and afterwards broiled or fried.

CARBONATE OF SODA, the union of carbonic acid with soda, as a base. This commercial product is manufactured on a very large scale from sulphate of soda, or common salt. *See* SODA.

CARBONIC ACID, a fixed air or gas, which imparts that pleasant effervescence or briskness to aerated mineral waters, and light sparkling wines. It extinguishes flame, and suffocates animals, hence it is called by miners choke-damp.

CARBOY, a large green-glass bottle, cased in basket work, varying in size from five to ten cubic inches, used for conveying distilled waters or liquid acids of too powerful a nature to be carried in casks.

CARBUNCLE, a precious stone, the *Almandine* of mineralogy. Fine large garnets cut with a rounded face are those known as carbuncles.

CARCANET, a chain or collar of jewels.

CARCASS, the dead body of an animal; the external shell or skeleton of a house or other building, roofed, partitioned, and floored, but not lathed and plastered.

CARCASS-BUILDER, one who merely constructs the shell or framework of houses, leaving other workmen to complete the interior fittings of the building.

CARCASS-BUTCHER, one who sells and slaughters cattle wholesale; a dealer who receives meat from the country for sale in metropolitan towns.

CARCASS-ROOFING, an unfinished roof, the mere frame of timber, on which to place the tiles, slates, &c., to complete the covering.

CARCEL LAMP, a lamp of French invention, in which the oil is wound up by a kind of clock-work pump, which forces it up to the wick. It is now generally known as the moderator lamp.

CARDAMOMS, the capsules of various not very clearly defined species of *Amomum*, *Elettaria* and other plants; the acrid, pungent seeds of which are used in medicine as aromatic tonics, and carminatives, and to give an artificial strength to spirits, wine and beer. In the East they form a universal ingredient in soups, curries, pilaus, ketchups and sauces, &c.

CARD-BASKET, an ornament for a table made of various materials, in which are deposited visiting-cards.

CARD-BOARD, a very stiff paper substance, or pasteboard, for cutting cards from, for making boxes and for other uses.

CARD-BOARD-CUTTING-MACHINE, a machine which cuts card-board into slips of an uniform size, and sometimes prints and numbers them for railway tickets or other purposes.

CARD-BOX, a box for keeping playing cards in.

CARD-CASE, a portable fancy case for holding visiting cards.

CARD-CASE-MAKER, a maker of small receptacles for ladies' visiting cards—which are constructed of various fancy materials, leather, tortoiseshell, ivory, &c.

CARDE, CHARDE, a name on the Continent for the white beet, *Beta cicla*.

CARDER, one who combs or clears wool or flax.

CARDIER (French), a card-maker.

CARDINAL-CAPE, a lady's article of dress, usually of silk.

CARDING-COMB, a cast-steel implement for cleaning wool, cotton, &c.; cards in the carding engine seem to lay all the fibres in one direction, accumulating it into a loose mass called a fleece, preparatory to the process of spinning.

CARDING-MACHINE, a mechanical engine with toothed revolving cylinders for separating and cleaning wool, flax, cotton and other fibres.

CARDINELLO, the Spanish name for verdigris, and verditer.

CARD-MAKER, one who makes cards, of which there are two classes, pasteboard cards and metal cards or mounted wire dents for machinery.

CARDOLE, a thick black oily substance obtained in the East Indies from the pericarp of the cashew nut. It is a powerful vesicating agent.

CARDOON, a culinary plant, the *Cynara cardunculus*, resembling the artichoke, but larger; the blanched stems of the young leaves are stewed or used as an ingredient in soups and salads on the Continent.

CARD-RACK, a receptacle for address, visiting, or business cards.

CAR-DRIVER, the driver of a jaunting or other car.

CARDS, shaped pieces of cardboard, used for various purposes;—when painted with figures, &c., for games and subject to a duty; when printed or engraved used for visiting or business purposes. Conversation cards with sentences or mottos, &c., form a pleasant pastime for young persons, &c.; metal dents fixed in an elastic band for teazing and separating the fibres of wool are called cards.

CARD-TABLE, a light folding-top table covered with baize.

CARD-SETTING-MACHINE, a beautiful and efficient piece of mechanism, for inserting the ends of forked wires into holes in a leather or other strap and bending them to the required inclination.

CARD-TRAY, a small salver for a servant to deliver a card on.

CARD-WIRE CLOTH, cloth in which fine iron wire is inserted for combing and unharling the fibres, &c., of wool, cotton, flax, and hemp.

CAREEN, to heave a ship down on her side in order to examine her bottom, for cleaning or paying it with pitch; when a vessel lies over with the wind in sailing, she is said to careen.

CAREENAGE, a careening ground, a place suitable for placing a ship high and dry.

CARE-TAKER, a person employed at a wharf, quay, or exposed store to look after goods.

CAREY, the Spanish name for tortoise-shell.

CARGA, a standard Spanish liquid measure, equal in some parts of that kingdom to 32¼ gallons, but in others only 27¼ gallons; also a Spanish weight, ranging from 177¼ lbs. to 338¼ lbs. In Candia and Milan the carga as a grain measure is equal to 4 1-6th bushels. A commercial weight in Central America equal to 81 lbs.

CARGADOR, a Dutch shipbroker who obtains freight for vessels.

CARGASON, the freight or lading of a ship.

CARGO, a ship's lading, the merchandise, &c., taken on board for conveyance. That which cannot be stowed in the hold is termed deck cargo.

CARGO-BOAT, a luggage-boat or barge for the conveyance of heavy goods on rivers or in harbours.

CARIACA, a small and esteemed variety of maize grown in British Guiana.

CARICA, a Venetian weight of 266¼ lbs.; also another name for the carga a grain or dry measure.

CARICO (Italian), the cargo of a ship.

CARIOLE, a carriage for general use.

CARIOLLA, a weight for salt in the Ionian islands rather more than 104 lbs.

CARIPPU, a name in Southern India for the refuse cuttings or knotty pieces forming the worst kind of sandal wood.

CARIVAL, a money of account in the Deckan, India, worth about a halfpenny; also a variable grain measure in the same locality.

CARK, an old name for a quantity of wool.

CARKOON, a revenue officer.

CARL D' OR, a gold coin of Brunswick worth about 16s. 4d.

CARLE, a kind of hemp.

CARLIN, CARLINE, a small silver coin current in some parts of Italy and worth about 4d.

CARLINGS, short small square pieces of timber which lie fore and aft in a ship, in tiers from beam to beam, and which receive the ends of the ledges for framing the decks.

CARLOCK, a kind of isinglass obtained from the air-bladder of the sturgeon in Russia.

CARMAN, a carter, one who conveys goods. The fellowship or fraternity of carmen has the exclusive privilege of cartage within the city of London.

CARMEL, a cover for sweetmeats.

CARMENIA-MAUND, a weight for wool in Persia of 5 lbs.

CARMEN'S COMPANY, one of the companies of the city of London, not on the livery, which, having no hall of its own, transacts its business at Guildhall.

CARMINE, a beautiful lake pigment, a fine bright crimson inclining to scarlet, formed by a combination of cochineal, alumina, and oxide of tin. In consequence of being more transparent than other colours, it is chiefly used for miniature painting, artificial-flower tinting, and water-colour drawing.

CARNAUBA, the Brazilian name for a palm the *Copernica cerifera*; the leaves yield a vegetable wax which is made into candles; the fruit is eaten raw or boiled; a farina is obtained from the trunk, and the wood is very durable.

CARNELIAN, a variety of quartz from India used for decorative ornaments of the person, of which the agate and chalcedony are varieties.

CARNET, in French commerce a bill book.

CAROBA, in Tunis the sixteenth part of a piastre; and equal to rather more than a penny. [used in France.

CAROBE, the small pound or prime formerly

CAROB-FRUIT, the leguminous pods of the carob-tree (*Ceratonia siliqua*), which contain a succulent sweetish pulp and are often eaten in Spain and the countries bordering on the Mediterranean. They are a large article of import at Taganrog, are occasionally sold in this country to singers under the impression that they improve the voice, and have recently been largely imported for feeding cattle. *See* ALGARROBO.

CAROCHE, a pleasure carriage.

CAROLIN, a German gold coin worth about 20s.; there are also double carolins, and half and quarter carolin pieces.

CAROLUS, a gold one-pound coin struck in the reign of Charles I., but subsequently of the value of 23s.

CAROMEL. *See* CARAMEL.

CAROOB, a money of account in Tunis, the 48th part of a piastre, a little more than a penny; also a weight in Barbary.

CAROON, a kind of cherry.

CAROTEEL, the commercial name for a tierce or cask, in which dried fruit and some other commodities are packed, which usually averages about 7 cwt.

CARP, the *Cyprinus carpio*, a river fish. In the rivers running into the Black Sea, the carp sometimes attains 60 lbs. in weight. There are eighteen or twenty species of carp, some of which are very abundant; they are caught with nets and dressed in different ways.

CARPATHIAN BALSAM, an oleo-resin or essential oil distilled from the fresh cones and green tops of *Pinus Cembra*, in Germany.

CARPENTER, a worker in woods, who usually combines the business of a joiner; a ship's officer who has charge of the boats and repairs. [carpenter.

CARPENTER'S-BENCH, the work-table of a

CARPENTER'S-COMPANY, one of the minor livery companies of London, whose hall is situate in London Wall.

CARPENTER'S-MATE, the assistant to a carpenter in a ship.

CARPENTER'S-RULE, a two-feet folding rule for the pocket, sub-divided into inches and parts for measuring work.

CARPENTER'S-SQUARE, a tool for squaring wood-work.

CARPENTER'S-TOOLS, planes, saws, chisels, hammers, &c., used by carpenters.

CARPENTRY, the trade of a carpenter, the art of cutting, framing, and joining timber, for house or ship building.

CARPET-BAG, a portable sack for travellers, made of carpet, capable of holding a few essential articles or changes of linen. The name has got to be applied also to black varnished linen bags resembling leather.

CARPET-BAG-MAKER, a workman who sews and finishes off carpet-bags. In this as in many other articles of trade there are many sub-divisions. Some workmen make the iron frame-work alone, others sew the handles, &c., on.

CARPET-BEATER, one who takes carpets to shake and beat the dust from them.

CARPET-BROOM, a long-handled stiff brush for sweeping the carpets of rooms, made of strong fibre, bristle, grass, &c.

CARPET-BROOM-MAKER, one who makes carpet sweeping brushes.

CARPET-HAMMER, a tool for nailing down a carpet.

CARPETING, a general name for the material for carpets; but often applied to small lengths or floor pieces for the sides of beds in a sleeping room.

CARPET-MANUFACTURER, a weaver of carpets.

CARPET-MERCHANT, an agent for carpet-weavers; the keeper of a carpet warehouse.

CARPET-PLANNER, a cutter of carpets; a workman who measures rooms, and makes a plan on paper, of the breaks, doorways, windows, &c., to ascertain the quantity of material required, and the best mode of cutting, adapting, and laying it down with the least waste.

CARPETS, ornamental floor coverings of woollen material, woven in fancy patterns or devices, of which there are many kinds. The ordinary descriptions are Kidderminster or Scotch, Brussels, Turkey, Velvet-pile, Tapestry, Felt, Dutch, and Hemp carpets.

CARPET-CLEANING, the process of scouring and removing grease stains from carpets.

CARPET-LOOM, a frame for weaving carpets.

CARPET-SLIPPERS, easy slippers, covered with carpet for indoor use.

CARPET-SHUTTLE, a weaver's implement.

CARPET-STRAINER, a kind of metal rake or tool for holding and stretching carpets tight on the floor of a room, when laying them down.

CARPET-WAREHOUSE, a wholesale establishment where a large stock of carpets is kept for selection and sale.

CARPET-WAY, an interval of turf or grass left unploughed in a field.

CARPET-WEAVER, a workman employed in making carpets by hand or by machinery.

CARPMEALS a kind of coarse cloth formerly made in the North of England.

CARRACK, a large Spanish ship.

CARRAGEEN, a purplish-white nearly translucent sea-weed, the Irish moss of the shops, obtained from the *Chondrus crispus*, which is used for jellies, for feeding cattle, for dressing the warp of webs in the loom, and for sizing pulp in the paper-maker's vat.

CARRAPATO, a name in Brazil for the castor-oil-tree.

CARRARA-MARBLE, a fine white marble.

CARRARA-WATER, an aerated beverage.

CARRATA (Italian), a cart-load, a ton weight of marble; a solid measure in Carrara of 12⅘ cubic feet.

CARRAWAY. *See* CARAWAY.

CARRE, a superficial measure in the French West India islands of 3 1-5th acres; also a former French grain measure. *See* CARSE.

CARREAU, a land measure in Hayti, nearly two acres; also a solid and superficial measure formerly used in France; a carreau of stone in Paris being 63·032 cubic feet.

CARREGADOR (Portuguese), the freighterer and charterer of a ship.

CARRIAGE, a carrying vehicle of any kind, whether for private use or for the conveyance of goods; part of a printing-press or machine on which the forms of type are placed to be worked; the frame work to support a piece of ordnance; the charge made for the conveyance of goods from one place to another.

CARRIAGE-AXLE. *See* AXLE.

CARRIAGE-BREAK, the drag or retarder applied to the wheel for stopping a carriage.

CARRIAGE-BUILDER, one who designs and constructs carriages.

CARRIAGE-FITTINGS, the iron or other metal parts of a vehicle, made by a coach-ironmonger.

CARRIAGE, HAND, an invalid's wheel chair, or child's perambulator.

CARRIAGE-RETARDER, a break for carriage-wheels.

CARRIAGE-RUG, a sheep-skin mat, fur, woollen or other wrapper or rug for the feet and legs in travelling.

CARRIAGE-SPRING, a series of metallic banded plates; steel springs to lessen the motion of a carriage, and give elasticity.

CARRIAGE-TIME-PIECE, a chronometer, with compensating balance adapted for a travelling carriage.

CARRIAGE-UPHOLSTERER, a tradesman who furnishes braid, lace, buttons, silk, straps, &c., for the interior fittings of carriages.

CARRIAGE-WHEEL. *See* WHEEL.

CARRICK-BEND, a peculiar kind of knot made in cordage.

CARRICK-BITTS, the windlass bitts in a ship.

CARRIER, a carter, one who conveys goods.

CARRIER'S CART, a parcels' delivery cart, in suburban places and country towns.

CARRION, the carcass of an animal; slaughtered meat unfit for human food.

CARRO, a wine measure of Italy, in Naples equal to 290½ English gallons. As a dry measure, it is 5⅔ to nearly 7 imperial quarters, and as a superficial measure about ten acres.

CARRONADE, a short piece of ordnance carrying a 32 or 42 pound shot.

CARROON, a kind of cherry; money paid for licensing a cart.

CARROT, a well-known esculent root, the *Daucus Carota*, used largely for human food, and for feeding stock.

CARRUCA, an old name for a plough.

CARRYING TRADE, the business of transporting merchandise, &c., from place to place by sea or land.

CARSE, rich alluvial land on the bank of a river; a grain measure formerly used in France, equal to 3½ to 3¾ gallons.

CARSHA, an ancient Hindoo weight equal to 107 1-5th grains.

CART, a vehicle on two or four wheels, adapted for conveying loads, light or heavy, according to the peculiar build or construction of the cart.

CARTABAC, a river fish of Demerara, the *Tetragonopterus latus*, which is excellent when dried and smoked.

CARTAGE, the act of conveying goods by carts; the charge for the same.

CARTE, QUARTE, a grain measure formerly used in France, very variable in different departments, ranging from 1½ up to 18½ gallons. Also a superficial measure about the seventh of an acre.

CARTE, a French name for the bill of fare at an eating-house; the list of wines, &c.

CARTE-BLANCHE, an unlimited or unconditional power or authority given to a person to act at discretion for another.

CARTEL, a grain measure formerly used in France and Belgium of from 4½ to 7 gallons, according to the locality.

CARTER, one who drives a cart or team, an inferior farm servant, having the care of driving and foddering the draught cattle.

CARTIERE, a grain measure formerly used in some parts of Spain and France, about 2¾ bushels.

CART-GREASE-MAKER, a preparer and vender of fatty mixtures for lubricating the axles of wheels of vehicles.

CARTHAMUS OIL, an oil obtained in Egypt from the seeds of the safflower, *Carthamus Persicus*, and in Bombay from *Carthamus tinctorius*.

CART-HORSE, a draught horse of which there are several kinds, the principal being the Cleveland, Clydesdale, Northamptonshire, Suffolk Punch, and the dray horse, or heavy black.

CART-HOUSE, a shed to shelter carts, farm implements, &c., from exposure to the sun and rain.

CART-LADDER, a kind of rack thrown out at the head or tail of a cart, to enable it to carry a larger load of light goods, as hay, straw, &c.

CART-LOAD, the quantity that a cart will hold, or a horse can draw. A single horse will convey a load of two tons over the paved streets of a town. The Scotch carters, in carts weighing seven cwt., will with one horse, convey a ton of goods twenty-one miles in a day. The French carriers in Normandy will convey in two-wheeled carts drawn by four horses, four tons of goods a distance of from fourteen to twenty-two miles in a day. A cart-load of grain is five quarters, or forty bushels. *See* LOAD.

CARTOCCIO, a Roman liquid measure, ranging from a pint to a quarter of a pint, according to locality, and the fluid measured, as oil, wine, &c.

CARTON, CARTONNAGE, thin paste-board or paper boxes.

CARTONATE, CARTONNEE, a superficial measure used in Perpignan, about the third of an English acre.

Cartonné, a book bound in boards.

Cartonnerie (French), a paste-board manufactory. The manufacture of stiff paper boxes is largely carried on in France. In Paris 4000 persons are employed in it, and the trade is divided into six distinct branches, each making special kinds of boxes.

Carton-pierre, a species of papier-mâché, imitating stone or bronze sculpture. It has been used for roofing, and is composed of the pulp of paper mixed with whiting and glue. This is pressed into plaster piece-moulds, backed with paper, and when sufficiently set, removed to a drying room to harden.

Cartoon, a stiff paper or cardboard box, used by linen-drapers and others; a rough sketch or outline in chalk made on stout paper in order to be transferred on a fresh plastered wall to be painted in fresco.

Cartouch, a case filled with shot to be fired from a bomb or howitzer.

Cartouch-box, a soldier's wooden case for holding cartridges.

Cartouche, an architectural ornament representing a scroll in carved work; it is sometimes made to receive a motto or inscription.

Cartridge, a woollen or paper case or bag filled with powder, the proper charge for a musket or piece of ordnance; when unaccompanied with ball it is termed a blank cartridge.

Cartridge-case, a box with cells for holding cartridges, suspended by a belt over the shoulder. The paper in which the powder of a cartridge is enclosed.

Cartridge-maker, one who makes and fills cases with charges of powder for guns.

Cartridge-paper, a very stout paper for drawing rough designs on, or for making cartridge cases, &c.

Cart-saddle, the harness-support on a horse's back to which is attached the breeching, chains, traces, &c., of a cart.

Cart-shed, a covered house or shelter for protecting carts from the weather.

Cart-wheels, large stout wheels made for carts, capable of supporting heavy loads.

Cart-whip, a stout strong whip used by carters; in the colonies the long bullock whips are made of strips of hide.

Cart wright, an artificer who makes or repairs carts.

Caruto, a name for the Lana dye, a permanent and beautiful bluish-black colour, obtained in British Guiana from the juice of the fruit of the *Genipa Americana*.

Carved-work, sculptured, or open work in stone, wood, &c.

Carvel, **Caravel**, a small vessel.

Carver, one who designs and works on sculpture, or who cuts wood and stone in the form of figures or other devices as ornaments and in enrichments of mouldings. The trade of a carver in wood and gilder is often combined.

Carver and gilder, a picture and looking-glass frame maker and decorator.

Carvers, large pointed knives for cutting up joints of meat and poultry.

Carver's-tools, the cutting tools necessary for a carver.

Carvi (French), caraway seed.

Carving, the art and process of cutting wood, stone, ivory, shell, &c.

Carving-fork, a large fork with a protecting guard for carving joints of meat.

Carving-knife, a pointed knife made on a larger scale than the ordinary knives for table use.

Carwal, **Carval**, a grain measure of India, ranging in different localities from 900 to 1784lbs. avoirdupois.

Carwar, a grain measure on the Malabar coast equal to 12 maunds of barley or paddy, about 8 cwt.; but 15 maunds (half a ton) of other grain.

Cascalho, a name in Brazil for the sediment or deposit after the first washing of the sand, &c., for gold.

Cascarilla, an aromatic bark, the produce of *Croton Cascarilla* and *eleuteria* of the Bahamas and other islands of the West Indies.

Casco (Spanish), the hull of a ship.

Case, a box of any kind, the outside of a watch; a printer's box with partitions for letters or type; printers' cases generally go in pairs on the top of a frame, or case rack; a cover for the cushions of chairs and sofas.

Case-brandy, brandy of a superior kind sold in case bottles.

Cased-goods, in the glass trade articles in which coloured metal has been added to flint glass.

Cased-sash-frame, a leaded window, opening sideways.

Case-hardening, the process of converting the surface of iron into steel, by heating it with charcoal for a short time. Iron may be hardened by the flame of gas, by immersing it in oil, or in boiling water. Metals are also hardened by exposing them wrapped in a cement or composition paste in a forge to a red heat.

Casein, the curd or coagulable portion of milk.

Case-maker, a carpenter who makes wooden packing cases for shipping goods.

Casement, a moveable window turning and opening on hinges.

Case-rack, a printer's frame for placing the wooden cases of type on.

Case-shot, pieces of iron, musket balls, or other projectiles enclosed in a case for firing from a cannon.

Caseum, the purified curd of cheese.

Cash, the general name for coin and bank notes, sometimes applied to cheques, bills, bonds, and other property easily convertible into money. The only coin of the Chinese is the cash, also called le; which is nominally divided into ten haous. These cash are made of a very base alloy of copper, are round, about the size of an English farthing, and have a square hole in the middle, by which a hundred or more are usually strung together. On one side are Chinese characters, denoting the reign under which they were cast; and on the other side, in those of the present dynasty, are either Chinese or Mantchou characters, designating the place of coinage. Under preceding dynasties, two, five, and ten cash pieces were in use, as well as other coins of various descriptions; but the single cash is the only coin now current throughout the Empire. It is cast also in Japan, Corea, and Cochin China; and is clandestinely imported from the last-named place to a large amount. In Madras, 80 cash formerly made one fanam, worth about twopence.

CASHAW-TREE, a West India tree, the *Prosopis juliflora.*

CASH-BOOK, the book in which a trader enters his receipts and payments.

CASH-BOX, a metal or wooden case for keeping money in.

CASH-CREDIT, the privilege of drawing money from a bank, obtained by personal or deposited security.

CASHEW NUT, a nut attached to the fruit of *Anacardium occidentale*, the sweet kernels of which are used as an edible fruit. An oil is obtained from the inner shell, and the bark of the tree has been used for tanning.

CASHIER, CASH-KEEPER, an officer in any establishment who has the charge of moneys received, and dispenses payments, &c.

CASHMERE, a stuff made of goats' hair, also a fancy woollen fabric.

CASHMERE SHAWLS, a fine and costly kind of shawl made in the East of goats' hair, of which there are three kinds, the border shawl; the rizayee, or shawl of the finest texture; and the ordinary cashmere shawl. Some of these are valued at £100 and upwards, according to the delicacy of the workmanship, and beauty of the pattern.

CASH-TAKER, the receiver of money at a place of amusement, or public resort, shop, &c.

CASIMIR (French), kerseymere.

CASING, the act of packing in a case; also the process of plastering a building-frame or timber work, and indenting into squares, &c., while moist, so as to resemble stone; a name for dried cow-dung used as fuel in many localities.

CASINO, a French term for a club-house; in England, applied to public dancing-rooms.

CASK, a wooden hooped vessel, or barrel, of staves and headings, of variable shape and dimensions, for holding liquors. *See* Hogshead, Puncheon, Barrel, Butt, Pipe, Tierce, &c.

CASKEVAL, a kind of cheese made in the Danubian provinces.

CASKET, a small jewel case or box for ornaments, &c.

CASK-LIFTING-FRAME, a tilter for facilitating the drawing off liquids when the cask gets low.

CASSABA, an Arab measure of about 4 yards.

CASSADA. *See* CASSAVA.

CASSAREEP, the inspissated juice in which the starch of the bitter cassava, *Janipha Manihot*, has been washed; it forms a delicious sauce in the tropics, and is the foundation of the far-famed pepper-pot of the West Indies.

CASSATION, COURT OF, a supreme tribunal in Paris, consisting of the most eminent judges of the French Bench, whose function is to watch over the correct application and interpretation of the law, in all judicial decisions pronounced by the Imperial Courts.

CASSAVA, a starch obtained by grating and washing the roots of species of *Janipha*, *J. Manihot*, the bitter cassava, and *J. Lorflingii*, the sweet cassava.

CASSAVA-CAKES, thin cakes baked on a griddle or the embers of a wood fire, made of the pulp or starchy matter of the roots of the cassava or mandioc, which form a considerable article of food in tropical countries.

CASSAVA-JUICE, a poisonous principle, believed to be hydrocyanic acid, in the root of the bitter cassava, which is, however, driven off by heat. Mixed with molasses and fermented, it is made into an intoxicating liquor. It also furnishes an esteemed seasoning for culinary purposes. *See* CASSAREEP.

CASSAVA-SIFTER, a sieve for separating the coarse fibrous parts from the finer starch of the cassava.

CASSE (French), cassia bark; also breakage.

CASSELA, a name for the Jhinby bark.

CASSENA, a name for the *Ilex vomitoria*, a species of holly, native of Carolina, used for the purpose of correcting the flavour of water.

CASSENEY, a superficial measure in some parts of the presidency of Madras=1⅓ acre.

CASSE-PAPER, broken or damaged paper.

CASSEROLLE, a cooking utensil; a bordering of rice to a dish.

CASSIA-BARK. A large number of trees of the Cinnamomum family are stated to furnish the cassia-bark of commerce in the East, although it is usually ascribed to *Cinnamomum Cassia*. Cassia bark is easily distinguished from cinnamon by its very mucilaginous character when chewed. It appears, however, probable that cassia bark is merely an inferior kind of cinnamon obtained from the larger branches and trunk of the true tree in Ceylon and other islands of the East.

CASSIA-BUDS, the immature flowers (perianth and ovary), gathered and dried, of several species of cinnamon, chiefly used in confectionery, having the flavour and pungency of cassia.

CASSIA-FISTULA, the commercial and botanical name for the legumes or cylindrical pods of the pudding pipe tree; the cells are filled with a sweetish pulp which is an agreeable laxative and the base for purgative electuaries.

CASSIA-LIGNEA. *See* CASSIA-BARK.

CASSIA-OIL, a volatile oil obtained from cinnamon bark.

CASSIMERE, KERSEYMERE, a thin fine woollen cloth.

CASSINETS, a light mixed cloth, the warp of cotton and the weft of very fine wool, or wool and silk, made for summer wear.

CASSIUS-PURPLE, a beautiful pigment used for staining glass and painting porcelain; a mixture of oxide of tin and gold.

Cassock, a clergyman's black gown or vestment.

Cassonade (French), coarse brown moist or muscovado sugar.

Cassumanur, Cassumur, an aromatic root, the yellow zedoary, *Zingiber Cassumanur*, of the East Indies, somewhat resembling ginger, but the rhizoma much larger, of a pungent bitter taste.

Cast, a mould or copy taken from a pattern.

Castanets, a pair of small concave shells, of ivory, bone, or hard wood, held on the thumbs and rattled by the fingers to make music, or to mark time by dancers and others.

Castellano, a weight for gold used in South America of about 71 grains. The marc of gold is equal to 8 troy ounces of the Netherland pound, or 3608 grains English. The Indians in collecting gold-dust place it in an eagle's quill, which is marked in grains and castellanos.

Caster, a founder, one who makes castings in metals.

Caster, a bottle frame or stand for holding cruets.

Castile Soap, a hard mottled curd soap.

Castine, the French name for limestone.

Casting, the process of giving to steel a better quality, by pouring it into moulds or ingots while in a liquid state. A foundry operation, the process of running metal into a shape, the taking impressions from medals, figures, &c. The metal so shaped.

Casting-net, a net to be thrown in the water from a boat, and drawn instead of left.

Casting-pot, a pot adapted for melting metals.

Casting-pot and Crucible Maker, a special trade in the iron districts.

Casting-up, a printer's term for estimating the number of thousands of letters in a sheet of any work, or in a job, in order to fix the price for composing it.

Cast-iron, iron run from the furnace into pigs or ingots, instead of being beaten or wrought.

Castle, one of the carved pieces used in playing the game of chess.

Castor, Castoreum, an animal substance possessing a disagreeable odour, obtained from the beaver, *Castor fiber*, and once much used as an antispasmodic in medicine.

Castor-oil, a mild purgative fixed oil, obtained from the seeds of *Ricinus communis*, used in medicine, for lamps, and other purposes.

Castors, small roller-wheels fixed to the feet of heavy household furniture, such as beds, tables, arm-chairs, couches, &c., to admit of moving them with facility. There are plate castors, square and round, socket castors, claw castors, &c. Cruets or bottles for holding sauces.

Castrating, the operation of gelding animals to make them more docile, or for fattening.

Cast-scissors Manufacturer, a trade in Sheffield, where cheap and comparatively worthless scissors are made for sale.

Cast-steel, broken bars of iron fused in a crucible and poured into moulds.

Cat, a wild and domestic animal (*Felis catus*) whose skin is largely used for furriers' purposes; a kind of tackle used to hoist the anchor to the fore part of a ship.

Catacomb, a cave or grotto for burying the dead.

Catalogue, a written or printed list of books or articles.

Catalogue Raisonné, a classed or arranged catalogue, in which the articles are placed under regular heads or divisions.

Catamaran, a rude surf-boat or shaped log for a single individual, used to reach the shore at Madras in the East Indies. The Madras surf boats consist of thin flattened timbers eight or ten feet long, tied together horizontally, and sharpened a little at the point. Also a light raft used at Bahia and other places on the coast of Brazil for landing goods through the surf.

Cataract, a lock-gate; a contrivance to regulate the number of strokes per minute of an engine.

Catasta (Italian), a pile of wood, and a measure by which cord-wood is sold.

Catawba Wine, an American wine made from the catawba, a variety of grape grown in the United States.

Cat-block, a large block with two sheaves, used in hoisting up an anchor to the ship's side.

Catch-drain. *See* Catch-work.

Catch-penny, any thing worthless or of little value, made merely to sell.

Catch-word, the first word of the ensuing page, formerly printed isolated at the foot of the preceding page, but now seldom used.

Catch-work, the process of draining meadow lands on hill sides, by a successive series of drain channels.

Catechu, an inspissated extract from the wood, &c., of several Indian trees, chiefly the Areca palm and the *Acacia catechu*, used in medicine as an astringent, and by dyers as a source of tannic acid. *See* Cutch and Gambier.

Catena, an Italian measure of length, from 14 to 20 yards.

Caterer, one who has to purchase, provide, or purvey for others; the manager of a mess; the word cates signifying niceties or choice articles of food.

Cat-fall, a pulley for hoisting the anchor of a ship to the cat-head.

Catgut, the name applied to strings made from the peritoneal coverings of the intestines of the sheep. The greatest care is necessary to prepare these strings for the violin, the harp, and similar instruments, to secure the strength necessary for the great tension required for the high notes. The best strings are made in Naples, because the Italian sheep, from their leanness, afford the best raw material, for it is a well-ascertained fact, that the membranes of lean animals are much tougher than those of animals in high condition.

Cathartic Medicines, those which have purgative properties.

CATHARINE-WHEEL, a pyrotechnic which revolves and throws out radiations as it turns. Also the circular compartment of a Gothic window with radiating divisions or spokes.

CAT-HEAD, a miner's name for a small capstan; a projecting timber or beam on each side of a ship's bow, to which a pulley is attached, to assist in heaving up the anchor, and securing it to the side.

CATHEDRAL GLASS, stained or painted glass for church windows sold either in sheets or small squares.

CATHETER, a surgical instrument for relieving obstructions in the bladder, made of various materials.

CATJANG, the Malabar name for *Cajanus flavus*, a leguminous plant, the seed of which is much eaten by the poorer classes, and esteemed a wholesome pulse.

CATLINGS, a commercial name for the dried twisted intestines of animals, used for the strings of harps, fiddles, and other musical instruments. Indian and Persian catlings are sold by the 1000 strings. *See* CATGUT.

CAT-MINT, the *Nepeta cataria*, which has some stimulating qualities, and is a remarkable feline aphrodisiac.

CATO, a name for baskets in some of the Pacific islands, which are very neatly and elegantly made from coir and other palm fibres, and grasses.

CAT-O'-NINE-TAILS, a whip for corporeal punishment with nine lashes.

CATOPTER, CATOPTRON, a mirror, a reflecting optical glass.

CAT-ROPES, the pulleys employed in hoisting a ship's anchor over the bows by the cat-heads.

CAT-SALT, a granulated coarse salt formed from the bittern or leach brine, used in the manufacture of hard soap.

CAT-SKINS, the skins of wild or domestic cats, bought by furriers and others. Wild cats with a long and valuable fur abound in the forests of Hungary and are not uncommon in Wales and Scotland.

CAT'S-EYE, a variety of opal or fibrous quartz, enclosing asbestos. The finest kinds are obtained in Ceylon.

CAT'S-PAW, a kind of hitch made by sailors in a rope.

CATSUP, KETCHUP, a seasoning or sauce for meat, made of mushrooms, tomatoes, walnuts, or other vegetable substances.

CATTEMUNDOO, CALLEMUNDOO, an elastic gum or hydro-carbon, obtained in India from the *Euphorbia antiquorum*, and other species.

CATTIES, a name given in Ceylon to bill-hooks for cutting down underwood.

CATTLE, a collective name for all quadrupeds used by man for food, or for tilling the ground; they are divided into two principal classes, large or black cattle, which comprises horses and the bovine tribe; and small cattle which includes sheep and goats, &c. In America the term does not include horses.

CATTLE-DEALER, a grazier, one who buys and sells the live stock reared on a farm.

CATTLE-MARKET, the place of resort for graziers and dealers, where cattle are bought and sold.

CATTLE-MEDICINES, strong drastic medicines, used by veterinary surgeons, and owners of live stock.

CATTLE-PENN, an enclosure for folding cattle for the night.

CATTLE-RUN, an extent of grazing ground in the colonies.

CATTLE-SHED, a place for housing cattle.

CATTLE-SHOW, an assemblage of domestic animals, held periodically to compete for superior breeds and conditions.

CATTLE-TRAIN, a set of railway trucks conveying cattle to market.

CATTLE-TRUCK, an open car or partially closed carriage for conveying live stock on a railway.

CATTLE WEIGHING-MACHINE, a weigh-bridge on which cattle and sheep are placed to be weighed.

CATTY, an Eastern weight, the hundredth part of the picul, and equal to 1⅓ lb. avoirdupois; 84 catties being about 1 cwt. The Chinese catty weighs 22½ Spanish dollars, the Malayan catty 24 dollars or rather more than 2 lbs. The catty of silk in the East is equal to about 2⅘ lbs. The catty is sometimes called a kin.

CAUDLE, gruel; a mixture of wine and other ingredients as a drink.

CAUF, a perforated chest to keep fish in under water.

CAUK, a mining name for sulphate of barytes; a weight and measure in Sumatra, the fifth part of the bamboo, which is 3 lbs. 10 oz.

CAUL, a net for the hair worn by ladies; a cabinet maker's term for a piece of solid wood, shaped and smoothed to fasten veneers on.

CAULIFLOWER, a well-known esculent or pot herb, the *Brassica oleracea cauliflora*, a variety of the common cabbage.

CAULKER. *See* SHIP-CAULKER.

CAULKING, COCKING, the process of filling the seams between the planks of a ship's deck or sides with oakum, and wh... is afterwards covered with pitch to keep out water.

CAULKING-IRON, a kind of cold chisel used by the caulker.

CAULKING-MALLET, a mallet used by the caulker for driving in the iron to force the oakum between the seams.

CAUNTER-LODE, in mining, a lode which inclines at a considerable angle to the other contiguous veins.

CAUSALTY, a mining name for light particles of ore carried away in the process of washing.

CAUSEWAY, a raised footpath or artificial embankment in low land.

CAUSTIC, a corroding substance. Lunar caustic is a nitrate of silver.

CAUSTIC BARLEY, a name for the seeds of the *Veratrum album*, &c. *See* CEBADILLA.

CAUTERY, a farrier's searing iron.

CAUTH, a name in Canara for the Terra Japonica of commerce, which is extensively employed in many manufactures.

It is also used in the east with the pan or betel leaf instead of lime, especially by elderly people, being considered beneficial to the gums. *See* BETEL NUT.

CAUTHEE, a coarse Indian cotton cloth.

CAUTIONNEMENT, in France a sum lodged by way of guarantee or security—as by a newspaper proprietor to the government as a surety,—to be forfeited in case of misconduct.

CAUTIONER, in Scotland one who becomes bond or security for another.

CAUZ, an ancient Arab measure about an English pint.

CAVA, a name for an intoxicating beverage made in the Pacific islands by first chewing the root of the *Macropiper methysticum*, and letting it ferment.

CAVALCAVIA, the Italian name for an arcade or piazza.

CAVALLARO, an Italian carrier or courier.

CAVALLERIA. *See* CABALLERIA.

CAVALLO, a very petty copper coin of Italy worth but the 24th part of a penny; the Italian name for a horse.

CAVALLOCCHIO, a mounted exciseman in Italy.

CAVALRY, a mounted body of troops, either light horse or dragoons.

CAVAN, CABAN, a dry measure and weight used in the Philippine islands for grain; a cavan of paddy, or rice in the husk, will weigh about 96 lbs., of cleaned rice, 130 to 135 lbs.

CAVANA, the Spanish name for a flock of sheep.

CAVANNA, a name in Barbados for the logger-head turtle, *Caretta cephalo*, (Schopff.)

CAVATION, CAVAZION, hollowing the earth for the foundation of a building or for cellarage.

CAVE, a name for the space under the fire of a furnace.

CAVEACHING, a mode of pickling fish.

CAVEAR, CAVEER, a money of account at Mocha worth about a halfpenny; a nominal division of the Spanish dollar, forty caveers being reckoned equal to one dollar.

CAVEAT, an admonitory prohibition or protest, entered by the holder of a patent, against the granting of another applied for, which appears likely to infringe his existing rights.

CAVENDISH, a kind of tobacco.

CAVENGA, a name in the Pacific islands for the burthen or freight of a canoe or vessel.

CAVETTO, in building, a simple concave moulding used for cornices, &c.; a quarter of a circle, the reverse of the ovalo.

CAVEZON, CAVESSON, a severe nose band of various materials to punish or subdue an untractable horse.

CAVEZZINA, the Italian name for a bridle.

CAVEZZO, an Italian measure of length of variable dimensions in different cities, the minimum being about 2½ yards, the maximum 4½. It is analogous to the French toise.

CAVIAR, a preparation of the dried spawn or salted roe of fish; a single sturgeon will sometimes yield as much as 120 lbs. of roe. Caviar is principally consumed in Russia, Germany, and Italy, by the Greeks during their long fasts; and also in England. The black caviar is made from the roe of the sturgeon; a cheaper and less prized red kind is obtained from the roe of the grey mullet and some of the carp species, which are common in the rivers and shores of the Black Sea.

CAVING, in mining a sinking or falling in of the superincumbent earth or rock of a tunnel.

CAVING-RAKE, a barn-floor rake with long teeth and a short head to separate the chaff from grain.

CAWK, an opaque massive variety of barytes, found in Staffordshire and Derbyshire.

CAWNEY, an Indian land measure of 57,600 square feet or 1⅓ acre, chiefly used at Madras.

CAXO, a Spanish measure of ore containing many quintals, but varying in bulk at different places; at Potosi equal to about 5000 lbs.

CAXON. *See* CAJON.

CAYA, a bastard satin-wood shipped from St. Domingo.

CAYELAC, an aromatic wood obtained in Siam.

CAYENNE PEPPER, a pungent seasoning made from the pounded red bird-pepper or small shrubby capsicum seed-vessels. It is used medicinally in gargles and as a stimulant.

CAYENNE POTTAGE, a mess made in the West Indies termed pepper-pot.

CAYMAN, another name for the alligator, which is killed sometimes for its oil and its skin; it also yields musk.

CAYTONGEE, a name given in Sumatra to the second quality of pepper.

CAZAL, another name for the concadi, an agrarian measure of France.

CAZZONS, a provincial name for the dried dung of cattle collected for fuel.

CAZZUOLA, a trowel or tool for spreading mortar, used in Italy.

CEBADILLA, CEVADILLA, SABADILLA, names for the follicular fruits of *Stenanthium frigidum*, *Asagrea officinalis*, and *Veratrum Sabadilla*, which contain the alkaloid veratrin, used as an emetic and purgative in mania, and which has also been administered in cases of gout, rheumatism, and neuralgia. *See* SEVORJA.

CECCHIA (Italian), a kind of vessel; a snow or bylander.

CECILS, a name for hashed beef.

CECOGRAPH, a French writing apparatus for the use of the blind.

CEDANT (French), one who assigns over or surrenders his right or property.

CEDAR, a name given to several woods, but properly belonging to the almost incorruptible wood obtained from two species of *Cedrus*, *C. Deodara* and *Libani*, which grow to a great height, and furnish fine timber. The wood of the common *Cedrela* is far less valuable. The name of red cedar is given to the *Juniperus Bermudiana*, a wood used for pencils, and also recognised by the Committee of Lloyds for some parts of ship-building.

Cedar Gum, a gum resin obtained in the Cape colony, from the branches and cones of the *Widdingtonia juniperoides*, much resembling gum olibanum. It is used for various medicinal purposes, for compounding plasters, and preparing varnish.

Cedazo (Spanish), a hair sieve or strainer.

Cedra, Cedrat, a species of Italian citron having a thick rind which contains much essential oil, and is used for making perfumes, and for flavouring liqueurs.

Cedrium, the resin of the cedar tree used to preserve books and to protect other articles from insects.

Ceiling, the upper surface of an apartment, usually formed of laths and plaster; the inside of a roof.

Ceiling-floor, the joists or frame-work on the lower surface of an apartment, upon which the ceiling is made.

Ceiling Laths, the thin strips of wood nailed to the joists for receiving the plaster.

Celemin, a Spanish dry measure, the 12th of a fanegada, ranging in different places from 3½ to 11 pints. The name was also formerly given to the Portuguese selamim.

Ceinture, a waist-belt, scarf or girdle of gauze or muslin, cotton, linen, or silk.

Celature, the art of engraving, cutting, or embossing metals.

Celery, an esculent (*Apium graveolens*), the blanched footstalks of the leaves are eaten in England, and in many countries the leaves and seeds are used for soup. The seeds are also employed as a stimulant by the native medical practitioners of India.

Celestine, a name for native sulphate of strontia. The nitrate is used for red lights in theatres.

Cellar, an underground room beneath a building, often used as a wine store, or for other commodities not injured by damp.

Cellarage, the area beneath a building laid out in a series of vaults or cellars.

Cellaret, a wooden cabinet, case, or bureau, for holding liquor bottles.

Cellar-flap, the wooden lifting door which closes a cellar.

Cellarman, Cellarer, one who attends to the business of a cellar.

Celonaio, a carpet maker.

Celone, a carpet in Italy.

Cembalo (Italian), the harpsichord.

Cement, any substance that serves to bind or unite by cohesion, as glue, solder, mortars, &c. In building, cement is a concretion of rubble mortars; the name is also applied to hydraulic mortars, impervious to water, such as Roman and Portland cements, puzzolano, &c. A composition for uniting metals is called solder, and the name cement is given to a lute or paste surrounding bodies in pots or crucibles for chemical purposes.

Cementation, in metallurgy, the application of cement to substances; the union of carbon and iron when exposed to heat forms steel.

Cementitious, agglutinating; having the quality of cementing.

Cement-stone, nodules of calcareous matter a species of septaria, obtained at Harwich, Sheppey, and other localities, for making cements.

Cemetery, a detached enclosure set apart for the burial of the dead; pieces of ground attached to churches, however, are sometimes called cemeteries.

Cenere, the Italian name for ashes.

Cenotaph, an empty tomb; an honorary monument erected in memory of some person whose body has been entombed elsewhere.

Censer, a chafing dish or pan attached to a chain, used for burning incense in religious ceremonies.

Censor, an officer in despotic countries appointed to revise MSS. &c. for press, having the power to expunge passages, so as to prevent the publication of unpleasant truths, or of information not deemed politic to be generally known.

Census, an enumeration, or statistical account taken occasionally or periodically, of persons or things; as of population, land under crop, stock and produce. In many countries these returns are by law made at decennial periods; in others more frequently.

Cent, the hundredth part, an abbreviation of the Latin *centum*; used as a prefix to many words, weights, coins, &c. As a nominal money division the cent is in use in the United States and various parts of the Continent where decimal coinage is current. The American cent, the hundredth part of the dollar, is worth about a halfpenny. The cent is an old superficial measure of Belgium, the hundredth part of the bonnier. The great cent or solive as a solid measure for wood in France contains 868,168 cubic feet. The great cent or centaine is also a provincial salt measure of France and equal to 115 quarters.

Centage, a rate by the hundred; *per centage* being a commission or allowance at so much per cent.

Centass, a weight of Baden, the hundredth part of the local pound, and weighing 77·17 grains.

Centenaar, the Amsterdam hundredweight or quintal, equal to nearly 109lbs. avoirdupois. *See* Centner.

Centering, the temporary wooden framing on which an arch or any vaulted work is shaped and constructed.

Centesimal, a division into hundredth parts.

Centiare, the metre superficial, the hundredth part of the French are, and equal to 1·19 square yards.

Centigrade, the division into grades or degrees by hundredth parts, called also centesimal; a name for the thermometer of Celsus, used chiefly in France. The distance between the freezing point of water and the boiling point, is divided into 100 degrees, each being equal to 1 4-5th of Fahrenheit's scale. Reaumer's thermometer has only 80 degrees on its scale. *See* Thermometer.

Centigramme, the hundredth part of the present French grain in the decimal pound, and equal to 0·15 English grain.

Centilitre, the hundredth part of the pint or litre of France—0·017 English pint, also 0·017 cubic inch. In Holland the centilitre bears the name of vingerhoed or de.

Centime, an existing French copper coin though rarely seen, the tenth part of a penny; 100 centimes making a franc. The centime is also used in accounts in Belgium, Switzerland, Italy and Austria, and as a division of the Dutch guilder.

Centimetre, a linear measure in France and Belgium—the hundredth part of the metre equal to 0.39 inch. In Holland the legal name of the centimetre is duim or pouce; in Venetian Lombardy it is called dito or doight.

Centinajo, the Italian quintal, of varying proportions in different towns; in Florence only 75lbs., in Milan 220½; a salt measure in the Ionian islands of 4410lbs avoirdupois.

Centinarius. *See* Centum-pondium.

Centistere, the hundredth part of the French stere, 0·353 cubic feet.

Centlit, a Dalmatian liquid measure, the eighty-fourth part of the baril, and equal to 1·8 pint.

Centner, the commercial hundred-weight or quintal of the Continental States which varies in most. The toll centner of the German States is 110¼lbs. avoirdupois, the trade centner 113⅜lbs. In Vienna it is 123¾lbs.

Centre-bit, a carpenter's tool for boring circular holes.

Centre-piece, a table ornament; also a workman's tool.

Centres, the plain parts of shawls prepared in Bradford, &c., to which the Paisley weavers attach ornamental borders.

Centrifugal-machine, a whirling machine for drying sugar or clearing it from molasses, on the principle of trundling a mop. The sugar is enclosed in cylindrical strainers, a rapid rotary motion is imparted, by which the moisture is thrown off more speedily than by the old process of leaving the molasses to drain away from the sugar gradually in flat coolers and casks. Also, a machine so constructed as to raise water by centrifugal force, aided by the pressure of the atmosphere.

Centrifugal-pump, an engine for raising water by steam power.

Centripetal-press, a mechanical contrivance for pressing square in all directions.

Centum, a hundred.

Centum-pondium, **Centinarius**, an ancient Roman weight corresponding to the modern quintal, and equal to about 72lbs. avoirdupois.

Centurie, an ancient Roman land measure equal to 123½ acres.

Ceol, **Chol**, a ship or vessel.

Cephalic, a name applied to snuffs, or medicines which relieve headache.

Ceralacca (Italian), sealing wax.

Ceramic, a term often applied to ornamental pottery.

Cerasin, a name given to such gums as cherry-tree gum, which swell in water but do not readily dissolve.

Cerate, an ointment made of wax and oil, of spermaceti, or lard and wax; used for outward applications or plasters.

Cerbonea (Italian), sour or vapid wine.

Cerchiaio (Italian), a cooper, one who hoops casks.

Cereal, pertaining to edible grain; the grasses which produce bread-corn and are the object of a continuous culture for food, as wheat, rye, barley, maize, oats, rice, and millet, are called cereals.

Cerine, the chief constituent of wax; bees' wax containing nearly eighty per cent. of cerine.

Ceroon, the American mode of spelling seroon, a bale or package made of skins.

Ceroxyline, the resin of palm-wax.

Certificate, a testimony given in writing; a paper granting some particular privilege. A bankrupt's certificate is the legal document issued by the Commissioner of the Bankruptcy Court, certifying that he has surrendered his estate, passed the examinations and forms required, and, being released from his pecuniary obligations, is permitted to recommence his trading operations. A certificate of origin is a Custom-House document, testifying to particular articles being the growth of a British colony.

Certificated Bankrupt, one who is freed from his liabilities, and holds a certificate from the Bankruptcy Court, in contradistinction to an uncertificated bankrupt, who has no right to trade.

Ceruleum, a blue Roman pigment, a silicate of copper.

Ceruse, a name given to white-lead paint, a preparation from thin plates of lead exposed to the hot vaporous exhalations of vinegar or other acid.

Cerussite, a valuable ore of lead.

Cervesa, the Spanish name for beer or ale.

Cess, a rate or tax.

Cessio Bonorum, a process in Scotland similar to assignment of the property of a debtor for the benefit of his creditors, in England.

Cession, a voluntary assignment or surrender of a person's effects or estate to his creditors, to avoid imprisonment.

Cessionnaire (French), an assignee or receiver.

Cess pool, a cavity or receptacle for drainage; the name is, however, often applied to the grating which covers the cavity.

Cesta (Spanish and Italian), a basket or pannier, ceston being one of large dimensions.

Cestaio (Italian), a basket-maker.

Cetwert, **Cetvert**. *See* Tchetwert.

Cevadilla. *See* Cebadilla.

Cevadine, a name for hordeine, the starch of barley, *Hordeum distichon*.

Ceventeria, a name in Tuscany for rouge, or paint for the face.

Ceylon Moss, a small and delicate fucus, believed to be the *Gracelaria lichenoides*, obtained in the salt lakes, on the coasts of Ceylon; which contains a large proportion of true starch, and is used for jellies.

CEYLON STONE, a general name given to many fine minerals and jewels obtained in the island of Ceylon; specially applied, however, to a species of black spinelle.

CHA, a kind of tea rolled up like tobacco, which goes to the interior of Asia.

CHABBA, an old Arabian weight, nearly equal to one English grain.

CHABENA, CHABINI (Hindustani), parched grain.

CHABLIS, a kind of French white wine.

CHABOOK, an Indian name for a whip.

CHABUTARAH, CHUBOOTURA (Hindustani), a market-place, custom-house, or police-station in India.

CHACCAR, a period of rest for refreshment, accorded three times a day to miners and other labourers in South America.

CHACO, an unctuous earth of La Paz, South America, which is made into little pats, and eaten with chocolate.

CHACOE, SHACO, a military cap or helmet.

CHAD, a name for the young of the sea bream, *Pargus centrodontus.*

CHADAM, an imaginary money of account in some parts of Asia, equal to one paysa, of the value of twenty-five cowries, and worth about half a farthing in English money.

CHADAR, CHUDUR (Hindustani), a sheet or cloth.

CHAFE, to rub or damage the surface of any thing.

CHAFF, the pericarp or dry calyx of grain removed by thrashing and winnowing, which has many medicinal and economical uses. It is occasionally mixed with mortar, and employed as a substitute for hair in making plaster for rooms, and sometimes used for stuffing beds.

CHAFF-CUTTER, CHAFF-ENGINE, a straw-cutter or chopping machine, with knives for dividing straw into small lengths, or "*chaff*" as it is termed, for feeding cattle.

CHAFFER, a small portable furnace.

CHAFFERER, one who bargains for wares.

CHAFFERY, that part of a foundry where the forges are placed for hammering iron into bars.

CHAFING DISH, a vessel for holding charcoal or coals to give heat.

CHAGREEN, SHAGREEN, a rough tuberculated leather; also the prepared skin of the dog-fish.

CHAHAR (Mahratta), an Indian superficial measure for land, ranging from 120 to 150 biggahs.

CHAHI, a money of Georgia and Persia, the fourth part of an abassi, and the half of an uzaltum.

CHAHORA (Hindustani), a fine variety of transplanted rice in India.

CHAHOTRA, CHAHUTRA (Mahratta), interest taken at four per cent. per month.

CHAIN, a line of connected links of any kind; a British lineal measure used in surveying or plotting, made of links of iron wire united together. The surveyor's chain contains 22 yards or 792 inches, which, being divided into 100 links, gives 7·92 inches for each link. The square chain is the tenth of an acre, or 484 square yards. The chain as a land measure in Tinnevalley, and some other parts of India, is equal to 3 7-11th acres. In France, Belgium, and Holland, the chain represents the double decametre, equal to 65·61 feet, nearly the same as the British.

CHAINA, CHENA (Hindustani), an inferior kind of grain or millet, *Panicum pilosum.*

CHAIN-BOAT, a substantial boat used in harbours, for getting-up mooring chains or anchors.

CHAIN-BOLTS, the large bolts used to secure to the ship's side the links, or dead-eyes, through which the standing rigging is rove.

CHAIN-BRIDGE, a suspension-bridge.

CHAIN-CABLE, a mooring or anchoring cable made of stout iron rings.

CHAIN-CABLE MANUFACTURER, a maker of iron cables for ships and other purposes.

CHAIN-PLATES, strong thick plates of iron used in merchant vessels, bolted to the ship's side, instead of chains to the dead-eyes, for holding the blocks by which the rigging of the mast is secured. They take their name from the mast, and are hence called fore-chains, main-chains, or mizen-chains.

CHAIN-PUMP, an hydraulic machine for raising water, employed in ships, and for draining land.

CHAIN-SHOT, large iron balls or bullets chained together, used in sea-battles to destroy the spars, rigging, &c., of an enemy's vessel.

CHAIN-STITCH, work made with open spaces like chain links.

CHAIN-TIMBER, large joists used in the middle stories of a building, to bind and give it strength.

CHAIN-WORK, a style of fabric, of which tambouring, net, and hosiery are examples.

CHAIR, a heavy cast-iron socket for receiving and securing the bars of a railroad; a moveable seat of which there are numberless kinds made to suit special uses, such as light and ornamented drawing-room chairs, heavy and substantial office chairs, dining-room chairs, and folding, rocking, and reclining chairs, hall chairs, shop chairs, garden chairs, &c.

CHAIR AND SOFA STUFFER, a workman who fills, pads, and covers seats.

CHAIR-CARVER, one employed in carving the upright posts and other parts of beds, arm-chairs, sofas, &c.

CHAIR-MAKER, a workman who makes the frames or parts of chairs, sofas, and other seats.

CHAIRMAN, the presiding officer of a company, board of directors, or public meeting.

CHAIR-WEBB, a kind of saw.

CHAIS (French), wine vaults.

CHAISE, a two-wheeled carriage drawn by one horse, of which there are many varieties, such as headed chaises, pony chaises, &c.

CHAISE-LONGUE (French), a couch or sofa with one arm or end.

CHAKA (Bengalee), the upper portion of a salt boiling furnace.

CHAKAN, CHAKKALA (Malabar), an oil presser.

CHAKI (Bengalee and Hindustani), a handmill or grinding stone; an apparatus for spinning twine suspended from the hand.

CHAKKARA (Malabar), coarse sugar made from the tari or juice of the coco nut and other palms.

CHAKKU (Karnatic), a pack or bale of raw cotton.

CHAKHAND, an Indian measure of length, the half of a cubit; about nine inches.

CHAKKILI (ordinarily corrupted to Chucklar by Europeans); the Tamil and Malabar name for a currier, shoemaker, or worker in hides and leather. In the Hindustani and some other Indian dialects, the worker in skins is called a chamar.

CHAKRAMU, a coin formerly current in the South of India, the 16th part of a pagoda.

CHAKRI, a dealer in oils in India.

CHAKSOO, an Indian name for the small flat shining black seeds, of *Cassia absus*, Linnæus, which are employed in all parts of the East against inflammation of the eyes.

CHALAN, CHELLAUM, CHULAN, a common Indian name for an invoice, pass, voucher, or way-bill.

CHALAND (French), a customer, one who deals with another; a large barge or lighter used on the French rivers for the transport of goods and towed by steam or horses.

CHALCEDONY, CALCEDONY, a general term for a semi-transparent siliceous mineral, comprising several well-known varieties of stones, as the onyx, sardonyx, &c. *See* AGATE and CARNELIAN.

CHALCOGRAPHY, the art of engraving on brass and copper.

CHALCOUS, CHALCUS, an ancient Greek weight of 1·04 to 1·44 grains, corresponding to the *tassondj* of the Arabs.

CHALDER, a dry measure in the old Scottish system, containing nearly 8 imperial quarters of wheat or flour; for other grain, fruit, potatoes, &c., 11¾ quarters; an old mode of spelling chaldron.

CHALDRON, a heaped measure for various dry goods, formerly in use but now prohibited. It is, however, still employed as a weight for coals; the London chaldron being 25½ cwt., the Newcastle chaldron of 3 wains 52½ cwt, but for boats estimated at 53 cwt. In the transatlantic ports, the coal chaldron varies—at Pictou, Nova Scotia, it is nominally one ton and a quarter, but the average weight of the Pictou chaldron is 3456 lbs. The ordinary weight required in the markets of the United States, is 2940 lbs., but at New York the chaldron of coals is only 2500 lbs.

CHALDRON-WAGON, a wagon which conveys the coal from the pit's mouth to the place of shipment, and holds a chaldron of coals.

CHALIAS, a distinct caste of natives in Ceylon who are employed as cinnamon peelers, stripping the bark twice annually. They derive their name from chawl the Sanscrit name for bark.

CHALICE, a sacramental cup used in the celebration of the eucharist.

CHALIES, a petty money of account, in Ceylon the fourth part of a pice.

CHALK, the carbonate of lime, a white calcareous deposit occurring with flint, nodules. Chalk forms the basis of whiting, crayons, and some white colours. In agriculture, chalk is perhaps the most extensively employed of the limestone species, being added in many instances to the soil to alter the constituents and to fertilize land. In medicine it is used in the form of prepared chalk and compound chalk powder, as an astringent and antacid.

CHALK-CEMENT, an hydraulic cement made of chalk which hardens under water in a few minutes.

CHALK-CUTTER, a workman employed in digging chalk.

CHALK-DRAWING, a drawing sketched and filled in with black and coloured crayons.

CHALK-LIME, the burnt carbonate or chalk from which heat has driven off the carbonic acid.

CHALK-LINE, a carpenter's line which is chalked so as to leave a mark for working by.

CHALK-PIT, a pit from which chalk is dug.

CHALLENGE, in law an exception taken to jurors by a person to be tried, or by his counsel.

CHALLIS, a fine printed soft woollen fabric, used for ladies' dresses.

CHALLIS-PRINTER, a printer of challis.

CHALLY, an old Dutch copper coin still occasionally found in circulation in Ceylon. *See* RIDDY.

CHALON (French), a lighter or barge.

CHALOT, a mode of spelling the shallot, *Allium ascalonicum*, an article of diet in some countries.

CHALOUPE (French), the long-boat of a ship.

CHALTER, a dry measure of Stettin, equal to 84¼ Winchester bushels.

CHALTICK, a native kind of rice grown in Russia.

CHALU (Telugu), rice cleaned for cooking.

CHALUMEAU (French), an ancient rustic flute.

CHALYBEATES, mineral waters and medicines which hold iron.

CHALYBITE, a very valuable sparry iron ore, the Styrian steel is made from it.

CHAMA, the Malabar name for the *Panicum miliaceum*; the seed of which is sometimes used as a substitute for rice; also a very large bivalve found in the Indian ocean, the shells of which are used for *benitiers*.

CHAMAR, CHUMAR, a worker of skins in India. *See* CHAKKILI.

CHAMBARD FABRICS, stuffs made from soft worsted yarn in Saxony, by hand weavers at their houses.

CHAMBER, the inside of a piece of ordnance. Chambers are also suites of rooms in a house, occupied as offices by gentlemen and members of the learned professions. The inside of a lock, a partition in a canal.

CHAMBERLAIN, a receiver of public rents and revenues; the treasurer of a corporation.

CHAMBER-HANGINGS, the curtains or tapestry of a sleeping-room.

CHAMBERMAID, a servant who has the charge of sleeping apartments, or attends on a lady.

CHAMBER OF COMMERCE, a committee of

merchants, or influential manufacturers and traders, appointed in a port or inland town, to take cognisance of matters affecting the general or special interests of trade, to memorialize the government, to diffuse useful information, &c.

CHAMFERED, curved, grooved, or inflexed; any thing of which the edge is bevelled or sloped.

CHAMOIS LEATHER, leather made from various kinds of skins, dressed with fish-oil. The oil is hammered or beaten by a mill into the pores of the skin, which is afterwards partially dried, and washed in strong alkali, when it becomes very soft and pliable.

CHAMOMILE, an indigenous plant of Britain, (*Anthemis nobilis*), cultivated for its flowers, which are largely employed in medicine.

CHAMPAGNE, a pleasant effervescing French wine.

CHAMPAGNE-BOTTLE, a strong and particular shaped bottle, which has the cork secured with wire, when holding champagne.

CHAMPAGNE-GLASS, a long, narrow glass, made for drinking effervescing wines from.

CHAMPIGNON, an edible mushroom (*Agaricus oreades*), which is nutritious, stimulant, and rather fragrant. Champignons are frequently strung on thread, dried in the shade, and pounded as an addition to rich gravies and sauces.

CHANA, a kind of yam grown in Cochin.

CHANAPPAN, a weaver of hempen cordage in some of the Indian districts; a maker of coarse cloth for sacks.

CHANCACA, a name in Costa Rica for coarse sugar.

CHANCELIER, CHANCELLOR, the keeper of the records of a consul general.

CHANCELLOR OF THE EXCHEQUER, the finance minister of Great Britain.

CHANCERY, the official abode of a consul in a foreign country.

CHANCERY BARRISTER, a lawyer who practises in the chancery courts.

CHANDELIER, a hanging or fixed lamp with branches, or a frame with branches to hold candles for lighting a room.

CHANDELIER-MAKER, a manufacturer who makes metal suspensory lamps, for candles or gas.

CHANDLER, an old name for a dealer, as corn-chandler, tallow-chandler, ship-chandler, &c.

CHANDLER'S SHOP, a petty huckster's shop; a place where small articles of provisions, &c., are vended.

CHANDO, a species of prepared opium.

CHANGE, to barter; to give one kind of money for another; also an abbreviated mode of designating an exchange or place where merchants and men of business assemble.

CHANKARI, an Indian grain measure, the fourth of a Chauthia; about half a pound.

CHANKS, the Indian name for the large white massive shells of *Turbinella pyrum*, which are much prized and extensively used in India for the manufacture of bangles or shell-bracelets and anklets, &c. Chanks cut in segments of circles form ornaments for the fore arms and wrists of women. The chief supply of these shells is from Ceylon, and when the volutes turn to the right the shell is held in peculiar estimation, and fetches a very high price. When the end is cut off the shell is used as a kind of sounding-horn, both in the East and the West Indies; "Shell blow," at the sugar plantation being the time for drawing off from labour, or for adjourning to meals.

CHANNELS, CHAINWALES, strong projecting planks at the sides of a ship, over which the shrouds are spread, to obtain a greater angle. *See* CHAINS.

CHANNEL-PILOT, a skilled officer who takes charge of the navigation of ships in the English Channel.

CHANNEL-STEAMER, a steamer employed in running across the channels around the British islands.

CHANTA (Malabar), a fair or market.

CHANTEUR (French), a male singer; chanteuse being a female vocalist.

CHANTERELLE (French), the *Chantarellus cibarius*, one of our best eatable mushrooms.

CHANTIER (French), a timber yard or naval dockyard.

CHANTILLY LACE, a fine and rich French hand-made lace, which from its price can only be obtained by the wealthy.

CHANVRE (French), hemp.

CHANWAN (Hindustani), a small sort of millet.

CHAP, the upper and lower parts of the mouth in animals, the jaw; hence pigs' cheeks smoked and dried are vended as Bath chaps.

CHAPATA (Hindustani), a thin unleavened cake of flour and water, toasted or baked over a fire.

CHAPE, the back piece or catch by which a buckle is attached to the article or garment; a thin plate at the point of a scabbard.

CHAPEAU (French), a bonnet or hat; in maritime commerce a primage.

CHAPELIER (French), a hatter.

CHAPEL-MASTER, a director of music.

CHAPEL-WARDEN, the warden of a chapelry.

CHAPLAIN, an honorary or paid officiating clergyman, having no see or incumbency; thus there are chaplains to regiments, to hospitals, to ships, to masonic lodges, to Lord Mayors, and to British chapels in foreign countries.

CHAPITER, in architecture, the capital of a column.

CHAPLET, a pair of stirrup leathers; a little moulding.

CHAPMAN, a pedlar or itinerant dealer.

CHAPPRASSER, an Indian messenger.

CHAPRA (Hindustani), dried cakes of cow-dung used as fuel.

CHARACTOGRAPH, a philosophical instrument.

CHARBON (French), coal, charcoal, bituminous fuel.

CHARBONNIER (French), a collier; a coal-man, one who supplies or deals in fuel.

CHARCOAL, ANIMAL, a form of carbon obtained by burning bone or the chippings of hides, leather, &c., which is used for filtering or decolorizing vegetable solutions.

CHARCOAL-BURNER, a workman employed in the preparation of charcoal.

CHARCOAL-FILTER, a fountain or other filter for water, filled with charcoal.

CHARCOAL-MAKER AND DEALER, a trader who manufactures and vends charcoal for fuel, &c.

CHARCOAL, VEGETABLE, charred or burnt wood, which is largely used for fuel on the Continent, and is also valued for making glass, steel, and as a deodorizer when powdered: cylinder charcoal obtained by distilling non-resinous woods, is used in the manufacture of gunpowder.

CHARCUTERIE, formerly *Chair cuit*, the French name for cooked flesh, such as dressed hams, cold meats and fowls, toques, sausages, &c.

CHARDOON. *See* CARDOON.

CHARGE, an onset or attack; a grain measure of 16 decalitres formerly in use in some of the departments of France; in Marseilles it was nearly 4½ bushels; 180 charges being equal to 100 quarters. The quantity of coal a gas retort will take, or of ore for a furnace, powder for a gun, &c; 30 pigs of lead.

CHARGED, burthened or loaded; trusted or debited for payment.

CHARGÉ D'AFFAIRES, a subordinate foreign minister, one intrusted with diplomatic affairs in a foreign country in the place of an ambassador.

CHARGEMENT (French), the cargo, bulk, or lading of a ship.

CHARGER, a soldier's horse trained for duty; a large sort of dish.

CHARGEUR (French), a shipper.

CHARIOT, a light coach of which there are many kinds, as for travelling, Britzka chariots, post chariots, dormeuse post chariots, dress chariots, and chariots for town use, &c. In France the term generally implies a wagon.

CHARKANA, an Indian name for a checked Dacca muslin.

CHARKEY, CHARKA, TSCHARKEY, the hundredth part of the Russian vedro, a liquid measure equal to 0.21 of a pint, 100 vedro are equal to 270½ imperial gallons.

CHARMS, amulets, fancy ornaments and articles of various kinds sold to wear, from an imaginary belief that they ward off evil.

CHARNECO, a sweet Spanish wine.

CHARNLEY FOREST STONE, a description of whetstone or hone obtained from Leicestershire, some of the best substitutes for the Turkey hone stone.

CHARPOYS, small portable stretcher beds used in India, consisting of a wooden frame resting on four legs, with tape across to support the bedding.

CHAR, a small and esteemed fish of the salmon family (*Salmo salvelinus*), not very common in this country.

CHARRED-WOOD, the surface of posts and other pieces of wood, are often exposed to fire to render them more durable under ground.

CHART, a hydrographical map; a representation on paper of the seas, rivers and seacoasts of countries, &c., for the guidance of mariners.

CHARTER, a grant of exclusive rights by the Crown to a company.

CHARTERED, a ship hired for a voyage.

CHARTERER, one who engages a ship and causes it to be laden wholly with his own goods, or partly with merchandise or produce belonging to others.

CHARTERING-BROKER, a shipping agent who negotiates the charter of vessels.

CHARTERING-CLERK, a clerk employed in a chartering broker's office.

CHARTERMASTER, in the mining districts, one who raises coal or iron stone by the ton, at a contract price.

CHARTER-PARTY, a contract in writing between the owner or master of a ship and the freighter, for the use of the ship for a determined voyage upon certain specified conditions to some particular place; occasionally it is for part of a ship.

CHART-MAKER, an artist who draws or engraves charts on metal plates.

CHARTOMETER, an instrument for measuring maps and charts.

CHART-PUBLISHER, a tradesman who keeps and sells charts.

CHARVEDAR, a mule driver with a caravan in Persia or Turkey.

CHARVOLANT, a carriage drawn by kites.

CHARWAHA (Hindustani), a herdsman or grazier.

CHARWOMAN, one who goes out to work by the day or job.

CHASE, to hunt or pursue game; an iron frame to fasten forms of type in, to print from; chases are made of either cast or malleable iron.

CHASER, one who ornaments or embosses metals by punching or driving out the surface so as to form bas-relief figures, &c.

CHASNI (Hindustani), a pan for boiling sugar in.

CHASSE-MARÉE, a French shallop or coasting vessel.

CHASSEUR, a light-armed French trooper.

CHAT (French), a prefix for any thing small—as chat-potatoes, chat-wood, chat-moss.

CHATA (Spanish), a lighter or pontoon.

CHATELAINE, a steel chain worn at a lady's waist-belt to suspend keys, scissors, and fancy ornaments to.

CHATHWA, another name for the seer, an Indian dry measure. *See* CHAUTHIA.

CHATIGNA, a name in France for boiled chestnuts mashed or beaten up for food.

CHATS, a mining term for the second stratum or centre portion of a mass of ore in the process of washing; small heaps of ore; small potatoes used for feeding pigs, &c.

CHATTAH, an umbrella-hat, or sun screen, made in the East of the leaves of the *Licuala peltata* palm of Roxburgh, sometimes of a dried talipot or plantain leaf. These chattah hats are much worn by the ploughmen, cowkeepers, and coolies, of Bengal, Assam, &c. The Chinese umbrellas or *kittysols* are exceedingly popular, they are made of paper stretched on ribs of bamboo and varnished black.

CHATTE, a sort of ship classed in the Veritas or French Lloyds.

CHATTELS, choses in action, all goods and real or personal property except freehold estates.

CHATTY, a porous earthen water-pot used in India.

CHATWOOD, small sticks collected for fuel.

CHAUDRONNIER (French), a French coppersmith.

CHAULE, the Hindustani name for the *Dolichos sinensis*, a species of pulse largely cultivated; also the ceremony of tonsure.

CHAULI, CHAWALI, a small silver coin in the Mahratta country, worth about two annas, or threepence.

CHAUTHIA, a common grain measure in the north-west provinces of India, about equal to a seer, or 2 lbs.; five chauthias make a pansiri. [nearly 11 feet.

CHAVERKALU, a Telugu measure of 7½ cubits,

CHAWAR, a Mahratta land measure, consisting of 120 square biggahs.

CHAWKE, CHOWKE (Hindustani), an open square or market-place in an eastern city.

CHAWL, a weight for precious metals in Malwa, about the fourth of a grain. Also a vernacular name in India for rice.

CHAY, a red dye-stuff obtained in India from the root of *Oldenlandia umbellata*, and used by dyers for the same purposes as madder.

CHEAP-JACK, the common name for a travelling hawker or a stationary vender of refuse or cheap articles.

CHEAT, any thing false or defrauding; also a kind of fine bread.

CHEBACCO, a small boat in Massachusetts.

CHEBEC, a kind of naval craft.

CHECK, an order for payment on demand. *See* CHEQUE.

CHECK-BOOK, CHEQUE-BOOK, a printed book of blank forms, for writing orders or drafts on a banker, for money lodged to his credit by the drawer.

CHECK-CLERK, an officer employed to examine and scrutinize the work, time of labour, or the accounts of others.

CHECKER-WORK, any kind of work in which crossed or angular patterns occur.

CHECKRUM, an Indian money equal to 1¼ rupee, or 3s. sterling.

CHECKS, a kind of Venetian blind used as screens or sun shades in India. They are formed of very narrow strips or laths of bamboo, four to six feet long, and are hung before the windows or doors of dwellings. Cords and fancy checks are cambric muslins with stripes and cords placed chequerwise, by thick threads being introduced into the warp or weft. A trousers material, a cross-barred fabric, chiefly black and white worsted and cotton; but some is made all of cotton; pieces of wood which correspond to each other in machines, &c., or which enclose other parts.

CHECK-SHIRTS, cross-barred shirts of various colours, much used by seamen.

CHECK-STRING, a cord leading to the inside of a carriage, to enable the occupant to signalize to the coachman.

CHECK-TAKER, a person employed to receive pass-tickets, &c., at places of transit or amusement.

CHEDAM, the fourth of a pice, a nominal subdivision of a petty coin in Malwa.

CHEDDAR, a rich fatty cheese, of a spongy appearance, made from new milk, of a very nutritious quality.

CHEESE, a commercial product from milk, of which there are many kinds made for home use and export; we also receive large quantities from America and the Continent: those made in England taking their name from counties, &c., are Cheshire, a large rich solid cheese; Derbyshire, a small, rich, white variety; Gloucester, rich and mild, of two kinds, single and double; Lincolnshire, a small and soft cheese made of new milk and cream; Norfolk, a dark yellow coloured; Suffolk, a skim-milk cheese; and Cottenham, a broad-shaped and superior flavoured Stilton. Other prime home-made cheeses are Cheddar, Wensleydale, cream pine, and loaf cheese. The esteemed foreign cheeses are Parmesan, Gruyere, &c. Other kinds of cheese will be found mentioned in their alphabetical order.

CHEESE-CAKE, a sweet custard cake made of grated cheese, flour, sugar, &c.

CHEESE-COLOURING. *See* ANNOTTA.

CHEESE-DAIRY, a cool room where cheese is made.

CHEESE-FACTOR, CHEESE-MONGER, a dealer in cheese, a provision-merchant.

CHEESE-KNIFE, a large spatula made use of in dairies to break down the curd whilst in the cheese tub.

CHEESE-LEP, a bag in which rennet is kept for making cheese. [cheese.

CHEESE-MAKER, one employed in making

CHEESE-PRESS, a screw press employed in cheese-dairies to force the whey from the curd in the cheese-vat.

CHEESE-RENNET, a wild flower, the yellow bedstraw, *Galium verum*, sometimes used for colouring milk to make cheese.

CHEESE-SCOOP, CHEESE-TASTER, an auger instrument for boring and tasting cheese.

CHEESE-TASTER MANUFACTURER, a maker of metal scoops or augers for boring cheese, in order to test the quality.

CHEESE-TOASTER, an instrument hung at the bars of a grate to toast cheese.

CHEESE-VAT, the case in which the curd is placed to be pressed in cheese making.

CHEH, the tenth part of the Chinese tael.

CHEI, a land measure used in rice culture in Mysore equal to 1·322 acre.

CHEKI, a jeweller's weight in Persia of 7200 grains.

CHEKMAK, a fabric of silk and gold thread, mixed with cotton, made in Turkey.

CHELLAUN (Hindustani), a way-bill for checking the time on a journey between the different rests or stages. [powder.

CHEMIC, a commercial name for bleaching

CHEMICAL-BALANCE, a very accurate balance for assays, and other nice operations.

CHEMICAL-COLOUR-MANUFACTURER, a maker of artificially compounded pigments.

CHEMICAL-INSTRUMENT-MAKER, a manufacturer of apparatus for chemists, and also occasionally of mathematical and philosophical instruments.

CHEMICAL-PAPER, paper prepared for chemical operations, as filtering paper, paper for photographs, &c.

CHEMICALS, substances used in chemistry.

CHEMICAL-STOPPERER, a manufacturer of stoppers for glass bottles.

CHEMISE, a French name for the lining of a furnace; a female inner garment.

CHEMISETTE, a lady's lace or net stomacher.

CHEMIST, a scientific manufacturer of substances used in chemistry; also a drug-seller. Sometimes the business of operative and retail chemist is combined.

CHEMISTRY, the study of the various elementary bodies of nature; their affinity, properties, laws and combinations and their useful applications to the arts and manufactures.

CHEMIST'S-LABORATORY, the place where the manipulations and analytical operations of a manufacturing chemist are carried on.

CHEMIST'S-SHOP, a shop where chemicals and pharmaceutical preparations are retailed.

CHEMITYPY, a mode of printing from metal plates with ordinary presses, which is intended as a substitute for wood-cutting. The process enables casts in relief to be taken from an engraving.

CHEMKE, a name given to the razor carp (*Cyprinus cultratus*), the young of which are dried and consumed in the Black Sea. See CARP.

CHEMMARI. See CHAMAR.

CHENA, a name in India for millet (*Panicum miliaceum*); also ground covered with underwood; a bushy thorny jungle of low growth.

CHENDI, an Eastern name for the fermented juice of the date palm.

CHÊNE (French), an oak.

CHENEVIS, a name for hemp seed in France.

CHENICA, a small dry measure of Persia, the half of a capicha.

CHENILLE, a loose silk trimming.

CHENNA, corrupted from Chana (Hindustani), a kind of pulse (*Cicer arietinum*), commonly known as gram; when parched and mixed with lime juice and pepper chenna forms an esteemed condiment among the Hindoos.

CHENVUKOTTI, from Chenva, copper; the Malabar name for a coppersmith or brazier.

CHEOH, a long measure in Sumatra, about 14½ inches.

CHEQUE, a written order for payment to bearer of a specified sum of money on some bank or individual, by a depositor or person having the necessary funds or credit. Sometimes the cheque is "crossed," that is, made payable only through a banking firm, instead of on demand by presentation at the counter.

CHEQUEE, a weight in Turkey; that for precious metals contains 100 drachms, and is equal to 4950 troy grains; that for opium 250 drachms, or 1⅞lb; and the heavy chequee for wool, &c., 800 drachms, about 5 1-6th lbs. In Smyrna 22½ chequees make 1 cantaro.

CHEQUERS, the armorial coat of the Earls of Warren and Surrey; from being used on their hostels or inns it was afterwards adopted as a sign for public houses; chequers are also uniformly-shaped stones in the faces of walls.

CHERAMELLA, a vernacular Indian name for the subacid fruit of the *Cicca disticha*, universally used as an article of food, raw or cooked, or in pickles or preserves.

CHERANG, a lac varnish used in Cambodia for lackering cabinets, cases, &c.

CHERASSE, a gold coin of different values struck for distribution on coronations in Persia. Some have been for 4s., some for 12s., some for 30s.

CHERIMOYA, an esteemed fruit of Peru and New Granada, the produce of *Anona Cherimolia*.

CHERMES (Italian), cochineal. See KERMES.

CHEROOT, a rough and loosely made cigar, the best kind come from Manila.

CHERRAY, a commercial weight of Persia, 78·85 of which are equal to 100lbs. avoirdupois, or 88·31 to the English cwt.

CHERRIES, the well-known fruit of the *Prunus cerasus*, of which there are now several hundred varieties. The wood of the cherry-tree is worked up into common chairs and other articles, being stained to imitate mahogany, and is also used for musical instruments.

CHERRY-BRANDY, a sweetened or cordial spirit in which cherries are steeped.

CHERRY-COFFEE, the planters' name for the fruit of the coffee as picked from the tree, before it has undergone the operations of pulping, drying, &c., to prepare the berry for shipment.

CHERRY-WINE, a sweet wine made from cherries. The liqueur called maraschino made in Italy and Dalmatia is prepared from a variety of cherry. The kernel of the cherry is also much used for communicating its peculiar flavour to brandy and cordials.

CHERT-STONE, a mineral sometimes called hornstone, quarried in Derbyshire and Cornwall for making the stones of pottery mills to pulverize flints. The North American Indians formerly used chert or hornstone for the heads of their spears and arrows.

CHERTWERT, the principal corn measure of Russia equal nearly to 5¾ bushels.

CHERUMAH, CHEROOMER, a slave labourer in Malabar.

CHERVICE, a fine kind of tallow shipped to Constantinople from the Black Sea ports, and used for culinary purposes.

CHERVIL, a common potherb with edible roots, the *Anthriscus cerefolium*, also much used as a salad on the Continent.

CHESHIRE-ACRE, a linear measure of 28 yards, as used in some parts of the country; but in Barnsley it is used as a superficial measure of 10,240 square yards.

CHESHIRE-CHEESE, a large-sized rich cheese, weighing from 100 to 200 lbs.

CHESS-BOARD, a board with sixty-four chequers or squares of alternate light and dark colours, for playing the game of chess on.

CHESSEL, the perforated wooden mould or vat in which cheese is pressed.

CHESS-MEN, sets of turned pieces or carved figures, with which the game of chess is played.

CHESS-TABLE, a small pedestal table with inlaid squares on the top for playing the game of chess on.

CHESS-TREES, pieces of wood bolted to the sides of a ship to secure the clews of the mainsail.

CHESSYLITE, a species of copper ore which is valuable when found in sufficient quantity.

CHEST, a wooden box or package of no certain dimensions. The chest of opium weighs 141¼lbs. the tare allowance for leaf and dust being 1¼lb. A chest of tea varies: the chest of Pekoe contains but seven catties, of souchong and pouchong 25, and of hyson 60. The chest of sugar from Brazil is about 13 cwt.; of indigo from Bengal about 260 lbs. The chest of olive oil contains 60 flasks, or a little over two gallons.

CHESTERFIELD, a kind of loose coat.

CHEST-EXPANDER, an application of fixed or pliable materials for keeping back the shoulders.

CHESTNUT, the fruit or nuts of the *Castanea vesca*. In some countries chestnuts constitute a considerable part of the general food of the inhabitants. From the horse chestnut excellent flour, starch and vermicelli have been made: the wood is cheap, strong, and durable, and has a very handsome natural colour and grain which is greatly heightened by varnishing.

CHEST OF DRAWERS, a set of drawers for keeping clothes or other articles in, made of mahogany, deal, or other wood.

CHEST-PROTECTOR, a hare skin or any covering for the chest worn by persons suffering from pulmonary complaints.

CHEST-UPON-CHEST, a double set of drawers that divides in the middle for the convenience of moving or travelling.

CHETTERKARAN, the Malabar name for a grass cutter and a drawer of Tari, or the juice of the coco-nut palm.

CHEVAL-GLASS, a lady's dressing room looking-glass, in which the full length figure may be seen.

CHEVALIER BARLEY, an esteemed kind of malting barley, named after the gentleman who first brought it into notice.

CHEVERIL, leather prepared from kid skin.

CHEVILLE (French), the peg of a violin, tenor, &c.

CHEVRETTE, an engine for raising pieces of artillery into their carriages.

CHEVRON (French), a rafter; a Gothic architectural ornament, sometimes called a zig-zag.

CHEW-STICK, the branches and twigs of the *Gouania Domingensis*, which are used in the West Indies for cleaning the teeth, and also powdered as a dentifrice.

CHEWING-BALL, a medicinal bolus for a horse.

CHHAKRA (Hindustani), a cart.

CHHALA (Bengalee), a pair of sacks or panniers slung across the back of a bullock.

CHHAP, CHOP (Hindustani), an official mark on weights and measures, to indicate their accuracy; an eastern Custom-house stamp or seal on goods that have been examined and have paid duty.

CHIAN TURPENTINE, a resinous juice obtained in small quantities from the *Pistacia Terebinthus*, used medicinally, and employed in the East as a masticatory to sweeten the breath and preserve the teeth.

CHIATTA (Italian), a kind of flat-bottomed boat.

CHIBOUK, a Turkish pipe, usually with an ebony or cherry-wood stem, and an amber mouth-piece, the bowl being of baked clay.

CHICA, a fermented intoxicating beverage made in South America, usually from maize steeped in warm water; that most prized is, however, first chewed and then mashed in hot water; sometimes it is made from other vegetable substances.

CHICK, a name for the inspissated juice of the poppy, three pounds of which will make one of opium.

CHICKEN, CHICKLING, a young fowl.

CHICKEN-WEED, a name under which the dyeing lichen, *Rocella fuciformis*, has been imported into Liverpool from Lisbon.

CHICKLING VETCH, the *Lathyrus sativus*, used in Germany as food.

CHICK-PEA, a leguminous plant, the *Cicer arietinum*, which is a common crop in India, where it is known as grain. It is also cultivated in the South of Europe. In some places it is roasted as a substitute for coffee.

CHICORY, the powdered root of *Cichorium intybus*, used either alone or with coffee as an infused beverage. Chicory is largely imported from the Continent and the Channel islands, and is also extensively grown at home.

CHICORY-CUTTER, a machine for slicing and preparing the chicory roots previous to drying, roasting, and grinding.

CHIEF TRADER, the name of certain superior officers employed by the Hudson's Bay Company in their North American territories.

CHIFFONIER (French), a collector of rags, bones, and shreds, &c.

CHIFFONIERE, a neat chest of drawers, a lady's work table.

CHIK, a bamboo mat to hang at the entrance of a room in India; they are sometimes lined with cotton.

CHIKAN, the Hindustani name for embroidering and working flowers on muslin.

CHIKSA, a fragrant Indian powder composed of sandal wood, andropogon, benzoin, and other aromatic ingredients.

CHILGOZA, a local Indian name for the seeds in the cones of *Pinus Gerardiana*, which form one of the principal articles of subsistence for the natives in Kunawur.

CHILIAN PINE, the *Araucaria imbricata*, a handsome lofty tree, valuable not only for its beauty, but for the large seeds in the pine-cones which supply the natives with a great part of their usual food; the fruit of one tree being sufficient to support eighteen persons for a year.

CHILLAW, a Persian name for plain boiled rice.

CHILLIES, a name given to the small pungent pods or fruit of the *Capsicum annuum*, which, when pounded and ground, form Cayenne pepper.

CHILLO, a name in the Ionian islands for the imperial bushel.

CHIMES, the ends of the staves of a cask, which come out beyond the head; the ringing of church bells.

CHIMNEY, a tube or funnel to a stove, a passage or aperture in the wall of a dwelling-house or building, leading from the fire-place to the top of the house, or some outer wall to carry off the smoke. In factories and machine-shops, &c., chimneys were formerly required to be carried to a great height; but the compulsory consumption of smoke by law now obviates this in a great measure.

CHIMNEY FILTER-DRAIN, a peculiar kind of drain pipe, which can be lifted out at pleasure.

CHIMNEY-GLASS, a looking-glass fixed over a mantel-piece.

CHIMNEY-JAMB, the side of a chimney reaching from the top of the grate to the entrance of the chimney.

CHIMNEY-PIECE, a projection over the front of the fire-place of a room, sometimes called mantel-piece.

CHIMNEY-POT, an addition to the top of a chimney, of metal or pottery ware.

CHIMNEY-STACK, a tall chimney for carrying off smoke from a furnace or manufactory.

CHIMNEY-SWEEPER, a workman who cleanses chimneys by sweeping away and removing the soot deposited about the sides.

CHIMNEY-SWEEPING-MACHINE, a series of connecting rods, by which a stiff whale-bone brush is raised through the chimney to cleanse it from soot.

CHUNO, a nutritive food made in Peru from potatoes, which are first frozen and afterwards reduced to powder.

CHIMON, the Spanish name for an extract of tobacco.

CHIN, CHINI, a name in some parts of India for a coarse kind of sugar.

CHINA, CHINA-WARE, a fine kind of earthen-ware originally made in China, from whence small quantities are still occasionally imported. The name has been very generally transferred to many kinds of porcelain made in Europe.

CHINA CLAY, decomposed felspar of the granite, a fine potter's clay largely used in ceramic manufactures, being first artificially cleaned and prepared in Cornwall.

CHINA CRAPE, a very fine kind of silk crape.

CHINA-DEALER, one who keeps glass, earthenware, porcelain, and pottery for sale.

CHINA-GRASS CLOTH, a beautiful fine fabric made from the fibre of an Indian nettle, the Rhea or Ramee, the *Boehmeria nivea* of Gaudichaud.

CHINA INK, a black pigment made from oil and lampblack thickened with gelatine or isinglass, and scented with musk or camphor. It is ordinarily known as Indian ink, and many cheap and poor imitations of it are made.

CHINA-ORANGE, the sweet orange, *Citrus aurantium*, so named from our having received the plant originally from China.

CHINA-RIVETTER, a mender of broken china ware or porcelain.

CHINAROO, an Indian name for the apricot.

CHINA-ROOT, a species of sarsaparilla, *Smilax China*, largely imported into Calcutta from the eastward, and much employed by native practitioners. *S. glabra* and some other species also pass in the bazaars as China root.

CHINA-SHOP, a common name for any shop where earthen-ware or crockery-ware is sold.

CHINCHEW, a name in China for sugar-candy.

CHINCHILLA, a fur obtained from the *Chinchilla lanigera*, a South American rodent, which is remarkably soft, and extensively used both in America and Europe.

CHINCHORRO (Spanish), a yawl or skiff.

CHINDAWAN, the Malay name for mushrooms.

CHINE, a piece of meat cut near the back-bone of an animal; the ridge of a cask where the ends of the staves are united; the part of the waterway of a ship left above the deck.

CHINE', goods of worsted, cotton, silk, and linen, with printed warps.

CHINE-HOOP, the last hoop at the extremities of a cask.

CHINESE BEER, a fermented drink made by the Chinese, from barley or wheat, with a bitter added to the wort.

CHINGALL, a land measure of Mysore in India of 101 feet.

CHINGHEI, the Malay name for cloves.

CHINKA, the name in India for a temporary bridge of a single cable, often made of stout grass, upon which a seat traverses, in the shape of an ox-yoke.

CHINSING, a temporary caulking or stopping of the seams of a ship's deck or sides with oakum, which is thrust in with a small iron.

CHINTZ, a variety of print in which the figure has at least five different colours. Chintzes often possess great beauty of design and richness of colour.

CHINTZ-PATTERN, any thing having a running or fancy pattern of divers colours, as cottons, paper-hangings, &c.

CHINTZ PRINTER, one who forms or stamps chintz patterns or prints.

CHINUM, a weight in Mysore of eight grains.

CHIODAIUOLO (Italian), a nail maker.

CHIP, a small slip or thin cutting of wood, a kind of straw plait, the leaves of *Thrinax argentea*, a Cuban palm prepared for hats.

CHIP BONNET, a lady's bonnet made of fancy straw plait, or palm leaves.

CHIP PLATTING, prepared and twisted straw, &c., used for hats and bonnets.

CHIQUETER (French), to untangle, and lengthen wool.

CHIRAGON, a writing frame for the blind.

CHIRETTA, the Indian name of the *Agathotes chirayta*; all the parts of the plant are extremely bitter, and highly esteemed as a tonic and febrifuge.

CHIRISH, a mucilaginous liquor used by the weaver in the East for saturating his yarn, said to be procured from the root of a plant of the Asphodel family.

Chirogymnaste, a square board with contrivances for exercising the fingers of a pianist; an instrument of a similar kind for guiding the hands of a piano-forte player is called a Chiroplase.

Chiropodist, one who removes corns, and attends to callosities of the feet.

Chirurgeon, an old mode of spelling surgeon.

Chisel, a mechanic's sharp cutting tool for shaping or gouging wood and stone, of which there are many kinds; as firmer chisels, coach-maker's chisels, mill-wright's chisels, long paring chisels, ripping chisels, blunt chisels, best mortice chisels, sash chisels, mortice-lock chisels, socket chisels, &c.; cold chisels are stouter tools of steel, for cutting iron, &c.

Chiselled-work, wood or stone shaped with the chisel; sculptured work.

Chiselling, the process of shaping a block of stone by a sculptor or stone-worker; a slang name for cheating.

Chit, an abbreviation for the Hindoo term chitthi; a note or letter.

Chitak, Chittack, the lowest denomination of the gross Indian weights; the 16th part of the seer, and equal to 1 oz., 17 dwts., and 12 grains troy; a land measure of 45 square feet, the 16th of the cottah; the fifth part of the koonkee, a small grain measure weighing about 2 oz.

Chitarah, a cotton and silk stuff made in Turkey.

Chite, a kind of Spanish cotton stuff.

Chittagong Wood, a common commercial name for several woods of Southern India, the most valuable is the *Cedrela toona*; another is the *Chickrassa tabularis*.

Chittamootyaloo, an Indian name for a species of seed paried rice.

Chitterlings, Chitlings, parts of the smaller intestines of some animals, cleansed and prepared for food.

Chitthi, Chittie, ordinarily abbreviated to chit, a common Indian name for a bill, bond, draft, or order for payment, note, &c.

Chives, an alliaceous plant, *Allium Schœnoprasum*, the leaves and young tops of which are used as a pot-herb.

Chivoka, the Telugu name for an Indian coin worth about 6d.; the quarter of a rupee.

Chlorate of Potash, a combination of chloric acid with potass. It forms an ingredient of the composition for tipping lucifer matches, is used for bleaching fats and oils, and has lately been introduced into medicine as a tonic and valuable remedy for nervous complaints.

Chloride of Lime, the chemical name of the bleaching powder of commerce, which is now manufactured on a very extensive scale. It is an efficient disinfectant in a high degree, and is therefore much used to destroy fetid odours and poisonous qualities.

Chlorimetry, the process of ascertaining the proportion of chlorine in bleaching powder.

Chlorite, a dark-green compact mineral, which is soft and easily worked. By the moderate action of fire, it becomes very black and quite hard, and then forms the famous pipe stone of the Indians of New Brunswick.

Chloroform, a valuable anæsthetic agent, and therefore largely prepared as a commercial product.

Chlorometer, an instrument for determining the relative decolouring value of samples of bleaching powder.

Choadany, Choradany, an Eastern measure for oil in Malabar, equal to 3¾ gallons. In Travancore, 30 choradanies make one candy of 8 13-64th gallons.

Chobdar, in India, a retainer of some consequence, the bearer of a chobe, or silver stick; a superior class of footman, being, as it were, the silver-stick in waiting.

Cho'ca, a mixture of coffee and chocolate.

Chock, Chuck, a piece of wood for stopping or raising any thing.

Chock and Block, a nautical and mining term, signifying closely wedged, or tightly filled up.

Chock-full, Choke-full, any thing quite full, and into which no more can be put.

Chocolate Cake, pulverized and prepared cacao beans, flavoured with sugar and other ingredients.

Chocolate Maker, one who grinds and prepares the cacao beans of commerce into rolls or cakes, termed chocolate.

Chocolate Nut, a name given to the beans or seeds of *Theobroma Cacao*. *See* Cocoa.

Choir, that part of a church or chapel allotted to the choristers; a band of musicians, &c., who sing in a place of worship.

Choka, a Hindustani name for rice.

Choke, to stifle or stop up.

Choke-damp, a miner's name for carbonic acid gas and other dangerous gases.

Chokeedar, an Indian watchman, a collector of dues at a Custom House.

Choky, Chowkee, an Indian chair or seat; the station of a guard or officer appointed to collect customs' dues.

Chola (Hindustani), a species of gram, *Cicer arietinum*; also, one who cuts sugar canes.

Chollu, a name in some of the Indian dialects for a kind of grain, *Cynosurus coracanus*.

Cholum, the Tamil name for the great millet, *Sorghum vulgare*.

Choo'a, a name in Kumaon for *Amaranthus frumentaceus*, called in Bombay razgeera. *See* Choua.

Choochock, a name for the candareen in Sooloo, one of the Sunda islands.

Choolah, a cooking hearth or fire-place in India.

Choon, a linear measure in Sumatra of 1¼ inch.

Choopah, an Eastern measure of capacity, the fourth of a gantong, and equal to 2¼ pints.

Chop, a slice of meat; a trade term in China for the entire bulk of a certain kind of tea brought to market, or the quantity made; usually comprising 600 chests of Congou, but sometimes reaching 1000 chests. The East India Company offers a part of its tea in London at a time, and this is called a "break." *See* Chhab.

CHOP-HOUSE, an eating-house; a place of refreshment in towns and cities.

CHOPINE, a high kind of shoe formerly used in Europe; a former French measure of capacity, the half of the old pint of Paris. The chopine was also half of a Scotch pint.

CHOPNIES, a kind of shovel or spade.

CHOPPER, an edge tool or small hatchet for domestic use.

CHOPPING-BLOCK, a large solid block of wood, used by butchers and others to chop meat, &c. upon.

CHOPPING-KNIFE, a knife with a handle at each end, for mincing meat and chopping suet, &c.

CHOPPING-MACHINE, a rotary machine for mincing sausage meat.

CHOP-STICKS, small pieces of wood used by the Chinese to convey food to the mouth, in the place of the knife and fork or spoon of other nations.

CHORISTER, a trained public singer; the member of a vocal or ecclesiastical choir.

CHOROGRAPHER, one who lays down maps or plans descriptive of a country.

CHOROGRAPHICAL-APPARATUS, a machine for measuring heights, invented by Baron Klein.

CHORUS, a band or company of singers.

CHOTANA, an uncertain and variable liquid measure in Malabar.

CHOUA, a vernacular name for *Amaranthus oleraceus* or *frumentaceus*, a plant used as a potherb in some parts of India. In Ghurwal, Kumaon, &c., the small grains are also largely used for food.

CHOULTRY, an ornamental stone or other covered building in the East, an inn for accommodating travellers.

CHOUTE, a black mail or tribute levied by the Bheels, a predatory race inhabiting the ghauts of peninsular India. The fourth part of net revenue.

CHOW, corrupted from Chaver or Chau, the nominal weight by which pearls are valued in India, the 6th part of the grain as a weight for silver. The chow is nominally divided into 320 fractional parts. The term has also reference to the quality and value of the gem, ascertained by the size, colour, and weight. *See* KALLINGEE and MANDAJA.

CHOW-CHOW, a Chinese word applied to any mixture; but in trade circles usually applied to mixed pickles.

CHOWDER, a soup made with fish; a term sometimes used to signify trash or rubbish.

CHOWDER-BEER, an infusion of black spruce in water sweetened with molasses, used by the fishermen of Newfoundland as an antiscorbutic.

CHOWDRY, a former receiver of the land revenues in India, now replaced by the Zemindar.

CHOWKEE, a kind of cane chair made in India of rattans, the *Calamus rotang* and *arborescens*.

CHOWKEEDAR, CHOKEEDAR, a custom-house officer, toll collector, village watchman or policeman in India.

CHOW-PATTIES, baked cakes of unleavened bread made in India of wheat or barley meal, used by the lower classes.

CHOWRY, a horse-hair whisk or Indian fly-flapper, the handle of which is made of ivory, sandal wood or other material.

CHRETIEN, BON CHRETIEN, a variety of pear.

CHRISTIAN D'OR, a Danish gold coin worth about 16s. 6d.

CHRISTMAS-BOX, a gratuity formerly given to various classes of servants, by tradesmen, &c.; but now growing into disuse.

CHRISTMAS-TREES, small growing firs or artificial trees sold to decorate with bon-bons, fancy ornaments, &c., on festive occasions.

CHROMASCOPE, an instrument for exhibiting colours.

CHROMATYPE, a process of photography on chemically prepared paper.

CHROME, CHROMITE, CHROMIUM, an important mineral. The green oxide furnishes a valuable colour for oil-painting, enamel, and porcelain. Chrome iron ore forms the basis of many of the coloured preparations of chrome used in dyeing, and for the production of chromate of potash.

CHROME-YELLOW, the chromate of lead, a rich pigment of various shades from deep orange to the palest canary-yellow.

CHROMIC-ACID, a chemical preparation in the form of an orange red coloured powder much used by bleachers and calico printers.

CHROMO-LITHOGRAPHY, the art of printing tinted and coloured lithographs.

CHROMO-TYPOGRAPHY, a new French process of letter-press printing in colours.

CHRONOGRAPHER, a maker of clocks worked by electricity.

CHRONOMETER, an exact time-keeper, any instrument used for determining the longitude at sea or for other purposes, where great accuracy is required. The construction of these time-keepers for marine use has been carried to a high degree of perfection in this country and some are made to go without re-winding about a month.

CHRONOMETER-MAKER, a maker of very accurate-going watches for scientific purposes.

CHRONOMETER, POCKET, an expensive kind of watch noted for its precision and superior make.

CHRONOSCOPE, an instrument for the exact mensuration of time.

CHRYSAMMIC-ACID, a newly invented colouring matter obtained from aloes, which is also called polychromate.

CHRYSOBERYL, a hard, green, semi-transparent aluminous stone obtained from Brazil.

CHRYSOLITE, a yellow gem stone obtained in the Levant.

CHRYSOPHRASE, a highly prized species of chalcedony, of a semi-opaque green colour, used for jewellery.

CHUCK, an appendage to a turner's lathe.

CHUCKRUM, a money of account in Malabar, 28½ going to the rupee of 2s.

CHUCKUNDOJEE, an Indian name for gold embroidery work.

CHUDDER, a wrapper for a female, in India, used to envelop the upper part of the person. It is worn in loose folds and the material may be either silk, muslin, or cambric, &c.

CHUKA, the Malay name for vinegar.

CHU-LAN, a name in China for the spikes of flowers of *Chloranthus inconspicuus*, which are there used to scent tea.

CHUMBALEE OIL, an Indian name for the essential oil of jasmine.

CHUMMY, an associate or companion; popular name for a chimney sweeper.

CHUMP, a short thick block of wood, a bony part of the loin in meat.

CHUN, CHOONU (Hindustani), pea-meal; pulse coarsely ground.

CHUNAM, an Indian name for lime made from sea-shells or coral; a small weight for gold in Masulipatam, nearly 6 grains.

CHUNAM-MAKER, a lime-burner, a cement maker.

CHUNDIGAR (Guzarattee), a bracelet-maker, one who makes armlets of glass or ivory for married women.

CHUNDOO, a small dry measure of Ceylon, about a quarter of a pound; the fourth part of a seer.

CHUNGAH, a bamboo liquid measure used in Commercolly, India, containing about one-sixth of an imperial gallon.

CHUNO, a name in Peru for potatoes frozen and dried.

CHUPAH, a Malayan grain measure, the fourth part of a guntong, 80 chupahs make one bushel of rice, equal to 56 lb. *See* COYAN.

CHUPASSY, the Hindustani name for a peon or messenger.

CHUPATTIES, small unleavened cakes eaten by the lower classes in India.

CHUPPA-KHANEH, an Indian name for a printing-office.

CHURAP, a weight of Central Asia about 2¼ lbs.

CHURCH-FITTER, a tradesman who attends to the interior fittings of places of public worship.

CHURCH-PLATE, the utensils for the administration of the Eucharist.

CHURCH-RATE, a tax levied on parishioners for the repairs and maintenance of the Church.

CHURCH SERVICE, a book of common prayer, and daily lessons of the church.

CHURCH-WARDEN, a parish officer chosen by the vicar or rate-payers to attend to the disbursements and other affairs connected with a church.

CHURCHYARD, the area round a church, in many instances set aside for the burial of the dead.

CHURKA, corrupted from the Bengalee charaki, a wheel or rotatory machine; a rude handmill with rollers for cleaning cotton from the seed in India.

CHURN, an agitating instrument for separating the butter from milk, of which there are several kinds.

CHURN-DRILL, a large drill several feet long, with a chisel point at each end, used in the mining districts.

CHURN-STAFF, the revolving staff of a barrel or other churn.

CHURRANG, CHERAGG, a small earthenware lamp for burning coconut-oil in India.

CHURRUS, the Indian name for a crude resinous exudation obtained from the Indian hemp plant, *Cannabis Indica*.

CHUSPA, a leathern pouch used by the South American Indians to carry their coca-leaves, an important masticatory.

CHUTA (Hindustani), a receiver for cane juice, as it flows from the mill, when expressed from the cane.

CHUTE, a river-fall or rapid over which timber is floated in North America.

CHUTE, CHUTUL, in some of the East Indian dialects a roll of tobacco or cigar.

CHUTNEY, CHUTNEE, a condiment or pickle made in India, compounded of sweets and acids of which there are several local kinds, as Cashmere chutney, Madras chutney, Bengal chutney, sweet chutney, green mango chutney, &c. It is much eaten in the East with curries, stews, &c.

CIACCO (Italian), a hog.

CIALDONE, thin rolled wafer cakes made in Italy.

CIBARIOUS, good for food, esculent.

CICERCHIA (Italian), chick-pease.

CIDER, a wholesome beverage obtained from the fermented juice of apples, and of which there are two kinds, sweet cider and rough cider.

CIDER-APPLES, common kinds of orchard apples grown for making cider, which are usually distributed into three classes, the sweet, the bitter, and the sour.

CIDER-BRANDY, a beverage made in some of the States of North America.

CIDERKIN, a weak kind of cider.

CIDER-MILL, CIDER-PRESS, the mash press in which the heavy squeezing roller traverses to express the juice from the apples.

CIDER-VINEGAR, vinegar made in Devonshire and America from refuse cider.

CIE, the French abbreviation for Company synonymous with the English Co.

CIELING, another mode of spelling ceiling, the upper part of a room.

CIGAIE, a classification term for prime quality wool in the Danubian Provinces, strosse being the second quality.

CIGAR, a quantity of tobacco rolled in a leaf for smoking; the consumption of cigars is very large.

CIGAR-BOX, a wooden box, usually of cedar, in which cigars are packed.

CIGAR-CASE, a pouch or fancy receptacle to hold cigars for the pocket.

CIGAR-DIVAN, a place of public resort for smoking, &c.

CIGARETTES, fine tobacco rolled in paper for smoking like cigars.

CIGAR-HOLDER, a mouth-piece or tube for holding cigars; also a cigar-case.

CIGAR-MAKER, a tobacco merchant, one who makes or employs persons to make cigars.

CIGAR-MAKING MACHINE, a machine patented by Mr. Adorno for making cigars and cigarettes; of the latter it will make 80 to 100 per minute, and much neater than those made by hand.

CIGAR-TUBE, an amber, bone, or other mouth piece used for smoking cigars.

CIMATORE (Italian), a cloth shearer.

CIMITER, another mode of spelling scimitar, a short curved sword.

CIMOLITE, or KIMAULIA-EARTH, a hydrous silicate of alumina, occurring in volcanic districts, which has the property of cleaning cloth, and bleaching linen.

CINCHONA, the barks of various South American trees, broadly distinguished in commerce by their colour, which yield the bitter alkaloid quinine.

CINDERS, the small refuse pieces left after the combustion of coal.

CINDER-SIFTER, a perforated shovel or sieve for separating the fine dust or coal ashes from large cinders.

CINNABAR, sulphide of mercury a red pigment, generally known as vermilion.

CINNAMON, a well-known spice, the aromatic pungent inner bark of the *Cinnamomum verum* or *Zeylanicum*.

CINNAMON-OIL, a fragrant purified oil obtained from the *Cinnamomum verum*, and from Cassia bark.

CINNAMON-PEELER, a labourer employed in stripping the cinnamon bark, and preparing the spice for shipment.

CINNAMON-PLANTATION, the sandy ground or garden in which cinnamon plants are reared in Ceylon.

CINNAMON-PLANTER, a tropical cultivator who invests capital in the growth of cinnamon.

CINNAMON-STONE, a massive rounded stone found in Ceylon, named from its colour. It is occasionally cut and polished for jewellery purposes.

CINQUEFOIL, a common hedge-weed, the *Potentilla reptans*, which having astringent, tonic, and febrifugal properties, is used medicinally.

CINQUE PORTS, five privileged and chartered ports on the coasts of Kent and Sussex, comprising the towns of Sandwich, Dover, Hythe, Romney, and Hastings. The Lord Warden of these ports still has special jurisdiction and important marine powers.

CIOPPA (Italian), an under-petticoat.

CIPHERING-BOOK, a child's book for working arithmetical questions.

CIPHERING-SLATE, a common framed slate for schools or for the use of children.

CIPOLINO, a variety of green marble with white veins; a mixture of talcose schist with white saccharoidal marble.

CIRCUIT, the space traversed by a machine, &c., in moving round; a district visited by a Judge.

CIRCULAR, a printed or lithographed handbill, note, or address, issued by tradesmen to customers, &c.

CIRCULAR-BOLT, a machine employed by the Nottingham lace manufacturers in making net.

CIRCULAR-NOTE, a letter of credit granted by London bankers for the convenience of travellers, payable at different Continental or foreign towns, and accompanied by a letter of indication.

CIRCULAR-SAW, a very useful machine tool, a revolving disc of steel with serrated edges or teeth, for cutting wood and metal.

CIRCULATING LIBRARY, a library from which books are sent out on loan to subscribers.

CIRCULATING MEDIUM, cash and bank notes payable on demand.

CIRCULATOR, one employed in distributing bills.

CIRCULUS, an instrument for cutting off the neck of glass.

CIRCUMFERENCE, the boundary line of a circle or plot.

CIRCUMFERENTOR, a surveyor's instrument for measuring angles.

CIRCUMNAVIGATION, the act of voyaging round the globe.

CIRCUMPOLAR, lying around the pole.

CIRCUMVENTOR, a surveying instrument, having a compass-box at the top for taking angles.

CIRCUS, a building or enclosure in which feats of horsemanship are exhibited.

CIRE (French), bees-wax.

CIST, any thing for holding, as a bag, basket, case, or chest.

CISTERN, a reservoir or receptacle for water, or other fluid.

CITHARA, an old kind of harp.

CITHERN, an Austrian stringed instrument.

CITOLE, an instrument like the dulcimer.

CITRIC ACID, the juice of limes neutralized with chalk, and the citrate of lime thus formed decomposed by sulphuric acid. It is largely made for domestic use and for calico-printing.

CITRON, the fruit of the *Citrus Medica*, a large species of lemon, less acid than that fruit, imported chiefly from Madeira.

CITRONELLA, an essential oil obtained from the grass *Andropogon Citratum*, and chiefly imported from Ceylon. Another species, *A. schœnanthus*, or *Cymbogon schœnanthus*, furnishes the lemon-grass oil. *See* LEMON GRASS.

CITTERN, an ancient musical instrument resembling the lute.

CITY ARTICLE, the portion of a newspaper specially devoted to the consideration of matters of commerce and finance.

CITY EDITOR, the employee of a daily or weekly London journal, whose special duty it is to report upon the prices of public securities, the state of the money market, and other matters of commerce and finance.

CITY-PORTER, a ticket-porter, one licensed by the Corporation of London.

CIVAIA (Italian), pulse, beans, pease, &c.

CIVANZO, the name in Italy for interest.

CIVET, a perfume analogous to musk, obtained from some species of *Viverra*.

CIVIL ENGINEER, a scientific man, one who attends to the business of engineering as applied to the economic or useful purposes of civil life.

CLACK, in mining phraseology the valve of a pump; clack door being the aperture through which it is fixed and removed; a bell that gives warning of more corn being required in a mill.

CLAFTER, a name given to the fathom of six feet in Germany, Russia, and Switzerland; in Hamburgh it is only equal to 68 English inches.

CLAIE, a long bed or couch of split canes or reeds used in silk-worm establishments in France, to deposit the worms and leaves on.

CLAM, a large species of shell-fish or conchiferous mollusc, which exists only in very deep water. Clams are used on the

North American coasts as bait for cod, which are exceedingly fond of them. Some of the species are of gigantic size, and the shells are occasionally used in Catholic churches as receptacles for the holy water. *See* BENITIER.

CLAMP, an iron holdfast; a kiln or pile of bricks placed for burning.

CLAMPING, a union of boards at right angles.

CLAMP-NAILS, nails suited for clamp-work.

CLAMP-SHOES, heavy shoes for rough work.

CLAPBOARDS, a kind of thin weather-board used for the outer covering of houses; rough cask staves before they are properly shaped.

CLAP-MATCH, a fisherman's name for an old female seal.

CLAP-NET, a bird catcher's net.

CLAPPER, the tongue or striker of a bell; a mill clack.

CLARENCE, a kind of carriage.

CLARET, the name given in England to the red wines of Medoc in France, mostly shipped from Bordeaux.

CLARET-GLASS, a large shallow wine glass for drinking claret from.

CLARET-JUG, a fancy glass decanter with lip and handle for holding claret.

CLARICHORD, CLAVICHORD, an old small keyed musical instrument in the form of a spinnet.

CLARIFY, to clear or fine a liquor by a chemical process.

CLARINET, a musical reed instrument larger than the oboe.

CLARION (French), CLARINO (*Italian*), a shrill kind of octave trumpet now out of use.

CLARY-WATER, a spiced and highly perfumed sweet cordial or medicinal drink, made from the flowers of the clary (*Salvia Sclarea*), which is a stimulant aromatic bitter.

CLASP, a fastening.

CLASP-KNIFE, a large folding knife for the pocket, or one to suspend by a cord to the neck.

CLASP-KNIFE MANUFACTURER, a workman who makes clasp knives.

CLASP-NAIL, a nail with a head.

CLASSE (Italian), a fleet of ships.

CLAVICEMBALO (Italian), the harpsichord.

CLAVICHORD. *See* CLARICHORD.

CLAVIER, the key-board of an organ or piano.

CLAVIOLE, a finger keyed viol.

CLAY, aluminous or argillaceous earth which disintegrates in water and forms a plastic ductile mixture. Clay, from its tenacity, is of great importance both in an agricultural and commercial point of view. Various descriptions of clay are used in the manufacture of pipes for smoking, for pottery and porcelain, bricks, crucibles, &c.

CLAYED, a term applied to sugars which have been purified or bleached by water filtered through superimposed clay.

CLAYING, a process of bleaching sugar by water passed through a layer of clay; also the operation of puddling.

CLAY-KILN, a stove for burning clay.

CLAY-MERCHANT, a dealer in fire and other clays.

CLAYMORE, a large two-handed double-edged sword formerly used in England and Scotland.

CLAY-PIPE, a pipe for smoking tobacco moulded from clay.

CLAY-SCREENING MACHINE, a machine for preparing clay for the manufacture of bricks, tiles, pipes, &c.

CLAY-STONE, a grayish mineral, a species of indurated clay, resembling calcareous marl.

CLEAN PROOF, a slip or sheet of printed matter sent to an author from a printer.

CLEARANCE, a document from a Custom-House officer, or other qualified person, permitting a ship to depart on her voyage.

CLEARING, a removal, as a clearing sale; an open space in forest land.

CLEARING HOUSE, an establishment for the convenience of certain bankers, where drafts and accounts on each other are mutually exchanged without the individual presentation of each at the banks, and a balance struck and agreed upon is settled by a draft on the account of the clearing bankers at the Bank of England.

CLEARING NUT, a name given to the seed of *Strychnos potatorum* from its property of clearing water.

CLEARING-SALE, a disposal of stock, remainder, or rummage.

CLEAR STARCHER, a laundress who washes fine linens and stiffens them with starch.

CLEATS, pieces of wood used to strengthen, resist, or support great weights; on board ship cleats are a kind of belaying pins to fasten ropes to.

CLEAVER, a name in some places for a hatchet, but principally applied to a butcher's metal axe or chopper.

CLEDGE, a mining term for the upper stratum of fuller's earth.

CLEET, a wedge or belaying pin, &c.

CLEFT, a space or opening made by a wedge.

CLENCHING, CLINCHING, the process of fastening securely, as in doubling over the point of a nail when it has passed through a plank.

CLERESTORY, the upper part of the nave of a church, the windows in the tower.

CLERK, an assistant; a subordinate officer in a public or private office. The name was originally given to learned men, hence it is still legally applied to clergymen of the established Church. A clerk of the court is a judicial officer in law or county courts; a clerk of the peace, a law officer in counties and at Quarter-Sessions, &c.

CLERK OF THE WORKS, a general superintendent during large building operations.

CLEW, the lower corner of the sail of a ship.

CLEW-GARNETS, CLEW-LINES, brails or rope tackle, to hoist up the ends of ships' sails to the yards.

CLEVVY, a provincial name for the draught iron of a plough, &c.

CLICKER, in the shoe trade, a cutter out of leather for the uppers and soles of boots and shoes; in the printing profession, one who, under the overseer, has the charge of any particular work, making up and imposing the matter, and presenting it to the reader in a proper form for revisal.

Client, a customer; usually applied to those who deal with bankers, brokers, and solicitors.

Clinch, a nautical term for a half hitch, stopped to its own part.

Clincher-work, planks laid to overlap each other in the manner of slating roofs. Boats built in this manner are termed clincher or clinker built.

Clinker, the accumulated cake or refuse of coal, a vitreous scoria which forms in grates or furnaces; an exceedingly hard Dutch or Flemish brick, six inches by three broad, and one thick, used for paving yards and stables. Clinkers are more thoroughly burnt than ordinary bricks.

Clinker-built. *See* Clincher-work.

Clink-stone, a German mineral, consisting of felspar and zeolite, yielding a metallic sound under the hammer.

Clinometer, a surveyor's instrument for measuring the slopes of cuttings and embankments, and ascertaining the dip of strata.

Clinquant (French), oraidew or Dutch gold leaf.

Clip, the wool sheared from a sheep; a clasp or spring holder for letters and papers.

Clip-fish, also called Baccalau, a name in Norway, and some other countries, for cod-fish salted and cured in the manner of the Newfoundland cod.

Clipper Ship, a fast-sailing vessel, one built on fine sharp lines, and adapted more for fast sailing than for carrying large cargo.

Clit-bur, a common name for the burdock (*Arctium lappa*), all the parts of which have some medicinal properties.

Clives, a hook with a spring to prevent its unfastening.

Cloak, a large loose wrapper of cloth or other material.

Cloaking, a woollen dress material, of which there are plain, mixture, and fancy kinds.

Cloak Pin, a brass or iron pin to hang garments on.

Clobberer, the lowest class of cobblers, who patch and botch up old shoes and boots, rubbing in ground cinders and paste, termed "clobber," into the crevices and breaks of the leather.

Clock, a well-known horological instrument for measuring time, which is moved by a pendulum.

Clock-case, the wooden or other framing in which the clock works or machinery is fixed; an old-fashioned tall case for enclosing a pendulum clock.

Clock-case-maker, a branch trade connected with clock-works.

Clock-chain-maker, a maker of metallic chains for clocks.

Clock-dial, the face of an elevated or turret clock, on which the figures are marked, and over which the pointing hands or indicators travel.

Clocked Stockings, hose which have a worked pattern or embroidery on the ancle.

Clock-face, the enamelled dial of a house or turret clock.

Clock-hands, the metal revolving pointers which traverse the clock face.

Clock-maker, a constructor of clocks, and of the machinery which keeps them in motion.

Clock-maker's Company, one of the livery companies of London which has no hall.

Clock-making Machines, wheel-cutting engines, and other special machines used to facilitate the manufacture, and cheapen the cost of clock-work.

Clock-tool-maker, a workman who prepares the working tools used by clock-makers.

Clock-tower, Clock-turret, a more or less lofty erection for placing clock-work in, so that the dials or plates may be visible from a distance.

Clock-winder, one appointed to attend to a church or other elevated clock.

Clock-work, the wheels and various complicated machinery, for the interior of a clock.

Clod-crusher, a heavy roller for pressing down and smoothing the surface of land.

Cloff, a further reduction of 2 lbs. in every 3 cwt., on certain goods, after the tare and tret are taken. It is an allowance now almost obsolete.

Clogger, a workman who repairs clogs.

Clog-maker, one who makes pattens and clogs for use in wet weather.

Clogs, heavy wooden shoes worn in tanneries and other manufactories where the feet are exposed to wet; also lighter raised supports for the feet, worn by females.

Clog-soles, thick soles of wood for clogs, of which about 2½ millions are made in the northern counties, chiefly for workmen, and they sell at about 1s. the dozen.

Close-hauled, a marine term applied to a vessel with her yards braced up, and sailing as near to the wind as possible.

Close-stool, a bed-room commode for invalids.

Closet, a cupboard, a place for keeping articles in; also a small private room.

Closh, a provincial name for nine-pins.

Closing an Account, balancing the items by an adjustment of the debtor and creditor sides.

Cloth, a wrapper or towel of any kind; a woven, textile woollen fabric broad or narrow, of which garments are made.

Cloth-cutter, one who cuts out garments, or who serves customers with lengths of cloth.

Clothes, Clothing, a general name for articles of dress for animals; also personal attire; apparel.

Clothes-brush, a stiff hair brush, used for brushing garments of cloth.

Clothes-horse, a wooden frame to hang garments or linen on, before a fire.

Clothes-line, small strong cord used in gardens, &c., for suspending wet clothes on to dry.

Clothes-man, a fixed or itinerant dealer in old clothes.

Clothes-pegs, wooden divided pegs, used by laundresses to secure washed linen on a line to dry.

CLOTHES-PRESS, a wardrobe or cupboard for hanging clothes in.

CLOTH-FAIR, a locality set apart for the sale of garments, &c. A periodical fair held in some parts of the Continent for the sale of woollen goods.

CLOTH-HALLS, meeting places at Bradford, Halifax, Huddersfield, Leeds, and other places where the clothiers and purchasers of woollens assemble periodically to transact business.

CLOTHIER, a maker of or dealer in cloth.

CLOTH-PAPERS, coarse papers glazed and unglazed for pressing and finishing woollen cloths.

CLOTH-PRESSER, one engaged in preparing cloth.

CLOTH-SHEARER, a workman employed to remove the imperfections of woollen fabrics after weaving; this is now done to some extent on the Continent by cloth-shearing machines.

CLOTH-WATER-PROOFER, a workman who renders cloth impervious to water.

CLOTH-WORKERS' COMPANY, one of the twelve great livery companies of London—whose charter dates from the time of Edward IV. It is the last in precedence. Their hall is in Mincing Lane.

CLOUD-BERRY, a name for the fruit of the *Rubus Chamæmorus* which is acid and pleasant to the taste. The Scottish Highlanders and the Laplanders esteem it as one of the most grateful and useful fruits.

CLOUDING, an appearance given to ribbons and silks in the process of dyeing.

CLOUGH, an engineering appliance for dividing the fall of water into two parts, applicable to drains in tideways, &c.

CLOUS, French for nails.

CLOUT, an iron plate on an axle tree; a kind of heavy nail.

CLOUTED-CREAM, CLOTTED-CREAM, thick cream obtained on the surface of milk by the application of slight heat.

CLOUTED-SHOES, heavily nailed shoes worn by agricultural labourers, carters and workmen.

CLOUTERIE, a manufactory for nails.

CLOVE, an English weight for wool, equal to seven pounds or the half of a stone.

CLOVE-BARK, a commercial name given to the barks of two different trees, one being the *Cinnamomum Culilaban* growing in the Eastern archipelago, and the other the *Dicypellium caryophyllatum*, found in Brazil.

CLOVE-HITCH, two half hitches round a spar or rope.

CLOVER, one of the most valuable of the artificial grasses for fodder, of which there are many varieties. Clover seed, such as American and French red clover and German white clover, are largely imported.

CLOVES, the unexpanded flower buds of the *Caryophyllus aromaticus*, which form a well-known spice. In the East fancy models and toys are often made with cloves.

CLUB, a weapon of attack, a stout stick; a benefit society; a place of resort for discussion and refreshment. The west-end club-houses of London are of a highly respectable character—and in many of them a candidate must be proposed several years before there is a vacancy for his admission.

CLUBBING, uniting together for some object; a sea term for a vessel drifting down a current with an anchor out.

CLUE, CLEW, the lower corner of the square sail of a ship; hence the ropes by which it is lifted are called clue-garnets or clue-lines.

CLUMP-BOOTS, heavy boots for rough wear, such as shooting, excavators' work, &c.

CLUNCH or CURL-STONE, a local name in Staffordshire for a mineral substance from which tripoli is made.

CLYSTER-PIPE, a medical instrument for injecting into the rectum.

CNASTER, KANASTER, a coarse kind of tobacco made from Havana leaf, and which derived its name originally from being imported from America in rush or cane baskets.

COACH, a pleasure carriage, a vehicle on springs of which there are many kinds, as dress coaches, driving coaches, &c.

COACH AND CART GREASE-MAKER, a manufacturer of fatty compositions for lubricating the axle-trees of vehicles.

COACH AND HARNESS-MAKERS' COMPANY, one of the livery companies of London, whose hall is in Noble-street, Cheapside.

COACH-AXLE-TREE-MAKER, a tradesman who supplies axle-trees to carriage-builders.

COACH-BEADER. *See* COACH-PLATER.

COACH-BLIND-MAKER. *See* COACH-JOINER.

COACH-BODY-MAKERS, workmen in a coach factory who construct the delicate framework and panelling of coaches, in contradistinction to a separate class of mechanics, who make the heavier and stronger part or carriage to support the body, and to connect it with the wheels, pole, &c.

COACH-BOLT-MAKER, a coach-smith, a manufacturer of the iron parts of coaches, &c.

COACH-BOX, the driver's seat on a coach.

COACH-BROKER, a tradesman who makes a business of dealing in carriages.

COACH-CARVER, a workman who carves the beadings and mouldings of the body of a carriage, and the foliage and ornamental tracery on state coaches and elaborately decorated vehicles.

COACH-CURRIER, a mechanic who supplies and makes the leather parts of carriages.

COACH-DRAUGHTSMAN, a designer of the forms, &c., of carriages.

COACH-FOUNDER, a workman who supplies the iron materials for coach-builders.

COACH-HERALD-PAINTER, an artist who paints arms, crests, and devices on the panels of carriages.

COACH-HIRE, the fare or charge for a coach.

COACH-HORSE, a horse adapted for carriages.

COACH-HOUSE, the stable, building, or shelter-house, where a carriage is placed under cover to secure it from the influence of the weather.

COACH-IRONMONGER, a tradesman who supplies the smaller kinds of iron work, bolts, nails, screws, &c., for carriages.

COACH-JOINER, a workman employed in making blinds, glass-frames, and German shutters, as well as seat-boxes for carriages.

COACH-LACE-MAKER, a maker of woven worsted or silk lace for carriages.

COACH-MAKER, a carriage-builder.

COACH-MOUNTING-FURNISHER, a tradesman who supplies plated work, and other materials to carriage-builders.

COACH-OFFICE, a booking-office for passengers and parcels, a place where coaches and omnibuses stop.

COACH-PAINTER, a workman who paints and varnishes carriages.

COACH-PLATER, a tradesman who supplies plated work, beading and other similar articles for carriages.

COACH-SMITH, a workman who forges and finishes the iron work used in carriages.

COACH-SPRING-MAKER, a manufacturer of steel carriage-springs.

COACH-STAND, the place where hackney-coaches and cabs are permitted to remain for hire.

COACH-TRIMMER, a workman who prepares and finishes the lace, linings, and other trimmings for carriage-builders.

COACH-WHEELWRIGHT, a maker of carriage-wheels, &c.

COAKING, in mast-making a process of joining or uniting timber to the inside spar. Generally the word implies a union of two pieces of wood, by letting in a small projection of one piece into the hollowed end of the other.

COAL, fossil fuel, which enters largely into commerce for domestic, manufacturing, and propelling purposes for steam-engines, on land and on sea. At the present time not less than 40,000,000 tons of coal are annually raised in the United Kingdom.

COAL-AGENT, the manager for a colliery proprietor.

COAL-BARGE, a flat-bottomed river-boat for transporting coal short distances to wharves, &c.

COAL-BOX, a scuttle to hold coals in a room.

COAL-CELLAR, a vault where coals are kept for convenient access for domestic use.

COAL-DROP, a staith or contrivance for shooting or lowering coals into the hold of a vessel.

COAL-DUST, the small broken or fine coal, after the larger masses have been screened.

COAL-DUST-MAKER, a manufacturer of artificial fuel.

COAL-EXCHANGE, a central market in London, situate near Billingsgate, where coal-factors, captains, and others resort, and the wholesale coal business of the metropolis is carried on. The imports of coal into London in 1856, by sea, railway, and canal, amounted to 4,100,000 tons.

COAL-FACTOR, an intermediate agent between the buyers and sellers of coals.

COAL FACTORS' SOCIETY, an association of traders who meet at the Coal Exchange, London, and are specially interested in the carrying and vending of coals.

COAL-FISH, a name on the British and Irish coasts for the pollack.

COAL-GAS, the common illuminating gas made from coal.

COAL-HAMMER, a servant's instrument for breaking lumps of coal in a coal cellar.

COAL-HEAVER, a porter who loads and unloads coal wagons.

COAL-HULK, a vessel kept as a receptacle for coal, usually on some foreign station, to supply steamers.

COAL-METER, a corporation officer in London, charged with the inspection of coals sent from a wharf.

COAL-MEASURE-MAKER, one who makes and vends measures for coals.

COAL-MINER, a workman engaged in a colliery.

COAL-PIT, the mouth of a coal mine, or the descent to a colliery.

COAL-PORTER, a carrier of coals.

COAL-SACK-MAKER, a manufacturer of coarse stout bags holding 2 cwt., used for conveying coals.

COAL-SCALES, a weighing-machine which by law is compulsorily carried by every coal wagon delivering coals.

COAL-SCOOP, a shovel for taking coals from a scuttle to throw on a fire.

COAL-SCUTTLE, a portable metal receptacle for coals in a room.

COAL-SHED, a retailer's depository for coals.

COAL-SHOOT, a metal scuttle or vase for holding coals.

COAL-SHOVEL, a small shovel for filling a coal scuttle from the cellar; a larger kind are used by coal-heavers.

COAL-SHOVEL-MAKER, a manufacturer of iron shovels for unloading coals from ships, and for filling coal bags, &c.

COAL-STAITH, a drop or machine on an elevated wharf for shipping coal.

COAL-TAR, a product of gas-making which furnishes the chief ingredient of printers' ink in the shape of lamp black; it is made into asphalte for pavements, and mixed with red-hot clay forms a charcoal that acts as a powerful disinfectant; with coal dust it forms by pressure an excellent and compact artificial fuel.

COAL-TRIMMER, a labourer who arranges the cargo of coal on board a ship.

COAL-VASE, a fancy coal scuttle for a parlour.

COAL-WAGON, a large cart capable of carrying about three or more tons of coals.

COAL-WHARF, a landing pier where coals are deposited.

COAL-WHIPPER, a London porter who unlades coals from ships at the wharves, &c.

COAMINGS, raised borders of wood round the edges of hatches and scuttles, to prevent water flowing down from the deck, and to receive and support the hatches, &c.

COASTER, a vessel employed in the trade along shore, and which does not sail far from land.

COAST-GUARD, a department of the Customs, the men and officers of which are employed on the coast to prevent the smuggling of contraband goods, and excisable articles; smugglers and their boats, carts, &c., being liable to seizure, confiscation, and penalties.

Coat, a covering of paint, varnish, or other material given to any substance; an outer garment for men.
Coatee, a short cut-away body coat.
Coat-link, a pair of buttons or studs joined by a link to close a coat with button holes.
Cob, in mining, the process of crushing ore with hammers to separate the worthless parts; the hard stalk from which the grain of maize has been removed; when chopped, it is given as provender to live-stock in America; a hazel nut; a wicker basket; a name given in some places to the hard dollar; a kind of horse.
Cobalt, a mineral, the oxides of which are used for colouring glass and porcelain blue.
Cobalt Bloom, the red arseniate of cobalt; a beautiful mineral found with the ores of cobalt, and used in the manufacture of smalt.
Cobang, a gold coin of Japan of about 27s.
Cobbing, a mining name for old furnace bottoms, pieces of brick, &c., thrown into a smelting furnace.
Cobble, a kind of paving stone.
Cobbler, a jobbing shoemaker, one who undertakes repairs; a cooling drink, a mixture of sherry, sugar, ice, &c.
Cob-crushing Machine, a mill for breaking the cobs of maize for cattle food.
Cobechi, a stamp, made of strong dry leaves in the Pacific islands, marked with patterns for impressing dyes or colours on fibrous materials.
Cobido, another name for the covid; a long measure of 19 inches in Mosha.
Cobenga, a name in some parts of the Pacific for a fishing net.
Cob-iron, an andiron with knobs.
Coble, the name of a kind of pilot and fishing boat used on the northern sea-coasts, having a low square stern and little or no keel on the after body.
Cob-nut, an improved variety of the common hazel-nut, of which there are two or three British kinds cultivated.
Cobourg, a thin worsted fabric, a lady's dress material composed either of wool and cotton, or of wool and silk.
Cobre, a name for the covid in China of 14·625 inches.
Cobres, an European name for a superior quality of indigo made in Central America.
Cob-wall, a wall made of straw, lime, and earth.
Coca, the leaves of the *Erythroxylon Coca*, largely used as a masticatory by the miners and others in the interior of South America.
Cocco, the Maltese name for a grain, 72 cocchi being equal to one ottavo.
Cocculus Indicus, the small berry of several species of *Cocculus* imported from the East. From the bitter principle which they yield, these berries are said to be used to adulterate beer.
Cochenilla Wood, the heart of a tree shipped from St. Domingo, furnishing a handsome furniture wood.
Cochin, a grain measure of Siam of 65 lbs.
Cochineal, the dried carcases of the female *Coccus cacti*, an insect which feeds on several species of *Opuntia*. Cochineal is a brilliant scarlet colour, and also furnishes the beautiful carmine pigment. In 1855, 1875 tons of cochineal, valued at £608,000 were imported into the United Kingdom.
Cock, the hammer of the lock of a pistol or musket, &c. *See* Cocks.
Cockade, an ornament worn in the hat, which used to be very common in many ranks of society, but this rosette is now confined to men-servants; a bunch of ribbon worn by recruiting - sergeants, electioneering agents, and others.
Cockade-maker, a workman who makes cockades.
Cock-boat, a very small boat.
Cocket, a warrant from the Custom House, on entering goods, showing that the duty on them has been paid.
Cock-founder, a caster in brass, one who makes metal spigots.
Cockle, an edible mollusc, the *Cardium edule*, extensively found in the sands of the sea-shore.
Cock-loft, an elevated loft over a barn, stable, &c.
Cocks, Stop-cocks, metal taps or escapes for gas and fluids, some of which are turned on and off by the hand; others, acted upon by a floating or air ball, are self-regulating.
Cockspurs, small clay wedges used in the potteries to separate articles of pottery ware, after the process of glazing, and to prevent them adhering.
Cockswain, Coxwain, the steersman of a boat.
Cockup, a large fish of the Indian seas, resembling the jack, which is not unlike cod in flavour. They are brought to market sometimes weighing 12 lbs. *See* Begti.
Coco, Eddoe, a name in the West Indies for the root of the *Colocasia esculenta*.
Cocoa, the commercial name for the dried seeds or beans contained in the fruit pods of the *Theobroma Cacao*. In commerce these seeds are sold raw or roasted, and crushed and powdered; prepared in the form of rock or flake cocoa; deprived of the husk as cocoa nibs, or sweetened and flavoured made into cakes under the name of chocolate.
Cocoa Plum, a name in the Colonies for the fruit of the *Chrysobalanus icaco*.
Cocoa-wood, the mottled wood of the cocoa palm, *Cocos nucifera*, which is occasionally used for inlaying.
Cocoma (Italian), a tea-kettle or boiler.
Coco-nut, the well-known edible fruit of the *Cocos nucifera* palm, largely grown in most tropical countries for the milk, the pulp, and for oil. Many thousands of these nuts are imported as dunnage in ships, and sold by hawkers in the streets, and by fruiterers.
Coco-nut Coir, the outer husk of the coco-nut, which, when macerated, is woven into fibre of various kinds.
Coco-nut Fibre, the husk of the yarn spun and manufactured into rope, lashing, matting, &c. *See* Coir.

COCO-NUT OIL, oil expressed from the ripened kernel of the nut, which contains 71 per cent of oil. The commerce in this oil is very large, more than 10,000 tons being annually imported.

COCO-NUT SHELLS, the hard shells of the *Cocos nucifera*, which, when fully ripe, are often carved and made into drinking cups, ladles, and other articles of use or ornament.

COCOON, the nest formed by the silk-worm, as its embryo or chrysalis, which is a hollow envelope of light tissue-like texture, from which the silk of commerce is obtained, in one continuous thread, of two filaments, agglutinated by a gummy liquid. Each cocoon yields about 300 yards of silk, and 230 average-sized cocoons will weigh about a pound.

COCOS, PETITS (French), cocoa beans.

COCUM-BUTTER, a pale greenish-yellow solid oil, obtained from the seeds of *Garcinia purpurea*, and used in India to adulterate ghee or fluid butter. In England it is sometimes mixed with bear's grease in pomatums.

COCUS-WOOD, a wood obtained in Cuba and other West India islands, from *Lepidostachys Roxburghii*, much used in turnery for making flutes and other musical instruments.

COD-FISH, the *Morrhua vulgaris*, a very valuable and esteemed fish of commerce, which is caught largely on the British coasts, and sold extensively both fresh and salted. The chief cod fishery is on the banks of Newfoundland, whence millions of salted fish are annually shipped. When cod cannot be dry-cured, they are salted in pickle and packed in barrels, and then called pickled cod. About 3½ millions cwt. of cod are shipped annually from Newfoundland, by the British, French, and Americans.

CODILLA, the coarse tow of flax and hemp.

CODINIAC, a quince marmalade.

COD-LINE, an eighteen-thread line.

CODLING, a small cod-fish; a kind of apple suited for cooking.

COD-LIVER OIL, a valuable medicinal oil obtained from the liver of the cod, *Morrhua vulgaris*, of which large quantities are made in Newfoundland and in the United Kingdom.

COD-ROES, the melt or spawn of the cod-fish, salted and dried, which are shipped from Norway to France, to the extent of 20,000 to 30,000 barrels and used as ground bait, chiefly in the Bay of Biscay.

COD-SOUNDS, the air-bladder of the cod-fish; the pickled tongues and sounds are esteemed delicacies of food, and are sold by fishmongers.

COESTEAD, a small building at the mines.

COFE, a name in the Pacific for the bamboo.

COFERING, in the mining districts, a mode of protecting the shaft from an influx of water, by rammed clay, &c.

COFF, the waste or offal in the pilchard fishery.

COFFEE, the beans or berries of the *Coffea Arabica*, in which an immense traffic is carried on among all civilised nations. Our imports annually are about 60,000,000 lbs.

COFFEE-CANISTER, a tinned receptacle for holding ground roasted coffee.

COFFEE-EXTRACTOR, a machine for making coffee.

COFFEE-FILTER, a percolator or straining machine for clearing coffee when prepared as a beverage.

COFFEE-HOUSE, a place of resort for refreshment, where coffee, tea, and other dietetic beverages are prepared and sold.

COFFEE-LEAVES, the leaves of the coffee tree have lately been recommended for use, as affording, by infusion, a beverage like tea, forming an agreeable, refreshing, and nutritive article of diet.

COFFEE-MILL, a machine for grinding the coffee berries.

COFFEE-PLANTER, a tropical agriculturist who attends to the culture and preparation of coffee.

COFFEE-POT, a metal vessel in which ground coffee is boiled or infused.

COFFEE-PULPER, a machine for preparing coffee berries for shipment, by removing the pulp and parchment.

COFFEE-ROASTER, a tradesman who prepares the raw coffee berries for use; also the revolving machine in which coffee is roasted.

COFFEE-STALL, a street stall where coffee is vended at night or early in the morning.

COFFER, a chest; the lock for a barge.

COFFER-DAM, a water-tight enclosure, within which the construction of hydraulic works, such as the foundations of bridges and sea-walls can be securely carried on.

COFFIN, a mining term in Derbyshire for old exposed workings; a wooden or other shell or receptacle for the dead. Coffins, although usually made of wood or lead, have been made of glass and slate.

COFFIN-FURNITURE, the handles, metal ornaments, &c., affixed to a coffin for decoration, which are usually white or black, though occasionally gilt.

COFFIN-MAKER, a carpenter who makes wooden coffins.

COFFIN-PLATE ENGRAVER, a workman who engraves the name, age, &c., of deceased persons on coffin plates.

COFFLE, a gang of negro slaves.

COFFOLA, an Arabian weight, of about 2 pennyweights troy.

COFFRETIER (French), a trunk-maker.

COG, the tooth of a wheel or rack.

COGGING. See CAULKING.

COGNAC, a name for the best distilled brandy.

COGNAC-OIL. See ŒNANTHIC ETHER.

COGNASSE, a wild quince.

COGNOIR (French), a printer's wooden mallet; a shooting stick.

COGNOVIT, a document signed by a defendant to an action, in the presence of his attorney, admitting the cause of action and his liability thereon.

COGWOOD, a name for the *Laurus chloroxylon*, which from its durability in water is used in the West Indies for mill-framing and cog-wheels.

COHONG, the Chinese name for a company,

Cohosh, one of the American names of the black snake-root (*Cimicifuga racemosa*, or *Macrotys serpentaria*), which has some anodyne properties.

Cohune-palm. *See* Cahoun.

Coi (Spanish), a hammock; plural, coyes.

Coif, the cap of a serjeant at law.

Coiffeuse (French), a tire-woman; a milliner.

Coiffure, a head-dress, coiffeur being a hairdresser.

Coil, a circle of pipes, rope, or chain; to lay a rope up in a ring with one turn or fake above another.

Coin, pieces of metal, most commonly gold, silver, or copper, stamped by authority, and in many countries made a legal tender for their respective values, when not exceeding certain specified amounts. *See* Legal Tender.

Coinage, minted money. *See* Copper-Coinage, and the different coins.

Coining-press, a powerful lever screw, for impressing devices, legends, &c. on current coin, medals, &c.

Coins, Quoins (French), wooden or metal wedges placed under the breech of a gun, to elevate it; pieces of wooden furniture in a printing-office; the clocks of stockings. Coins are also stamped money, current or uncurrent.

Coir, the commercial name of the short fibre obtained from the dry husk or covering of the cocoa-nut, which is now largely used in the manufacture of cordage, matting, &c., and to stuff beds, chair bottoms, &c. From Ceylon alone more than 60,000 cwt. is shipped annually. The varieties of coir entering the market are coir yarn, coir junk and coir fibre. Matting is made here of coir.

Coke, the residue left after the distillation of bituminous coal. Coke is largely used as fuel for domestic purposes, for furnaces, and for the generation of steam in locomotive engines.

Coke-burner, a labourer employed in attending to the conversion of coal into coke.

Coke oven, a brick structure or enclosed chamber where coal is burnt to be deprived of its gas and converted into coke. It is usually 8 or 10 feet high, having a flat roof with an opening at which to introduce the coal, and another by which to remove the coke.

Coker-canvas, a kind of sail-cloth made in Crewkerne, Somersetshire.

Coker-nut, a modern mode of spelling cocoa-nut, in commercial circles, in order to make a broader distinction between the numerous articles spelt much in the same manner.

Colachon, an Italian lute.

Colaga, a variable Eastern grain measure; that used in Canara is nearly equal to a bushel; in Seringapatam it is 11 Winchester bushels; in Bangalore it is but 11 lbs. 13 oz. 6½ drachms; it is also called a coodom and is divided into four bullahs.

Colander, Cullender, a metal or earthenware strainer.

Colcothar, a chemical preparation from oxide of iron, the brown peroxide. *See* Rouge.

Cold-chisel, a strong iron tool for cutting metal.

Cold-cream, a cooling application for the lips or skin made of melted white wax and almond oil flavoured with rose water. Pure glycerine is however now more generally used.

Cole-seed. *See* Colza.

Colewort, a kind of cabbage.

Collijeerah, a native name, in India for black cumin seed.

Colis (French), a package or bale of goods.

Colisse (French), the opening of the warp through which the shuttle passes.

Colla, from the French Colle, a name for glue.

Collana (Italian), a necklace.

Collar, a circlet for the neck. There are collars of various kinds manufactured—horse collars, which are iron, frames covered with leather and padded or stuffed. Men's collars of stitched linen; ladies' lace, muslin and other worked collars. The part of a garment which fits close round the throat is called the collar.

Collar-check, a rough cross-barred woollen material for saddlery purposes, made either broad or narrow.

Collar-maker, a tradesman who makes collars of any kind.

Collate, to collect and examine the sheets of book-work, &c., before being sent out, or previously to their being arranged for binding.

Collation, an afternoon luncheon.

Colle (French), glue, size, paste.

Colle de Poisson (French), isinglass.

Collector, an authorized receiver who applies for or is paid certain moneys, whether for individuals, societies, corporations or the State; as of poors-rate, customs, city-dues, market revenues and toll, gas and water rates, &c. Sometimes collectors are paid fixed salaries; at other times they are paid a commission or poundage on the sums received.

College-cap, a silk or cloth cap, of a particular shape, worn by academicians and students at universities.

College-pudding, a kind of small plum dumpling.

Collerage (French), a feudal tax paid for broaching casks of wine.

Colleret, a drag-net.

Colletier (French), a buff-collar maker.

Colleur (French), a paper-hanger, a sizer or dresser.

Collier, a miner, one engaged in a coal mine; also the name for a vessel which carries coals.

Collier Bead, a large bead, usually white, a principal article of trade on some parts of the coast of Western Africa; they are sometimes called Bokoia beads.

Colliery, a seat of coal seams; the place where coals are mined.

Collocation (French), a financial investment.

Collodion, a solution of gun-cotton in alcohol and ether for cementing purposes and for wounds; used also for taking portraits.

Collop, a cutlet or small slice of meat; a term for four or five sheep.

Collum, a grain measure in Coromandel of 70 to 80 quarts.

Colly, a shepherd's dog, much esteemed by the Scottish drovers for his sagacity.

Colmar, a kind of pear.

Colocynth, a purgative medicinal extract, prepared from the pulp and seeds of the fruit of *Cucumis colocynthis*.

Cologne-earth, a kind of colour.

Cologne-water, Eau de Cologne, a volatile spirituous perfume, compounded of various essences with ten times its weight of spirits of wine, frequently distilled.

Colombier, a large sized paper 23½ inches by 34.

Colombine, (French), pigeons' dung, or the dung of fowls.

Colombo-root, Calumba-root, an esteemed medicinal root obtained in eastern Africa from the *Cocculus palmatus* of Lindley, the *Menispermum palmatum* of others, and which is a most valuable antiseptic and tonic.

Colonata, an Italian name for the Spanish pillar dollar.

Colonel, the commanding officer of a regiment.

Colonial Agent, a merchant or factor, who transacts business connected with the colonies, or acts as agent for colonists.

Colonial Secretary, the secretary of State for the Colonies; a member of the British cabinet, to whom is deputed the management of all affairs connected with the outlying dependencies of the empire.

Colonist, a native of, or resident in, a colony or dependency.

Colonnade, a range of columns.

Colony, a distant settlement; the possession or dependency of a nation.

Colophony, a name for the ordinary resin or resin of commerce, being the residuum remaining in the body of the still after common turpentine has been submitted to distillation, for the manufacture of the oil of turpentine. The black colophony is the cooled brittle mass, in the state in which it leaves the still; the amber or yellow-coloured, is the same resin, mixed with about one-eighth part of water, while it is yet fluid. It is used in soap-making, as a varnish, and for plasters, &c.

Coloquintida, a Continental name for colocynth.

Color, Colour, a dye or pigment; a flag or standard. The colours of a ship or regiment are the national ensign or some special distinguishing flag. *See* Ensign.

Color-box, a box with cakes of water-colours.

Colored-glass, stained glass for windows; Bohemian or fancy glass articles.

Colored-saucer-maker, one who manufactures what are termed pink saucers, used by ladies for rouging purposes, and to give a flesh tint to silk stockings when washing them.

Color-extractor, an apparatus patented by M. Bourra, and shown at the Great Exhibition in 1851, for removing colours from fabrics.

Color-man, a vender of paints, &c., who is usually styled an oil-and-colour man.

Color-manufacturer, one who prepares and compounds colours.

Color-serjeant, a non-commissioned military officer, who supports the ensign-bearer of a regiment.

Colporteur (French), a news-hawker, a pedlar or itinerant vendor or distributor of wares.

Colrake, a shovel used to stir lead ore when it is being washed.

Colt, a young male horse.

Colter, Coulter, the sharp iron cutting-knife of a plough, fixed over the share, to prevent, or remove, the accumulation of grass or rubbish. In fen lands it is in the form of a wheel.

Coltre, Coltrone (Italian), a quilt or counterpane.

Coltrice (Italian), a feather bed; a woman employed in husbandry.

Colt's-foot, a name for the *Tussilago Farfara*, a wild herb, the leaves of which are emollient, demulcent, and tonic. They were formerly smoked in troublesome coughs, but are now used in decoction.

Columba-root. *See* Colombo-root.

Column, a cylindrical post; a divisional body of type, running from top to bottom of the page of a newspaper, or of a book, when the lines do not run the full width of the page; a large body of troops drawn up in order.

Column Rules, thin pieces of brass used in printing-offices to separate longitudinally the columns of type.

Colunaria, a Spanish term applied to the half and quarter peseta or dollar.

Colza, the French name for rapeseed.

Colza Oil, a valuable oil manufactured to a large extent in Europe, by expression from the unctuous seeds of a species of wild cabbage, the *Brassica napus sativa*, or *B. campestris*. It is much used for lubricating machinery, for burning in the carcel, moderator, and similar lamps; and in the French light-houses it is preferred to any other oil in use, on account of its greater brilliancy and steadier flame, with less charring of the wick, as well as for its greater cheapness.

Comaca, a name given by the Indians of Demerara to the silk cotton or down of the *Bombax ceiba*.

Comasco, a kind of plum in Italy.

Comb, the wax-cell of bees; a sharp or toothed thin plate; an instrument for separating the hair, &c. Hair-combs are made of various substances, bone, ivory, horn, tortoiseshell, and latterly moulded of elastic gums. Metallic combs are used for carding or cleaning wool, cotton, and other fibres, and for rubbing down the coat of horses.

Combaruckoo, a resin made in some parts of India from lac.

Comb-broach, the tooth of a wool-comb.

Comb-cutting-machine, an apparatus for shaping and forming the teeth of combs in ivory and other substances.

Combination, in trade, an illegal union of workmen on strike, to prevent others taking the places they have quitted. In chemistry combination means the union of particles of different matter.

Comble (French), a heaped measure.

Comb-maker, a manufacturer or cutter of combs, with which is often combined the making of bone spoons, and other articles.

Comb-maker's Company, one of the livery companies of London which has no hall.

Comboy, a name in Ceylon for the waist-cloth of the herdsmen. It is about three yards long, and is wrapped several times round the body, being then fastened by a broad band or strong belt.

Combriere (French), a large fishing-net.

Comb-tray, a small wooden or other tray for a lady's toilet table.

Combustible, any thing that will ignite, but properly applicable to those dangerous substances which consume spontaneously with the emission of heat and light, and which railway companies, carriers, and vessels therefore refuse to carry.

Combustion, the act of taking fire or burning.

Comedian, a stage actor who plays humorous parts.

Comestibles (French), provisions; eatables.

Cometary, a machine or apparatus to show the revolutions of comets.

Comfit, a dry sweetmeat; seeds coated or crusted with sugar.

Comfit-maker, a confectioner, a preparer of comfits or sugar plums.

Comfrey, the root of the common comfrey, *Symphytum officinale*, has been used medicinally; that of the prickly comfrey, *S. asperrimum*, a gigantic species, is favorably spoken of as a green food for cattle.

Cominos, the Spanish name for cumin seed.

Comite (French), the officer of a galley.

Commander, a leader; the commodore or chief naval officer of a small squadron.

Commanderia, a kind of wine made in the island of Cyprus.

Commanditaire, a dormant or sleeping partner in a French joint-stock company, one who supplies the capital requisite to carry on business, but is only liable for the sum he invests.

Commandite, a French partnership or association, in which some supply money, others talents, services, or special knowledge.

Commassee, a small Arabian coin, about the size of a sixpence, consisting of seven carats; it contains little silver, and may be taken to be worth one penny. From 40 to 60 commassees generally pass for a dollar at Mocha.

Commeator, a messenger.

Commedador Balsam, a compound tincture of benzoin used in Brazil.

Commercants (French), merchants, traders, or dealers.

Commerce, the business of exchanging one commodity or production for another, or of buying merchandise with the view of gaining by the transaction; mercantile business in general as carried on between different countries.

Commercial, pertaining to commerce or trade.

Commestibile (Italian), food; any thing eatable.

Commettant (French), a principal or constituent; one who employs.

Commings, a maltster's name for the shoot of the barley after being kiln-dried.

Commis, a clerk or shopman in France.

Commissariat, the provisioning department of an army or other large body.

Commissary, an officer charged with the supply of provisions, medical stores, and clothing for troops, bodies of travellers, &c.

Commission, a charge given or undertaken; a percentage allowed to agents or factors by their employers upon business transacted; a written warrant granting powers or privileges, and authorizing the performance of special duties.

Commission of Bankruptcy, a power granted by law to a commissioner to inspect the effects and investigate the affairs of a bankrupt for the benefit of his creditors.

Commission-broker, a produce or other broker who acts on trust for another.

Commissioner, a high public officer of some department.

Commission-merchant, **Commission-agent**, one who executes general commissions, and attends to the supply of goods.

Commissionnaire, a French factor or merchant who buys and sells goods for others; one who attends to the transport of goods; a porter.

Committee, a delegated or selected body of persons appointed to act for a society or company; and which may be either provisional or permanent.

Commitment, a warrant of committal to prison.

Commode, a piece of bed-room furniture; a night-stool; a set of drawers.

Commodore, the commander of a yacht squadron.

Common, a public unenclosed ground.

Commonage, the right of feeding cattle on a common.

Common-council, a body of councillors elected by citizens or burgesses to represent and attend to municipal interests.

Common-hall, the hall or meeting-place of a town council, guild, or corporate body.

Common-pitch, a building term implying that the length of the rafter is ¾ of the span.

Common-place Book, a memorandum or jotting book.

Common Pleas, one of the superior law-courts of Great Britain.

Common Prayer, a book containing the forms used in the services of the Church of England.

Communion Service, a book containing the order of the Eucharist or Holy Sacrament of the Lord's Supper.

Communion Table, a piece of church furniture at the east end of a church, within the railed altar.

Compadore, in India a butler or purveyor.

Companion, the wooden covering or hood of the ladder way leading to the cabin in a merchant ship; an associate, fellow traveller or workman.

COMPANION-LADDER, the steps leading from the poop to the main deck, or from the deck to the cabin of a ship.

COMPANIONSHIP, a body of compositors working together.

COMPANY, a joint-stock association; a partnership in trade or any public concern; the subdivision of a regiment, the soldiers under the command of a captain.

COMPARATEUR, a Prussian instrument for accurately ascertaining the length of measures after Bessil's mode. The micrometers are placed on a strong mahogany beam; and the slide, which carries the two measures to be compared, is so arranged that it moves them exactly behind one another in the micrometer line, and there retains them.

COMPARTMENT, a specific division of the intermediate spaces. Warehouses are frequently built in compartments for precaution against fire. Ships are often built with water-tight compartments for greater security against accidents.

COMPASS, a well-known instrument, contrived to indicate the magnetic meridian, and for telling the course of a vessel, of which there are several varieties, as the mariner's compass, the azimuth compass, the variation compass, &c.; a workman's measuring tool, a pair of dividers of which many kinds are made, as wing, rack, club, millwright's, drawing, curb, and proportionate compasses, and compasses with cutting leg for paper.

COMPASS-BOX, a case in which to keep the compass card and magnetic needle on board ship.

COMPASS-BRICK, a kind of brick made for forming the walls of wells.

COMPASS-CARD, the suspended card on which the points of the compass are drawn.

COMPASSES, a drawing instrument with two legs for making circles. *See* COMPASS.

COMPASS-HEADED, round.

COMPASS-MAKER, a nautical instrument maker, who manufactures and repairs compasses.

COMPASS-PLANE, COMPASS-SAW, workmen's tools, the latter for cutting circles.

COMPASS-SIGNALS, flags which denote the points of the compass.

COMPENSATING-BALANCE, a spring or other contrivance to equalize temperature, or to recover error from inequality of movement.

COMPENSATION, a remuneration or reward; a recompence for injury, breach of agreement, &c.

COMPERA (Italian), a purchase or bargain.

COMPETITION, a rivalry, the contention for a contract, for business, for supremacy in workmanship, &c.

COMPILATION, a collection of laws; a selection of passages, &c.

COMPLAISANCE (French), accommodation; *billet de complaisance* is an accommodation note or bill.

COMPLEMENT, the full amount; a complete set of any thing.

COMPO, a concrete or mortar.

COMPONITORE (Italian), a type-setter or compositor at a printing-office.

COMPOSER, a musical author; a type-setter.

COMPOSING, the practical business of picking up and arranging the letter types for printing, spacing, and justifying the lines, &c.

COMPOSING-DRAUGHT, an opiate or soothing draught.

COMPOSING-FRAME, a printer's elevated working-frame, on which the cases of type are rested obliquely.

COMPOSING-MACHINE, an ingenious and complicated machine, invented for setting and arranging type, which is worked by keys like a piano-forte. These machines, however, have always some practical defects, the spacing and making up into lines still requiring to be performed by hand.

COMPOSING-RULE, a printer's adjusting measure.

COMPOSING-STICK, an iron, brass, or wooden frame, held in the hand by a compositor or type-setter, in which he arranges the letters and words into lines for book or newspaper work.

COMPOSITION, the union of several substances or parts; a musical production; in printing the act of setting up type; the commercial name for an arrangement or legal compromise with creditors, made by a debtor who is unable to pay his liabilities in full, a portion of the debt being taken in lieu of the full demand; in French this is called Concordat.

COMPOSITION CANDLES, stearine or other hard candles which do not waste or burn too freely.

COMPOSITION CLOTH, a material made from long flax, and dressed with a solution, which renders it waterproof. It is used for railway luggage, trunk covers, &c.

COMPOSITION METAL, a kind of sheathing for vessels, which, being cheaper, is used instead of copper.

COMPOSITION NAILS, nails suited for fastening composition metal.

COMPOSITION ORNAMENT-MAKER, a manufacturer of plaster or stucco ornaments.

COMPOSITOR, a type-setter engaged in picking up, arranging, and distributing letters or type in a printing-office.

COMPOST, a collection of fertilizing substances for manuring land.

COMPOT, a jar or box of preserves, or dried sweets.

COMPOTE, stewed fruits or fowls.

COMPOUND, a mixture; the garden or fenced enclosure around houses and buildings in India; a corruption of the Portuguese *campana*.

COMPOUNDER, a distiller or rectifier; a preparer of sweetened cordials.

COMPRADOR, the name in China for a collector or accountant.

COMPRESS, to condense or squeeze into a smaller compass; a linen pad.

COMPROMISE, an adjustment of differences between parties by individual or mutual concession; an arrangement with creditors.

COMPTANT (French), ready money, cash, specie.

COMPTOIR (French), a counting-house, shop-counter or general factory.

COMPTROLLER, CONTROLLER, a supervisor or check officer; thus there are controllers of accounts, controllers of customs, &c.

CONCAVE-BRICK, a sort of brick chiefly used in making drains and water-courses.

CONCENTRATED MILK, solidified milk prepared to keep without spoiling.

CONCENTRIC CIRCLES, in turnery, circles, that are drawn from one common centre but have different radii.

CONCERTINA, a small hexagonal musical instrument, the bellows of which are usually of an octagonal shape, and the reeds and keys are contained in both boards, so as to be played on by pressing the fingers of each hand. *See* MELODEON.

CONCESSION, an American and Canadian name for allotments or portions of land in a township; on the Continent a privilege or right granted by the government to do certain acts, such as to form companies, construct railways, &c.

CONCESSIONNAIRE, the grantee to whom a privilege or concession has been made.

CONCHOLOGIST, one versed in the natural history of shells and their inhabitants; a dealer in ornamental shells. [shells.

CONCHOMETER, an instrument for measuring

CONCH-SHELL, a common name in the West Indies for the helmet or casket shells, which are there used (a mouth hole having been made at the spiral end), to blow as trumpets, to call in the labourers from work. Hence the term "shell-blow" there implies a period for refreshment, or a withdrawal from labour.

CONCHUM, a dry measure in Mysore of 8 lbs.

CONCIATETTI (Italian), a tiler.

CONCIATOR, a workman who assorts and allots the proportion of salt required in glass-making.

CONCIERGE, the doorkeeper of a house on the Continent.

CONCORDAT (French), a bankrupt's certificate. *See* COMPOSITION.

CONCRETE, an artificial cement formed of lime, sand, pebbles, or other materials, frequently used for the foundations of buildings. *See* BETON.

CONDENSER, a pneumatic engine; a mechanical contrivance for cooling liquids in brewing, for making vinegar, spirits, &c., for condensing steam generated in boilers, gas for the purposes of illumination, the fumes and noxious vapours from furnaces, &c.; a machine performing by power the manual labour of the slubbing machine.

CONDER, a person at the herring fishery, who from an elevated position by signal directs the course of the boats, so that they may enclose the schools of fish in their nets.

CONDIMENTS, seasoning or flavouring substances for food, as mustard, pepper, vinegar, sugar, salt, &c.

CONDIT (French), sweetmeats, preserves, pickles.

CONDITIONING SILK, a trade term for the assaying of silk, in order to test the proportions of moisture it contains.

CONDITIONING HOUSES, trade establishments in London and Manchester, where silk is assayed.

CONDITIONS OF SALE, certain stipulations and agreements which are usually stated on catalogues of property to be disposed of by auction, and which are frequently read out previous to the sale, and considered binding on the bidders, purchaser, and vender.

CONDITOR (German), a confectioner.

CONDONGO, a long kind of Spanish raw silk of low quality.

CONDORIN, a Japanese and Chinese coin, the tenth part of a mass, and worth about 1d.

CONDUCTA, a convoy or caravan of mules or horses, in Mexico, &c., conveying money or the precious metals from one place to another inland, or to a seaport for shipment to Europe.

CONDUCTOR, a guide; a person employed in taking up and setting down passengers by omnibus, and who receives their fare; the guard of a stage coach in France; a metallic rod affixed to any great elevation, to carry off the lightning fluid without doing damage to the ship or building; any substance which attracts electricity, and transmits it.

CONDUIT, CONDUCT, a pipe or channel for conveying water; the term was formerly applied to stone buildings erected in some central place over a fountain to supply water to the inhabitants.

CONES, the seeds of pine-trees; beautiful and very valuable species of shells, some being exceedingly scarce.

CONESSI BARK, the bark of *Wrightia antidysenterica*, which is astringent and bitter, and also deemed febrifuge.

CONEY, CONY, another name for the rabbit.

CONFECT, a comfit.

CONFECTION, a medicinal conserve or soft electuary, of which there are many kinds, as opiate confection, aromatic confection, confection of senna, &c. Saccharine matter enters into the composition in different proportions for various objects.

CONFECTIONER, a pastry cook; a maker of sweetmeats.

CONFECTIONER'S-MOULDS, metal or earthenware shapes for general use.

CONFECTIONERY, sweetmeats and pastry in general.

CONFERENCE, the legal term for a meeting for the purpose of consultation.

CONFETTATORE, an Italian confectioner.

CONFETTI, preserves, sweetmeats, comfits, in Italy.

CONFIRE (French), to preserve with sugar; to pickle.

CONFIT (French), a tub or vat; also dogs' excrements prepared for dressing leather; in England termed puer. [ments.

CONFITURES (French), preserves, sweet-

CONFLUENCE, the junction of two rivers.

CONFORTINO, the Italian name for ginger bread.

CONGER EEL, a well-known coarse fish, *Muraena conger*, forming a considerable article of commerce in Cornwall and Devonshire. These fish, besides being sold fresh in our markets, are exported in a dried state to Spain and Portugal, where, being reduced to powder, they are used for making soup.

CONGEE, an Indian name for boiled rice.

CONGIUS, the pharmaceutical name for a gallon; an ancient measure containing 10 pounds.

CONGOU, black tea; a superior kind of Bohea, larger leaf and less dusty, and that which is most extensively imported from China, the consumption exceeding 50 million pounds per annum.

CONGREVE-MATCH, a kind of lucifer or phosphoric match.

CONGREVE ROCKET, a formidable projectile and missile of war named after its inventor, Sir W. Congreve.

CONICOPOLY, the name for an accountant or clerk in some of the Indian presidencies.

CONIMA, a very fragrant gum-resin suitable for pastilles, &c., obtained in British Guiana from the hyawa or incense tree, *Icica heptaphylla*.

CONNAISSEMENT (French), CONOSSEMENT (German), a bill of lading.

CONNECTING-ROD, part of a steam-engine.

CONQUINTAY, a Creole name in the West Indies for meal prepared from the core of the sun-dried fruit of the plantain.

CONSERVATOIRE (French), a public school of music.

CONSERVATORY, a large glazed greenhouse for exotics.

CONSERVATORY-MAKER, a builder of greenhouses and hothouses.

CONSERVE (French), a tender or convoy; in ordinary parlance a preserve; in pharmacy a confection or electuary, a sweetened pulp containing the virtues of flowers, herbs, or fruits.

CONSIDERATION, a bonus or sum given on account or for any thing; the motive or material cause of a bargain or contract, expressed or implied.

CONSIGN, to send goods to an agent or factor for sale.

CONSIGNATURE, a joint signature.

CONSIGNEE, a person who receives goods in trust, or to dispose of for another.

CONSIGNMENT, a despatch of goods for sale to a correspondent for disposal on the best terms; merchandise in a state of transport.

CONSIGNOR, the party who consigns or transmits goods.

CONSOLE, an elbow truss or projecting shoulder piece, a bracket or support mostly fixed between two windows in a building; a small fancy side-table for a sitting-room with bracket-shaped projecting legs.

CONSOLS, the leading English funded government security; a fund formed by the consolidation of different annuities, and on which 3 per cent. interest is now paid. It forms the largest portion of the public funds, amounting at present to £[illegible], and in it are absorbed from time to time other public securities. It is that stock in which there is most speculation and jobbing among the dealers—hence the price at which it stands generally regulates the rise and fall of other public securities.

CONSOLS-ACCOUNT. *See* ACCOUNT-DAY.

CONSOLS-MARKET, the Stock Exchange, where sales of public securities are transacted.

CONSOMME' (French), jelly broth, gravy soup.

CONSORT, a partner or ship sailing in company with another.

CONSTABLE, a policeman or petty peace officer; the officer of a sheriff.

CONSTANTIA, a sweet Cape wine.

CONSTITUENCY, a body of burgesses or electors who send a member to parliament.

CONSTRUCTOR, a builder.

CONSUL, the commercial representative of a State in a foreign country, whose duty it is to protect trade and superintend commercial transactions, of shippers, merchants and others. There are Consuls-general, Vice-consuls, and Consular agents.

CONSULAR FEES, the privileged fees or perquisites charged by a consul for his official certificates and notarial legalizations.

CONSULAR SEAL, the distinctive seal appertaining to a consul, which is required to be affixed to commercial and other documents which he attests.

CONSULATE, the office or residence of a consul.

CONSULTATION, a council of lawyers, physicians, &c., met to advise or confer together.

CONSUMER, one who uses or expends goods, &c.

CONSUMPTION, a using up; the quantity consumed.

CONTADOR (Spanish), a purser.

CONTAGAH, an eastern grain measure about 98½ cwt.

CONTAILLES (French), coarse silk.

CONTANGO, a Stock Exchange term, signifying a sum of money paid for accommodating either a buyer or seller by carrying the engagement to pay money or deliver shares over to the next account-day.

CONTEMPT OF COURT, any slight paid to a presiding law-officer in a civil court, or disobedience to the rules and orders, which is a punishable offence with pains and penalties.

CONTENTED-GOODS, an old Custom-house term applied to linens and other fabrics which had the number of lengths or yards they contained fixed to the piece.

CONTENTS, what is contained in bales, casks, or packages of merchandise.

CONTERIE, coarse glass of Venice.

CONTEST, to dispute or litigate.

CONTINGENT, a share or portion arising from an adventure or partnership in trade; the quota which each is to furnish or receive; a supply of men, money, or munitions of war.

CONTINUATION, a connection: the carrying over of stock, &c., by a stock broker or dealer.

CONTO, a Portuguese word for million; a conto of reis (1000 milreis) is usually expressed thus, 1000$000; and is worth about £150.

CONTRA (Latin), on the other side. *Per contra* in commercial phraseology means a credit or writing off on the opposite page.

CONTRABAND-GOODS, articles which are either wholly prohibited or only legally permitted to be imported or exported on payment of certain heavy duties. In time of war articles of ammunition, &c., calculated to be useful to the enemy, are contraband. Articles subject to customs or excise duty attempted to be smuggled in are contraband, or unlawful.

CONTRACT, a covenant or agreement between parties for a lawful consideration as in the case of a sale, the acceptance of a tender for the supply of goods or work to be executed, letting, &c. See CHARTER PARTY.

CONTRACTOR, one who bargains; an undertaker of work upon contract.

CONTRACT-TICKET, an agreement between shipowners or ship-brokers and passengers required to be given to the latter by law.

CONTRA-MAESTRE (Spanish), the boatswain of a ship.

CONTRATE-WHEEL, one of the wheels of a watch.

CONTRAYERVA, a South American plant, the *Dorstenia Contrayerva*; the rhizoma are stimulant, sudorific, and tonic, also emetic. It has a Spanish reputation for being an antidote to poisons.

CONTREBANDIER (French), a smuggler.

CONTREFAÇON, CONTREFACTION, the French term for pirating or counterfeiting.

CONTRIBUTION, a joint payment of money to an undertaking; the individual proportion of a general average.

CONTRIBUTORY, one called upon to pay in his share to the common stock, as a call in the winding up of a company.

CONTROLE, a French term applied to stamped silver or gold.

CONTROLLER. See COMPTROLLER.

CONVENER, one who has to call persons together; a common term in Scotland for a person appointed to summon a meeting of the members of a society or association.

CONVENTION, an agreement or treaty between States.

CONVENTIONARY-RENT, a stipulated or agreed rental charge.

CONVENTION-DOLLAR, or THALER, a German silver coin worth nearly 4s. In Italy the convention dollar passes current for 6 Austrian lire of 8d. each.

CONVERSATION-TUBES, conducting pipes of elastic gum or metal for conveying sound or for delivering messages to distant parts of a building.

CONVERTIBLE-CARRIAGE, a vehicle which can be used either open or closed.

CONVERTING-MILLS, works at Sheffield for making the crudest form of steel.

CONVEYANCE, a legal document transferring land or property from one person to another; the transport of goods or passengers by land or sea.

CONVEYANCER, a person educated to the law, and practising under or at the Bar, who draws up the conveyance or assignment of property from one person to another.

CONVITTO (Italian), a boarding-house.

CONVOY, one or more ships of war, specially appointed by authority of the government, or by the commander-in-chief of a naval station, to accompany merchant vessels for protection and defence in time of war; a name for the brake of a railway carriage.

COOCOO, a local native name in some of the Pacific islands for the mussel shellfish.

COODEE, an Indian name for the corge, or score.

COODOM, another name for the Colaga.

COOK, a kitchen servant, any one who prepares and dresses food.

COOKING-ACCOUNTS, a term applied to falsely represented accounts; statements prepared for deceptive purposes.

COOKING-APPARATUS, a complete cooking stove.

COOKING-APPARATUS-MAKER, a manufacturer of such stoves.

COOKING-UTENSILS, the stew-pans, gridirons, ladles, and other necessary articles for kitchen use in dressing and preparing food.

COOK-ROOM, the galley or place set apart for cooking in a ship.

COOKS' COMPANY, one of the livery companies of London; having no hall, their business is transacted at Guildhall.

COOK'S MATE, the assistant or help to a cook on board ship.

COOK'S-SHOP, a place where ready-dressed meat is sold, or viands can be had.

COOL, a tub cut in two, in which butter is sometimes sent to market by farmers; it weighs from ½ cwt. to 1 cwt.; a kind of gruel made by the Singhalese from the flour or meal of the young plants of the palmyra, termed kelingoos and odials.

COOLER, in the West Indies, a flat wooden receiver for syrup after boiling to settle and granulate; a vessel used in breweries and distilleries to cool the wort in.

COOLING APPARATUS, a refrigerator; a freezing machine.

COOLOO, a land measure in Trichinopoly of 21 English feet.

COOLTIE, a name in Bellary for one of the varieties of horse-gram, the pulse of *Dolichos uniflorus*.

COOLY, a porter or carrier in the East.

COOM, the soot at the mouth of an oven.

COOMB, an English grain measure, containing 4 bushels or half a quarter.

COOMIE, an extensive present in the shape of customs-duty, demanded by the king and chiefs from supercargoes in the Bonny and other rivers of Western Africa for permission to trade with the natives.

COON, an abbreviated name for the racoon in America.

COONCHA, a Malayan grain measure. See COYAN.

COONCHUM, an undefined Indian land measure.

COONDEE, a weight for the precious metals in Bencoolen of 1½ grain.

COONTAH, an undefined Indian land measure.

COOP, a wooden pen for poultry on board ship; for sheep, &c., on shore; a twig fish-pot used in the Humber.

COOPER, one who makes casks, barrels, &c., with staves bound by hoops.

COOTHAY, a striped satin made in India.

Cooperage, money paid to a cooper who attends on the quays to repair casks, and to open them for sampling; also the workshop of a cooper.

Cooper's-company, one of the livery companies of London, whose hall is in Basinghall-street.

Cooper's-mate, an assistant to a cooper on board ship.

Cooper's-tool-maker, a manufacturer of articles used in the coopery trade.

Coortah, a tight-fitting jacket worn by some of the native women in India.

Coosumba, an Indian name for white paddy or rice.

Coottinad, a kind of coarse boiled rice sold in Canara.

Cop, a head; a bundle or ball of yarn on a spindle.

Copaiva, Capivi, Balsam, a yellow medicinal stimulant oil obtained from *Copaifera officinalis* and other species in Tropical America.

Copal, an important pure resin of commerce, forming the basis of most varnishes; a general name for most clear resins.

Copalche-bark, an aromatic, bitter medicinal bark, the produce of *Croton pseudo-china*, a Mexican bush. Copalche bark is also obtained from the *Strychnos pseudoquina*, reputed to be the most valuable of all remedies for the intermittents of Brazil.

Copal-varnish, an important and useful varnish much used in the arts and manufactures.

Copang, a money of account and weight in some parts of the Eastern archipelago; the fourth part of a mace; in Sumatra, the copang is 2½ grains, in other parts 7 to 10 grains.

Copartner, one who is united in partnership with another.

Cope, a priest's vestment; the archwork over a door. The word also signifies to barter or change away.

Copeck, Kopeck, a Russian copper coin, the hundredth part of the rouble; 3 copecks are equal to one penny. The coined copper money is in pieces of 10, 5, 2, 1 and half copecks. There are silver pieces current of 5, 10, 15, 20, 25, 30, 50, 75 and 150 copecks.

Copeman, a merchant; one who barters.

Coper, in lead mining one who contracts to get ore at an agreed sum per dish or load, &c.

Copey, a Cuba dye-wood obtained from *Clusia rosea*.

Copfstuck, a name given to the twenty kreutzer piece in Austria and Bavaria.

Cop-house, a place where tools are kept.

Coping, the upper course of masonry on a wall or parapet, &c., which forms a projecting or covering course.

Coping-stones, long plates of stone laid on a wall, and projecting a few inches beyond the wall to carry off rain.

Copper, a well-known, brownish-red metal, obtained largely in this country, in North America, the Cape Colony, Australia, and the West Indies, &c. It enters into commerce in the form of ore, regulus, old plates, and coin; in manufactures, unwrought in bricks and pigs, rose copper, sheets, nails, wire, rods, &c. According to the estimates of M. Leplay, the secretary of the commission of mining statistics, in France, the whole amount of the smelted copper produced in the world is 52,400 tons, the amount consumed by various countries being as follows:—Great Britain, 10,000 tons; France, 9200; the German Customs Union, 5400; the Austrian Empire, 2600; the Russian Empire, 2000; Sweden and Norway, 400; other European States, 6600; the United States, 5000; other States of America, 1100; the Asiatic continent (India and Oceanica), 3800; and Japan, 1200.

Copperah, Copra, an eastern name for the dried oily pulp of the cocoa-nut, used for expressing oil from.

Copperas, a popular name for the beautiful green crystals forming sulphate of iron, also called green vitriol.

Copper-bottomed, a term applied to vessels sheathed with copper sheets or yellow composition metal below the water-mark.

Copper-coinage, the petty British coinage for mercantile transactions, and for the convenience of small traders, consisting of pennies, halfpennies, and farthings. In the seven years, ending 1854, 371½ tons of copper were coined into about 30½ million pieces. The principal portion of this was in 1854, when 275 tons of metal were coined chiefly at Birmingham, under contract with Messrs. R. Heaton and Son. Copper money is coined in the proportion of 24 pence to the pound avoirdupois, and is not a legal tender for more than one shilling.

Copper-fastened, a term applied to vessels or boats which have rivets and bolts of copper to secure the timber and planks, &c.

Copper-founder, one who casts copper-metal into moulds or shapes.

Copper-mine, the works where the ores of copper are obtained.

Copper Nickel, an ore found on the Continent, which consists of a compound of arsenic with nickel.

Copper-ore, the crude ore from which metal is obtained by smelting. In 1855, there was raised in Cornwall 161,375 tons of copper ore; in Devonshire, 34,024; in Ireland, 15,063 tons. In the year ending June 1856, the copper ore raised in Cornwall amounted to 200,305 tons, valued at £1,283,630.

Copper-plate, a flat sheet of copper, highly polished, on which a line engraving has been cut, or is to be etched; also a name-plate for a door, &c.

Copper-plate Engraver, one who etches or designs patterns or drawings, &c., on copper.

Copper-plate Maker, a workman who shapes, smooths, and prepares metal plates for engraving.

Copper-plate Press, a roller press for striking off impressions on paper from a metal plate.

Copper-plate Printer, one who works off copies or impressions of cards, bill heads, &c., from a metal plate.

COPPER-PYRITES, the most important and ordinary ores of copper, which are sulphurets of copper and iron.

COPPER-SHEATHING, thin sheets of copper for nailing on ships' bottoms to preserve the timber.

COPPER-SMELTER, one who melts copper ore.

COPPER-SMITH, a worker in copper, who frequently combines the trade of brazier and tin-plate worker.

COPPER-WIRE, fine drawn wire of copper, used for various purposes. Copper wire is now largely in demand for electric telegraphs.

COPPICE-WOOD, small brushwood; underwood.

COPPIN, a cone of thread or yarn formed on a spindle.

COPPO, a measure for oil at Lucca, containing nearly 200 lbs. avoirdupois.

COPRA. *See* COPPERAH.

COPROLITES, the fossil excrements of extinct animals, which, from the large quantity of phosphate of lime they contain, 50 to 55 per cent., when digested with sulphuric acid, form a valuable fertilizer for land.

COP-SPINNER, an American invention combining the qualities of the throstle and mule in one frame, which, it is asserted, will spin 100 per cent. more yarn than the flyer spindle, with one half the power, compared to the quantity produced.

COPY, a printer's term for any thing furnished him to compose in type, whether manuscript or printed matter.

COPY-BOOK, a ruled book for practising writing in.

COPY-HOLD, a legal term for manorial lands held on a tenure by copy of court-roll.

COPYING, taking a fac-simile or impression; hence the terms copying-clerks, copying-machine, copying-paper, &c.

COPYING-CLERK, a clerk in a merchant's, lawyer's, or other office, whose duty it is to make transcripts of letters and other documents.

COPYING-INK, adhesive ink prepared with gum and other substances for taking one or more impressions or copies from the manuscript.

COPYING MACHINE, a press for taking duplicate or manifold impressions on damped paper from manuscripts by a lever.

COPYING-MACHINE MAKER, a mechanic who manufactures presses for taking copies of letters.

COPYING-PAPER, thin unsized paper used damp for taking impressions from writings.

COPYING-PRESS. *See* COPYING-MACHINE.

COPYRIGHT, the sole legal right of printing and publishing any thing which belongs to the author, unless assigned or made over to another.

COQUEMAR (French), a boiler; a tea kettle.

COQUILLAGE (French), shell fish, shell work, &c.

COQUILLA NUT, the fruit of the *Attalea funifera*, a South American palm. These hard mottled nuts, which take a fine polish, are largely imported for the purposes of the turner, who shapes them into various small ornamental and useful articles, especially the handles of bell-pulls, the knobs of walking-sticks, umbrellas, &c. The same palm furnishes the piassaba fibre of commerce.

COQUO, a kind of sheep met with in Angola in Africa.

COR, a pottle measure; a French horn.

CORACLE, a rude boat made of wicker-work and hide used for salmon-fishing in the rivers of Wales.

CORAH, a measure of length in the East, varying for different goods from 41 to 52½ inches; an Indian pattern silk handkerchief.

CORAH-GRASS, CORAY, a species of *Cyperus*, probably *C. textilis*, from which the corah matting of Madras is made.

CORAH PRINTER, one who prints imitation Indian handkerchiefs.

CORAILLEUR (French), a coral fisher.

CORAKAN, a name in Ceylon for the meal of *Eleusine coracana*, the flour of which is baked and eaten.

CORAL, the natural skeleton or organ of support of a species of polypi of which some varieties are imported for ornaments. The chief coral fisheries are in the Mediterranean and Red Sea, and the Persian gulf.

CORAL AND JET WORKERS, mechanics who carve these substances for ornamental purposes, and for decorations.

CORAL WOOD, a hard, fine red cabinet wood, easily polished.

CORAMOUR, a West Indian name for the king-fish when taken young, which is esteemed a delicacy.

CORATCH, a sauce made of ketchup, soy, and essence of anchovies.

CORAWA, a strong silky fibre, obtained from a species of *Bromelia*, used by the Indians of Demerara to make bow-strings, nets, fishing-lines, cordage, &c.

CORAZZA (Italian), a breast-plate or cuirass.

CORBEILLE (French), a little osier basket.

CORBEL, a stone or other projection from the face of a wall, to sustain some superincumbent object; a bolster or support to shorten the bearings on a bridge.

CORBELING, in building, a projection of stones "oversailing" or overlapping each other, out of the vertical direction, the centre of gravity being, however, still preserved.

CORD, a measure for firewood, equal to 1000 billets or four loads; so called because it was formerly measured by a cord. The dimensions of a cord of wood are stated to be eight feet long, four feet high, and four feet broad; the weight being about half a ton. The French cord for measuring wood is replaced by the stere. Cord is also a name for small rope

CORDAGE, small rope used for lashing, cording, or other purposes.

CORDELINE (French), the edge or listere of silk stuff.

CORDELLA (Italian), tape, ribbons, and small cords.

CORDIAL GIN, sweetened gin.

CORDIAL MAKER, a manufacturer of liqueurs, syrups, and sweet drinks.

CORDILLA, an American name for a kind of felt hat, covered with camel or goat hair.

CORDILLAS, a kind of kersey.

CORDING-QUIRES, the outsides of a ream of paper.

CORD-MAKER, a manufacturer of twine or small fasting.

CORDON, a band or wreath; a guarded line or circuit kept by appointed officers, to prevent the breaking of quarantine, blockade, smuggling, &c.

CORDONNET (French), coarse silk.

CORDONNIER, a shoemaker or cordwainer.

CORDOVAN, leather made in Spain from goat skin; the term here is always applied to leather made from horse hide.

CORDOVANIERE (Italian), a tanner or shoemaker.

CORDS. *See* CHECKS.

CORDUROY, a kind of ribbed stuff. *See* FUSTIAN.

CORDUROY-ROAD, the name for a species of plank road in America, consisting of logs of wood.

CORDUROY-TROUSERS, male garments made of fustian.

CORDWAINER, the old name for a shoemaker.

CORDWAINERS' COMPANY, one of the livery companies of London, whose hall is in Cannon-street.

CORD-WOOD, a name for firewood in many colonies; stacks of firewood were formerly measured by a cord.

CORE, the interior of any thing; the mould on which a metal pipe is formed; a miner's name for the period of labour which extends to six hours. The twenty-four hours are therefore divided into four cores, commencing with the "forenoon core," at 6 a.m., and ending with the "last core by night," which commences at midnight.

CORF, in the mining district a basket for carrying coals; a square frame of wood to load the coals on; a sledge to carry ore from the miners to the shaft bottom, to be raised to the surface.

CORF-BOW, the handle of a coal-basket or corf.

CORF-HOUSE, a temporary building or shed erected in Scotland for curing salmon and for keeping the nets in.

CORFT-FISH, a Scotch term for fish boiled with salt and water.

COROK, from the Portuguese *Corja*. The common Indian name for a score, by which many kinds of dry goods are vended in the bazaars.

COROKE, a term in Canara, India, for 212 moodahs, or rush mat bundles of rice, the mode in which that grain is usually sold there.

CORIAH, a species of Indian canoe.

CORIANDER, an umbelliferous plant, the *Coriandrum sativum*, grown for its pungent fruit, used as a seasoning in India, and for the essential oil expressed from the seeds, which are a warm and agreeable aromatic.

CORK, the modified liber of the *Quercus suber*, largely used for stoppers of bottles and casks, and many other purposes.

CORK-CUTTER, a manufacturer of cork bark for commercial purposes.

CORK-CUTTER'S KNIFE-MAKER, a cutler who prepares the particular cutting tools required in the cork trade.

CORKER, a wedge used to stretch women's boots and shoes.

CORK-HAT, a man's hat in which parts of the body, for lightness, are made of cork.

CORK-JACKET, a belt of corks, worn to float the person in water.

CORK-LEG, an artificial leg.

CORK-SCREW, a lever for extracting the cork from a bottle, which is either simple or complicated.

CORK SOCK-MAKER, a cutter of soles of cork for shoes, &c.

CORK-SOLE, a thin slice of cork bark, used for the inside of slippers and shoes, and sometimes between the soles of walking-boots, to keep the feet dry; cork-soles are also now placed between the iron shoe and frog of a horse.

CORN, a general commercial name for the grain or seed of plants, which is used for human food. In England the bread corn is chiefly wheat; in the United States the name corn applies specially to maize; in Scotland the name is given to oats before they are ground; in Sweden, Iceland, &c., it denotes barley; hence it may be inferred that the term is generally applied to that species of grain which is most commonly used for food, in any particular region.

CORNAMUSA (Italian), the bagpipe.

CORN BAGGING, sacking suited for grain bags.

CORN-BIN, a corn-chandler's deposit for grain; the place in a stable where horse food is kept.

CORN-CHANDLER, a retail dealer in grain, meal, and seeds.

CORN CLEANING AND DRESSING MACHINE, a mechanical contrivance for preparing grain for market, by removing imperfections.

CORN DRYING MACHINE, an aërator or kiln.

CORNE (French), horn.

CORNED-MEAT, flesh slightly salted, intended for early use, and not for keeping for any time.

CORNEL, the cornelian cherry, a common tree furnishing a durable wood, used for wheel-work, wedges, pins, &c., obtained from the *Cornus mas*. The austere subacid fruit was formerly fermented for a beverage; the bark is said to have power in intermittents.

CORNELIAN, CARNELIAN, a precious stone used for ornaments. *See* AGATE.

CORNEO, a Spanish ore of quicksilver.

CORNEOUS, horny, resembling horn in colour or texture.

CORNER-STONE, the union stone of the two angles of a wall; the first or foundation-stone laid of a building.

CORNET, a paper bag or cap used by retailers to enclose small wares; a pipe or flute; a cavalry officer who bears the colours.

CORNET-A-PISTON, a musical instrument, a kind of brass horn, or trumpet with valves.

CORN-EXCHANGE, a place of meeting for farmers, corn-factors, and dealers generally, where business is transacted by samples.

CORNEY, a grain measure in Ceylon, of 4½ seers, about 9½ lbs.

CORN-FACTORS, CORN-MERCHANTS, agents who buy and sell grain and meal, &c., on behalf of others.

CORN-FIELD, a space of land devoted to the culture of grain.

CORN-HARP, a wire instrument used in Scotland for freeing grain from the seeds of weeds.

CORN-HUSK-FIBRE, the sheaths of the ears of maize, which have been turned to use in America, for stuffing mattresses.

CORNICE, an upper moulding, or finished ornamental projection; a gilded or other ornamental work within which window curtains are suspended.

CORNICHON (French), horn tips.

CORNING, a name given to the process of granulating gunpowder; salting and curing meat.

CORNING-HOUSE, the place where gunpowder is granulated.

CORN-LIFT, an elevator or contrivance for raising corn to the upper floors of a granary or mill.

CORN-LOFT, an elevated storehouse or depository for corn.

CORN-METER, one who measures grain and seed.

CORN-MILL, a grinding and crushing mill for grain, worked by wind, water, or steam. There are also hand-grinding mills for domestic use.

CORNO (Italian), a horn.

CORNOPEAN, a musical wind instrument.

CORN-SACK, a coarse canvas bag for holding grain, containing about 240 lbs.

CORN-SHELLER, a machine for removing the grain of maize from the cob or stalk.

CORN-STACK, a pile or rick of corn.

CORN-STORE, a place where grain is housed; a retail shop for grain.

COROKAN, the meal of a pulse, the *Eleusine coracana*, of which cakes are made in the East.

COROMANDEL-WOOD, a cabinet wood of a red hazel brown colour, obtained from the *Diospyrus hirsuta;* imported chiefly in logs and planks from Madras.

CORONAL, a lady's ornament for the head.

CORONER, an officer whose chief duty is that of taking inquisitions when any person dies suddenly or by violent means.

CORONER'S INQUEST, a jury of twelve persons, summoned by authority of a coroner to investigate into the cause of the sudden death of a person.

CORONILLA, a Spanish name for the gold dollar of 20 reals vellon, about 4s. 6d.

COROZALE (Spanish), a grove or ridge of cohune palms.

COROZO, COROSSO, CORUSCO-NUTS, commercial names for the fruit of a species of Brazilian palm, *Phytelephas macrocarpa*. The hardened albumen of these nuts has obtained for them the name of vegetable ivory, and they are much used for small articles of turnery-ware. Several hundred tons of these nuts are now annually imported. The Corozo colorado of Central America is the American oil palm, *Elais melanococca*, so named from its red fruit.

CORPORAL, the lowest officer in an infantry company.

CORPORATION, a body politic, or incorporated association.

CORPS, a body of troops, a minor division of an army.

CORRAL, the Spanish name for a cattle enclosure, also called a craal or kraal.

CORRALOO, a name in Masulipatam and other parts of India for Italian millet.

CORRECTING, in printing, the rectification of errors, whether literal or accidental, from wrong type being taken up, or verbal alterations made by the Reader or Author.

CORREGIDOR, a Spanish judge.

CORRESPONDENT, one at a distance who carries on commercial intercourse with another; the news-writer for a periodical journal.

CORRIDOR, a covered passage from one part of a building to another; a gallery or long aisle round a building, leading to several apartments.

CORROI, COUROI (French), a coating stuff for paying a ship's bottom.

CORROSIVE, having the power to eat away.

CORROSIVE-SUBLIMATE, the bichloride of mercury, an extremely acrid and virulent poison, but not unfrequently used medicinally.

CORRUGATED-IRON, iron wrinkled or fluted, with alternate elevations and depressions, used for roofing and other purposes. It is mostly galvanized, but sometimes painted.

CORSAGE, a lady's waist-dress or bodice.

CORSAIR, a piratical vessel which cruises about, attacking and plundering merchant ships.

CORSETS, stays or supports for the waist worn by females.

CORSICAN MOSS, a nutritious strong-scented sea-weed, the *Plocaria Helminthochorton*, found on the coasts of the Mediterranean, recommended medicinally for removing worms. As sold in the shops this moss consists of various marine productions, with a very little *Plocaria* intermixed.

CORTICAL, belonging to the bark.

CORT-STOP, the name in Scotland for a vessel for holding a quart.

CORUNDUM, a mineral, composed of crystalline alumina, in great request for grinding and polishing machinery, plate-glass, pebbles, &c. There are several kinds, as common corundum, or adamantine spar, obtained in the East, the sapphire and ruby, which are termed precious corundum, and emery.

CORVER, a man who makes and repairs corves or coal baskets. See CORF.

CORVES, the mining name for baskets of coal.

CORVETTE, a sloop of war which does not carry more than twenty guns.

COSAQUES, a French fancy paper for wrapping sweetmeats.

COS-LETTUCE, an esteemed variety of lettuce with leaves of an oblong shape.

COSMETICS, nostrums and preparations for improving the hair and beautifying the skin, many of which are at best of doubtful utility.

Coss, a corrupted term for the Karoh or Kros-ah, an Indian itinerary or road measure, which varies in different places, averaging however about 1¼ mile. It is generally distinguished into the common coss, and the standard coss. The standard coss ranges from 35 to 45 to the degree; the common coss, from 1 to 2½ British miles. The Bengal coss of 1000 fathoms is 1 British mile, 1 furlong, 3 poles, and 3½ yards. Major Rennell estimates 190 statute miles to be equal to 100 cosses. In Seringapatam the coss or hardary is 3 miles and 5 1-6th furlongs.

Cossa, a grain measure of the Deccan, India, rather less than 1 lb.; the 60th part of the carwar.

Cossas, a kind of plain Indian muslin.

Cossets, a name on the Continent for slices of beet-root, from which spirit has been distilled.

Cossumba, safflower; a red dye much used among the Malays.

Costal (Spanish), a sack or large bag used in South America; those for carrying ore are made of pita or aloe fibre. It is also a rammer or beetle.

Costard, an early summer apple, which being hawked about, gave to the venders the name of costardmongers, now changed to costermongers.

Cost-book, an old system on which Cornish mines are conducted, by which the adventurers can ascertain and determine their liability. Meetings are held of the shareholders every two months, and the accounts and liabilities made up to that time. A shareholder can withdraw when he pleases on paying his fair proportion of the existing liabilities, when his name is written off the cost-book.

Costeaning, in mining, a search for mineral lodes, by sinking pits, and driving transversely in their supposed direction.

Coster, a piece of arable land in Scotland.

Costermonger, an itinerant hawker or street dealer; originally costardmonger, one who sold apples, but now applied indiscriminately to hawkers of fruit, vegetables, fish, &c.

Costiere (Italian), a coasting pilot.

Costrel, a kind of bottle.

Cost-sheet, a statement of the two-monthly expenses of working a mine.

Costume, a term usually applied to a fancy or character dress.

Costumier, a dealer in fancy dresses.

Costus, a name for the putchuk root, a kind of Indian orris, obtained from *Costus Arabicus*, used in China as an incense.

Cosy, the name given to a small kind of omnibus recently introduced.

Cot, a swinging canvas bed or hammock; a cottage or small house.

Cote (French), the quotation in a prices-current.

Cotgare, refuse wool.

Cothon, a landing quay or dock.

Cotillion, a woollen material, in black and white for ladies' skirts.

Cotman, a term for a fisherman in Ireland; in Scotland a cottager. *See* Cottar.

Cotogno (Italian), the quince tree.

Cotonnade (French), cotton check.

Cotswold-sheep, a long-woolled breed of sheep, so named from the cots or sheds in which they were housed; which at one time were peculiar to the counties of Gloucester, Hereford, and Worcester.

Cotta, a measure used in the Maldives for selling cowries, containing about 1200 of these shells. *See* Cowry.

Cottah, an Indian land measure, the 20th part of the beegah or biggah; equal in Bengal to 720 square feet.

Cottar, Cotter, one who inhabits a cottage dependent on a farm.

Cottenham-cheese, a name in the London market for new cheese.

Cottier, a weaver in Ireland who works for the flax manufacturers without holding land.

Cotton, the wool or down surrounding the seeds of various species of *Gossypium*, of which the commerce is enormous. The quantities of raw cotton consumed in the chief manufacturing countries in 1856 were as follows, in millions of pounds:—Great Britain, 920; Russia, Germany, Holland, and Belgium, 256; France, 211; Spain, 48; countries bordering on the Adriatic, 80; United States of North America, 265; Mediterranean and other countries, 56. Total 1793 million pounds.

Cotton-bagging, a coarse wrapping material for baling cotton wool, and for sacking. *See* Gunny-bags.

Cotton-broker, an agent in a seaport town for the sale of cotton.

Cotton-dyer, one who dyes cotton.

Cottonee, a Turkish fabric of cotton and silk satinet.

Cotton-floaters, an India-rubber envelope or casing, in which bales of cotton are floated down some of the American rivers.

Cotton-gin, a machine for clearing cotton wool from the seeds, husks, and other impurities: there are several kinds, among which are the Indian churka or foot-roller, the hand-gin, saw-gin, &c.

Cotton, Gun. *See* Gun-cotton.

Cottonier, a provincial name for the wild asparagus of Canada, the fibre of which is believed to be of importance as a substitute for flax or hemp.

Cotton-manufacturer, a maker of cotton fabrics by machinery. The declared value of our cotton manufactured goods in 1856 was £20,632,713 and of that consumed at home the value is estimated at £23,000,000.

Cotton-mills, works where cotton wool is spun by machinery into yarn, &c. The number of spindles at work in Great Britain was estimated at 27 millions in the end of 1856.

Cotton-mill-furnishers, machinists who supply the fittings for mills.

Cotton-printer, a machine-printer, who stamps and dyes cotton fabrics.

Cotton-seed Oil, a bland dark oil extracted from the seed which is separated from the cotton wool.

Cotton-spinner, a workman at a cotton-mill; the owner of cotton works.

COTTON-TICK, a material for bed and pillow cases, &c., which is either plain or twilled, and sometimes composed partly of linen, as in union tick.

COTTON-WASTE-DEALER, a trader who buys the refuse from cotton mills

COTTON-YARN-MEASURE. In the cotton trade a thread is equal to 54 inches; a skein or rap of 80 threads, equal to 120 yards; a hank of 7 skeins, 840 yards; a spindle of 18 hanks, 15,120 yards.

COTTON-YARN-MERCHANT, an agent or dealer in cotton yarn. In 1856 we exported about 187½ million pounds of yarn and thread, valued at £8,652,000, and double that quantity in manufactured articles; while about 273 million pounds of yarn were used at home.

COTTON-YARN-TWISTER, a preparer of yarn for spinning, &c.; the waste of cotton in spinning is about 1¼ oz. in the pound.

COTTREL, a hook and trammel to hang a boiler or pot on for cooking purposes.

COTWAL. See CUTWAL.

COUCH, a frame on which barley is malted; a kind of sofa or long soft reclining seat.

COUCHER, a workman in a paper manufactory.

COUCH-GRASS, a name for various creeping roots troublesome to the farmer. Some of these are now employed for paper stuff, and as food for cattle in Italy. See GRAMIGNA.

COUCOU, a wooden clock.

COULAGE (French), leakage.

COULEUVRE (French), snakewood.

COULISSE, CULLIS, a groove or channel, the gutter in a roof.

COULTER, part of a plough. See COLTER.

COULTREE, a kind of Indian grain.

COUMATCH, a red twill made in Russia.

COUMIA-RESIN, a resin obtained in the West Indies and South America from *Icica Guianensis*.

COUNCIL, a civic court.

COUNSELLOR, an American advocate or barrister.

COUNTER, part of the stern of a vessel; a shopboard, a table or bench on which money is counted; an imitation money; the back leather or heel part of a boot.

COUNTERBRUSCK, a plane for working out the groove which unites the two sashes of a window in the middle.

COUNTER-JUMPER, a contemptuous name sometimes given to a linendraper's shopman.

COUNTERMAND, a contrary order; a stoppage in transitu.

COUNTER-PANE, COUNTER-POINT, a bed-covering woven with little protuberances of various patterns. A more elegant species is the *Marseilles quilts*. These have a double cloth with a softer fabric quilted between them in the loom.

COUNTERSIGN, a military watchword or private pass signal.

COUNTER-TURNER, a workman who makes button moulds, and bone, ivory, shell or other markers.

COUNTERVAILING-DUTIES, excise duties chargeable on the receipt of goods from the Isle of Man and other specified places, equal to those which would be paid from other quarters.

COUNTESSES, a kind of slate measuring 20 inches by 10. See SLATES.

COUNTING-HOUSE, a merchant's office, a place where business is transacted.

COUNTRY, a Derbyshire mining term for a rock through which the mineral vein traverses.

COUNTRY-CLOTHS, a name for mats, and textile fabrics, &c., made in Africa by the natives. Some are made of grass, which look cool and pretty but cannot be washed; others are of long coloured strips of cotton cloth, blue and red, woven about the breadth of a ribbon, and then sewed together.

COUNTY-COURT, a civil district court, presided over by a Judge, for the summary trial of small causes, where the debt or damage sued for is not above £50.

COUP, a Scotch term for exchanging or bartering, buying and selling.

COUPE, a Swiss grain measure, in Fribourg equal to 7 gallons, in Geneva to 17; in Lyons the coupe is but 1¼ gallon. In Germany this measure bears the name of kopf.

COUPEE, the glazed front part of a French diligence or other carriage.

COUPLINGS, the connecting link by which motion is added from one machine to another from the same motive power; also the rod or chain which unites railway carriages.

COUPLING-BOX, a connection for joining the ends of shafts.

COUPON, an order or warrant for the payment of periodical dividends on public stocks, which is usually attached to foreign bonds.

COUPON-SHEET, a connected series of coupons given in advance, which have to be detached from time to time as the dividends fall due, and are paid.

COURBARIL, a kind of clear resin. See ANIME and COPAL.

COURIDA, a wood obtained in Demerara from *Avicennia nitida*. It is perishable when much exposed, but is useful as foundations for buildings. The bark is used for tanning.

COURIER, an express or special messenger.

COURSE, a continued range of stones or bricks in the wall of a building.

COURSES, the lower square sails of a ship; course is also the term for the track or direction a ship is to take in prosecuting her voyage.

COURSE OF EXCHANGE, the sum merchants pay to each other for bills to enable them to make remittances from one country to another.

COURTAGE, the business or remuneration of a courtier or broker in France.

COURT-GUIDE, a fashionable directory of the names and residences of the gentry and nobility in a town.

COURTIER, a French broker. On the Continent as in England there are many kinds, as bill-broker, courtier de change; ship-broker, courtier de navire; share-broker, courtier d'actions; custom-house broker, courtier de douane; and different produce brokers.

COURTLAGE, the court or yard of a shop or dwelling-house.
COURT-MARTIAL, a military or naval tribunal, taking cognizance of offences committed by officers or men in the Queen's service, and having penal jurisdiction.
COURT OF CHANCERY, a superior equity court of law, over which the Lord Chancellor presides, to which legal decisions, or the administration of disputed property is referred, or, in popular parlance, "thrown into chancery."
COURT OF REQUESTS, a summary judicial court for the trial of small causes.
COURT PLASTER, an adhesive plaster of black sarcenet silk, strained and brushed over several times with a gummy preparation of isinglass, benzoin, and turpentine. It is used chiefly for closing wounds.
COURT-PLUME, a bunch of white ostrich feathers, worn by ladies on the head on state visits at Court.
COUTT, a superior kind of Catechu, said to be made in Southern India from the areca or betel nut.
COUSCOUS, COUZ-COUZ, KOUS-KOUS, African names for the pounded grain of *Penicillaria spicata*, a species of millet.
COUS-O-BRODEUR, a French sewing machine.
COUSTIC, an old Prussian coin of 5 groschen, and worth rather more than 2d.
COUTABALLI, a common wood of British Guiana, principally used for house frames. It is very hard and durable when not exposed to the weather. It will square 12 inches, from 30 to 40 feet long.
COUTEAU, the French term for a knife.
COUTELIER, the French name for a cutler.
COUTIL (French), canvas, ticking, drill or duck.
COVA, in Italian a tortoise shell.
COVADO, the Portuguese cubit, and measure of length for cloth, containing 3 palms, equal to 2·15 feet, or 26¾ inches.
COVEACHING, a mode of marinating Spanish mackerel and other fish in the West Indies, for keeping and export. The fish are cut into junks, fried with onions and oil, and afterwards potted with vinegar, spices, and some of the fried onions and oil.
COVED-CEILING, a roof arched at the junction with the walls.
COVER, a miner's box in which ore is removed from the rock or strata; the moveable top of anything.
COVERLET, a counterpane or quilt; the upper covering for a bed.
COVETTA, a plane used for moulding framework, called also a quarter-round.
COVID, an eastern cloth measure of variable length; in Calcutta and Bombay it is 18 inches; in Madras 18 3-5ths; in Arabia 19; in Malacca 18¼; and in China 14⅝ inches.
COVING, the sides of a fireplace; a projection in houses beyond the foundation or outer wall.
COW, a miner's name for a wedge placed behind a crab or gin-start to prevent it from revolving; the female of the bovine tribe of animals. In Scotland this word has a variety of significations. It is applied to a rude shed erected over the mouth of a coal pit; to a besom made of broom; to the fuel used for a temporary fire; to a scarecrow, and to the act of pruning or lopping.
COWAGE. See COWHAGE.
COWAN, a Scotch fishing boat; a builder of dry walls, one who does the work of a mason but has not been regularly trained to it.
COWBECK, a mixture of hair and wool for hats.
COW-BELLS, bells hung round the neck of cattle and sheep to notify their locality to the agriculturist, especially in mountainous districts, and in low underwood.
COW BEZOAR. See BEZOAR.
COW-BLAKES, dried cow-dung used as fuel, which bears different names in various counties and foreign countries. In parts of Scotland it is called cow's backrin, cow-plats, and cow-sharn. See ARGOLS.
COWDACH, COWDY, a small cow or heifer; in some parts a Scotch runt without horns.
COWDIE PINE, KOWRIE, or KAURI, the *Dammara australis*, a splendid coniferous tree, a native of New Zealand, furnishing valuable timber, and from the fossil deposits of which the kowrie resin of commerce is obtained.
COWDUNG, the excrement of the ox tribe. Besides its value as manure, and when dried for fuel, cowdung is much used in the process of calico-printing, after the fabric has been mordanted.
COW-FEEDER, an attendant on cows; in Scotland, a dairyman, who sells milk.
COWHAGE, COW-ITCH, a name given to the small hairs on the pods of *Mucuna urens* and *pruriens*, climbing plants of the East and West Indies. They are used in medicine as a vermifuge.
COWHAIR, the hair taken from the hides of slaughtered cattle which is useful for various purposes, for making rope, for stuffing, and for mixing with mortar. The white hair is employed in blanket-making, and the brown hair by felt makers, and for ship's sheathing, &c.
COW-HEEL, the foot of a calf or cow boiled for jelly.
COW-HIDE, the skins of cattle used for making leather, for rope and for packing bales, &c.
COWIE, a name given to the seal in the Frith of Tay, from its round head resembling a cow that has no horns.
COWKEEPER, a dairyman who keeps cows for milking.
COW-[illegible], COW-HOUSE, a shelter for milch cows or other cattle.
COWL, a revolving chimney-pot or cover to facilitate the escape of smoke. In India, a contract or lease to a zemindar or large farmer.
COWP, a mining term for exchanging places, or for an over turn. See COUP.
COWRIES, the small white glossy shells of *Cypræa moneta* and other species, which are used in several parts of Africa and India for money. In the eastern bazaars they are made use of for minute fractional payments and their value rises and falls

according to the demand and the quantity in the market; 6000 to 7000 being equal to a rupee or two shillings. In the interior of Africa they bear a higher value, five strings or 200 being worth about eightpence. Some kinds of cowries are ground to make the glaze on the enamel plate of clocks, others are used for ornamental purposes.

COWSLIP, the *Primula veris*, the flowers when fermented with sugar form a domestic wine, used for wheys.

COWS-MILK. The milk of the cow is that ordinarily supplied to towns, &c.; it contains by analysis about 87 per cent. of water, 4½ of caseine or curd, 4¾ of sugar of milk, about 3 per cent. of butter, and the remainder is made up of various salts. The proportion of solid matter to that of water is rather less than in the milk of the ewe and goat.

COWSOONG, COOSONG, a kind of nankeen dyed black; an article of trade in the Philippine and Sunda islands.

COXSWAIN, a steersman or chief boatman; one who has the charge of a boat.

COYAN, a dry measure of common use in Asiatic and eastern countries, containing more or less piculs, according to the articles measured and the locality. In some parts it is reckoned 3000 lbs. In Java it is 27 piculs or 3581 lbs. avoirdupois, in Amboyna 25 piculs or 3255¼ lbs.; in Singapore 40 piculs of 133⅓ lbs. each.

COZ, COZBAUGUES, a small Persian copper coin, worth rather more than a farthing.

COZINNEIRO (Spanish), a ship's cook.

CRAB, a small portable crane or lifting machine, with a single or double purchase; a capstan used by miners for raising or lowering pumps in a pit; a wild sour apple; a well-known crustaceous animal (*Cancer pagurus*). Sea crabs are taken in large quantities for consumption in towns; land crabs (*Gegarcina ruricola*) are also much esteemed as a delicacy in the West Indies.

CRABS'-EYES, concretions found in the stomach of the cray fish before it casts its shell in July. They were formerly in great repute as antacids, and at Astracan large quantities of crayfish were bruised with mallets, and allowed to putrify in heaps, after which the flesh was washed, and the two concretions picked out; but chalk answers every purpose for which these stones were used.

CRAB-WOOD, a light wood obtained in Guiana from the *Carapa Guianensis*, which takes a high polish, and is used for masts and spars, floorings, partitions, and doors of houses. There are two varieties, the red and the white. It may be cut from 40 to 60 feet in length, with a square of 14 or 16 inches. The bark is used for tanning, and the seeds yield a valuable oil, which is used for burning, and is highly esteemed as a hair oil, preventing it turning grey, and curing scalpy eruptions.

CRACK, a flaw or fissure.

CRACKER, a kind of small dry hard water biscuit chiefly made in the United States; a firework.

CRACKIE, a small low three-legged stool, with a hole in the middle for lifting it, used in cottages.

CRACKLINGS, the refuse of tallow when prepared by the chandler or candle maker.

CRACKNELLS, a kind of crisp sweet biscuit.

CRADLE, a strong frame of timber, &c., placed under the bottom of a ship to conduct her steadily in her ways when being launched; a child's cot, moving on rockers; a gold sifting machine; a miner's name for a suspended scaffold used in shafts.

CRADLE-SCYTHE, a rake or support to a scythe for receiving the straw as it is cut.

CRAFT, a trade; a name given to small vessels.

CRAFTSMAN, a skilled mechanic or artificer.

CRAIG (Scotch), a rock or cliff.

CRAIG-FLOOK, a species of flounder.

CRAIG-HERRING, a Scotch name for the shad.

CRAIGSMAN, one who climbs cliffs overhanging the sea in Shetland for the purpose of procuring sea birds, or their eggs.

CRAIL-CAPON, a name in the Lothians for a haddock dried but not split, named from Crail, a town in Fife.

CRALLS, CRAWLS, enclosures made with stakes near the shore for confining turtle.

CRAM, CRAME, a Scotch term for a market stall; a pack of goods for sale.

CRAMBOO, a name in some parts of India for cloves.

CRAMPS, bent irons for holding things together; metal ties or holdfasts for securing large stones in a wall.

CRAN, a fish measure, equal to about 37½ gallons; as many fresh herrings as will fill a barrel; an iron support for a pot or kettle over a fire; a name in the shoe trade for any secret method of performing work.

CRANAGE, the money hire of a crane for loading and unloading ships, and warehousing goods.

CRANBERRIES, the acid red fruit of *Oxycoccus palustris*, and other species of the same genus, imported preserved in spring water from Newfoundland and the United States. They are largely used for tarts and puddings. Cranberries are cultivated in many parts of North America; they are sown broadcast on wet land, and on drier soils the plants are drilled in, and bear fruit the third year, yielding on the average about 150 bushels to the acre, which sell at 8s. or 9s. the bushel.

CRANE, a powerful lifting machine, moved by a winch, of great use on wharves and docks, &c., for hoisting heavy goods. Small iron cranes are used at private stores and warehouses, and on ships.

CRANE-HOUSE, the covering or weather-shelter for a crane.

CRANE-MANUFACTURER, a maker of lifting-machines.

CRANE POTATO, a wild root eaten by the Indians of the north-west parts of America.

CRANG, a name for the blubber or carcase of the whale.

CRANIOMETER, an instrument for measuring the skulls of animals.

Crank, an elbow-shaped piece of iron; a nautical term for vessels which have not sufficient breadth of beam, and are in danger of upsetting; an angular connection or bend for a bell wire.

Crank-axle, a driving axle.

Crank-pin, the joining arm of a crank.

Crap, a name for buck-wheat, darnel, &c.

Crape, a kind of thin gauze made of raw silk woven without crossing and stiffened with gum water; mourning crape is black, aerophanes, crape-lesse, and gauze are either white or coloured.

Crape and Feather Dresser, one who crimps and curls those articles, and restiffens crape with gum water.

Crape-dyer, a tradesman who re-dresses and improves black crape.

Crap-leather, **Crops**, leather made from thin cow hides, used chiefly for pumps and light walking-shoes.

Crare, a small sea vessel.

Crash, a heavy low-priced linen fabric; coarse Russian packing cloth, sold in bales and pieces.

Crat, a Mocha weight of three grains.

Crate, a large wicker hamper with strong wooden supports.

Cravalli, **Cavalla**, a name in the West Indies for several species of *Caranx*. The green cavalla, *C. Bartholomæi*, is very good eating, and much in demand, but this fish is sometimes poisonous.

Cravat, a neck tie or kerchief made of various material.

Crawl, **Craal**, a fish-pond or turtle inclosure in the West Indies.

Cray, a small sea vessel.

Crayfish, **Crawfish**, a well-known crustacean, the *Astacus fluviatilis*.

Crayon Board, thick drawing paper or card board for crayon drawings.

Crayon Maker, a manufacturer of crayons for artists.

Crayons, coloured cylinders of pipe clay, used for drawing on paper.

Craze Mill, a crushing or grinding mill for tin ore.

Crazia, a money, the eighth part of a Tuscan paul, and subdivided into five liards; as a weight the twelfth part of a Tuscan pound; also a Tuscan measure of length of nearly two inches.

Creaght, a name for herds of cattle.

Creah, a raised dorey, in Honduras; the hollow log out of which the canoe is shaped, is partially decked and rigged for sailing.

Cream, the oleaginous portion of milk which rises to the surface.

Cream Cheese, a soft easily digested cheese, made entirely from the cream of milk.

Cream of Tartar, crystallized supertartrate of potash.

Cream Slice, a wooden knife for parting cream.

Creance, a book debt in France.

Creancier, **Crediteur**, the French term for creditor; one to whom money is due.

Creases, in mining, divisions of buddled work. See **Creaze**.

Creasote, a product of the distillation of vegetable and of most animal substances, a powerful antiseptic. What is usually sold as creasote is a false product, obtained from coal tar.

Creaze, a mining name for tin, in the washing tub or buddle.

Credit, a giving trust; goods supplied without prepayment.

Creel, a fishing or potato basket.

Creeper, a kind of small grapnel for dragging in search of any thing lost in a harbour or river.

Crese, **Crease**. See **Cris**.

Cremerie, a breakfast or refreshment house in French towns.

Cremon, the French name for a new shutting piece for a window.

Cremona, a valuable violin.

Crenoline, **Crinoline**, a horsehair and cotton fabric used for ladies' petticoats and bonnets, &c.

Creosote. See **Creasote**.

Crequillas, a textile cotton fabric of light and low-priced quality, made for export.

Cress, the general name of a number of plants possessing pungent and aromatic qualities. The garden cress, *Lepidium sativum*, is a hardy and esteemed salad plant.

Cresset, a light shown upon a beacon, watch-tower, &c.

Creutzer, a German coin. See **Kreutzer**.

Creuset, a crucible or melting pot.

Crew, a gang or party; the complement of sailors for a boat or ship.

Crewel, worsted twisted in knots, and sold for tapestry, and embroidery work; now called Berlin wool.

Crib, a child's bed or cot, of iron, cane, or wood; the rack or manger of a stable; a reel for winding yarn in Scotland; a small raft of timber in Canada. A crib of white pine generally contains 1500 cubic feet; of red pine, 1000 cubic feet.

Cribbage-board, a marking board with holes, on which players score the game of cribbage with pegs.

Cribbie, a Scotch term for as much yarn as goes half round the reel or crib in winding yarn.

Cribble, a sieve.

Cricket, a game played with a bat and ball, and stumps or wickets.

Cricket-bat-maker, a workman who manufactures wooden bats for cricketers.

Crimping-iron, **Crimping-pin**, an instrument for pinching or puckering the border of a lady's cap, or frill, &c.

Crimping Machine, a laundress's roller or iron, which is heated for crimping borders.

Crimson, one of the red colours used by dyers.

Crin, the French name for horsehair.

Cringle, a nautical term for a ring or thimble fitted or spliced into the bolt-rope of a sail.

Cris, **Creese**, a Malay dagger. [fabric.

Cristale, the name of a white worsted

Cristallier (French), a glasscutter.

Crochet, a contrivance used by French street porters for throwing the load off the spine, and causing it to rest on the limbs; a figured ornamental needle-work.

Crochet Case, a case for keeping the knitting needles and other requisites for crochet work.

Crochet Lace, hand-knitted lace, remarkable for cheapness, durability, delicacy, and elegance of design; qualities which have caused it to take the place, to a considerable extent, of the Honiton, Valenciennes, and Brussels laces.

Crochet Needle, a lady's bone or metal knitting hook, for working crochet.

Crock, an earthen vessel; a name in Scotland for an old ewe past bearing.

Crockery-ware, earthenware and pottery.

Crocus, a commercial name for a polishing powder made from oxides of iron.

Croft, an inclosure near a dwelling-house, for pasturage or other purposes; the name for a bleach-house.

Croft-land, in Scotland, land which is successively cropped.

Crogan, a bowl or earthen vessel used in Scotland for holding milk.

Crony, a name in some parts of Scotland for a potato.

Croobacks, panniers borne by horses, and used in some of the mountainous districts of Scotland, for carrying home corn, peats, &c.

Crook, a shepherd's hook; a bent-headed instrument; the iron chain with its appropriate hooks by which the vessels for cooking are hung over a fire.

Croom, a husbandman's fork with long prongs.

Crop, a miner's term for the best ore; in the leather trade, the commercial name for an entire hide; a fixed weight in different localities for sugar, tobacco, and other staples.

Crop-hogshead, the usual recognised weight of a crop-hogshead of tobacco is from 1000 to 1800 lbs. nett.

Cropping-out, in mining, an exposure of the seam or lode to the surface.

Croquettes, fried forcemeat balls, made of pounded chicken meat and butter, much used in India.

Crore, in Hindoo enumeration, 100 lacs of rupees, or 10 millions, and equivalent to one million pounds sterling. *See* Lac.

Cross-buns, sweet spiced cakes sold on Good Friday, marked with a cross on them.

Cross-course, in mining, a lode or vein which intersects or crosses another lode at an angle, and generally throws the lode out of its regular course.

Cross-cut, in mining, a lode level, driven at right angles to the direction of the vein.

Cross-cut Saw. *See* Saw.

Crossed Cheque, an order for payment of money on demand, which being crossed with the name of a banker, requires to be paid by, or through a bank, instead of being presented at the banker's counter for payment; the object being greater security, and the more readily tracing its payment.

Cross-piece, a wooden rail over a windlass.

Cross-sill, a block of stone under a railway sleeper.

Cross-somer, a beam of timber.

Cross-springer, in groined vaulting the rib which extends from one pier to another.

Cross-staff, a surveyor's instrument for measuring offsets.

Cross-tie, a railway sleeper; a connecting band in building.

Cross-trees, pieces of wood at the mast-head of a vessel.

Crotalo, a musical instrument.

Crotches, forked pieces of mahogany or other timber; not straight logs.

Croton Oil, a powerful purgative obtained from the seeds of *Croton tiglium*.

Crottles, a Scottish name for certain mosses and lichens used in the Highlands for dyeing woollen stuffs brown, &c.; *Parmelio physodes* is the dark brown crottle; *Sticta pulmonacea*, the light-brown crottle; *Isidium corallinum*, the white crottle, used in the preparation of a red or crimson dye. The isidiod form of other crustaceous lichens may be used in a similar way. *Lecanora parella*, is another; *Parmelia omphalodes* is the black crottle; and *P. saxatilis* is one of the crottles most frequently used in dyeing yarn.

Crow-bar, a wrought iron lever for lifting or prizing.

Crow-berry, a name given to the fruit of the bilberry, *Vaccinium Myrtillus*.

Crowdie, a general name in Scotland for porridge; in some parts of the north it is applied to a preparation of milk-curds with the whey pressed out, and an equal proportion of butter, flavoured with salt.

Crowle, an old English wind instrument.

Crown, a kind of paper 15 inches by 20; a British current silver coin worth 5s., weighing 18 dwt. 4·36 grains. Of this silver piece very few have been coined lately; the only issue from the mint in the last eight years was 466 crowns in 1851. The half-crown is also giving place to the florin, shilling, and smaller silver coins. On the Continent the crown piece is known under the various names of patagon, couronne, scudo, and écu. The silver crown of Copenhagen passes for 60 schellings.

Crown-glass, sheet glass for glazing purposes, made in a circular form called tables; of crown and sheet glass upwards of 15,000 tons are made annually in Great Britain by about ten companies.

Crown-lands, lands in the United Kingdom or the colonies reserved or held by the Crown.

Crown-piece, a five-shilling silver coin.

Crown-saw, a circular saw.

Crown-wheel, the upper wheel in the works of a watch.

Crow-quills, feathers of the crow which are used for pens, where very fine writing is required, as in lithography and tracing, &c.; those of the Hudson's Bay ducks are used for the same purpose.

Crows-nest, a look-out house at the main top-gallant mast head in arctic vessels, consisting of a cask or other screen or shelter for a man.

Croy, an enclosure for catching fish; a mound or quay projecting into a river for breaking the force of the stream or preventing encroachments.

CROZE, a cooper's tool.
CRUCHON, a stone bottle in France.
CRUCIBLE, a small chemical melting-pot made of various substances.
CRUE, a sheep pen or small fold in Scotland.
CRUEL-RIBBAND, a kind of caddis or lint for bandaging and dressing a wound.
CRUET-STAND, a metal frame for holding bottles of sauces and condiments.
CRUISE, CRUIZE, a short voyage.
CRUIVE, CRUVE, formerly a box resembling a hen-coop, placed in a dam or dike that runs across a river, for confining the fish that enter it; the term has now a broader application to any thing placed in a river for stopping fish.
CRUMB-BRUSH, a curved shaped brush with short handle for sweeping crumbs from a table cloth.
CRUMB-CLOTH, a linen or holland carpet-cover for a living-room.
CRUMPET, a slightly-baked soft thin cake requiring to be toasted at the fire before eating.
CRUMPET AND MUFFIN MAKER, one who makes and vends such cakes.
CRUPPER, a leather strap from the saddle to the horse's tail.
CRUSADO, CRUZADA, a Portuguese gold coin; the old crusado being worth 400 reis, and the new 480, being worth 2s. 4d. There are, however, silver crusadoes of 240, 120, and 60 reis.
CRUSE, an Arabian money consisting of 40 duanies and worth about 1s. 8d. or 2s.; a cup or cruet.
CRUSET, a goldsmith's crucible.
CRUSHING, in mining the process of pulverizing or grinding the ores without water.
CRUSHING-MILL, a mill of various kinds for crushing ore, malt, or other substance.
CRUTCHES, wooden supports made to assist lame persons or cripples in walking; knees of timber.
CRWTH, a Welsh musical instrument with six strings, played upon with a bow.
CRYOLITE, a mineral only found on the west coast of Greenland, lately imported as a source of aluminium; which it is said can be afforded at a price as low as silver. Besides this metal and crystals of soda, a clay is obtainable which will be valuable to calico printers as a substitute for a compound of alum and sugar of lead.
CRYSTAL, the common name for quartz, or pure crystalline silex.
CRYSTALLOGRAPHY, the science which treats of the formation, shape, and peculiarities of crystalline bodies.
CUARE, a quarry of stones.
CUARTAL, a dry measure of Arragon = 0·213 Winchester bushel.
CUARTANE, the twelfth part of the cuartera, a Spanish weight.
CUARTAS, the most valueless kind of tobacco in Cuba, fit only for filling cigars.
CUARTELLA, a variable dry measure in Spain, ranging from 0·077 to 0·388 bushel. As a liquid measure for wine it is generally equal to 1·065 gallon, and for oil 0·829 gallon; 4 cuartellas make an azumbre. The Arragonese cuartella as a weight is 0·016 lb.
CUARTERA, a Spanish corn measure; 2¼ cuarteras make one carga; 100 cuarteras of Barcelona = 24½ imperial quarters.
CUARTERON, an oil measure of Madrid = 0·033 gallon.
CUARTO, a Spanish weight = 0·0158 lb.; also a liquid and dry measure of Spain of very variable dimensions; the minimum as a dry measure being 0·113 bushel, the maximum, 2·52 bushels; as a liquid measure the minimum is 0·085 gallon for wine, and 0·272 gallon for oil, the maximum 0·778 gallon.
CUB, the young of a wild animal, as of a bear or a seal.
CUBA, a liquid measure of Abyssinia, containing 62 cubic inches, and rather more than two pints.
CUBA SABICA, a building wood. *See* SABICU.
CUBEBS, the fruit of the *Cubeba officinalis* and *canina*, which is used medicinally as a diuretic, and in diseases of the genital organs.
CUBE-YARD, a solid British measure of 27 cubic feet.
CUBICA, a kind of shalloon.
CUBIC-FOOT, a solid English measure. The cubic foot of water is the quantity that a vessel a foot square and a foot deep will hold.
CUBIC NITRE, another name for nitrate of soda, or American saltpetre.
CUBIT, a measure of length in England equal to 18 inches; a cubit was originally the distance from the elbow to the extremity of the middle finger, which is the fourth part of a well-proportioned man's stature. The Egyptian cubit is 22¾ inches; the Turkish 26½ inches; the Burmese 19 inches. The common cubit of Persia is 25 inches; the royal Persian cubit 37½ inches.
CUBSHA, an Indian drug.
CUCCHIARO, a dry measure of Turin = 0·0034 bushel.
CUCHA, a weight in Muscat of about 6 ounces.
CUCITRICE, an Italian sempstress.
CUCUMBER, a well-known and extensively cultivated genus (*Cucumis*), chiefly reared for culinary purposes. *C. colocynthis* produces the colocynth of the druggists' shops; *Momordica elaterium* is the edible cucumber; large quantities of cucumbers are pickled for exportation.
CUCUMBER-SEED-OIL, a bland oil obtained in the East from the seeds of plants of the cucumber family, which is used as a lamp oil, and for cooking.
CUCURBIT, a chemical vessel of glass, for distillations and rectification.
CUCUTO, a petty Spanish coin of four maravedis. *See* MARAVEDO.
CUDA, a liquid measure of Arabia, equal to 2 gallons.
CUDBEAR, a red powder sometimes called perels, obtained from the *Lecanora tartarea* and other lichens, by steeping in ammoniacal liquor, and which yields a rich purple colour, employed in dyeing yarn. *See* ARCHIL.
CUDDOCH, a yearling cow or young heifer in Scotland.

Cuddy, properly a cabin in the fore part of a boat, but frequently applied to an after cabin built under the poop of a ship; a liquid measure on the Arabian coast of 2 gallons, also called a gudda.

Cudgel, a heavy stick.

Cudreme, **Chudreme**, in Scotland a stone weight.

Cue, a straight rod or stick used by billiard players; the last or catch word of a speech, by which one actor knows he has to follow another in action or discourse.

Cueillette, the French name for a mixed or general cargo in a ship.

Cuerda, a Spanish long measure of uncertain dimensions, in some places represented to be 7·65 yards, in others as much as 39¼ yards.

Cugnatella, an oil measure of Rome, 2·17 gallons.

Cuinage, the making up of tin into pigs, &c. for carriage.

Cuir, in French, leather or hide.

Cuirass, a piece of soldiers' armour, a metal breast-plate which extends also to the back.

Cuirassier, a soldier armed with a metal breast-plate.

Cuirass-maker, a manufacturer of soldiers' breast-plates.

Cuir de laine, double-milled cloth in France.

Cuisinier, a cook, an attendant in a kitchen.

Cuivre, French for copper.

Culah, a dry measure of Sumatra equal to 0·0618 Winchester bushel.

Culaka, **Cutaka**, Eastern names for the seeds of the *Strychnos nux vomica*. See Nux vomica.

Culblank, a name for a variety of wild sheep found in California.

Culilaban-bark, an aromatic bark obtained in flat pieces from the *Cinnamomum Culilabàn*, sometimes called Clove bark.

Culinary utensils, vessels used for cooking, or belonging to the kitchen.

Cullender, a sieve or large strainer.

Culler, a sampler; a selector of wood, staves, deals, &c. in Canada.

Cullet, a technical name for broken crown or flint glass, with which the crucibles are replenished, for the purpose of being re-melted; the pad on a saddle.

Culling, picking out or selecting the best quality.

Cullingey, a small weight in the southern division of the Carnatic in India, equal to 81¼ grains troy.

Cullis, a brown gravy; broth or jelly strained from boiled meat.

Cullishiay, a grain measure of the Malabar coast, the third part of the mudi or moray which is about 1¼ bushel.

Cullock, a species of shell-fish in Scotland.

Culls, refuse timber in Canada which brings an inferior price.

Culm, a valuable species of Welsh stone-coal or anthracite, containing 92½ per cent. of carbon.

Culaey, a measure of capacity in the East, about 113 gallons.

Cultch, **Cutch**, the spawn of oysters.

Culter. See Coulter.

Cultivator, a husbandman or agriculturist; an instrument for tilling land.

Culver-house, a dove-cote.

Culverin, a long gun.

Culvert, an arched passage or substantial brick-work drain carried beneath a road, railway, or canal.

Culy, an Indian land measure, the 100th part of the cawny, which is about an English acre, though in some parts 1¼ acre.

Cumbi, a superior kind of cloth, made from the wool of the alpaca in Peru and Bolivia.

Cumblies, a kind of native-made woollen rug or blanket in India.

Cumboo, an Indian name for the grain of the spiked millet, *Penicillaria spicata*, or *Holcus spicatus*.

Cummer-bund, a sash or waist-band formed of folds of white muslin always worn by the superior class of natives in India, and by the lower classes in towns on holiday occasions. Sometimes they are embroidered and trimmed with lace and pearls, &c.

Cummin, the *Cuminum Cyminum*, a plant grown for its aromatic seeds and for the yellow essential oil they yield. The fruit is mildly stimulant and carminative, and is used in the preparation of plasters in veterinary practice, and in liqueurs. The pungent seeds of *Nigella sativa*, known as black cummin, are used as a condiment instead of pepper, and pounded as a stimulatory.

Cumming, a vessel for holding wort.

Cundaloo, **Cundooloo**, an Indian name for the pigeon pea, in Masulipatam; also for red grain in Nellore.

Cundapoors, cloths made in Canara for wearing by both sexes.

Cundy, a name among the Singhalese for the hair turned up in a knot behind by both sexes; the men wearing one or two tortoiseshell combs above their cundies.

Cunner, a name for the sea perch.

Cuoiaio, a leather-dresser in the Italian States.

Cuoio (Italian), leather, skin, or parchment.

Cup, a small hollow vessel of various materials.

Cup-board, a framed inclosure or piece of furniture, in a room, usually with shelves to place articles on.

Cupel, a shallow vessel made of bone-earth for purifying metals by exposing them to a strong heat and oxidation.

Cupellation, a mode of analysing metals by fusing them in a cupel, and oxidizing them with lead.

Cupelo, a small furnace.

Cuppa, an Indian name for mat bags sold by the hundred.

Cupper, a surgeon, one who uses cupping instruments to let blood.

Cupping-glass, a small glass vessel with a wide mouth, into the neck of which a brass syringe is screwed for the purpose of exhausting the air. It is used for drawing blood, or milk from the breasts; to prevent the absorption of snake and other poisons from wounds, and for many other purposes.

CUPPRA, the Hindustani name for pieces of cloth.

CUPS, small drinking vessels of earthenware.

CUPULE, the cup of the acorn, which enters into commerce as a tanning substance, under the name of valonia.

CURAÇOA, a sweet cordial or liqueur.

CURANDAIO, the Italian name for a bleacher.

CURATOR, a guardian; in Germany a trustee, or assignee; in England the term is usually applied to a person in charge of a museum.

CURB, the mouth-piece of a bridle; the outer edge of a foot pavement or wall.

CURBA, a species of tub, basket, or earthen pot, used by the negroes, on the west coast of Africa, as a measure of capacity in the sale of palm oil, grain, pulse, &c., and which varies according to the locality. The curba of Ajuda, contains 18 gallons, and of Onim only 7½ gallons.

CURB-CHAIN, a small chain passing from the bridle under the head of a horse; a kind of gold watch-guard.

CURB-ROOF, a roof with a double slope on each side.

CURBS, Cornish granite or other stone, prepared for paving, flat or edged, usually 12 inches by 6 inches; the flag stones at the outer edge or roadside of a pavement, are those usually called curbs or kerbs.

CURD, the common name for the caseine of milk, a solid substance separated from milk by acids, which resembles albumen in several of its properties. It is the basis of cheese, contains nitrogen, and is highly nutritious.

CURD-CUTTER, a machine with revolving knives on a spindle or axis, for cutting the curd, and separating the whey from the curd in cheese-making.

CURDEE, an Indian name for safflower seed.

CURD-MILL, a cheese press, for forcing the whey from the curd.

CURDOWER, a tailor or sempstress who goes from house to house in Scotland to mend old clothes.

CURDS AND WHEY, coagulated milk sweetened.

CURING, the process of slightly salting meat, &c.; also the operation of freeing sugar from its molasses.

CURING-HOUSE, the building on a sugar estate, where the hogsheads of newly potted sugar are placed to harden, and drain off the molasses prior to shipment.

CURLED HAIR MANUFACTURER, a trader in horse hair, who bakes and prepares the rough material for use by others.

CURLING, an amusement in Scotland on the ice, in which two contending parties push or slide forward heavy stones. The object of the player is to lay his stone as near the mark as possible, to guard that of his partner, which has been well laid before, or to strike off that of his antagonist.

CURLING-IRONS, iron tongs for twisting the hair, requiring first to be heated in the fire.

CURLING-STONES, large stones of a hemispherical form, of from 40 to 70lbs weight, with iron or wooden handles at the top, used for playing on the ice.

CURLY-MAPLE, a variety of the *Acer saccharinum*, a North American maple.

CURRAGH, in Ireland a swamp or marsh; an ancient Celtic boat, still in use for fishing on the north-west coast of Ireland.

CURRANT-JELLY, a preserve made by boiling down black or red currants with sugar.

CURRANTS, a small seedless variety of the grape, largely consumed for confectionery and culinary purposes.

CURRENCY, paper money and coin, established as, and passing for, the circulating medium of a country. In the British North American provinces and West Indian colonies, and in some parts of Germany, the term currency is applied to the moneys of account only. In the Canadian currency, £1 sterling is equal to £1:4:4 currency. The following is a statement of the ordinary currencies of the chief countries:—France, Belgium, and Switzerland, francs of 100 centimes; Prussia, thalers of 30 silver groschen, 1 groschen equal to 12 pfennings; Austria, florins of 60 kreutzers; Hamburg, marks-current of 16 shillings; Russia, roubles of 100 kopecks; East India Co.'s territories, rupees of 16 annas; United States, dollars of 100 cents; Great Britain, sovereigns of 20 shillings.

CURRICLE, an open two-wheeled chaise, drawn by a pair of horses.

CURRIER, one who dresses skins, and prepares leathers after they are tanned.

CURRIERS' COMPANY, one of the livery companies of London, whose hall is in Curriers'-court, London Wall.

CURRY, a seasoned dish, flavoured with curry-powder, and of which boiled rice is a necessary accompaniment.

CURRY-COMB, an iron scraper for rubbing down and cleaning the coats of horses.

CURRYING, the art of preparing leather and skins for shoes and other manufacturing purposes.

CURRY POWDER, a seasoning or condiment, originally prepared in the East Indies, and compounded of various pungent and aromatic ingredients, coloured yellow by turmeric root.

CURRY STUFF, a name for the various condiments used to form curries, many of which are transported from place to place in the East, forming extensive articles of commerce. The principal ingredients used by the lower classes for their rice is red pepper, salt, lime juice, and the dried skin of the gorka. The components of a more elaborate curry stuff in Ceylon, are a piece of green ginger, two cloves of garlic, a few coriander and cummin seeds, six small onions, one dry chilli or capsicum, six or eight corns of pepper, a small piece of turmeric, half a dessert spoon of butter, half a coco-nut, and half a lime.

CURTAIN, the hanging for a window, a cloth contracted or expanded at pleasure, made of various material, muslin, merino, damask, &c.

CURTAIN-BAND, a metal rest or support for a curtain.

CURTAIN-MANUFACTURER, a maker of curtains and hangings.

Curtain-paper, a peculiar kind of paper-hangings made in the Western States of America, about 35 inches wide. An ornament within a panel is printed, extending to the length of about 1½ yard, and these are cut off and used as substitutes for roller blinds by a large class of people.

Curtain-rings, rings to which curtains are hung by hooks sewn to the material.

Curtain-rod, a support on which the rings of curtains traverse.

Curvaila Gum, an Indian name for gum arabic.

Curve, a gradual bend in a railway or canal.

Cusco Bark, a variety of Peruvian bark, with a white epidermis, and orange-red cortical layers, yielding an alkaloid called Aricina.

Cuscus Root, sometimes written kuskus, a commercial name for the fragrant rhizoma obtained from a grass, the *Anatherum muricatum*, which, when wetted, emits a strong, penetrating agreeable odour, and is used for making mats, ns, &c. Cuscus root is occasionally im-rted into London. The leaves, like ose of the lemon grass, yield an aromatic stimulant essential oil, known as vitever.

Cush, one of the Indian names for the *Sorghum vulgare*, a species of millet.

Cushion, the padded side of a billiard table; a pillow or air case for the seat of a chair, sofa, carriage, &c.

Cusk, a name for the torsk (*Brosmus vulgaris*), a fish which is sometimes salted and dried.

Cusnee, an Indian drug.

Cusparia Bark, a name for the Angostura bark, obtained from *Galipea Cusparia*, a tree of South America, which is powerfully aromatic and stimulant, and is esteemed for its useful medicinal properties.

Custard, a sweetened cream made of milk, eggs, and spice.

Custard Apple, the yellowish succulent fruit of the *Anona reticulata*, a native of the West Indies and South America, which is of the consistence of custard, and much esteemed by some persons.

Custard Powder, a dry material for making custards, used instead of eggs.

Custode, a chief civil public officer in the West Indies, having the custody of writs, warrants, and other county and parochial legal affairs.

Custodier, one who has any thing in trust in order to its safe keeping.

Custom, a tax or revenue duty levied on goods exported or imported; the patronage or support accorded to a tradesman.

Customer, the supporter of a tradesman, &c.; one who deals with him and purchases his goods.

Custom House, the place appointed by the Government at each port, for the receipt of all duties levied under existing tariffs.

Custom House Agent, one who attends for firms and individuals, to the business of passing and clearing goods at the custom house and docks.

Custom House Entry, a statement made and fees and expenses paid in clearing out a ship.

Custom House Officer, a legally appointed officer of the Customs, to examine and assess goods for duty, &c.

Custos, a name in the West Indies for the chief civil officer of a county. *See* Custode.

Cut, a Scotch term for a quantity of yarn.

Cutch, Kutch. *See* Catechu.

Cutcha, Kucha, a word applied to temporary erections or inferior buildings in India; a weak kind of lime made in the East by burning kunker, a species of flinty chalk.

Cutchall, a kind of Indian snare for fish, made of the stalks of a plant.

Cutcha Maund. *See* Bombay Maund.

Cutcha Seer, a weight in Mysore, 0·59 lb.

Cutcherry, an Indian court of justice.

Cut Glass, glass with sharp edges, which has been shaped by cutting instead of being simply moulded.

Cutie-stone, a stone used in the amusement of curling.

Cutlah, a large Indian river fish, of a dark colour; a species of bream.

Cutlass, a broad curving sword used chiefly by seamen.

Cutler, a dealer in knives and forks; one who makes cutting instruments.

Cutlers' Company, one of the livery companies of London, whose hall is in Cloak-lane.

Cutlers'-spring-maker, a workman who prepares the springs for folding-knives.

Cutlery, a general name for all edged-tools. The British cutlery trade chiefly centres in Sheffield.

Cutlery-manufacturer, a wholesale maker of knives and edged tools.

Cutlet, a fleshy slice of meat usually from the leg.

Cutlings, a name for groats, bruised oat seeds freed of the pericarp, used for gruel, porridge, &c.

Cut-meats, an American term for certain cured meats, hams, shoulders, &c.

Cut-nail-manufacturer, a maker of cut nails.

Cut-nails, nails made by machinery, instead of wrought by hand.

Cutra, a weight in Persia for indigo, of about 139 lbs.

Cuttee, a box to hold weavers' quills.

Cuttemundoo, Cuttemundoo, a hydro-carbon, differing somewhat in its physical qualities from the true elastic gums of commerce, but possessing useful properties. It is obtained in the Peninsula of India, from several species of Euphorbia (*E. antiquorum*, *Tirucalli*, and *neriifolia*).

Cutter, a small boat, a swift-sailing vessel with one mast; a tailor's assistant; a piercing instrument used in boring for water.

Cutter, Revenue, a sloop belonging to the Customs, employed on the coast to prevent smuggling.

Cutters, a description of brick, also called firsts or marle-stocks, 8¾ inches long, by 4¼ broad, and 2½ thick, chiefly used for the arches of windows, doorways, quoins, &c.

Cuttie, Cutty, a Scottish term for short; hence it is frequently applied as an adjective, as cutty-pipe, cutty-stool, &c.

CUTTIES, an Indian name for blooms of iron.

CUTTIE-STOOL, a low stool or seat.

CUTTIE-STOUP, a pewter vessel holding the eighth part of a Scotch chopin or English quart.

CUTTING-PLANE, a carpenter's smoothing tool.

CUTTLE-BONE, a name given to the calcareous plate which strengthens the back of the cuttle fish (*Sepia officinalis*). It was formerly much prized in medicine as an absorbent; it is now almost solely employed for polishing of paint, varnish, wood, or the softer metals, and for making pounce and tooth powder. Large supplies are received at Bombay from the Persian gulf.

CUTTORAH, a metal cup used in India.

CUTTRA, a weight in use at Bassora equal to 136¼ lbs.

CUTTY-PIPE, a short tobacco pipe.

CUTWAL, the chief police officer in an Indian city; also a superintendant of the markets.

CUTWATER, the knee of the head of a ship; the foremost part of the prow which projects forward off the bows.

CUVES. *See* KEAVES.

CUYUPA, an Indian name for the large tubers of a species of Leguminosæ, discovered in the Upper Essequibo by Sir Robert Schomburgk.

CWT., the commercial abbreviation for centum and weight. The Hessian hundredweight is nearly equal to the English, 112 lbs.; the Vienna cwt. is one tenth heavier, or about 123¼ lbs. A cwt. of potatoes is 120 lbs. For the centner and hundred-weight of the Continent, see QUINTAL.

CYANIDE POWDER, a salt of potassium, much used in the electrotype processes; a brilliant white tasteless powder, the cyanide of zinc.

CYANITE, a massive and crystallized mineral; a silicate of alumina, with a trace of oxide of iron.

CYANOMETER, an instrument for determining the deepness of the tint of the atmosphere.

CYANOTYPE, a process of taking solar portraits in Prussian blue, by a wash of cyanogen on the prepared paper, whence the name.

CYATHUS, an ancient Greek and Roman liquid and dry measure of 0.0118 gallon.

CYDER, CIDER, a beverage made from apples.

CYGNET, a young swan.

CYLINDER, a long round case or body; a hollow vessel for steam.

CYLINDER-BOX, CYLINDER-PLATE, parts of a steam cylinder.

CYLINDRICAL-CEILING, a vaulted ceiling.

CYMBALS, musical clappers, concave brass plates used in military bands for producing a clashing sound.

CYPHER, a mode of secret writing

CYPHON, SYPHON, the name of the largest cane-juice receiver in the boiling house of a sugar plantation, capable of holding from 300 to 500 gallons.

CYPRESS-TREE, the *Cupressus* of botanists, a very durable and valuable wood; the tree grows to a great size.

CYPRUS, a thin stuff; a kind of wine.

D.

D. the abbreviation for pence, from the Latin word denarius, a penny: as a Roman numeral D represents 500, and with a dash over it, 5000.

D-TRAP, or VALVE, a trap shaped like a D.

DAB, a moist lump, as of butter, &c.; a small flat fish about eight or nine inches in length; the *Pleuronectes limanda*.

DABOU, a small weight of Masulipatam on the coast of Coromandel, equal to 191 grains.

DABS, refuse forms of sugar.

DACE, a river fish, the *Cyprinus leuciscus*.

DACKAJEE, a Persian silver coin worth about 3s.

DACTYLUS, a Greek measure of length, the sixteenth part of an English foot.

DAFFER, DAPPER, provincial names for small crockery ware.

DAGA (Spanish), the stove of a brick-kiln.

DAGGER, a short dirk or poniard.

DAGING, the Malay name for meat or flesh.

DAGUERREOTYPE, a process of taking sun pictures on plates of iodized silvered copper, highly polished.

DAGUERREOTYPIST, an artist who takes pictures by the daguerreotype process.

DAHAB, a money of account of Abyssinia, worth about 9d.

DAHLIA, a large showy and much esteemed garden flower, of which there are numberless varieties.

DAIKCHEES, metal boilers, used in Hindustan.

DAIKER, from the old Swedish deker, a term applied to twelve hides; the long hundred of 120, or six score, is still used in the sale of oysters and many other articles.

DAIN, the Burman league equal to two miles and two furlongs.

DAINTY, a delicacy; in Scotland the term is applied to any thing large or fine.

DAIRY, part of a farm-building devoted to the making of butter and cheese. In towns the word dairy is applied to milk-houses, and places where milch cows are kept.

DAIRY-FARM, a farm chiefly devoted to meadow and pasture.

DAIRY-MAID, a female domestic employed about the business of a dairy, and in making various kinds of food from milk.

DAIRYMEN, DAIRY-KEEPERS, persons who keep milch cows for the supply of milk, or who attend to the sale of dairy produce.

DAK, or DAWK, a mode of travelling by post in the East.

Dalby's Carminative, a popular nostrum given as an opiate or soothing draught to young children.

Dali, Dari, a large and majestic tree growing in Demerara, the *Virola sebifera*: the wood is light, and splits freely, and is used for staves and headings of casks. From the seeds candles equal to wax are made.

Dalim, Darimba, vernacular names in India for the pomegranate, large quantities of which are imported into the north of India from Cabul and Cashmere. The rind on account of its great astringency is used in medicine, in tanning, and in dyeing yellow. The roots are considered a good vermifuge.

Dall, a large cake made of sawdust, mixed with the dung of cows, used by some of the lower classes in Scotland for fuel.

Daller, a money of account in Sweden, of two kinds, the silver and the copper; three of the latter being equal to one of the former. *See* **Dollar**.

Dalnee, a name in Scotland for damask cloth.

Dam, a wall or mole built across a river, to confine or elevate the water for irrigation purposes, or for impelling mill-wheels, &c.; the mother, as applied to beasts or inferior animals.

Dam, Daum, an Indian copper coin, the fortieth part of a rupee, and therefore worth rather more than a halfpenny.

Damage, in law mischief done by collision, &c.; any injury inflicted or sustained.

Damaged Goods, articles of merchandise or produce which have been injured in transit. The Customs make an abatement of the duties on sea-damaged goods.

Damages, the amount awarded to a plaintiff by a jury for libel, seduction, false imprisonment, or other injury or grievance.

Damar-batu, the Malay name for rosin.

Damascus-steel, a very choice steel made directly from the ore, principally a red oxide of iron, used chiefly for sword-blades.

Damask: washing damask is a fine-twilled linen fabric much used for table cloths, chiefly made at Dunfermline and in Ireland. Brown damask is the same article unbleached. Silk damask is a twilled variegated fabric made in the same manner as linen damask with raised flowers, birds and other ornaments worked into its texture; it was formerly used for dresses, but is now chiefly employed for furniture and upholstery. Worsted damask is also used for the same purposes.

Damassin, a name for silk damask containing gold or silver flowers in the fabric.

Dammar, a valuable clear resin obtained in India from the *Pinus dammara*, and in New Zealand from the kauri pine.

Dammer, a name sometimes given in Scotland to a miner.

Dammour, a coarse cotton cloth which passes current at a fixed value in Nubia.

Damp, a mining name for noxious and explosive gases, the choke-damp being carbonic acid, and the fire-damp carburetted hydrogen.

Damper, an iron sliding plate or valve for shutting off fire in a chimney, or lessening the draught in the flue of a furnace; the Australian name for a baked cake of flour and water; parts of the pianoforte covered with leather acted on by a pedal.

Damson, a small useful black plum, a variety of the *Prunus domestica*.

Damson-cheese, a conserve of dried damsons pressed into a cake.

Dan, a kind of small truck or sledge used in coal mines; a name for the grain for weighing silver, &c., in Calcutta.

Dancing-master, one who gives instruction in the steps and figures of dances.

Dancing-room, a public room licensed for music and dancing; a ball-room in a public or private building.

Dandies (a corruption of Daundee, Hindustani), an Indian name for the boatmen of the Ganges.

Dandy-brush, a hard whale-bone bristle brush.

Dandy-rigged-cutter, a peculiarly rigged sloop.

Dandy-roller, a woven wire sieve for a paper-mill.

Danim, a petty money of Bussorah, in Persia, the twelfth part of a mamoodie, and worth about a halfpenny.

Dannemora-iron. *See* **Oregrund-iron**.

Darah, the Malay name for blood.

Dare, another name for the dace fish.

Darger, a day labourer in Scotland.

Darning-needle, a long needle for mending holes or rents.

Darsena (Spanish), a place in a harbour for laying up and repairing ships.

Dash, a flourish in writing; a bold effort; in Scotland a cant term for a hat or cap; on the West coast of Africa, a present made by traders to headmen or native chiefs.

Date, that part of a writing or letter which expresses the day of the month and year in which it was written.

Dates, the fruit of the date palm (*Phœnix dactylifera*, Linn.), largely used as food in Africa and the East. They enter into commerce as a succade or dried. Wine, spirit, and sugar are made from the date by the Arabs. The hard stones are even ground up as food for their camels, and of the leaves they make baskets and bags.

Datum-line, a given level or line from which to calculate elevations, &c. In the construction of a plan, as of a railway or canal, the surface points are reckoned or measured from the datum level.

Daub, a smear, or rough covering of paint or plaster.

Daucus, a name for Cretan birds' nests imported into Spain.

Daugh, in Scotland a division of land, capable of producing 48 bolls of grain; sometimes written Dawache.

Daum, an imaginary Indian money, the fortieth part of a rupee, which is 2s.

Daunder (Hindustani), a waterman.

Davenport, a piece of furniture in which to keep music books, &c.

Davit, a projecting wooden crane at the bow of a ship for hoisting the flukes of the anchor to the gunwales; davits are also pieces of timber or iron protruding over a ship's side or stern, having sheaves or blocks to hoist a boat up to.

DAW, a cake of coal dross and dried cow's dung, used as fuel in Scotland.

DAWAMESK, a confection of the inspissated juice of hemp and aromatics used by the Arabs.

DAWK, quick Indian travelling by runners, or express.

DAY, the interval between two midnights; but in ordinary acceptation the time of sunlight and period of labour. The period of a day's labour varies in different trades and countries; in the British factories by law it must not exceed ten hours. In navigation, in demurrage clauses the word "day" means working or running days, and does not comprehend Sundays or holidays.

DAY-BOOK, a tradesman's journal of sales and business transactions.

DAY-LABOURER, one hired or working by the day.

DAYLIGHT-REFLECTOR, a shade or screen with a polished metal surface, placed at or over a window to throw more light into a room.

DAY'S JOURNEY, an eastern mode of computing the distance that can be accomplished in the 24 hours, or in such portion of the day as can be fairly given to travel. The Day's Journey of a traveller on foot may be estimated at from 20 to 24 English miles by the road or about 18 geographical miles by the direct distance, if for a very few days, but for many successive days about 17½ miles. In Turkey and Western Persia, though the Tatar couriers ride fast, yet travellers only walk their horses, and their day's journeys may be taken at about 26 to 30 English miles by the road, or as 18 to 23 geographical miles in direct distance. In caravan journeys across the deserts, the day's journey (with camels) is about 16 geographical miles per day, in direct distance for short intervals, but on an extended line, only 15 to 15½; their hourly rate by the road being about 2½ English miles or 2¼ geographical miles. With mules the day's journey is 17 or 18 miles. The mean rate of the daily marches of armies is equal to about 14 British or 12 geographical miles by the road; or, if reduced to direct distance, about 10½ geographical miles on a line of 8 or 10 marches; but a single march or even 2 or 3 taken together will be equal to about 11 geographical miles per day.

DAYS OF GRACE, the period allowed by law or custom, beyond the fixed day of payment, to meet an acceptance or note. In England the days of grace extend to three days.

DAY-TICKET, a railway or steam boat pass available for return on the same day.

DE, another name for the Dutch vingerhoed, a liquid measure used in Holland and the Netherlands. It is the 100th part of the litron or kan, and contains 0·0176 imperial pint.

DEACON, a church officer in Scotland; a clergyman of the Established Church, who has not yet taken priest's orders; the master of a Scotch incorporated company.

DEAD-EYES, oblate solid blocks of wood, with a groove and three holes bored through them, fixed to the channels of a ship, for reeving the lanyards of the shrouds through.

DEAD-LEVEL, a surveyor's term for a flat country, offering no obstructions to road-making.

DEAD-LIGHTS, strong shutters or ports for the stern lights or cabin windows of a ship in boisterous weather.

DEAD-RECKONING, a nautical computation of a ship's position, by the distance run according to the log line in a given time.

DEAD WEIGHT, heavy merchandise forming part of a ship's cargo; a name given to an advance made by the Bank of England to Government on account of the half pay and pensions of the retired officers of the Army and Navy. At the end of the French war in 1815, this sum amounted to nearly five millions per annum; but Government wishing to relieve the revenue of this heavy yearly burden, and to spread it more equally over the forty-five years, which it was calculated the average duration of the lives of the claimants would be, proposed to exchange it for annuities, continuing that period, of £2,800,000 per annum. The bank, after a time, advanced to Government £13,089,419, for which they received an annuity of £585,740 for forty-four years, ending Oct. 10, 1867.

DEAD WOOL, wool taken from the skin of the carcase instead of being shorn from the live animal.

DEAL, a plank of fir or pine timber, for carpenters' use, above seven inches wide; differing from a batten, which must not exceed seven inches; a whole deal is usually 1¼ inch thick, a slit-deal half that thickness.

DEALDER, DAALDER, another name for the Hamburgh thaler, worth about 2s. 7d.

DEALER, a trader in goods of any kind, the specialty indicated by the prefix, as tea-dealer, wholesale-dealer, retail-dealer, &c.

DEBALLER (French), to unpack.

DEBARQUEMENT (French), landing.

DEBARQUER (French), to unlade.

DEBASE, to lessen in value by adulteration or inferior admixtures.

DEBENTURE, originally a writ or note drawn upon government; but the term has now got to be applied to railway companies', municipal, and other bonds or securities for money loaned; a Custom-house certificate.

DEBIT, to charge in an account of a sum due for goods sold on credit. In French it implies a sale or market.

DEBITANT (French), a retailer.

DEBIT-SIDE, in book-keeping, the left-hand page of the ledger.

DEBOUCHE' (French), a market or mart.

DEBRIS, a word adopted from the French, signifying rubbish, waste, or refuse.

DEBT, that which one person owes to another for goods, or money had, &c.

DEBTOR, one indebted for money or wares.

Deca, a term derived from the Greek, signifying ten, and used as a prefix in the French decimal system of weights and measures, to express a weight or measure ten times the amount of the unit which follows it, as décagramme, décamètre, &c.

Decade, a measure of time now applied to a period of ten years.

Decagramme, a French weight represented by a centilitre of pure water. It is the 100th part of a kilogramme, and is divided into 10 grammes, = 100 décigrammes, = 1000 centigrammes, = 154·3402 English grains. In Holland it bears the name of lood, and in Venetian Lombardy gros or grosso.

Decalitre, a French measure of capacity, of ten litres or 2·201 imperial gallons, the tenth part of the hectolitre. It is the new French bushel for grain, and velto for liquids. As a dry measure it is rather more than the English peck, viz: 1·10 peck. In Holland where the decimal system of measures is adopted, they give the name of schepel (boisseau) to the décalitre, and in the kingdom of Venetian Lombardy they call it a mina or mine.

Decamalee-gum, an East Indian gum obtained from the *Gardenia lucida* of Roxburgh.

Decametre, a measure of length, the old French perch, also used in surveying. It is still called the rood or perch in Holland. The décamètre is 1.9884 English poles. It is the hundredth part of the kilomètre, and is divided into 10 metres = 100 décimètres = 1000 centimètres = 10,000 millimètres = 10·936389 yards.

Decant, to pour off gently.

Decanter, a clear glass bottle for holding wine, &c., for the table, or at a tavern bar.

Decapode, another name for the acene, an ancient measure of length, nearly four yards.

Decare (French), an agrarian or superficial measure, equal to the tenth part of the hectare, and divided into ten ares. It is never legally used, being considered superfluous, and fully expressed by ares, hectares, and centiares.

Decastere, a French solid measure, of ten stères = 353·1741 cubic feet.

Decennial, occurring every ten years.

Decharger (French), to unload.

Decheance (French), a forfeiture.

Deciatine, a Russian land measure, usually containing 117,600 English square feet, 2·7 acres; but in Kazan it is greater by one half. *See* Desiatine.

Decigramme, a nominal French weight, the tenth part of the gramme = 1·5434 grains.

Decilitre, a French measure of capacity for liquids, often called a verre, the tenth part of the pint or litre = ·704 gill. As a dry measure the décilitre is equal to ·176 English pint (6.1028 cubic inches).

Decimal, a tenth part, multiplied by ten. The decimal numeration and division of coins, weights, and measures, is becoming very general now in many countries.

Decime, a copper coin and money of account in France of ten centimes, and nearly equal to one penny.

Decimetre, a French measure of length, the palm = 3·9371 inches.

Decistere, the French name for the new solwi = 3·531741 cubic feet.

Deck, the planked flooring of a ship, resting on the beams, which is called upper or lower according to its situation; large vessels have several decks.

Deck-beams, cross beams on which the deck planks are laid.

Decked-boat, a covered boat with a hold or cabin sheltered from the weather.

Deckle, in paper-making, a thin frame of wood fitting on the shallow mould in which the paper pulp is placed; also the rough or raw edge of paper.

Deck-passenger, one who goes a short channel journey at a cheaper fare, and has not the privilege of the cabins.

Declaration, a report of entry; an official affirmation or statement made before a properly authorized officer; in law that part of the process or pleadings in which a statement of the plaintiff's complaint against the defendant is set forth.

Declinator, an instrument used in dialling, for taking the declination and inclination of a plane.

Declinometer, an instrument for measuring the variation of the magnetic needle.

Decoction, a medicinal solution or extract of vegetables, obtained by boiling.

Decomposition, a wasting away or spoiling; compounding a second time.

Decorator, an ornamenter; one who adorns or paints and embellishes houses.

Decorticate, to peel off the bark.

Decoy, a lure; a place for catching wildfowl.

Dedit (French), a forfeit; a consideration.

Dedo (Spanish), a finger's breadth, the forty-eighth part of a Spanish yard or vara.

Dee, Dey, a name in some parts of Scotland for a dairymaid.

Deed, a written or printed legal instrument of agreement between contracting parties, executed under seal.

Deed-box, a tin case for keeping deeds in a lawyer's office.

Deed-poll, in law a deed made by one party only.

Deeds, a name in Scotland for the gravel or coarse soil, &c., which is taken out of the bottom of a ditch.

Deemster, Demster, a judge in the Channel islands and Scotland.

Deep-sea-line, a line with a plummet, shot, or other attachment for taking soundings at great depths at sea.

Deer, a general name for animals of the Cervus family, which have deciduous horns or antlers: their flesh is termed venison. Deer's horns enter largely into commerce.

Defaced Coin. On the 20th August, 1853, a new Act, 16 and 17 Vict., chap. 102, to prevent the defacing of the current coin of the realm, came into operation. It enacts that if any person shall deface any of the Queen's current gold, silver, or copper coin, by stamping thereon any name or words, whether such coin shall or shall not be thereby diminished or lightened, or shall use any machine or instrument for the purpose of bending the same, every such offender shall, in England and Ireland, be guilty of misdemeanour, and in Scotland of a crime or offence; and, being convicted thereof, shall be liable to fine or imprisonment, at the discretion of the court. The second provision is of such general importance that it may be given at length: "No tender of payment in money made in any gold, silver, or copper coin, so defaced or stamped as aforesaid, shall be allowed to be a legal tender; and, if any person shall tender, utter, or put off any coin so defaced, stamped, or bent as aforesaid, he shall, on summary conviction thereof, before two justices, be liable to forfeit and pay any sum not exceeding 40s., provided always, that it shall not be lawful for any person to proceed for any such penalty as last aforesaid, without the consent (in England or Ireland) of her Majesty's Attorney-general for England or Ireland respectively, or (in Scotland), of the Lord Advocate." A notice was subsequently issued from the Treasury, "that it was not the intention of the Government, in passing the act to impose any difficulty in regard to such coin as may become defaced by ordinary wear and use; or in relation to persons who, in the ordinary course of business, pay coins which are defaced. The immediate object of the Government in obtaining the act, was to put a stop to a practice of stamping the names of persons, firms, &c., upon coins by way of advertisement or otherwise, and the intention of the Government was to reach by penalties the persons who in this or in any other wilful or malicious way injured the coin."

DEFAULT, a failure of payment of instalments, &c., agreed upon, or in the due execution of a contract.

DEFAULTER, one who makes away with public moneys intrusted to his care; a trader who fails in his payments, or is unable to meet his engagements.

DEFECATION, the act of cleaning or separating liquors from the lees or dregs.

DEFECT, a failure or blemish.

DEFENCE, a justification; a legal reply to a plaintiff's declaration.

DEFENDANT, the person accused or summoned in a court of law, to answer the charges of a plaintiff.

DEFICIENCY BILLS, a kind of short loan or advance made to the Government by the Bank of England, whenever the taxes received are insufficient to pay the public dividends due on Government stocks.

DEFICIT, a deficiency, something wanting.

DEFINITION, an explanation given; the description of a thing.

DEFORMITIES-APPARATUS MANUFACTURER, a mechanic who prepares metal fittings for injuries or defects in limbs and parts of the body.

DEFRAUDER, a cheat; an embezzler; one who wrongs another.

DEHANA (Spanish), a farm and farm buildings.

DEGREE, 60 geographical miles, the 360th part of the circumference of a circle. The French degree is now the 400th part of the circle. A degree of the meridian and of longitude, necessarily varies, in measurement with the locality.

DEJEUNER (French), luncheon, a morning meal.

DE LAINE, a sort of thin figured muslin, sometimes made entirely of wool, at other times of a mixed fabric.

DELAISSEMENT (French), an abandonment.

DEL CREDERE, an Italian commercial term, implying a guarantee for the solvency of a purchaser.

DELE, to strike out, or omit; in Scotland the term is used synonymously with deal, to divide or share out.

DELF, DELFT-WARE, a coarse species of pottery or imitative porcelain, originally manufactured at Delft in Holland, and covered with a white enamel or glaze. Blue and green clay are those chiefly used for this ware.

DELFINA (Spanish), a kind of light drugget.

DELINEATION, a draught, or outline sketch.

DELIVERY TAP, an outlet pipe.

DELVE, to dig, to open the ground with a spade.

DEMAND, a claim made for a debt due; the asking or requiring of a price for goods offered for sale.

DEMESNE, a manor-house and lands contiguous to it.

DEMI, a prefix signifying *half*.

DEMI-CULVERIN, a large gun carrying a ball of from 9 to 12 lbs. according to size.

DEMIJOHNS, taken from the French *damejeanne*, large round glass bottles, which are generally encased in osier baskets or wicker work to prevent fracture; they hold about two gallons.

DEMISE, in law, a conveyance or transfer, as of a ship, tenements, &c.; to bequeath by will.

DEMPLE, a dibble or instrument for setting potatoes. [Channel Isles.

DEMPSTER, a judge in Scotland, and the

DEMURRAGE, a delay or detention in loading or unloading a ship, beyond the time stipulated; also the payment to be made for it. Legal holidays and Sundays are not included in demurrage charges. The term is also applied to land carriage by wagons, railways, &c. The railway clearing-house has fixed a tariff of demurrage for the detention of trucks, horse-boxes, wagons, and carriages belonging to other companies.

DEMY, the name for a particular size of paper, which is about half the size of columbier; drawing demy is the smallest, 15 inches by 20; printing demy is 17½ by 22½; also an ancient gold coin of Scotland, worth about 12s.

DEMYOSTAGE, a kind of tammy or woollen stuff used in Scotland.

DENARE, a money of account at Leghorn, about a penny sterling.

DENARIUS, an ancient Roman silver coin worth eight-pence of our money; also a former name for the English penny.

DENDENG, a name in the east for the muscles and sinews of the deer, ox, buffalo and wild hog, dried in the sun, which form an article of export from Siam and the Indian islands chiefly to China.

DENDROMETER, an instrument constructed for measuring the heights and diameter of growing timber.

DENEGRIDA, a Mexican name given to the blackened carcases of the cochineal insect, which have been killed by water.

DENIER, a Prussian piece of money, the twelfth part of a silver bon gros. It is also called a pening. A weight in Denmark, the fourth of a quintin; a French scruple; an ancient French penny; in Italy, a small weight equal to about a grain, by which silk is weighed.

DENIER-LUBS, a current coin and money of account in Hamburgh, the sixth part of a denier gros. At Hamburgh there are many debased pieces of 6 and 3 deniers in circulation, the first of which are called suchslings and the second drellings.

DENIER-TOURNOIS, an old copper coin and money of account in France, the twelfth part of the sou, which answered to our penny.

DENIZEN, a free-born subject, the native of a country or state, as distinguished from an alien, who does not possess civil rights.

DENMARK-SATIN, a stout worsted stuff used for covering ladies' shoes, &c.

DENNET, a two-wheeled carriage.

DENNUM, a land measure of Candia or Crete equal to about forty square yards.

DENREE (French), commodity or produce.

DENSITY, compactness.

DENT, a mark, an impression.

DENTELLE (French), lace.

DENTIFRICE, a powder or wash for cleansing the teeth.

DENTILS, architectural ornaments, consisting of small square blocks or projections resembling teeth, in the bed-mouldings of cornices.

DENTIST, an operator on the teeth, who repairs or extracts them; one who makes and fits false teeth.

DENTS, the French name for teeth; applied by manufacturers to the teeth of a comb or metallic brush or "card," and the canes or wires of the reed frame of a weaver's loom.

DENY, a kind of woollen.

DEODAR OIL, an empyreumatic medicinal oil obtained from *Erythroxylon areolatum*; deodar is also the name for a species of pine of the Himalayas, the turpentine of which is used as a stimulant to foul ulcers.

DEODORIZE, to purify, to remove unpleasant smells.

DEPA, a land measure in Prince of Wales Island equal to two English yards.

DEPARTMENT, a classified range or branch of duties assigned to one or more persons; a subdivision of official work, a separate allotment of business.

DEPENSES (French), expenditure.

DEPILATORY, any substance employed to remove hair from the skin.

DEPOH, a long measure of Sumatra equal to seventy-two inches.

DEPONENT, one who makes a deposition, or gives in a written statement.

DEPORT, the French stock-exchange term equivalent to our word Backwardation. *See* BACKWARDATION.

DEPOSANT (French), a depositor in a bank.

DEPOSIT, a lodgment; money paid on account of a purchase; a pledge or pawn; any thing intrusted to the care of another.

DEPOSITION, the written statement made by a deponent.

DEPOSITOR, one who has money lodged in a savings' or other bank, &c. The owner of goods, &c. entrusted to the care or safe keeping of another.

DEPOSIT-RECEIPT, a note or acknowledgment for money lodged with a banker for a stipulated time, not less than three months, upon which an agreed rate of interest is allowed.

DEPOT (French), a railway station; an agency, warehouse, or temporary repository for goods.

DEPRECIATION, a diminished value; a reduction of worth.

DEPTH, the measure of any thing from the surface downwards.

DEPURATOR, a French machine for cleansing and preparing cotton for spinning; the exhibitor of which received a Council medal at the Great Exhibition in London in 1851.

DEPUTATION, a body of persons delegated to represent and to wait on others upon matters connected with public affairs.

DEPUTY, a subordinate officer; one commissioned to act for another, as deputy-commissary, deputy-lieutenant, &c.

DERAA, an Arabian cloth measure. The ancient "deraa belledi," used for local purposes, in measuring linen, &c. made in the country, is 22⅔ inches; but the deraa Stambouli employed to measure European cloths, is 26⅔ inches. Another deraa, the "Hindazeh" of 25 inches, is used to measure goods coming from the East Indies.

DERBYSHIRE SPAR, fluoride of calcium, which occurs in beautiful cubic crystals of a blue, white, or variegated colour.

DERELICTS, goods found at sea, relinquished or abandoned by the owner.

DERHAM, a weight in Persia, of 150 troy grains, by which gold and silver are weighed.

DERHEM SEGAR, a petty copper coin current in Algiers; the twenty-ninth part of the mouzonah.

DERHM, DERHIM, the Egyptian name for the drachm.

DERI, a name in the East for goat's hair from the dead skin.

DERRICK, a temporary crane, consisting of a spar supported by stays and guys, carrying a purchase for hoisting in or unloading goods, &c. on board ship.

DERRICK-CRANE, an improved iron crane, the projecting beam or derrick of which can be raised or lowered to different angles from the upright.

DERSETINE, DESATINE, a land measure of Russia. *See* DESSATINE.

DESA, a name in Java for a village.

Desabollador, a tin worker; an instrument used by the tin-man in Spain.

Desbagar (Spanish), to extract the flax seed from the capsule.

Descamino, in Spain, contraband goods seized for non-payment of duty.

Descarga (Spanish), a clearance at the custom-house; a discharge, the unloading a ship.

Desertion, an absconding from service, as in the case of an apprentice or seaman, soldier, &c., which involves forfeiture of wages due, and other civil disabilities; and in the government service, the penalty of death.

Deshabille (French), an undress.

Deshollinador (Spanish), a chimney-sweeper.

Desiatine, a Russian land measure, sometimes written deciatine; 104 desiatines make a square verst, three versts being equal to two English miles. As a superficial measure it is ordinarily equal to 270 English acres or 117,600 square feet, but in Kazan it is greater by one half. As an imperial measure in Russia the desiatine is 2400 square sachine or sagene = 21,600 square arsheens = 13066⅔ square yards. In some districts the domestic desiatine is 3200 square sachine.

Desiccation, the process of driving off water by heat or exposure.

Design, a draught or plan; an invention; a pattern, drawing, or figure.

Designer, an inventor or draughtsman; one who sketches figures and patterns for enriching stuffs, &c.

Designer and Stamper, an artist who invents patterns for lace workers, and cuts them upon wooden blocks, by which he sends out the pattern slightly stamped on the material with some coloured pigment.

Desire', a kind of dress material imported into Hayti.

Desk, a writing-flap or inclined table with enclosures; in counting-houses and offices it is usually fixed; but in private rooms or studies it is generally moveable.

Desk and Dressing-case Manufacturer, a maker and fitter of these portable boxes.

Desmarojador, one who takes off the glutinous rind from olives in Spain.

Despalmador, the Spanish term for a careening place for cleaning and paying the bottoms of ships.

Despampanador, a pruner of vines in Spain.

Despatch, to transmit or forward goods, invoices, or other advices.

Despensero, a Spanish butler; a ship's steward or providore.

Dessert, a service of fruit and sweetmeats at the close of an entertainment.

Dessert-knife-maker, a manufacturer of silver fruit-knives, and other fancy mounted dessert knives.

Dessert-service, the china or glass requisites for the after-dinner confections.

Destrados, a coarse woollen carpet.

Destral (Spanish), a small axe.

Detaillant (French), a retailer.

Detainer, a writ or legal notice lodged with the keeper of a debtor's prison, for continuing a person in custody after a former debt is discharged.

Detective, a police officer.

Detenteur (French), a holder or possessor of funds, bills, &c.

Detents, stops in clock-work machinery.

Deterioration, damage done; wear and tear.

Determa, a native wood of Guiana, which is used for masts, booms, and planking for colonial craft; and as it is not infested by insects, it is well adapted for chests, wardrobes, &c. It will square from 14 to 16 feet.

Detonating-powder, fulminating mercury, silver, or other compounds which explode when struck or heated. Gun-cotton also explodes.

Deviation, a departure from a ship's authorized course; also applied to an irregularity of the compass.

Devil, a spiked mill employed in Yorkshire for reducing to fragments woollen rags intended for the manufacture of shoddy; also a highly seasoned dish; a printer's boy; a fire-work.

Devis, a French word for estimate.

Devisee, one entitled to a bequest of real estate.

Devonshire Batts, a valuable fine-grained porous sandstone obtained from quarries in the vicinity of Collumpton.

Dew-retting, the exposure of flax in the fields to the action of the rain, dew, or snow, to effect by maceration the decomposition of the gum or resin which coats the fibre.

Dextrine, a chemical name for what is termed British gum, the calcined starch of wheat or potatoes. It is largely used for stiffening fabrics, and also for the adhesive substance on postage and receipt stamps, and envelopes. About fifty or sixty tons are used weekly in the print-works of Glasgow and Manchester.

Dha, a name for the bamboo, a long measure of 7 royal cubits, the thousandth part of the Burman league. *See* Dain.

Dhadium, a commercial weight in some parts of the East of 3 lbs 5 ounces 8 drachms.

Dhal-baat, an Hindustani name for rice and yellow pease stewed together.

Dhan, a vernacular name in parts of Hindustan for rice.

Dharanum, a weight of Mysore in India equal to 40 grains.

Dharoos, a Bengalee name for the *Hibiscus esculentus*, the edible mucilaginous fruits of which are much esteemed in the tropics.

Dhenroos, a name in Bengal for the fibre of the *Hibiscus esculentus*, known in the West Indies as the ochro, and in parts of Asia as the bayndie.

Dhie, Dhye, an Indian wet-nurse for a European child; a lady's attendant.

Dhobie, Dhoby, an Indian washerman usually attached to a household, and paid a monthly wage according to the number of the establishment.

Dhoby's-earth, an unctuous earth used in scouring and washing in India.

Dholl, the Indian name for the pigeon pea, *Cytisus Cajan*; an eastern commercial term for a bale or package; also beads of carnelian made at Cambay in India.

DHOLUCK, a large Indian drum.

DHONEY, a native coasting vessel in India, sloop-rigged or with two masts, seldom more than 150 tons.

DHOONA, an Indian name for the dammar or resin obtained from the *Shorea robusta.*

DHOOP, an eastern name for the *Vateria Indica*, a tree the fruit or nut of which, about the size of a large walnut, furnishes a fine solid oil known as Piney tallow, which is wholesome and edible, and also used for lamps.

DHOTEE, DHOTY, a waistcloth or loose wrapper; a long narrow strip of cotton or gauze worn by the male Hindoos, instead of pantaloons; it is sometimes ornamented with a silk border.

DHOURIA, an Indian name for wormwood.

DHOW, DOW, an Arabian coasting vessel trading between the Persian gulf, the Red sea, and the peninsula of India.

DHURRA, a variable eastern measure of capacity; in the Bombay presidency it contains 10 seers, and is equal to 19lbs. 11 ounces 6¾ drachms; occasionally it is 12 to 18 seers. In some parts of Guzerat the dhurra or dhurree is only 12lbs. 8 ounces 7½ drachms, and in Malwa it is but 3lbs. 12 ounces.

DHURRA, DOURAH, a species of *Holcus*, the principal grain crop of Egypt after wheat, which is largely used there by the labouring classes for food, and also forms the currency of Nubia. Varieties of this grain are grown in many parts of Africa, and cargoes often reach the London market from the Levant.

DHYE. *See* DHIE.

DIACHYLON-PLASTER, a medicinal adhesive plaster used as a strapping; the basis of which is litharge and olive oil.

DIACITRON (Spanish), candied lemon-peel.

DIAGRAM, a rough delineation, an explanatory sketch or drawing.

DIAGRIDIUM, an old commercial name for scammony.

DIAL, an instrument for registering time by the sun's rays falling upon an index or gnomon, whose shadow marks the progress of the hours. There are a variety of dials, horizontal, oblique, or vertical, and also depending on their aspect with reference to the sun.

DIAL-PLATE, the face of a clock or watch, on which the hours are marked, or of a dial on which the lines are drawn.

DIAMANTAIRE (French), a diamond cutter.

DIAMETER, width; measurement across the centre.

DIAMOND, the smallest kind of regular printing-type that is cast in British foundries; the hardest and most valuable of gems; a tup or shearling ram.

DIAMOND-BORT or POWDER, the crushed refuse fragments of the gem, which is used by lapidaries, seal-engravers, watch-jewellers, and others.

DIAMOND-CUTTER, a lapidary; one who cuts, sets, and works gems.

DIAMOND-PENCIL, a cutting instrument used by glaziers and glass-cutters.

DIAMOND-WEIGHT. Diamonds are weighed by carats, 151½ of which make an ounce troy; this carat is therefore equal to 3 1-5th troy grains.

DIAPER, a fabric made of flax; damask of small size and simple patterns, used for napkins, towelling, &c., is chiefly made in Dunfermline in Scotland, and the north of Ireland.

DIAPHANE, a woven silk stuff with transparent and coloured figures.

DIAPHORETICS, sweating medicines.

DIARY, a note-book or journal; a register or record of daily business or events.

DIASTASE, a chemical substance extracted by water from crushed malt, which possesses the remarkable property of converting starch into sugar in an hour or two.

DIASTIMETER, a philosophical instrument for measuring distances.

DIBBLE, a small spade; a pointed garden instrument for making holes in the ground for planting.

DIBS, a sort of treacle made in Syria from grapes.

DICE, to weave or form figures of waved pattern; small cubical pieces of ivory or bone, numbered with dots on the sides, for casting in games of chance. There is a duty of £1 on each pair of dice.

DICE-BOX, a leather, bone or other case for holding dice to throw at hazard, or games of chance.

DICKER, a commercial term for ten of some things, and for the long hundred of others, as ten skins make a dicker of hides; ten bars a dicker of iron, ten dozen a dicker of gloves; and so on. *See* DAIKER.

DICKEY, a loose shirt front to be worn over a soiled shirt.

DICOTOLI, the eighth part of a gallon in Corfu.

DICTIONARY, a book of reference for the orthography and definition of words, or for terms of art, science, &c.

DIE, a stamp or reversed impression, used for striking medals, coining, &c.; an ivory cube, one of a pair of dice used in gaming.

DIE-SINKER, a maker of metal dies.

DIETARY, a table of rations supplied daily, on board ship, or to soldiers, persons in prisons, workhouses, &c.

DIET-DRINKS, beverages prepared with various medicinal ingredients.

DIGEST, an abstract of a speech or decision; a compendium or summary of mercantile law, disposed under proper heads.

DIGESTER, a metal vessel with a detached cover to be screwed down, and some elastic interposing substances to prevent the loss of heat by evaporation. It is chiefly used in chemical operations to raise the boiling fluid to a higher temperature than 212 degrees, the better to act on solids, by softening and preparing them.

DIGESTIVE BISCUITS, coarse brown biscuits.

DIGGING, the operation of turning up or loosening the earth by hand labour with a spade or fork.

DIGGINGS, a popular name for the localities where gold is found, in Australia and California.

DIGIT, a Roman letter, or character, which represents a numeral as I for one; V for five; L for fifty, &c. As a measure the digit is three-fourths of an inch.
DIKAMALI, DECAMALEE, a fragrant resinous gum which in India exudes from the tops of the branches of the *Gardinia lucida*. It is extensively used as a dressing for slight injuries and wounds, and is sold in some parts as googul.
DIKE, DYKE, the Scotch name for a stone fence; in engineering, a hydraulic embankment similar to those employed in Holland to keep out the sea; in mining, a kind of faulty vein; a ditch or channel for water.
DILAPIDATION, waste or decay in buildings, &c.
DILIGENCE, a lumbering French passenger carriage.
DILLOCK, a seasoning made of cayenne, salt, and a little pea-meal used in Abyssinia.
DILL-OIL, a yellow oil, obtained from the seeds of *Anethum graveolens*, which are stimulant and carminative.
DIME, a small silver coin and money of account of the United States, the tenth part of a dollar, and worth five-pence; there are also half dimes.
DIMENSION, the extension of a body considered as capable of being measured; bulk, extent, capacity.
DIMITY, a fabric of cotton, used for bed-furniture and other purposes, which is made both plain and striped or cross-barred; it was formerly imported from Damietta.
DINAR, a petty imaginary money of Persia.
DINERAL (Spanish), a large sum of money; a measure for wine and oil; also a weight used by assayers.
DINERO, a money of account in Alicant, the twelfth part of a sueldo; twenty sueldos making one libra or peso, worth 3s. 3d.
DINGO, the wild dog of Australia, which is a great pest to the stock-keeper, destroying his sheep.
DINGY, a small ship's boat.
DINING-ROOMS, an eating-house, where diners are served to casual customers.
DINING-TABLE, a massive solid table usually supported on four legs, sometimes extensible and capable of being materially enlarged by extra leaves or flaps.
DINMONT, DIAMOND, the name in Scotland for a shearing tup or ram, a year and a half or two years old.
DINNER, the most substantial meal of the day.
DIORAMA, a scenic exhibition embracing the union of transparent and opaque painting, with a judicious use of light before and behind the picture represented.
DIPIN (Scotch), part of a herring net.
DIPLEIDOSCOPE, an instrument for observing the transit of the sun over the meridian by day, or of the stars by night, so as to correct a time-keeper.
DIPLOMA, a medical licence, or honorary document, conferring some power, privilege, or honour.
DIPPA, a Malayan measure equal to the breadth across the body with the arms extended; the dippa is divided into four hastas or short cubits.
DIPPEL'S OIL, an empyreumatic oil produced during the destructive distillation of bones.
DIPPER, an utensil for taking up fluids in a brewery; the vatman in a paper-manufactory.
DIPPING, a composition of boiled oil and grease used in Scotland by curriers for softening leather and making it more fit for resisting dampness; in England it is called dubbing. Also the process of washing sheep to cleanse the fleece before shearing.
DIPPING-NEEDLE, an instrument for indicating the direction of magnetic force; a needle which dips or inclines to the earth.
DIPS, a common name for small or store candles, which are made by merely dipping cotton wicks repeatedly in a cistern of melted tallow.
DIRECTOR, a manager; a member of a board, one appointed to superintend the affairs of a private establishment or public company.
DIRECTORY, an alphabetical address or guide-book to the inhabitants, trades, &c. of a city, with their places of abode.
DIRHEM, a small weight used at Angora; 400 make one oke, which is equal to 2¾ lbs. *See* DERHM.
DIRK, a short dagger.
DIS, a name in Algiers for the fibrous stems of *Festuca patula* and *Arundo festucoides*, which are used for cordage, &c.
DISBURSEMENTS, money paid out.
DISCALE (French), a shrinkage.
DISCHARGE, a release, as when a soldier or sailor is released from his period of servitude, a prisoner dismissed, &c.; the unloading of the cargo of a vessel.
DISCOLORATION, the art of altering the colour of any thing; injury or damage to walls or goods, &c.
DISCOUNT, an allowance, or rebate for prompt payment on a bill or debt not yet due; the sum paid by way of interest, for the advance of money, as on a bill of exchange, &c., not due till a future period.
DISCOUNT-BROKER, one who cashes bills of exchange, or makes advances on securities.
DISCOUNT-DAY, the day of the week on which a bank discounts notes and bills.
DISH, a broad open vessel of earthenware or metal, for holding food; a large trough in which miners measure ore.
DISH-COVER, a metal or earthenware cover for retaining the heat; metal covers are made of silver, block tin, and Britannia metal.
DISH-MAT, a straw, oiled cloth, or other table [mat.
DISHONOURED, a commercial term for the return, unpaid, of a draft or acceptance legally due when presented.
DISINFECTING LIQUOR, chloride of soda or lime in solution.
DISMANTLED. A vessel laid up in dock with her spars, upper masts, rigging, &c., removed, is said to be dismantled.
DISMASTED, a vessel which has lost one or more masts. [express messenger.
DISPATCH, a letter, &c. forwarded by an

DISPENSARY, a public institution for the sale of medicines, where they are often dispensed free to the poor.

DISPENSATORY, an authorized book on pharmacy, emanating from a College of Physicians, containing the properties of drugs, and directions for the use and compounding of medicines.

DISPENSER, one who distributes or administers; usually applied to medicines.

DISPONER, a person who legally transfers property from himself to another.

DISPOSE, to sell or get rid of, to apply to any purpose or use.

DISSECT, to investigate, to cut in pieces.

DISSELBOOM, the pole of a wagon in the Cape colony.

DISSERTINE, an extent of land in Syria, as much as can be ploughed by a pair of oxen in eight hours.

DISSOLUTION, a breaking up, as of a contract or partnership.

DISTEMPER, a kind of size or body-colour painting, with colours to which some unctuous or glutinous matter has been added; a disease incident to dogs, horses, &c.

DISTIL, to extract by heat; to separate spirit or essential oils from liquor by evaporation or heat.

DISTILLER, a manufacturer or preparer of spirits, one who distils from malt, or prepares perfumes; a rectifier and compounder.

DISTILLERS' CHEMIST, a chemist who supplies materials used in distillation.

DISTILLERS' COMPANY, one of the livery companies of the city of London, which has no hall, but transacts its business at Guildhall.

DISTILLERY, a building in which distillation and the rectification of spirits is carried on.

DISTINGUISHING PENNANT, the special flag of a ship, or a particular pennant hoisted to call attention to signals.

DISTRAIN, to seize for debt, or levy upon goods, &c., for rent or taxes.

DISTRESS, a levy or distraint for rent, &c.

DISTRIBUTION, in printing, the breaking up of a form, or page, &c. of type; and replacing the letters in their proper cells in the compositor's cases.

DISTRICT SURVEYOR, a local officer legally appointed to superintend repairs, examine buildings, &c.

DISTRINGAS, a writ commanding the sheriff to distrain on a person for debt, or for his appearance at a certain day.

DISTY-MELDER, in Scotland, the last quantity of meal made of the crops of one year.

DITCH, a trench in the earth made by digging.

DITTO (abbreviated to Do., in books of accounts and bills), denotes the aforesaid, or the same thing.

DIURETICS, medicines which operate by increasing the discharge of urine.

DIVER, a man who descends under water; one employed in fishing for pearl oysters, chank shells, sponge, or in other submarine operations.

DIVIDEND, the commercial name for the interest allowed on government stocks, foreign bonds, and various other public securities, which are usually payable half yearly. The dividend on consols and a few other government securities is due on January fifth, and July fifth, and is receivable four or five days afterward. On the Reduced 3 per cents., of Bank Stock, April fifth and October tenth. On East India Stock, January sixth and July sixth; and on India Treasury bonds, April first and October first. Dividend is also the proportionate payment made to creditors out of the estate of a bankrupt, and the profits received by stock and share holders in public companies and associations at stated periods.—*Ex div.* is a Stock Exchange abbreviation, implying that a security is dealt in without the dividend due or accruing.

DIVIDEND WARRANT, an order or authority upon which shareholders or stockholders receive their half-yearly interest.

DIVIDERS, a trade name for compasses.

DIVI-DIVI, a commercial name for the wrinkled pods of the *Cæsalpina coriaria*, used in tanning.

DIVING-BELL, an apparatus for carrying on submarine operations; the men who descend being supplied with air from the surface by means of pipes or tubes worked by a force-pump.

DIVING-DRESS, a waterproof helmet and clothing, supplied with air for submarine operations.

DIVIT, DIVOT, a thin flat oblong turf used in Scotland for covering cottages, and also for fuel.

DIVIT-SEAT, a turf bench at the door of a cottage.

DIWANI, a name for the para in Abyssinia, a petty money, of which five are worth about a halfpenny.

DJUNG, a large superficial measure for land in the Eastern archipelago, equal to four bahus or about 28¼ acres.

DO. *See* DITTO.

DOBRA, DOBRAON, the doubloon, a Portuguese obsolete gold coin, worth about £6 10s. to £6 14s.

DOCENO (Spanish), a kind of cloth; to cut short, to curtail.

DOCK, an artificial enclosure or basin for the reception of ships. Wet docks and basins are for loading and unloading cargoes, or laying up vessels; dry docks and slips, for building or repairing ships. The latter are called graving docks.

DOCK-CHARGES, certain dues payable on vessels and goods entering or leaving the docks.

DOCK COMPANY, the corporate body or association owning docks.

DOCKET, to label; a memorandum affixed to papers implying their meaning; a ticket attached to goods specifying their measurement; also what is tied or fastened to a bundle, as a direction where to deliver it. To strike a docket is a term frequently used for entering a declaration of bankruptcy against a person.

DOCK-MASTER, a resident officer who has the superintendence of docks.

DOCK-RENT, charges for storing and warehousing goods in a dock.

DOCK-WAREHOUSES, stores and sheds within the docks.

DOCK-YARD, a private or government yard, near a harbour or roadstead, where naval stores are kept, and ships built and repaired.

DOCRA, a nominal weight in Bombay, of 16 buddams or almonds.

DOCTOR, a local name for the knife in a print-machine which cleanses the surplus colour from the surface of the engraving cylinder; a medical man holding the degree of M.D.

DOCTORING, a term applied to injuring or adulterating, as doctoring seed, horses, &c.; the operation of removing with a knife the excess of colour from the cylinder in calico-printing.

DOCUMENT, an official or authoritative paper containing instructions or proof for information, and the establishment of facts.

DOCUMENT-BILL, an Indian bill of exchange drawn on London, having as collateral security the bill of lading and policy of insurance on the goods; against a part or the estimated value of these the bill is drawn.

DODD, to cut the wool from the tails of sheep.

DODDER-CAKE, an oil cake made in Lubeck from the marc of the seed of the *Camelina sativa*.

DODRANTE (Spanish), a weight of nine ounces; a measure of twelve inches.

DOE, the female of the fallow deer; the wooden ball used in the game of shinty in Scotland.

DOER, a Scotch name for an attorney, manager, or steward; synonymous with factor.

DOESKIN, woollen for trowsers; a name for deerskin prepared for gloves.

DOFFER, part of a carding machine.

DOG, an iron grab or hook with crooked teeth, used by ship-wrights for driving into timber, to move or hold it; a name for the andiron which is used to support logs of wood on a fire hearth; a name in the West Indies for the three-halfpenny piece, formerly current there; a well-known domestic animal, in many varieties of which there is a considerable trade carried on; the skin and fat of the dog have also commercial uses.

DOGANIERE, a custom-house officer in Italy.

DOG-BISCUIT, coarse, waste or broken biscuits sold for feeding dogs.

DOG-CART, a sporting carriage with a box for carrying pointers; also a light jaunting car.

DOG-FISH, a species of shark, the *Scyllium catulus*. On the North American coasts the catch of these fish is large for the oil their livers yield, and other commercial products. If of good size a dog-fish will yield a barrel of oil of 31½ gallons. The dried bodies are sold in Nova Scotia at 2s. 6d. the hundred for feeding pigs during the winter from November till May: two fish broiled or roasted are given per day to a good-sized store pig. The rough skin of the dog-fish is used for polishing wood and other substances.

DOGGAR, coarse iron stone.

DOGGER, a one-masted Dutch fishing-vessel resembling a ketch, often fitted with a well for fish.

DOGGRANE, a kind of cloth known in Scotland.

DOG-KENNEL, a building for housing hounds, or other dogs kept for coursing, &c.; a wooden hutch for a house dog or watch dog.

DOG-LOAF, the name for the small three-halfpenny loaf or roll of bread in many of the West India islands, which varies in weight from 6¼ to 2¼ ounces, according to the official assize of bread, regulated by the price of flour.

DOG-SHORES, pieces of wood fitted to the upper end of the bilgeways on a building-slip, which are knocked away to facilitate the sliding or launching of a vessel.

DOG-SKIN, gloves, &c. are made of the skin of the dog.

DOG'S-MEAT, paunches, boiled horseflesh, offal, &c. vended as food for dogs.

DOG-STONES, rough, shaped or hewn pieces of stone imported to make millstones.

DOG-VANE, a small vane on the mast-head to show the direction of the wind.

DOG-WATCH, a short watch or spell of duty on shipboard of only two hours.

DOGWOOD, the produce of *Piscidia erythrina*, a deciduous tree indigenous to the tropics; the bark of the roots is used as a narcotic to stupefy fish. The dogwood of America (*Cornus florida*) is used for inlaying by cabinet-makers; the bark is also an esteemed tonic, and used in the manufacture of ink.

DOH, a name in Java for the horsehair-like fibre of the Ejoo or Gomuti palm, (*Arenga saccharifera*, Labill.).

DOIGT, the hundredth part of the French metre.

DOIT, half a bodle; the old Scotch copper halfpenny, twelve of which made a penny sterling. Doit or duit was also a Dutch copper coin, the eighth part of a stiver, worth little more than a farthing; it is not current now.

DOLADOR (Spanish), a joiner.

DOLCINO, DULCINO (Italian), a small bassoon formerly much in use.

DOLE, to mete out in small quantities.

DOLEY, a part, a division of the Russian pound, 96 doleys making 1 zolotnik, and 96 zolotniks 1 Russian pound: 10 Russian pounds are equal to about 9¼ English pounds.

DOLL, a child's baby toy; a name for pigeons' dung in Scotland.

DOLLAR, a coin current in the United States of America, parts of South America, China, and some of the Continental States of Europe. It is usually the largest silver coin of a country. The American dollar is divided into 100 cents, and is valued at 4s. 2d. There are Sicilian, Austrian, and Spanish dollars, which are estimated according to their weights and fineness. The following figures show the relative weight and fineness of some of the principal dollar coins:—

	Weight. Grains.	Fineness. Thousandths.
United States dollar 1792-1836	424	892½
United States dollar after the year 1837	417	900
The new United States dollar since 1853	386	—
Mexicans of all dates about	416¾	899
Chilian dollars	416¾	901
Peruvian, mixed	415	905
Bolivian 1827 to 1837	416½	905
do. 1840 vary in weight	416½	900
Spanish Carolus 1772-1808	412	893
do. Ferdinand 1808-1821	414	909
Brazilian restamped	412	896

To convert sterling money into dollars and cents, reduce the former to pence, double the amount and call it cents, and mark off by a decimal point the two right-hand figures of the product for dollars and cents. *See* DALLER AND THALER.

DOLL-MAKER, one who makes sham infants as playthings for children.

DOLL'S-EYES, glass beads which are extensively made in Birmingham, and also imported from Austria, the trade being valued at about £15,000 per annum.

DOLLY, in mining parlance a perforated board, placed over a tub containing ore to be washed, and which being worked by a winch-handle, gives a circular motion to the ore.

DOLOMITE, a variety of magnesian limestone, admirably adapted for mortar, as it absorbs less carbonic acid than the common limestone; a white variety of dolomite was used by ancient sculptors.

DOLPHIN, a spar or buoy, with a large ring in it secured to an anchor, to which vessels may bind their cables.

DOMBA OIL, a fragrant fixed oil obtained in India from the seeds of the Alexandrian laurel (*Calophyllum inophyllum*). It is used for burning and for medicinal purposes, being considered a cure for the itch.

DOME, an arched or spherical roof raised over the centre of a building.

DOMESTICATE, to tame, to make familiar.

DOMESTICS, a strong bleached sheeting, or cotton manufacture of America; household servants or hired labourers. *Domestic* is also a carriage for general use.

DOMETT, DOMMETS, a mixed cotton and woollen fabric for baize; also a kind of white flannel made in Germany.

DOMICILE, a dwelling; a place of permanent residence.

DOMICILED BILL, a bill not made payable at the residence or place of business of the acceptor, but directed for payment by the acceptor at the time of his acceptance.

DOMINO, a masquerade dress, a long silk mantle or loose wrapper with a hood and wide sleeves; a marked piece of bone or ivory used in playing a game.

DONATION, a gift or bequest.

DONEY, a kind of Indian river ferry-boat, made of basket-work of a circular form, eight or ten feet in diameter, covered with leather; also a larger coasting vessel. *See* DHONEY.

DONKEY, an ass for the saddle or for draught.

DONKEY-ENGINE, a kind of steam-pump to feed boilers.

DOODOO, DOODY, an old Indian copper coin the eighth part of a fanam, worth less than a halfpenny.

DOOGANY, a petty Indian copper coin of Arcot; worth about one farthing.

DOOLOO, a name in Bootan for the roots of the small-stalked variety of rhubarb.

DOOLY, an Indian covered litter or palanquin, often used for conveying the sick or wounded.

DOOMAULAH, the Indian name for a two-storied house.

DOOM-PALM, the *Hyphæne Thebaica*, which is highly valued in Egypt for its fruit. The wood is used for various domestic purposes; the rind of the fruit, which resembles gingerbread in appearance and taste, is eaten, and the kernel turned into beads for rosaries.

DOON, an Indian land measure, equal to about 6·85 English acres.

DOOPADA RESIN, a resin obtained in considerable quantities in the East Indies, from the *Vateria Indica*; which is used as a fragrant incense in the temples, makes an excellent varnish, and is sometimes called *East Indian copal*, or gum Piney.

DOOR, any moveable opening or entrance for access to a building, room, or closet; a frame of boards that shuts the opening, &c.

DOOR AND DRAWER KNOB MAKER, a turner, or one who prepares and sells wooden, porcelain, and metal handles for the doors of rooms and for articles of furniture.

DOOR-FASTENER, the catch for a door.

DOOR-FURNITURE, the iron work required for doors.

DOOR-HANDLE, the knob of a door.

DOOR-HINGE MAKER, a worker and dealer in hinges for hanging doors with.

DOORIAHS, a cotton fabric made in India.

DOOR-KEEPER, one who has the charge of the entrance-way in a house or public building; a gate porter.

DOOR-KEY, the latch or lock key for a street or other door.

DOOR-KNOB, a handle for turning the latch of a door.

DOOR-KNOCKER, a hand rapper for a street door or outer door on a stairway.

DOOR-LATCH, an iron bolt or catch for fastening a door.

DOOR-MAT, a coarse rough mat placed at door-ways or entrances from the street, to clean the shoes on.

DOOR-PLATE, a metallic engraved name plate.

DOOR-PLATE MAKER, one who prepares metal name-plates, and gets them engraved.

DOOR-SPRING MAKER, a maker of elastic and other springs for doors.

DOORVAGER, a Turkish mason.

DOOSOOTEE, thick tent cloth of cotton made in India.

DOPPIA, another name for the pistole, an Italian gold coin, worth about 18s. 6d. In Rome the doppia consists of three crowns and thirteen bajocchi, or 318 bajocchi.

DOPUTTA, a wrapper or garment of cotton, worn by the natives of India.

DOREEA, a petty money of account of Bombay worth about a halfpenny.

DOREMAL, a kind of flowered muslin made in Spain.

DOREY, the colonial name, in the Gulf of Mexico and the West Indies, for a canoe hollowed out of a log of wood.

DORMER, the upper or attic window on the sloping roof of a house.

DORMEUSE POST CHARIOT, a travelling carriage.

DORMITORY, a sleeping-place.

DORNAR, a small Spanish fishing-boat.

DORNICK, a stout figured linen made for table-cloths, used in Scotland.

DORSOUR, cloth for hanging on the walls of a hall or chapel in Scotland.

DOSE, a variable quantity or portion of medicine to be swallowed; the proportion of any thing liquid applied in manufactures.

DOSS, in Scotland a tobacco pouch.

DOT, a small point or spot, made with a pen or other sharp-pointed instrument.

DOTCHIN, a Chinese portable balance for weighing coins and merchandise, made somewhat after the plan of the English steel-yard. In Hong Kong, and other ports open to British trade, it is doubly graduated with circles of brass pins to mark British and Chinese weights.

DOUANIER, a French Custom-house officer.

DOUBLE-BARRELLED, a gun having two barrels.

DOUBLE-ENTRY, a mode of book-keeping which offers facilities for detecting errors in accounts.

DOUBLE-MANUFACTURER, a maker of galloon and double, a kind of silk material for shoe ties and binding.

DOUBLE PICA, a type one size larger than paragon, and one size smaller than two-line pica.

DOUBLE SOVEREIGN, a British coin, of which some were minted a few years ago, but none have been coined these ten years past.

DOUBLETS, a pair; a name given to counterfeit gems, crystals in two thicknesses, with a colour between them; a kind of netted silk; a waistcoat or jacket.

DOUBLOON, a common Spanish and South American gold coin, which weighs 417·70 troy grains, of which 365·40 grains are pure. By the bullion dealers of London the Spanish doubloon, full weight, is taken at 65s. to 67s. 6d.; the Mexican, Patriotic, and South American doubloons, 64s. to 65s.; the Sun or Tree doubloons, at 58s. to 61s. There are also half and quarter doubloons of proportional value. This coin being the form generally given to gold in the mining countries of South America, is, like the dollar, extensively circulated as bullion.

DOUCEUR, a gift or bonus.

DOUGH, flour or meal which has been kneaded with water, and leavened with yeast ready for baking.

DOUGHLAGHMAN, the name given to an esculent sea weed, *Fucus vesiculosus*, which is held in high estimation by the peasantry on the coast of Donegal.

DOUGH-NUT, pastry fried or boiled in lard.

DOUSE, a sudden lowering.

DOUZAIN, an old French coin worth a sou; douzaine is also a dozen.

DOVE-COT, a small building or box in which domestic pigeons breed.

DOVER'S POWDER, a valuable diaphoretic preparation, the compound powder of ipecacuanha.

DOVE-TAILING, a neat and secure method of joining wood-work.

DOVETTY, a wrapping cloth or garment of silk, or some mixed fabric, worn by rich natives in Madras.

DOW, an Arabian coasting vessel, with one mast, carrying a lateen sail.

DOWEL, a pin of wood or iron used at the edges of boards, in laying floors, to avoid the appearance of nails on the surface.

DOWELLING, a method of corking or joining by letting pieces into the solid, or uniting two pieces of timber together by tenons.

DOWLAS, a strong coarse kind of bleached linen for sheeting, &c., made chiefly in Yorkshire, Dundee, and Forfarshire. It is now much superseded by calico.

DOWN, the fine short breast plumage of the eider duck and other birds; a large open plain on the top of a hill.

DOWNHAUL, a rope attached to a staysail or jib to pull it down by.

DOWN-TRAIN, a departing railway train.

DOWSING, a superstitious mode of discovering a mineral lode by the divining rod.

DOYLEY, a small fancy napkin or plate cover, of different materials.

DOZEN, the number twelve.

DRAAIBORD, a sort of turn-table to a colonial-made wagon in the Cape colony.

DRAB, a woollen cloth of a dun colour, made in Yorkshire, generally woven thick and double milled, for great coats; a kind of wooden box used in salt-works for holding the salt when taken out of the boiling pans.

DRABBETS, a coarse linen fabric or duck, made at Barnsley, &c.

DRACHM, DRAM, the principal silver coin and money of account in Greece, worth 8½d. sterling. In Britain, the term dram is applied to two weights; in apothecaries weight, to the eighth part of the troy ounce, or 60 troy grains; and to the one-sixteenth part of the avoirdupois ounce, or 27 11-32nd troy grains. The latter, however, is seldom used. In medicine, the drachm weight is expressed in prescriptions by the symbol ʒ, equal to 3 scruples, or, in liquids, the eighth part of an ounce measure. In Turkish weight, the drachme is the hundredth part of the ordinary cheque, and = to 49 3-5th grains troy.

DRAFF, a common name in Scotland for refuse or dregs, and for brewers' grains used for feeding cattle.

DRAFT, a check or order for money on a banker or other person; a deduction allowed from the gross weight of goods; a plan of a building; a rough copy of any writing. The draft of a ship is the number of feet she sinks in the water.

DRAFT-NET, a seine or hauling net.

DRAFTS, DRAUGHTS, turned pieces of wood or bone, &c. for playing the game of drafts on a chequer board.

Drag, a dredging machine; a kind of hook for recovering dead bodies under water; a skid or chain to lock the wheel of a vehicle in descending hills; a four-horse coach.

Dragon Cane, a thick kind of rattan imported from China, with long internodes and a hard bark, less flexible than the common rattans, but strong, springy, and much valued. A variety with soft bark is called Manila dragon cane, and is believed to be the stem of *Calamus Draco*.

Dragon's Blood, a resinous astringent extract, of a deep red colour, obtained from the fleshy fruits of the *Calamus Draco*, a plant of Sumatra and the Malay Islands. It is chiefly used as a colouring ingredient for spirit and turpentine varnishes and paints, for staining marble, preparing gold lacker, dentifrices, &c.

Drag-rope, a rope attached to a ship, canal boat, or any object for traction.

Drain, to draw off or filter; also a sink or water channel.

Drainage, the systematic process employed for carrying off water from land.

Drainage Company, a joint-stock association empowered by Act of Parliament to carry out drainage operations for improving the estates of a landowner, and to charge the lands with the gradual repayment by certain instalments.

Draining-pipe Maker, a manufacturer of draining pipes and tiles, &c.

Draining-tiles, burnt clay tiles, usually horseshoe-shaped, one foot long, by two to three inches broad, about half a million tons of which are annually manufactured.

Drain-pipe. *See* Stone-ware.

Drain-traps, contrivances for preventing the escape of foul air from drains, but allowing the passage of water into them.

Drake, the male of the duck.

Dram, a small quantity of an alcoholic draught.

Drama, a play, whether comic or tragic.

Dramatist, a writer of plays.

Dram-bottle Manufacturer, a tradesman who cases with leather or straw, and sells glass bottles for travellers and others, for the pocket.

Drape (French), woollen cloth; to make cloth, to barter.

Draper, a dealer in cloth, as a woollen-draper or a linen-draper.

Draper's Company, the third of the twelve great London livery companies. The first charter of the guild was granted in the thirty-eighth year of Edward III. The hall of the company is in Throgmorton street.

Drapery, an artist's term for the clothing or dress of a figure or statue; by upholsterers it is applied to bed and window curtains, tapestry, and hangings of any kind. Also a general name for the woollen and linen fabrics retailed by drapers. In its primary sense, from the French word "drap," it means woollen goods only, but has been extended to cotton prints and linens. Thus we call a dealer in calicoes a linen-draper, to distinguish him from what is called a draper, but the goods of both are alike denominated "drapery."

Drapier, a French clothier, or cloth manufacturer.

Draping, the ancient name for making cloth; whence the word draper.

Drappiere, an Italian weaver.

Drappit Eggs (Scotch), fried eggs.

Drappo, a name for silk stuffs and cloth in Italy.

Draps d'été, summer cloths twilled like merino.

Drastics, medicines which are rapid and powerful in their operations.

Draught, a term applied to the depth of water which a ship displaces when she is afloat; a drench for cattle; a drastic purgative.

Draught-bar, an agricultural implement; a swing-tree.

Draught-board, a folding chequered board for playing the game of draughts.

Draught-horse, a cart-horse; one employed in husbandry.

Draught-ox, an ox employed in ploughing, or drawing a wagon; in the Cape colony it is called a trek ox.

Draughtsman, a delineator, one who designs from instructions, or prepares drawings, plans, and elevations of buildings, diagrams for lectures, &c.

Draw, to haul or pull along; to sketch, or design; to raise water from a well, or liquors by a tap.

Drawback, an allowance or return of the duty on exporting goods that had previously been imported.

Drawbar, an iron rod used to connect a locomotive with a tender.

Drawboys, assistants to the shawl weavers at Paisley.

Drawbridge, a bridge that can be lifted or swung, placed over a dry moat or water channel at the gate of a fortified city, over a dock entrance, canal, or navigable river.

Drawee, the person upon whom a bill is drawn.

Drawer, the person who draws a bill.

Drawer-handle, a knob or metal handle for attaching to drawers.

Drawers, sliding boxes for holding articles which can easily be drawn out and returned to their places; light under-clothing for the legs.

Drawing-board Maker, a manufacturer of boards for artists.

Drawing-knife. *See* Knife.

Drawing-instrument Maker, a manufacturer of the mechanical appliances for painters.

Drawing-master, one who teaches the art of drawing.

Drawing-room, the chief apartment or reception-room of a dwelling-house or mansion.

Drawing-room-chairs, light fancy and highly ornamented chairs, suited for a drawing-room.

Drawing-slate. *See* Black Chalk.

Draw-link, a contrivance for connecting railway carriages together.

Draw-plate, a stout plate of shear steel pierced with one or more holes, for drawing wire through.

DRAY, a low heavy luggage cart, a kind of brewer's vehicle on which barrels of beer are transported.

DRAYMAN, the driver of a dray.

DREDGE, a drag-net for taking oysters and other mollusca; a machine for clearing mud in a river; a mixture of oats and barley sown together.

DREDGER, one engaged in working a dredging machine; a ballast lighter.

DREDGING-BOX, a tin box with perforations in the lid for sprinkling flour on meat, &c.

DREDGING-MACHINE, an engine used to clear away sandbanks, and to take up mud or gravel from the bottoms of rivers or harbours.

DREGS, the lees or sediment of liquors; the refuse in the manufacture of tallow.

DRENCH, a medicinal draught for horses and cattle; the horn scoop by which it is forced down the throat.

DRESSED, a term applied to stone or other material, shaped and smoothed; ore prepared and fitted for use.

DRESSER, a piece of kitchen furniture, a fixed side-board with shelves, &c. for plates and dishes; an officer in an hospital.

DRESSING, a starch, or gummy stiffening, glaze, or other application to linen, silks, &c.; manures applied to land; trimming and smoothing rough stones for masonry; cleaning or preparing grains, ores, &c.

DRESSING-CASE, a box fitted with apparatus and toilet utensils for a dressing-room.

DRESSING-CASE-INSTRUMENT MAKER, a maker and vender of such articles.

DRESSING-GOWN, a loose morning robe or wrapper.

DRESSING-ROOM, a small ante-room attached to a sleeping apartment.

DRESSING-ROOM TABLE, a table for a dressing glass and other conveniences.

DRESS-MAKER, a mantua-maker, one who makes ladies' dresses.

DREYLING, an Austrian liquid measure containing thirty Vienna wine eimers.

DRIERS, a material added to oil paints. *See* DRYERS.

DRIESTACH, the dross of a turf fire, which glows when stirred.

DRIFT, a hardened steel tool; a horizontal passage in a mine; a drove of cattle.

DRIFT-NET, a fishing net about twenty feet deep, by 120 feet long, well corked at the top, but without lead at the bottom. The size of the mesh is 2½ inches or upwards; frequently a dozen or more of these nets are attached to each other lengthwise by a drift-rope.

DRILL, an agricultural implement used for dibbling or sowing grain and seeds. There are many combined machines, as drill-harrows, drill-ploughs, &c.; an instrument for boring holes; a stout white linen twill used for trowsers; a machine for cutting circular holes in metal; the act of training soldiers to their duty.

DRILL-BOW, the moveable handle of the drill.

DRILL-GRUBBER, an agricultural implement for cultivating land.

DRILL-MANUFACTURER, a maker of drills.

DRILL-SERJEANT, a military non-commissioned officer who trains soldiers.

DRILL-STOCK, the holdfast for a metal drill.

DRINKING-HORN, a cup made out of pressed horn.

DRIPPING, the fat that falls from baked and roast meat.

DRIPPING-PAN, a tin dish for receiving the gravy and fat, which drops from meat in roasting before the fire.

DRIPSTONE, a filter for water.

DRITTLE, a silver money of Prussia, worth about 1s.

DRIVER, a coachman, one who drives beasts; the manager of a locomotive engine; a storm sail, a sailor's name for a spanker; the after sail of a ship or bark; a piece of wood upon a weaver's spindle which impels the shuttle through the opening in the warp.

DRIVING-BAND, the strap, belt, or gearing for uniting, turning, and carrying machinery.

DRIVING-WHEELS, the large wheels of a locomotive engine.

DROG, a name given in Scotland to a buoy attached to the end of a harpoon line.

DROGHER, a West Indian cargo boat employed in coasting, having long light masts and lateen sails.

DROGUISTE (French), a dealer in drugs.

DROIT, a division of the troy grain used by moneyers; a legal claim or title, duty, &c.

DROP, a machine for lowering coals from railway staiths into the holds of colliers.

DROSHKI, DROSKY, DROITSKA, a Russian pleasure carriage or sledge.

DROSOMETER, an instrument for measuring the fall of dew.

DROSS, the refuse or scales from metals, slag, cinders, &c.; impure matter.

DROUD (Scotch), a codfish; a kind of wattled box for catching herrings.

DROVE, a description of tooling by parallel perpendicular flutes on the face of hard *stones*; a narrow irrigating channel; a herd of cattle, or a number of animals driven in a body; the broadest pointed iron instrument used by a stone-mason in Scotland in hewing stones.

DROVER, one who drives cattle or sheep to market.

DRUG BROKER, a licensed broker who deals in drugs.

DRUGGET, a coarse flimsy woollen fabric, printed or plain, used for carpeting, packing, and for rough female garments in Scotland.

DRUGGIST, properly one who buys or sells drugs; a wholesale dealer; but commonly applied to one who combines the retail business of chemist and druggist, and sells surgical instruments and various miscellaneous articles in common demand.

DRUG-GRINDER, one who pulverizes drugs in a mill for the chemist and druggist.

DRUG-MILL, a mill where drugs, &c. are crushed and ground.

DRUGS, animal and vegetable products used in pharmacy; the raw material from which medicines are compounded.

Drum, a well-known musical instrument, consisting of a hollow cylinder covered at the end with vellum skin, there are side drums, large bass drums, and double or kettle drums. Also a circular box in which dried fruit is sent here for sale, weighing when full, from ¼ to ½ of a cwt. The large flat tubs in which fish are packed in New Brunswick for the Brazil markets are called drums; each drum contains exactly 128lbs. of pressed codfish, that being the Portuguese quintal. The drums are shaped to suit the convenience of the Brazilians, who transport them into the interior of South America, slung in pairs upon mules. Also the hollow short cylinder revolving on an axis, over which the driving bands or ropes of machinery pass, setting in motion several small wheels.

Drumhead, the top of a capstan containing holes in which the capstan bars are fixed; the parchment or vellum skin stretched on the top of a drum.

Drum-maker, a manufacturer of drums.

Drummock, in Scotland meal and water mixed.

Drummond-light, an intense light procured by the combustion of coal gas and oxygen on lime.

Drum-sticks, a pair of short sticks with which the drummer beats his drum.

Dry-dock, a graving dock; one which can be laid dry in order to examine and repair the bottom of a ship.

Dryers, litharge, sugar of lead, white copperas, and other desiccatives, added to oil paints to cause them to dry quickly.

Dry-goods, a commercial name for textile fabrics, cottons, woollens, laces, hardwares, and some few other articles; in contradistinction to groceries.

Dry-goods-store, an American name for a warehouse or shop devoted to the sale of cotton and other manufactured articles for personal use.

Dry-goose, in Scotland a handful of fine meal pressed very close together, dipt in water, and then roasted among the ashes of a kiln.

Drying-oils, linseed and other oils which having been heated with oxide of lead; dry quickly on exposure to the atmosphere and retain their transparency on solidifying. Drying-oils are essential for the purposes of the painter and for the manufacture of printing-ink; they also form the basis of many paints and varnishes. Castor-oil, linseed-oil, poppy-oil and walnut-oil are among the drying-oils.

Drying-stove, a stove used by laundresses; also one employed by founders and others.

Dry-rot, a decay in timber; a disease which attacks wood, and renders it brittle, by destroying the cohesion of its parts.

Dry-salter, a dealer in the minerals used in pickling, salting and preserving various kinds of food. Also in gums, drugs, dye-stuffs, mineral colours, tanning substances, artificial manures, &c.

Dry-stove, a place constructed for the plants of dry, arid climates.

Duanie, an Arabian money, worth about a halfpenny, 40 of which make up a cruse. *See* Diwani.

Dub, to reduce the end of timber; a division of the rupee in Mangalore also called a dudu, equal to about 2½d; a weight in Mysore about ¼ an ounce.

Dubash, an Indian interpreter or commissioner, employed by ships and Europeans at the seaports.

Dubbeltje, a division of the rixdollar in the Eastern archipelago equal to about 6d.

Dubber, **Dupper**, a leather bottle or skin bag, used chiefly in India for holding oil, ghee, and other liquids, and capable of holding, according to size, from 20 to 80lbs. weight.

Dubbing, a sea term for working with an adze; a greasy composition used, and the process employed, for softening hard shoes and other articles of stiff leather. *See* Dipping.

Dubble, a monetary division of the florin in Batavia, equal to about 2½d.

Ducape, a rich silk.

Ducat, a gold coin current in several European States, generally of the value of about 9s. 4d. There are also silver ducats in some of the Italian States, worth only about a third of this value.

Ducatoon, a Dutch silver coin of the same value as the rixdollar, and passing for nearly 4s. in Sweden and Denmark. In Holland and the Netherlands it is about 5s. 6d.

Duchesses, **Duchess-slates**, large-sized slates, 24 by 12 inches.

Duck, a fabric lighter and finer than canvas, made of flax, used for small sails, seamen's trowsers, &c; a water-fowl, wild and domesticated, much esteemed as food.

Duckling, a young duck.

Ductilimeter, an instrument for comparing the ductility of lead, tin, &c.

Duddah, a name for the fourth part of the maund in Bangalore.

Duddie, a wooden dish with two ears used in Scotland, which is generally of an octagonal form on the brim.

Dudu, another name for the Dub, an Indian money.

Duffadar, a subordinate officer in an Indian army; thus there are quarter-master duffadars, pay duffadars, &c.

Duffels, **Duffields**, a thick coarse kind of woollen cloth having a thick nap or frieze.

Dugong, a name in Australia and the Indian ocean for the *Halicore Dugong*, which is taken for the oil obtained from the blubber. This oil is asserted to be equal to cod-liver oil, and is a cure for diseases of the ear. The bone of the animal in fineness and hardness of grain, specific gravity, and appearance, approaches nearly to the nature of ivory. The flesh of the dugong is often eaten.

Duim, a Dutch long measure; the Netherlands duim or centimètre is 1½ square inches. In cubic measure it is the third of a cubic foot.

Duk, **Doh**, a name in Java for the material, like *horse-hair*, covering the petioles of the Ejoo or Gomuti palm, *Arenga saccharifera*, Labill.

Dukkun, a small species of millet raised in Socotra.

DULCIMER, a triangular chest, strung with wires, which are struck with a little rod held in each hand.

DULLAUK, a Persian barber who attends the baths.

DULSE, DYLISK, an edible alga (*Rhodomenia palmata*), which is sold in the Irish markets, it is eaten raw by the peasantry.

DULSHIT, the name for a small bundle in some parts of Scotland.

DUMAREE, a petty nominal money on the Malabar coast, of 4 cowry shells; the third part of the copper pice.

DUMB-BELLS, heavy metal weights swung in the hands for exercise, to open the chest and increase muscular strength.

DUMB-SINGLES, a kind of silk merely wound and cleaned.

DUMB-WAITER, a dining-room stand, with shelves and conveniences for holding various requisite articles.

DUMMY, a sham package in a shop; a hatter's pressing iron; a name given by firemen to the jets from the mains or chief water pipes.

DUMPLING, a kind of pudding of wheaten flour; in cookery usually a casing or cover of paste, enclosing apples and boiled; in Scotland it is a bannock made of oatmeal and suet boiled in broth.

DUMPY, short and thick.

DUMPY LEVEL, a spirit level with a telescope for surveying purposes.

DUMRIE, an imaginary money of account in Malwa, the eighth part of a pice.

DUN, a persevering person; one employed in soliciting the payment of debts

DUNBAR WEDDER, a name given by some of the lower classes in Scotland to a salted herring.

DUNDER, the fermenting lees of cane-juice, used in the distillation of rum.

DUNG, the excretory deposit of animals; a general name for farm-yard or stable manure. The dung of most animals possesses a commercial value; that of dogs and of pigeons is used in tanning; horse dung in foundries; that of cows in calico-printing: under the names of album-græcum, argols, guano and other heads, the uses of most of these are noticed.

DUNGALLY, a small liquid measure in the East; 11½ dungallies making one chora-dany, = 1 3-32nd quart.

DUNGAREE, DUNGARY, a coarse kind of unbleached Indian calico.

DUNGHILL, a waste heap of ashes, refuse substances or manure, &c.

DUNGHILL-FORK, a prong for lifting or turning straw, manure, &c. in a farm or stable yard, &c.

DUNGING, manuring land; the term is also applied to the act of steeping printed calicoes in a bath of cow-dung, at a certain stage of the process.

DUNLOP CHEESE, a quality of cheese made in Scotland, very like the Derbyshire; namely, a sweet, rich, white variety.

DUNNAGE, loose articles of merchandise permitted to be shipped for the convenience of stowing, securing and filling up cargo, such as billet-wood, coco-nuts, &c.

DUNNING, a common term for urgent pressing for the payment of a debt; also a mode of curing cod-fish in New Hampshire, so as to give them a particular colour.

DUNNOCK, a kind of boat used at the head of the Persian gulf.

DUNSTABLE STRAW, wheat straw used for bonnet plaits. The middle part of the straw above the last joint is selected; it is cut into lengths of about ten inches, which are then split by a single machine into slips of the requisite width. Whole Dunstable signifies that the plait is formed of seven entire straws, while patent Dunstable consists of fourteen split straws.

DUNTER, a cant term in parts of Scotland for the porpoise.

DUNTER-GOOSE, a name given to the eider-duck.

DUODECIMO, a volume formed by folding the sheet into 12 leaves, making 24 pages. It is written for shortness, 12mo.

DUPICHO, an elastic bitumen obtained about the roots of *Siphonia elastica*, in Brazil.

DUPION, a double cocoon formed by two silkworms.

DUPLEX, a double or compound movement in a watch.

DUPLICATE, a second article of the same kind; a copy or transcript; a pawnbroker's ticket for a pledge deposited, being a fac-simile of a similar ticket fastened to the article left in pledge.

DUPPER, DUBBER, a skin bottle or leather bag for liquids, used in the East, holding ordinarily about 80 lbs. of oil.

DURMA MATS, mats made in India of the split stalks of the nul or nar, a grass of Bengal.

DURO, the hard dollar of exchange of Spain, of 20 reals, and worth about 4s 2d.

DUROY, a kind of figured serge, very commonly worn by the lower orders in the West of England some years ago.

DURRA, a kind of Egyptian millet. *See*, DHURRA.

DURZEE, an Indian tailor.

DUSSOOTEE, a species of Indian calico.

DUST-BRUSH, a light feather or hair brush for cleaning rooms and furniture.

DUST-CART, a scavenger's cart.

DUST-CONTRACTOR, one who leases from the authorities the right to remove the waste substances, street sweepings, and refuse deposits in a parish or district.

DUSTERS, a common linen material, white; twilled with coloured borders, or blue checked with red borders, for servants' use.

DUST-HOLE, an ash-pit; a place for rubbish.

DUSTMAN, a street-cleaner, and contractor for the removal of filth, dirt, and accumulated refuse of any kind.

DUSTOOREE, an Indian term for commission or perquisites.

DUST-PAN, a broad, flat, tin shovel.

DUTCH-CARPET, a mixed material of cotton and wool, used for floor-coverings.

DUTCH-CHEESE, a small round cheese made on the Continent from skim milk.

DUTCH-CLINKERS, long narrow bricks of a brimstone colour, very hard and well-burnt, imported from Holland. They appear almost vitrified by heat.

DUTCH-DROPS, a balsam or popular nostrum, prepared with oil of turpentine, tincture of guaiacum, nitric ether, succinic acid, and oil of cloves.

DUTCH-GOLD-LEAF, a mixture of copper and zinc, in the form of thin leaves or foil, in the proportion of eleven parts of copper to two of zinc. *See* LEAF METAL and BRONZE-POWDER.

DUTCH-METAL-LEAF MAKER, a preparer of leaf metal.

DUTCH-OVEN, a tin hanging screen for cooking before a kitchen range or ordinary fire-grate.

DUTCH-PINK, a painter's colour, obtained from the plant *Reseda luteola*.

DUTCH RUSH, a plant; the horsetail or shave grass, *Equisetum hyemale*, which from its hard and rough exterior surface is found useful for polishing marbles, hard woods, ivory, brass, and other substances. The rhizomes are nutritious, and have been used as food in times of famine.

DUTCH-RUSH IMPORTER, a merchant who receives Dutch-rushes from the Continent for sale.

DUTCH-TILES, glazed and painted ornamental tiles; formerly much used to plaster up in the jambs of chimneys.

DUTTON, a variety of Indian corn or maize grown in America.

DUTY, a tax on goods or merchandise; the work done by a steam engine; the business of a soldier or marine on guard.

DUVET (French), down or fine feathers.

DWANG, a large iron bar used by blacksmiths in Scotland, for screwing nuts for bolts, and by quarrymen and others for raising large stones.

DWELLING-HOUSE, a tenement intended to be inhabited, as contra-distinguished from a store or office.

DWT, the abbreviation for pennyweight.

DYE, a colour, stain, or tinge.

DYEING, the process of colouring substances by immersion; the art of developing and extracting the colouring particles from any substance, and of uniting and fixing them afterwards upon cloth, stuff, or any other material.

DYER, one whose occupation is to dye fabrics, &c., and who practises the art of staining or colouring cloth.

DYERS' COMPANY, one of the livery companies of London, whose hall is situate in College-street, Dowgate-hill.

DYERS'-WEED, the *Genista tinctoria*, *Reseda luteola*, and *Isatis tinctoria*, native plants which are sometimes used by dyers.

DYE-SAUCER MAKER, a preparer of pink saucers and rouge colouring substances.

DYESTER, a Scotch name for a dyer.

DYESTUFFS, a collective trade term for the dyewoods, lichens, powders and dye-cakes entering into commerce for dyeing and staining purposes.

DYE-WOODS, various foreign woods, used by the dyer and stainer, when cut and ground, to extract colours from.

DYKE, a ditch; in Scotland a stone wall; a dry-stone dyke is one built without mortar; a fail dyke is a wall of turf.

DYKER, one who attends to the ditches; in the North a builder of stone walls about 5 or 6 feet high for enclosures.

DYMMOND, a name in Scotland for a wether of the second year.

DYNAMETER, an instrument for ascertaining by a simple process the magnifying power of telescopes.

DYNAMOMETER, an instrument which measures any thing to which the name of power has been given, whether of animal bodies, or machinery, &c. Reignier's dynamometer consists of two plates of steel of a curved form, increasing in thickness towards the ends, which unites into solid cylindrical loops; the curved sides of the plates being placed opposite to each other, and the whole forming an entire elliptic spring. On the application of this instrument as a *link* in the line of draught, the oval becomes lengthened in proportion to the degrees of force acting on the loops in opposite directions, and the curved sides approach more nearly towards each other, accordingly. The degree of approximation in the plates, is shown on a scale in divisions corresponding to half and whole hundred-weights, by means of a cross rod secured to one plate acting on a crank attached to the opposite one, thus communicating its effect to the lever index, which, moving over the divisions of the scale, marks the varying degrees of force exerted each moment by the draught to which the instrument is subjected. Messrs. Cottam and Hallen, of London, and Mr. R. Clyburn of Uley, have invented dynamometers, which are improvements on those previously in use, as they also register the space through which the power is exerted.

DZERD, an Algerine measure of length, of which there are two kinds, the dzerd-a-Torky = to 2·099 English feet, and the dzerd-a-Raby = to 1·574 feet.

E.

EAGLE, the principal gold coin of the United States, which is a legal tender for 10 dollars. The new eagle, since 1843, weighs 258 troy grains, 9-10ths fine, and contains 232 1-5th grains pure; and, estimating British standard gold 11-12ths fine at £3 : 17 : 10½d. per ounce, is equal to £2 : 1 : 1 1-6th sterling. The half eagle, the most common gold coin of the States, is of proportional value; there are also quarter eagles.

EAGLES' FEATHERS have a commercial value, being used for ornament in Scotch bonnets, and the large quills for making artists' hair pencils, &c.

EAGLE-STONE, a description of clay iron ore.

EAGLE-WOOD, a fragrant wood said to be obtained in the East from *Aloexylum agallochum*, and used for incense by the Asiatics. It is the calambak or lignum aloes of commerce. *See* AGALLOCHUM-WOOD.

EARING, a rope attached to the cringle or ring of a ship's sail, by which the sail is bent or reefed.

EAR-MARK, a mark made by slitting or notching the ears of sheep, pigs, dogs, and other domestic animals, to identify them.

EARNEST, a certain sum of money paid to the seller by a purchaser, to bind a verbal bargain. In France, the parties are at liberty to withdraw from such a bargain on the following conditions:—the intending purchaser forfeiting his deposit, and the intending seller repaying double the amount deposited.

EARNINGS, wages gained by servitude, or for work and labour done.

EAR-PICK, a small instrument for cleansing the ear of the cerumen.

EAR-RING, a jewel or ornament suspended from the ear by a gold or other ring passing through the lobe. Ear-rings are mostly worn by females; but they are often worn by European or Oriental males.

EAR-SHELL, a flattened univalve, species of *Haliotis*, much prized for the enamelled iridescence of its inner nacreous coating, which renders it useful for inlaying papier-maché work, &c.

EARTH-BOARD, the mould-board of a plough; that which turns over the furrow.

EARTHEN-WARE, the common name for the ordinary classes of cheap crockery and pottery ware for domestic service, which is not so hard as stone ware.

EARTHEN-WARE MANUFACTURER, a potter, a dealer in crockery, &c.

EARTH-FLAX, a name sometimes given to asbestos.

EARTH-NUT, a name for the seeds of the *Arachis hypogæa*, described under the head ground-nut. In America it is called pea-nut.

EARTH-WORK, an engineering term applied to cuttings, embankments, &c.

EARTH-WORM OIL, a green medicinal oil obtained from the common species of *Lumbricus* and used as a remedy for ear-ache.

EAR-TRUMPET, a funnel-shaped tube, made of various sizes, to assist the hearing of persons partially deaf.

EASEL, a painter's wooden frame or rest, on which the canvas is supported for painting.

EAST INDIA COMPANY, an incorporated association of merchants established about two centuries and a half ago, having now the entire political and civil government of India, under the supervision of the Board of Control. The Court of Directors, consisting of 24 members, holders of not less than £2000 stock each, are chosen by the proprietors.

EASY-CHAIR MAKER, a manufacturer of arm-chairs or reclining couches.

EATCHE, ETTCH, the Scotch name for an adze.

EATING-HOUSE, a dining-house or place of refreshment where cooked provisions are sold.

EAU-DE-COLOGNE, an aromatized alcohol, used as a perfume and toilet article; so named from being originally and principally made at Cologne. *See* COLOGNE-WATER.

EAU-DE-JAVELLE, chlorine in solution with water.

EAU-DE-LUCE, a volatile preparation consisting of a mixture of alcohol, caustic ammonia, and a small quantity of oil of amber.

EAU-DE-PARIS, a substitute for eau-de-Cologne and other similar cosmetics which is sometimes taken in sweetened water as a cordial and stimulant. It takes out spots, and preserves woollens from moths. There are many other local waters in the commerce of the Continent, as eau d'arquebusade, eau gazeuse, &c.

EAU-DE-VIE (French), brandy.

EAVES, the lowest tiles, slates, &c., of the roof of a house; which usually project over the side walls and throw off the water.

EBANISTA (Italian), a cabinet-maker.

EBAROUISSAGE (French), the separation of staves or planks.

EBAUCHE (French), a rough draught or sketch.

EBAUCHOIR (French), a large chisel used by statuaries to rough-hew their work; a great hatchel or beating instrument used by rope-makers.

EBB, the reflux or return of the tide after it has reached its full flood; *ebb-tide* being the receding tide towards low water.

EBE'NISTE (French), a cabinet-maker.

EBONY, a heavy hard black wood, obtained from the *Diospyrus ebenus*, much used by turners, and for inlaying work by cabinet-makers. Green ebony is used as a dye-wood, and comes principally from the West Indies.

EBONY, BROWN. *See* WAMARA.

EBOUQUEUSE (French), a burler; one who picks the knots, &c. from new cloth or silk.

EBROUDEUR (French), a wire-drawer.

EBURE, Italian for ivory.

ECACHEUR (French), a gold-beater.

ECANGUEUR, in France a cleaner of flax or hemp

ECARLATIN, a kind of red cider made in France. [cod.

ECHAMPEAU (French), a hook for catching

ECHANDOLE, the French name for a shingle to cover the roof of a house.

ECHANTILLON (French), a sample, pattern, or specimen.

ECHANVROIR, in France a hatchel or flax-beating instrument.

ECHARSETER (French), to coin money below the standard.

ECHE'ANCE (French), a specified day for payment; the falling due of a bill of exchange, &c.

ECHELLE (French), a ladder; a scale.

ECHETS, skeins or hanks of worsted, &c. in France.

ECHEVEAU, the French name for a skein, knot, or hank of thread or silk.

ECHEVETTE, a small hank, the tenth part of a large skein of cotton thread or yarn, and the twenty-second part of an ordinary skein of wool.

ECHINUS, in building, a moulding resembling the ovalo; but its outline is elliptical instead of circular.

ECHOMETER, a musical scale or rule for determining the ratio and duration of sounds, &c.

ECKA, a light pony-gig used by the natives of India, having cloth cushions on which they squat cross-legged.

ECKLEIN, a dry measure of Wurtemberg, nearly 1½ pint.

ECONOMY, prudence and care in the management or distribution of materials, &c.

ECOSSINE'S, the name of a sort of grey limestone in France.

ECOUAILLE (French), coarse wool.

ECRIVAIN, a French copyist or scribe.

ECRITOIRE (French), an inkstand.

ECU, a French name for the crown-piece, a silver coin worth six livres; there were two kinds of écus in France, the écu of six francs, and the *petit écu* of three francs; also a Swiss piece of 40 batzen. The écu is a money of account in Rome, passing for 10 jules or paules, and, as a coin, is worth 10 jules or paules; the crown of Sicily is 12 tarins.

ECUELLE (French), a porringer or basin.

EDDAS, EDDOES, names in the West Indies for species of *Colocasia*, the tubers of which are roasted and eaten like the potatoe; they are also called cocos. When deprived of acridity by boiling, the leaves are eaten as spinach, and the corms are used for soup.

EDGE, the thin cutting extremity of an instrument; hence knives, scythes, adzes, planes, chisels, cleavers, saws, &c., are called edged tools.

EDGE-TOOL MAKER, a manufacturer of iron and steel cutting-instruments, table cutlery, and workmen's implements.

EDGING, any thing used for a border to garments, &c., as lace, fringe, ribbon-edging; a bordering of box, plants, &c. for a garden-plot, &c.

EDIBLE, any thing wholesome or nutritious; esculent, or fit for eating.

EDICT, an official decree.

EDIFICE, a large structure, or stately building.

EDITION, the impression of a work; the publication or republication, as the first, second, or third issue, &c., of any book, newspaper, &c.

EDITOR, the chief literary superintendant of a newspaper, serial, or periodical; one who revises and prepares a book for publication.

EDITORIAL, appertaining to an editor; the leading article of a newspaper.

EDUCTION-PIPE, the pipe from the exhaust passage of the cylinder to the condenser.

EEL, an esteemed table fish, the *Anguilla vulgaris*, inhabiting chiefly fresh water. The consumption of eels in our large cities is very great, and they are considered exceedingly nutritious; on the average 700 tons a year are brought over from Holland, while the total consumption of eels in Great Britain is estimated at 4500 tons per annum.

EELA, a name in Shetland for a fishing-ground near the shore.

EEL-POT, a basket for catching eels.

EEL-PUNT, a flat-bottomed fishing-boat to spear eels from.

EEL-SPEAR, a pronged instrument used for catching eels.

EEN-CAKE, a name in Scotland for a thick oatmeal cake, made with yeast, and baked in an oven.

EFFECTIVE, a term used in many parts of the Continent to express coin in contradistinction to paper money. Thus bills on Vienna are generally directed to be paid in *effective*, to guard against their being paid in paper money of a depreciated value. Effective money is reduced to paper, by saying: As 100 munies, the discount, is to 100, so is the effective sum to the sum in paper. Paper money is reduced to effective by reversing this operation.

EFFECTS, goods or moveable property; available funds.

EFFENDI, a Turkish lawyer.

EFFERVESCENCE, a chemical ebullition or ferment in liquids, which is common in gaseous or aërated waters and wines.

EFFERVESCING DRAUGHTS, pleasant gaseous drinks or sweetened beverages.

EFFIGY, a portrait or likeness; the representation of the sovereign on coins.

EFFILE' (French), a kind of trimming; fringed linen.

EFFLORESCENCE, a powdery coating, which forms on the surface of certain substances.

EFOURCEAU (French), a truck; a large two-wheeled cart to transport heavy burdens.

EGG-CUP, a small cup of earthenware, glass, metal, &c., for holding an egg.

EGG-FLIP, a drink made of warmed beer, flavoured with a little sugar, spirit, spices, and eggs beaten with it.

EGG-GLASS, a small sand glass, running about three minutes, for boiling eggs by.

EGGIBA, EGEBBA, a weight of the west coast of Africa, the third part of a benda, which is 989¼ grains troy; in some places it is represented as the fourth part of the benda, or 247·4 grains.

EGG-LADLE, a kind of spoon for taking eggs from a saucepan.

EGG-MERCHANT, an importer and wholesale dealer in eggs, of whom there are a large number in London, making a business of supplying the retailers by means of travelling carts.

EGG-NOG, a drink composed of wine or spirits, mixed with sugar and eggs.

EGG-PLANT, the *Solanum melongena*, a plant cultivated in warm climates for its fruit, used as a vegetable; in the East it is called the brinjol. In French and Italian cookery, the fruit is used in soups, like its kindred species the tomato, but in the tropics it is mostly fried, after being cut in slices.

EGG-POACHER, a metal vessel with stands to place eggs in a boiler for cooking.

EGGS, the ovum of domestic poultry, which are largely used as food by all nations, and form considerable articles of commerce in most countries. Besides our home produce, from 100 to 120 millions of eggs are annually imported from the Continent. Eggs are used in glove-making, tanning, bookbinding, and other manufacturing processes. The eggs of the ostrich, the turtle, and various species of wild-fowl are also used when obtainable.

EGG-SLICE, a kitchen utensil for removing omelets or fried eggs from a pan.

EGG-SPOON, a small spoon with a narrow bowl for eating eggs with.

EGG-WHISK, a wire bunch or brush for beating up eggs.

EGOHINE, a kind of French hand-saw.

EGRET, EGRETTE, a tuft of feathers; the feathers of the little egret heron (*Herodias garzetta*) are much esteemed for ornament.

EGRIOT, a species of sour cherry.

EGYPTIAN, a kind of type; also a large-sized [paper.

EIDAM, a kind of Dutch cheese.

EIDER-DOWN, the fine soft feathers obtained from the eider-duck (*Somateria mollissima*). The elasticity, lightness, and resistance to wet, of this down, are prominent among its other advantages; it is used for the insides tuffing of muffs, and on the Continent eider-down quilts are largely made, and preferred by the luxurious to every other article for beds and coverlets.

EIDOGRAPH, an instrument for copying [drawings.

EIGHTEENMO, a sheet of paper folded into eighteen leaves, usually written 18mo.

EIK (Scotch), a liniment for greasing sheep.

EIKING, a piece of wood fitted to make good a deficiency in length.

EIMER, a German liquid measure, the third of an oxhoft, which varies considerably in different localities. The Munich eimer is only 8½ gallons, while the Swiss eimer is often more than 25. The Prussian eimer or rundlet is rather more than 18 English gallons. The eimer represents, however, in general, the half of the ahm or aum.

EJECTMENT, a forcing out; the dispossession of house or land.

EJOO FIBRE, a strong black horsehair-looking fibre, obtained from an eastern palm, the *Arenga saccharifera*. It is very durable and tenacious, and universally employed, in the countries where the trees are indigenous, for making cordage, for nets and seines, for the rigging of vessels, and for cables.

EKKA, an Indian single horse native car.

ELAINE, the liquid principle of oils and fats, after the stearine has been pressed out. *See* OLEINE.

ELASTIC-BANDS, belts, braces, gaiters, &c., made with threads of caoutchouc, either naked or covered.

ELASTIC-GUMS, a common name given to those vegetable extracts, such as caoutchouc and gutta percha, which may be elongated by heat, &c.

ELATCHEE, an Eastern name for cardamoms, a much esteemed Indian spice.

ELBOW-CHAIR, a chair with rests or arms to support the elbows.

ELCE, the Italian name for the holm oak.

ELDER, the *Sambucus nigra*, a tree common in Britain and the South of Europe. The wood, which is remarkable for its hardness, is often used for carpenters' rules, weavers' shuttles, meat skewers, &c. The light pith of the branches is used for electrical purposes. From the juice of the deep purple berries a wine and spirit are made, and various kinds of medicine are obtained from the inner bark and other parts of the tree.

ELDER-FLOWER-WATER, a cosmetic made from the flowers of the elder-tree.

ELDER-WINE, a wine made from elder berries, sweetened and flavoured with spices, which is generally drank hot, or mulled with toast.

ELDIN (Scotch), fuel of any kind.

ELECAMPANE, the aromatic bitter roots, &c. of *Corvisartia helenium*, which are much used in some quarters, made into a syrup, for colds and coughs; from its pungency it was formerly in repute as a stomachic; a sweetmeat is also made from it.

ELECTRIC TELEGRAPH, a mode of transmitting messages and intelligence by means of electricity over wires, for long and short distances. Great progress has been made of late years in the extension of the electric telegraph over the principal countries of Europe, Asia, and America; and submarine wires are also now being largely resorted to, to connect countries for commercial purposes.

ELECTRIC-WIRES, a popular name for the wires of the magnetic telegraph on land, or those of the submarine cable.

ELECTRO-GILDER and -PLATER, one who gilds or plates metal goods by electricity.

ELECTROMETER, an instrument for determining the presence and quantity of electricity.

ELECTRO-PLATE, a precipitation of silver or gold on a surface of copper, or German-silver metal.

ELECTROTYPIST, one who coats metals with [silver or gold.

ELECTRUM, a name for German-silver plate; a compound metal, a mixture of gold and silver.

ELECTUARY, a sweetened medicine, of conserves and powders, of the consistence of thick honey.

ELEMI, a gum-resin obtained in the East from *Balsamodendron zeylanicum*, and in America, from a species of *Icica*.

ELEPHANT, the largest of quadrupeds, which is domesticated in the East and trained to service. The wild animals are also hunted for their tusks, which furnish the ivory of commerce, and their back teeth or grinders are also useful. The feet, trunk, &c. are eaten by the hunters; the tail is used for a fly-flapper.

ELEPHANT PAPER, a very large kind of drawing paper, 28 inches by 23.

ELEVATION, a plan; a perspective representation of a building.

ELEVATOR, a lifting machine in the large corn and flour mills of America for grain. It consists of an endless band to which are fixed a series of metal cans revolving in a long wooden trough, which is lowered through the respective hatchways into the vessel, and is connected at its upper end with the building, where its belt is driven. Also a contrivance for raising a person to a height, for the purpose of cleaning, painting, or taking observations, &c.

Eleve (French), an apprentice, a pupil.

Elingues (French), can-hooks to sling a bale of goods, &c.

Elinguet (French), a capstan-bar.

Elixir, in pharmacy a compound tincture; in popular parlance an invigorating cordial.

Elk, a North American quadruped, hunted for its flesh. The horns and skin enter into commerce. The hair is used for stuffing saddles in America, and the hoofs at one time were held in repute in pharmacy for epileptic complaints. Elks' feet still occur in some of the Continental tariffs.

Elk-nut, a name for the oily nut of *Hamiltonia oleifera*.

Ell, an English measure of length equal to 45 inches, but now superseded by the imperial yard. The term is however still employed in designating the width of certain goods. The ell varies in length on the Continent; the Dutch or Flemish ell is 27 inches. The proportion between Dutch ells and English yards is generally taken at 3 yards to 4 ells; but the real rate is 100 yards to 129.2 27-th ells. In Leipsic the ell is 22¼ inches; in Prussia 26¼ nearly; the French ell is 54 inches. In Trieste the woollen ell is 26·6 imperial inches; that for silk 25·22 inches. The German ell is 21 5-9 inches; the Scottish ell rather more than 37 inches. *See* **Braccio**.

Elm, a useful forest tree, the several species of which are natives chiefly of Europe and North America. The timber of elm for constructive purposes ranks next to the oak, and is much used in building; for the keels of vessels, pumps, coffins, &c. It does not split, and therefore bears the driving of nails and bolts well.

Elne, the Scotch ell of 37 inches.

Elsyn, Elson (Scotch), an awl.

Elvans, a mineral stone intermediate between porphyry and granite.

Elvas-plums, a kind of dried prune, a dessert fruit sold in boxes.

Elve, a mining name for the shaft or handle of a pick.

Elytra, the wing-sheaths or outer coverings of the beetle tribe, many of which, from their elegance, are used to ornament articles of dress, fans, &c. in the East and in Brazil.

Emancipate, to liberate or set free from feudal servitude or slavery.

Embale, to pack up or bind goods in a bale or package.

Embank, to enclose with a mound; the term is applied chiefly to banks of earth, by which water is kept out from land that has been reclaimed, or that is liable to inundation.

Embankments, artificial mounds of earth, raised by the sides of rivers, fens, &c., or for levelling the line of road for a railway.

Embar, a liquid measure of Sweden, equal to 20¾ gallons.

Embargo, a restraint or arrest; an order from Government, preventing ships from quitting a port. This State prohibition is usually in time of war, and may be enforced on either native or foreign ships, or merchandise.

Embark, to ship; to proceed on board a vessel or boat; to engage or take part in any business.

Embauchure, the utensils for a salt manufactory in France.

Embden Groats. *See* **Groats**.

Embellishment, the act of adorning or enriching; ornament, decoration.

Embers, small lighted coals or the ashes of burning wood.

Embezzlement, the fraudulent appropriation of the money or goods of another.

Embossing, a kind of raised sculpture, or ornamental carving in relief.

Embossing Press, a machine used by bookbinders for ornamenting cloth and leather for covering books.

Embouchoir (French), a boot-last or boot-tree.

Embouchure, the mouth of any thing, as of a river or harbour; of a cannon, a bottle, a wind instrument, &c.

Embrocation, a pungent oil or medicinal spirit used as an external application to moisten or rub diseased parts of the body.

Embroider, to adorn with raised figures of needle-work in fancy patterns, &c.

Embroidered - muslin Manufacturer, a wholesale dealer in fancy muslin-work done by the needle.

Embroiderer, a person who does ornamental or fancy work with the needle.

Embroidery, variegated needle-work on cloths, stuffs, or muslin, figured in gold, silver, coloured silks or thread.

Embroidery-silk Manufacturer, a dealer in articles worked with silk.

Emerald, a valuable gem for ornamental purposes. The finest stones, which are of a pure green, come either from Peru or the East Indies; a new kind of printing type, intermediate between minion and nonpareil.

Emery, a grey or blackish variety of corundum, used to polish hard bodies. The powder is prepared by sieves, &c., from the size of pepper-corns to superfine flour, or impalpable dust. It is stuck on paper, cloth, and sticks.

Emery-paper, a rough scouring paper for brightening metals, smoothing wood, &c.

Emery-paper Maker, a manufacturer of scouring paper.

Emetics, medicinal compounds which cause vomiting, and are therefore given to disgorge the stomach.

Emigrant, one who removes from or quits his country to settle or take up his residence in another. The emigration from the United Kingdom to the British colonies and foreign countries, is always extensive, averaging nearly 1000 a day.

Emigrant Ship, a passenger ship.

Emigrate, to depart from a place permanently.

Emine, an old French liquid measure, containing a little more than 4 gallons. As a dry measure, it was exceedingly variable, ranging in different localities from 5¾ to 10¼ gallons.

Emissary, a secret agent; a person sent on a private message or business.

EMOLUMENTS, perquisites, fees, or salary; the profits arising from an office or employment.

EMOTTOIR, a scuffler or clod-crusher, used in France. [nine inches

EMPAN, the French name for the span of

EMPENNELLE, in France a kedge-anchor.

EMPESEUR (French), a starcher.

EMPIRIC, a quack, a pretender; an uneducated or irregular practitioner.

EMPLETTE (French), a bargain or purchase.

EMPLOYÉ, a clerk; one engaged in the service of another.

EMPLOYER, a master; one who hires and directs the labour of others.

EMPOIS, potato or wheat starch.

EMPOLDER, a name in Demerara for the extension of an estate inland, 3100 yards backwards from a canal or river frontage.

EMPORIUM, in a large sense a trading mart, or town of extensive commerce; but in the more common and restricted use, a general shop and depot for various goods.

EMPTY-CASE, a compositor's case of type, which is deficient in some of the letters; hence he cannot proceed with his work, until the exhausted sorts are replenished.

EMPTYING, a discharging or pouring out the contents of a package or vessel.

EMPTY-PACKAGES, returned cases from the purchaser to the sender of the goods, consisting, for the most part, of casks, crates, hampers, sacks, &c., which are transported free, or at a very low charge, by the railway companies.

EMU, the Australian ostrich (*Dromiceus Novæ Hollandiæ*); its feathers are used for ornament, and the skin produces six or seven quarts of oil which is used medicinally.

EMULSIONS, medicines made of bruised oily seeds and fluid.

ENACTMENT, a decree, or legislative measure.

ENAMEL, a thin opaque or partially transparent coating of glass of various colours on a metallic surface; a porcellaineous surface is thus given to the interior of iron cooking utensils. The white glass for pottery is also called enamel. The process of painting with coloured glass, and with different mineral colours on gold and copper, is termed enamelling. The basis of all kinds of enamel is a pure glass, which is rendered either transparent or opaque, by the admixture of metallic oxides. White enamel is made by melting the oxide of tin with glass.

ENAMELLED-CARDS, pieces of pasteboard, one surface of which has been coated with white lead and size, and then glazed by passing between highly polished rollers.

ENAMELLED-LEATHER, glazed leather for patent boots and shoes, belts, &c., prepared from calf or seal-skin, by means of sumach; the gloss or enamel is given by several coats of a peculiar varnish.

ENAMELLER, one who lays on enamels or inlays with mineral colours.

ENCAUSTIC, a method of painting in heated or burnt wax. The term is also now very generally applied to all kinds of painting, where the colours are laid on or fixed by heat, so as to be rendered permanent and brilliant.

ENCAUSTIC-TILE, a variegated paving-tile, on which patterns have been formed in coloured clays on the ordinary buff-tile, and fired, which brings out the colours more vividly.

ENCHASE, or CHASE, to enrich or beautify any work in metal by an embossed design, &c. in low relief. [ding.

ENCHÈRE (French), an auction, an outbid-

ENCLOSURE, land fenced in or hedged round for separation or for the protection of crops.

ENCRE (French), printing or writing ink.

ENCYCLOPÆDIA, a dictionary or descriptive work of reference, which treats of the various branches of the arts, sciences, and manufactures.

ENDASSE, ENDRAZE, names for the short ell or pike in Turkey, by which cotton goods and carpets are measured; it is equal to 27·00 inches.

ENDAZEE, a Turkish measure of length for silk equal to 25¼ inches; a similar measure used for cloth is 26¾ inches.

ENDIVE, a hardy annual, the *Cichorium endivia*; the blanched leaves of which are used as a salad.

ENDLESS-CHAIN, a perpetually revolving chain, much used in machinery.

ENDLESS-TAPE, the connecting bands for some light machinery.

ENDORSE, to transfer or make over: on a bill of exchange this endorsement is often made in blank, but renders the endorser liable for the payment of the bill, if not met by the acceptor or person on whom it is drawn, or any other endorser.

ENEMA, a clyster, or syringe.

ENFRAYURE (French), the first combing of wool.

ENGA, a name in some of the Pacific islands for turmeric root.

ENGAGE, to retain or employ a person.

ENGAGEMENT, an obligation, contract, or undertaking entered into.

ENGEL, a Dutch money-weight formerly used in Belgium, &c., the 160th part of the troy marc, = therefore to 23¾ grains. It was also called an esterlin.

ENGINE, the general name for any mechanical machine which produces or regulates motive power, such as a fire-engine, steam-engine, &c. Engines are of three great classes, locomotive, marine, and stationary, and in their motion are either oscillating or rotary.

ENGINEER, one skilled in mechanism, or the construction and management of complicated machinery, and the uses of motive power, repairs of mill work, &c.

ENGINEER, CIVIL, a skilled designer, architect, and mathematician, who delineates plans, and superintends the construction of large industrial buildings and public works.

ENGINE-MAN, a machine man; one who attends to the engine in a mill, steam-boat, locomotive, &c., he is often loosely called an engineer.

ENGINE-OIL MAKER, a preparer and vender of oil for lubricating machinery.

ENGINE-TURNER, one who practises a peculiar kind of complex turning.

Engrais (French), pasture-ground; food on which cattle or poultry are fattened; manure.

Engraver, a carver, sculptor, or cutter of devices; thus there are wood-engravers, steel and copper-plate engravers, seal cutters, &c.

Engraver's-tool Cutter, a maker of metal gravers, &c.

Engraving, the process of incising or cutting letters, designs, &c. on metals, stones, or wood, with a chisel or graver; a drawing or impression taken from a copper-plate.

Engrossing, the act of making a fair copy of a draught in a bold plain hand.

Eno, the name of a New Zealand tree, the bark of which furnishes a valuable black dye, used by the natives for colouring their grass mats.

Enouer (French), to pick the knots from cloth, &c.

Enrichment, the builder's name for the figuring and mouldings of a cornice.

Ensayador (Spanish), an assayer.

Ensign, a military or naval banner. The regimental ensign is a piece of silk borne on a staff, having figures, colours, and arms thereon. The naval ensign is usually suspended over the poop or stern of a ship, and is used to distinguish vessels of different nations. Also the lowest commissioned officer in a company of infantry, who takes his name from having to bear the colours of the regiment.

Ensimage (French), the oiling of cloth, in order to dress it more freely.

Ensouple (French), a weaver's beam or roller.

Enstatine, a bisilicate of magnesia, augite in crystallization, and having some resemblance to scapolite.

Ente (French), a grafted tree, a scion; the handle of a painter's brush.

Enter, to register, to set down in writing; to lodge a manifest of goods at the custom-house.

Enterprise, a projected scheme; a hazardous adventure.

Entertainment, a public dinner; amusement of any kind, a concert, dancing-room, &c.

Entire, the name for a kind of beer, combining the appreciated properties of two or three esteemed qualities of malted beverage; a stallion, or ungelded horse.

Entoir (French), a grafting-knife.

Entr'acte, the time between the acts of a play; an interlude.

Entrebandes (French), the fag end of woollen stuffs.

Entrebas (French), an unequal distance between the threads of a warp.

Entre-cote (French), a piece of beef cut between the ribs.

Entrée, an admission or introduction; the first course of dishes.

Entrelacs (French), threads, twine, or string.

Entremets, side-dishes; dainties.

Entreposer (French), to store or warehouse goods.

Entrepot, a mart; a store-room for the deposit of goods; a bonded warehouse.

Entrepreneur, a French contractor; one who executes or undertakes constructive works.

Entresol (French), a suite of rooms between two floors; a low apartment, usually placed above the ground-floor.

Entry, the record made in a merchant's books of any business transaction; the lodgment of a ship's papers in the custom-house on arrival, when permission to land cargo is obtained.

Enumerator, a calculator, one employed to count over or reckon up figures or things.

Envelope, the outer cover or enclosure case for a letter; the wrapper on which the address is written.

Envelope-machine, a cleverly constructed machine by which envelopes are cut and folded.

Envelope-maker, a wholesale manufacturer of letter enclosures.

Envoy, a deputy or messenger; a diplomatic agent.

Epais, Epaisseur (French), thickness; density.

Eparcet, in France, a kind of hay.

Epars (French), a flagstaff.

Epaulet, a shoulder ornament or badge of rank worn by naval and military commissioned officers.

Epaves (French), goods found floating at sea without owner; flotson and jetson.

Epergne, an ornamental stand for a large dish in the centre of a table.

Ephah, an ancient Jewish dry measure, of about four gallons.

Epicerie (French), grocery wares, spices, &c.

Epidemic, a murrain among cattle.

Epidermis, the cuticle or scarfskin; the membranous or fibrous horny covering of some shells.

Epincoir, a pavior's hammer in France.

Epingare (French), a small cannon.

Epingle (French), a pin; any small pointed instrument.

Epinglier, a maker or dealer in pins.

Epissoir (French), a marline-spike.

Epitome, an abstract, abridgment, or compendium.

Eplaigneur, a French cloth-dresser.

Epoussetoir (French), a soft light brush.

Eprouvette, a French instrument for testing the strength of gunpowder.

Epsom-salts, a popular name for sulphate of magnesia, a well-known cooling purgative. It is met with as a bitter saline efflorescence, and is also obtained by chemists from magnesian limestone.

Epure (French), a model; an enlarged plan of a building.

Equatorial, an astronomical instrument with a telescope, for taking celestial observations.

Equestrian Statue, a mounted figure of a horseman.

Equipage, the fittings and furniture used by an army in the camp or field. Camp-equipage includes marquees, tents, &c., field equipage artillery, wagons, tumbrils, &c. Equipage is also often applied to a vehicle or carriage of state; and to the attendants or retinue of a person of rank.

Equipet (French), a small open locker used in a ship, to prevent things falling about the decks.

Equipments, the clothing, accoutrements, arms, &c. of a soldier; hence there are artillery equipment, for field and garrison, and engineer equipments, &c.; also the fitting out of a ship for sea.

Eraser, an instrument for scratching out writing, and obliterating errors.

Erect, to raise or build up, as a house, pier, &c.

Erenda, the Sanscrit name for the castor-oil plant.

Erf, the Dutch name in the Cape colony for a piece of garden land of variable extent, usually about half an acre; plural, erven.

Ergot, a morbid development of the seed of rye (*Secale cornutum*), and of some other gramineous plants, produced by the growth upon them of a microscopic fungus. It is used medicinally as an agent for accelerating parturition.

Eriometer, an instrument for measuring the fibres of wool.

Ermailli, a foreman in a cheese manufactory of Gruyere and Berne.

Ermellino (Italian), ermine.

Ermin, an import duty in the Levant.

Ermina, a name sometimes given to the mine or mina, a measure for grain used in Italy; which ranges from about a quarter to half a bushel in different towns.

Ermine, the short soft silky white fur forming the winter clothing of the stoat, *Mustela erminea;* which is sought for extensively over northern Europe and America. It is worn by the Judges, and for articles of ladies' dress. The black tuft from the tail is sewed to the skin at regular intervals.

Erminette (French), a plane; an adze.

Erqoo8os, liquorice water sold as a drink in the streets of Alexandria, as coffee and tea are in other towns.

Errand-boy, a lad kept to deliver messages, or to do jobs of all kinds.

Errata, a published list of mis-prints or typographical errors, which have escaped the eye of the Author and press Reader

Errhines, sternutatories; medicines which cause sneezing or mucous discharges when snuffed up the nose.

Eruginous, green with a blue tint; the colour of verdigris.

Erunda, a name for the seed of the castor-oil plant in the East.

Erva Lenta, the farina or meal of the common lentil (*Ervum Lens*).

Esagio, the sixth part of the Italian ounce.

Esame, Esciame (Italian), a swarm of bees.

Esca, a land measure in use at Bordeaux; the acre (of three roods six perches,) being divided into 216 escas.

Escaladon (French), a small mill for winding silk.

Escalin, a Dutch and Flemish shilling: a base silver coin and money of account, worth about sixpence sterling.

Escandal, a liquid measure of Marseilles; 400 escandaux = 1 millerolle, which is about 17 English wine gallons.

Escandole (French), the cabin for the serjeant of a row-galley.

Escapement, part of a clock or watch movement; a mechanical contrivance in a chronometer, for transmission at equal intervals of the maintaining power to the regulator. Its office is to allow a tooth of the wheel to escape or pass onward, at such intervals of time as are measured by the regulator.

Escarballe (French), a scrivello or elephant's tusk under 20 lbs. weight.

Escarbilles (French), coal cinders.

Escargatoire, a nursery of esculent snails (*Helix pomatia*); snails are esteemed an edible dainty on the Continent.

Escarpin (French), a light pump or shoe with a thin sole.

Eschen, a division of the gold and silver pound weight in Hamburgh; 544 eschens make one troy pound.

Eschevin, a name formerly given to the older or warden, the principal of the ancient guilds.

Eschio (Italian), the beech-tree.

Escompte (French), discount; money deducted for interest.

Escort, a body of armed men sent for security or convoy, as with a gold freight from the mines to a sea-port for shipment.

Escritoire, a writing-desk; a chest of drawers with a flap and convenience for writing.

Escropulo, the 192nd part of the Portuguese and Spanish marc. The scruple is used in Brazil for weighing precious stones, consisting of 3 carats, or about 9½ English grains.

Escudo, a money of account in Bilboa; also a gold coin of Spain and Portugal. *See* Scudo.

Esculent, something that is wholesome and eatable; good as food for man.

Escutcheon, a shield for a key-hole on a door, &c.; the part of a merchant vessel's stern where her name is written.

Espade (French), a wooden bat or beetle used by rope-makers for towing or teasing the hemp.

Espagnolette, a sash-window fastening.

Espalement (French), gauge; the difference between the old and new measures.

Espalier, a low lattice-work for training dwarfed fruit trees on; the first rower of a French galley.

Esparto, a name given in Spain to the herbaceous stalks of the *Machrochloa* (*Stipa*) *tenacissima*, a grass which is used for mats, sandals, cordage, and for paper pulp.

Espato (Spanish), spar.

Esplanade, in military parlance, the void space between the glacis of a citadel and the first houses of the town, but now ordinarily applied to any open level public walk or drive near the sea; a grass plot in a garden.

Espiotte, a species of rye.

Esquif (French), a small skiff or ship's boat.

Esquiman, in France, a boatswain's mate.

Esquisse (French), a sketch; a rough outline drawing.

Essencia, a common name for the volatile or essential oils, which have the special perfume or odour of plants; diluted flavourings for drinks, &c., containing the peculiar taste of fruits.

Essette (French), a heavy adze.

Estacarocin, a Spanish name for *Peganum Harmala*, used as a spice, and for dyeing red.

Estada, the Spanish fathom of six feet.

Estadal, a Spanish measure of 100 varas, equal to 274·800 feet.

Estadio, a furlong, the eighth part of the Portuguese and Spanish mile, usually subdivided into 125 paces, each of five feet; but in Spain the stadio measures 190½ yards, and in Portugal, 281¼ yards.

Estado (Spanish), a statement or account.

Estafette, a French courier or express.

Estame (French), worsted; woollen yarn.

Estamin, a woollen stuff made in Prussia, used for cartridges, sackcloth, plush caps, &c.

Estaminet, a French ale-house or coffee-house, where smoking is allowed.

Estancia, the Spanish name for a grazing-farm or pasture-ground.

Estano (Spanish), tin.

Estate, the lands or tenements to which a person has a clear title and interest.

Esterlin, a French name for the Dutch engel, the 20th part of an ounce; the 160th part of the troy mark, and equal to about 23¾ grains. *See* Estlin.

Estimate, to appraise or value; to judge of by inspection. An estimate is an approximate calculation made of the probable cost or charges of any undertaking, as of a contract for work and labour to be done, a building to be constructed, &c., quantity of materials required for any work, &c.

Estimator, an appraiser; one who computes or values.

Estimo, in Italian, an impost, tax, or customs duty.

Estivage, Estive, a French term applied to the stowage or trimming of a ship; a mode of pressing or screwing cargoes into vessels, practised in America and the Mediterranean ports, by means of a capstan machinery, for the better balancing of the ship.

Estlin, a French weight, in the old ponderary system: the twentieth part of an ounce. *See Esterlin.*

Esto, Etto, a long measure used in Sumatra, equal to about 18 inches.

Estopilla, a kind of long lawn or mixed linen fabric, made in Silesia.

Estray, or **Stray**, a domestic animal found wandering without owner.

Estridge, the fine soft down which lies under the feathers of the ostrich; which was formerly used as a substitute for beaver in hat-making, and of the coarser kind a stuff was fabricated.

Estrique (French), a tool used in a plate-glass manufactory to flatten the plates of crown glass.

Estriqueux (French), a pipe maker's paring-knife.

Etabli (French), a tailor's shopboard, a carpenter's work-bench; a stage on which tallow-chandlers dry their candles.

Etadou (French), a comb-maker's tooth cutter.

Etagere, a piece of cabinet furniture; a what-not, side-board, dumb-waiter or set of shelves.

Etaim (French), the finest part of carded wool.

Etain (French), tin; pewter, or an alloy of tin and lead.

Etal, a butcher's or fishmonger's stall in France.

Etalon, the French name for the standard for weights and measures; also a stallion.

Etalonneur, a French officer appointed to officially mark or stamp weights and measures.

Etami, an Indian sieve for bolting the meal of cassava, made from the fibres of the Ita palm, *Mauritia flexuosa*.

Etamine (French), a thin stuff made with wool; a filtering cloth or bolter; a sieve.

Etamure, tin used for coating iron saucepans in France.

Etape (French), a storehouse, where goods are landed; a staple mart.

Etaux (French), a butcher's shambles.

Etavillon, kid, sheep, or other skins prepared for glove-making.

Etching, a process of engraving on copper, by corroding in the lines of the drawing &c. with nitric acid, or on glass by fluoric acid; also a pen-and-ink line drawing.

Etching-needle, a stylus or steel graver, with a fine point, for tracing lines through the varnish on the metal plate.

Etendeur (French), a flattener of crown-glass.

Etendoir, a kind of flat shovel or peel with a long handle, used by French printers to spread their damp printed sheets on lines to dry; a drying loft.

Ether, a general name for any volatile spirit or compound, consisting of an acid and an organic radical.

Etherins (Scotch), the cross ropes of a thatched roof or stack.

Ethiopian-pepper, a name for the fruit of *Xylopia aromatica*, used as a pungent condiment in Africa.

Etier, a ditch or canal which brings sea-water to the salt-pits in France.

Etiquette, ceremony; in France a label or ticket affixed to a package.

Etire, a French currier's stretching iron.

Etna, a table cooking-utensil, heated by a spirit lamp.

Etoupe (French), tow; lint; the coarsest part of flax or hemp; oakum.

Etourdeau (French), a young capon.

Etrape, a small sickle for cutting stubble, used in France.

Etrasse, Estrasse (French), floss-silk.

Etreignoir (French), a cramp or hand-screw.

Etrein, litter for horses in France.

Etresses (French), paper doubled and pasted for cards.

Etrier (French), a stirrup.

Etrille (French), a curry-comb.

Etterlin (Scotch), a cow which has a calf when only two years old.

Etuvée (French), stewed fish or meat.

Eudiometer, an instrument for ascertaining the purity or salubrity of air, or rather for determining the quantity of oxygen in any given bulk of elastic fluid.

Euphorbium, a concrete gum-resin obtained from several species of *Euphorbia* in the East, and used medicinally.

Eupion, a product of the destructive distillation of vegetable substances.

Evaporameter, a hygroscope or atmometer, an instrument for ascertaining the evaporation of fluids.

Evaporation, the conversion of substances into vapour by heat.

Evener, a name in the Lothians for an instrument used by weavers for spreading out the yarn: in other parts called a raivel.

Even Keel, a vessel which is loaded so as to draw the same water abaft as forward.

Even Lines, Make Even. Technical terms in newspaper printing. When copy has to be cut into pieces to be distributed among many compositors, they have frequently to space out the words very irregularly, so as to fill a line; hence the common instruction, from one printer to another who follows or precedes him with copy, to "make even."

Eventail (French), a fan, a screen.

Eventoir, a large ozier blower or fan used in France to light coals with instead of bellows.

Evergreens, plants which retain their verdure throughout the year, such as pines, laurels, hollies, &c.

Everlasting, a striped cotton material; also a common name for the American cudweed, of the genus *Gnaphalium*, which has been recommended as a material for paper-making.

Ever-pointed Pencil-maker, a manufacturer of sliding screw pencil-cases, by which the lead is replenished as required.

Evidence, oral or written testimony given by a witness.

Evidoir (French), a clearing or hollowing tool used by flute-makers to scoop out the centre of the wood.

Evilasse, a name in France for Madagascar ebony.

Evitee (French), room for a ship to swing in a river or channel with the turn of the tide.

Evolutions, the movements of a vessel or fleet.

Ewe, a female sheep.

Ewe-cheese, cheese made from the milk of sheep.

Ewer, a water pitcher with a wide spout.

Ex, a Latin preposition, which denotes out of, or from.

Examination, a careful search or inspection; a judicial trial, enquiry, or proceeding.

Examiner, an inspector or investigator; one appointed to test or scrutinize accounts, or to assay by experiments.

Excavation, a digging or hollowing out.

Excavator, a machine for excavating; also one who cuts or digs out earth. See Navigator.

Exchange, the balance of money of different countries, each of which has a certain regulated par of exchange; a place of public resort, in commercial cities, where merchants meet to transact business; the bartering of one commodity for another.

Exchange-broker, a person who attends on 'Change to negotiate foreign bills for merchants, for which he receives a small commission.

Exchequer, the principal receptacle for money paid to the State arising from taxes.

Exchequer Bill, a promissory note or credit bill, issued by the Treasury under the authority of Parliament, for defraying portions of the current financial expenses of the Government, and usually forming a large portion of the floating or unfunded National Debt. Exchequer bills are circulated for sums varying in amount from £100 to £1000. The small bills, as they are called, of £100, are printed in red ink; the bills for £200 in yellow ink; those for £500 in blue ink; and the largest amount bills, £1000, in black. From their convenience, as a ready and secure investment, not liable to fluctuation like the funds, and being redeemable at par at short fixed periods, they are much in request by bankers and capitalists, and the Government is usually able to keep a large amount afloat at an exceedingly low rate of interest; they therefore commonly bear a premium. Of late years the rate of interest paid by Government on Exchequer-bills has fluctuated from 2½d. to 1d. per diem; that is from £3 16s. 0½d. to £1 10s. 5d. per cent. per annum. They are usually renewed or paid off yearly, and bear interest from their date until the period fixed for their payment; which is always announced by public advertisement.

Excise, an inland duty or tax levied on certain articles of home manufacture and consumption, as on beer, British spirits, malt, &c.; excise duties therefore differ from customs duties, which are levied on imports and exports. The excise also grant licences for certain trades and occupations which bring in a duty to government.

Exciseman, an officer appointed to look after excise duties, and to carry out the regulations enforced by the Excise Commissioners.

Excortication, the stripping off the bark of a tree.

Excursion-train, a pleasure train of railway carriages, usually dispatched at fares below the ordinary rates of charge for travelling.

Execution, a judicial writ issuing from some court of law against the body, lands, or goods and chattels of a person.

Execution-Creditor, one who has a preferential claim for costs incurred, or who holds a judgment.

Executor, a person appointed by the testator to administer to his estate, to carry into force the appropriations of his will and testament, after his decease.

Exemplaire (French), a pattern or specimen.

Exempt, privileged; free from charge or duty.

Exhibit, any voucher or document produced in a court of law, or before arbitrators, &c.
Exhibition, a public display of works of art, industry, manufactures, &c.; such collections have of late years been held periodically in most civilized countries.
Ex-officio (Latin), by virtue of the office.
Exotic, a plant or product of a foreign country.
Ex-parte, a partial or one-sided statement.
Expectant, a junior excise-officer; one not fully confirmed, or upon trial.
Expectorants, medicines which promote discharges from the lungs, and hence relieve a cough.
Expedient, a contrivance.
Expenditure, a charge or disbursement; outlay; that which is consumed or used on board ship is said to be expended.
Experiment, a trial or effort; an attempt to analyse or determine by a chemist.
Exploitation (French), the improving of lands, the felling of woods, the working of mines, or other undertakings.
Exporter, a shipper of wares, commodities, or merchandise of any kind to a foreign country or colony.
Exports, goods, wares, or manufactures, transmitted abroad.
Expositeur (French), one who tries to pass counterfeit money.
Express, to force out by pressure; a courier or special messenger.
Expressed Oil, oil obtained by the mechanical operation of pressing or squeezing, as contradistinguished from that which is obtained by boiling; cold-drawn castor-oil is obtained by expression; so are olive, almond, and coco-nut oils.
Extentour (Scotch), an assessor, one who apportions a general tax; the word stent-master is now generally used.
Exterior, the outside.
Externat (French), a day-school.
Extinguisher, an inverted hollow cone for putting out a candle.
Extirpation, destroying or removing, as in weeding, &c.
Extortion, an exaction or overcharge; an illegal demand enforced.
Extract, a substance abstracted; an epitome; a passage taken from a book, &c.; an evaporated decoction; an inspissated or expressed vegetable juice.
Extra-parochial, without the legal limits or assigned boundary of a parish.
Extravagance, recklessness and improvidence; a waste of materials.
Eyalet, a Turkish government or principality, under the administration of a vizier or pacha of the first class.
Eye-blinds, bandages for a horse's eyes when being singed, bled, &c.
Eye-bolt, a small ring-bolt used on ship-board, to which ropes are fastened.
Eyebright, a meadow plant, the *Euphrasia officinalis*, used medicinally.
Eye-flap, a blinder on a horse's head stall.
Eye-glass, a single spectacle glass worn by near-sighted persons; the outer glass of a telescope, which is placed against the eye.
Eyelet, a small hole for reeving a lace or cord in parts of dress, &c.
Eyeleteer, a small pointed instrument for piercing eyelet holes.
Eyelet-hole, a hole in a sail for a cringle or ribbon to go through.

F.

Fabric, the texture or structure of a manufactured article; the material or woven goods themselves; a building, or erection; a frame or workshop.
Fabricant (French), a manufacturer, a working tradesman.
Fabricateur (French), a coiner or forger.
Fabricator, a handicraftsman; one who constructs or makes.
Fabrilia, workmen's tools.
Façade (French), the front view or elevation of an edifice.
Face, the edge, surface, or front of any thing; the dial of a watch.
Face-Guard, a wire gauze mask used by workmen, as in stone-breaking, in chemical or manufacturing processes, &c.
Facets, the various sides into which a precious stone, &c. is cut.
Facing, a covering; a superficial layer or coating of better material laid over anything to improve its appearance, or to mask it.
Fac-simile, a true likeness, or representation of any thing; an exact copy of a handwriting.
Factitious, artificial.
Factor (Scotch), a land steward; one who has the charge of an estate, lets the land, collects the rents, &c.; a mercantile agent who transacts business for others on commission, and is empowered to buy and sell goods in his own name, in this respect differing from a broker.
Factorage, the commission paid to a factor by his employer for business done.
Factory, a common abbreviation for manufactory, &c.; a workshop, a mill, &c.; usually applied to buildings on an extensive scale, where complicated machinery, worked by motive power, is used. In these the great textile products of the country are made.
Factory-hand, a manufactory workman; a person employed about a mill.
Factory-maund, a commercial weight of India, of 74 lbs. 10 oz. 10⅔ drachms avoirdupois, and less ponderous than the ordinary bazaar maund.
Factotum, a useful person; one who can turn his hand readily to any thing.

Facture (French), **Factura** (Spanish and Portuguese), **Fattura** (Italian), an invoice or bill of parcels; a written account of the particulars of merchandise shipped, or sent to a purchaser.

Faculty, a privilege or dispensation; a body of masters or professors of law, physic, &c.

Fade, to wear away; to wither or lose colour or distinctness, as in silks, daguerreotypes, &c.

Fadge, a name amongst leather sellers for a covering of undressed leather inclosing a bundle of patent or other valuable leather, corded, &c.; in Scotland a bundle of sticks; a large flat wheaten loaf or bannock.

Faduj, an Arab name for bezoar.

Fag, one who works hard; a knot in cloth.

Fag-end, the refuse part or worst end of a web of cloth or any fabric; the untwisted end of a rope.

Fagot, a quantity of steel in bars, equal to 120 lbs.; a bundle of sticks of wood about 3 feet long and 2 feet round.

Fagotto, a musical instrument. *See* Bassoon.

Faham-tea, a name given in the Mauritius to the dried leaves of the *Angræcum fragrans*, a fragrant orchid which owes its odour to the presence of coumarin. The infusion is drunk to promote digestion, and is useful for certain diseases of the lungs.

Fahrenheit, a thermometric scale, in which the freezing point of water is fixed at 32 degrees, and the boiling point at 212. *See* Thermometer.

Faience, **Fayence**, delft-ware; china or pottery embellished with painted designs.

Faik (Scotch), to grasp, to fold or tuck up; a stratum of stone.

Fail-Dyke, **Fald dyke** (Scotch), a wall built of sods or turf, surrounding the space appropriated for a fold.

Failure, a commercial term for the suspension of payment; insolvency, bankruptcy, &c., of an individual or firm.

Faints, **Feints**, the impure spirit in the process of distillation passing over at first and at last from the still; the former being called strong and the latter weak faints.

Fair, an assemblage of buyers and sellers at a fixed place on certain fixed days. Fairs are being gradually abolished in this country, but are still held on the Continent and in India. *See* Market.

Fairing, a gift or present purchased at a fair.

Fairntosh, a peat-flavoured spirit formerly distilled in Ross-shire.

Fairway, the mid-passage in a short channel, the navigable part of a river.

Faisselle, **Fesselle** (French), a cheese-frame.

Faisseur, **Fessier** (French), a basket-maker.

Faitiere (French), a tile for a ridge or gutter.

Fake, a sailor's name for one of the coils or circles made in winding a rope.

Falcated, bending like a hook.

Falchion, a short crooked sword.

Falcon, a hunting-hawk, one trained to sport; a piece of ordnance of 5½ inches' bore, carrying a 2½ lbs. shot.

Falconer, one who breeds and trains hawks, and has the charge of falcons for pursuing game.

Falconet, a small cannon whose bore is 4½ inches and the shot 1¼ lb. weight.

Falding, a coarse cloth.

Fald-stool, a portable seat made to fold up in the manner of a camp stool.

Fall, a border of lace to the neck-part or body of a lady's evening dress; a short veil for a lady's bonnet or hat; a superficial measure in Scotland equal to a perch; 6 ells of 37 inches; a trap for animals; a descent of water; the loose end of a tackle, that part to which the power is applied in hoisting.

Fall-board, the wooden drop shutter of a window that is not glazed, which moves backwards and forwards on hinges.

Fallow, untilled land; ground lying at rest, not under a grain crop. A naked fallow is when it has been ploughed and harrowed and left; while a green fallow is when some intermediate crop of roots or forage has been taken from it.

Fallow-deer, the *Cervus dama*, an animal kept as an ornament in parks, of which there are two kinds, the dappled and the very deep brown variety. The venison is very rich and delicate, and the horns and skin are used commercially.

Falot (French), a large lantern fixed to a pole; a burning beacon.

Falotier, a French lamplighter.

False-core, a name among brass-founders for a loose piece of the mould not intended for holes; by the iron-founder it is called a drawback.

False-keel, pieces of timber secured under the main keel of vessels.

Famine, dearth, or destitution; a scarcity of food or provisions for sustenance.

Famis, a kind of Spanish gold cloth or brocade.

Fan, an apparatus for winnowing grain; a hand ornament or instrument chiefly used by ladies to cool themselves. Ladies' fans are made, of various materials, coloured paper, feathers, bone or ivory carved, &c. China and France are the chief seats of the manufacture. The manufacture in Paris is a very extensive branch of industry, supplying all civilized nations with these useful and ornamental articles. The Chinese are noted for their chaste and elegantly carved ivory fans. It is the nature of the decoration of the leaf or surface of the fan which increases its costliness. It is often made of paper, vellum, parchment, satin, gauze, or crape.

Fanal (French), a ship's lantern, or watch light; a light-house.

Fanam, an old Indian copper coin worth from 2d. to 3d., of which there are also double ones. The gold canteroy fanam of North Arcot and other parts ranged from 6d. to 9d. in value.

Fan and Sky-light Maker, a manufacturer of semi-circular windows and glazed-roofs.

Fancy-box Maker, a manufacturer of card-board and other boxes, for linen-drapery goods, or confectioners' use, &c.

FANCY-CHECK MUSLINS, cambrics marked with cords and stripes, by heavy threads introduced into the warp and weft.

FANCY-GOODS, fabrics made of various patterns, as ribbons, silks, satins, &c., differing from those which are of a plain or simple colour.

FANCY-PAPER MAKER, a manufacturer of coloured or ornamental papers.

FANCY-REPOSITORY, a shop where various articles for ladies' use are vended, often termed a Berlin warehouse.

FANEGA, a Spanish measure used for different purposes. As a dry measure in Spain, it varies from 1½ to 2½ bushels. In South America, the fanega of Chile, for grain, ranges from 153 lbs. weight to upwards of 200 lbs.; in Central America the fanega of maize weighs 400 lbs.; in Monte Video, it is as much as 3¾ bushels; but the average computation may be taken at 5 fanegas to the English quarter of 8 bushels. As a land measure the fanega is 40.000 varas of about 2¾ feet each.

FANEGADA, a Spanish land measure; as much ground as may be sown with a fanega of grain; about 153 square yards, = 170 varas.

FANEUR (French), a hay-maker.

FANG, the bend of a rope; a long nail.

FANGO, a native name in some parts of the Pacific for oil.

FANGOT, a quantity of wares, as raw silk, &c., from 1 to 2½ cwts.

FANK, the name, in some parts of Scotland, for a sheep-cot or pen; to coil a rope.

FANLIGHT, a framed window shaped like an outspread fan, usually placed over doors.

FAN-MAKER, a manufacturer of ladies' fans.

FAN MAKERS' COMPANY, one of the minor livery companies of London, which has no hall.

FANNER, a revolving instrument with vanes, which creates wind for winnowing the chaff from grain; a cooling apparatus.

FANTAIL, a joint; a gas burner.

FARANDAMS, a mixed fabric of silk and wool.

FARANZULA, a weight of Lohela on the Red Sea of 20 lbs.

FARCE, to stuff with mingled ingredients; a laughable or grotesque dramatic piece.

FARCEL. *See* FRAZIL.

FARCOST, a Scotch trading vessel.

FARD (Scotch), to paint or embellish.

FARDAGE (French), the tonnage of a ship.

FARDEL, a bundle or little pack; a term used in reckoning in Germany, equal to 45 barchets or pieces of cloth of 22 or 24 ells each; the fourth part of a yard of land.

FARDING-DEAL, an old term for the fourth part of an acre of land.

FARE, a word of wide application; food or provisions for the table; the price of passage for travelling; the sum paid or due for conveying a person by land or water.

FARGOT, a term employed in parts of France to designate a bale of manufactured goods weighing 150 to 160 lbs.

FARINA, the flour or meal of any species of corn or starchy root.

FARINACEOUS, containing meal.

FARINA-MANUFACTURER, a grinder and preparer of meal, or fine powder from grain, pulse or roots.

FARINIER (French), a corn-chandler, a dealer in meal and flour.

FARM, to take or hire at a certain rate per cent.; a monopoly, licence, or permission to vend certain articles subject to duty; a portion of land with suitable buildings, &c. devoted to agricultural operations.

FARMER, a tenant; a lessee; a person employed in the cultivation of land, breeding and rearing live-stock, and the management of the commercial products they yield.

FARMER-GENERAL, a contractor for taxes.

FARM-HOUSE, the dwelling-house on a farm.

FARM-LABOURER, a person employed about a farm.

FARM-MEAL (Scotch), meal paid as part of the rent.

FARM-YARD-MANURE, the excrements of cattle, and other fertilizing substances collected from stables, cattle sheds, &c. for spreading on land; and largely used.

FAROODEEYEH, a turban for Arab females.

FARRA, a kind of salmon in Spain.

FARRAM, a tobacco cutter in Alexandria.

FARRIER, originally a blacksmith, one who forged and fitted horses' shoes—but now applied to a horse doctor; although they often take the more ambitious title of veterinary surgeon.

FARRIERS' COMPANY, one of the minor livery companies of London which has no hall.

FARRO (Spanish), peeled barley.

FARSAKH, an itinerary measure of Mocha of 3 miles; the fourth part of a baryd.

FARTHING, a land measure representing 30 acres; a small English copper coin, the fourth part of a penny, and weighing 4 dwt.: from 1848 to 1850 the coinage of farthings averaged about one million pieces per annum; but in 1854, owing to the want of small copper coin, 6,500,000 farthings were coined. A few half farthings have also been issued.

FARTHINGALE. *See* FARDING-DEAL.

FASCET, a tool for bottles.

FASCIA, a bandage or fillet.

FASCO, a liquid measure of Paraguay, equal to 34 pounds.

FASHION, shape or form; a custom, the style or mode.

FASHIONER, one who fashions or shapes things; a tailor.

FASS, a measure of capacity used in Germany, of a very variable character, ranging as a dry measure from 1½ gallons in Dusseldorf, to 11½ in Altona. For charcoal it is 59 gallons at Treves, in Prussia. As a liquid measure it is equally variable and difficult to define, and differs with the nature of the contents. In Vienna the fass of wine is about 127½ gallons, in Leipsic it is 83½, and so on. One Hamburgh last of 60 fass is equivalent to 11 Imperial quarters; 1 fass = 2 himpten.

FAST, the rope by which a vessel is secured to a wharf; in nautical language attached to; as when a boat is secured by a rope; a vessel aground is said to be "hard and fast."

FASTENING, a stop or holdfast; a bolt or bar; a screw or spring-catch for window-sashes; also a security for doors.

FAST-TRAIN, an express railway train.

FATA-MORGANA (Italian), the name applied to an optical illusion which occurs in the Straits of Messina; the Fairy Morgana.

FATHOM, an English nautical measure of six feet, employed in sounding mines, &c., and measuring cordage. It is also used in India, being divided into four arms or cubits of eighteen inches each. A fathom of fire wood is six feet wide by six feet high.

FAT-LUTE, a mixture of pipeclay and linseed-oil for filling joints.

FATS, solid oily substances found in the animal and vegetable kingdoms, which enter largely into commerce, and are described under their several heads.

FAUCET, a pipe; a spout with a peg or spigot for drawing liquor from a cask.

FAUCHARD, a small sickle with a long handle, used in France.

FAUCHET (French), a wooden hay-rake.

FAULDS (Scotch), the part of a farm manured by folding sheep or cattle on it.

FAULX, FAUX (French), a scythe or reaping-hook.

FAUTEUIL, a large elbow-chair.

FAUX, a Swiss land measure of 7,855 English square yards, or 65 2-3rds French acres: 6 1-6th faux = 10 imperial acres.

FAUXBOURG, FAUBOURGS (French), the suburbs of a town.

FAVO (Spanish), a cake of yellow wax.

FAVOUR, a bunch or knot of ribbons worn at weddings or other festive occasions.

FAWAL, an Arab vender of boiled beans for breakfast, which are eaten with butter and lemon juice.

FAWN a young deer under one year old.

FAYING, in maritime phraseology, the union of two pieces so close that no intervening space occurs.

FEAL, a provincial name for sward or turf; hence feal-dyke, feal-manure, &c.

FEARNOUGHT, a thick shaggy woollen stuff, used for draymen's coats, sailors' pea-jackets, and for lining the portholes and the outside door of a powder-magazine in a ship. It is also known as dreadnought.

FEAST, a sumptuous repast; a public banquet or entertainment.

FEATHER-DRESSER, a cleaner or preparer of feathers.

FEATHER-DRIER, FEATHER-BEATER, one who beats feathers, to cleanse and make them light or loose.

FEATHER-DUSTER, a light brush made of feathers.

FEATHER-EDGED, planks, or any wrought substance in which one side is much thicker than the other.

FEATHER-FLOWERS, artificial flowers made of feathers, which are used by ladies for head ornaments, and for fancy plumes and groups for rooms.

FEATHERING, in rowing, a term applied to the uniform turning of the edge of an oar horizontally, when raised from the water.

FEATHER-MERCHANT, an importer or wholesale dealer in feathers, who sells to feather-dressers and plumassiers.

FEATHER-PURIFIER, one who boils or steams feathers, to fit them for bedding or upholstery purposes.

FEATHERS, the light portion of the wings and plumage of birds. The kinds most used for dress and military purposes, are those of the ostrich, marabou stork, American or three-toed ostrich, emu, heron, birds of paradise, ibis, and domestic fowls. The feathers of the emu, of the white egret heron, and of the osprey, or fish-hawk, are used in military costume, and for ladies' ornaments. The tail feathers of the domestic cock, either dyed or in their natural colours, are much used for military plumes. The manufacture of feathers into ornaments employs great numbers of females. Grebe and loon skins, and swan's down, are also used for muffs, and trimmings of ladies' dresses. Feathers from common birds, and the soft fine down from aquatic birds of cold climates, from their elasticity, softness, and non-conducting powers, are eminently useful to man. *See* BIRDS OF PARADISE, MARABOU-FEATHERS, OSTRICH-FEATHERS, &c.

FEAUK, a Scotch plaid.

FECKET (Scotch), a woollen shirt or under waistcoat.

FECULA, the starch or meal of different plants; the pulverulent matter extracted from vegetables by grinding them in water, and allowing the fluid to settle; the fecula then subsides.

FEDDAN, a land measure of Egypt and Turkey, equal to about an acre; it is divided into 24 gerats; among the Arabs it is about one and a third acre.

FEDELINI, a kind of dried Italian paste in a pipe form, of a smaller size than vermicelli.

FEE, a gratuity or reward given to a professional man, as a physician or barrister, for advice or service; a perquisite claimed by official personages under legal authority, or by prescription; a Scotch term for small domestic cattle, such as sheep, goats, &c.; also wages and property.

FEEDER, the stream supplying a river or canal; a branch railway, running into the main-trunk line; a large head or supply of fluid iron to a runner or mould in heavy castings.

FEEDING-BOTTLE, a glass bottle for supplying milk or liquid nutriment to an infant in the absence or indisposition of its mother.

FEED-PUMP, the force-pump which supplies the boiler of an engine with water.

FEE-FARM-RENT COLLECTOR, a person in Scotland employed to wait upon tenants of land, for the rent due to the owner of the property. *See* FEW-FERME.

FEE-SIMPLE, in law, the largest estate which a man can have, and which may be disposed of by deed or by will; a property acquired by inheritance.

FEET, a commercial name given to the twenty-five small plates of tortoise-shell, from the edges of the carapace; the superior plates being called "the head."

FEEZE-NAIL (Scotch), a screw.

Feint, another name for the viertel, a German grain measure, representing the quart.

Feints. *See* Faints.

Fe'latier, Fe'ratier, a glass-blower's assistant in France.

Felin, a weight for gold and silver, formerly used in France, the 80th part of the ounce, and the 4th of the esterlin; nearly 6 English grains.

Fell, a skin, the hide of an animal; in Scotland, high pasture land.

Fellahs, the peasants or labouring classes in Egypt.

Fell-monger, a dealer in hides; a dresser of skins; a part of the business of the fellmonger is to separate the wool from the sheep's skin, the wool being sold to the woolstaplers, and the pelts, or stripped skins, sent to the leather-dressers and parchment-makers.

Felloes, the circular parts of a wheel, generally made of ash, framed and supported on the extremities of the spokes, and joined one to another, so as to form a circle.

Fellow, to match; one of a pair.

Fellow-craft, a freemason of the second rank; one above an entered apprentice.

Fellowship, a companionship or guild; an association.

Fellowship-porters, a body of enrolled porters; one of the companies of London not on the livery, whose hall is in St. Mary-at-hill.

Felly, the exterior part or rim of a wheel, supported by the spokes. *See* Felloes.

Felony, in law, every crime which entails, besides punishment, the forfeiture of lands or goods; murder, manslaughter, arson, robbery, burglary, and offences against the coin, are felonies.

Felpilla (Spanish), corded silk for embroidering.

Felspar, a silicious mineral, of which there are several varieties, displaying elegant and varied iridescent colours. Cornish stone or porcelain clay is one of the products of decomposed felspar.

Felt, matted hair, wool, and other substances, first carded and delivered in the form of a fine bat or lap, and then converted into a stout mass or cloth by a peculiar rubbing that causes the interlocking of the fibres, or felting. Felt is used for hat bodies, for heavy cloths to resist water, and for other purposes.

Felting, the operation of matting or uniting different substances into one compact mass.

Felt-maker, a manufacturer of felt, of which there are two kinds: that used for hat-making and for cloth, and a more stout and coarse material, used for flooring, roofing, &c.

Felt-maker's Company, one of the livery companies of London, which has no hall, but conducts its business at Guildhall.

Felucca, a small coasting vessel in the Mediterranean, carrying two masts with latean sails; often propelled with oars, as well as sails.

Fen, a moor or marsh.

Fen-boat, a boat used in the creeks of marshes, and lands overflowed with water.

Fence, the guard of a carpenter's plane; a rail, or bordering protection for a field, such as a wall, ditch, bank, &c.; live fences are hedges of quickset; a slang term for a receiver of stolen goods; to thrust, parry, or guard off a blow.

Fencing, wooden or metallic casing, as a protection for machinery in factories, required to be placed by law, to prevent injury to the workman about the machinery.

Fend, to ward off.

Fender, a thick piece of rope or solid wooden guard or protection hung over the side in vessels, to prevent injury to the bulwarks, &c., by chafing or collision; a solid or open ornamented metal casting placed before a fireplace, for enclosing the cinders and ashes of the grate.

Fenester, Fenetre, a window, an opening in a building, by which air and light are admitted.

Fenim, a petty money of account in Switzerland, 540 making a rixdollar.

Fenks, the ultimate refuse of the blubber of the whale, which forms an excellent manure when available, and might be used in the manufacture of Prussian blue, and also for the production of ammonia.

Fennel, an umbelliferous plant, the *Anethum fœniculum dulce*, cultivated on the Continent as a pot-herb, and for the seeds and essential oil obtained from them. The seed is used in the manufacture of gin, and in medicine as a carminative. Another species, the common fennel, *Fœniculum officinale*, is cultivated in gardens as a garnish for fish, &c., and as a pot-herb for flavouring sauces.

Fenugreek, a plant, native of the South of France, the *Trigonella Fœnum Græcum*, the seeds of which are emollient; poultices made of the flour are employed in veterinary practice, and the Arabs use it in fomentations.

Feoffee, one vested with the fee of land.

Fer-blantier (French), a tinker; one who works or sells tin.

Ferde, a piece of coarse cotton cloth; a nominal medium of value among the Berbers in Nubia.

Ferding, a small money of account in the Russian ports of the Baltic, the 80th part of the rixdollar.

Feret, a glass-blower's rod. *See* Ferret.

Ferlino, the sixteenth part of the ounce in Italy.

Ferlot. *See* Firlot.

Ferment, a name for yeast or barm, the scum which collects on beer.

Fermentation, an effervescence or ebullition in fluids, which is either vinous or acetous; a decomposition in animal and vegetable substances.

Fermoir (French), a clasp; a joiner's ripping-chisel.

Fern, Fearn (*Scotch*), prepared gut.

Fernandina, Fe'randine, a stuff made of silk and wool; a weaver.

FEROSH, an Indian servant who has the care of tents, furniture, &c.
FERRADO, a corn measure of Spain, the third part of the Castilian fanega, and containing about four gallons.
FERRAILLE (French), old iron.
FERRET, an animal of the weasel tribe (*Mustela furo*), kept for the purpose of hunting rabbits, and destroying rats, &c. in corn stacks and out-buildings; in French, a tag for a lace or point; in glass-making, an iron used to make the rings at the mouths of bottles, or to try the melted matter.
FERRONNERIE (French), a warehouse for iron; a blacksmith's shop.
FERRUGINOUS, containing particles of iron.
FERRULE, a metal ring or case, fixed on the handle of a tool, or at the end of a stick or umbrella, to prevent the wood from splitting.
FERRY, the place in a river, lake or harbour, where a boat plies for the conveyance of goods or passengers from shore to shore.
FERRY-BOAT, a boat employed in crossing a ferry.
FERRY-COW, FARROW-COW (Scotch), a cow that has brought forth; a cow not in calf.
FERRYMAN, a waterman who plies at a ferry.
FERTILE, rich or fruitful; having abundant resources.
FERTILIZER, a manure; an application to the soil, organic or inorganic.
FERULE. *See* FERRULE.
FESTIVAL, a holiday; a day set apart for rejoicing, public or private. *See* PUBLIC HOLIDAY.
FESTOON, a kind of ornamental hanging drapery, suspended in a curve with ends passed over; a garland of flowers.
FETLOCK-BOOT MAKER, a manufacturer of protections or supports for the pastern joints of horses.
FETTER, a shackle or chain for the feet; iron links for spanning horses' feet, when grazing in open grounds, to prevent them straying to a distance.
FETTLE, order, good condition; any thing neatly bound or tied; in Scotland a horse's girth made of straw; a handle in the side of a large basket.
FEU, heritable property held on the condition of a certain return in grain, money, &c.
FEU-DUTY, a land-tax; annual rent paid in Scotland by a vassal.
FEU-FERME, the rent or duty paid by a tenant for lands in Scotland.
FEUILLAGE (French), foliage; a row of leaves; branched work.
FEUILLANTINE, pastry made of puff-paste.
FEUILLE (French), a leaf or sheet of paper; a bill.
FEUILLE-MORTE, the colour of a faded leaf.
FEUILLETON, that part of a French newspaper, devoted to literary and dramatic criticism; a small public journal.
FEUILLETTE (French), a half-hogshead.
FEUTRIERE (French), felted cloth.
FEVERFEW, the popular name of the *Pyrethrum Parthenium*, a wild plant, a decoction of which is a favourite popular remedy for slight fevers. It contains much tannic acid, and in Germany has been usefully employed in tanning and currying leather. A medicinal extract is also made from the *Matricaria chamomilla*, which was formerly classed as a fever-few.
FIACRE, a French hackney-coach.
FIARS, the average prices of grain legally fixed for the year in Scotland.
FIASCO, a liquid measure of Italy; for wine about four pints, and for oil somewhat less.
FIBRE, a general name for the cotton, flaxen, and hempen raw material, which forms so important a class of our textile manufactures.
FICELLE (French), pack-thread or twine.
FICELLIER, a roller for pack-thread.
FICHEUR (French), a brick-layer.
FICHU (French), a sort of neckerchief worn by ladies.
FICHURE (French), a spear or trident to catch fish.
FICTILE, moulded into form by art; manufactured of clay by the potter.
FID, a tapered wooden pin, used by seamen in splicing large ropes, opening eyes, or holes, &c.; an iron support passed through a hole in the heel of a mast.
FIDDLE, a violin, a stringed instrument so called.
FIDDLE-BLOCK, a block with two sheaves; one over the other; the lower one smaller than the upper.
FIDDLE-BOW, FIDDLE-STICK, the stringed bow with which a fiddler draws sound from his instrument.
FIDDLER, one who plays on a violin.
FIDDLE-STRINGS, the catgut cords, stretched across a violin, fastened at the ends, and elevated in the middle by a bridge.
FIDDLE-WOOD, a durable wood used for mills framing, carriage-wheels, &c.; the produce of *Citharexylum melanocardium*; a useful timber tree of the West Indies.
FIDEOS (Spanish), vermicelli.
FIEF, an estate in lands held from a superior.
FIEL (Spanish), a clerk of the market; a wharfinger.
FIELD, a portion of arable land; a large extent of compact ice.
FIELD BED, a portable or folding camp-bed for an officer.
FIELD-BOOK, a land surveyor's plotting book, in which the angles, distances, stations, &c. are noted down for mapping or reference.
FIELD-CORNET, the magistrate of a township in the Cape colony.
FIELD-GUN, a piece of cannon mounted on a two-wheel carriage, and drawn by horses, which can be carried into the field of battle.
FIELD-MARSHAL, the highest military rank in England; one who takes the command of an army. A field-marshal may command two regiments at once.
FIELD-OFFICER, a military officer above the rank of captain.
FIELD-PIECE, a portable cannon for service with an army, throwing a shot of from 3 to 12 pounds.
FIERDINGAR. *See* FURDINGAR.

FIFE, a very small wooden flute or pipe giving acute piercing sounds.
FIFER, one who plays on a fife, a musician to a regiment.
FIFE-RAIL, the rail round a ship's mast.
FIG-CAKE, a preparation of figs and almonds worked up into a hard paste, and pressed into round cakes like small cheeses, which is vended about the streets.
FIGON, a Spanish eating-house.
FIGS, the dried fruit of *Ficus carica*, chiefly imported from the Mediterranean ports. In 1855 we received upwards of 2200 tons, nearly all of which were for home consumption.
FIGURANTE (French), a female ballet-dancer.
FIGURE, a number; an artist's model; any representation made of things in wood, stone, or other solid material; the steps of a dance; to goffer, to emboss, to ornament a stuff with gold, silk, &c.
FIGURE-HEAD, a carved bust, statue, or full-length figure, placed over the cutwater or bow of a ship.
FIGURE-MAKER, a modeller; one who practises the most refined part of the art of moulding, and casts busts, animals, and many ornaments consisting of branches, foliage, &c.; a maker of wooden anatomical models for artists.
FIGURED-MUSLIN, a thin fabric in which a pattern, design, or representation is wrought. *See* MUSLIN.
FIGURE-WEAVING, a process differing from plain weaving; patterns or designs being produced in the damask, velvet, or other stuff, by employing threads of different colours or of different appearance, in the warp or in the weft.
FIL (French), thread, hair, wire; a small twist of silk, hemp, or flax.
FILADIERE, a small flat-bottomed fishing-boat used on the river Garonne.
FILAMENT, a string; a long fibre or fine thread.
FILASSE (French), hemp or flax ready to be spun.
FILASSIER, a flax or hemp dresser.
FILATURE, a silk-yarn, or cotton-twist, manufactory; a workshop where silk is reeled from cocoons and spun.
FILBERT, the fruit of the cultivated hazel (*Corylus avellana*), of which there are several varieties grown in this country.
FILCH, to steal or purloin.
FILE, a workman's metal rubbing or abrading tool, of which there are many kinds, as rubber, handsaw, pitsaw, rattail, bastard, half-round, &c. The difference between files and rasps, is that the latter have angular indentations, and the former have only straight cuts. Files are of the first importance to every worker in metal, from the engineer builder to the maker of the most delicate watch movement; they require great skill in hardening to prevent their warping. Small files are made of the best cast steel and cut by hand; those of larger size are manufactured from ordinary steel, and usually machine-made; these are frequently deficient in their "bite." Also the name for a rank or row as a file of soldiers; also for a wire or string which retains and secures documents or receipts for reference.
FILE (French), fine wire-thread of gold or silver.
FILE-CUTTER, a maker of files.
FILERIE (French), a spinning-house where hemp or flax is spun; a rope-walk.
FILET, a small thread of fibre; a string or lace.
FILEUR (French), a spinner, a wire drawer.
FILINGS, fragments or raspings of metal, ivory, &c.; particles rubbed off in the process of filing.
FILLE-DE-CHAMBRE, a French chambermaid.
FILLET, a band for the hair; a chine of meat; the fleshy part of the thigh, boned, rolled together, and tied round.
FILLIGREE, FILIGRANE, FILAGREE WORK, ornamental kinds of jewelry, statues, &c., made from delicate threads of gold or silver wire; the filaments being braided and festooned in various ways, according to the taste and design of the artist, and with a very light and beautiful effect.
FILLINGS, a brewer's term for prepared wort, added in small quantities to casks of ale to cleanse it; the woof in weaving
FILLISTER, a plane used for making the outer part of a window sash fit for receiving the glass.
FILLY, a young mare.
FILOCHE (French), a large rope used by millers and others.
FILOSEDA (Spanish), a silk and worsted fabric.
FILOSELLE, ferret, or floss silk; grogram-yarn.
FILOTIER (French), a dealer in thread.
FILTER, a small strainer of unsized paper used in chemical operations; an earthenware, or other vessel, with a tap for purifying water, in a house or on shipboard.
FILTERING, the process of straining and purifying.
FILTER-MAKER, a potter; one who moulds and makes filters.
FIN, a membraneous winglike appendage to fish; the trade name for a blade of whalebone: sharks' fins enter into eastern commerce dried, being eaten as food.
FINANCE (French), ready money or cash; a type in printing to imitate writing.
FINANCIER, a treasurer; an accountant; a capitalist or monied man skilled in financial operations; a public officer who manages the funds or revenues of the Crown.
FINDINGS, the wax, thread, and tools which a journeyman shoemaker has to supply himself with for his work.
FINDING-STORES, an American name for what are termed in England grindery-warehouses; shops where shoemakers' tools, &c. are vended.
FINE-ARTS, the arts of design, music, &c.; any business or pursuit requiring taste, skill, and judgment in the execution
FINE-DRAWING, the art of sewing up cloth so finely, that the rent cannot be perceived.
FINEER (Scotch), to veneer.
FINERY, a small forge used in making iron wire; showy articles of dress; jewels, trinkets, &c.

Fine-stilling, the distillation of spirit from molasses or other preparations of sugar.

Fine-stuff, the second coat of plaster for the walls of a room, composed of finely sifted lime and sand, mixed with hair; the first coat is of a coarser material.

Finger, an ancient measure, the fourth part of the palm of hand, nearly an inch; still used in parts of India.

Finger-board, part of a fiddle.

Finger-glass, a coloured or plain glass vessel to hold water for rinsing the fingers after dessert.

Fingerin, worsted spun in Scotland from combed wool, on a small wheel.

Finger-plate, an ornamental piece of metal or porcelain fixed on the edge of a door, to keep off finger marks from the paint-work.

Finger-post, a guide-post or directing-post at cross roads.

Finger-stall, a workman's protection for the finger.

Finger-watch, a species of clock-work.

Fingroms, woollen cloth made of combed wool.

Fining pot, a vessel in which metals are refined.

Finings, a preparation of isinglass, gelatine, or other substances for clarifying beer.

Finisher, one who completes work for sale, as in watch-making, the boot and shoe trade, &c.

Finnack, a Scotch name for a white trout.

Finner-whale, the *Balænoptera boops*; this cetaceous animal, the fin-backed whale, furnishes the shortest and coarsest plates of baleen or whalebone.

Finnin Haddock, a mode of pronouncing Findon haddock, a species of smoke-dried fish, chiefly prepared in Scotland; but largely vended in London and other great towns.

Fir, a general name for the trees of the genera *Abies* and *Pinus*. *See* Pine.

Fire-annihilator, an apparatus holding a chemical composition, which has the effect of extinguishing fire, flame, and smoke.

Fire-arms, a collective name for the smaller kinds of offensive weapons from which destructive missiles are discharged; such as rifles, muskets, and pistols.

Fire-ball, a grenade filled with combustibles to be thrown among enemies.

Fire-balloon, a balloon sent up at night with fire-works, which ignite at a regulated height.

Fire-bars, moveable wedge-shaped iron bars in the fire-box of a locomotive engine; the bars of a grate.

Fire-basket, an iron receptacle for holding a small portable grate with coals, &c., for a bed-room.

Fire-box, a copper receiver for a locomotive engine, in which the fire is placed; having an outside casing of iron, thus forming an intermediate receptacle for water.

Fire-bricks, bricks 9 inches long, by 4½ broad, and 1¼ thick; used for lining chimneys, ovens, and furnaces, being capable of resisting intense heat; they are known in commerce by the names of Bristol, Stourbridge, Newcastle, Welsh, and Windsor bricks.

Fire-brigade, a body of firemen; persons in large towns trained to do duty at conflagrations, and held in constant readiness to proceed with fire engines and buckets, to assist in extinguishing fires.

Fire-brush, a hair sweeping-brush for the hearth of a room.

Fire-bucket, a light canvas or leather pail used by firemen to convey water.

Fire-clay, a refractory clay, nearly a pure silicate of alumina, abounding under the coal-measures, which is used for the manufacture of fire-bricks and gas retorts.

Fire-cock, a plug for obtaining water from the main pipes in a street to extinguish fires.

Fire-crackers, a preparation of gunpowder, &c., discharged for amusement. A large trade is carried on in fire-crackers from China to the United States. They are shipped from Canton, in boxes of 40 packs each, and sell at about 12s. the box; the imports from China to New York averaging £50,000 per annum in value.

Fire-damp, impure carburetted hydrogen; foul air found in coal mines.

Fire-dog, an andiron or rest for wood on a fire hearth.

Fire-engine, an hydraulic machine or force-pump, for raising water to a great height to extinguish conflagrations.

Fire-escapes, contrivances of various kinds to facilitate exit from a burning building; as iron chains, link ladders, &c. The most generally adopted public fire-escape is a wheel-carriage, supporting a lofty canvas sheet or trunk, attached to a ladder or frame, which can be raised to the upper story windows of a building, and parties can slide safely down it to the ground.

Fire-guard, a wire frame to be hung before a fire-grate to prevent sparks and burning coals, &c. flying out and endangering furniture.

Fire-insurance, an indemnity against loss from fire, obtained by payment of a small percentage annually to an insurance company.

Fire-irons, the utensils for a fire grate; tongs, poker, and shovel.

Fire-kiln, an oven or place for heating any thing.

Fire-lock, a musket.

Fireman, a stoker; the feeder of a furnace, marine or locomotive engine; a member of a fire-brigade.

Fire-office, an office where insurance against loss from fire can be effected.

Fire-place, the place within a chimney-piece where fuel is burnt, usually an open grate.

Fire-plug. *See* Fire-cock.

Fire Policy, the official certificate or document received from an insurance office, guaranteeing the payment of a certain sum in the case of loss of property by fire.

Fire-proof, a vault, safe, or building, so constructed as to be secure from the ravaging effects of fire, should it break out.

FIRE-PROOF-BOX MAKER, a manufacturer of iron safes for securing books and papers.

FIRE SCREEN, a wire guard or protection against fire. *See* FIRE-GUARD.

FIRE-SET, the metal articles, poker, shovel, and tongs for a grate; usually made of steel or wrought iron.

FIRE-SHIP, a vessel filled with combustibles sent into an enemy's fleet to injure it.

FIRE-SHOVEL, the coal shovel for a fire-place.

FIRE-TUBE, a pipe flue.

FIRE-WARDEN, a head fireman: the officer in America who directs the operations of a fire brigade.

FIRE-WOOD, small bundles of wood, in different shapes, prepared by machinery, for lighting fires: the sale of fire-wood has now become a very important and extensive trade in London and other populous towns.

FIRE-WORK MAKER, a pyrotechnist; a manufacturer of explosive articles for amusement, signals, &c.

FIRE-WORKS, pyrotechnic preparations; such as squibs, rockets, serpents, crackers, and other more elaborate, explosive, and combustible compositions of powder, &c. for brilliant display.

FIRING-IRON, a farrier's cautery.

FIRKIN, an English measure of capacity, the fourth of a barrel, now disused; but the name is still applied to a cask containing nominally 9 gallons of beer or 8 of ale, but truly only 7½ imperial gallons. A firkin of soap is 64 lbs.; of butter usually considered 56 lbs; but Irish butter firkins weigh nearly ¾ of a cwt. gross, the cask weighing about 14 lbs.

FIRLOT, a Scotch dry measure, the fourth part of the boll; the Linlithgow wheat firlot is 2211 cubic inches, very nearly equal to the imperial bushel, but the barley firlot contains 31 standard pints only, = 1074·429 cubic inches.

FIRM, a co-partnership; a house of business; the abbreviated title under which a trade is conducted, or a body of partners is known

FIRMAN, an edict or legal authority from the Turkish government.

FIR-PINE FRUIT, a name in the Ionian islands for the seeds of the pine cones, used as food.

FIRST, a kind of brick or marl-stock. *See* [BRICKS.

FIRST-CLASS PASSENGER, a traveller in the best fitted carriages on a railway line; contradistinguished from the second and third class passengers, who pay lower fares, and have inferior accommodation.

FIRST-HAND, obtained direct from the maker, shipper, or wholesale dealer.

FIRST LORD, the chief commissioner or lord of the admiralty board.

FIRST-MATE, the chief officer of a merchant vessel; the next in rank to the captain.

FIRST-RATE, excellent; of superior quality; one of the largest ships of war, a vessel carrying 100 or more guns.

FISANELLA, a water fowl, *Colymbus major*, or great diver.

FISCAL, a public officer in Scotland, who prosecutes in petty criminal cases; an attorney or solicitor general in Spain; an exchequer officer in Ceylon; one who has charge of the fisc or treasury of a prince, State, &c.

FISH, a general name for marine swimming animals, in the capture and sale of which a large trade is carried on: a sea-term for strengthening a weakened spar by fastening another piece on; to raise the flukes of an anchor on the gunwale, or vessel's side; to catch fish by net, or by hook and line.

FISH-BASKET, a large flat or deep wicker basket for holding or transporting fish.

FISH-CARLE, a Scotch fisherman.

FISH-CARVER, a silver knife for helping fish at a dinner table.

FISH-CURER, a salter and smoker of fish.

FISHER, a name for the *Mustela Canadensis*; the skin is principally used for trimmings and linings, the fur being long, fine, and lustrous, but not so valuable as the sable. The tail is extensively used by the Jews.

FISHERMAN, one who follows the business of catching fish for sale.

FISH-FAG, a fishwoman.

FISH-FLAKES, erections in the North American colonies, for drying fish on.

FISHGARTHS, a dam or weir in a river, for catching and retaining fish.

FISH-GIG, a kind of harpoon or spear, with several barbed prongs attached to a line, used for striking fish at sea; often called a dolphin-striker.

FISH-GLUE. *See* ISINGLASS.

FISH-HOOK MAKER, a manufacturer of metal hooks for catching fish.

FISH-HOOKS, barbed instruments, of various size and form, for catching fish. In making them, straight wires of the proper length are flattened at one end, and the barb is formed by a single blow with a chisel. The point having been sharpened, the proper curve or twist is given to the hook; the soft iron is then case-hardened, to give it the stiffness and elasticity of steel, by immersion in hot animal charcoal. The hooks are subsequently brightened by friction, and tempered.

FISHING-BOAT, a small decked or undecked boat, in which the pursuit of fish is carried on. [Scotch rivers.

FISHING-CRUIVE, an enclosure for fish in the

FISHING LINE, small cord of different sizes, with, in some instances, gut or chain attached, to which a hook is appended, for river or sea-fishing.

FISHING-NET, twine or cord formed into meshes of different sizes, for enclosing fish. There are various kinds of nets made, the bag-net for the angler, the shrimping-net, the drag-net, the trawl and the seine for sea-fishing; the casting-net, &c.

FISHING-ROD AND -TACKLE MAKER, a manufacturing tradesman who keeps on sale the appliances for angling.

FISH-KETTLE, an oblong metal boiler for cooking fish in.

FISH-KNIFE, a broad flat silver, or plated, knife for serving fish with at table.

FISH-MARKET, the place where fish is sold; in large towns it is usually a covered building with arranged stalls, and has the convenience of water for washing the fish.

FISHMAW, the sound of a fish. In the eastern seas, a large trade is carried on in fishmaws, which are sent to China and used as glue, &c.

FISH MEASURES, the customary measures used in selling and estimating fish, which vary with the kind of fish, thus:—Salmon is sent to market in boxes of 120lbs to 130lbs, containing about 14 fish; codfish in barrels, containing about 50 fish, and is sold by the quintal or cwt.; a barrel of herrings is 26⅔ gallons, and contains about 700 fresh fish, or 500 smoked; a basket of bloaters contains about 150; a cran of herrings is 37½ gallons; a mace or mease of herrings is 600 fish; a cade of herrings, 500 fish: a long hundred, 132; a cade of sprats, 1000; a barrel of pilchards is 41⅔ gallons, and 3000 pilchards weigh about 40lbs; a barrel of haddock contains about 300 fish; a stone of fish is 14lbs; a last of cod fish is 12 barrels; a last of herrings 100 long hundred, or 13,200; a barrel of anchovies, 30lbs. Native oysters are sold in kegs of 16lbs., containing about 5 score; or in barrels of 1600. Dried sprats are sold in bundles of 30; cockles and whelks wholesale by the bushel; shrimps by the gallon; periwinkles and mussels by the basket.

FISHMONGER, **FISH-SALESMAN**, a general dealer in fish.

FISHMONGERS' COMPANY, one of the principal incorporated companies of London, the fourth in order of the 12 great livery companies, whose hall is in Adelaide-place, London bridge. This company obtained its first charter in the 17th year of the reign of Edward I, A.D. 1289.

FISH-OIL, a general name for the oil obtained from various marine animals and fishes—from the black and white porpoise in the gulf of St. Lawrence; from the livers of sharks in warm regions; from pilchards, ray, cod, and other large and small fish; from the seal, sea-elephant, dugong, &c.

FISH-POT, a wicker basket or enclosure sunk with a cork float attached, for catching crabs, lobsters, &c.

FISH-SALESMAN, one who receives consignments of fish for sale to retail dealers.

FISH-SAUCES, anchovy, soy, and other condiments used as flavourings for cooked fish.

FISH-SCALES, the coating of some fish: the hard scales are now frequently used for making brooches, bracelets, and ornamental flowers, &c. The scales of the bleak are dissolved to coat the inner surface of glass beads or artificial pearls.

FISH SLICE, a silver perforated table instrument for serving fish.

FISH-SKIN, the covering of the flesh of marine animals. The rough skin of the dog-fish or shark, is used by the cabinet-maker, type-founder, and others, as an abrasive material for smoothing wood-work and metals. A kind of shagreen is made of fish-skin. The skin of the porpoise, beluga, seal, &c., are tanned; eel skins are used for making strong ropes, for connecting the swiple and hand-staff of a thrashing-flail, and for other purposes. Sole skins and some others, are used for clarifying coffee and liquors.

FISH-SOUND, the swimming-bladder of a fish, many of which are prepared for isinglass; others, as cod-sounds, are salted for food; some are sold to the Chinese under the name of fishmaws.

FISH-STRAINER, a metal cullender with handles, for taking fish from a boiler; an earthenware slab with holes, placed at the bottom of a dish, to drain the water from cooked fish.

FISH-TAIL BURNER, a gas jet of that shape.

FISH-VAN, a light spring-cart for transporting fish; a railway truck set apart for fish.

FISH-WEAR, a dam in a river, or on the sea shore, for stopping fish.

FISOLIERE (French), a Venetian sculler.

FIT, to join, to dove-tail, to clamp; Scotch a custom.

FITCH, a common name for the polecat, an animal of the weasel tribe, the skin of which is much used for fur; a Scotch term for moving any thing a little way from its place.

FITCHES, another name for vetches or tares.

FIT-GANG (Scotch), as much ground as one can move on.

FITTER, a coal-broker; a weigher at the mint; a tailor, one who tries on and adjusts articles of dress; a gas-fitter, is one who lays on pipes to houses, &c.; an out-fitter, is a shopkeeper who keeps ready-made garments on sale, or procures them properly made to order.

FITTIOK, a piece of dammour or coarse cotton cloth, which is a medium of currency in Nubia.

FITTINGS, shop-fixtures, tackle for a ship; equipment, &c.

FIXATURE, a gummy composition for the hair. *See* BANDOLINE.

FIXTURE-DEALER, a furniture-dealer; a vender of shop-counters, desks, drawers, &c.

FIZ-GIG, a harpoon; a small firework of moistened gunpowder. *See* FISH-GIG.

FLACK, **FLAIK** (Scotch), a square plaid.

FLACKET, a barrel-shaped bottle.

FLACKIE, a truss made of straw for protecting a horse's back from the creel or basket for carrying fish, potatoes, &c.

FLACON, **FLAGON**, a flask or decanter, a carafe; a vessel with a narrow mouth; a smelling-bottle.

FLAG AND COMPASS MAKER, a manufacturer and retailer of these articles for ships' use.

FLAGEOLET, an English flute; a small wooden musical instrument, played on by means of a mouth-piece, and furnished with holes or keys for fingering.

FLAG-OFFICER, the commander of a squadron; an admiral, of whom there are three ranks, bearing respectively the distinguishing flags of red, white, or blue.

FLAGON, a jug; a measure of two quarts.

FLAGS, large flat thin stones for paving, from 1½ to 3 inches thick, and of various lengths and breadths, obtained in the quarries of the north of Scotland, Yorkshire and Lancashire, and also imported from Hamburgh, for the foot-walks of streets, the floors of houses and factories, and for paving yards and wharves, &c. The aggregate excavations of flags throughout the United Kingdom have been estimated at one million tons per annum. Flagging stones are obtained from all the sandstone formations below the coal measures.

FLAG-SHIP, the commanding vessel of a fleet or on a naval station; that which bears the admiral's flag at the mast-head.

FLAG-SIDE, a Scotch term for the boneless side of a split haddock.

FLAG-STAFF, the pole or spar on which a banner or flag is elevated.

FLAIL, a wooden instrument for thrashing corn by hand.

FLAKE-WHITE, a sub-nitrate of bismuth: oxidised carbonate of lead in the form of scales or plates; when levigated, it is called body white.

FLAMBEAU, a link or torch.

FLAN (French), a custard, a kind of tart made with cream.

FLANCHET (French), part of a sirloin of beef.

FLANDERS-BRICK, a soft brick used for cleaning knives. *See* BATH-BRICK.

FLANG, a two-pointed pick used by miners.

FLANGE, part of a wheel, of a railway-bar, of a gas-pipe, &c.; something screwed on to another piece.

FLANGE-MAKER, a manufacturer of iron girders, joints for gas-pipes, and other perforated metal pieces to be attached to other pieces or parts.

FLANNEL, a soft open woollen stuff, of which there are many kinds, milled, gauze, coloured and checked, cricketing and house flannel, blankets, &c.; upwards of 54 million yards are made in this country annually.

FLANNEL-SHIRT, a woven worsted or woollen inner garment.

FLASK, a metal or other pocket dram-bottle; a measure for holding gunpowder; a shallow iron frame or casting-box, without top or bottom, used in foundries for moulding; the lower flask is called a drag; a globular glass vessel for holding liquids containing about half a gallon: in Holland 16 flasks make an anker. The flask of quicksilver from California is about 75lbs.

FLASKET, a long shallow basket with two handles.

FLAT, a description of river boat for conveying merchandise, which usually carries from 80 to 120 tons; those worked by the captains or owners are termed No 1 flats. Also a basket or hamper in which the English farmers usually send their butter to market, containing from 3 to 6 dozen pounds; a rough piece of bone for a button mould; to preserve gilding by size; a story or floor of a building, sometimes constructed so as to accommodate a family having the necessary suite of rooms. In Scotland and some other large towns, houses are specially built for letting in these kinds of flats or floors with one common staircase.

FLAT-BOTTOMED, a vessel with an even lower surface and but small depth.

FLAT-IRON, FLATTENING-IRON, a laundress's or workman's smoothing-iron.

FLATTING, the operation of smoothing; a mode of house-painting in which the colour on the surface is left without gloss.

FLATTING-MILL, a mill for rolling out metals by cylindrical pressure.

FLAUCHT (Scotch), a flake of wool, a handful; when applied to land, a croft.

FLAUCHTER, a term in Scotland having various significations in different localities; in some parts it is a man who pares turf; in Fife it is a skinner, one who scrapes skins; in the South of Scotland a person employed in carding wool.

FLAUCHTER-SPADE, a long two-handed tool for cutting turf.

FLAUCHTS, instruments for carding wool used in Scotland.

FLAUTIST, a player on the flute.

FLAVINE, a vegetable extract from the United States, in the form of a light brown or greenish yellow powder, which contains much colouring matter and tannin, and takes the place of quercitron bark. It gives a fine olive yellow colour to cloth.

FLAW, a crack; a fracture or defect in metals, gems, timber, &c.

FLAWN, custard or pastry. *See* FLAN.

FLAX, a plant; the *Linum usitatissimum*, and the textile fibre obtained from it. From the seed an oil, known as linseed oil, is expressed, which is largely used in the arts. Our foreign supplies of flax come chiefly from Russia; we imported in 1856, 84,832 tons of dressed and undressed flax and tow.

FLAX-COMB, a hatchel or heckle for preparing flax.

FLAX-DRESSER, a cleaner of the fibre of flax.

FLAX-GROWER, a cultivator of the flax plant. Flax is chiefly grown in Ireland; in 1856 there were 106,826 acres under culture with flax, there calculated to produce 27,000 tons of fibre valued at £1,350,000, exclusive of the seed.

FLAX-MILL, a factory where flax is spun into linen goods.

FLAX-SEED, the boll of flax, generally termed linseed. In 1856 our imports were 1,180,179 quarters. *See* FLAX.

FLAY, to strip or cut off the skin.

FLEAK, a twist or lock; a hurdle or grating.

FLEAM, a large strong instrument, used by veterinary surgeons, for letting blood from horses and other animals.

FLEASOCKS (Scotch), the shavings of wood.

FLECKET (Scotch), a small pocket flask; a little portable dram barrel.

FLEECE, as much wool as is shorn from one sheep; the weight varies according to the breed and the climate.

FLEET, a navy; a collection of ships or sailing boats; an inlet or creek; swift, shallow.

FLEET-DYKE, an embankment for preventing inundation.

FLEETING-DISH, a skimming bowl.

FLEMISH-BRICKS, paving bricks of a yellowish colour, harder than the ordinary bricks.

FLEMISH-HORSE, in mariners' parlance, an additional footrope at the ends of topsail-yards.

FLENCH, FLINCH, to strip off in layers.

FLENCH-GUT, the blubber of a whale laid out in long slices in the hold before barrelling.

FLENCING, the operation of cutting the blubber from the whale.

FLESH, butcher's meat; the carcase of any animal killed for food.

FLESHARY, FLESHING, in Scotland the business of a butcher.
FLESHER, the common designation of a butcher in Scotland.
FLESH-BRUSH, a brush for rubbing the surface of the body, of which there are several kinds, made either of horsehair, or fine wire, &c.
FLESH-FORK, a cook's fork for trying meat, and taking it from the boiler.
FLESTOIR (French), a small hammer.
FLET, FLEAT, a mat of plaited straw for protecting a horse's back from injury by the load; a saucer. See FLACKIE.
FLETADOR (Spanish), the freighter of a ship.
FLETCHER, an old name for an arrow maker.
FLETCHERS' COMPANY, one of the minor livery companies of London, whose hall is in St Mary Axe.
FLET-MILK, skimmed milk.
FLETTE, a French passage boat or wherry.
FLEUK, FLOOK, a flounder.
FLEURAGH (French), oatmeal or bean meal for gruel.
FLEURET (French), a sort of coarse silk; a kind of narrow ribbon; ferret-ribbon.
FLEWS, in Scotland a sluice for letting off the water from an irrigated meadow.
FLIES, artificial insects which are very dexterously made of bright feathers, silk, &c., for the use of anglers for fish in rivers and lakes.
FLIGHT, a set of stairs.
FLINGIN-TREE (Scotch), the lower part of a flail; that which strikes the grain.
FLINKING-COMB, a dressing-table comb for the hair.
FLINT-GLASS, common table glass, which was originally made of flint.
FLINT-LOCK, a musket lock, with a flint fixed in the hammer, for striking on the steel pan.
FLINTS, nodules of silica occurring in the chalky strata, which are largely used for pottery. Flints for guns are now to a great extent superseded by the percussion cap, but common muskets for shipment are still supplied with flint locks. Sharpened flints are seldom used now for producing fire; congreve matches, or lucifers, having taken the place of the flint and steel with the tinder box.
FLINTY SLATE, a silicious schist containing about 75 per cent. of silica, which is used under the name of touchstone, for testing gold, by a comparison of colours.
FLISK, a large tooth comb.
FLITCH, a side of bacon.
FLITTERN BARK, the bark of young oak-trees, as distinguished from that of old oak-trees which is called timber bark and is less valuable to tanners. There is a third sort called coppice bark, which is the bark stripped off oak grown as coppice from stems or stools.
FLITTING (Scotch), removing from one place of residence to another; a moonlight flitting is synonymous to moving without paying one's debts or rent.
FLOAT, the water-gauge of a steam-boiler attached to the valve in a feed pipe; the buoy of a fishing line; a plasterer's tool; a coal cart; a raft of timber 18 feet square by 1 foot deep.
FLOAT-BOARDS. See FLOATS.
FLOATING-BRIDGE, a flat-bottomed ferry steam-boat in harbours or rivers running on chains laid across the bottom, and constructed for the conveyance of passengers, goods, and vehicles.
FLOATING-LIGHT, a life-buoy carried at a ship's stern, with a light or lanthorn, which can be dropped into the sea, in order to save any one falling overboard at night; a pyrotechnic; a stationary light-ship.
FLOATING-PIER, a landing-stage which rises and falls with the tide.
FLOATS, the boards fixed on the paddle-wheels of steamers, and to undershot water wheels, by which they act.
FLOATSAM, goods found floating on the sea from a wreck. See FLOTSAM.
FLOCK, an indefinite number of sheep, kept together under one shepherd; in Australia a shepherd will manage several thousand sheep.
FLOCK-MANUFACTURER, a grinder of wool; one who pulverizes and colours it for the use of the paper stainer wherewith to make flock paper.
FLOCK-MASTER, an owner of sheep.
FLOCK-PAPER, wall hangings in which finely pulverized and dyed wool is laid on the surface of paper and attached by size.
FLOCK-RAIK, a range of pasture-ground for sheep.
FLOCKS, a name given to the refuse or waste of cotton and wool, which is used for stuffing mattresses, seamen's bedding, and common furniture.
FLOKKIT (Scotch), having the nap raised or thickened.
FLOOD-GATE, a sluice in rivers, canals, or docks that may be opened or closed at will, to admit or exclude water.
FLOOD-TIDE, the advancing tide increasing towards high water.
FLOOK, a popular name in Scotland for various kinds of flat fish, but most generally applied to the common flounder; the broad plate on the arm of an anchor.
FLOOKAN, earth or clay of a slimy consistence; in mining, the shifting of the vein or lode by a cleft, &c.
FLOOR, the timber, bricks, &c. of the platform which forms the base or surface of any story of a house, and on which the planks or flooring is laid; the name in a general sense applies to all that part of a building on the same level, and varies, according to the height from the ground, as ground floor, first floor, second floor, &c.; the bottom of a vessel on each side of the kelson.
FLOOR-CLOTH, the name for printed oiled canvas used for covering entrance halls and floors, &c. The material is made partly of hemp and partly of flax. Six or seven coats of thick oil paint are applied on both sides to give it consistence, and the patterns are impressed by machinery or with blocks by hand. The value of this manufacture is about £1,500,000 annually.
FLOOR-CLOTH CANVAS, a coarse fabric manufactured chiefly at Dundee, and made of the width of eight yards or more. The oiling, painting, and finished manufacture principally centre in London.

FLOOR-CLOTH MANUFACTURER, a maker of oil-cloth or painted canvas.

FLOORING, the boards which are laid across the joists of a room for walking on.

FLOOSE, the tenth part of a danim, a petty money of Bussorah and other parts of Arabia. *See* DANIM.

FLORAN, a mining term for fine-grained tin, ore scarcely perceptible in the stone, or stamped very small.

FLORES. powder blue or indigo.

FLORENCE, a gold coin worth 6s.; a kind of wine.

FLORENCE-LEAF. *See* LEAF-METAL and BRONZE-POWDER.

FLORENCE-OIL, olive oil sold in flasks.

FLORENTINE, meat baked in a dish with a cover of paste; a kind of wrought satin made in Florence; a lake colour extracted from the shreds of scarlet cloth.

FLORES, a commercial classification of indigo, the best quality of dye from Nos. 7 to 9.

FLORETONNE, a Spanish wool.

FLORETTA, refuse or floss silk.

FLORIN, a British silver coin worth 2s., first minted in 1849, and since that period nine or ten million pieces have been put into circulation. The florin is a coin circulating in many Continental countries, ranging in value from 1s. 6d. to 2s. 4d.

FLORIST, a dealer in flowers; one who grows or sells them.

FLOSS, fluid glass floating in a puddling furnace.

FLOSS-SILK, the external soft envelope of the silk worm's cocoon; the ravelled downy silk broken off in the filature. It is carded and spun into coarse yarn or thread, suited for various purposes.

FLOTE-BOAT, in Scotland a yawl or pinnace.

FLOTILLA, a fleet of small vessels.

FLOTSAM, the portion of a ship or cargo wrecked which remains floating upon the water. *See* JETSAM and LAGAN-GOODS.

FLOUNCE, a loose appendage or trimming to the skirt or lower part of a lady's dress.

FLOUNDER, a well known flat fish, the *Pleuronectes flesus*, which is obtained on the British coasts and large rivers.

FLOUR, in ordinary parlance the meal of wheat finely ground and sifted, and in which a large trade is carried on by land and by sea. The term flour is, however, also applied to the meal of rice, potatoes, &c. Flour is usually put up in packs or loads of 240 lbs., or sacks of 280 lbs. In 1856 we imported four million cwts. of flour chiefly from the United States and Canada.

FLOUR-BARREL, a light cask, in which wheat meal is imported from America. The barrel of flour weighs 196 lbs.

FLOUR-DEALER, an agent for millers; one who sells flour to bakers.

FLOUR-DREDGE, a tin for sprinkling flour. *See* DREDGE.

FLOUR-DRESSER, a cylinder for dressing flour, instead of passing it through bolting cloths.

FLOURICE (Scotch), a steel for striking fire from flint.

FLOUR-SACK, a coarse bag for flour, holding usually 280 lbs.

FLOWER, an old Scotch name for an edged tool used in cleaving laths.

FLOWER-BASKET, a fancy stand or basket for holding flowers in a room.

FLOWER-GARDEN, an ornamental plot of ground, devoted to the culture and raising of flowers; a kitchen-garden, being that devoted to the culture of pot-herbs, fruit, &c.

FLOWER-POTS, earthenware or china pots for holding flowering plants.

FLOWERS, the blossoms of plants. A large trade is carried on by florists in ornamental plants and cut flowers. Imitation flowers, for personal decoration, &c., have already been alluded to under the head of Artificial flowers. In chymistry, the fine mealy matter formed in the process of sublimation is called flowers, as flowers of sulphur, zinc, benjamin, &c.

FLOWER-SHOW, a floricultural display, or competitive show for prizes, &c.

FLUATE, a salt from fluoric acid.

FLUE, a chimney tube or shaft; soft down or loose fur.

FLUID, a liquid or gas, any thing that flows; not solidified.

FLUKES, the broad, projecting, triangular hooked plates at the extremity of the arms of an anchor, one or other of which, according as it is tilted, enters the anchorage ground as a holdfast; a name for the plaice fish.

FLUME, a water-channel; a stream or run for gold washing.

FLUMMERY, a food of flour meal.

FLUNKIE (Scotch), a livery servant.

FLUOR-SPAR, fluate of lime, used as a flux for the metallic ores, whence its name. The coloured specimens are turned into vases and other ornaments, in Derbyshire.

FLUORIC ACID, a corrosive liquid prepared from fluor spar, used for etching upon glass, roughing the shades of table-lamps &c.

FLUSE, a copper coin of Morocco. *See* FLOOSE.

FLUSH (Scotch), full; as, affluent, flush of money; a flow or run of water, as in flushing a sewer; a workman's term for an even surface; any thing on the same level.

FLUSH-DECK, an even-deck, one running the whole length of the vessel from stem to stern, without a forecastle or poop.

FLUTE, a pipe or wind instrument, with lateral holes, made of various materials, hardwood, ivory, glass, metal, and even vulcanized India rubber; a long thin French roll eaten at breakfast; a store-ship.

FLUTED, grooved, furrowed, or channelled.

FLUTE-MAKER, one who makes flutes.

FLUTER, one who grooves or channels metals; a flautist; a person who goffers or plaits.

FLUTING-MACHINE, a goffering-iron.

FLUTINGS, hollow channels cut in the shafts of columns; piping or frill ornaments to a lady's cap or dress, &c.

FLUTTER-WHEEL, a peculiar kind of wheel to a water-mill.

FLUX, any substance used to cause the fusion and reduction of a metallic ore, or for pottery. Limestone, fluor spar, protoxide of lead, carbonate of potash, and charcoal, are various fluxes used.

FLY, that part of a ship's flag which extends from the union to the extreme end; a public carriage so named; the regulating moving power of a machine, as the weight in a jack.

FLY-BOAT, a long narrow boat used on canals; also a larger class of Dutch vessel, flat-bottomed, of several hundred tons.

FLY-FISHING, trolling in streams with a rod and line, and artificial flies.

FLY-FLAPPER, a fan or other instrument for keeping off flies.

FLYING-BRIDGE, a temporary bridge.

FLYING-FISH, the oceanic variety, *Exocetus volitans*, a native of the Indian and American seas; is esteemed in some parts a culinary delicacy.

FLY-LEAF, a spare blank leaf in a bound book.

FLY-PENNING, a mode of manuring land practised in the colonies, by folding cattle or sheep in rotation over different parts of it.

FLY-POWDER, an insect-destroying powder.

FLY-SHUTTLE, the shuttle impelled by the weaver.

FLY-WHEEL, a heavy regulating wheel, revolving on an axle, for equalizing the motion, and increasing the effect of machines.

FOAL, the young of the horse kind; a colt or filly; a Scotch bannock or soft cake.

FOB, a small pocket.

FOCUS, a centre; a hearth or fireplace; the point where the rays meet or converge, after passing through a convex glass.

FODDER, a general name for the dry food given to cattle, or stored for the winter; a weight by which lead is sold, varying from 19½ to 25 cwt., according to the custom of the district.

FOGE, a name in Cornwall for a forge for smelting tin.

FOGLIETTA, an Italian liquid measure varying from half an English pint to a pint.

FOG-SIGNAL, a detonating powder placed on a railway, which, when the engine passes over the rails, explodes with a loud report, and gives warning to the driver and guard of danger, &c.

FOILING, a division of tracery.

FOILS, books of gold or silver leaf; thin leaves of metal placed under artificial gems, to heighten their brilliancy; an amalgam of quicksilver and tin at the back of a looking-glass; guarded weapons for fencing.

FOIL-STONE, an imitation jewel.

FOIRE (French), a stated market in a town or city; a fair.

FOLD, a temporary enclosure for sheep or cattle; a farm.

FOLDING, the operation of doubling one part of a substance over another; putting sheets of printed matter in order for binding; in agriculture, penning sheep or cattle on land to feed and manure.

FOLDING-DOORS, a pair of doors to a room, which throw back.

FOLDING-MACHINE, a machine which delivers newspapers or printed book-work folded.

FOLDING-NET, a net for trapping small birds.

FOLDING-SCREEN, an upright portable screen, in several leaves or parts, which shuts up, and can be put away when not in use.

FOLDING-STOOL, a portable or camp stool.

FOLD-YARD, an enclosure for keeping cattle.

FOLE, a leather bottle used in Spain.

FOLILET (French), a shoulder of venison.

FOLIO, a volume; a printing term for the index letter or number of a sheet; the right and left hand pages of a ledger or account-book; a law stationer's term for 72 words of manuscript, but in exchequer proceedings it runs to 80 words, and in chancery proceedings, to 90 words.

FOLIOING, the operation of paging or marking a book.

FOLLETA (Spanish), a wine measure used in Italy, the fourth of the boccale. *See* FOGLIETTA.

FOLLOWER, a law-stationer's name for a sheet of parchment, which is added to the first, or indenture, &c. sheet.

FONCET (French), a long flat-bottomed barge.

FONDA, the Spanish name for an inn or tavern.

FONDIQUE, a hall for merchants, an exchange; a customs' warehouse in Spain and Portugal.

FONG, a coin current in Siam, the eighth of a tical, and worth about 4d.

FONOO, a name in some parts of the Pacific for the turtle.

FONT, a stone basin or vessel in a church, for holding water for the purposes of baptism.

FONTAH, an apron fabric of cotton and silk made in Turkey.

FONTANGE, a knot of ribbons on the top of a head-dress.

FOO, the Chinese name for a department.

FOOCHI, or FOOJI, a name in the Pacific for the plantain.

FOOD, victuals for man or beast; what is taken for nourishment.

FOO-FOO, a negro name for dough made from plantains; the fruit being boiled and then pounded in a mortar.

FOOL, a compound of gooseberries.

FOOLSCAP, a long folio writing-paper for official use, about 13½ by 16½ inches; a foolscap millboard is 18½ by 14½ inches.

FOOT, a lineal measure in Great Britain of 12 inches, or the third part of a yard. As a measure of length the foot varies in different countries; an ancient measure of two gallons; a weight for tin, now merely nominal, of 60 lbs.; a measurement for grindstones of 8 inches. The size of a stone is found by adding the diameter and thickness together, and dividing by 8, which gives the number of "foots;" the bottom of any thing, as of a shoe or stocking; the lower end of a mast or sail; the rest or support on which a machine or any thing heavy stands.

FOOT-BALL, a large ball to be kicked about.

FOOTMAN, a man-servant; an iron or brass stand with feet, or with a hook, for keeping any thing warm before a fire.

Foot-bath, a pan in which to wash the feet.

Foot-board, a support for the feet in a boat, gig, &c., or at a workman's bench.

Foot-iron, Foot-plate, a step for a carriage.

Foot-muff, a receptacle to keep the feet warm in travelling.

Foot-pan. *See* Foot-bath.

Foot-passenger, a pedestrian.

Foot-path, a beaten track, conferring by long usage a right of way through lands; the pavement, or side walk of a street.

Foot-rope, a rope stretched loosely along a ship's yard, for the seamen to stand on in furling the sails.

Foot-rule, a twelve-inch measuring stick.

Foots, refuse or sediment, as at the bottom of a sugar or oil cask, &c.

Foot-scraper, an iron scraper at an entrance door to remove the dirt from the feet before entering.

Foot-stall, the stirrup of a woman's saddle.

Foot-step, an inclined plane under a printing-press.

Foot-stick, a printer's tool.

Foot-stool, a small cushion or stool to rest the foot upon.

Foot-valve, a valve, so named, between the condenser and air-pump.

Foot-waling, the inside planks or lining of a vessel over the floor timbers and below the lower deck.

Foot-warmer, a heated stool for the feet; a chafing dish.

Footing, the finer detached fragments of the fenks, or refuse whale blubber, not wholly deprived of oil.

Forage, provender or food suited for horses and domestic cattle, as hay, straw, beans, grass, clover, &c. In French, *forage* is a duty on wine; the operation of boring guns, muskets, &c.; the opening in the trench of a quarry for the extraction of slate.

Forage-cap, a loose, rough-made military cap.

Forage-contractor, one who supplies horse provender to cavalry regiments, mounted police, or large bodies of horses.

Foraging-party, persons sent out from an encampment in search of cattle, food, or provender.

Forbidden Fruit, a species of *Citrus*, something like the shaddock, brought to this country in small quantities from the West Indies.

Forçage (French), applied to coin that is above weight.

Force-majeure, a French commercial term for unavoidable accidents in the transport of goods, from superior force, the act of God, &c.

Force-pump, a syringe pump with a solid piston, and two valves or a side-pipe, through which the water is forced; the plunger pump for supplying the boiler of a locomotive engine.

Forceps, tweezers, or holders of various kinds; medical instruments used in midwifery, craniotomy, and for other purposes.

Forcing, a method of producing fruit, flowers, and vegetables, before their ordinary season of maturity, by artificial heat; the process of fining wines, so as to render them fit for immediate draught.

Forcing-house, a hot-house.

Forcing-pit, an enclosed hot-bed or frame, with a glass roof, containing a fermenting mass of dung for accelerating the growth of plants, &c.

Ford, the narrow and shallow part of a stream or frith, which may be passed through on foot by wading, or crossed on horseback.

Fore, a maritime term for any thing near, or pertaining to, the bow or stem, the forward part of a ship; as foremast, forefoot, &c.

Fore and Aft, a seaman's term for "in the direction of the ship's length;" from head to stern.

Fore-cabin, the cabin in the front part of a ship, which has inferior accommodation for passengers.

Forecastle, a short deck in the bow of a ship, above the upper deck, in advance of the foremast; the forward part of the ship under the deck, where the sailors live in merchant vessels.

Forefoot, a piece of wood at the foremost extremity of the keel of a ship.

Foreganger, a short piece of rope grafted on a harpoon, to which the line is bent.

Foreign-going Ships, vessels trading to ports beyond the limits of the United Kingdom, and the nearer Continental ports, which are comprised between Brest and the river Elbe.

Forelock, a flat piece of iron driven through the end of a bolt to prevent its drawing.

Foreman, an overseer; a chief workman; the president or spokesman of a jury; an inferior seaman.

Foremast, the first or forward mast in a ship; that nearest the bow.

Forensic Wig, a legal wig worn by judges and counsellors, made of horse hair, sitting in stiff rows of curls.

Foreright, coarse wheaten bread.

Forerunner, a piece of rag terminating the stray line of the log line of a ship.

Fore-sail, the large lower square sail on the foremast of a ship; the first triangular sail before the mast of a sloop or cutter.

Forest, a great wood; ground [illegible] with a natural growth of trees, [illegible] for hunting.

Foresters, one connected [illegible]; a member of a secret [illegible] benefit society so named.

Forestalling, the act of [illegible]; buying up or preventing the arrival of grain and provisions [illegible]; formerly an offence at common [illegible].

Forestay, the rope supporting the foremast of a ship.

Foret (French), a gimlet or drill.

Foretop, the platform erected at the head of the foremast.

Foretopmast, the mast erected over the foremast, and above which is fixed the foretop-gallant-mast.

Foretopman, a seaman whose duties relate to the foretop of a ship.

Forfaro, a name in some parts of Egypt for the rottolo, equal to about 15 ounces.

Forfeiture, a penalty incurred or paid.

Forge, a smithery; the furnace where wrought metals are heated, to render them soft and more malleable.

Forge-bellows Maker, a manufacturer of the large blowing apparatus for forges.

Forge Furnace, a blacksmith's open furnace, urged by a powerful bellows.

Forge-man, a superior class of coach-smith, having a hammer-man under him. The forger judges of the quality of the metal, regulates the curvatures, and exercises his skill in combining elegance with strength in the various iron fittings required for the coach.

Forge-manufacturer, a maker of portable forges for smiths' use.

Forger, in the cutlery trade, one who forms or fashions a tool or implement from the bar or rod of steel; one who counterfeits coins, or issues false documents.

Forgery, a fraudulent or counterfeit imitation or deception, practised in the making or uttering a false instrument, or by altering a note, cheque, or order, with a fraudulent intent.

Foring, an Iceland weight of 11 lbs. avoirdupois.

Fork, a farm-workman's prong; a table utensil for taking up food; a turner's tool; a piece of steel fitting into the socket or chuck of a lathe.

Fork-grinder, a smoother or sharpener and finisher of forks.

Fork-guard Maker, a manufacturer of metal pieces for carving-forks.

Fork Manufacturer, a branch of the cutlery trade.

Fork-tail, a salmon four years old.

Forlo, a small copper coin formerly current in Egypt; a subdivision of the medino, the half of an asper, and worth scarcely a halfpenny.

Forlon, a Spanish chaise or carriage with four seats.

Form, shape; a mould in which any thing is wrought; a mass of type, in pages or columns, ready for press; the arrangement of newspaper columns or the pages of a book in an iron chase, for machining or printing; a long wooden bench.

Formers, pieces of wood used for shaping [illegible] wads.

F[illegible], the acid of ants, chiefly obtained from the red ant; it is also made by [illegible] tartaric acid, sulphuric acid, and [illegible] manganese.

Formula, a prescription; a set of instructions.

Forpet, the fourth part of a Scotch peck; 64 [illegible] make one boll.

Forrid, a kind of [illegible].

Fo[illegible] (French), a manorial tax on paving-stones.

Fortin, a dry measure of Constantinople, 4 kilows; rather less than 4 bushels.

Forward, the fore[illegible] of a ship.

Forwarder, Forwarding Agent, a merchant who attends to the transmission of goods and produce from one point to another.

Forwarding-house, Forwarding-merchants, a name assumed by many mercantile firms in America, who attend to the receipt and transmission of merchandise and produce by railways and canals, from the interior to the coast, or to market-towns, and *vice versâ*.

Fosse d'Aisances (French), a cesspool.

Fosset, a small chest.

Fossils, petrified shells, animals, plants, &c.

Fostel (Scotch), a cask.

Fother, Fodder, in navigation, to draw a sail filled with oakum under a ship's bottom in order to stop a leak; a cart-load; a large quantity; a weight for lead, ordinarily 2184 lbs. or 8 pigs, but variable. *See* Fodder.

Fotinellio, a weight of lead of ten stone.

Fotmal, a commercial term for 70lbs. of lead.

Fou (Scotch), a pitchfork; a firlot or bushel.

Fouace (French), a dough cake; a bun baked under hot cinders.

Fouang, a coin of Siam, the half of a mace, called by the natives phuani, worth 800 cowries; a weight, the 8th part of the tical, and equal to 29¼ grains. *See* Bat.

Fouat (Scotch), a buttered currant cake or bun.

Foudre, a large cask or vessel; a liquid and dry measure used in Germany; as a grain measure, it is about 7¼ quarters; for liquids it varies from 142 up to 644 gallons.

Foul, unfair; twisted; unclean; as the foul bottom of a ship, a foul wind, a foul anchor, &c.; also, in navigation, to run against another vessel.

Foul-anchor, a term applied when the cable has a turn round the anchor.

Foulard, a kind of silk material for ladies' dresses, plain, dyed, and printed; a silk kerchief or cravat.

Foulemart, a name given to the polecat.

Foul-proof, an uncorrected printed slip, before the typographical and other errors have been rectified.

Found, artillery of molten metal; hence founder, the designation of the tradesman who casts metals.

Foundation, the basis on which a superstructure rests, as of a bridge or building.

Foundation-muslin, an open-worked gummed fabric, used for stiffening dresses and bonnets.

Foundation-stone, the first or corner-stone of a building in large erections, usually laid in public, and with some ceremony.

Founder, one who establishes; a caster of metals; the act of a ship sinking; Scotch, to fill.

Founders' Company, one of the livery companies of London, whose hall is situate in Swithin's Lane.

Founders' Dust, charcoal powder, and coal and coke dust ground fine, and sifted for casting purposes in foundries.

Founders' Sand, a species of sand obtained from Lewisham, Kent, and other districts, for making foundry moulds.

Foundry, the place where masses of metals are melted and run into moulds.

Fount, Font, a complete assortment of a particular set of printing-type.

Fountain, an artificial receptacle for water; a machine by which water is spouted out, generally consisting of pipes or jets of water flowing from statues, vases, &c., in public squares, gardens, or private conservatories, &c.

Fountain-pen, a writing pen with a reservoir for ink larger than usual.

Four (French), an oven, kiln, or stove.

Fourbisseur, a sword-cutler.

Fourchette (French), a table fork.

Fourgon, a tumbrel or ammunition wagon; a kind of French baggage cart; a fire poker; an oven-fork or coal-rake.

Four-in-hand, a coach driven with four horses.

Fourneau, a stove or kiln in France.

Fournil, a French bakehouse or oven.

Fourpence, a British silver coin (29 1-11th grains), also known as a groat, of which upwards of £60,000 worth have been coined and put into circulation in the ten years ending with 1856.

Four-poster, a large square bedstead, with upright pillars at each corner, supporting a canopy or curtains.

Fourth-rate, a vessel of war carrying from 50 to 70 guns.

Fow (Scotch), a mow or heap of corn in the sheaf.

Fowl, a very general name for the denizens of the poultry yard; but for the most part restricted to the cock and hen, *Gallus domesticus*, of which the breeds are now very numerous. [fowl.

Fowler, one who pursues or traps wild

Fowling-piece, a light long-barrelled gun.

Fox, a seaman's name for a kind of strand of two or more rope-yarns, twisted together; to put new soles on boots; a carnivorous animal (*Canis vulpes*), hunted in this country by sportsmen. The skin of some of the Northern foxes forms an article of commerce, as many as 70,000 or 80,000 being imported annually by the Hudson's Bay Company. The most valuable are those of the black fox, and silver fox, which are purchased for the Russian and Chinese markets. The red fox is that chiefly brought to market.

Fox-hound, a dog kept for chasing the fox.

Fox-hunter, a sportsman who follows a fox with hounds.

Fox-trap, a gin for catching foxes.

Fracture, a severance; damage or injury done.

Fragile, brittle, easily broken, as glass, pottery, &c.

Frail, a package or basket made of rushes, in which dried fruit is occasionally imported, varying from 32 to 56 lbs. in weight.

Fraise, a pancake with bacon; the French name for a strawberry.

Fraisil (French), cinders remaining in forges; charcoal dust.

Frame, a word of varied signification; the border or enclosure for a picture; the woodwork in which panes of glass are placed for windows; the outward work of doors or window shutters, enclosing panels; the strong work which supports the boiler and machinery on the axles of a locomotive engine; a support for printers' cases of type; a mould; the ribs or stretchers for an umbrella or parasol; the timbers or skeleton of a house or ship.

Frame-maker, a name applied to several mechanical trades, &c., as a picture-frame maker, printer's-frame maker, &c.

Frame-work Knitter, an operative in the hosiery trade, who weaves the worsted or cotton thread up into a knitted fabric.

Frame-work Knitter's Company, one of the minor livery companies of London which has no hall.

Franc, the principal French silver coin, of 100 centimes, worth 9½d. or 10d., the unity of the French coinage. It weighs five grammes, and contains one-tenth part of alloy; 200 francs in silver is the exact weight of the French kilogramme.

Francarte, a former grain measure of France, about 5¼ gallons.

Francatu, a russetin-apple.

Francescone, another name for the Leopoldo, a principal silver coin of Tuscany worth about 4s. 6d.

Franchipane, Frangipane, a kind of pastry, a cake of cream, almonds, spice, [illegible] a perfume.

Franchise, the right of voting at elections for knights of the shire, &c.; in law, a privilege or exemption from ordinary jurisdiction.

Francisation, entering a vessel on the French register.

Franc-real, a kind of baking pear.

Frangipane, a perfume of jasmine. See Franchipane.

Frangollo, a Spanish pottage made of boiled wheat and milk.

Frangote, a bale of goods in Spain.

Frankfort-black, a pigment said to be prepared by burning vine branches, grape stones, and the refuse lees of the wine manufacture, &c., used for copper-plate printing.

Frankincense, a name for the gum olibanum of commerce, an odoriferous resin obtained from several species of *Boswellia*; the European frankincense is a resinous exudation from the spruce fir, and is used in the composition of plasters.

Franking, the privilege of freeing letters from postal charge, formerly enjoyed by members of the Legislature and certain departments of the State, but now abolished; a carpenter's term for window-sashes, in which the cross pieces of the frame intersect each other.

Franklinite, an ore of iron, zinc, and manganese.

Frasco, the name for a flask or case bottle in Brazil, containing about 3½ pints.

Frazil, Frazil, the Arabian name for a bale of variable weight, ranging from 18½ lbs. to 30 lbs. In Beetlefakee the frazil is 20½ lbs.; in Judda, rather more than 22 lbs.; in Mocha, 20 lbs.

Fraud, a dishonourable transaction; adulteration, deception; a cheat, &c.

FRAUGHT (Scotch), the freight of a vessel; the fare.
FRAY, to fret or rub; to unweave.
FREDERICK D'OR, a gold coin of Prussia, worth about 16s. 6d.
FREEBORD, ground outside a fence.
FREEDOM, liberty of action; the right to enjoy the immunities and privileges of a corporation.
FREEHOLD, lands or tenements held by free tenure in fee-simple, for tail or for life; an estate held for ever free from restrictions.
FREEMAN, one who is his own master, not a bondsman; a person enjoying the freedom, liberty, or privileges of a city.
FREE-MARTIN, a heifer incapable of breeding; the barren twin calf whose mate is a bull calf.
FREEMASON'S APRON, an ornamented apron of different material, and bearing various devices, according to the degree the wearer has attained in the craft, or the office he holds, or has served, in a lodge or chapter. There is also a large business done in jewels and collars for freemasons, both in craft and arch masonry, and some of the higher orders.
FREE PUBLIC-HOUSE, one not belonging to a brewer; the landlord has therefore free liberty to brew his own beer, or purchase where he chooses.
FREE-SCHOOL, a charity school; one open to all.
FREE-STONE, a durable kind of oolite or sandstone, much used in building; having no grain it can be easily cut into blocks, and worked with the chisel.
FREE-TRADE, in a political sense, the liberty of trading with any country for corn, &c.; the removal of restrictions compelling the dealing only with certain kingdoms; unrestricted action in banking operations.
FREE VINTNER, a member of the vintners' company; one who can sell wine without a licence.
FREEZING MIXTURE, a compound of muriate of ammonia, nitrate of potash, and phosphate of soda, or other salts, used by confectioners and others, to produce cold, by the liquefaction of their solid ingredients.
FREEZING-POWDER-AND-MACHINE MAKER, a tradesman who devotes attention to the manufacture and sale of refrigerators and freezing mixtures.
FREIGHT, a load; the sum agreed on for the hire of a ship, or the carriage of goods by water.
FRELUCHE (French), a small silk tuft.
FRENCH-BEAN, a dwarf variety of the *Phaseolus vulgaris.*
FRENCH-BERRIES, berries used in dyeing. See AVIGNON-BERRIES.
FRENCH-CHALK, indurated talc; a magnesian mineral used to remove grease, stains, &c.
FRENCH-ELL, a measure of 4½ feet.
FRENCH-HORN, a musical wind instrument of copper, having several curves.
FRENCH-LEAF. See LEAF-METAL and BRONZE-POWDER.
FRENCH-MASTER, a teacher or professor of the French language.
FRENCH-PLUM, a table prune, a fine variety of the *Prunus domestica.*
FRENCH-POLISHER, a varnisher and cleaner of tables, chairs, and other articles of cabinet furniture.
FRENCH-POLISH MAKER, a manufacturer of spirit varnish for articles of furniture.
FRENCH-ROLL, a light breakfast milk bread.
FREQUIN, a cask used in France for holding sugar or treacle.
FRESCO, a kind of painting upon newly plastered walls, when the colour becoming incorporated with the soft stucco, is hence exceedingly durable.
FRET, to fray; to unweave; in French, the hire of a ship; the cargo; the sum paid for the transport of goods.
FRET WORK, carved or open wood-work, in ornamental devices and patterns.
FRIARS'-BALSAM, a popular specific for wounds, so named.
FRIARS'-CHICKENS, FRIED-CHICKENS, a name in Scotland for chicken broth with eggs dropped in it, or eggs beat up and mixed with it.
FRICANDEAU, a slice of veal larded and stewed.
FRICASSEE, a savoury dish of cooked meat; usually chickens, rabbits, &c., cut into small pieces and fried.
FRICKLE, a bushel-basket.
FRIENDLY-SOCIETY, a kind of club or association among operatives, for affording relief to each other when out of work, or in time of sickness; and also for extending assistance to widows and orphans.
FRIGARD (French), a pickled herring.
FRIGATE, a fast-sailing ship of war, carrying from 36 to 60 guns.
FRIGATOON, a small Venetian vessel with a square stern, carrying only a main mast, mizen and bowsprit.
FRIJOLES, a Spanish name for several varieties of pulse.
FRILL, a ruff or edging round the neck, sleeves, &c. of a lady's dress.
FRINGE, an ornamental bordering or edging; trimming for articles of dress and drapery; as, to bed-furniture, window-curtains, table-covers; made of various material, silk, worsted, gold, &c.
FRINGE AND LACE MANUFACTURER, a maker of edging ornaments, of various kinds, according to the purpose for which they are to be used.
FRINGER, one who sews on fringe.
FRIOLET, a kind of pear.
FRIPERIE (French), old garments or furniture; a second-hand clothes shop; brokers' trade; brokers' row.
FRISADO (Spanish), silk plush or shag.
FRISEUR, a hair-dresser.
FRISKET, the iron frame of a printing-press, which keeps the sheet on the tympan.
FRIT, in glass-making, the calcined materials; an imperfectly fused mass of silica, &c. having to be re-melted.
FRITTER, a kind of small pancake.
FRIZONS, a name for silk waste in France.
FRIZZLE (Scotch), the hammer of a gun or pistol; the fire-steel for a tinder-box.

Frock, a child's gown; a monk's dress; a Guernsey frock is a sailor's or boatman's worsted netted shirt. In Scotland the name for a pair of oxen in the team of a plough, which are distinguished as the hind-frock, fore-frock, mid-frock, &c. A gentleman's surtout or square-tailed long walking-coat.

Frog, in Scotland a young horse; an amphibious reptile; the flesh of the hind thighs of the green frog (*Rana esculenta*) is eaten on the Continent and in America; a portion of the foot of a horse; a loose trimming or braid for a gentleman's coat; an ornament for a sword hilt.

Fromage (French), cheese.

Froment (French), wheat; the best kind of bread-corn.

Front, a set of false hair or curls for a lady; the dickey for a shirt.

Front-door, the entrance door at the best part of the house.

Frontignac, a rich, luscious, muscadine white wine, made in Herault, in the south of France.

Frontispiece, the illustration in a book which faces the title-page; in architecture, the principal face of the building.

Frontlet, a bandage for the forehead.

Frosting, loaf-sugar prepared to coat plum cakes with.

Frow, Frower, an instrument for splitting staves; a tool with which to cleave laths.

Frowy-stuff, a builder's name for short, or brittle and soft, timber.

Fruit, the edible seed of many trees; a large commerce is carried on in green and dried fruit, as well as in nuts, and pickled and preserved fruit.

Fruiterer, a dealer in foreign and domestic fruit; a business most generally combined with that of greengrocer.

Fruiterers' Company, one of the minor livery companies of London, which has no hall.

Fruit-essence Manufacturer, a maker of different sweet flavouring substances, many of which are obtained from fusel oil.

Fruit-knife Maker, a manufacturer of ornamental knives for dessert use.

Fruit-stall, a stand on the pavement where fruit is sold in the streets.

Frumentaceous, pertaining to wheat or other grain.

Frumentazzo, a name in the Mediterranean ports for damaged grain unfit for human food.

Frumenty. See **Furmenty**.

Frundele, a dry measure of two pecks.

Fruslera, a metal made in Spain of latten filings.

Frustratoire, negus; a drink made in France of spiced and sweetened wine.

Fry, small fish; any thing cooked in a pan; a sieve.

Frying-pan, a flat open iron cooking vessel with a handle, for frying meat, &c. over a fire.

Fuchsia, a handsome flower, a great favourite for conservatories and gardens.

Fucus, a name for many kinds of sea-weed, some of which are eaten raw as food by man and beast; while others afford soda, iodine, and glue.

Fuddea, a name in the Bombay presidency for the double pice; a money of account, worth about 3 farthings.

Fuel, any substance used for making a fire to obtain heat, as turf, wood, coal, coke, charcoal, lignite, &c.

Fuel, Patent, Manufacturer, a maker of artificial combustibles for heating purposes.

Fuller, a scourer and cleanser of woollen cloths.

Fullers'-earth, a variety of oolite clay, containing about 25 per cent. of alumina, which removes stains of grease from cloth. About 6000 tons a year are used in this country.

Fullers'-thistle, a name for the teasels or heads of the *Dipsacus fullonum*, used in the wool trade for carding.

Fulling-mill, a water-mill where woollen cloths are cleansed from the grease, by beating with hammers and scouring ingredients.

Full-pay, the entire wages; not under stoppages or deductions.

Fulminating-powder, the salts of fulminic acid, which have detonating properties. The fulminate of mercury is largely used for priming percussion caps.

Fumigation, the employment of vapours or gases, &c. to purify a room or building.

Fumier (French), dung or manure.

Fumific-impeller, a machine for applying effectively the hot products of combustion.

Fun, another name for the candareen, a Chinese weight. See **Candareen**.

Function, an employment; a duty.

Functionary, one who holds an office.

Fund, a stock or capital; that by which any expense is supported. Established stocks or public funds are the loans advanced to Government, on which interest is regularly paid. These are too numerous and complex to be entered into here. In 1861, the capital debt of the United Kingdom was £782,869,388, of which £765,126,562 were funded. A *sinking fund*, is a regular appropriation, by a Company or State, for reducing a public or other debt.

Funda, a name for the Russian pound. See **Funt**.

Fund-holder, an owner of Government stock or public securities; one who has property in the funds.

Fundi, Fundungi the African name for the grain of *Paspalum exile*, grown on the western coast, and in some places known as hungry rice.

Fundook, an Indian name for Spanish nuts.

Funduclee, the name of a species of gold sequin, formerly current in Suez at 146 medines, and worth about one guinea.

Funeral, an interment; a common name for the carriages or procession attending the burial.

Funeral-carriage Master, the owner of hearses and mourning coaches with black horses, who lets them out for hire.

Funeral-feather Merchant, a maker of mourning plumes for hearses, horses, and bearers, who lets them out to undertakers.

FUNERAL-PALL, a hearse-cloth. *See* PALL.

FUNERAL-PLUME, an elaborately prepared and expensive set of sprays of ostrich feathers, mounted on wires for fixing on horses' heads, hearses, or coffin-lid boards, borne by mutes.

FUNERAL-UNDERTAKER. *See* UNDERTAKER.

FUNGIBLES, a Scotch law term for moveable goods, which may be valued by weight or measure, as grain or money; in contradistinction to those which must be judged of individually or by number.

FUNNEL, a hollow conical vessel, usually of tin or earthenware, with a pipe at the apex, for pouring liquids into small-mouthed vessels; the iron chimney of a steamer, or of a stove.

FUNT, the Russian pound weight of 14 oz. 7½ drachms.

FUR, the fine soft short hair on the skin of some animals, which is worn for warmth or ornament; a scaly deposit, or calcareous incrustation in steam boilers, to prevent the accumulation of which a boiler compound is used; and a salinometer or gauge has been adopted for marine boilers. *See* SALINOMETER.

FUR AND SKIN DRESSER AND DYER, a tradesman who softens and prepares rough skins for the use of the furrier.

FURBELOW, a plaited border; the flounce for a dress.

FUR-CAP, a seal or other skin cap.

FUR-COAT, a wrapper for cold weather made of bear-skin, beaver, seal, or other fur.

FUR-CUTTING MACHINE, a mechanical contrivance for shaving peltries at the back of the skin, so as to loosen the long hairs, leaving only the fine under-fur.

FURDINGAR, FIERDINGAR, a liquid measure of Finland, about 7½ pints, the fourth part of the tonna.

FURLING, in naval parlance, the wrapping or rolling a sail up snugly to the yard or boom, and binding or securing it.

FURLONG, an English measure of length, 40 poles, the eighth part of a mile.

FURLOUGH, a leave of absence given to soldiers.

FURMENTY, a pottage of wheat boiled in milk, flavoured with sugar, spice, &c

FURNACE, a large fuel-holder; the enclosed fire-place in which ore is put for the purpose of smelting or *reduction*. There are many kinds of furnaces, as reverberatory, assay, evaporating, and forge furnaces.

FURNACE-FEEDER, a stoker or fireman; one who supplies fuel to the furnace.

FURNISHED, a term applied to any thing completed or having the necessary appurtenances; a house which is properly filled with necessary goods, upholstery, cabinet-ware, culinary utensils, and garniture; fit for occupation.

FURNISHING-SHOPS, an ironmonger's, or furniture broker's shop.

FURNITURE, a word of wide signification, but chiefly applied to the moveable articles of upholstery, decoration, and use in a dwelling-house, as curtains to windows and beds; tables, chairs, sofas, and other cabinet-work; likewise to the wooden or metallic materials in use among printers for securing the pages of type and allowing a proper margin for the book; also to the masts and rigging of a ship; and, among builders, to the metal work of locks, doors, windows, &c. The value of the household furniture manufactured in the United Kingdom has been roughly estimated at £15,000,000 per annum.

FURNITURE-BROKER, a dealer in second-hand goods, shop fixtures, &c.

FURNITURE-CLEANER, a dyer and renovator of curtains, &c.

FURNITURE-JAPANNER AND POLISHER, a workman who oils, varnishes, and prepares for sale new cabinet articles, and cleans and repolishes old worn pieces of room furniture.

FURNITURE-POLISH, a kind of spirit varnish, or oil, used for articles of room furniture. It is often sold under the name of French-polish. Bees' wax is sometimes used.

FURNITURE-PRINTER, a maker of fabrics for covering articles used in rooms.

FURNITURE-WAREHOUSE, a repository where household furniture is sold.

FURNITURE-WOODS, hard ornamental woods, used for cabinet work.

FURRIER, a dealer in skins; a manufacturer and vender of various articles of fur.

FURRING, fixing thin scantlings on the edges of timber to make the surface even; double planking the sides of a ship; encrusting a boiler with a scaly deposit.

FURROW, the trench made by a plough.

FURROW-DRAIN, a deep open channel made by a plough to carry off water.

FURROW-SLICE, the narrow slip of earth turned up by a plough.

FURSOCH, another name for the augage, a Persian land measure of 4½ miles.

FURSUNG, PHARSAK, other names for the parasang, a Persian land measure of about 4 English miles, but variable.

FUR-TRADE, the commerce in the skins of wild animals, which is largely carried on in several countries. The most valuable furs are chiefly obtained in Russia and Arctic America, and we import from 3 to 4 million skins of different kinds annually, either to be used here, or to be dressed and prepared for export. The annual value of the fur trade of the world is estimated, on good data, to be from 5 to 6 million pounds sterling.

FURZE, the common gorse or whin (*Ulex Europæus*). When chopped it is used as food for cattle; and in many parts of the kingdom it forms the main dependence for the supply of fagots for the poor man's hearth, and the baker's oven.

FUSE. *See* FUZE.

FUSEE, a squib; the conical part of a watch or clock, round which the chain or cord is wound; a lighter or slow match, used by smokers for igniting tobacco.

FUSEE-ENGINE, a clock-maker's machine for cutting and shaping fusees.

FUSEL-OIL, the refuse from distillation; a deleterious component of alcohol used in the manufacture of various fruit essences.

FUSIBLE-METAL, a compound consisting of about 50 per cent. bismuth, 20 per cent. tin, and 30 per cent. lead.

FUSIL, a light musket; hence probably the term fusilier, a foot soldier armed with a fusil; the fire steel of a tinder box.

FUSILIER, an infantry soldier, armed with a light gun.

FUSION, a melting; the converting of a solid into a liquid by heat.

FUST, the shaft of a column.

FUSTA (Spanish), a small vessel with lateen sails; a kind of woollen cloth.

FUSTETE (Spanish), the red sumach shrub, *Rhus cotinus.*

FUSTIAN, a coarse stout twilled cotton fabric, including many varieties, as corduroy, jean, velveteen, thickset, &c., used by working men. Plain fustian is called pillow; strong twilled fustian, cropped before dyeing, is known as moleskin; when cropped after dyeing, beaverteen.

FUSTIAN-JACKET, a working man's garment.

FUSTIC, a well-known hard strong yellow dye-wood. The old fustic of commerce is obtained from the *Maclura tinctoria*, a tree of South America. The wood is admirably adapted for the felloes of carriage and cart wheels. The young fustic of commerce is procured from *Rhus cotinus*. Our supplies of the former come from Cuba, Tampico, Puerto Cabello, and the Spanish Main.

FUSTO (Italian,) a sort of light galley.

FUT, the French name for a cask, a vessel for liquids; a stock for a gun, or tool; a bookbinder's plough.

FUTAILLE (French), a cask of any kind for wine, water, or provisions.

FUTAINIER (French), a fustian-weaver.

FUTFAILL, FUTFELL, a name in Scotland for the dressed skins of a slink lamb, or one prematurely dropped.

FUTIER, in France, a trunk-maker.

FUTKEE, an Indian name for alum.

FUTTOCKS, the upright curved timbers or ribs of a ship, springing from the keel, upon which the outer frame-work, the horizontal strakes or planking, &c., is laid.

FUZE, a short metallic tube, charged with an explosive composition, and having a slow match attached, for firing a shell or blast charge.

FUZEE-MAKER, a manufacturer of parts of watch-work. See FUSEE.

FWEN, another name for the candareen in China. See FUN.

FYRKE, a petty copper coin, and money of account in Denmark.

FYRTEL, a mode of spelling the viertel; a liquid measure.

G.

GAB, a hook for a pot in Scotland.

GABAN, a coarse cloak.

GABARAGE, coarse packing-cloth; a term formerly used for the wrappers in which Irish goods were packed.

GABARDINE, a coarse smock-frock, or blouse.

GABARE, a French lighter; a fishing-boat; a kind of net.

GABARIER (French), a boatman; a lighterman; to mould timber.

GABBANO (Italian), a felt cloak.

GABBART, GABERT, a name in Scotland for a canal barge or lighter.

GABBIAIO (Italian), a cage-maker.

GABELLE, a tax formerly levied upon salt and other provisions.

GABELLIERE (Italian), a custom-house officer.

GABILLA, a finger or parcel of tobacco in Cuba, consisting of about 36 to 40 leaves. The bales are usually made up of 80 hands, each of four gabillas.

GABION, a basket filled with earth, used in fortification.

GABLE, the upright triangular end of a house.

GACHEUR (French), a mason's boy who mixes mortar; one who undersells.

GAD, a small iron punch, with a wooden handle, used by miners to break up ore; in Scotland a fishing-rod; a bar of metal.

GADELLE, a kind of currant grown in France.

GADESDEN-PAN, an evaporating sugar pan, named after the inventor.

GADING, the Malay name for the elephant's tusk or ivory.

GADOUARD (French), a nightman; one who removes *gadoue* or ordure.

GAFF, a spar to which the head of a fore and aft sail is bent; in Scotland, a sort of net.

GAFF-TOPSAIL, a light sail set over a gaff.

GAGAT, an Austrian name for black amber.

GAGE, a pawn or pledge; a token; the depth of water displaced by a ship; also applied to her position in relation to the wind with another vessel as weather-gage, lee-gage.

GAGE, GAUGE, a measure or standard; the name given to a variety of measuring instruments, as for measuring the state of rarefaction in the air-pump, variations in the barometer, &c. The gauging rod is a measure by which the capacity or contents of a cask or vessel may be ascertained. See GUAGE.

GAGGER, a lifter used by the founder, consisting of a light T-shaped piece of iron.

GAGNE-DENIER, a labourer; a wharf-porter.

GAIN-GEAR, in Scotland the moving machinery of a mill, as distinguished from the fixtures.

GAINIER (French), a maker of sheaths or cases.

GAISEL, GAISSLE, a grain measure of Bavaria, from 3½ to 4½ pints.

Gait, a charge made for sheep and cattle taken at a pasture to graze for the season; sometimes termed agistment; a sheaf of grain tied up.

Gaiters, leather or cloth wrappings; spatterdashes, for the upper part of the foot and ancle.

Gajah, the Malay name for the elephant.

Gajum, a long measure used by cloth merchants in parts of the East Indies; rather more than an ell, but variable. *See* Guz.

Gala, a Scotch cotton fabric; a grand entertainment.

Galactite, a newly-named white mineral, found in Perthshire.

Galactometer, an areometer or glass instrument, for testing the density of milk, consisting of a stem, enclosing scales; of a cylinder serving to float it, and of a bulb charged with shot, serving as a ballast, so that the instrument floats upright in the milk. It is centesimally graduated.

Gala-gala, the Malay name for pitch.

Galage, Galoche, Galosh, a shepherd's clog; a shoe worn over another.

Galam-butter, a reddish white solid oil obtained in India and Africa from the *Bassia butyracea*.

Galana (Italian), the sea-tortoise.

Galangal, a commercial name for the root-stocks of the *Alpinia Galanga* and *A. racemosa*, which have the same properties as ginger.

Galbanum, a yellowish brown fetid resin obtained in Persia from *Galbanum officinale* and used medicinally.

Galea, a Tartar name for the barbot (*Gadus jubatus*), a fish of an exquisite flavour.

Galeac, a French white wine.

Galeace, Galeasse, a Venetian galley.

Galeas, a heavy low-built French galley worked with both sails and oars.

Galena, a native sulphuret of lead, called also lead glance.

Galette, a thick flat cake made in France of chestnut meal and milk.

Galiot, Galliot, a light galley, a Dutch ship.

Galipot, white pine resin; the residue of the turpentine, which has lost its volatile oil by spontaneous evaporation; when purified it is called Burgundy pitch.

Gall, a small piece of silver with characters on one side, used as a coin in Cambodia, and worth about 4d. sterling; the bitter fluid secreted by the liver; ox-gall is used for scouring cloth; and, when refined, by artists to fix chalk and pencil drawings before tinting them. *See* Galls.

Galleon, a large four-decked vessel formerly used by the Spaniards in trading to South America.

Gallery, in mining, an under-ground excavation, vertical or horizontal; a long narrow room in the wing of a building; the upper places or seats in a church or theatre; a raised balcony or walk in a room; a railed projection at the stern or quarter of a ship.

Galletta (Italian), a kind of grape; a sea-biscuit.

Galley, a printer's long frame with a ledge on which the compositor empties the contents of his stick as often as it is filled, so that the composed lines, or arranged letters may be made up into columns on pages; there are newspaper, book, and job galleys; the place set apart for the fire hearth and the use of the cook in a ship; a long sharp boat; a low flat-built decked vessel used in the Mediterranean.

Gallic-acid, a peculiar acid obtained from nut-galls, divi divi, and other vegetable substances, rich in tannin. It is used in photography and as a test to detect iron: and is well known as an ingredient of black dye and ink.

Gallinha, literally a hen; a nominal money of account on the West coast of Africa represented by cowries. *See* Cabeca.

Gallipoli-oil, a general name for the best olive oil imported from Gallipoli, in Naples; but much better oil is now made in other quarters.

Gallipot, a small white earthenware pot or jar, used by chemists, &c.

Gallivat, a large rowing boat in the East Indies.

Gallon, an English measure of capacity of 4 quarts. The imperial gallon is 277·2738 cubic inches, and should contain 10 lbs. avoirdupois of distilled water.

Galloon, a narrow kind of lace of cotton, silk, &c., used for binding shoes, hats, and for other purposes.

Gallo-tannic-acid, a name for the pure tannin of nut-galls employed for chemical purposes.

Galloway, a horse under 14 hands high.

Gallows-bitts, a strong frame in the centre of a ship's deck to support spare spars when in port.

Galls, Nut-galls, spherical concretions and excrescences formed upon the leaves and leaf stalks of several species of oak and tamarisk in the South of Europe. They are made by the puncture of the female gall fly. There are blue or black, green and white galls; the last are of little value. Those from Aleppo are the best. In India, myrobalons and the fruit of different species of *Terminalia*, are called galls. The imports of galls have been increasing lately, and about 1200 bags of 1 or 2 cwt. are imported in some years.

Gall-stone, a calcareous concretion found in the gall-bladder of animals; it is sometimes used by painters as a yellow colouring matter, on account of its brightness and durability.

Gallygaskins, leather protectors for the legs of sportsmen during shooting excursions, &c.

Galoshes. *See* Goloshes.

Galt, in Scotland, a young spayed sow.

Galvanic Battery, an apparatus employed in accumulating galvanism.

Galvanized Iron, iron tinned by a peculiar process, whereby it is rendered less liable to be acted upon by moisture. It is made in corrugated sheets, and ranges from 800 square feet per ton, to 2170 feet or more. It is either curved, step-corrugated, or corrugated with small flutes or channels,

Galvanoglyphy. *See* Glyphography.

Galvanometer, an instrument constructed to measure minute quantities of electricity in galvanic operations.

Gama Grass, a tall and esteemed fodder grass, the *Tripsacum dactyloides* of Linnæus, native of the south-eastern coasts of North America. It yields from 70 to 90 tons of green hay to the acre.

Gamass, a name for the bulbs of the squamash or biscuit-root (*Gamassia esculenta*) of the North American Indians.

Gambadoes, a name given to mud boots.

Gambier, an extract prepared at Singapore from the *Uncaria Gambir*, and used as a dye and tanning substance. It is misnamed in trade circles *Terra Japonica*. The imports in the last few years have averaged 6000 tons per annum.

Gamboge, a yellow resin used as a pigment, and in medicine as a purgative; obtained in the East from species of *Hebradendron* and *Stalagmites*; our supplies, come chiefly from Siam.

Gambroon, a kind of twilled linen cloth for linings.

Game, a collective name for wild birds and animals which are coursed or shot by sportsmen, &c.

Game-keeper, a servant on a gentleman's estate who has the charge of the preservation of the game from poachers.

Gamel, a rice measure on the east coast of Africa, of 38 lbs. weight.

Gammon, to deceive; in Scotland, the feet of an animal; a piece of bacon.

Gammoning, a strong lashing, by which the bowsprit of a ship is secured to the cut-water.

Gandang, a bale of 25 pieces of cloth in the Philippine islands.

Gander, a male goose.

Gang, a body of men employed together on any work.

Gang-board, a plank from a boat's side, resting on the shore to step on.

Gang-casks, small casks for bringing off water in boats.

Ganger, the foreman or manager of a gang of platelayers and labourers on a railway.

Gangue, the matrix or portion of a rock in which an ore is deposited; also protogene granite.

Gangway, the passway or entrance into a ship by the steps on the side; a narrow passage among the cargo in the hold, to facilitate inspection, examine leaks, &c.

Ganitrus-Beads, a kind of berry or seed used for ornamental purposes.

Ganjah, Ganza, an Indian name for the dried leaves and flowers of the hemp plant. *See* Gunjah.

Gannister Stone, a species of slaty stone used around Sheffield for keeping the macadamized roads in repair.

Gant (French), a glove.

Gantang, Gantam, Ganton, a Malayan measure of capacity, containing 256 cubic inches. For grain it is divided into 4 chupahs. In Malacca the gantang of rice weighs 6¼ lbs. avoirdupois; in Macassar it is 8 lbs. 5 oz.; and in Java and Borneo it is even more. *See* Coyan.

Ganza, a small base coin in some parts of India beyond the Ganges, worth about 1½d.; also a name in India for the dried leaves and flowers of hemp, an article of export from Bombay. In 1851, 10,254 lbs., valued at £874, were shipped thence to the United Kingdom. *See* Gunjah.

Ganze-kopf, a coin current in Vienna for 20 kreutzers, and worth about 8d.

Gaoler, a guardian of prisoners.

Garam, the Malay name for salt.

Garancine, a dyeing powder, prepared in France from madder root.

Garaye, a grain measure of Syria, equal to about 5 imperial quarters.

Garbage, waste animal substances; the entrails of animals.

Garbanzos, the Spanish name for the chick pea, the grain or vetch of the *Cicer arietinum*; largely used as an ingredient in the famous olla podrida.

Garbelled, a commercial term for sorted or picked.

Garbeller, originally a sorter of spices; but garbelling is now applied to any kind of sorting.

Garbling, a commercial term for picking or sorting, hence the worst or refuse of any staple is called "garblings."

Garbure, a cabbage soup with bacon, made in France.

Garce, an Indian measure of capacity for grain, oil, seeds, &c., containing 128 maunds, or 400 marcals, and equal to 9250¼ lbs. The garce of Masulipatan is 156¼ bushels.

Garden, a cultivated piece of land, usually near a dwelling-house, for raising fruit, flowers, or vegetables.

Garden-engine, a watering machine, with a small hose attached.

Garden labels, wooden, metallic, or porcelain labels for the names of plants to be fixed in the earth.

Garden-seat, a rustic chair, or cast-iron seat.

Garden-tools, spades, hoes, forks, rakes, and other appliances for cultivating and keeping a garden in order.

Gardener, one who has the charge, and attends to the management, of a garden.

Gardeners' Company, one of the companies of London, which has no hall, and is not on the livery.

Garole, a wash for the throat.

Gar-fish, a West Indian name for the *Belone*, esteemed as food notwithstanding the green colour of the bones. The European species, *B. vulgaris*, is the well-known mackerel guide of the fisherman.

Gargantiglia (Italian), a necklace.

Gari, an Indian term for 4000 rupees or £400.

Garland, a large rope or strap lashed to a spar when hoisting it on board a vessel; a wreath of flowers.

Garlic, a plant, the *Allium sativum*, having an acrimonious taste; the small cloves or minute bulbs are used for flavouring food, and also for medicinal purposes.

Garner, to store up.

Garnet, a corn measure of Russia, the 64th part of a chetwert; a purchase or description of tackle on the mainstay of a ship.

for hoisting cargo in and out: a precious stone of a beautiful red, colour, like the seed of the pomegranate, whence the name.

GARNIEC, a measure of capacity in use in Poland fixed legally at about 7 pints, but which varies in some parts of Russia.

GARNISH, to embellish or beautify; also a Scotch law-term, signifying to give notice or warn.

GARNISHEE, in law, a person in whose hands money or property belonging to a third person is attached; who is warned by a garnishment or notice not to pay the money, but to appear and answer to the suit of the plaintiff creditor.

GARNITURE, ornamental appendages or trimmings; the furniture or fittings to finish or embellish any thing.

GARRAFON, the Spanish name for a large stone jar in which spirits or cordials are sometimes shipped.

GARRET, an uppermost room in a house, sometimes termed an attic.

GARRETING, small splinters of stone inserted into flint walls, or the joints of coarse masonry.

GARRET-MASTER, a maker of household furniture on his own account, who sells his goods to the furniture-dealers for the best price he can obtain.

GARRISON, a body of troops, stationed in a fort or town, for protection or defence.

GARRIWAN, the driver of a bullock-cart or hackery in India.

GARTER, a knee-band; a support for the stockings.

GARTH, a weir or enclosure for catching fish in a river.

GAS, an aeriform, inflammable, elastic fluid, furnishing artificial light: the manufacture of coal-gas is carried on upon a large scale in populous places for illuminating purposes.

GASALIER, a gas-burner for a private room.

GAS-BURNER, the beak or mouth-piece for a gas-pipe, of which there are many kinds; as the common jet with a single small hole, the argand with a circle of holes, the fish-tail, the bat's-wing, &c.

GAS-BURNER MANUFACTURER, a metal founder; one who casts jets and burners for gas consumers.

GASELITE, GAZIVERE, an apparatus for making aerated waters.

GAS-FITTER, a workman who lays on pipes and fits burners for gas.

GAS-GLASS MAKER, a manufacturer of upright glass tubes and globes, &c. for gas-burners.

GAS-HOLDER, a large reservoir for containing gas; a gasometer.

GASKETS, plaited cords, or small ropes, used to secure a sail to the yard, or boom, when it is furled.

GASKINS, packings of hemp; wide open hose.

GAS-LANTERN MAKER, a manufacturer of glazed frames for enclosing gas-burners at street doors, or the fronts of taverns, &c.

GAS-LIGHT, a jet of flame from ignited coal gas.

GAS-MAINS, the large iron supply pipes, by which the gas is distributed from the manufactory to different localities in a town.

GAS-METER, an apparatus for measuring and registering the volume of gas, which passes from the main-pipe to the burners, in any given period. These meters are either on the wet or dry principle.

GAS-METER DIAL MAKER, a manufacturer of the dial-plates and indicators, &c. for gas-meters.

GASOMETER, a large receptacle suspended in water and counter-balanced by weights, for holding the gas made in the retorts when purified, for after-distribution from the gas-works through the mains and service pipes for illumination.

GASOMETER-MAKER, a constructor of large circular receivers made of iron plates for holding gas.

GAS-OIL MANUFACTURER, a purifier of the essential oil obtained in the process of gas-making.

GASOSCOPE, the name given to an apparatus for indicating the presence of bicarburetted hydrogen gas in buildings, mines, &c.

GASPEREAUX, a name in North America for the alewife, a small species of shad exported in pickle to the Southern States of America and the West Indies, where they are eaten by the negroes. It is very dry when salted, but tolerably good if eaten fresh. *See* ALEWIFE.

GAS-PIPE MAKER, a manufacturer of metal tubing to be fixed in buildings for the conveyance of gas from room to room; or of iron service pipes and mains, for holding gas in roads and streets.

GAS-REGULATOR, a governor or apparatus for equalizing and regulating the flow of gas.

GASS, GASSA, a money of account in Persia, the twentieth part of a mamoodi, and worth rather more than ½d.

GASSING, the process of singeing net, lace, &c., in order to remove the hairy filaments from the cotton. It is performed by passing the material between two rollers, and exposing it to the action of a large number of minute jets of gas.

GASSOUL, a mineral soap exported from Morocco, to the value of about £1000 annually.

GAS-STOVE, a stove heated by gas, for cooking, or for other purposes.

GAS-TAR, the bituminous substance which distils over in the manufacture of coal gas; which, from its offensive smell, is only used for common purposes.

GAS-WATER, water through which illuminating gas has passed from the retorts to the gasometer; sometimes used as manure.

GAS-WORKS, the plant and general buildings belonging to a gas-company.

GATE, a doorway or entrance, of which there are various kinds. The term is now chiefly applied to any light swinging wooden or metal construction, as a park-gate, wicket-gate, garden-gate, turnpike-gate, &c.; in founding, the gutter or hole through which the molten metal is poured; also a founder's name for a ridge in a casting, which has to be sawn off.

Gate, Fence, and Hurdle Maker, a manufacturer of iron rails and enclosures, &c. for fields and park lands.

Gate-hinge, a long strong hinge for suspending a gate by.

Gateman, the attendant at a swing-gate on a railway crossing; the lessee or collector at a toll-gate; the porter at a park lodge.

Gateway, an entrance to some enclosed place.

Gatherer, in printing and book-binding, the person who collects the sheets to make a perfect book; a sempstress who plaits or folds.

Gatine, a common in France; waste uninclosed land.

Gattie, the name of an East Indian soluble gum, obtained from the common babool, or *Acacia Arabica;* it is very similar to the African gum arabic.

Gaub, an Indian name for the fruit of *Diospyros embryopteris*, which, when expressed, exudes an excessively astringent juice, yielding 60 per cent. of pure tannic acid. It is used in medicine as an astringent and styptic, and is employed in Bengal for paying the bottom of boats.

Gaude, Guelda, Spanish names for weld, the yellow dye obtained from *Reseda luteola.*

Gaufres, French cakes or crumpets, made in iron moulds.

Gaufreur (French), one who figures stuffs.

Gauge, to measure the charge of a furnace; in founding, the calibre of a gun; the size or dimensions of metal wire; a workman's tool: thus there are, mortice, cutting, and marking gauges; in a printing-office, a measuring rule; on railways the width of the road from rail to rail, which, on the broad-gauge lines, is 7 feet; on the narrow-gauge lines, 4 feet 8½ inches.

Gauge-instrument Maker, a constructor of gauging tools for excisemen, harness-makers, and others.

Gauger, an excise-officer; a measurer of the contents of casks, &c.; an instrument used by leather cutters.

Gauging, determining the amount of liquid contained in casks, vats, &c., by internal measurement.

Gauging-rod, an exciseman's measuring [staff.

Gauntlet, a long glove, worn by ladies or soldiers.

Gausabey, a village committee or petty court in Ceylon, to which is referred, for decision, all disputes respecting paddy (rice) cultivation, water-rights, cattle-trespass, &c.

Gauze, a thin transparent textile fabric, woven of thread and silk, and sometimes of thread only; it is made either plain or figured.

Gauze-dresser, a stiffener of gauze.

Gauze-dyer, one who colours gauze fabrics.

Gauze-loom, a loom in which gauze is woven.

Gauze-manufacturer, a weaver of gauze.

Gauze-ribbon, a thin kind of ribbon worn by ladies, made of gauze.

Gavada, a land measure in Mysore, being the day's journey of 4 hardary or coss, and equal to from 11 to 14½ miles.

Gavel, a small parcel of grain; toll or custom.

Gayal, a name in some parts of India for the *Agave vivipara*, a cordage plant.

Gaze-à-blutoir, a very thin kind of silk gauze, used by millers in France for bolting cloths, which has been made as fine as 220 threads to the inch.

Gazette, an official newspaper published in each of the three capitals in the United Kingdom, London, Edinburgh, and Dublin; in which legal and State notices are required to be published by law for general information. The title of gazette is, however, adopted by many provincial journals.

Gazlich, a cotton fabric made in Turkey.

Gazzies, mixed caravans in Africa, on a smaller scale than kafilahs, and comprising camels, mules, asses, and men and women.

Gea, a name in some of the Pacific islands for the bread-fruit.

Gear, accoutrements; apparatus; harness.

Gear-cutter, a manufacturer of the toothed wheels for conducting motion in machinery, known as spur-gear and bevelled-gear.

Gearing, a series of toothed wheels, either spurred or bevelled, for communicating motion to machinery.

Gebook, a hamper of edible birds' nests in the East, weighing 25 catties.

Gebraude, a name in Germany for the quantity of beer brewed at one time; in Berlin it is a liquid measure of about 106½ gallons.

Ged, a Scotch name for the pike fish.

Geelim, Gillem, a name in some parts of Scotland for the joiner's rabbit-plane.

Geira, a land measure of Portugal, about 7000 square yards.

Gelatin, an animal jelly, obtained in considerable quantity from different parts of a great variety of animals; from the skin, from the cartilage, tendons, membranes, bones, and horns. Isinglass and glue are examples.

Gelatin-capsule Maker, a manufacturer of small hollow soluble capsules, enclosing a few drops of nauseous medicines.

Gelatin-maker, one who makes and prepares glue and gelatin from animal tissues.

Gelding, a castrated horse.

Gelso (Italian), the mulberry-tree.

Gems, a name given to certain minerals which have become valuable as precious stones, from their colour, hardness and lustre, or rarity.

Gen, a kind of manure obtained in Persia, Arabia, and other eastern countries, from the camel's thorn, *Hedysarum alhagi* of Linn. It is collected from the branches by the Arabs and caravans which cross the desert, and is used as food.

Genappe, a worsted yarn or cord used in the manufacture of braids, fringes, &c.; its smoothness enabling it to be well combined with silk.

Gendarme (French), a street-official; a *military policeman*; a civic and departmental guard, mounted and armed.

GENDA-SING, an Indian name for the horn of the rhinoceros. [common.

GENERAL, the chief commander of an army;

GENERAL POST-OFFICE, the head office in London, situated in St. Martin's-le-Grand, for the collection and transmission of all mailable matter, and for the general management of the metropolitan, provincial, and foreign post-office arrangements; under the superintendence of a Postmaster-general, Secretary, and various subordinate officers. The post office gives employment to a larger number of persons than the customs' and inland revenue departments combined. In 1855, 22,000 persons were employed; and the letters carried, exclusive of newspapers and books, &c., numbered 456,000,000.

GENET, a small horse.

GENEVA, a pure rectified grain spirit, with juniper berries added; the best is made in Holland; and hence it often bears the appellative name of Hollands.

GENEVRETTE, a wine made on the Continent, of juniper berries.

GENTIAN ROOT, the root of several species of *Gentiana*, obtained in the European Alps, used medicinally for their pure bitterness. The root contains a good deal of sugar and mucilage, which enables the Swiss to prepare from it a liquor, held in high esteem among that people.

GEOMETRIC PEN, an ingenious instrument for drawing curves.

GERAH, an Indian cloth-measure, the eighth part of a cubit, and equal to 2¼ inches; an ancient Hebrew coin worth about 1d.

GERANIUM, an extensive genus of handsome flowers, in which a large trade is carried on by nurserymen. The root of *G. maculatum* is considered a valuable astringent, and *G. Robertianum* is used in nephritic disorders.

GERANT, the responsible manager of a joint-stock association, or newspaper establishment, &c.; the acting partner.

GERLE, a wine measure of Switzerland, about 16 gallons.

GERLOANTICO, a fine, rare, and rich flesh-coloured marble, used for statuary purposes in Rome.

GERMAN-CLOCK MAKER, a manufacturer of small cheap hanging clocks largely made in Germany.

GERMAN-MILLET, the *Setaria Germanica*, a grass cultivated in Southern Europe and India, the seed being employed as food where better grain cannot be had.

GERMAN-PASTE, a food sold for certain kinds of cage birds, as blackbirds, thrushes, larks, &c. made of pea-meal, hemp-seed, maw-seed, lard, and honey or treacle.

GERMAN-SARSAPARILLA, a name for the sweetish rhizomes of the *Carex arenaria*, which are used on the Continent as a substitute for American sarsaparilla.

GERMAN-SAUSAGE, a polony; a bladder or cleaned gut stuffed with meat partly cooked.

GERMAN-SILVER, an alloy of about 60 per cent of copper, 25 of zinc and the remainder nickel; sometimes lead is added.

GERMAN-SILVER CASTER, GERMAN-SILVER FOUNDER, a maker of articles of alloyed metal, passing under the commercial name of German silver.

GERMAN-STEEL, a metal made of pig or white plate iron in forges where charcoal is used for fuel. The ore from which it is obtained is bog-iron or the sparry carbonate.

GERMAN TINDER, a soft amadou; a fungal, *Polyporus fomentarius*, growing on old trees, which stanches light wounds, forms small surgical pads, and is used as tinder. See AMADOU.

GERRA, JARRA, a liquid measure of Minorca; rather more than 2¼ gallons.

GESCHEID, a grain measure of Germany, the 64th part of the malter; and ranging from 3 to 3½ pints.

GHARK, a name in parts of the east for the best descriptions of eagle-wood, which, after being buried for a time, when dug up, is dark, glossy, and sinks in water.

GHARR, an Indian name for carnelian in the rough state.

GHARRY, a native Indian carriage drawn by oxen.

GHAUSKARRAH, an Indian grass-cutter.

GHAUT, a pass through a mountain; in India a chain of hills.

GHAUT-SERANG, a crimp in the eastern ports.

GHEE, liquid butter made from the milk of buffaloes and clarified; it is an article of very considerable commerce in various parts of India, and is generally conveyed in dubbers or large bottles made of hide, holding from 10 to 40 gallons each. Ghee will keep sweet a considerable time.

GHERIAH. See GERAH.

GHERKIN, a small cucumber used for pickling.

GHERLINO (Italian), a hawser.

GHETCHOO, an Indian name for the *Aponogeton monostachyon*, the roots of which are nearly as good as potatoes, and as much liked by the natives.

GHET-KOL, a vernacular name in Bengal for the acrid tubers of *Arum orixense*, used for poultices, applications to snake-bites, and inwardly as a powerful stimulant.

GHIAZZERUOLA (Italian), a cock-boat.

GHOONT, a small surefooted Indian pony, used in the mountain ranges as a pack or saddle-horse.

GHURREE, GHURRY, a division of time in India; 24 minutes.

GIARA (Italian), a flagon.

GIBELOTTE, a fricasee of rabbits or chickens.

GIBERNE, a French soldier's cartridge-box.

GIBIER (French), game; articles pursued or taken in the chase; venison.

GIBLETS, the liver, gizzard, feet, &c. of geese or ducks, which are often sold separately, for stews or pies.

GIDDAH, GIDUAH, an eastern grain measure of 2 lbs. 1 oz. 14 drachms; in some places it is only 2 oz., two giddahs making one arsolah, or the eighth part of the pucca seer.

GIES, strong mats made of bark or horsehair-looking fibres, worn by native boatmen in the Pacific to keep off the wet.

Gig, a shearing-frame used for cropping the nap or wool from cloth; a long light boat; a light two-wheeled carriage for general use.

Gig-mill, the cylinder in a cloth manufactory on which teasles or wire teeth are fixed, to card the cloth, which is stretched on beams.

Gigot (French), a leg of mutton.

Gilbacker, a fish of British Guiana, the *Silurus Parkerii;* from the sound isinglass is made and exported to some extent.

Gilbert, a measure for fire-wood in Frankfort; it consists of two or three stecken, each 3½ feet square.

Gilder, one who applies gold to substances. There are many kinds of gilders, as book and card-edge gilders, electro-gilders, china-gilders, French-gilders, water-gilders, screw-gilders, and gilders of glass, leather, &c.

Gilder's-material Dealer, a vender of gold-leaf, size, brushes and other articles for the use of the gilder.

Gilding, the process of laying thin gold over any surface.

Gilding-size, a pure description of size for the use of gilders.

Gill, a liquid measure, the fourth part of a pint, and weighing 5 ounces avoirdupois of water. In London the gill is usually called a quartern, but in the North of England it is a noggin, and the half pint is termed a gill; a pair of wheels and a frame on which timber is carried.

Gilly, in Scotland, an errand boy or messenger.

Gillosanto, a pastel or colouring substance made of argol and rhamnus, or yellow berries.

Gilt-jeweller, a manufacturer of gilded ornaments to represent gold.

Gilt-metal Worker, one who overlays metals with gold; an electro-plater.

Gimbal, Gimmal, the brass ring by which a ship's compass is suspended in its box.

Gimblet, a carpenter's boring instrument; to screw round, to turn any thing on its end, as an anchor round by its stock.

Gimblette, a kind of hard French cake in the form of a ring.

Gimlet-maker, Gimblet-maker, a manufacturer of workmen's small boring instruments with screw points.

Gimmer, a name given to a female sheep; a gimmer lamb is one unweaned; a shearing gimmer, a ewe that has been sheared.

Gimp, Gymp, silk thread or twist, usually interlaced with a metallic wire, used for dress trimmings, in coach-lace making, and for fringes.

Gin, a Chinese name for the catty; the machinery by which men, coals, or ore are raised from the pit of a mine; a cotton-cleaning instrument; a trap for catching vermin; a British spirit of large consumption, distilled from grain, and flavoured with juniper berries.

Gingal, an Indian match-lock.

Gingan (French), cloth for mattresses.

Gingelly, a name in India for the *Sesamum orientale*, the small seeds of which are largely used for making oil. It is often called teel seed.

Ginger, a pungent condiment obtained from the rhizomes of *Zingiber officinale*, grown in the East and West Indies. It is occasionally imported green, but usually comes dried, and sometimes preserved in syrup.

Ginger-beer, a popular bottled drink made by fermenting ginger, cream of tartar, and sugar, with yeast.

Ginger-bleacher, one who dries and scrapes off the epidermis of ginger, and steeps inferior ginger in cream of lime, or a lye of wood-ashes, to render it white for sale, and to prevent insects from attacking it.

Gingerbread, a baked cake made of flour, treacle and butter with ginger and other spice; which will keep for some time.

Gingerbread-nuts, small cakes made of the same materials as the above.

Gingham, a thin chequered linen for women's dresses; there are also umbrella and fancy ginghams.

Gingleman, the driver of an old-fashioned one horse covered car having two wheels, called a gingle, and confined to the city and county of Cork. It is sometimes improperly spelled Jingle in accordance with its pronunciation.

Ginko, a name for the maidenhair-tree (*Salisburia adiantifolia*), a native of Japan, the fruit of which is said to be eatable, and the tree is extensively cultivated in China for the purpose of procuring it.

Ginning, the operation of cleaning cotton wool from the seeds, by an apparatus called a gin.

Ginseng, the root of the *Panax quinquefolium* of America, which fetches an enormous price in China, from its imaginary stimulating properties.

Ginting, the Malay name for tiles.

Giomella, Giumella (Italian), a me[illegible] of two handfuls.

Gipsey-cart, a kind of heavy vehicle [illegible] which gipsey families live, and move fr[illegible] place to place.

Girandole, a branched burner or chandelier for gas; a stand for candles or flowers.

Girders, beams of wood or iron for supporting the superincumbent weight in any erection; as in houses, bridges, &c.

Girdle, a belt; a circular plate of malleable or cast iron, used in Scotland for toasting cakes over a fire.

Girdler, a brazier.

Girdler's Company, one of the livery companies of London, whose hall is in Basinghall-street.

Girdling, a mode of killing trees by cutting circles round them with a hatchet, and so leaving them to perish by time.

Girn, Gyrne, in Scotland, a noose, snare, or trap of any kind.

Girri, an instrument used in Ceylon for cutting up the areca-nut.

Girth, the circumference or round measurement of timber, &c.; the belly strap for a saddle.

Girth and Girth-web Manufacturer, a maker of webbing straps for horses.

Giuncata (Italian), cream cheese.
Glace' Silk, a kind of shaded silk for ladies' dresses.
Glaire, the white of eggs used in bookbinding. *See* Albumen.
Glaire-dealer, a vender of broken eggs, albumen, &c.
Glance, a rich ore of iron.
Glance-coal, uninflammable coal; close-burning coal.
Glareous, viscid and transparent, like the white of an egg.
Glass, a drinking vessel of various shapes; a transparent substance formed by the fusion of siliceous and alkaline matter. The principal commercial kinds are, crown-glass, formed of silicate of potash and lime; window-glass, of silicate of soda and lime; bottle-glass, of silicate of soda, lime, alumina, and iron; flint-glass of silicate of potash and lead; perforated glass, coloured glass, &c. *See* Plate-glass.
Glass-bender, a workman who moulds glass into certain forms by heat.
Glass-blower, a workman who shapes glass by blowing through an iron tube into the ductile and plastic material.
Glass-coach, an old-fashioned four-wheeled public carriage, now almost obsolete since the introduction of cabs.
Glass-cutter, a glazier or dealer in glass, who cuts sheets of glass to the requisite sizes for window-panes, &c.
Glass-embosser, an ornamenter of glass.
Glass-engraver, a workman who cuts figures on glass.
Glasses, spectacles for assisting the sight.
Glass-gall, the neutral salt skimmed from the surface of melted crown-glass, also called sandiver. *See* Sandever.
Glass-grinder, a rubber, or reducer of glass.
Glass-manufacturer, an operative in a glass-work; the owner of an establishment where glass is made.
Glass-mender, a workman who joins and rivets fractured articles of glass.
Glass-painter, a workman who stains glass.
Glass-paper, pulverized glass fastened on paper with glue, for abrasive purposes.
Glass-paper Maker, a manufacturer of emery and touch-glass papers, for polishing wood and metals.
Glass-riveter, a mender and repairer of glass.
Glass-rougher, a workman who dulls the surface, or removes the polish from glass.
Glass-sellers' Company, one of the minor livery companies of London, which has no hall.
Glass-shade Maker, a manufacturer of hollow glass shapes, &c. used as ornamental cases, and protections for articles.
Glass-silverer, one who coats glass with quicksilver, for mirrors, &c.
Glass-stainer. *See* Glass-painter.
Glass-staining, the process of colouring or painting glass.
Glass-stopperer, a maker of stoppers for chemical and other glass bottles.
Glass-wort, species of *Salicornia*, natives of the sea-shore, from which is obtained the alkali, so extensively used in the manufacture of soap and glass.
Glass, Writer and Gilder on; a glass-painter.
Glauber-salts, sulphate of soda, a compact massive white mineral, which effloresces rapidly, originally named after the discoverer, Glauber, a German chemist.
Glauconite, a green sand of Rhenish Westphalia.
Glaucous, having a sea-green colour.
Glave, a falchion.
Glaze, a powder applied to the external surface of pottery-ware, which vitrifies by heat.
Glazer, a wooden wheel for polishing knives, coated on the edge either with leather, having a rough surface of emery powder glued on, or with a ring of metal, consisting of an alloy of lead and tin; a calenderer, or calico smoother; a workman who applies the vitreous incrustation to the surface of earthenware.
Glazier, a workman who sets panes of glass in sashes or window-frames.
Glaziers' Company, one of the minor livery companies of London, which has no hall.
Glaziers'-diamond Maker, a manufacturer of the cutting-tool used by glaziers, consisting of a small diamond, mounted in a handle.
Glazing, the operation of putting window panes in frames; applying a varnish or vitreous coating of any kind to articles.
Gleaner, one who gathers up the loose ears of wheat in a corn-field after it has been reaped.
Glebe, the land belonging to a parish-church; a piece of earth with ore.
Glengarry, a Scotch bonnet; a man's cap.
Glenlivet, a fine kind of Scotch highland usquebaugh, or whisky; named from the district in which it is made.
Globe, a ball; a glass shade for lamps; a receptacle for small fish in a room; a sphere, on which is represented a map or delineation of the constellations and celestial bodies, or of the parts of the earth, showing the divisions of land and water, &c.; a very large model of the earth, in Leicester-square, London, made by Mr. Wyld, the geographer.
Globe-maker, a constructor of terrestrial and celestial globes, of various forms and sizes.
Gloss, a lustre, or varnish; a polished or shining surface.
Glossary, a book of provincialisms, or hard words and scientific names.
Gloucester Cheese, a kind of cheese for which the county of Gloucester has become famous, and of which there are two varieties, known as single and double Gloucester. The thin cheese is mostly made from April to November; the thick in May and June. Much of the so-called "double Gloucester" is, however, made in Wiltshire.
Glove, a covering for the hand, usually of prepared skin; but sometimes of worsted, thread, silk, or other material.

GLOVE-BAND, a protection for the glove round the wrist.

GLOVE-BOX, a long paper-box for holding gloves.

GLOVE-CLASP, a kind of hook-and-eye, or stud, for fastening gloves at the wrist; a contrivance for buttoning gloves.

GLOVE-CLEANER, a person who removes grease and other soils from kid gloves, by benzole or some other chemical application.

GLOVE-MANUFACTURER, GLOVER, a maker of gloves.

GLOVERS' COMPANY, one of the minor livery companies of London, which has no hall.

GLOVE-STRETCHERS, instruments for opening the fingers of gloves, that they may be drawn on the hand the easier.

GLOY (Scotch), oaten straw.

GLUCOSE, a potato starch used instead of gum arabic for dressing, in weaving and printing woollens, cottons, or silks. It is also advantageously employed by paper-stainers, and for stiffening gauzes, glazing of paper, &c. See DEXTRINE.

GLUDEN, a name in Baden for the florin.

GLUE, inspissated animal gluten, a hard and brittle substance, made from the parings of hides and horns, the pelts obtained from furriers, the hoofs and ears of horses, oxen, calves, sheep, &c., the raspings and trimmings of ivory, the refuse pieces and shavings left by button-mould makers, and from other kinds of hard bone. It is extensively used as a cement for its adhesive quality. Marine glue is a solution of caoutchouc in naphtha, with some shellac added.

GLUE AND SIZE MAKER, one who boils and prepares these substances for the use of operatives.

GLUE-PIECES, cuttings of hides of various kinds, sometimes termed scrowls, used to prepare glue from.

GLUE-POT, a metal pot containing an earthenware vessel immersed in boiling water, to heat the glue in it, when required to be used.

GLUTEN, the nutritious part of wheaten flour and other grain; the constituent of blood which gives it firmness.

GLUTINOUS, viscid or tenacious; having the quality of glue.

GLUTTON, an animal hunted for its fur, which is described under the head wolverine.

GLYCERIN, a kind of syrup, the sweet principle of oils; a product in the manufacture of stearin candles: it has many valuable commercial and medicinal uses.

GLYPHOGRAPHER, an engraver; a worker in galvanoglyphy.

GLYPHOGRAPHY, GALVANOGLYPHY, a process to cheapen or simplify wood engraving. A drawing is etched on a zinc plate, coated with varnish; several coats of ink are spread over the plate by a small composition-roller, being deposited only on those parts where the varnish has not been broken through by the graver. When the hollows are deep enough, the plate is placed in connection with the galvanic battery, and the result is another plate, in which the hollows of the engraving are produced in relief.

GNAPA, a name for the fathom in the Pacific islands; the measure of the extended arms.

GNATOO, the name in some of the Pacific islands, for clothing made from the bark of the Chinese paper mulberry.

GNOMON, the hand or style of a sun-dial.

GO, a slang term for a dram or glass of spirits.

GOAD, GODE, an ell 27½ inches long, by which Welch flannel, frieze, &c., were formerly measured; a pointed stick for driving cattle.

GOAT, a genus of animals, the *Capra*, furnishing many articles to commerce, in the flesh of the young kid, goats' milk, hair, &c. The skin of the kid forms the softest and most beautiful leather for gloves. The long wool of the Cashmere and Angora goats is much esteemed for manufacturing purposes. Goat is also the name for a rough surveying instrument used in road-making in Ceylon. It consists of a ten-feet rod attached to one permanent leg, with a leg graduated to inches, moving in a socket at the other extremity; in Scotland, a cavern or small inlet of the sea; a trench.

GOAT-CHAISE, a child's carriage, drawn by a goat in harness.

GOAT-HERD, an attendant on goats.

GOAT-MILK CHEESE, a cheese sometimes made from goats' milk.

GOATS'-HAIR, the fine fleece or hair of several species of foreign goat, imported chiefly through Turkey. See ANGORA and MOHAIR.

GOAT-SKINS, the skins of goats, in which a large trade is carried on; the imports into this country numbering above 300,000 a year.

GOBBING, rubbish remaining after coal [has] been extracted from the coal mine.

GOBBO, another name for the ochro, [a] culinary plant, the *Abelmoschus esculentus* of Wight and Arnott.

GOBELINS, the superior class of French tapestry, which derives its name from the brothers Gobelin, the first manufacturers.

GOBERGE (French), the largest species of the cod-fish.

GOBILLARDS, planks for staves.

GOBLET, a tankard or drinking cup; a name for the bechar, a dry measure of Switzerland, 64 of which make a sack of corn.

GO-CART, a small machine or frame without a bottom, running on casters or rollers, for teaching infants to walk.

GOCK, a name in parts of Scotland for a deep wooden dish.

GOCKROO, an Indian name for a drug, the *Ruellia longifolia*.

GODAVEZ, an Indian name for the *Calamus aromaticus*, or sweet cane.

GODFREY'S-CORDIAL, a quack medicine; a kind of soothing syrup given to infants, composed of sassafras, caraway, coriander, and anise seeds, infused in water, with treacle and tincture of opium added.

GODIVEAU (French), a veal-pie; force-meat.

GODOWN, a warehouse, store, or cellar for goods in the East Indies. See GUDANG.

GODRON, plaits on sleeve ruffles, or on ladies' caps.

GOELACK, a weight in Java, principally used for pepper, about 2 lbs.; in some parts 200 goolacks make a bahar.

GOELETTE (French), a schooner.

GOFFERED-ROUCHE MANUFACTURER, a maker of plaited quillings or trimmings for widows' caps.

GOFFERING, the operation of plaiting, puckering, or fluting linen, lace, &c.

GOGAR, whey boiled with a little oatmeal, and used as food in Scotland. In Fife it is termed whillins.

GOGGLES, eyeblinds for horses.

GOGLET, a sort of pottery jar, or earthenware vase, for keeping water cool.

GOGUL, a kind of bitumen used in India for painting ship bottoms.

GOHTAN, an Indian name for upland rice.

GOLABA, a rose-water sprinkler used in India, made of silver, &c.

GOLADUR GOLDER, an Indian store-keeper.

GOLAH, the Hindustani name for a warehouse.

GOLKEAH, the bowman of a boat plying on the Ganges.

GOLD, a precious metal, and next to platinum the heaviest known. It is however very malleable. Within the last ten years large quantities of gold have been discovered in Australia and California. The imports of gold into the United Kingdom, in the five years ending with 1855, according to the Customs' returns, were as follows, but quantities are also brought in privately which are unrecorded:—

1851	£11,500,000
1852	15,500,000
1853	21,000,000
1854	19,800,000
1855	17,300,000
	85,100,000

See CALIFORNIA GOLD.

GOLD-AMALGAM, a yellowish white mineral; a mixture of gold and quicksilver, found in West Mariposa, California.

GOLD AND SILVER BEATER, a worker in those metals, who hammers them out into very thin sheets or leaves.

GOLD AND SILVER BURNISHER, a workman who polishes and brightens articles made of the precious metals.

GOLD AND SILVER CASTER, one who moulds, or runs, the precious metals into different shapes and articles.

GOLD AND SILVER CHASER, a workman who embosses the precious metals.

GOLD AND SILVER FISH DEALER, a vender of the small ornamental species of carp, *Cyprinus auratus*, which are kept, in tanks, globes, or ponds, for their beauty and gentleness.

GOLD AND SILVER LACE-CLEANER, a reviver of tarnished lace and bullion.

GOLD AND SILVER LACE-MAN, a dealer in bullion and articles made of gold and silver wire.

GOLD AND SILVER MOUNTER, one who ornaments, frames, or sets articles in gold and silver.

GOLD AND SILVER PAPER-MAKER, a fancy paper manufacturer.

GOLD AND SILVER REFINER, one who purifies the precious metals from alloy.

GOLD AND SILVER THREAD-MAKER, a manufacturer of fine wire of those metals.

GOLD AND SILVER WIRE-DRAWERS' COMPANY, one of the minor livery companies of London, which has no hall.

GOLD-BEATER, a hammerer of gold into leaves or sheets. See GOLD AND SILVER BEATER.

GOLD-BEATERS' MALLET, a heavy iron hammer, weighing from 8 to 16 lbs., used in beating out gold into leaves.

GOLD-BEATERS' MOULD, a collection of about 850 leaves of parchment, vellum, and gold-beaters' skin, each of double thickness, fixed upon a metal mould; between the leaves flattened pieces of gold are placed to be hammered out to the full size of the leaf.

GOLD-BEATERS' SKIN, the peritoneal or serous membrane separated from the intestinal tube of the ox, prepared, stretched, varnished, and guarded from putrefaction by gums, spirit, and spices.

GOLD-BEATERS' SKIN-MANUFACTURER, a preparer of gut for the use of gold-beaters and others. The trade is limited to a very few persons. One person in London uses the gut of 10,000 oxen a week in the process of his manufacture.

GOLD-CHAIN MANUFACTURER, a maker of watch protectors and neck chains of gold, of different patterns.

GOLD-CLOTH MANUFACTURER, a weaver of cloth of gold wire.

GOLD-COINAGE, the current gold coins of the realm; these at present are sovereigns and half sovereigns. Guineas were formerly current, and a few double sovereigns have occasionally been struck; but these are now seldom met with. The value of the gold coined at the British mint, in the fifteen years ending with 1854, was £65,624,328.

GOLD-CUTTER, a workman who prepares gold for the use of others.

GOLD-DIGGER, a seeker for gold.

GOLD-DUST, gold ore met with in fine grains, as washed from the earth and clay in the gold fields.

GOLD-FIELDS, auriferous deposits and diggings, in Australia, California and other localities where gold is found.

GOLD-FISH. See GOLD AND SILVER FISH DEALER.

GOLD-FOIL, thin sheets of gold used by dentists and others.

GOLD-FRAME MAKER, a manufacturer of gilt picture and looking-glass frames.

GOLD-LACE MAKER, a weaver of silver-gilt wire or lace, and articles of bullion.

GOLD-LEAF, gold beaten into a thin film, varying in thickness according to the use for which it is to be applied. It is largely employed in gilding frames, cornices, projecting letters, shop fronts, &c., and is sold in books containing a certain number of leaves.

Gold of Pleasure, the *Camelina sativa*, a plant much cultivated on the Continent for its seeds, which produce a fine oil; the stems also yield a coarse fibre used for making sacks, sail-cloth, coarse packing-paper, and are employed for thatching.

Gold-pen Maker, a manufacturer of pens with iridium points for writing, or of gilded metal or imitation-gold pens.

Gold-plate, dishes or table service of gold; race cups or plates given away as rewards.

Gold-printer, a printer who does ornamental printing, letter-press, or lithography, in gold.

Gold-refiner. *See* Gold and Silver Refiner.

Gold-ring, a wedding or ornamental ring for the finger.

Gold-size Maker, a manufacturer of a kind of gold paint or bright varnish.

Goldsmith and Jeweller, a worker in gold; a dealer in articles of gold and silver, and ornaments and jewellery in general.

Goldsmiths' Company, the fifth in rank of the twelve great livery companies of London. Their first charter was granted in the first year of the reign of Edward III. The skinners' and merchant tailors' charters were also granted in the same year; whose hall is in Foster Lane, near the General Post-office.

Gold-swivel Maker, a manufacturer of the swivels or twisting links for gold chains.

Gold-thread, thread used for embroidery, consisting of flattened silver-gilt wire closely twisted, or wrapped over a thread of yellow silk by machinery.

Gold-thread Root, a name for the roots of some species of *Coptis*. In the United States, the root of *C. trifoliata* is a popular remedy for aphthous affections of the mouth, in children. In India the golden thread root of *C. Teeta* of Assam, which is intensely bitter, brings a very high price, being deemed a tonic remedy of the greatest value.

Gold-weaver, a maker of gold thread.

Gold-wire Drawer, a preparer of fine gold wire.

Golette, an Italian vessel.

Golf, a club used in a well-known game in Scotland, for striking balls stuffed very hard with feathers, from one hole to another.

Gollah, a station of brinjarries, or carriers of grain in India.

Golos-shoes, an over-shoe of caoutchouc or leather for keeping the feet dry, generally called goloshes.

Golpathun, an Indian striped silk.

Golsch, a name in Wurtemberg for a piece of cloth measuring 72 aunes or ells.

Golt-shut, a gold or silver ingot.

Gomastah, a native factor or agent in the East Indies.

Gombetta, a dry measure used in Genoa, equal to 2¼ pints nearly.

Gome, grease for cart-wheels.

Gomee, in India, a handful; literally as many rice stalks, with ears attached, as can be grasped by the hand.

Gomelin, a kind of German dextrine (starch from potatoes), in crystals and in powder, used as weavers' glue for cotton warps, and for dressing printed calicoes.

Gomia, a species of Caucasian millet.

Gommer, a very favourite and wholesome agricultural product, much used in the neighbourhood of Darmstadt in the preparation of soups. It is manufactured from black amel wheat (*Triticum amyleum*), which for this purpose is deprived of its skin by millstones.

Gonda, a nominal division of the anna, a petty Indian coin.

Gondola, a Venetian galley; an American flat-bottomed boat.

Goneometer, an instrument for measuring the angles of crystals.

Gonfia (Italian), a glass-maker or glass-blower.

Gong, a Chinese sounding instrument serving the purpose of a bell.

Gongonah, a variety of maté or Paraguay tea used in Brazil, prepared from the leaves of *Ilex gongonah* and *I. theezans*, species of holly.

Gonje, a small weight used in India for precious metals, nearly two grains.

Goods, a general name for moveables, but usually restricted to merchandise; heavy traffic; property; wares.

Goods Repository, a class of warehouses established for storing furniture, plate, &c., belonging to families leaving town, or for housing merchandise.

Goods-shed, a cover or shelter for luggage at railway stations, docks, or landing wharves.

Goods-train, a train of carriages on a railway, conveying only, or chiefly, luggage and merchandise.

Goods-truck, an uncovered railway-carriage for merchandise.

Goodwill, in trade, a saleable custom; the right and title to take up a trade or business connection, purchased of an outgoing occupier or tenant.

Goodul, a resinous substance resembling myrrh, met with in India, believed to be the bdellium of commerce, and probably the produce of *Commiphora Madagascarensis*.

Goolcund, a conserve flavoured with roses, made in the East.

Goolo, a pottery vessel made in the Feejee islands.

Gooloochund, a name in Scinde for a mixture of purree, a pigment, and sandal-wood, used to produce the yellow forehead mark of the Hindoos.

Goomala, a name in some of the Pacific islands for the sweet potato, *Batatus edulis*.

Goonch, a Hindoo name for the beautiful seeds of the *Abrus precatorius*, which are used as weights by the jewellers; also for necklaces, bracelets, and other trinkets. The roots abound in sugar, and are a perfect substitute for liquorice.

Goond, an Indian name for gum.

Goondooming, a seed or bead used, in some parts of the East, as a weight for gold and silver, three of these make one canteroy or fanam, which is about 5·875 grains.

GOONER, the grain, or weight for silver of six chows, used in Bombay.

GOOPTEE, a name in India for a sword-stick.

GOOR, the Indian name for coarse or half-made sugar: the concentrated syrup or juice of the date palm, *Phœnix dactyliferus*. It is also called jaggery; 12 pints of the sap are boiled down to one of goor, and four of goor yield one of good powder sugar.

GOORGOORY, a small kind of portable hookah, less massy and elaborate than the one smoked when seated.

GOOROOCHUNDUN, an Indian name for bezoar.

GOORTOO, an Indian superficial measure, a little more than 8 acres.

GOOSE, a genus of web-footed birds; the tame goose is well known, and is largely reared for its flesh, quills, and feathers. Wild geese in the winter are often brought to market. Also, a tailor's smoothing-iron.

GOOSEBERRY, a well-known and esteemed fruit, the produce of *Ribes grossularia* and *R. Uva-crispa*, of which there are several varieties.

GOOSEBERRY-FOOD, GOOSEBERRY-FOOL, a mess of boiled gooseberries with milk and sugar.

GOOSE-GREASE, the dripping or fat from a goose, which is considered an emollient application for chapped hands.

GOOSE-NECK, an iron ring fitted at the end of a yard or boom, for various purposes.

GOOSE-QUILL, the wing-feather of a goose, used for pen-making.

GOOSE-WING, the wing of the goose with the feathers on, which is often used as a dusting brush, and in cottages to sweep up hearths.

GOOSHT (Hindustani), flesh-meat.

GOOWA, the Bengalee name for the betel nut, *Areca Catechu*.

GORACOO, prepared tobacco, a paste smoked in their hookahs by the natives of [illegible]tern India. The tobacco having been [illegible] very fine, molasses, cinnamon, musk, and other aromatics and perfumes are added, until the mass assumes the form of an electuary.

GORD (French), a fishery set up in a river.

GORE, a narrow strip of any fabric to let in to another piece; an angular or oblique piece of canvas which increases the breadth or depth of a sail.

GORET (French), a young pig; a shoemaker's clicker; a swab or mop.

GORGERETTE (French), a tucker; a woman's kerchief.

GORGORALLA, a Dutch cloth.

GORIA, a nominal division of the anna.

GORSE, another name for furze or whin.

GORSE BRUISER, a machine for cutting and crushing gorse or furze as food for cattle.

GOSLARITE, a name for sulphate of zinc, used in medicine and in dyeing.

GOSLING, a young goose.

GOSSAMER, a very thin gauze.

GOSSAN, a miner's name for oxide of iron and quartz, generally occurring in lodes at shallow depths.

GOTAH, an Indian name for tissues.

GOTAH-HAR, an Indian state garland of gold and silver tissue, with imitation precious stones.

GOTON (French), the tiller-wheel of a ship.

GOUDA, a kind of Dutch cheese.

GOUET, a French wood-cutter's bill-hook or chopper.

GOUGE, a round hollow scooping chisel.

GOUGE-SLIPS, oil-stones or hones, for sharpening chisels.

GOULARD'S EXTRACT, GOULARD WATER, a common name for the solution of acetate of lead, used as an external lotion.

GOULDE, GULDE, another name for the florin in Austria.

GOURDE, a name in Hayti for the dollar.

GOURDS, cucurbitaceous plants, several of which have commercial uses. The bottle or trumpet gourd, and the colocynth gourd have already been mentioned. The squash gourd or pumpkin (*C. Melopepo*), and the common gourd (*C. Pepo*), are agreeable culinary fruits, and used for making pies. The vegetable marrow is a variety of the common gourd. The very large Spanish gourd (*C. maxima*), is met with in gardens under the French name of *potiron jaune*, and used in soups, or mashed. The young fruit of the gourd are used for pickles.

GOURREAU, a kind of long violet-coloured fig: Madona-fig.

GOUREUR (French), an adulterator of drugs; one who cheats in selling.

GOURMANDINE, a sort of pear grown in France.

GOUZE, a name in Bombay for the grain weight, used in weighing gold and silver; the 100th part of the tola.

GOVERNESS, a female teacher of young persons, who is either resident, or makes periodical visits; in the latter case she is termed a day governess.

GOVERNESS INSTITUTION, an establishment where a register is kept of vacant situations, or of governesses out of place.

GOVERNOR, part of a steam-engine regulating the supply of steam from the boiler to the cylinder, and insuring the uniform velocity of the piston; one who directs; a subscriber of a prescribed sum to a public charitable institution, who receives in return certain privileges of votes or nomination.

GOW, a Singhalese measure for computing distance, equal to five miles; five gows making a day's journey.

GOWAN, decomposed granite.

GOWAR, GOW, the Hindoo name for *Triticum æstivum*.

GOWLAND'S LOTION, the essential oil of bitter almonds, mixed with [illegible] spirits, and corrosive sublimate.

GOWN, a woman's long [illegible] garment; a man's official loose [illegible] dressing wrapper.

GOWN-PIECE, enough material for a dress.

GOWNSMAN, a lawyer; a professor; a student.

G. P. O., abbreviation for the General Post-Office.

GRAB, a Malabar ship.

GRACE. *See* DAYS OF GRACE.

Graddan, a kind of Scotch snuff.

Grade, a step or rank; to lay the permanent way of a railway.

Gradiator, Gradiating Engine, an instrument for dividing scales.

Gradient, the gradual acclivity or declivity upon a railway, which affects the speed at which a train can travel.

Gradine, a toothed chisel used by sculptors.

Grading. *See* Grade.

Graduate, a scholar who has taken his degrees in a university.

Grafting, covering a rope by weaving together yarns; the process of inserting a shoot or scion of one tree into the bark of another, to make it yield fruit; a bit put into a stocking.

Grah, an Indian long measure; in Guzerat, the sixteenth part of the guz, and rather more than two inches.

Grain, small seed of any kind of grass; chiefly, however, cereals. The smallest British weight in troy or avoirdupois weight; in apothecaries weight the 20th part of the scruple; in troy weight the 24th part of the penny-weight; a very small copper coin, minted here for circulation in Malta; the third part of a farthing.

Grain-dealer, a corn-dealer.

Grainer, a workman who ornaments woodwork with fancy devices; the brush with which he works; an infusion of pigeons' dung in water, used for giving flexibility to skins in the process of tanning; a knife used by tanners and skinners for taking off the hair from skins.

Graining, a process in tanning, which consists in immersing the skin in an alkaline solution, of which sal ammoniac is the most active constituent; a mode of painting.

Grain-leather, a name for dressed horse-hides; goat, seal, and other skins blacked on the grain-side for women's shoes, &c.

Grain-market, a corn market; the metropolitan market is the Corn Exchange in Mark Lane.

Grainoir (French), a granulating sieve used in gunpowder-mills.

Grains, the refuse or husks of malt from a brewery, or of any grain after distillation; usually purchased to feed cows and pigs with; a kind of iron harpoon, with four or more barbed points to it, used for striking small fish.

Grains of Paradise, the aromatic pungent seeds of the Malaguetta pepper (*Amomum Grana Paradisi*), obtained on the coast of Guinea; a spicy condiment, used in veterinary practice, and in the illegal preparation of malt liquors, &c.

Grain-tin, crystalline tin ore; metallic tin, smelted with charcoal; the purest kind of metal, that reduced from the loose grains of tin stone.

Grain-weigher, a corn meter; a person employed at the docks to measure cargoes of corn.

Graip, a dung-fork; a tool for lifting or digging potatoes from the ground.

Graith (Scotch), the furniture of a house; accoutrements of a horse; apparatus of any kind; wearing apparel.

Gram, a common name in India for several kinds of pulse, the produce of varieties of *Dolichos* and *Phaseolus*. Gram is distinguished by its colour; and one variety, *Dolichos uniflorus*, is known as horse gram; green gram and black gram or moong are varieties of *Phaseolus radiatus* and *P. Mungo*; *P. trilobus* and *aureus* are other varieties. Red and white gram are *Dolichos catjang* and *Soja hispida*. *See* Chola and Dholl.

Gramashes, garters reaching to the knees; a kind of stockings worn in Scotland instead of boots.

Gramigna, a name in Italy for the long under-ground shoots of couch grass (*Triticum repens*), which is extensively collected after the plough and harrow, and used as food for horses. Colonel Maceroni, in his Memoirs, states that upwards of £40,000 sterling worth of this root is annually sold by the peasants to the inhabitants of the city of Naples alone. It has been recommended as a material for paper manufacture.

Gramme, the proper unity of French weight; a cube of one hundredth of a metre on a side, and equal to 15·4339 troy grains. The kilogramme, which is the weight of a cubic decimètre of pure water, is, however, practically used as the unity of weight in France.

Gramola (Italian), an instrument for beating or bruising flax.

Gram-pot, a boiler in which pulse is cooked by the natives in India.

Granadilla, a climbing plant of the tropics, *Passiflora quadrangularis*: the sub-acid pulp of the fruit is esteemed, and the root is emetic and narcotic.

Granary, a warehouse or place where grain is stored.

Granary-keeper, the owner, or person in charge, of a corn-store or warehouse for grain.

Grand-jury, the first or principal jury, to which is referred the examination of indictments against criminals.

Grand-piano, a long piano-forte, shaped like a harpsichord.

Grand-stand, the principal erection on a race-course, whence a view of the race can be obtained.

Grange, a farm having suitable barns, stables, and other necessary buildings for stock, &c.

Granger (French), a barn-keeper; the foreman of a farm.

Granite, a plutonic or igneous rock, consisting of quartz, mica, and felspar; being of great strength, hardness, and durability, it is much used for building. The colour is chiefly light gray, but there are also white, red, and mottled granites. The best is obtained near Penryn in Cornwall, but some comes from Aberdeen, the Channel Islands, and other quarters. The principal uses of this stone are for laying door-ways, court-ways, railway stations, floors of manufactories and warehouses, kitchens, cellars, churches, engineering-works, the columns and foundations of buildings, &c.

GRANITE MERCHANT, a stone dealer; one who supplies builders and contractors for paving.
GRANO, a money of account in Italy, the hundredth part of the ducat; there are silver pieces of 10, 20, and 50 grani.
GRANOTINO, a minute weight of Italy, the 24th part of the grain.
GRANULATED, formed into small grains, as in sugar, grain tin, &c.
GRAPES, the fruit of the vine, forming a large article of commerce in different countries, either ripe, dried as raisins, or when collected, for making wine.
GRAPE-SHOT, small shot confined in a canvas cartridge to be discharged from a gun.
GRAPE-SUGAR, the sweet substance of the chestnut, of the brewers' wort, and of all fermented liquors. It gives sweetness to most fruits, and may be prepared from starch.
GRAPHIOLITE, a description of writing slate.
GRAPHITE, a valuable mineral used for black-lead pencils, melting-pots, and as a polish for iron stoves; also as a lubricator for fine machinery. It is better known as plumbago.
GRAPHOMETER, a mathematical instrument for measuring angles.
GRAPNEL, a small boat's anchor with several claws or hooks instead of flukes.
GRAPPLING-IRONS, crooked irons used to seize and hold fast another vessel.
GRASS-CLOTH. See CHINA-GRASS CLOTH.
GRASS-CUTTERS, attendants of an Indian army, essentially requisite to provide provender for the large quantity of cattle usually required in transporting munitions, baggage, &c.
[illegible]-DOUBLE, the French name for tripe
[illegible]SELLO (Italian), a kind of very fine [illegible]
[illegible]-OIL, a name given to some essential [illegible] obtained from scented grasses in [illegible]ia, as that from the lemon grass; the [illegible]ss oil of Nemaur, from another *Andro*[illegible]*on*, &c. It is sometimes called ginger-grass oil.
[illegible]ASS-PLOT, a lawn of trimmed grass.
GRASS-TREE, a name in Australia for some liliaceous plants, species of *Xanthorrhœa*, from which a resin is obtained, known in commerce as gum acroides.
GRATE, a register-stove, or cast-iron frame with fire-bars for a sitting-room, &c. for holding fuel, and making a fire in. A grate, or grid, is also a plate with iron bars for sewers, drains, &c.
GRATE AND FENDER MAKER, a caster of register-stoves, kitchen-ranges, fenders, and other iron articles.
GRATEAU, a burnisher or scraper; a tool used by gilders in France.
GRATERS, rubbing or scratching utensils of metal for domestic use, such as nutmeg-graters, arrow-root graters, raspers, &c.
GRATICULATION, the division of a drawing into squares.
GRATING, an open lattice work of wood or iron; a cross-barred covering for the hatchways of a ship.
GRAVECEMBALO (Italian), a harpsichord.
GRAVE-DIGGER, a digger of trenches for burying corpses in churchyards or cemeteries.
GRAVEL, small water-worn stones, used for covering garden-walks, roads, footways, &c.
GRAVEL-CAR, a railway ballast-wagon.
GRAVEL-PIT, the place whence gravel is dug.
GRAVER, a watchmaker's tool; a burin used in engraving.
GRAVES, GREAVES, the refuse or marc left by tallow-chandlers.
GRAVE-STONE, the head-stone to a grave; usually bearing an inscription recording the name, age and date of death, &c. of the person buried.
GRAVE-STONE CUTTER, a worker in stone, who chisels out letters, &c. upon tomb-stones, or sarcophaguses.
GRAVIMETER, an instrument for measuring the specific gravity of bodies. See HYDROMETER.
GRAVING-DOCK, a dock into which vessels are taken to have their bottoms examined, and breamed or graved.
GRAVY, the juice of cooked meat.
GRAVY AND GRUEL STRAINER, a small wire or hair sieve, used for culinary purposes.
GRAVY-DISH, a large table dish for a joint, with a well for gravy.
GRAVY-SPOON, a large spoon used at table for helping gravy to guests.
GRAWATHA, the Brazilian name for a species of *Bromelia*, from which excellent cordage is made.
GRAZIER, one who rears or feeds stock; a cattle-dealer.
GREASE, animal fat of any kind; melted tallow, with soda, palm oil and water, used as a lubricator for the axles of railway carriages.
GREASE-BOX, the receptacle over the axle of a railway carriage holding grease; the portable box in which grease is carried to replenish the above.
GREASE-MAKER, a manufacturer of lubricating substances for railway carriage axles, machinery, engines, &c.
GREAT-COAT, an overall, or outercoat.
GREAT-HUNDRED, the long hundred of six score. See HUNDRED.
GREAVE, to clean a ship's bottom by burning.
GREAVES, the sediment of melted tallow made into cakes, and used for feeding dogs and cattle.
GREBE, an aquatic bird (*Podiceps cristata*) inhabiting most of the lakes of Europe. The feathers are of a rich silver-white colour, variously shaded with brown. They are very durable, are worn as trimmings for the trains of court and drawing-room dresses, and are made into muffs, cuffs, boas, &c.
GREEN-CLOTH, baize, &c., for covering tables.
GREEN-CROPS, plants which are grown on a farm to be consumed before they are fully ripe or come to maturity, as tares, turnips, carrots; sometimes green crops are ploughed into the soil to fertilize it.
GREEN-EBONY, a wood obtained from the *Jacaranda ovalifolia*, a native of the West Indies, and used both as a hard turning wood and as a dye-stuff: about 600 or 700 tons are imported annually. See EBONY.

Green-finch, a common British bird, the *Chlorospiza chloris*), which is frequently caged, but its note is not admired.

Green-gage, a kind of plum of a green colour; a choice variety of the *Prunus domesticus*.

Green-grocer, a retail dealer in vegetables and fruit.

Greenheart, a common tree of Guiana, the *Nectandra Rodioei*; its timber, squaring from 18 to 24 inches, can be procured without a knot from 60 to 70 feet long. It is a fine-grained hard wood, well adapted for the planking of vessels, house frames, wharves, bridges, and other purposes, where great strength and durability are required. It is the best timber for resisting tensile and compressive strains, and is therefore well adapted for kelsons of ships, and beams of all kinds. The black greenheart is considered more durable than the common greenheart. The bark yields biberine, the sulphate of which is used like the sulphate of quinine.

Green-house, a conservatory or glazed house for rearing and protecting plants from changes of temperature.

Green Paints, oil-colours, of which the chief varieties are emerald, mineral, green copperas, mountain sap, and Brunswick greens.

Green-room, the actors' retiring or meeting room in a theatre.

Greens, a common name for small young cabbages, which have not formed the leaves into full hearts.

Green-sand, a silicious stone found in the Blackdown Hills, Devon, used as a whetstone for scythes, &c.

Green-stone, a stone containing native copper, found in Renfrewshire; an igneous rock, in which felspar is combined with hornblende or augite; stone walls are made of it in parts of Scotland.

Greensward, a grass-plot.

Green-tea, a commercial variety of tea imported from China, of which there are several kinds; the principal being Twankay, an inferior description; Hyson-skin, Hyson, and young Hyson, imperial, and gunpowder.

Green Turtle, the *Chelone midas*, imported as a luxury for making turtle soup. The imports vary, but may average 15,000 a-year.

Green Vitriol, crystallized sulphate of iron used in making ink, Prussian blue, and sulphuric acid; also employed in dyeing.

Greeur (French), a ship-rigger.

Greffier, a registrar, or recorder in a French court of justice.

Gregarious, herding together, or living in flocks, as domestic cattle, birds, &c.

Grege, a French term applied to raw silk.

Grelet, a mason's hammer in France.

Grelin (French), a small cablet or line for a boat.

Grenade, a hollow ball or shell of metal, filled with powder, having a burning fuse attached, thrown by hand amongst enemies; in France a small shrimp used by fishermen for bait.

Grenadier, a tall foot-soldier wearing a high cap; one originally employed to throw grenades.

Grenadillo, a tropical fruit. *See* Granadilla.

Grenat (French), dried lemon-peel.

Grenetine, a French name for gelatin.

Greyhound, a slim-made dog kept for coursing, remarkable for swiftness, strength, and sagacity in pursuing game.

Gribane, a small French vessel.

Griblette (French), a pork-chop broiled.

Gridiron, a kind of frame for drawing up a ship on to be docked and repaired; a frying and grilling iron grated frame for cooking chops, steaks, fish, &c., over a fire.

Griddle, Riddle, a miner's wire-bottomed sieve for separating the ore from the halvans.

Grigs, a variety of eel found in the Thames.

Grilling, the operation of broiling meat over a fire.

Grilse, a young salmon.

Grimellino, a small money of account in Tripoli, of 4 aspers.

Grinder, a sharpener and polisher of edge-tools; the large teeth that masticate food. Elephants' grinders are used for making knife handles.

Grindery Warehouse, a shop where the materials and tools for shoemakers and other leather workers are kept on sale.

Grinding-slips, hones; a kind of oil-stone.

Grindstone, a circular-shaped sandstone, moved by a handle, for sharpening and grinding edge-tools.

Griotte, the French name for the morella or black cherry; a speckled marble.

Grip, a small French vessel.

Gripes, bars of iron with lanyard-rings [illegible] claws, by which a large boat is lash[illegible] the ring-bolts of the deck.

Grippe-sou, a French house-agent; [illegible] of broker.

Grisar, the name in France for a very [illegible] kind of sandstone, like Purbeck ston[illegible]

Griscio, an Egyptian coin of 30 paras.

Grisette, a common brown French stuf[illegible] fabric, worn by females of inferior class; whence the transfer of the name to the wearer.

Grist, wheat-flour, divested of the coarse bran only.

Grist-mill, a name in North America for a flour-mill.

Grit, hard sandstone employed for millstones, grindstones, pavement, &c.; gravel; the coarse part of meal.

Gritty, earthy; containing sand or grit; flour or meal having pieces of stone, &c. mixed with it.

Grive, Griwin, a debased coin passing in Russia for 10 kopecks, about 3½d.; the tenth part of a rouble.

Groat, a small English silver coin, equivalent to 4d., first minted in the reign of Edward I. A very large quantity of groats were coined in 1854, weighing 29 1-11th gr. each. *See* Fourpence.

Groat Manufacturer, a preparer of oats into groats; one who removes the husks or shells from the grain.

GROATS, decorticated oats; hulled and peeled barley. In commerce there are several varieties, as Embden groats, which are crushed oats; pearl barley, &c. *See* CUTLINGS.

GROCER, a dealer and vender of sugars, spices, dried fruits, and other comestibles, or articles of food for the table; usually combined with the sale of coffee and tea, &c. A green-grocer is a vender of vegetables, ripe fruit, &c.

GROCERIES, the comestible wares, or general commodities sold by a grocer.

GROCERS' COMPANY, the second in rank of the twelve great metropolitan livery companies, or guilds; its original charter dates from 27th Edward III. Their hall is in Grocers' Hall Court, Poultry.

GROCER'S MATERIAL MANUFACTURER, a maker of most of the requisites for a grocer's shop.

GROCER'S SHOP-FITTING MANUFACTURER, a fixture dealer; a maker of tinned canisters, scoops, &c. for grocers.

GROESCHEL, a copper coin of Austria, in value one third less than the kreutzer.

GROG, a sailor's name for rum, whisky, or other spirituous liquor, diluted with water, and unsweetened.

GROGRAMS, a fabric made on the Continent of silk and mohair; also a name for a silk called gros-de-Naples.

GROIN, a framework of wood across a beach to retain the accumulated shingle; the point of junction in two semi-cylinders or arches.

GROMA, GRUMA, an ancient measure of length, about 20 feet.

GROMMET, a ring formed of rope, by laying round a single strand; used to fasten the upper edge of a sail to its stay.

GROOM, a stable attendant; one who has the care of horses; a gentleman's servant, or outrider.

GROOMETRY. *See* GOONDOOMING.

GROOPER, GROUPER, a common name in the West India markets for several species of *Serranus*, fish belonging to the perch family; the best known is the *S. chrysotomus* of Cuvier.

GROOVE, a channel or long hollow furrow cut by a tool; a shaft or pit sunk by miners.

GROOVED, furrowed, or channelled.

GROS, a money of Venice, the 24th part of the ducat about 1½d.; also a money in Bavaria and other parts of 2 florins and 24 kreutzers; the eighth part of the old French ounce, 59·07 troy grains.

GROSCHEN, a small silver coin and money of account in various parts of Germany, worth about 1½d.; the gutgroschen is half as much again as the marien groschen.

GROS-DE-NAPLES, a plain silken fabric made of organzine silk, and woven with much neatness and care.

GROSS, in merchandise the whole weight of goods, including box, package, bailing, &c.; the number of 12 dozen, which is the small gross, but the great gross is 12 times 12 dozen.

GROS-SOU, a French copper coin of ten centimes, about 1d. sterling.

GROT, GROOTE, a petty money of Germany, worth about a halfpenny. [piastre.

GROUCH, GOOROCH, a Turkish name for the

GROUND, land; the colour first put on, the surface; the prevailing colour of a fabric, building, &c.; the first layer of colour in a painting; dregs; in navigation, to touch the bottom; an Indian land measure, the 24th part of a cawney, 60 feet long by 40 broad, and containing 2,400 square feet.

GROUND-BAILIFF, a superintendant of mines, who makes periodical visits to report upon their condition.

GROUND-BAIT, pasty bread, or other substances, cast to the bottom of the water to entice fish.

GROUND-FLOOR, the story or floor of a house level with the ground.

GROUND-IVY. *See* ALE-HOOF.

GROUND-NUTS, the seed of *Arachis hypogæa*, from which oil is expressed.

GROUND-PLAN, the surface representation of the divisions of a building.

GROUND-PLOT, the land on which a building stands; the plan of the ground.

GROUND-RATTAN, a kind of cane, the stem of *Rhapis flabelliformis*.

GROUND-RENT, the rent paid by a lessee to the owner of the freehold, or for the privilege of building on another man's land.

GROUND-RICE, pulverized rice; the grain ground into flour or meal.

GROUNDSEL, a common wild plant, the *Senecio vulgaris;* the stalks, containing the young buds, seeds, and leaves, are collected and sold to feed cage-birds, particularly goldfinches and linnets; the timber or sill of a building resting on the earth.

GROUNDS, the dregs or feculencies deposited at the bottom of liquids.

GROUND-TACKLE, a general name for the appliances and gear used in securing a vessel at anchor, comprising cables, warps, springs, anchors, &c.

GROUND-TIER, the lowest tier of casks in a vessel's hold; the pit range of boxes in a theatre.

GROUND-WORK, the earth-work or foundation; the commencement of any operation.

GROUSE, a large family of birds, many of which are much esteemed, and seeking them affords salutary amusement to the keen sportsman in the north. The black grouse is the *Tetras tetrix;* the red grouse, or moor-cock, is the *Lagopus Scoticus*. There are several species common in North America. For the wood grouse, or cock of the wood, *see* CAPERCAILZIE.

GROUT, coarse meal; pollard; a thin mortar, a mixture of quicklime and fine sand, used for mouldings and finishing ceilings.

GROVE, a small shady wood; a Derbyshire name for a mine.

GROWAN, a miner's name for rock, or for decomposed granite.

GROYNE, a sea wall, or defence against the encroachments of the tide. *See* GROIN.

GRUAU (French), oatmeal; water-gruel; a crane (both bird and machine).

GRUAUX, wooden vessels used in salt manufactories in France; wheat flour coarsely ground, so as to free it from the husk.

GRUB-AXE, a hoe or field tool for digging up weeds.

GRUBBER, an agricultural machine for cultivating; an extirpator or scarifier, for loosening the earth.

GRUBB-STONE MORTAR, a concrete cement. *See* BETON.

GRUEL, a thick nutritive porridge or food prepared from oats or pearl barley, forming an article of diet for invalids and convalescents.

GRUNT, a West-Indian name for various species of *Hæmulon*, a common fish in the markets.

GRUNTER, an iron rod bent like a hook, used by iron founders.

GRUYERE, a kind of Swiss cheese.

GUACHO, a South American mounted herdsman, or cattle hunter.

GUADE (Italian), a kind of fishing-net.

GUAIACUM, an acrid resin obtained from the wood of the lignum vitæ (*Guaiacum officinale*, and *G. sanctum*), used medicinally.

GUANA, a common name for a large species of tree lizard, the *Iguana tuberculata*, which is esteemed for its delicate flesh, and the skin is often tanned.

GUANACO, a variety of the alpaca, the *Auchenia huanaca*.

GUANO, a valuable fertilizer, imported from various quarters, chiefly from Peru, consisting of the excrements of sea-fowl, and the decomposed carcases of marine animals. In the last sixteen years we have received upwards of two million tons: the average annual imports of the four years ending with 1856, having been 215,000 tons.

GUARANA BREAD, a name in Brazil for cakes made from the seeds of the *Paullinia sorbilis*, and used like cocoa for making a beverage; it contains a bitter principle, identical with caffeine.

GUARANTEE SOCIETIES, certain joint-stock companies, which, upon payment of an agreed premium, guarantee to the employer the honesty of a person employed, or, at least, undertake to make good any deficiencies in his accounts.

GUARANTY, GUARANTEE, an engagement to perform some act, or pay some debt in case another person primarily liable fails to do so.

GUARAPO, a common beverage of the lower orders in Venezuela, made from the juice of the sugar-cane, or with sugar and water which has undergone the vinous fermentation.

GUARD, a watchman or sentinel; the conductor of a coach or railway train; an escort or protection; the part of the handle of a sword which covers the hand.

GUARD-BOAT, a row-boat in a harbour, or among vessels at anchorage.

GUARD-HOUSE, the building where a guard of soldiers is kept.

GUARDIAN, a protector; a warden; an officer of a poor-law union or workhouse board.

GUARD-SHIP, a vessel of war stationed in a harbour or river, to superintend marine affairs, and to receive seamen.

GUARNELLO (Italian), fustian.

GUASTADA, in Italy, a decanter.

GUAVA, a common name for the *Psidium pyriferum*, the fruit of which is much esteemed, either stewed in wine, or made into a jelly. The aromatic leaves are used in the Eastern islands medicinally, and as a substitute for the leaf of the betel pepper. The wood, when old, is tough and close-grained, taking a good polish: in India it is used for gun-stocks.

GUAVA-JELLY, a favourite preserve or jam made in the West Indies from the fruit of the guava.

GUDANG, GADONG, the Malay name for a storehouse, Anglicised godown.

GUDDA, an Arabian measure of capacity, of 8 noosfias, and equal to 1⅜ gallon.

GUDDOK, a rustic violin, with three strings, used among the Russian peasantry.

GUERILLA, an insurgent; a border invader.

GUIDE, a conductor or director; a regulator.

GUIDE-POST, a finger-post or directing-post at cross roads.

GUILD, an old commercial association; a fraternity or corporation possessing special privileges; a company of merchants in Scotland who are freemen of the royal burghs.

GUILDER, GULDER, a silver coin current in many of the States of the Zollverein, and worth about 1s. 8d., but variable; in some places it is called a florin.

GUILDHALL, the place of meeting of the corporation of the city of London; the great court of judicature for the civic part of the metropolis.

GUILDIVE (French), rum; a spirit distilled from molasses.

GUINDRE, a French reel for winding silk.

GUINEA, a British gold coin first struck in the reign of Charles II., and worth 21s. It is now seldom met with. There were also gold pieces of half-a-guinea, two guineas, and five guineas.—(5 dwt. 9½ gr.)

GUINEA-CORN, a name in the West Indies for several species of *Panicum*, including *P. pyramidale*, *scabrum*, and *tenellum*, cultivated for their seeds.

GUINEA-FOWL, the *Numida meleagris*, a bird wild in the West Indies, but now domesticated in our poultry yards. The flesh is considered by many persons to equal that of the pheasant.

GUINEA-GRAINS. *See* GRAINS OF PARADISE.

GUINEA-GRASS, a tall strong forage grass, the *Panicum maximum* of Jaquin; naturalized in the West Indies and Southern States of America, having been introduced from the Western coast of Africa.

GUINEA-PEPPER. *See* ETHIOPIAN-PEPPER.

GUINEA-PIG, a small tailless quadruped, the *Cavia cobaya*, a native of South America, which is often domesticated, and kept as a pet.

GUINEA-YAM, a name for the *Dioscorea bulbifera*.

GUINGUETTE, a suburban tea-garden in France; a low public-house out of town, whither the lower classes resort; a coarse linen made in Normandy.

GUIPURE, an imitation of antique lace, which is durable, less expensive, and equally beautiful. It is made in Limerick by cutting out the pattern from cambric, the flowers and heavy parts being made of the cambric, and the open parts of stitches closely resembling the antique lace. In France a guipure lace, much resembling the Honiton, is made, which is very fine and white, and of a moderate price; a kind of gimp.

GUITAR, a musical stringed-instrument, larger than the violin, and played with the fingers. The modern Spanish guitar has six strings, three being of silk, covered with silver wire, and three of catgut.

GUITAR-MAKER, a manufacturer of stringed instruments.

GUJORATZ-CLOTH, black and white cloth made in Transylvania.

GUL, an Eastern name for the Provence red rose.

GULIVANDA, an Eastern weight; also called a patika, and equal to 2 grains.

GULLIES, a name sometimes given to iron rails or tram-plates.

GULLY, a worn water-channel.

GUM ARABIC, a general trade name for several descriptions of clear soluble gums. The best, or true white gum, is yielded by *Acacia verek* of Guillemin, the red gum arabic by *A. Adansonii*: *A. vera* also yields gum arabic and a part of the senegal gum. Our imports of gum arabic are about 5000 tons a year.

GUM-LAC. *See* LAC.

GUM-MANUFACTURER, one who prepares dextrine or gum substitutes from calcined meal of different kinds.

GUM-RESINS, substances which are a compound of gum, oil, and resin.

GUMS, exudations from plants which soften in water. The true gums are very few in number. Gum is consumed in immense quantities by dyers and glaziers, and enters into a great number of pharmaceutical preparations. The value of the British trade in gums, resins, balsams, and other vegetable inspissated extracts, is nearly two millions sterling a year.

GUM-WOOD, a species of *Eucalyptus*.

GUN, a fire-lock, a piece of ordnance. *See* GUNS.

GUN-BARREL, the tube of a gun.

GUN-BARREL MAKER, a metal-caster and borer of the tubes for gun and pistols.

GUN-BARREL PROVER, one who tests the strength of gun-barrels by charges of gunpowder.

GUN-BOAT, a small vessel formerly fitted to carry one or two guns at the bow; but they are now very differently constructed.

GUN-CARRIAGE, the frame-work or moveable support for a piece of ordnance.

GUN-CARRIAGE MAKER, a manufacturer of wooden or metal supports for great guns.

GUN-CASE, the box or receptacle for a rifle or fowling-piece.

GUNCHA, a weight used in Acheen, the tenth part of the coyan; about 290 lbs. avoirdupois.

GUN-COTTON, purified cotton wool steeped for a short time in equal parts of nitric and sulphuric acids, and dried, by which it becomes explosive. For gunnery and fire-arms it has not been found so useful as predicted, but it is admirably adapted for mining and blasting. Dissolved in ether, gun-cotton forms a good varnish for covering wounds, or giving a thin film to any surface, and is a powerful deoxidizer.

GUNDA, the sum of four cowry shells, used by the poorer natives of India as a medium of currency in smaller or fractional payments and purchases. *See* COWRIES.

GUNDAUR, the Hindustani name for the rhinoceros.

GUNDUCK, the Indian name for brimstone.

GUN-FLINT MANUFACTURER, a shaper of flints for musket-locks.

GUN-FLINTS, shaped flints for fire-locks; since the introduction of percussion caps to rifles and pistols, flint-locks are now seldom used, except among a few barbarous tribes.

GUNJAH, a name in India for the dried hemp plant (*Cannabis sativa*), which has flowered, but from which the resinous juice has not been removed. It is chiefly sold for smoking with tobacco, and is made up in bundles about 2 feet long and 3 inches in diameter, containing 24 plants.

GUNJES, grain markets in India.

GUNJUN, an Indian balsam. *See* GURJUN.

GUN-LOCK MAKER, a manufacturer of the percussion or flint-locks for muskets, rifles, pistols, and other small arms. The polishing of these is often another branch of trade.

GUN-MAKER, a gunsmith, a manufacturer of muskets or rifles; a founder or caster of pieces of ordnance.

GUN-MAKER'S COMPANY, one of the livery companies of London, which, having no hall, transacts its business at Guildhall.

GUN-METAL, an alloy of copper and tin.

GUNNA-ASH, the ashes of a Cape tree, which contain 56 or 60 per cent. of soda.

GUNNALA, an Indian name for the *Cassia fistula*.

GUNNEL. *See* GUNWALE.

GUNNER, a cannonier; an officer on land or sea appointed to manage pieces of artillery.

GUNNERY, the science of constructing and using large and small fire-arms.

GUNNY-BAGS, GUNNY-CLOTH, GUNNIES, a name for coarse strong sacking made in India, and much used for bags and bales for wrapping rice, spices, and other dry goods. In Bengal gunny cloth is made of jute, the produce of species of *Corchorus*, and is exported either in pieces or made up into bags. The gunny bags of Bombay and Madras are, however, made of different kinds of sunn fibre, the *Crotalaria juncea*.

GUNPOWDER, a well-known explosive substance prepared from nitre, charcoal, and sulphur: the compound consists usually of 75 parts of saltpetre, 10 of sulphur and 15 of charcoal, mixed and reduced to a fine powder, then granulated and dried; but the proportion of the ingredients varies in different countries, and according to the purpose for which it is to be used.

GUNPOWDER-BARREL MAKER, a manufacturer of small light casks for securely holding gunpowder and keeping it dry.

Gunpowder Flask Maker, a manufacturer of small metal cases for sportsmen, to hold gun-powder. [gunpowder.

Gunpowder Manufacturer, a maker of

Gunpowder-tea, a kind of green tea.

Gun-room, the mess room of the lieutenants in a large ship of war.

Guns, explosive instruments, of different sizes, consisting of a barrel of strong metal fixed in a stock or mounted on carriages. The smaller and portable kinds are named muskets, rifles, carbines, fowling-pieces, &c. The heavy descriptions of guns, called cannon, ordnance, field-pieces, swivels, carronades, howitzers, and mortars, are described under those several heads. They usually take their distinguishing name from the weight of the ball that will fit them.

Gun-shot: "within gun-shot" is, within the distance a piece of artillery will carry.

Gun-smith, an armourer; a maker of small fire-arms; a repairer of guns.

Gun-stock, the wood in which the barrel of a gun is fixed: usually walnut.

Gun-stock Maker, a manufacturer of the shaped wooden stocks for gun-barrels.

Gun-tackle, the blocks and pulleys of a gun-carriage affixed to the side of a ship, by which it is run in and out of the port-hole.

Gun-tackle Purchase, a purchase or pulley made by two single blocks.

Guntang, an Indian dry measure rather more than 15 lbs.

Gunter's Chain, a surveyor's measure named after the inventor, consisting of a series of iron links, usually 100, of 7·92 inches each. At every tenth link is fastened a small brass plate, with a figure engraven upon it, or else cut into different shapes, to show how many links it is from the end. The length of the chain is four poles of 5½ yards each, or 66 feet.

Gunter's Scale, a large plane scale, chiefly used by seamen, having various lines relating to trigonometry and navigation engraven on it.

Gun-wadding, circular pieces of card-board, cloth, felt, and chemically prepared substances, used to keep down the charge of ball or shot, &c. in a gun. In large guns rope wads are used.

Gun-wadding Maker, a manufacturer of wads of different kinds for guns.

Gunwale, the upper rail of a boat or vessel.

Gura nut, a species of large red bean, with a bitter taste, growing on the West coast of Africa, much prized by the natives of the interior for its tonic properties.

Gurge, an old term, signifying a gulf or gorge of water, for the preservation of fishes.

Gurjun, an oleo-resin; a thin balsam or wood oil, obtained in Burmah and the Eastern archipelago, from *Dipterocarpus lævis*, and other species. It is used medicinally; and forms an excellent substitute for linseed-oil. In the coarser kinds of house and ship painting. Mixed with dammar or resin, it preserves wood from the attacks of white ants.

Gurmies, in mining, levels or workings.

Gurnet, a popular name for the gurnard fish. Several species of *Trigla* are taken on the British coasts. In Ireland and Scotland they are often called crooners.

Gurrah, a plain coarse Indian muslin.

Gurry, a small fort in India.

Gursay, a name for the garce in some parts of Madras.

Gursoonder, a name in Bengal for the *Acacia Arabica*, yielding the babool gum of commerce. The bark of the tree is a powerful astringent.

Gurt, a gutter, or channel for water.

Gusset, an insertion or piece let into a fabric or garment.

Gutah, the Malay name for bird-lime, or for any elastic gum.

Gutta-percha, a concrete milky juice, forming a gum-resin, obtained in the Eastern archipelago from *Isonandra Gutta*; of extensive use in the arts, and for various economical purposes, being easily shaped, and retaining the form given to it.

Gutta-percha Dealer, a vender of gutta-percha soles, and articles made of this elastic gum.

Gutta-trap, the inspissated sap of an *Artocarpus*, obtained in the East, which, from its glutinous properties, is used for making bird-lime.

Gutter, a channel, or sewer.

Gutter-spout, a spout for carrying off water from a roof.

Gutties, dry cakes of cow-dung, used for fuel and other purposes in India.

Gutto (Italian), a cruet for oil.

Guy, a rope for steadying or guiding any thing that has to be hoisted or lowered.

Guz, an Indian name for the yard or cloth measure, which varies in length in different places, from about 2 to 3 feet.

Gybe, a nautical term for the shifting over of the boom of a fore-and-aft sail in tacking, &c.

Gyle, a brewer's vat or utensil; a name given by the vinegar-maker to the fermented wort which he uses.

Gymnasium, a public place or school-yard, where feats of strength, agility, &c., are practised, such as climbing, leaping, &c.

Gymnast, an athlete; an instructor in exercises of the body.

Gynahs, gold and silver ornaments used by the natives of India.

Gypsum, a well-known mineral, softer than limestone, which, when calcined and powdered, forms plaster of Paris. In the crushed state it is used as manure in North America. The large blocks are wrought into alabaster ornaments.

Gyves, fetters or shackles for the legs.

H.

HAAF-BOAT, a deep-sea fishing-boat in Scotland, probably a corruption of half-decked boat.

Haaf-fishing, the fishery for cod, ling, tusk, &c. off Orkney and the Shetlands.

Habbie', a Syrian dry measure; 100 habbies of Jaffa being equal to 39 quarters.

Habeck, a clothier's tool.

Haberdasher, a dealer in small wares, such as sewing threads, laces, and *tapes, fringes* and twists, buttons, hooks-and-eyes, trimmings, &c. It is often combined with the woollen-drapery trade. Haberdasheries formerly included numerous articles now dealt in by other trades, as hats, clothes, glasses, spoons, &c.

Haberdashers' Company, one of the twelve great livery companies of London, ranking the eighth in order. Its charter was granted 26th Henry VI. The hall of the company is in Gresham-street.

Haberdine, a dried salted cod-fish.

Habillement (French), garments, clothing, gear.

Habilleur, a hemp-dresser; a preparer of skins in France.

Habit-maker, a tailor who makes long cloth riding-coats, or dresses for ladies, termed habits.

Habit-shirt, a thin muslin or lace garment, worn over the breast and neck by females.

Habu, the Malay name for ashes.

Hache-paille, a chaff-cutter in France.

Hacienda, the Spanish name for a farm or plantation.

Hack, a worn-out horse; to use much; to hew or cut; in Scotland, a fodder for cattle; a frame suspended from the roof for drying cheeses; the wooden bars in the tailrace of a mill; a framework for drying fish; a dung fork; a large pick used in working stone.

Hackberry, the *Celtis occidentalis*, an ornamental tree of the United States, of medium size. The wood is hard, close-grained, and elastic, and makes the best of *hoops*, whip-stalks, and thills for carriages; the Indians formerly made great use of it for their bows.

Hackbrett, the German name for the dulcimer.

Hackery, an Indian bullock-cart, capable of carrying a load of about 12 maunds, or from 900 to 1000 lbs.

Hackia, a wood of Demerara, known in the colony as lignum vitæ, but a much larger tree than the *Guaiacum officinale*, attaining a height of from 50 to 60 feet, and squaring 16 to 18 inches. It is used for mill cogs and shafts.

Hackle, a flax-comb; a fly for angling, dressed merely with a cock's feather.

Hackle-maker, a manufacturer of glittering artificial flies for anglers, made of bright-coloured feathers, silk, &c. disguising a fish-hook.

Hackler, a flax-dresser.

Hackles, the long shining feathers from the cock's neck, used to make artificial flies.

Hackmatack, a name for the American larch (*Larix Americana*), a useful building wood.

Hackney-coach, a public carriage plying for hire, now almost obsolete, from the general introduction of cabs and omnibuses.

Hackney-coachman, the driver of a hired carriage called a hackney-coach.

Hackney-coach Stand, a cab-stand; the appointed place where public carriages wait to be hired.

Haddock, a small fish, the *Morrhua Æglifinus*, which is exceedingly fine when eaten fresh, or when slightly salted and smoked, in the same manner as the Finnan haddocks of Scotland.

Hadned, a cloth measure in Turkey, of about 34 inches.

Haft, a handle; in Scotland, to fix or settle; a dwelling.

Hafter, in the cutlery *trade*, a workman who forms and fixes the solid handles for knives.

Haft-and-scale Cutter, one who shapes, cuts, or presses, bone and horn handles, for cutting instruments.

Hafts, the solid handles of knives, cut from ivory, bone, &c.; into a drilled hole, in which the tang or iron end of the knife passes, and is fixed. In other knives, there are flat side-pieces rivetted to a central plate, which are called "scales."

Hag, **Hagger**, in Scotland, one who uses a hatchet or axe; a person employed in felling timber, or who cuts up a quantity of wood.

Haggis, a baked mess of sheep's entrails, thickened with oatmeal and seasoned.

Haggis-bag, the maw of a sheep, used to make a haggis in.

Hagman, in Scotland, a wood-cutter, one who sells wood; a local name for a bark-cutter, who, with a ripping-saw and hatchet, prepares the bark for being subsequently stripped by the skinners or barkers (generally women and children), who follow him.

Ha-ha, a kind of sunk fence, made of the Ha palm; a shield used by the Indians of Guiana.

Hail, to speak loud or call to another.

Hailoh, a long measure of Sumatra, equal to 4 feet.

Haim (French), a fish-hook.

Hair, a filament, an integument of the skin covering many animals, or parts of the body. Hair of various kinds enters largely into trade: horse-hair, camels'-hair, ox and cow hair, pig-hair, goats'-hair and human-hair, being all extensively employed for different purposes. Even the stout bristly hair of the elephant's tail is worked into bracelets in India.

Hair-breadth, a nominal measure of length, the 48th part of an inch.

Hair-broom, a long-handled sweeping-broom for servants.

Hair-brush, a toilet brush for smoothing and dressing the hair.

Hair cloth, a woven fabric of horse-hair. Horse-hair seatings or coverings for furniture, &c. have a mixture of cotton interwoven.

Hair-dresser, an artist who trims and arranges the hair; a perruquier, who often combines the sale of perfumery and toilet articles.

Hair-dye, a preparation used for darkening or altering the colour of the hair. Almost every hair-dresser has a nostrum of his own; many of these are extremely injurious, containing oxide of lead, which is absorbed by the skin.

Hair-gloves, horsehair gloves used for rubbing the skin in bathing, &c.

Hair-line, a horsehair fishing-line.

Hair-merchant, a dealer in hair.

Hair-net, a net for enclosing a lady's hair.

Hair-oil, scented oil for moistening the hair.

Hair-pencils, small brushes used by artists made of the fine hairs of the marten, badger, polecat, &c. mounted in quills or white iron tubes. *See* Camel-hair-pencil Maker.

Hair-pin, a double pin or bent wire for confining a lady's hair.

Hair-plume Maker, a manufacturer of black horsehair plumes borne by mutes, or for horses drawing funeral carriages, or hearses, &c.

Hair-powder, flour applied to the hair, worn by old men and footmen; in this country a tax is levied on the privilege of wearing hair-powder.

Hair-seating, woven horse-hair, used for covering chairs, couches, and cushions.

Hair-sieve, a sieve or strainer with a woven horsehair bottom.

Hair-worker, a fancy workman in hair, who makes ornaments for wear; bracelets, lockets, pictures, &c. in human hair.

Hake, a shed for drying draining tiles; a large fish, the *Merluccius vulgaris*, frequently found three feet in length: in North America it is split and dry-cured like cod, and often passes under the name of stock-fish, but on the British coasts it is usually sold fresh.

Hakeem, an eastern physician.

Haken, a wooden frame-harrow without teeth, used in parts of Belgium.

Halberd, a military spear or pole-axe; the cross-bar on a horse-shoe.

Halbe-kopf, a piece of Austrian money of 18 kreutzers.

Halfa, a name in Algeria for the *Lygeum Spartum* and several species of *Stipa*, which are used in the manufacture of cordage, bagging, paper, &c. [or pale.

Half-and-half, a mixture of beer or porter

Half-boarder, a day-boarder at a school; a scholar not permanently resident.

Half-bred, a mongrel; a race horse not pure-blooded; a coursing dog not completely trained.

Half-crown, the second in value of the British current silver coins, worth 2s. 6d.; weighing rather more than 9 dwts. 2 grains (9.2·1818). The number of these pieces coined at the mint in the last few years has been as follows:—

1848	91,872.	1850	483,120.
1849	261,360.	1851	1,403.

Half-farthing, a British copper coin, the 8th part of a penny, of which a few tons have been struck within the last three or four years; the number of pieces issued between 1852 and 1854 was 2,021,784: 192 half-farthings weigh a pound avoirdupois.

Half-holiday, the half of the day taken from work, and devoted to rest or amusement.

Half-hundred, a weight of 56 lbs.

Half imperial, a kind of mill-board 22½ by 16½ inches; whole imperial is 32 by 22.

Half-ounce, the moiety of the ounce, which in avoirdupois is 218¾ grains; in troy weight 240 grains.

Half-pay, a moiety of the usual pay.

Half-penny, a piece of two farthings, the second in value of the British current copper coins; weighing 146 grains; 48 weigh a pound avoirdupois. The following numbers of these pieces have recently been issued:

1848	329,560	1854	12,461,648
1851	215,040	1855	7,455,837
1852	637,056	1856	1,942,080
1853	1,559,040		

Half-pike, a boarding-pike used in ships.

Half-pint, a measure of two gills, the fourth part of a quart, and = 17·329 cubic inches.

Half-pound, 6 ounces troy, or 8 ounces avoirdupois.

Half-price, half the cost; a reduced charge for admission to a theatre, late in the evening.

Half-quarter Day, a period of six weeks, from the last rent day.

Half-round, in building, a semi-circular moulding.

Half-royal, a kind of mill-board, of which there are two sizes, small 20½ by 13 inches, and large 21 by 14; large whole royal is 26½ by 20½; long royal is 34 by 21, double royal 46 by 21.

Half-sovereign, the second in value of the English current gold coins, weighing 2 dwts. 13.63724 grains, and worth 10s. The following is a return of the number of half-sovereigns coined at the British mint since 1848:—

	No.		No.
1848	410,595	1853	2,708,796
1849	845,112	1854	1,125,144
1850	179,595	1855	1,120,362
1851	773,573	1856	2,391,909
1852	1,377,671		

Half-stuff, in manufactures any thing half-formed; the name for a partially-prepared pulp for paper-making.

Half-way, mid-way; equi-distant from the extremes.

Hali, a weight used in Malacca, about 32 lbs. avoirdupois.

HALIBUT, a large flat fish of the flounder family, the *Hippoglossus vulgaris*, which often reaches the weight of 200 lbs. or more. The flesh is dry and coarse. It is lightly salted and smoked by the North American fishermen. The fins and flaps are esteemed delicacies. The halibut is also cut into slices and pickled in barrels, in which state they sell at half the price of the best herrings.

HALL, a large room in a town-guild for public business; a spacious building attached to inns of court; a name usually applied to the first room or open space after entering the doorway in a large dwelling-house.

HALL-DOOR, the street door or entrance.

HALLE, a French market-place.

HALLIARD. *See* HALYARDS.

HALLIER, a birding-net.

HALL-LAMP, a suspending lamp for a lobby, hall, or passage; for burning oil or candles, &c.

HALL-MARK, the official stamp affixed by the Goldsmiths' Company and the assay offices of particular districts, to articles of gold and silver, as a test of their legal quality. The hall-mark of Birmingham is an anchor; of Chester, three wheat-sheaves or a dagger; Dublin, a harp or figure of Britannia; Edinburgh, a thistle or castle and lion; Exeter, a castle with two wings, Glasgow, a tree and a salmon with a ring in its mouth; London, a leopard's head; Newcastle-on-Tyne, three castles; Sheffield, a crown; York, five lions and a cross. The date mark is a letter of the alphabet, which is changed every year, and differs in different companies. *See* STANDARD-MARK.

HALLOW-FAIR, a market held in November.

HALSTER, a measure of capacity, formerly used in Sweden, ranging from 5¼ to 11¼ gallons.

HALTER, a rope or strap and headstall for leading a horse; a rope for hanging malefactors.

HALVANNER, a miner who dresses and washes the impurities from crude ores.

HALVANS, impure ores, which require to be washed and freed from impurities.

HALVE, to divide or share into equal portions.

HALVE-NET, HAAVE-NET, in Scotland, a fixed bag-net, placed within water-mark, to prevent fish returning with the tide.

HALYA, the Malay name for ginger.

HALYARDS, ropes or tackles used for hoisting and lowering yards and sails on their respective masts.

HAM, a cured or smoked leg of pork, mutton, &c.

HAMALS, porters in Constantinople, who carry immense weights between them, suspended on poles supported on their shoulders.

HAMBEL, a species of woollen blanket or carpet used in Algeria.

HAM-CURER, a salter and smoker of hams.

HAME, the collar for a draught-horse or ox; the crooked pieces of wood which form the collar.

HAMEÇON (French), a fish-hook.

HAME-MANUFACTURER, a collar-maker.

HAMLET, a small village.

HAMMA, the lesser or leeward boat of the double canoe used in the Pacific.

HAMMEL, a small shed with a yard.

HAMMER, a workman's tool; a well-known striking instrument, used in various trades; thus there are blacksmiths' hammers, glaziers', carpenters', and upholsterers' hammers; claw, rivetting, sledge, smiths', wrench, and veneer hammers; part of a gunlock.

HAMMER-AXE, a double tool, having a hammer at one side of the handle, and an axe at the other.

HAMMER-BEAM, a tie-beam.

HAMMER-CLOTH, an ornamental covering to the coachman's seat, principally used for the more elegant kinds of coaches.

HAMMER-DRESSED, a term applied to building stone which has been hewn with a pick or pointed hammer.

HAMMERER, a blacksmith; a worker on metals at an anvil.

HAMMER-HEAD, the solid shaped piece of iron which is fitted to a handle for striking with, and which is sent in large quantities or strings, packed in casks, to different parts.

HAMMER-MAKER, a manufacturer of hammer-heads.

HAMMERMAN, a name in Scotland for a smith.

HAMMER-RAIL MAKER, a manufacturer of parts of the machinery for a piano-forte.

HAMMOCK, a hanging bed, or a swinging cot; those used to sleep in on board ship are strips of canvas sewn together, hung by cords or lines to cleets in the upper-deck beams. On shore they are frequently made of plaited or twisted grass.

HAMPER, a wicker-work pannier.

HAM-SHOP, a provision shop; an eating-house where cooked victuals are sold.

HAM-SANDWICH, a slice of ham between bread and butter.

HAMSTER, a small rodent animal, the *Cricetus frumentarius*, the fur of which is used for many purposes; the animal is very plentiful in parts of the Continent.

HAN, a caravansary or inn in the Levant.

HAND, the palm; a measure of four inches, used for ascertaining the height of horses; a set of cards; a workman; the form of writing or penmanship; a bundle or head of tobacco-leaves tied together, without the stem being stripped.

HAND-BALL, a small stuffed ball for children's amusement.

HAND-BARROW, a frame or tray with handles at each end, carried between two persons.

HAND-BASKET, a portable basket with handle.

HAND-BELL, a small portable sounding instrument, rung by the hand, often kept on a table for summoning servants or attendants.

HAND-BILL, a chopper or pruning hook; a small printed sheet distributed by hand to persons, or delivered from house to house.

HAND-BOOK, a manual of reference.

HAND-BRACE, a boring tool. [hand.

HAND-BREADTH, the palm; the size of the

Hand-bucket, a small leather bucket or wooden pail that is easily lifted.
Hand-churn, a box for making butter, worked by the hand.
Hand-crank, a crank turned by the hand.
Handcuffs, iron shackles or manacles for the wrist.
Hand-fork, a prong; an agricultural implement.
Handful, a small quantity of any thing; as much as can be grasped in the hand.
Hand galloon and double Maker, a workman who makes those articles by hand.
Hand-gallop, an easy pace of a horse.
Hand-gear, the contrivances for working steam-engine valves.
Handglass, a small glazed frame for sheltering and forwarding out-door plants.
Hand-grenade, a grenade to be thrown by the hand.
Hand-guide, an instrument for insuring to the player a good position of the hands and arms on the pianoforte.
Hand-hammer, a workman's tool; a small light hammer. *See* Hammer.
Hand-hook, a smith's tool.
Handicap, a kind of race.
Handicraftsman, a mechanic or artificer; an artisan or hand-worker.
Handiness, neatness, skill, dexterity.
Hand-kase, a kind of cheese made in Germany from sour milk.
Handkerchief, a silk or linen cloth to wipe the face, or wear about the neck.
Handle, the haft; the part of any thing taken in the hand, by which it is used or lifted, as of a saucepan, a knife, a sword, &c.
Hand-lead, a small lead fastened to a line, used for sounding, in rivers and harbours, or for ascertaining the depth of wells, &c.
Hand-light, a portable lantern; a blue light.
Hand-line, a small fishing-line.
Hand-mallet, a wooden hammer or beater.
Hand-mill, a quern; a small iron mill for grinding grain, pepper, coffee, or other articles, worked by the hand.
Hand-plane, a carpenter's smoothing or facing plane.
Hand-rail, a leaning support in a ship; a stair rail supported by balusters.
Hand-rail Maker, a manufacturer of patent shaped rails for stairs, &c. made by machinery.
Hands, a sea-term for the sailors or available force of a ship; factory-workmen; dock-labourers, &c.
Hand-saw, a small saw. *See* Saw.
Handsaw-file. *See* File.
Hand-screen, an ornamental screen for keeping off the heat of the fire.
Hand-screw, a jack or engine for raising heavy timbers or weights.
Hand-screw Maker, a manufacturer of lifting jacks.
Handsel, an earnest money paid to close a bargain. *See* Earnest.
Handsomely, in nautical language, dexterously, slowly, carefully.
Handspike, a long wooden bar used for turning a windlass, &c.
Hand-staff, a stout walking-stick; the upper or holding part of a flail.
Hand-vice, a small portable vice.
Hand-writing, the cast or form of writing peculiar to a person.
Handy-Billy, a watch-tackle in a ship.
Hangar (French), a shed; a cart-house; coach-house.
Hanger, a seaman's cutlass, a short round curved sword.
Hanger-on, a miner employed at the bottom of the shaft, in fixing the skip or bucket to the chain.
Hangings, tapestry or curtains; room papers.
Hanging-shelf, a suspended shelf in a pantry or room to avoid rats.
Hanging-sleeves, large loose sleeves to a lady's dress.
Hangman, a public executioner.
Hang-net, a net with a large mesh.
Hank, a coil; a skein or head of thread, silk, or cotton, &c.; two or more threads twisted and tied together; a yarn-measure which, for cotton yarn, consists of 7 leas, or 480 yards; for worsted yarn the leas are longer, making the length of the hank 560 yards.
Hanks, rings or hoops of wood, rope or iron round a stay in a ship, to secure a sail to.
Hansard, the name of the books which contain the official printed records of the proceedings in Parliament, and named after the printer.
Hanse, a trading corporation, anciently synonymous with the term guild.
Hansom's Cab, a superior kind of light two-wheeled street carriage. *See* Cab.
Haou, a name in China for the tenth part of a dollar.
Hapse. *See* Hasp.
Haque, a French name for herrings prepared for bait.
Haquetier, a French drayman, the driver of a haquet, a kind of low cart.
Harbaia, a measure of capacity, used in Tripoli, Barbary, and other parts of Northern Africa, = about 20½ lbs.
Harbour, a technical name, in the glass trade, for a chest 6 or 7 feet long, to hold the mixed ingredients, previous to being put in the pot for fusion; a safe port, or haven, for ships to lie at anchor in.
Harbour-dues, the charges made to ships, for using a harbour and moorings, &c.
Harbour-light, a light to guide ships on entering a harbour.
Harbour-master, the officer in charge of a port, who has the superintendence of the shipping.
Hardary. *See* Coss.
Hardbake, a kind of sweetmeat, of baked sugar with blanched almonds.
Hardener, one who brings tools up to the required temper.
Harders, a kind of mullet about eight inches long, caught near the coasts of the Cape colony, which are cured in brine, and sent up the country in small casks, for the use of the farmers.
Hardes (French), clothes, luggage, apparel.
Hard-fish, a name in Scotland for cod, ling, &c. salted and dried.
Hard-roe, a female fish or spawner.

HARDWARE, goods manufactured from metals; articles of ironmongery in particular.

HARDWARE-DEALER. HARDWAREMAN, a vender of hardware.

HARDWOOD-MERCHANT, a dealer in mahogany and turnery woods.

HARDWOODS, in the timber trade, birch, beech, maple, mahogany, ebony, &c.; heavy, close-grained woods, chiefly used by the turner.

HARE, a rodent animal, widely distributed, which is hunted and shot for its flesh and for its skin.

HARE-SKIN, the skin of the hare, vended for its fur, which forms a large article of commerce.

HARICOT, French or kidney beans: a dish consisting of mutton stewed with turnips and carrots.

HARKEM, a Belgian rake or harrow.

HARLE, the reed or brittle stem of flax, separated from the filament.

HARLEQUIN, a clown, or buffoon; the principal performer in a pantomime.

HARMONEON. *See* MELODEON.

HARMONICON, a musical instrument, whence the sound is obtained by striking with a cork on pieces of glass loosely suspended.

HARMONIUM, a modern wind instrument.

HARMONIPHON, a small instrument with a key-board, in which the sounds are produced from small metal tongues, acted upon by blowing through a flexible tube.

HARMONOMETER, an instrument for ascertaining the harmonic relation of sounds.

HARNESS, the gear and trappings for a draught-horse; furniture or equipment for a carriage; for a loom, &c.

HARNESS BOOK-MUSLIN. *See* MUSLIN.

HARNESS-CASK, a cask or high tub with a lid guarded by a rim, which comes a small way down the cask; used on board ship for keeping salted meats ready at hand for daily use.

HARNESS-CURRIER, a dresser of leather for harness saddlery purposes.

HARNESS-MAKER, a saddler; a manufacturer of furniture for carriages, and horse-trappings.

HARNESS-PLATER, a workman who electro-plates the metal work for harness.

HARNESS-POLISHER, a brightener of the harness of carriages.

HARNESS-ROOM, a store-place where harness is kept.

HARNESS-SMITH, a metal worker who forms the iron-work for saddlery.

HARNESS WEAVERS, operatives employed in Paisley in weaving the more complicated patterns of shawls.

HARP, a musical instrument, consisting of a triangular frame, furnished with a set of strings, and pedals: a scarce or sifting implement for cleansing grain.

HARP-LUTE, a musical instrument.

HARP-MAKER, a manufacturer of harps.

HARPOON, a kind of spear with a barbed point, thrown by the hand, used in whale fishing, and for killing porpoises and other fish. It is attached to a line, in order to recover it, and secure the prey to which it becomes fastened.

HARPOONER, the seaman in a whale-boat who uses the harpoon.

HARPOON-MAKER, a manufacturer of whaling [spears.

HARP-SEAL, the *Phoca Groenlandica* and *P. oceanica*, about 6 feet in length. *See* SEALS.

HARPSICHORD, an old kind of musical instrument, provided with quills in place of hammers to sound the strings, now superseded by the pianoforte.

HARP-STRING MAKER, a manufacturer of gut and wire strings for the harp.

HARRA, a weight of Surat about 787½ lbs. avoirdupois.

HARRIER, a small hound for coursing hares.

HARROW, an agricultural implement; a frame with teeth, for scarifying or loosing the surface soil; of which there are two kinds, heavy and light.

HARSELA, a name sometimes given to the oke, a Turkish weight, rather less than 3 lbs.

HARSLET, the pluck of a pig; the heart, liver, and lights.

HART, the stag or male of the deer.

HARTALL, another name for orpiment in the Eastern markets.

HARTE-BEEST, an African antelope.

HARTSHORN, raspings from the horn of the deer, which are used medicinally. When boiled to a jelly it is nutritive, and a pungent volatile spirit was formerly obtained by distillation from the horn, but it is now made from carbonate of ammonia and similar products of bone.

HARTSHORN-SHAVER, a preparer of hartshorn raspings.

HARVEST, the time of reaping grain, or gathering in any crop.

HARVESTER, an American machine for cutting clover and timothy seed, &c.

HARVEST-HOME, the festival of celebrating the completion of the grain harvest.

HASH, a ragout; meat cut up into small pieces and cooked.

HASP, a fastening; a clasp for a staple.

HASSOCK, a footstool or cushion to kneel on; originally a rush-mat cushion, but now of more general signification.

HASSOCK-MAKER, a manufacturer of footstools.

HASTENER, a metal kitchen-stand for keeping in the heat of the fire to the joint while cooking.

HASTER, a Belgian grain measure, containing about 360 French bushels.

HASTY-PUDDING, boiled dough which has been leavened with yeast.

HAT-BAND, a cloth or crape band for the hat, worn by persons in mourning for a relative.

HAT-BAND MAKER, a manufacturer of galloon or binding for the outer edge of the brim, or the outside of the crown of hats; a cutter and maker of cloth or crape bands.

HAT-BLOCK MAKER, a manufacturer of the solid wooden shapes used in blocking or forming hats.

HAT-BOX, HAT-CASE, a paper, leather, or tin box for a man's hat.

HAT-BRUSH, a soft brush for smoothing the nap of a hat.

Hat-case Maker, a manufacturer of thin wood or leather boxes for holding hats.

Hatch, a railway flood-gate or half-door; a crib or cruive in the weir of a river to stop fish; to incubate; to rear chickens from eggs.

Hatch-boat, a kind of half-decked fishing boat; one which has a hatch or well for keeping fish.

Hatchel, a beating instrument for dressing flax. *See* Hackle.

Hatches, the coverings of the hatchway or openings to the hold of a ship.

Hatchet, a chopper or cleaver.

Hatching-apparatus, an artificial incubator for bringing forth chickens from eggs, by steam and hot water.

Hatchment, an escutcheon or panel representing the armorial bearings of a deceased person, which is placed on the front of the house for a twelvemonth after the funeral.

Hatchway, an opening in the deck to afford a passage up or down.

Hat-dyer, a workman who dyes beaver hats black.

Hatreau (French), a dish of sliced liver sprinkled with pepper and parsley.

Hat-frame, cross-bars of wood placed round three or four dozen hats in sending them out for home sale.

Hat-lining and-leather Cutter, a shaper of silk, calico, leather, and other inside trimmings for hats.

Hat-manufacturer, one who has a factory or place where hats are made on a large scale.

Hats, covers for the head, chiefly worn by men, made of silk or felt, and sometimes beaver or other material.

Hat-shag Maker, a maker of imperial or silk plush for covering the bodies of hats.

Hat-spring Maker, a manufacturer of springs for light opera or closing-up hats.

Hatter, a maker or vender of hats.

Hatter's-bow-string Maker, a manufacturer of the fitted gut cord used in bowing or felting the materials for beaver hats.

Hatter's-furrier, a tradesman who prepares and keeps on sale the wool and different furs used for felting into hat bodies.

Hat-tip Maker, a manufacturer of silk pieces for the lining of the crowns of hats.

Hattock, a shock of corn containing 12 sheaves.

Hat-varnish Maker, a manufacturer of shellac varnishes, and other chemical preparations, for hatters.

Haugh, a little meadow.

Haul, to drag or pull; a catch, as of fish, &c.; a ropemaker's term for about 400 threads of yarn warped off the winches with a slight turn in it, to be tarred.

Hauler, a workman engaged in drawing ore out of a mine; a fisherman who pulls in a cast-net to the shore.

Haunch, the hip or thigh; the hinder quarter of a small animal; sometimes applied to a joint of mutton or venison dressed.

Haunkus. *See* Ankoose.

Hauser. *See* Hawser.

Hausil (Hindustani), a tax or duty on goods.

Haut, a name for the cubit in some parts of the East Indies, about 19 inches; a weekly market held on stated days.

Haut-a-bas, a French pedlar; a travelling foot trader.

Hautboy, a wild strawberry; a musical wind instrument. *See* Oboe.

Haute-lice (French), tapestry hangings; an upright loom.

Haute-mare'e (French), high-water.

Havana, Havannah, a Cuban cigar.

Havelee, an enclosure or dwelling in India, sometimes called Bakhur or Bukree.

Haven, a port for shelter. *See* Harbour.

Haversack, a soldier's knapsack; a gunner's case for ordnance.

Havildar, a native sergeant of sepoys in India.

Haw, the berry of the hawthorn, used on the Continent in cookery.

Hawk, a small quadrangular tool used by a plasterer.

Hawk-boy, a plasterer's assistant.

Hawker, a pedlar or petty chapman; a travelling vender of small wares, usually holding a licence.

Hawk's-bill Turtle, the *Chelone imbricata*, valued for its shell which is employed for manufacturing purposes.

Hawse-block, the wooden plug or stopper fitted into the hawse-hole when the ship is at sea.

Hawse-hole, the hole in the bows of a ship through which the cable runs.

Hawser, a large rope used for warping and other purposes.

Hay, dried grass, kept as fodder; a hedge or enclosure; to lay snares for rabbits.

Hay and straw Dealer, a vender of forage and fodder for horses, &c.

Hay-band, rope made of twisted hay.

Hay-bote, a fine for breaking fences; an old allowance of wood to a tenant for repairing hedges or fences.

Hay-cock, a pile or heap of hay in a field.

Hayessine, the borate of lime, so called from its discoverer Mr. Hayes. It is found abundantly on the Western coast of America, and is of great value in the manufacture of glass.

Hay-fork, a pronged instrument for turning over hay, or lifting it from the cart to the rick.

Hay-knife, a long sharp cutting instrument for taking hay from a hay-rick.

Hayloft, a loft for hay over a stable or barn.

Hay-maker, an agricultural labourer; one who cuts grass and turns it over from time to time in the sun to be dried for hay.

Hay-making Machine, a grass-cutting apparatus taking the place of the scythe.

Hay-market, a place in a town whither hay is brought for sale; one of the principal places in London for the sale of hay is Whitechapel.

Hay-rake, an agricultural implement; a cross piece with teeth, and a long handle, for collecting grass in hay-making.

Hay-rick, a pile or stack of hay.

Hayward, a warden or overlooker of fences and foot-paths.

Hazel, a small underwood; the *Corylus avellana*, producing the common hazel nuts; being very elastic it is used for the hoops of casks and in turnery.

Hea, the local name for an undefined tree in the Pacific islands, the fruit of which furnishes a glutinous red varnish, with which fibres are stained.

Head, the chief or principal; the state of a deer's horns by which his age is known; the blade of an axe; the striking-part of a hammer; the upper part of a bed or bedstead; the top of a nail; a bundle of flax measuring probably two feet in length, and weighing a few pounds; in the North of Europe 18 head of hemp or flax are about 1 cwt.; the work at the prow or foremost part of a ship.

Head-band, a bookbinder's material of narrow silk or other substance, sold in pieces of a certain number of yards.

Head-board, the cross-board of a bedstead near the head.

Head-borough, a constable; the chief officer of a township.

Head-dress, a cap, feathers, or any ornament worn on the head by females.

Header, a cooper who closes casks; a workman who heads nails or pins; a brick with a short face in front.

Headers, a building term for bricks or stones placed lengthways across the wall instead of in the direction of the wall.

Head-fast, a rope to secure a ship's bows to the wharf or shore.

Head-gardener, the chief or principal gardener.

Heading, pieces of wood suited for closing sugar hogsheads, and other casks of merchandise.

Head-lines, in printing, lines conspicuously displayed at the top of a page, or to a chapter, which are set in small capitals; in navigation, ropes next the yards.

Head-man, a principal workman; in the West Indies the chief of a gang of negro labourers.

Head-master, the principal teacher in a [school.

Head-quarters, the depot of a regiment.

Head-rope, that part of the bolt-rope fastened to a sail.

Head-sails, the various sails of a ship which are set on or before the foremast.

Head-man, a putter or labourer in a colliery, who conveys the coals from the workings to the horseway.

Head-stall, the part of a horse's bridle, which goes over the head.

Head-stone, an upright tombstone erected at the place where the head of the corpse lies, and usually bearing an inscription.

Head-sword, a miner's term in Cornwall for water running through the adit.

Head-teacher, the chief assistant in a school.

Head-waiter, the superintendant or principal table servant at an inn.

Headway, the progress made by a ship or boat in the water; a passage in a mine driven in the direction of the layer of coal.

Head-workman, the principal operative in an establishment.

Heal, to tile or cover as with a roof.

Healds, the harness for guiding the warp-threads in a weaver's loom.

Heap, a pile, as of stones, dung, &c.

Heap-keeper, a miner who overlooks the cleaning of coal on the surface.

Hearse, a funeral carriage for conveying a corpse to be buried.

Hearse-cloth, a coffin pall.

Hearth, a floor for a fire.

Hearth-broom, **Hearth-brush**, a sweeping brush for the hearth or grate.

Hearth-rug, an ornamental rug of carpet-work laid before a fire-hearth.

Hearth-rug Maker, a carpet-weaver, one who manufactures ornamental rugs for rooms.

Hearth-stone, soft stone for whitening door steps or paving stones in a yard, &c.

Hearth-stone Maker, a stone worker; a manufacturer of the flat stones laid down before fire-grates or stoves in the rooms of dwelling-houses.

Heart-wood, the central part of the trunk of a tree; timber within the sap-wood.

Heater, a triangular mass of iron, which is heated in the fire, and put into a box-iron to smooth clothes.

Heave, to throw; to employ force in lifting or moving resisting substances or weighty goods.

Heavers, a class of men employed about docks, taking goods from barges and flats; short wooden bars tapering at each end, used as a purchase or prising lever.

Heavy, weighty; ponderous.

Heavy-laden, vessels sitting deep in the water, which have a full cargo; vehicles carrying a large burthen.

Heavy-metal, guns of large size, carrying balls of heavy weight.

Heck, a door latch; a fishing-net; an apparatus for warping; a cattle-rack.

Heckle, a flax-dresser's comb, consisting of several rows of long metal spikes or teeth, fixed into round or oblong blocks of wood, for cleaning and subdividing the fibre of flax; also, a flax-dressing machine of a similar nature, consisting of combs of iron teeth arranged on cylinders, which separates, straightens, cleanses, and in some cases splits the fibres.

Heckling, **Hackling**, a rough process of combing flax with a heckle.

Hectare, the principal French land measure or new arpent, consisting of a square of 100 metres on every side, equal to 2·471 English acres, or 2 acres, 1 rood, 35 square poles, 11½ square yards: 17 hectares are nearly 42 imperial acres.

Hecto, a Greek prefix to French weights and measures, signifying a hundred times greater.

Hectogramme, the new name for the ounce of the French decimal pound; a weight for jewels and precious metals, equal to one hundred grammes, or rather more than 3½ avoirdupois ounces (3.5277).

Hectolitre, a French measure of capacity, the new setier, containing one hundred litres, equal to 2·75 bushels: 2 9-10th hectolitres are about one English quarter. The hectolitre of wheat is equal to 11½ pecks imperial measure.

HECTOMETRE, a French measure of length of 100 mètres, containing 109 yards and 13 1-10th inches, or 19·884 poles.
HECTOSTERE, 100 stères, or French cubical mètres, = 3531·741 cubic feet.
HEDDLE, a part of the weaver's loom. *See* HEALDS.
HEDDLE-MAKER, a manufacturer of flax combs, and of weavers' utensils.
HEDGE, a fence of bushes or living plants; a bank or mound.
HEDGEHOG, a dredging-machine, employed in harbour works and rivers, for removing shoals, formed by accumulated mud or silt; an animal, the *Erinaceus Europæus*, sometimes kept in bake-houses and kitchens to eat up cockroaches.
HEDGER, a workman who has the charge of repairing hedges and ditches.
HEDGE-SCISSORS, shears for trimming quick-set hedges.
HEDGING-GLOVES, strong leather gloves.
HEEL, the after-part of the keel; a nautical term for the lower end of any thing, as of a rafter, a tool, a mast, boom, stern-post, &c.; the hinder part of the sole of a boot or shoe.
HEEL-BALL MAKER, a maker of a hard wax or polishing substance, used by shoemakers, to give a shining black surface to the leather of new boots or shoes.
HEELING, in navigation, a vessel leaning over; putting new heel-pieces to boots.
HEEL-TIP, an iron plate or protection for the heels of boots and shoes.
HEEN, the Chinese name for a district.
HEER, a yarn measure; a heer of 24 cuts, or 240 threads, is 600 yards.
HEERABOLE, an Indian name for myrrh.
HEERACUSSEE, a name for copperas or sulphate of iron in India.
HEERADACUN, a name in the Bombay tariff for dragon's blood.
H.E.I.C., the abbreviation for the "Hon. East India Company."
HEIFER, a young cow.
HELAHA, a tree in the Pacific islands, the seed of which is used to make necklaces.
HELBEH, an agricultural seed with a somewhat bitter taste whose flour is mixed with dourah or dhurra by the labourers of Egypt.
HELIOMETER, a kind of telescope, with two object glasses, for measuring the diameter of the sun, moon, and planets.
HELIOSCOPE, a telescope for viewing the sun through coloured glass without injury to the eyes.
HELIOSTAT, a philosophical instrument for reflecting an image of the sun into the telescope of a theodolite at a distant station: a train of clock-work so rotates a mirror that on being once adjusted it follows the sun's motion, requiring only winding and occasional adjustment to give a constant vivid station-signal when the sun shines.
HELIOTROPE, green quartz with blood-red spots and veins; a flower. *See* BLOODSTONE.
HELLER, a former money of account at Aix-la-Chapelle, the fourth part of a busche, 6 busches making one mark, and 54 marks the rixdollar: a German weight about 7 grains imperial; the half of a Danish denier, and of the Austrian pening; also, the eighth part of a kreutzer of Vienna.
HELLIER, a slater or tiler.
HELM, the tiller of a ship, but also applied to the collective apparatus or machinery by which a vessel is steered, comprising the rudder, wheel, tiller-ropes, &c.
HELMET, a horse-soldier's headpiece, a protection for the head; the upper part of a retort.
HELMET-MAKER, a maker of defensive coverings for the head, worn by soldiers, firemen, &c.
HELMET-SHELL, a common name for several species of *Cassides* which are used for cutting cameos from; the principal being *Cassis cornuta*, *C. rufa*, and *C. tuberosa*.
HELMSMAN, the man at the wheel who steers a ship.
HELP, aid; assistance; an American name for a hired servant; in Russia the name for an aid or assistant at a furnace.
HELPMATE, an assistant.
HELVE, the long handle of a tool.
HELVE-HAMMER, a large, ponderous blacksmith's hammer for manufacturing wrought iron.
HEM, the border of a garment doubled and sewed over, to strengthen it and prevent the ravelling of the threads.
HEMATIN, the colouring principle of logwood.
HEMATITE, a rich ore of iron of which there are several varieties, the red, black, purple, brown, &c.
HEMATOSIN, the red colouring matter of blood; in its dried state it is sold for making Prussian blue.
HEMI, a Greek word used as a prefix, signifying half.
HEMLOCK SPRUCE, the *Abies Canadensis*, the wood of which is not held in much estimation. It has, however, been used for railway sleepers in England, and is much used for laths. The bark is largely used for tanning in the United States, although inferior to oak bark.
HEMMEL, a shed or hovel for cattle.
HEMMING, HIMMING, a shoe or sandal made of raw hide.
HEMP, a fibre obtained from the *Cannabis sativa*, which is stronger and coarser than flax. It is used for making cordage, canvas for sail-cloth, towelling, &c. The foreign imports are very large. In 1870, we received, chiefly from Russia, 777,936 cwts. of dressed and undressed hemp, besides 15,233 cwts. of tow or codilla. In previous years we had received much more than this, but jute and several other foreign fibrous substances now come in in immense quantities.
HEMPEN, made of hemp.
HEMP-SEED, the seed of the hemp plant, sold for feeding cage birds. A useful oil is obtained from it by expression, which is employed for paints, for lamps, and for making soft soap.
HEM-STITCH, a particular mode of sewing by drawing the threads of the fabric and separating them.

Hen, a female fowl.

Hencoop, a latticed or barred cage for poultry on ship-board.

Hen-house, **Hen-roost**, an enclosed poultry house on a farm, or private residence.

Henna, an Indian colouring substance obtained from the shoots of the *Lawsonia inermis*. The Mahometan women use it for dyeing the nails red; the manes and tails of the horses in Arabia and Barbary, are also stained red in the same manner. The distilled water of the flowers is used as a perfume.

Hen-roost, a perch on which poultry roost at night.

Herald-chaser, an engraver of heraldic emblems, &c.

Heraldic Engraver, a die sinker; a seal engraver.

Herald-painter, an artist who emblazons arms and crests on carriage-panels, hatchments, &c.

Herald's College, the authorized office in Benet's Hill, Doctors Commons, where genealogies, pedigrees, and coats of arms of families are ascertained and registered.

Herbage, pasturage for cattle.

Herbal, **Herbarium**, a book or case in which dried specimens of plants are preserved.

Herbalist, one skilled in the properties of herbs; a collector and dealer in medicinal plants.

Herb-shop, the place where medicinal herbs are sold.

Herbon, **Boutoir**, a French currier's knife.

Herd, to tend cattle, or take care of a flock; the person who looks after live stock; a troop or body of cattle.

Herds, **Hards**, the refuse of flax.

Herdsman, a cattle keeper.

Heriot, an old obnoxious custom which still prevails in several English counties, by which the lord of the manor is entitled to the best beast or chattel belonging to a deceased copy-hold tenant at the time of his death.

Herling, a fish. *See* Hirling.

Hermilique, a Turkish coin and money of account, ranging in value from 14 to 18 piastres, according to the rate of exchange.

Hermitage, a French wine.

Hernant-seeds, a commercial name for the seeds of the *Hernandia ovigera*, imported into Liverpool from India for tanning [illegible].

[illegible]ane, a Ceylon coco-nut rasp or scraper.

Herring-barrel, a cask for fish; those for white herrings are made of staves of Norway birch and ash; those for red or smoked herrings of fir. *See* Fish Measures.

Herring-boat, a fishing-boat employed in netting herrings.

Herring-bone, a kind of cross-stitch in seams, mostly used in woollen work.

Herring-curer, a gutter and salter of herrings.

Herrings, a common fish, the *Clupea harengus*, in the capture and sale of which a large trade is carried on, on both shores of the Atlantic. In North America the fall herrings are fat, and fully equal in every respect to the best Scotch herrings; but the spring herrings, being taken in the very act of spawning, are thin and poor, and of little value whether fresh or salted.

Herse, the French name for a harrow; a lattice; a church candlestick.

Herst-pan, a frying-pan.

Hessian-boots, a kind of long boots.

Hew, to cut by blows with an edged instrument; to shape with an axe.

Hewer, a worker in wood; a stonemason; one who cuts or shapes the rough material.

Hexachord, a musical instrument with six strings.

Hhd., the commercial abbreviation for hogshead.

Hiccatee, a fresh-water tortoise of Central America, esteemed for its liver and feet, which are gelatinous when dressed.

Hickory, the wood of *Carya alba* and *C. glabra*, North American trees, which possesses probably the greatest strength and tenacity of any other of the indigenous trees. It is used for making handspikes, and for a variety of purposes, but unfortunately it is liable to be eaten by worms, and lacks durability. The small white nuts are sometimes imported as a table fruit.

Hide, an old English land-measure of about 100 acres; but Dugdale computes it at 96 acres only; the skin of any large or full-grown animal, as the ox, the horse, the buffalo, &c. Hides are imported or brought to market dry, green, dressed, or undressed. *See* Peltries.

Hide-rope, rope made of strands of cow-hide plaited, which is very durable, and used for wheel-ropes, traces, jigger and purchase-ropes.

Higgler, a chaffer; a travelling dealer in provisions or small wares.

High-bailiff, the chief officer of a town.

High-pressure Engine, a steam-engine in which the steam is not condensed but admitted into the cylinder at a very high temperature, and therefore an exceedingly strong boiler is required.

High-road, a public way for vehicles, &c.

High-seasoned, flavoured with spices or other seasoning.

High-water, the highest state of the tide; the turning-point just before the ebb commences.

High-water Mark, the mark made on the shore when the tide is at its highest.

Highway, a public thoroughfare or road for traffic.

Highway-rate, a road-rate for the maintenance of the public roads in good order.

Hilsah, an esteemed native fish of the Ganges. It is very oily and bony; when marinaded, baked with vinegar, or preserved in tamarinds, it is very fine.

Hilt, the upper part or handle of a sword or other weapon or tool.

Himt, **Himten**, a German corn measure, varying in different localities. It ranges from 5¼ up to nearly 10 gallons. In Hanover 96 himtens are equal to 62 imperial bushels.

Hin, a Hebrew measure of capacity equal to one gallon and 3¼ pints imperial, nearly.

HINA, the name for a gourd or melon in the Pacific islands.
HIND, the female of the red deer, of which the male is the stag; a farm-servant; a peasant.
HING, the Indian name for asafœtida; hingda being the coarsest kind of the drug.
HINGES, moveable metal ligaments, or connected plates, for the joints of doors, gates, &c. to turn on.
HINK, a reaping-hook.
HINTAM, another name for the ochava, the eighth part of the Spanish ounce.
HIP-KNOBS, ornaments at the gable end of houses.
HIPPOCRAS, an aromatic cordial or spiced wine, formerly in high repute in England.
HIPPODROME, a circus for feats of horsemanship.
HIPPOPOTAMUS-HIDES, the tanned skin of this pachyderm is used by mechanical engineers, and also formed into shields and other articles.
HIRE, wages or compensation for services.
HIRING, an engagement: in many country districts there are periodical markets for hiring farm and domestic servants for half-yearly engagements.
HIRLING, a small sea-trout like a salmon, with reddish flesh.
HIRSELL, a flock of sheep; the act of classing or sorting into breeds or flocks.
HISSA, an Indian term for a share or division.
HISTA, an arbitrary Malayan measure of length, the fourth of the dippa; about half a yard. *See* DIPPA.
HISTRIONIC, a dramatic performer.
HITCH, a knot or noose in a rope for fastening it to any thing, of which there are many kinds: as a half-hitch, clove-hitch, Blackwall-hitch, magnus-hitch, timber-hitch, &c.
HITHE, an old Saxon word for a port or small harbour, where goods were landed and shipped.
HIVE, a box or rush basket for a swarm of bees to lodge and work in.
H.M.C., H.M.S., abbreviations for "her Majesty's customs—her Majesty's ship—her Majesty's service."
HO, a Chinese measure of capacity, about 7¾ gallons.
HOARDING, a boarded enclosure or fence, fixed about any building which is being erected or repaired; the act of accumulating or saving.
HOASTMAN, a coal-fitter, one who vends coals at a seaport.
HOB, the flat iron projection at the side of a firegrate; the nave of a wheel; a boor.
HOB-NAIL, a clout-nail; a short nail with a large head, used for nailing strong country boots.
HOCK, a light Rhenish wine, which is either sparkling or still.
HOD, a bricklayer's or plasterer's box or tray, fixed at the end of a staff, in which to carry bricks and mortar on the shoulder.
HODGE-PODGE, an Irish stew; a mixture of vegetables and meat.
HODMAN, the bearer of a hod; one who carries mortar or bricks in a hod to other workmen on a building.
HOE, an agricultural implement of iron, for farm or garden use, employed to turn up weeds, and loosen the soil round plants.
HOE, HOIOS (Scotch), stockings; hose.
HOG, a flat rough broom, used by seamen for scrubbing the bottom of a vessel; a castrated boar.
HOGG, young sheep that has not been shorn: hence the terms ewe-hogg, wedder-hogg, and tup-hogg.
HOGGED, a term applied to a ship, which, through some defect or strain, droops at each end.
HOGGER-PUMP, the top pump in the sinking pit of a mine.
HOGGERS, stockings without feet, worn by coal-miners when at work.
HOGGETT, abbreviated into hog, or tup-hog; a weaned male sheep; if castrated, he is called a wether-hog.
HOG-PEN, a pig-stye or enclosure for swine.
HOG-REEVE, a parish officer in some of the colonies, who adjudicates upon the trespasses of swine.
HOG-RINGER, one who puts rings in the snouts of hogs, to prevent their rooting up the ground.
HOGSHEAD, a British measure of capacity: prior to the introduction of the imperial system, the ale hogshead contained 1½ barrel, or about 54 liquid gallons, = 54·12 imperial gallons; the wine hogshead 63 gallons, = 52·48599 imperial gallons. The hogshead is at present a large cask used for transporting various articles; for sugar ranging from 14 to 18 cwt. in weight; for tobacco, *see* CROP-HOGSHEAD.
HOGS'-LARD, the purified fat of pigs. *See* LARD.
HOG-SKIN SADDLE, a superior kind of saddle made from tanned hogskin.
HOG-STY, a house or pen for pigs.
HOG-WASH, the refuse of a kitchen or brewery; a collection of vegetables and fluids for feeding pigs.
HOHONI, a name for large coco-nut shells, used in the Pacific islands to hold water.
HOIST, to lift up.
HOJA-DE-LATA (Spanish), tinned iron—hoja-de-laton being sheet brass.
HOLD, the whole interior of a vessel, below the decks; the space where the cargo is stowed.
HOLDFASTS, flat-headed nails; stout, bent pieces of iron; catches or clamps for driving into walls, &c. as supports for attached pieces.
HOLDING, a quantity of land held from the Crown in the colonies.
HOLD-WATER, staying the progress of a boat, by keeping the oars submerged.
HOLIDAY. *See* PUBLIC HOLIDAY.
HOLING, undermining coal beds; dibbling in plants; digging trenches to plant pieces of sugar cane.
HOLLA, an Algerine measure of capacity, equal to about 17 pints.
HOLLAND, a kind of linen which, when brown or unbleached, is used chiefly for window-blinds and children's garments; bleached is used for finer purposes.

HOLLANDS, a superior kind of gin. See GENEVA.
HOLLOW-GIRDER, an iron girder not solid.
HOLLOW-WARE, a general trade-name given to various articles, such as cast-iron kitchen utensils, earthenware, &c.
HOLLY, a tree; the *Ilex Aquifolium*, the leaves of which are astringent and tonic, the root and bark having also medicinal uses. The bark yields bird-lime. The boughs with the red berries are sold at Christmas time in towns, to decorate rooms. A species of holly furnishes the Paraguay tea.
HOLLYHOCK, a tall-stemmed plant (*Althea rosea*), with a gaudy flower, cultivated in gardens; the flowers are mucilaginous and demulcent, and the leaves dye blue.
HOLM (Saxon), a river islet; the level low ground on the banks of a river.
HOLOMETER, a mathematical instrument for taking measures both on the earth and in the heavens.
HOLSTER, a leather case for pistols fixed at the saddle of a horseman.
HOLSTER-PISTOLS, pistols carried in the holster.
HOLYSTONE, a large stone used with sand, for scouring a ship's decks by hand.
HOMARDS (French), lobsters.
HOME-BREWED, beer made at a private house; not purchased from a brewery.
HOME-FARM, that part of a farm on which the mansion-house and principal buildings are erected.
HOMER, an old measure of about 3 pints.
HOME-SECRETARY, a State officer who has the management of affairs connected with the civil jurisdiction of the kingdom, separate from the Colonial or Foreign departments.
HOME-SPUN, made at one's own dwelling.
HOMESTEAD, the mansion-house on a farm, and a few acres of land adjoining.
HOME-TRADE SHIPS: in the official returns these comprise ships trading on the coasts of the United Kingdom, or to the Continental ports between the limits of the River Elbe and Brest.
HOMEWARD-BOUND, on the way home.
HOMINY, Indian-corn meal, one of the breadstuffs of the United States; also a dough cake made from it.
HOMMÉE, a French land-measure; as much ground as a man can turn up with the spade in a day.
HOMŒOPATHIST, an irregular practitioner; one who professes to cure diseases by very minute doses of medicine, and upon the great principle of *homœopathy*, viz.:—"*Similia similibus curantur*," to which *allopathy* is antagonistic.
HONAY, a name in Canara for the *Calophyllum inophyllum*.
HONES, HONE SLATES: a name given to different kinds of talcy slate-stone, native or foreign, cut into smooth slabs for whetstones, &c. for setting razors, penknives, and tools.
HONEY, the thick sweet substance obtained from flowers, and deposited in the wax comb by bees: several thousand tons are annually imported, besides what is obtained at home.
HONEY-BEE, the *Apis mellifica*.
HONEY-COMB, the waxen cells made by bees in their hive, for depositing their honey, forming when purified the bees' wax of commerce; a flaw in a metal casting. See BEES' WAX.
HONEY-DEW, a kind of tobacco which has been moistened with molasses.
HONEY-SUGAR, the saccharine extracted from flowers by bees, and converted into wax.
HONGNETTE, a French marble-carver's chisel.
HONGS, the name for certain licensed merchants, who had, until of late years, the monopoly of foreign trade at the chief Chinese ports.
HONITON LACE, a pillow, or cushion, lace made in Devonshire, remarkable for the beauty of its figures and sprigs, which are sewed on to net by the needle.
HONORARY SECRETARY, one who voluntarily undertakes secretarial duties, without being paid.
HOOBOBALLI, a close fine-grained wood of Guiana: it is easily worked, takes a high polish, and is much used in the Colony for furniture. It may be had from 16 to 20 inches square, 40 to 70 feet long.
HOOD, a young seal; the covering for a carriage head; a companion-hatch, sky-light, &c.; a slight covering for the head, worn by females.
HOODING, a piece of rough leather, connecting the hand-staff and couple of a flail.
HOOF, the horny protection that covers the feet of many domestic and wild animals, as the horse, ox, deer, &c.
HOOHOO, a piece of checked cotton, used in the African trade.
HOOK, the fastening for a garment; a sickle; a bent nail; a curved piece of metal of various sizes: thus there are meat-hooks, fish-hooks, small brass hooks, boat-hooks, breast-hooks, can-hooks, cat-hooks, &c. See FISH-HOOKS.
HOOKAH, an Indian pipe, of several parts; the bowl is of silver, shell, earthenware, &c.; the stem or tube, of coco-nut, or some other wood, which a snake or pliable ornamental tubing lengthens out into several coils, and the smoke passes through a glass water-vase, while the mouth-piece is of amber, silver, &c.
HOOK-AND-EYE MAKER, a manufacturer of the metal catches for fastening into each other, which are bent and cut in a press.
HOOKER, HOWKAH, a small Netherlands ship. See HOWKAH.
HOOK-LADDER, a small ladder with hooks at the top.
HOOK-PIN, a carpenter's tool, so named.
HOONDEE, an Indian draft or bill of exchange, drawn by or upon a native banker or shroff.
HOOP, a circular band of wood or iron, for binding the staves of casks together; a frame of whalebone to spread out petticoats.
HOOP-BENDER, an iron worker.
HOOP-IRON, narrow thin strips of iron, for hooping casks with; a child's toy for trundling a hoop.
HOOP-MAKER, a cooper; a manufacturer of hoops.

HOOP-TONGS, implements used in forging.

HOP, a climbing plant, the *Humulus lupulus*, cultivated for its bitter principle, which forms an important element in brewing; the fine hops being used for pale ales, the common, or less fine, for porter. There were, in 1855, nearly 38,000 acres of hop gardens under cultivation in England, which produced about 83,250,000 lbs. of hops. Hop-vines, abounding in fibre, have often been proposed to be turned to useful account for cordage or paper, but as yet to little extent.

HOP-BACK, a brewer's vessel.

HOP-BAG, a coarse heavy wrapper for hops: the bag of hops weighs about 2½ cwt. The finest description of hops are put into fine light pockets, weighing about 1½ cwt. each.

HOP-DUTY, a tax of about twopence per pound, levied on hops by the government. This duty netted, in 1855, £698,750.

HOP-FACTOR, a dealer in hops; a salesman: the Borough is the chief location of the hop trade in London.

HOP-GARDEN, a field where hops are grown.

HOP-HORNBEAM, a name for the American iron-wood (*Ostrya Virginica*).

HOP-OAST, a kind of kiln for drying hops.

HOPPER, in the glass trade, a conical vessel suspended from the ceiling, containing sand and water for the use of the cutter; a kind of cake made of rice flour in Ceylon; the trough in a flour-mill, into which the corn is put to be ground; a seed-basket for carrying grain, used by the sower; a popular name for an insect breeding in hams.

HOPPLE, a mode of fettering the fore-legs of animals to prevent them from straying.

HOP-POCKET. *See* HOP-BAG.

HOP-POLE, a support for the hop vine.

HOP-SETTER, an instrument for planting hop sets; the labourer so employed.

HOP-VINE, the climbing stem of the hop.

HORDEINE, the starchy matter of barley.

HOREHOUND, a wild plant, the *Marrubium vulgare*, which is used medicinally for coughs, and in uterine and hepatic affections.

HORLOGER (French), a maker or vender of clocks and watches.

HORN, the hard pointed bodies growing on the heads of some animals. The horns of the ox, buffalo, &c. are hollow, and never shed. They are deposited in layers or bony cores, their constituents being albumen with a little gelatin, and a small proportion of lime. They are not brittle like bone, and may be moulded when softened by heat. The antlers of the deer are solid processes from the frontal bone, and possess the chemical and physical properties of true bone, they grow rapidly and are periodically shed. Also a wind-instrument originally made of horn, but now for the most part of brass.

HORNBEAM, the wood of the *Carpinus Americana*, which is used for the cogs of mill wheels, and for agricultural implements; the inner bark dyes yellow.

HORN-BOW, a bow made of horn, used in the East.

HORN-COMB MAKER, a manufacturer of pocket, dressing, and mane combs of horn.

HORN-CUTTER AND -PRESSER, a worker in horn; an artificer who moulds and shapes horn into various articles.

HORNEL, a fisherman's name, in Scotland, for the sand launce, *Ammodytes Tobianus*.

HORNER, a worker in horn; in olden times an outlaw, one who had been denounced by the formality of blowing a horn.

HORNERS' COMPANY, one of the minor livery companies of London, incorporated in 1638; it has no hall.

HORN-FISH, a name for the gar-fish.

HORN-LANTERN, a lantern having plates or sheets of thin pressed horn in the frame, instead of glass.

HORN-MAKER, a workman who moulds horns into drinking-cups.

HORN-MERCHANT, a dealer in horns.

HORNO (Spanish), a furnace.

HORN-PIKE, a common fish in the Black Sea, the *Esox Belone*, caught every where.

HORNPIPE, an animated dance.

HORN-PLATE, a transparent sheet of horn for lanterns, &c.

HORN-PRESSER, one who softens and prepares horn for working, by heat, &c.

HORNS, a miner's name for the guides for the ropes on the drum.

HORN-SILVER, a native chloride of silver which is often found in the mines of Mexico and Peru.

HORN-STONE, a kind of quartz resembling horn, used for forming the grinding blocks of flint mills, in the pottery manufacture. *See* CHERT-STONE.

HORN-TIPS, the solid pointed tops of horns, which are used for umbrella-tops, knife-handles, and many other purposes.

HOROGRAPHY, the art of constructing dials.

HOROLOGER, a watchmaker.

HOROMETER, an instrument for measuring the hours.

HOROMETRY, the art of measuring time by hours and subordinate divisions.

HORSE, a wooden frame for towels or clothes; a stool or tressel used by many workmen; the carrying part of a machine, as in tile-making; a foot-rope from the middle of a ship's yard; a well-known animal, valued for its docility and usefulness to man.

HORSE-BARGE, one towed by horses on a canal or narrow river.

HORSE-BAZAAR, a place for the sale of horses.

HORSE-BEAN, a species of *Faba* extensively grown in fields for feeding horses. There are several varieties, as the Scotch horse-bean, the tick, or field-bean of different kinds, &c. Our imports of foreign-grown beans average 360,000 quarters a year.

HORSE-BLANKET, a coarse woollen rug with which to clothe horses.

HORSE-BLOCK, a foot-stone or step in country towns for mounting a horse.

HORSE-BOAT, a ferry-boat for transporting horses across rivers or harbours, &c.

HORSE-BOX, a closed carriage or vehicle for transporting horses by railway; an enclosure for a horse to be slung into a vessel.

HORSE-BREAKER, one who tames and trains young horses for the saddle or draught.

HORSE-CHESTNUT, a tree, the *Æsculus hippocastanum*; the white wood is used for the backs of brushes, and for making the ornamental articles of Tunbridge-ware. The bark is used on the Continent as a febrifuge, and of the nuts or seeds starch and vermicelli have been made.

HORSE-CIRCUS. *See* CIRCUS.

HORSE-CLOTH, a blanket or wrapper for a horse.

HORSE-COLLAR MAKER, a maker of stuffed collars and hames for draught-horses.

HORSE-COMB, a strong comb used by grooms for combing the mane and tail of horses.

HORSE-DEALER, a trader in horses.

HORSE-DOCTOR, a farrier; a veterinary surgeon.

HORSE-DRENCH, a drastic purge for a horse; the horn by which the medicine is administered.

HORSE-DUNG, the droppings from horses, in stables, &c. collected for manure.

HORSE-FAIR, a market for the sale of horses.

HORSE-FETTLER, a workman in mines who provides for, and attends to, the horses kept underground.

HORSE FLESH, a name for a species of Bahamas mahogany; the carcase of horses sold to the knackers.

HORSE-GRAM, a name in India for a variety of pulse, the produce of *Dolichos uniflorus*, also called Coollie and Gahut in some parts.

HORSE-GUARDS, mounted soldiers; a fine British cavalry regiment.

HORSE-HAIR, the long hair of the mane and tail of the horse, which is valuable for many trade purposes.

HORSE-HIDE, the skin of the horse, which, when tanned, makes the strong cordovan leather, and is also used for covering large board-room or office tables.

HORSE-HOE, an agricultural implement drawn by a horse, used to weed turnips, or to extirpate weeds, and loosen the soil in other crops.

HORSE-JOCKEY, one who rides a race-horse.

HORSE-KEEPER, a groom or stableman; one who looks after horses.

HORSE-KNACKER, a purchaser of diseased or worn-out horses, who kills them for their commercial products.

HORSE-LOAD, the weight which a horse can draw.

HORSEMAN, an equestrian.

HORSE-MILL, a mill worked by a horse.

HORSE-POWER, the strength of a horse in draught; the dynamical unit employed to express the force of the working action of a steam-engine. Estimating that a horse will walk with a load of 200 lbs. at the rate of 2½ miles an hour, this gives 44,000 feet per minute as the average value of a horse's power; 1 lb. could therefore be raised that height in a minute.

HORSE-RACE, a running match between horses to test their speed and endurance.

HORSE-RADISH, the pungent root of the *Cochlearia Armoracia*, used as a condiment, on account of its pungent, acrid, and stimulant qualities.

HORSE-RADISH TREE, a common name for the *Moringa pterygosperma*, the seeds of which furnish the fluid watchmaker's oil, known as oil of ben; the bark yields a gum like tragacanth, and the acrid leaves are used in curries and also as sinapisms.

HORSE-REPOSITORY, a place where horses are kept on sale and view, or put up at auction periodically.

HORSERUG. *See* HORSE-BLANKET.

HORSE-RUN, a contrivance in deep earthworks for drawing up and lowering a man with a wheelbarrow.

HORSE-SHOER, a blacksmith who puts shoes on horses' feet.

HORSE-SHOES, semicircular plates of iron nailed to the hoofs of horses, to protect the frog or sole of the foot.

HORSE-STABLE, a shelter and house for horses.

HORSE-TAIL, the long hair of the tail of the horse is of considerable commercial value, being applicable to many uses. *See* HORSE-HAIR. A plant used for polishing. *See* DUTCH-RUSH.

HORSE-TRAINER, one who trains horses for running races.

HORSE-TRAPPINGS, the saddlery and harness for a horse.

HORSE-TROUGH, a wooden cistern, kept filled with water before road-side inns, for wagoners' or wayfarers' horses to drink from.

HORSE-WHIM, a machine for raising ore from a mine-shaft, worked by a horse.

HORSE-WHIP, a light whip for a horseman; those for ladies are often very elegantly mounted.

HORTICULTURAL SHOW, a public exhibition of fruit and vegetables.

HORTICULTURIST, a gardener; one who cultivates vegetables and fruit.

HOSE, socks, stockings, or coverings for the legs; leather or canvas pipes for conveying water on shore or afloat.

HOSHENS, HOSHINS (Scotch), stockings without feet.

HOSIER, one who deals in stockings, shawls, gloves, braces, laces, and under garments, &c.

HOSIERY, the articles dealt in by a hosier; the manufacture of which, in the United Kingdom, has been estimated at £4,000,000 annually.

HOSPITAL, an infirmary; a public institution for the reception of sick persons.

HOSTESS, the landlady of an inn.

HOSTLER. *See* OSTLER.

HOT-BATH, a bath of hot-water; a vapour bath.

HOT-BED, a forcing pit containing horse-dung and other manure, and covered with glass for raising early plants.

HOTCH-POTCH, an Irish stew, or broth, made with mutton and vegetables.

HOTEL, an inn; a house for lodging and entertaining travellers; in France the term is applied to a private house or large mansion.

HOTEL-DE-VILLE, the town-hall or guild-hall of a French town.

HOTEL-KEEPER, the landlord of an inn.

HOT-FLUE, an apartment heated by stoves, or steam pipes, where goods are dried.

HOT-PRESSED PAPER, paper of which the sheets have been smoothed and glazed by passing them between heated rollers of polished steel.

Hotteau, a measure of capacity formerly used in Hainault, from 3 to 4 gallons, according to the articles measured.

Hot-water Bottle, an earthenware jar filled with hot water, for keeping the feet warm in bed.

Hot-water Heating Apparatus, a system of pipes, for conveying steam or hot water for warming churches, and other public institutions, dwellings, and horticultural buildings, &c.

Hot-water Jug, an earthenware mug, capped with a metal cover, for bringing boiling water to table.

Hot-water Plate, a deep metal-covered plate, filled with boiling water, to keep victuals warm.

Houille (French), pit-coal.

Houisson, Houssoir (French), a whisk; a hair-broom; a feather-broom.

Hounds, projections at the mast-head of a ship, on which the top or trestle-trees rest; dogs kept for coursing.

Houppelande, a kind of great-coat worn in France; a riding-coat.

Hour, a division of time; the 24th part of the day.

Houarce (French), a small cable; the vang of a mizen-yard, in rigging.

Hour-glass, a sand-glass running for an hour: this instrument is now chiefly used by seamen, for measuring time by the fall of sand in a glass tube, during the period of heaving the log, and is only constructed to run a certain number of seconds or minutes.

Hour-hand, the short index hand of a clock or watch; that which points to the hour, while the long hand indicates the minutes.

House, a sea-term, implying to protect or secure any thing, as housing a gun, mast, &c. House is also the general name for a dwelling. *See* Houses and Housing.

House-agent, a person entrusted with the letting of houses or apartments, estates, &c.

House-breaking, entering a house for unlawful purposes in the day-time; a felonious entry at night is termed burglary.

House-decorator, one who combines the business of several trades, painting, paper-hanging, white-washing, &c.

House-dog, a terrier, mastiff, or some other dog kept chained up for the protection of a dwelling.

House-factor, an agent in Scotland for the sale or letting of houses.

Householder, the occupier and renter of a house.

Households, a technical name among millers for the best flour made from red wheat, with a small portion of white wheat mixed.

House-joiner, a carpenter who does work for the interior of houses.

House-keeper, the head woman-servant or manager of a household; one who has the charge of the ménage.

House-lamb, a lamb brought up by hand, and fed at home.

House-maid, an indoor domestic, one who attends table, and has the care of the furniture, rooms, &c.

House-maids' Gloves, stout, coarse, leather gloves used by servants to clean grates, and perform other dirty work.

House of Call, a public-house, where journeymen connected with a particular trade or calling assemble when out of work; and where the unemployed can be hired by masters, or those seeking hands. Each particular trade has one or more special houses of call in the metropolis.

House-rent, the yearly amount paid for the hire or occupation of a house.

Houses, places of residence; buildings of various forms, styles, and dimensions, occupied as dwellings.

House-tax, a tax on buildings levied by [government.

House-warming, a feast, entertainment, or carousal, given to friends or customers, on taking possession of a new house.

House-wife, a kind of needle-book or case, for holding thread, needles, buttons, &c., often taken to sea by sailors.

Housing, a covering or protection to any thing, as to a vessel laid up in harbour or dock; a small cord used at sea, made of three small yarns, and used for seizings, also termed house-line.

Howdah, the body of an Indian carriage; a small pavilion or car, with trappings, on the back of an elephant.

Howdy, in Scotland, a midwife.

Howitzer, a kind of mortar or short gun, mounted on a field carriage, for throwing spherical shells filled with gunpowder and musket-balls.

Howker, a two-masted Dutch vessel; a kind of hulk; also a small fishing-smack, used on the Irish coasts.

Hoy, a small passenger sloop employed on the sea-coast, or in conveying cargo from a ship in a roadstead or bay.

H.P., the abbreviation for "horse-power," and "half-pay."

Hubble-bubble, the bottom of a hookah, or snake-pipe.

Hubla, a weight for pearls and diamonds, used in Sinde; about 2 grains troy.

Huckaback, a species of very coarse diaper, made of flax, used for towelling.

Huckster, an inferior dealer or minor trader; a hawker or itinerant vender of goods with a pack, box, or tray. The term is very generally used in the West Indies, where a licence is imposed for trading.

Hudang, the Malay name for shrimps.

Hudson's Bay Company, a trading corporation, having jurisdiction and exclusive right of trade over the greater part of Arctic or Northern America. It collects and trades in furs, from which it derives a large annual revenue. [leather.

Huffling, a process of ornamenting gilded

Huile (French), oil.

Huissier, an usher or door-keeper in a French court; a public officer, a process-server, whose duty it is to draw up and deliver, at the residence of parties concerned, official legal documents, &c.

Huitre (French), oyster.

Hujaum, an Indian barber.

Huldee, in the East Indies a name for turmeric, the *Curcuma longa*.

Hulk, the old hull of a vessel, employed for various purposes; in naval harbours for a receiving-ship, to which the officers and crew are turned over, while their own vessel is refitting. Hulks are also used for marine police-stations, hospitals, coal-depots, &c.

Hull, the body of a ship; to decorticate oats, or other grains.

Hull-down, a nautical term, signifying that only the masts and sails of a vessel are seen in the distance, the hull or body of the ship being concealed by the convexity of the sea.

Hulling, the process of cleaning grass-seeds and cereal grains.

Hulwaee, a Persian sweetmeat or baked jelly made of fruit, candied sugar, and butter, much used in Western India.

Hum, the milt or soft roe of a codfish, esteemed a delicacy in Scotland.

Humall, a class of servants in Bombay, employed either as a palanquin-bearer or for domestic purposes.

Human-hair Manufacturer, a wig-maker; an ornamental worker in hair.

Humbalau the Malay name for lac.

Humbles, **Umbles**, a name given to the entrails of the deer.

Hummaul, an Indian porter or palanquin-bearer. *See* Humall.

Hummeler, an instrument for clearing barley of the haums or avels. *See* Barley Aveler.

Humming-top, a hollow spinning-top; a child's toy.

Hummocks, pieces of ice thrown up by pressure from large fragments coming in contact.

Hummums, a house where sweating baths can be had.

Hump-backed Whale, a species of whale of which there are two principal varieties, the *Megaptera longimana*, and *M. Americana*, which yield some of the whalebone of commerce.

Humulin, the narcotic principle of the hop.

Hundred, in numeration twice fifty; but in commerce, a variable amount of different goods; usually 112lbs. In Belgium, the hundred of articles sold at market is invariably 104 pieces. The hundred of planks or deals in Sweden is 120, in Westewyck 124, in Christiana 127, and in some other northern ports 132. In Riga and Elsinore the great hundred is 20 gross, or 2880 pieces. It is also the name of a district or division of a county. *See* Great Hundred.

Hundred-weight, the chief British measure of weight for bulky articles, containing 112 lbs. avoirdupois; the 20th part of a ton. It is generally written for shortness' sake, *cwt.* *See* Cwt.

Hundua, a measure in Ceylon equal to a handful.

Hungary-water, water distilled from the tops of rosemary flowers with some spirit of wine.

Hunt, a chase with dogs; the portion of country hunted with hounds.

Hunter, **Huntsman**, a pursuer of wild animals for sport or sustenance; also a strong heavy horse suited for the chase.

Hunting-boots, long boots with white tops.

Hunting-box, **Hunting-seat**, a temporary residence when hunting.

Hunting-coat, a scarlet or green coat, or some particular costume worn by a company of hunters.

Huntsman, the whipper-in or manager of a pack of hounds.

Hurda, a name for myrabolams or country galls in India.

Hurdle, a moveable wooden frame of split timber, or wattled osiers; an iron fence for protecting trees, enclosing land, or folding cattle and sheep.

Hurds, the refuse of flax; any waste tow or oakum.

Hurdy-gurdy, a droning musical instrument; a kind of rude hand grinding street organ.

Hurkaru, a running footman in the East; a Calcutta daily paper so called.

Hurler, in Scotland, one employed in carrying stones, peats, &c. on a wheel-barrow.

Hurries, timber stages, having spouts, by which coals are shot into vessels.

Hurse-skin, a name for the hard tuberculated skin of a fish, from which shagreen is made, to cover lancet-cases, pocket-books, sword-hilts, &c.

Hurtal, an Indian name for yellow arsenic, or orpiment. *See* Hurtall.

Husbandage, the agent or managing owner's allowance or commission, for attending to a ship's business.

Husband-land, an old Scotch term for a division of land containing 26 acres; that is, as much as could be tilled by a plough, or mowed by a scythe by the husbandman.

Husbandman, an agriculturist; a farmer.

Husband, Ship's. *See* Ship's Husband.

Hussar, a light horse-soldier.

Hussar-saddle, a saddle with holsters and furniture for a lightly mounted horseman.

Hussey, **Huswife**, **Housewife**, a case containing a set of sewing materials, thread, needles, buttons, &c. for a man's use.

Hutan, the Malay name for a jungle or wood.

Hutch, a box or cistern; a cage for tame rabbits; a basket in which coals are brought from the mines; a measure of two Winchester bushels: six hutches of coal make a cart-load of about 14 cwt.

Hutte (German), a foundry or smelting-house; a kiln.

Hwun, a Chinese nominal weight; the tenth part of a sze.

Hyacinth, a kind of gem-stone; also a flower. *See* Zircon.

Hyawaballi, a colonial name for the zebra wood of Guiana, which is used for furniture; the tree is scarce.

Hydrangea, a very pretty dwarf shrub, prized for its large flowers.

Hydrant, a water plug; a pipe or spout for discharging water at a fire.

Hydrate, a compound containing water.

Hydraulic-cements, cements which have the power of hardening under water, and are prepared by the calcination of argillaceous limestone.

HYDRAULIC-MACHINE MAKER, an engineer or iron-founder who superintends the manufacture of hydraulic presses.

HYDRAULIC-PRESS, a heavy iron machine worked by water-power for acquiring great pressure.

HYDRAULIC-RAM, a kind of force-pump, originally invented by Montgolfier, for raising small quantities of water to heights considerably above the source of supply.

HYDROCYANIC-ACID, another name for prussic acid; a deadly poison.

HYDRO-EXTRACTOR, the name given to a machine for wringing and drying clothes.

HYDROGRAPHER, one who makes or plans charts; a public officer, so named, at the Admiralty.

HYDROGRAPHIC-OFFICE, the department of the Admiralty where the results of naval surveys are received, and official charts prepared therefrom, and published at a low price for the use of navigators.

HYDROMEL, a species of mead, consisting of fermented honey and water.

HYDROMETER, an instrument for determining the specific gravity or density of fluids by floating in them.

HYDROSCOPE, an instrument intended to mark the presence of water in air.

HYDROSTAT, an apparatus for preventing the explosion of steam-boilers.

HYDROSTATIC-BALANCE, a very delicate balance employed in finding specific gravities.

HYDROSTATIC-BED MAKER, a manufacturer of water-beds for invalids.

HYDROSTATIC-PRESS, a press invented by Mr. Bramah, and hence often called the Bramah-press.

HYPOTHECATION, the pledging of a ship or goods for advances made. *See* BOTTOMRY-BOND.

HYSON, an esteemed kind of green tea, of which there are two or three varieties, as hyson-skin, young hyson, &c.

I.

IBEX, an animal of the goat kind, of which there are several distinct species.

IBIS, a genus of birds resembling the storks: the plumage of several is used for ornamental purposes.

ICA, a general name for fish in some of the Pacific islands.

ICE, crushed ice flavoured, sold as a confection; congealed water, which enters into commerce for cooling liquids and for confectioners' purposes: large quantities are shipped from America to other countries. The city of Boston is the chief port of shipment; 150,000 tons were exported thence in 1856, while the large cities of New York and Philadelphia consume more than half a million tons yearly.

ICEBERG, an insulated mountain of ice.

ICEBOUND, vessels blocked up in the ice.

ICE-CREAM, iced confectionery.

ICED, cakes frosted with sugar; water chilled with ice.

ICE-DEALER, a collector and vender of ice.

ICED-WATER, water with ice in it to cool it in summer weather.

ICE-HOUSE, an under-ground storehouse or cellar where ice is kept for use in warm weather.

ICELAND-MOSS, a lichen, the *Cetraria islandica*, yielding a nutritious starch, used in medicine, and forming an important article of commerce. It has to go through a long process before it can be rendered sufficiently palatable to be used as food; it is first soaked in water till the bitterness is extracted, and then boiled with milk, a kind of bread is also said to be prepared from it.

ICELAND SPAR, a transparent calcareous stone, the best of which is obtained in Iceland.

ICE-PAIL MAKER, a cooper who makes buckets for holding ice.

ICE-PLANE, an instrument for smoothing away the rough surface of ice in winter, before cutting and carting it away for storage.

ICE-PLOUGH, an instrument used in America for cutting grooves in the ice on ponds and lakes, to facilitate the removal of blocks of 1 to 2 cwt. which are stored for summer use.

ICE-SAFE, a chamber for cooling water, &c.

ICE-SAW, a long saw, with a heavy weight attached at the lower end, for cutting channels in the ice to liberate vessels which have been frozen in.

ICE-TONGS, utensils for taking up ice at a table.

ICICA RESIN, resinous exudations of value in the districts of South America where the *Icica* trees occur, and furnish the elemi, carana, and tacamahaca resins.

IDOL, an image; a heathen god: idols were formerly cast at Birmingham to some extent for shipment abroad.

IDWALL-STONE, a Welsh oil-stone obtained from the Snowdon district.

IGUARIAS (Spanish), viands dressed and served up.

IKAN, the Malayan name for fish: telor ikan being fish roes; sirip ikan, fish fins; sisek ikan, fish scales.

ILLEGAL, any act contrary to law, such as the use of false weights and measures, smuggling, &c.

ILLICIT, unlawful; prohibited; as secret distillation, &c.

ILLIPE OIL, ILLOOPOO OIL, a solid oil expressed in India from the seeds of *Bassia longifolia*.

ILL-MANNED, short-handed; a vessel that has not a proportionate number of seamen to her size and tonnage, is said to be ill-manned.

Illuminating, a mode of painting, or emblazoning, books and manuscripts with ornamental letters; placing lights at the windows or in front of a house on festive occasions, or days of rejoicing.

Illustrated Newspapers, printed journals containing woodcut illustrations, of which there are now several issued in London, and others published in the principal foreign cities. The old-established illustrated papers of London are the *Illustrated London News*, the *Illustrated Times*, and *Punch*.

Illustration, a woodcut or stereotype block; an impression taken therefrom.

Illustrator, a commentator; a draughtsman or designer.

Imadas (Spanish), sliding planks.

Image-maker, a manufacturer of plaster casts and figures, or statues.

Imal, a provincial grain-measure formerly used in France, about 5½ gallons.

Imamea, a Turkish name for amber mouthpieces for pipes.

Imbricated, overlapping, like the tiles or slates upon the roof of a house.

Imbuto, a grain and land measure of Sardinia, for grain = 5½ pints.

Imitation, a counterfeit; a copy in inferior materials.

Imitator, a copyist; one who follows a set pattern.

Immi, a dry measure of Baden, a little more than 6 pints.

Immersion, the act of plunging or dipping into a fluid.

Immigrant, a passenger who arrives in a country; the term is only used when large bodies of passengers arrive together in vessels; when quitting they are termed emigrants, as they go forth.

Immovables, lands; houses; fixtures.

Immunity, a freedom from tax, office, or obligation, &c.

Impannel, to form or constitute, a jury for the trial of any cause.

Impediment, an obstacle or hindrance to progress; an obstruction to navigation, or to any undertaking.

Imperative, a positive command; *absolute*; compulsory.

Imperial, relating to royalty; any thing large, as a large decanter; a large kind of slate; *large-sized* paper, 27 inches by 23; in Spanish the roof of a coach, hence a case for luggage on a coach top; a species of pointed dome; a dried plum; a gold coin of different dates and values, current in Russia for 10 silver roubles, nearly £1 12s; a cooling drink so called.

Imperishable, not subject to decay; indestructible; calculated to last long.

Impermeable, any textile substance rendered water-proof by the application of some solution.

Impinge, to fall or strike against.

Implicate, to embarrass; to connect with.

Important, urgent; of great consequence.

Imports, a collective name for all goods and merchandise introduced by sea.

Importer, one who receives goods, produce, manufactures, or merchandise from abroad.

Imposing-stone, the stone in a printing-office on which the pages or columns are arranged, and locked up in the chases for press.

Imposing-table. *See* Imposing-stone.

Imposition, an overcharge; a fraud.

Impost, a tax or toll levied on goods imported.

Impostor, a cheat; one who defrauds.

Impressing, taking a copy of any work by printing; stamping, or marking with a die.

Impression, an effect made on any substance by a *tool*; the copy taken from a die or seal; the total number of sheets printed of a book or journal; the copy of an engraving taken from a plate or wood block.

Impressment, a compulsory mode of obtaining seamen, for service in the navy, by a press-gang; sometimes resorted to in time of war.

Imprest, an advance on loan: a department of the Admiralty in Somerset House is called the Imprest-office, from attending to the business of loans or advances to paymasters, and other officers.

Imprimador (Spanish), one who primes or lays the first colours on a piece of linen or board to be painted.

Imprimatur, a licence to print.

Imprint, the printer's name and address attached to the first or last leaf of a book or printed sheet.

Imprison, to incarcerate; to deprive of liberty.

Impropriator, a layman who holds possession of church lands or an ecclesiastical living.

Improvement, an alteration in any thing for the better; as, an increase in custom; an advance in prices, &c.; turning to profit or advantage; making land productive.

Improver, a learner; one who shapes or finishes work.

Improvident, thoughtless, careless, inconsiderate.

I.N. an abbreviation for "Indian Navy."

Inah, an Indian jewel, consisting of a very small mirror mounted in a finger-ring.

Inarching, a mode of grafting by uniting a stock to the parent tree without separating it.

Inc, Ink, a long measure of Japan, about 4 Chinese cubits, and nearly 6½ English feet.

Incandescence, a white heat; the appearance of metals when intensely heated.

Incendiary, one who sets fire to a dwelling-house, which crime in law is termed arson.

Incense, a name for odoriferous resins used to fumigate Roman Catholic churches. *See* Frankincense.

Inch, in Scotland, an island: to drive or advance by slow degrees; the twelfth part of a *foot*, and the smallest lineal measure to which a commonly recognised name is given; but subdivisions are used for many purposes. Among mechanics, the inch is commonly divided into eighths. By the officers of the revenue and by scientific persons, it is divided into tenths, hundredths, &c. Formerly it was made to consist of 12 parts, called lines; and anciently it was subdivided into 3 barleycorns.

Inch-stuff, deal plank sawn to the thickness of an inch.

Incinerate, to burn to ashes.

Incision, a cutting-mark, or impression made on any thing; the separation of the surface by a sharp instrument.

Incisor, a cutting-tooth: those of the walrus, wild boar, hippopotamus, and some other animals, enter into commerce for ivory.

Incline, to lean over; to slope gradually, as an inclined plane.

Inclosure, commonable or waste land, taken in for culture. *See* Enclosure.

Inclusa (Spanish), an hospital for foundlings.

Inclusive, comprehended in the number or sum.

Incombustible Cloth, is made either of asbestos fibres, or linen dipped in a solution of alum, or sal-ammoniac.

Income, a stipend; the receipts or gains derived from labour, business, or property of any kind; as from the produce of a farm; the rent of houses or land; the proceeds of literary or professional business; the profits of commerce or of occupation; the interest on funded property; or joint-stock securities.

Income-tax Collector, a government official, who collects the property and income tax, levied by the State; receiving a percentage commission for his labours.

Income-tax Commissioners, responsible persons appointed to assess incomes for taxation, and to adjudicate upon appeals relating thereto.

Incomings, receipts; money paid on entering upon a business, &c.

Incoming Tenant, the person who goes into possession of a house, or who succeeds another on a farm.

Inconvertible, not transmutable or changeable; some securities or investments are convertible into stock, &c.; others are not so.

Incrustation, a fur or sediment; an accumulation of lime, &c. on the inside of steam-boilers; in building, work fixed with cement or cramp irons into notches made to receive it.

Incubator, a machine for hatching eggs by artificial heat. *See* Hatching Apparatus.

Incumbency, the state of holding a benefice, or being in possession of an office.

Incumbent, the holder of a benefice; a clergyman who is resident on his benefice, having the spiritual charge of his district or parish.

Incumbered Estate, a landed property burdened with mortgage charges, for which provision has lately been made in commissions, taking over the management of such from proprietors. Thus there is an Irish Encumbered Estate Commission; a West Indian Encumbered Estate Commission, &c.

Indelible, a fast colour; what cannot be blotted out.

Indemnification, securing against loss, damage, or penalty. *See* Insurance and Guarantee.

Indentation, a notch or mark cut in any thing—running in and out like a row of teeth.

Indenture, an obligation by writing, a contract as of apprenticeship. Originally the deed or writing was strictly an indenture; the two copies were fac-similes, one being written or indented over the other.

Index, an alphabetical table of reference to the contents of a book; a pointer or needle which turns on a pivot; the exponent of a power; a directing post.

Index-hands, the pointers of a clock, watch, or other registering machine.

Index-maker, one who makes indexes of subjects, or catalogues of convenient reference, &c.

India-matting, grass or reed mats, made in the East from *Papyrus corymbosus*; large quantities of which are imported.

Indiana (Spanish), chintz.

Indian-ink, a black pigment used for water-colour painting. *See* China-ink.

Indian-madder. *See* Chay.

Indian-oak, a name sometimes applied to the teak-wood, *Tectona grandis*.

Indian-red, a purple earth; a variety of ochre.

Indian-shot, a name for the *Canna Indica*, which furnishes a useful fibre.

Indian-yellow, a dye of questionable origin, said to be procured from the urine of the cow, after eating decayed and yellow mango leaves; other authorities refer it to camels' dung. Analysis shows it to be composed chiefly of purreic acid, combined with magnesia. Its name, in some parts of the East, is Purree.

India-rubber Manufacturer. *See* Caoutchouc Manufacturer.

Indicator, an index machine for various purposes; a water-gauge in a steam-engine; a stone-block for marking boundaries of land, &c.

Indictment, a written accusation or charge in a public court, made in the first instance by a grand jury.

Indigo, a blue dye-stuff of commerce, obtained principally from the leaves of various species of *Indigofera*, largely cultivated in India; but other plants yield it in small quantities.

Indigo-blue, washing blue prepared in small lumps for laundresses, who use it to tint the water for rinsing their linen.

Indigo-manufacturer, a preparer of the colouring substance by maceration, &c. from the leaves of the indigo plant.

Indigo-planter, a cultivator of indigo, which is now chiefly grown in the East Indies; but was formerly largely cultivated in the West Indies and Central America.

Indisputable, undeniable, not open to cavil; policies of insurance which are not to be questioned when once granted, are termed indisputable.

Indite, to commit words to writing; to direct or dictate to another.

Indorsement, a writing at the back of a deed or note.

Indorser, one who writes his name at the back of a promissory note, or bill of exchange, and thus makes himself responsible for its payment. *See* Endorse.

Indrain, the Hindustani name for colocynth.

INDRAJOW, INDURJAW, INDRUJOB, Indian names for the intensely bitter seeds of *Wrightia antidysenterica*, used as a vermifuge. The bark furnishes the conessi-bark of commerce.

INDUCT, to introduce; to put in actual possession, or instal in office.

INDUGA, an Indian name for the clearing nut, *Strychnos potatorum*.

INDUSTRIAL, relating to industry; those identified with the manufacturing pursuits, or producing arts, are said to be industrially occupied.

INDUSTRIAL EXHIBITION, INDUSTRIAL SHOW, a public display of objects of utility, industry, and skill.

INDUSTRIAL SCHOOL, a trade school; one where some of the mechanical arts or useful occupations are taught.

INELEGANT, plain; wanting polish or beauty; not handsome.

INFANCINO (Spanish), oil made of green olives.

INFANCY, strictly childhood; but in law, a person under the age of 21, who is not considered answerable for debts incurred.

INFANTRY, foot soldiers in an army.

INFERIOR, of second-rate quality; not the best of any thing.

INFIRMARY, an hospital for the sick; generally one free to the public, and supported by charitable contributions.

INFLAMMABLE, easily set on fire.

INFORMAL, not regular, or customary; contrary to instructions.

INFORMATION, intelligence given; a judicial enquiry and process; an accusation laid against a person in a civil court of some breach of the law.

INFORMER, one who lays an information charging a party with some breach of the customs or excise laws; and who receives a moiety of the penalty recovered.

INFRACTION, a breach or violation of a rule, law, or ordinance.

INFRINGEMENT, a violation of an agreement, or right; an infraction of copyright, or of the patent rights of another.

INFUSIBLE, incapable of fusion, or of being melted.

INFUSION, a preparation obtained by pouring boiling water on a substance, as on tea in tea-making.

INGA BEANS, a Brazilian name for the pods of the horse cassia or bastard cassia.

INGATE, an aperture in a mould for pouring in metal; technically called the tedge.

INGENIO (Spanish), a steam-engine; a sugar-boiling house.

INGENUITY, ready invention; dexterity, skill in any operation.

INGLE (Spanish), a groin; (Scotch), a fire-side.

INGOT, a small wedge-shaped mass of metal, as of tin, copper, gold or silver, &c. of an indefinite size and weight. About 40 ingots of tin go to the ton. In some countries ingots of the precious metals pass current, as silver in China. In Burmah gold and silver ingots, of half an ounce weight avoirdupois, form part of the local currency. In South Australia, by a recent provincial law, coined ingots of gold pass current at 71s. the ounce.

INGREDIENT, a component part of a compound body; one of many substances.

INGRAIN, a name given to yarns, wools, &c., dyed with fast colours before manufacture.

INGROSSING, purchasing large quantities of corn or other merchandise on speculation, with an expectation of increasing their value.

INHABITABLE, fit for occupation; a dwelling-house in good tenantable condition.

INHABITANT, an occupier; a dweller or resident in a house, or city, &c.

INHERITANCE, that which is possessed or enjoyed; lands invested in perpetuity in a person and his heirs.

INHIBITION, a process in the law of Scotland, interdicting a party from disposing of his real estate, in prejudice of the debt claimed.

INIS (Irish), an island.

INITIALS, the first or capital letters of a name.

INITIATE, to instruct in the rudiments of an art; to acquaint with.

INJECTION, a medicated liquor thrown into a cavity by a syringe.

INJECTION-PIPE, a pipe for injecting cold water into the condenser of an engine.

INJIBAR, an Indian name for bistort root, used in hæmorrhage.

INJUNCTION, a legal prohibition or restraint, as upon the infringement of a patent right.

INJURY, damage done to goods, fixtures, or rights, &c.

INK, a Japanese long measure, nearly 75 inches; a pigment or fluid for writing or printing with, of which there are several kinds. Black writing-ink is commonly made from salts of iron, with various astringent vegetable infusions. The best materials are sulphate of iron and nutgalls, suspended by mucilage of gum arabic; other ingredients, as logwood, sulphate of copper, and sugar, are sometimes added. Blue ink is made with sulphate of indigo; red ink with Brazil wood infused in vinegar or alcohol, alum and gum. Black printing-ink is made of lamp-black, linseed oil, rosin, brown soap, and a small quantity of indigo. See INK.

INKBOTTLE, a receptacle for ink of various forms.

INKING-ROLLER, a composition roller with handles, used by printers for spreading ink over type, wood-cut blocks, or engraved plates.

INKING-TABLE, a table of a peculiar construction, used by letter-press printers to supply the roller with the requisite quantity of ink during the process of printing.

INKLE, a species of broad linen tape; wrought inkle is principally used in Manchester; unwrought inkle, or short upinel, is bleached yarn.

INK-POWDER MAKER, a manufacturer of a dry composition for making ink with.

INKSTAND, a tray or stand for holding an ink bottle, pens, &c.

INKSTAND-MAKER, a manufacturer of ink-holders and the wooden or other ornamental stands in which the bottles are fixed.

Inland-bills, drafts and bills of exchange, drawn and payable in the same country.

Inland-trade, interior or domestic trade; the home transport and supply of goods over the country, and which does not pass the sea.

Inlayer, a mosaic worker; a cabinet-maker who ornaments work with veneers or devices in various-coloured woods; a manufacturer of papier-mâché who inserts nacreous shell into a prepared ground.

Inlet, an entrance; a creek or bay; inserted materials.

Inmate, a lodger; an occupier; the member of a household; one who lives with a family.

Inmeats (Scotch), those parts of the intestines used for food.

Inn, a tavern or hotel; a place of lodging and entertainment; differing from a public or ale house, which does not usually provide beds or food for travellers.

Innholders' Company, one of the livery companies of London, whose hall is in College-street, Dowgate-hill.

Innings, in cricket, or other games, the turn to play; a spell at work.

Inn-keeper, a tavern-keeper.

Innovation, a novelty or change; a departure from old practices, laws, or customs.

Input (Scotch), the share in a contribution; the balance in change of money.

Inquest, a judicial inquiry or examination. *See* Coroner's Inquest.

Inquilino (Spanish), a tenant.

Inquiry, a scrutiny, or investigation; a close examination.

Inscribe, to write or engrave on any thing; to mark with characters; to address or dedicate.

Inscription, a writing or title on a tomb, or on an address; a piece of plate presented, &c.

Insertions, narrow strips of lace, embroidered muslin or cambric, sold for inlets in handkerchiefs, dresses, &c.; work in general added or joined, to enlarge or ornament ladies' fancy-work.

Insides, passengers in the interior of a vehicle; perfect paper, from which the outsides or faulty sheets have been removed.

Insignia, badges of office; decorations.

Insolvent, incompetent to pay all just demands; in pecuniary difficulties.

Insolvent Court, a specially appointed law court in London and the provinces, having jurisdiction over the affairs of insolvents; and in which causes are heard before a commissioner, who adjudicates upon them, and discharges or remands the insolvent, according to the features of the case, as brought before him by documents or evidence.

Insolvent-petitioner, an insolvent who claims to be heard and relieved from his debts.

Inspan, to yoke draught oxen.

Inspection, a surveillance; an examination.

Inspector, a superintendant or overseer; an officer of a public company, as a gas inspector. There are also inspectors of schools, of police, &c.

Instalments, a debt divided into several parts, and paid at different times.

Instant, the present or current month.

Institor (Spanish), a factor or agent.

Institution, an establishment, public or social, as a Mechanics' institution, a Banking Company, &c.

Instructor, a teacher; one who imparts knowledge or skill of any kind.

Instrument, a law term for a written document or deed; a tool used for any purpose; an artificial machine, as mathematical, nautical, philosophical, and electro-magnetic instruments.

Instrumental, pertaining to musical instruments.

Instrument-maker, a manufacturer of instruments of any kind.

Insulate, to isolate or detach; to separate or cut off, as in electricity.

Insulator, a non-conductor of electricity.

Insurance, an indemnification for loss averted, obtained by paying a percentage on ships or goods; also against fire on houses or furniture.

Insurance-broker, an intermediate agent between the marine insurance-offices and the insurers, who effects policies upon ships, cargo, and passengers' effects, &c.

Insurance-clerk, an assistant officer employed in an insurance-office.

Insurance-company, a joint stock association, which grants policies of insurance against fire, wreck, window-breaking, &c.

Insurance-office, the office or building where an Insurance Company conducts its business.

Insurance-policy, the legal document or contract given by an Insurance Company, to a party who has paid the premium required, as a guarantee against risk.

Intaglio, a name given to small gems in which the design is indented, or engraved, instead of being raised, as in cameos.

Intan, the Malay name for the diamond.

Integer, a whole quantity number, in contradistinction to a fractional part.

Intelligence Office, a telegraph office; a servants' registry; an office where information may be obtained. In the United States there are many of these offices established for different purposes; for the transmission of news; for registering the addresses of individuals; for forwarding news, advices, &c.

Intendant, in France, an inspector or superintendant.

Inter, to bury, to cover with earth.

Intercourse, communication or correspondence; trade.

Interdict, a prohibition.

Interest, a sum paid for the use of money lent; a right or share in a business or undertaking.

Interim, the meantime; the interval between two periods.

Interjoist, a middle joist or cross beam.

Interlacing, mixed or joined together.

Interleave, to place blank leaves of paper, in binding, between the printed leaves or sheets of a book.

Interlineation, additions or corrections made in manuscript between the previously written lines.

INTERLOCUTION, an intermediate act or decree before final decision.

INTERLUDE, a farce or light piece performed at a theatre between the first play and the after-piece.

INTERMEDIATE, interposed, lying between.

INTEROCEANIC, lying between two seas; a communication connecting two oceans—as a railway, road, &c.

INTERPOLATE, to add to an original; to alter a book or manuscript.

INTERPRETER, a linguist; a translator of languages in law courts, or for travellers, &c.; one who explains between two parties.

INTERSECT, to divide into parts; to meet and cross each other.

INTERSTICE, a small intervening space; the space between one thing and another.

INTERTIE, horizontal timber framed between two posts.

INTERVALE, an alluvial deposit on the bank of a river; low land near a stream, or on the border of a swamp; in the West Indies, a pathway or narrow strip of grass, or space between the sugar-cane fields.

INTERVIEW, a meeting of parties; a conference.

INTERWEAVE, to insert together; to intermix or unite in texture, or construction

INTESTATE, dying without having made a will.

INTIMATION, an indirect suggestion or notice given; a declaration or remark.

INTOXICATE, to make drunk.

INTRODUCE, to bring into notice or practice.

INTRODUCTION, a preface or preliminary dissertation to a book; the act of bringing into a country; ushering an individual into the presence of another personally or by letter.

INTROMISSION, a Scotch term for moneys passing through a person's hands; an intermeddling with the effects of another.

INTRUDER, one who forces his way in uninvited; a person who enters a manufactory or place of business without permission previously obtained.

INVALID, weak, worn out, or disabled; of no weight or cogency.

INVALIDITY, the absence of legal right; informality.

INVALID'S-CHAIR MAKER, a manufacturer of what are termed Bath-chairs, for wheeling out infirm or sick persons in the open air.

INVENTION, the skill or ingenuity displayed in the contrivance of any thing new; the article invented.

INVENTOR, a contriver; a discoverer or maker of something new.

INVENTORY, a catalogue of stock in business; of a ship's fittings and furniture, or of goods intended for sale; an account taken of fixtures, &c., on taking possession of a house, shop, or farm.

INVERNACULO (Spanish), a green-house for preserving plants in winter.

INVESTIGATION, a searching inquiry.

INVESTIGATOR, an examiner; one charged to look into any thing, or the state of affairs of a company or firm.

INVESTMENT, money put out at interest in some public fund or association, or in the purchase of houses or land, &c.

INVOICE, a bill of parcels containing particulars of quality, quantity, and price of goods remitted to an agent or factor for sale, or on approval.

INVOICE-BOOK, the book in which are copied or posted the originals of bills and invoices of merchandise purchased or received. [loss.

INVOLVE, to embarrass; to render liable to

IODIDE OF POTASSIUM, a medicinal preparation for scrofulous diseases.

IODINE, a valuable chemical preparation from kelp or the ashes of sea-weed.

I. O. U., an acknowledgment for money or goods lent.

IPECACUANHA, a medicinal powder, prepared from the root of the *Cephaelis Ipecacuanha*, containing an emetic principle.

IPLIK, the common Turkish word for thread or yarn.

IPSOLA (Spanish), a kind of wool.

IRASA, a dry measure of Mysore of 16 lbs.

IRIDIUM, a rare white metal found in combination with platinum and osmium; being a very hard substance, it is used for tipping or pointing metallic pens.

IRISH-MOSS, a marine plant brought from Ireland, and obtained from the *Chondrus crispus*, which being nutritive, emollient, and demulcent, is used medicinally, and for various economic purposes. *See* CARRAGEEN.

IRISH-STEW, a kind of hash consisting of potatoes and meat boiled together.

IRLANDA (Spanish), fine Irish linen.

IRON, the most common and most important of the useful metals: of iron there are at least forty kinds of ores, but the most valuable are the oxides and carbonate. It enters into commerce in its manufactured state under various forms, the principal kinds being bar and bolt iron; iron castings, hoop iron, nails, pig, tube, rivet, plate or sheet, railway, and rod iron.

IRON AND TIN-PLATE WORKER, a worker in *malleable iron*, who shapes articles from the thin plates of metal.

IRON-BEDSTEAD MAKER, a manufacturer of bedsteads or frames of iron

IRON-CHAIN MAKER, a manufacturer of chain cables for vessels, or for suspension purposes.

IRON-FASTENED; vessels whose planks and timbers are rivetted with iron nails and bolts instead of copper, are said to be iron-fastened.

IRON-FENCE AND HURDLE MAKER, a manufacturer of articles so named.

IRON-FOUNDER, a metal caster who runs iron into various shapes.

IRON-FOUNDERS' PATTERN-MAKER, a manufacturer of moulds, &c. for metal-founders.

IRON-FOUNDRY, a place where iron castings are made.

IRON-HEATER, the piece of metal which is heated in the fire for a laundress's box-iron or Italian-iron.

IRON-HOLDER, a stand for a laundress's smoothing-iron.

IRONING-BLANKET, a coarse blanket used as a smooth surface by laundresses when ironing linen.

IRONING-BOARD, a tailor's board for pressing cloth on with an iron to smooth the seams, &c.; a laundress's board, covered with flannel, for ironing ladies' dresses; a table.

IRON-LIQUOR, a solution of acetate of iron used as a mordant by calico printers. It is usually called printers' liquor.

IRON-MASTER, a manufacturer of raw and bar iron; the owner of smelting works, or blast furnaces for making iron from the ore.

IRON-MERCHANT, a wholesale dealer in iron.

IRONMONGER, a shop-keeper who vends hardware, and iron tools and utensils.

IRONMONGERS' COMPANY, the tenth in rank of the twelve principal livery companies of London; their first charter was granted in 3 Edward IV., A.D., 1463. Their hall is in Fenchurch street.

IRONMONGERS' TOOLS, the tools used by many trades sold by ironmongers; such as hammers, axes, saws, chisels, gimlets, &c.

IRONMONGERY, miscellaneous articles of iron, consisting of fenders, fire-irons, grates, ovens, pans, kettles, pots, spades, shovels, and other articles of hardware, usually sold by ironmongers.

IRON-MOULD, a mark on linen made by the rust of iron.

IRON-PLATE WORKER, a manufacturer of plates of iron for boilers, bridges, iron ships, &c.

IRONS, tools for heating at a fire, as laundresses' flat and box smoothing-irons for clothes; tailors' and hatters' irons, &c.; the poker, tongs, and shovel, for a grate; shackles or manacles for the legs.

IRON-SCRAPS, the cuttings and parings of iron work which are saved, collected together, and melted again in the puddling furnace.

IRON-SMITH, a worker in iron.

IRON-SPOON, a kitchen spoon used by cooks.

IRON-STEAM-BOAT BUILDER, an engineer who constructs vessels of plates of iron rivetted together. Iron ships and steamers are now coming very generally into use.

IRON-STONE, the argillaceous carbonate of iron, commonly known as clay iron-stone.

IRON-WIRE, metal drawn into slender bright threads from wire iron, and used for making rope, fencing, riddles, bird-cages, flower-stands, &c.

IRON-WIRE WEAVER, a manufacturer of articles with iron wire.

IRON-WOOD, a common name for many trees, producing hard, ponderous, close-grained woods; in America, for the *Ostrya Virginica*, a tree which only grows to a small size, but the white wood is compact, finely grained and heavy. There is an iron-wood in Brazil, but the tree yielding it is not defined. Another iron-wood entering into commerce is the *Metrosideros verus*, brought from China. The *Argania sideroxylon*, of Morocco, is another close, hard wood which sinks in water.

IRON-WORK, any thing made of iron; the parts or pieces of a building or machine which consists of iron.

IRRIGATION, the practice of flooding land in arid countries.

ISELOTTE, another name for the zlote, a Russian silver coin of 15 silver copecks, about 6d.

ISINGLASS, the commercial name for the purest form of animal jelly obtained from the swimming-bladder of various fish. It is a substance well known in commerce, and employed both in the arts and domestic economy, being used in confectionery and cooking, and for clarifying wine and beer. The best isinglass is obtained in Russia from the sturgeon, and is divided into leaf and book (first and second), and staple. About 300 lbs. of isinglass are obtained from 1000 fish. Brazilian isinglass is probably obtained from species of *Pimelodus* and *Silurus*. It is in the form of pipe, block, honey-comb, cake, and tongue isinglass; the last formed of a double swimming-bladder. East-India isinglass is obtained from a species of *Polynemus*, viz. *P. plebeius*.

ISINGLASS MANUFACTURER AND DEALER, a purifier and preparer of rough isinglass into the saleable article of trade.

ISPRUK, a coarse powder made from a species of *Delphinium*, growing in Affghanistan, used in dyeing.

ISTUMRAR, a tenure of land in India.

ITALIC, a kind of inclined type used by printers; that in which the scientific names of plants are given in this dictionary.

ITALIAN-IRON, a laundress's heater for fluting and smoothing frills, &c.

ITALIAN MAPLE, a noble tree (*Acer opalus*), much prized in Italy as a shade tree, for avenues and public walks.

ITALIAN OAK, the *Quercus Esculus*, a native of the South of Europe; where the sweet acorns are often ground and made into bread along with wheat flour.

ITALIAN RYE-GRASS, a plant, the *Lolium Italicum*, which produces a coarse kind of seed.

ITALIAN WAREHOUSEMAN, an oil-man; a vender of macaroni, vermicelli, olive oil, dried fruits, provisions, and such like comestibles.

ITEM, a Malay name for ducks; a memorandum; a new article; one of the particulars of an account.

ITIKIBOURA-BALLI, a wood chiefly used in British Guiana for cabinet work, believed to be obtained from *Machaerium Schomburgkii*.

ITINERANT, a wanderer; a pedlar; a workman who travels from place to place.

ITINERARY, a distance guide, &c. for travellers; an account or description of a country.

ITZIB, a Japanese gold coin worth about eight shillings and ninepence.

IVORY, the commercial name for the bony matter of the tusks of the elephant, the teeth of the hippopotamus and walrus, the horn of the narwhal, &c. Elephant ivory is the most esteemed, and that obtained in the largest quantity; our imports are nearly 300 tons a-year. Ivory is largely used for various purposes, by cutlers, turners, comb-makers, instrument-makers, and others. Ivory is also the name for a pass-ticket on a railway, or subscriber's admission to a theatre, public gardens, &c.

IVORY AND BONE STAINER, a workman who colours these substances.

IVORY-BLACK, animal charcoal; a powder prepared by heating ivory shavings in an iron cylinder; when from bones, it is called bone-black. *See* BONE-BLACK.

IVORY-BLACK MANUFACTURER, a maker of animal charcoal from calcined ivory refuse. It is used as the basis of the finer black pigments, and for ink for copper-plate printers.

IVORY-CARVER, a maker of various carvings in ivory, either by hand or by the lathe; such as figures, chessmen, fans, brooches, combs, chains, signets, dice, knife-handles.

IVORY-MERCHANT, an importer or wholesale dealer in elephants' tusks, and the teeth of animals, supplying the ivory of commerce.

IVORY-TURNER, a worker in ivory: one who shapes ivory into various forms and articles with a turning-lathe.

IVORY-WORKER AND CUTTER, a turner and carver in ivory.

IVORY, VEGETABLE, a name given to the nuts of *Phytelephas macrocarpa*, a dwarf South-American palm; which, from their resemblance to ivory, are used by turners for making small articles.

J.

JABB, a net used in Scotland for catching the fry of coal fish.

JABBLE (Scotch), a large blunt needle; a knife.

JACARANDA, a Brazilian name for a fine lofty tree, the *Jacaranda Brasiliana*, from which rosewood is obtained.

JACINTH, another name for the hyacinth; a gem stone.

JACK, a name for a male ass; a sailor; an instrument for pulling off boots; a powerful machine for raising great weights, its ordinary power being about 5 tons; a kitchen machine for turning a spit, the moving power being either a weight, or the smoke and rarefied air of a chimney; a wooden frame for sawing timber on; a wedge; a flag carried on the bowsprit of a vessel; in the Orkneys, a term for taking off the skin of the seal.

JACK-BLOCK, a block used in a ship when sending the higher masts up or down.

JACK-BOOTS, heavy long boots for riding.

JACK-CHAIN, the chain that revolves on the wheel of a kitchen jack.

JACKET, a short coat.

JACK-KNIFE, a large clasp knife.

JACK-MAKER, a maker of lifting-screws; or of roasting bottle-jacks, &c.

JACK-PLANE, a smoothing plane about 18 inches long, used to prepare wood for the trying-plane.

JACKS, wooden wedges used in coal mining.

JACK-SCREW, a screw used for stowing cotton in the hold of a ship.

JACK-STAFF, a staff, fixed on the bowsprit cap of a ship, upon which the Union Jack is hoisted.

JACK-STAYS, ropes or strips of wood or iron stretched along the yard of a ship to bind the sails to.

JACK-TOWEL, a long towel placed over a roller, and fixed to a wall.

JACKWOOD, an excellent furniture and fancy wood obtained from the *Artocarpus integrifolia*: the fruit of this tree is occasionally eaten.

JACOB'S-LADDER, a ship's ladder made of rope with wooden steps.

JACONET, a light open and soft kind of fabric, rather stouter than muslin used for dresses, neckcloths, &c.

JACQUARD-CARDS, perforated patterns used in weaving figured fabrics.

JACQUARD-LOOM, an ingenious mechanism employed in weaving silk and muslin, carpets, and other figured goods.

JACQUARD-MACHINE MAKER, a manufacturer of Jacquard looms.

JADE, a stone (*nephrite*) used by lapidaries, of a light green colour, and an oily appearance when polished, remarkable for its hardness and tenacity. It is worked into elegant boxes, cups, and saucers, bottles, &c. in India. Scalping-knives, and other weapons bearing a fine cutting edge, are made of it by the Indians of North America.

JAG, a small load of hay; a wallet; a notch.

JAGGED, cut in a coarse manner.

JAGGER, in Scotland a pedlar; the bearer of a leather bag or wallet called a jag.

JAGGERY, the Indian name for a coarse dark kind of sugar made from the sap of the coco-nut, the palmyra, the kittool, and other palms, and from the sugar cane. Jaggery is often used to mix with lime as a cement in the East, and it takes a very fine polish.

JAGGING-IRON, a pastry-cook's tool.

JAGHIRE, in India a fief or lordship for life.

JAGONG, the Malay name for Indian-corn or maize.

JAIL, a prison; a penitentiary.

JAILER, the keeper or guardian of a jail.

JALAP, the tuberous root and powder of *Exogonium Purga*.

JALE (French), a large bowl.

JALOUSIES, a name for Venetian blinds in the West Indies.

JAM, a conserve of fruits; a thick bed of stones: a block or squeeze.

JAMAICA-PEPPER, one of the names given to allspice.

JAMALGHOTA, the Hindustani name for croton oil and seed.

JAMBEE, a species of cane imported from China, having a stiff stem with large knots.

JAMBETTE (French), a clasp-knife: JAMBETTES, jambs, in architecture.

JAMBIRA, a Sanscrit name for the lemon, the *Citrus Limonum*.

JAMBOLON, a species of the myrtle from India.

JAMBON (French), a ham; a gammon of bacon;—Jambon de Mayence, a Westphalia ham.

JAMBS, projections; the side or vertical posts of any opening in a wall, &c. which bear the pieces that discharge the superincumbent weight; as the posts of a door, the sides of a fire-place or window.

JAMDANEE, a flowered Dacca wove muslin.

JAMES'-POWDER, a medicinal preparation used in fevers, consisting of 38 per cent. of antimonious acid and 62 of bone earth.

JANAPA, a name in Madras for the sunn hemp of India, *Crotalaria juncea*, which also furnishes a valuable fodder; gunny cloth is also said to be made from it. *See* GUNNY-BAGS.

JANGADA, a sort of rude log, float, or raft used on the Brazilian coasts and rivers.

JANITOR, a door-keeper.

JANKER, a long pole on two wheels, used in Scotland for transporting logs of wood.

JANNOCK, a bannock; oaten bread made into loaves.

JANTONG, the Malay name for a leaf of the plantain.

JAPAN, a varnish for metallic and other articles, made of linseed oil, umber, and turpentine; another kind is made of seedlac and spirits of wine with a colouring substance added.

JAPAN-EARTH, TERRA JAPONICA. *See* GAMBIER.

JAPAN-MAKER, a manufacturer of the varnish termed japan.

JAPANNED-LEATHER, enamelled or varnished leather prepared with several coatings of a mixture, consisting of linseed-oil, Prussian-blue and lamp-black, rubbed in with the hand and then dried in a stove.

JAPANNER, a varnisher: one who lays japan upon substances.

JAR, an earthenware pot or vessel, of variable shape and dimensions: as a measure of capacity for oil it contains from 18 up [illegible] gallons.

JARDINIER (French), a gardener.

JAREE, a name in Hindustan for the jujube fruit.

JARGONELLE, a large and esteemed kind of pear.

JARGOON, a gem, constituting a variety of Zircon.

JASERON (French), braid; fine gold chain.

JASEY, a worsted peruke or wig.

JASMINE OIL, a yellowish essential oil obtained from the flowers of several species of jasmine. The genuine oil of jasmine of the shops, is the produce of *Jasminum grandiflorum* and *officinale*, but a similar perfume is obtained from *J. Sambac*.

JASPER, a species of quartz, apparently coloured by iron; a precious stone, nearly as hard as agate, which occurs of many colours and varieties. The ancient arrow-heads, spear-heads, and other Indian implements of stone for use in war or in the chase, were chiefly formed of native blood-red jasper, exceedingly fine and hard, and often times emulating the appearance of the semi-pellucid gems.

JATAI, a Brazilian name for the locust-tree *Hymenæa courbaril*.

JATAMANSI, the Indian name for spikenard, *Nardostachys Jatamansi*.

JATEE, the common Indian name for *Jasminum grandiflorum*.

JATIPATRI, an Eastern name for mace.

JATIPHALI, a Sanscrit name for the nutmeg.

JATROPHA-OIL. *See* PHYSIC NUT.

JATTE (French), a porringer; a wooden bowl.

JAUGEUR (French), a gauger.

JAULINGITE, a new mineral resin obtained from the lignite of Jauling.

JAUNTING-CAR, a light car used in Ireland.

JAVA RUPEE, a Dutch silver coin, passing current in the Eastern Archipelago for about 1s. 8d.

JAVELAGE (French), laying corn in heaps to dry.

JAVELIN MAN, a sheriff's guard at assizes.

JAWATRI, a name in Hindustan for mace.

JAW-LEVER, an instrument for opening the mouth and administering medicine to cattle.

JAWS, the inner ends of the booms or gaffs of a ship hollowed in.

JEAN, a twilled cotton made both striped and white. Satin jeans are woven like satin, with a smooth glossy surface, and are used for stays, shoes, children's frocks, &c.

JEDDART-JUG, an old brass vessel, holding about 8 Scotch gills, still used as a standard measure, being kept in the custody of the Dean of Guild.

JEEAPOOTRA, a name in Hindustan for the nuts of *Putranjiva Roxburghii*, which are strung by the natives round the necks of their children, as an amulet to keep them in health.

JEERA, an Indian name for cumin-seed.

JEERS, tackles used in a ship, for hoisting the lower yards.

JEGGET, a sausage.

JELLY, a homogeneous mass. The principal animal jellies are gelatin, glue, and isinglass; the vegetable jellies are those in which the syrups of fruits are made into preserves.

JELLY-MOULD, a confectioner's shape for making jelly in.

JEMIDAR, a subaltern native officer in India.

JEMMIES, a species of woollen cloth made in Scotland, also called shafts; house-breakers' tools.

JENMY, an owner of slaves in Malabar.

JENNET, a Spanish horse.

JENNETING, an early apple.

JENNY, a spinning machine.

JEROATCHEREE, an Indian name for nux vomica seeds.

JERKED BEEF, beef hung or dried in the sun.

JERMAHEE, an Indian name for *Cocculus Indicus*.

JERQUER, a custom-house officer; a searcher.

JERQUING, the search of a ship by a custom-house officer, called a jerquer, to ascertain if there are any unentered goods, concealed.

JERSEY, one yarn of wool.

JERUSALEM ARTICHOKE, the *Helianthus tuberosa*: the tubers have a culinary value, and the stems abound in useful fibre.

JERUSALEM OAK, a name for the *Chenopodium Botrys*, a fragrant plant, said to be a powerful expectorant.

JESSE, a large branched candlestick.

JET, a variety of soft bituminous coal, admitting of a fine polish, which is worked up into many kinds of ornaments, such as brooches, bracelets, earrings, &c.; a spout of water; a tube for melted metal in a mould.

JETEEH, an Indian name for the *Marsdenia tenacissima*, a small climbing plant, from the fibres of which the Rajmahl mountaineers make their bow-strings.

JETHIMADH, a vernacular name in Hindustan for liquorice. [polishing grates.

JET-LUSTRE, a Bohemian black-lead for

JETSAM, goods cast into the sea from a ship, in stress of weather, &c., which sink and remain under water. *See* FLOTSAM and LAGAN-GOODS.

JETTIMADH, a name in India for liquorice root.

JETTY, the projecting part of a wharf; a mole or timber pier of slight construction, to land goods and passengers on.

JET-WORKER, a turner who shapes ornaments from jet.

JEWEL, a precious stone; a gem.

JEWEL-BLOCKS, blocks at the yard-arms of a ship, for the studding-sail halyards to pass through.

JEWEL-CASE, a lady's case for keeping gems and ornaments in.

JEWELLERS'-GOLD, gold with an alloy of copper or silver in variable proportion. For trinkets the alloy is about 25 per cent. of copper added to the gold.

JEWELLERS'-ROUGE, a kind of red putty powder used for polishing jewellery.

JEWELLERS'-SWEEPS, a general name for the scraps, dust, and washings remaining in jewellers' workshops, gold-pen manufactories, &c. which are collected by persons who separate the gold and silver from the refuse.

JEWELLERY, a general name for ornaments for the person, of silver, gold, enamels, precious stones, &c.

JEW'S HARP, a metal instrument for music, played in the mouth.

JEW'S-MALLOW, a name for the plant yielding the jute fibre.

JEWUL, JHEWUL, the name in Bengal for a gum-resin that exudes from the bark of *Odina wodier*.

JHAPEES, peculiar umbrella-shaped hats, worn by the lower class of Assamese, made from the coarse leaves of the Toko-pat palm (*Livistonia Jenkinsiana*, Griffith). The leaf of the talipot palm (*Corypha Taliera*) is used for the same purpose.

JHOOL-DOOM, a kind of white or black blanket, made by the natives of India, worth about 6s.

JHUGGERY, a mixture of tobacco, molasses, and opium, which is smoked by some of the lower class natives in the East.

JIB, the projecting frame of a crane; a triangular ship's sail set on a stay, forward.

JIB-BOOM, the spar rigged out beyond the bowsprit; the flying jib-boom is another added spar.

JIB-DOOR, a door made flush with the wall on both sides.

JIGGER, a potter's wheel, by which earthenware vessels are shaped, &c. by a rapid motion; a small ship-tackle used about decks or aloft; a miner who cleans ores in a wire sieve; a machine to steady a cable.

JIGGING, in mining, the process of sorting ore, by passing it through a griddle or wire-bottomed sieve. [GIGOT.

JIGOT, the hip joint of lamb or mutton. *See*

JIQUILITE, a Spanish name in Guatemala for the indigo plant.

JINGALL, a small portable piece of ordnance, fired on the ground, which rests on a long slender butt-end and a pair of legs.

JINGLE, GINGLE, a covered two-wheeled public car used in Cork. *See* GINGLEMAN.

JINGUN, the name in Upper India for a gum-resin that exudes from the bark of *Odina wodier*, called in Bengal, Jewul.

JINTAN, the Malay name for seeds.

JIPPO, a kind of women's stays.

JIRA, the Hindoo name for cumin seed.

JOANESE, another name for the Joe, a Portuguese gold coin.

JOAR, a vernacular name in India for the farinaceous seeds of *Holcus sorghum*: the stalks afford sugar, but in less quantity than the *Holcus saccharatus*, which has recently been introduced into culture in Europe and North America for extracting sugar from.

JOB, a piece of work; casual employment; to buy and sell as a broker; to let out horses and vehicles for hire.

JOBBER, a person who undertakes small pieces of work; an outside or wholesale dealer on the Stock Exchange, who makes the price at the market value for joint-stock or public securities between the buyer and seller; being the intermediate agent between the stock-broker and the public; a petty-dealer in cattle, &c.

JOBBING-OFFICE, a printing-office, where small jobs are undertaken, as the printing of hand or posting bills, circulars, cards, &c.

JOB-MASTER, a livery stable-keeper; one who lets out horses and carriages.

JOB-PRINTER, a printer in a small line of business.

JOB'S TEARS, a popular name for the stony bead-like seeds of a grass, the *Coix lachryma*, used for making necklaces, &c., and valued for supposed medicinal qualities.

JOCH, an Austrian land-measure equal to 1·[illegible] acre or [illegible] square yards.

JOCKEY, a horse-dealer or trainer; one who rides a horse in a race.

JOE, a Portuguese and Brazilian gold coin, worth about 36s.

Joggles, pieces of hard stone introduced in a joint; particular kinds of connecting joints in masonry.

Johannes, a Portuguese gold coin of eight dollars.

Johannisberger, a name for a kind of hock wine.

Johannis-brod, a German name for the pod of the carob-tree. *See* Carob-fruit.

John Dory, an excellent table fish, the *Zeus faber*, common in the European seas.

Johnny-cake, a West-Indian name for small meal-cakes, toasted on the embers.

Joiner, a carpenter who does the neat or fine woodwork in ships and buildings, and is therefore distinguished from the shipwright and carpenter; sometimes, however, the trades are combined.

Joiners' Company, one of the minor incorporated livery companies of London which has no hall.

Joint, a junction of wood, &c.; the limb of an animal cut up by the butcher.

Jointing-plane, the largest plane used by carpenters and joiners.

Joints, places where two parts are united, or where pieces are articulated with each other, as in gas-pipes, &c.

Joint-stock, a common fund or stock formed by the contributions or paid-up shares of different persons.

Joint-stock Company, an association with a capital formed of shares or contributions, to carry on any undertaking requiring large funds.

Joists, beams or cross pieces; the timber on which the flooring of buildings is laid; there are bending-joists and bridging-joists.

Jolly-boat, a small boat, usually hoisted at a ship's stern, and sometimes termed a yawl.

Jolt, to jerk or shake.

Jondeland, a land-measure of Denmark, equal to 6627 English square yards.

Jones (French), rushes.

Jornaleros (Spanish), day-labourers.

Jorum, a full bowl.

Joseph (French), very thin paper; silver or blotting paper.

Jostick, aromatic or fumigating wood, used in China for matches, &c.

Jostiks, a name in Cuddapah and other parts of India for pastiles.

Joucatte, Jucat, a Scotch liquid measure synonymous with gill.

Jour (French), [illegible]; a Japanese beverage.

Journal, a ship's log-book; a day-book; a diary or register of daily transactions in business; a daily newspaper; the bearing portion of the shaft in machinery; that which revolves on a support situated between the power and the resistance.

Journalist, a news' writer; an editor.

Journeyman, one who works for hire by the day; a mechanic employed to work for another in his particular trade.

Jow, a minute linear measure in the East Indies, represented by a grain of rice; 8 jows making 1 angle of 2 11-80th inches; a name in India for barley.

Jowl, Jole, the cheek or head of a pig salted.

Judge, a measuring staff for estimating excavating work done in coal-mines; a civil officer appointed to try causes, or preside over a court of justice.

Judges' Chambers, the private offices of a judge, in the inns of a court, &c.

Judge's Order, an order supposed to be signed before a judge in chambers, in which the defendant to an action admits the sum named in the order to be due by him to the plaintiff, and undertakes to pay it, as well as the costs of the action, in the manner and at the time specified on the face of the order.

Judgment, a compulsory decree; the sentence pronounced in a cause by a judge.

Judgment-debt, a security debt, legalized by a judge's order, under which the creditor can at any time issue execution against the debtor's goods and chattels. These debts have the preferential claim for payment in full out of an estate, before bond or simple contract debts.

Judiega, Spanish olives, not fit for eating, but used for making oil.

Judwar, an Arab name for the round zedoary (*Curcuma zerumbet*), which resembles ginger in flavour, though less pungent and agreeable.

Juephul, the name in Hindustan for nutmeg.

Juft, Youft, a Russian name for hide.

Jug, a pitcher, or water vessel.

Jugere, an ancient measure of about half an acre.

Jugged-hare, hare cut into pieces, and stewed, with wine and other flavourings.

Juggler, a conjurer.

Juice, the succulent or fluid part of meat; the water of fruit; the sap of vegetables.

Jujube, the fruit of the *Zizyphus vulgaris* and *jujuba*, which nearly resembles a small plum, and is sweet and mealy; the former are brought into this country from the South of Europe, in a half dried state, and were formerly much used in pectoral decoctions. The bark and root are used medicinally in the East. The term jujube is, however, very generally applied by chemists and confectioners to a thickened mucilaginous lozenge.

Juk, Juz, a name in Constantinople for the sum of 100,000 aspers.

Jule, a name for the paul, a Roman coin worth about [illegible].

Julep, an American drink, consisting of a solution of sugar in an aromatic water, with a seasoning of mint, &c.

Julienne, a kind of light, thin, vegetable soup.

Jullalya, an Indian name for hard wheat.

Jumalgoota. *See* Jamalgota.

Jumba, a Malayan land-measure, 12 feet square, or 144 feet superficial; in Prince of Wales Island, the umba is the 400th part of the orlong, which is 1⅓ acre.

Jumboo, a brass glass for wine, used in India.

Jument (French), a mare; a mould for casting money.

Jumento (Spanish), an ass; a beast of burthen.

Jumfras, a liquid measure in Lapland, equal to about three-quarters of an English pint.

JUMPER, an iron punch, with a steel-like chisel point, used for boring rocks before blasting; a name for the maggots of the cheese-fly, *Piophila casei*.

JUNGLE, a general name in the tropics for thick brushwood, or very high grass; land covered with forest trees.

JUNIPER, a name for gin.

JUNIPER-BERRIES, the fleshy galbules of *Juniperus communis*, employed in medicine; but their chief consumption is for flavouring the spirit called gin.

JUNIPER-GUM, a name for African incense, or olibanum resin, commonly attributed to the *Juniperus Lycia*; also for gum sandarac, the produce of *Thuja articulata*. *See* ARAR.

JUNIPER-OIL, a volatile oil, obtained from the berries of *Juniperus communis*. It is white or yellowish, light, very liquid, of hot and acrid juniper taste, and very strong smell. It is prepared on a large scale in Holland, and often adulterated with turpentine.

JUNK, hard salted beef supplied to ships; old and condemned pieces of rope and cordage, cut into short lengths, and used for making mats, swabs, and oakum, &c.; a Chinese vessel.

JUNK-DEALER, a marine store-dealer; one who vends old rope.

JUNKERITE, a name given by some mineralogists to spathic iron.

JUNKET, a dish of curdled cream and milk.

JUNK-RING, a steam-tight packing round the piston of a steam engine.

JUPE, a sort of pelisse or short mantle, formerly worn by women and children; a flannel shirt or jacket.

JUPON (French), an under-petticoat.

JURERB, a land measure in Cabul, half an English acre.

JUREMA-BARK, an astringent bark, said to be obtained from the *Acacia jurema*, a native of Brazil.

JUROR, a member of a jury; one of a body summoned to try a cause.

JURY, a body of men sworn to decide upon facts according to the evidence produced before them.

JURYMAN, a person summoned to attend on a jury.

JURY-MAST, a temporary spar rigged as a mast, in place of one lost or carried away by storm, &c.

JUSSI, a delicate fibre produced in Manila from some undescribed plant, and of which dresses, &c. are made.

JUSTICOAT, a waistcoat with sleeves; a close coat.

JUSTINE, an Italian coin worth about 5s.

JUTE, an annual plant common in Bengal, the *Corchorus olitorius*. There are two varieties of the plant, the green and the reddish, known by the local names of pat and bun-pat. A coarse kind of cloth is woven from the jute, and affords the materials of the well-known gunny-bags of India. *See* GUNNY-BAGS.

JUVANEE, a name in India for the *Ptychotis ajowain*. *See* AJOUAN.

JUVIA, a South American name for the Brazil nut (*Bertholletia excelsa*).

JUWANSA, a name for the camels' thorn (*Alhagi maurorum*), a thorny shrub used for making tatties or screens, to hang at windows and doors to keep out the heat and dust. It also furnishes the manna of the desert.

JYNTEE, a name, in India, for the *Æschynomene Sesban*, which yields an excellent charcoal used for making gunpowder.

K.

KABAK, an inn in Russia.

KABAN, a weight of Ternate, one of the Molucca islands. *See* CABAN.

KABANI, an attorney in the Levant.

KABBELOW, codfish salted and hung for a few days; a name in parts of Scotland for a mess of cabbage and potatoes.

KABOB, a Turkish dish.

KABONG, a name in Malacca for the Gomuto palm, the *Arenga saccharifera*, cultivated there chiefly for its sap, to make jaggery or coarse sugar; but which also yields a strong fibre. *See* EJOO-FIBRE.

KABOOK, a name for clay iron-stone, the decomposition of which forms a productive reddish loam in Ceylon.

KABOOKA, an African caravan of slaves and merchandise in the Congo, Loando, and neighbouring districts.

KACHAH, the Malay name for glass.

KACHEL, a Dutch tile; an earthen vessel.

KADI-KANE, an Indian name for millet, *Panicum miliaceum*.

KADUKAY, in India, powdered myrabolams.

KAFA, a name in the Friendly islands for sinnet made from cocoa-nut coir.

KAFFAK, a Turkish shoe merchant or dealer in slippers.

KAFILAH, an African caravan consisting of from 1800 to 2000 camels.

KAGNE, a kind of vermicelli.

KAHAWON. *See* CAHUN.

KAHOO, an East Indian name for the lettuce.

KAI, a Malayan grain measure. *See* COYAN.

KAHN (German), a boat.

KAIL-BROSE. *See* KALE.

KAIL-YARD, a common term in Scotland for a kitchen-garden.

KAIMESTER (German), a wharfinger.

KAIN-KANI, the Malay name for linen; kain-kalambu, being gauze; kain-layer, canvas; kain-kipri, diaper; kain-panas, flannel.

KAJAWEHS, panniers for a camel in which women ride in Persia.

KAKABALLI, a common wood of Demerara, which is very durable in salt water, possessing the quality of resisting the depredations of the sea-worm and barnacle. It may be had from 6 to 14 inches square.

KAKOON, one of the Hindoo names for *Panicum italicum*.

Kalamkari, the Malay name for calico.

Kalande, a native goldsmith's weight in Ceylon, almost obsolete, equal to 24 of a large red seed used for its subdivisions. The kalande represents about 73¼ grains.

Kalauy, the eighth part of a paw or seer in the southern Mahratta country, the paw being 1 5-16ths quart.

Kaldei, the Malay name for the ass.

Kale, Kail, the generic name for colewort, a kitchen plant; a kind of pottage made with greens.

Kaleidoscope, a highly ingenious optical instrument, showing, by the change of position of small pieces of coloured glass, a great variety of beautiful designs, which have been found very useful to pattern-drawers. It was invented by Sir David Brewster of Edinburgh.

Kalfaterer (German), one who caulks seams.

Kallingee, a weight in Ceylon used for pearls, supposed, like the chow, to contain 320 fractional parts. One kallingee is equal to 20 manjadies, each containing 7⅛ grains troy.

Kalmuck, a kind of shaggy cloth or bear-skin; a coarse cotton fabric made of various colours in Prussia.

Kambing, the Malay name for a sheep or goat.

Kambou, a name in the Kurile islands for the *Fucus saccharinus*, called by the Russians sea-cabbage; a favourite article of food among all classes in the Japanese empire.

Kamisol (German), a waistcoat or jacket.

Kammerer (German), a chamberlain or treasurer.

Kan, a liquid measure in Batavia of 91 cubic inches: 83 are equal to about 10½ gallons; 388 Batavia kans make one leaguer or 100 English gallons.

Kanasterre, a rush basket.

Kangan. *See* Cangan.

Kangaroo, a marsupial animal peculiar to Australia, which is hunted for its flesh and its skin. The tail makes excellent soup, and the skin when tanned forms a soft and durable shoe leather.

Kaninchen (German), a rabbit.

Kanna, a dry and liquid measure of Sweden, 100 being equal to 57·60 gallons.

Kanne, the unit for liquid measure in the Netherlands, corresponding to the French litre, and equal to 1¾ imperial pint; about 4½ go to the imperial gallon.

Kaolin, a porcelain earth derived from the decomposition of the feldspathic granites, and much used for fine pottery. This earth is met with in Assam, Bangalore, Madras, China, and other parts of Asia, whence the name is derived.

Kapak, the Malay name for a hatchet or axe.

Kapas, a name in the East for cotton wool, and for the herbaceous cotton plant.

Kaper, Caper, a name, in Scotland, for an oat-cake buttered, with a slice of cheese on it.

Kapitia, a resin or lacquer obtained in Ceylon from the sap of the *Croton lacciferum*.

Kapok, a name, in the Eastern archipelago for the cotton down enveloping the seeds of the silk cotton-tree, *Bombax pentandrum*. It is used by the poor inhabitants for stuffing chairs, pillows, &c., but is seldom or never used for beds, it being thought unwholesome to sleep upon.

Kapp, a dry measure used in Sweden, equal to an English gallon, but in some places rather more.

Kapulaga, the Malay name for cardamoms.

Kapur-barus, the name for the best camphor in the East.

Kapur-tohor, the Malay name for lime; kapur-makan being fine or shell lime.

Karbi, a Hindoo name for the *Sorghum vulgare*.

Karch, an Austrian weight of 403·80 lbs. avoirdupois. *See* Charge.

Karman. *See* Buck-wax.

Karmesses, fairs held in Belgium and Holland.

Karocawn, a term applied to a species of money on some parts of the West coast of Africa, consisting of gold drawn out into a fine wire, and cut afterwards into small pieces.

Karoh, another name for the coss, an Indian itinerary measure.

Karoo-vailum Gum, an Indian name (at Madura) for the gum of *Acacia Arabica*.

Kaross, a skin cloak very neatly made by the Kafirs, and which are much esteemed for driving wrappers, railway and carriage rugs, &c.; they are made of the wild cat, silver and red jackal, mixed jackal, antelope, and weasel.

Kas, a horse-hair sieve; a negro drum.

Kassa, a kind of fine catechu in cakes, made in India from the nuts or seeds of the *Areca catechu*.

Katchung-oil, an Eastern name for ground-nut oil, expressed from the seeds of *Arachis hypogæa*.

Katumbar, the Malay name for coriander.

Kauf (German), a purchase or bargain.

Kaufmann, a merchant or tradesman in Germany.

Kava. *See* Cava.

Kavaroo, the Tamil name for *Eleusine coracana*, a species of millet.

Kavel-mell, a large sledge-hammer used in Scotland for breaking stones.

Kayla, the Hindoo name for the banana.

Kayu-manis, the Malay name for cinnamon.

Keatib, a Turkish scribe, who writes letters, petitions, contracts, &c.

Keaves, Cuves, chemical vessels employed to contain salts.

Keb, a term in Scotland for a premature birth in animals; a slink lamb, &c.

Kebabs, small pieces of roasted meat, dressed with fresh parsley and celery, sold in the Turkish bazaars for dinner.

Kebbuck, a common name for cheese in Scotland.

Keckling, a sailor's name for old rope wound round cables to keep them from chafing.

Keckling-pins, a name in Scotland for wires or needles used in knitting stockings.

KEDGE, a small anchor with an iron stock, used for warping, or for riding in a harbour or river.

KEEL, the lowest and principal timber of a vessel, running the whole length and supporting the frames and hull; a lighter or barge, a flat-bottomed vessel used in the Tyne for carrying coals to colliers. It contains about 8 Newcastle chaldrons = 15½ London chaldrons or 21 tons 4 cwt; but is commonly taken at 21 tons 1 cwt. 8 quarters.

KEELAGE, duty paid for a ship entering the port of Hartlepool.

KEELER, one who manages coal-barges and colliers.

KEELFAT, a vessel in which liquor is set to cool.

KEELING, a name in some places for the codfish, *Morrhua vulgaris*.

KEELSON, a timber placed over the keel on the floor timbers, and running parallel.

KEEN, sharp; having a fine edge.

KEEPER, a preserver, a defender; one who has the custody of prisoners, or of deranged persons; one who has the care of a park or other enclosure, or the custody of beasts; a guard ring worn by married females, above the wedding ring.

KEEPSAKE, a remembrance or gift-token.

KEESLIP, a name in Scotland for the stomach of the calf used in curdling milk for cheese; also for the *Galium* plant or cheese rennet, used as a substitute. *See* KESLOP.

KEEVE, a large vat used in the mining districts; a mash-tub or vessel employed in brewing; to tilt a cart, to unload it.

KEFKE, the Turkish name for a purse of silver, = 500 piastres.

KEG, a small wooden cask or barrel containing 4 or 5 gallons: paint, lard, Dantzic beer, oysters, &c. are packed in kegs, and will weigh about 28lbs.

KEHEL, a powdered frankincense or rosin, with which the Arab women darken their eyelids and eyebrows.

KEHLING (German), fresh cod-fish.

KEIR, a kind of boiler used in a bleachery.

KEITH, in Scotland, a bar laid across a river or stream to prevent the ascent of salmon.

KELINGOO, an Indian name for sweet potatoes, of which there are many varieties; as velly kelingoo, sury kelingoo, aivully kelingoo, linevully kelingoo, &c.

KELKEL, a slice of sole dried and salted.

KELLA, an Arabian dry measure, the fortieth part of the tomand; and equal to 4 1-5th lbs.

KELLACH, a kind of sledge or wicker cart used in Scotland.

KELLAT, a weight at Suez, of four grains, the 18th part of a dram.

KELLEK, a kind of raft used on the river Euphrates.

KELLOW, a name for black-lead.

KELONTER, a Persian magistrate.

KELP, the commercial name for the ash obtained by the incineration of various sea-weeds. Kelp was largely manufactured on the northern shores of Scotland until about the year 1817, when the removal of the salt-duty made the manufacture unprofitable.

KELSON. *See* KEELSON.

KELT, a name in Scotland for cloth with the nap, generally made with native black wool; a spawning salmon.

KELTER, a wine-press in Germany.

KEMELIN, a brewer's vessel.

KEMENGEH, an Arab violincello with two strings.

KEMESTER, the name in Scotland for a wool-comber.

KEMO SHELLS, an eastern name for the large heavy shells of *Tridacna gigas*. *See* CLAM.

KEMP, KEMPTY, the coarse rough hairs of wool, which is avoided by the manufacturer in his purchases of wool, deteriorating, as it does, the appearance of even common fabrics by its inferiority and harshness, and not taking dye readily. The kemp of Cashmere goats' wool is now, however, made into coarse cloth.

KEMPER, a well-known name in Scotland for a competitor among reapers; one who strives to outrun the others in the quantity of work done.

KEMPLE, in Scotland, 40 wisps or bottles of straw or hay.

KEMP-SEEDS, a Scotch term for the sifting or refuse of oats, in making oatmeal.

KEN, a long measure of Siam, the half of the vouah, and equal to 37½ inches.

KENDOO, a vernacular name in Bengal for Indian ebony, the *Diospyros Melanoxylon*. The bark is astringent.

KENGUEL, the seeds of a species of *Gundelia*, which are roasted and used as coffee in parts of Turkey.

KENNEL, a watch-dog's house; a building for a pack of hounds; the channel or water-course in a street.

KENNEL-COAL. *See* CANNEL-COAL.

KENNEL-RAKER, a rag-gatherer; a bone-grubber.

KENNETS, a coarse cloth made in Wales.

KENT, a long shepherd's staff or leaping pole.

KENTLEDGE, pigs of iron used for ballast in a ship.

KEORA-OIL, KETOKE-OIL, an essential oil obtained in the East from the *Pandanus odoratissimus*.

KEPER, KOPER, a name in Germany for marsella, a kind of twilled linen.

KEPOOR, a Hindoo name for amber.

KEPPING, a division of the Spanish dollar in Sumatra, which is divided into 400 keppings; eight therefore are worth about 1d.

KERAN, a Persian silver coin worth about 1s.

KERAT, the Egyptian name for the carat.

KERBSTONE, the edge flag-stones of a paved footway or causeway. *See* CURB.

KERCHIEF. *See* HANDKERCHIEF.

KERF, a notch or slit made in wood by cutting.

KERIEH, a Turkish gold coin of 21 piasters under the old coinage, but the kerieh of the reigns of the sultans Mahmoud and Abdul Mejid is worth only 18 piasters, or the 6th of a pound sterling.

KERMES, an insect obtained from the *Quercus coccifera*, which furnishes a red colouring matter. Also the name for a brick-red mineral powder, a factitious sulphuret of antimony, for dyeing, and formerly used in medicine.

KERNED-LETTER, those letters of printing-type which hang over the shank.

KERNEL, the edible substance contained in the shell of a nut.

KEROSENE, a liquid hydro-carbon obtained from a species of bituminous shale in New Brunswick.

KERSA, a name in Cambay for a large package.

KERSEY, a very coarse stuff usually ribbed, woven from long wool; chiefly manufactured in the North of England.

KERSEYMERE, a thin fabric generally woven plain from the finest wools, and made chiefly in the West of England.

KESHOOR, the Bengalee name for *Rottleria tinctoria*.

KESLOP, a name for rennet, the substance used in curdling milk. *See* KEESLIP.

KESME, a name in Berber, Nubia, for the sum of 2 dollars.

KESSEL-BIER, home-brewed beer in Germany.

KESSKIKER, a German brazier or tinker.

KESTING, KESLING, a small green plum; a bullace.

KETCH, a two-masted vessel with the main mast placed amidships, and a mizen-mast, ranging from 100 to 250 tons burden.

KETCHUP. *See* CATSUP.

KETTEL (German), a little chain.

KETTFEIDE (German), thrown-silk.

KETTLE, a metal boiler, saucepan, stewpan, or other cooking vessel for heating and boiling water for domestic purposes.

KETTLE-DRUM, a musical instrument used in military bands, consisting of two basins of copper or brass with goatskin, or vellum stretched over them.

KETTLE-DRUMMER, the musician who plays on the kettle-drum.

KEUFTER, a paste made from raisins exported from Turkey.

KEVEL, a strong piece of wood bolted to a stanchion for belaying ropes to; a frame for spreading the main-sail.

KEVINS, a term in Scotland for the refuse separated from grain.

KEY, an instrument by which the bolt of a lock is pushed backward or forward, or clock-work machinery is wound up; an index; that which serves to explain any thing difficult to be understood; in flooring, the board last laid down.

KEY-BUGLE, a brass horn or musical instrument.

KEY-HOLE, the perforation in a door or lock for receiving a key.

KEYL, a local name in Scotland for a bag or sack.

KEYS, small shoals or uninhabited islets; the stops of a musical wind instrument; the fingering notes of a piano-forte.

KEY-SCREW, a lever for turning screws.

KEY-STONE, the middle voussoir, or centre-stone of an arch.

KHALSAH, a government rent-roll in India.

KHAM, a name in Turkey for cotton cloth not dyed.

KHANCHAA, an Indian weight, ranging from 231 to 236 grains.

KHANSAMAH, an Indian butler.

KHEL-BOAT, a boat in Assam, the roof of which is covered with the leaves of the *Livistona Jenkinsiana*, a palm.

KHENNA, a Persian dye for the hair, used in the baths of Constantinople.

KHISMIS, the Malay name for raisins; also a preserve or sweetmeat. *See* KISSMISS.

KHORMA, a Malay name for the date.

KHUNDER. *See* KUNDER.

KHUS-KHUS. *See* CUSCUS.

KHUSREH SURVEY, a private or native survey of land in India.

KHWAY, a Burmese measure of capacity, equal to about one gallon.

KIABOOCA-WOOD. *See* KYABOOCA.

KIAT, a name in Rangoon for the tical, a piece of silver money weighing 10 dwts. 10½ grs.

KIBKAR, a small currency of Abyssinia, consisting of 8 borjookes, or glass beads.

KIBBLE, a bucket, usually of iron, for raising ore to the surface from a mine-shaft.

KIBBLING-MILL, a hand-mill of steel, attached to a post, for crushing or grinding beans, pease, malt, &c.

KIBITZKA, a one-horse vehicle on two wheels, used in Siberia.

KID, a young goat; a fagot or bundle of heath and furze.

KIDDER, an engrosser of corn or other merchandise. *See* FORESTALLING.

KIDDERMINSTER, an ingrain carpeting, originally named from the town where it was principally made, but the largest quantity is now manufactured in Scotland. Kidderminster is composed of two webs, each consisting of a separate warped woof; the two are interwoven at intervals, to produce the figures, as the two webs are passed at intervals through each other, each part being at one time above, and at the other below. When different colours are used, the figure will be the same on both sides, but the colours will be reversed: these are made entirely of wool.

KIDDLE, a kind of weir in a river, for catching fish.

KIDNAPPING, enticing away persons to enter the army or navy, &c.

KIDNEY-BEAN, the common name of plants of the genus *Phaseolus*, much used as a vegetable.

KIDNEYS, glands lying in the lumbar regions of animals; ox and sheep kidneys are often sold separately by butchers.

KIDS, a technical name for bundles of sticks and bushes planted on a sea beach, around which collect the waifs and strays of the ocean, sand, and other matters.

KIEN, a German name for the fir or pine, and rosin obtained from it.

KIERA, a name in India for the seeds of *Amarantus frumentaceus*, which are ground into flour. The leaves and tender tops of another species are much esteemed by the natives, and eaten by them in their curries, or as a substitute for asparagus.

KIFFEKIL, a name for meerschaum.

KIJANG, a Malay name for the roe or hart.

KIKUEL OIL, the produce of the solid part of the seeds of *Salvadora Persica*, imported into Bombay from Guzerat, for local consumption.

KILDERKIN, a beer-cask, containing 2 firkins, or 18 gallons.

KILIARE, a measure of 1000 ares, equal to 119,604·6 square yards, or 24·71 imperial acres.

KILL, KEIL, the Turkish word for bristle, and for the coarse hair on goat-skins.

KILLAS, a name for clay slate.

KILLOW, KILO, a Turkish dry measure of very variable dimensions in different localities; in Constantinople equal to the Winchester bushel, and divided into 22 okes. In Alexandria, however, it is about 4·603½ bushels; in Bucharest nearly 11 bushels; and in Ibrail as much as 17½ bushels.

KILL-PAIN, an American specific or quack medicine, so called.

KILN, an oven for roasting or drying malt and grain, burning bricks, tiles, lime, &c.; a furnace for annealing glass and pottery ware.

KILOGONE, a geometrical figure, having [1000 sides.

KILOGRAMME, the French new pound, a measure of weight of 1000 grammes, equal to about 2 1-5th lbs. avoirdupois, or more exactly 2·2046 lbs.; 100 kilogrammes, or a quintal, is equal to 1·9686 cwt., 1000 kilogrammes, or the tonneau, to 19·686 cwt. To convert pounds avoirdupois into kilogrammes, or *vice versa*, divide or multiply by 2·2046.

KILOLITRE, a French dry and grain measure, the new muid = 35·3171 cubic feet.

KILOMETRE, a French itinerary measure, nearly 5 furlongs; also called a mille, the tenth of the new league, containing one thousand metres, equal to 1093·633 yards, or 4 furlongs, 213 yards, 1 foot, 11 inches.

KILOSTERE, one thousand stères, = 35,317·41 cubic feet.

KILT, a Highlander's petticoat; a loose dress extending to the knee.

KIMDIN, a name in Cambay for a bamboo basket.

KIMMEL, a name in Java and the Eastern archipelago, for a liqueur made from aniseed.

KIMMEN, KYMMOND, a name in Scotland for a milk pail, and for a large shallow brewer's tub.

KIN, another name for the catty, a Chinese weight. *See* CATTY.

KINCHIN, an Indian metal kettle.

KINE, an ancient collective name for cows.

KING, one of a set of chessmen, used in playing the game of chess.

KING-FISH, a common name given to several fishes; for instance, to the *Cybium Solandri*, and the *Polynemus plebeius* in the East Indies.

KING-POST, the middle post of a roof.

KING-WOOD, one of the most beautiful of the hard-woods imported; which reaches us from Brazil in trimmed logs, from 2 to 7 inches in diameter. It is believed to be derived from a species of *Triptolomea*. It is also called violet-wood, being streaked in violet tints of different intensities, finer in the grain than rosewood, and is principally used in turning and small cabinet-work, being generally hollow in the heart, and therefore too unsound for upholstery.

KINK, a twist or bend in a rope.

KINO, an astringent substance obtained from various Australian and Indian trees, and containing a large proportion of tannic acid. It occurs in shining grains of a rich ruby-red colour. In India, kino is used for dyeing cotton a nankeen colour, and is also employed in medicine.

KINRO, a small cake made in India of the mucilaginous seeds of *Salvia plebeia*, R. Brown, which, moistened with water, is used to plaster back women's hair, and to keep it glossy and in its place.

KINSH, a lever or bar for quarrying or raising stones.

KINTAL. *See* QUINTAL and CWT.

KIP, a weight for tin in Malacca, of 15 bedoors or 30 tampangs, and containing 40 lbs. 11 oz. avoirdupois.

KIPAS, the Malay name for a fan.

KIPE, a basket for catching fish.

KIPPERED FISH, salmon or other fish, salted, peppered, and dried.

KIPS, a name among tanners for the skins of young animals, though many kips belong to full grown cattle of small breed.

KIRBIAU, the Chinese name for a pipkin, also used by the Malays.

KIRK, the Scotch name for their Presbyterian or National church.

KIRLACHE, a kind of Turkish lighter, navigating the Danube, ranging from 30 to 100 tons.

KIRLANGHISH, a small Turkish vessel; a tender to the Admiral's ship.

KIRN, a churn; the last handful of grain cut down on the harvest-field in Scotland.

KIRN-MILK, a Scotch name for butter-milk.

KIRSCH, KIRSCHWASSER, cherry-water; a spirit distilled from cherries in Germany.

KISHMISH, a small kind of grape, from which the Shiraz wine is made in Persia. When dried in the form of raisins, it constitutes a large article of commerce in the Indian markets.

KIST (Hindustani), a stated or agreed payment or instalment; a portion of a tax paid by the ryot.

KISTBUNDEE, an Indian contract or agreement for payments of rent, duties, debts, &c. by instalments.

KISTNER, a trunk-maker in Germany.

KISTNAKAZ-BULLAH, a grain-measure in Bangalore, of 2 pucca seers, or 4 lb. 3 oz. 5½ drams.

KIT, a small fiddle; a large bottle; a milk-pail or churn; the tools, &c. of a workman; an outfit, as the chest of clothes of a seaman, the knapsack of a soldier; a small wooden vessel, in which fish is occasionally sold.

KITCHEN, the cooking-room or servants' room in a house.

KITCHEN-DRESSER, a frame with shelves and drawers, for keeping crockery ware, &c. for ready use.

KITCHEN MAID, a cook or servant.

KITCHEN-RANGE, a fire-grate and stove with oven and boiler, &c. for cooking.

KITCHEN-STUFF, a name for the fat and grease, or dripping, collected and sold by servants, and forming an ingredient in the common kinds of soap.

KITE, a boy's plaything for flying, with a string; sometimes used to carry a line over rivers, or elevated heights for engineering purposes; a name given to an accommodation bill.

KITKUTGAR, a table-servant in India.

KITTYSOLLS, paper parasols made in China, which are exported to India and the Straits settlements, packed in boxes of 100 each.

KITZE, the Turkish name for a purse of gold of 30,000 piastres.

KLACK, in Scotland, fishing-ground near the shore, as opposed to the haff or deep-sea fishing.

KLAFTER, an Austrian measure of length, containing 6 Vienna feet, and equal to 6·23 imperial feet, used also for timber.

KLAPA, the Malay name for the coco-nut.

KLEIN-SCHMIED (German), a white-smith.

KLEIN-WAARE, KLINGEN-WAARE (German), hardware.

KLEMPNER, a German tinker or tinman.

KLINGENSCHMIED, a German sword-cutler.

KLINGEN-WAARE. *See* KLEIN-WAARE.

KLIPSPRINGER, a Dutch name in the Cape colony for the *Antilope oreotragus*.

KLIPP-FISCH (German), lub-fish, salt-fish.

KLIP-SWEET, a species of bitumen oozing from the rocks of the Winterberger in the Cape colony, used by the natives to cure convulsions, &c.

KLOPPLER (German), a lace-maker.

KNACKER'S YARD, a horse-killer's yard; a place where dead carcases are taken to be cut up for their commercial uses.

KNAG, the shoot of a deer's horns.

KNAPPING HAMMER, a stone-breaker's hammer in Scotland.

KNEAD, to work off a soft mass, as of dough or clay.

KNEADING-MACHINE, an apparatus for working dough by means of a revolving spiral.

KNEADING-TROUGH, a deep tray, in which dough is mixed by bakers, and bread-makers.

KNECHT (German), a man-servant; a workman or journeyman.

KNEE, to elbow or bend in the middle; a crank; a bent piece of timber, or metal.

KNEE-CAP, a cover or protection for the knee of a stumbling-horse.

KNIFE. *See* KNIVES.

KNIFE-BASKET, a tray for holding table-knives.

KNIFE-BLADE, the metal or cutting part of the knife.

KNIFE-BOARD, a piece of wood, plain, or cased with leather for cleaning and polishing table-knives.

KNIFE-BOX, a box with partitions for keeping superior table or dessert-knives.

KNIFE-CLEANING MACHINE, a labour-saving machine for polishing knives. It consists of a series of brushes or leather pads which are made to revolve vertically. The knives are arranged in slits on the circumference of the case, and are subjected on each side to the revolving brushes.

KNIFE-HANDLE, the holding part of the knife; that to which the blade is affixed.

KNIFE-REST, a metal or glass article for a dinner table to rest carving-knives on.

KNIFE-SHARPENER, a steel or tool for giving a cutting edge to knives.

KNIFE-TRAY, a servant's tray for depositing knives in.

KNIGHT, a mounted horseman; one of the pieces used in playing the game of chess.

KNISTIR-GOLD, a German name for gold leaf or tinsel.

KNIT, to weave by the hand.

KNITTING-MACHINE, a machine for weaving and making knitted work, as nets, open curtains, &c.

KNITTING-NEEDLE, KNITTING-PIN, a metal, wooden, or bone pin for knitting.

KNIVES, cutting instruments for table use, and for various trades, &c. as clasp, drawing, putty, and pallette knives, pocket, or spring knives, desk knives, sportsmen's and gardeners' knives, pen-knives, fruit, ham, oyster, bread, butter, cooks', shoe, pruning, paring, plough knives, and other kinds; all of which differ in form or shape.

KNOB, a boss or protuberance; the handle for a door or drawer, &c., made of wood, brass, glass, slate, or some other material.

KNOCKER, an iron rapper or instrument for summoning at a door; a piece of wood to deaden the recoil of a wheel.

KNOLLS, a German name for lead ore separated from the smaller parts as they are raised from the shafts.

KNOPF-MACKER (German), a button-maker.

KNOT, a mark or division of the log-line, and name for the nautical mile of 2208 yards, 3 knots making a marine league, and 60 knots a degree. The line knots are placed at distances of 50 feet from each other. Now, as 120 times half a minute make an hour, and 120 times 50 feet make almost a geographical mile, so many knots will run from the reel in one experiment, as the vessel sails miles in an hour. The knot is used for ascertaining the speed of a ship's sailing, and answers to half a minute by the sand-glass, as the log-line runs out, as a mile does to an hour; that is, it is the 120th part of a mile; hence we say the ship is going nine knots, equivalent to nine nautical miles per hour. *See* LOG LINE. Knot is also a fastening in a rope. *See* HITCH and BEND.

KNOT-GRASS, the *Polygonum aviculare*, the small rugose nuts of which are reported to be emetic and purgative.

KNOUT, the ball or piece of wood that is struck in the game of shinty; a kind of Russian leather whip.

KNUBS, a name for the offal or waste silk, in winding off from the cocoon. A large quantity is imported under the names of "knubs and husks," which is carded and spun up into various common silk stuffs.

KOARK, a name in the interior of Persia for the shawl wool obtained from the double-coated goat of Angora.

KOARY, a fine kind of Indian grass, used for making mats.

KOB, KOBA, a species of African antelope, the *Antilope Senegalensis*.

KOBANG, a gold coin of Japan, the old Kobang of 100 mas being valued at 42s. 8d., the new one at 27s. 4d. There are half pieces of corresponding value.

KOBER (German), a basket or dorser.

KOBIL, a small boat. *See* COBLE.

KODA, a grain measure of Georgia, about 27 lbs.

KODAMA, a money of Japan, consisting of a round, thick lump of silver, passing in trade, and weighed in payment from one individual to another.

KODEE, a name in Sinde for various species of cowry; the shells are calcined, and the powder sprinkled over sores.

KODIE, a name in Java for the candy or bahar, a weight, of which there are two kinds, the large = to 610 lbs. avoirdupois, and the small to 407 lbs.

KOFF, a small two-masted Dutch vessel.

KOFFER-MACKER, a trunk maker in Germany.

KOFFO-HEMP, a name in the Moluccas for the fibres of the *Musa textilis*, a wild species of plantain, which yields the Manila hemp cordage of commerce.

KOHL, the German name for cabbage or colewort.

KOHL-RABI, a curious variety of cabbage, with a bulbed stalk, the rapecole (*Brassica oleracea*, var. *caula-rapa*).

KOIJANG, a name in Java for the coyan, equal to about 60 imperial bushels.

KOKF, a revenue measure of Japan, of 3 600 bags or bales of rice.

KOKRA-WOOD, another name for cocus-wood.

KOKUM-OIL, a concrete oil, obtained in India from the dried fruit of the *Garcinia purpurea*. It is used as an article of food, and as a medicine. *See* COCUM BUTTER.

KOLAS, glazed earthenware pans, used in the East by sugar-boilers and sweetmeat-makers.

KOLA-SEED, COLAS, the brown seed of the *Sterculia acuminata*, about the size of a pigeon's egg, which are so highly esteemed in Africa. When chewed or sucked, they are said to enhance the flavour of any thing eaten afterwards, and also to purify putrid water.

KOLE, a Malabar long measure for timber, equal to 28½ English inches.

KOMMODE (German), a chest of drawers.

KOMPOW, a strong white Chinese linen made of flax, passing as a medium of currency in some of the Philippine islands.

KOMST (German), curdled milk.

KONGPU, CONGPU, a name for the builders' foot measure in China, about ¾ of an inch more than the English foot.

KOODO, a large African antelope, the *Damalis strepsiceros*, which has fine long horns, with three elongated spiral turns.

KOOL, a Bengalee name for the fruit of the *Zizyphus jujuba*. *See* JUJUBE.

KOOLINJAN, a name in Hindustan for the Galanga root. *See* GALANGAL.

KOOLTOO, a name in Bengal for a species of buckwheat, *Fagopyrum esculentum*.

KOONGOONIE, a name in Bellary for the Italian millet, *Panicum Italicum*.

KOONGOO-TARO, an Indian name for the flowers of a species of *Tamarix*, used in dyeing.

KOONKEE, a grain-measure of India, of 5 chittacks. *See* CHITAK.

KOORA, a measure of capacity, in the South Mahratta country, of 31½ gallons.

KOORINGA-FIBRE, a good substitute for flax, prepared in Tanjore from the *Tylophora asthmatica*.

KOOROOMBA, a name in Ceylon for the young or green coco-nut.

KOOSUM, KOOSUMBA, a name in India for safflower; also for the *Schleichera trijuga*, a tree on which the best lac resin is formed.

KOOT, KOOTH, a name in Lahore and the Bengal bazaars for putchuk or costus root.

KOP, the Dutch unit of measures for dry wares, and the cube of the palm, answering to the French litre.

KOPECK. *See* COPECK.

KOPFEN, an Austrian liquid measure, 70 of which make up the wine eimer. *See* EIMER.

KOPF-STUCK, a silver coin of Bavaria, worth 8¼d; also called a shuster; in Brandenburg it passes for 24 kreuzers.

KOPRA. *See* COPPERAH.

KOQUERETTE-BALLI, a native wood of Demerara, which forms excellent rafters and beams for cottages, growing from 20 to 30 feet long, and from 4 to 6 inches in diameter.

KORB (German), a basket or hamper.

KORETZ, a Galician measure equal to 3¼ bushels.

KORREE, a Flemish weight corresponding to the French decigramme, or rather more than 1½ grain (1·543.)

KORSEC, KORZEC, a Polish weight equal to nearly 2 cwt.; also a corn-measure of about 3¼ to 3½ bushels.

KOSKOSSOO, in Tunis, a dry preparation of semola, or coarse meal.

KOSSANG, a petty money of account in the Malay peninsula; the fourth part of the mace.

KOST (German), board, food, or diet; hence the compound words kostganger, a boarder; kosthaus, a boarding-house; kostschule, a boarding-school, &c.

KOTAR, an eastern weight of 15½ lbs.

KOU, an ancient Chinese measure about 17½ gallons.

KOUBANKA, a kind of wheat grown in Russia.

KOUKAN, an ornamented silver bracelet.

KOU-KOU, a Tartar name for the St. Ignatius bean, the seeds of a species of *Strychnos* (*S. Sancti Ignatii*, the *Ignatia amara* of some authors), which enjoys a high reputation in the Chinese Materia Medica. It is bitter, and believed to be a good vermifuge, but is dangerous from the quantity of strychnine it contains.

KOUMIS, a liquor made in Tartary, from mares' and camels' milk, which has undergone a certain degree of vinous fermentation.

KOURIE, KOWRIE. *See* COWDIE PINE.

KOUSSO, a medicinal plant, the *Brayera anthelmintica*, a native of Abyssinia; which is reported to be a very effectual vermifuge.

KOVIORE, an Indian agrarian measure equal to 4 acres.

KOYAN, a variable weight for dry goods in the East; at Lombok it is equal to 33 piculs, at Batavia to 28, at Samarang, to 30, and at Singapore to 40. *See* COYAN.

KOYPUL, an Indian name for wild nutmegs.

KRAAL, an enclosure for cattle in the Cape colony; also applied to the huts of the natives.

KRAMA, a woman's wooden clog or sandal.

KRAMER, a German shopkeeper; a merchant trader.

KRAMERGEWICHT (German), avoirdupois weight.

KRAMERMEISTER, an alderman of the Grocer's guild in Germany.

KRAMMES (German), retail wares; commodities; articles of trade.

KRAMPLER, a German wool-carder.

KRANG, a name given by fishermen to the fleshy part of the whale after the blubber has been taken off.

KRAUT (German), colewort or cabbage.

KRAUTER-TABAK (German), herb tobacco.

KRAUTER-THEE, herb tea.

KREAT, CREAT, an infusion of the root of *Andrographis paniculata*, which is much esteemed as a tonic and stomachic bitter in the Peninsula of India, and also used in cholera and dysentery.

KREIDSCHNUR (German), a chalk-line or plumb-line.

KREISAMTMANN, the bailiff of a circle in Germany.

KREMSERWEISS, a pure carbonate of lead, of remarkably bright colour, made in Germany.

KREOSOTE. *See* CREASOTE.

KREUZER, KREUTZER, a German coin of variable value, in some places worth about the seventh part of a penny, in others, 30 kreuzers are equal to one shilling. In Frankfort, and the southern part of Germany, 4 pfennings make a kreuzer, and 3 kreuzers are equal to 1 penny sterling; and 35 to one shilling. In Bale, the kreuzer passes for 5 deniers, in the canton of Berne, for 6. The Austrian paper, marked zehn (10) kreuzers passes for 12 kreuzers. The larger kreuzer is worth 1 kreuzer and 1 pfenning.

KRIS, the Malay name for a dagger.

KRON-THALER, a German money; the crown-piece.

KROO, KROU, a measure of capacity on the west coast of Africa, varying from 4 to 12½ imperial gallons, in different localities; for palm oil it is 4 gallons, and weighs about 30 lbs.; in Accra and other parts, 50 lbs. A krou of rice weighs from 25 to 30 lbs.

KROOMEN, labourers employed at Sierra Leone, chiefly in boats and vessels; originally natives of the Kroo country, 150 miles to the southward and westward, whence their name.

KROSSAH, another name for the coss, an Indian itinerary measure.

KRUSE. *See* CRUSE.

KUCHEN (German), a cake or tart; a kitchen.

KUCHEN-MEISTER, the steward of a kitchen in Germany.

KUCHEN-ZETTEL, a German bill of fare.

KUCHOO, a name in Bengal for the large tuberous roots of *Arum Colocasia*, in the West Indies known as cocos or eddoes.

KUCHOORA, a name in Hindustan for the long zedoary, the root of *Curcuma Zerumbet*.

KUDA, a Malay name for the horse.

KUDAKUDA, the Malay name for spars.

KUDDIAKHAR, a local name in India for borax.

KUDEI, the Malay name for shop.

KUEPHUL, a name, in Hindustan, for the aromatic and stimulant bark of *Myrica sapida*, a favourite native medicine.

KUGEL-THEE (German), imperial tea.

KUJOOR, an Indian name for dates.

KULACK, COULACK, a Chinese grain-measure, in use in Java, = 7½ catties, of 46 measures, each of 5 gantangs, or about 9·83 lbs. avoirdupois. It is also another name for the bamboo.

KULIT, the Malay name for skin or leather.

KULLANGEE, CULLINGEY, an Eastern weight of about 78 grains, but in the Carnatic a little more. *See* CULLINGEY.

KULMET, a dry measure of Riga: 84 kulmets = 3½ English gallons.

KUMERA, the Maori name in New Zealand for the sweet potato.

KUMKUMA, an aromatic drug and perfume, obtained from *Didymocarpus aromaticus*; also the Malay name for saffron.

KUMLA, a name in Bengal for the sweet orange.

KUMMEL (German), cumin, or caraway seed.

KUMMEL-WASSER, brandy flavoured with cumin seeds.

KUMNYIAN, the name among the Malays for frankincense, or gum olibanum.

KUMOON, an Indian name for cumin seed.

KUMPF, a German dry measure of 1½ to 1⅗ gallon.

KUMUT, a kind of bark cloth, made in the Eastern archipelago, from the fibre of a species of *Artocarpus*.

KUNCHOORA, KUNKHOORA, Indian names for the China-grass cloth.

KUNDALOO, a large kind of nettle growing in the Himalayas, from the fibres of which the natives make rope for tying up their cattle, and snow-sandals.

KUNDE (German), a customer; a chapman.

KUNDEE, KHUNDEE, an Indian dry measure used for salt, grain, and some other goods, equal to 611 pounds avoirdupois.

KUNDEL, a name in Hindustan for the fetid gum-resin sagapenum.

KUNDOO, a name in Bengal for the seeds of the *Panicum Italicum*.

KUNJOO, a red powder made by steeping turmeric-root in an alkali, used in India for the forehead marks of the Hindoos.

KUNKUR, a variety of nodular limestone found in India, which is not easily calcined, and forms but a poor cement.

KUPFER (German), copper.

KUPOE, a Malayan grain measure. *See* COYAN.

KUPOOR, the Hindustani name for camphor.

KUPPAS, a name in India for cotton in the seed.

KURA-KURA, the Malay name for a land-tortoise.

KURBAU, the Malay name for the buffalo.

KURDEH, CURDEE, Indian names for safflower.

KURREE, a coarse kind of blanket, made by the hill people of India, from a curious downy substance, obtained from the leaves of plants.
KURSCHNER (German), a furrier; a skinner.
KURTAS, the Malay name for paper.
KURTAU, a Malay name for the mulberry.
KURUNDA, the Hindústani name for the *Carissa carandas*, an Indian plant, the acid fruits of which afford the well-known and favourite caranda-jelly.
KURUNJ-OIL, an oil expressed from the nut of the *Pongamia glabra*, and used in India externally as a stimulant; by some authorities this oil is said to be the produce of *Dalbergia arborea*.
KUSHMUT, an Indian name for the root of *Costus speciosus*, used to adulterate colombo root.
KUSHNEEZ, the Persian name for coriander [seed.
KUROFS, an Eastern name for celery seed, sold in all the bazaars as a stimulant.
KUSTENFAHRER (German), a coasting vessel.
KUTCHOORA, a general Indian name for the roots of *Curcuma longa* or turmeric.
KUTEERA, a gum obtained in India from the *Sterculia urens*, which has but a limited use, the want of adhesiveness rendering it unsuitable for the arts, while its difficult solubility renders it inferior to most of the gums for medicinal purposes. A similar gum, called kutira, is afforded by the *Cochlospermum gossypium*. This is the Bussora gum of Guibourt, in his Histoire de Drogues.
KUTKARANGA, KUTKULEGA, Indian names for the seeds of the *Cæsalpinia Bonducella*, which are a powerful tonic, and a valuable febrifuge.
KUTRAN, an Indian name for pitch.
KUX (German), a share in a mine.
KWAN, KOUAN, the Cochin China name for a string of about 600 "cash," the popular coin. Each kouan makes 10 heaps, or "tiens," each of 60 cash. The Spanish dollar averages about 4 kouan; in Upper Cochin China being worth 3 to 4 kouan, and in Lower Cochin China, 5 or 6 kouan. As a weight, 500 kan or catties, of 1¼ ounce each, make one kouan.
KWART, KWARTI, a measure of capacity in Poland and Gallicia, ranging from 1¼ to 1¾ pint.
KWARTEEL, KWARDEEL, a Dutch liquid measure, by which whale and seal oil is vended; ranging from 51 to 88 gallons.
KWATERK, a Polish liquid measure, the fourth of the kwarti.
KYABOOCA, an ornamental fancy wood obtained in the Eastern archipelago, from the knotty excrescences or burrs of *Pterospermum Indicum*. It is also called amboyna wood. It is much esteemed in China and India, where it is made into small boxes and writing-desks, and other ornamental works.
KYANIZING, a process of preserving vegetable fibre, by forcing a solution of corrosive sublimate into the pores of the timber. Several other processes have been carried into successful practice since that of the late Mr. Kyan of New York.
KYAR. *See* COIR.
KYAT, another name in Burmah for the tical, = 252 grains troy.
KYLOES, a name in Scotland for highland cattle, which are usually of small size and black.
KYPOO, an astringent extract made in Ceylon, resembling catechu.

L.

L, a Roman numeral denoting 50.
LA, LA, a name in the Pacific for the sail of a canoe, or other vessel, which is usually made of leaves sewed together.
LABDANUM, a scarce and expensive medicinal resin, obtained from the surface of the leaves of *Cistus Creticus* in Candia, &c. It is used in plasters, in perfumery, for pastiles, and as an expectorant.
LABELS, narrow slips of parchment, paper, &c. for writing names for articles, especially for chemists' preparations.
LABERDAN, a German name for salted codfish.
LABOR, a Mexican land-measure of 177 acres; work of any kind; a handicraft or trade.
LABORATORY, the workroom of an experimental chemist.
LABOURER, LABOURING-MAN, a workman, a journeyman, one who earns his living by toil and the use of his hands at some work; not a craftsman or artisan.
LABOUR-SAVING MACHINES, inventions which economize or diminish human toil.
LABRADOR-STONE, a kind of feldspar, exhibiting a play of colours, supposed to be produced by microscopic crystals of quartz included in the labradorite. It receives a good polish, and is valued for ornamental purposes on account of its beautiful colours.
LABRADOR TEA, a popular name for the leaves of the *Ledum latifolium*, which, from their narcotic properties are used medicinally, and to render beer heady.
L. A. C., an abbreviation used by the dispensing surgeon or chemist, implying that he is a "licentiate of the Apothecaries Company."
LAC, in Hindoo numeration, 100,000; a lac of rupees is therefore £10,000; a crore is 100 lacs; a resinous incrustation produced on the boughs of trees by the punctures of the *Coccus lacca* insect; and which forms the basis of dyes, varnishes, and sealing-wax, entering largely into commerce. Our imports of crude lac, and lac dye, amount to about 1500 tons a year, worth about £88,000.
LAC-DYE, small square cakes of lac, for dyeing red colours.

Lace, a tie or string; a delicate kind of net-work, consisting of silk, cotton, or flax; fine threads woven into narrow strips for ladies' use, as an ornament in dress, and for trimmings. The annual value of the home manufacture has been estimated at £3,000,000. *See* the different kinds of lace under their separate names.

Lace-bark, the reticulated bark of the *Lagetta lintearia*, a West Indian tree, which splits into layers with delicate transverse fibres, exactly resembling beautiful lace.

Lace-boot, a boot which laces at the side or in front.

Lace-cleaner, a laundress; one who renovates the colour of antique or choice lace, or brightens gold or silver lace.

Laced-stocking, a bandage-support or laced protection for weak legs, varicose veins, &c.

Lace-dyer, a dyer of lace in common with other fabrics.

Lace-frame, a machine for making lace.

Laceman, a dealer in gold lace, or in lace for ladies' wear.

Lace-manufacturer, a weaver of lace; one who has looms and workmen engaged in making lace.

Laceret, **Lasseret** (French), a borer or auger; a sort of gimblet.

Laceron, **Laiteron**, *sonchus*, sowthistle.

Lace-runner, a female who embroiders patterns on net, stretched on a frame, following the stamped device imprinted on it.

Lace-warehouse, a shop where lace is sold, usually combined with the trade of silk-mercer and linendraper.

Lachs the German name for salmon.

Lachter (Scotch), a lock or flake of wool; the eggs laid by a fowl at one time; a fathom measure employed in the German mines, varying in different districts, from 6¼ to nearly 7 feet.

Lacker, **Lacquer**, a varnish for metals; lac-resin dissolved in alcohol, and coloured.

Lacksa, a weight in the Sooloo islands, the half of the picul, or 66⅔ lbs.

Lac-lake, a kind of lac dye.

Lacquered-ware, articles coated or varnished with lacquer, which stand the effect of washing well.

Lacquerer, one who varnishes metals or wood.

Lacquer-maker, a manufacturer of thick varnishing substances, termed lacquers.

Lacsan, a money of Java, the tenth part of a catty.

Lactarene, a preparation of casein from milk, in extensive use among calico-printers.

Lactometer, an instrument for determining the proportion of cream in milk, consisting of four or five glass tubes, about half an inch in diameter, and eleven inches long, fitted into an upright mahogany frame, each tube having a fine line drawn round it, ten inches from the bottom; three inches from the line downwards it is graduated into inches and tenths of inches. After standing twelve hours, the quantity of cream which floats upon the surface of the milk, is shown by the scale of inches and tenths; each division will therefore represent one per cent. of the whole.

Lactoscope, a kind of eye-glass; an instrument invented by M. Donne, of Paris, for ascertaining the opacity of milk, and thus estimating the richness of the fluid in cream.

Lada, the Malay name for pepper.

Ladang, a name in the Eastern archipelago for a newly cleared piece of ground; a plantation for pepper.

Ladanum-gum. *See* **Labdanum**.

Ladder, a frame of wood or iron with connecting rounds; a flight of wooden or rope steps for climbing.

Ladder-maker, a manufacturer of ladders, of which there are many kinds, as long round ladders, step ladders, rule-joint ladders, rope ladders, chain ladders, &c.

Ladder-work, among artificers, painting, stuccoing, &c., which has to be done on a ladder, and is generally charged double.

Lade, to load; a freight; in Germany, a trunk or box.

Lademan, in Scotland, a man who has the charge of a pack-horse; the servant of a mill who returns the loads of meal to the owners of the corn sent to be ground.

Laden, a shop or stall in Germany.

Laden-meister, in Germany, the master of a company; one who has the charge of the chest or funds.

Laden-preis, the publication or announced price in Germany.

Lading, a freight or cargo for a ship, barge, lighter, &c.

Lading, Bill of. *See* **Bill of Lading**.

Ladle, a dipping spoon for serving soup at table; an iron founder's utensil for removing molten metal; an instrument for drawing the charge of a cannon.

Ladle-board, a mill-wheel float.

Ladrone (Italian), a pirate; a robber.

Lady's Boot-maker, a maker of kid, cloth, or other boots for females.

Lady's-maid, the personal dress attendant on a lady.

Lady's-saddle, a quilted side-saddle, with a pummel for lady equestrians.

Laegel, **Lagel**, a weight for steel used in Germany; in Styria, 154·34 lbs.; in Prussia, 108·11 lbs.

Lagan-goods, a name given to merchandise thrown overboard, and sunk with a buoy attached for recovery. *See* **Ligan**.

Lagatenie, a money of account in Cochin China, of fluctuating value; two lagatenies are generally, however, equal to one dollar.

Lager (German), a camp; a harbour; a warehouse, or resting-place.

Lager-beer, a popular strong German beer, now largely manufactured in the United States.

Lager-miethe, warehouse rent.

Lager-wine, old bottled wine, that has been kept in the cellar.

Lagoon, a salt-water pond; land occasionally covered by the sea.

Lahn, a German name for plated wire; tinsel, thin metal foil.

LAID-PAPERS, writing papers with a ribbed surface, which are either cream laid, blue-laid, &c.

LAIR, a covered shed for cattle.

LAIZE (French), a width of manufactured stuff.

LAKE, a pigment of a fine crimson red colour, of which there are several kinds. Common lake is obtained from Brazil wood, which affords a very fugitive colour. Superior red lakes are prepared from lac, cochineal, or kermes, and the best from madder root. *See* GARANCINE.

LAKHIRAJ, lands held rent-free in India, or of which the dues are assigned or appropriated to some public or private object.

LAMANEUR (French), a coasting pilot.

LAMB, the young of the sheep kind.

LAMBSKINS, the skins of the lamb, which with the fleece on are extensively used for clothing, for door-mats, &c.: the grey and black Russian lambs are mostly used for coat and cloak linings, collars, caps, &c. the Astracan lamb is a rich glossy, black skin, with short fur, having the appearance of watered silk. The Hungarian lamb is produced in that country in immense numbers; of it is made the national coat; the woolly part is worn outside in summer, inside in winter; they are often highly decorated. The Spanish lamb furnishes the well-known short jacket of that country. About a million of lambskins a year are imported from abroad, chiefly for glove-making.

LAMBS'-WOOL, the fleece of the lamb; a kind of woollen stuff; a name for a beverage composed of ale with the pulp of roasted apples added.

LAME-DUCK, a slang term applied to a member of the Stock Exchange who fails to meet his engagements.

LAME-MAKER, a foil maker.

LAMENTINE, the manati or sea-cow.

LAMETTA, brass, silver, or gold foil or wire.

LAMEY, LAMYEH, a small Burmese measure of capacity, about half a pint.

LAMINATED, disposed in layers or plates.

LAMP, a utensil or apparatus for giving light, of which there are many kinds, as the argand lamp, the sperm-oil lamp, the moderator for vegetable oil, the camphine lamp, the spirit lamp for chemical operations; the reflecting lamp for light-houses, the miner's safety-lamp, &c.

LAMP-BLACK, the carbon or smoke formed by burning vegetable substances in confined air. It constitutes the basis of lithographic and printing inks, and also of an oil paint.

LAMP-COTTON MANUFACTURER, a maker of cotton wicks for lamps. These are chiefly made in London.

LAMPERN. *See* LAMPREY.

LAMP-GLASS, the upright glass tube, or chimney for a lamp; the circular glass shade for a lamp, or gas-burner.

LAMP-LIGHTER, an itinerant employed by gas companies or individuals to light lamps.

LAMP-MAKER, a manufacturer of various kinds of lamps.

LAMP-POST, the iron column or pillar for carrying a lamp.

LAMPREY, a small eel-like fish, the fresh-water species of which, *Petromyzon fluviatilis*, was formerly of great importance as a delicacy, and also largely used as bait by fishermen. In Germany they are taken in large quantities, fried, packed in barrels by layers, with bay leaves and spices, and sprinkled with vinegar; and thus exported to other countries.

LAMP SELLER, a vender of lamps, often combined with the trade of gas-fitter.

LAN, the Burmese name for the fathom.

LANA, a close-grained wood obtained in Demerara from *Genipa Americana*, which is not liable to split. The tree will frequently square from 14 to 18 inches. The fruit yields the pigment known as Lana dye, with which the Indians stain their faces and persons. Lana is also the Italian for wool; and a Russian weight of 526½ grains.

LANA-DYE, a bluish-black colour used by the Indians of Guiana for staining their persons. *See* CARUTO.

LANAIUOLO (Italian), a clothier.

LANCASTER-GUN, a gun with a very long range named after the inventor. The bore is slightly oval, and some of these guns in use will throw a conoidal projectile, weighing 100 lbs., to an enormous distance.

LANCE, a long spear, or sharp-pointed offensive weapon.

LANCE-CORPORAL, a soldier from the ranks, fulfilling the duties of a corporal, with temporary rank as such.

LANCER, a horse soldier armed with a spear or lance.

LANCET, a surgeon's instrument for letting blood.

LANCET-CASE, a case for keeping lancets in.

LANCEWOOD, a slender tree, the *Duguetia quitarensis*, of Lindley, the *Guatteria virgata* of others; found in tolerable abundance in the interior of Guiana, and also imported from Cuba and Jamaica. The wood possesses much toughness and elasticity, and is used for gig shafts, archery bows, billiard cues, and other purposes. Its native name is yarri-yarri.

LAND, ground; soil; real estate; also to disembark.

LAND-AGENT, a bailiff or assistant to the steward of an estate; a manager of landed property.

LANDAU, a carriage which may be opened.

LANDAULET, a small landau.

LAND-CHAIN. *See* CHAIN, and GUNTER'S-CHAIN.

LANDED-ESTATE, property in land.

LANDED-PROPRIETOR, an owner of houses or land.

LANDER, a miner who attends at the mouth of a shaft to receive the kibble or bucket with ore, &c.

LAND-FALL, the first land seen after a voyage.

LANDIER (French), a large kitchen-grate or range; a kitchen andiron.

LANDING, a quay or steps, &c. for disembarking from a boat; the level space of a staircase at the top of a flight of stairs; a platform at a railway station.

Landing-pier, Landing-stage, a jetty or wharf for landing passengers or goods.

Landing-surveyor, a customs-officer; one who has the superintendence of landing-waiters, or of the discharging of vessels in docks.

Landing-waiter, a custom-house officer, or searcher who examines and registers the articles of a ship's cargo discharged in the docks or harbour.

Land-jobber, a dealer in land; one who buys to sell again at an enhanced price.

Land-mark, a boundary stone; some object seen from the sea which guides a navigator.

Land-reeve, an assistant to the steward on a large landed estate.

Land-roll, a clod-crusher and seam-presser.

Land-sales Fund, the money accruing in the colonies from the sale of Crown lands, a large portion of which is usually applied to the introduction of labourers and useful settlers.

Landscape, a picture representing the scenery of nature.

Landscape-gardener, an artistic gardener; one who plots and lays out flower-gardens, shrubberies, park-grounds, &c.

Landscape-painter, one who practises the art of landscape-painting.

Landsman, a new hand at sea; not an able seaman, or conversant with the routine of ship's work.

Land-steward, the agent of a land-owner.

Land-surveying Chain-maker, a manufacturer of the chain-links used by surveyors

Land-surveyor, one who measures and draws plans of landed estates, parishes, &c.

Land-tax, a government impost on rent. *See* Property-tax.

Land-tortoise, a tortoise that lives on land, several species of which are sought for as food, or for their shell, which is used for inlaying work, while others form excellent scavengers in wells.

Land-warrant, a title to a lot of public land; an American security or official document for entering or settling upon government land, much dealt in among jobbers.

Langoustine (French), prawns.

Langrage, Langrel, pieces of iron of any kind used as shot for great guns; chain-shot.

Lanificio (Italian), woollen manufactures.

Lantern, Lanthorn, a circular case or frame for holding a light; a light-house frame.

Lanthorn-leaf and horn-plate Manufacturer, a horn-presser.

Lanyard, a piece of small line or rope used for fastening tackle, &c.

Lanzo, a German foot-soldier.

Lap, a roll or sliver of cotton for feeding the cards of a spinning-machine; a wooden disk or metal wheel, on which leather, &c. is secured, used for grinding, burnishing, or polishing by the turner.

Lapel, a facing; the part of a man's coat turned over.

Lapidary, a jeweller; a gem cutter; one who shapes and smoothes precious stones.

Lapis-lazuli, a valuable deep-blue ornamental stone. It was formerly the only source of ultramarine, but this beautiful pigment is now artificially manufactured.

Lappa, a kind of Indian brocade.

Lappet, a broad string to a lady's cap or head-dress.

Lappet-muslin, a white or coloured, sprigged or striped, muslin for dresses, &c.

Lappet-wheel-cutter, a machine for making welds.

Lapping, a kind of machine blanket or wrapping material, used by calico-printers &c. and made either plain, twilled, or fine.

Lapping-engine, a doubling machine; an engine for making folds or welds.

Lappior, a miner who dresses the refuse ores which are left.

Lapmude, a dress made of reindeer's skin.

Lapstone, a shoemaker's stone for hammering his leather on.

Larboard, the left hand side of a ship, looking forward.

Larceny, theft; the stealing any thing below the value of a shilling is termed petty larceny.

Larch, a tree of the fir tribe, (*Abies Larix*), which has been introduced and largely cultivated in Scotland, where its timber is useful for many purposes, and the bark is employed in tanning. From the inner bark very excellent soft gloves are made in Russia. The tree also yields Venice turpentine, Orenburgh gum, and larch manna.

Lard, the fat of the omentum and mesentery of the pig, which enters extensively into commerce, being used in pharmacy and for culinary purposes; our imports from the United States in some years exceed 11,000 tons.

Lard and Grease Manufacturer, a melter and purifier of animal fats.

Larder, a pantry; a room where victuals are kept.

Lard-oil, the oleine from lard, after the stearine has been removed, which is used for burning, and for lubricating machinery.

Larin, a money of silver wire, formerly current in several Eastern countries, and worth about 6d. In Arabia and Persia it was the eighteenth part of the toman, and in Goa passed for about 94 bazaruchi.

Lark, a singing bird, sometimes kept as a cage bird, and often caught and spitted by the dozen, and sold for eating.

Larry, an empty wagon or truck on a railway.

Lascar, a Hindoo seaman, employed on board vessels trading to the East Indian ports; menials employed to do the dirty work of the artillery, and the arsenals in India. The term is derived from lushkur, literally, an army man.

Lase, a land-measure of 324 square feet, used in Cornwall.

Lashes, the thongs of whips, made of cord, or twisted strips of hide.

Lashing, baling cord; rope for binding packages.

Lasso, a strong rope with a noose, carried by the gauchos or mounted herdsmen, in Patagonia and Buenos Ayres, for catching wild cattle.

LASSUN, LUSHOONA, Indian names for garlic and onions.

LAST, a metrical term of German origin for a load; hence in commerce it is applied to various quantities of merchandise: as 12 barrels of tar or pitch, ashes, codfish, white herrings or meal. A last of flax is 17 cwt.; of gunpowder, 24 barrels, of 100 lbs. each; of wool, 12 sacks of 364 lbs. each. As a grain-measure in England, the last usually consists of 10½ imperial quarters; 12 sacks, or 4363 lbs. For wheat and rape-seed, it is calculated at 8 loads or 10 quarters. On the Continent it varies, the last of grain in several parts being as much as 14 quarters. The last of ballast in Amsterdam is but 2000 lbs. The Prussian ship last is 4124 lbs.; the last of timber at Dantzic, 80 cubic feet.

LAST AND BOOT-TREE MAKER, a maker of wooden moulds, or shapes, for boots and shoes.

LASTING, the process of drawing the upper leather smooth and straight in shoe-making; a woollen fabric, used in making women's shoes.

LASTING-MANUFACTURER, a maker of the woollen fabric termed lasting.

LATAKIA, a fine kind of Turkish tobacco, taking its name from the port of shipment.

LATCH, a door catch or fastening.

LATCHET, a shoe-buckle.

LATCH-KEY, a small private key for a street-door.

LATEEN-SAIL, a triangular mainsail.

LATER, a brick or tile.

LATERITE, a conglomerate, mineral substance used for road-making in Madras, and ground up to form a chief ingredient in hydraulic cements.

LATH, a thin cleft strip of wood, used in house-building; a runner nailed to a roof to support tiles.

LATH-BRICK, a long kind of brick, 22 inches by 6, used in hopoasts or kilns instead of laths or spars.

LATHE, a revolving machine used for turning, drilling, or burnishing.

LATHERKIN, a glazier's tool; a tringlette.

LATHING, small wooden bars to fix mortar in; bed staves for the centre-frame of a bedstead, to rest the bedding on.

LATH-RENDER, LATH-SPLITTER, a cutter of wood into laths.

LATH-WOOD, straight-grained wood, the outside cuttings of fir-trees, used for splitting into laths. Lathwood is sold by the fathom, and varies in length from 3 to 8 feet; 4000 to 5000 tons are annually imported.

LATH-WORK, thin battened work at the sides of rooms, or at the ceilings, for receiving plaster.

LATITUDE, in navigation, the distance from the equator north or south.

LATTA (Italian), tinned iron; tin.

LATTE (Italian), milk.

LATTEN, sheet or plate brass, or thin plates of mixed metal: black latten is brass in milled sheets, composed of copper and zinc, used by braziers, and for drawing into wire. Shaven latten is a thinner article: roll latten is polished on both sides ready for use.

LATTEN-WIRE, wire made from the plates.

LATTICE, a trellis or cross-barred work; a net-work window.

LATTICE-MAKER, a maker of light cross-barred wooden frames for training creeping plants to, for the sides of walls or footpaths, or of windows for dairies, &c.

LAUDANUM, a preparation of opium; a soporific and anodyne tincture used medicinally.

LAUNCE, a fish. *See* HORN-PIKE.

LAUNCH, the long-boat, or large boat of a ship; the sending of a new vessel into the water, which is usually attended with some ceremony.

LAUNDERS, in the mining districts, wooden tubes or gutters for the conveyance of water; a long shallow trough to receive the powdered ore from the stamping-mill.

LAUNDRESS, a washerwoman.

LAUNDRY, the place where washing is carried on; an ironing-room.

LAUNDRY-MAID, a servant who attends to the laundry.

LAUOK, the Malay name for a curry, stew, &c.

LAUREATE (Scotch), to confer a literary degree.

LAUREL, a handsome and interesting genus of trees, furnishing many important articles of commerce, as benzoin, sassafras, &c. *See* also BAY-BERRIES and BAY-LEAVES.

LAUREL-WATER, the leaves of the *Cerasus Lauro-cerasus*, distilled with water, which is used medicinally, as a substitute for hydrocyanic acid, in palpitation of the heart, &c.

LAVA, the scoria from active volcanoes, which is used for several purposes.

LAVA-MILLSTONES, hard and coarse basaltic millstones, obtained from quarries near Andernach on the Rhine.

LAVANDARA (Italian), a washerwoman.

LAVARET, a species of salmon.

LAVATORY, a washing-place.

LAVENDER, the floral leaves of the *Lavandula vera*, which are very fragrant. The compound spirit or tincture of lavender, is given in faintness or lowness of spirits, as a stimulant cordial. It is known as red lavender drops.

LAVENDER, FRENCH. From the floral leaves of *Lavandula spica*, the oil of spike is obtained, which is used by painters on porcelain, and by artists in the preparation of varnish.

LAVENDER-OIL, a yellow essential oil, distilled from the leaves and flowers of various species of lavender.

LAVER, the name for an edible sea-weed. *See* SLOKE.

LAVUNCHA, an Indian name for *Andropogon muricatum*, which is esteemed for its medicinal properties.

LAWEK, a Polish long measure, equal to 1·7 inch.

LAWN, a species of very fine linen, approaching cambric in texture; a grass-plot in a garden, or in front of a dwelling-house; an open green space between trees.

Law-bookseller, a vender of books relating to jurisprudence; often also a publisher of legal works.

Law-stationer, a shopkeeper who keeps on sale the articles required by lawyers, such as parchment, tape, pounce, foolscap and brief paper, &c.; one who takes in drafts or writings to be fairly copied for lawyers.

Law-wig-maker, a manufacturer of the horse-hair powdered wigs worn by barristers and judges, &c.

Law-writer, an engrosser: a clerk employed by a law-stationer to make copies of briefs, cases, deeds, &c. in a round legible hand.

Lawyer, a name indiscriminately applied to any one practising law, whether attorney or solicitor, barrister or judge.

Lawyer's-clerk, an assistant engaged in a lawyer's office, to write or attend to out-door business.

Lawyer's-office, the business rooms of a solicitor; the chambers of a barrister.

Lax, a name in Aberdeen for salmon.

Laxar, Luxur, Loxar, a weight used on the coast of Pedir, Acheen, by which betel nuts are sold. It weighs about 168 lbs, and consists of ten thousand nuts, with from 10 to 25 per cent. added, according to the bargain previously made, for nuts which may be worm-eaten or otherwise damaged.

Lay, to produce eggs; a share of the freight of a ship; land in the state of grass or sward; a Scotch term for to smear sheep with a mixture of tar and grease in winter.

Lay-days, a certain number of days allowed to the merchant or charterer to load or unload cargo.

Layering, in gardening, binding down the shoots of shrubs, in order that they may strike roots.

Lay-figure, an artist's model: a figure made of wood or cloth in imitation of the human body.

Laying, the process of twisting the strands of hemp into a rope; producing eggs; smearing sheep. *See* Lay.

Laying-on-tool, a bookbinder's tool.

Lay-stall, a place where milch cows are kept in London.

Lazaretto, a pest-house or building, in which quarantine has to be performed in the Mediterranean; where passengers and goods have to be landed; an hospital ship.

Lazulite, a blue spar, found in crystals, and in masses in Europe and the Brazils.

Lazzaroni, a class of beggars and idlers in the Italian States.

Lb., the abbreviation for the pound weight.

Le (French), the breadth of cloth between the two lists or edge borders.

Lea, a meadow; a yarn measure, sometimes called a rap, containing in cotton yarn 80 threads, or 4,320 inches; for linen yarn 120 threads, or 10,800 inches; for worsted yarn 80 threads, or 2,880 inches. The lea, as applied to foreign linen yarn, contains 3,420 Ermland inches, and 40 threads; 7,200 Hamburg inches, and 90 threads; 7 German skeins, 100 threads in a skein.

Leach, the border or side edge of a sail; to form lye from ashes.

Leach-line, a rope used for hauling up the leach of a sail.

Lead, a poisonous bluish-white metal; principally obtained from galena. Lead occurs in commerce under the several names of pig, sheet, or rolled lead, and shot; besides which there are red and white lead, chromate of lead, and litharge. On shipboard the "lead" is a cone or pyramid of this metal, with a small hole at the base, attached to a line for taking soundings at sea. The hand lead for shallow depths weighs about 7 lbs.; the deep-sea lead two or three times that weight.

Lead-ash Smelter, a purifier of the slag of lead.

Leader, a principal or editorial article in a newspaper; a branch of ore leading to the lode.

Lead-line, the line attached to a sounding-weight used in ships, which is marked or divided into fathoms.

Lead-mill, a circular plate of lead, used by the lapidary for roughing or grinding.

Lead-pencil, a pencil containing black-lead, or compressed plumbago.

Lead-pipe Maker, a manufacturer of lead tubes of various thicknesses, for conveying water or gas, &c.

Leads, shaped pieces of metal used by the compositor for spacing and arranging lines of printing-type; a flat roof covered with lead.

Lead-shot, shot for fire-arms, for sportsmen's use.

Lead-spar, a sulphate of lead.

Leadwort, the common name for several species of plants, belonging to the genus *Plumbago*, which have extremely acrid properties; the roots and leaves are used for raising blisters, and as a stimulating wash for ulcers.

Leaf, the green blade of plants. A large commerce is carried on in many kinds of prepared leaves, as of tea, tobacco, and senna; for forage, as in hay; for culinary purposes, as cabbage; and for fibrous use, as many palms. The term leaf is also applied to any thing foliated, as the flap of a table, the side of a folding door, the double page of a book; a thin plate of metal or horn. The leaf of a fan is the surface which is cut in the shape of the segment of a circle.

Leaf-metal. There are four different kinds of Dutch bronze leaf; common, which is soft, and of a reddish cast, made of one part of zinc to three of copper; French, which contains more zinc, is, therefore harder, less ductile, and has a purer yellow colour; Florence, which contains a large proportion of zinc, and is of a greenish gold colour; and lastly, white leaf, composed of tin. Leaf metal is chiefly used for giving a cheap and brilliant metallic surface to metal and other substances.

Leaf-lard, lard from the flaky animal fat of the hog.

LEAGUE, an itinerary measure, varying in different countries. The English league is three geographical miles, or 6076 yards. The French astronomical league is 4860 yards; but the French legal or posting league is 4263 yards; and the marine league 6076 yards. The Portuguese league is 6751 yards. The Spanish common league 7419 yards; and the judicial league 4637 yards. Also a confederacy or union for some specific object, as the anti-corn-law league.

LEAGUER, LEGGER, an old Dutch measure for liquids still used in the Dutch eastern colonies; at Amsterdam it was about 126 gallons; in Batavia it is about 133 gallons.

LEAK, a hole or breach in a vessel at which the water comes in, or goes out.

LEAKAGE, an allowance made for waste or loss in liquors.

LEAM, an artificial cut or drain in a fen district.

LEANG, another name for the tael, a Chinese weight.

LEAN-TO, a shed attached to another building.

LEASE, to let for a term upon rental.

LEASEHOLD, a house, a landed estate, &c. held for a term of years at a rent.

LEASEHOLDER, one who holds property under a lease.

LEASH, a leather thong to hold birds or dogs by; among sportsmen three birds or animals, as pheasants, partridges, and hares.

LEASON, a pasture.

LEAT, an artificial water-course or channel.

LEATHER, the skins of animals, which have been prepared for commercial use by tanning, tawing, or other processes. The foreign imports of leather are valued at about 3 million sterling per annum, while the home production and the manufactured products bring up the annual value of the leather trade to nearly 18 millions. Leather enters into commerce in the form of hides, alumed leather, oiled or chamois leather, rough tanned leather, curried leather, enamelled leather, dyed leather, embossed or stamped leather, shoes and boots, saddlery and harness, &c.

LEATHER, AMERICAN, a kind of japanned and enamelled cloth imitating leather, used as a seating material for chairs, couches, &c. See AMERICAN-LEATHER.

LEATHER-APRON, an apron used by different persons, as blacksmiths, freemasons, &c., but of different texture.

LEATHER-BREECHES, men's strong garments of leather for riding or for hard service.

LEATHER-BUCKET, a bucket made of leather, used, for irrigation in India, by firemen and others.

LEATHER-CAP MAKER, a manufacturer of seal-skin caps and other coverings of leather for the head.

LEATHER-COAT, a popular name for a fish in the West Indies, a species of *Chorinemes;* a tough-skinned apple.

LEATHER-CUTTER, a worker in leather.

LEATHER-DEALER, a vender of leather of various kinds.

LEATHER-DRESSER, a currier; one who prepares leather for use in various ways.

LEATHER-DYER, a stainer of leather; one who colours the outer surface.

LEATHER-EMBOSSER, one who stamps leather in patterns for bookbinding, covering furniture or room hangings.

LEATHER-ENAMELLER, a varnisher of leather; the workman who gives the glossy surface for which patent leather is remarkable.

LEATHER-GILDER, an ornamenter of leather.

LEATHER-JAPANNER. *See* LEATHER-ENAMELLER.

LEATHER-MERCHANT AND CURRIER, a wholesale dealer in leather, sometimes combined with the business of tanning or currying.

LEATHER-PIPE-AND-BUCKET MAKER, a manufacturer of leather hose and pails.

LEATHER-SELLERS' COMPANY, one of the livery companies of London, whose hall is in St. Helen's Place.

LEATHER-SPLITTER, a mechanic, who divides the skin, splitting it into thin sections by a machine-cutting knife.

LEATHER-STAINER, one who dyes leather.

LEATHER-STRAP MAKER, a cutter of leather into strips, for straps of different kinds.

LEATHER-STRIPER, a workman who marks leather with coloured lines for the use of shoe-binders and others.

LEAVEN, dough in a state of ferment; yeast.

LEBAN, a fermented liquor, or milk-beer, similar to the koumiss made by the Arabs.

LEBO, in the Pacific islands, leaves of the bread-fruit tree sewed together, for the purpose of covering food in cooking to keep in the steam.

LECTURER, a professor; one who instructs or amuses a public audience by a discourse.

LEDGER, the principal account-book kept by tradesmen, banks, or companies, for entering the debit and credit transactions of individuals; a large flat tombstone; horizontal timber used in scaffolding.

LEE, in navigation, the side of the ship under shelter, and opposite to that from which the wind blows.

LEE-BOARD, a board fitted to the lee side of flat-bottomed boats, to prevent their drifting to leeward.

LEECH, a worm used for drawing blood, the *Hirudo medicinalis;* eleven or twelve millions a-year are annually imported into France, and fully as many into this country.

LEECH, ARTIFICIAL, a mechanical contrivance for drawing blood in place of the worm usually employed.

LEECH-ROPE, that part of the bolt-rope at the side of the sails.

LEEFANGE, an iron bar upon which the sheets of fore and aft sails traverse.

LEEK, a well-known pot-herb, the *Allium porrum*, used in soups.

LEER, an annealing furnace in a glass-house; a long arched building, in which glass articles are placed to assume hardness and temper.

LEER-BOOM, a Dutch name in the Cape colony for the tops of the sides of a wagon.

Leet, one portion of many; a court-leet is an assemblage of persons to nominate for an election to some office; a jurisdiction for a township; a petty inquest for local police.

Leeward, the side towards which the wind blows. *See* Lee.

Leeway, a deviation from the course laid down on the chart; a drifting with the current and wind to leeward.

Legacy-duty, a government tax on bequests, or the transfer of property; which varies in amount, according to the consanguinity of the receiver.

Legalization, an authoritative document issued from the office of the chief secretary in Malta.

Legal-tender, the authorized coins or payment that can be lawfully offered and received in a country; which varies. In 1816 gold coins were declared to be the only legal tender for Great Britain in all payments of more than 40s.; silver is therefore now a merely subsidiary currency below that sum, and a legal tender up to 40s., and no higher. Copper coins are only a legal tender to the extent of a shilling in any one payment. Bank of England notes are a legal tender without limit, except for payments due by the bank itself. In France silver is the legal tender.

Legatee, one to whom a legacy is left.

Legation, an embassy; a deputation.

Leggers, large casks. *See* Leaguer.

Leggings, Leggins, long garters reaching to the knees.

Leghorn, one of the names for a Tuscan plait for bonnets and hats, obtained from the straw of a variety of bearded wheat, cut when green, and bleached.

Leghorn-hat Presser, a cleaner and presser of hats made of straw plait.

Leghorn-plait Dealer, one who sells straw chip and plait for hats.

Legista (Italian), a lawyer.

Leguminous, pertaining to pulse; plants that produce pods, as pease, beans, &c.

Leister, Lister, a pronged fish spear.

Lemon, a fruit. *See* Lemons and Limes.

Lemonade, a cooling drink made from the juice of lemons, or some acidulated compound.

Lemonade-maker, a manufacturer of aerated waters, who makes a pleasant beverage with citric acid, or tartaric acid, and essence of lemon, &c.

Lemon-grass, a name for the *Andropogon citratum* of Decandolle. From its fragrant smell and pleasant taste, it is in common use in the West Indies as a substitute for Chinese tea, and is frequently employed as a sudorific in febrile diseases. The white succulent centre or pith of the leaves is used in India to give an agreeable flavour to curries. It is largely cultivated in Ceylon and the Moluccas, and the otto obtained by distillation, and known in commerce as citronella oil, is employed for perfuming soaps and grease, and making artificial essence of verbena.

Lemon-juice, the expressed juice of limes and lemons, justly esteemed as a valuable antiscorbutic remedy, and which is therefore required to be included in all ships' stores in regulated quantities.

Lemon-kali, a drink made from citric and tartaric acid.

Lemon-peel, the rind of the lemon sold either dried or preserved and candied. The rind of the *Citrus Bergamia* is forced by violent pressure in the shape of proper moulds into small boxes.

Lemons and Limes, acid fruits, the produce of *Citrus Limonum* and *C. acida*. The rind is aromatic, and the pulp or juice refrigerant and antiscorbutic.

Lending-library, one which gives books out to be read.

Lenitive-electuary, an agreeable confection, prescribed as a mild laxative.

Leno, a kind of cotton gauze, used for window-blinds, which is thinner and clearer than buke muslin, and is made bordered and figured for long curtains.

Lenses, magnifying glasses for conveying light to a focus, in telescopes, &c.

Lentil, a pulse, the *Ervum lens*, the seeds of which are amylaceous and nutritious, but difficult of digestion. It is much used as food in southern countries, and the meal forms the base of a popular substance vended under the name of *Revalenta Arabica*.

Leopard-wood, a fancy wood obtained from one of the palm tribe.

Lepta, Lepton, a small Greek copper coin, and money of account, the hundredth part of the drachma. There are pieces of one, two, five and ten lepta. *See* Lipta.

Lesh-pund, a weight used in Orkney, containing 36 lbs. Scots Troye, = 32·6806 lbs. avoirdupois.

Lessee, one to whom a lease is given.

Lesson, a piece of instruction.

Let, to lease; to put to hire.

Letter, a type; an epistle; the transmitted correspondence through the post is very large. *See* General Post-office.

Letter-box, a post-office box for receiving letters; a box in a street-door for depositing letters.

Letter-carrier, a post-office distributor; a postman, who delivers letters.

Letter-case, a box for holding letters; a compositor's case of type.

Letter-clasp, Letter-clip, a kind of spring-file or hold-fast, for letters or papers.

Letter-copying-machine Maker, a manufacturer of copying machines.

Letter-cutter, a die-sinker; a type-cutter; a maker of projecting letters, in brass, glass, porcelain, or wood.

Letter-founder, a founder who casts printing-type.

Lettering, marking books or pages with letters, &c.

Letter of Advice, a letter giving notice of any transaction.

Letter of Attorney, a power of legal authority to act for another, and to proceed with his affairs. The power may be special for a particular purpose, or general.

Letter of Credit, an order or circular note from a bank or mercantile firm, on some foreign correspondent, given to a traveller (who requires to be identified); to advance money to a specified amount, to the bearer or a third party named; usually in return for money deposited, or security lodged.

LETTERS OF HORNING, a Scotch law term for a species of outlawry.

LETTER OF LICENCE, a customs permit; a permission from a patentee to make goods, or to use an invention, of which he has the property or right; an instrument granted to a person in embarrassed circumstances by his creditors, granting him time for payment, or permission to continue his business.

LETTER OF MARQUE, a public or private licence, or extraordinary permission granted to subjects for reprisals; a kind of privateering.

LETTER-PAPER, foolscap or post paper, for writing letters on.

LETTER-PRESS, print or impression taken from type.

LETTER-PRESS PRINTER, one who uses type in printing, contradistinguished from a copper-plate or lithographic printer.

LETTERS PATENT, a royal grant; a patent right.

LETTER-SORTER, a subordinate employed in a local or colonial post-office, or at the general post-office, looking out and classifying letters for despatch or delivery.

LETTER-WEIGHER, a poising scale or steelyard, for weighing letters, to ascertain the postage they will be subject to on being mailed; a balance for calculating the rate of postage chargeable on English and foreign letters. The rate is uniform in the United Kingdom at 1d. for letters under half an ounce; and so on in proportion for every further half-ounce, the weight allowed by the post-office for a single rate, being 218¾ grains. The sea-postage to the Colonies is also now pretty general at 6d. The following facts may be borne in mind:—a sheet of common 4to letter paper weighs about 120 grains; a sheet of thick 4to, 180 grains; a sheet of small foreign post, 65 grains; the usual quantity of wax, 6 grains; 20 dips of ink from a steel pen, when wet, 4 grains—reduced when dry to 1 grain; a drop of water will add another grain. A letter exposed to a slight rain for 5 minutes, will gain in weight 15 grains.

LETTER-WOOD, one of the costliest woods which Guiana possesses, obtained from *Piratinera guianensis*. It is very hard, of a beautiful brown colour, with black spots, which have been compared to hieroglyphics. The spotted part is only the heart-wood, which is seldom more than 12 or 15 inches in circumference. It is adapted for cabinet work of small size, and for veneering only.

LETTER-WRITER, one who writes official or other letters, for persons less skilled in correspondence. In India, Turkey, and other countries, where education is less general, this is a recognised profession.

LETTUCE, the *Lactuca sativa*, a cooling and agreeable vegetable, used as a salad plant, of which there are two principal varieties, the coss lettuce, and the cabbage lettuce.

LEVEE, a public assemblage, or official gathering; in the United States an artificial embankment near rivers or the sea, for the convenience of commerce.

LEVEE-DUES, shipping or landing dues paid at a levee.

LEVEL, a gallery in a coal mine, named in fathoms according to its depth below the surface; a workman's tool with a plumb-line or a plummet; a surveyor's instrument for determining the height of one place with another. The spirit-level is a more accurate mode of determining the plane of the sensible horizon.

LEVELLING, removing the inequalities of the surface for roads, railways, &c.

LEVELLING INSTRUMENTS, the spirit-level, theodolite, staves, and other instruments used by the surveyor.

LEVER, a bar for raising a weight; a footmat; a basket.

LEVERET, the young of the hare, during the first year of its age.

LEVER-WATCH, a watch with a lever balance.

LEVIGATION, the process of grinding or reducing hard bodies to an impalpable powder.

LEVY, a name in Pennsylvania for the eighth part of a dollar, about 6d.; it is called in New York a shilling; a distraint; an assessment; raising recruits for military service.

LEWER, a local name in Scotland for a lever; a hatter's name for a smoothing pad of silk, properly velour from the French.

LEWIS, a mechanical appliance for raising stone; thin wedges of iron indented into the stone forming a dove-tail.

LEY, a detergent wash composed of urine, soap, &c. for freeing wool from the animal grease; a standard of metal; grass sward or herbage for cattle.

LI, another name for the Chinese copper cash, ten of which make a candareen, 100 a mas, and 1000 a tael worth about 5s. See CASH. Also a Chinese linear measure equal 0·360 mile.

LIARD, the French farthing, a copper coin; the quarter of a sou, 3 deniers, and equal to half an English farthing.

LIAS, a division of the hank of cambric yarn spun by hand; a hank of 30 to the pound contains 360 lias; hydraulic lime used for making cement.

LIBBRA-GROSSA, the Italian name for the avoirdupois pound used in the Ionian islands and other localities; libbra-sottile being the troy pound.

LIBDAH, a brown felt-cap worn by the poorer class of Arabs.

LIBEL, a malicious publication reflecting on character, &c.

LIBI-DIBI, a name for Divi-divi. See DIVI-DIVI.

LIBRA, the best kind of tobacco grown in the western part of Cuba, selected for its good colour, flavour, elasticity, and the entireness of the leaves; a Continental name for a pound weight, a balance or pair of scales; also a money of account, varying in different provinces. In medicine when the abbreviation for libra is preceded by

Arabic figures, avoirdupois weight is meant, but when succeeded by Roman numerals, troy weight or pint measure is intended.

Libra-piccola, the silk measure of Austria.

Librarian, the custodian of a public or private library; the owner of a circulating library who lets out books on hire to subscribers.

Library, a collection of books; one or more rooms appropriated to books, arranged or classified.

Libretto, the words of an opera; a small book.

Licence, a grant; an official authority to act; a permission to sell exciseable articles, or to keep a public-house.

Licensed Victualler, an innkeeper who sells wines and spirits.

Licensed Victuallers' Society, an association supported by the subscriptions of the licensed victuallers of London and the Provinces, which supports a metropolitan daily paper, the *Morning Advertiser*, and large schools for the children of its members, as well as almshouses for decayed victuallers, &c.

Licenser, one authorized to grant licences or permits; an officer appointed by the Crown to read plays, and who, if they contain nothing immoral or objectionable, permits them to be publicly represented.

Licensing-day, the annual day on which the county magistrates sit to grant spirit licences to publicans.

Licentiate, a graduate; one authorized to follow a profession; a medical man; a barrister.

Lichenine, a starch prepared from lichens.

Lichens, cryptogamous plants, several of which enter into commerce, as the Iceland moss, liverwort and the orchella weeds.

Lichnite, a transparent and brilliant white marble obtained in the island of Paros; it is sometimes found flesh-coloured.

Liciter (French), to sell a house or an estate by auction.

Licorice. *See* Liquorice.

Lienchello, the name in Venezuela for a striped cotton handkerchief.

Lieue, the French league; a measure of length. *See* League.

Lieutenant, a deputy; as Lieutenant-colonel; Lieutenant-governor; Lieutenant-general; a commissioned officer in the army or navy next to a captain.

Lif, Lief, Loof, a name for the fibre by which the petioles of the date palm are bound together. All sorts of cordage is made of it, and it serves for a rubber or drying towel after the bath.

Life-annuity, a pension receivable during life.

Life-assurance, a money payment secured to relatives or creditors, after a person's death, by a yearly premium paid during life to an assurance office, varying in percentage amount according to age, health, or risk of accidental death.

Life-belt, an air-inflated or cork belt for floating in the sea. *See* Life-preserver.

Life-boat, a boat constructed to float in a stormy sea, and many of which are kept at certain parts of the coast to proceed to the assistance of vessels in distress.

Life-buoy, an apparatus thrown overboard from a ship to a person in the water, consisting of a pair of hollow copper cylinders with an erect pole, bearing a flag by day and a light at night; and on which a person can rest till released by a boat.

Life-guard, a heavy mounted soldier, the Queen's cavalry-guard.

Life-lines, ropes carried along yards, booms, &c., or any part of a vessel, for men to hold on by.

Life-preserver, a cork or other floating buoy; an air jacket or belt, to be worn on the person as a protection at sea; a loaded weapon; a sword-stick.

Lift, a hoist; a support or tackle running from the yard-arms to the mast-head; an elevator for sending dishes, &c. up or down from a kitchen.

Lift-hammer, a large hammer.

Lifting-bridge, a swing or draw-bridge over a dock entrance, moat, or canal.

Lift-pump, a pump acting by the pressure of the atmosphere on the external body of water.

Ligan, goods cast into the sea, from a ship in stress of weather, and sunk, but having a float or buoy attached by a line, in order that they may be subsequently found and recovered. *See* Lagan-goods.

Ligature, a bandage.

Light-dues, passing tolls levied on ships navigating certain waters, towards the maintenance of the lights, shown for their guidance or warning.

Lighter, a small licensed vessel or large barge, employed in the transhipment of goods; a taper.

Lighterage, the charges paid for conveying goods in a lighter.

Lighterman, the owner of a lighter, or a sailor employed in one.

Lighthouse-builder, an engineer; a maker of iron structures for transport to rocks, capes, &c. for erection.

Lighthouse-keeper, the resident in a lighthouse, who attends to the lamps.

Lighthouse-lamp Manufacturer, a constructor of the reflecting plates, lantern, and other apparatus necessary for the brilliant light required in a lighthouse.

Light Infantry, sharp-shooters; soldiers not heavily armed.

Lighting-rate, a public rate for maintaining the lamps or gas-lights in a parish.

Lightning-conductor, a rod or wire from the top of a chimney-stack, steeple, or mast-head, to carry off the electric fluid.

Lights, the lungs of animals, some of which are cooked and eaten as food.

Light-ship, a vessel bearing a light at night, anchored by moorings on a bank, or in the proximity of shoals, to guide navigators.

Lignite, fossil wood carbonised. It is found in various parts of England, and on the Continent, and supplies, in the districts in which it occurs, a bad substitute for coal.

Lignum-vitæ, a very hard and heavy wood, the produce of two species of *Guaiacum*, obtained in the West Indies. It is much used in machinery, for rollers, presses, mills, pestles and mortars, sheaves for ship-blocks, skittle-balls, and a great variety of other works requiring hardness and strength.

Lille Lace, Lisle Lace, a light, fine, and transparent white thread hand-made lace, sometimes called "clear foundation," taking its name from the French town where it is made. It has a diamond-shaped mesh, formed by two threads plaited to a perpendicular line.

Lima-bean, the *Phaseolus Limensis*, an esteemed kind of pulse cultivated in the tropics; the perennial kidney-bean, *P. perennis*.

Liman, a shallow narrow lagoon, at the mouth of rivers, where salt is made.

Lima-wood, the finest description of Nicaragua wood, produced in South America.

Limbello, Limbelluccio (Italian), the shavings of leather.

Limber, a two-wheeled carriage, bearing boxes of ammunition, fastened to a field-piece, which can be "unlimbered," or detached, when in action.

Limber Tar, the bilge-water, or refuse found in the hold of a ship that imports tar, which has drained from the casks during the voyage.

Lime, cement; calcined chalk or limestone, also called quick lime; a fruit so called. *See* Lemons and Limes.

Lime-burner, one who prepares lime for cement, &c., in a kiln.

Lime-juice. *See* Lemon-juice.

Lime-kiln, a furnace of different kinds, but usually a funnel-shaped chamber, in which limestone is mixed with coal or wood, and ignited, to prepare lime for mortar and manure, by driving off the carbonic acid and water which it contains.

Lime-merchant, a wholesale dealer in lime.

Lime-quarry, a pit or quarry where limestone is dug.

Lime-stone, calcareous spar, chalk, or other mineral substance, used for making lime.

Lime-tree, Linden-tree, the *Tilia Europea*, an ornamental lofty tree. The white soft wood is fine and close-grained, and is used for harps and piano-fortes, &c., and is particularly suitable for carving. The charcoal is not inferior to that of the alder and willow, for making gunpowder. The bark, when stripped off, is made into shoes, cordage, sacks for corn, matting, &c. *See* Bass.

Lime-wash, a coating given with lime water; whitewash.

Lime-water, water impregnated with lime, used as a steep for skins in tan-yards, for whitewashing, and for various other purposes.

Limonadière, a barmaid at a French coffee-house; a maker or seller of lemonade.

Limonite, a name for bog iron ore; the hydrous oxide of iron, which, containing upwards of 50 per cent of metal, is much worked in France, and makes excellent iron.

Limoo, a name in some of the Pacific islands for sea-weed.

Limpet, a marine edible mollusc, the common species of which, *Patella vulgaris*, is well known on the British coasts.

Linch, a boundary wall; an unploughed ridge of land.

Linch-pin, a small iron pin put into the end of the axle-tree, to confine the wheels on carts, &c.

Linden Tree. *See* Lime.

Line, the tenth or twelfth part of an inch; a row of type, or of soldiers, &c.; a railway track.

Linear Measures, the measures of length used in a country. *See* Inch, Foot, Mile, &c.

Lined Gold, gold lined with copper, used for jewellery and ornamental articles. It consists of a standard gold leaf, affixed to a leaf of some other metal, either by means of pressure when hot, or by a chemical process.

Line-maker, a manufacturer of rope, sash-lines, clothes-lines, &c.

Line-men, men employed on a railway; persons carrying the measuring line for a surveyor.

Linen, under clothing; a woven fabric made of flax. Our exports of linen are now large. The shipments in 1856, reached about 146½ million yards, besides about 4½ million yards of thread for sewing, and lace thread.

Linen-agent, a factor or agent for Irish linen manufacturers.

Linen-draper, a retail dealer in linen, calico, and other articles usually purchased by females.

Linen-yarn, spun flax. Besides our large home consumption, we exported, in 1856, about 25 million pounds of linen yarn.

Linen-yarn-measure. *See* Yarn-measure.

Line-of-Battle-Ship, a vessel of war large enough to have a place *in the line of battle*; a vessel with two or more gun decks, and carrying, at the lowest, 64 guns.

Liner, a person who measures land, or marks out intended roads, railways, or plots of land for digging trenches for sugar cane, or for planting; one of a line of ocean traders; a vessel of war.

Lines, small cordage or large twine, used for various purposes.

Ling, a valuable fish of the cod tribe, the *Lota molva*, Cuv.; besides those consumed fresh, considerable quantities are cured for exportation. The name lings also applied to the hake, when cured.

Lingan, Lingel, a name for shoemakers' thread in Scotland.

Lingeria (Italian), linen.

Lingot (Spanish), an ingot.

Liniment, an ointment, a balsamic lotion.

Lining, any covering for an interior surface, as to garments, &c.

Link, a torch; a ring or connection; a portion of a chain; each link of Gunter's surveying chain with the connecting ring measures exactly 7·92 inches. *See* Chain and Gunter's Chain.

Link-boy, the bearer of a light or torch in foggy weather or dark nights.

LINK-MOTION, an apparatus for reversing steam engines.

LINSEED, the seed of the flax-plant which is largely imported for sowing, and for crushing into oil for painters' use, the refuse cake is employed to feed cattle and sheep. Our imports have been largely increasing of late years. *See* FLAX-SEED.

LINSEED-MEAL, the meal of flax-seed which is used for poultices.

LINSEED-OIL, a well-known commercial yellow oil obtained from the seed of the flax-plant (*Linum usitatissimum*).

LINSEED TEA, a mucilaginous drink; an infusion of linseed sweetened with liquorice root, and sometimes with honey.

LINSEY, LINSEY-WOOLSEY, a material made from flax and wool, formerly much used by the middle classes for aprons and petticoats; now chiefly worn in union workhouses and charitable institutions. Linseys are made either plain blue, or plain white, or striped blue and white.

LINSTOCK, a gunner's match.

LINT, linen cloth scraped so as to raise a nap or pile, in order to make a soft and smooth surface suited for bandages for wounds. It is usually prepared by hand, but has sometimes been done by machine.

LINTEL, LINTOL, a horizontal piece of timber or stone, placed over a doorway, to bear the superincumbent weight.

LINT-MANUFACTURER, one who gets lint scraped for supplying large quantities to hospitals and army surgeons, &c.

LIPP, a delicate fish, the *Labrus*, of which there are eight or nine species, much esteemed about the Crimea.

LIPPIE, a term in Scotland for the fourth part of a peck, also called a forpet, = 137·3334 cubic inches.

LIPSALVE, glycerine or cold cream; some softening solution applied to chapped lips.

LIPTA, a Greek copper coin, the hundredth part of the silver phoenix; which is worth eightpence halfpenny. *See* LEPTA.

LIQUEUR-MANUFACTURER, a maker of cordials or sweet liquors, compounded of alcohol, water, sugar, and different aromatic flavouring substances.

LIQUEUR-STAND, a metal frame for holding spirit bottles.

LIQUIDATION, an arrangement or settlement of the affairs of a merchant or company; the clearing up or paying off accounts.

LIQUID-MANURE, urine; a solution of guano or some other fertilizer to be applied to land.

LIQUID-MANURE CART, a watering cart to diffuse liquid manure over a field.

LIQUOR, strong drink; a name among workmen for dyes or solutions used; any thing flowing.

LIQUORICE, the roots of *Glycirrhiza glabra*, a perennial plant common to the south of Europe, considerable quantities of which are imported. Liquorice is much used in the Levant in making a decoction which is drunk cold in summer, and liquorice water is a favourite beverage in this country with children.

LIQUORICE-JUICE, the inspissated juice of the liquorice root, boiled to a consistency for rolling into paste, and used for confectionery purposes. It is often termed Spanish juice.

LIQUORISTE, LIQUEURISTE (French), a compounder of liqueurs.

LIRA, a Venetian coin worth about 10d.

LISBONNINE, another name for the moidore, a Portuguese coin, and worth about 27s.

LISLE-GLOVES, fine thread gloves for summer wear.

LISLE-LACE. *See* LILLE-LACE.

LISPFUND, LISPOND, a Dutch weight, also used in Norway, Sweden, and Denmark, varying from 14 to 18 lbs.; in Hamburgh, the eighth part of the centner, which is equal to 112 lbs.

LISSE' (French), silk; boiled sugar; "amandes lissées" is sugared almonds, almond comfits.

LIST, an inventory; detailed particulars; a narrow selvedge strip torn from the edge of cloth, used for various purposes.

LIST-DEALER, a piece-dealer, also called a fent dealer; one who vends strips of cloth.

LIST-SHOES, a kind of easy slippers made of pieces of cloth.

LITCHI, an elegant scarlet fruit, the produce of *Euphoria* (*Dimocarpus*) *Litchi*.

LITER, a name for the rottolo in Abyssinia, rather more than 10 ounces.

LITHARGE, semi-crystalline or fused protoxide of lead, obtained in separating silver from lead ore, which enters largely into the composition of flint glass.

LITHOGRAPHER, a writer or designer on stone; a workman who takes impressions from lithographic stones.

LITHOGRAPHIC-PAPER, gelatinous or sized paper, tinted with gamboge and rolled very smooth.

LITHOGRAPHIC-PRESS MAKER, a manufacturer of the presses for lithographic work.

LITHOGRAPHIC-PRINTER, a workman who takes impressions on paper, from drawings, maps, plans, and writings previously traced upon stone.

LITHOGRAPHIC-ROLLER, an inking roller for a lithographic press.

LITHOGRAPHIC-STONE, a fine oolite or granular limestone used in lithography: good stone should be of a uniform yellowish gray hue, free from veins and spots, cut by a steel point with difficulty, and in splintering it should show a conchoidal fracture. The best stone was long obtained exclusively from Germany, but it is now found in other quarters.

LITHOGRAPHIC-STONE IMPORTER, a merchant who receives for sale the fine yellowish gray limestones suited for the purpose of the lithographer.

LITHOSTROLE, a sort of mosaic pavement.

LITHOTINT, a tint obtained by a brush used on the lithographic stone instead of a crayon.

LITMUS, cakes of blue dye prepared in Holland from the *Lecanora tartarea* and other lichens, and chiefly used for chemical tests.

LITMUS-PAPER, unsized paper stained with litmus, used as a delicate test of acidity.

LITRAMETER, an instrument for ascertaining the specific gravity of liquids.

Litre, a cubic decimètre, the unit of measures of capacity in the French metrical system; about 1¾ pint (1·760).

Litron, a French dry measure, the sixteenth part of the old French bushel.

Litter, a carriage with a bed for an invalid or wounded person, conveyed by hand or by horse; scattered straw, &c., as a couch or bed for beasts; the young produced by small animals at one birth; confusion or a careless arrangement.

Littoral, belonging to or growing on the shore of the sea; extending along a coast.

Liva, a Turkish division of territory, under the jurisdiction of a Mirmiran or Pacha with two tails.

Liver, an organ of the body of animals, which is eaten as food; as the liver of calves, of lambs, of codfish, &c.

Livery, the particular dress or uniform worn by male servants in a gentleman's household; the garb worn by citizens of high rank, or officers; the body of liverymen or superior freemen of a city.

Livery Company, any incorporated company of London having the right of livery.

Livery-lace Maker, a manufacturer of the lace for state liveries, and for official servants, &c.

Livery-stable Keeper, a job-master; one who lets out horses and carriages, or takes in horses at livery and bait.

Live-stock, animals kept for use, to be dealt in or vended, or for their produce; the term chiefly applies to cattle, but includes poultry, and even rabbits, in some districts; while in many countries, fish, game, bees, silk-worms, &c., are of sufficient importance to be included in the category of live stock.

Live-stock Dealer, a dealer in cattle, sheep, and other animals vended for food.

Living, maintenance; a clergyman's benefice.

Livraison (French), a serial issue; the number or part of a literary work published and delivered periodically; the commercial name for a partial transfer of goods, in contradistinction to the actual receipt and acceptance by the purchaser, which constitutes a delivery.

Livre, the integer of account in the old system of France, equivalent to 9½d. nearly. At first the livre was divided into 20 solidos, afterwards into 10 sous. The revolution changed the name into franc. Also the name for a pound weight. The French livre usuelle, was equal to 7717 grains, but it was prohibited to be used after 1st January, 1840.

Livre Tournois, a money of Tours, formerly in use, which was one-fifth less than that of Paris.

Lizard-stone, a name for the serpentine marble stone obtained in Cornwall, in the vicinity of the Lizard Point, which is worked up into chimney-pieces, ornaments, &c.

Lloyds, an establishment in London for the classification and certifying of British merchant ships; also a place where underwriters and merchants, engaged in marine insurance, &c. assemble.

Lloyds' Agent, an agent acting for the committee of underwriters at Lloyds, who transmits all kinds of maritime information; reports upon accidents, and performs other duties.

Lloyds' Register, a society formed from among the underwriters, shipowners, and others, established in London for the purpose of obtaining a faithful and accurate classification of the mercantile marine of the United Kingdom, and of the foreign vessels trading thereto. They publish a corrected register-book annually, for the use of subscribers, containing ample details, respecting the character of ships, and these books are periodically posted up, with the necessary alterations and changes. The affairs of the society are managed by a committee of 24 members.

Lloyds' Surveyor, a skilled shipwright, or person having a thorough knowledge of ship-building, employed by the committee of Lloyds' Register to survey ships, or superintend their construction.

Lloyds, The Committee of, the managing body elected from among the shipowners, underwriters, and subscribers to Lloyds, to manage, in conjunction with a secretary, clerks, and outlying agents at seaports, the general business affairs of the mercantile marine. They receive notice of, and register in their books, all movements of vessels, arrivals, departures, accidents, &c.; and publish these each evening in a daily sheet, termed "Lloyds' List," for the information of subscribers and the public. The business affairs of Lloyds occupy the upper part of the Royal Exchange, and includes a reading-room, underwriters'-room, captains'-room, and suites of offices.

Load, the charge of a gun; a burthen or freight; a defined quantity of different commodities or bulky merchandise: namely, 5 quarters, or 40 bushels of corn; 36 trusses of hay or straw; 18 cwt. of old hay; 19 cwt. 32 lbs. of new hay; 11 cwt. 64 lbs. of straw; 500 bricks; 1000 tiles; 9 dishes, or nearly 3 cwt. of lead ore; 63 bundles of bulrushes; 27 feet of mortar. In the North American colonies, a load of coals is half a chaldron; of grain, 15 bushels; of coffee in bags, 12 cwt. of flour, 6 barrels; of rice, half a ton; of dried fish, a hogshead, or 15 cwt. In Marseilles, 3 loads are equal to two English quarters. All timber is bought and sold by the load, and a load or quarter of a cord, is estimated at 40 cubic feet of unhewn or rough timber, and 50 feet of hewn or squared timber, which is supposed to weigh a ton. A load of 1 inch plank is 600 square feet; of 1½ inch, 400; of 2 inch, 300; of 2½, 240; of 3 inch, 200; of 3½, 170; and of 4 inch, 150 square feet. In the Cape colony, two loops of wagon wood; 50 planks of yellow-wood, and 10 planks of stink-wood; each make a load. See Cart-load.

Loaded Cushion, a lady's table pincushion, for fastening work to, and which is loaded with lead.

Loading Turn, the successive rotation for ships to approach the quays, to take in cargo.

Loadstone, a magnet.

Loaf, a thick mass of any thing; a large cake or shape of bread, of different weights and kinds; as the quartern, or 4 lb. loaf; the half-quartern; the cottage loaf; tin loaves; bricks, &c.

Loafer, an American term for an idler or vagrant.

Loaf-sugar, solid white or refined bleached sugar, which has been run into long moulds or shapes, and purified from the molasses.

Loam, a clay containing a large proportion of silex, and occasionally used for polishing common articles by manufacturers.

Loan, a national debt; money lent at interest; any thing lent.

Loan-office, an office, of which there are many now established in town and country for lending sums of money to individuals, at high rates of interest, to be repaid by weekly or other instalments, guaranteed by the security of one or more sureties.

Lobby, a small hall or waiting-room; the entrance into a principal apartment.

Lobelia, a handsome genus of plants, some of the American species of which, although dangerous in their properties, are used medicinally, especially *L. cardinalis* and *L. siphilitica*; spirit or ethereal tinctures of the Indian tobacco herb (*L. inflata*) are medicinally prescribed in spasmodic and asthmatic attacks, as an expectorant, and as an emetic; but should only be given in very small doses, or may else prove fatal.

Lobster, a crustaceous animal, the *Astacus gammarus* (*A. marinus* of Fabr.), in the capture and sale of which a large trade is carried on, from 2½ to 3 millions being brought to London annually.

Locandiere (Italian), one who lets furnished lodgings.

Location, a colonial name for surveyed land; a settlement; leasing on rent.

Loch, the name in Scotland for a lake; a French ship-building wood; also a French sea-term for the log.

Lock, part of a gun; an instrument to secure doors, &c.; a tuft of hair or wool; part of a canal between a sluice and a flood-gate to confine water, and to facilitate the ascent or descent of barges.

Lock and Hinge Manufacturer, a maker of mechanical metal contrivances for fastening and hanging doors.

Lock-chamber, the space on a canal between two lock-gates.

Locker, a small fixed chest or closet to stow any thing away in on board ship; a custom-house officer.

Locker's-order, a customs order, the counterpart or slip of which is delivered to a warehouse-keeper, being his authority to deliver goods to a searcher. There are two kinds of these orders, one for wet goods, and the other for dry.

Locket, a small neck ornament worn by a lady, to keep a lock of hair or small miniature or other memento in.

Lock-gate, the entrance into a lock-chamber on a canal, for the admission, &c. of boats or vessels.

Lock-keeper, one who opens a canal lock.

Lock-maker, a constructor of patent or ordinary locks.

Lock-saw. *See* Saw.

Lock-smith, a fixer and repairer of locks, who usually combines with it the business of bell-hanger.

Locomotive, a self-moving travelling steam-engine, running by inward machinery on land; one that propels or draws a train of railway carriages, or ballast vans, &c.

Locomotive-engine Builder, a mechanical engineer; a constructor of steam-engines.

Locust, a predatory insect, the *Gryllus migratorius*, which, in many countries, commits great devastation on crops, devouring every green herb that it comes across. In Africa locusts are largely consumed in many districts for food, either roasted, or pounded and baked into bread. They are also salted. A common West-Indian tree, the *Hymenæa Courbaril*, which often attains a height of from 60 to 80 feet, with a trunk from 7 to 8 feet in diameter. The wood is hard and compact, and its durability recommends it for mill-rollers and similar purposes. Also a name for the *Robinia pseud'-acacia*.

Locust-beans, a name for the sweet pods of the carob tree. *See* Carob-fruit.

Lode, a mining term for a regular vein producing or yielding ore or metal.

Lodge, a porter's room; a cottage at the entrance-gate of a park; a small dwelling-house.

Lodge-gate, a park or entrance-gate, situated near the lodge.

Lodger, one who occupies an apartment, and lives in another person's house; a tenant of part of a house.

Lodging-house, a house let out by the owner or tenant in apartments.

Lodging-house Keeper, the tenant of a house who makes a profit or living by letting lodgings, casual or permanent.

Lodgings, rooms which are for hire in a house, and are let either furnished or unfurnished.

Lof, Loof, a Russian weight and dry-measure: as a weight in Russia it is 92·17 lbs.; as a measure it ranges in different localities from one to 1⅝ bushel. It is also called a looper in some districts.

Loft, a storehouse on an elevated story; a room immediately under the roof.

Log, a large shapeless junk of wood; a journal kept on board ship, in which the situation of the vessel, weather, and every thing of importance is noted down; a flat piece of wood loaded with lead at one of its edges to make it float upright, to which is attached a line about 150 fathoms long, divided into equal lengths by little pieces of knotted twine rove into it. The line is wound upon a reel, and cast into the sea, for ascertaining the ship's rate of sailing by the time a certain quantity takes in running off the reel. *See* Knot.

Log-book, a journal of proceedings. *See* Log.

Loggans, a local name in Scotland for stockings without feet.

LOGGER-HEAD, an iron for heating tar.
LOG-GLASS, a half-minute sandglass, used on board ship in timing the speed of sailing, by the quantity of line run out in a given time.
LOG-HUT, a settler's rude cabin in the backwoods, &c.; a lime burner's shanty.
LOG-LINE, a line thrown over the stern of a ship with a float attached, to measure the rate at which she is proceeding. The line is usually marked with a knot at each 120th part of a mile, and when measured by a half-minute sandglass, the number of knots carried off during that time shows the number of miles the vessel runs in an hour. *See* LOG and KNOT.
LOG-REEL, the reel on which the log-line of a ship is wound.
LOGWOOD, a dye-wood used by the calico printer and others, obtained from the *Hæmatoxylon Campechianum*, which affords the most durable deep red and black dye. Our imports have been on the increase of late years, and in 1856 we received about 30,000 tons.
LOHER (German), a tanner.
LOHNARBEITER, a labourer in Germany.
LOLO, the name in some parts of the Pacific for coco-nut oil.
LOMBARD, on the Continent a banker or money-lender.
LOMBARD-HOUSE, a public pawnbroking establishment; a mont de piété.
LOMBARD-STREET, the chief street of banks, discount-brokers, and bullion-dealers, in the City of London; a term for the money-market.
LONGAN, an agreeable fruit, the produce of *Nephelium Longan*, sometimes imported from China for the sake of the sweet subacid vinous pulp which covers the seed.
LONG-BEARD, a name for a kind of moss or epiphyte brought down the Mississippi. *See* BARBA HISPANICA.
LONG-BOAT, the largest boat of a merchant [ship.
LONG-BOW, an archery bow for shooting.
LONG-BOW-STRING MAKERS' COMPANY, one of the minor incorporated companies of London, not on the livery, and which has no hall.
LONG-CLOTH, a peculiar kind of fine calico or cotton fabric, which is made milled and plain.
LONG-DOZEN, thirteen articles to the dozen.
LONG-HUNDRED, six score, or 120.
LONGITUDE, in navigation the distance of a place on the earth's surface east or west from a meridional point. The Royal Observatory at Greenwich has been for many years taken as the point of departure in English maps and charts. The French take theirs from Paris.
LONG-MEASURE, the measure of length of a country.
LONG-PRIMER, a printing-type intermediate in size between small pica and bourgeois.
LONG-ROOM, the principal room in the London Custom-House, where shipping business is transacted.
LONG-SHOREMEN, a name given in London to a large body of liverymen, of the lower class, who have the reputation of taking bribes to vote at civic elections.
LONG-TOM, a cradle used for washing out gold by miners at the gold fields.
LONG-VACATION, in law the intervening period between Trinity and Michaelmas term.
LONTAR, one of the names of the palmyra [palm.
LONTAR SUGAR, sugar made from the sap of the Palmyra palm (*Borassus raphis flabelliformis*).
LOOBS, tin slime or sludge containing ore.
LOOF, a Russian corn-measure, nearly equal to the chetwert, which is now generally used instead; 48 loof are equal to 11¼ imperial quarters.
LOOFIES, a name in Scotland for mittens for the hands.
LOOKING-GLASS MANUFACTURER, a maker of looking-glasses and mirrors, &c. for bedroom or parlour use.
LOOKING-GLASS MOUNTER, a frame maker and gilder.
LOOKING-GLASS SILVERER, a workman who covers the back of glass with quicksilver for mirrors, &c.
LOOL, a vessel used in the mining districts to receive the washings of the ore.
LOOM, one of the most useful of machines, employed by weavers for crossing and weaving threads. There are various kinds of looms according to the pattern and fabric to be worked; some are still worked by hand, although the larger number are now moved by water or steam power; the part of an oar held in the hand and within the boat, contradistinguished from the blade.
LOOM-CARDS, perforated cards with patterns for jacquard weaving.
LOOM-MAKER, a manufacturer of frames for weaving, worked either by hand or by steam-power, &c.
LOONGHIE, an Indian waist cloth; a mixed fabric of rich-coloured silk and cotton, made in Sinde, about four yards long by two feet wide.
LOOP, a noose; a double or fold of string; a dry measure of Riga—48 going to the last—60 loops being equal to 14 imperial quarters; part of a row of cast iron; in the Cape colony sufficient wood to make a wagon out of, two loops going to a load.
LOOP-LINE, a connecting line of railway; one running into the trunk line.
LOOT, an Indian name for theft or plunder.
LOO-TABLE, a round table for a sitting-room; originally so named from its convenient adaptation for a circle of persons playing the game of loo.
LOOTAH, a brass water vessel used in India of variable dimensions, holding from a pint to half a gallon.
LOP, the cuttings or branches from a tree; thus in a sale of standing timber trees they are advertised with their "lop, top, and bark."
LOPATNY, a description of Russian tallow, known as second candle tallow.
LORCHA, a peculiar class of trading vessel on the Eastern seas.
LORD MAYOR, the chief magistrate of the cities of London, Dublin, and York, each of whom has the title of lord.

LORGNETTE, a spy-glass; an opera-glass.
LORIMER, LORINER, a bridle-cutter; a bit-maker.
LORINERS' COMPANY, one of the minor livery companies of London which has no hall, but simply oiled.
LORRIE, a coal cart.
LOSH HIDE, a hide not dressed in any way,
LOT, a division; a share, a term much used in the United States, as for instance, timber-lot, water-lot, residence-lot, garden-lot, building-lot, &c.; a parcel of goods offered for sale at an auction, &c.; a liquid measure of Dunkirk, equal to half a gallon.
LOTH, a Dutch light weight used for quills and other small commodities, equal to half an ounce; the sixteenth part of the Prussian marc; in Russia it is the thirty-second part of the bercheroot.
LOTION, a wash.
LOTMAN, in Scotland, one who thrashes corn for an agreed proportion of the grain.
LOTTERY, an allotment; a distribution of prizes and blanks by a chance drawing.
LOUIS, LOUIS D' OR, a French gold coin; the old Louis was 24 francs; the new one is only 20.
LOURDIER, a kind of mattress.
LOUVRE, a lantern; an opening in the roof of a house for smoke to escape.
LOVAGE, a liqueur or cordial; a plant, the *Ligusticum Scoticum*, the acrid leaves of which are eaten crude as a salad, or boiled as greens, and, though aromatic and stomachic, are very nauseous; the stem yields English opoponax, and the roots are reported to be carminative.
LOVE-APPLE, another name for the tomato, *Lycopersicum esculentum*, Miller. See TOMATO.
LOVE-BIRD, a name for the small parroquet, *Psittacus passerinus*, found in both Continents, and esteemed as a cage bird.
LOVE-RIBBON, a thin gauze ribbon.
LOWER-CASE, in letter-press printing, an oblong case of about a yard long, and half a yard broad. It is composed of about 50 boxes of different sizes, in which are separately deposited the whole letters of the alphabet, as also the points, double letters, and, in some offices, the figures. The case containing the capital letters, small capitals, and accents, is placed on a frame directly above, and called, in contradistinction to the other, the Upper-case.
LOW-PRESSURE ENGINE, an engine where the steam is drawn off into a condenser.
LOW-WATER MARK, the lowest state of the tide, after the ebb is completed.
LOW WINES, the weak spirit remaining after the first distillation of alcohol.
LOXA, a measure for betel nuts. See LAXAR.
LOXA BARK, a pale Peruvian bark, also called crown bark, the produce of *Cinchona Condaminea*. There is another kind with a white epidermis.
LOY, a long narrow spade used in the stony lands of Munster, Ireland.
LOZENGE, a rhomb or oblique four-sided figure, as a glass quarry in a casement; a cake or sweetmeat rolled and cut into such a shape.

L.R.C.S., "Licentiate of the Royal College of Surgeons."
LUBBER'S HOLE, a hole in the top of a vessel next to the mast.
LUBRICATION, the oiling of the joints and bearings of machinery, axles, &c. in order to diminish friction
LUBRICATOR, an oil-cup or other contrivance for supplying grease, &c. to ease the friction of rubbing surfaces.
LUCERNE, a name formerly given to the skin of the lynx; an artificial fodder grass, the *Medicago sativa*.
LUCET, a lady's lace loom, made of bone, ivory, or wood.
LUCIFER-BOX, a box or case with phosphoric matches.
LUCIFER-MATCHES, splints of wood, dipped in a solution of phosphorus, chlorate of potash, gum, or glue.
LUCIFER-MATCH MAKER, a manufacturer of the matches so named.
LUFFER, a frame of laths to admit air or light; the turret on a hall or kitchen roof; the wooden window in a church steeple.
LUFF TACKLE, a purchase, composed of a double and single block.
LUG, the projecting slip of a mould or flask, used in casting operations; a local name for the pole or perch; in Gloucestershire, a land-measure of six yards; a square sail used in large boats.
LUGGAGE, personal baggage; any thing cumbrous carried about by a traveller, but now applied to goods of any kind or quantity transported, belonging to an individual.
LUGGAGE-TRAIN, a slow or night train on a railway; that by which goods and merchandise are transported.
LUGGAGE-VAN, a baggage-wagon, for conveying heavy goods and merchandise.
LUGGER, a decked boat for fishing; a vessel with two or three low masts and lug sails.
LUGGIE, the name for a measuring cord or chain in Bengal; in some places six feet; in Tirhoot and Sarun, 8½ to 10 feet; in the northern and western parts, from 12 to 14 feet.
LUG-MARK, a mark cut in the ear of a sheep or dog to identify it.
LUGS, a classification of American tobacco; thus there are factory lugs and planters' lugs.
LUM, a name in Scotland for a cottage chimney.
LUMACHELLA, a kind of shell marble in Florence.
LUMBARDAR, a cultivator of the poppy in Bengal, who has signed articles with the government.
LUMBER, a name in North America for rough timber.
LUMBER-DEALER, a wood merchant; a dealer in hard and soft woods.
LUMBERER, a backwoodsman in North America; one who fells and shapes timber.
LUMBER-WHARF, a timber-yard.
LUMPER, one who furnishes ballast for ships.
LUMPS, a kind of brick or tile; dock-yard barges.

LUMP-SUGAR, white or loaf sugar broken into small pieces.
LUNAR CAUSTIC, a name for nitrate of silver, used medicinally outwardly and inwardly.
LUNATIC ASYLUM, a house for the insane.
LUNATIC ASYLUM PROPRIETOR, the keeper of a licensed house for the care of insane persons.
LUNCHEON, a mid-day meal; a refreshment taken between breakfast and dinner.
LUNETTE, the rim of a watch glass: a small opening in the roof of a house; an eye-glass.
LUNETTIER, a spectacle-maker.
LUNT (German), a match-cord for firing guns.
LUPINE, a leguminous plant, the seeds of which are eaten in Turkey.
LUPPE (German), a microscope or magnifying glass.
LURCH, the sudden heavy rolling of a vessel at sea to one side.
LURCHER, a hunting dog that lies in wait, or watches for his game.
LUSTRE, a sconce or chandelier.
LUSTRED SEAL, a furrier's name for a dyed and prepared skin of the fur seal.
LUSTRE-MANUFACTURER, a lamp-maker.
LUSTRING, a shining silk; often corruptly written and pronounced lutestring. *See* LUTESTRING.
LUSTROUS, having a shining or glossy appearance, like silk.
LUST-SCHIFF (German), a pleasure-boat or yacht.
LUTE, a cement; a pasty or loamy and fatty matter, used to keep the joints of tubes and chemical apparatus, &c. tight. It is made either with pipe-clay and linseed-oil, or chalk, flour, and water; but the material varies with the substance to be cemented; a musical instrument so named.
LUTESTRING, often but very erroneously so spelled for lustring, a shining silk; the string of a lute.
LUTESTRING-MAKER, a silk manufacturer; a maker of strings for lutes or harps.
LY, a Chinese land-measure, about the third part of an English mile.
LYANG, another name for the Chinese tael.
LYCEUM, a theatre; a grammar-school; a literary institution.
LYCOPODIUM, a cryptogamous plant, the puff ball; a decoction of it is used in Sweden to destroy vermin in cattle. It is also employed for dyeing purposes, to fix the colour of woollen cloth, and also by pyrotechnists.
LYDIAN-STONE, a name for the blood stones, and jaspery varieties of quartz, used by jewellers as burnishing stones, and also as a touchstone, to determine the amount of alloy in jewellers' gold. The best pebbles are obtained from Lydia. *See* BASANITE.
LYE, LEY, water alkalized with wood ashes.
LYNX, the skin of this animal is of a greyish white, with dark spots. Being very soft, warm, and light, it is much used by the Chinese, Greeks, Persians, and others, for cloaks, linings, facings, &c. When dyed and prepared, the skins of the lynx and lynx cat, are exported in large numbers to the United States.
LYRE, a musical instrument.
LYSPUND, SETTEE, an Orkney weight. *See* LESH-PUND.

M.

MAAFEE, a term in Bengal for land exempt from revenue duty.
MAANAH, an Eastern grain-measure, about 34 lbs. 8 oz.
MAAP, a liquid measure used in Baden, rather more than a gallon.
MAAS, a division of the wine-measure in Bavaria, 48 making a muid of 15·08, and 60 a wine eimer, of 8·12 imperial gallons. In Frankfort and the South of Germany, the maas, or gescheid, is a little more than 3 pints. A Persian name for curds of milk dried in the sun, which are mixed with water, to make an acidulous beverage.
MAATJE, the Netherlandish name for the French decilitre.
MACADAMIZED ROAD, a road prepared and made durable, level, and firm, by pounded granite, &c. which binds the earth into a solid mass: named after the introducer.
MACARONI, a paste of flour. *See* MACCARONI.
MACAROONS, small sweet wine cakes.
MACAW-FAT, a West-Indian name for the oil palm, *Elais guineensis*.
MACAW-PALM, the *Acrocomia sclerocarpa* of Martius, occurring in considerable abundance in some of the West-India islands, and the eastern parts of South America. The fruit yields an oil of a golden yellow hue, of the consistence of butter, which has an odour like violets, and a sweetish taste. It enters into the composition of toilet soaps. The nuts, which are susceptible of a high polish, are sometimes fancifully carved by the negroes. The tree is also called the grougrou palm by the negroes.
MACCARONI, a delicate food-product made from wheat flour, the dough of which is dried in the shape of pipes. It is often termed Genoese paste. We receive imports in small boxes of from 6 to 28 lbs. from the Mediterranean, for consumption at table, with cheese, in soup, and for puddings, &c. Vermicelli is the same substance, rolled smaller than maccaroni.
MACCARONI AND VERMICELLI MAKER, a manufacturer of the dough paste in pipes so named.
MACCO, an Italian mess, which consists of beans boiled to a mash.
MACCOBOY, MACCUBAU, a kind of snuff.

Mace, the arillus, or branching membrane covering the nutmeg, used as a spice; an ornamented staff borne before a magistrate, and some other functionaries. A Chinese money and weight; the former is the tenth part of the tael, nearly 7½d., and consists of 100 to 140 copper cash; as a weight, it is about 58 grains; a fish measure, a mace or maize of herrings being 500 in number.

Macellaro, an Italian butcher; macello being a slaughter-house or shambles.

Macerate, to wear away by steeping in water; to make lean; to mortify or fret.

Machbat, Machette, the negro name for a cutlass.

Macheta. a kind of violin used in Brazil.

Machine, an engine, a piece of mechanism or contrivance for performing some work; of which there are numberless kinds employed for different purposes.

Machine-maker and Mill-wright, an engineer; a constructive builder, who designs or supplies machines and engines to order.

Machine-ruler, a machine which lines or rules paper, according to patterns.

Machinery, engines of all kinds, which are put into action to perform certain effective work which supersedes manual labour; such as for spinning and weaving, wire-drawing, making lace, rope, paper-making and printing, sawing, &c. There were stated to be, a few years ago, 15,000 stationary engines in the kingdom, working in mines, &c. valued at £25,000,000; 4000 wind, water, and steam mills, and 5000 horse, and other small mills. Besides what is used at home, we export machinery and mill-work, to the value of £2,500,000 a-year.

Machine-strap Maker, a manufacturer of leather and other connecting bands, &c. for the moving power of machinery.

Machining, working off newspaper or book sheets at a steam press, often contracted for at an agreed rate per thousand.

Machinist, one engaged in the manufacture of machines; an employé at a theatre, who attends to the working of the moveable scenery.

Macho, a Spanish weight, equal to about 150 French pounds.

Machooti, a name in Hindustan for the knot-grass.

Macinatoio, an oil-mill in Italy.

Macintosh, a solution of caoutchouc in coal naphtha, applied to linen cloths and other substances, to render them waterproof; so called from the name of the patentee.

Mack, the Burmese name for a hand's-breadth or measure of 6 inches.

Mackerel, a well-known useful fish, the *Scomber scombrus*, which frequents the British coasts, and is either netted or caught by the hook; about 24,000,000, weighing nearly 10,500 tons, are brought to Billingsgate in a year.

Mackerel-boat, a boat pursuing the mackerel fishery.

Mackle, to sell weavers' goods to the shopkeepers.

Macon, a kind of wine.

Macuquina, a silver cut money of debased quality, circulating in Guatemala.

Macuto, a money of account in Sierra Leone, equivalent to about 9d. There are silver coins current, circulating for 2 and 10 macutos.

Mada, an Indian weight of 1 drachm 20 grains.

Madapollam, a kind of fine long cloth, shipped to the Eastern markets.

Madder, the root of *Rubia tinctoria*, which enters largely into commerce, furnishing a fine scarlet colour to dyers and calico-printers.

Madega, a Spanish name for a skein or hank.

Madeira, an esteemed dry light wine, produced in the Portuguese island from which it receives its name.

Mad-house, an asylum for the insane.

Madhouse-keeper, the licensed registered owner of a private lunatic asylum; an attendant on insane persons.

Madooka, an Indian name for the *Bassia latifolia*. *See* Mowha.

Madrepore, a petrifaction, or species of coral; a variety of limestone.

Madriers (French), thick boards or planks.

Magazine, a warehouse or store-room; a secure place for keeping powder in, ashore or afloat; a periodical publication.

Magazine-day, the publication-day for monthlies and serials when they are supplied to the trade; the last day of the month.

Magic Lantern, an optical machine, with a lamp and lenses for reflecting magnified pictures on the wall from painted glass slides.

Magistrate, a public civil officer who has legal jurisdiction in certain cases.

Magnanier (French), the manager or proprietor of a nursery for silkworms.

Magnano, an Italian locksmith.

Magnesia, one of the primitive earths, having a metallic base. The sulphate is Epsom salts—the carbonate is compounded with carbonic acid gas. Magnesia is now generally prepared artificially, and is used to purify oils; in the manufacture of glass, and for medicinal purposes.

Magnet, a kind of rich iron-stone, which has the property of attracting light pieces of iron towards it; a bar of iron made artificially magnetic by electricity.

Magnetic-needle, *See* Magnet.

Magnetic Telegraph. *See* Telegraph.

Magnetometer, a measurer of the force of magnetism.

Magnifying-glass, a lens that magnifies or enlarges the object looked at.

Mahallah. a petty brass coin current in some parts of Arabia, the 66th part of a dollar.

Maharmah, a muslin wrapper worn over the head, and across the mouth and chin, by Turkish and Armenian ladies when they appear abroad.

Maharunga, a name in the Himalayas for the *Onosma emodi*, which furnishes a dye-stuff like alkanet.

Mahaseer, a delicious fresh-water fish of the Indian rivers.

Mahlib, Mklub, the fragrant kernels of *Prunus Mahaleb* of Linnæus, strung as necklaces, which are much valued by the women of Sinde and other parts of India.

Mahoe, an *Hibiscus* furnishing a useful fibre. The common mahoe of the West Indies is *H. elatus* of Swartz; the East Indian mahoe, *H. latifolia*; the sea-side mahoe, *H. tiliaceus*. The strong fibre is used in the East for making cordage, coffee-bags, &c.

Mahogany, a well-known valuable furniture wood, chiefly imported from Honduras, where it is obtained from a large forest tree, the *Swietenia Mahagoni*. African mahogany is the wood of *Khaya senegalensis*. The wood of the Toon-tree (*Cedrela Toona*) is sometimes called Indian mahogany. Our imports of mahogany average about 38,000 tons per annum. The astringent bark is used in the West Indies as a substitute for cinchona, but contains no alkaline principle.

Mahogany Broker and Merchant, an importer or dealer in mahogany.

Mahone, a large Turkish ship.

Mahoree, a name for aniseed in Bengal.

Mahouib, Mahboub, a name in Tunis for the sequin, a small thin gold coin of 4½ piastres, worth about 3s. 9d. sterling. In Egypt the mahoub passes for 90 paras.

Maidan, a market-place in the Levant.

Maid of Honour, a kind of bun or cake sold at Richmond.

Maid-servant, a female domestic.

Mail-coach, a travelling-carriage which carries the mails for the post-office from one town to another. The great bulk of the inland mails are now, however, forwarded by railway, except on a few bye-roads to cross post towns or villages.

Mailloir (French), a piece of marble on which bleachers beat the linen.

Mails, a common term for communications and matter transmitted by the post-office, comprising letters, newspapers, books, &c.

Main (French), the hand; the chief or principal; hence a common prefix to some sails, yards, and parts of a ship; a great channel or ditch; a large cast-iron supply-pipe under ground for distributing water or gas over a town or district; a banker's shovel; the gross or bulk of any thing.

Main-boom, the spar of a small vessel's main-sail.

Main-chains. *See* Chain-plates.

Main-hamper, a hand-basket for grapes.

Main-mast, the chief or middle mast of a ship; the after-mast of a brig.

Main-sail, the lower course or largest sail in a ship; that set on the main-yard, and extending towards the deck.

Main-sheet, the rope attached to the lower corners of the main-sail.

Maintenance, support, as of seamen, paupers, prisoners, or apprentices.

Main-top, the resting-place or junction between the main-mast and the main-top-mast.

Main-yard, the largest or principal yard in a ship; that on which the main-sail is extended.

Maiolica (Italian), earthenware.

Maisonnage (French), timber for building.

Maistrance (French), warrant-officers; non-commissioned-officers.

Maize, the general name for the seeds of Indian corn, (*Zea Mays*); the principal grain crop of the United States; a Scotch fish-measure of 500 herrings. *See* Mace.

Majoon, a confection of hemp, being a compound of butter, sugar, flour, milk, and bhang. It is largely consumed as an intoxicating drug by all classes of natives in the East.

Major, a field-officer in the army above a captain.

Major-domo, a house-steward.

Makara, a name in Bengal for the *Emyale ferox*, found in lakes and ponds. The seeds of the berry being farinaceous, are a favourite article of diet among the natives: they are deemed powerful tonics.

Malaboorong, a small weight used in Borneo, equal to about 3 grains.

Malacca-bean, a name in the East for the marking-nut.

Malachite, a valuable green ore or massive carbonate of copper, much prized by the lapidary in consequence of the beauty of its colour and marking, and the high polish it will take.

Malaga, a kind of wine; also called mountain.

Malaguetta Pepper. *See* Grains of Paradise.

Malambo-bark, a bark found in Colombia, possessed of strong, bitter, and aromatic properties, supposed to belong to a *Quassia*, or some allied plant. It is also called Matias bark.

Malee, a gardener in India.

Male-fern, a wild plant, the *Aspidium Filix-mas* of Swartz, which has astringent and emetic properties, and is used as an anthelmintic.

Male-screw, a screw which has the spiral threads on the outside of the cylinder.

Malet, a portmanteau.

Maletent, a heavy tax levied on the export of wool some centuries ago.

Malgoozaree, a name in India for land subject to assessment; unassessed land is termed Minhaee.

Malkungee, an Indian name for the *Celastrus paniculatus*, from the seeds of which an empyreumatic black oily fluid is distilled, used beneficially in rheumatism. Large quantities would doubtless yield paraffine and creasote.

Mall, a public walk.

Mallard (French), a small grindstone; a drake.

Malle-molle (French), mull-muslin; very thin muslin.

Mallet, a small maul made of wood, used for caulking, serving rope, &c.

Malletier (French), a portmanteau-maker.

Mallier (French), a sumpter horse; a pack-horse.

Malms, Marle-stocks, a kind of brick. *See* Cutters.

MALMSEY, a luscious and high-flavoured wine made in Madeira and Teneriffe from grapes in the last stage of ripeness.

MALT, prepared barley, which has been steeped in water and then kiln-dried. It is used for making malt-liquors. Malt is subject to a duty of 2s. 7d. per bushel and 5 per cent. The quantity made in 1856 was about 34½ million bushels.

MALT-DISTILLER, one who makes a decoction or preparation from malt.

MALT-DUST, the remains of malt.

MALTER, a German grain-measure, varying in different localities, but usually reckoned, in the southern parts of Germany, to be equal to 3 bushels and 1¼ gallon.

MALTESE STONE, a soft stone quarried in Malta, used for carving, and for making large jars, &c.

MALT-FACTOR, a dealer in malt.

MALT-FLOOR, a perforated floor in the chamber of a malt-kiln, through which the heat ascends from the furnace below, and dries the barley laid upon it.

MALT-GRINDER, a machine for crushing or cutting malted barley.

MALTHA, mineral pitch; thickened petroleum or rock oil.

MALT-LIQUORS, ale, beer, and porter, which are prepared with malt.

MALT-ROASTER MAKER, a manufacturer of machines for roasting barley on a small scale.

MALT-SHOVEL, a large flat wooden shovel for turning over malt.

MALTSTER, a manufacturer of malt from barley; there are about 9000 maltsters in the kingdom.

MALT-VINEGAR, the ordinary kind of vinegar made for domestic use in this country.

MALVADA, a small Spanish coin, thirteen of which make an English farthing.

MALVAGIA, the Italian name for Malmsey wine.

MALWA OPIUM, one of the leading descriptions of Indian opium, which is inferior in quality to the Benares and Behar kinds.

MAMALIGA, a sort of hasty pudding or grout made from maize, on which the lower classes in the Danubian provinces almost exclusively subsist.

MAMMEE, a tropical fruit, the *Mammea Americana*, which has a sweet and very agreeable taste, accompanied with an aromatic pleasant odour.

MAMMOODIS, a coarse muslin.

MAMMOTIE, a road hoe, used in Ceylon.

MAN, a corrupted name for the Indian maund.

MANAGER, a director; a superintendant; the lessee or director of a theatre.

MANCHESTER AND GLASGOW WAREHOUSE, a sale depository for all kinds of cotton goods.

MANCHINEEL, a large tree, the *Hippomane Mancinella*, a native of the West Indies, the wood of which is hard and durable; very close, yellow-brown, and beautifully clouded. The sap is, however, a most deadly poison.

MANDANDOO, a mixture of the buds and fruits of an aromatic plant, used in Ceylon in the preparation of betel.

MANDATAIRE, a French agent or attorney.

MANDATS, a national paper-money, issued in the early part of the century, in France to replace the assignats which had become wretchedly depreciated.

MANDAVALLI, an Indian name for the *Convolvolus reptans*, affording a milky juice, which, when dried, is equal to scammony in purgative effect. The tops and leaves are eaten in stews by the natives.

MANDEEL, a name in Turkey for black and coloured cotton handkerchiefs.

MANDEL, a term in Germany for 15 articles of any kind.

MANDILION, a loose garment; a sleeveless jacket.

MANDIOC, a Brazilian name for the root and starch of the cassava. *See* CASSAVA.

MANDOLA (Italian), a cithern, a musical instrument; an almond.

MANDOLINE, a sort of guitar.

MANDORE, a four-stringed lute.

MANDRAKE, the root of *Mandragora officinarum*, an old ingredient in philtres, but of dangerous properties.

MANDREL, a pulley in a turner's lathe.

MANEGE, a French riding school.

MANEH, a Scripture weight equal to 2 lbs. 3 ounces, 10 dwts., 3 grains: when applied to money it consisted of 60 shekels, and was worth £6 16s. 7½d.

MANEQUIN, an artist's model of wood or wax.

MANGAL, a kind of portable copper stove or brasier used in Turkey.

MANGANESE, a black metallic ore, consumed to the amount of 4000 to 5000 tons per annum, being used in glass-making, for glazing black earthenware, giving colour to enamels, making oxymuriatic acid for forming bleaching liquor, as a dryer for painters' colours, and preparations are used in medicine.

MANGEL WURZEL, one of the common names of a variety of the beet-root grown for feeding cattle; the *Beta vulgaris*, var. *macrorhiza*.

MANGER, a trough or rack for feeding horses.

MANGLE, a machine or rolling-press for smoothing linen by pressure.

MANGLE AND PRESS MAKER, a manufacturer of machines so named.

MANGLE-KEEPER, the owner of a mangle; a smoother of linen.

MANGO, a tropical fruit, the produce of trees of the *Mangifera* family, of which there are many cultivated varieties, although only two distinct species of tree. The fruit of the finer kinds have a rich perfumed grateful flavour; while others are so stringy and unpleasant as not to be eatable. The fruit is pickled and preserved, and made into a chutney.

MANGO-FISH, a small fish eight or nine inches in length and two in depth, the *Polynemus longifilis* of Cuvier, the *P. paradisius* of Linnaeus, esteemed as a delicacy in India, where it is also called the Tupsee. Isinglass is made of the swimming-bladder.

MANGO-GINGER, an Indian name for the *Curcuma amada*, used as an article for seasoning food.

MANGOSTEEN, a delicious eastern fruit, the produce of *Garcinia Mangostana*. The rind of the fruit furnishes small quantities of gamboge.

MANGROVE, a tropical tree frequenting the borders of seas and swamps, the *Rhizophora Mangle*, the bark of which is used for tanning. The mangrove or tree-oyster attaches itself to the boughs which droop in the water. The wood of this tree is used for making sugar hogsheads, and for ship-building.

MANGUERA, a canvas shoot, used at the Chincha islands for discharging guano into the holds of ships, or into boats.

MANHOLE, an opening in the top of the boiler of a locomotive engine, made to admit a person to clean the interior.

MANI, MANIBILLA. See BUCK-WAX.

MANICRISTO, an Italian confection.

MANIFEST, the list of a ship's cargo, containing the mark, number, and description of each package of goods, the shipper's name, &c.

MANIFOLD-WRITER, a writing apparatus, for taking several copies of a letter or document at once by a stylus, upon thin tissue or tracing paper interleaved with black oiled sheets.

MANIKA, MANNIKAH, an Indian grain-measure of 2 seers or about $4\frac{1}{2}$ pints.

MANILA-HEMP, a name given in commerce to the fibre of the wild plantain, *Musa textilis*, brought from the Philippines, and from which the white rope so much prized is made.

MANILAS, a name for a kind of cheroots made in the Philippines, so called from the name of the city from which they are shipped.

MANILLA, a piece of copper, of a horse-shoe shape, passing as money among the natives on parts of the West African coast: a metal ring worn as an ornament on the small part of the leg, or on the thick part of the arm above the elbow, by African chiefs and others.

MANIOC. See CASSAVA.

MANIVEAU, a small flat basket, used in France for fish.

MANJADA, a Ceylon weight for pearls, of $7\frac{1}{2}$ troy grains, and divided into 320 fractional parts.

MANJEE, the helmsman or superintendant of a boat in the river Ganges.

MANJHIKA, an Indian name for the small seeds of the sweet bazil (*Ocymum Basilicum*, used in disease of the kidneys, &c.

MAN-MILLINER, a man who makes or sells millinery.

MANNA, a sweet gummy exudation from several plants; the Calabrian manna is produced in tears from a species of ash, the *Fraxinus rotundifolia*, while some is obtained from another species, the *F. florifera*. The oriental manna of the desert is from *Alhagi Maurorum*. Manna is used medicinally.

MANNA CROUP, a preparation of wheat imported from Russia to compete with semolina.

MANNETTE (French), a small hamper.

MAN OF WAR, an armed vessel belonging to a Government or State.

MANOMETER, an instrument intended to measure the rarefaction and condensation of elastic fluids in confined circumstances. It is also called a manoscope.

MANONIM, a name for wild rice in Minnesota, America.

MANOSCOPE. See MANOMETER.

MANOVALE, MANUALE, a bricklayer's labourer in Italy; a hodman.

MAN-ROPES, side ropes to the gangway of a ship.

MANSANA, a division of land in some of the States of Central America, equal to 100 Spanish or 88 8-9th English square yards.

MANSARDE (French), an attic or garret with a curved roof, so called from Mansard, the architect who introduced them.

MANSE, a Scotch parsonage; a farm-house and land.

MANSION, a large dwelling: a manor-house.

MANSIONNAIRE, the porter to a Greek church.

MAN'S-MERCER, a vender of small articles of men's dress, such as braces, hose, gloves, handkerchiefs, &c.

MANTEL-PIECE, MANTEL-SHELF, a projecting beam or ledge in a room, resting on the jambs of a fire-place. Mantel-pieces are of wood, marble, slate, or iron.

MANTILLA, a small mantle.

MANTLE, a lady's wrapper or cloak.

MANTLE AND CLOAK WAREHOUSE, a show-room, or repository for ladies' wrapping garments, cloaks, shawls, and mantles.

MANTUA-MAKER, a sempstress, a maker of women's dresses and gowns.

MANUAL, a hand-book or instruction-guide; a book of reference.

MANUFACTORY, a building where a manufacture or trade is carried on.

MANUFACTURE, to make up goods; to work up raw material.

MANUFACTURERS, fabricators, or makers of goods by hand or with art; employers of workmen and machinery.

MANUFACTURING CHEMIST, a working chemist; one who has a laboratory and prepares chemicals, &c.

MANUGUDU, an Indian weight of 30 lbs.

MANURE, any thing applied to fertilize land. In this and some European countries where the soil has been much exhausted by repeated cropping, a large trade is carried on in natural and artificial manures. Several of these, as guano, super-phosphate of lime, &c., are noticed under their separate heads.

MANURE MANUFACTURER, a maker of artificial manures, such as super-phosphate of lime and other compounds used as fertilizers.

MANURE MERCHANT, an agricultural agent; a vender of guano or artificial manures to farmers.

MANUSCRIPT, a letter or document written by the hand.

MANY-ROOT, a name for the *Ruellia tuberosa*, a native of Jamaica, the roots of which are emetic.

MANZANA, a Spanish term for a solid square of buildings formed by the intersection of streets and right angles. It varies in extent from 150 to 350 yards' frontage.

Map, a delineation of the surface of the earth, or part of a country, with its position, boundaries, and geographical peculiarities defined.

Map and Chart Seller and Publisher, a vender and preparer of maps, charts, and plans.

Map and Print Colourer, a person who defines more clearly the boundaries, districts or states on a map by different colours; a tinter and colourer of black prints or engravings.

Map-dissecter and Puzzle-maker, a manufacturer of maps and drawings, &c. in pieces, mounted, which can be united into one whole by children.

Map-engraver and Printer, a worker on copperplate, who draws or engraves maps and prints, &c.

Map-maker, a constructor of maps from the information of travellers or of published works.

Map-mounter, a workman who backs maps with canvas, varnishes and fixes them on rollers, &c.

Maple, a family of trees, of which several have a commercial value. The common maple (*Acer campestre*) is much used in America for house carpentry and furniture. *A. saccharinum*, furnishes the bird's eye maple and curled maple. *See* Bird's Eye Maple. *A. pseudo-platanus* is used in making Tunbridge-ware, and for boxes, butter-prints, &c.

Maple-honey, a name in British North America, for the uncrystallizable portion of the sap of the sugar-maple, which is consumed in the form of molasses.

Maple-sugar, sugar prepared from the sap of the *Acer saccharinum*, which is largely made for home consumption by the settlers in parts of the United States and British North American Provinces: usually it is of a dark treacle colour, as it does not granulate readily; but it is occasionally refined and bleached.

Maquila, a term used in Mexico for reducing ores for mine-owners who do not possess hacienda or mill power, and for which a certain sum, according to agreement, is paid by the mine-owner to the proprietors of the reduction establishment.

Marabou-feathers, the under tail coverts of the *Ciconia argala* and *C. Marabou*; the former, the adjutant-crane of tropical India, furnishes the best; the latter inhabits Africa and Asia; both birds are very large, being sometimes six feet high. The feathers are very light, and are much worn for head-dresses, the white kinds being exceedingly valuable.

Marabout (French), a very large coffee-pot.

Maracaura, a furniture-wood imported from the Brazils, in appearance between mahogany and tulip-wood.

Maraicher (French), a kitchen gardener.

Maharajah, Maharajah, a Hindoo sovereign prince.

Marany Nuts, a name under which the [illegible]-nut has been occasionally imported into Liverpool.

Maraschino, a liqueur prepared in Italy and Dalmatia from a variety of cherry. The fruit and seed are crushed together, one part to the hundred of honey added, and the whole subjected to fermentation, and then distilled and rectified. Sugar and water are subsequently added to flavour it, and it is then stored for some months to free it of empyreumatic flavour.

Maravedi, a Spanish copper coin and petty money of account, the 6th of a penny and the 272nd part of the dollar: 34 maravedis make a real, which is the legal money of account.

Marble, a description of variegated limestone used for ornamental purposes by builders, sculptors, and others. Large quantities are imported in blocks or slabs, and consist of statuary, vein, and Sicilian. Some of the commercial varieties used are Sienna, Bardiglio, black, and dove, St. Ann's, Emperor's red, and Sarplan, Brocatella, amber, verd antique, serpentine, rouge royal, black, and gold. In Spain three-fourths of the mountains are composed of beautiful marble and alabaster. In Catalonia alone there are 177 kinds. The green marble of Granada and the flesh-coloured, have a brilliancy to the eye, and a fineness to the touch, which rank them with the most recherché oriental substances.

Marble-cutter, a stone-mason, a worker in marble.

Marble-paper Manufacturer, a maker of veined or marbled paper for covering boxes, books, wall-hangings, &c.

Marbler, one who veins paper, paint-work, or other material in imitation of marble.

Marbles *for Children*, are made of clay baked and glazed, of alabaster, of glass, of marble, and of a hard stone found near Coburg in Saxony, which is broken into small pieces with a hammer, and then ground in a mill and reduced to accurate smooth spheres in about a quarter of an hour.

Marc, the cake or refuse after expressing the oil or juice from fruits or seeds, as of apples, olives, grapes, &c., mostly used for manure; the half pound of 8 ounces in the old weights of France.

Marcal, an Indian dry-measure containing 8 measures or puddies: 400 marcals make one garce of 9256 lbs.

Marceline, a thin silk tissue called Persian.

Marcella, a quilted cotton fabric.

Marchand, a French shopkeeper or dealer.

Marchetto, a current money of Venice, 124 making a ducat.

Marcite Meadows, a name for irrigated fields in Italy.

Marcos, a weight for silver in South America of eight ounces.

Marcus, a large iron-headed hammer.

Mare, the female of the horse.

Marena, a kind of dry salt fish in Turkey.

Marengo, a name for the 20 franc gold piece in Piedmont.

Mare's-milk. The milk of the mare is richer in sugar than that of the cow, and is usually employed by the Kalmucks and others for the manufacture of milk beer. By distillation, ardent spirits are obtained from this koumiss, and, when carefully made, a pint of liquor will yield half an ounce of spirit. To this milk-brandy, when only once distilled, they give the common Eastern name for spirit, of arraca, and from the residue in the still a kind of hasty-pudding is made.

MAREYEUR (French), a fish-carrier or fish-monger.

MARGIN, an edge or border; the blank unprinted sides of a book page.

MARGOSA-OIL, a native name for the oil expressed in India from the seeds of *Melia azadirachta.*

MARICHU, a Sanscrit name for pepper.

MARILLE, a kind of vessel employed at Naples in the coasting or foreign trade.

MARIEN-GROSCHE, a coin of Hamburgh worth about 1d.

MARFIL (French, Italian), an elephant's tusks. [fagots.

MARGOTIN (French), a small bundle of

MARGUILLIER, a churchwarden in France.

MARIGOLD, a genus of showy plants; the well-known common marigold, *Calendula officinalis*, was formerly used in soups and broths, and employed as a carminative, but is now chiefly used to adulterate saffron.

MARIGRAPH, a French machine for registering, in a permanent manner, the height of the tides, &c.

MARINADE (French), pickled meat fried; fish salted and prepared; or baked in vinegar with spice.

MARINARE (Italian), to pickle.

MARINE, frequenting or appertaining to the sea. A general collective term for shipping, as the mercantile marine, the Royal marine, &c.

MARINE-ENGINE, a steam-engine for use in ships at sea.

MARINE-ENGINE BUILDER, a mechanical engineer who makes engines for steamers.

MARINE-ENGINE BOILER-MAKER, a manufacturer who contracts for the construction of boilers made of iron plates.

MARINE-GLUE. *See* GLUE.

MARINER, a seaman.

MARINES, soldiers who serve on board ship. The Royal Marine corps has also an artillery branch.

MARINE-SOAP, soap suited for washing in sea-water, which is made chiefly with cocoa-nut oil.

MARINE-STORE, a place where old ships' materials are bought and sold, as canvas, junk, iron, &c.

MARINE-STORE DEALER, a purchaser and vender of marine stores, who is permitted to deal in certain articles.

MARIONETTES, a puppet-show; dancing-dolls.

MARI-BALLI, a South American tree, which is used chiefly for spars. It will square from 13 to 14 inches, from 30 to 40 feet in length.

MARITIME, naval; relating to the sea.

MARJORAM, the *Origanum vulgare*, used as a seasoning in cookery, the powder as an errhine, the tea for nervousness. This plant also yields what is called the oil of thyme in the shops, a common remedy for tooth-ache.

MARK, a stamp; a badge; a letter, number, or device, put upon boxes or packages shipped; in archery or gunnery a butt or point aimed at; a Spanish half-pound weight; a coin of 1s. 4d. in Germany.

MARKER, a counter; one who registers the score at a billiard-table.

MARKET, a public place in a city or town, where provisions and merchandise are sold: the right to hold a market was formerly a chartered right or privilege.

MARKETABLE, what may be readily sold.

MARKETAINE, a name in the Danubian Provinces for nails, locks, kettles, and other small wares. [to market.

MARKET-BOAT, a boat which conveys goods

MARKET-CART, a cart travelling to a market with goods for sale.

MARKET-DAY, the fixed day on which a market is held in towns under a chartered privilege.

MARKET-GARDENER, one who raises vegetables, fruit, and flowers for sale. Flowers are usually, however, cultivated by nurserymen and florists.

MARKET-PLACE, an open square or ground, where stalls are pitched, or goods exposed for sale in a town.

MARKING-INK MAKER, a maker of indelible inks for linen, the basis of which is nitrate of silver, although there are various compounds and ingredients used.

MARKING-NUT, a name for the seed of the *Semicarpus Anacardium*, the pure black acrid juice of the pulp is universally employed in the East, for marking cotton cloth, the colour being improved and prevented from running by its being mixed with lime water. The fleshy receptacle on which the seeds rest, is roasted and eaten, and tastes very like roasted apples.

MARL, an earthy carbonate of lime, forming a valuable addition to many soils; a term among sailors, to wind or twist a small line or rope round another.

MARLE-STOCKS, a builder's name for a kind of brick sometimes called firsts or cutters. *See* CUTTERS.

MARLI (French). Scotch gauze.

MARLINE, a fine kind of spun-yarn; small two-stranded stuff, used for twisting or winding round rope.

MARLING-HITCH, a kind of hitch used by sailors in winding or twisting spun-yarn.

MARLING-SPIKE, a pointed iron pin, suspended to a lanyard, used by sailors and others to make an opening in rope, &c.

MARMALADE, a confection; preserved or sweetened fruit. Scotch marmalade is presumed to be of oranges, and there are also marmalades of lemon, quince, and shaddock.

MARMALADE-TREE, the *Lucuma mammosa*, which yields a delicious fruit, like marmalade. The hard tough wood is used for making pestles.

MARMALA-WATER, a fragrant liquid distilled in Ceylon, from the flowers of the Bengal quince, *Ægle marmelos*, and much used as a perfume for sprinkling by the natives.

MARMORATUM, a cement of pounded marble.

MARONE, a brownish crimson or claret colour.

MAROOL, a name for the long fine fibre of the *Sanseveira zeylanica*.

MAROUCHIN (French), an inferior sort of woad, a plant used by dyers.

MARQUEE-MAKER, a manufacturer of strong field booths or tents, of a long form, differing from the small circular tents.

MARQUETERIE-MANUFACTURER. *See* BUHL-CUTTER.

MARQUETRY, a general name applied to inlaid works of various materials, as buhl, reisner, parquetry, mosaic, &c.; a kind of cabinet work, in which the surface of the wood *is* ornamented with inlaid pieces of gold, silver, pearl, tortoiseshell, ivory, horn, or rare woods.

MARQUETTE, a cake of bee's-wax.

MARQUIES, an Indian coin worth about 3s. 4d.

MARRON, a large chestnut; a work printed clandestinely. [in Italy.

MARRONETO, an orchard of chestnut trees

MARROW, the fat in the long hollow bones of animals. Beef marrow is eaten as a culinary delicacy, and also considered useful as a pomatum for the hair.

MARROW-FAT, a choice but late variety of pea.

MARROW-PUDDING, a pudding made with beef marrow.

MARROW-SPOON, a long thin shaped bone or metal spoon, for scooping out marrow.

MARRYAT'S SIGNALS, a particular code of marine signals, very generally adopted by merchant vessels, as laid down in Marryat's Signal Book.

MARSALA, a kind of French light wine.

MARSEILLES QUILT. *See* COUNTERPANE.

MARSEILLES SOAP. Marseilles is the chief seat of the soap manufacture in France, and olive oil is principally used in this manufacture.

MARSELLA, a kind of twilled linen.

MARSH-MALLOW; the leaves of the *Althæa officinalis*, being demulcent and pectoral, are used by herbalists, and like those of the common mallow. *Malva sylvestris*, made into poultices for use in external inflammation.

MARSILIANE, a Venetian vessel.

MARTELLO TOWERS, buildings formerly erected along the coast, within sight of each other, for observation and defence.

MARTINGALE, a perpendicular spar under the bowsprit end, for guying down the head-stays of a ship; part of a horse's bridle, a strap from the noseband to the girth, to prevent him tossing up his head and rearing. [Naples.

MARTINGANE, a kind of vessel employed at

MARVEL OF PERU, a very handsome flower, the *Mirabilis*. The roots of one species, *M. Jalapa*, are drastic and purgative, when old.

MARZUOTO, a kind of Tuscan spring corn, supplying straw for bonnets.

MAS, a money of account, by which calculations are made in Cochin China, equal to about 3d. In Indian numeration, the mas is 100 crores of rupees, the crore being one million pounds sterling. Mas is also the Malay name for gold; mas-urai being gold dust.

MASCULIT, a vessel used on shipboard in the East Indies.

MASDEU, a kind of red wine.

MASH, the Hindustani name for a species of pulse, *Phaseolus mungo*; a mixed food for horses; malt and water.

MASHA, an Eastern weight of 15·375 troy grains, used for the precious metals by native goldsmiths.

MASH-TUN, one of the most important vessels in the brew-house, made of cast iron, in a circular shape, and provided with an inner pierced bottom.

MASK, a cover for the face

MASLIN. *See* MESLIN. [in stone or brick.

MASON, a stone-cutter; a worker or builder

MASONS' COMPANY, one of the livery companies of London, whose hall is situated in Basinghall-street.

MASQUERADE AND FANCY-DRESS WAREHOUSE, a shop where dresses, masks, and disguises are sold for revels, fancy-dress balls, &c.

MASSICOT, a manufacturing name for a tolerably pure oxide of lead, the protoxide used by glass-makers.

MASSOY BARK, a bark obtained from a lofty tree in New Guinea and Java, which has tonic properties, and is rich in essential oil.

MAST, a spar set upright from the deck to support yards, sails, and rigging. *See* MASTS. The fruit or nut of the beech-tree, on which swine are extensively fed in Europe and America, but the pork is not much esteemed.

MASTELLO (Italian), a bucket or pail; a liquid measure of Italy, in *some* places 12 gallons; in others 23.

MASTER, a manager or superintendant; as respects vessels, it applies to the person who has the permanent command or charge; a chief officer in many public departments, as master of the mint, master of the rolls, &c.; an employer of labourers; a chief teacher; the head of a shop or school; the commander of a trading vessel; a departmental superintendant in a theatre, as a property-master, chorus-master, ballet-master, &c.

MASTER-BAKER, MASTER-BRICKLAYER, MASTER-BUILDER, &c., persons who carry on trades on their own account, and employ workmen.

MASTER-KEY, a key that opens many locks.

MASTER-MARINER, the commander of a merchant vessel; a skilled mariner holding a certificate of competency to take charge of a vessel.

MASTER-WORT, a common name for the *Imperatoria Ostruthium*, the root of which is acrid and bitter; it has been used for tooth-ache, and commended as a remedy for intermittent fever.

MAST-HOUSE, MAST-LOFT, a large roofed building, in which masts are shaped, bound, and fitted, which is usually situated near a mast-pond so that the masts can be easily floated in and out.

MASTIC, a choice and valuable white resin obtained from the *Pistacia lentiscus*, which forms the basis of a varnish for paper; a building cement made from Portland stone, sand, and a small quantity of litharge.

MASTICOT, a light yellow pigment prepared from tin.

MAST-MAKER, one who shapes, joins, and prepares spars for masts; often combined with the manufacture of oars, sculls, and ships' blocks.

MASTS, the erect spars of a ship or boat on which the yards and sails are suspended, of which a vessel has one, two, three, or more, according to her rig; and large vessels have several tiers of masts, rising one above another. For the lower-masts of ships one spar is seldom thick enough; it has, therefore, to be padded or fitted at the sides with other pieces of timber fastened and banded together by iron hoops.

MASUR, MUSOOR, the Hindoo name for the [*Cicer Lens*.

MAT, a floor-cloth for wiping the feet, of yarn, or sheep's skin, &c.; a texture of flags or rushes; a protection for yards and shrouds from chafing, made of strands of old rope and oakum. *See* MATS.

MATADORE, the officer in a Spanish bull-fight, who kills the animal when disabled.

MATAPI, the Indian name in Guiana for a cassava squeezer to press the juice from the root.

MATAR, MUTTIR, an Indian name for pease.

MATARA, a Turkish water-bottle made of leather, often embroidered in gold.

MATCH, a game or contest; as a rowing-match, a cricket-match; a lucifer; something that will readily ignite.

MATCH-BOARDS, a kind of plank used for flooring.

MATCH-BOX, a box or case to hold matches.

MATCH-CLOTH, a coarse kind of cloth.

MATCHLOCK, a long musket fired by a rope-match; still used by many of the natives of the East.

MATE, a helper or companion; in the mercantile marine an officer under the master as first-mate, second-mate, &c.; in the Royal Navy a midshipman who has passed his examination for lieutenant; an assistant, as a carpenter's mate, boatswain's mate, gunner's mate; a name for the beverage made from the Paraguay tea.

MATELASSIER (French), a mattress-maker.

MATELOT, a seaman; the tender to a large vessel.

MATELOTE (French), a stew of different fishes.

MATERIALS, the substances or fabrics from which any thing is to be made up. Raw materials is a trade term for products imported or sold for subsequent preparation and use in manufactures.

MATERIA-MEDICA, a knowledge of drugs and their uses; a dispensatory or work treating of the properties and uses of pharmaceutical preparations, animal or mineral, and medicinal plants.

MATHEMATICAL-INSTRUMENT MAKER, a manufacturer and vender of the various instruments and machines used by scientific men, in which there is a large trade, and much skill and precision is required in their construction. The manufacturing part of the trade is divided into different hands, some making only parts, as the lenses, brass work, &c.; others mounting and finishing, while other workmen merely make the cases.

MATHEMATICAL INSTRUMENTS, a collective trade name for a variety of instruments, including compasses, slide-rules, theodolites, chains, &c., and the sale of which is usually combined with philosophical instruments, or those used in the physical sciences.

MATIAS-BARK. *See* MALAMBO-BARK.

MATICO, the leaves of a Peruvian plant, the *Artanthe elongata* of Miquel, used as a powerful styptic, and for other medicinal purposes.

MATIES, a name for the first quality of Scotch cured herrings, being those fish in which the roes and melts are perfectly but not largely developed.

MAT-MAKER, a weaver of mats; a worker in rope, yarn, or rushes. *See* MATS.

MATRIX, plural MATRICES, a mould for casting, used by type-founders and others; a cavity or shape in which any thing is formed.

MATRON, a female superintendant.

MATS, floor covers, of which various kinds are imported from Africa, India, and China. The grass mats from Africa are of all sizes, and very neatly made of fancy-coloured patterns. Rattan floor mats from China, are usually made 7 feet long by 5 broad. Those of rushes are of various sizes and colours, some beautifully checkered. Plain and coloured table mats to stand dishes on are made in sets of six, of three different sizes, both plain and coloured.

MATT, a name given to the bale of flax; the Russian matt is about 5 or 6 cwt., the Dutch matt is only 126 lbs.

MATTARO, an oil measure of Tripoli, considered equal to 47 lbs. weight.

MATTING AND HASSOCK MAKER, a manufacturer of the articles so named.

MATTOCK, a pickaxe with broad ends.

MATTONIERO, an Italian brickmaker.

MATTRESS, a hard under-bed filled with flocks, horsehair, straw, or other stuffing.

MATTRESS-MAKER, a manufacturer of mattresses.

MATY, a servant of all work in Southern India; usually a native servant is required for each special class of work.

MAUD, a species of wrapping plaid or shawl, made of undyed or natural brown wool, of different kinds and countries. Mauds are used as a wrapper for the shoulders in walking, or for the knees in driving; also, a gray striped plaid, worn by shepherds in the south of Scotland.

MAUL, a heavy wooden hammer; also an iron hammer used in driving bolts.

MAULSTICK, a writing-painter's stick to steady his hand.

MAUN, a Persian weight of about 7½ lbs.

MAUND, a hand basket; 8 bushels of apples; a variable Indian weight in different localities, but divided into 40 seers. The ordinary Indian bazaar-maund is 82 2-7th lbs. The Bengal factory-maund is 74 lbs. 10 oz. 10 drachms. The Madras-maund is only 25 lbs., the Bombay-maund is 28 lbs., while the Surat-maund is 41 lbs.

MAUNDRILL, a pick with two shanks.
MAUNDY MONEY, a name given to certain special small silver coins, distributed as alms by the sovereign on Maundy Thursday, or the day before Good Friday.
MAUNEY, an Indian land-measure of 2400 square feet; the 24th part of a cawney; it is also called a ground.
MAURITIUS WEED, a name for the *Rocella fuciformis*, a dye-lichen.
MAW, the stomach of an animal: the stomach of the calf furnishes rennet; the stomach of fishes enter into commerce in the East, under the name of fishmaws.
MAXIMILIAN, a gold coin of Bavaria, worth about 13s. 6d.
MAY-DUKE, a kind of cherry.
MAY-FLIES, the *Ephemera vulgata*, which are used in some parts of Hungary and Carinthia as manure, many farmers in some seasons using more than thirty cart loads on their farms.
MAYO, a Brazilian dry measure of 15 fanegas, and equal to 22½ bushels; as a liquid measure the Spanish mayo is 16 cantari.
MAY-POLE, a decorated pole, &c. carried about and danced round by chimney-sweepers on the first of May.
MAYOR, the chief magistrate of a town.
MAZAGAN, a kind of bean.
MAZARD, a small dark black cherry.
MAZARINE, a deep blue.
MAZE, a place made with many windings and turnings.
MAZER, a drinking cup made of maple-wood.
MAZI, the Turkish name for galls.
MAZZACAVALLO, an engine used in Italy to draw water.
M.C.P., the abbreviation for a "Member of the College of Preceptors," and for a "Member of a Colonial Parliament."
M.C.S., "Member of the Chemical Society."
M.D., "Doctor of Medicine;" also, in Roman numerals, 1500.
MEAD, a drink made with honey; metheglin.
MEADOW, a field under grass cultivation; grass land mown for hay.
MEADOW-SWEET, a wild plant, the *Spiræa Ulmaria*, or, queen of the meadows, the roots of which are astringent, and the flowers yield a fragrant distilled water, which is said to be used by wine-merchants to improve the flavour of home made wines.
MEAK, a hook with a long handle.
MEAL, the flour of corn or pulse, which has been ground for food.
MEALIES, an African name for Indian corn or maize.
MEALMAN, a miller; a dealer in meal.
MEAR, a boundary.
MEASE, 500 herrings. See MACE.
MEASURE, a standard; an instrument for finding weight or length; the size of a suit of clothes, or shoes, hat, &c.; applied to strata or beds, as the coal measures; an Indian term for the puddy, a dry measure, but used also for oil and ghee.
MEASUREMENT-GOODS, light goods taken on freight by bulk or the cubic dimensions of the packages, in contradistinction to ponderous goods, which are usually charged by weight.
MEASURER, one who computes dimensions; a surveyor.
MEASURING-LINE, MEASURING-TAPE, measures of length, used for different purposes.
MEAT, food; the flesh of animals. Preserved meat is meat parboiled, prepared, or potted.
MEAT-BISCUIT, a portable or concentrated preparation of meat, pounded and dried, and mixed with meal and baked.
MEAT-DISH, a large dish of crockery-ware or metal, for serving meat at table.
MEAT-HOOK, a hook for holding meat.
MEAT-PIE, MEAT-PUDDING, meat covered or encased with dough.
MEAT-SALESMAN, an agent for cattle breeders; one who receives in towns carcases from the provinces for sale, or vends them whole, or dissected, to retail-butchers.
MEAT-SCREEN, a metal screen placed behind meat roasting at the fire, to keep in the heat.
MECCA BALSAM, a choice oleo-resin, obtained from the *Balsamodendron Gileadense*.
MECHANIC, a skilled workman or artisan; a handicraftsman; one who plans or makes machinery.
MECHANICAL ENGINEER, a practical mechanist; an engineer who understands the construction and working of machinery.
MECHANICS' INSTITUTE, an institution for the instruction and amusement of working men, supported by small subscriptions from the members.
MECHLIN LACE, a beautiful light Belgian lace, which has a six-sided mesh, of three flax threads, twisted and plaited to a perpendicular line, the pattern being worked in the net, and the plait thread surrounding the flowers.
MEDAL, an ancient or imitation coin; an honorary reward given for scientific merit; a distinction granted for public service, to be worn on the breast.
MEDALLION, a small painting or carving; a medal of a large size.
MEDALLION-WAFER MAKER, a manufacturer of stamped adhesive wafers; imprinted from a die, with some fancy device.
MEDALLIST, one skilled in the art of making medals; a seal engraver; a coin-dealer, &c.
MEDAL-MACHINE, a coining press, with dies, for striking medals.
MEDICAL-AGENT, a person who makes a business of buying or selling the good-will, &c. of chemists and surgeons, keeping a register for reference of business transfers open for negotiation.
MEDICAL-BOOKSELLER, a vender or publisher of works on pharmacy and medicine.
MEDICAL-GALVANIST, a person who applies galvanism for the cure of diseased action.
MEDICAL GLASS-DEALER, a vender of glass jars, bottles, and other fittings for surgeries and chemists' shops.
MEDICAL-LABELLER, a maker of labels for bottles; a painter who writes the names on drawers, jars, and other surgeons' and chemists' fixtures.
MEDICAL-MAN, a physician or surgeon.

MEDICAL-RUBBERS, a coarse unbleached flax towelling, used for drying the body after bathing. *See* BADEN RUBBERS.
MEDICATED-SPIRITS, alcohol flavoured with some strong ingredient, and permitted to be imported duty free.
MEDICINAL-WATERS. *See* MINERAL-WATERS.
MEDICINE, a drug or tincture prescribed, or taken, for ailments of the body.
MEDICINE-CHEST MAKER, a manufacturer of cases with bottles, &c. to hold drugs and chemicals, for ship or family use.
MEDIDA, a Portuguese wine measure, nearly five pints.
MEDINE, an old Turkish money of 3 aspers, worth 1½d. *See* MEIDEN.
MEDINO, another name for the Egyptian para, 40 of which go to the piastre in Alexandria and 33 in Cairo.
MEDIO, a Spanish silver coin, worth about 6d.
MEDIUM-SIZED, a kind of paper 22 inches by 17 inches.
MEDLAR, the fruit of the *Mespilus Germanica*; the white soft wood of the tree is used for walking-sticks.
MEDLEY, a mixture.
MEDLEYS, a technical term which includes all wool-dyed colours, excepting blue and black.
MEDOC, a French red wine; a shining pebble found in France.
MEERSCHAUM, a hydrated silicate of magnesia, largely used for making ornamental pipe bowls. When found it is usually pressed into moulds, dried by heat, boiled in milk, and afterwards rudely polished with soft leather. Before being moulded into pipe bowls, it is soaked in a liquefied unguent.
MEET, an appointed place for fox-hunters, and a pack of hounds, &c. to assemble.
MEETING-HOUSE, a dissenter's chapel or place of worship.
MEGAMETRE, a French instrument for determining the longitude by measurement of the stars.
MEGASCOPE, an optical instrument for representing objects on a large scale.
MEGASS, a name given to the dried cane stems after the juice has been expressed, used as fuel in the furnaces of sugar boilers, and also called trash. *See* BAGAZO.
MEGISSIER, a French leather dresser.
MEIDEN, a former coin of Constantinople, consisting of 3 aspers, and 30 making a Spanish dollar. *See* MEDINE.
MELARANCIO (Italian), an orange-tree.
MELASSE. *See* MOLASSES.
MELATA, an apple marmalade made in Italy.
MELAYE, MELAZE, a Turkish woman's silk veil.
MELET, the French name for the sprat.
MELICOTOON, a peach grafted on a quince stock or tree.
MELICA, a name in Italy for millet or dhurra, the corn grown in Turkey.
MELILOT, a sweet-scented clover.
MELLAGHOO, a common Indian name for pepper.
MELLAROSA, a name for the bergamot orange, the *Citrus Bergamia* of Risso, which yields the essential oil of bergamot.
MELLIFEROUS, producing honey.
MELODEON, a reed organ; the keys open valves, by which the wind from the bellows, worked by the feet of the performer, is allowed to act on the reeds. Seraphine, harmoneon, reed-organ, &c. are names for essentially the same instrument. The concertina is much on the same principle, with a different arrangement of details.
MELODRAMA, a play with songs, music, or pantomime.
MELOE, the Indian name for one of the blistering flies (*Mylabris cichorei*), the Telini of the Hindoos.
MELON, a grateful and delicious fruit, the *Cucumis Melo*, of which there are several cultivated varieties, as the water-melon, musk-melon, &c.
MELON-FRAME, a glazed frame for raising melons.
MELT, to make or become liquid; the soft roe of a fish; the spleen of an animal.
MELTED-BUTTER, boiling water with butter and flour added, used for sauce.
MELTER, a soap boiler; a purifier of lard; a tallow-chandler.
MELTING-POT AND CRUCIBLE-MAKER, a manufacturer of the utensils so named. *See* CRUCIBLE.
MELTON, a kind of broad cloth.
MEMBER, one of a fellowship or society; the representative in Parliament for a borough or county.
MEMBRURE, a French frame for measuring cord-wood; a pannel square; the rib or frame of a ship.
MEMOIR, a statement; a biographical notice.
MEMORANDUM, a reminder; a note to refresh the memory.
MEMORANDUM-BOOK, a note-book; a common-place book.
MEMORIAL, a statement of facts and petition.
MENDEE, an Indian name for henna. *See* HENNA.
MENDICANT, a beggar; one who solicits alms.
MENDICITY SOCIETY, a society established in London to suppress begging, and to put a stop to fraudulent impostors preying upon the charitably disposed.
MENDO, a wild sweet potato of North America.
MENIAL, a hireling; a domestic servant.
MENSURATION, the art of measuring.
MENTOOLOO, an Indian name for *Trigonella Fœnum Græcum*. *See* FENUGREEK.
MENUISIER, a French joiner.
MERCAL, an Indian grain-measure. *See* MARCAL.
MERCANTILE, relating to trade.
MERCATOR'S CHART, a chart where the earth is treated as a cylinder or long round body.
MERCER, a dealer in silks and cloths, laces and small wares.
MERCERIE, a French commercial Customs classification for a variety of goods, not including merely small haberdashery wares, as hooks and eyes, knitting-needles, buckles, necklaces of berries, wooden beads, reels, &c. but comprising under common mercerie, a very wide range of articles, too numerous to particularize, including, for instance, such things as sabots, snuff-boxes, mariners' compasses, spectacles snuffers, whips, &c. Fine

mercerie includes more costly manufactured articles—those to which a greater degree of finish, polish, and ornamentation have been given.

MERCERS' COMPANY, the first in rank of the twelve great livery companies of London; their original charter dates from the 17th Richard II., A.D. 1393-4.

MERCHANDISE, trade goods or wares; the stock dealt in, received, forwarded, or kept for sale.

MERCHANT, a wholesale dealer; one who trades abroad. The word is, however, often affixed to special home trades, as coal-merchant, wine-merchant, vinegar-merchant, timber-merchant, &c.

MERCHANT CAPTAIN, the master of a trading vessel.

MERCHANTMAN, a cargo vessel, a foreign trading ship.

MERCHANT-SERVICE, the mercantile marine of the country.

MERCHANT-SHIP, a trading vessel; one carrying passengers and cargo.

MERCHANT-TAILOR, one who supplies cloths, &c. for garments; a name lately assumed by many clothiers and outfitters.

MERCHANT-TAYLORS' COMPANY, the 7th in rank of the twelve great livery companies of London, whose first charter was granted by Edward III.

MERCURY, a white silvery fluid, also known as quicksilver, of great value in the arts and medicine. It is found under the name of cinnabar, in union with sulphur.

MERIDIAN, an imaginary circle passing through the north and south poles of a place, and defining its position relatively with other situations. *See* LONGITUDE.

MERINO, a fine-woolled sheep; a thin fabric made of fine wool.

MERLUCHE (French), stock-fish; haddock.

MERRY, a small wild black cherry.

MERRY-ANDREW, a buffoon at a fair-booth; a clown in a pantomime.

MERRY-QUILTS, cotton fabrics made in Assam.

MESHES, the interstices or open spaces between the lines of a net.

MESLIN, METEIL, wheat and rye grown together for home consumption, a very common crop in France.

MESQUITE, a French name for American oak; a kind of gum. *See* MEZQUITE.

MESS, a dish; a meal; a number of men who take their meals together; thus in vessels of war there are ward-room and gun-room messes, comprising commissioned and subordinate officers. The seamen and marines' messes consist of a dozen or more under the superintendence of a non-commissioned or petty officer.

MESSAGE, an errand; a telegram or despatch.

MESSENGER, an office-servant; the bearer of a message; a despatch-carrier in the employ of the Foreign office; a rope used for heaving in a cable by the capstan.

MESSMATE, a companion at meals, one of a mess.

MESSUAGE, a tenement.

MESS-UTENSILS, eating and cooking apparatus.

MESTOLA (Italian), a ladle; a trowel.

MESTOUR, a name in the silk trade for a package.

MET, MET JANGREE, a species of fuller's earth found in Sinde, used for scouring the hair, and for cleansing calico cloths preparatory to dyeing.

METAGE, the charge made for measuring goods in bulk from a vessel.

METAL, a sweetmeat or confection in India.

METAL, a technical name for glass in a state of fusion; a mineral substance; broken stone for roads; the effective power of guns borne by a vessel of war.

METAL-BROKER, a dealer in metals and minerals.

METALLIC-CURRENCY, the coins forming the circulating medium of a country.

METALLIC-STANDARD. *See* STANDARD.

METALLING, an engineering name for stone and other material applied to give firmness and solidity to railways and common roads.

METALLURGIST, a worker in metals.

METALLURGY, the process of separating metals from their ores, and converting them into articles of commercial value.

METAL-PERFORATOR, a workman who bores or makes holes in metals.

METAL-PLANER, a smoother; a polisher of metallic substances.

METAL-REFINER, a smelter of ores, one who separates the dross from copper, lead, and other ores.

METAL-SASH-MAKER, a constructor of frames of metal for holding panes of glass.

METAL-TURNER, a turner and driller of metals.

METAL-WAREHOUSE, a store where metals are warehoused or sold.

METAYER, a cultivator who pays rent partly in produce.

METER, a measurer out of fruit, corn, &c. *See* also GAS-METER.

METHEE-SEED, an Indian name for *Trigonella Fœnum Græcum* seed. *See* FENUGREEK.

METHEGLIN, another name for mead, a sweet drink of honey.

METHOD, a plan or system; order or classification.

METHYLATED SPIRIT, spirit of wine of 5½ per cent. over-proof, mixed with not less than one-ninth part of its bulk measure of wood naphtha, or methylic alcohol, for use in manufactures, and to prevent its consumption as a beverage.

METRE, the unity of French long measures, = 39·3710 inches.

METROGRAPH, a controller of the speed of railway trains; this apparatus indicates at every moment and every mile the speed of the train, and the hour of arrival and departure at each station.

METRONOME, an instrument for beating and dividing the time in music.

METTAR, MATARO, a variable liquid measure of Tunis; for oil about 4½ or 5 gallons; in weight 40½ lbs; as a measure for wine it is one-half less.

METZE, a variable German grain-measure, about the fourth part of a bushel.

MEUBLES (French), furniture.

MEULARD, in France, a large grindstone.

MEULARDE (French), a grindstone of a middle size.

MEWS, a range of stables; a locality for stabling horses. Originally the word meant a coop for hawks; hence, when falconry was patronized and practised, there were royal mews, which are, however, now only stables, although the name remains.

Mezereon-bark, the bark of *Daphne Mezereum*, which is employed medicinally, having acrid, laxative, and poisonous qualities. It is also used as a masticatory.

Mezquite, a soluble gum obtained from the *Robinia*, a species of acacia in Texas, and other parts of North America.

Mezzaiuolo, a farmer in Italy.

Mezzo, an Italian word for half.

Mezzonine, a small intermediate story or floor.

Mezzotint, a particular mode of engraving on copper plates by punching and scraping.

Mica, a transparent mineral in flakes, largely used in America, and, to some extent, in this country, for the openings of stoves, in order to afford a view of the fire. It is commonly known as talc.

Michaelmas Day, one of the usual quarter-days of the year, falling on the 29th September.

Michaelmas Term, among lawyers the interval between November 2nd and 25th.

Mico, Mijo, a vegetable butter or solid oil, made from *Soja hispida*, in Japan.

Micrometer, an instrument employed for measuring very small spaces; usually attached to a telescope, microscope, &c.

Microscope, an instrument for magnifying and examining minute objects.

Midden, a dunghill.

Middle-man, one who stands in the middle, as, between buyer and seller, or landlord and tenant.

Middling, of mediocre quality; passable.

Midlings, a miller's name for the finest kind of bran. *See* Sharps.

Midship, in the middle of the vessel, equidistant from the bulwarks.

Midshipman, a non-commissioned naval officer in a vessel of war, or in an East Indiaman.

Midsummer's-day, one of the quarter-days of the year, falling on the 24th June.

Midwife, a female accoucheur.

Migliaccio, a kind of millet pudding, eaten in Italy.

Migrate, to pass or remove from one region or climate to another; the term is generally applied to birds and fishes, many species of which are migratory. Emigrate implies to go out, and immigrate, to come in.

Milch-cow, a cow yielding milk.

Mild ale, mellow ale; not sharp or hard-flavoured.

Mildew, a disease in plants; a blight or rust in wheat, &c.

Mile, an itinerary or long measure; in England, the statute mile is 1760 yards: in Holland, [illegible]; the nautical or geographical mile is the third of the marine league, or 2025·66 yards; in Scotland, 1984 yards; in Spain, 1521·97 yards; in France, 2131·53; in Italy, 2025·66; in Portugal, 2250·74; in Rome, 1628·97. The linear measure corresponding to the British mile bears different names in various countries, and must therefore be looked for under the special title.

Mileage, the rate of fare per mile; fees paid for travelling, when posting or proceeding by rail.

Mile-post, Mile-stone, a mark for a mile.

Milho, a Brazilian name for maize.

Military-accoutrement Maker, an army outfitter; one who supplies belts, sashes, swords, shacoes, &c.

Military-embroidery, gold and silver lace and other ornaments for the facings, collars, and skirts, of soldiers' coats, &c.

Military-musical-instrument Maker, a manufacturer of horns, kettle-drums, fifes, or other instruments.

Military-plume Maker, a maker of feather ornaments for the hats of field and staff officers, army-surgeons, &c.

Militia, a kind of volunteer troops, not an embodied corps; citizens trained to arms for local defence.

Milk, a fluid secreted by certain glands of mammiferous animals to nourish their young; it is sold raw, or skimmed, and is also artificially imitated for sea voyages.

Milk-can, a large tin vessel holding several gallons, in which milk is brought by railway or other conveyance from the farms to dairies. There are also other smaller cans of a quart or less carried round daily for supplying families.

Milk-maid, a woman who milks cows, or carries round milk for sale.

Milk-pail, a large tin bucket with a handle, used for carrying out milk for sale.

Milk-pan, a shallow dairy vessel for holding milk.

Milk-punch, a luscious liqueur.

Milk-score, a bill for milk supplied.

Milk-walk, the district served by a milkman, often yielding a large and profitable return, and the good-will of which is frequently sold.

Milk-wood, a common plant in the West Indies, the *Brosimum spurium*, which furnishes a useful fibre.

Milk-wort, a wild plant with bitter properties, the *Polygala vulgaris*, used in pulmonary affections, and as a remedy in spitting of blood.

Mill, an engine for grinding, &c.; a building or factory containing machinery; the 1000th part of a dollar; a lapidary's term for his different wheels, which are called roughing-mill, cloth-mill, &c.; to serrate or dent the edge of coin; to mill or throw silk before it is dyed.

Mill-band Maker, a manufacturer of bands for machine shops, and for driving wheels.

Mill-board, a stout pasteboard.

Mill-board-box Maker, a manufacturer of stout paper or card-board boxes for the trade. Under this name are comprehended paper-boxes, hat and bonnet boxes, pill-boxes, snuff-boxes, match-boxes, fancy-boxes, muff-boxes, linen drapers'-boxes, &c. *See* Carton-pierre.

Mill-cog, the tooth of a water-wheel.

Mill-croft, a small field or enclosure near a mill.

Mill-dam, a mound or embankment to keep up water to turn a mill.

Miller, one who grinds corn.

Millerole, a liquid measure of Marseilles, Tunis, &c., = 14·15 imperial gallons.

Millet, a common name for several species of small-seed corn. In the Mediterranean the millets are generally called Dhurra. On the Western African coast the chief millets grown are *Holcus lanatus*, *mollus*, and *spicatus*. In the West Indies millet passes under the name of Guinea corn.

Millet Beer, a drink made of fermented millet-seed, with substances added to render it astringent, used by the Crim-Tartars, and also called murwa or bouza.

Millet Rice, a grain grown in India, the *Panicum colonum*.

Mill-gearing, the shaft, wheels, &c. by which the motion of the first moving power is communicated to any manufacturing machine.

Mill-hand, a workman employed in a factory.

Millilitre, the thousandth part of the litre.

Millimetre, a nominal French lineal measure, the thousandth part of a mètre, and equal to 0·039371 inch.

Milliner and Dressmaker, one who makes bonnets, head-dresses, and gowns, and other articles of female attire.

Milling, a process of rolling steel into bars; denting the edge of coin.

Mill-maker, a constructor of grinding or pulverizing machines of different kinds, chiefly of steel.

Milloço, a tuberous plant growing in Ecuador, which has the taste and shape of the best potatoes.

Milsey, a sieve for straining milk.

Millstone-grit, a coarse-grained quartzoze sand-stone.

Millstone-maker, a shaper and binder of stones for grinding purposes in mills.

Millstone, a stone for grinding corn, minerals, paints, drugs, &c., which forms an important branch of trade. There are upwards of thirty makers of millstones in the United Kingdom, who produce about 1100 pairs of large millstones annually, besides about as many more smaller makers spread over the country, and others who are engaged in preparing burr-stones, making and dressing the millstones, &c. The weight of the stones annually made is estimated at 2,500 tons. An ordinary sized pair of millstones measures 4 feet diameter, by 10 inches thick, is composed of twenty to thirty burr stones, and weighs probably 12 to 15 cwt. or more. Good millstones will last 30 or 40 years, and when worn, can be fresh cut. In America, millstones are largely obtained from the conglomerates of the coal measure, from red sandstone, and the finer stone, shales, and syenites.

Millwright, an engineer, or one skilled in the mechanical construction and repairs of machinery.

Milrea, the integer of account in Brazil and Portugal, consisting of 1000 reis. The value fluctuates according to the rate of exchange on England, but is usually equivalent to a dollar. *See* Conto. Also a Portuguese gold money, coined in 1775, for its African colonies, and worth about 5s 8d.

Milt, the soft roe of fish. *See* Melt.

Milter, a male salmon.

Mina, Emina, an Italian grain-measure of 4 stari, and equal to 3·145 bushels.

Minage, a duty on grain brought to market in France.

Mince-meat, meat chopped up fine, with sweets added.

Mince-pie, a small pie made of mince-meat.

Mincing-machine, a chopping-machine.

Mine, a workman's term in the iron districts, for the crude ore or iron-stone, which is variously designated raw-mine, green-mine, burnt-mine, &c.; an underground work for obtaining minerals, or for blowing up with gunpowder; another name for the asper, a nominal petty money of account in Turkey, 120 making a piastre. The mine was also a dry-measure used in France.

Mine-captain, the overseer of a mine.

Miner, a searcher for ores; a workman underground.

Mineral Charcoal, a combination of charcoal and coal, which is sometimes met with.

Mineralogist, one possessing a knowledge of minerals.

Mineral Surveyor, an inspector of mines; one who understands the appearance of lodes, and the prospects of working for ores.

Mineral-teeth Maker, a manufacturer of artificial teeth of ground quartz, China clay, and other substances, pressed into moulds, coloured, and then burnt to harden them. Mineral teeth are largely made in the United States.

Mineral-water Warehouse, a manufactory or depot of mineral aerated waters.

Mineral-waters, waters impregnated with any mineral, many of which are prescribed medicinally.

Minestra, pottage or soup in Italy.

Mingel, a German liquid measure, about 2 pints, 13 of which make a steckan.

Minhare, a term for unassessed land in India. *See* Maafee.

Miniature Painter, an artist who takes likenesses on a small scale.

Minim, in apothecaries' weight, a division of the fluid drachm, which is made up of 60 minims; a measure of time in music.

Mining Agent and Broker, a dealer in shares; a secretary or manager for mines.

Mining Company, a joint-stock association for carrying on operations in a mine.

Minion, a kind of type intermediate between brevier and nonpareil; a piece of ordnance, the bore of which was 3½ inches diameter.

Minister, a high officer of state; a priest; an ambassador.

Minium, a kind of red lead obtained by exposing lead or its protoxide to heat, till it is converted to a red oxide.

Miniver, the white fur of the ermine, prepared spotted with black tails, which is a distinguishing mark of nobility.

Mink, Minx, a commercial name for the fur of the *Mustela vison*, a species of weasel, which is extensively used in the manufacture of ladies' victorines, muffs, capes, &c. From 150,000 to 250,000 skins are imported annually.

Minoomooloo, an Indian name for *Phaseolus Mungo.*

Minot, an old French grain-measure, chiefly used in Lower Canada, equal to 1·073 bushel, but by some stated to be 1-8th less than a bushel.

Minstrel, a vocalist who accompanies himself on an instrument.

Mint, an official place for coining money. There is a British mint in London, at Calcutta, and in Sydney. There is a mint at San Francisco, California, and several other mints in the American States. Almost every civilized country coins money for local circulation. A plant, the *Mentha viridis*, which has a strong, peculiar, and pleasant odour. The leaves are used as a culinary sauce and salad; and being aromatic and carminative, are prescribed medicinally, and an essential oil is obtained from them.

Mint-julep, an American drink; spirit and water flavoured with mint-leaves.

Mint-sauce, mint chopped up with vinegar and sugar, used as a flavouring for lamb.

Minute, the 60th part of an hour.

Minute-book, a rough entry-book containing a sketch or note of the proceedings at committee-meetings, or the operations of public companies.

Minute-glass, a sand-glass running for a minute.

Minute-hand, the long hand or pointer of a watch or clock, which registers or indicates the minutes and seconds, as the short hand does the hours.

Minyak, the Malay name for oil.

Mira, an Italian measure for oil, about 3¼ gallons.

Mirabilite, an efflorescence on the soil among salt springs in some countries, used as a substitute for soda in the manufacture of glass. *See* Glauber Salt.

Mirbane, Essence of, a mixture of benzole and nitric acid; an artificial oil of bitter almonds, used for scenting soaps, and for flavouring confections and cookery.

Mirror, a looking-glass, usually of an oval or circular form.

Misalta, the name for pickled pork in Italy.

Miscal, an Oriental weight used in Arabia, of 73·37 troy grains.

Misou, an Indian tooth-powder.

Mise en-scène, getting up for the stage.

Miser, an instrument for earth-boring.

Miskrable, a name in the chocolate manufactories of the Italian ports, for the husk of the cocoa bean; it is imported thence in large quantities, and partly ground up in the inferior cocoas, and partly dispatched to Ireland, where it is said to yield a wholesome and agreeable beverage to the poorer classes.

Mishk, an Eastern name for musk.

Mishmee Teeta, a name in India for the gold thread roots, which are sent to Assam in neat little open-work rattan baskets, containing about an ounce. *See* Gold Thread Root.

Mishmish, one of the Indian names for the apricot.

Mispickel, a white granulated iron ore; an alloy of iron with arsenic.

Misselto, Mistletoe, a parasitical plant, the *Viscum album*, which grows on the oak, used at Christmas for decorating rooms, and from its viscid berries birdlime is made.

Missile, a weapon for throwing.

Missive, a letter sent by a messenger.

Missoy-bark, an aromatic bark obtained in the Eastern archipelago.

Mistach, a liquid measure in Crete or Candia; for oil, it is equal to 3 imperial gallons; for wine, it varies from 3 to 5 gallons.

Misteca, Mistequr, a local name for the cochineal insect in Mexico.

Mistic, a kind of sailing-vessel.

Misura, a Maltese corn-measure, of 10 minti.

Mite, a division of the troy-grain, used by moneyers; a small coin.

Miter-box, a joiner's tool.

Mithkal, a name in Nubia for 4 dollars.

Mitre, an angle of 45 degrees; a junction of two boards at an angle by a diagonal fitting; a bishop's crown.

Mitre Mushroom, the *Helvella crispa*, Scopoli, a nutritious fungus, found in woods, and esteemed a delicate article of food.

Mittens, Mitts, thin ladies' gloves without fingers, of silk, net or lace; men's warm wrappers for the hands made of cloth, worsted, &c., differing from gloves in having no separate divisions for the fingers.

Mix, to mingle.

Mixture, a compound; one or more articles combined.

Mizen-mast, the aftermost mast of a ship.

M.N.I., "Madras native infantry."

Moachiro, a name for the cotton plant in some of the Pacific islands.

Mocassins, rough deer-skin sandals.

Mocha, a weight in Abyssinia, equal to a troy grain.

Mocha-coffee, the best description of Arabian coffee.

Mocha-stone, a species of quartz, with the appearance of mosses in it.

Moche (French), a bale of raw silk.

Mochilica, a memorandum or agreement in India.

Mock-lead, a miner's name for blende.

Mock-turtle, a soup made with calf's head, veal, and condiments, which, as it solidifies upon cooling, is also sold in the solid form for private use, by confectioners and at cooks' shops.

Mocuddum, the Hindustani name for the head ryot in a village; a collector of government rents; he is sometimes called a mundul in Bengal.

Modehandlung (German), a fancy trade; a milliner's shop.

Model, a miniature plan of any thing; an original pattern to work from; a specimen; a person who stands to a sculptor.

Modeller, a designer; a moulder in wax, clay, or plaster; a sculptor in stone; a constructor of models of ships, buildings, &c.

Modelling-loft, a place in a dock-yard, or shipwright's yard, where the parts of a ship are laid down.

Model Mapping, a mode of showing the features of a district or country by accurate representations on a raised surface of the elevations, depressions, &c. in relief.

Modillions, small inverted consoles forming ornaments in a cornice to support the larmier.

Modiste, a milliner.

Moduga, a name in India for the flowers of the *Butea frondosa*, used to dye red.

Moellon (French), rough stones fit for building.

Moët's Champagne, the finest quality of champagne, named after the maker.

Mofe, a silk stuff made in Caucasia.

Moggio, a variable Italian dry-measure, in some places, 2 quarters, in others only 4 bushels; a land-measure of Naples, of 37,898 square feet, or 0·8700 English acre.

Mogree-oil, a name in Western India for oil of jasmine.

Moha, a name for the German millet (*Setaria Italica*, Palisot).

Mohair, the long silky hair or wool of the Angora goat, *Capra Angorensis*; also, a fabric made from the wool dyed.

Mohair-manufacturer, a worker of mohair; the manufacture is principally carried on in Bradford by those who weave alpaca wool. Mohair is worked up into plush, lace, fringes, &c.

Mohair-yarn, the wool of the Angora goat, combed and spun into yarn or thread.

Mohsul, a native form of legal process in India, which consists in sending a peon, horse or foot, to demand the revenue; the peon remains until he receives payment, the defaulter being charged with his subsistence.

Mohulla, Mohullah, a ward or district of a city in India.

Mohullahdar, the head man or warden of an Indian city.

Mohur, an East Indian gold coin, equal to 15 rupees; as it contains 165·92 grains pure gold, and 15·08 grains alloy, it is worth intrinsically £1. 9s. 2d. sterling.

Mohurir, an Indian policeman.

Moidore, a Portuguese gold coin of 6 dollars, and worth about 27s. It contains 48 testoons, of 100 reis.

Moiety, the half of any thing.

Moio, Moyo, a Portuguese grain-measure of 2¾ quarters; also a wine measure in Spain, of 56·827 gallons.

Moire, watered or clouded silk; mohair.

Moire-Antique, a species of watered silk.

Moisonnier, a tenant-farmer in France, who divides the produce of the land with the owner.

Mokka, a vernacular name in Bengal for Indian corn (*Zea Mays*).

Molasses, the drainage from sugar, in the process of granulation; the syrup which will not crystallize forms the treacle of the shops.

Mole, a name given in America to the draining plough; a kind of pier.

Mole-skin, a substitute for low woollen cloths; a strong twilled fustian. *See* Fustian.

Mollebaert, a Flemish agricultural instrument, consisting of a kind of large shovel drawn along by a horse and guided by a man. *See* Mouldebaert.

Molleton (French), swanskin; a kind of blanket or flannel.

Molunghee, a salt-maker in India.

Momeea, a name in Nepaul for the waxen churrus or resinous exudation of the hemp plant.

Moncha, a grain-measure for rice, used in Madagascar, containing about 7 pints, or 6 lbs. weight of that grain.

Mondello, Modillo, a Maltese grain-measure, nearly a gallon.

Money, coin or stamped pieces of metal, the legalized circulating medium of civilized countries, issued from a mint, and usually bearing on the face an impression of the monarch in whose reign it was coined. In general acceptation the word money is not, however, restricted to coin, but also includes paper money, notes being the chief medium of exchange in some states. *See* Bank-note and Coin.

Money-bag, a small leather or canvas purse for the pocket.

Money-box, a child's closed box with a slit at the top for hoarding or saving money.

Money-broker, Money-changer, Money-dealer, names for exchange-brokers and bullion dealers.

Moneyers, workmen employed in the royal mint to forge shear, round, mill, and stamp coin.

Money-market, a general term for the transactions in Lombard-street, the Stock Exchange, &c., where discounts, loans, and payments are transacted. It was estimated, in 1856, that there were about 130 millions of money in circulation among the London banks.

Money-order, a convenient form of transmitting small sums of money, carried on to a great extent by the English General Post-office through its branches, receiving deposits and granting orders, payable at sight, for any small sums up to five pounds, on payment of a graduated fee of threepence for any sum under one pound, and sixpence beyond. This mode of remittance has recently been extended to most of the British colonies and possessions abroad, where the necessary arrangements could be carried into effect. In 1854, the number of money-orders issued in England was five-and-a-half millions, representing nearly £10,500,000 sterling.

Money-scrivener, one who obtains money on loan for others.

Money-taker, a waiter at an hotel, &c.; a cash clerk in a retail shop; a door-keeper at a public place of amusement, who receives the payment for admissions.

Monger, a small vessel used by fishermen.

Mongrel, an animal of a mixed breed.

Moning, a fine black tea.

Moniteur, the official gazette of Paris.

Monitor, a school-boy set to teach or watch others.

Monkelsee, a name in Persia for the royal guz, a measure of length of 37½ inches.

Monkey, an apparatus for disengaging and securing again the ram of a pile-driving machine.

Monkey-block, a small single block strapped with a swivel.

Monkey-boat, a boat employed in the docks.

Monkey-bread, a name for the large fruit of the *Adansonia digitata*, the slightly acid pulp of which is used as an article of food by

the natives of Africa. The leaves dried and reduced to powder constitute Lalo, a favourite article with the Africans, which they mix daily with their food, for the purpose of diminishing the excessive perspiration to which they are subject.
MONKEY-JACKET, a short spencer, or thick pea-jacket.
MONKEY-WRENCH, a spanner with a moveable jaw.
MONKSHOOD, a wild plant, the *Aconitum Napellus*, the roots of which yield aconitine, an acrid, narcotic poison, the most virulent known. It is, however, used in medicine. The plant is also called wolfsbane.
MONKS'-SEAM, a seam made by laying the selvages of sails one over the other.
MONOCHORD, a one-stringed instrument.
MONOCLE (French), a reading-glass for one eye.
MONONGAHELA-WHISKY, a popular home-made spirit in the United States.
MONOPOLIST, one who engrosses all; a person who holds exclusive possession; an opposer of free-trade.
MONOPOLY, the exclusive possession of any thing, as of a patent right, a sole licence to manufacture or sell; a special market, &c.
MONSOON, a species of periodical strong trade-wind in the Eastern seas, blowing for a portion of the year in one direction, and for the remainder in a contrary direction.
MONT DE PIÉTÉ, a public pawnbroking office on the Continent, kept in general by the Government.
MONTEFIASCO, an Italian wine.
MONTERO, a Spanish horseman's cap.
MONTEURS, a class of French workmen who arrange artificial flowers into wreaths and trimmings, &c.
MONTHLY, a magazine or periodical, published every month.
MONTHLY-NURSE, an attendant on females during childbirth, and until convalescent.
MONTILLADO. See AMONTILLADO.
MONTON (Spanish), a miner's name for a heap of ore; a batch under the process of amalgamation, varying in quantity in different localities, from 15 to 32 quintals.
MONUMENT, a column; a memorial of the living or dead; a tomb.
MOO, a Burmese weight, rather more than half an ounce.
MOOABADUL, an Hindustani name for sponge.
MOOCHEE, an Indian shoemaker.
MOOCHERUS, a gum-resin obtained in India from the *Bombax Malabaricum*, Decand.
MOOCHY, a saddler, bookbinder, or any worker in leather in India.
MOODAH, a bundle or bale of rice in the East, packed in straw or rush-matting, tied with coir.
MOOHOOK, a weight in the Sunda Islands, the tenth part of the candareen.
MOOLANEE, an Indian name for the *Phaseolus trilobus*.
MOOM, the name in Persia and Hindustan, for wax.
MOONG, varieties of pulse or gram, (*Phaseolus radiatus* and *P. Mungo*), cultivated in India.
MOON-RAKER, MOON-SAIL, a small uppermost sail, occasionally carried by American vessels in light winds, above the sky-sail.
MOONSIFF, an assistant native magistrate in India.
MOONSHEE, a Mussulman linguist; one employed as an interpreter or scribe.
MOOQL, an Arab name for gum bdellium. See GOOGUL and BDELLIUM.
MOOR, to secure a ship by two anchors.
MOORA, MOORAH, an Eastern long measure; that used by stone-cutters being rather more than 33 inches, and that employed by carpenters, 34 1-15 inches. Cotton twist is measured by the moorah; a bundle in India; in Bombay, a weight or measure for paddy, of 863 lbs. 12 oz. 12 drs.
MOORINGS, a ship lying with more than one anchor out; moorings are also buoys in a harbour, securely anchored, for the convenience of ships to make fast to.
MOORSTONE, a miner's name for granite.
MOORY, a brown cloth made in India.
MOOSE, a large species of elk, the *Cervus alces*: this fine animal furnishes an excellent hide for mocassins and snow-shoes, and the flesh supplies food to the Indians.
MOOT, a piece of hard wood, hooped with iron at each end, used in making blocks.
MOOTER, a maker of tree-nails or wooden bolts, for fastening the planks of a ship.
MOOTHAS, an Indian name for species of *Cyperus*, the roots or rhizomes of which are used there as a diaphoretic and diuretic.
MOOTHE, METHA, Indian names for fenugreek-seed.
MOOZONAT, MOUZOUNAH, a small silver coin current in Morocco, and equivalent to 7-10ths of a penny.
MOP, a country fair for hiring servants; pieces of cloth, or rope fastened to a handle, for wiping up wet, or cleaning stones, boards, &c.
MOP-AND-BROOM-STICK MAKER, a shaper of wood for handles.
MOP-HEAD, MOP-STICK, the separate parts of a mop.
MOQUETTE, a tapestry Brussels carpet of a fine quality; a species of Wilton carpet.
MOR, the Malay name for myrrh.
MORA, a valuable South American wood, obtained from the *Mora excelsa*, a tree which, in Guiana, frequently reaches 100 feet in height or upwards. It is tough, close, and cross-grained, and is peculiarly adapted for ships' timbers and planks, for which purpose it is extensively used, being recognised as a first-class wood by Lloyd's. When of the height of from 40 to 50 feet, the trunk will square from 18 to 20 inches, but when grown to that size it is generally faulty. The bark is used as a tanning substance. The seeds of the tree contain starch, and are used by the Indians as food in times of scarcity.
MORAH, a footstool used in India made of *Calamus rotang*; a weight in Mysore consisting of about 80lbs.
MORAU, an Indian grain-measure equal to 84·56 cubic inches.
MORAY, an Indian measure of 88 seers, about 1 8-10ths bushel, also called a Mudi.

Morcellement, in France, a compulsory division of land among the sons, on the death of the father.

Morchal, an emblem of state in India of gold and silver tissue, spangles, feathers, &c.

Mordant, a chemical base used in calico-printing to fix the colours, such as alum; a liquid mixture, used in dyeing, which enables the colour to combine permanently with the textile fabric.

Moreen, a kind of worsted stuff, chiefly used for hangings, covering furniture, and ladies' petticoats.

Morell, a variety of cherry; the smallest and most delicate kind of wild mushroom, the *Morchella esculenta*, found in woods.

Morfil, a kind of coarse woollen material used in France for making sacks or bags to contain the oil-cake of flax seed; elephants' teeth. *See* Marfil.

Morgen, a German land-measure, varying in different localities, but usually about two-thirds of an acre.

Morgenblatt, Morgen-zeitung (German), a morning newspaper.

Morillons, fine black grapes grown in France; rough emeralds.

Morisque, an Algerine coin worth about [4½d.

Morita, a Spanish name for the fustic-tree, *Maclura tinctoria*. *See* Fustic.

Morling. *See* Mortling.

Morning-gown, a lady's loose undress wrapper for morning wear.

Morocco-dresser, Morocco-leather-Dresser, a preparer of leather of the kind called true morocco, or in imitation.

Morocco Leather, a light fancy leather tanned with sumach and dyed, used for coach-linings, chair-covers, book-binding, ladies' shoes, &c. True morocco is made from goat skins, but imitation morocco is made from split sheep-skin. It is usually grained.

Morocco-leather-case Maker, a maker of pocket-books, writing-cases, and other articles covered with morocco.

Morphia, an important principle of opium, used as an anodyne, &c.

Morse, a name for the walrus, and sometimes applied in trade to the hippopotamus; the teeth of both enter into commerce for ivory purposes.

Mort, a three-year-old salmon.

Mortadella, the Italian name for Bologna sausages.

Mortar, a utensil for pounding or bruising drugs, &c. in, made of various materials, porcelain, agate, brass, stone, earthenware, or glass: marble ones are often used for domestic purposes in the kitchen; a thick candle or chamber light; a cement for joining bricks and stone; a short cannon with a large bore for throwing shells, in shape somewhat resembling an inverted bell.

Mortgage, a pledge of land to a creditor, until the debt is paid; a lien on land, houses, ships, &c. for money advanced.

Mortgagee, the person who holds a mortgage on property.

Mortise-chisel, a joiner's tool of different kinds, square, round, or pointed.

Morticed-block, a single block of wood, morticed out to receive a sheave.

Mortice, a hole cut into wood for another piece to fit into.

Mortising-machine, a machine for cutting holes in wood.

Mortling, pelt wool; wool from the fleece of a dead sheep.

Moruno Saul, a timber, recognised as a ship-building wood by Lloyds; a species of *Shorea*. *See* Saul.

Mosaic-gold, a bisulphuret of tin imported from Germany under the name of bronze powder, used for ornamental work, especially paper-hangings; an alloy of equal proportions of copper and zinc. A common composition for trinkets, is 75 parts gold, 25 parts copper, and a little silver.

Mosaics, inlaid patterns or pictures. There are several kinds of mosaic, but all of them consist in embedding fragments of different-coloured stones, gems, marbles, and even glass in a cement, so as to produce a fancy pattern, or the effect of a picture.

Moscosque, a Russian money of account, the half of a copeck, and the 200th part of a rouble.

Moselle, a French white wine, and one of the most acid of the light wines imported.

Moslings, a name for the thin bibulous shreds of leather shaved off by the currier in dressing skins.

Mosque, a Mahometan temple.

Moss. The New Orleans long moss is the produce of *Tillandsia usnoides*: it possesses considerable elasticity, is prepared as a substitute for horse-hair in upholstery purposes, and is used by naturalists for stuffing birds. *See* Barba Hispanica.

Moss-agate. *See* Mocha-stone.

Moss-basket, a fancy basket for a room, conservatory, &c., covered with moss.

Moss-rose, a choice and esteemed variety of rose, extensively cultivated for sale.

Mostahiba, a Brazilian wood. *See* Mustaiba.

Most-presse (German), a wine or cider [press.

Mote, an imperfection in wool, which has to be cleansed of burrs and motes by machine; a name for the nut of the *Carapa guineensis*, used for extracting oil in Sierra-Leone.

Mother, dregs, lees or feculencies; a thick slimy substance found in liquors.

Mother-cloves, a name in the East for the fully expanded flower-buds of the *Caryophyllus aromaticus*, which, when they thus reach maturity, are only fit for seed or for candying.

Mother-of-Pearl, the commercial name for the iridescent shell of the pearl oyster and other molluscs.

Mother-of-Vinegar, a name for the vinegar plant (*Mycoderma aceti*).

Motion, the moving part of a watch, or of machinery; the cross-head, &c. in a locomotive.

Motto, a sentence, emblem, or device.

Motto-kisses, sweetmeats having poetry, mottoes, &c., rolled up in fancy papers for the amusement of a party.

Moturpha, an Indian tax on houses, ships, looms, trades and professions.
Moud, a wooden grain-measure used in Natal, holding about eighteen handfuls.
Moulage, a French name for segments of stone, cemented together and bound by iron hoops, used as mill-stones.
Mould, a shape for jellies or sweet pastries; a form for casting type, &c.; fine earth.
Mould-board, the part of a plough above the share, which turns over the earth or lays the furrow-slice.
Mouldebaert, a farming implement in Flanders, drawn by a pair of horses, for taking up and dropping compost, earth, &c.
Moulder, a founder; a former or shaper.
Moulding, a small border or edging to a panel or to a picture-frame.
Moulding-mill, a saw-mill or shaping mill for timber.
Moulding-plane. *See* Plane.
Mould-maker, a maker of casts or shapes of different kinds: thus there are moulds for making glass bottles, for gold-beaters, for iron founders, for sugar-refiners, for casting tobacco-pipes, for making tassels and fringes, &c.
Mould-turner, a maker of metal frames or shapes.
Moules (French), mussels.
Moulin, a French mill.
Moulinage (French), the last dressing of silk before it is dyed.
Mountain, a kind of wine.
Mountain-green, a carbonate of copper; malachite.
Mountain-pepper, a name for the seeds of *Capparis sinaica*.
Mountain-rice, an upland description of rice, grown without irrigation, on the edge of the Himalayan range, in Cochin-China, and some parts of Europe and the United States.
Mountebank, a cheat or charlatan.
Mounter, an ornamenter; a picture or glass framer; one who stuffs and sets up birds and animals.
Mount-guard, to do duty as sentry; to be on the watch or look-out.
Mounting, the setting to a gem; the frame to a picture; the harness or tackle used in weaving.
Mourning-brooch, a jet brooch.
Mourning-coach, a carriage with black horses and trappings to attend at a funeral.
Mourning-reglet, a broad metal bordering for black columns in a newspaper.
Mourning-ring Maker, a manufacturer of finger rings which are worn as mementoes of deceased friends.
Mounhy, a Tartar name for koumiss or fermented mare's milk, which is said to cure consumption.
Mouse, to wrap a hook and its standing part with yarn to prevent its slipping.
Mouse-trap, a trap baited to catch mice.
Moussache, a name for the fecula of the manioc.
Mousseline (French), muslin.
Mousseline de Laine, muslin made of wool.
Moustache, hair worn over the upper lip by males: artificial moustaches are sold for the use of actors and masqueraders.
Mouth, the opening of a vessel; the muzzle of a gun; the lip of a jug; the aperture of a furnace, boiler, or funnel.
Mouth-glass, a small hand-mirror for inspecting the teeth and gums, &c.
Mouth-piece, the part of a bugle or other wind instrument, applied to the lips.
Mouzah, an East Indian term for a township, or tract of land, with known limits and a separate name.
Moveables, dress and personal goods, household furniture, books, farming-stock and implements; things that can be moved.
Movement, the train of wheel-work in a clock or watch.
Movement-maker, a manufacturer of the internal machinery of watches or clocks.
Mow, Mau, a Chinese land-measure, equal to about a rood; a heap of corn or hay.
Mowha, Muohwa, the flowers of *Bassia latifolia*, dried as they fall off, which, abounding in saccharine matter, are eaten in the East, by the natives. Subjected to fermentation, they yield a spirit, which forms the common arrack of a great part of India. Its flavour is compared by some to that of whisky.
Mowing, the operation of cutting grass with a scythe.
Mowloo, the Bengalee name for a species of yam, *Dioscorea aculeata*.
Moxa, a shrub, the *Artemisia Moxa*, Decand.; a native of China, which is used in paralysis of the nerves, and other affections. The loose wool or the beaten tops, forms an inflammable substance, employed to produce eschars, instead of the actual cautery.
Moyau, a minute Burmese measure of length, 4 making a finger's-breadth, or about an inch.
Moyo, a liquid measure of Spain, 56·827 galls.
Mozing, an operation in preparing cloth in the gig-mill.
M.R.C.S., "Member of the Royal College of Surgeons."
M.S.A., "Member of the Society of Arts," F.S.A. being "Fellow of the Society of Antiquaries."
MSS., abbreviation for "Manuscripts."
Mucchero, an infusion of roses and violets, made in Italy.
Mudar, the *Calotropis gigantea*, R. Brown; which is alterative and sudorific, and used in medicine in the East.
Mud-cart, a scavenger's cart for removing filth from the streets.
Mudde, Mudd, a Dutch and Belgian grain-measure, corresponding to the French hectolitre, and equal to 2·7522 imperial bushels, but variable. It is also called a zak.
Mudi. *See* Moray.
Muff, a soft cover of fur or feathers, &c. to wrap the hands in.
Muff-box Maker, a maker of paper boxes to hold ladies' muffs.
Muffin, a cake of plain paste, with hard sides for toasting.
Muffin and Crumpet Baker, a maker of the light tea-cakes so named.
Muffineer, a covered dish to keep toasted muffins hot.
Muffin-man, an itinerant vender of muffins.

MUFFLE, to wind something round, so as to deaden the sound, as muffling the oars of a boat, muffling a knocker, &c.; a hollow arched vessel of fire-clay, closed at the extreme end, used in a furnace, and for silver assaying.
MUFFLER, a throat-wrapper, made of tartan, woollen, or some other warm or soft material; a Turkish or Arab woman's veil for the lower part of the face.
MUFF-MAKER, a furrier: one who makes of skins ladies' case coverings for the hands.
MUG, properly a jug or vessel without a lip; but indifferently applied to both.
MUGGET, the entrails of a calf.
MUGNAIO, MOLINARO, an Italian miller.
MUID, a Dutch grain measure. *See* MUDDE.
MUKE, MEUK, a Belgian grain-measure, 4½ to 5 gallons.
MUKKI, an Indian native name for gamboge.
MUKUER, the Hindustani name for Indian corn or maize.
MULBERRY, a tree, one species of which, the *Morus nigra*, is cultivated for its fruit: the other, *Morus alba*, and its varieties, for the leaves, which form the food of silk-worms: the wood, in some of the varieties, is esteemed for its toughness.
MULCH, half-rotten straw, litter, &c.
MULCT, to stop wages; to inflict a fine or penalty.
MULE, a name for the spinning-jenny, a machine for drawing or elongating the fibres of cotton, and twisting or winding the yarn for the shuttles of the loom: a hybrid canary; a mongrel animal of any kind; a serviceable cross between the ass and the mare, forming a sure-footed beast of burden.
MULE-LOAD, the travelling burthen for a mule; in South America the medium pack-load for a mule is 270 lbs.
MULE-SPINNER, a machine-spinner.
MULETEER, a driver of mules.
MULETTE, a kind of sailing-vessel.
MULL, a very thin and soft muslin, used for dresses and trimmings, of which there are several kinds made, under the names of Swiss-mulls, India-mulls, starched-mulls, &c. A snuff-box made of a ram's horn.
MULLED-WINE, wine heated over the fire, with sugar and spices added.
MULLER, a hand-stone for grinding down oil paint on a slab; a vessel for heating wine over a fire.
MULLET, the rowel of a spur; a sea-fish, of which there are several species belonging to two genera, the red and the gray mullets. The former (*Mullus barbatus*) is still as esteemed as it was among the Romans; the latter (*Mugil capito*) is not so fine a fish, being generally taken out of season when it ascends the rivers.
MULLIGATAWNY, a kind of curry soup, the stock of which is made of veal with ham, vegetables, &c. added.
MULLIGATAWNY-PASTE, a curry paste, used for flavouring mulligatawny-soup.
MULLION, the upright bar dividing the lights of a window.
MULSE, wine boiled with honey.
MULTIPLYING-GLASS, one which repeats the same object several times at once.
MULTIPLYING-WHEEL, a wheel which increases the number of movements in machinery.
MULTUM, a name under which a stupefying mixture, of cocculus indicus and other ingredients, for adulterating beer is sold.
MULTURE, a toll for grinding; grist.
MUM, a kind of spruce beer, or ale brewed with wheat, oat malt, and ground beans, and flavoured with aromatic herbs. It requires to be stored about two years.
MUMMY, a dead human body embalmed and preserved, kept in museums, or the cabinets of the curious.
MUN, a local name for the maund in parts of India.
MUNDIC, iron pyrites.
MUNDIKEL, the Malay name for the water-melon.
MUNDIL, an embroidered turban richly ornamented in imitation of gold and silver.
MUNGPALLI, the Bengalee name for the ground nut, *Arachis hypogæa*.
MUNIMENT, a deed or charter; a strong-hold.
MUNJANDIE, an Indian weight nearly 4 grains.
MUNJEET, the commercial name for the root of *Rubia munjista*, largely used for the same purposes as madder.
MUNTEGA, the Malay name for butter.
MUNTZ'S-METAL, a composition for sheathing, &c. consisting of 50 per cent. of copper, 41 of zinc, and about 4 of lead, named after its inventor, the late Mr. Muntz of Birmingham.
MURAL-CIRCLE, a quadrant fixed in a wall.
MUREX, the handsome shell of a mollusc, many varieties of which are esteemed by collectors. Some species of Murex, and Purpura, yielded the Tyrian purple dye of the ancients.
MURIATE, a salt formed by muriatic acid combined with a base. Muriate of soda and chloride of sodium, are chemical names given to common salt.
MURIATIC-ACID, hydrochloric acid; a compound of hydrogen and chlorine.
MURLINS, another name for the *Alaria esculenta*, also called badderlocks.
MURRAIN, a disease among cattle.
MURRAYA-WOOD, a name for boxwood.
MURSIE, a liquid measure used in Batavia, ten making a rand, which is about the third of a gallon.
MURUTE, a name in Ceylon for the *Lagerstrœmia regina*, the wood of which is used for building and making casks.
MURWA. *See* MILLET-BEER.
MUSADA, a native name in parts of India for the *Strychnos nux-vomica*.
MUSCADEL-WINE, MUSCADINE, a rich wine of Languedoc in France.
MUSCARDINE, a fungus or rot, the *Botrytis Bassiana* of Montagne, which kills silk-worms in great numbers.
MUSCATEL, a choice species of grape, which is dried into fine table raisins.
MUSCOVADO, the ordinary dark-coloured, raw, unrefined sugar of commerce; moist-sugar.
MUSCOVITE, MUSCOVY-GLASS, a name for mica.
MUSCOVY-DUCK, a variety of the duck-species so named.

MUSEUM, a building appropriated to objects connected with science and art, of which there are several mixed or special ones in the metropolis: as the British Museum, taking in the whole range of objects of natural history, antiquities, literature, &c.; the Museum of Economic Geology; the Museum of Botany and Vegetable Products at Kew; the East India Company's Museum, at the India House, Leadenhall-street; and the South Kensington Museum, including animal products, Paintings, Fine Arts, and other illustrations.

MUSH, an American name for a porridge made of Indian meal.

MUSHROOM-KETCHUP, a flavouring for viands; a sauce made of mushrooms.

MUSHROOMS, a name for edible fungi, some of which, as the *Agaricus campestris* and *A. oreades*, the mitre mushroom, and the morell, are esteemed as delicacies.

MUSHROOM-SPAWN, the seed of the mushroom sold in mass by gardeners.

MUSICAL-BOX, a small barrel-organ machine which is often made to play a large number of popular tunes. They are principally manufactured on the Continent.

MUSICAL CLOCK, a clock which plays tunes at the hours.

MUSICAL-INSTRUMENT-COVER MAKER, a maker of leather-cases for wind instruments, or of boxes for violins, &c.

MUSICAL-INSTRUMENT MAKER, a manufacturer of one or more kinds of musical instruments: several of these are special trades.

MUSICAL-INSTRUMENT STRING-MAKER, a maker of catgut, or the prepared twisted intestines of sheep, &c., for the strings of harps, violins, guitars, and other instruments.

MUSICAL REED-MAKER, a manufacturer of the pipes for reed-organs, &c.

MUSICAL-TUBE MAKER, a maker of parts of certain musical instruments.

MUSIC-COPYIST, a transcriber of the score of music, for large bands or orchestra use, where a number of copies are required.

MUSIC-ENGRAVER, an artist who engraves the score of music on metal or stone, for taking impressions from.

MUSIC-FOLIO, MUSIC-WRAPPER, a case or book for holding loose music.

MUSICIAN, an instrumentalist; one who plays or composes music.

MUSICIANS' COMPANY, one of the minor livery companies of London, which, having no hall of its own, transacts its business at Guildhall.

MUSIC-LICENCE, a permission from the magistrates to hold concerts and vocal entertainments, &c. at a room or house.

MUSIC-LOFT, a raised balcony or gallery for a band.

MUSIC-MASTER, MUSIC-MISTRESS, a teacher of music; a professional who gives lessons to learners.

MUSIC PAPER, lined paper, ruled in a particular manner, for copying music on.

MUSIC-PLATE, an engraved plate with music notes, for taking impressions from.

MUSIC-PLATE MANUFACTURER, a preparer of sheets of metal to engrave music on.

MUSIC-SELLER, a shopkeeper who keeps a stock of popular songs, opera scores, &c., and vends printed music.

MUSIC-SLATE, a slate for writing music on.

MUSIC-SMITH, a workman who makes the metal parts for pianofortes, &c.

MUSIC-STAND, a light frame for holding a piece of music or book; a Canterbury, or other article of furniture, for holding music-books.

MUSIC-STOOL, a round-seated screw, pivot stool for a pianoforte player.

MUSIC-TYPE, the symbols or notes of music, cast for printing from.

MUSK, an odoriferous substance, one of the most powerful, penetrating, and lasting of perfumes, obtained from the musk-deer, *Moschus moschiferus*. Our imports average 9,000 to 10,000 oz. a year.

MUSKET, a hand-gun for a soldier: the barrel, lock, and stock are all made by separate hands.

MUSKET-BARREL, the metal tube of a musket, which is sometimes browned or bronzed, and sometimes plain.

MUSKET-LOCK, the hammer or striking part of a gun; the nipple, &c., of a percussion lock.

MUSKETOON, an American weapon, a kind of blunderbuss.

MUSK-MELON. *See* MELON.

MUSK-RAT. *See* MUSQUASH.

MUSK-ROSE, a variety of rose, from which a very odoriferous oil is obtained in the regency of Tunis.

MUSK-SEED, the seeds of *Abelmoschus moschatus*, of Wight and Arnot; the *Hibiscus abelmoschus* of Linnæus, which are stimulating, cordial, and stomachic, and made into a tincture by the Arabs, against serpent bites. *See* ABELMOSCHUS.

MUSK-WOOD, a pretty veined dotted wood, useful for the cabinet-maker, obtained from *Emebra argophylla*, (?) in Tasmania.

MUSLIN, a very thin cotton material, of which there are numberless kinds; book, mull, jaconet, bishops'-lawn, saccharillo, harness, leno, nainsook, seerhand, foundation, cambric, cord, and fancy checks, &c. Figured muslins are wrought in the loom to imitate the tamboured muslins. Muslin is only distinguished from calico by its superior fineness. The India muslins are remarkably fine, and very rich, soft, and durable. Machine-made muslins are, however, deficient in some of these properties.

MUSLIN AND LACE PRINTER, a manufacturer of muslin and lace.

MUSLIN BLIND, a thin short curtain for the lower part of a window.

MUSLIN CURTAINS, long curtains of muslin for a drawing or sitting room, for summer wear.

MUSLIN-EMBROIDERER, a sempstress who overlays or embroiders muslin with figures or patterns.

MUSLINETS, a kind of muslin of which there are several varieties, as single cord, and fancy satin stripes and figures.

MUSOOR, a common Indian name for *Cicer Lens* and *Ervum hirsutum*.

MUSQUASH, a burrowing animal, the *Fiber zibethicus*, commonly called the musk-rat, native of North America, sought for its skin, the fur resembling that of the beaver. It is chiefly used for hat-making. Rather more than a million skins are annually imported, which are for the most part sent to the Continent.

MUSQUASH-ROOT, a tuberous-rooted plant, the *Claytonia acutiflora*, eaten by the Micmac Indians, in the British American Lower Provinces.

MUSQUITO-CURTAIN AND NETTING, thin muslin hung round beds in the tropics, to keep out the troublesome mosquitoes.

MUSROLL, the noseband for a horse.

MUSSAUL, a useful male general servant employed in Bombay.

MUSSEL, a common mollusc, the *Mytilus edulis*, eaten by the lower classes. The shells are used to hold gold and silver paint or size for artists. In several species of river-mussel pearls are found.

MUSSUCK, a large skin or leather bag, used for supplying water in India.

MUSSULCHEE, an Indian link-bearer.

MUST, the juice of the grape, before fermentation has commenced.

MUSTAIBA, a close sound heavy wood imported from Brazil, and used for turning, and at Sheffield for making the handles of glaziers and other knives. The veins are of a chestnut brown, running into black.

MUSTANG, a wild horse.

MUSTARD, pulverized mustard-seed, made into a paste with water, as a condiment for meat, or used for stimulating poultices.

MUSTARD-MANUFACTURER, a preparer of mustard meal or flour, an extensive manufacture, the quantity made annually exceeding 2000 tons.

MUSTARD-SEED, the fruit of various species of *Sinapis*, largely imported as oil seeds for crushing, and varieties are cultivated at home for the meal, which is used as a pungent condiment.

MUSTER, a sample; a review; a drawing together.

MUSTER-BOOK, a book for entering attendance in.

MUTCHKIN, a Scotch liquid measure of 4 gills, = 25·831 cubic inches; the fourth of the Scotch pint.

MUTH, an Austrian and an Italian corn-measure consisting of 30 metzen; 100 metzen = 21 1-6th imperial quarters.

MUTIARA, the Malay name for pearl.

MUTTER, an Indian name for pease (*Pisum sativum*).

MUTTON, the flesh of sheep.

MUTTON-BROTH, a thin soup of mutton.

MUTTON-CHOP, MUTTON-CUTLET, pieces from the ribs or leg of a sheep.

MUTTON-HAM, a leg of mutton salted.

MUTTON-SUET, the fat from the vicinity of the kidneys of the sheep.

MUTTY-PAL, a resinous exudation from *Alianthus Malabaricus*.

MUZZLE, a gag or headstall put on dogs to prevent them biting, or on calves to prevent them sucking; the mouth of a gun.

MYA, the name for a cord or rope in some of the Pacific islands.

MYAM, the sixteenth part of the buncal, a weight for gold and silver, used in the East Indies. *See* BUNCAL.

MYRIAGRAMME, a French weight of 22·0486 lbs.

MYRIALITRE, a French measure of capacity; 10,000 litres, = 34·3901 imperial quarters.

MYRIAMETRE, the new French league of ten thousand mètres, 10936·330 yards = 6 miles, 1 furlong, 28½ poles.

MYROBALONS, a commercial name for the dried wrinkled fruit of various species of *Terminalia*, largely imported from India for the use of tanners and dyers.

MYRRH, an aromatic medicinal gum-resin obtained from the *Balsamodendron myrrha*.

MYRTLE, a well-known shrub, the *Myrtus communis*. The fragrant and aromatic dried fruit and flower-buds were formerly used as a spice, and are said to be so still in Tuscany: a kind of wine is formed of them, and the flowers yield a distilled water called Eau d'Ange.

MYRTLE-WAX, a green solid vegetable fat obtained in the Cape colony and North America from the berries of several species of *Myrica*.

N.

N. an abbreviation for North, one of the four cardinal points; and for Number, in medical prescriptions.

NAARTOE, a name in the Cape colony for a small kind of orange.

NABEE, a powerful poison made in the East Indies from *Aconitum ferox*, called also Bish and Bikh.

NABIT, powdered sugar-candy.

NACCHERA, the Italian name for the castanets; a kettle-drum.

NACKER. *See* KNACKER.

NACODAR, the master of an Arab-vessel on the Malabar coast.

NACRE, the lustrous substance which lines the interior surface of shells yielding mother-of-pearl.

NACREOUS-SHELLS, iridescent shells; those which have an exterior or interior layer of pearl, of which several kinds are used for manufacturing purposes, as some species of *Meleagrina*, *Turbo*, *Nautili*, &c.

NAG, a small saddle horse.

NAHOOR, a species of medium-sized wild sheep found in Nepaul, the *Ovis Nahoor*.

NAIB, a deputy law-officer in an Indian court of justice.

NAIL, a stamping instrument: a measure of length, 2¼ inches, or the 16th part of a yard: a metal spike. Nails are made of variable weight and length, and are usually named from the price at which they are sold. Nails are either cut or hammered; the former are preferable on account of their sharp corners and true taper, and the facility with which they may be driven without the danger of splitting the wood.

NAIL-BRUSH, a toilet brush for scrubbing and cleaning the finger nails.

NAILER, a workman employed in nail-making.

NAIL-FILE, a small file for smoothing the finger nails.

NAIL-MAKER, a manufacturer of nails.

NAIL SCISSORS, small short scissors, with files on the sides, for trimming the finger nails.

NAIL-TRIMMER, an instrument for cutting and paring the finger nails.

NAINSOOK, a thick sort of jaconet muslin, plain or striped; it was formerly made in India.

NAKED-FLOORING, the parallel floor-joists or timber work for supporting the boarding of a floor.

NAKHOUDA (Persian), the master of an Arabian or eastern coasting vessel.

NALEE, a land-measure in Kamaon, India, of 240 square yards, or as much land as can be sown with 2 seers of seed wheat.

NALI, a weight used in Malacca. See HALI.

NALKEE, a litter used by the higher class of native princes in India.

NALLIE, a Malayan grain-measure. See COYAN.

NAMAD, a coarse woollen cloth or blanket, made in Persia.

NAME-PLATE, a metal door-plate; a visiting-card-plate of copper for taking impressions from.

NAMUR OIL, NEMAUR OIL, a fragrant deep yellow grass oil, obtained from the *Andropogon Iwarancusa*, in the East Indies.

NANDIOGIN, a silver coin of Japan worth about 4s. 7d.

NANKEI, a name in Canara for the *Bassia latifolia*, from the seed of which a good oil is obtained.

NANKAH, the Persian name for ajouan. See AJOUAN.

NANKE, NANQUE, a small weight in use in Madagascar for gold and silver, equal to about 5 grains; another weight, nearly the same in name, the Nanqui, is twice the weight of the Nanque.

NANKEEN, a buff-coloured cotton cloth, made in China from a species of yellowish cotton grown in the Nankin district.

NAP, in Scotland, a milk-vat; a small round wooden dish made of staves; the pile of cloth; the down of a hat.

NAPATALM, a vernacular name in parts of India, for the physic-nut.

NAPAULAH OIL, an Indian name for croton oil.

NAPHOLONITE, a variety of felspar.

NAPERY, table-linen.

NAPHTHA, a mineral oil obtained from petroleum, shale, and other substances, used for burning in lamps, and, when containing paraffine, for lubricating machinery: coal-naphtha consists principally of benzole. This aromatic bituminous oil is found oozing out of clefts in the rocks, or the ground; it soon solidifies when exposed to the atmosphere. See PETROLEUM.

NAPHTHA-DISTILLER, a rectifier and preparer of naphtha from crude coal tar, one of the residues of the manufacture of coal gas.

NAPHTHA-LAMP, a table-lamp constructed to burn naphtha in.

NAPKIN, a small damask cloth for table use, for a tray, for breakfast, dinner, or fish, or for tying up infants.

NAPKIN-RING, a small ring of ivory, shell, wood, or some other substance, to enclose a dinner napkin in.

NAPLES-YELLOW, a pigment prepared by calcining antimony and lead, with alum and salt. It was employed in oil-painting, and, also for porcelain and enamel, but is now superseded by chromate of lead.

NAPOLEON, a French gold coin of 20 francs, about 16s. There are also double Napoleons. See LOUIS.

NAPOOTA OIL, an oil made in Eastern Africa, from the Agaiti, and used like olive oil in the Indian markets. See AGAITI.

NARCOTICS, opiates; medicines that induce sleep.

NARD. See SPIKENARD.

NARGAS, a pillau, or prepared dish of lamb, eggs, and spices, &c. in India.

NARGHEEL, a small hookah pipe.

NARGIL, a name for the cocoa-nut-tree in Southern India.

NARGILE, a Turkish pipe, for smoking through water, by means of a long flexible pidge or tube.

NARIKEL, NARIYUL, Indian names for the [cocoa-nut.

NARROW-CLOTHS, in the woollen trade, those under 52 inches wide; cloth beyond that width being termed broad-cloth.

NARROW-GAUGE, a railway, where the rails are placed 4 feet 8½ inches apart.

NARUNGEE, a vernacular name in parts of India for the sweet orange.

NARWHAL, a fish, the *Monodon monoceros*, the long spiral horn or tusk of which furnishes ivory, although seldom used in manufacture.

NASI, the Malay name for boiled rice.

NASTURTIUM, a name for Indian cress, *Tropaeolum orthoceras*. Gardner.

NATCHENY, NATCHINE, another name for corokan in Ceylon. See COROKAN.

NATIONAL SCHOOL, a free school for the young, supported by members of the Church of England.

NATIVE IRON, massive ore with minute crystalline grains, free from carbon, found in Liberia.

NATRON, a native sesqui-carbonate of soda, of which two kinds are obtained in Egypt, the white and the ash-coloured substance. It is employed in the manufacture of soap and glass, for bleaching and other purposes.

NATURALIST, a collector and dealer in objects of natural history.

NATURALIZATION, a legal grant to a resident alien of the rights and privileges of a British-born subject.

NAUT, a marine measure of length, used in the Mediterranean: 124 nauts = 145 miles.

NAUTCH-GIRL, an Indian dancing-girl.

NAUTICAL, relating to ships, navigation, or seamen.

NAUTICAL-INSTRUMENT MAKER, a manufacturer of quadrants, telescopes, and other instruments, for the use of navigators.

NAVAL, belonging to shipping.

NAVAL STORES, a name for certain articles used in ships, such as cordage, turpentine, spirits of turpentine, rosin and tar, &c.

NAVE, a short block of wood, usually elm, forming the middle of a wheel, and pierced with a hole, to receive the axle or axle-tree; the body of a church.

NAVETTE, a smaller kind of colza, cultivated in France, for the seed, for making oil. The seed is less abundant but more valuable than the larger kind.

NAVICELLE, a kind of ship.

NAVIGATION, the art of managing a ship at sea.

NAVIGATORS, seamen; also men employed upon heavy earthwork-cuttings, &c. for railways, canals, and docks.

NAVY, the war ships of a nation.

NAVY-BILLS, bills issued by the Admiralty in payment of stores for ships and dock-yards; short-dated bills drawn by officers of the Royal Navy, on the Accountant-general for pay due to them, and which on foreign stations are readily purchased as convenient remittances on London.

NAW, a kind of ironwood met with in Ceylon.

NAWAB, a deputy or viceroy in India; a title often given by courtesy to persons of high rank in the East.

N. E., "North-east."

NEAD-END, a trade-name for the show end of woollen cloths, kerseymeres, &c.

NEAP-TIDES, the lowest tides of the month, which fall at the middle of the moon's second and fourth quarters; the lowest neap-tide occurs four days before the full or change of the moon.

NEAT-CATTLE, kine; animals of the ox kind.

NEAT'S-FOOT OIL, oil obtained from the feet of cattle.

NEB, the beak or mouth; a slot in a copper cylinder for printing fabrics; the point of a pen.

NEBBEK, a name in Arabia for the fruit of the jujube.

NEB-NEB, NIB-NIB, the pods of the *Acacia Nilotica*, which are used for tanning in Egypt.

NEBOO, an Indian name for the lemon.

NECK, the narrow throat of a bottle; the part of an animal connecting the head with the body.

NECK-BAND, the collar of a shirt.

NECK HANDKERCHIEF, a tie for the throat.

NECKLACE, an ornament or circlet for the neck worn by females, made of various materials, pearls or other gems, beads, glass, &c.

NECROMANCER, a conjuror.

NECTAR, a pleasant cooling drink.

NECTARINE, a peach-like fruit; a variety of the apricot.

NEEDLE, a sewing instrument, made of the best steel wire. The needles of English manufacture are decidedly superior to those of any other country, and are extensively used in every civiliz d part of the globe; the pointer of a magnetic compass.

NEEDLE-BOOK, slips of flannel to stick needles in, with covers in the form of a book.

NEEDLE-BOX, a small fancy box for keeping papers of needles in.

NEEDLE-CASE, a lady's workcase, in which needles are kept according to sizes or numbers.

NEEDLE-MAKER, a manufacturer of needles.

NEEDLE-MAKERS' COMPANY, one of the minor livery companies of London, which has no hall.

NEEDLE-WOMAN, a sempstress.

NEEDLE-WORK, embroidery, lace, all articles worked by the needle; but the term is chiefly applied to fancy or ornamental work.

NEELA, an Indian name for indigo blue.

NEEM, NIM, vernacular names in India for the Margosa-tree (*Melia Azadirachta*). The astringent bitter bark is used as a tonic; the leaves are used for poultices; from the ripe pericarp of the fruit a very bitter fixed oil is expressed; the trunk of the tree yields gum; and the young trees when tapped furnish a saccharine sap or toddy, capable of undergoing the vinous fermentation, and which is believed to be stomachic. [Margosa-berries.

NEEM-OIL, an oil expressed in India from

NEEMOOKA, a vernacular name for the *Cissampelos hexandra*, used medicinally in India like the *Pareira brava*.

NEESBERRY, NISBERRY, a West Indian fruit, the *Achras sapotilla*.

NEFT, an Arabic name for petroleum.

NEGALHO, a Portuguese name for a hank or skein of cotton.

NEGLIGEE, a long necklace, usually of coral.

NEGOCIANT, a French merchant or trader.

NEGOCIATE, to transact business; to bargain or exchange; to put securities into circulation.

NEGRO-CORN, a West Indian name for the Turkish millet or dhurra.

NEGROHEAD-TOBACCO, tobacco softened with molasses or syrup and pressed into cakes, generally called Cavendish.

NEGUS, a drink of wine and warm water, sweetened with sugar, lemon, and nutmeg.

NEIGELLA-CLOTH, a fabric made in India of jute or sunn hemp, *Crotalaria juncea*.

NELLIE, a grain-measure of Sumatra, of eight bamboos, the tenth part of the gun-cha, and equal to 20½ lbs., but by some authorities given at less.

NELLO, NELLY, a weight for gold and silver in the East; in Pondicherry, equal to 0·867 grain; in Bengal to 0·28 grain.

NEOZA, a vernacular name in India for some edible pine seeds. *See* CHILGOZA.

NEPAUL-PAPER, a strong unsized paper, made in Nepaul from the pulverized bark of the *Daphne papyracea*. Sheets have been made many yards square, and bricks of the pulp are sold at 1s. to 1s. 6d. for three seers.

NEPE, a square piece of blanket, used by the Indians, to wrap the foot and ancle before mocassins are put on.

NEPHRITIC-STONE. See JADE.

NEPTUNE, a large brass pan used in the West African trade.

NERFS (French), sinews of animals.

NEROLI-OIL, an essential oil obtained by distilling orange-flowers, which is colourless, but becomes red in presence of air.

NESHISHTA, an Indian name for wheat-starch.

NEST, a number of buckets, tubs, baskets, or boxes, placed one within the other; a set of drawers.

NET, the clear amount without any further abatement for discount, &c.; open mesh work of any kind; a snare to catch fish, birds, or insects; an open or thin lace work fabric, of which there are many kinds, as plain or fancy broad net, plait, wire ground, quilling-net or edging, bobbin-net, &c.

NET-MAKER, a maker of fishing-nets.

NET-PROCEEDS, the amount or sum which goods produce after every charge is paid.

NETTING, the process of forming meshes, whether for fancy-work or for fishing, garden, and other nets of a larger kind.

NETTING-BOOK, a lady's book of instructions or patterns for netting.

NETTING-BOX, NETTING-CASE, a lady's case to keep meshes, pins, needles, and netting materials, cotton, silk, &c. in.

NETTING-NEEDLE, a long needle with a slit at each end to pass the thread through, used by females for netting.

NETTLE-CLOTH, a new German material, consisting of a very thick tissued cotton, which is japanned and prepared as a substitute for leather, particularly for the peaks of caps, waistbelts, &c.

NETTLE-TREE, the *Celtis australis*, which yields a compact wood between oak and box for density. It takes a high polish, and is used by the French, under the name of Micocoulier and Perpignan wood, for flutes, and for carving.

NETTY, a name sometimes given to the tutty, a variable weight in Bengal.

NET-WEIGHT, the true weight of merchandise, after allowance has been made for the cask, bag, or enclosure. The gross weight is the actual weight of goods and package.

NEVE, a weight on the coast of Coromandel of 256 grains.

NEWEL, the upright post of the hand-rail of a staircase.

NEWEKEEN, an African money term applied to the ounce, or 16 ackies. See AKEY.

NEW-LAID EGGS, fresh laid eggs, not those imported from France.

NEW-ORLEANS MOSS. See BARBA HISPANICA.

NEWS-AGENT. See NEWSPAPER AGENT.

NEWS-BOY, an itinerant vender of newspapers.

NEWS-EXCHANGE, a central meeting-place for news-venders, where trade matters are discussed, and surplus papers exchanged or bought and sold.

NEWS-GALLEYS, long metal frames of iron or brass, or with wooden sides and metal bottom, to contain columns of type, which are lodged thereon by the compositor for the purpose of pulling proofs in slips.

NEWSPAPER, a periodical journal, published daily, weekly, or at other specific intervals, and furnishing the news of the day.

NEWSPAPER-AGENT, NEWS-VENDER, one who supplies newspapers to the public.

NEWSPAPER-CHASE. See CHASE.

NEWS-WRITER, a casual reporter; a contributor to a newspaper.

NEW ZEALAND FLAX, the *Phormium tenax*, a plant of New Zealand, the leaf of which furnishes a strong and valuable fibre.

NHON, a minute Burmese measure, equal to ten lines or hairs'-breadths, and locally represented by a small seed, the *Sesamum orientale*.

NHUT, a nose ornament or jewel worn by women in Hindustan.

NIB, the point of a pen; the handle of a scythe.

NIBO, a coarse powder used in some parts of India for washing silk, obtained from *Anticharis Arabica* of Endl.

NICARAGUA-WOOD, an inferior kind of Brazil-wood, the produce of *Cæsalpinia echinata*, used to dye a bright fugitive fancy red. It is also called peach-wood.

NICHE, a hollow recess in a wall for a statue to stand in, or for other purposes.

NICK, an incision or mark in the shank of printing-types, which guides the compositor in arranging the letters properly in his composing stick.

NICKEL, a durable white metal easily malleable, resembling silver, usually procured from speise, a compound of the metal with arsenic, found associated with cobalt, in Germany. Nickel is used to a very large extent in the arts, being remarkable for the peculiar whiteness and silver-like lustre which it communicates to other metals when alloyed with them.

NICKNACKERY, trifles; toys.

NICOTINE, a colourless limpid oil, the poisonous principle of tobacco: a single drop of it is sufficient to kill a dog.

NIDGED ASHLAR, hard granite hewn with a pick or pointed hammer instead of a chisel.

NIELLO, an engraved gold or silver plate, the lines of which are filled permanently with a black enamel.

NIGGED. See NIDGED ASHLAR.

NIGHT-BELL, a surgeon's or chemist's door bell leading to a sleeping room, to be rung at night.

NIGHT-CAB, a cab which plies for hire at night.

NIGHT-CAP, a covering for the head to sleep in: many are open-woven of worsted or cotton; those for females are of different materials trimmed with borders.

NIGHT-CART, a covered dung-cart for removing human ordure from privies.

NIGHT-CLOTHES, a bed-gown and night-cap; garments to sleep in.

NIGHT-GLASS, a telescope for use at night.

NIGHT-GOWN, a child's or female's long loose garment to sleep in.

NIGHT-HOUSE, a tavern or public-house permitted to be opened at night.

NIGHT-LIGHT, a small mortar taper, for burning in a sleeping-room, and which stands in water for safety.

NIGHTMAN, one who empties privies in towns; always performed at night.

NIGHT-PAN, NIGHT-STOOL, a bedroom close-stool or commode; a bed-pan; a portable water-closet.

NIGHT-PORTER, a servant who sits up in attendance at an hotel at night.

NIGHT-SHIRT, a plain loose coarse man's shirt for sleeping in.

NIGHT-TRAIN, a railway train running in the night.

NIL (Latin), nothing; a commonly used term for cancelling, in accounts or book-keeping; meaning to pass it over or take no notice of it.

NIMBOOKA, an Indian name for the lemon.

NINE-PINS, the wooden pins used in the game of skittles, which are aimed at with a heavy wooden ball.

NINZIN, a variety of ginseng obtained in Corea. *See* GINSENG.

NIP, a short turn in a rope; a pinch with something sharp; a small cut; a vessel caught between icebergs; a small cup; a draught of ardent spirits.

NIPAH, the leaves of the *Nipa fruticans* palm, which are used generally in the East for thatching; also called atap.

NIPPERS, a pair of pincers; instruments for cutting up loaf sugar; tweezers, wire-pliers; in ships a number of yarns twisted together to secure a cable to the messenger.

NIPPES (French), clothes; apparel, furniture.

NIPPLE-SHIELD, a protection for the breast worn by females.

NISFIR, the half of a zermahboub or Turkish sequin.

NISHAN-BURDAR, an Indian standard-bearer.

NITRATE, an oxygenated base combined with nitric acid.

NITRATE OF LEAD, crystallized nitric acid and oxide of lead, which is much employed in the chrome yellow style of calico-printing.

NITRATE OF POTASH. *See* NITRE and SALTPETRE.

NITRATE OF SILVER, nitric acid and silver, much used as an indelible ink for writing upon linen with a pen.

NITRATE OF SODA. *See* CUBIC NITRE.

NITRATE OF STRONTIA, crystals which, when mixed with charcoal and chlorate of potash, afford the brilliant red light of the theatres.

NITRATINE, a nitrate of soda found in crystals in Peru.

NITRE, nitrate of potassa, a natural efflorescence on the surface of the earth in several countries, which is used as saltpetre in the manufacture of gunpowder and of nitric acid.

NITRIC-ACID, a preparation from nitrates of potash and soda; which is popularly called aquafortis. *See* AQUAFORTIS.

NITROMETER, a measure to value nitre.

NITTLES, in Scotland, the small stunted horns of sheep.

NIVET, in French commerce an abatement, allowance, or commission.

NIVETTE, a kind of peach.

NIZAM, the governor or administrator of an Indian province.

N.N.E., the nautical abbreviation for the compass point of "North-north-east;" N.N.W. being "North-north-west."

NO., the commercial abbreviation for "number."

NOBBLER, an American slang term for a dram of spirits.

NOBLE, a former gold coin worth 6s. 8d.

NOCHER (French), a pilot or steersman.

NOCTOGRAPH, a writing-frame for the blind.

NOG, a piece of wood shaped like a brick; square blocks of wood piled on each other to support the roof of a mine.

NOGGIN, a name in the north of England for the gill or quartern, the fourth part of a liquid pint; a little mug.

NOGGING, brick-work in panels carried between quarters.

NOILS, the short pieces and knots of wool, left after combing out the "tops," by the combs, or when the sliver is drawn off; noils being only fit for coarse woollen yarn or for cloth manufacture.

NOISERAIE (French), a plantation of walnut-trees.

NOISETTES, hazel-nuts; the French name for filberts.

NOLIS, NOLISSEMENT (French), freight; the chartering or hiring a vessel.

NOMINEE, one appointed or chosen by another.

NON-COMMISSIONED OFFICER, in the army a corporal or sergeant, one under the rank of ensign; in the navy a warrant officer, a paymaster's clerk, or any one under the rank of a lieutenant.

NONNETTES, a kind of French ginger-bread.

NONPAREIL, a small kind of printing-type; a choice variety of apple; a small sugar plum; a narrow ribbon.

NONSUIT, the relinquishment of a suit or action at law, by reason of the plaintiff failing to prove his case, or not wishing to proceed from doubt of success, &c.

NOOSE, a running or slip knot; a lasso.

NOOSFIA, a liquid measure used in Arabia on the coasts of the Red sea, about a pint.

NOPAL, the Spanish name for the cactus, on which the cochineal insect breeds; the *Opuntia Cochinillifera*.

NOPALLERIE, a cochineal field where cacti are cultivated, and the cochineal insect bred thereon.

NORIA (Spanish), a machine for raising water; an endless chain with buckets attached revolving round a wheel for discharging water from a shaft.

NORMA, a model or pattern; a square for measuring right angles, used by carpenters, masons, and other artificers to make their work rectangular.

NORWAY RAGSTONE, the coarsest variety of the hone-slates, or whetstones.

NOSEBAG, a feeding bag with oats, &c. suspended to a horse's head.

NOSEBAND, part of a horse's bridle.

NOSEGAY, a bunch of cut flowers; a bouquet.

NOSE-PIECE, the nozzle of a hose or pipe.

NOSE-RING, a gold or other ornament worn by natives of the East; a ring for the snouts of swine.

NOSES, a name given to some of the smaller shell plates from the edges of the carapace of the sea-tortoise.

Nosfwokye, a name in Nubia for the half ounce.

Nosing, a moulding on the upper edge of a step.

Nostrum, a quack medicine; a secret remedy.

Notarial Seal, the official seal of a notary placed on a writing to legalize it, as in protests and other public and legal documents.

Notary-public, an officer authorized to attest documents and writings, to present dishonoured bills of exchange, and protest and note their non-acceptance or non-payment; a French solicitor.

Notation, the art of representing musical sounds and their various modifications by notes, signs, terms, &c.

Note, a brief minute of any business transaction, &c. taken at the time; a foot-note, mark, or reference in printing. A promise to pay, a bill of exchange, or bank note.

Note-book, a small memorandum-book.

Note-paper, small-sized paper for writing notes or short letters on.

Notice, a warning; information given.

Notice-board, one on which bills, placards, or announcements may be stuck.

Nougat, a cake made in France of almonds and honey or treacle.

Noulet (French), the gutter on a roof.

Noust, in the Orkneys, a landing-place for a boat; a small creek or opening in the rocks.

Novel, a work of fiction.

Novelist, a writer of novels.

Novillos (Spanish), young oxen or bulls.

Nowel, the inner part of a large loam mould used in a foundry.

Nowtauk, a commercial weight in India = 1½ oz., and forming the eighth part of the catcha seer.

Noyale (French), sailcloth or canvas.

Noyau (French), the stone of a fruit: hence the name of a white liqueur or cordial which is flavoured with the kernel of a cherry, the produce of *Cerasus occidentalis*.

Nozzle, the end of a bellows or spout.

Nozzola, a name for the stones of the olive, in Malta.

N.P., "Notary-Public."

Ntaba, the Gaboon name for a species of wild blood red grape, large and very palatable, found on the west coast of Africa.

Nubbin, an imperfect ear of maize.

Nude-figures, statues without drapery.

Nugga, a weight for cotton in India of 12 maunds, equal to 313 lbs. 15 oz. 10 drs.

Nuggadtykrerin, a term in India for rateable lands, those which have to be assessed.

Nugget, a lump of gold in its pristine state, as taken from the mine. In olden times it was spelt niggot, a transposition of ingot. The gold mines of the Ural mountains yielded, some years ago, a mass of this description, weighing 70 lbs. which is now in possession of the Emperor of Russia: previous to this, the largest nugget or *pepita* did not exceed in weight 35¼ lbs. troy. In the Colony of Victoria, many very large masses have been from time to time discovered, far exceeding in size and value any previously known. The Dascombe nugget, found at Bendigo, weighed 27 lbs. 8 oz.; another, of 28 lbs. weight, was discovered in the same locality, and purchased by the local government for presentation to the Queen. After some interval, a third mass, much larger than the others, was discovered, weighing no less than 45 lbs. troy. Several masses, of even larger dimensions, have been found in Canadian Gully, Ballaarat. The largest of these weighed, in gross, upwards of 134 lbs., of which it was estimated that at least 126 lbs. consisted of solid gold.

Nuisance, any occupation or trade tending to endanger public health.

Nullah, a water-course in India.

Number, a figure; a numeral character; a portion of a serial; the quantity reckoned or told.

Numbering-machine Maker, a constructor of paging machines.

Numismatist, one skilled in coins and medals, and keeping a collection for sale.

Nummud, a carpet of felt, much used in Persia.

Nun-buoy, a buoy tapering at each end.

Nung, a large package or bale, generally applied to cloves.

Nun's Thread, a kind of thread formerly made to a large extent in Paisley.

Nurse, a female attendant on children, sick persons, or the insane: the attendant on a lying-in woman is called a monthly nurse.

Nursemaid, a girl who has the care of children.

Nursery, a plantation for raising shrubs, young trees, and plants; an apartment in a house set aside for children.

Nursery-garden, Nursery-ground, a garden for raising young plants, flowers, &c. for sale or transplantation.

Nursery-governess, one who teaches young children.

Nurseryman and Seedsman, a floriculturist and gardener; a cultivator of flowers and shrubs for sale.

Nursing-apron, an apron of flannel, or mackintosh, worn by females who attend to infants.

Nushtur, a sharp instrument, consisting of four narrow bars of iron, used in the poppy fields of India, to scarify the capsule, and cause the juice to exude.

Nut, the fruit or kernel of many trees and shrubs, several of which, being edible, form large articles of commerce; such are almonds, cob-nuts and hazel-nuts, filberts, Brazil-nuts, coco-nuts, pistachio-nuts, hickory-nuts, walnuts, &c. See these respective words. Also a piece of iron screwing on to secure a bolt.

Nut-crackers, a metal wrench, with two handles working on a hinge, for breaking the hard shells of nuts.

Nut-galls. See Galls.

Nutmeg, the hard aromatic seed of the *Myristica moschata*, a valuable spice, which is chiefly cultivated in Penang and some of the other Eastern islands. Wild nutmegs of a longer shape, are the produce of *Myristica tomentosa*, and are often imported.

NUTMEG-BUTTER, a solid oil in cakes, extracted from the nutmeg by expression; a yellow and volatile oil is also obtained.

NUTMEG-GRATER, a metal rasp for grating spices, made of different sizes; sometimes in small fancy cases for the pocket.

NUTMEG-WOOD, another name for palmyra-wood.

NUT-OIL, a commercial name for oil expressed from the ground-nut; but oil is obtained from many species of nut strictly so called, as the almond, walnut, &c.

NUT-PINE, a new species of pine, the *Pinus monophyllus*, inhabiting the Rocky mountains, the seeds in the cones of which are oily, agreeable, and nutritious, and constitute the principal subsistence of some of the Indian tribes.

NUTRIA, the commercial name for the fur of the coypu (*Myopotamus coypus*), which is imported from South America, sometimes in large quantities. Formerly, upwards of a million skins were received annually from the River Plate, but of late years the imports have declined below 200,000. The skin is either dressed as a peltry, or shorn as a hatting fur.

NUT-SCREW, a tumbler screw.

NUTTOO, a nose-stud, or ornament, which is worn by Indian women, often set with brilliants, rubies, emeralds, and pearls.

NUT-WRENCH, an instrument for fixing or removing the nuts on screws.

NUX VOMICA, a drug, the seeds of the *Strychnos nux vomica* and *S. Ignatia*, used for poisoning rats, and adulterating beer.

O.

OAK, an important genus of forest trees, of which there are a great many species. As a building wood its timber is most valuable, and for naval architecture there is no other timber equal to it. The bark, leaves, and fruit of all the species abound in astringent matter and in tannin. Under the heads of Cork, Quercitron, and Valonia, other products of oak will be found noticed.

OAK-BARK, the bark of the oak which is largely used for tanning; the inner cortical of young trees being preferred, as containing a larger proportion of tannin. Besides our home supplies of oak-bark, estimated at 200,000 to 300,000 tons per annum, 4000 to 5000 tons more are imported from the Continent for use in the tanneries. *See* FLITTERN-BARK.

OAK, LIVE, the *Quercus virens*, a native of the Southern States of North America, which is used with the red cedar for ship-building.

OAK-PAPER, paper-hangings stained, like oak.

OAKUM, rope-yarns picked to pieces, used for caulking and other purposes.

OAKUM-MERCHANT, a collector and dealer in oakum.

OAKUM-PICKER, a pauper employed in a workhouse in separating junk into oakum.

OAR, a long wooden paddle with a flat blade, used for propelling boats.

OAR-MAKER, a manufacturer of oars and sculls for boats. Large quantities of the largest and best kinds of oars are made in the United States.

OAST, a drying-kiln or stove for hops. *See* HOP-OAST.

OAT-CAKE, a thin flat cake made of oatmeal, baked on a girdle.

OATMEAL, flour made by grinding oats, used for making porridge, bread, and poultices.

OATS, the seed of the *Avena sativa*, the hardiest of all the cereal grasses, of which there are many cultivated varieties: it is extensively used as a horse-food, and also for bread and porridge in the northern counties, being hardy and containing a large amount of nutritive matter.

OAT-STRAW, the dried stem of oat-grass.

OBAN, the principal gold coin of Japan, worth about £4 2s.

OBELISK, a quadrangular slender stone pyramid, raised for monumental purposes, or for ornament; sometimes as a support for lamps in streets; a reference mark to a foot-note in printing.

OBIT, a particular length of slate.

OBITUARY, a register of deaths; a detailed account of dead persons.

OBJECT-GLASS, in an optical instrument, the glass at the extreme end which is placed towards the object; the reverse of the lens which is placed against the eye.

OBLEA (Spanish), a wafer.

OBLIER, a Spanish confectioner.

OBLIGATION, a bond or indenture, an agreement; a contract with a penalty attached for non-fulfilment.

OBOE (Italian), the hautboy; a musical wind instrument sounded through a reed.

OBOLE, a small weight of twelve grains; a mite.

OBOLO, a copper coin worth about a halfpenny, circulating in the Tonian islands.

OBRADA (Spanish), as much ground as two mules or oxen can plough in a day.

OBSERVATION, in navigation, a sight of the sun, moon, or stars, in order to determine by their altitude, the latitude, and the ship's position.

OBSERVATORY, a look-out building for carrying on astronomical observations. Besides the chief one at Greenwich, observatories have been established in many of the principal British colonies.

OBSERVER, a watchman; one stationed to look out; an astronomer; a person occupied in an observatory.

OBVERSE, the face of a coin or medal; in a tool, having the smaller end towards the stock.

OC, a Turkish arrow.

OCA, a Turkish weight equal to 2 1-8th pounds.

OCA, plural OCOES, a kind of tuberous root or potato, grown in tropical America, the *Caladium esculentum*, sometimes called tanier; also a name for the acid tubers of *Oxalis crenata* growing in the mountains of South America, which, after exposure to light, sweeten and become a useful food.

OCAL (Spanish), a cocoon spun by two silkworms; coarse silk.

OCCA, OOCHA. *See* OKE.

OCCASIONAL-OFFICER, a temporary officer employed in the Customs.

OCCUPANCY, a possession or tenancy.

OCCUPATION, a business pursuit or livelihood; action; settled land.

OCCUPATION-BRIDGE, an engineer's name for a bridge carried over or under a line of railway, to connect the parts of a farm or estate severed by the line.

OCEAN-STEAMER, a large sea-going steamship, carrying passengers to distant quarters.

OCHAVA, a Spanish light weight of 5547 grains, used for the precious metals; the eighth part of the Spanish ounce; and the sixty fourth part of the marc.

OCHAVILLO, a dry-measure of Spain, the fourth part of the ochavo; a Castilian measure, and equal to ·2303 pint.

OCHAVO, a Spanish dry-measure, the sixteenth part of the celemin and = 0·3026 pint. It is also called a racion in some localities; a small brass coin.

OCHO, in Spain, the fourth part of a pint of wine.

OCHRE, an argillaceous earth of different colours, which, when finely ground, is used as a pigment: a name given to the oxides of various metals. Red ochre is a form of specular iron ore; brown ochre a variety of hematite.

GOMBO, a name given in the West Indies to the *Abelmoschus esculentus*, cultivated in gardens for its mucilage; the young capsules being used to thicken soups. The seeds may also be added like barley to soups, and have been roasted as a substitute for coffee. The bark of the plant furnishes, like all the tribe, a strong fibre. The dried capsules would form a valuable basis for soups on long sea-voyages. The leaves are used as poultices.

OCKA, OCQUE. *See* OKE.

OCOZOL (Spanish), liquidamber; a fragrant gum.

OCTAVA, a Spanish long measure, the eighth part of the vara, and = 4·1094 inches.

OCTAVE, the keynote of a pianoforte; a small cask for wine, the eighth part of a pipe.

OCTAVILLA, an excise of half-a-pint taken in Spain upon vinegar, oil, and wine retailed.

OCTAVO, a book folded into eight leaves or sixteen pages to the sheet; usually written 8vo.

OCTROI, a grant; a small fiscal import duty levied in the French towns on all goods entering the gates or barriers of the city.

OCULIST, a surgeon who attends to diseases of the eyes.

ODD-FELLOW, a member of a charitable society, which affords assistance and relief to distressed members.

ODDS-AND-ENDS, miscellaneous things; fragments; scraps; refuse.

ODOMETER, a road measurer to be attached to carriages, for showing the distance over which the wheels pass.

ODONTOGRAPH, an instrument constructed to measure, draw, and design the teeth of wheels.

ODOUR, a scent; a perfume.

ODRE, a liquid measure used in Majorca, of about 10·679 gallons, but variable, containing more or fewer cortans.

ODRECILLO (Spanish) a small leather or goat-skin bag.

ŒNANTHIC-ACID, a solid, resembling butter, found in union with ether in wines, to which it gives the bouquet or pleasant flavour.

ŒNANTHIC-ETHER, the name given to the essential oil, or substance to which the smell and a great part of the taste of many wines are due, and which, being volatile, is distilled over in the manufacture of brandy from such wines, contributing largely to the flavour of cognac.

ŒUF (French), an egg.

ŒUVRE, a land or superficial measure used in France, also called a journal, varying from 4 to 5½ French ares; about an English acre.

OFFAL, waste meat or refuse; the entrails of an animal. In the cattle trade, applied to the trimmings of the crops, the shoulders, bellies, shanks, heads, tails, and pieces of the carcase.

OFFER, a bid or tender; a proposal: a price named.

OFF-HAND, in driving, the right hand; the left being termed the near side.

OFFICE, a counting-house; the place of business of a merchant, law-agent, broker, or professional man; a departmental branch of government administration. A situation or post of trust; the station or employment of a functionary. The offices of a detached dwelling-house are the pantry, scullery, wash-house, store-rooms, and necessary out-houses, conveniences, and subordinate buildings.

OFFICE-COPY, an official copy.

OFFICER, a man in command; a person appointed to perform some public duty civil, naval, or military. The classes of officers are various, but most of them are mentioned under their specific designations.

OFFICIAL, an officer; *relating to an office*; done by virtue of an office.

OFFICIAL ASSIGNEE, a public officer of the Bankruptcy Court, appointed to manage the estate of a bankrupt.

OFFICIAL MANAGER, an officer appointed to wind up the affairs of a joint-stock company.

OFFICINAL, a frequent prefix to the ordinary drugs and preparations of the chemist; implying that they are ready prepared, kept in the shop for sale.

OFFING, a good distance from the shore; deep water.

OFFSET, a contra-account or set-off to a demand made; the shoot or sucker of a plant; a surveying staff.

OGEE, or O. G., a species of moulding used by carpenters and cabinet-makers, consisting of two parts, a concave and a convex. The term is also applied to a pointed arch, the sides of which are formed of two contrasted curves.

OHM, another name for the ox-hoft, a German liquid measure, varying in different localities; generally the average may be taken at thirty gallons: a measure or cask at Dantzic, equal to 32·97 imperial gallons. In English it is generally written aum. See AUM.

OHMASS. See KANNE.

OHRT, a German dry-measure. See ORT.

OIL, a greasy liquid; a term applied commercially to two distinct and dissimilar organic products, called fixed or fat oils, and volatile or essential oils. They are further divided into solid butters or fats, and fluid fixed oils. The number of oils now entering into commerce is very large; those of any importance will be found noticed in their alphabetical order.

OIL AND ITALIAN WAREHOUSE. See ITALIAN WAREHOUSEMAN.

OIL-BAG MAKER, a manufacturer either of oiled-silk bags used for holding toilet sponges, and for covering the hair in bathing; or of another kind of bag of horse-hair, or coco-nut fibre, used to press out the stearine from the oleine in fats and oils.

OIL-BEETLE, the *Meloe proscarabeus*, an insect from the joints of the legs of which exudes a deep yellow oil, used in rheumatic complaints.

OIL-BROKER, a merchant or agent who receives oil on consignment.

OIL-CAKE, the marc or refuse after oil is pressed from flax-seed, rape-seed, coconut pulp, &c., which is imported for feeding cattle, and for manure, to the extent of about 83,000 tons a-year, besides fully as much more made at home.

OIL-CAKE MAKER, a preparer and compounder of slabs of oil-cake from the refuse mass from the oil-mills.

OIL-CAN, a tin vessel for holding oil to supply lamps, &c.

OIL-CLOTH, a tarpaulin; canvas for flooring having a thick coat of paint. See FLOOR-CLOTH.

OIL-CLOTH MANUFACTURER. See FLOOR-CLOTH MANUFACTURER.

OIL-COLOUR PRINTER, a printer in colours, a branch which is now brought to a high state of perfection.

OIL-COLOURS, painters' colours or pigments, formed of mineral substances worked up with oil, for ornamenting and preserving wood, stone, &c. Besides the large quantity used at home, painters' colours, to the value of nearly half a million sterling, are exported.

OIL-CRUET, a small glass bottle for holding salad-oil.

OIL-CRUSHER, a preparer of oil; a mill or press for crushing oil-seeds.

OILED LEATHER. See CHAMOIS-LEATHER.

OILED PAPER, transparent paper used for tracing purposes, by surveyors, draughtsmen, and others.

OILED SILK, silk prepared to prevent perspiration from passing, used for lining men's hats, ladies' bonnets, &c.

OIL-LAMP, a table or other lamp, in which oil is burned.

OILMAN, one who deals in oils, pickles, &c.; often termed an Italian warehouseman.

OIL-NUT, a name for various butyraceous nuts and seeds yielding oil, as the butter-nut, the ground-nut, coco-nut, oil-palm-nut, &c.

OIL OF VITRIOL MANUFACTURER, a maker of sulphuric acid.

OIL-PAINTING, a picture painted with oil colours, and which may be washed and cleaned, which a water-colour drawing cannot be.

OIL-PALM, the *Elais Guineensis*, the fruit of which furnishes the palm-oil of commerce.

OIL-PRESS, a mill or machine for squeezing out oil from seeds or pulp.

OIL-REFINER AND SEED-CRUSHER, a maker of oil.

OIL-SHOP, a place where oil is sold; an Italian warehouse; an oilman's shop.

OIL-SKIN, waterproofed cloth; prepared leather or linen for making garments to keep out the rain.

OIL-STONE, a description of hone slate, of which there are two varieties, black and white, imported from Turkey.

OILY-GRAIN, a name for sesame seed, the *Sesamum orientale*.

OINO (French), cart-grease.

OINTMENT, an oleaginous compound usually having as its basis lard or suet, for smearing, or for dressing sores.

OITAVA, a Brazilian weight, 1 oz. 19 9-10ths dwts. troy.

OKATKA, a name for bristles in Russia.

OKE, a weight used chiefly in the Levant, of 400 drams, which varies, but may be taken to be about 2¾lbs. In Turkey the quintal or cantaro usually consists of 45 okes, except for cotton, wool, and tin, when it is only 44 okes; in Egypt it is 36 okes. As a measure of capacity in Hungary and Wallachia the oke is about 2¼ pints.

OKIE, a name in parts of Northern Africa for the ounce.

OKTHABA, a Burmese long-measure of 70 feet.

OLAS, OLLAS, the leaves of palms prepared in the East for writing on with a stylus.

OLD-CLOTHESMAN, an itinerant who collects half-worn out garments and old attire, which, when renovated and mended, are sold to poor persons. Those too bad for further wear are sold to rag dealers for making into paper pulp; to the Dewsbury woollen manufacturers for making into shoddy; or to the hop growers for manure.

OLD TOM, a kind of strong London gin.

OLEAGINOUS, unctuous; having the quality of oil.

OLEANDER, a fine shrub, the spurge laurel (*Nerium Oleander*), which has large handsome blossoms. The leaves and bark are used in skin diseases, and the charcoal of the wood in the East for making gunpowder.

OLEINE, the fluid portion of fats and oils, after the stearine or solid part has been removed.

Olibanum, a stimulating gum-resin, obtained in India from *Boswellia thurifera*, used medicinally and as a perfume. *See* Frankincense.

Olick, a name in Shetland for the torsk or tusk fish (*Brosmius vulgaris*).

Olinde (French), a thin sword blade.

Olio, a mixture; a medley.

Olive, a brownish green colour; the fruit of the *Olea Europæa*, which is pickled in salt and water, and eaten as a dessert relish with wine, and also crushed for oil.

Olive-oil, oil obtained by expression from the pericarp of the fruit of *Olea Europæa*, which forms an extensive article of commerce, and is used largely for food, in liniments, and in calico-printing. The average imports of 1855 and 1856 were 23,400 tuns. [foot.

Oliver, a small lift-hammer worked by the

Olivet, a kind of mock pearl or white bugle made for the African trade and prized by the negroes of Senegal.

Olive-wood, the yellowish wood of the olive-tree which takes a good polish and, being beautifully feathered, is worked up into small ornamental fancy articles: in France and other parts of the Continent, it is used as a building wood.

Olla, a measure of capacity for liquids in Spain, the fourth of the canada and equal to 2·172 gallons. *See* Olas.

Olla Podrida, a medley hash; a mixture of stewed meat and vegetables, forming a favourite dish in Spain.

Olliks, an Indian name for bars of iron, drawn out from clay crucibles.

Olluck, an Indian dry-measure, the eighth part of a puddy, and the 20th part of a gallon.

Olunda, a name in some parts of the East for the Dutch pound, equal to 1lb. 1 oz. 8 drams avoirdupois.

O.M., "old measurement."

Omander-wood, a variety of Coromandel or calamander-wood, obtained in Ceylon from *Diospyros Ebenaster*.

Ombre, a kind of damask.

Ombrometer, an instrument for measuring the fall of rain. *See* Rain-gauge or Hygrometer. [of muslin.

Ombres, the name for a particular quality

Omelet, eggs beaten up and fried, sometimes with herbs.

Omelet-pan, a cooking utensil for frying egg-cakes.

Omer, a Hebrew measure which contained about 2¼ pints.

Omnibus, a long public four-wheeled passenger carriage, plying periodically for hire along certain routes in or to large towns.

Omnibus-box, a large box at the opera.

Omnibus-builder, a coach-maker; a constructor of omnibuses.

Omnibus-conductor. *See* Conductor.

Omnibus-driver, the coachman of an omnibus.

Omnibus-passenger Register, a tell-tale of the number of passengers conveyed.

Omnibus-proprietor, an owner of omnibuses.

Omnium, all the securities of which a government loan is composed, consisting sometimes of 3 per cent. Consols, long annuities, &c.

Oncia, the Maltese ounce of 14 drams, 25·52 grains avoirdupois.

Onder (French), to water or wave stuffs, &c.

Onfacomeli (Spanish), oxymel; a drink made of honey and the acid juice of unripe grapes.

Onion, a well-known edible bulb, the *Allium cepa*. The onions of Spain, Portugal, and the South of France are much superior to those grown in Great Britain, being of a larger size and more mild and succulent. The onion is used either raw, cooked as a flavouring for made dishes, or pickled.

Onquyah, an Algerian weight equal to 2 drams.

Onstead (Scotch), the building on a farm; probably a corruption of homestead.

Onyx, a variety of agate or chalcedony with alternate bands of brown and white.

Oo, in the Pacific islands the name for a bundle. [catechu.

Ood-beg, a name in Bengal for the *Areca*

Ookh, Uch, a vernacular name in India for the sugar-cane.

Oolong, a peculiar description of black tea, possessing many of the qualities of green tea.

Oome, a name for the seal (*Phoca*) in the Pacific islands.

Oomiak, a large Esquimaux boat.

Oondee-oil, a name in Bombay for an oil obtained from the nut of the *Calophyllum inophyllum*, imported from the Somali coast, and used as a stimulant externally and internally.

Oono, a name, in some parts of the Pacific, for tortoise-shell and the scales of fish.

Oopack, a black tea.

Oord, an Indian name for a species of *Dolichos*.

Ootrum, the Indian name for the fibre of *Dæmia extensa*, a promising substitute for flax.

Ooze, soft mud or slime; a tanner's name for a solution of oak-bark, or other tanning material, in a cistern, in which the hide or skin is immersed.

O.P., "out of print:" in the books of the Veritas or French Lloyds, O.P. attached to a vessel's name implies that she has no deck.

Opal, a beautiful iridescent gem, a species of quartz, always cut with a rounded face.

Opening Knives, strong blunt metal instruments of various kinds, for opening oysters, and tin cases of preserved meats, vegetables, sardines, &c.

Opera, a musical drama, consisting of recitatives, airs, choruses, &c. combined with scenery, decorations, and action; the building where the representation takes place; the music or words printed and sold.

Opera-dancer, a ballet-girl.

Opera-glass, a lorgnette; a short single or double telescope for a theatre.

Opera-hat, a gibus; a folding hat.

Operameter, a machine for measuring work done; as the quantity of broadcloth dressed.

Opera-singer, a vocalist, who takes part in the music of an opera.

Operative, a mechanical workman of any kind.

Operative Chemist, one who has a laboratory, and prepares chemicals himself.

Operculum, a lid or cover; the horny plate which closes the mouth of certain univalve shells, and was formerly esteemed in medicine.

Ophicleide, a kind of trumpet, a loud-toned brass serpent-shaped instrument, chiefly used in military music: it forms the bass wind instrument in a brass band.

Ophthalmic Hospital, an hospital where attention is paid to the cure of diseases of the eyes.

Opiate, a soporific; a narcotic.

Opiate Confection, a medicine given in purging, colic, &c.

Opium, the inspissated juice of the white poppy, (*Papaver somniferum*), which is extensively prepared in India, for shipment to China: the exports from Bombay and Calcutta are about 11,500,000 lbs. In 1856, the consumption of Indian opium in China was about 63,000 chests of 140 lbs. The average imports of opium into Great Britain are about 100,000 lbs.

Opium-clipper, a quick-sailing vessel engaged in smuggling opium from India into China, where its import is prohibited.

Opobalsam, an oleo-resin obtained from the *Amyris Gileadensis*, and *A. Opobalsam*, which has a fragrant odour, and is used medicinally. It is sometimes called balm of Gilead, and is chiefly used as a cosmetic by the Turkish ladies.

Opodeldoc, a camphorated soap liniment, used as a remedy for sprains.

Opoponax, an acrid medicinal gum-resin, obtained from the juice of the roots of *Opoponax Cheronium*, in the Levant. In most of its properties it closely resembles asafœtida.

Oporice, a conserve of fruits.

Opossum, the *Didelphis Virginiana*, the skins of which, having a mixed black and white fur, have been prepared in America for ladies' use.

Optical Brazier, a metal worker who furnishes the brass-work and mountings for optical instruments.

Optical-case Maker, a workman who supplies opticians with the wooden or leather cases required to hold or forward optical instruments.

Optical-square, a surveyor's instrument for laying out perpendicular lines.

Optical-turner, a workman who shapes parts of instruments for opticians.

Optician, a maker of, or dealer in, instruments for the eyes, such as telescopes, microscopes, opera-glasses, spectacles, reading-glasses, magnifying glasses, &c.; but who often vends philosophical and other instruments.

Optic-lens, a ground glass for a telescope, or other optical instrument.

Option, a stock-exchange term for a percentage paid for the privilege of the "put and call;" that is, the liberty to sell or buy stock in a time-bargain, at an agreed price.

Optometer, Opsiometer, an instrument for ascertaining the length of sight in trying spectacle glasses.

Or, the French for gold.

Orache, an old-fashioned pot-herb, the *Atriplex hortensis*, cultivated for its insipid nutritious leaves, which are boiled and eaten as spinach.

Orafo. Orefice (Italian), a goldsmith.

Orange, a colour composed of equal parts of red and yellow; a fruit.

Orangeade, a drink made of orange-juice, water, and sugar; a sherbet, or cool sweet beverage, flavoured with orange essence.

Orange-flower-water. *See* Neroli.

Orange-marmalade, the crushed fruit of the Seville orange, boiled in sugar, and vended in small pots.

Orange-merchant, an importer or wholesale dealer in oranges and lemons, who frequently also deals in nuts, Spanish onions, and other dry fruit and vegetables.

Orange-peel, the outer skin or rind of the orange, candied or preserved.

Orange-peel Cutter, a slicer of Seville orange-peel, for drying or candying.

Orange-pekoe, a black tea from China, so named, of which there is also a scented kind.

Orange-pippin, a kind of apple.

Oranges and Lemons, the fruit of several species of *Citrus*, in which a large trade is carried on. The common sweet orange is the fruit of *Citrus Aurantium*; the Seville orange is the acid and bitter fruit of *C. Bigaradia*; the Bergamot orange is obtained from *C. Bergamia*; the common lemon from *C. Limonum*; the sweet lemon from *C. Lumia*; the lime from *C. acida*; the sweet lime from *C. Limetta*; the citron from *C. Medica*; and the shaddock from *C. decumana*. Some of these have already been noticed under the heads of Citron, Lemons and Limes, Mellarosa, &c. The imports of oranges and lemons range from 700,000 to 800,000 bushels annually.

Orange-woman, a street vendor of oranges, perambulatory, or having a fixed fruit-stall.

Oratorio, a vocal representation of some Scripture story.

Orcanett. *See* Alkanet.

Orchal. *See* Orchilla and Archil.

Orchard, an enclosure devoted to the cultivation of fruit-trees; a plantation of apple, plum, or cherry trees, &c.

Orchestra, an enclosed place for musicians in a theatre, immediately in front of the foot-lights of the stage; a balcony or raised gallery in a ball-room; collectively, the instrumental performers themselves.

Orchids, curious ornamental plants esteemed by cultivators. The roots of some form the agreeable diet called salep.

Orchilla, a name for various dye-lichens, varieties of *Roccella* and *Lecanora*; *R. fuciformis* and *tinctoria*, and *Lecanora tartarea*, imported from the Canary and Cape de Verde islands, Angola and Lima.

Orcio (Italian), an earthen oil jar or wine vessel; some of which are made of an immense size.

ORDER, the condition of any thing; a commission given to supply goods; a dealing or sale transaction: a demand made; a free admission to some public amusement.

ORDER-BOOK, a shop-book for entering roughly the orders of customers, or directions for purchase: a book collector's list of works to be obtained in his circuit.

ORDER IN COUNCIL, an official announcement or new regulation published in the *Gazette* by the Privy Council of the Board of Trade.

ORDERLY, a non-commissioned military officer attending on a field-officer, whose duty it is to bear the orders of his superior; a street sweeper.

ORDERLY-BOOK, a small book containing regimental, garrison, or general orders, which is carried round and shown to the officers concerned.

ORDINARY, a place where dinners are served at a fixed hour and price. A ship in ordinary is one laid up in harbour, dismantled, or not rigged, and often housed over; a clergyman officiating at Newgate.

ORDINARY-SEAMAN, an inferior seaman in the navy, not rated as an able seaman.

ORDITORE (Italian), a weaver.

ORDNANCE, a name for cannon and all description of large guns.

ORDNANCE-MAP, a map made from the national survey carried on by the Royal engineer corps under the direction of the ordnance office.

ORDURE, dung, filth, manure.

ORE, a crude mineral or metal as found in the earth; a Swedish coin, sometimes called a whitten, worth about 1½d.: 2⅔ ores or 8 orts make a copper mark.

OREALA, a decomposed rock of British Guiana, valuable in the manufacture of pottery.

OREGRUND-IRON, a name for the iron obtained from the magnetical ore of the celebrated mines of Dannemora, Sweden, which derives its name from the port of shipment. This iron is valued for its peculiar adaptability for the manufacture of steel. It is also known as Dannemora iron, and bears the distinguishing brand of the letter L within a hoop.

OREILLONS, ORILLONS (French), parings of skins, &c.

OREJON (Spanish), a preserved peach.

ORENBURGH-GUM. *See* LARCH.

ORERIA (Italian), gold-plate.

ORFÈVRE (French), a goldsmith or jeweller.

ORFROI (French), broad bands or welts of gold lace or fringe.

ORGAN, a large complicated powerful musical instrument, chiefly used in places of divine worship. There is a small common barrel-organ, which is carried by Italian and other street musicians.

ORGAN-BLOWER, one who blows the bellows of an organ.

ORGAN-BUILDER, a constructor of organs.

ORGANDI, a clear muslin.

ORGANEAU, ARGANEAU (French), the ring of an anchor.

ORGANIST, the instrumental performer who plays on an organ.

ORGAN-KEY-MAKER, a manufacturer of the moveable keys, which are pressed down by the organist to open the valves.

ORGAN-LOFT, the elevated gallery in which an organ is usually fixed.

ORGAN METAL-PIPE-MAKER, a constructor of the metal air-tubes for organs, both wood and metal pipes being used.

ORGAN-PIPES, the tubes of an organ into which air rushes, when the valve is opened, from a chamber where it has been condensed by bellows.

ORGAN-STOP, a particular set or collection of pipes, differing in pitch, but having the same character of sound.

ORGANZINE, a kind of silk which has been twisted or thrown twice, the first twist being like the yarns which form a strand, and the second like the strands which form a rope; thus constituting a hard and compact thread, which is used as the warp or long threads for the same kind of goods as those which have tram in the weft. Organzine is used for tulle blonde, for ribbons, for plush, and for satin.

ORGE (French), barley.

ORGEAT, a refreshing drink made with orange-water, sugar, and almonds.

ORIEL-WINDOW, an upper story bay or projecting window.

ORIGANUM OIL, an essential oil obtained from the leaves of the wild marjoram (*Origanum vulgare*), the oil of thyme of the shops; a common remedy for the pain of carious teeth, and also used as a liniment.

ORIGIN, CERTIFICATE OF, a custom-house document required to be produced, showing that the commodity imported is of British growth, and introduced from some of our colonies.

ORIGINAL, a first copy; that from which a thing is copied.

ORILLON, a mound of earth faced with brick.

ORLAN (Spanish), cambric.

ORLEANS, a cloth made of worsted and cotton used for dresses, &c.

ORLEANS-PLUM, a large and common variety of plum.

ORLO, a kind of Spanish musical instrument.

ORLONG, a Malay land-measure of 400 square jumbas, and equal to 1⅓ acre.

ORLOP, the deck of a ship of the line over the hold; that on which the cables are stowed.

ORME (French), the wood of the elm.

ORMOLU, an alloy of equal parts of copper and zinc, made to resemble fine gold, and known among jewellers as mosaic gold; an imitation bronze.

ORMOLU-FRAME MAKER, a maker of gilt bronze frames, or of imitation ones.

ORMOLU-LACQUER. *See* ORMOLU-VARNISH.

ORMOLU-RESTORER, a lacquerer; one who bronzes articles with ormolu varnish.

ORMOLU-VARNISH, a copper, bronze, or imitation gold varnish.

ORNA, another name for the eimer, a variable liquid measure. In Trieste, the wine orna is 12·45, that for oil 14·17 gallons.

ORNAMENT, a decoration or embellishment; a jewel.

ORNAMENTOR, a decorator; a finisher of articles.

Oropel, in Spain, a thin plate of brass; tinsel.

Orpheon, a musical instrument.

Orpiment. *See* Arsenic.

Orrery, a planetary; a representation, on a small scale, of the revolutions of the planets, invented by Graham, but named after its patron, the Earl of Orrery.

Orris, a peculiar pattern, in which gold and silver lace is worked. The edges are ornamented with conical figures placed at equal distances, with spots between them.

Orris-root, the fragrant, bitterish, acrid rhizomes of two species of Iris (*I. Germanica* and *I. Florentina*). It is employed in scenting violet-powder, hair powder, and articles of perfumery, and for flavouring liqueurs.

Orsedew, leaf metal, sometimes called Dutch gold. It is imported in small boxes, or in papers containing 5 books, of about 21 leaves each.

Orseille. *See* Archil.

Ort (French), the gross weight; garbage or refuse; a Norwegian coin of 24 skillings, also called a mark, and equal to 9½d.; an Hungarian coin, containing 12 kreutzers; in Poland, 5 orts make a rix-dollar; also a Swedish money equal to 2 farthings, sometimes called a runstick. *See* Poole.

Orthopedist, one who cures deformities of the limbs.

Ortolan, a delicate small bird, the *Emberiza hortulana*, famous in the annals of gastronomy, which is found in some of the islands and shores of the Mediterranean. From the island of Cyprus, 400 casks, containing about 14,000 of these birds, are often shipped yearly, prepared with spice and vinegar.

Orvietan (French), a quack medicine; an antidote against poison.

Oscillating-engine, a marine engine, with a vibrating cylinder.

Osella, a Venetian coin of two kinds, silver and gold, the former worth about 1s. 10d., the latter nearly 40s.

Oshak, the Persian name for the *Dorema Ammoniacum*, the stem and fruits of which yield the fetid gum-resin ammoniacum.

Osier, a willow with bending flexible shoots, used for basket-making. The fine basket osier grown in the eastern part of England, is *Salix Forbyana*. *S. purpurea* is also valuable for basket work, and *S. Helix* is used for the coarser kinds. The common osier, *S. viminalis*, and *S. caprea*, are cultivated for hoops.

Osier-ait, a small island for growing osiers.

Osier-holt, a portion of fen or marsh land, planted with osier-willows for basket-rods.

Osmond-iron, bars of iron specially made for the manufacture of wire.

Osmic, an old Turkish coin, the half of a beshlik and worth about 4d.

Osmazome, the savoury portion or essence of meat, soluble in water.

Osmin, a Russian grain-measure, the half of a chetwert = about 2¾ bushels.

Osnaburghs, coarse linen made of flax and tow, chiefly consumed among the negroes in the West Indies, Brazil, and America, and the native population of Africa and the East. They derive the name from having been originally made at Osnaburgh in Germany.

Osseter, a species of sturgeon, which is said to yield one of the best kinds of Russian isinglass.

Ostellano, an Italian innkeeper.

Ostrich-eggs, the large eggs of the African bird, *Struthio camelus*, which are collected as food by the natives, and the hard strong shell serves for water-pitchers and drinking-vessels. They are sold in most curiosity-shops, are often mounted as cups, and sometimes engraved and ornamented.

Ostrich-feathers, the tail, back, and wing feathers of the ostrich, brought from Africa, which are worn as articles of decoration, and for dress, and are also used for making funeral plumes, both in their native state, and variously coloured. The feathers of the American, or three-toed ostrich, *Rhea Americana*, are extensively worn on bonnets, and as military plumes.

Oswego Starch, a very fine kind of starch made from Indian corn or maize, in the town of Oswego, in the state of New York, whence it takes its name.

Otaheite Apple, a kind of West Indian plum, the *Spondias dulcis*, Forster.

Otaheite Gooseberry, a fruit, the produce of an euphorbaceous tree, the *Cicca disticha*, a native of India.

Otaheite Salep, the fecula produced by the large fleshy roots of the *Tacca pinnatifida*, in the Pacific islands.

Otho, a Greek silver coin of 5 drachmas, and worth about 3s. 6d.

Ottavo, a small weight, the eighth of the Maltese ounce. *See* Oncia.

Otter, a name for two distinct animals, the land-otter, *Lutra vulgaris* and *L. Canadensis*, and the sea-otter, *Enhydra marina*. Both are caught for their fur; of the former we receive about 20,000 skins a-year. The latter, more like the seal in its habits, is obtained in much smaller numbers, but being the royal fur of China is highly valued there and in Russia.

Otto, from the Arab otr, an essence. *See* Attar of Roses.

Ottoman, a couch or sofa; a stuffed stool or hassock; a reclining or easy seat.

Ottone (Italian), brass.

Oublie, a wafer cake.

Ouch, the socket or setting of a precious stone; a carcanet.

Ouchad, an Algerian land-measure of 2¼ English acres.

Ouchain, a variety of young hyson; a green tea.

Ounce, a weight, a common division of the pound, derived from the Latin uncia, a twelfth part. In Great Britain the troy pound is twelve ounces, but the avoirdupois or commercial pound contains sixteen ounces; and is so divided in most of the countries of northern Europe. The troy ounce in England weighs 480 grains, but varies considerably in other countries. The avoirdupois ounce is 437½ grains. The onco, (onza, the eighth part) is a term in several Continental countries for long, superficial, and dry measures. In some parts of the West Coast of Africa, the ounce is a nominal money of account, often represented by 16,000 cowry shells.

OUT, a printer's term for an omission from the copy, given to be set in type.

OUT-BUILDING, a detached erection; one not connected with the main-building.

OUT-CROP, an exposure of strata, or a bed or vein of mineral at the earth's surface.

OUTCRY, the name in India for a public sale by auction.

OUTFIT, the equipment for a voyage or journey; the habiliments, &c. of a workman, soldier, &c.

OUTFITTER, one who supplies ready-made clothes, packages, cabin-furniture, &c. for travellers or emigrants.

OUT-HOUSES, barns, sheds, stables, and other out-lying offices, adjoining a dwelling-house, or on a farm.

OUTILLAGE, a stock of tools.

OUTILS (French), tools.

OUTLAWRY, a legal proscription of a person who is out of the country, and has left debts unpaid; a deprivation of civil rights and privileges, and the forfeiture of his goods and chattels to the Crown.

OUTLET, a passage of any kind.

OUT OF PRINT, publications that are sold off; not to be obtained.

OUT-PARISH, a suburban parish of a large town.

OUT-PENSIONER, an invalid soldier or sailor; a pensioner belonging to Chelsea or Greenwich Hospitals, who is at liberty to live where he pleases.

OUTPORT, a harbour some distance from the chief town or seat of trade; a port away from the chief custom-house.

OUT-POST, an advanced military guard; a picket.

OUT-PUT, a term in the iron trade for the make of metal or annual quantity made.

OUTRE (French), a sewed goat's-skin; a leather sack to hold liquids.

OUT-RIDER, a mounted horseman in advance of a party.

OUTRIGGER, a projecting spar for extending sails; a spar rigged out from the cross-trees to spread the breast back-stays; a light boat for river matches.

OUT-SHOT, a name in Scotland for pasture-land or untilled ground; the second quality of Russian hemp, the bundle of which weighs less than the clean.

OUTSIDES, the exterior sheets of a ream of printing or writing paper; spoiled sheets.

OUT-SPAN, a colonial term in the Cape colony for unyoking ox-teams from waggons.

OUTSTANDING, book-debts, liabilities, accounts, &c. not closed or settled.

OUTWARD-BOUND, merchant ships departing on a distant voyage.

OUVRIER (French), a workman, an artificer.

OVALO, a moulding merely exposing the quarter of a circle; it is generally sunk upon the solid angle of a piece of work.

OVEN, a furnace for baking bread; making coke, &c.

OVEN-BUILDER, a mason who constructs ovens for bakers or others.

OVEN-FORK, OVEN-RAKE, a tool or stirrer for ashes in a stove or oven.

OVERALLS, a kind of leggings worn to keep the wet from the legs.

OVER-BOARD, thrown into the sea.

OVER-CHARGE, an exorbitant or unreasonable price for work or labour done.

OVERCOAT, a great-coat, or wrapper worn over another.

OVERDRAW, to draw on a banker or merchant for a larger sum than stands to the credit of the drawer.

OVERDUE, beyond the date or assigned limit; as an unpaid account or bill of exchange; a vessel, train, &c. past time.

OVERHAUL, to search, to examine; to gain on another vessel in sailing, at sea.

OVERLAPPING, lying one over another, as the slates or tiles on a roof.

OVER-LEATHER, the upper leather of shoes and boots.

OVERLOAD, to put too much goods or lading on an animal, or in a vessel.

OVERLOOKER, an inspector of workmen, a superintendent.

OVER-MASTED, top-heavy: a vessel is said to be over-masted when her masts are too lofty, or too bulky for her size, or for her hold of the water.

OVERPLUS, surplusage; something left; more than is requisite.

OVERSEER, an inspector; a parish officer having the charge of paupers; the resident manager of a sugar estate in the West Indies.

OVERSHOES, goloshes; India-rubber shoes for wet weather, worn over others.

OVERSHOT-WHEEL, the wheel of a water-mill driven by the weight of water falling in the upper buckets, while those on the lower circumference are empty.

OVER-TIME, OVER-WORK, extra labour done beyond the regular fixed hours of business.

OVER-TRADING, speculating or purchase beyond one's capital, or available means.

OVER-WEIGHT, beyond the prescribed or legal weight.

OVER-WORK. *See* OVER-TIME.

OVINE, pertaining to sheep.

OVOLO, a carpenter's name for a kind of moulding. *See* OVALO.

OWITTE, alluvial flat lands in Ceylon, between the hills, generally cultivated with rice.

OWNER, a possessor; a proprietor.

OX, a male animal of the bovine tribe.

OXALIC ACID, a dry poisonous acid, obtained from wood sorrel, resembling Epsom salts, used for removing ink-stains and iron-moulds, and often sold as salts of lemon.

OX-BOW. *See* OX-YOKE.

OX-EYE BEAN, another name for the horse-eye bean, or *Mucuna urens* of Decandolle.

OX-GALL, the bile or bitter fluid secreted by the liver of the ox, which is used for scouring cloth, cleaning carpets, and, when refined, by artists.

OX-GANG, a parcel of land of about 15 acres, on the average; as much as a pair of oxen could plough in a year or season. It varied according to the nature of the land from 6 to 40 acres.

OX-HIDE, the dried or tanned skin of the ox; a measure of land, as much as could be encircled by a hide cut into narrow strips.

OXHOFT, a German name for the cask we call a hogshead, derived from ox-head. It varies from 44 to 52 gallons.

OXIDATION, the rusting of metals by damp, or from exposure to the atmosphere.

OXIDES OF IRON, the rust on iron from which various pigments and polishing powders are prepared by chemists, bearing special commercial names.

OXIDIZED SILVER, more properly sulphuretted silver; a process of turning the surface dull and dark by washing it with a solution of sulphuret of sodium or potassium. It is much used by the French in the manufacture of bijouterie.

OXONIANS, a kind of men's shoes.

OX-PLOUGH, a plough drawn by one or more pairs of oxen.

OX-REIMS, narrow strips of prepared hide, about 9 feet long, extensively used in the Cape colony for halters for horses, for passing round the horns, close to the head, of draught oxen, to keep them together; twisted for ropes and traces and various other purposes.

OXYGEN, a manufacturing name for bleaching-powder.

OXYGENATOR, a contrivance for throwing a current of air on the flame of an argand lamp.

OXYHYDROGEN-BLOWPIPE, an instrument much employed by chemists, mineralogists, and others, for the reduction of metallic ores, &c., from which, by the combustion of a mixture of oxygen and hydrogen gases, a very intense heat is obtained, and substances the most intractable have been fused.

OXYHYDROGEN-MICROSCOPE, a very powerful microscope for reflecting objects by an intense light.

OXYMEL, a mixture of honey and vinegar, which is prescribed as an expectorant and demulcent. It is frequently combined with other medical ingredients, and then named from them, as oxymel of squills, &c.

OX-YOKE, OX-BOW, a piece of curved wood put round the neck of a draught ox, as a kind of collar to attach the traces to.

OXYRRHODINE, a mixture of oil of roses and vinegar.

OYSTER, an esteemed, edible mollusc, the *Ostrea edulis*, largely consumed in cities. About 800,000 bushels a year are sold in London. There are various species of edible oysters found in different seas.

OYSTER-BED, a bank in a river or harbour, &c., where oysters are planted and fattened for sale.

OYSTER-DREDGE, a small drag-net for bringing up oysters from the bottom of the sea.

OYSTER-KNIFE, a strong blunt knife for opening oysters.

OYSTER-OPENER, an apparatus of French invention, something like a pair of sugar-nippers, for opening oysters at the hinge.

OYSTER-PATTY, a pasty with oysters baked.

OYSTER-ROOM, a metropolitan supper-room; a shell-fish shop.

OYSTER-SAUCE, melted butter with oysters added.

OYSTERS, SCALLOPED, oysters baked with crumbs of bread in a scallop shell or tin.

OZ., abbreviation for "ounce."

OZMAZOME. *See* OSMAZOME.

P.

PAB, in Scotland the refuse of flax.

PACE, a degree of speed, and in measurement the length of a stride. The military pace is 2½ feet, the geometrical pace, 5 feet; in Scotland, the weight of a clock.

PACHA, the governor of a Turkish province.

PACHANA, a bitter tonic prepared in the East from the stems, roots, and leaves of *Cocculus cordifolius*.

PACK, the load for an animal; a large hand-packed bale of goods, lashed with cord, of variable size: a pack of flour or Indian-corn meal, flax, &c. weighs 280 lbs.; of wool 240 lbs. net; formerly, in many parts of the country it was 252 lbs.; a parcel of hounds kept for hunting or coursing; a set of suits of playing cards, 52 in number.

PACKAGE, PACKET, a small parcel.

PACKALL, PAGALA, a kind of basket made of the outer rind of the Ita palm (*Mauritia flexuosa*).

PACKCLOTH, a coarse baling material; the wrapper for a pack of goods.

PACKER, a person who makes a business of receiving goods from merchants, to pack for forwarding inland or for shipment abroad.

PACKET, a small bundle of letters or loose papers tied together.

PACKET-DAY, the mail-day; the day for posting letters, or for the departure of a ship.

PACKET-SHIP, a regular trader; a vessel that carries mails or passengers at stated periods.

PACK-FONG, a Chinese name for Argentine, or German silver. *See* PAKFONG.

PACK-HORSE, a horse which carries bales or packs.

PACK-HOUSE, a warehouse for receiving goods.

PACK-ICE, in the Arctic regions, an assemblage of large floating pieces of ice, as far as the eye can reach.

PACKING, a quantity of wood or coals piled up to support roofs in a mine or for other purposes; the stuffing round a cylinder, &c.

PACKING-CASE, a deal or other box for moving and protecting goods.

PACKING-CASE MAKER, a carpenter, who makes rough deal boxes.

PACKING-OFFICER, an excise-officer who superintends or watches the packing of paper, and other excisable articles.

PACK-LOAD, the average load an animal can carry on its back. The load for an ass, for a camel, and a mule, have already been stated. The pack load for a man is about 60 lbs., for a pony 125 lbs., for a bullock 210 lbs., and for an elephant, 1000 lbs. The loads of pack animals and of carriages, will however necessarily vary, according to the nature of the goods, the road, or the season.

PACKMAN, a pedlar; one who carries a pack.

PACKMAN-RICH, in Scotland, a species of bere or barley having six rows of grains on the ear.

PACK-SADDLE, the saddle for a pack-horse.

PACK-SHEET, a baling material, a large cover for goods in a wagon.

PACK-THREAD, strong twine; small cordage that has been thrice twisted.

PACO, one of the names given to red silver ore.

PACOU, a river fish of Demerara (the *Myletes pacu*), which is excellent food when dried and smoked.

PAD, a basket of soles; a fish measure, which varies in number—60 mackerel go to a pad; a soft stuffing; a bolster or saddle; to impregnate with a mordant; to travel on foot.

PADAR, groats; coarse flour.

PADDINGS, a cloth worked out of old rags for stuffing collars and other parts of coats.

PADDLE, a furnace tool; a small scull, or broad-ended oar for propelling a boat or canoe; the fly of a steamer's wheel; to row.

PADDLE-BOARDS, floats fixed round the circumference of a steamer's paddle-wheel for propelling her through the water.

PADDLE-BOX, the upper case or cover of the paddle-wheels in a steam vessel; sometimes removeable, and forming a kind of available life-boat.

PADDLE-HOLE, in building, a clough arch.

PADDLE-SHAFT, the shaft upon which the paddle-wheel is fixed and connected with the crank shaft.

PADDLE-WHEEL STEAMER, a steamer propelled by side paddle-wheels—not a screw propeller.

PADDLE-WHEELS, the dipping wheels on each side of a steam boat, armed with floats for propelling her through the water.

PADDLE-WOOD, a light, elastic, and very strong wood obtained from *Aspidosperma excelsa* in Guiana, which is preferred to any other for cotton-gin rollers. The fluted projections of the trunk are used by the Indians for the construction of their paddles.

PADDOCK, a small field or fold for a horse or deer, &c.; in Scotland, a low sledge for removing stones.

PADDY, unhusked rice.

PADDY-BIRD FEATHERS, ornamental feathers, smaller and finer than those of the ostrich, of a cream colour, imported in limited quantities from the East, obtained from a small species of crane, which frequents the rice fields, whence the name.

PADDY-FIELD, a field under rice culture.

PADEGUM, a brass spittoon used in Madura and other parts of India.

PADELIN, a kind of crucible.

PADELLA (Italian), a small frying-pan; a kind of oven.

PADELLARO (Italian), a maker or seller of frying-pans.

PADEN. *See* BADDAN.

PADESOY, a kind of silk.

PADLOCK, a lock with a link to hold on to a staple.

PADOU, a sort of silk ferret or ribbon.

PADOUK, the Burmese name for the *Pterocarpus Indicus*, a valuable forest tree.

PADRA, a black tea.

PADRE, a Romish priest.

PADS AND POTS, a kind of fish-hamper.

PAE, a grain-measure of some parts of India, eight of which go to the koora. The pae of cleaned rice weighs about 3 lbs.

PAFFLER, one who occupies a small farm in Scotland.

PAGACK, a measure for ten gallons.

PAGARE (Spanish), a bond or agreement to pay a certain sum.

PAGATORE (Italian) a paymaster.

PAGE, a boy servant in livery, who attends on a lady; one side of the leaf of a book or writing.

PAGE-CORD, thin twine used by printers to tie together the pages or columns previous to printing.

PAGING-MACHINE, a machine for consecutive paging or impressing numerals on the sheets of blank account and other manuscript books; and also for numbering railway and other tickets.

PAGLIONE (Italian), chopped straw.

BAGNON (French), superfine sedan cloth, named after the maker.

PAGODA, the name of numerous gold coins formerly current in India. They mostly weighed about 52·85 troy grains, containing 44·39 troy grains of pure metal; the standard of the star pagoda, the former integer of account at Madras, which passed for 3½ Arcot rupees, and was worth 7s. 10d. to 8s. Government, the banks, and all the houses of agency, kept their accounts at 42 fanams the star pagoda; the shops and bazaars at 44 or 45. The pagoda is used as a weight in Madras, ten making a pollam.

PAIL, a bucket; a wooden or tin vessel, carried by a moving handle, for holding water, milk, &c.

PAILA, a large metal pan in Italy.

PAIL-BRUSH, a hard brush to clean the corners of vessels.

PAILLASSE (French), a straw bed; PAILLASSON being straw matting.

PAILLE (French), straw or chaff.

PAILLET (French), the spring of a door-lock.

PAILLIE, an Indian dry-measure for grain, &c., equal in weight to 2·057 lbs.

PAIN (French), bread; a loaf.

PAINA, bracelets of zinc worn by the native women of India.

PAINT, a popular general name for all colouring substances used as pigments; to lay on colours.

PAINT-BOX, a child's box containing cakes of water-colours.

PAINTER, a workman who lays on oil-colours, and who often combines the trade of a glazier. Painters are subdivided into numerous classes, following separate branches, and include, among others, coach and chaise painters; house, sign, and fancy painters; herald painters; marine and ship painters; miniature and portrait painters; ornamental and standard painters; glass painters, &c. Painter is also the name for a rope attached to the bow of a boat to make her fast to a ship or pier with.

PAINTERS'-BRUSH-MAKER, a manufacturer of hair brushes for oil-painting.

PAINTERS'-COLOURS. *See* OIL-COLOURS.

PAINTER-STAINERS, one of the livery companies of London, whose hall is situated in Little Trinity Lane.

PAINTERS' TOOLS, brushes, pallets, paints, pots, and other utensils and implements used in painting.

PAINTING-ROOM, an artist's studio, a large well-lighted room for working in; a gallery of paintings.

PAINTINGS, pictures worked in oil; those in water-colours are usually styled drawings.

PAIR, a couple or brace; two articles that are fellows, as a pair of stockings, gloves, &c. A pair of stairs is one flight of stairs.

PAIXHAN GUN, a howitzer of long bore, named after its inventor, which will carry enormous projectiles to a great range.

PAJACK, PAJOCK, a Russian measure for corn of about 1½ bushel English.

PAJOLE (Italian), straw and rushes woven together to cover fruit-trees and plants.

PAKFONG, the white copper of the Chinese, an alloy of 40·4 parts of copper, 31·6 of nickel, 25·4 of zinc, and 2·6 of iron.

PAKU, the Malay name for nails.

PALA, a name in India for the *Wrightia tinctoria*, from which a species of indigo is obtained; in Italy, a wooden shovel of any kind; a battledore; the blade of an oar.

PALACE, a large house; the dwelling of a prince or bishop, &c.

PALAMENTA, the oars of an Italian galley.

PALAMITA (Italian), a pilchard; a kind of tunny fish.

PALAMOUD, an alimentary substance used by the Turks and Arabs, and very much esteemed. It consists of acorns which have been burned to destroy the bitterness, dried, and toasted, and reduced to powder, with sugar and aromatics added.

PALANDOO, an Eastern name for onions.

PALANDRA (Italian), a bombship.

PALANDRANO (Italian), a great-coat.

PALANKEEN, PALANQUIN, an Indian portable couch; a litter or covered carriage borne on men's shoulders.

PALASA, a local name in India for the *Butea frondosa*, from which gum is obtained.

PALASS-GOOND, a name for the Bengal kino, the produce of *Butea frondosa*.

PALATINE (French), a tippet; having royal privileges.

PALAY, a local name in India for a climbing plant, the *Cryptostegia grandiflora*, which yields a strong fibre.

PALE, a flat stake of wood stuck into the ground, and secured to a rail at the top; a cheese scoop.

PALE ALE, a light-coloured pleasant bitter ale, brewed principally at Burton-upon-Trent. *See* BITTER ALE.

PALEMPORES, a species of Indian dimity, of elegant patterns, used for bed-coverlits. They are sometimes flowered with gold made of silk, and worked in shawl and other patterns of coloured woven cotton.

PALENDAR, a foreign coasting vessel.

PALETOT, a loose thin overcoat.

PALETTE. *See* PALLET.

PALFREY, a lady's horse.

PALING, a fence made of stakes.

PALING-BOARDS, in Customs' definition, the outside parts of a tree, taken from the four sides, to square the log, and fit it to be sawed into deals. They should not exceed an inch and a half in the thickest part.

PALISSANDER, a name in France for rosewood or jacaranda. There is considerable irregularity in the employment of this name, which is sometimes applied to striped ebony, and in other cases to violetwood.

PALITA, a trowel; a small shovel.

PALITO, a light-yellow ochre.

PALKIE, an Indian carriage shaped like a palankeen. *See* PALANKEEN.

PALL, a covering thrown over a coffin; a cloak; a detent or click to catch a racket-wheel.

PALLADIUM, a metal which occurs in rolled grains with platina, and particles imbedded in and combined with gold. It does not tarnish, and has therefore been used by dentists, and by mathematical-instrument makers, particularly for balances.

PALLAMPOOR, an Indian chintz counterpane. *See* PALEMPORES.

PALLAR (Italian), to extract the pure metal from ores or minerals.

PALLET, a painter's board, or porcelain slab with a thumb-hole, on which the colours are mixed and held for use; a piece connected with a pendulum; a sort of shovel; a gilding-tool; a weight of 8 ounces.

PALLET-KNIFE, a painter's knife for scraping up paint.

PALLIASSE. *See* PAILLASSE.

PALLON (Italian), an assay of gold or silver.

PALM, an ancient measure of length, taken from the dimensions of the hand; the breadth of the hand indicating the small palm, the length of it the longer palm. This last was the Roman palm, understood to be 8¼ inches. The Roman palm is now considered equal to 0·733 English feet; 1 English foot is equal to 1·364 Roman palm. The former is the English palm or hand, of 4 inches, now used only for the measurement of horses. The palm, as used in different countries, is an exceedingly variable measure. In Russia, a palm is used of 2·026 inches; in others, it is 8, 10, or 11 inches. Also a leather protection for the hand in sail-making, on which a thimble is fixed; an Indian name for a bar of iron; the fluke, or triangular-shaped piece of iron, at each end of the arms of an anchor, the point of which enters the ground.

PALMA CHRISTI, a name for the castor-oil shrub, the *Ricinus communis*.

PALM-CABBAGE. *See* CABBAGE-PALM.

PALMETTE ROYAL, the *Sabal umbraculifera*, Martius.

PALMETTO, a common name for several small palms. One species, the dwarf fern palm, *Chamærops humilis*, common in the countries bordering on the Mediterranean, is now largely used in Algiers for many economic purposes. It furnishes a fibre resembling horsehair, which is largely employed in France in making common carpets, and has been prepared into a kind of flax-cotton. Paper and pasteboard are made of it: and it is spun into sail-cloth. The leaves are also used for making brooms, seats of chairs, hats, thatch for cottages, &c. The leaves of another class of short palms, the *Thrinax*, have many economic uses. *T. argentea* furnishes the chip which is woven into hats, and made into baskets and wicker-work, while other species of the genus furnish the palmetto-thatch, which forms an article of export from North America. The name is sometimes applied to the cabbage-palm.

PALM-FIBRE, fibre obtained from the leaves of the palmyra, carnauba, and other palms. Palm-leaf is sold in Salvador, Brazil, in bundles of 60 leaves, at 3¾ to 4 dollars, or about 16s.

PALM-HOUSE, a glass building for sheltering and raising palms and other tropical plants in cold climates.

PALMO, a long-measure in Genoa, equal to 9¾ inches; in Malta it is rather more, 3¼ palmi being about a yard.

PALM-OIL, a dark-yellow oil obtained from the fruit of the oil-palm of the west coast of Africa, the *Elæis Guineensis*. It is used with other solid oils for making soap and candles. Our imports amount to about 40 000 tons a year.

PALMS, those chiefly of interest for their commercial products, are the areca or betel-nut palm, the cabbage, cocoa, date, fan, oil, and wax palms.

PALM-SUGAR. *See* JAGGERY.

PALM-TREE WOOD, the stems or trunks of palms, obtained from the East and West Indies, and imported to a small extent for fancy use. They furnish a great variety of wood, black, brown, prickly brown, and speckled, and are used for cabinet and marquetry work and for billiard cues.

PALM-WINE. *See* TODDY.

PALMYRAH-WOOD, the trunk of a palm-tree (the *Borassus flabelliformis*), which is largely used in Ceylon and Southern India for rafters, joists, reapers, and other building purposes. The fruit and the fusiform roots of the young trees are used as food by the poorer classes. The leaves are used for thatching, and from the coarse fibre very neat baskets are made. Jaggery, course sugar, and toddy are made from the sap. Palmyrah is sometimes called nutmeg-wood by turners.

PALO, an Eastern medicinal preparation from the *Cocculus cordifolius*, the stem of which is macerated, and the solution evaporated to dryness.

PALOMBARO (Italian), a diver.

PALOMBINA, a sort of grape grown in Italy.

PALUNG, a name in Bengal for a native variety of beet-root cultivated for food.

PALUNGOO, a name in the East for the fibre of the stems of *Hibiscus cannabinus*.

PAMPE (French), a load of wheat or barley.

PAMPELMOUSE, POMPELMOOSE, the *Citrus Pompelmos*, a species of large orange grown in Siam.

PAMPHLET, a small unbound book; stitched printed sheets.

PAMPHLETEER, a writer of pamphlets.

PAMPIROLADA, PAPIROLADA, a sauce made in Italy of garlic, bread, and water.

PAN, a broad and shallow earthen or metal vessel; the hollow part of a gun-lock that holds the priming powder; the name for the famous eastern masticatory, a narcotic which takes the place of opium and tobacco in many Asiatic countries. Slices of the areca nut are wrapped in the fresh leaves of the betel-pepper vine, with a small quantity of quicklime. The masticatory has an herbaceous and aromatic but astringent taste. All classes, male and female, chew it, and they allege that it strengthens the stomach, sweetens the breath, and preserves the teeth. It gives the lips, tongue, and teeth a reddish tinge; a general name in Italy for bread or paste of any kind, whether of seeds, figs, &c.; a wafer; a leaf of gold or silver.

PANABASE, copper ore.

PANACHE (French), a plume, a bunch of feathers; a manufacturing name in France for the two outermost brins or radiating sticks of a fan, which are wider and stronger for the protection of the rest.

PANADA, boiled bread.

PANADERO (Spanish), a bread maker; a baker.

PANAMA-HATS, very fine plaited hats made from the fan-shaped leaves of *Carludovica palmata*, which are generally worn in the West Indies and American Continent, and fetch a high price. In Central America where they are made, the palm is called Jipijapa.

PANCARPEA, a garland of various kinds of flowers in Italy.

PANCONCELLO (Italian), a lath.

PANCONE (Italian), a plank or board; a joiner's bench.

PANCRÉAS (French), the sweet-bread of a calf.

PANDAL, a platform; a stage or erection in Ceylon.

PANDEAN-PIPES, a mouth reed-organ.

PANDORE, a rebeck, a kind of lute.

PANDOWDY, a pastry of bread and apples baked.

PANE, a separate sheet or panel of glass in a window; a piece in variegated work.

PANEL, a square; the space or compartment within a margin, as the sunken compartments of wainscoting, ceilings, &c.; a square of paper; in mining a heap of ore dressed and ready for sale; the face of a hewn stone; a roll of parchment containing the names of jurors; a prisoner at the bar; a name in Scinde for the leaves and stalks of the *Pogostemon Patchouli* of Lepellitier, which are used there, and in Europe, as a perfume.

PANELA, a cake made of Indian-corn meal.

PANEL-WORK, wainscoat oak laid out in panels.

PANER (French), to dress broiled or roasted meat with crumbs of bread.

PANIC, a monetary crisis; a sudden alarm.

PANILLA, a small measure of oil in Italy.

PANJAM, a name in the East for the resinous gum of the *Embryopteris glutenifera*, used for paying boats, &c.

PANJAROO, an Indian armlet; these are made sometimes of silver, of crystal, shell, &c. *See* BANGLES

PANMUG, the name of an earthenware crock, in which butter is sometimes sent to market by farmers, and which weighs, when filled, about ½ cwt.

PANNE, worsted plush made in France.

PANNEAU (French), a panel of thin wood.

PANNIER, a hamper or basket; two large baskets thrown across a horse's back.

PANNIERE, a woollen-draper in Italy.

PANNO (Italian), woven stuff of any kind.

PANNOCCHIA (Italian), an ear of Indian corn or maize.

PANNUSCORIUM, a name given to a species of leather cloth, used for shoes and boots for those who have tender feet.

PANORAMA, a general view; a large cylindrical painting seen from the inside, or rolled along, so as to be seen from the outside.

PANSWAY, a small boat used on the Ganges, and Hooghly rivers, with an awning of matting over the stern.

PANTAGRAPH. *See* PANTOGRAPH.

PANTALOON, the name for an old buffoon, an actor in a pantomime; a kind of trousers tight at the ancles.

PANTALOON STUFF, material for men's trousers.

PANTECHNICON, a bazaar in London for the sale of carriages, furniture, &c.; a place where all kinds of workmanship are sold.

PANTECH, a stretcher for carding.

PANTHEON, a large bazaar for light wares in London.

PANTIERE (French), a draw-net to catch birds.

PANTILE, a gutter-shaped tile, about 13½ inches long, by 9½ wide.

PANTILE LATHS, laths of 1½ inch wide and one inch thick, sold in bundles of twelve; one bundle being sufficient for a square of pantiling.

PANTINE (French), a lot of silks tied for dyeing.

PANTOGRAPH, PENTOGRAPH, an instrument for copying maps, charts, and drawings of all descriptions, on a reduced scale; also one for producing an exquisite embroidery on plain silk goods, after weaving.

PANTOMETER, an instrument for measuring dimensions.

PANTOMIME, a humorous or grotesque representation; buffoonery in dumb show.

PANTOMIMIST, a writer or actor of pantomimes; a buffoon or mimic.

PANTRY, a butler's room; a closet in a house where provisions are kept, or plate and knives are cleaned.

PANYALA, a name in Behar, India, for the small leaves and shoots of the *Flacourtia cataphracta*, which resemble rhubarb in flavour, and are used as gentle astringents.

PAO CRAVO, a name in Brazil for the *Dicypellium caryophyllatum*, which produces clove-bark.

PAOLO, an Italian silver coin of 10 baiocchi, worth about 5d. The ten-paoli piece of Tuscany, is worth rather less than a dollar. There are also five-paoli pieces.

PAON (French), a peacock.

PAP, a child's food; a piece of whalebone about 18 inches long, used by fishermen in Shetland, to connect the balls of lead with the lines to which the hooks are attached.

PAPAW, a tropical fruit, the produce of *Carica Papaya*.

PAPETA, an Indian name for the St. Ignatius bean.

PAPER, a material made from flexible fibres, reduced to a pulp by minute division, by the cutters of a revolving cylinder. The pulp is bleached by chloride of lime, small quantities of which often remain in the paper, and injure its quality. Writing papers are either laid or woven, as cream or blue laid, yellow and blue wove. There are a great variety of papers forming articles of trade, as tissue, blotting, and tracing-papers; stout drawing-papers; gold and silver paper; coloured-papers; lace-paper; bank-note paper; China rice-paper; wrapping-paper; printing; foolscap; pot; demy; and other different sizes.

PAPER AND BANDBOX MAKER, a maker of wood and paper boxes.

PAPERASSE (French), old dusty writings; waste paper.

PAPER-BAG MAKER, a maker of small bags for bakers, confectioners, meal-men, and other retailers.

PAPER-BORDERER. *See* BLACK-BORDERER.

PAPER-BOX MAKER, a workman who makes card-board, or light wood papered boxes.

PAPER CAP, a cap worn by some workmen at their labour.

PAPER-CASE, a case for holding writing and note paper, &c. on a table.

PAPER-CUTTER. *See* PAPER-FOLDER.

PAPER-CURRENCY, the issue of bank notes and bills of exchange.

PAPER-CUTTING-MACHINE MAKER, a manufacturer of press ploughs for cutting the edges of paper even. There are also mill-board and card-cutting machines. *See* CARD-BOARD-CUTTING-MACHINE.

PAPER-FOLDER, PAPER-KNIFE, a piece of bone, ivory, wood, shell, or metal, in the shape of a knife for folding sheets. *See* PAPER-KNIFE.

PAPER-GLOSSER, a card hot-presser; one who gives a smooth surface to paper.

PAPER-HANGER, one who covers rooms with paper, pasting lengths on the walls.

PAPER-HANGING-MANUFACTURER, a paper-stainer; a maker of paper-hangings.

PAPER-HANGINGS, stained or printed paper for covering the walls of rooms. A piece of paper contains about 63 superficial feet. French room-papers, however, vary in length and breadth, according to quality.

PAPER-HOLDER, an upright inclined frame to stretch a newspaper for reading.

PAPER-KNIFE, a knife for smoothing or folding paper, and for cutting the leaves of books.

PAPER-MAKER, a manufacturer of paper.

PAPER-MARBLER, one who veins or marbles paper for bookbinding, hangings, and other ornamental purposes; a bookbinder who sprinkles the edges of books.

PAPER-MILL, the works where a paper-manufactory is carried on.

PAPER-MOULD-MAKER, a manufacturer of shapes, or machine-wire frames, for placing paper pulp in, which are of various kinds, according to the paper to be made, whether writing-paper, printing-paper, or bank-note paper, &c.

PAPER-RULER, a workman who lines paper by hand. *See* RULER.

PAPER-SHADE, a cover or shade for a table-lamp glass, or a paper frame on wire for a gas-light burner, to moderate the intense light.

PAPER-STAINER, a manufacturer of paper-hangings.

PAPER-STAINER'S-BLOCK-CUTTER, a cutter of wood blocks for stamping colours on paper-hangings; he often also makes blocks for calico-printers.

PAPER-WAREHOUSE, the stores of a paper-maker; a retail shop for the sale of paper, often carried on combined with the trade of bookseller and stationer.

PAPER-WEIGHT, a fancy ornament for keeping loose letters or papers on a table or desk from blowing about.

PAPETERIE (French), a paper-mill; the stationery trade; a fancy case with a stock of writing-paper.

PAPIER (French), paper; a book; a writing.

PAPIER-MACHÉ, paper pulp and fancy articles made therefrom. Papier-mâché is made in two ways; one consists in pasting together on a mould different thicknesses of paper; the other is by pressing in moulds the paper reduced to a pulp. The former produces the best quality, the latter the inferior kinds. It is sized, covered with lamp-black, varnished, and placed in a heated oven.

PAPILLOTES, a lady's curl-papers; these are sold ready for use of leather and other material, to roll the hair on.

PAPPEN (German), paste-board.

PAPPIN, a soft paste used by weavers in Scotland for dressing their warps or webs; generally, however, called batter.

PAP-SPOON, a spoon for feeding an infant.

PAPYRUS, a species of *Cyperus*, about 15 feet high; the exterior tunic of the stems cut in bands, and pressed, formed the paper of ancient Egypt and Europe; the leaves which are several feet long, served for the same purpose, but were of inferior quality.

PAQUAGE (French), packing of fish in barrels.

PAQUEUR (French), a herring packer.

PAR, a state of equality; the original nominal price or full value of a security or money. In stocks and shares, "above par" means at a premium, or above the original value; "below par," at a discount.

PARA, a nominal Turkish coin, also called a medino. In Constantinople and Alexandria, 40 paras go to the piastre of 2¼d. sterling, and but 33 in Cairo. In Greece the para passes for about the third of a penny, and 100 make a drachma. *See* PIASTRE.

PARACHUTE, an apparatus shaped like an umbrella, with a suspended car, in which an aeronaut descends from a balloon.

PARADE, military display or procession; a drill ground.

PARADIS (French), a wet dock or inner harbour; the upper gallery in a playhouse.

PARADISE-BIRD. *See* BIRDS OF PARADISE.

PARADISE-FISH, a species of *Polynemus*, which is esteemed excellent food in India, and the sound furnishes isinglass.

PARADISE-GRAINS. *See* GRAINS OF PARADISE.

PARAFFINE, a light transparent oil or solid fat, obtained from bituminous coal, by distillation, which, mixed with other oils, is used for lubricating purposes in the cotton-mills. It is also obtained from peat, and has been made into candles.

PARAGE (French), a roadstead near a harbour.

PARAGRAPH, a short piece of news, or notice in a newspaper; a distinctive subdivision of a book, sometimes marked thus ¶.

PARA-GRASS, a name for the fibres of the leaves of the *Attalea funifera*. *See* PIASSAVA.

PARAGUAY-TEA, the leaves of the South American holly, *Ilex Paraguensis*, largely used for making the dietetic beverage termed mate in South America. The consumption of this leaf in the various South American republics, is estimated at 40 million pounds.

PARAH, an Indian measure of capacity, two feet square and six and a half inches deep. The internal measure of a standard parah is a cube of 11·57-100ths inches. The weight for various goods according to the Ceylon Custom-house practice is, for coffee, 38 to 50 lbs.; pepper 27 to 60 lbs.; salt 52 to 55 lbs.; paddy, 30 to 33 lbs.; husked rice 42 to 46 lbs. In Bombay eight parahs make a candy, by which seeds, grain, &c. are measured; the parah contains 7 pailies, and weighs 19 lbs. 9 oz. 9·6 drs. The parah measure for salt is 1,607·61 cubic inches.

PARALLEL GUIDES, PARALLEL RULER, a mathematical instrument formed of two flat equal rulers, connected by moveable cross-bars, and used for drawing parallel lines.

PARAMATTA, a kind of bombazine, the weft of which is worsted, the warp of cotton.

PARANGON (French), long primer type; black marble.

PARA-NUT, a name for the Brazil-nut.

PARANZELLE, a Neapolitan vessel.

PARAPET, a balustrade; a breast-high wall or paling on the edges of bridges, flat roofs, &c.

PARAPLUIE (French), an umbrella.

PARASANG, the Persian league, an itinerary measure, equal to 6086 English yards, or 3½ English miles.

PARASOL, a silk sun-shade or complexion-protector, carried by ladies, being an umbrella on a smaller scale, and more tastefully made.

PARASOL-HANDLE, the stick or support for the frame, &c. of a parasol, which is made of wood, bone, or ivory.

PARASOL-MAKER, a tradesman who employs persons to make ornamental hand sun-shades for ladies. Parasols are usually sold by linendrapers.

PARASOL-RING, a ring to keep the frame-work of a parasol closed, made of metal, ivory, or other substance.

PARBOIL, to cook partially.

PARBUCKLE, single ropes passed round a spar or cask to hoist or lower it by.

PARCAGE (French), the time during which sheep are folded.

PARCEL, a small package or bundle of goods; a lot or portion.

PARCEL-BOOK, a merchant's register book of the despatch of parcels.

PARCELLING, a nautical term for wrapping ropes, &c., with pieces of tarred canvas, to protect them from friction.

PARCELS DELIVERY COMPANY, a company in London which receives and delivers by vans, packages and small parcels over the metropolis; receiving-houses being appointed in all the principal localities.

PARCHMENT, a writing material for lawyers, made from the prepared skins of sheep and goats.

PARCHMENT AND VELLUM MAKER, a preparer of the skins of sheep, calves, &c. for writing and other uses.

PARCHMENT-COFFEE, coffee stripped from the pulp, and prepared in a particular manner in the West Indies.

PARCHMENT-CUTTINGS, the trimmings and clippings of prepared skins, which are used for making size.

PARCHMENT-DEALER, a law-stationer; a vender of parchments.

PARDESSUS, a lady's over-garment of fur, &c.

PARDO, a money of account of Goa, in the East Indies, of 4 or 5 tangas, and worth about 2s. 6d.

PARE, to peel; to thin down; to cut off gradually.

PAREGORIC, a soothing syrup for coughs.

PAREMENT (French), free-stone; pavement on the sides of streets, curb-stones; the facings of garments.

PAREPIEDS (French), fenders or protections for the side of a ship.

PARERE (French), the opinion of merchants on questions of trade.

PARGET, gypsum or plaster-stone; rough plaster, as for the interior of a chimney or roof.

PARIAN, a white marble; a white porcelain.

PARIAN-CEMENT, a fine or coarse cement, according to the purpose for which it is to be used.

PARIAN-WAREHOUSE, a shop where fine pottery and fancy articles of biscuit-ware are sold.

PARING-KNIFE, a bookbinder's tool; a knife for thinning down or paring any thing.

PARISH-CLERK, a subordinate officer in a church, who gives out the responses to the minister, and attends to other official duties.

PARISH-CLERKS' COMPANY, one of the London incorporated companies not on the livery. Their hall is in Silver-street, Wood-street.

PARK, a public or private inclosure or pleasure ground; a piece of woodland and meadow enclosed for keeping deer; a train of artillery.

PARK-KEEPER, a warden; one who has the care of a park.

PARK-PHAETON, a small low carriage for general use.

PARLOUR, a sitting or living room on the ground floor in a private house; a sitting-room or meeting-room for customers in a public-house or tavern.

PARLOUR-BOARDER, a scholar who takes his meals with the schoolmaster's family.

PARMESAN-CHEESE, a choice Italian cheese.

PAR-OF-EXCHANGE; when two things of different denominations are equal to each other in value, they are then said to be at par. *See* EXCHANGE.

PAROIR (French), a parer or scraper.

PAROQUET, PARRAKEET, a small parrot with a long pointed tail, of which there are many species.

PARQUET (French), an inlaid floor; a chimney frame; the bar in a court of justice; the place close to the orchestra in a play-house.

PARQUETRY. *See* MARQUETRY.

PARR, a salmon under two years old.

PARRAL, a collar of greased rope supporting yards to the mast in a ship.

PARRILLA, an earthen jar with two handles used in Italy.

PARROT, a well-known talking bird, a species of *Psittacus*, several of which, as the gray and the green, are favourite cage birds, and largely dealt in by bird fanciers.

PARROT-COAL, a kind of coal that burns very clearly.

PARSLEY, a well-known culinary herb, the *Petroselinum sativum*, with its varieties, *P. hortense* and *P. crispum*.

PARSLING, a nautical term for wrapping or covering ropes, &c. with coarse canvas.

PARSNIP, PARSNEP, a culinary root, the *Pastinaca sativa*.

PARSON, a common name for a clergyman.

PARSONAGE-HOUSE, the vicarage or rectory-house; the residence of a clergyman.

PART, a portion or share; a character or personage in a play.

PARTERRE, a flower-garden; a garden bed with walks between; the pit in a French playhouse.

PARTICATE, in Scotland, a rood of land.

PARTING, the operation of separating silver from gold by an acid; in paper-making, separating the moistened sheets; in navigation, a ship breaking her cable, and leaving her anchor in the ground.

PARTNER, an associate; the member of a firm; one who has a joint-share, interest, or business-stake with another in any concern or speculation.

PARTNERSHIP, a firm or joint-stock association; common property or interest in matters or things.

PART-OWNER, one who has a share in a ship, house, or other property.

PARTRIDGE, a well-known game bird, the common partridge, *Perdix cinereus*, shot in large quantities by sportsmen, and sold in the London markets to the number of about 150,000 a year.

PARTRIDGE-WOOD, a name for the wood of several trees coming from South America and the West Indies. The West Indian is the produce of *Heisteria coccinea*. It is used for walking-sticks, umbrella and parasol handles, and a variety of it in cabinet-work and turning. The colours are variously mingled, and most frequently disposed in fine hair-streaks of two or three shades, which in some of the early specimens resemble the feathers of the bird; other varieties are called pheasant-wood. Some authorities believe partridge-wood to be the produce of *Andira inermis*.

PARTY-WALL, a partition or separation wall between two or more buildings.

PARURE (French), a set of pearls and brilliants; articles of ornament, dress, or attire; in bookbinding, parings or shreds.

PASAMINILLO, a name for narrow lace in Italy.

PASAR, the Malay name for a market.

PASCHER (German), a smuggler.

PASS, a name for the third classification or quality of Russian hemp; a free journey-ticket on a railway; an unpaid admission to a place of amusement.

PASSAGE, a narrow lane or corridor in a house or building; a voyage taken by water.

PASSAGE-MONEY, the fare paid for conveyance by sea.

PASS-BOOK, the account-book in which entries and payments are made for the information of depositors, by banking-institutions, saving-banks, &c.

PASS-CHECK, a ticket of admission given to some exhibition or place of amusement in exchange for money, or for re-entrance.

PASSEMENT (French), trimmings, lace, or tape, of gold, silver, silk, or thread.

PASSEMENTIER, a dealer in lace or trimmings in France.

PASSENGER, a traveller by land or sea.

PASSENGER-AGENT, a broker, licensed to engage passages in ships for emigrants.

PASSENGER-SHIP, a steamer or merchant-vessel which has accommodation for passengers; an emigrant-ship.

PASS-HOLDER, one who holds a free pass, or a paid season ticket.

PASS-KEY, one that will open several locks.

PASS-NOTE, in the manufacturing districts, a certificate from the occupier or manager of a factory, that the bearer has legally left his last employment.

PASSOVER-BREAD, PASSOVER-CAKE, a thin unleavened cake, used among the Jews at the festival of the Passover, near Easter.

PASSPORT, an official licence or permission to enter or leave a country, required in most of the Continental States of Europe.

PASTE, flour and water mixed for cooking; a soft, sticky, adhesive substance, prepared by boiling wheaten-flour, largely used in many trades, especially by paper-hangers, bookbinders, &c. A little alum added, prevents paste from turning sour for some time. A kind of paste, or maccaroni, is imported into Malta from Italy, to a large amount. In commerce, the term paste is applied to the inspissated juice of liquorice, and some other vegetables. Paste is also the technical name for a kind of glass used to manufacture imitation precious stones. It is composed, according to Professor Ansted, of pounded rock crystal, melted with alkaline salts, and coloured with metallic oxides.

PASTE-BOARD, a wooden board on which dough is rolled out for pastry; thick stiff paper pasted together.

PASTE-BOARD MAKER, a manufacturer of card-board, mill-board, and other stout paper substances.

PASTE-BRUSH, a bookbinder's, or paper-hanger's brush; a cook's brush for varnishing pastry.

PASTE-CUTTER, PASTE-JAGGER, kitchen utensils used in making pastry.

PASTEL, the colouring pulp obtained from the *Isatis tinctoria*.

PASTELLIERE, PASTICCIERE (Italian), a pastry-cook.

PASTE-ROLLER, a rolling-pin of wood or glass, for spreading dough.

PASTICCERIA, a pastry-cook's shop in Italy.

PASTILLE, a small fragrant roll of paste; a small perfumed taper to burn in a room; an aromatic lozenge or drop.

PASTING-LACE, a narrow kind of coach lace, employed to cover and hide rows of tacks.

PAST-MASTER, one who has been master of a civic company, or has filled the chair of a freemason's lodge.

PAST-MASTER'S JEWEL, a freemason's honorary distinction or decoration, worn on the breast in a lodge, by one who has filled the master's chair.

PASTOORMAH, PASTURMA, PASTRAMA, beef preserved in Asia Minor, with garlic and pepper, and dried in the sun for winter food. It is prepared in Wallachia and Moldavia, and largely shipped from Varna. Besides providing all Anatolia, Aleppo, and Damascus, 6000 cwt. or more is yearly sent from Kaissariah to Constantinople.

PASTRY, food made of paste, such as pies, puddings, tarts, &c.

PASTRY-COOK, a dealer in tarts and pastries; a confectioner.

PASTRY-CUTTER, a cook's or confectioner's utensil for cutting dough.

PASTRY-MOULD, a shape of metal or earthenware, for pastry.

PASTURAGE, grazing-ground.

PASTURE, meadow; grazing-land for horses and cattle; food for cattle.

PASTURMA. See PASTOORMAH.

PASTY, a pie of dough, baked without a dish, and enclosing meat, potatoes, or the like.

PATACA, a copper coin; the Algerine name for the piastre of 24 tomins, which is valued at 1s. 6d.

PATACHE, a light vessel; a stage-coach.

PATACK, a former silver coin of Brazil, worth about 1s. 9d.

PATACOON, a Spanish dollar.

PATAGON, the silver crown-piece of Berne, worth about 4s. 9d.; a Spanish coin worth about 2s. 6d.

PATAK, an Egyptian money worth nearly 6d., 17 being equal to 8s. 1d.

PATARASSE (French), a caulking-iron used on board ship.

PATASCIA (Italian), a look-out boat; a ship's cutter.

PATATES, a name in the French colonies for sweet potatoes. See BATATAS.

PATCH, a piece sewed on to repair a hole; a small parcel, as of land.

PATCH-ICE, pieces of ice in the sea overlapping or nearly joining each other, extending but a short distance.

PATCHOULY, an Indian herb, the *Pogostemon Patchouli:* the dried tops, with the leaves and flowers, are imported to distil an essential oil from, which is esteemed by some as a perfume.

PATCHWORK, a union of pieces of different kinds or colours; patchwork quilts and table-covers were formerly in estimation, as displaying the economy and taste in arrangement of the pieces by the good housewife.

PATE (French), paste or dough; a pie or pasty.

PATENA, a large medal worn by country women in Italy.

PATENT, a protective right granted to an inventor, against piracy; a writ or privilege given by authority for the sole right to a new invention or discovery for a term of years. The word patent is often prefixed to articles vended, as patent sea cot; patent grease; patent barley, &c.

PATENT-AGENT, a person who acts for inventors and patentees; making searches, enrolling their designs, &c. at the patent-office, and securing their rights at home or abroad.

PATENTEE, one who holds a patent right.

PATENT-FUEL MANUFACTURER, a maker of compressed coal; a composition-material for burning in fires.

PATENT-MEDICINE, a secret nostrum, pills, draught, or ointment, &c., these articles requiring to bear a government stamp.

PATENT-MEDICINE VENDER, a dealer in patent medicines, usually a chemist, but there are a few wholesale houses in London who keep stocks of the different patent medicines, and supply retailers.

PATENT-OFFICE, the government office where patents are enrolled, and privileges obtained upon payment of certain fees.

PATERNOSTER ROW, the chief locality for the shops of wholesale booksellers and publishers in London; usually spoken of in brief as "the Row."

PATH, a walk in a garden; a narrow footway through a field, &c.

PATIE, a name in Cambay for a large box.

PATINA, a basin or bowl; a name in Ceylon for grass land, for the most part rock, barely covered with a superstratum of soil, but producing long grass, and here and there a stunted and thorny bush or tree. Like the prairies of America these patinas are burned off every year.

PATISSIER, a French pastry-cook.

PATON, paste with which poultry is fattened in France.

PATROL, a mounted policeman; a watchman who goes his rounds.

PATRON, a protector; the owner of a church living; in France, the master of a passage boat; a pattern or model.

PATRONAGE, custom; favour; support.

PATTEN, a clog of wood standing on a ring of iron, worn to elevate the feet from the wet; a socket for a column.

PATTEN AND CLOG MAKER, a maker of these articles for the feet.

PATTEN-MAKERS' COMPANY, one of the minor livery companies of the city of London, which has no hall.

PATTEN-RING MAKER, a maker of the iron supports for pattens.

PATTERN, a model to be copied; needle-work or lace-work marked out to be executed by the needle; a design submitted for imitation.

PATTERN-BOOK, a book with designs for selection.

PATTERN-CARD, a set of samples or pieces, &c.

PATTERN-DRAWER, one who designs patterns.

PATTERN-MAKER, PATTERN-READER, one who arranges textile patterns for weaving.

PATTERN-MOULDER, a designer and maker of models for cast-iron foundries.

PATTERN-SETTER, a workman who decides on the manner in which a lace or other pattern, which has been designed and stamped, is to be embroidered or filled up.

PATTY, a little baked pasty.

PATTY-PAN, a small shallow tinned vessel for baking patties in.

PAUL, a small tent used in military camps in India; a Tuscan coin worth about 5d. See PAOLO.

PAULIE, in Scotland, an unhealthy sheep; the smallest lamb in a flock.

PAUMELLE, a kind of French barley.

PAUNCH, the bowels of an animal, which is sold to feed dogs.

PAUPER, an indigent person; one unable to obtain his own livelihood, or who is supported in the workhouse at the expense of the parishioners.

PAVE, to cover or floor with brick or stone.

PAVEMENT, a flagging of flat, smooth, square cut stones, mostly granite, laid on a footway or path.

PAVEMENT-MERCHANT, a dealer in paving materials, granite, flags, curb stones, &c.

PAVILION, a large park or lawn tent; a summer-house; a building with a dome.

PAVILLON (French), a flag, a tent bed.

PAVING BOARD, a parochial committee or board of commissioners in whom is vested the superintendence and management of the paving, lighting, and cleansing of the streets of a district or parish.

PAVING-RATE, a parish rate levied on the householders for maintaining or extending the pavements.

PAVING-STONES, large flat stones for pavements.

PAVIOR, a workman who lays stones and bricks in streets and yards, &c.

PAVIORS, a building term for bricks used for paving, which are made nine inches long, four and a half broad, by one and three quarters thick.

PAVIORS' COMPANY, one of the London incorporated companies, which is not on the livery, and has no hall.

PAVIOR'S-RAMMER, a heavy mallet, or iron-bound wooden maul, used by a pavior, for forcing down paving-stones level.

PAW, PAO, an Indian word signifying fourth; another name in the East for the seer, = 1 5-16 quart. See SEER.

PAWL, a short bar of iron which prevents the capstan or windlass from turning back; a piece of money in Guinea.

PAWN, a pledge; one who has temporarily sold himself as a slave in Africa for debt, or for money advanced, &c.; a piece belonging to the game of chess; in Scotland, a narrow hanging or curtain fixed to the roof or to the lower part of a bed.

PAWN-BROKER, a shopkeeper licensed to take in goods on pledge, who advances money thereon at a fixed rate of interest.

PAWN-TICKET, a dated receipt of particulars, given by a pawn-broker, for an article received in pledge.

PAY, salary or wages earned; hire; to give what is due, to discharge a debt.

PAY-BILL, a list of persons to be paid.

PAY-CLERK, one who makes payments, or pays wages.

PAY-DAY, the day fixed for payments to be made; or when wages or salary is receivable; on the Stock Exchange, the last day for closing and settling a stock or share account, usually the fifteenth and thirtieth day of the month.

PAYREE, a measure of capacity in the Southern Mahratta country, of 2 adholies and = 5¼ quarts.

PAYMASTER, a naval commissioned officer, ranking with a lieutenant, who has charge of all cash payments of the vessel, and of the victualling stores. He keeps all the ship's accounts, and makes whatever disbursements are requisite. He was formerly called a purser. There are also paymasters to regiments.

PEA-BOILER, a peculiar cullender or strainer to boil peas in.

PEA-HAUM, the dry stalk or stem of pease.

PEACH, a choice fruit, the produce of *Amygdalus communis*, of which there are more than 200 cultivated varieties; a colour; a miner's name for chlorite.

PEACH-BRANDY, a spirit made in parts of the United States, especially in Pennsylvania and Indiana.

PEACH-WOOD, a name for the Nicaragua-wood (*Cæsalpinia echinata*), a concentrated decoction of which is largely used as a dye-stuff. See NICARAGUA-WOOD.

PEACOCK, a well-known domestic fowl, the *Pavo cristatus*, which has a beautiful spreading tail. The ocellated feathers are esteemed in the East, being worn by the Chinese mandarins in their caps, and made into fly-flappers, fans, and other ornaments in India.

PEAGER, a French toll-collector: A turnpike-man.

PEA-HEN, the female of the pea-cock.

PEA-JACKET, a loose, warm short-coat, made of rough pilot-cloth for use at sea.

PEAK, the pointed bill of the palm of an anchor made to enter the ground; the upper corner of a sprit-sail; the leather front of a cap; a name for the great Constantinople foot, = 0·7317 English yard; an old word for lace.

PEA-MEAL, ground pease, used for soup, and to make bread in the north.

PEA-NUT, an American name for the ground-nut, *Arachis hypogæa*.

PEAR, a choice fruit, of which there are between 600 and 700 varieties grown for table use. The fruit is sometimes pressed for making perry.

PEARL, a kind of printing-type; the seam stitch in a knitted stocking; a well-known nacreous gem, formed by several molluscs of the mussel and oyster families, and for obtaining which, extensive fisheries are carried on by divers in the Persian Gulf, Bay of Panama, and coasts of Ceylon. Imitation pearls are largely made for ladies' ornaments.

PEARL-ASH, potashes purified by solution in water, filtration, and ignition.

PEARL-BARLEY MAKER, a preparer of husked barley for soups. See BARLEY.

PEARL-BUTTON, a nacreous shell button, made of different sizes and shapes, according to the use to which it is to be applied.

PEARL-DIVER, one engaged in bringing up oysters, to search them for pearls.

PEARLED, having a border of lace; made in shape and appearance like pearls, as barley, sago, &c.

PEARL-EDGE, a projection at the sides of ribbons, which is formed by making some of the threads of the weft project beyond the rest. Pearl-edge is also the name for a narrow kind of thread edging to be sewn to lace.

PEARL-MERCHANT, a dealer in pearls.

PEARL-MOSS. See CARRAGEEN, and Irish-moss.

PEARL-OYSTER, a species of *Avicula*, the *Meleagrina margaritifera*.

PEARL-SAGO, sago in the form of small hard grains, not larger than a pin's head. Common sago is in large grains, about the size of pearl barley, and brownish white.

PEARL-SHELL. See MOTHER-OF-PEARL.

PEARL-STRINGER, one who threads pearls, imitation or real, for necklaces or other ornaments.

PEARL-WEIGHT. The troy ounce contains 600 pearl grains, and hence one pearl grain is 4-5ths of a troy grain. See CHOW.

PEARL-WHITE, a colour; a powder made from nitrate of bismuth, and sometimes used by ladies as a cosmetic.

PEARL-WORKER, a workman who cuts up mother-of-pearl shell, or forms it into buttons, papier mâché, or other ornamental and useful articles for sale.

PEAR-MAIN, a kind of apple.

PEAR-TREE, the *Pyrus communis*, the light brown wood of which is much used for the engraved blocks for calico-printers, paper-stainers, and pastry-cooks; and also for carving, and by the Tunbridge-ware turner.

PEASANT, a rustic or country person; one who lives by rural labour.

PEASE, the seeds of varieties of the leguminous plant, *Pisum sativum*, esteemed as a culinary vegetable, and the plant is largely grown both as a field and garden crop. Peas are sold fresh gathered or green, and dried or split, to be used for making soup.

PEASE-PUDDING, a pudding made of dried split peas, boiled to be eaten with meat.

PEA-SHOOTER, a small metal tube for blowing peas through.

PEA-SOUP, a meat soup flavoured or thickened with dried peas boiled.

PEA-STICKS, climbing supports for the vines or stems of garden pease.

PEAT, turf, or the decaying roots and stems of plants. In many localities turf is cut and dried for fuel, and frequently containing peculiar resins, various commercial products have been obtained from it.

PEAT-MOSS, the place where peats are dug.

PEAT-REEK, the smoke of peat, as communicated to Highland whisky, distilled by means of peat.

PEAT-RICK, a stack of peats piled to dry for [fuel.

PEAT-STONE, the corner-stone at the top of the wall of a house.

PEAUX-BRUTES (French), raw hides.

PEBBLES, a name given to various ornamental stones, worked by the lapidary, which, though differing much in colour and appearance, may be regarded as varieties of agate.

PEBRE, a sauce made in Italy of garlic and spice.

PECA, a former gold coin of Brazil, of 6 dollars 400 milreis, weighing 4 octavas, equal to 9 dwts. 5 grains, and of the fineness of 22 carats. At the par of exchange of 67½d. per mil., its intrinsic value was 36s. sterling.

PECCAN-NUT, the seed of the *Carya oliveformis* growing in North America.

PECK, a British dry-measure of 2 gallons, the fourth part of a bushel; 4 lbs. of flour, or a 4lb. loaf. There are, however, some local pecks of variable dimensions.

PECUL, PICUL, a Dutch measure of capacity, the principal heavy weight used in most of the markets of the Eastern archipelago. At Macao the Portuguese distinguish it into three kinds, viz:—the pecul balanca of 100 catties, = 133 lbs. 5 oz. 5·33 dwts. avoirdupois: the pecul seda of from 111 to 115 catties, = 146·2 lbs. avoird.: the pecul chapa of 150 catties, = 200 lbs. avoird.: at Singapore 16 peculs and 80 catties make a ton, and 40 peculs a coyan. Ninety catties seda = a Canton pecul, or pecul balanca. By the first or p. balanca are sold cotton, and valuable articles; by p. seda, alum, pepper, and coarse goods; and by the p. chapa, rice.

PEDAGE, a toll paid in crossing a bridge.

PEDAGGIERE (Italian), a collector of tolls from foot passengers; a turnpike-man.

PEDAL, the lever of a harp, organ, or pianoforte, moved by the foot.

PEDDLE, to carry about goods for retail sale.

PEDESTAL, the foot or base of a column or statue.

PEDLAR, a hawker; one who carries about small wares for sale in a box or pack.

PEDOMETER, a distance-measurer, made in the form of a watch, by the use of which the number of steps or paces the wearer takes when walking, may be ascertained. When affixed to a saddle, it indicates the number of paces the horse makes, and to a carricle, or other carriage, the number of the revolutions of the wheels.

PEDOTO (Italian), a pilot or helmsman.

PEDRENAL, a kind of small firelock.

PEDRIZA, PETRIERA, a quarry in Italy; a heap of loose stones.

PEEL, a baker's wooden slide, with a long handle, for putting loaves in the oven, and taking them out; a broad shovel; a printer's tool for hanging up damp printed sheets on a line to dry; the skin or rind of fruit. *See* ORANGE-PEEL.

PEEN, the sharp point of a mason's hammer.

PEEROGRUG, an Indian name for the *Cissampelos glabra*, the acrid roots of which are used in medicine by the natives.

PEETHA, a name in India for the *Benincasa cerifera*, a cucurbitaceous plant.

PEET SAL, a name in Bengal for the *Pterocarpus marsupium*, a tree from which a red juice exudes, that hardens into an astringent, brittle gum-resin, of a dark-red colour.

PEG, a wooden nail, a small marker for a cribbage-board; a pin in a hat-rack. A large trade is carried on in North America in the manufacture of wooden pegs for shoes; quantities of which are shipped to this country.

PEGALL, a description of basket made by the Indians of Guiana.

PEGGED BOOTS, boots with wooden pegs in the soles, instead of metal nails or brads.

PEGOLA (Italian), pitch; tar.

PEGOTE, a fricassee with a sauce.

PEG-TOP, a child's plaything for spinning, made of wood.

PEIGNE (French), a comb; a card or weaver's reed.

PEIK, a long plummet, or piece of lead used for ruling paper.

PEILLER (French), a rag-picker.

PEJEPALO, an Italian name for salted-fish or stock-fish.

PEKOE, a fine black tea, so named.

PELACANE (Italian), a tanner.

PELADILLA, a sugared almond in Italy.

PELAGE, a wild beast's skin.

PELERINE, a lady's long cape with ends.

PELETERO, in Italy a furrier.

PELLUCREEE, an Indian name for the root of *Thalictrum foliolosum* of Wallich, a native of the Himalayas, which is used as a febrifuge and a tonic aperient. Another species (*T. flavum*), is common in France, where it is termed "the poor man's rhubarb."

PELISSE, a lady's silk cloak; a furred robe for men; a dress of sheep-skin made at Kaboushan, north of Khorassan, in Persia, sometimes called a posteen.

PELLERON (French), a small shovel.

PELLET, a name in Scotland for the skin of a sheep without the wool. *See* PELT.

PELLICIA (Italian), a fur coat.

PELLICO (Italian), a garment made of skins or furs.

PELLITORY, a name for the root of *Anthemis Pyrethrum*, which is used as a masticatory to relieve toothache; it enters into the composition of certain snuffs, and the powder is used in large quantities by the Mohammedans to excite transpiration, being rubbed upon the skin.

PELLON, a long fur robe.

PELOTAGE, packs or bales of Spanish wool.

PELTRIES, PELTS, the commercial name given to the skins of animals before tanning.

PELTRO (Italian), pewter.

PELUQUERO (Italian), a wig or peruke maker.

PEMETTOFORO, a machine for carrying heavy burdens.

PEMMICAN, dried and pounded meat, prepared with fat and raisins in a concentrated or portable form, for the use of Arctic voyagers.

PEN, a shaped quill or metal instrument for writing with; a coop for poultry; a fold for cattle; a reservoir of water; a name in Scotland for the dung of fowls.

PENANG LAWYERS, a commercial name given to walking-sticks made from the stems of a small palm, the *Licuala acutifida*.

PENCASE, a receptacle for keeping pens in.

PENCIL, a black lead, slate, or other instrument, or brush, for writing or drawing.

PENCIL-CASE, a small pocket-case holding a pencil point, &c. for ready use.

PENCIL-CASE MAKER, a manufacturer of gold, silver, or alloyed metal cases for holding pencils for the pocket. Some of which, as Mordan's pencils, have reserve cases for spare leads, and a spiral which sends down the lead to the point.

PENCIL-RULER. *See* RULER.

PEND, PENOCK, Eastern names for oil-cake.

PENDANT, a hanging burner for gas.

PENDICLER, a name in Scotland for an inferior tenant.

PEND-STANE, in Scotland, a stone suited for building an arch.

PENDULE, PENDULUM, a swinging weight or time-regulator to a clock.

PEN-FOLD, a fold of hurdles for enclosing cattle.

PENGUIN, a sea-fowl exclusively found in the Antarctic seas, deriving its name from its pinguidity or excessive fatness. The skin of the breast of some species is used for making muffs, and other articles of ladies' dress; a species of *Bromelia*, *B. Penguin*, much used in the West Indies, as a fence to gardens and fields; its sharp spiny leaves keeping out cattle and hogs.

PEN-HOLDER, a handle, holdfast, or support for a steel-pen, made of different materials.

PENING, a small money of Holland; the eighth of a denier gros.

PENITENTIARY, a house of correction, for criminals.

PEN-KNIFE, a small sharp knife for shaping quills into pens.

PEN-MANUFACTURER, a maker of steel or other metal pens; a cutter of quill-pens by machinery.

PEN, originally a palisadoed enclosure for cattle in the West Indies, but now applied to a pasture-farm for grazing and cattle-breeding in the colonies.

PENNANT, a rope to which a purchase is hooked; a long narrow streamer borne at the mast-head by vessels of war.

PENNISTONE, a coarse woollen frieze.

PENNON, a small banner or flag. *See* PENNANT.

PENNY, the largest and most ancient British copper coin, weighing one ounce. It was at first composed of silver, and minted with a deep cross, weighing the 240th part of a lb. When broken into two parts, each was called a halfpenny, and when into four, each was called a fourth-thing, or farthing. It was gradually diminished till the time of Elizabeth, when its value was reduced to the 62nd part of an ounce. Pennies are still minted in silver to a small amount (under 8000 a-year); but those in ordinary circulation have been for a long time made of copper. The pennies coined since 1845 have been as follows in number:—

1848	161,280	1852	263,424
1849	268,800	1853	1,021,440
1851	268,800	1854	6,827,520

—*See* COPPER COINAGE.

PENNY-A-LINER, a chance contributor to the columns of a newspaper, who is paid at the rate of 1d. or 1½d. a line for whatever portion of the matter is published.

PENNY RECEIPT-STAMP, a stamp required by law to be affixed and given on bills settled for sums above £2.

PENNY-ROYAL, an aromatic plant, the *Mentha Pulegium*. The distilled water is much used as a vehicle for medicines for children, and in flatulent colics; a popular emmenagogue.

PENNY-STAMP, a postal-stamp affixed to letters under half an ounce weight, which frees them by the post throughout the United Kingdom.

PENNYWEIGHT, a British weight, equal to 24 grains, or the 20th part of an ounce troy. It is so called because such was the weight of a silver penny in the reign of Edward I., when the pennyweight was first adopted.

PENNY-WHIP, a name in Scotland for weak small beer, sold at a penny a bottle; a child's toy.

PEN-RACK, a support for pens.

PEN-REED GRASS, a name for the *Saccharum Sara*, which is beaten into a rude fibre, and twisted into rope, which is esteemed as a tow line, for its strength and durability, by the boatmen on the Upper Ganges.

PENSION, a French boarding-house or school; a salary or allowance accorded to ex-public functionaries, and retired soldiers or sailors, for past services.

PENSIONER, a soldier receiving a pension, but who has to make his appearance at certain times, and do certain duties.

PEN-SLIDES, an instrument for writing, used by surveyors and map drawers.

PENSTOCK, PENTROUGH, the floodgate of a mill-pond; an instrument to supply water to a mill.

PENTAGRAPH, PANTOGRAPH, an instrument for enlarging or reducing plans.
PENT-HOUSE, a shed with a sloping roof.
PEN-TRAY, a small wooden tray for holding pens.
PEN-WIPER, a fancy ornament of patch-work, cloth, &c. for cleaning pens of the ink.
PEON (Italian), a day-labourer; a foot soldier; a hive of bees.
PEONERIA, PEANIA (Italian), as much land as can be ploughed in a day; a Spanish superficial land-measure, 500 paces long, by 300 broad; the half of a caballeria.
PEORREE, PURREE. *See* INDIAN YELLOW.
PEPINIERISTE (French), a nurseryman.
PEPITAS, the Spanish term for small rough masses of gold, as discovered in the mines, and which are called by our miners nuggets. *See* NUGGET.
PEPLAMOOR, an Indian name for the long pepper root.
PEPON, POPONE (Italian), the water-melon.
PEPPER, a name for the hot pungent berry or fruit of different plants, used for seasonings. The ordinary kinds of commerce are, black pepper, the fruit of a climbing plant, the *Piper nigrum*, grown in the East, of which we import on the average about seven million pounds a-year; white pepper made by blanching the black pepper; and Cayenne pepper produced by several species of Capsicum. The common long pepper of the shops is the produce of *Chavica Roxburghii* and *C. officinarum*. Pimento is sometimes called Jamaica pepper. *See* CAYENNE PEPPER, and GRAINS OF PARADISE.
PEPPER, AFRICAN, the fruit of the *Xylopia aromatica*; which is used as pepper in Sierra Leone, and other parts of Africa.
PEPPER, BIRD, the fruit of *Capsicum baccatum*. the seeds of which are ground to make Cayenne pepper. *See* BIRD PEPPER.
PEPPER-BOX, a cruet for holding ground pepper for table use.
PEPPER-BRAND, a disease in wheat, the *Uredo caries*.
PEPPER-CORN, the seed of the pepper vine. These pass current as money in some parts of Africa.
PEPPER-CORN-RENT, a nominal rent or perpetual lease.
PEPPER-CURN (Scotch), a hand-mill for grinding pepper.
PEPPER-DREDGE, a kitchen pepper-box.
PEPPER-DULSE, a pungent nutritious sea-weed, the *Laurencia pinnatifida*, used as a condiment, when other sea-weeds are eaten.
PEPPER-ELDER, a species of the pepper tribe, *Piper amalago*, abundant in Jamaica, the aromatic seeds of which afford a good substitute for the black pepper of the East Indies.
PEPPERERS, a name formerly given to the grocers.
PEPPER, GOAT, a name for the *Capsicum frutescens*.
PEPPER-MILL, a hand-mill for grinding pepper.
PEPPERMINT-CORDIAL, PEPPERMINT-WATER, an aromatic drink, flavoured with peppermint.
PEPPERMINT-OIL, a greenish essential oil, obtained by distillation from the *Mentha piperita*.
PEPPER-POT, a mucilaginous soup or stew of vegetables and cassareep, in high repute in the West Indies.
PERADA, a conserve made of pears.
PERAK, the Malay name for silver.
PERALEDA (Italian), an orchard of pear-trees.
PERAMBULATOR, a surveying instrument for measuring distances; termed also the pedometer and surveying-wheel; a wheel carriage for children, propelled by the hand from behind.
PERAMBULATOR-MAKER, a maker of the surveying instruments termed perambulators; also a coach-maker who constructs children's carriages.
PERBENDS, a building term for stones carried through the whole thickness of a wall.
PERCALINE (French), fine cotton print.
PER-CENTAGE, a rate or commission per hundred.
PERCEPTEUR, a French tax-gatherer or rate-collector.
PERCH, a linear-measure of 5½ yards; a square perch is equivalent to the 160th of an acre, or the 40th of a rood; a term applied to the French decamètre. Also the name of a fish, one species, the Sander (*Perca Lucio-perca*), is very common in the rivers which empty themselves into the Black sea. It is cured like cod, and might readily supply the place of it. The roe is much in request in the Levant; the oil is also more in esteem than that of other fish, and might very well be used for burning; for purposes of tanning; for the manufacture of soap; for the preparation of common colours, &c.
PERCHA (Italian), a snare for catching partridges; the sign-post of a barber's shop.
PERCOLATOR, a filter coffee-pot.
PERCUSSION-CAPS, small detonating copper caps for exploding the charge of a gun or pistol. Besides those made at home, large quantities are imported from the Continent.
PERCUSSION-POWDER. *See* DETONATING-POWDER.
PERCUSSION-STOP, a piano-forte stop to the harmonium, which renders the touch precisely like the piano-forte.
PERDRIGON, a kind of French plum.
PERELLE, a name for the crab's-eye lichen, the *Lecanora Parella*, found on rocks in mountainous countries, which yields a purple dye equal to that of archil.
PERFECT, to render complete, as finishing the printing of both sides of a sheet; making the sheets of a quire or ream of paper correct; to elaborate, to finish off.
PERFECTING-MACHINE, a printing-press for making perfect copies.
PERFORATE, to make full of holes; to bore or pierce through.
PERFORATED-PLATES, brass stencil plates for making letters or figures on paper; or for marking linen.
PERFUME, an essential essence; an agreeable scent. A good perfume should leave no residue on evaporation, and the ingre-

dients should be combined so harmoniously that no particular one should be perceptible. Hence well-prepared eau-de-Cologne may be considered the perfection of perfumery.

PERFUMER, one who makes or sells perfumes.

PERGAMENA (Italian), a parchment skin dressed for writing.

PERGOLA, PERGOLESE (Italian), a kind of late grape; a gallery or balcony.

PERGUM, an African money.

PERGUNNAH, a name in India for the largest division of land in a zemindaree; a subdivision of a district answering to the English hundred.

PERIDOT, a name given by French mineralogists to the chrysolite, a yellow gem, supposed to be the topaz of the ancients; a kind of emerald.

PERIER, a metal-founder's iron rod.

PERIGORD, an ore of manganese.

PERIGORD-PIE, an epicurean dish.

PERILLA, a small pear.

PERILLO, the Italian name for gingerbread.

PERINE-VIERGE, a French name for turpentine.

PERIODICAL, any publication that appears at stated intervals; a weekly, monthly, quarterly, or serial.

PERIOT, a division of the troy grain, formerly used by moneyers; the 11-520th part of the grain, and divided into 24 blanks.

PERIWIG, a peruke; a wig to cover a bald head.

PERIWINKLE, a species of mollusc, the *Turbo littoreus*, largely used as food when boiled, being collected and sold by measure. The quantity consumed in London has been estimated at 76,000 baskets, weighing 1900 tons, and valued at £15,000.

PERJURY, a wilful false oath, taken in some judicial proceeding.

PERMA, a Russian weight of 8665 lbs.

PERMAGY, a Turkish boat.

PERMANENT-WAY, the finished ballasted road of a railway.

PERMAYRUTIE, an Indian name for the Malabar cat-mint, *Anisomeles Malabarica*; an infusion of the bitter and somewhat aromatic leaves of the plant, is given in dysentery and intermittent fever.

PERNIO (Italian), a kind of hinge for hanging doors and windows.

PERMIT, a licence to remove exciseable articles; a let-pass granted by the excise-officers, customs, or other fiscal department.

PERMIT-WRITER, an excise-officer.

PERNAMBUCA-WOOD, a name for the *Cæsalpinia echinata*. *See* BRAZIL-WOOD, and PEACH-WOOD.

PERO, a kind of apple.

PEROGUE, a name in New Brunswick for a canoe hollowed out of a large pine log. Some are made large enough to carry twenty persons.

PEROL (Italian), a boiler or kettle.

PERPENDICULAR-LIFT, a contrivance on canals for passing boats from one level to another.

PERPIGNAN-WOOD. *See* NETTLE-TREE.

PERQUISITE, a privileged grant; an extra allowance or fee, beyond a salary.

PERRIER, an engine for throwing stones.

PERRON (French), a flight of steps before the doors of a house.

PERRY, a drink made of the juice of pears, which, when bottled, makes a very good imitation champagne.

PERSE (French), chintz.

PERSIAN, a thin inferior silk chiefly used for lining garments.

PERSIANA (Italian), a silk with large flowers; Venetian-blinds.

PERSIAN-BERRIES, the seeds of *Rhamnus infectorius*, used as a dye in calico-printing, also called yellow berries.

PERSIAN-BLINDS, jalousies or Venetian-blinds.

PERSIAN-TOBACCO, the leaves of *Nicotiana Persica* which are very fragrant and agreeable for smoking in pipes, but the tobacco is not suited to cigars from the difficulty of making it burn.

PERSIAN-WHEEL, a revolving wheel with buckets for raising water in a river or stream for irrigating or other purposes.

PERSICOT, a liqueur.

PERSIS, a colouring matter prepared from lichens, the mass being of a drier character than archil.

PERSONAL-PROPERTY, money and moveable goods—not landed property or houses.

PERUVIAN-BALSAM, a fragrant oleo-resin, obtained from the *Myroxylon Peruiferum*.

PESADA, a variable Spanish weight, used in the River Plate, from 35½ to 40½lbs.

PESANTE, an Italian weight of half a drachm.

PESATA, an Italian measurement for fire wood, equal to 3 cantari.

PESATORE (Italian), a weigher.

PESCATORE, an Italian fisherman.

PESCEDUOVA (Italian), an omelet; an egg pancake.

PESETA, a Spanish silver coin; a name for the fourth part of the Mexican dollar; the provincial peseta is however only 1-5th of the dollar. The peseta varies in value according to the purity and weight of the dollar; it may, however, be generally reckoned at about 10½d.

PESHKAR, PAISKKAR, in India, a tributary officer or collector; a chief agent, assistant, or manager.

PESILLO, small scales used in Italy for weighing gold or silver coin.

PESINALO, a dry-measure of Venetian Lombardy, rather more than 2 gallons.

PESO, a Spanish name for the dollar of exchange; a common name for the pound weight.

PESO-DURO, the hard dollar of Spain.

PESON (French), a steelyard.

PESSALOO, an Indian name for the *Phaseolus Mungo*.

PESSARY, a surgical instrument for supporting the vagina.

PESTLE, a solid pounder for crushing things in a mortar.

PETAQUILLA (Italian), a small trunk or hamper covered with hide or leather.

PETARD, an explosive for blowing up gates, &c.

PETATE, a name in Central America for dried palm leaves or grass, used for platting into hats and mats.

Peter-boat, a Thames fishing-boat.
Petersham, a rough woollen-cloth used for great coats.
Petit-canon (French) a kind of type, two-line English.
Petites-affiches, a small French journal of advertisements.
Petit-grain, an essential oil obtained from the fruit and leaves of *Citrus Bigaradia*.
Petit-gris, the name for miniver fur in France.
Petit-lait (French), whey.
Petit-texte, the French name for brevier type.
Petit-toes, the feet of sucking pigs.
Petricon, a liquid measure of Barcelona of nearly half a pint.
Petroleum, a rock oil or mineral naphtha; a solution of paraffine. *See* Naphtha.
Petticoat, a woman's loose lower garment, many kinds of which are kept ready-made in shops, as flannel, red, skeleton, stiff, and other petticoats.
Petty Cash-book, a book for entering small receipts and payments.
Petty-jury, a jury of twelve, summoned and empanelled to try offenders.
Petty-officers, the subordinate or warrant officers of a vessel of war.
Petty-rice, a name in Peru for the white seeds of *Chenopodium quinoa*, which make good porridge and cakes.
Petun, a common French name for tobacco and snuff.
Petunse, a clay-stone used in making porcelain.
Peum, a Cambodian land-measure of six feet; 20 peums make a sen.
Peverada (Italian), meat broth.
Pew, an enclosed seat in a church or chapel.
Pew-opener, an attendant in a church.
Pewter, an alloyed metal, of which there are several kinds; the best consists of 100 parts of tin and 17 antimony. That used for plates and dishes is formed of 89 parts of tin, 7 of antimony, and 2 of copper: tin and zinc and lead and tin are sometimes used to make pewter. Ley pewter for wine measures is an alloy of 1 part of lead to 3 of tin.
Pewterer, a workman who casts pewter in a mould, and afterwards hammers it out.
Pewterers' Company, one of the livery companies of London, whose hall is in Lime-street.
Pewter-pot, a publican's measure for serving malt-liquors; a quart, pint, or half pint pot.
Pezza, Pezzo, a land-measure of Rome 0·6521 acre; a nominal Italian coin passing in Malta for 30 tari or one dollar.
Pfand-leiher, Pfand-verleiher, a pawnbroker in Germany.
Pfanne, a salt measure of Prussian Saxony = 004·84 gallons.
Pfarrer, a German minister or curate.
Pfees, a name in Sinde for the *Chamærops Ritchiana*, of the fibre of which twine and ropes, sandals, baskets, and mats are made.
Pfeiler-spiegel (German), a pier-glass.
Pfenning, a small coin in Germany, the fourth part of a kreuzer, 3 kreuzers being equal nearly to an English penny: 80 German kreuzers are, however, about one shilling sterling.
Pferd (German), a horse.
Phaeton, a four-wheeled open carriage.
Pharmaceutist, Pharmaceutical Chemist, an apothecary; one skilled in the choice, preparation, and mixture of drugs and medicines.
Pharmacopœia, an official dispensatory; a book of authorized recipes and directions for dispensing drugs, emanating from a College of Physicians, and in Great Britain sanctioned and adopted by an order in Council. There are different ones in use in Scotland, Ireland, and England —a matter to be regretted,—uniformity in prescriptions, &c. being highly desirable.
Pharsang. *See* Parasang.
Pheasant, a well-known bird, the *Phasianus Colchicus*, preserved as a game-bird in Britain. The feathers of the gold and silver pheasants, and Argus pheasant, have commercial uses for ornament and artificial fly-making.
Pheasant-wood. *See* Partridge-wood.
Phial, a small bottle chiefly used for medicine.
Philadelphia Bark. *See* Quercitron.
Philibeg, the plaid petticoat of a Celt.
Phœnix, another name for the drachma, a Greek silver coin divided into 100 lepta, and worth about 8d.
Phonography, the art of expressing sounds by peculiar abbreviated characters or types.
Phosphate of Lime, a salt obtained from bones; a combination of phosphoric acid and lime.
Phosphoric Acid, an acid formed by the combustion of phosphorus, and also made by heating bones in a furnace to whiteness, and by distilling phosphorus with nitric acid, or with sulphuric acid, or chlorine. It is combined with sulphur in dipping lucifer matches.
Phosphorus, an elementary substance, a chemical product obtained from bones, which is extensively employed in the manufacture of lucifer matches.
Photograph, a sun-painting; a daguerreotype, or talbotype.
Photographic-apparatus Maker, a manufacturer of the appurtenances and materials for taking sun-pictures.
Photographic Artist, Photographer, one skilled in the art and manipulations of photography.
Photographic Paper, a chemically prepared paper, brushed with a solution of nitrate of silver, for receiving and fixing sun-impressions.
Photography, the process of taking facsimile impressions on paper, by the influence of light upon salts of silver.
Photometer, an instrument for measuring the intensity of light.
Phurra, a name for the leaves of the *Chamærops Ritchiana*, which are brought from Beloochistan into Sinde, and made into a variety of articles, baskets, fans, brushes, sieves, sandals, pouches, platters, and ropes.

PHYSICIAN, a doctor of medicine who holds a diploma from a College of Physicians or University; one who practises the art of healing.

PHYSIC-NUT, a name for the seed-capsules of *Curcas purgans* and *C. multifidus*. The milky juice of the plant dyes linen black. The oil obtained by expression from the seeds is largely used in India for lamps, and has been introduced into this country for the purpose. It is odourless, colourless, and limpid, and burns well; when cold it deposits a considerable quantity of stearine. It has the same qualities and uses as the croton-oil, but in large doses is a dangerous poison.

PIALLA (Italian), a carpenter's plane.

PIANELLAIO, an Italian shoemaker.

PIANO-FORTE, a well-known and popular stringed instrument played by keys; it is generally made in one of three forms, grand, square, or upright. There are, however, many fanciful and trade names given to them, as cabinet and cottage, piccolo, &c.

PIANOFORTE-FRET CUTTER, a maker of the open, ornamental wood-work for the front of a cabinet or upright piano.

PIANOFORTE HAMMER AND DAMPER-CLOTH MAKER, a workman who prepares the interior parts of the instrument so named.

PIANOFORTE-KEY MAKER, a turner who shapes and prepares the ivory and ebony keys, with which the instrument is played.

PIANOFORTE-MAKER, a manufacturer who employs workmen to construct and finish pianos.

PIANOFORTE-RAIL MAKER, a workman who makes the hammer-rails for the interior of the instrument.

PIANOFORTE-RESTERS, glass insulators, on which the legs of a pianoforte are sometimes placed.

PIANOFORTE SILKER, a workman who fits the ornamented silk to the front or open part of cottage and other upright pianos.

PIANOFORTE-STRING MAKER, a preparer of the wires and strings for the interior mechanism of the pianoforte.

PIANOFORTE-TUNER, a person who attends occasionally, or periodically, to tighten the strings, and put the instrument in tune for the player.

PIASSAVA, PIACABA, the footstalks of a species of South-American palm, the *Attalea funifera*, an important article of commerce in Brazil, and shipped to this country for making brushes and street-sweeping machines.

PIASTA (Italian), a thin plate of metal.

PIASTER, the dollar of exchange in Spain, where it is also called the peso de plata: an imaginary money estimated at eight reaux old plate, or fifteen reaux two maravedis vellon; and as the hard dollar is worth twenty reaux vellon, the piastre is equivalent at par to 3s. 1½d. sterling. The piastre, or piece of eight, was formerly a silver coin worth about 4s. 6d., being in fact the old dollar. Also a coin and money of account in Turkey, of 40 paras. The Turkish moneys, however, have been so depreciated and altered, that the value of the piastre has varied considerably. In 1773, it was worth about 1s. 8d.; in 1801, 1s. 8d.; in 1818, 9d.; while in the present coinage it is only worth about 2½d. The piastre of Tunis has, however, a higher value, and is divided into sixteen carabas, or twenty-five aspers. The value of the Turkish piastre fluctuates, being governed by the rate at which bills of exchange on London are sold at Constantinople.

PIATTA, a flat boat used in Italy.

PIAZZA, a square open space surrounded by buildings, or a walk roofed in; a market.

PIC, PIK, a variable Turkish cloth-measure, ranging from twenty-eight inches the long pic, to eighteen inches the short pic.

PICA, a species of printing-type, larger than long primer, of which there are several kinds cast, as large and small, four line, fourteen line, twenty line, double, and double small.

PICA-PEDRERO, an Italian stone-cutter.

PICAYUNE, an American coin worth threepence.

PICCALILLI, an imitation Indian pickle of various vegetables, with pungent spices.

PICCOLO, a small pianoforte; a small flute.

PICCONE (Italian), a pickaxe.

PICCOZZA (Italian), a hatchet.

PICE, a small East Indian copper coin, the fourth of an anna, precisely an inch in diameter, weighing 100 grains troy, which is a legal tender there for one sixty-fourth of the Company's rupee, and the double pice weighing 200 grains for one thirty-second of the rupee. This name is also applied to a weight, a variable division of the seer, ranging in different localities from 156½ grains up to 276½ grains.

PICHEL, the Italian name for a pewter tankard.

PICHELA, an Italian wine-measure.

PICHOUNE, a wine-measure used in Marseilles, the 60th part of the escandel, = to 0·4695 pint.

PICHURIM BEANS, a name for the isolated lobes of the drupe of *Ocotea Pichurim*; the sassafras nuts of commerce.

PICK, PICK-AXE, an implement with two slightly curved points or prongs, used in mining, agriculture, &c. to loosen the soil, or pick out paving stones.

PICKAGE, a charge or toll for breaking up ground to plant booths or stalls at a fair.

PICKER-BENDS, pieces of buffalo hide, limed, but not tanned or otherwise dressed, imported for the use of power-loom weavers, who attach them to the shuttle.

PICKETS, small sticks stuck in the ground in lining or surveying. In America the term is applied to stakes or narrow boards of cypress and other wood; outposts or guards placed as watchmen.

PICK-HAMMER, a pointed hammer for dressing granite.

PICKINGS, cullings; pounded oyster-shells for gravel walks; hard burnt bricks.

PICKLE, a name for brine, a liquor used for salting or preserving; also any fruit or vegetable preserved in vinegar or salt. A large trade is carried on in the sale of pickles and preserves.

PICKLE-BOTTLES, particular shaped thin glass bottles, made for holding pickles for sale.
PICKLE-DISH, a small glass or porcelain dish for holding pickles at a dinner table.
PICKLED-FISH, herrings, cod, &c. salted.
PICKLE-JAR, an earthenware vessel for preserving or holding pickles.
PICKLE-WAREHOUSE, a wholesale depot where pickles are manufactured and sold.
PICKLING, preserving flesh or vegetables by brine or vinegar; a workman's name for placing any thing in a steep.
PICKLING-TUB, PICKLING-PAN, vessels for keeping salted meat in.
PICK-LOCK, an instrument for picking locks; a term in the wool trade for a superior description of wool.
PICKTHA, another name for the viss, an Indian and Burmese weight of 140 tolas, about 3¼ pounds.
PIC-NICS, a kind of small sweet fancy biscuit, so named.
PICON, small charcoal burnt in braziers in Italy.
PICOTE, the name in Italy for a coarse stuff made of goats' hair, and for a glossy silk fabric.
PICOTINE, a name in some parts of the Continent for a peck, a measure used principally to serve out the quantity of oats, &c. for a horse's meal.
PICTURE, a painting; though the word is sometimes applied to a print or engraving. Large sums of money are laid out annually on the works of living artists, or ancient masters, and the public exhibitions of paintings do much good.
PICTURE-BOOK, an illustrated work for children.
PICTURE-CLEANER, a restorer of the brightness of colours, &c. in oil-paintings.
PICTURE-DEALER, a purchaser of pictures for re-sale.
PICTURE-FRAME, a setting, or frame for a picture, made of different materials, either wood, solid or veneered, leather, papier-mâché, gutta-percha, metal, &c.
PICTURE-FRAME MAKER, a workman who makes square frames for prints or for looking-glasses. Oval frames are either turned, or moulded of some composition.
PICTURE-GALLERY, a place for hanging or exhibiting pictures.
PICTURE-LINER, one who prepares and fixes the inner canvas of a picture.
PICTURE-RESTORER and CLEANER. *See* PICTURE-CLEANER.
PICTURE-ROD, a kind of brass tubing for affixing to the tops of walls in a room, to suspend pictures from.
PICUDELLA, a variety of olive.
PICUL: in Batavia it is 135 lbs. 10 oz.; in Japan, 133⅓ lbs; in Manila, 1¼ cwt. (140 lbs.) *See* PECUL.
PIE, a dish of baked meat or fruit, with a crust top.
PIE, a printer's term for a confused mass of letters or type, broken up by accident; a small nominal Indian money, the third part of the pice, 12 of which go to the anna, of 1½d.
PIECE, a picture; a play; a patch; a part or length of any thing, or the whole, of variable dimensions. A piece of muslin is 10 yards, of calico 28 yards, of Irish linen 25 yards, of Hanoverian linen 100 double ells, or 128 yards.
PIECE-BROKER, a person who buys shreds and remnants of woollen cloth from tailors, to sell again to others who want them for mending, or for other purposes.
PIECE-GOODS, the articles usually classed under this category are grey cotton, mulls, jaconets, shirtings, madapollams, printers' cambrics, long-cloths, sheetings, drills, &c.
PIECING, mending; making additions; joining two things together.
PIECE-WORK, task-work; work paid for by the job.
PIE-DISH, an oval, flat deep dish of crockery ware, for baking pies in.
PIEDOUCHE (French), a bracket-pedestal.
PIEGGIERIA (Italian), a surety; bail, or security.
PIEGO (Italian), a packet of letters.
PIEL, an iron wedge for boring stones.
PIELAGO, a kind of sailing-vessel.
PIE-MAN, one who makes and carries pies about the streets for sale.
PIENSO, a daily allowance of barley, &c., given to horses and mules in Spain.
PIER, a projecting quay, wharf, or landing-place; a strong marine erection running out into the sea from the shore, on a shallow coast, for the facility of passengers, shipping, &c.; a projection or column on which the arch of a bridge is raised.
PIERAGE, money paid by ships for the use of a pier or wharf; a toll demanded of passengers for walking or landing on certain piers.
PIERCED-WORK, perforated or filigree-work.
PIERCEL, PIERCER, a kind of awl or gimlet for giving vent to casks of liquor.
PIERCER, a lady's eyeletteer for fancy-work, made of ivory, bone, pearl, or a porcupine's quill.
PIER-GLASS, a large looking-glass between windows.
PIERRIER (French), a swivel-gun.
PIETRA DURA, a name for any hard stone, such as onyx, chalcedony, and arno pebbles, &c., used for cutting, and for representing flowers, animals, &c. on.
PIEZGO, a leather bottle or skin, used for carrying liquors.
PIG, a well-known domestic animal, whose valuable commercial products are noticed under Bacon, Pork, Lard, &c.; an earthen pitcher; a chimney-pot; a common name for a large mass of unforged metal; an ingot of iron or lead, weighing ⅞ to 1¼ cwt.
PIGEON, a common name for several varieties of birds, several of which enter largely into commerce, both for food, and as fancy-birds. The carrier pigeon, formerly so much prized, is now replaced by the electric wires on land and in the sea.
PIGEON-EXPRESS, the transmission of intelligence by a slip or note attached to a carrier pigeon, set loose to return to its home.
PIGEON-HOLE, a receptacle for letters, &c.

Pigeon-house, a dove-cot, or elevated shelter for pigeons to roost and breed in.

Pigeon-match, a competitive trial of skill among sportsmen, in shooting at pigeons let loose from a trap.

Pigeon-pie, a pastry made of pigeons.

Pigeon-trap, a trap in which pigeons are confined, in order to be shot at when liberated and on the wing.

Pigeon-wood, another name for zebra-wood, of which there are several kinds; one from Jamaica is the produce of *Guettarda speciosa*; others come from the Brazils.

Piggin, a small wooden or earthen vessel, without a handle.

Pigione (Italian), house-rent.

Pignons, **Pinones**, the edible seeds of the cones of various pines. Those of the *Pinus Pinea*, are consumed in Italy. In Chile, they are considered a great delicacy, both by the Indians and Spaniards. They are sometimes boiled, ground down on a stone into a kind of paste, and made into pastry. The cone of a magnificent Australian pine, containing as many as 150 edible seeds, furnishes at certain seasons, a rich harvest to the aborigines.

Pigment, a paint; any colour used by painters.

Pig-nuts, a North American name for a variety of the hickory-tree, *Carya glabra*. The nuts are smaller, and not quite so pleasant as those of the shell-bark variety of hickory. The hog-nut is the *Carya porcina*.

Pig's-face, **Pig's-cheek**. *See* Bath-chaps.

Pig's-fry, the entrails of a pig sold for food.

Pig's-head, the head of a pig, sold fresh or salted.

Pig-skin, the skin of the hog prepared as leather for saddles, binding, or other purposes.

Pig-stye, an enclosure, with a house for pigs to fatten in.

Pig-tail, a dark kind of tobacco twisted into a long rope or cord, which is afterwards wound into a hard close ball.

Pike, a long lance; an iron spring for fastening work to a turning-lathe; a fresh-water fish, the *Esox lucius*; the sea-pike is the gar-fish, *E. belone*; an abbreviation for a "toll-gate," or "turnpike-gate;" a measure of length used in Egypt, Syria, Servia, and the adjoining countries; about 26¾ inches; 1 9-24ths pike are, according to Dr. Bowring, 1 yard. *See* Pic.

Pike-head, the spear, or arrow-pointed part of a pike.

Pike-staff, the pole of a pike.

Pilaster, a square column set in a wall.

Pilch (Scotch), a gown made of silk; a petticoat open in front, worn by infants; an apron of protection for the thighs, worn by men digging peat; a child's flannel napkin.

Pilchard, a small fish resembling the herring, the *Clupea pilchardus*, which is caught in large numbers on the western coasts of England; the take of the Cornish fisheries being, on the average, 63,000,000 fish, or 21,000 hhds., of which the greater portion are shipped salted, to the Mediterranean ports.

Pile, a pale or pointed stake; a sharpened log of timber driven a considerable depth into the ground, in the bed of rivers, or in marshy land, to build upon; an erection or superstructure; the shag, nap, or surface of velvet, plush, broad-cloth, &c.; a galvanic battery.

Pile-driver, a workman occupied in sinking piles for the foundation of a superstructure; a machine used for the purpose.

Pile-driving Machine, **Pile-engine**, a heavy rammer, or mass of iron, raised by a leverage, and descending repeatedly with force by gravity, on the head of a pile or log of wood, to be driven into the earth. Nasmyth's steam hammer, applied to the pile-engine, raises the rammer again, by the action of steam.

Pilentum, a light vehicle; a combination of the cab and carriage.

Pilewort, a common field plant, the *Ranunculus Ficaria*, the leaves of which are sometimes used as a potherb.

Pill, a medicine rolled into a small globule.

Pillar, an upright column or support of wood, iron, stone, &c.

Pillar Dollar, a Spanish silver coin with two columns supporting the royal arms on the obverse, which is at a high premium for the Chinese market.

Pillau, a Turkish dish of rice with fowl or mutton, raisins, almonds, chillies and cardamoms, boiled or stewed together, and served up with sweet gravy and fried onions.

Pill-box Maker, a manufacturer of small round pasteboard, or thin wooden, boxes of different sizes, for chemists' and surgeons' use.

Pillez, a kind of naked barley.

Pillicciaio (Italian), a furrier.

Pillion, a soft saddle for a woman; a pad for a horse's back; tin in slags.

Pillmaking-machine. *See* Pill-tile.

Pillococia, a drug for pills.

Pillow, a bag filled with feathers to rest the head on in bed, &c.; a name for a kind of plain fustian. *See* Fustian.

Pillow-lace, lace worked by hand on a small cushion or pillow.

Pillow-slip, an outer covering or case of linen or calico for a feather pillow.

Pill-tile, a corrugated metal plate for rolling pills on, so as to divide them accurately.

Pilot, a qualified licensed mariner, employed to navigate ships through intricate channels into or out of a river, port or road-stead.

Pilotage, the authorized fees paid to a pilot for navigating a vessel.

Pilot-balloon, a small balloon sent up to try the wind.

Pilot-boat, a small strong-built cutter, belonging to a pilot, employed in beating about the coasts and approaches to ports, awaiting vessels requiring the services of a pilot.

Pilot-bread, a name in the West Indies for hard or ship biscuit. The whiter and finer kind of sea-biscuit is often called captains' biscuit.

PILOT-CLOTH, an indigo blue woollen cloth, used for great coats, and for the clothing of mariners and others.

PILOT-ENGINE, an engine sent before to clear the line or to attend on a railway train.

PILOTIN (French), the apprentice to a pilot; the wire of an organ pipe.

PILOT-JACK, a union or other flag hoisted by a vessel for a pilot.

PIMENT, spiced or honeyed wine.

PIMENTO, the dried berries of a West Indian tree, the *Eugenia Pimenta*, used as a spice in cookery, which have a flavour intermediate between pepper and cloves. The tree is exclusively cultivated in Jamaica, but of 36,061 cwts. imported thence in 1855, only 3,535 cwts. were entered for home consumption.

PIMENTO-OIL, an aromatic yellow oil obtained from the covering of the fruit of the *Eugenia Pimenta*.

PIMPLE, a name given to calcined copper in a certain state; also called sponge regulus.

PIMPLOES, a West Indian name for the prickly pear (*Opuntia Tuna* and *O. vulgaris*), which is much used as a hedge plant.

PIMIENTO, the Spanish name for capsicums.

PIN, a peg or bolt of wood or metal; a short piece of wire used by females for fastening articles of dress, &c. These are made of brass wire reduced by the usual process of wire drawing; the old "spun head," which was liable to get loose, is now giving way to those with solid heads; the axis on which the sheave of a block turns; a short piece of wood for belaying or fastening ropes to in a ship; a vulgar name for the half of a tub or anker of smuggled spirits.

PINA (Spanish), amalgamated silver; pine-apple leaf fibres.

PINA-CLOTH, an expensive fabric made by the natives of the Philippines from the fibres of the pine-apple leaf, *Ananassa sativa*; the texture is very delicate, soft, and transparent, and generally has a very slight tinge of pale yellow. It is made into shawls, scarfs, handkerchiefs, dresses, &c., and is most beautifully embroidered by the needle.

PINAFORE, a child's apron; an outer dress covering.

PINANG, a Malay name for the betel-nut palm (*Areca catechu*).

PINAZA, a kind of fine Indian fabric.

PIN-BOX, PIN-CASE, a small fancy box for holding pins.

PINCEL (Spanish), an instrument for tarring a vessel.

PINCELERO (Spanish), a pencil-maker.

PINCERS, small tongs, or nippers.

PINCHBECK, a brittle alloy consisting of 85 per cent. of copper and 15 per cent. of zinc. It is sometimes called tomback.

PINCO, a Neapolitan vessel.

PINCHINA (French), coarse woollen cloth.

PINCUSHION, a cushion for sticking pins in for a dressing-table, sometimes made of small size for a lady's pocket.

PINDALS, PINDARS, American and West Indian names for the ground-nut, *Arachis hypogaea*.

PINE, a well-known useful evergreen tree, furnishing the deals generally used for building purposes.

PINE-APPLE, a tropical fruit, the *Ananassa sativa* and *lucida*, of which large quantities are now imported in bulk from the Bahamas islands and the West coast of Africa. There are many distinct kinds now cultivated in hot-houses in this country, some of which are brought to high perfection, and being matured are far superior in flavour to those imported, which have to be picked green, or before they are fully ripe.

PINE-APPLE CHEESE, a kind of cheese shaped and formed in a mould like a pine-apple, which is principally manufactured for export.

PINE-APPLE FIBRE. *See* PINA-CLOTH.

PINE-BOARDS, PINE-PLANKS. *See* DEALS.

PINE-FISH, a name in the Shetlands for fish dried in the open air.

PINE-HOUSE, PINERY, a hot-house or stove for growing pines.

PINE-KERNELS, the seeds of the stone pine (*Pinus pinea*), which are commonly sold in foreign markets as an article of dessert. They taste somewhat like hazel nuts. *See* PIGNONS.

PINE-KNOTS, a name in the United States for the cones of pines, large quantities of which are brought down the Mississippi to New Orleans.

PINE NEEDLE-WOOL, PINE WOOD-WOOL, a fibrous vegetable substance obtained in Prussia by treating the buds and leaves of coniferous trees with a strong solution of carbonate of soda. The fibre is used there for upholstery purposes, such as stuffing for mattresses, intended as a protection against insects, and for wadding; blankets are made with it; and oil and soap are also obtained from it.

PINEY, an Indian resin or dammer obtained from the dhoop tree (*Vateria Indica*).

PINGLE-PAN, in Scotland, a small tin goblet with a long handle for preparing children's food.

PINGO, an elastic stick loaded at both ends poised on the shoulder, used in Ceylon for carrying burthens.

PINGUIN, PEN-GWYN, a fence plant used in the West Indies for hedge-rows, the *Bromelia Pinguin* and *B. Karatas*.

PIN-HEAD, the wire added to the top of a pin.

PINION, a pivot; a small toothed wheel, connected with, and receiving motion from a larger one; the quills from the joint farthest from the body of the wing of the goose or swan, used for making pens.

PINK, a painter's colour, a yellowish or pale red, or light crimson, of which the chief varieties are rose-pink, Dutch, and English-pink; a garden-flower; a vessel with a round stern and bulging sides, capable of carrying a large cargo; to slash cloth; to work in eyelet holes.

PINKER, one who stabs or cuts out flounces and borders, &c. with a machine, for ladies' dresses.

PINKIE, a name in Scotland for the weakest kind of table-beer.

PINKING-IRON, a cutting instrument for scolloping the edges of ribbons, flounces, paper for coffin trimmings, &c.

PINK-ROOT, a name for the worm-grass (*Spigelia marilandica*), a poisonous narcotic and purgative, and a very powerful vermifuge; the fresh leaves and stems of *Spigelia anthelmia*, and *S. marilandica*, are used as an anthelmintic.

PINK-SAUCER, a little saucer, containing safflower prepared with a small portion of soda, and used for giving a flesh tint to silk stockings, &c.

PINK-STERN, a ship with a high, narrow stern.

PIN-MAKER, a manufacturer of pins.

PINNACE, a ship's barge, intermediate in size between a launch and a cutter, and never rowing more than eight oars.

PINNACLE, a small turret or spire on the angle of a building.

PINNACOTTAY-OIL, a name in some parts of India for an oil obtained from the seeds of *Calophyllum inophyllum*. In other districts it is called Domba-oil.

PINOCCHIO (Italian), the edible seeds from pine-cones; the kernel of the pine apple.

PINOLA, PINULA (Italian), a spindle; the detent of a repeating watch.

PINOLE, an aromatic powder used in Italy for making chocolate.

PINONATA, a conserve or paste made of the kernels of pine cones.

PINSTICKER, a person who fixes pins in paper; a machine which performs the same operation.

PINT, a British liquid measure; ⅛ of an imperial quart, and ⅛ of a gallon; a pint of distilled water weighs 1¼ pound avoirdupois; a Scots pint contains three English pints, and is 103·404 cubic inches.

PINTLE, a metal bolt on which the rudder of a ship is hung.

PINT-STOUP, a tin-measure in Scotland containing very nearly three English pints.

PIOCHE (French), a pickaxe or mattock.

PIONEER, a settler or colonist who penetrates into the wilderness; a backwoodsman; a working soldier provided with hatchet, &c., who precedes and clears the way of obstructions, for an army, repairs the roads, and works at intrenchments, &c.

PIPE, a leather or canvas hose; a long tube or cylinder of metal, earthenware, or glass for conducting water, gas, steam, &c. When large, water and gas pipes are called mains, and the smaller ones, supply pipes and services; a tube for smoking; a boatswain's whistle; a cask for liquids of variable dimensions, but considered ordinarily to hold 105 gallons. In different countries and localities it varies considerably, ranging from 48 up to 160 gallons.

PIPE-CASE, a smoker's pocket-case for holding a short meerschaum or clay tobacco-pipe.

PIPE-CLAY, an adhesive and plastic unctuous earth, containing about 30 per cent. of alumina with [illegible] silica, which is used for moulding clay tobacco-pipes, for smokers, for making various kinds of earthenware, and as a detergent for scouring cloth. From Kingsteignton, in Devonshire, nearly 20,000 tons are obtained yearly.

PIPE-LAYER, a workman who lays gas mains, water, or draining-pipes.

PIPE-MANUFACTURER, a maker of metal tubes, clay, or glass cylinders, or of tobacco smoking-pipes.

PIPER, one who plays on the bag-pipes.

PIPE-STAVES. *See* STAVES.

PI-PI, the legumes of *Cæsalpinia Pipai* used as a tanning material, but inferior to Divi-divi.

PIPIAN, an Indian fricassee.

PIPING, a kind of cord trimming or fluting for ladies' dresses.

PIPING-IRONS, fluting-irons.

PIPING BULLFINCH, a bullfinch that whistles tunes.

PIPKIN, a small earthen saucepan.

PIPOTE (Italian), a keg; a small barrel.

PIPPIN, a name for some varieties of small choice apples.

PIPSISSEWA, a wild plant of North America, the *Chimaphila umbellata*, which being diuretic, acrid, and narcotic, is used in medicine.

PIQUEE (French), marcella; a cotton stuff used for waistcoats.

PIQUETTE, sour acid wine; a drink made in France by pouring water on the husks of grapes.

PIRAMETER, the name given to an instrument for ascertaining the power required to draw carriages over roads.

PIRATE, a sea-robber; a vessel which attacks others at sea for the sake of plunder.

PIRATING, counterfeiting; copying any thing without permission; stealing the copyright of a work.

PIRL, to twist or twine, as in forming horse-hair into a fishing-line.

PIRN (Scotch), a quill or reed; yarn wound on a shuttle; the bobbin of a spinning-wheel; the wheel on a fishing-rod.

PIRNIE, a woollen nightcap made in Kilmarnock, of different colours or stripes.

PIROGUE, a rough canoe formed out of the trunk of a tree.

PISANG, one of the Malay names for the plantain. *See* PINANG.

PISE, blocks of clay rammed into moulds; rammed earth, used in some countries to build the walls of cottages.

PISMIRE, a name in the Orkneys for the steel-yard.

PISTACHIO-NUTS, the small almonds or nuts in the drupe of the *Pistacia vera*, and its varieties, natives of Syria, which are imported in small quantities from Messina, Sicily, and other ports in the Mediterranean, either shelled or unshelled. The kernels are small, pale green, with a flavour like sweet almonds. They are used as a dessert fruit, in confectionery, and also to make a sort of cosmetic-powder for the face. In [illegible], we imported [illegible] cwts. of these nuts.

PISTAREEN, a Spanish silver coin, worth about 8d. or 9d. The "head" pistareen is worth about 1d. more. There are also quarter and half pistareen silver pieces. The double pistareen is current for about 1s. 6d.

Pistera, in Italy, a round jug with a spout.

Pistol, a well-known hand weapon; the smallest fire-arm used.

Pistol-case, a box for keeping one or more pistols in.

Pistole, a gold coin of the European States, varying in different countries, and in different coinages. The Spanish pistole is the fourth of the doubloon. The coinage of 1813 to 1822, weighed 4 dwts. 8 grs., of which 3 dwts. 18·6 grs. were pure gold. The previous coins of 1745, 1774, and 1782, contained 2 to 3 grains more pure gold. The doppia, or pistole of Milan, coined in 1783, weighs 4 dwts. 1·5 grs., of which 3 dwts. 16½ grs. are pure gold. The later pistoles of Switzerland, weigh 4 dwts. 20 grs., of which 4 dwts. 8 grs. are pure gold. On the average, the pistole may be valued at 16s.

Pistol-routers, the name for a kind of carpenter's plane.

Piston, the sucker, or part of a pump which fits the bore; the short cylinder or disk of a steam-engine, acted upon by the air or steam, and causing suction.

Piston-rod, the rod by which a piston is forced down and drawn up.

Pit, a well, or deep hole; the sunken shaft of a mine; the floor, or chief audience part of a play-house; a place for sawing wood.

Pita, a name for aloe-fibre, obtained from the leaves of the *Agave Americana*, which is made into a strong and white cordage, and also manufactured into paper in Mexico.

Pitch, the resin of pine extracted by fire and inspissation; or the residuum of boiled tar, made in England, and of which about a thousand tons a year are imported from Russia; in mining, the limit of ground set to those who work on tribute; an inclination, or elevation; the sloping side of a roof; the rising or falling of a vessel in a heavy sea; to set in array, as to pitch a tent; to pave with stones.

Pitch and Tar, Manufacturer, a maker of those commodities, largely used for smearing or covering ships' bottoms, palings, &c.

Pitch-back Wheel, a kind of wheel used in a mill, propelled by water.

Pitch-blende, a valuable ore for the porcelain painter, producing a fine orange colour, and also a black, found in Saxony, Bohemia, and Cornwall.

Pitcher, an earthen water-jug.

Pitch-fork, a prong with which hay, &c. is lifted from a cart to the rick.

Pitching, a market term for unloading, and for the small charge paid to the carrier for looking after the empty packages and cloths, and returning them correctly; fixing a tent or booth; covering a ship's bottom, a roof, or palings with pitch or tar.

Pitching-stables, a kind of shaped Cornish granite, 4 or 6 inches long, for paving.

Pitch-ladle, an iron ladle for lifting out pitch from a boiler.

Pitch-pipe Manufacturer, a maker of pipes used for giving the key-notes for music.

Pitch-plaster, a plaster of Burgundy pitch.

Pitch-stone, a vitreous lava which occurs in veins and beds, and sometimes in whole mountains.

Pitch-wheels, toothed wheels in machinery or clocks, which work together.

Pitch-work, work done in a coal-mine, by those working on tribute.

Pit-coal, the common bituminous coal used throughout the country. *See* Coal.

Pith, the cellular or spongy substance of plant stalks, used for various purposes, for making light models, &c. The pith of the elder is used for electrical purposes; that of the sago palm is converted into starch. *See* Shola.

Pit-man, a collier; one who looks after the mine-gear; the sawyer who stands in the pit.

Piton (French), a screw-ring; a staple.

Pit-pan, a long flat-bottomed river-boat used in Central America. It is deep and wide in the middle, but shallow at the ends, which are square. It not unfrequently contains 60 paddlers.

Pit-saw. *See* Saw.

Pit-saw File. *See* File.

Pittore (Italian), a painter or limner.

Piuma, the name given to a new and mixed fabric of light texture, used for gentlemen's coats.

Pivot-gun, a piece of ordnance turning freely on a pivot, to alter the direction.

Pix, the name given to a box kept at the British Mint, in which a small sample of the coins struck are deposited, in order to be assayed and compared with a standard preserved in the Exchequer. This operation, called "the trial of the pix," is performed in the presence of certain members of the Privy Council, the officers of the Mint, and a jury of the Goldsmiths' Company, and now usually takes place on the appointment of a new Master of the Mint, before his predecessor receives a discharge.

Pizza (Italian), a sort of cake.

Pizzicagnolo (Italian), a cheese-monger; a pork-shop.

Placage (French), veneering; inlaying.

Placard, a written or printed notice stuck up; to advertise by posted bills.

Placard-bearer, a man walking about the streets or thoroughfares, carrying notices on boards.

Place, a public or private employment; a public square in a city; a name in Scotland for the mansion-house on an estate; to arrange or dispose.

Place-brick, a builder's term for an inferior kind of brick, which, from being on the outside of a clamp or kiln, is only imperfectly burnt.

Placer, a gold field; a position or locality in an auriferous country.

Plack, a small copper coin, formerly current in Scotland, equal to the third part of an English penny.

Plaice, a flat fish, the *Pleuronectes platessa*, which, when of a moderate size, is good eating, but inferior to the turbot and sole.

Plaid, an outer loose tartan wrapper, worn by the Highlanders. *See* Maud, Tartan, and Tweeds.

PLAIN, simple, without ornament or beauty.

PLAINBACKS, a term in the weaving trade for bombazettes.

PLAIN-CHART, a chart laid down on Mercator's projection.

PLAINT, a written statement of a suit in a Court of Requests, County Court, &c.

PLAINTIFF, a suitor; one who commences a law-suit.

PLAIT, PLAT, PLEAT, a fold or double in cloth, linen, &c

PLAN, a scheme; an outline drawing or design; a ground-plan of a building; a horizontal section.

PLANCHET, in coining, a piece of metal intended for a coin, with a smooth flat surface, to be placed in the mill for receiving the die impression.

PLANCHETTE, a small plank or board; a circumferentor.

PLANE, a carpenter's cutting and surface-smoothing tool, of which there are great varieties, named after the purposes they are intended to fulfil; as smooth-plane; beading-plane; jack-plane; trying-plane; long-plane; jointer-plane; moulding-plane; panel-plane; rounding-plane; toothing-plane; fork-staff-plane; ovolo; lamb's-tongue, astragal and hollow-sash-planes; bead-plane; match-plane; grooving-plane; hand-rail-plane; table-plane; single and three reed-planes; side-fillisters; sash-fillister; dovetail-box; side-round; side-rabbit; side-snipe; square-rabbit; skew-rabbit; and numerous others.

PLANE-IRONS, cutting irons to insert in a plane, and which are either double or single.

PLANE-MAKER, a manufacturer of the wood cases for workmen's planes.

PLANER, in printing, a flat, square-made piece of wood, used by the compositor for forcing down the type in the form, and making the surface perfectly even.

PLANE-TABLE, a surveyor's instrument for taking angles.

PLANETARIUM, a machine for showing the motions of the planets.

PLANE-TREE, the sycamore, *Platanus occidentalis*, a large North American tree, the wood of which is used for musical instruments, and other works requiring a clean light-coloured wood.

PLANIMETER, an instrument for calculating the area of plane figures.

PLANING-MACHINE, PLANING-MILL, a facing-machine for smoothing boards, &c., and economizing time and labour; an application of the slide-rest to a traversing-table.

PLANISH, to smooth wood; to polish metals.

PLANISHER, a tool used by turners for smoothing brass work; a workman who smooths or planes.

PLANK, a liquid measure used in Lubeck, Rostock, &c., also called a noessel, about ⅞ of a pint; a long flat piece of timber. *See* BOARD, DEAL, and LOAD.

PLANK-ROAD, a road formed upon planks laid transversely, much used in America.

PLANK-SAWER, a sawyer.

PLANT, railway engines and machinery; utensils; the machinery, apparatus, or fixtures by which a business or manufacture is carried on, as a builder's plant; the plant of a brewery, &c.; to set in the ground; to cultivate.

PLANTADO-PASADO, the sun-dried fruit of the plantain, which forms a considerable article of internal commerce in some of the districts of Mexico.

PLANTAIN, a succulent shrub or tree, the *Musa Paradisiaca*, largely cultivated in the tropics for its fruit, eaten boiled or roasted, or prepared into dough and meal; bags are made of the leaves, and the stalk furnishes a large quantity of useful fibre for paper making or for cordage. Another species, *M. textilis*, furnishes a valuable fibre for rope. *See* MANILA-HEMP.

PLANTATION, a woodland of young trees, an estate for growing coffee, sugar, indigo or spices in the tropics; formerly the term was applied to our foreign possessions, now generally known as colonies.

PLANT-CANE, a first crop of sugar-canes raised from cuttings, not a ratoon or second-shoot crop; the former yielding more juice and sugar.

PLANTER, the manager or overseer of a sugar estate; the superintendant of a coffee plantation or an indigo estate.

PLAQUETTE, a small French coin; a farthing.

PLAQUEUR (French), one who veneers or lays on plates.

PLASHING, binding and interweaving branches of trees for low fences, &c.

PLASM, a mould or matrix.

PLASMA, a transparent chalcedony of a grass-green or leek-green colour, found in India and China.

PLASTER, a common name in America and other quarters for gypsum, used as a manure; a composition of lime and hair; a substance for casting ornaments and figures; an ointment or salve spread on skin or paper.

PLASTERER, a workman who covers the walls, ceilings, &c. of a house or other edifice with plaster.

PLASTERERS'-COMPANY, one of the minor livery companies of London, which has no hall.

PLASTERERS'-HAIR MANUFACTURER, a collector and preparer of cow hair, and other waste hair, for mixing in mortar.

PLASTER-FACTORY, works where gypsum is ground and prepared, or where cements are made.

PLASTER-IMAGE MAKER, one who makes figures, medallions, and other casts in plaster of Paris.

PLASTER-OF-PARIS, a common name for sulphate of lime or gypsum, from its occurrence in the Paris formation.

PLASTERS, external medical applications, the base of which is generally metallic or alkaline soaps.

PLATA, the Spanish name for silver, applied to both ore and money.

PLATA-PINA, amalgamated silver.

PLATE, a common name for articles made of the precious metals for table use; a horizontal timber placed on a wall to receive other pieces; a small round flat food platter; a flat piece of metal, such as a copper-plate, door or name plate, boiler-plate, &c.

Plateau, a large ornamental centre dish for a table: a tea tray or salver.

Plate-basket, a basket lined with tin for removing plates which have been used from a dinner table: a small basket lined with baize for holding knives, forks, and spoons.

Plate-bending-machine, a rolling machine for bending plates of metal to any required curve, for making iron boiler plates, water-wheel buckets, &c.

Plate-carrier, a servants' tray for bringing plates to table; a moving apparatus in the wall, with a series of shelves rising and falling, to take up and bring down plates, &c. in an eating-house or hotel from and to the kitchen.

Plate-case-maker, **Plate-chest-maker**, a manufacturer of boxes of various kinds and sizes, to hold dessert knives and forks, spoons, and other articles of plate.

Plate-cover, a small metal cover for keeping toast, meals, &c. warm on a plate.

Plate-cutting-machine, a machine for cutting metal into plates.

Plated-ware, electrotyped articles; articles silvered over, or gilt.

Plate-glass, sheets of a superior kind of thick glass, used for silvering for mirrors, and also for large panes in drawing-room windows, shop-fronts, &c. It contains about 76 per cent. of silica. A superficial foot, one-tenth of an inch in thickness, is considered to weigh 1 lb.

Plate-glass-manufacturer, a manufacturer and polisher of thick sheet glass.

Platel, a small dish.

Plate-layer, a workman who lays down the iron rails, and fixes them to the sleepers of a railway.

Plate-leather, a kind of wash leather; chamois leather used for rubbing and cleaning silver or plated articles.

Plate-marks, special marks or emblematic representations stamped on gold or silver plate: thus, for London the local mark is a lion; Birmingham, an anchor; Sheffield, a crown and lion; Newcastle, three castles; Exeter, king's head, lion and castle; Edinburgh, castle, thistle and king's head; Glasgow, a tree, with a bell and salmon; Ireland, a harp and the figure of Britannia. There are also certain letters to distinguish the date of manufacture, for the convenience of the custom-house officers in assessing the duty.

Plate-polisher, a brush for cleaning plate; a workman who smooths copper or steel plates for engraving, &c., or polishes plate-glass.

Plate-powder, a rouge or polishing powder for brightening plate.

Plater, an electrotyper; one who coats metal articles with silver or gold.

Plate-rack, a wooden frame fixed in a scullery to stand plates and dishes in to drain after they are washed.

Plates and *Dishes*, articles of crockery ware for table use, usually sold in sets; sometimes in a complete or full dinner service of so many pieces.

Plate-warmer, a japanned metal or linned case with shelves, for standing plates in before a fire to warm.

Platform, a landing stage; an elevation of earth, wood, or stone; a hustings; the raised part of a railway station.

Platillas, the name of a white linen fabric made in Silesia for export to America.

Platina, twisted silver wire; an iron-plate for glazing stuff.

Platinum, a valuable white metal like silver, very ductile and of great tenacity. In Russia it is used for coinage, in England it is employed for making large vessels in the sulphuric acid manufacture, and gold pens are also tipped with it.

Plat-menage (German), a cruet-stand; a set of castors for the table.

Platrage (French), plaster-work.

Platrier, a French plasterer.

Platter, a large wooden plate or dish; in Germany one who irons linen.

Plattin, **Platen**, the flat superincumbent part of a printing-press, which, when brought down on the types, gives the impression.

Plaustro (Spanish), a cart or wagon.

Play, a drama; a story told by actors.

Play-actor, one who performs a part in a drama or play.

Play-bill, a printed guide to the amusements of the evening in a play-house.

Play-book, a book containing the words of a play, as acted.

Play-house, a theatre; a building for dramatic representations.

Playing-card-makers' Company, one of the minor livery companies of London, which has no hall.

Playing-cards, pieces of cardboard made in 4 suits of 13 each, with painted figures and devices on them, for playing games with.

Play-wright, a dramatist; an adapter of plays.

Plea, an allegation; a legal act or form of pleading.

Pleader, one who draws pleas in technical form; an advocate; one who argues in a court of justice.

Pleasure-boat, a small boat for use on a river or lake.

Pleasure-ground, a small park or shrubbery contiguous to a dwelling-house; an ornamental garden.

Pleasure-train, a railway excursion-train.

Pleat, to crimp linen or lace in narrow folds.

Pledge, an article put in pawn.

Pleita (Spanish), a plaited strand of bass.

Plenshing-nail, a large nail for fastening planks or floor boards to the joists.

Pleurisy-root, a name in North America for the *Asclepias tuberosa*, which is expectorant, diaphoretic, and a mild tonic and stimulant.

Plett, a kind of ship.

Pliant, a French folding seat or chair.

Pliers, **Plyers**, small nippers or pincers to hold wire, &c. to bend it; of which there are several kinds made, for the use of bell-hangers, saddlers, and others; there are also fishing pliers, bottling pliers, &c.

Plisson (French), a kind of custard pudding.

PLOC, a mixture of hair and tar for covering a ship's bottom.

PLOCAGE (French), the operation of carding wool.

PLOMBAGE, lead work.

PLOMBAGINE, plumbago, black-lead.

PLOMBARIO (Italian), lead and silver ore.

PLOMB-BRUT, rough lead.

PLOMBE (French), a kind of varnish; goods sealed by the douaniers or Custom-house officers.

PLOMBEE (French), red lead.

PLOMBIER, a plumber and glazier in France.

PLONKET, a coarse woollen fabric.

PLOQUE (French), a bundle of carded wool.

PLOT, a small piece of land; the story of a play; to lay out ground.

PLOTTE, a Swedish silver coin worth about 1s. 6d. There are double, half, and quarter plottes.

PLOTTIE, in Scotland, mulled wine flavoured with ice.

PLOTTING-SCALE, a mathematical instrument used in plotting ground, which is a foot or a foot and a half long, and an inch and a half broad.

PLOUGH, an agricultural implement for turning up the soil, of which there are several kinds, adapted either for light or heavy land, as swing, wheel, or turn-wrist ploughs, and draining or subsoil ploughs, &c. Also a plane; a bookbinder's knife or press for cutting paper.

PLOUGH-GATE, PLOUGH-GANG, an extent of land equal on an average to about 40 Scotch acres. *See* OX-GANG.

PLOUGHMAN, a labourer who holds the handles and guides the plough.

PLOUGH-SHARE, the cutting part of the plough; the plate which turns over the soil.

PLOUGH-WRIGHT, a workman who repairs ploughs.

PLOUT-NET, POUT-NET, a small river fishing-net shaped like a stocking, attached to two poles.

PLUCK, a two-pronged dung-fork used in Scotland with the teeth placed at right angles to the shaft; the heart, liver, and lights, &c. of an animal, as of a sheep, calf, &c. used for food; to strip the feathers from poultry.

PLUCKER, a machine used in a worsted factory, consisting of a pair of spiked rollers fed by an endless apron, for cleansing and straightening the fibres of wool.

PLUG, a peg of wood; a metal bung; a water-tap or any substance that serves to stop a hole or breach; a stopple for the hole in the bottom of a boat, by which water may be let out.

PLUG-ROD, an air-pump rod.

PLUM, a well-known fruit, the produce of the *Prunus domesticus* and its varieties, which is eaten when ripe, or made into pies, &c. *See* PRUNES.

PLUMAIL, PLUMEAU (French), a feather dusting broom.

PLUMASSIER, a feather dresser, seller, &c.

PLUMBAGO, a carburet of iron commonly known as black lead, and also called graphite, used for making crucibles and leads for pencils; we import large quantities from Ceylon. A genus of plants with acrid, caustic properties. *See* LEAD-WORT.

PLUMBER, one who works in lead.

PLUMBERS' COMPANY, one of the livery companies of London, whose hall is in Great Bush-lane.

PLUMBIC-ACID, the binoxide or brown oxide of lead.

PLUMB-LINE, a line with a plummet attached to ascertain whether any work is perpendicular.

PLUMB-RULE, a narrow board with a plumb-line.

PLUME, an ornament or bunch of feathers for the head, or for decorating a hearse or the coffin-lid borne by mutes.

PLUME-MAKER, a feather-dresser; a manufacturer of funeral plumes. *See* FUNERAL PLUME.

PLUMET, a French coal porter; a feather worn for ornament.

PLUMETA, a sort of Spanish woollen cloth.

PLUMMER'S-PILL, a well-known alterative medicine; a preparation of mercury.

PLUMMET, a pencil of solid lead, a lump of lead for sounding, or for the line of a plumb rule.

PLUMPER, a vote given at an election for one candidate only, by a voter who has the right to split his vote, or to give one for each of the number of candidates required to be returned.

PLUM-PIE, PLUM-TART, pastries with plums in.

PLUM-PUDDING, a solid mixed pudding containing dried raisins and currants, with suet and flour.

PLUM-TREE, a species of *Prunus*, the wood of which is used principally in turning.

PLUNDERSACK (German), a knapsack.

PLUNDER-WAGON, a lumber or baggage wagon in Germany.

PLUNGER, the piston of a forcing-pump.

PLUNGING-BATH, a public bath, where a person can dive and swim.

PLUNKET, a blue colour.

PLUSH, a shaggy cloth or velvet; a fabric of silk and cotton for upholstery, for making or trimming bonnets, cloaks, &c.

PLUSH-HAT, a hat made of silk plush, dyed drab, black, &c.

PLUSH-MANUFACTURER, a maker of silk or cotton velvet plush.

PLUTEO (Spanish), the compartments of book-shelves in a library.

PLUVIOMETER, an instrument to measure the quantity of rain that falls. *See* RAIN-GAUGE.

PLY, a fold, twist, or plait; to work between two points.

PLYERS, a kind of nippers; the balance for a drawbridge. *See* PLIERS.

P. M., abbreviation for "postmaster." Also "post meridiem," or the afternoon; "past mid-day."

P. O. "post-office."

POACH, to steal game; to soften or boil by cooking; to stab or spear.

POAK, waste from the preparation of skins.

POCAN-BUSH, a name in the United States for the *Phytolacca decandra*. The young, tender, blanched shoots are boiled as a pot-herb, the pulp of the black berries is used to adulterate wine, and the root is an emetic, approaching nearly to Ipecacuanha.

POCOSON, one of the American names for *Sanguinaria Canadensis*. See BLOODROOT.
POCKET, a pouch or small bag in a garment; a mass of rich ore; a large bag for holding ginger, cowry shells, hops, &c. In the wool and hop trade, a pocket contains half a sack, or 12 stone, of 14 lbs. each; but it is a variable quantity, the articles being sold by their actual weight. See HOP-BAG.
POCKET-BOOK, a small portable diary or memorandum-book with a tuck or strap.
POCKET-BOOK MAKER, a manufacturer of the leather cases, &c., for binding pocket-books.
POCKET-COMB, a small folding hair-comb for the pocket.
POCKET-COMPASS, a small portable compass for pedestrians and travellers.
POCKET-EDITION, POCKET-VOLUME, a small size book.
POCKET-GLASS, a small compact telescope to be carried in the pocket; a magnifying-glass; a small dram-glass in a case.
POCKET-HANDKERCHIEF, a handkerchief of silk or cotton, carried in the pocket for use. Some of the dress pocket-handkerchiefs for ladies, of thin muslin or cambric, are highly embroidered and ornamented, and more for show than use.
POCKET-INK, a wooden screw-box holding an ink-stand, for carrying in the pocket.
POCKET-KNIFE, a useful knife with several blades, for general use, or one for making pens carried in the pocket.
POCKET-LEDGER, a small private abstract ledger, with a lock or clasp, kept by bankers, merchants, and others, for their own reference.
POCKET-PISTOL, a small revolver or single-barrelled pistol, carried in the pocket for self-defence; a spirit-flask or dram-bottle.
POD, the capsule or seed-case of legumes.
PODDISOY, a rich plain silk.
PODDOCK (Scotch), a rough wooden sledge for carrying stones on.
PODERE (Italian), a manor; an estate or farm.
PODESTA, an Italian magistrate.
POEGEL. See POGLE.
POET LAUREATE, a pensioned officer who has been elected by the Government or State to the post of honour of national poet.
POGLE, PAEGEL, a Danish liquid measure, the fourth part of the pott, also called an ort, = 0·425 pint.
POHEGAN, a name in the North American fisheries for a kind of paste-bait for mackerel, &c., made of damaged and frequently putrid fish, chopped or ground in a cutting-mill. See BAIT-MILL.
POIDS (French), weight.
POIDS-DE-MARC, a Continental name for avoirdupois or gross weight; the former legal weight of France: it contained 7080 grains, while the British avoirdupois pound is but 7000 grains.
POIDS ROMAIN, troy weight.
POIGNÉE (French), a handful; the sixth of the kante of flax.
POINT, the sharp end of a tool or instrument; a degree of the horizon or mariner's compass; a railway switch; to insert lime with a small trowel between the stones of a wall already built; to aim a gun; to twist and bind the end of a rope, and protect it from ravelling.
POINTER, the index hand of a watch or clock; a setter, a kind of sporting dog; a graving-tool.
POINT-LACE, fine lace wrought with the needle.
POINTSMAN, a railway officer whose duty it is to shift the switches or moveable guiding rails on the approach or departure of trains, near junction lines and stations.
POIRE (French), a pear; perry, the drink made from pears; a powder-horn or flask.
POIRÉE, the white beet grown in France.
POIS (French), pease.
POISONS, many vegetable and mineral substances dangerous to life, some of which, however, in the hands of skilled practitioners are used as powerful remedies in disease.
POISSON (French), a fish; the fourth part of a chopin, and the eighth part of the old Paris pint, or setier. The ancient pint of Paris was the ½ of the velte, or setier, and = 1·6398 pint English: 8 poissons made the French pint; the poisson was = 1·161 decilitre, = 0·205 English pint.
POITRON (French), a kind of yellow plum.
POIVRADE, a pepper and vinegar sauce.
POIVRE (French), pepper.
POIX (French), pitch.
POJACK. See PAJOCK.
POKE, a bag. See POCKET.
POKE-BOY, POKE-PULLER, persons engaged in bagging hops.
POKEL-FLEISCH (German), pickled or salted meat.
POKER, a long iron bar used in mast-making to drive on the hoop; a polished metal bar for stirring the fire in a grate.
POKE-WEED, the American name for the *Phytolacca decandra*. See POCAN BUSH.
POLACCA, POLACRE, a lateen-rigged vessel, common to the Mediterranean.
POLAR-BEAR, the white bear, *Thalassarctos maritimus*, the skin of which is of the greatest value to the Arctic tribes, and of it trousers, boots, gloves, &c. are made. In this country it is sometimes used for wrappers, and carriage or other rugs.
POLAR-HARE, the *Lepus glacialis*, the fur of which is used for making boas, muffs, linings, &c.
POLARISCOPE, an instrument for showing the polarization of light.
POLBA, a Russian name for spelt-wheat.
POLDAVY, a coarse kind of canvas.
POLDER, a name given in Holland to a marshy plot of land, often enclosed and drained. There are kleipolders (clay or marl), dollerdpolders (hollows or dells), and wadpolders.
POLE, a prop; the tall stock of a tree planted in the ground; a land-measure. See PERCH.
POLE-AXE, a boarding axe used on shipboard.
POLEMIT, a sort of French camlet.
POLEMOSCOPE (French), a spy-glass; an oblique perspective glass.
POLE-NET, a net attached to a pole for illegal fishing in rivers; a shrimping net.

POLENTA, a thick porridge made in France of chestnut meal boiled with milk. In Italy it is a sort of pudding made of Indian-corn meal.

POLICE-CONSTABLE, an ordinary policeman: one charged to see the peace kept, and whose duty it is to perambulate on a certain beat for a fixed period.

POLICE-INSPECTOR, a superintendant of police.

POLICE-MAGISTRATE, a stipendiary law-officer who presides at a police-court, and tries and sentences offenders brought before him, upon charges preferred by the police.

POLICEMAN, POLICE-OFFICER. *See* POLICE-CONSTABLE.

POLICE-SERGEANT, a superior police-officer.

POLICE-STATION, the receiving house where offenders are taken by the police; the place where the police assemble for orders, and to march out on duty.

POLICY, the certificate issued to an insurer by a life, fire, or marine insurance office: a gentleman's pleasure ground.

POLICY-BOOK, a book kept at an insurance-office for making entries of policies granted.

POLICY-HOLDERS, the persons insured in an office.

POLIGAR, the head of a village district in India.

POLIMITA, a stuff of variegated colours.

POLISHING, the art of giving brightness to any substance, as wood, metal, glass, &c.

POLISHING-BRUSH, a hand brush for shining stoves or grates with black lead. *See* PLATE-BRUSH.

POLISHING-IRON, a smoothing iron.

POLISHING-PASTE, a kind of blacking or paste for harness and leather; a substance compounded of oil, beeswax, and spirit varnish, for giving a polish to articles of household furniture.

POLISHING-SLATES, a name for hone-slates or whet-stones.

POLISHING-SNAKE, a tool used by lithographers.

POLISHING-[illegible], a bookbinder's tool.

POLISH-POWDER, a preparation of plumbago for stoves and iron articles; rouge or other substances for brightening articles of plate. *See* PLATE-POWDER.

POLKA-JACKET, a hand-knitted worsted jacket.

POLL, the name in Germany for a sort of coarse meal; a list of persons voting at an election.

POLLACK, an ocean fish, the *Gadus pollachius*, found on both sides of the Atlantic; on the British coasts it is often known as the coal fish, and the whiting pollack. In North America it is so plentiful that it is salted and sold by the quintal.

POLLAM, an Eastern weight, used at Aden and in India, about 527 troy grains.

POLLAME (Italian), poultry.

POLLARD, a coarse product of wheat from the mill, but finer than bran; in many counties it has particular local names; also a lopped or polled tree.

POLL-BOOK, a register of voters exercising their franchise.

POLL-CLERK, a clerk who enters the names of voters at elections as they appear and vote.

POLLED-CATTLE, a mixed breed of Scotch cattle, including the polled Angus or Aberdeen, and the polled Galloway.

POLLEGADA, a Portuguese name for the inch.

POLLEN, a fresh-water herring.

POLLERIA, a poultry market or shop in Italy.

POLLICE, a Maltese linear measure.

POLLINARO (Italian), a poulterer.

POLLING, a process by which copper is changed from a highly crystalline mass into a metal which may be beaten into thin leaves.

POLONICK, a dry measure of Trieste, = 0.6836 gallons.

POLONY, a dried sausage.

POLPOLTIN, a Russian coin of two denominations, one equal to 25 copecks, worth about 10d., the other of 5 grives or 50 copecks.

POLST, a term in the leather trade in Electoral Hesse for the half of a dicker or five pieces.

POLSTER, the German name for a soft cushion or pad; a bolster. [1s. 7d.

POLTIN, a Russian silver coin worth about

POLTUROCK, a petty Hungarian coin of 1½ kreutzer, less than a halfpenny in value.

POLTUZAC, a small Polish coin, about the same value as the polturock.

POLUSCA, a very minute Russian coin, the half of a moscosque or denusca, and worth about the twelfth part of a penny.

POLVERINE, glass-makers' ashes.

POLYCHORD, having many strings; an apparatus which couples two octave notes, and can be affixed to any piano-forte or similar instrument with keys.

POLYGLOT, a Bible in several languages.

POLYGRAPH, a copying machine.

POLYSCOPE, a multiplying glass or lens.

POMACE, a builder's name for pumice-stone; the refuse of apples after they have been pressed for cider.

POMADE, a scented ointment for the hair; pomatum.

POMADE-POT, a porcelain or other ornamental jar for holding pomatum for the toilet-table.

POMATUM-BOTTLE, a bottle for holding pomatum, often enclosed in polished box-wood cases.

POMEGRANATE, the fruit of the *Punica Granatum*, the juice of which is acidulous and sweet, and makes a pleasant sherbet for fever patients. The tree is common now in almost all warm climates. *See* [illegible].

POMEGRANATE-BARK, a name for the rind of the pomegranate fruit, which is used in medicine, and in dyeing, on account of its astringency. It is also said to be employed for tanning Morocco leather. The bark of the root is emetic and purgative, and administered for worms.

POMELLOES, a name under which forbidden fruit is sometimes sold in this country by fruiterers.

POMERANZE (German), the orange.

POMFRET, an Indian fish, of which there are two kinds, the black and the white.

Pomfret-cake, a liquorice-cake.

Pomme (French), an apple.

Pommel, the knob on the hilt of a sword; the protuberant part of a saddle bow.

Pommelle (French), a round leaden plate, pierced with holes, placed at the end of a tobacco-pipe, to hinder the dirt from going through the bowl.

Pommes-de-terre (French), potatoes.

Pompelmouse, a name for the shaddock (*Citrus Pompelmos Decumana*). *See* Pampelmouse, and Pumplenose.

Pompet, a printer's inking-ball.

Pompier (French), a fireman, one who pumps water; a maker of fire-engines.

Pompion, a name for the common gourd, *Cucurbita Pepo.*

Ponceau (French), a deep scarlet.

Poncho, a woollen cape, cloak, or outer garment, without sleeves, which is merely a length of cloth with a slit made in it, for the head of the wearer to pass through; thus leaving the arms at liberty. The design was taken from an article of clothing used by the natives of South America; fine ponchos are there made of vicunna skins. Poncho is now a trade name for camlets, or stout worsted.

Poncire, a large thick-rinded lemon.

Pongee, a coarse silk.

Poniard, a dagger.

Pont, Punt, a linear measure of China, the tenth part of the covid, equal to nearly 1½ inch; pont is also the French name for a bridge, and the deck of a ship.

Pontac, a kind of Constantia wine, made in the Cape colony.

Pontee, a workman's instrument for taking hot glass out of the pot.

Pontoon, a ferry-boat; a lighter for careening ships; a flat-bottomed boat, covered and lined with tin or copper, used in forming bridges over rivers, for armies to cross.

Pony, a small horse; in betting on horse races, the sum of £25.

Pony-chaise, a small four-wheel carriage, to be drawn by a pony.

Pooah, a local name for a species of wild hemp, obtained from the *Bœhmeria frutescens*, in Nepaul, which is used for fishing-nets and twine.

Pood, a Russian ordinary commercial weight, of which 63 make a ton. A pood contains 40 Russian pounds, and is ordinarily reckoned equal to 36 pounds avoirdupois; but is 36 lbs. 1 oz. 11 drs.

Poodina, Podeena, Indian names for *Mentha sativa* and *viridis*.

Poodle, a shaggy water-spaniel; a lady's small French lap-dog.

Pool-balls, ivory balls, 9 or 12 to the set, about 2 inches in diameter, for playing a kind of billiards.

Pooyah, an instrument used in a tan-yard, for stirring up the vats.

Poolooo-odials, a name in Ceylon for the young shoots of the Palmyra palm boiled, when eaten raw, they are termed odials; and are also called kelingoes.

Poonac, a name for the caky left after expressing the oil from the cocoa-nut pulp, which is used as a manure, and for feeding stock.

Poonay-oil, Poonseed-oil, a bitter lamp oil, obtained from the seeds of *Calophyllum inophyllum*, which yield about 60 per cent. of their weight of oil. It is also called Plunnaoltay-oil.

Poon-wood, an Indian wood, the produce of one or two species of *Calophyllum*, used for ship-building, for planks, and also for spars.

Poor-house, a work-house; an house for the reception of the indigent, supported by the poors-rate.

Poor law, a law for the support of the poor, those infirm and distressed, or able-bodied out of employ.

Poor-law Board, a commission which has the superintendence and regulation of all matters in the kingdom, relating to the relief of the poor, and the administration of union work-houses.

Poor-law Office, the metropolitan office, where the Poor-law Commissioners meet.

Poor-rate, a poundage-tax levied on parishioners who are householders, for the relief of the poor.

Poose, a name for a charge of oil; a measure in Brussels, about 27 gallons.

Pop, the name for some varieties of maize in the United States, as red, blue, white, yellow, and mixed pop; parched corn; a vulgar name for pawning.

Pope Joan-board, a fancy painted board for a card-table, with marked divisions, for playing the game at cards, called Pope Joan.

Pop-gun, a child's plaything; a small wooden tube with a ramrod and pellet.

Poplar, a tree, the *Populus*, of which there are several species, and the soft wood is used for carving, for toys, and common turnery. The wooden polishing wheels of the glass-grinder, are made out of horizontal slices of the stem. The bark of the white poplar is used by fishermen, for floats to support their nets. The buds of the black poplar are aromatic and bitter, and are considered diuretic and antispasmodic. Tacamahac is obtained from the buds of *P. balsamifera*, in the United States.

Poplin, a stuff of silk and worsted, of which there are many varieties, as watered, figured, brocaded, tissued, &c. The manufacture chiefly centres at Dublin and Norwich.

Popped-corn, the green ears of maize roasted on the stalk or cob.

Poppin. *See* Pappin.

Poppy-head, the capsule of the poppy.

Poppy-seed, the seed of the *Papaver somniferum*, which enters into commerce as an oil seed.

Poppy-seed Oil, a bland drying oil, obtained from poppy-seed, which is more extensively used in the Madras presidency, and some other parts of India, than any other, both in lamps and for food. Exposed to the rays of the sun, it becomes perfectly colourless.

Population-returns, the official details of a census.

Porcal, a kind of large plum grown in Spain.

PORCELAIN. *See* POTTERY.

PORCELAIN-CLAY, a fine and white clay suited for pottery and earthenware purposes.

PORCELAIN-JASPER, beds of clay which have been partially vitrified by contact with trap rocks.

PORCELAIN-LETTER MAKER, a preparer of the ornamental coloured letters of pottery-ware, to be affixed to shop-fronts.

PORCELAIN-PAPER, a kind of French-made fancy paper, which is sometimes figured, painted and gilt.

PORCH, a covered way to an entrance, as to a church or dwelling-house; a portico.

PORCUPINE-WOOD, a species of palm so named, because, when cut horizontally, the markings of the wood assimilate to the quills of the porcupine.

PORK, the flesh of the hog sold fresh or salted. [pork.

PORK-BUTCHER, one who kills pigs and sells

PORK-CHOP, a slice from the rib of a pig.

PORKERS, young pigs.

PORK-SAUSAGES, minced pork, seasoned and cased in gut.

PORPHYRY, a hard stone of a reddish colour, having a basis of felspar or clay, &c., with other mineral crystals dispersed through it.

PORPOISE, a cetaceous animal. the varieties of which, *Phocœna communis*, and *Americana*, and especially the *Beluga catodon* of Gray, are useful to man for their skin and oil. The leather made from porpoise skins is said to be the strongest known. Their skins are dressed for traces, and the Canadian mail-bags are made of them. These bags are very white, thick and soft; they stand much chafing, and effectually resist the wet. The blubber yields a large quantity of oil of fine quality.

PORRIDGE, a thick food made by boiling flour, pease, or oatmeal in water.

PORRIDGE-POT, a saucepan for making gruel or porridge.

PORRINGER, a kind of bowl of pottery or glass.

PORRON, a liquid measure of Catalonia, nearly half a pint.

PORSE (French), twenty-six leaves of paper.

PORT, a harbour, bay, inlet, or cove, forming a shelter for vessels; an embrasure or opening in the side of a ship for running out cannon; the lid which shuts the port-hole; the left or larboard side of a ship looking forward. An important commercial red wine, the produce of the vineyards of the Upper Douro, and shipped from Oporto, in pipes of 115 gallons, of which we import to the extent of from 3,000,000 to 4,000,000 gallons a-year.

PORTABLE, handy, that may be carried with ease; in French the word implies any thing wearable.

PORTABLE-FORGE MAKER, a manufacturer of forges that can be easily transported.

PORTABLE-GAS, gas made from resin and oil, and carried about in iron cylinders.

PORT ADMIRAL, the officer having charge of a naval port, and the vessels of war resorting thither.

PORTAGE, sailors' wages in port; also the amount of a sailor's wages for a voyage; an interruption to river navigation; a carrying place round rapids and waterfalls, or from one water communication to another; a charge for carriage.

PORTAL, a small gate.

PORT-CRAYON, a lithographer's writing-pencil; a pencil-case.

PORTCULLIS, a sliding gate to close a doorway.

PORT-DUES, certain tolls levied on shipping, entering or quitting a port.

PORTE-AIGUILLE (French), a needle-case; a surgeon's needle-bearer.

PORTE-ALLUMETTES (French), a match-box.

PORTE-BALLE (French), a pedlar.

PORTE-CHAISE (French), a sedan-chair.

PORTEFAIX, a street-porter in France.

PORTEFEUILLE (French), PORTFOLIO, a pocket-book; a case for holding loose papers, drawings, &c.

PORTE-LETTRE, a letter-case.

PORTE-MONNAIE, a kind of leathern purse, or fancy money-holder, for the pocket.

PORTE-MOUCHETTES (French), a snuffers-tray.

PORTE-PRESSE (French), a bookbinder's shaving-tub.

PORTER, a weaver's term in Scotland for twenty splits, or threads, in plain linen work; in England it is termed a beer; a door-keeper; a carrier of burdens; a fermented malt liquor, which is distinguished from ale or beer by its darker colour, arising in some degree from an incipient charring of the malt, which also imparts an agreeable bitter taste to it. Burned sugar and Spanish juice or liquorice, are also added to heighten the colour. In London porter is often termed beer, in contradistinction to ale.

PORTER AND ALE DEALER, a vender or shipper of malt liquors.

PORTERAGE, the hire of porters.

PORTER'S LODGE, a small house for a gate-keeper; a room at the door of a set of offices.

PORTEUR (French), a carrier; a postilion's horse.

PORTFIRE, an inflammable composition rolled in paper for discharging guns, instead of by a match.

PORT-HOLES, holes in the side of a vessel for pointing cannon out of. *See* PORT.

PORTIA-NUT OIL, a new oil obtained in India from the *Thespesia Populnea*.

PORTICO, a porch, hall, or gateway; a sheltered walk; any disposition or series of columns, which forms a sort of gallery.

PORTLAND-CEMENT MAKER, a manufacturer of cement for builders.

PORTLAND-STONE, a coarse earthy limestone used for building purposes in London, obtained from the quarries of Purbeck and Portland.

PORTMANTEAU, a small leather case for holding a change of linen, &c.; literally a cloak-bag.

PORTMANTEAU-MAKER, a trunk-maker.

PORTOR, a marble with deep yellow veins.

PORTRAIT AND MINIATURE PAINTER, an artist who takes pictures of persons, or of the face from life.

Portrait Gallery, a collection of likenesses of persons.

Portulan (French), a ship-master's guide; a book containing the situation and description of sea-ports, &c., with instructions for navigation.

Port-warden, the officer in charge of a port; a harbour-master.

Posada, Posaderia, a Spanish inn or tavern.

Posca (Spanish), a mixture of vinegar and water.

Pose, a land and superficial measure of Switzerland, ranging, in different localities, from 27 to 45 French ares.

Poseur (French), a stonemason; a pavior.

Posnett, a kitchen utensil; a small skillet or pan.

Posset, a pleasant drink; milk with spice or wine. There are treacle possets, sago possets, &c.

Posson, an old liquid measure of France, which is defined under its more common name of Poisson.

Post, a continental road measure, generally calculated in France and Germany at two leagues, in Italy two miles; a piece of timber or stone set upright; in Scotland, a stratum in a quarry; a situation of office; to register; to enter particulars in account-books; to travel express with relays of horses.

Postage, an official charge for the transmission of letters, or other mailable matter carried by the mails by land or by sea.

Postage-book, a memorandum-book in an office of postal expenditure.

Postage-stamp, an adhesive Government stamp of variable value, for affixing to letters to pay the postal charge; in England—1d. 2d. 4d. 6d. 10d. and 1s.; in India and the Colonies for different sums, according to the local postal rates in force.

Postal-districts, the assigned divisions of the metropolis, within which letters are delivered at certain regular intervals of the day.

Postal-knocker, a door rapper.

Post-and-job-master, a person who keeps post-horses, and lets out horses and carriages on job hire.

Post-bag, a bag for holding the mails.

Post-bill, a post-office way-bill placed in the mail bag, or given in charge of the guard or driver.

Post-boy, a postilion; a person who rides post-horses, and takes charge of them back when arrived at the end of the stage.

Post-captain, a common unofficial title given to a captain of the Royal Navy, to distinguish him from a commander, who is often styled by courtesy a captain.

Post-chaise, a carriage travelling with post-horses or relays.

Post-date, to afterdate, or date a document in advance of the real date.

Poster, a large printed hand-bill or placard; a legal announcement.

Postern, a small gate in a military fortification; a back door.

Post-horn, a horn or tin tube blown by a mail guard to clear the road for his vehicle, mail carts having the precedence of the roads.

Post-horse, a horse let out to travellers or carriers.

Post-house, a house where relays of post-horses are kept for the convenience of travellers; a post-office.

Postilion, the rider on one of the leading horses of a coach.

Postman, a letter-carrier.

Post-mark, the date and place stamp affixed to letters in a post-office.

Post-master General, the chief officer of the general post-office, usually a member of the Cabinet, who has the superintendence of all matters connected with the interior and exterior postal arrangements of the kingdom, the transmission of the mails, and the appointment to vacant offices in his department.

Post-obit, a contract made by an heir to pay a certain sum on his coming into his property, after the death of the existing possessor.

Post-office, a head depot, or branch receiving-house, for the despatch and delivery of letters. *See* General-post-office.

Post-office clerk, a subordinate employed in a post-office.

Post-office-directory, an old-established London directory, based upon the returns of the post letter-carriers, of the residents in the metropolis, comprising officials, private individuals, traders, companies, streets, and a variety of other useful information.

Post-office-order. *See* Money-order.

Post-wood, wood suited for gate-posts and other purposes. *See* Prop-wood.

Pot, a mug; a pewter vessel used by publicans for supplying malt liquors to customers; a general vulgar name for the imperial quart measure, the fourth of a gallon; a dry and liquid measure used in many parts of the Continent, ranging, for liquids, from 1¾ pint in Denmark and Norway, to 6½ pints in some parts of Belgium. As a dry measure it is about 2½ to 3 pints. In Sardinia the pot for oil is 17 pints. As a local liquid measure in Jersey, 200 pots are computed to yield 92 imperial gallons, equal to a loss of 8 per cent on the gallon. Also a kind of paper and millboard, 17½ by 14½ inches.

Potador, an officer in Spain who examines and marks weights and measures.

Potage, broth with vegetables in it; soup or porridge.

Potager (French), a kitchen-garden; a soup pan; a stove for cooking.

Potal, distiller's grains.

Pot and Pearl-ash Dealer, a dealer in wood ashes, exported in large quantities from America.

Potash, such constituents of burned vegetables as are very soluble in water, and fixed in the fire; the lixivium of the ashes of wood fuel evaporated in iron pots. These ashes are principally used in the manufacture of flint glass, prussiate of potash, and soft soap. The imports of pot and pearl ash range from 4000 to 9000 tons a-year.

POTATOES, a highly esteemed edible root, the tubers of the *Solanum tuberosum*, which enter into commerce in their fresh state, under the form of preserved potatoes, dried, and as starch. There are about 2½ million acres under potato cultivation in the United Kingdom, and the weight of food annually raised from these must be enormous. We also import 3000 or 4000 tons a-year from the Continent.

POTATO-FLOUR, meal or farina prepared from the potato tubers.

POTATO-LIFTER, a prong; also a kind of digging machine to save labour in raising potatoes from the ground.

POTATO-MERCHANT, a wholesale dealer in potatoes.

POTATO-PASTY, a pasty made of potatoes and flour.

POTATO-PASTY-PAN, a shallow tinned pan for baking pasties in.

POTATORE (Italian), a pruner of trees; a wine dresser.

POTATO-ROASTER, a tin machine carried about by an itinerant vender, who sells hot baked-potatoes in the streets in cold weather.

POTATO-SALESMAN, an agent for potato growers, who receives quantities from the country on sale.

POTATO-SMASHER, a cook's wooden utensil for mashing potatoes for the table.

POTATO-STARCH, the fecula prepared from the potato root, and forming a gum substitute, used extensively by calico-printers and cotton manufacturers. *See* DEXTRINE.

POT-AU-FEU (French), meat, consisting of gravy soup, and bouilli, or boiled meat.

POTBOY, POTMAN, a messenger who takes out beer from public-houses, and collects the pots and cans again.

POTDAR, an Indian money-changer, many of whom sit in the open markets changing cowries for rupees, and *vice versa*.

POTE, CANTARO, OR ALQUIERE, a liquid-measure of Portugal and Brazil, of 6 canadas, = 14·8647 English pints; the alquiére as a dry measure is = 6·000 gallons imperial.

POTÉE, a French liquid-measure, the fourth of a pint.

POTELOT (French), black-lead.

POT-GUN, a small mortar used for firing salutes.

POT-HANGER, POT-HOOK, a hook for suspending an iron pot over a fire.

POT-HERB, any culinary vegetable suited for soups or stews, &c.

POT-HOUSE, a petty public or ale-house.

POTICHOMANIE, articles of glass coated or ornamented in imitation of old chinaware, with paper or linen flowers and devices, and varnished.

POT-METAL, a kind of stained glass; an alloy of lead and copper for making pots.

POT-PLANT, a name for the *Lecythis ollaria*.

POT-POURRI, hotch potch; a kind of pie; a perfume made of orris powder, lemon-peel, lavender flowers, rose-petals, and essence of musk.

POTSTONE, a magnesian mineral allied to serpentine and steatite, susceptible of a high polish; it is a coarse and indistinctly granular variety of prismatic talc, and, from its softness and tenacity, may be readily turned. It is used for the manufacture of cooking utensils and other vessels; for fire stones in furnaces; in a powder, for diminishing friction in machinery, and for removing oil stains in cloth.

POTTAGE, soup; a mess of food boiled in a pot.

POTTE, a Danish liquid measure, the krug, of 4 pogles: 100 pottes = 21·25 imperial gallons: 1·7010 pint = 1 potte.

POTTED-MEATS, viands preserved by parboiling, &c. in small jars covered with grease, or enclosed in hermetically sealed tin cases.

POTTER, a maker of earthen pots and ware.

POTTER'S-CLAY, plastic clay; clay suited for the manufacture of pots or earthenware.

POTTER'S-WHEEL, a wheel used by the potter.

POTTERY, the generic name for all kinds of clay ware; the manufactory of a potter.

POTTERY-MANUFACTURER. *See* POTTER.

POTTING, the operation of pouring soft sugar into earthen moulds, and placing wet clay saturated on the top to refine it; pouring new made muscovado sugar into casks to cure it, or drain off the molasses.

POTTINGER, an earthen jar.

POTTING-HOUSE, a place where plants are shifted into pots.

POTTLE, an English dry-measure, containing 2 quarts or the half of a gallon. Also a small cone-shaped basket in which fruit is sold, and which should hold about 12 ounces of strawberries or raspberries.

POU, a linear and itinerary measure in China; the former is 5¼ feet, the latter 8·5792 miles.

POUAH, PAO, an Indian liquid-measure nearly 2-5ths of a pint.

POUCE, the French name for the inch.

POUCH, a small bag; a shot-belt; a case with tin divisions in which a soldier carries his cartridges. *See* CARTRIDGE-CASE.

POUCHONG, a black tea; a superior kind of souchong.

POUCH-ROLLER, a leather pocket-case for holding toilet articles, such as tooth, nail, and shaving brushes, &c., or for any other article that will roll up.

POU-DE-SOIE, a stuff or farandine of silk; padesoy.

POUDRETTE, a French artificial manure, consisting of solid excrement dried in the air, and mixed with copperas, gypsum and charcoal for the purpose of neutralizing the odour; this prepared manure, though originally manufactured in France, is now also made in New York and other large towns, and consists of about two-thirds night-soil, and one-third decomposed vegetable matter, finely sifted.

POUL, a copper coin of Bokhara worth rather more than a farthing; in Georgian money it is the 10th part of a chaui.

POULARDE (French), a pullet.

POULOU, a close woollen fabric manufactured in Thibet, of various qualities and colours, used for garments.

POULT, a young chicken; a pullet.

POULTERER, a dealer in eggs, poultry, and game, who usually sells other articles, such as sausages, butter, rabbits, &c.

POULTERERS' COMPANY, one of the minor livery companies of London, which, having no hall of its own, conducts its business at Guildhall.

POULTICE, an external application for promoting the suppuration of tumours, or abating painful inflammation: poultices are made of bread, of linseed-meal, mustard-meal, &c. *See* SPONGIO-PILINE.

POULTRY, a general name for every kind of domesticated fowls, reared about a house or farm, embracing a large variety of birds which are eaten as food.

POULTRY-SALESMAN, a wholesale poulterer, who receives hampers of poultry from the country on consignment for sale.

POULTRY-SHOW, a competitive exhibition of poultry for prizes.

POUNCE, a resinous powder used to sprinkle over fresh written documents, consisting of gum sandarac, pounded and sifted very fine, and mixed with the calcareous bone of the cuttle-fish crushed.

POUNCE-BOX, a receptacle for holding pounce.

POUNCE-PAPER, a transparent paper for drawing, or tracing, &c. made in Carlsruhe; it is free from oily, greasy, or other objectionable substance, and will therefore bear sketching and painting on.

POUND, the sovereign of 20s., the principal current gold coin of Great Britain; a place where cattle which have been distrained, or taken trespassing, are lodged and kept till redeemed; a weight of many countries. Two different pounds are used in England; the troy and the avoirdupois. The avoirdupois is divided into 16 ounces (each 437·5 grains); each ounce into 16 drachms; each drachm is 27·34 grains, consequently the avoirdupois pound contains 7000 grains. The troy pound, used in weighing the precious metals, drugs, &c. contains 96 drachms and 5760 grains; the Baden pound is equal to 1-10th lb. avoirdupois. *See* APOTHECARIES-WEIGHT, AVOIRDUPOIS, and TROY-WEIGHT.

POUNDAGE, a commission allowed to collectors and assessors, to the clerks of the local commissioners of taxes, to distributors and subdistributors of stamps, &c. under various acts of Parliament; a charge for penning stray cattle.

POUND-BEADS, a kind of bead, white or red, used in West African trade with the natives.

POUND-CAKE, a rich sweet cake, so named, from a pound or an equal quantity of different ingredients being used in making it.

POUNDER, a term used to express the weight of a shot, as a six-pounder, or to distinguish the size of a cannon, as a 32-pounder.

POUND-KEEPER, one who has the charge of a cattle-pound.

POUPELIN, a kind of French pastry or pancake.

POUPETIER, a doll-maker in France.

POUPETON (French), hashed meat.

POURIE, a jug with a spout.

POURPIER, a French name for purslain.

POUT, the young of some fish and birds, as a chicken, a young partridge, a whiting-pout, a caller-pout, a small haddock.

POUT-NET. *See* PLOUT-NET.

POWDER, any thing ground down to dust; perfumed dust for the hair or skin; pulverized drugs; an explosive compound. *See* GUNPOWDER.

POWDER-BARREL MAKER, a cooper who makes substantial small oak barrels for holding gunpowder, capable of containing 8, 10, 12½, 20, 25, 50, 90, or 100 lbs., which is the maximum weight allowed by Government to be contained in a single package.

POWDER-BELT, a leather belt to carry gunpowder in.

POWDER-BLUE, a name for smalts.

POWDER-BOX, a lady's toilet-table box for holding violet-powder and a puff.

POWDER-CART, a carriage for conveying gunpowder and shot for artillery.

POWDER-FLASK, POWDER-HORN, a metal or other case with a spring, carried by sportsmen, holding gunpowder to charge a rifle or fowling-piece.

POWDER-MAGAZINE. *See* MAGAZINE.

POWDER-MILL, the place in which gunpowder is made, of which there are about two dozen in the United Kingdom.

POWDER-MONKEY, a boy employed in carrying powder from the magazine to the gunner.

POWDER-PUFF, a pad of swan's down used by ladies to powder the skin.

POWDERS, pulverized drugs, as rhubarb, jalap, or mixtures, &c., sold as medicines by chemists and surgeons.

POWE, an Indian weight and measure. As a weight for the precious metals it is 1056·6 grains troy; for merchandise, 21 ounces avoirdupois; as a dry-measure, it is equal to 3698·1 grains. *See* ADPAO.

POWER-LOOM, a weaving machine worked by steam or water power. *See* LOOM.

POWER OF ATTORNEY, a letter or warrant, forming a legal authority to act for another.

POY, a rope-dancer's balancing pole; a steering pole.

POYA, a duty paid in Spain for baking bread in a public oven.

POYAL, a kind of striped stuff with which benches and seats are covered.

POYNDING, a Scotch law term for distraining.

POZERO, a Spanish well-digger.

POZO, a Spanish mining term.

POZZOLANO, a species of cement for building and stucco-work. *See* PUZZOLANO.

PRAAM, PRAME, a French lighter or small barge; a flat-bottomed vessel, on which cannon are mounted, to form a floating battery.

PRACTICE, to carry on a profession; the employment of a medical man or lawyer. The good-will of a medical man's practice or patients, is often sold.

PRAGER (German), one who stamps or coins.

PRAHU, PROA, a Malay ship or lugger.

PRAIRIE, undulating grass land in North America; a large natural meadow without trees.

PRAISS (French), tobacco juice.

PRALINE, burnt almonds; sugared almonds.

PRALL-STEIN (German), a curb or corner-stone.

PRAMMERANT (German), a subscriber.

Präsentirteller (German), a waiter or salver.

Pratique, a certificate of having performed quarantine.

Prawn, a kind of large shrimp.

Praya, an embanked road or public walk.

Prayer-book, a book containing the forms of prayer and services of the Established Church, authorized to be used in churches and chapels by the State.

Prebendary, a priest holding a stipend or stall in a Cathedral church.

Precentor, a church clerk; a priest who leads a choir, next to the dean in a cathedral.

Precept, the mandate or official summons of a mayor, sheriff, &c.

Preceptor, a head master or teacher.

Precious Metals, gold and silver coin and bullion, in which there is a considerable import and export trade, the bulk of the supplies of gold coming from our own colonies in Australia, and indirectly from California, through the United States' Atlantic ports. The aggregate value of our imports of gold and silver, in the five years ending with 1855, was nearly £115,000,000.

Preen, a clothier's forked tool; a bodkin.

Preface, the introductory observations to a published work.

Prefect, the governor of a province; a chief of police.

Prefecture, a French police office.

Preference-shareholder, one who is a holder of preference stock, and entitled to first dividends.

Preference-stock, that which takes the first dividend, before other share capital, in a company.

Pregonero (Spanish), a common crier.

Prelude, a preliminary flourish of music.

Premier (French) a chief or prime minister; the head of a cabinet.

Premises, names, titles, &c., at the beginning of a deed; lands or houses.

Premium, a rate paid for insurance; something given to invite a loan or bargain; an advance paid by purchasers of shares, stock, &c., above the par price; a reward or bonus offered by Government to stimulate trade.

Prendero, a pawnbroker in Spain.

Prerogative-office, the office for registering wills.

Presburgers, a kind of sweet fancy biscuits.

Prescription, a direction; a memorandum or receipt, from a medical man, of medicines to be made up.

Prescriptive-right, a title acquired by long use, time, or custom.

Preserve, a cover for game; a river set apart for the preservation of fish; fruit kept in sugar.

Preserved-meat-can, a tin vessel that can be closed from the air.

Preserved-provision Merchant, a preparer or dealer in dried vegetables, bottled fruits, and animal substances for food, hermetically sealed to exclude air.

Preserving-pan, a stew-pan of copper, bell-metal, or enamel, for boiling down fruit to make preserves.

Preserving-spoon, a spoon used for stirring fruit when making preserves.

Press, a machine by which any thing is pressed or an impression taken, as a coining-press, a printing-press, a cider-press; an hydraulic-press; a collective name for newspapers and their writers; a closet for clothes; a chest of drawers. *See* Printers' Press-maker.

Press and Mangle-maker, a manufacturer of rolling-presses for linen, and clothes-presses for keeping table-cloths, towels, and napkins smooth.

Press-bed, a stretcher bed that shuts up in a case.

Pressed-glass, articles of glass forced into a mould, by a machine, which thence take the required form and markings, and differ from blown glass.

Presser and Packer, one who bales and packs goods for warehousemen and merchants. *See* Packer.

Press-gang, a detachment, formerly authorized to seize men to serve as sailors in the Royal navy, in time of war.

Press-indicator, an instrument made of different kinds; a register of impressions thrown off, some with 4 dials indicating to 10,000.

Pressing-board, a tailor's ironing board for smoothing seams of garments on.

Press-keys, small shaped pieces of brass used by bookbinders to hold the strings tight in a sewing press.

Press-man, a mechanical printer, who works at the press, and takes off impressions on paper, whether from type, stone, woodcuts, or metal plates.

Press-piercer, a metal perforator.

Press-pin, an iron bar or prizing lever for turning the screw of a bookbinder's press.

Pressurage, the juice of the grape extracted by the press; a fee paid to the owner of a wine-press for its use.

Pressure-gage, a register of the pressure of steam.

Prestinos, Pristinos, a kind of fritters cooked in a pan in Spain.

Preston-salts, bottles of smelling-salts used by females, containing carbonate of ammonia in small pieces, with a drachm of the following mixture added, viz. oils of bergamot, cloves, and lavender, and the strongest solution of ammonia.

Présure, Presame, the French and Italian names for rennet.

Preventive Service, a common name for the Coast guard, a department under the Customs for preventing smuggling.

Preyne, Prein, a pin or needle.

Price-list, a list of shares and stocks, with the quotations at which they can be bought and sold.

Prices-current, a published list of the ruling market-prices of the day for merchandise and produce.

Pricker, a bodkin; a toothed instrument used by workmen for stabbing or marking leather, paper, &c.; a small marline-spike with a wooden handle used in sail-making.

Pricket, a young male deer of two years old that begins to put forth his horns.

PRICKING-NOTE, a form of custom-house order (usually printed in red ink), delivered by a shipper of goods to the searcher. The name is derived from a practice of noting the tallies of goods taken into the ship, by pricking holes in the paper, corresponding with the number of packages counted into the ship.

PRICKLE, a sieve of filberts, containing about [½ a cwt.

PRICKLE YELLOW, a very common West Indian wood, the produce of *Xanthoxylon clava Herculis*, used for furniture, flooring, and inlaying, and said to afford a dye, and to possess medicinal properties. *See* YELLOW-WOOD.

PRICKLY PEAR, a name for the ripe fruit of the *Opuntia vulgaris*, which is occasionally imported from the South of Europe and the West Indies, but not much esteemed, being flat and insipid.

PRIE-DIEU, a kneeling-desk for prayers.

PRILL, a solid lump of metal from ore.

PRILLION, tin extracted from the slag.

PRIMAGE, an allowance to masters of vessels for the use of cables and ropes, and to mariners for their assistance in loading and unloading cargoes.

PRIME, superior, excellent; in French, a premium, money advanced; a small nominal weight, the 24th part of the troy grain; in Germany the tenth part of the inch, the 100th part of the lachter or fathom; a variable dry and liquid measure used in Switzerland; to charge the pan of a gun with loose powder; to lay a train to ignite a mine, &c.; to give a first coat of paint.

PRIMER, a name for some varieties of type, larger than bourgeois, as long primer, great primer, &c.; a child's first book.

PRIMICHON (Spanish), a skein of fine, soft silk used for embroidering.

PRIMING. *See* PRIME.

PRIMING-WIRE, an iron pricker for the vent-hole of a gun to pierce the cartridge.

PRINCE'S-METAL, an alloy of copper and zinc in the proportion of 72 parts of the former to 28 of the latter, or sometimes consisting of 75 per cent. of copper and 25 of zinc.

PRINCE'S-MIXTURE, a dark kind of snuff so called, which is scented with otto of roses.

PRINCE'S-WOOD, a light-veined brown-wood, the produce of *Cordia Gerascanthus*, obtained in Jamaica, and principally used for turning.

PRINCETTAS, a worsted fabric, which is sometimes made with a cotton warp.

PRINCEZA-SNUFF, a choice light-coloured snuff made at Bahia, of which many thousand pounds are annually shipped; but it is seldom imported here, owing to the heavy duty.

PRINCIPAL, the head of a school or business; capital laid out at interest; a main timber in a building.

PRINCIPELA, the name in Spain for a kind of light camlet.

PRINCIPESSA, a kind of cigar so named.

PRINCIPIERA (Spanish), a small metal saucepan in which broth is warmed.

PRINT, to stamp or impress; any thing printed, as a newspaper, engraving, calico stained with figures, &c.; a stamp for butter; to publish.

PRINT-COLOURER, an artist who tints or paints black engravings or prints.

PRINT-CUTTER, a workman who carves blocks of wood with figures, for printing calico, paper-hangings, &c., or who makes butter-prints, or other moulds.

PRINTER, one who prints with letter-press or copper-plates, or who stains calico.

PRINTERS'-AUCTIONEER, an agent who values stock for printers, and disposes of the good-will of their business; type, &c.

PRINTERS'-BLANKET MAKER, a manufacturer of stout plate roller-cloths and swanskins, used by copper-plate and letter-press printers, and of the plain and twilled lappings and machine blankets used by calico-printers.

PRINTERS'-FRAMES, upright wooden frames on which the letter-cases of type for compositors are placed.

PRINTERS'-INK MAKER, a manufacturer of printing-ink. *See* INK.

PRINTERS'-JOINER, a workman who makes the wood-work, &c., required in printing, such as frames, cases, &c., and cuts up the furniture used for making proper margin and in blocking the chases.

PRINTERS'-PRESS MAKER, a manufacturer of the presses used for taking impressions from type, which differ with the special purposes, whether for job-work, book-work, or newspaper-work. Hand-presses are now for the most part superseded in large establishments by steam-presses, generally called printing-machines. The kinds of presses used in different trades are very various, as the standing, cutting, sewing, finishing and arming presses, used by the bookbinder; the lithographic-press; copper-plate-press, &c.; and for letter-press printing there are the Columbian, Albion, Stanhope, Hoe's, Applegarth's; the platen power-press, cylinder-press, &c.

PRINTERS' LIQUOR, also called iron liquor, a liquid without spirit, thrown off the retorts as vapour, and then condensed through worms, which is used as a mordant by calico-printers.

PRINTERS'-ROLLERS, composition rollers used for inking the forms of type, by letter-press and other printers, made of treacle, glue, and other materials; roller-cloths, varying in width, weight, and fineness, used by calico-printers and others.

PRINTERS'-RULE CUTTER, a preparer of the lengths of brass, &c, rules, used by printers to divide columns of newspaper-type, or other work.

PRINTERS'-SMITH, a workman who makes iron work for printers.

PRINTERS' WOOD-TYPE CUTTER, an artist who shapes and carves the large fancy letters of wood, used in job-printing, and which are made from ten-line size, up to fifty-line and upwards.

PRINTING-INK. *See* INK.

PRINTING-MACHINE, a machine for taking impressions from type, or for staining calico, worked by steam-power.

PRINTING-PRESS. *See* PRINTERS'-PRESS MAKER.

PRINTING-TYPE, letter-press type of various kinds, used by printers for books, newspaper and job work. The weight of metal and stock of type required to be kept in a large printing-office is very heavy and extensive.

PRINT-SELLER AND PUBLISHER, a shopkeeper who vends engravings, lithographic, and coloured prints, &c.

PRINT-SHOP, a shop where engravings are kept on sale.

PRINT-WORKS, a factory where machine or block printing is carried on; a place for printing calicoes.

PRISCO, the Spanish name for a kind of peach.

PRISON, a jail; a place of confinement, for debtors or criminals.

PRISON-VAN, a police carriage for conveying prisoners to and from a court of justice.

PRIVATE, a soldier of the line or militia; a common soldier.

PRIVATE-BOX, an enclosed box at an opera or play-house, which can be engaged for a party.

PRIVATEERS, private ships commissioned against the enemy in time of war.

PRIZE, a slaver or pirate vessel taken; a capture made in time of war; a scholarship medal, money premium, or other reward gained by competition; money drawn by a lottery-ticket.

PRIZE-MASTER, an officer put in command or charge of a captured ship.

PRIZE-MONEY, a share or division of prizes captured, the proportion being regulated according to the rank of the recipient.

PROBANG, a surgical instrument, a probe for the throat.

PROBATE, a letter of administration to a will; an official document granted upon a proof of decease, to the nearest of kin, or properly authorized party.

PROBATE-DUTY, a government tax on property passing by will.

PROBE, a surgical instrument for examining wounds.

PROCÈS-VERBAL (French), a written declaration; a statement made before a magistrate; the minutes or written transactions of a society or association.

PROCHRAMETER, an instrument for registering the revolutions of a carriage-wheel, and thereby determining the distance travelled; also, applicable for counting with certainty the rotation of machinery, however high the velocity.

PROCLAMATION, a public declaration; an edict or official announcement from government.

PROCTOR, an attorney in an Admiralty or Ecclesiastical court; a college officer.

PROCURATION, authority or power to act for another. In mercantile affairs a foreign agent or correspondent is often authorized to sign for a firm, or to pledge its credit and authority; which is called procuration.

PROCURATORE (Italian), an attorney.

PROCURATOR-FISCAL, an official, the public prosecutor in Scotland.

PRODUCE, the yield of grain or other crop per acre; in mining, the per-centage of metal in the ore; a general name for the staple commodities imported, forming large articles of consumption.

PRODUCE-BROKER, a dealer in foreign imports, as of grocery articles, dye-stuffs, &c.

PRODUCE MARKET, Fenchurch-street, Mincing-lane, Tower-street, and their immediate localities, where the offices of the principal produce-brokers are situate, and where the principal sales and transactions in London are carried on.

PROFENDA, PROVENDA, a grain-measure used in Ancona, nearly two gallons.

PROFESSION, a trade or calling; usually, however, restricted and taken to designate those who are not traders, but skilled and learned men, as lawyers, medical men, and the clergy.

PROFESSIONAL, a term applied to a singer, musician, or actor.

PROFESSOR, a public teacher of any science or art.

PROFIT, money gain upon mercantile transactions; business pursuits or speculations in produce, the funds, &c.

PRO-FORMA-ACCOUNT, a model or sketch account; a pattern bill of particulars.

PROG, a slang sea-term for provisions.

PROGRAMME, a detail or outline guide of any thing to be done, as of a theatrical performance, musical entertainment, review public procession or festivity, &c.

PROJECTILE, a body, such as a rocket, ball, or shell, impelled through the air.

PROJECTING-LETTER MAKER, a manufacturer of porcelain, glass, wood, or other prominent letters to be affixed to shop-fronts or windows.

PROLATORE (Italian), an editor.

PROLOGUE, a preface in verse before a play.

PROLONGE, a gunner's instrument.

PROMETHEAN, a lucifer match.

PROMISSORY-NOTE, a note of hand acknowledging indebtedness; an engagement in writing to pay a defined sum at a time specified, to a person therein named, or sometimes to his order, or often to the bearer at large. Like a bill of exchange it can be made assignable and indorsable.

PROMPT, a trade term for a limit of time given for payment of the account for produce purchased; the limit varying with different goods.

PROMPTER, a person stationed near the actors at a theatre, who reminds them of their parts and duties when forgetful.

PROMPT-NOTE, a note of reminder of the day of payment and sum due, &c., given to a purchaser at a sale of produce.

PRON (Scotch), the bran of oatmeal, of which sowans or flummery is made.

PRONG, the spike of a fork.

PROOF, PROOF-SHEET, an impression taken from the type, for the purpose of correction before the final printing; a first impression of an engraving; a test or trial. *See* PROVER, and PROVING-PRESS.

PROOF-HOUSE, a place for trying the strength of guns, or gunpowder.

Proof-man, in Scotland, a person appointed to determine how much grain is in a corn-stack, by casting out a certain proportion of the sheaves, getting them threshed, the grain measured, and, by skilful calculation, determining the quantity which the whole stack contains.

Proof-sheet. *See* Proof.

Proof-spirit, is ordinarily equal parts of alcohol and water; all over that standard, being less in specific gravity, is considered above proof. The proportions of alcohol per cent., in some of the common varieties of commercial spirit, are as follows (at 62 degrees Fahrenheit): British proof spirit, by weight 50, by measure, 57 per cent.; Cognac, 50 to 54; rum, 72 to 77; Geneva, 50; whisky, 59. So that, on an average, the ardent spirits consumed contain only half their weight, or three-fifths of their bulk of absolute alcohol.

Prop, a support or pole for any purpose, as supporting a clothes-rope, &c.

Propagating-glasses, small hand-glasses to cover young seedlings or growing plants, cucumbers, &c. in a garden or nursery-ground.

Propeller, a screw for driving a steam-vessel; hence screw-steamers are termed screw-propellers.

Property-man, one having charge of the loose articles of furniture, table-fittings, &c. in a theatre, which are technically termed "properties."

Property-tax, a duty on the annual value of houses, land, &c. payable to government by the owner.

Prophet (German), a sort of thin cracknel [cake.

Proprietor, an owner or possessor of property; a holder of stock or shares in a public company.

Prop-wood, Post-wood, small saplings and copse-timber, suited for cutting into props; also short lengths of fir and other round pieces of timber, used in the collieries to prop the coal.

Pro-rata, an equitable division, or fair proportional distribution.

Proscenium, the front of the stage; before the scenes.

Prospecting, a miner's term for searching or examining for gold, preliminarily to settled or continuous operations.

Prospectus, in commercial parlance, the preliminary announcement, first details, or outline sketch of constitution, intended plans and operations of a new company, or a joint-stock association.

Prote, the foreman in a French printing-office.

Protection, a passport, permit, or exemption; a freedom from arrest granted to a bankrupt, pending the adjustment of his accounts, and previous to obtaining his certificate.

Protest, an official notice or remonstrance from a notary-public, preliminary to legal proceedings. Protesting a bill of exchange, or note, secures to the possessor a title of immediate claim on the parties concerned, and renders an oath or witness unnecessary, in further substantiating it.

Prothonotary, a chief notary; the clerk or registrar of a court.

Protocol, a record or registry; a first rough draft; the preliminaries for a treaty.

Protractor, a thin brass, ivory, or wooden instrument for laying down and measuring angles on paper with accuracy and despatch, and by which the use of the line of chords is superseded. It is of various forms, semicircular, rectangular, and circular.

Proved, fully tried or tested; as metals for strength. Gunpowder, fire-arms, pieces of ordnance, anchors, chain-cables, iron girders, or pillars, &c. are always proved, to test their efficiency or strength. A will which has been published or registered in the proper court is also said to be proved.

Provedore, Providore, a purveyor or steward; one who supplies provisions to large steamers, &c.

Provence-oil, an esteemed variety of olive-oil, the produce of Aix.

Provence Rose, a variety of rose esteemed for its beauty and fragrance, of which there are several varieties.

Provender, hay, chopped straw, or other dry food for cattle.

Proving-press, an apparatus for testing the strength of iron girders, and other castings, by pressure.

Provisional, holding office or place temporarily.

Provisional Registration, a preliminary and conditional registration, of a new public company, or joint-stock association, at the proper government office.

Provision-dealer, a grocer or shopkeeper; a retailer of hams, bacon, butter, cheese, and such articles.

Provision-merchant, a general dealer in articles of food.

Provisions, food and victuals of all kinds; live stock collected; the stores laid in for the crew and passengers of a ship.

Provost, the mayor of a royal burgh in Scotland; the head of a college, chapter, or other body.

Provost-marshal, the sheriff of an army.

Proxy, a deputy; a stamped power of attorney, or authority to vote or act for another.

Prunelet, a liquor made from sloes or wild plums.

Prunella Salt, Sal Prunell, fused nitre or saltpetre, moulded into cakes or balls and used for chemical purposes.

Prunes, Prunelloes, dried plums, which are imported, to the extent of about 1100 tons a-year, from France, as a table fruit, for pies and puddings; also for medicinal uses, their properties being laxative when stewed. The largest and finest kind, the French plum or table prune, is the Catharine variety of the *Prunus domestica*, and is usually packed in cartoons; the common kind, the Julian variety, being packed in barrels.

Prunello, a thin woollen or mixed stuff, formerly used for clergymen's gowns, but now chiefly employed for covering shoes, worn by elderly females.

PRUNING-KNIFE, a gardener's or arboriculturist's knife for lopping off the superfluous branches of trees and shrubs.

PRUSSIAN-BLUE, a well-known fugitive colour, used in dyeing, for tinting paper, and by washerwomen. It is obtained by mixing a solution of sulphate of iron and yellow prussiate of potash.

PRUSSIAN-BLUE MANUFACTURER, a manufacturing chemist who prepares this pigment, which is chiefly made at Newcastle, Birmingham, Hull, and London.

PRUSSIAN-DOLLAR, a German money, worth about 3s. See THALER.

PRUSSIATE OF POTASH, a chemical substance consisting of cyanogen united to iron and potassium, with animal refuse added to supply nitrogen. This salt is remarkable for the beauty of its crystals, and the brilliant colours of many of its compounds.

PRUSSIC-ACID, a name for hydrocyanic-acid; one of the most powerful of poisons.

PSYCHE (French), a cheval dressing-glass.

P. S., a theatrical abbreviation for the "prompter's side" of the stage; also for "postscriptum," the postscript to a letter; "past steward," &c.

PSA, an Algerian dry-measure, equal to 51 3-7th pints.

PSALMODICON, a Norwegian musical instrument.

PSALTER, a psalm-book.

PTARMIGAN, a name for the white grouse (*Lagopus mutus*), found in most of the northern parts of Europe.

PUBLICAN, an ale-house keeper.

PUBLICAN'S-BAR FITTER, a tradesman who fits up the enclosed counters, beer engines, shelves, &c., forming the bar of a public-house or tavern.

PUBLICAN'S BROKER, an appraiser and intermediate agent between an outgoing and incoming tenant of a public-house.

PUBLICATION, the act of publishing or printing any thing for diffusion.

PUBLIC HOLIDAY, a day set apart by the legislature, or by magisterial authority; when places of business are ordered to be closed. They are generally days of festivity or humiliation. The public holidays which are universally kept, are Good Friday and Christmas-day; and at most of the government offices, the Queen's birthday. Some of the public establishments have special holidays. Thus the Bank Transfer-office, and the Stock Exchange, close on May 1st, and November 1st; the Excise-office, May 29th and June 28th, the former being the accession of Charles II., the latter the anniversary of the Queen's coronation; the Stamps and Taxes-office keep May 12th, 13th, and 29th; June 28th, and November 10th; the Chancery-offices, March 21st, 24th, and 25th. The Common Pleas and law-offices, March 21st, 22nd, 24th, and 25th; May 12th and 13th; June 28th; December 26th, 27th, and 29th.

PUBLIC-HOUSE, in Scotland an inn or tavern; but in England more generally applied to a beer-shop or ale-house; one that has not a spirit licence.

PUBLICIST, a writer on international law, &c.

PUBLISH, to print and offer for sale.

PUBLISHER, one who prints books, and supplies the public and the trade with copies.

PUCCA SEER. See PUCKA-SEER and SEER.

PUCCOON, a name for the blood-root. See BLOODROOT.

PUCHA-PAT, the leaf of the *Marrubium odoratissimum*, used as an ingredient in India, in tobacco for smoking, and for scenting the hair of women. The essential oil is also in common use for imparting the peculiar fragrance of the leaf to clothes, among the superior class of natives.

PUCHECILLA (Spanish), a thin batter made of flour and water.

PUCHERO (Spanish), a glazed earthen-pot; a pitcher.

PUCHETTE, a drag-net for fishing.

PUCHEUX, a copper ladle used in sugar-boiling.

PUCKA, PUKKAH, a better class of building in India than the temporary cutcha erections.

PUCKA-MAUND, an Indian measure of capacity, equal to 80 lbs. See MAUND.

PUCKA-SEER, an Indian weight for silk and other commodities, 1·8006 lbs.

PUDANG, the Malay name for a sword.

PUDDALUM, a weight of Masulipatam, of 1½ lb.

PUDDIE, a kind of cloth.

PUDDING, a mixed pastry of flour and dried fruit, &c., or a casing of dough enclosing meat or fruit, boiled.

PUDDING-BAG, PUDDING-CLOTH, a cloth to boil a pudding in.

PUDDING-MOULD, a tin or earthenware shape for boiling puddings in.

PUDDING-PAN, a flat tin dish, for baking batter puddings, or dough under meat in an oven.

PUDDING-PIPE TREE, a name for the *Cassia fistula*. See CASSIA FISTULA.

PUDDING-STONE, a conglomerate, compounded of rounded stones, imbedded in a paste.

PUDDLE, a mixture of tempered clay and sand, used for engineering purposes.

PUDDLE-ROLLS, a pair of large heavy rollers with grooved surfaces, between which iron is passed, to be flattened into bars.

PUDDLING, a mode of applying heat to the broken slabs of refined iron to drive off the remaining carbon and slag, and it is then turned out of the furnace in balls or blooms, weighing sixty or seventy pounds each.

PUDDY, an Eastern dry-measure for grain, consisting of eight ollucks, and forming the eighth part of a marcal. The puddy contains 1½ English quart, and the heaped puddy weighs about 3 lbs. 8 oz. 12 drachms. In the Carnatic the puddy is = 3¼ pints; in Madras, only 2⅞ pints; as a weight it is nearly 3 lbs. See MEASURES and MARCAL.

PUDRIDOR (Spanish), a vessel in which rags are steeped for making paper.

PURE, a tanner's name for dogs' dung, used as an alkaline steep in some of the processes, to remove the lime from the pores, and destroy the grease in the skin, in order to fit it for receiving the tannin.

Puffing, giving a notorious publicity, by advertisement or otherwise, of a man's business or wares.

Pugarre, an Indian turban-piece of muslin.

Pugging, working up clay for bricks; a coarse kind of mortar laid on the boards between joists.

Pugil, a handful, as much as can be conveniently taken up between the two first fingers and the thumb.

Pug-mill, a mill for mixing chalk with the clay for forming bricks, which are afterwards pressed into moulds.

Pukat, a Chinese trading vessel employed in the Eastern seas.

Pukeo, a money of account in the island of Lombok, equal to 5 attaks or 1000 cash; about 9s.

Pulas, a name in India for the *Butea frondosa*, and *B. superba*. Their fibre is used for cordage, or beaten to a kind of oakum, for caulking boats. It is also called dhak. The flowers are used for dyeing.

Pulgada, the Spanish name for the inch, the twelfth part of the Burgos foot.

Pullah, a commercial weight in India, ranging, in different localities, from 138¼ lbs. to 325¼ lbs. There is a difference in buying and selling: for instance, a selling pullah will be 120 seers, or 240 lbs. 6 oz. 9 drachms; and a purchasing pullah, 126 seers, or 252 lbs. 6 oz. 14 drachms.

Pulled Otter, otter skins from which the external or long hair has been pulled off, leaving the soft fine wool or down underneath. *See* Otter.

Pullet, a young hen.

Pulley, a general name for tackle or ropes moving on grooved blocks, for lifting or moving weights; a grooved wheel moveable about an axle, for carrying a line and weight for window sashes, &c.

Pullicate, a silk handkerchief.

Pullipunta, a name in Peru for the small palm which produces the vegetable ivory-nut (*Phytelephas macrocarpa*).

Pullom, a name on the African coast for the *Bombax Ceiba*, or silk cotton-tree, the trunk of which is converted into canoes.

Pulp, the soft part of fruit; the covering of a coffee-berry; half stuff, or the macerated materials for making paper.

Pulpero (Spanish), a chandler; one who keeps a retail shop for provisions.

Pulpit, a clergyman's rostrum in a church or chapel of wood, iron, or stone.

Pulpit-builder, a wood-carver, or stonemason, who constructs the elevated rostrums for ministers.

Pulp-strainer, a kind of sieve used in paper-making.

Pulqueria, a shop where pulque, or the fermented beverage made from the sap of the aloe, is sold.

Pu-lu, a species of brown thistle-down imported from the Sandwich islands, to mix with silk in the manufacture of hats.

Pulver (German), powder.

Pulverine, barilla ashes.

Pulveriser, a quartz-crusher; any machine for pounding substances to dust.

Pulvertonne (German), a barrel of gunpowder.

Pumice-stone, a vesicular species of lava which floats on water; a volcanic product obtained principally from one of the Lipari islands. It is employed in various branches of the arts. The dome of the church or mosque of St. Sophia is built of pumice-stone for lightness.

Pumicin (French), palm-oil.

Pummel, the knob of a saddle.

Pump-brake, the handle or arm of a ship's pump.

Pump-dale, a waste pipe for carrying off water pumped up.

Pumping-engine, a steam-engine applied for draining fens or lifting water from mines, and for supplying towns.

Pumpkin, a species of gourd (the *Cucurbita Pepo*) of which there are numerous varieties, varying in the shape and colour of the fruit. *See* Gourd.

Pumplenose, a name for the shaddock, *Citrus Decumana*. *See* Pompelmouse.

Pump-maker, a manufacturer of pumps of different kinds, as of the sucking or common household-pump, the forcing-pump, the lifting-pump, the chain-pump for ships, &c.

Pump-room, a place for drinking mineral waters, where there is a mineral spring.

Pumps, machines for raising fluids either upon the lifting or forcing principle; men's thin shoes worn by sailors, or for dancing.

Pump-stock, the solid body of a pump.

Pump-valve, the moveable interior part or lid of a pump.

Pump-wood Bark, a tanning bark, obtained from an undescribed tree in British Guiana; also called Baramilla.

Pun, a name in Sinde for the leaves of *Typha elephantina*, used for making mats and baskets; a nominal species of currency in India calculated by cowry shells; in Hindostan, a handful or about 80 shells; five puns or 400 cowries making an anna or 1½d.

Punal (Spanish), a poniard or dagger.

Punatoo, a name in Ceylon for the preserved pulp of the fruit of the palmyra, washed, pressed, and dried on mats in the sun. It is the chief food of the poorer inhabitants of the peninsula of Jaffna for several months of the year; and also enters largely into the composition of soups, puffs, cakes, and various other preparations.

Punch, an instrument for stamping holes; a shape for cutting pasteboard wads for guns; a stone cutter's tool for chipping; a die for making printing-type; a well-known metropolitan weekly humorous publication; an iron lever; a puppet show; a strong mixed beverage made of spirits, wine, water, sugar, lemon, and other flavouring ingredients.

Punchagah, a grain-measure in the East Indies, = 24 cwts. 2 qrs. 16 lbs.

Punch-bowl, a china bowl for bringing punch to table in.

Puncheon, a cask made of oak staves, iron hooped, supposed to contain 84 gallons, but varying with different liquors.

Punching-machine, Punching-press, a machine for stamping holes through thick metal plates.

PUNCH-LADLE, a small ladle for dipping out punch into glasses, made of silver, hard-wood, or other material.

PUNJUM, an unbleached, strong, fine cotton long cloth made in India.

PUNK, a name for touchwood or vegetable tinder. *See* AMADOU.

PUNKAH, a hand, or swinging, fan used in India. Punkahs are frequently richly ornamented with gold and silver, beetles' wings, peacocks' feathers, &c.

PUNKHO, a weight for the precious metals used in Bengal, = 0·14036 grain troy.

PUNNET, a small round basket for fruit, about 2 inches deep, and of various diameter, holding from half a pound to two pounds of strawberries.

PUNNY, a name in parts of the East for the bamboo as a measure.

PUNSARRY, a weight for grain in the Nizam territory, India, of 5 seers, or 9 lbs. 14 oz. 12 drs.

PUNT, a small ship's boat; a gunner's flat-bottomed boat for wild-fowl shooting.

PUNTILLA (Spanish), a narrow point-lace edging; a graver.

PUNTO, a petty Maltese linear measure, the 12th part of a linea, and the 24th part of a palmo, which is 10¼ inches.

PUNTY, a long solid iron rod fixed to a piece of glass, to enable the workman to move it, and mould it easily.

PUNYU, a Malay name for the tortoise.

PUP, the whelp of a dog; a young seal.

PUPIL, a ward or scholar.

PUPLA, a local Indian name for the bark of an undefined scandent shrub used for dyeing an orange colour.

PUPPET, the upright supports of a mandrel; a little doll moved by wires in a show.

PURBECK-STONE, a harsh rough alkaline sandstone, of an ash colour, used for buildings in London, and obtained from Purbeck in Dorsetshire.

PURCHASE, any thing bought; in seamen's language to haul or draw; also a tackle or lift; any mechanical power which increases the force applied.

PURDAH, an Indian cotton cloth, with white and blue stripes used for curtains, &c.

PURE-FINDER. *See* PUER.

PURÉE (French), soup made of pease or lentils.

PURGERIE (French), a bleaching or refining house for sugar.

PURKALAH, cambric of various colours made in India.

PURL, boiled beer with gin, sugar, and spice added; two rounds in knitting.

PURLINS, timbers lying across the main-rafters of a building.

PURNS, the dried dung of horses and cattle collected for fuel in some parts of Scotland.

PURMATA, the Malay name for a jewel.

PURPLEHEART, a local name for trees of Essequibo, the *Copaifera pubiflora* and *bracteata*, which yield a timber possessing great strength, durability, and elasticity. It is used for windmill shafts, rollers, and machinery.

PURPLE-WOOD, an undefined Brazilian wood, principally used for ramrods, and occasionally for buhl-work, marquetry, and turning: varieties of king-wood are sometimes called purple and violet woods; but these are variegated, while the true purple wood is plain.

PURPURINE, a substance extracted from garancine by alum.

PURREE, a yellow pigment obtained from India. *See* INDIAN-YELLOW.

PURRELA (Spanish), a name for wine of a very inferior quality.

PURSE, a money-bag, of which there are various kinds, leather, netted, &c.; a Turkish sum of money equivalent to 500 piastres, or £5 sterling. In Persia the purse is 50 tomans of 10s. each. *See* PORTE-MONNAIE.

PURSE-CLASP, a snap and catch for a purse.

PURSE-LOOM, a lady's machine for weaving or netting fancy bead and silk purses.

PURSE-MAKER, a manufacturer of leather and other money pouches.

PURSE-NET, a net placed over the burrows of rabbits to snare them, when hunted out of their holes by a ferret.

PURSER, a kind of cabin steward or providore in a passenger ship; the cashier of a mining adventure. *See* PAYMASTER.

PURSE-SLIDES, small rings of vegetable ivory, pearl, steel, or ivory to slip over a netted silk purse.

PURSE-STRETCHER, a piece of satin-wood or rose-wood for distending a purse.

PURSE-TASSELS, steel or other pendants for the ends of a purse.

PURSILL, a name in Scotland for an edible fucus. *See* BADDERLOCKS.

PURSUER, a law term for a plaintiff.

PURSUIVANT, a herald's officer at arms.

PURTALLAH, an Indian name for a leather belt.

PURVEYOR, one who supplies provisions; a providore.

PUSSERREE, an Indian weight of 5 seers, each 2 lbs. 6 oz. troy, but varying considerably in different localities, and analogous to the vis or dhurra.

PUSTULATUS MOSS, a dye-lichen, the *Umbilicaria pustulata*.

PUT-AND-CALL, a Stock-exchange term. *See* OPTION.

PUTCHUCK, an Eastern name for the roots of *Aucklandia Costus*, the *Costus Arabicus* of the ancients. About two million pounds are annually collected on the mountains of Cashmere. It is chiefly exported to China, where it is used as incense.

PUTERA, an Indian name for *Typha elephantina*, the leaves of which are employed in the East for making mats and baskets.

PUTERBRATEN (German), a roast turkey.

PUT-KUTNELLUM, an Indian name for holdings, or lands which have been assessed and farmed out.

PUTOO, an esteemed dish made by the Singhalese, of kelingoo flour, or meal from the young shoots of the palmyra-palm, scraped cocoa-nut, and unripe Jack-fruit, and steamed over a boiler.

PUTTAH, a name in India for a double-edged sword, with a guard-handle, or basket-hilt.

PUTTEN, a Cochin-Chinese coin of the value of ten pice (4d.), which has recently become the general circulating medium, available for all ordinary purposes. Eighteen puttan and six pice, should go to the rupee, but it varies two or three pice, according to local circumstances.

PUTTOO, a coarse thick fabric made of the refuse wool and long hair from the shawl goat, *Capra changra*.

PUTTY, a cement composed of fresh powdered chalk, or whiting, and raw linseed-oil, kneaded to the consistency of dough, which is largely used by glaziers to fix panes of glass in sashes, and by painters to stop crevices in wood, &c. About 16,000 tons are annually made in the United Kingdom.

PUTTY-KNIFE, a blunt round-pointed knife, used by glaziers and painters, to spread putty.

PUTTY-POWDER, a white powder, the pulverized oxide of tin, or of tin and lead mixed, used in polishing metals, glass, &c.

PUTWA, an Indian name for string and ropes made from the fibre of *Bauhinia racemosa*.

PUTWARREE, a registrar or collector under an Indian zemindar, or land-holder.

PUYOU, the Malay name for the quail.

PUZZLES, various articles of turnery ware and carving; dissecting maps, and pictures for children.

PUZZOLANO, volcanic ashes imported from the Mediterranean, much used in mixing with mortar, to make hydraulic cement.

P. Y. C., an abbreviation in the tallow-trade, for "Prime Yellow Candle" tallow, imported from Russia.

PYDLE, the name in Scotland for a kind of bag-net for catching fish.

PYLA, a wooden cup used for measuring grain in some parts of the Bengal presidency; the average weight of which in cleaned rice is about 1¼ lb.

PYLEE, a dry-measure used in India; in Bombay only 2·800 lbs., but in most other localities, 10 to 12 lbs.

PYRITES, fire-stone; a term applied very indiscriminately to many of the metallic sulphides, especially to sulphuret of iron.

PYROGALLIC-ACID, an acid obtained by cautiously distilling either gallic or tannic acid. Among other uses it is employed to stain the hair brown.

PYROLIGNEOUS-ACID, the vinegar obtained from hard woods, by destructive distillation. *See* ACETIC-ACID.

PYROMETER, a chemical instrument for registering very high temperatures, depending on the uniform and permanent contraction of pure clay. Daniell's is now considered the best.

PYROTECHNICS, a name for rockets, squibs, and various kinds of fireworks.

PYROTECHNIST, a maker and vender of fireworks.

PYSA, a coin current in Central Asia, the 50th part of a Mahmoud-Shahi rupee.

PYSSEE, a name for the soft wheat of India.

Q.

QUACK, a pretender to a knowledge of physic.

QUACK MEDICINES, nostrums which have a fictitious reputation for wonderful cures.

QUADRANT, a mathematical instrument for taking astronomical observations and measuring altitudes and angular distances.

QUADRANT COMPASSES, a carpenter's tool.

QUADRANT-STAND, the rest or support for a quadrant.

QUADRAT, a thick space or square of metal to represent a space in printing. There are m quadrats and n quadrats.

QUADRILLE-BAND, a small band of musicians attending at evening parties, to play the popular airs for quadrilles, and other dances.

QUAICH, a small shallow drinking-cup with two ears, formerly used in Scotland.

QUAICK, the Indian name for a basket in Guiana.

QUAILS, birds resembling the partridge, the *Coturnix vulgaris*, which are sometimes obtained in prodigious numbers in the South of Europe, and imported to this country.

QUALITY-BINDING, a kind of worsted tape used in Scotland for binding the borders of carpets.

QUALLY, a small elliptical iron pan, capable of holding about five gallons, used in Singapore for manufacturing sago over a fire.

QUAN, an imaginary coin of Cochin-China, worth about 3s. 6d. It consists of 10 mas (nominal money), or 600 sapeks, a zinc coin.

QUANNET, a tool for working horn and tortoise-shell.

QUANTAR, the Egyptian term for cwt., equal to 110 lbs., but it varies for different commodities, for coffee 108 lbs.; pepper, &c. 102; cotton 120; gums, &c., 150 lbs.

QUARANTINE, a surveillance for forty days over an infected ship, which is not permitted during that interval to communicate freely with the shore, but has to lie at a quarantine ground, or else the crew and passengers are transferred to a lazaretto.

QUARREE, a Spanish land-measure used in surveying, equal to 2 1-5th English acres, consequently 100 quarrees are equal to 320 acres.

QUARREL, a stone quarry in Scotland; a glazier's diamond.

QUARRIER. *See* QUARRYMAN.

QUARRY, originally a place where stones were squared; but now applied to a stone-bed or chalk-pit whence building materials are dug or cut; a diamond-shaped pane of glass, usually framed in lead; a small square stone for paving. The total number of quarries worked in the United Kingdom exceeds 1,500, and the annual products are worth more than £10,000,000.

QUARRY-MAN, QUARRIER, a workman engaged in a stone or slate quarry.

QUART, an English measure of capacity, the fourth part of a gallon, and weighing 2½ pounds avoirdupois of distilled water.

QUARTANA, a liquid-measure of Sardinia of 12 quartucci, = 7·395 pints.

QUARTARO, an Italian dry-measure of 1 gallon; for liquids about a third more.

QUARTAUT, a quarter-cask; the fourth part of a hogshead.

QUARTER, the fourth part of any thing, as a quarter of lamb; an English measure of capacity, usually applied to grain, and containing 8 bushels of corn, weighing about 540 pounds avoirdupois of water. A quarter of maize or Indian corn weighs 420 lbs; also the part of a vessel's side between the main chains and the stern.

QUARTERA, a Spanish corn-measure equal to about the fourth of an English quarter.

QUARTER-DAY, the day which terminates a quarter, or when rent is due. The usual quarters are 25th March, 24th June, 29th September, and 25th December.

QUARTER-DECK, the part of the upper deck of a vessel of war abaft the main-mast, reaching from the stern to the gangway, appropriated to the use of the captain and commissioned officers.

QUARTER-GALLERY, a sort of balcony on the stern sides or quarters of a ship.

QUARTERLY, a literary publication issued every three months; payments made three-monthly.

QUARTER-MASTER, a petty officer in a vessel of war.

QUARTERN, a name given in London to the gill, the fourth of a pint; also the fourth part of a peck; a 4lb. loaf.

QUARTERON, a name in several countries of Europe for a quarter of a pound; also for the tale of some goods or a quarter of a hundred with one added in; a very variable liquid and dry measure.

QUARTERS, the place occupied by troops; the assigned stations of men and officers on ship-board, when prepared for action.

QUARTIER, a German wine-measure, about one-fourth less than an English quart; a Sardinian liquid-measure equal to 1 1-10th gallon.

QUARTIL, the fourth part of a real.

QUARTILLO, a Spanish liquid-measure, very variable; in some localities only half a pint, in others more than 7 pints; as a dry-measure about 2 pints.

QUARTINO, an Italian liquid measure, = 0·3630 pint; as a dry-measure variable: at Ferrara, 0·888 pints; at Milan, only 0·303 pint.

QUARTO, a Portuguese corn-measure ranging from 1½ to 3½ gallons: a Maltese weight, the fourth of the ounce; a book of 4 leaves to the sheet, usually written 4to.

QUARTUCCIO, a Maltese wine-measure equal to an imperial quart: an oil quart is there equal to 1 1-8th wine quart.

QUARTZ, a common name for several forms of silica occurring in primary rocks.

QUARTZ-CRUSHER, a pulverizing machine to reduce quartz, in order to obtain gold from it.

QUAS, a fermented beverage, made in Russia from barley-meal.

QUASSIA, a name for some bitter woods—the Surinam quassia is the produce of *Quassia amara*, and the Jamaica quassia of *Picræna excelsa*. They furnish a pure and simple bitter, and brewers are said to use the chips freely as a substitute for hops, although they have narcotic properties. *See* SIMAROUBA.

QUATEMBER (German), quarter-day.

QUATTRINO, a petty coin of Italy, the fifth part of a bajocco; an Italian long measure, = 0·3829 inch.

QUAY, a landing-place or wharf for loading and unloading goods from ships.

QUAY-BERTH, a loading or discharging berth for a ship in a public dock.

QUEBEC-OAK, a ship-building wood, obtained from the *Quercus alba*.

QUEEN, one of a set of chessmen, the principal piece in the game of chess.

QUEEN'S-COUNSEL, a counsel learned in the law, who assists the Attorney-general in cases on behalf of the Crown, and is not allowed to appear on behalf of claims adverse to State interests.

QUEEN'S-METAL, an alloy, imitating silver, which has a fine lustre, and is composed of 9 parts tin and 1 part each of lead, antimony, and bismuth.

QUEEN-WOOD, a term applied, occasionally, to woods of the greenheart and cocus character, imported from the Brazils.

QUENELLE, a kind of forcemeat-garnishing for a dish.

QUENT, a German weight, 64 making 1 Augsburg marc, equal to 3643 troy grains; 128 quent make 1 light German pound of 15 1-20th troy ounces.

QUENTCHEN. *See* QUINTIN.

QUERCITRON, a name for the black oak (*Quercus tinctoria*) of the United States, the wood of which is valuable for building, and for cutting into staves: the bark is used for tanning, while the cellular integument is extensively employed in dyeing wool, silk, and paper hangings, and forms an important article of export from Philadelphia.

QUERN, a hand-mill for grain.

QUESADILLA (Spanish), a sort of cheesecake or fritter.

QUESERO, a cheesemonger in Spain.

QUEY, the name in Scotland for a young heifer; a cow of two years old.

QUICKLIME, caustic-lime; calcined limestone, which has lost its carbonic acid by exposure to a strong heat.

QUICKSET, a name given to white-thorn, &c. hedges.

QUICKSILVER, the commercial name for mercury: our imports average 2½ to 3½ million pounds a year, chiefly from California and Spain. Alloyed with tin-foil, quicksilver forms the reflecting surface of looking-glasses, and by its ready solution of gold or silver, and subsequent dissipation by a moderate heat, it becomes the great instrument in the arts of gilding and silvering copper and brass. The same property makes it so available in extracting these precious metals from their ores. It is also the basis of many very powerful medicines.

QUILATA, a Brazilian weight for precious stones, = 4·23-50th dwts. troy.

QUILL, the name for a pivot or axle on a shuttle, which is loaded with weft yarn; the hard and strong feather of the wing in geese and swans—imported in large quantities for making writing pens. The barrels of the feathers of turkeys, ducks, and crows are also used to a limited extent. We imported in 1855 nearly 26½ millions of foreign goose and swan quills, but feather pens are much superseded now by the very general adoption of metallic pens.

QUILLAI-BARK, the bark of *Quillaia saponaria*, used in South America to make a lather instead of soap, when washing woollens and silks.

QUILL AND PEN MERCHANT, an importer of quills; one who prepares them for use as pens by baking and stripping them.

QUILL-BITS, instruments for boring wood.

QUILLING, a narrow bordering of net.

QUILL-NIBS, small pens for placing in holders.

QUILOT, a variable grain-measure in use in the Levant. At Salonica, it is nearly double that of Smyrna and Constantinople.

QUILT, an outer bed-covering, of which there are many kinds, as Marseilles summer quilts, white or coloured, damask quilts, cot or crib quilts, &c.

QUILTING, a kind of figured material, made plain or coloured, for bed covers, toilet quilts, and vestings; a padding or lining.

QUINCAILLE (French), hardware; articles of copper, brass, and iron.

QUINCE, the fruit of the *Cydonia vulgaris*, which, when stewed, forms an agreeable food, and is used to flavour apple pies.

QUINCE-SEED, the seeds of the quince, which are sold to some extent for making a gummy fixature for the hair, and for a mucilage to be applied to cracked lips, &c.

QUINCE-TART, a pastry made or flavoured with quinces.

QUINCE-WINE, a pleasant beverage made of the fermented juice of the quince.

QUININE, a valuable alkaloid, extracted from Cinchona bark, and used as a stimulant and tonic in intermittents. The sulphate of quinine is used to a great extent in medicine, for a medicinal wine, and in other forms.

QUINITS, a kind of Spanish camlet.

QUINONS (Spanish), fine printed cotton.

QUINOA. See PETTY-RICE.

QUINQUILLERO, a hawker of ironmongery, &c. in Spain.

QUINQUINO, a South American tree, the *Myrospermum peruiferum*, which yields the balsam of Peru, a stimulant expectorant analogous to storax.

QUINTAL, a gross weight, which, in general, signifies 100 lbs., corresponding to the cwt. and centner of Great Britain and Germany in its uses, but of various weights in different States. The Castilla quintal of Spain consists of 4 arrobas, 100 lbs. Spanish, or 101·43 avoirdupois. The metrical quintal of France is 100 kilogrammes or 220·49 lbs.

QUINTALADA, a commission of 2½ per cent. on the freight, paid to masters of Spanish vessels.

QUINTERIA, a farm or grange in Spain.

QUINTERNO, a Spanish and Italian name for the fifth of a quire of paper, about 5 sheets.

QUINTIN (Spanish), a kind of fine cloth of a loose texture; the quintin or quintchen is also the fourth part of the lotir, a weight in Denmark.

QUIRATE, a name for the carat in Egypt.

QUIRE, a defined quantity of paper, of outsides, 20 sheets; but, if perfect, 24 sheets; in printing-paper 25 sheets.

QUIRK, in building, a narrow angular indentation in a moulding; a moulding increased by an additional twist.

QUITANZA (Spanish), a receipt.

QUITASOL (Spanish), a parasol.

QUITCH, a name for couch grass, the *Triticum repens*, a common weed, the rhizomes of which are, however, diaphoretic, aperient, and refreshing, and are made into diet drinks, and used as a substitute for sarsaparilla. For other uses *See* COUCH-GRASS and GRAMIGNA.

QUIT-RENT, a rent paid by the tenant of a freehold, discharging him from any other rent.

QUITTANCE, a recompence, release, or receipt.

QUITTE (German), the quince.

QUODDY, a kind of scaled herring, which are smoked or salted in the North American provinces.

QUOINS, wedge-like pieces of wood, used by printers to block up the forms in the chase, and keep the type firmly secured; also a name among builders for the corners of stone and brick walls; a wooden wedge for the breech of a gun to rest upon.

QUOIT, a flat iron ring for throwing at a mark in the game of quoits.

QUORUM, a legal or sufficient number of a committee, or board of directors, to hold a meeting and transact business.

QUOTATIONS, current prices for stock and shares, or for articles of produce in the market for sale; printers' marks, as follows, " ", showing passages have been cited or quoted.

QUOY, a name in Scotland for enclosed common land.

QUOYANE, a measure used in Malacca of 800 gantons, each 6½ lbs. For rice, the quoyane is 40 Chinese peculs, and is supposed to weigh 5,400 lbs.

R.

R. A., an abbreviation for "Royal Academician, Rear-Admiral, or Royal Artillery."

RABA (Spanish), bait used in the pilchard fishery.

RABADAN, the principal of a sheep-walk in Spain.

RABANO (Spanish), a radish.

RABATO, a neck-band or ruff.

RABATTAGE (French), a deduction or tare; the picking of wool.

RABAZUZ, a Spanish name for the inspissated juice of liquorice.

RABBET, a part of the keel, stern, and sternpost of a ship; a groove in the edge of a board.

RABBET-PLANE, a carpenter's tool for making grooves or rabbet-joints.

RABBIT-HUTCH, a box or cage for keeping tame rabbits in.

RABBITS and HARES, prolific rodents, species of *Lepus*, which, besides their employment as food, furnish to commerce useful articles in their skins. In Spain the hair of the skins is shaved off, and put to the same purpose as down. Nearly a million rabbits are sold annually in London, and we export about a million and a half rabbit and hare skins yearly; while about a quarter of a million hare skins are received from the Continent.

RABBIT-WARREN, an open common or preserved enclosure for wild rabbits to breed in.

RABBLE, a furnace tool; an iron rake for skimming off the slag in calcining metals.

RACAHOU, RACAHOUT, an Arabian substitute for chocolate; a preparation of roasted acorns, powdered, with sugar and aromatics. *See* PALAMOUD.

RACE, a distinct or particular breed of animals; a contest for speed between horses, &c.; a strong current or rippling tide; a form of root, as of ginger.

RACE-COURSE, the canal along which the water is conveyed to and from a water-wheel; a level ground on which horse-races are run.

RACE-CUP, a prize-plate run for in a match or race by horses over a course.

RACE-HORSE, a thorough-bred horse, trained to run for prizes, of which there are some 1,500 to 2,000 kept in Great Britain.

RACHI, arrack, a spirituous drink made in Turkey.

RACINAGE (French), a decoction of rind and walnut-tree leaves for dyeing.

RACION, a Spanish dry-measure, the fourth of the quartillo, and rather more than half a pint.

RACK, a wooden frame for hay in a stable, or for bottles, plates, &c. to drain in; a toothed wheel or bar of metal; an inclined plane on which ore is washed; an abbreviation for arrack, and often applied as a prefix to punch, of which it forms a principal ingredient.

RACKAY, a weight for the precious metals in Sumatra, about 1½ grain troy.

RACK-CHASE, in printing, the frame in which the chases are kept.

RACKET, a stringed battledore for striking a racket-ball: a snow-shoe.

RACKET-COURT, a tennis court.

RACKET-MAKER, a maker of stringed battledores.

RACKING, clearing wine, &c.; in mining, washing off the earth and impurities from the ore.

RACKING-CAN, a metal vessel containing sour beer in which iron wire is steeped for wire-drawing; a vessel for clearing wine from the lees.

RACK-RENT, the full yearly value of land: a high rate of rent without any deductions.

RACK-SAW, a wide-toothed saw.

RACLOIR (French), a scraper; a grater; an instrument to strike off the heaped corn in a measure.

RACOON, the *Procyon lotor*, an animal inhabiting chiefly the northern parts of America. The dark skins of some are very handsome and valuable. We import about half a million skins yearly, which are sent to the Continent, being used in Russia for sledge-wrappers, and lining coats, and the common kinds for hat-making in Germany.

RACOONDA, an old name for the fur of the coypu. *See* NUTRIA.

RADEAU (French), a raft; a float of timber.

RADEUR, a salt meter in France.

RADIOMETER, a forestaff; an instrument for taking the altitudes of the celestial bodies.

RADISH, a small well-known esculent root, the *Raphanus sativus*, and its varieties, which are sub-acrid, succulent, and tender, when young.

RAEDERA (Spanish) a scraper; a cylinder for reducing lead into sheets.

RAFFES (French), the cuttings or clippings of leather in glove-making, &c.

RAFFLE, the disposition of an article by lottery, according to throws of dice.

RAFF-MERCHANT, a lumber-merchant.

RAFT, a rough float of spars, or planks; an extensive collection of rough or squared timber logs drifted or floated down a stream. Some of the timber rafts which descend the Rhine, the Mississippi, the Ohio, and the St. Lawrence, are of immense size, and worth £20,000 to £30,000.

RAFTERS, the ribs of the roof of a house; the beams on which the roofing rests.

RAFTSMAN, the manager of a raft of timber.

RAG, stone that breaks into jagged pieces; a large kind of slate; a torn, worn, or waste piece of linen or woollen cloth. *See* RAGS.

RAGA, a grain-measure of the Sooloo and Sunda isles, in weight 5½ lbs.

RAG-BROKER. *See* RAG-MERCHANT.

RAG-DEALER, a marine store-dealer.

RAGEE, the Hindustani name for a species of millet, *Eleusine coracana*.

RAG-FAIR, a metropolitan market for vending old clothes, and cast-off garments.

RAG-GATHERER, an itinerant collector of rags from the streets, dunghills, and sewers.

RAGGED-SCHOOL, a free school for the education of the children of the poor.

RAGGING. *See* STRAGGLING.

RAGMAN, RAG-MERCHANT, a wholesale purchaser of rags from collectors, marine-store dealers, and individuals, for re-sale to paper manufacturers, farmers, and others.

RAGOUT, a high-seasoned dish.

RAGS, the fragments and shreds of worn-out garments and drapery, woollen or linen, collected for various purposes throughout the kingdom, and amounting, with those imported, to more than 70,000 tons a-year, worth fully a million sterling. Woollen rags are used for manure, for working up into shoddy, or coarse cloths and druggets, and for flock-paper; linen rags for making lint, and paper; and cotton rags for paper-pulp.

RAG-SHOP, a place where rags, bones, kitchen grease, scrap metal, and other refuse articles are purchased in small quantities.

RAGSTONE, a description of hone-slate, used as a whetstone; a kind of sandstone or limestone found in Kent.

RAG-WHEEL, a wheel with a notched edge.

RAHAL, an Arabian name for a camel-load, about 5 cwts.

RAHMEL, REMEL, a German term for a bundle of flax of 20 lbs.

RAI, RAKE, names in Hindostan for some species of mustard-seed, as *Sinapis nigra*, and *S. ramosa*.

RAIK, a weight and measure for grain in Bengal of 20 chittacks, and weighing 2½ lbs.

RAIL, a long narrow bar of iron used for railways; a horizontal timber in a piece of panelling; a piece of wood resting on stakes or posts, forming part of a fence of wooden rails.

RAILROAD, RAILWAY, levelled and prepared roads, laid with iron bars, for locomotives and carriages to travel easily, of which there are many thousand miles laid throughout the United Kingdom, and a large number in other countries. In the United Kingdom there are about 8,500 miles of railway; in the United States, 24,500 miles, in operation. On the Continent, in India, and in the Colonies, they are also spreading.

RAILWAY-BARS, long wrought iron bars, 15 feet by 2½ to 3 inches broad, and 5 inches deep, laid down and fixed on a prepared road for locomotive engines, railway carriages, and waggons to travel on.

RAILWAY-BLANKET, RAILWAY-RUG, a traveller's warm wrapper.

RAILWAY-CARRIAGE, a passenger carriage drawn by an engine on a railway line, which are variously fitted for the accommodation of first, second, and third class passengers.

RAILWAY-CARRIAGE-SPRING MAKER, a manufacturer of the metal springs for railway carriages.

RAILWAY-CHAIR. *See* CHAIR.

RAILWAY-CHAIRMAN, the head of a railway-board.

RAILWAY-COMPANION, a pocket-case for a traveller on a railway, for holding sandwiches or other refreshments.

RAILWAY-CROSSING, the place where an ordinary road crosses a railway line.

RAILWAY-DEPOT, the goods station of a railway.

RAILWAY-DIRECTOR, a managing member of a railway board or committee.

RAILWAY-ENGINE, a locomotive steam-engine for drawing a railway train.

RAILWAY-GREASE MANUFACTURER. *See* GREASE, and GREASE-MAKER.

RAILWAY-LINK, a draw-link.

RAILWAY-MARKET, the Stock-exchange; where shares are dealt in.

RAILWAY-PLANT, the locomotives, carriages, trucks, and general machinery, for working a railway.

RAILWAY-SCRIP, the first or preliminary certificate issued on account of money paid for railway shares.

RAILWAY-SIGNAL, a telegraph, light, or combustible to give notice of the approach or departure of trains. *See* FOG-SIGNAL.

RAILWAY-SLEEPER, a cross timber for carrying the iron rails.

RAILWAY-SLIDE, a turn-table.

RAILWAY-SPECTACLES, wire-gauze shades for the eyes, to protect them from dust, &c. when travelling.

RAILWAY-STATION, the place whence railway trains start.

RAILWAY-STOCK, the capital invested in a railway.

RAILWAY-SUPERINTENDANT, the general traffic-manager of a railway, or a special officer at a station.

RAILWAY-SWITCH, an instrument for moving the diverging points of the rails at a station, and thus changing the route of the trains.

RAILWAY-TICKET, a pass given at a railway office in return for the money fare paid.

RAILWAY TIME-TABLE, a printed list of the hours of arrival or departure of trains, fares, &c. on a railway.

RAILWAY-TRACK, the line of iron rails on which the train travels.

RAILWAY-TRAIN, a connected set of carriages and breaks, drawn by a locomotive engine.

RAILWAY-TRUCK, a wagon for conveying baggage or merchandise on a railway.

RAILWAY TURN-TABLE MANUFACTURER, a maker of the circular revolving platforms or sliding frames, called turntables, by which carriages, &c. are transferred from one set of rails to another, at a depot or station.

RAILWAY-WHEEL MAKER, a manufacturer of the peculiar metal wheels required for carriages and engines travelling on a railway line.

RAILWAY-WHISTLE, a mechanical contrivance on the locomotive, by which a loud, shrill, warning sound is given, to call attention in tunnels, or at the approach of the train to stations.

RAILWAY-WRAPPER, RAILWAY-RUG, a blanket to cover the legs in travelling.

RAINETTE (French), a compositor's knife; a rennet apple.

RAIN-GAUGE, an instrument for registering the fall of rain in a given period. It has also various other names, as hygrometer, ombrometer, pluviometer, &c. Its principles and construction are of the simplest nature, but it is made of a variety of shapes.

RAIN-WATER-CASK, RAIN-WATER-TANK, a receptacle for rain-water, for domestic washing purposes.

RAIN-WATER-HEAD, a hollow receptacle of iron at the top of a rain water pipe, receiving the water from the gutter.

RAIN-WATER-PIPE, a hollow tube of cast or wrought iron, made in lengths, for carrying off rain water from the eaves of a roof.

RAISED PIE, a solid meat pie, baked without a dish, served at suppers, déjeuners, &c. *See* PORK PIE.

RAISINS, dried grapes, imported chiefly from Malaga and Smyrna, to the extent of 12,000 or 13,000 tons annually, as a dessert fruit, and for puddings.

RAISIN-WINE, a British home-made sweet wine from raisins.

RAJADILLO (Spanish), a comfit of sliced almonds crusted with sugar.

RAJETA, a kind of Spanish coarse cloth of mixed colours.

RAJIKA, a Sanscrit name for black mustard seed.

RAKE, a gardening or agricultural tool with teeth and a handle; several of these, as horse-rakes, stubble-rakes, hay-rakes, and drag-rakes, are drawn by horses; the inclination or slope of a mast from the perpendicular.

RAKEE, a common Russian brandy.

RAKITZER, a first-quality flax in some of the provinces of Russia.

RAM, the male of the sheep.

RAMA (Spanish), a rack; a chase for holding printing-type.

RAMASSEUR (French), the driver of a mountain sledge termed a ramasse.

RAMBERGUE, a kind of galley.

RAMBIYA, a Malay name for the sago-palm.

RAMBOOSE, a mixed drink of ale, milk, &c.

RAMBOUR, a large French baking apple.

RAMBUT, a Malay name for hair.

RAME (French), a scull or oar; a stick for pease; a ream of paper.

RAMEQUIN (French), a Welsh rabbit, or toasted cheese.

RAMILLETE (Spanish), a nosegay; a pyramid of sweetmeats and fruits.

RAMMER, a heavy pavior's hammer.

RAMONEUR (French), a chimney-sweeper; a contrivance for sweeping chimneys without the necessity of climbing boys.

RAMROD, an iron or wooden stick for ramming down the load or charge of a gun.

RAMSAWMY, an Indian silver cigar lighter.

RAM'S-HORN, the crooked horn of a ram, often mounted for a mull or snuff-box.

RAM-TIL, black til, the *Guizotia oleifera* of Decandolle; the *Verbesina sativa* of Roxburgh; grown in Bombay and Madras, which yields a large quantity of bland oil like olive oil.

RAMTURAI, a name in Hindustan for the ochro.

RANCHER (French), a ladder.

RANCHERIA (Spanish), a hut or cottage.

RANCHERO (Spanish), the steward of a mess.

RANCHO, a Spanish cattle station.

RANCID, applied to fat that has become rank or sour.

RANCIO, Spanish red wine turned yellow by age.

RAND, a border or shred; a shoemaker's name for a thin inner sole or cover of cork, leather, &c; a small Dutch liquid-measure, 396 of which go to a leaguer of 160 wine gallons.

RANDAN, a miller's name for the finest parts of the bran or outside skin of the wheat. In some counties it bears other names.

RANDY, an Indian weight of 80 dhurras, weighing ordinarily 493 5-7ths. lbs., but variable.

RANFORSEE, an obsolete name for a kind of black silk made in former years.

RANGE, a fire-place and cooking-stove for a kitchen, cottage, &c.; the step in a ladder; the compass or reach of a cable, gun, or piece of ordnance.

RANGER, the chief keeper of a forest or park; one who inspects and regulates woods and forests; a dog that beats the ground.

RANK-AND-FILE, the soldiers in an army who carry firelocks.

RAPATELLE, the French name for tammy; a kind of horse-hair cloth.

RAPE, the refuse raisin stalks and skins left after making British wines, used by vinegar makers, the vinegar being filtered through the mass in large wooden vessels; a name for several fusiform varieties of *Brassica*, as the summer rape, *B. campestris*; the winter rape, *B. napus*; and others, cultivated for their seed, from which oil is expressed. *See* COLZA-OIL. A debased coin current in Basle, Switzerland, for 2 pennings.

RAPE-CAKE, the mass left after rape seed has been pressed for oil, dried, and prepared as food for cattle and for manure. *See* OIL-CAKE

RAPE-OIL. *See* COLZA-OIL.

RAPE-SEED, the seed of plants of the cole kind, threshed out for making oil, or for planting. In 1855, we imported from the Continent 162, 853 quarters of rape-seed.

RAPE-WINE, a poor thin wine from the last dregs of raisins, which have been pressed.

RAPID, the fall of a river; "shooting the rapids," is descending the stream over these strong river currents.

RAPIER, a long thin fencing sword.

RAPPADURA, a very coarse kind of sugar made in Mexico; it is met with in long cylindrical pieces of about one pound weight, each piece carefully covered with flag leaves.

RAPPEE, a kind of snuff of either a brown or black colour, which is sometimes scented. It is made from the darker and ranker kind of tobacco leaves moistened.

RAPPEL, the beat of the drum to call soldiers to arms.

RAPPEN, a Swiss coin, the tenth part of a franc, the same as a batz, nearly 1d.

Rarak, the Malay name for the soap-berry, *Sapindus emarginatus*.

Rasa, the Malay name for quicksilver.

Rasamala, an Eastern name for the *Liquidambar altingia*, which affords the balsam called liquid storax.

Rase (French), pitch for caulking seams.

Rasete (Spanish), satinet.

Rasette (French), a reed-spring in an organ.

Rash, a measure of capacity for salt used in Bombay, weighing about 40 tons; nearly 14½ lasts.

Rasher, a thin slice of bacon for frying, &c.

Rasiere, a heaped corn-measure formerly used in Belgium and Flanders, 1½ to 5 bushels in different localities; in Sardinia 8½ starelli, very nearly 4⅓ bushels. The French rasiere (now 2 hectolitres) was 5½ bushels.

Raso, (Spanish), satin; a long measure of Piedmont and Sardinia, 21½ to 23½ inches.

Rasp, a large rough coarse file. *See* File.

Raspberry, the fragrant subacid fruit of the *Rubus Idæus*, employed for the dessert, and also in very general use for jams and tarts: it is likewise converted into a kind of vinegar.

Raspberry-vinegar, a pleasant acid beverage or flavouring liqueur, made from the juice of raspberries: diluted with water it forms a refreshing drink in fevers.

Rasper, a kind of scraping or kitchen grater for rasping loaves, &c.

Rasping-mill, a species of saw-mill.

Rasp-maker, a manufacturer of rough files.

Rassade (French), hollow glass beads or bugles.

Rassy, a kind of boiled coarse rice in India.

Ratafia, a kind of liqueur flavoured with apricot kernels; cherry or raspberry brandy; a sweet fancy wine-biscuit.

Rat-bane, a poison sold to kill rats.

Rat-catcher, a man who makes a business of trapping and clearing premises of rats.

Ratch, a bar containing small angular teeth; a ratchet-wheel being a circular ratch, with teeth like a saw.

Ratchell, loose stones.

Rat-dealer, one who buys and sells rats to be baited by dogs; or for their skins.

Rate, a tax levied rateably on persons assessable to it; a standard or comparative price.

Ratekanuj, an Indian name for tar and colophony.

Ratego (Spanish), articles or goods carried in carts.

Ratlines, pieces of small rope fastened across the shrouds, forming steps whereby to ascend the rigging.

Ratmara, a vernacular name for a dyeing lichen in India.

Ratoon, a colonial name for a fresh shoot from the stool of the sugar cane; which is called first or second ratoons, according as it is the first or second year's sprout, after the crop, from the first planting of the cane, has been reaped.

Rattail-file. *See* File.

Rattanas, a species of coarse sacking, made of a long st[illegible] fibre in Madagascar, about five feet square, and largely used, in the island of Mauritius, to dry sugar on.

Rattan-dealer, a stick merchant, or dealer in canes, &c.

Rattans, a commercial name for the long trailing stems of the *Calamus Rotang*, *C. rudentum*, and various other species of palms, which form a considerable article of import from India and the Eastern archipelago. They are extensively used, when split, for caning chairs, and for making rough brooms, and, when dyed black, as a substitute for whalebone for umbrella ribs, and for stiffening bonnets. The imports, in 1855 exceeded 80,000 bundles, of 100 canes each, besides one million reeds, canes, and other sticks.

Rattany-root, **Rhatany**, a powerful astringent root, the produce of *Krameria triandra*; used medicinally, and for tooth-powder and mouth-washes.

Ratteen, a kind of woollen stuff.

Rattle, a policeman's or watchman's alarm, made double or single; a child's toy of different kinds; a division of the maund or commercial weight in Bangalore, where 24 rattles make 1 maund of 25lbs.; in Travancore 25 rattles or rauttals = the maund of 18lbs. 12 oz. 13 grs.; an Arab weight. *See* Rottolo.

Ratureur (French), an eraser for parchment.

Raughan, the name in Persia for butter made from sheep's milk, and preserved in a liquid state.

Ravelled, thread tangled or twisted.

Ravenchenny, an Indian name for gamboge.

Ravensara-nuts, the produce of *Agathophyllum aromaticum*, found in Madagascar, where they are used as a spice, and from thence occasionally exported to France.

Ravensduck, a kind of canvas or sail-cloth.

Raverdoir (French), a brewer's oval vat.

Ravigote (French), a sauce made of shallots and other seasonings.

Raw materials, a commercial name for goods and articles in their rough or undressed state, previous to manufacture; such as raw silk, raw cotton, raw or unrefined sugar, raw hides, &c.

Rawund, **Rewund**, Indian names for rhubarb.

Ray (French), a quantity of wool from 30 to 40lbs.; a kind of net; a genus of cartilaginous fish, the *Raia*, some of which are edible.

Raza, a salt-measure used in Portugal; nearly 1½ bushel.

Razago, coarse cloth made of tow in Spain.

Razchive, a small vessel employed in Russian trade, on the Caspian sea, of 70 to 140 tons burthen.

Raze, an old dry-measure of Brittany; 1·378 bushel.

Razee, a vessel of war which has had one deck cut down.

Razor, a kind of scraping-knife or sharp-edged instrument for shaving.

Razor-blade Maker, a forger and manufacturer of the metal part of razors.

Razor-case Maker, a workman who makes the small cases to hold one or more sets of razors.

Razor-fish, the *Solen siliqua*, a bivalve, whose shell is shaped like a razor. It is very common on the sands and dug up for sale as food.

Razor-grinder, a knife-grinder; one who sets edge tools.

Razor-maker, a manufacturer and finisher of razors for sale; the trade is chiefly carried on at Sheffield and Birmingham.

Razor-scale Presser, a maker of the side pieces of horn, bone, tortoise-shell, &c., used for the handles of razors.

Razor-strop Maker, a manufacturer of leather or other strops for setting and sharpening razors.

Razor-strop-paste Maker, a maker of a composition for rubbing on razor-strops.

Reaction Water-wheel, the wheel of a mill where the water reacts on the curved vanes or buckets, producing a backward rotatory motion.

Reader, a corrector of the press in a printing-office.

Reading-boy, one who reads the copy to a press corrector.

Reading-desk, a clergyman's rostrum; a stand for reading at in a library.

Reading-hook, a book-marker, made of bone or ivory, plain or carved.

Reading-room, a public room where newspapers and periodicals, &c. are consulted; the principal room of public reference for books in the British Museum.

Ready-made, articles prepared beforehand, and kept in stock; not made to order or pattern.

Ready-made Linen Warehouse, an outfitter's or shirt-maker's shop; a juvenile warehouse for baby-linen, &c.

Ready Money, a prompt payment for articles; not credit.

Ready-reckoner, a book of tables and figures, giving the prices of articles or quantities, without the trouble of arithmetical calculation.

Real, Rial, plural **Reaux**, a silver coin of the southern and central American States, worth from 3d. to 6d. The pure 8 real pieces are worth a dollar, those of base, or alloyed metal, less. In Mexico, there are quarter reals worth about 3 cents; the twenty-fourth part of the piastre divided into 34 maravedi.

Realejo, a chamber-organ in Spain; a small real.

Realgar, one of the names of bisulphide of arsenic.

Realillo, a small Spanish silver coin of the value of 2½d.

Real Property, Real Estate, property in houses and land, contra-distinguished from money or goods, which are termed personal or moveable property.

Ream, a package of paper containing 20 quires, 500 sheets of damaged or outsides; 480 of writing-paper; and 500 of printing paper; a bale is ten reams; a leather rope or strap. *See* **Reins**.

Reaper, a labourer employed in cutting corn; also the name for a machine used for harvesting grain; a building lath in the East. *See* **Reepers**.

Reaping-hook, a sickle for cutting corn.

Reaping-machine, a machine which cuts and lays corn, and thus economizes hand labour.

Rear-admiral, a naval officer ranking below a vice-admiral.

Reas, a former subdivision of the rupee at Bombay; 100 reas were = 1 quarter; and 4 quarters = 1 rupee; also a Portuguese coin.

Rebano (Spanish), a flock of sheep.

Rebate, a discount; a groove or channel sunk on an edge; a kind of free-stone; a tool to beat up mortar.

Rebate Plane, Rabbet Plane, a tool like a chisel. *See* **Plane**.

Rebenque, a name in Cuba for thin pieces of jerked beef cured in Central America.

Rebocino, a short cloak worn in Spain.

Rebotadera, an iron plate or card used in Spain for raising the nap on cloth to be shorn.

Rebotica, the back room behind an apothecary's shop in Spain.

Recamo (Spanish), embroidery of raised work.

Recaudador, a collector of rents and taxes in Spain.

Receipt, an acquittance; an acknowledgment of money or other articles, handed over from one person to another.

Receipt-book, a book containing instructions or prescriptions.

Receipt-stamp, a penny government stamp, affixed to settled accounts, which is either adhesive or impressed on the paper; when the former is used, it must be cancelled by the written initials of the party receiving the money.

Receiver, a cashier; one who knowingly takes stolen goods from a thief.

Receiving-house, a depot or store; a place where parcels are left to be collected for transport.

Recel (Spanish), a kind of striped tapestry.

Recipe, a medical prescription; a receipt for cooking.

Reciprocity Treaty, a treaty concluded between two countries, conferring equal privileges, whether for Customs' charges on imports, or other purposes.

Reckoning, the settlement at an inn or tavern; the estimated position of a ship at sea.

Reclining-chair, an easy chair for invalids.

Record, a state paper; an official register.

Recorder, a chief law-officer of the corporation of London; a local judge in a borough or municipality; the chief justice of an East Indian settlement; also a flageolet.

Record-office, a place for keeping state papers and official government documents.

Recruit, a newly enlisted soldier; one who has taken the government fee or bounty.

Recruiting Sergeant, a non-commissioned officer deputed to enlist recruits.

Rectified-spirits, alcohol which has been re-distilled and flavoured.

Rectifier, one who prepares raw spirits for the market.

Rector, a clergyman of the Established church holding the great tithes of a parish; the head of a scholastic establishment.

Recuage (Spanish), a Customs' charge or duty for the passage of cattle.
Recuero, a muleteer in Spain.
Red, one of the primitive colours, of which the chief commercial varieties are fine Venetian, red lead, orange, Indian red, and vermilion.
Red-chalk, Reddle, a soft form of sesquioxide of iron used as a crayon in drawing.
Red-currant, the fruit of the *Ribes rubra*, largely cultivated for the dessert and for cooking. The juice is refrigerant and grateful to persons suffering from fever, and is made into wine.
Reddle. *See* Red-chalk.
Red-ink. *See* Ink.
Red-lead, a pigment. *See* Minium.
Red Ochre. *See* Red-chalk.
Red-root. *See* Blood-root.
Red Sanders-wood, an East Indian dye-wood, the produce of the *Pterocarpus santalinus*, a hard heavy wood imported from Madras and Calcutta. In 1856 117,901 Indian maunds (36·428 tons) of this wood were shipped from Madras. Besides its use as a dye-wood it is employed as the basis of various dentifrice mixtures.
Red-stuff, a name among watchmakers for some kinds of crocus, or the prepared powder from oxide of iron.
Red-vitriol, sulphate of iron.
Red-ware, one of the names of a nutritious alga, the *Laminaria digitata*, which, when young, is employed as food both for man and cattle.
Red-wood. *See* Red Sanders-wood.
Reed, part of a loom; thatch; a musical pipe.
Reed-maker, a manufacturer of the metal dents or whalebone reeds for looms.
Reed-organ. *See* Melodeon.
Reed-pen, a writing stylus made in India from the *Saccharum Sara*.
Reef, a coral bank; a ledge of rocks; to reduce the dimensions of a ship's or boat's sail, by bandaging it up.
Reef-cringle, the ring of a sail. *See* Cringle.
Reef-knot, a mode of joining the ends of ropes together by two overhand knots.
Reef-point, flat pieces of cordage on a sail for tying it up, or reefing the sail in stormy weather.
Reel, a turning frame for winding thread; a wooden roller or bobbin for cotton, of wood, of ivory, or pearl, with metal stems, plain or carved for a lady's work box; a yarn-measure; a cotton or linen reel is 54 inches in circuit; a worsted reel, 30 inches.
Reel-cotton, sewing cotton wound on reels, not made up into balls.
Reel-stand, a holder for cotton reels for ladies' use, made of ebony or rosewood, &c.
Reeming, opening the seams between planks with a caulking iron.
Reepers, laths or longitudinal sections of the palmyra palm, used for building purposes in the East; the trunk of the tree is split into 8 for reepers, and these are dressed with an adze. In Ceylon they are made of the kittool palm, and known as Nipera reepers; these are dearer than any other kind, they last, in many instances, for 50 or 60 years.
Reeve, a steward; the head of a township; in nautical parlance, to pass the end of a rope through a block or a loop.
Re-exchange, to re-barter; the second exchange.
Re-export, to ship again what has been brought in from abroad; a re-tran-it.
Referee, an arbitrator; one selected to give an opinion, or to settle points in dispute.
Refiner. *See* Gold and Silver Refiner.
Refiners'-sweeps, the refuse filings or dust collected from the workshops of silversmiths and jewellers to be re-smelted.
Refining, the process of purifying, as sugar, minerals, saltpetre, spermaceti, &c.
Refit, a putting in order; as the repairs of a ship; restoring damage or wear and tear; a renovating of that which is decayed.
Reflecting Telescope, a spyglass, in which the rays from the object to be viewed are first received on a speculum.
Reflector, any thing that throws back an image, as a looking-glass; a polished metal plate for reflecting the light in lighthouses, &c.; a reflecting telescope. *See* Day-light reflector.
Refleuret (French), the second quality of Spanish wool.
Refrigerator, a cooling or freezing machine; an apparatus for icing drinks, &c.
Regalia, a kind of cigar; the ornamental clothing, jewels, &c. worn by members of the masonic order, odd-fellows, knights-templar, and other societies, and by high officers and dignitaries.
Reganada, a kind of cake made in Spain.
Regaton, a Spanish huckster; one who keeps a retail shop.
Regatta, a contest of row-boats or sailing vessels for prizes.
Regents, a choice variety of potato.
Regiment, a body of troops, cavalry, foot, or artillery, usually 1000 strong, commanded by a colonel.
Regimentals, the official clothing, or uniform, worn by a regiment.
Register, a record; the title to a ship, indicating to whom she belongs, and at what port she is registered; a kind of door-lift or iron plate for regulating the draught in a stove or parlour grate; the correspondence of pages in printing a sheet.
Registered Company, a joint-stock association, not possessing a charter or special act of incorporation, but registered under the Joint-stock Act.
Registered Letter, a letter or packet on which a fee of 4d. is paid to the General Post-office to insure its safe transmission.
Registering, a rope-maker's phrase for twisting yarns into a strand; entering names or documents officially at some proper office, as when electors, or seamen, are registered.
Registering-instruments, machines or instruments which register or record, such as gauges, indicators, and tell-tales.
Register-office, a record-office; a place for registry, as a register for seamen, for servants, &c.

REGISTRAR, one who keeps a record or books of public reference; an officer of the Customs.

REGISTRAR'S-OFFICE, a district office for registering births and deaths, and celebrating marriages, &c.; a central office for the registration of seamen of the merchant navy. The registrar-general, in London who is under the Board of Trade, has his office on Tower-hill.

REGLET, a flat narrow moulding; a ledge of wood, which printers use to separate the lines in posters and pages widely printed; a black border for columns of type.

RÉGLISSE, the French name for liquorice-root.

REGULUS, a metallic sulphide, or the pure metal separated from the ore, as regulus of arsenic, or antimony, &c.

REHABILITATION, the restoration of a bankrupt or other person to his former civil rights.

REI, REA, a small money of account in Portugal and Brazil, the thousandth part of a milrea, which is 4s. 2d.; the rei is therefore worth about the twentieth of a penny. The dollar is sometimes, however, worth more than a thousand reis, and sometimes less. *See* MILREA.

REIMS, a name in the Cape colony for strips of ox-hide, unhaired, and rendered pliable by grease, which are used for twisting into rope, and for various other purposes. *See* OX-REIMS, and TREK-TOW.

REIN, a leather strap to guide a horse; the part of a bridle connected to the bit.

REIN-DEER, the *Cervus Tarandus*, one of the most useful animals to the Laplanders and Norwegians, serving as a beast of burden, and supplying them with food and clothing, while of its milk they make cheese.

REINE-CLAUDE, the French name for the green-gage plum.

REIS EFFENDI, a secretary or Turkish officer of state.

REISNER-WORK, a kind of inlaid work.

REJOINDER, a law term for an answer put in by a defendant to the replication of a plaintiff.

RELAY, a supply of fresh horses kept on the road to relieve others.

RELEASE, the remission of a claim or penalty; an acquittance or full discharge in law; an extinguishment of right or title; the discharge of a debtor from custody.

RELIEF, a relay; replacing a sentinel; assistance given to the poor in money or food, by the parish authorities.

RELIEUR, a French bookbinder.

RELIEVING-OFFICER, a poor-law officer to whom paupers apply for casual assistance.

RELOJERO, a Spanish watchmaker.

REMEMBRANCER, a recorder of the exchequer; a parliamentary agent of the corporation of London.

REMISSION, a forgiveness of fine, penalty, or punishment.

REMITTANCE, a sum of money or funds transmitted.

REMNANTS, the ends of pieces of linen, cloth, ribbon, &c.

REMOLAR, a master carpenter in Spain, who makes oars.

REMONTISTA, a commissioner for the purchase of cavalry horses in Spain.

REMORQUEUR, a French tug-boat, employed on the Seine.

REMOVE, a dish to be changed while the rest of the course remains.

REMPLISSEUSE (French), a mender of point-lace.

REMPUJO, the Spanish name for a sewing thimble of iron or brass.

RENDER, to furnish an account; to give up; a sea term for passing a rope through a place.

RENDERING, a kind of rough plastering. *See* PARGETING.

RENDEZVOUS, an appointed meeting-place for ships.

RENGUE, a kind of gauze which counsellors wear in Spain on their sleeves and collar.

RENNET, a variety of apple; the gastric juice or concreted milk found in the true stomach of a sucking quadruped, particularly of the calf, which is used for curdling milk. When required for this purpose it is prepared by salting in water for some weeks.

RENSETTY, an Italian stuff for summer wear, of different colours, variously figured and striped.

RENT, an income; a payment made to another for the use or occupation of house or lands.

RENT-CHARGE, a tax paid for tithes.

RENT-COLLECTOR, an agent who demands or receives rents for an owner of house property.

RENTES, perpetual annuities in the French government funds.

RENTIER, a French fundholder; one who has an income from an estate or invested capital.

RENTO, a country residence with a farm-yard in Spain.

RENT-ROLL, the income of an estate; a list of occupiers or lessees paying rent.

REOJAR (Spanish), to bleach wax.

REPASSETTE (French), a very fine card for combing wool.

REPEAL, to annul or abolish laws, &c.

REPEATER, a watch that strikes the time upon pressing a spring.

REPLICATION, in law, an answer put in by a plaintiff to a defendant's plea.

REPORT, an account given of proceedings; the result of an inspection or examination made.

REPORTER, a shorthand writer; one who gives in a report.

REPOSITORY, a depot; a name very generally applied now to several kinds of warehouses, as horse and carriage repository, goods repository, fancy repository, &c.

REPOUS (French), mortar made with brick-dust.

REPOUSSE, a kind of ornamental silver designing, produced by repeated operations of the hammer on either side of the metal.

REREE, a name for the *Typha angustifolia*, used in the North-West Provinces of India, for making mats.

RESCATADOR (Spanish), a purchaser of the ores from working miners, who refines them at reduction works.

RESERVOIR, a store; a fish-pond; a water enclosure for canals, or water companies.

Resins, various alkaline bases, or oxides of essential oils. The acid resins comprise rosin, dammar, gamboge, sandarac, benzoin, lac, &c.; the neutral resins elemi, guaiacum, dragon's-blood, and storax. They will be found described under their special heads.

Reshipment, goods re-loaded and sent back again.

Resist, a sort of paste or mixture used in print-dyeing, to keep portions white, when the fabric is dipped in the dye-vat.

Resolution, a declaration or special vote, or series of votes, passed by a public body.

Respirator, a mouth protector of wire-gauze, &c., worn by persons with delicate lungs.

Respondentia, money raised upon the security of the cargo or lading of a ship.

Ressemeler (French), to new sole boots or shoes.

Rest, a name given to a surplus or guarantee fund held in reserve by a bank, to equalize its dividends, when the profits made fall below the amount required for paying the usual dividend to shareholders.

Restaurateur (French), the keeper of a restaurant, an eating-house or refreshment saloon.

Retail, selling by small quantities, or at second-hand.

Retainer, a fee paid to a lawyer or counsellor to engage him to plead in a cause.

Reticule, a lady's small hand-bag.

Retorsoir (French), a rope-spinner's twisting-wheel.

Retort, an iron cylinder in a gas-works for charging with coal to convert into gas; an apparatus for distilling; a chemical glass vessel with a bent neck.

Retort-house, the portion of gas-works, where the gas is manufactured, and the retorts are situated.

Retratista, a Spanish portrait-painter.

Return-chaise, a carriage going back empty from a post station.

Returning-officer, a presiding officer at an election.

Returns, a light-coloured kind of tobacco, of a milder character than some of the other qualities vended; tabulated government statistics issued for general information; profits or receipts in business; the figures or state of the poll at an election.

Return-ticket, a ticket by steam-boat or railway, taken for the journey out and home, usually at a reduction of charge.

Rev., an abbreviation for "reverend," an honorary prefix to the names of clergymen.

Revalenta Arabica, the farina of the lentil freed from the outer husk, and sold as food for infants and invalids.

Revêche (French), woollen baize.

Revendage goods sold for the benefit of creditors in France.

Revente (French), a second sale.

Revenue, an income; the general receipts of a State; a French name for young shoots of coppice-wood.

Revenue-cutter, a Custom-house vessel stationed in the Channel to prevent smuggling, and commanded by a naval officer.

Revenue-officer, an officer in the service of the Customs; an exciseman.

Reverberatory-furnace, a furnace, in which the heat is applied, to the body heated, by a flame playing on its surface.

Reverse, the back of a coin or medal.

Reversible-coat, a coat which may be turned and worn either side outwards, usually of two different colours and materials.

Reversing-gear, apparatus for making a locomotive or marine-engine move backwards.

Reversion, a deferred annuity; the right to an estate or money, after the death of the present owner.

Reversionary Interest Society, a company which deals in reversions and annuities.

Review, a critical examination of a new book; a publication devoted to criticism; a survey or inspection of troops.

Revise, the second proof of a sheet, taken after the corrections on the first have been made.

Revolution, the circular motion of a mill or steam-engine; the speed or power calculated by the number of revolutions per minute.

Rhatany. *See* Rattany-root.

Rheedy. *See* Riddy.

Rhinoceros, a pachyderm animal, which is hunted for its hide and horns. The skin is so thick and coarse, that, when tanned, targets and shields made of it are almost sword and bullet proof. It is much used for making the whips or samboks of the African colonists; and of the horn, drinking cups, the hilts of swords, and other articles are made.

Rhodium, a grey powder; a silver-white brittle metal, obtained from platinum ore, used by dentists and others.

Rhubarb, a genus of plants, the *Rheum*, of extensive use, the stalks of some British varieties being used for making pies and wine. As much as 100,000 dozen bundles are annually sold in London; while the roots of many exotic varieties form an important drug. In 1855 we imported 86,891 lbs. of rhubarb.

Rhyne, a name for the best quality of Russian hemp, of which there are three kinds, Ukraine, Polish, and Druyaner.

Rhynland-rod, a Dutch measure of length, equal to 12·32 feet.

Ri, the Japanese league, about 30 of which go to a degree of latitude.

Rib, a pillar of coal left as a support in a coal mine. *See* Ribs.

Ribbon-block Maker, a cutter and shaper of wooden rolls for winding ribbons on.

Ribbon-dresser, one who stiffens, waters, and smooths ribbons.

Ribbons, Rubands, narrow lengths of silk, &c. used for trimmings, by ladies, which partake of the same varieties in general as the larger silk fabrics. They are frequently ornamented with a pearl edge.

Ribbon-waterer, an ornamenter of ribbons. *See* Ribbon-dresser.

Ribbon-weaver, a manufacturer of ribbons.

Riblette (French), a cutlet; a slice of meat broiled.

Ribola, a wine made in Zante.

Ribs, joints of beef from the sides of the animal with the bone in; the timbers or supports of a ship or roof; a kind of spars exported from the North of Europe; the whalebone, steel, or cane joints, used for the framework of an umbrella or parasol, usually sold wholesale, in sets of 8, 9 or 10.

Ribston-pippin, a choice variety of apple.

Rice, a name for the grain of the *Oryza sativa*, a cereal, largely cultivated in Eastern countries and other quarters, and in which a considerable export trade is carried on. Our imports, which have been gradually increasing, amounted in 1856 to 3,680,409 cwts., besides 32,941 qrs. of unhusked rice. About half of this quantity was retained for home consumption.

Rice-cleaner, one who husks paddy, and sifts and prepares it for sale as rice.

Rice-flour, ground rice for puddings.

Rice-merchant, a wholesale dealer in rice; one who imports cargoes from African and other parts, or ships it to Mauritius and other large consuming marts.

Rice mill, a machine or mill for breaking the husk of rice between mill-stones, and removing the red cuticle.

Rice-paper, a peculiar manufactured Chinese paper, used for painting, said to be made from the pith of the *Aralia papyrifera*.

Rice-pudding, a baked pastry made of parboiled rice, with milk, sugar, and spice.

Rice-starch, fecula prepared from rice, for the use of laundresses, now in very general use.

Rick, a pile or stack of corn.

Rick-cloth, a coarse tarpauling or tarred canvas, for covering a corn rick, and keeping out the wet.

Rickers, the stems or trunks of young trees, a kind of spars imported into Denmark, &c. from the north.

Rick-stones, supports of Purbeck or other stone for ricks, usually sold in pairs.

Rick-yard, an assemblage of corn ricks.

Riddle, a coarse iron-wire sieve, of different sizes, for sifting coals, lime, sand, ashes, grain, potatoes, &c.

Riddle-maker, a manufacturer of large coarse wire sieves.

Riddy, a Singhalese silver coin, worth about 7d., and equal to 64 challies; its form is singular; it resembles a fish-hook, and is merely a piece of thick silver wire bent.

Ride-officer, an exciseman.

Rider, a horseman; an additional clause or annex to an act of Parliament or deed, when nearly completed; a second tier of casks; a commercial-traveller.

Ridge-hoe, a field implement for row-culture, of which there are several combinations.

Ridge-tiles, tiles on the top of a roof.

Riding-habit, a long loose sweeping dress of cloth or other materials, fitting tight, however, about the upper part of the person, worn by ladies on horseback.

Riding-hat, a hat for lady equestrians.

Riding-master, a teacher or instructor in horsemanship.

Riding-school, a place where horsemanship and equestrian exercises are taught.

Riding-skirt, a long skirt worn by females when riding.

Riding-whip, a short whip: those for ladies are often made very elegant.

Riel (Spanish), a small ingot of gold or silver, unrefined, and unwrought.

Riflard, (French), a jack-plane; a carpenter's chisel.

Rifle, a gun with a grooved bore, the cylinder being furrowed with spiral channels to give the ball a rotatory motion about an axis; a whetstone for a scythe.

Rigger, one who fits the standing and running rigging, the cordage, sails, &c. of a ship.

Rigging, the shrouds of a ship, with their ratlines; a general term for all the ropes of a vessel. *Rigging the market* is a stock-exchange term for enhancing, fictitiously, the value of the stock or shares in a company, by the directors or officers buying them up out of the funds of the association.

Rim, the edge of any thing.

Rime, the round of a ladder; a hole or chink.

Rimer, a carpenter's tool for shaping rimes.

Rind, the skin of pork; the peel or bark of fruit, &c. The rind of oranges, of pomegranates, and some other fruits enters into commerce.

Ring, the betting arena on a race-course, or at Tattersall's; a circlet of metal; as articles of jewellery, finger-rings and ear-rings are largely manufactured and dealt in; the chime of a bell. [the eye.

Ring-bolt, an eye-bolt with a ring through

Ringer, a miner's name for a crow bar.

Ring-fence, the outer palings, or wall, enclosing a park or estate.

Ring-stand, an upright holder for rings made of wood, metal, &c. for a toilet-table. [a seam.

Rip, a wicker fish-basket; to tear; to undo

Ripiar (Spanish), to fill up the chinks of a wall with shingle, or small stone, and mortar.

Ripier, a fish-hawker or carrier.

Ripper, a slater's tool.

Ripping-saw, a saw with a blade tapering in width from the handle.

Ripple, a kind of comb with long wire teeth, through which the flax plants pass to remove the capsules containing the linseed.

Rip-rap, a foundation of loose stones.

Ris, a Madras weight of 5 seer: 8 ris are equal to 25lbs.

Riser, the upright piece of wood or stone which supports or carries a stair or step.

Rishta, Ritah, names in India for the *Sapindus emarginatus*. See Soap-nut.

River-craft, small vessels or boats, not sea-going ships.

Rivet, an iron-joining pin; a metal fastening clenched at both ends.

Rivetting-hammer, a hammer for driving and clenching rivets.

Rivetting-machine, a machine for making rivets.

Rix-dollar, a money of account; and also a silver coin, common in many parts of the Continent, and the value of which varies from 2s. 6d. to 4s. 6d.

R. M., an abbreviation for "Royal Marines."
R. M. S., "Royal Mail Steamer."
R. N., "Royal Navy."
ROAD AND DUST CONTRACTOR, a rubbish carter; a person who contracts to keep the streets and thoroughfares clean from mud, snow, &c.
ROAD-BOOK, a traveller's guide-book of towns and distances, &c.
ROAD-METAL, prepared stone for a macadamized road.
ROAD-SCRAPER, a large metal hoe or machine for cleansing highway roads.
ROADSTEAD, an open or exposed anchorage for vessels, at some distance from the shore.
ROAD-SURVEYOR, an officer who has the supervision of roads, and whose duty it is to see them kept in good order.
ROAN, a kind of leather used for shoes, slippers, and common bookbinding; prepared from sheepskins by tanning with sumach; a bay or sorrel horse marked with spots of grey, &c.
ROASTED CHESTNUTS, chestnuts baked in an oven, or on the bars of a grate.
ROASTER, a circular iron vessel, which revolves on a pivot for roasting coffee berries; a peculiar kind of calcining furnace, having a side door and small holes in the bridge to admit a current of air; a gridiron; a screen.
ROASTING-JACK, a clock-work contrivance with pulleys for keeping meat revolving before the fire in cooking. *See* BOTTLE JACK, and JACK.
ROASTING-ORE, a preliminary preparation to smelting, which consists in making ridges of alternate layers of coal and iron-stone, that are kindled and left to burn slowly for some days.
ROB, a name given to the extract or inspissated juice of a fruit, as of juniper berries, &c.
ROBADA (Spanish), a space of ground 400 square yards in extent.
ROBBIN, a package in which pepper and other dry goods are sometimes imported from Ceylon. The robbin of rice in Malabar weighs about 84 lbs.; the spring of a carriage; a rope having a loop or eye at one end.
ROBE, an official wrapper or loose overgarment; a female's gown or dress; an abbreviation for arroba.
ROBE-MAKER, a manufacturer of black silk and other robes for clergymen, barristers, aldermen and others.
ROCAMBOLE, an alliaceous plant (the *Allium Scorodoprasum*), used in the northern parts of Europe for flavouring food, like the shalot.
ROCHELLE SALTS, the tartrate of potass and soda, used in medicine as a mild aperient.
ROCK, a sweetmeat; a prefix to any thing massy or solid, as rock alum, or rock salt.
ROCKET, a firework made to project through the air.
ROCKET-CASE, a stout card-board or cartridge-paper case for holding the explosive materials for a rocket.
ROCKET-STICK, the guide and support for a rocket.

ROCKING-CHAIR, a reclining or easy chair on rockers.
ROCKING-HORSE, a wooden horse fixed on rockers for children to ride on.
ROCK-OIL, ROCK-TAR, petroleum or mineral naphtha.
ROCK-SALT, native common salt as found in mines.
ROD, a long measure of 16½ linear feet, or a square measure of 272¼ square feet.
RODAPIE (Spanish), a valance or foot hangings to a bedstead, table, &c.
RODENO (Spanish), a kind of porous stone.
ROD-IRON, iron for making nails, and other purposes, of which about 18,000 or 20,000 tons are made.
ROD-MERCHANT, a dealer in osiers or birch and alder rods for basket-making, &c. *See* OSIER.
RODOMEL, the juice of roses mixed with honey.
ROE, the female of the hart; the seed or spawn of fishes.
ROGHEN BALSAM, a Persian name for the balsam of Mecca or Gilead, an odoriferous liquid resin, the produce of *Protium Gileadense*.
ROHUN BARK, the bark of the *Soymida febrifuga*, which is said to be a good substitute for cinchona. The nux vomica bark is often sold for it in the East.
ROKO, a kind of small cigar smoked by the Malays and others in the East.
ROLL, a small loaf or twist; a lump of fresh butter; a twist of tobacco; a roller; any fabric rolled or folded up; 5 dozen skins.
ROLLER, a clod-crusher; a heavy presser of metal or stone for levelling gravel walks or land, and smoothing grass lawns; an inking cylinder used by printers.
ROLLER-JOINERS, children employed in certain processes of the woollen manufacture.
ROLLER-MAKER, a manufacturer of cylinders of different kinds.
ROLLEYWAY, a tram-way in a mine.
ROLLING-MACHINE, a machine for making brass mouldings.
ROLLING-MILL, a mill with cylinders for rolling out sheets of metal.
ROLLING-PIN, a small wooden or glass roller used by cooks to spread dough.
ROLLING PRAIRIE, undulating prairie land in the North-American States.
ROLLING-PRESS, a copper-plate cylinder printing-press.
ROLLOCKS, ROWLOCKS, places cut in the gunwale of a boat for the oars to rest in while pulling.
ROLLY-POLY PUDDING, a boiled pastry with layers of jam between the dough; also called a blanket-pudding.
ROMAL, an Indian silk fabric.
ROMANA, the Spanish name for the steelyard.
ROMAN-BALANCE, another name for the steel-yard.
ROMAN CANDLE, a firework so called.
ROMAN CEMENT, an hydraulic cement, an argillaceous carbonate of lime calcined, made from a dark-brown stone, brought from the Isle of Sheppy, and mixed with sand.
ROMAN-TYPE, the ordinary upright character of printing-type; that in which this Dictionary is printed; not italic.

Rombowline, a sea name for condemned canvas, rope, &c.

Rondelettes, a kind of sail-cloth made in Brittany.

Ronfea (Spanish), a long, broad sword.

Roobek, Rubek, an Egyptian corn-measure, the fourth part of a weybeck, and equal to 33 gallons.

Rood, an English land-measure, the fourth of an acre, 1210 square yards; also, a term applied by artificers to 36 square yards of stone, brick, or slate work; a rod or pole measuring 16½ feet. As a linear measure the rood varies from 21 feet in some parts of Lancashire, to 24 feet in Wrexham, and 36 yards in the vale of Leven.

Roof, a covering of timber, slate, or metal, &c. to a building; the part in a mine above the miner's head; the top of a coach or carriage of any kind.

Roof-tree, a beam or timber for a roof.

Rook, a name for the castle, one of the pieces of a chess-board; a common bird, the *Corvus frugilegus*, the young of which are sometimes made into pies.

Rookery, the crowded and poorer parts of a town; the haunt of birds; the name is applied by sailors to rocks and islets frequented by sea-birds for laying their eggs, and also to a resort for seals for breeding purposes.

Room, a fishing station in the British North American Provinces; an apartment in a dwelling-house or other building.

Rooman, a local name in India for the pomegranate.

Room-paper. *See* Paper-hangings.

Roosa-grass Oil, a volatile oil, extracted in India from the *Andropogon Schœnanthus*.

Root, the part of a plant striking into the earth; very many bulbs and tubers are edible, and enter largely into commerce.

Root-crops, turnips, beet, potatoes, yams, and other edible roots and tubers.

Root-cutter, a machine for slicing turnips, &c. for cattle.

Ropage (Spanish), wearing-apparel; drapery.

Rope, a large cord or cable of either twisted hemp, hide, or wire, above an inch in circumference; a row of things tied together, as a rope of onions.

Rope-ladder, a suspensory ladder made of ropes for a ship's side, or for descending from a height.

Rope-makers' mat, a strong iron chain-work protection, worn by rope-makers.

Rope-mat, a door or other mat made of oakum or cordage.

Rope-walk, a place where workmen are employed in twisting and forming small ropes.

Roquille, a gill; the fourth part of the poisson, an old liquid measure of France.

Rosaire, a French name for the large rose-apple, the *Jambosa Malaccensis*.

Rosary, a string or chaplet of beads.

Rose, a choice garden flower, of which there are numerous varieties, peculiarly fragrant in consequence of containing an essential oil; a red colour; the perforated nozzle of a watering-pot.

Rose-drop, an earring; a lozenge flavoured with rose essence.

Rose-engine, an appendage to the turning lathe for engraving a variety of curved lines or intricate patterns. It is also used in machinery for spinning, and for lace-making.

Rose-fish, a Norway haddock.

Rose-leaves, petals of roses which are imported dried, or preserved in salt for extracting the aroma, or distilling into rose-water; they are also laxative. Those of the French or Provence rose are gathered before becoming quite ripe, deprived of the calyx and central attachments, and dried in the sun, or in a stove. After being sifted, in order to separate the stamens and pistil, they are gently compressed, and kept in a dry place. From the cabbage-rose a fragrant distilled water is prepared; the petals furnish essential oil or attar in small quantities.

Roselle, a name for the *Hibiscus cannabinus* in India, also for *H. sabdariffa*. Its calyxes, as they ripen, become fleshy, are of a pleasantly acid taste, and are much employed for making tarts, jellies, and refreshing drinks; a fibre, also known as gayal fibre is obtained from the stem.

Rose-malloes, a name in Bombay for the liquid storax obtained from *Liquidambar orientale* of Miller.

Rosemary, a bush, the *Rosmarinus officinalis*, which yields an oil used in the preparation of unguents for the hair.

Rose-noble, an ancient gold coin of 22 carats fineness, ranging from 108 to nearly 140 troy grains in weight, and passing current in its time for 6s. 8d.

Rose-pink, a delicate pink colour.

Rose-quartz, massive quartz of a rose-red colour, common in Ceylon and some other localities.

Rosetta-wood, an East Indian wood, handsomely veined, of a lively red orange colour, and of a close and hard texture.

Rosette, a bunch of ribbons, or other materials, sometimes worn at weddings or elections; an ornament for a horse's head-stall.

Rosewater, a liquid scent distilled from roses.

Rose-wood, Rhodes-wood, a name for the candle wood of the West Indies, the *Amyris balsamifera*, or gum elemi tree. Rose-wood is a term as generally applied as iron wood, and to as great a variety of trees in different countries; sometimes from the colour, and sometimes from the smell of the wood. The rose-wood, imported in such large quantities from Brazil, is the *Jacaranda Brasiliana*, and some other species.

Rosin, the mass left after distilling off the volatile oil from turpentine, forming a large article of commerce. Yellow rosin contains some water, which black rosin does not. *See* Colophony.

Rosin-oil, an oil obtained from the resin of the pine-tree, used by painters, for lubricating machinery, and for other purposes, and in France for making printing-ink.

Rosolio, a red wine of Malta.

Roster, a list showing the turn or rotation of service or duty, as in the case of police-magistrates, military officers, and others, who relieve or succeed each other.

ROTARY-ENGINE, one for obtaining rotary motion.

ROT-STEEP, a weak alkaline lye used in calico-printing, to remove the weaver's dressing.

ROTTEN-STONE, a variety of English tripoli, found in large quantities in Derbyshire and South Wales, and used for polishing, &c.

ROTTOLO, a measure used in parts of the Mediterranean. In Malta, it is 2 Maltese pounds, or 30 ounces, = to 1·12 oz. avoirdupois. In Aleppo the ordinary rottolo is nearly 5lbs., but that for weighing silk varies from 1½ to 1 1-7th lb.

ROUANNE, a marking or branding iron.

ROUBB, the fourth part of a piastre, a coin current in Turkey for 10 paras.

ROUBBIE, a gold coin of Turkey, equal to a piastre.

ROUBLE, a Russian silver coin of 100 copecks, which is the legal standard of silver currency by which accounts are kept. It contains 4 zolotniks, 21 parts, Russian weight, of pure silver, with 61 14·25th parts of alloy, and is worth from about 3s. 1½d. to 3s. 7d. according to the coinage. The coined gold rouble contains 27 parts of pure gold, in coined pieces of 10, 5, 3 and 1 rouble each: 100 roubles of gold are enacted to be equal to 103 roubles of silver. Roubles of platina are current in Russia. The coined pieces are of 12, 6, and 3 roubles each, equivalent to the same number of silver roubles: a platina piece of 3 roubles contains 2 zolotniks, 41 parts of pure platina.

ROUCHE, RUCHE, a goffered quilling of net, ribbon, blonde, or any other material.

ROUCOU, ROUCOUYER, Spanish names for arnotto, the *Bixa orellana*.

ROUGE, a scarlet powder made from crystals of sulphate of iron, and used for polishing gold or silver; a colouring substance used by females for painting their faces, consisting of carthamine, the colouring principle of safflower, mixed with powdered talc. *See* CROCUS.

ROUGE AND CARMINE MAKER, a preparer of those colours.

ROUGE ROYAL, a kind of marble.

ROUGH-SHOD, a horse which has its shoes roughed or caulked to prevent slipping on icy or frosted roads.

ROUGH STUCCO, stucco floated and brushed in a small degree with water.

ROULIER, (French), a wagoner or carrier.

ROUNCE, a wooden cylinder, to which is attached a belt and handle, for rolling in and out the bed or coffin of a printing-press.

ROUNDS, brewers' vessels in the tun-room, which are filled with beer from the fermenting squares.

ROUND-TRADE, a term on the river Gaboon and neighbourhood for a description of barter, comprising a large assortment of miscellaneous articles, also called the bundle trade.

ROUP, a name in Scotland for a public sale by auction.

ROUSER, a rotating machine for stirring hops in the brewer's copper.

ROUSSABLE (French), a place for curing and smoking herrings.

ROUSSILLON, a wine made in the Pyrenees.

ROUT-CAKE, a rich sweet cake for evening parties.

ROUT-SEATS, slight cane-top benches let out to hire for dances and evening parties.

ROVE, a roll of wool drawn out and slightly twisted.

ROVING-MACHINE, a machine for hoisting or winding the slubbings on smaller bobbins for the creels of the spinning machine.

ROW-BALL, a name for some species of *Polynemus* in India, which are esteemed excellent table-fish.

ROW-BOAT, a harbour guard boat; a river police boat; a coast-guard boat keeping watch along the shore.

ROWEL, the wheel of a spur; the flat ring in a horse's bit.

ROWERS, ROUGHERS, workmen employed in certain processes of the woollen manufacture.

ROWLOCK, the hole or rest for an oar on the gunwale of a boat. *See* ROLLOCKS.

ROYAL, a very small mortar; or bomb gun; a large kind of paper, 21 inches by 19; a light upper sail set above the top-gallant sail.

ROYAL ACADEMICIAN, a member of the Royal Academy.

ROYAL ACADEMY, the principal exhibition or public school of first-class painting.

ROYAL SOCIETY, the oldest, most learned, and scientific incorporated society of the metropolis, instituted for the promotion of philosophy and science, and distinguished above all others for its high respectability and learning.

ROYALTY, a due claimed on mineral produce.

ROYAL-YARD, the fourth yard from the deck on which the royal is set.

RUBA, an Eastern measure, the 20th of an ardeb. *See* ARDEB.

RUBBER, a polishing substance of various kinds, as glass and emery paper and cloth, &c.; caoutchouc, for erasing pencil-marks; a coarse file or whetstone; a coarse towel.

RUBBIE, a name in India for a winter crop.

RUBBIO, an Italian oil-measure, which weighs 47½ lbs. avoirdupois; also a grain-measure, equal to about eight bushels English: 104½ rubbii are = 100 quarters in Ancona.

RUBBISH-CARTER, a scavenger.

RUBBLE, in building phraseology, unhewn stone; brickbats and small stones.

RUBBLES, a miller's name in some counties for the whole of the bran or outside skin of the wheat, before being sorted into pollard, bran, sharps, &c.

RUBY, a term applied to various minerals; but chiefly to varieties of spinelle or sapphire; a small-size printing-type, with which this Dictionary is printed.

RUBY-WOOD, a name for red sanders-wood.

RUCHE. *See* ROUCHE.

RUDDER, the moving projecting piece of machine at the stern, by which a vessel is steered.

RUDDLE, red ochre.

RUE, a common herb, the *Ruta graveolens*, which has acrid antispasmodic properties, and is used medicinally as a stimulant and anodyne in flatulent cholic, in hysteria, and infantile convulsions.

RUFFLES, puffings or wrist sleeves of lace.

RUG, a coarse woollen wrapper; a coverlet for a bed; an ornamental bordered square of carpet, for the front of a fire-place or hearth.

RUGGING, a coarse wrapping or blanket cloth.

RULE, printers' metal reglet, or dividing lines for type, and for forming diagrams; a workman's measure, made in size a foot, a foot and a half, or 2 feet, &c., straight or folding, in box-wood, or plain wood, or in ivory, and divided and ornamented; a formal regulation laid down for guidance

RULE-CUTTER, a printers'-smith who prepares brass column and page-rules for printers. *See* BRASS-RULE.

RULER, a stick used in drawing lines, made flat or round, from 9 to 24 inches, and of different materials, usually some hard wood, as green or black ebony, &c.

RULES, a double-jointed workman's measure, of two feet, or three feet in four joints. *See* PARALLEL GUIDES.

RULING and DOTTING PENS, a kind of metal pen for writing music.

RULING-MACHINE, a machine constructed for ruling systematically, neatly, and speedily, paper, account and other books.

RUM, a spirit distilled in the West Indies from the fermented saccharine wash left in the process of sugar manufacture. Our imports in 1855 were 8,714,387 gallons of proof spirit, of which 3,224,264 gallons were entered for home consumption.

RUMBIYA, a Malay name for the sago-palm.

RUMBLE, a revolving cask or shaking machine, used to clean small works of cast iron, which soon scrub each other bright by friction; the hind seat of a travelling carriage.

RUMINANT-ANIMALS, those which chew the cud, or masticate their food. Most of the cloven-footed animals are ruminant.

RUMMAGE-SALE, a clearance sale of unclaimed goods at the docks, or of odds and ends left in a warehouse.

RUMMER, a glass drinking vessel on a foot.

RUMPAT-RUMPAT, the Malay name for spices in general.

RUMP-STEAK, a tender slice of beef cut from the thigh.

RUM-SWIZZLE, the name given to a fabric made in Dublin from undyed foreign wool, which, while preserving its natural property of resisting wet, possesses the qualities of common cloth.

RUN, a range or extent of ground for feeding cattle in the colonies.

RUNDLE, the step of a ladder.

RUNG, a spoke; any long piece of wood.

RUNG-HEADS, the upper ends of the floor-timbers of a ship.

RUNLET, a small cask, which may contain an undefined quantity, usually about 14½ gallons.

RUNNING-DAYS, a chartering term for consecutive days occupied on a voyage, &c., including Sundays, and not being therefore limited to working days.

RUNNING-RIGGING, the loose ropes and gear, lifts, braces, &c. used about the masts, sails, and yards of a vessel during navigation; the standing rigging being the shrouds, stays, &c., which secure the masts to the hull.

RUNNING TITLE, the head-line title of a book on the upper margin of each page.

RUNT, a small kind of black cattle brought from Wales and Scotland; the trunk of a tree; an old cow that has left off breeding.

RUPEE, the principal coin circulating in British India. There were, until lately, two principal kinds current in calculations, the sicca rupee and the Company's rupee; 100 of the former were equal to 116 of the latter. It is ordinarily taken to weigh one tola or 180 grains, the standard being 11-12ths of silver and 1-12th of alloy. The E. I. Company's rupee, which was introduced in 1835 in place of the Sicca, Surat, and other rupees previously current, contains 165·92 grains pure silver, and 15·08 grains alloy; and is worth, reckoning silver at 5s. 2d. per ounce, 1s. 11d. sterling. Its diameter is 1-20th of an inch. It is ordinarily converted into sterling at the rate of 2s. The rupees of the Madras mint, previous to the coinage of 1835, and the different sorts of the Furruckabad rupee, are received and exchanged at par, provided they have not lost by fair wear more than the regulated limit of lightness, 1½ per cent.; if below that limit, they are only taken as bullion. Silver rupees are a modern currency, as there do not exist any in that metal struck anterior to the establishment of the Mahommedan power in India, while a great many in gold have been preserved of far higher antiquity.

RUSET-OFFAL, a name for kip or calf curried leather.

RUSH, a common plant, species of *Juncus*, several of which are largely used for making mats, baskets, and the bottoms of chairs, while the pith is employed for the wicks of rush-lights. Bulrushes are a different plant, used for polishing wood and metals, and also by coopers: 425 tons of them were imported in 1855.

RUSH-LIGHT, a tallow-candle with a rush wick.

RUSK, a kind of cake or small loaf which has been rasped.

RUSKIE, in Scotland, a twig or straw basket for corn or meal; a bee-hive; a coarse straw hat.

RUSOT, a watery extract prepared in the hilly districts of India from the sliced roots, stem, and branches of the *Berberis Lycium*, and *B. aristata*, used medicinally, and containing an alkaloid called berberine.

RUSSET, a kind of reddish-brown rough apple.

RUSSIA COMPANY, a trading company established by letters patent in the 1st and 2nd years of the reign of Philip and Mary. An Act of Elizabeth incorporated it as a perpetual body, under the above title; and an Act of William III. (A. D. [illegible]), was passed to extend the trade to Russia, and enacted, that every subject of the realm seeking admission into the company should pay £5 and no more. The dues received in London, on the importation of goods from Russian ports, are little more than nominal, and are not levied on trifling articles; nor are persons called upon to become free of the company unless engaged in the Russian trade. By far the greater amount of dues is paid by members of the Court of assistants. The Company have an agent at St. Petersburg, and one at Elsinore, from whom they receive information regarding the trade of the two countries. Her Majesty's consul at St. Petersburg is the commercial agent of the Company, and derives full half his official salary from this appointment. The Company contribute to the maintenance of chapels in the two capitals of Russia, at Cronstadt, and several other places.

RUSSIA-DUCK, a white linen fine canvas.

RUSSIA-LEATHER, fine curried leather, which has a peculiar smell, from being impregnated with an empyreumatic oil obtained from birch bark. The tanned hides of young oxen, coloured red, white, or black, are imported from Russia in rolls of about 10 hides. About 20,000 lbs. were imported in 1855.

RUST, a hydrous red oxide formed on iron when exposed to the atmosphere; the carbonic acid of the air mixing with the sesquioxide of the iron; a name for mildew in grain.

RUSTIC-CHAIR, a seat of twisted wood, &c. for a garden or shrubbery.

RUT, the track or furrow made by a wheel.

RUTA-BAGA, a name for the Swedish turnip, the *Brassica campestris ruta baga*.

RUTILE, an oxide of titanium, of variable colour, used in painting porcelain.

RUTTEE, a small Indian weight of 1·875 troy grain.

RYDER, a Dutch coin worth about 23s.

RYE, the seed of the *Secale cereale*. Although very little used in Great Britain for food, in the north of Europe and Flanders it forms a principal article of subsistence, generally mixed with wheat, and sometimes with barley. The meal, mixed with wheat-flour, is sometimes used here to make bread and gingerbread. In 1854 we imported as much as 28,000 quarters of rye.

RYND, a piece of iron in the upper millstone.

RYOT, a peasant in the East; an Indian cultivator of the soil.

S.

S, stands as an abbreviation for "south," and for "shilling."

SAA, SAHA, an Algerian dry-measure, = 1·596 bushel; in Tripoli, it is nearly 2 bushels. The oil saa is, however, but 2¼ pints.

SABADILLA. *See* CEBADILLA.

SABBATH-DAY JOURNEY, an ancient Hebrew itinerary measure, = 0·5432 English mile.

SABICU, a ship-building wood recognized at Lloyds.

SABLE, a much-prized fur; that from the Russian marten is so costly that it is rarely used, except by monarchs and high functionaries. The hair of the tail is used for artists' brushes or pencils. The American sable has a fur, varying in colour from tawny to black: it is often coloured to imitate Russian.

SABOT, a wooden shoe; an iron cap; a skid; a break.

SABRE, a long heavy sword for cavalry use.

SABUDANA, a name in Hindustan for sago.

SACARE, a weight used in Madagascar, of 20 grains.

SACATILLOS, a Spanish name for the dried carcases of the cochineal coccus, which perishing on the plant, and yielding but little dye, are comparatively valueless.

SACCA, a Tuscan corn-measure, containing 3 staji, each of [illegible] mine, or 4 quarti, and equal to about 2 bushels.

SACCATO, a superficial measure of Florence, = 56·191 French ares.

SACCHARILLA, a kind of muslin.

SACCHARINE, sweet, relating to sugar.

SACCHAROMETER, an instrument for testing the specific gravity of saccharine solutions.

SACHEL, SATCHEL, a small bag.

SACHET, a scent-bag, or perfume cushion.

SACHINE, SASHEN, other names for the sagene, a Russian linear-measure of about 7 feet.

SACK, a general name for a large bag, serving as a measure of capacity for grain and dry goods, which is common to all the languages of Europe, and some of those of Asia; a dry-measure of varying capacity, according to the article and country. The minimum sack of France is 2·18 Winchester bushels; the maximum, 4·20 ditto. The sack at Brussels is as much as 6·90 Winchester bushels. The American sack of salt, 215 lbs. The miller's sack of wheat in the United States is 3 Winchester bushels. A sack of wool in England is 2 weys or 13 tods, = 364 lbs.; of flour, corn, or meal, 280 lbs., or 2 cwt., 2 qrs. nett; but the foreign sacks of flour imported, are very irregular in size, varying from 140 to 200 lbs. The old sack of coals was equal to three bushels; it is now 2 cwt. by weight; a sack of dry goods is 3 bushels of heaped up, or 4 bushels strike measure. Sacks are made of very variable size, holding from 140 to 280 lbs. of flour; at Liverpool 8 sacks, or 10 barrels of flour, go to the ton. In France the sack of flour weighs about 157 kilogrammes; of wheat, from 100 to 120 kilogrammes; of rye, 1[illegible] kilogrammes; of barley and oats, 100 kilogrammes. Also a loose robe or coat; a kind of Spanish wine.

SACK-AND-BAG MAKER, a manufacturer of the coarse canvas bags used for holding different commodities.

Sackbut, a trombone, a musical instrument.

Sack-cloth Maker, a tarpaulin manufacturer; a makerof large coarse baling or wrapping sheets.

Sack-collector, an agent for millers, who collects the flour sacks from bakers and others.

Sack holder, an apparatus for holding sacks, to facilitate the filling them with corn or other materials; a small handbarrow for moving bags of coals, corn, &c. to or from a wagon.

Sacking, a coarse kind of flaxen or hempen fabric used for bagging, and for the frames of bedsteads, made chiefly in Dundee and Ireland. *See* Bagging.

Sacking and Pack-sheet Warehouse, a place where these articles are sold wholesale.

Sack-manufacturer, a tradesman who employs women to make sacks.

Sack-tree, a name given to the *Lepuranda saccidora*, the bark of which is formed into natural sacks in India, and used by the villagers for carrying rice.

Sacoleve, a kind of sailing vessel.

Sacred-bean, the *Nelumbium speciosum*.

Sacristan, a keeper of church furniture.

Sadang, Saundang, a measure of length in Pegu, = 0·001 yard.

Saddle, a leather seat or pad for the back of a saddle-horse; a joint of meat with the ribs on each side.

Saddle-back, the name for a kind of seal.

Saddle-bags, bags carried across a horse.

Saddle-cloth, a rug put under a saddle on a horse's back.

Saddler and Harness Maker, a worker in leather; one who makes up various articles for horses, as bridles, saddles, traces, reins, collars, harness, &c. There are some tradesmen who devote themselves more particularly to one branch, as army, hunting, or chaise-saddlers.

Saddlers' Company, one of the livery companies of London, whose hall is in Cheapside.

Saddlers'-currier, a preparer of leather for the use of saddlers and harness-makers.

Saddlers' Hair-skins, seal-skins obtained from old animals, the dozen skins weighing from 160 to 200 pounds. *See* White Coats.

Saddlers'-ironmonger, a smith or dealer who supplies the metal work required by saddlers, for saddles, harness, &c.

Saddlery, a collective name for various articles of horse-gear, made of leather. The value of the exports annually average a quarter of a million sterling.

Saddle-tree, the frame-work of a saddle.

Sad-iron, a tailor's flat-iron or goose, used, when heated, for smoothing cloth, and made of the weight of 1 lb. up to 10 lbs.

Sadrus, a name in Bengal for the aromatic bark of the *Laurus* [illegible] *malabathrum*.

Safe, a cupboard for meat; a fire-proof chest; a receptacle for books and valuable papers. Fire-proof safes are made of strong wrought-iron, lined with hard steel plates, the interval between the two being filled with some non-conductor of heat.

Safety-belt, Safety-buoy, a swimming belt or buoy, intended as a protection from drowning.

Safety-box. *See* Safe.

Safety-lamp Maker, a manufacturer of wire-gauze warning lamps, for use in mines where there is any danger of contact with fire-damp.

Safety-valve, a vent or valve to facilitate the escape of steam, and prevent the explosion of steam-boilers.

Safflower, the bastard saffron, the produce of the florets of the *Carthamus tinctorius*, largely imported as a dye-stuff. The seeds, yielding an abundance of fixed oil, are also imported for crushing.

Saffron, a commercial name for the dried stigmata of the flowers of the *Crocus sativus*. These are picked out, dried on paper in a kiln, or by the sun, and sold either compressed into cakes, or as hay saffron. Cake saffron, as now met with, contains none of the real article, being prepared from the florets of the safflower made into a paste with gum-water. Saffron is used as a colouring principle, and an ingredient in several culinary preparations. We imported 11,000 lbs. in 1855.

Saffron-cake, a pastry, coloured and flavoured with saffron.

Saga, a name in Siam for the red seeds of *Abrus precatorius*, 32 of which make a phainung, worth about 3d.; a gold and silver weight used in Malacca, the 12th of the mayam, and = 4·33 grains.

Sagapenum, a fetid gum-resin obtained from the *Ferula Persica*, which has a hot, nauseous, and rather bitter taste, and an odour resembling that of garlic and assafœtida. Its medical uses are the same as those of assafœtida, but it is considered less energetic, and is but little employed.

Sagathy, a mixed woven fabric of silk and cotton.

Sage, a culinary herb, the *Salvia officinalis*, used as a seasoning in its green or dry state. An oil is also obtained from it.

Sage-cheese, a green kind of cheese, simply coloured by a decoction of sage and other leaves being added to the milk. In Scotland, the seeds of lovage are added to cheese.

Sagene, Sachine, a Russian measure of length, = 1·167 English fathom: 1 English fathom = 0·856 Russian sagene.

Sage, Wild, a name in the Cape colony for the *Tarchonanthus camphoratus*, the leaves of which are chewed, smoked, and employed in the form of infusion.

Sagger, Seggar, a crucible or clay pot for baking earthenware, shaped like a band-box, and being piled in columns in the oven, each sagger covers the one beneath it, and protects the goods from the immediate contact of smoke and flame.

Sagging, a name applied to the bending of beams in the middle.

Saggina, a name for broom corn in Italy.

Sago, a granulated form of starch obtained from the pith of the trunk of *Sagus laevis*, and *S. Rumphii*, in Singapore, the former furnishing most of the sago sent to Europe. In India it is obtained from *Phœnix farinifera.* Our imports for home consumption, in 1855, were 5420 tons. Sago is made on the Continent in smaller grains from potato starch.

SAGO-PUDDING, a baked pastry made with sago, milk, sugar, and spice.

SAHEBA, an Indian name for worm-seed, the produce of *Artemisia judaica.*

SAHM, a measure for charcoal used in Austria and Hungary, = 6.768 bushels.

SAIDEL. *See* SEIDEL.

SAIL-CLOTH, a coarse flax or hempen fabric for sails, made to an immense extent in Dundee. *See* CANVAS.

SAILING-MATCH, a regatta; a race or contest for speed between yachts or sailing-boats.

SAIL-LOFT, the workshop of a sail-maker; a place where breadths of canvas are sewed into ship's-sails.

SAIL-MAKER, a workman who shapes and sews sails; one of a ship's crew who has the charge and repair of the sails.

SAILOR, a hired skilled seaman; one who assists in the navigation of a ship.

SAILS, shaped pieces of canvas for boats, ships, and windmills.

SAIN-DOUX (French), hogs'-lard.

SAINFOIN, a fodder-grass, the *Hedysarum onobrychis.*

SAIQUE, a vessel of the Levant.

SAJNA, SUJNA, Indian names for the *Moringa pterygosperma.*

SAKA, a colonial name for the bastard purple-heart tree, used in Demerara as a furniture wood; a Turkish water-carrier.

SAKACHERA, the Sanscrit name for henna.

SAKES, the Turkish name for gum mastic.

SAKHALAT, the Malay name for woollen cloth.

SAKUR, an Indian name for small rounded astringent galls, formed on some species of *Tamarix,* which are used in medicine and dyeing.

SALAD, lettuces, endive, and other herbs eaten raw, dressed with vinegar, oil, and other condiments.

SALAD-BOWL, a deep crockery-ware bowl used for mixing salad in.

SALAD-CREAM, a prepared dressing for salads.

SALADING, vegetables for making a salad.

SALAD-OIL, Florence or olive-oil, usually retailed in wicker-cased flasks, for mixing with salads.

SALAD-SPOON, a wooden, ivory, or other spoon, for mixing and serving salad.

SALÆRATUS, a name in the United States for prepared carbonate of soda and salt. Of this chemical product there are two kinds, one a bi-carbonate of soda, and the other of potash. Saleratus is used by bakers and housekeepers with cream of tartar, for mixing with flour, sour milk, &c. to evolve the carbonic acid gas on the addition of water, the dough expanding in the oven, and rendering the product light and spongy. It is also used for bleaching purposes.

SALAJIT. *See* SALARAS.

SALAMANDER, a vessel for cooking; a kind of salamander.

SALAMANDER-SAFES, an American name for patent fire-proof iron safes.

SALAMANIE, a Turkish flute.

SALAMIN. *See* CELEMIN.

SAL AMMONIAC, the hydrochlorate of ammonia, obtained by saturating the ammoniacal liquor of gas-works with muriatic acid, and afterwards sublimating it. It has many commercial uses; as for medicine, metallurgic operations, tinning and soldering, &c.

SAL VOLATILE, a smelling salt, the carbonate of ammonia.

SALAMIT, a small cured herring imported into the Ionian Islands.

SALAMIC, a Neapolitan name for salted provisions.

SALARAS, a native Indian name for the bitter stalks of the *Ophelia elegans,* which is often confounded with Chiretta.

SALARY, a stipend; wages paid periodically or annually.

SALE, an auction; the disposal of goods to public or private bidders; a wicker-basket.

SALE, BILL OF. *See* BILL OF SALE.

SALEP, the farinaceous portion of the tubers of the *Orchis morio,* formerly in much repute as a diet drink, but now less used. Twenty-seven cwt. were imported in 1856.

SALESMAN, a vender; a wholesale dealer, of whom there are various kinds in the metropolis and elsewhere; as butter, meat, poultry, cattle, and sheep, hide, oyster, game, fruit, hay and straw, potato and other salesmen.

SAL-GEM, a commercial name for native rock-salt or chloride of sodium.

SALIBREROS (Spanish), a maker of nitrate of soda.

SALICINE, an alkaloid; the crystalline bitter principle of the bark of the willow, which is used medicinally as a febrifuge. Besides what is made at home, we imported, in 1856, 646 oz.

SALICOQUE, SALICOT (French), a prawn or shrimp.

SALICOR, the ash of the *Salicornia annua,* which is often employed in France as a source of carbonate of soda, of which it frequently contains 15 per cent.

SALINAS, a name for salt marshes or salt ponds inclosed from the sea.

SALINOMETER, a salt gauge for indicating the density of the sea-water in the marine steam-boiler, and for keeping it free from salt or incrustation, by blowing off when required.

SALLOW, a name for species of *Salix,* which are not flexible like the osier, but furnish the best charcoal for gunpowder.

SALLY LUNN, the common name for a kind of sweet tea-cake, which is toasted and buttered.

SALMA, a measure of capacity used in the kingdom of the Two Sicilies, and other localities in the Mediterranean, of a variable character, ranging from 17 to 86 gallons; in Malta it is nearly 8 bushels. It is likewise a Maltese land-measure, equal to four acres, 1 rood, 38 poles nearly; in Sicily it is 5¼ acres.

SALMAGUNDI, a mixed dish of minced meat and condiments.

SALMIS (French), jugged hare.
SALMON, a choice edible fish frequenting the Northern seas and rivers, of which as much as 4000 tons weight has sometimes been taken in a season, in the Irish and Scotch rivers, and the greater part sent to London for sale.
SALMON-FRY, the *Salmo samulus*.
SALMON-PEEL, a young salmon.
SALMON-TROUT, a fine fresh-water fish, the *Salmo trutta*.
SALOON, a large room used as a place of entertainment; the state-room or main cabin of a passenger-ship or steamer; the refreshment-room in a theatre.
SALOOP. *See* SALEP.
SALPICON, a stuffing or larding put into beef.
SAL-PRUNELLA. *See* PRUNELLA SALT.
SALSAFY, a name for the *Tragopogon porrifolium*; the nutritious and sub-aromatic roots are sweet and tender, and much esteemed as an esculent.
SAL-SODA, an American commercial name for the carbonate of soda.
SALT, chloride of soda, an efflorescence, also found in beds and masses. Its uses for culinary purposes, for manure, for cattle, and for metallurgic operations, are well known. It also enters largely into the manufacture of soda, soap, earthenware, &c. The principal commercial varieties are rock-salt, common white salt, and stoved salt. *See* SALTS.
SALT AND CURED PROVISIONS, beef and pork prepared in pickle, or smoke-dried for use as food. A large trade is carried on in these articles, the estimated consumption in the Kingdom being 103 600 tons, valued at £2,800,000 sterling. The general weight of the packages may be stated as follows: Irish bacon is usually packed in matted bales of 3 cwt. nett, American bacon in boxes weighing about the same. American shoulders, hams, &c., in hogsheads of about 8 cwt. each, nett. Beef and pork, in tierces of 304, 320, and 336 lbs. nett, or in barrels of 200 lbs. nett.
SALT-BOX, a wooden box for a kitchen to keep salt in for ordinary purposes.
SALT-CAKE, a name for sulphate of soda made at alkali works, for the use of crown-glass manufacturers and soap makers. The consumption is about 12,000 tons a year.
SALT-CELLAR, a small vessel for holding salt at table.
SALTER, a dealer in salt, a dry-salter; one who cures meat or fish with salt.
SALTERS' COMPANY, the 9th in rank of the 12 great livery companies of London; whose first charter bears date 37 Edward III., A.D. [illegible]; their hall is in St. Swithin's Lane.
SALT-FISH, cod or ling, which has been salted.
SALTING-PAN, an earthenware vessel to stand meat in pickle.
SALTING-TUB. *See* PICKLING-TUB.
SALT-JUNK, hard, dry, cured beef.
SALT-MAKER, a preparer of salt in salinas or salt ponds; a salt boiler.
SALT-MERCHANT, an exporter or wholesale dealer in salt.
SALTPETRE, the nitrate of potash, imported chiefly from India, to the extent of about 20,000 tons a year; used in medicine, in making gunpowder, pickling, and other purposes.
SALTPETRE-REFINER, a purifier of the crude nitrate of potash.
SALT-RAKER, a collector of salt in natural salt-ponds, or enclosures from the sea.
SALTS, combinations of acids with oxide bases. English salt is chloride of soda; Epsom salt, sulphate of magnesia; Glauber's salt, sulphate of soda; Polychrest or Glaser salt, sulphate of potash.
SALTUS, an ancient Roman land-measure, = 493 4-5th acres.
SALT-WORT, the *Salicornia annua*, a source of soda. The shoots when young are pickled and sold under the false name of samphire. *See* SALICOR.
SALUNG, a money of account in Siam, the fourth of a tical, and worth about 7½d.
SALUP, a weight used in Sumatra of 2 lbs. avoirdupois.
SALUTE, a certain number of guns fired as a mark of respect or rejoicing: a royal salute is 21 guns.
SALVAGE, an allowance made for saving a ship or goods from danger of any kind; goods saved from a fire.
SALVE-MAKER, a manufacturer of ointments.
SALVER, a silver or plated tray.
SAMADU, an Indian name for corundum.
SAMAR, a grain-measure, used in Georgia, of 8½ bushels.
SAMBOK, a country riding-whip of hide, commonly used in the Cape colony.
SAMESTRE, a variety of coral.
SAMOREUX, a long Dutch boat.
SAMP, a preparation of Indian corn, largely used in the United States in preference to rice.
SAMPAN, a boat used in the Eastern seas.
SAMPHIRE, the aromatic, saline fleshy leaf of the *Crithmum maritimum*, a plant inhabiting rocky cliffs of the sea coasts, which is a favourite ingredient in pickles.
SAMPLER, a warehouseman, &c. who selects samples from bales, casks, or packages; a child's workpiece.
SAMPLING, taking small quantities of wine, spirits, &c. at the docks, or of merchandise from the bulk, to exhibit at public sales or privately.
SAMPLING-BOTTLE, a small glass bottle for bringing away samples of wines or spirits from the vaults, &c. in the docks.
SAMPLING-ORDER, an order from an owner of goods in the docks, serving as an authority to the dock-keepers to permit samples to be taken away.
SAMSHOO, a spirituous liquor extracted, by fermentation and distillation, from rice, by the Chinese.
SANAT, an Indian calico.
SAND, particles of silica mixed with other impurities. The commercial uses of sand are, for manure, as a disintegrator of the soil from its loosening properties; for scouring; for sand-baths; for glass-making; in chemical operations; for foundry moulds; for grinding and polishing, &c.

Sallyport, a postern gate, or passage under ground, from a fortified place.

Samian Stone, a kind of polishing stone used by goldsmiths, brought from Samos.

Sandal, a rough-made protection for the sole of the foot; a hide or skin shoe without uppers, bandaged or fastened round the ancle.

Sandal-wood, an odoriferous wood, the produce of several species of *Santalum*, in India and the Pacific islands, of which there are two commercial kinds, the white, probably the outer layers of the wood, and the yellow, or citron, the inner wood. The odour is very strong, rose-like, and enduring. The essential oil, to which this odour is due, is extensively used for the adulteration of attar of roses. Sandal-wood is very hard, heavy, and susceptible of a fine polish, and extensively used by cabinet-makers, in the fabrication of various articles of ornamental furniture. Sandal-wood is also a name among the Russians for the red wood of the *Rhamnus dahuricus*, used for dyeing leather.

Sandarac, a white juniper resin in round or long tears, not unlike mastic, but brittle, obtained from the *Thuja articulata* in Barbary and Central Africa.

Sand-bag, a long thin bag of sand applied to chinks in window-sashes to exclude draught; a larger bag filled with sand, used in field fortifications.

Sand-balls, soap mixed with sand, made into round balls for toilet use.

Sand-bath, a vessel filled with heated sand.

Sand-box, a box for sprinkling sand; a spittoon; a local West Indian name for the *Hura crepitans* tree, the seeds of which are a drastic purgative, and contain a very limpid oil.

Sanders wood, a red dye-wood obtained from *Pterocarpus santalinus*. See Red Sanders-wood.

Sandever, **Sandiver**, a corruption of the French "Saint de verre," the saline scum or alkaline sulphates formed on glass-pots, known as glass-gall. It is used as a flux in certain metallurgic operations.

Sand-merchant, a wholesale dealer in sand, for the use of glass-makers, founders, or for builders to mix with mortar.

Sandomirsk, a kind of Russian wheat.

Sand-paper, an abrading material for polishing; emery or glass paper used for rubbing wood or metals.

Sand-pattens, supports for the feet, used by fishermen in walking over soft or quick sands.

Sandstone, a valuable building material of many districts, equal to the freestone of Scotland.

Sandwich, thin layers of meat between slices of bread and butter.

Sandwich-box, a portable tin box for carrying sandwiches for lunch.

Sandyx, a mixture of realgar and red chalk.

Sangaree, a cooling drink in the West Indies; wine and water sweetened with sugar.

Sang-dragon (French); **Sanguis Draconis**, the Latin and pharmaceutical name for dragon's-blood.

Sans-peau, a variety of French pear.

Santa, a colonial name in Jamaica for the liqueur called shrub.

Santhee, an Indian measure for land, which varies all over the country. In some it is as much as can be ploughed by two bullocks, in others by three, and in some by four. In several districts this last is called a double santhee; in others, six bullocks per plough are necessary to form a double santhee; and in some, again, even three bullocks constitute a double santhee. Generally, a santhee of land is deemed to contain 3 prajas; each praja 30 weegas or beegas, and each weega a square of 35 cubits, or nominally 45 yards; but in reality reduced to 42 yards by the mode of applying the line; and in some districts to less.

Santonine, the vermifuge principle of the *Semen contra*, a medicinal substance obtained from the flower-heads of some of the *Artemisias*, and a most powerful anthelmintic. See Semencine.

Sanwuck, a name for *Panicum frumentaceum*, in the North-West provinces of India and Nepaul.

Saouari, an excellent wood for ship-building, mill timbers, and planks, obtained from the *Caryocar tomentosum*. It greatly resembles, in its properties, the *Mora*, and may be had from 16 to 20 inches square, and from 20 to 40 feet long. This tree yields the delicious nut known as the Souari.

Sapa, *a thick confection of grapes*.

Sapan-wood, a dye-wood obtained in Malabar, and the islands of the Eastern seas, from the *Cæsalpinia sappan*, *C. coriaria*, and *pulcherrima*. A decoction of the wood is used by calico-printers for red dyes.

Sapek, a Tartar money of account, equal to about 5d. sterling. See Sapeck.

Sap-green, a vegetable pigment composed of the colouring matter of the berries of the *Rhamnus catharticus*, and lime.

Sapin, the French name for the fir or pine.

Sapodilla-wood, a West Indian fancy wood used for furniture.

Sappers and Miners, a name applied to the men of the Royal Engineer Corps.

Sappadilla, a name for the soursop fruit, *Anona muricata*.

Sapphire, next to the diamond, one of the hardest of gems: it has several shades of colour and lustre, blue, yellow, green, red, and intermediate shades.

Sapsago, a dark-green cheese.

Sarangousty, a Belgian plaster, a composition for preventing the action of damp from old walls, statues, &c.

Sarbotiere (French), a mould for ice-creams.

Sarcenet, a thin silk used for ribbons, linings, &c.

Sarcocolla, a medicinal gum, now little used and scarce, obtained from the *Penæa mucronata*, a native of Persia and Arabia.

Sarcophagus, a stone coffin.

Sard and **Sardonyx**, varieties of chalcedony.

Sardine, the *Clupea sardina*, a small fish allied to the pilchard, caught in large quantities in the Mediterranean, and preserved in oil.

Saree, a cotton fabric worn by Indian women, to wrap around the person; also an embroidered long scarf of gauze or silk.

Sarinda, an Indian fiddle.

Sarking, shirting; the covering of wood above the rafters; usually of spruce and yellow pine.

Sarong, a sort of petticoat worn by females in the East; a woven or printed fabric imported into the Dutch ports of the Eastern archipelago. There are imitation Battick sarongs, and Turkey red sarongs.

Sarplar, a name given to a large bale or package of wool, containing 80 tods, or a ton in weight.

Sarrasin, a name in some parts of the Continent for buckwheat.

Sarsaparilla, the rhizomes of several species of the genus *Smilax*, chiefly imported from South America and Mexico, for making an extract for medicinal purposes.

Sarse, Searce, a fine sieve.

Sarshapa, a Sanscrit name for mustard-seed.

Sary, a dress, or simple wrapper, of cotton, worn by the females of India. *See* Saree.

Sash-door, a door with panes of glass to give light.

Sashes, silk or other waist-belts for females; scarfs worn by military men over the shoulder; long chequered window-frames for holding squares of glass. *See* Sash-frames.

Sash-fastenings, catches or bolts for the sashes of windows, to prevent their being opened from the outside.

Sash-frames, the wooden or metal borderings or frame-work, for setting squares of glass for windows.

Sash-line Maker, a manufacturer of stout cord, for attaching to the sliding-pulleys for window-sashes.

Sash-maker, a constructor of window-frames of different kinds, for houses, conservatories, and public buildings, of wood or iron.

Sassafras-nuts. *See* Pichurim Beans.

Sassafras-oil, a yellow volatile oil, obtained by either from the root of *Laurus Sassafras*.

Sassafras-wood, the wood and roots of the *Laurus Sassafras*, a native of North America, which are brought over in billets. They are highly aromatic both in smell and taste. The dried leaves contain so much mucilage that they are used for thickening soups.

Sassolina, a name for native boracic-acid, used in the manufacture of borax.

Sassy-bark, a poisonous bark obtained in Western Africa, from a leguminous tree, a species of *Erythrophlœum*, which natives, suspected of witchcraft, secret murder, &c. are put to the ordeal of swallowing.

Sat, Set, a grain-measure of Siam, weighing 3½ lbs., and holding about 3¼ pints.

Satilla, the half of a soco in Bencoolen and some parts of the Eastern archipelago.

Satin, a glossy silk twill, to which the soft and glistering appearance is given by rendering a great number of the threads of the warp visible in the process of weaving. The brilliant smooth lustre it bears is given by rolling on heated cylinders; a former weight of Brussels, = 112·78 grains.

Satin-de-laine, a black cassimere manufactured in Silesia, from wool.

Satin-dresser, a finisher of satin by rolling.

Satinet, a cheap and durable American mixed fabric, which is very largely worn by the labouring part of the community in the United States, taking the place of the fustians or velveteens worn in Great Britain. The warp of satinet is cotton, and the filling in is, to a large extent, the short waste of other branches of the woollen manufacture. This is mixed with a sufficient portion of long wool to enable it to be spun, and after being woven in a peculiar way, so as to bring the wool to the face of the cloth, it is then felted heavily, and the cotton is entirely hidden by the wool. Satinettes are also silky materials which are as cheap as, and more durable than, satins; their brilliancy being produced in the process of manufacture, without dress or any artificial means.

Satin-stone, a fibrous kind of gypsum used by lapidaries.

Satin-turk, a trade term for a superior quality of satinette.

Satin-wood, a beautiful veneering wood, of which there are several varieties, that obtained in the Indies, is from the *Chloroxylon Swietenia*.

Satisfaction, an entry upon the rolls of the court, to the effect that a debt owing by a defendant to a plaintiff in an action, has been paid and satisfied.

Satron, a small fish used by French fishermen as bait.

Satteau, a coral fishing-boat employed in the Mediterranean.

Sattranger, Sathringee, a kind of fibrous striped mat or carpet made in India.

Sauceboat, an earthenware or plated vessel with a lip for pouring out sauce.

Sauce-dish, a small crockery-ware tureen, or vessel with a cover and stand, for holding sauce.

Sauce-ladle, a kind of deep oval spoon, for dipping out melted butter, gravies, &c. at a dinner-table.

Sauce-maker, a preparer of condiments or relishes for food; sauces are usually vended at pickle-shops or Italian warehouses.

Saucepan, a small kitchen-pot or boiler, with a handle; a cooking utensil of iron or copper, sometimes tinned or enamelled.

Saucers, small, circular, shallow platters of china or crockery-ware, for standing tea-cups in.

Saucy-bark, a poisonous bark used on the West coast of Africa, by the natives. *See* Sassy Bark.

Saugamme (German), a wet nurse.

Saul, one of the most useful known Indian timbers for building and engineering purposes, the produce of the *Shorea robusta*. It yields in abundance the resin called dammar.

Saum, a liquid-measure used in Switzerland varying in different cantons, from 36 to 38 gallons; a weight used in Austria, 308½ to 442 lbs.; a name in Germany for 22 pieces of cloth of 32 ells each.

SAUMAY, a name in Tanjore for the *Panicum miliaceum*.

SAUMÉE, a French land-measure, about an acre.

SAUMER (German), a beast of burden.

SAUMON (French), a pig of lead, pewter, &c.

SAUNDAUNG, a Burmese long-measure of 23 inches, the 7th part of the bamboo.

SAUNDERS-WOOD. *See* RED SANDERS-WOOD.

SAURISSEUR, a French herring-curer.

SAUR-KRAUT, a German preparation of pickled cabbage. Slices of the large white cabbage are placed in layers with salt in a tub, and allowed to ferment. Previously to use it is washed from the salt.

SAUSAGE, a long roll of chopped meat, beef, or pork in a skin.

SAUSAGE-MACHINE, a chopping machine worked by steam for mincing meat.

SAUSAGE-PUDDING, SAUSAGE-ROLL, pastries enclosing sausages.

SAUTAGE (French), pressing herrings into barrels.

SAUTA-PAN, SAUTEE-PAN, a cook's stewing-pan.

SAUTÉE (French), a ragout.

SAUTERNE, a French wine so named.

SAUTIE, SALTIE, a name in Scotland for the dab, a species of *Pleuronectes*.

SAUVAGEON (French), an ungrafted slip of mulberry or other tree planted out.

SAVANNA, an open luxuriant grass plain or meadow.

SAVE-ALL, a small metal or other stand placed in a candlestick, to support the short candle ends while burning.

SAVELOY, a kind of dried sausage.

SAVINE, the plant *Juniperus Sabina*, whose stimulating and diuretic properties, as a drug, are well known.

SAVINE-OIL, an essential oil obtained by distilling the tops of the savine plant.

SAVINGS'-BANKS, certain provident institutions, established in Great Britain and other countries, to encourage frugality among the working classes, by receiving deposits, returnable, with interest, on demand. These funds have been placed under the control of Government, and identified with the public debt of the United Kingdom, a rather high rate of premium being allowed, as an inducement. In 1854, the total capital of the Savings'-banks was £33,742,620, of which £29,406,512 was lodged in Savings'-banks in England; £795,541 in Wales; £1,932,083 in Scotland; and £1,608,482 in Ireland. In the State of Massachusetts there was, in 1853, £[illegible],870,102 deposited in Savings'-banks by 117,404 depositors.

SAVONNETTE (French), a soap-ball for washing.

SAVONNIER, the French name for the soap-berry-tree (*Sapindus saponaria*).

SAVORY, an herb, of which there are two varieties, the summer savory (*Satureja hortensis*), and the winter savory (*S. montana*); being aromatic and carminative, they are used as an ingredient in culinary seasoning.

SAVOY, a species of small curled-leaf winter cabbage, the *Brassica oleracea major*.

SAW, a steel cutting plate with a serrated edge or teeth, which act as wedges to tear their way through an obstacle. Saws are either reciprocating or circular. The common hand-saw and the pit-saw are examples of the former. There are various kinds made, as half-rip, hand and panel, brass-back, iron-back, table-saws, lock-saws, gentlemen's hand-saws, frame, pit, and cross-cut saws, mill and circular saws, stonecutters'-saws, garden and pruning saws, keyhole-saws, woodcutters'-saws, bow saw and frames, metal saw and frames, &c.

SAW, SAHA, a grain-measure of Tunis and Barbary, = 4·846 pints.

SAWA, the Malay name for a rice field.

SAWDUST, the small fragments made in cutting wood, which is used in wine cellars for laying bottles in; as a stuffing material for dolls and cushions; for sprinkling floors in public-houses, the arenas of amphitheatres and riding-schools, and other purposes.

SAWING-BENCH, a carpenter's bench.

SAW-FILE, a mechanic's tool for sharpening saws, of which there are several kinds made, as hand-saw files, rip-saw files, tenant-saw files, frame-saw files, pit-saw files, &c.

SAW-HANDLE MAKER, a manufacturer of the wooden handles in which the saw blade is fitted.

SAWING-MACHINE, machinery for sawing wood, metal, &c. *See* SAW-MILL.

SAW-MANDREL, a holdfast for a saw in a lathe.

SAW-MANUFACTURER, a maker of saws.

SAW-MILL, machinery worked by steam or water-power, for cutting, moulding, or planing wood, by means of several saws; and for cutting veneers, and sawing stone, slate, and marble. Saw-mills are of two kinds: the circular, cutting by a continuous rotation, and the reciprocating, which operate as the common pit or frame saw.

SAW-PAD, a wooden handle forming a case for a small saw, which fits in at the end with a spring and screws.

SAW-PIERCER, a workman who cuts the teeth of saws.

SAW-PIT, a place for sawyers to cut logs of timber into planks and scantlings, by means of a frame saw.

SAW-SET, a triangular file, used by carpenters, sawyers, and others, for sharpening their saws.

SAWYER, one employed in cutting logs into planks, either by hand or machinery.

SAX-CORNET, SAX-HORN, musical wind instruments usually made of brass.

SAXON-BLUE, the sulphate of indigo.

SAXOPHONE, a brass instrument, soprano, alto, and bass, with a mouth-reed like a clarionet.

SAY (Scotch), a milk-pail, tub, or bucket; an old name for serge or bunting.

SAYER, a designation for variable Indian imposts, as town dues, tolls, licences, duties on merchandise, &c.

SAYETTE, a mixed stuff of silk and cotton, also called sagathy.

Sazer, another name for the Polish toise, = 5·669 feet.

Sazio, Sazo, a weight used in Venice, the 6th part of the ounce. There are two kinds of sazio, the heavy, weighing 102·26 grains, and the light, 64·89 grains.

Scabbard, the case or sheath for a sword, made of metal, leather, or wood.

Scabled, a building term applied to granite or other dressed or fine-axed stone, in contradistinction to plain-faced stone.

Scadding, a Scotch term for scalding; hence scadded beer, scadded whey, &c.

Scaffolding, a temporary erection raised on poles in the progress of building, or for white-washing, painting, &c.

Scaffold-pole, a long pole for supporting or building a scaffold.

Scagliola, an artificial surface to imitate marble, used for columns and pedestals, &c., which is made from a cement of the finest gypsum, in powder, mixed with aluminous matter, isinglass, and colours. It resembles fresco painting, in that the colours are laid on, and mixed in the wet state of the cement. The outlines of the work are traced with a sharp instrument, and the cavities are filled with the same material, of different colours, according to the veins to be imitated. Scagliola takes a fine polish, is as hard as marble, and very durable.

Scale, a graduated instrument for estimating measurements, making calculations, or ascertaining proportions; a comparative list of prices; a balance; the appendage to a weighing beam; the thin plates which cover the skin of certain fish, some of which, when hard, are made into very pretty flowers, brooches, and other ornaments.

Scale and Weight Maker, a maker of balances or weighing machines.

Scale-boards, a name given to thin veneers, or leaves of wood, which may be cut to thirty-two to an inch. There are 15 or 20 scale-board cutters in the metropolis. Also thin slips of wood, used by printers to make the pages register. See Veneers.

Scale-cutter, a workman who forms the thin pieces of horn or shell for the outer sides of knife-handles in Sheffield.

Scale-fish, a dealer's name for the pollack, the torsk, the hake, and the haddock, when dry-cured, which have only half the commercial value of the cod.

Scale-forger, in the cutlery trade, one who forms the inner metallic scales of a spring-knife, in which the blades lie.

Scale-preventer, a contrivance for blowing off, from the surface of the water in a boiler, the sediment, or particles of stony matter.

Scallion, a name for the shallot, the *Allium Ascalonicum*.

Scallop, a shell-fish; oysters with bread crumbs baked in a shell or tin; a hollow and round style of bordering to flounces, ribbons, &c.

Scalp, Scaup, a term in parts of Scotland for a bed of oysters or mussels; scalp is also the name for a small wig.

Scalpel, a surgeon's long dissecting knife, that tapers to a point.

Scalper, a tool for rasping bones.

Scammony, a cathartic gum-resin from the root of *Convolvulus Scammonia*, which is seldom to be obtained pure, being largely adulterated with chalk.

Scandal, Escandal, the fourth part of the millerolle, a wine-measure of Marseilles, and equal to 3¼ gallons.

Scantling, a local term in Ayrshire for the outline of a deed to be made; a rude sketch; the transverse dimensions of a piece of timber.

Scapple, to reduce a stone to a straight surface without working it smooth.

Scarf, a loose silk shoulder-belt; a light shawl; a wrapper for the neck.

Scarfing, the process of joining two pieces of timber to increase their length, by notching the ends into each other.

Scarf-shawl, a long narrow shawl worn by ladies.

Scarifier, a kind of harrow; an extirpator or cultivator; an instrument used in cupping.

Scarlet, a bright red colour, so named.

Scarlet-runner, a well-known climbing species of bean, the *Phaseolus multiflorus*, the young green pods of which are eaten boiled; and the ripe seeds, when stewed, under the name of haricot beans.

Scat, a tax paid in the Shetlands; a scot and lot duty.

Scavenger, a contractor for cleansing the streets; a street orderly.

Scavenger's-cart, a street-sweeping cart; a mud or dust cart.

Scene, a large painted view; the fixed or moveable paintings in a theatre.

Scene-painter, a theatrical painter, who designs and paints, on canvas or wood, the scenery required for a drama.

Scene-shifter, a mechanical workman employed in a theatre, to slide off and on, the moveable, or set-scenes and wings.

Scent, a common name for perfumes.

Scent-bottle, a fancy portable or toilet-table bottle for holding perfume.

Scent-packets, small perfumed cushions sold to ladies to place among their wearing apparel or in drawers.

Sceptre, a staff of royalty; an emblem of command.

Schabab (German), scrapings or refuse.

Schaff, a grain-measure formerly used in Germany; a name for the legal bushel of Bavaria, = 0·117 bushels; but the ordinary grain schaff of Bavaria is exceedingly variable; a weight used in Switzerland of 23·2 lbs.

Schaftmon, Shaftmon, an old Scotch term for a measure of 6 inches.

Schako (French), a military cap or helmet.

Schanel, in the Cape colony part of the side of a wagon.

Schappe, spun silk made from silk waste in Switzerland.

Schedule, an inventory or catalogue; the balance sheet of an insolvent; an appendix or tabular form added to a tract; a table of duties or tariff of charges.

SCHEFFEL, the German dry and grain measure, or bushel, varying considerably in different districts: in Prussia 1½ bushel; in Saxony about 3 bushels; at Oldenburg 0·844 bushel; in Rostock 1·070 bushel. For different kinds of grain the Prussian legal scheffel is estimated to weigh as follows: wheat 85½ lbs; rye 80½; barley 65; oats 45; meal 75; and pease 90½. The scheffel of salt is 54 lbs.

SCHEPEL, the Dutch and Spanish name for their bushel or grain-measure; like the scheffel, it is of very variable proportions; but the legal schepel is 0·275 bushel.

SCHERBETS, an Eastern beverage consisting of water in which jelly or syrup made from fruit has been dissolved, or of an infusion in water of the fruit itself. A kind of scherbet is also made with honey; and various ingredients, as vanilla, otto of roses, peppermint, vinegar, and even mastic are used to impart a flavour, while an agreeable colour is obtained by the employment of cochineal, the juice of the berries of *Phytolacca decandra*, and of *Cornus mascula*; the latter of which is an esteemed fruit in Asia Minor.

SCHERBETZIDES, itinerant venders of scherbet, the peculiar sound of whose little bells, struck by a machine which, at the same time, cools their glasses by a stream of water, may be heard far and near through the streets of an Eastern town, inviting customers to their trays, on which syrups, fruit, and sweetmeats are displayed.

SCHIEDAM, a name for Hollands gin.

SCHIFFPFUND. *See* SHIP-POUND.

SCHILLING, a small German coin worth about 1d.

SCHINEK, SCHINACK, a dry-measure of Hungary, nearly 3 bushels.

SCHISTE, a name for slate; also for shale; a mineral used in manufactures.

SCHNAPPS, a German name for drams of strong spirit.

SCHOCK, a German term for 60 pieces; 3 score, or 5 dozen of any thing.

SCHOLAR, a pupil or learner; a man of letters, or one devoted to books.

SCHOLASTIC, belonging to a school or schoolmaster.

SCHOOL, a place of study, for elementary teaching of different kinds, as day-schools, boarding-schools, free-schools, ragged-schools, grammar-schools, colleges, &c.; a shoal of fish; a herd of sea-lions.

SCHOOL-AGENT, SCHOLASTIC-AGENT, a person who negotiates the sale or purchase of the good-will of schools, the engagements of ushers or teachers, &c.

SCHOOL-DESK, a wooden desk for scholars to sit at.

SCHOOL-INSPECTOR, a visiting officer under the Education Board; a government overseer of schools.

SCHOOL-MASTER, SCHOOL-MISTRESS; persons employed in teaching in a school.

SCHOOL-SLATE, a slate framed in wood, used by school-boys for ciphering or writing on.

SCHOONER, a two-masted vessel with a fore and aft top-sail on both masts, but sometimes rigged with small square top-sails at the fore and main.

SCHOPPE, a German liquid-measure, the fourth part of a maas or gescheid, and somewhat less than an English pint.

SCHOT, a weight of Dantzic, representing the carat or the 24th part of the mark.

SCHREEF, SCHREVE, an old liquid-measure of Belgium, nearly 1½ gallon.

SCHROTT, SCHOOT, a German grain-measure, = to 0·197 pint.

SCHULL, SCHOOL, a shoal or large assemblage of fish.

SCHUTT, a vessel of a large class employed by the Russians on the Caspian sea, and ranging from 90 to 200 tons.

SCHWAREN, a nominal Bremen money. 5 of which go to the groat. There are 360 schwarens in the rixdollar.

SCIABECCHE, a kind of vessel employed in the trade of Genoa.

SCIEUR, a French sawyer.

SCIMITAR, a curved sabre.

SCISSEL, the clippings of various metals, or of slips or plates from which blanks for coins have been cut.

SCISSORS, metal cutting-instruments, consisting of two united blades, with holes at the handles for the fingers to pass through.

SCISSORS-CASE MAKER, one who makes the leather sheaths for scissors.

SCOBS, raspings; refuse dross; saw-dust.

SCOGIE, a Scotch term for a kitchen drudge; a female servant who performs the dirtiest work; also called a scuddle.

SCOLAZON, a manure so called.

SCOLLOP. *See* SCALLOP.

SCOLLOP-SHELLS, metal shapes for baking oysters in.

SCONCE, the hanging branch of a candelabrum, or of a wall candlestick; the socket in which a candle is placed.

SCOOP, SCOUP, an instrument for wetting the sails of boats; a kind of spoon; a wooden shovel; a large ladle; in Scotland a draught of liquor.

SCOOP-NET, a net for sweeping the bottom of a river.

SCORE, to mark or reckon; to draw a line with a sharp instrument, as in scoring the skin of pork; an account which, in former times, was often scored or chalked up on walls or boards, as a tavern-score, milk-score, &c.; 20 pieces; the original draught of a musical composition with all the parts marked.

SCORIA, slaggy lava; dross; the recrement or matter thrown off from metals in fusion; a slag of some vitrified or crystalline dross. *See* SLAG.

SCORZO, an Italian grain-measure, nearly 8 gallons; also a superficial measure, the 6th of the rubbio.

SCOT, a tax or reckoning.

SCOT AND LOT, bearing a fair share of taxes and offices; an inhabitant householder voting by olden rights and privileges.

SCOTCH-BONNETS, a name for the champignon; also for a variety of capsicum.

SCOTCH-CAMBRIC, a cotton fabric made in imitation of French cambric.

SCOTCHING, slightly lined; a drag or brake applied to the wheel of a carriage descending a declivity.

SCOTCH OATMEAL, the best kind of oatmeal.
SCOTIA, in building, a concave moulding, usually bounded by two narrow fillets.
SCOUP. *See* SCOOP.
SCOUR, to scrub or brighten; to remove grease spots.
SCOURER, a dyer and cleaner of fabrics.
SCOURING-PAPER MAKER, a manufacturer of emery and glass papers for brightening metals, &c.
SCOW, a flat-bottomed American lighter.
SCRAP-BOOK, a book for keeping miscellaneous prints or cuttings in; a kind of album.
SCRAPER, a small triangular iron tool, used for scraping the masts and decks of a ship; an engraver's instrument for working mezzotinto; a carpenter's tool for cleaning planks and casks; a long hoe for cleansing roads of mud. Also a fitted iron contrivance at a doorway to take off mud from the boots.
SCRAP-IRON, the cuttings and parings of iron work, which are saved, collected together, and melted again in the puddling furnaces.
SCRAPS, the residuum of melted fat.
SCRATCHER-UP, a bookbinder's tool.
SCRATCH-WIG, a thin rough wig.
SCREEN, a shelter of any kind; various articles bear this name, as a grate or sieve for separating stones or lumps from earth, and parting the dust from coal; a tin frame to reflect heat in cooking; a frame in leaves or folds to keep out draught; a hand-fan to keep off the heat of a fire; to sift.
SCREENED-COAL, sifted or large coal; that from which the breeze, or fine dust has been separated.
SCREENING-MACHINE, an apparatus for sifting earths, stamped ores, coals, &c. having a rotary motion, constantly changing the position of the article to be screened.
SCREW, a spirally grooved cylinder of metal or wood; that which works a screw press; a small metal fastening; a small paper packet of tobacco; in Scotland a small stack of hay; a blemished horse; one which, though useful as a hack, is unsaleable to persons who study the perfect appearance of the animal. *See* PROPELLER, and SCREWS.
SCREW-BOLT, a bolt secured by a screw.
SCREW-DRIVER, a tool for turning screws, in shape like a blunt chisel.
SCREW-GILDER, one who electrotypes or colours screws to imitate brass.
SCREW-GILL, part of a spinning mill.
SCREW-JACK MAKER, a maker of jack-screws. *See* JACK-SCREW.
SCREW-KEY, part of a lathe; a lever for turning the screw of a press. *See* PRESS-KEYS.
SCREW-PINE, the *Pandanus spiralis*, useful for its valuable fibre.
SCREW-PRESS, a press worked by a screw, used by bookbinders; a little machine for pressing table-linen, and other purposes.
SCREW-PROPELLER, the fan at the stern of a ship for propelling her through the water, and working on a screw.
SCREWS, spirally grooved metal fastenings made from iron rods. The head is raised in a die by pressure, flattened and split by a small revolving circular saw. Threading is effected by a saw which traverses the back of the spindle, and forces the blank iron against small cutters which groove out the thread; three runnings down suffice for making an ordinary-sized screw; the shape of the cutters regulates the fineness of the thread.
SCREW-STEAMER, a vessel propelled by a screw.
SCREW-WRENCH, a turn-screw; a bed-wrench.
SCRIBBET, a painter's pencil.
SCRIBBLING, a preliminary process to carding in the woollen manufacture.
SCRIBBLING-PAPER, rough foolscap or other waste-paper; outsides.
SCRIBE, a writer or clerk; a notary-public; to mark and adjust with compasses; to score with a scribing-iron.
SCRIBING-IRON, an iron-pointed instrument for marking casks and logs of timber.
SCRIP, an abbreviation of subscription, being the preliminary acknowledgment, or security, held for a certain amount paid up on a stock or share, which loses this distinctive term when the instalments are fully paid up, and the scrip is exchanged for a receipt in full; a bond, share, or other marketable security.
SCRIP-HOLDER, the holder of a scrip-certificate.
SCRIPT, a schedule; a kind of printing-type formed to imitate writing.
SCRIVELLOES, small elephants' tusks, those under the weight of 20 lbs.
SCRIVENER, a writer; a conveyancer, or money-broker. *See* MONEY-SCRIVENER.
SCRIVENERS' COMPANY, one of the minor livery companies of London, which has no hall.
SCROLL, a roll of parchment.
SCROW, a scroll; curriers' cuttings or small clippings from skins; the ears and other redundancies used for making glue or size.
SCRUB, dense underwood; stunted bushes; a name in Scotland for the jack-plane; to scour or rub hard; to clean by washing.
SCRUPLE, a small weight used in compounding medicines, the third part of a drachm, and equal to 20 grains troy, and thus expressed symbolically ℈.
SCRUTINEER, one who examines or assesses votes.
SCUD, in navigation, to drive before a gale with little or no sail set.
SCUDO, an Italian silver coin and money of account, worth about 4s.
SCUFE, a Scotch name for the racket or stringed battledore used in striking the ball at tennis.
SCUFFLER, an agricultural implement for cutting up weeds; the horse-hoe.
SCULL, a short oar.
SCULL-MAKER. *See* OAR-MAKER.
SCULPIN, a fish of the bull-head family, *Cottus octodecimspinosus*, common on the American coasts; also called "crapaud de mer." It is a favourite food of the Greenlanders.

SCULPTOR, a carver in wood or marble.

SCUM, the refuse or extraneous matters that rise on the surface of heated liquors, or melted metal.

SCUM-BOILER, a fat-melter, or tallow-chandler; one who refines the scum of sugar.

SCUPPER-NAIL, a large-headed nail.

SCUPPERS, holes in the side of a ship, to carry off water from the main deck.

SCURF-BRUSH, a hard hair-brush; a curry-comb for a horse.

SCURVY-GRASS, the *Cochlearia officinalis*, which is in repute for its antiscorbutic virtues.

SCUTCH, a wooden instrument used in dressing flax and hemp.

SCUTCHING STOCK, part of a flax-mill.

SCUTCH-MILL, a mill for preparing flax.

SCUTCH-RAKE, a flax dresser's implement.

SCUTTLE, a hole cut in any part of a vessel; an iron or copper pan or vessel for holding coals for a room.

SCUTTLE-BUTT, a cask with a hole cut in its bilge, and kept on the deck of a vessel to hold water for daily use.

SCYTHE, a long, sharp, curved instrument for cutting grass.

SCYTHE-MANUFACTURER, a maker of scythe-blades.

SCYTHE-STONE, a whetstone for sharpening gardening or reaping scythes.

SEA-COCK, a species of gurnard (*Trigla cuculus* and *T. Hirax*), much sought after by Russian epicures, and, being very scarce, they sometimes sell as high as 30 roubles.

SEA-COMPASS, a mariner's compass.

SEA-EAR-SHELL. *See* EAR-SHELL.

SEA-FOAM. *See* MEERSCHAUM.

SEA-GIRDLES, a name for the edible fucus, *Laminaria digitata.*

SEA-GREEN, a colour resembling the emerald green of the sea.

SEAH, a Jewish dry-measure, which contained nearly 14 pints.

SEA-HORSE TOOTH, a name given to the teeth of the walrus, and of the hippopotamus, which yield ivory.

SEAK, a preparation of the best mottled soap used in milling cloth.

SEA-KALE, an esteemed vegetable, the *Crambe maritima.*

SEAL, an engraved stamp for making an impression, used for private or public purposes.

SEALED-TEA, a kind of coarse tea, imported into Kiachta from China, so called from being pressed into solid sealed packages, weighing about 3 pounds each, so firmly compacted together that nothing less than hammer and chisel will break it. The leaves of this tea are old and tough as leather; the twigs and stalks are intermingled, and some fatty substance is mixed with it, to make it cohere.

SEAL-ENGRAVER, a die-sinker; a lapidary who cuts arms and crests on stones.

SEALING, the business of hunting and catching seals, and curing their skins; affixing a stamp to official documents.

SEALING-WAX, an adhesive resinous substance, made for sealing letters and documents, and covering the corks of bottles. The chief components of sealing-wax are shell-lac resin, and turpentine. In making red-wax, cinnabar is added, and for black wax, levigated ivory black.

SEAL-OIL, oil obtained from the seal fisheries, which is of two kinds, pale or cold drawn, and boiled or dark oil. The blubber is suffered to drain, for two or three months, into wooden pans, and this furnishes the pale seal oil of commerce, forming 60 to 70 per cent. of the whole. The putrescent refuse, and the clippings of the pelts, yield further quantities of dark oil by boiling. About 2½ millions gallons of seal-oil are shipped annually from Newfoundland.

SEALS, various species of *Phoca*, which are hunted for their skins, and the oil obtained from the blubber. The skins are sorted by fishermen into four qualities, young harp, young hood, old harp, bedlamer (year-old hood), and old hood; the most productive being young harp. Seals are found in immense numbers off the coasts of Newfoundland, Greenland, and Labrador, and we import from 500,000 to 700,000 skins annually. They are commercially classed into blue backs, white coats, and hair seal, small and large. Some of these are dyed and prepared as furs; others are used for leather, and, when tanned and varnished, they are employed by coach-makers and harness-makers, for accoutrements, and for patent or enamelled boots and shoes.

SEAL-SKIN MAKER, a tanner who prepares and varnishes seal skins for leather.

SEAM, a horse-load of timber, about 3 cwt.; a trade term for 24 stone of glass, = 120 lbs.; a name sometimes applied to the quarter of grain, or 8 bushels; a joint, the interval between planks in a vessel's deck or side.

SEAMAN, in a general sense all persons employed or engaged in any capacity on board a ship, although there are several classifications; able-bodied seamen, in the navy, are skilled and competent sailors, who know all the duties for which they are engaged.

SEA-MILE, the marine or geographical mile, the 60th part of a degree: it is often, however, applied to the marine league, or the 20th part of a degree. *See* MILE.

SEAMING-LACE, a coach-maker's lace, used to cover seams and edges.

SEA-HORSE TEETH, a name for the canines or tusks of the hippopotamus, which supply the most suitable ivory for the dentist.

SEAM-PRESSER, an abstract of a drill roller, consisting of two cylinders of cast iron, which, following the plough in the furrows, press and roll down the newly turned-up earth.

SEAN, SEINE, a large net for taking pilchards and herrings, varying from 200 to 300 fathoms in length, and from 10 to 14 fathoms in depth, and having cork buoys on one edge, and lead weights on the other.

SEANA, the head man of a village in India.

SEA-PIE, meat stewed in a saucepan, with a cover of dough.

SEARCHER, a Custom-house officer; a woman who examines female prisoners at a police station.

SEARCH-WARRANT, a legal authority for searching a house for stolen goods, or for concealed property belonging to a bankrupt, &c.

SEARSE, SEARCE, a fine wire sieve.

SEA-SALT, chloride of soda. See SALT.

SEA-SHAD, a delicious North-American fish, of from 2 to 5 lbs. which is split and pickled. The river shad are much inferior to those taken in the sea. See SHAD.

SEASIDE-GRAPE, the *Coccoloba uvifera*: the leaves, wood, and bark, are extremely astringent, and afford an extract termed Jamaica kino. The wood gives a red dye.

SEA-SLUG. See TRIPANG.

SEASONED, matured; food flavoured with condiments or spices.

SEAT, a chair, couch, or bench; a country house.

SEATING, horse-hair fabric, American leather, or other materials, made for covering the cushions of chairs, couches, &c.

SEAU, the French name for the eimer, of 7·337 gallons, formerly used in Antwerp.

SEA-UNICORN TOOTH, a name for the spiral horn or tusk of the narwhal (*Monodon monoceros*), which is often from 6 to 10 feet long, and is a beautiful ivory.

SEA-WALL, an embankment on the shore to keep off the encroachments of the tide.

SEA-WAND, SEA-WARE, names for a nutritious alga, the *Laminaria digitata*.

SEA-WEEDS, marine plants, many of which enter largely into commerce for food, for manure, for making glue or jelly, for barilla and iodine, and as a source of acetic acid.

SECCHIO, an Italian liquid-measure, ranging from 1½ to 2½ gallons in different towns.

SÉCHOIR (French), a clothes' horse; a drying room.

SECHSLING, SECHSTING, a Bavarian grain-measure, the 6th of the schaff, = 8·784 bushels.

SECHTER, a German grain-measure, of 4 gescheids, and = to 1·68 gallon.

SECKEL, a small pear.

SECOND, a measure of time of the 60th part of a minute, and represented thus ″. It is also a petty linear measure in England, the 12th part of a line; in Switzerland, the 10th part of a line; in Germany, the 10th part of the prime, or the 100th part of the inch.

SECONDARIES, those quills which rise from the second bone of the wings.

SECONDARIES' COURT, a small-debt court in the city of London.

SECONDARY, a judge and assistant of the sheriffs of London.

SECOND-HAND, not new or original; articles of clothing, &c. that have been used.

SECOND-MATE, a junior, or subordinate, executive officer in a merchant-ship.

SECOND-RATE, a ship of war carrying 80 to 110 guns.

SECONDS, a kind of flour manufactured from general runs of red wheat, and the flour made from sharps ground.

SECRETAGE, the application of a solution of nitrate of mercury with a sponge to rabbit and hare skins, and the fur of other animals, to communicate the property of felting which they do not possess.

SECRÉTARIAT (French), a secretaryship.

SECRETARY, a head clerk or writer; the acting official and record officer of a society or administrative board; a public functionary so named.

SECRET-SPRINGER, one who puts in watch-springs.

SECTION, an interior representation of a building; an indefinite portion of land; a railway cutting; a division of police.

SECTOR, a mathematical instrument, used in making diagrams and laying down plans.

SEDAN-CHAIR, a portable seat or hand-carriage for one person, carried by two footmen or bearers, with poles.

SEDIMENT, feculencies or refuse; a deposit of lees or dregs.

SEED-BROKER, an importer and dealer in oil and other seeds.

SEED-CAKE, a sweet cake containing caraway seeds. See OIL-CAKE.

SEED-CRUSHER, one who expresses oil from seeds; a machine with rollers.

SEED-LAC, small fragments of lac-resin, from which the colouring matter has been removed by boiling.

SEED-OIL, an indefinite name for several kinds of oil, which enter into commerce; especially for those made from the *Jatropha* nutteel, niver, poppy, and other Indian seeds. See GINGELIE.

SEED-PLANTER, the American name for the sowing-machine, which, in this country, is called a drill.

SEEDSMAN, a dealer in agricultural and garden seeds.

SEEKAKAI, an East Indian name for a species of soap-nut, obtained from the *Mimosa abstergens*.

SEER, a variable Indian weight, of which 40, however, usually go to the maund. It ranges from 3580 grains up to 33,650 grains. The seer should be a perfect cylinder, depth 4·35 inches, diameter 4·45 inches. In Bokhara the seer is 35½ lbs: in Trichinopoly the seer for metals is = 9 oz. 8¼ drachms. The East India Company's new seer of 80 tolas = 2·057 lbs. avoirdupois. The pucca seer is 1·866 lbs; 16 chittacks of 900 grains each, = 5 siccas or rupees, make a Calcutta bazaar seer; 60 siccas a Serampore seer; 82 a Hooghly seer; 84 a Benares and Mirzapore seer; and 96 an Allahabad and Lucknow seer. At Nagpore, 80 rupees' weight is a seer. The Calcutta factory seer is equal to 72 sicca weight, 11 annas, 2 puns, 10 gundas, and 2·63 cowries. Colonel Sykes and other Indian authorities give the Indian seer as 14,400 grains, = 2·057 lbs. avoirdupois, and the tola 180 grains. Also an Indian name for the fragrant aromatic root of *Hedychium spicatum*.

SEERHAND, a kind of muslin between nainsook and mull, particularly adapted for dresses, retaining its clearness after washing.

SEETOAH, a sort of concave iron trowel used to scrape and collect the juice of the poppy.

Segar. *See* Cigar.

Seggar, a fine clay receptacle, in which porcelain articles are placed to be fired or baked in the biscuit-kiln. *See* Saggar.

Seidel, Seitel, a German measure of capacity: for liquids ¾ to 1¾ pint in different localities; as a dry-measure about ¾ pint; for coal 4 bushels.

Seidlitz, an aperient powder, composed of equal parts of bi-carbonate of soda and Rochelle salts, which is taken dissolved in water; tartaric-acid being added to make it effervesce.

Seigle, the French name for rye.

Seigniorage, a duty paid for coining money. In 1816 a seigniorage of 6·45 per cent. was imposed on the silver coinage by the 56 George III.

Seil, the German name for the cord or surveyor's chain.

Seine-boat, a fishing-boat, about 15 tons burden, used in the fisheries on the west coast of England, to carry the large seine or casting-net. This boat is accompanied by two others, one a follower of about the same size, to assist in mooring the net, and a smaller boat, called a worker, for general purposes. *See* Sean.

Seitel. *See* Seidel.

Seizain, a sort of cloth of 1600 threads.

Seize, to fasten ropes together by turns of small stuff.

Selamim, a Portuguese grain-measure, nearly 1¼ pint.

Sell, to dispose of; to vend or traffic.

Sellier, a French saddler.

Seltzer-water, a mineral water; saline and slightly alkaline, and highly impregnated with carbonic-acid.

Selvage, the edge of any thing; a skein of rope yarns or spun yarn twisted together, used as a neat strap.

Semaine, the French name for a week or seven days.

Semaphore, an old-fashioned telegraph with arms.

Semencine, Semen Contra, names for the *Artemisia Sieberi*, and some allied species, the leaves and flower-heads of which are a celebrated remedy for worms. The vermifuge properties of this celebrated medicine reside in a volatile oil and resinous extract. *See* Santonine.

Seminary, a school for the young.

Semola, an Italian name for bran; but often erroneously applied by grocers, and other venders, to semolino.

Semolino (Italian), small seed; grains of rice; a kind of paste for soups. The commercial name for the fine hard parts of wheat rounded by attrition in the mill-stones, imported chiefly from Italy to the extent of 949 cwts. in 1855. In France, the name semolino is given to the large hard grains of wheat retained in the bolting machine, after the fine parts have been pressed through its meshes. With the semoule or gruau the fine white Parisian bread is made. The best semolino is obtained from the wheat of the southern parts of Europe.

Sen, a Siamese and Cambodian land-measure of 40 yards, and containing 20 [illegible].

Sendal, a thin kind of silk.

Senegal-root, a name for the diuretic and very bitter root of *Cocculus bakis*; used in intermittents, and in gonorrhœa.

Seneka-root, the root of *Polygala Senega* a native of the United States, which is diaphoretic, diuretic, and expectorant. It was introduced into medical practice as a remedy in snake-bites; but its efficacy in the treatment of these accidents is very questionable.

Seneschal, a high bailiff; a steward.

Senna, the leaflets of several species of *Cassia*, used in medicine for their purgative properties. *C. elongata* and *C. acutifolia*, furnish the Tinnevelly and Alexandrian senna, which are the best. The latter constitutes the bulk of the imports into Europe. It is much adulterated with the leaves of *Cynanchum Arghel*, *Tephrosia Apollinea*, and *Coriaria myrtifolia*. Our imports average about 150,000 lbs, although they are often much larger.

Sennit, a seaman's term for a coarse yarn or line for making rope; rope-yarns plaited, or flat braided cordage; plaited straw or palm leaves, &c., of which grass hats are made.

Sentinel, Sentry, a soldier, or guard; a watchman, or look-out.

Sentry-box, a small wooden house, serving as a shelter for a sentry in bad weather.

Sepeck, the current coin of Cochin China, cast of a compound brittle metal called tutenag, the base of which is zinc. It is about the size of a shilling, and pierced with a square hole, by which they are strung in numbers together; and as they are the only coin used, they form a very bulky and inconvenient medium: 60 sepecks are equal to one mas, an imaginary coin worth about 2½d.; and ten mas make a quan.

Sepia, a brown colour originally obtained from the ink-bag of a species of cuttle-fish.

Sepia Drawing, a neutral tinted picture coloured with sepia.

Sepoy, a bearer or messenger in Bombay; but in a general sense applied to the native soldiers serving under the East India Company.

Septaria, nodules of chalky marl, the well-known basis of Roman cement.

Sequestration, in Scotland, the process by which the effects of a bankrupt trader are realized and divided among his creditors, as by the process of bankruptcy in England. The law on the subject is contained in the statute 2 and 3 Vic. chap. 41.

Sequin, an Italian gold coin worth about 9s. 6d.; current in Algiers, at 8s. 6½d.; a Turkish money worth from 7s. 6d. to 7s. 8d.

Serafina, a sort of swan-skin used for waistcoats.

Seran (French), a hatchel to beat flax with.

Serancolin, a kind of red marble in France.

Serang, the Indian name for the boatswain of a ship.

Seraphine. *See* Melodeon.

Seraphine Maker, a manufacturer of musical instruments so named.

Seraskier, a Turkish general officer.

Serf, a Russian slave; an Hindustani name for exchange or discount. *See* Shroff.

Sergeant, an officer; the word is used in several senses, as for a police-officer, a non-commissioned military officer, &c.

Sergeants-at-Law are persons who, being called to the bar are, by the Queen's writ, commanded to take upon them the degree of the coif by a certain day. They rank after colonels, and before doctors and barristers.

Serge, a cloth of quilted woollen, extensively manufactured in Devonshire and other counties.

Sergette, a thin and slight serge.

Sericeous, silky; having a soft, smooth surface like silk; covered with silky hairs, as a leaf.

Serishtadar, a revenue officer in India.

Seron, Seroon, a kind of skin package; a bale formed of pieces of wood, covered or fastened with hide; cochineal, indigo, and various drugs are imported in this form. Sometimes a matted bale of almonds, or a pannier of raisins, weighing about 87½ lbs, is called a seron. An African weight of 185·55 grains.

Serpe (French), a bill-hook.

Serpent, a kind of fire-work; a brass musical wind-instrument, something like a serpent in its convolutions, chiefly used in military bands.

Serpentary-root, the root of *Aristolochia Serpentaria*, a native of North America, which is a valuable tonic, stimulant, and diaphoretic, and has been used as a febrifuge with considerable success.

Serpentin (French), the cock of a musket.

Serpentine, a handsome green magnesian limestone, so called from its spotted or snake-like markings, of which there are fine beds in Cornwall. Serpentine marble is now largely used for ornamental purposes and architectural decorations, being easily cut or turned, and admitting of a high polish. *See* Lizard-stone.

Serpette, a curved knife for pruning; a basket.

Serrated, notched; edged like a saw.

Serrurier, a French locksmith.

Servant, a household domestic; a farm labourer; a menial.

Servants' Register-office, a place where lists of vacancies are kept, and servants wait to be hired, who pay a fee to the registrar when suited with a place.

Service, duty or employment public or private; being engaged by another; a set of dishes and plates; an assortment of table linen; a seaman's term for layers of spun-yarn placed round a rope to protect it from friction.

Service-pipe, the junction or connecting pipe attached to water and gas mains leading to private houses, &c.

Serviette (French), a table napkin.

Serving, the process of binding or casing a cable or large rope with canvas or spun-yarn, to prevent friction or wearing in parts which are much exposed.

Serving-board, Serving-mallet, an implement used by sailors and riggers in winding tarred yarns around large ropes to protect them from friction or from undue wear.

Sesame, a plant, the *Sesamum orientale*, universally cultivated in the East Indies for the oil expressed from its seeds. We imported, in 1855, 652 quarters of sesame seed. In 1856, 22,700 cwt. of this seed were shipped from Madras alone, besides 2214 cwt. of oil. It is there called Gingely or Gingelie, and the seed is also known in commerce under its vernacular name of teel and til. *See* Simtrom.

Sessions-clerk, a clerk of the law courts in Scotland.

Sesspool, a reservoir for waste water; a hollow sunk for receiving drainage. *See* Cesspool.

Seste, a grain-measure of Siam, rather more than a picul; 135 lbs.

Sester, a name for the setier.

Set, a complete assortment; a measure of capacity in Siam. *See* Sat.

Seta, an ancient Hindoo weight of 225 grains.

Setee, a lateen-rigged vessel in the Mediterranean.

Seteree, an ancient variable land-measure of France, ranging from 0 to 113⅓ French ares.

Setier, a former French grain-measure of 1½ to 3½ bushels; but 1·8 setier of Paris may be taken as equal to a Winchester quarter of 8 bushels; a wine-measure of 8 French pints, 1·640 gallons. The new setier of France is the hectolitre.

Setine, a land-measure of Genova, about 4250 feet.

Set-off, a counterbalance; one demand placed against another.

Sett, a number of mines taken upon lease.

Settee, a large long seat with a back; a two-masted vessel; an Orkney weight. *See* Setee and Lesh-pund.

Settee-bed, a bed that folds up into a couch, chair, or sofa.

Setter, a useful sporting dog, the *Canis index*, trained to sit or crouch to the game he finds.

Setting-coat, the best kind of plastering.

Settlement, a new colony or township; the payment of a bill; the arranging or closing mercantile transactions; balancing of cross accounts; the location of a pauper on the parish to which he has a legal right; the sinking of a foundation; the dregs or feculencies deposited in liquors.

Settler, a colonist; one who locates on new land.

Settling-day, the prompt-day in the produce market; the half-monthly account-day for shares and stocks on the Stock-exchange.

Seville-orange, a bitter orange. *See* Oranges and Lemons.

Sevorja, a name for the *Stenanthium frigidum* of Kunth; the *Helonias frigida* of Schlecht, a native of the cool uplands of Mexico, and one of the sources of the poisonous sabadilla seeds of commerce, from which veratria is prepared. *See* Cebadilla.

Sew, to join by thread or fine fibre, and a needle; to drain a pond for the fish.

Sewed Muslin Manufacturer, a preparer of needle-work or embroidery.

Sewer-lamp, a safety-lamp for exploring sewers.

Sewers, subterraneous conduits; arched channels or water-courses constructed under-ground, to carry off the waste waters or filth of cities.

Sewers'-rate, a parish-rate levied for the keeping of the sewers in good order, usually chargeable to the landlord, unless agreed to be paid by the tenant or occupier.

Sewing-cotton, Sewing-silk, Sewing-thread, linen or silken threads prepared for the use of sempstresses, in balls or skeins, or wound on reels.

Sewing-machine, a labour-saving machine for stitching, adapted, according to its construction, for sewing or stitching woollen, linen, leather, &c.

Sewings, compound threads of silk, wound, cleaned, doubled, and thrown, with especial reference to their ultimate use as sewing-silk.

Sextant, an astronomical instrument made like a quadrant, but containing only sixty degrees.

Sexton, one who has the charge of a church, or of a graveyard, or cemetery.

Seyn, an Indian measure of capacity in use in Malwa, = to 34·137 lbs.

Shabby, damaged or faded; articles not new.

Shackles, links in a chain cable, fitted with a moveable bolt, so that the chain can be separated; iron fetters for the legs of prisoners, slaves, &c.

Shad, a common fish, the *Clupea Alosa*, caught principally in the Bay of Fundy. The shad of America having been found to differ materially from that of Europe, has received a distinct name, being designated *Alosa sapidissima* by Wilson, Dr. Storer, and others.

Shaddock, a West Indian fruit with a thick rind, the *Citrus decumana*.

Shade, a screen or sun-blind; a hollow glass cover for enclosing and protecting ornaments, &c.; a tint in painting.

Shaft, an engineering name for a large axle of machinery, a small one being termed a spindle; the pole of a carriage; the handle of a weapon; an arrow; the vertical access to a coal or other mine.

Shaft-bender, a person who bends timber by steam and pressure.

Shaft-horse, the horse which supports the poles or shafts of a vehicle.

Shaft-sinking, the process of boring or sinking excavations to mines.

Shag, a kind of cloth with a coarse nap; rough woolly hair.

Shagreen, a tuberculated or grained leather formerly prepared from the skin of a species of shark, and stained green; a kind of hard-grained leather, made in imitation of the above in Russia, from the skins of horses or asses.

Shag-tobacco, a very strong dark kind of tobacco, cut into fine threads, used both for chewing and smoking, which acquires its colour from being soaked or liquored.

Shahid, a Persian name for honey.

Shahee, an old Persian coin, the fourth part of an abushee, and worth about 4s.

Shake-willy. *See* Willying Machine.

Shale, indurated slaty clay. From bituminous shale a variety of commercial products are now obtained.

Shalli, a kind of twilled cloth, made from the native goats' hair at Angora.

Shalloon, a worsted stuff, the great staple of Halifax, where about 10,000 pieces are annually made for shipment to Turkey and the Levant.

Shalloon-maker, a weaver of shalloon.

Shallop, a large two-masted schooner-rigged boat; a light vessel with lug sails.

Shallot, a species of pungent small onion, the *Allium Ascalonicum*, used in cooking, for flavouring or seasoning food.

Shambles, a slaughter-house.

Shamiana, a gold throne cover of velvet, and gold embroidery, &c. used by native princes in India.

Shamie, a money of Bussorah.

Shammy, a common mode of writing or expressing chamois or oiled leather. *See* Chamois-leather.

Shampooer, a person in connection with the hot bath, who rubs the body and extends the limbs.

Shank, a double hand-ladle, capable of holding 2 to 4 cwt. of melted metal, carried in foundries by from three to five men; a part of type; the long part of a key or other instrument; the main piece of an anchor, the long iron bar connecting the flukes or arms with the stock.

Shank-painter, a rope or chain for securing the shank of the anchor to the ship's side.

Shanty, a woodman's hut in North America.

Shantyman, a lumberer or wood cutter; one who lives in a shanty.

Shape, form or figure; a pattern; a mould or cast, as a jelly shape, &c.

Shapere, a name given to the rupee when used as a weight in the Southern Mahratta country, and equal to 174 grains, but the new rupee is 180 grains.

Share, a part or portion, as of the property or stock in a joint-stock company; the cutting part or metal blade of a plough; to divide.

Sharebroker, a dealer in railway or other shares and securities.

Shareholder, one who owns a share in a joint fund or property.

Shark, a popular name for several species of *Squalus*, a voracious fish. The skin of some species is used by native workmen in India for polishing wood and ivory, and is made into shagreen. The dried fins are sent to China, where they are esteemed a food delicacy. A large quantity of oil is also obtained from the livers.

Shark-liver Oil, one of the common fish oils obtained in abundance, in some tropical localities, from sharks. It has a very low specific gravity.

Sharp, a term applied to instruments having a fine edge or thin point; also to vegetable substances which have a sour or acid flavour.

Sharps, a miller's name for the hard parts of the wheat, which require grinding a second time. By some millers sharps are called middlings.

SHATIR, a Persian name for a running footman.
SHAVE, a drawing knife used by coopers; to cut off thin slices; to clear the face of hair with a razor.
SHAVE-GRASS, a name for the Dutch rush, *Equisetum hyemale*. *See* DUTCH-RUSH.
SHAVING-BOX, a box with soap used for making a lather to shave with.
SHAVING-JUG, SHAVING-POT, a metal vessel or jug for holding hot water to shave with.
SHAVINGS, thin slices of wood, stripped off with a knife, plane, or other cutting instrument.
SHAWL, a gentleman's neck scarf; a lady's loose outer wrapper for the person, made of woollen or some other soft and warm material. Many of these, as Cashmere, Paisley, and Indian embroidered shawls, are held in high estimation.
SHAWL-BORDER MAKER, a manufacturer of the fancy borders for ladies' superior shawls, which are usually made separate, and afterwards attached to the middle.
SHAWL MANUFACTURER, a maker of shawls, of which there are numberless varieties, and fancy patterns and materials, barege, chenille, Paisley, Edinburgh, Cashmere, &c.
SHAWL-PIN, a lady's ornament, or fancy fastening for a shawl.
SHAWL-WAREHOUSEMAN, a wholesale dealer in shawls.
SHEA BUTTER, a solid fat obtained in Africa from the seed of *Passia Parkii*.
SHEADANA, SHALDANEH, Persian names for the seed of the hemp plant.
SHEADING, a tithing, or local subdivision of districts in the Isle of Man.
SHEAF, a bundle of corn bound up in the field; a bunch of 24 arrows; a quantity of iron or steel.
SHEALINGS, a name for the coarse husks of oats, taken off between mill-stones before the grain is kiln-dried in preparation for being ground into meal.
SHEAR, to clip or cut close, as a fleece of wool; the nap of cloth, &c.; to nap.
SHEARER, one who clips the fleece of wool.
SHEAR-HULK, a vessel fitted with shears.
SHEARING-FRAME, SHEARING-MACHINE, a screw-like machine in the manufacturing districts, through which woven fabrics are passed, to cut and level the surface.
SHEARING STEEL, a process of welding, or heating and hammering several pieces upon each other, to form a dense, compact, and tough mass, from which blister steel is made.
SHEARLING, a sheep that has been once [shorn.
SHEARS, spars elevated at angles and secured, for hoisting out masts, or fitting them in; cutting instruments, large, strong scissors, of which there are different kinds, as for shearing sheep, and for clipping hedges, &c.
SHEAR-STEEL, a prepared kind of steel, so named from its applicability for making scythes, clothiers', and shepherds' shears, and other cutting instruments. [a sword.
SHEATH, a case for a knife; a scabbard for
SHEATHING, a casing or covering for a ship's bottom of copper or yellow metal.
SHEAVE, the wheel in a pulley block, over which the rope travels. [Scotland.
SHEBEEN-SHOP, an illegal spirit-store in
SHED, a slight building; an erection with open sides; a shelter for cattle, carts, &c.; part of a weaver's loom.
SHED-STONES, a kind of granite.
SHEELING, a cottage.
SHEEP, the *Ovis aries*, a domestic animal, of high importance to man for its flesh and woolly covering. *See* WOOL.
SHEEP-COT, an enclosure or pen for sheep.
SHEEP-FARMER, a breeder of sheep, one who attends to the rearing of sheep for their wool or carcase.
SHEEP-GLUE PIECES and FLESHINGS, cuttings of sheep skins saved for making glue.
SHEEP-HOOK, a shepherd's crook for catching sheep by the legs.
SHEEP-PELTS, the skins of sheep, fresh or salted, intended for leather.
SHEEP-PEN, SHEEP-FOLD, an enclosure made with hurdles to confine sheep in some particular spot.
SHEEP-RUN, an extent of open country devoted to the grazing of sheep. In Australia the average requirement of pasture is an acre for each sheep.
SHEEP-SHEARER, a farm-labourer who clips the fleece of sheep.
SHEEP-SHEARS MAKER, a manufacturer of the steel clipping-instruments used in shearing sheep.
SHEEP-SKIN, the skin of a sheep; leather prepared from it.
SHEEP-SPLITS, the pelts or skins of sheep, split by a cutting knife or machine into two sections.
SHEEP-WASH, a liquid or smearing substance for the fleece or skins of sheep, either to kill vermin, or to preserve the wool; a mixture of arsenious acid and soft soap in water, in which sheep are dipped.
SHEERS, a triangular erection of spars, by which masts, &c. are lifted into a ship. *See* SHEARS.
SHEET, a rope attached to the lower part of the sail of a boat or ship; a piece of bed-linen of calico or linen; a thin plate or expanded surface of any kind, as a sheet of copper, iron, or glass; a broad piece of paper; an impression of printed paper folded to form part of a pamphlet or book.
SHEET-ANCHOR, the most important and reliable holdfast of a ship, the best bower being the second anchor.
SHEET-CABLE, the strongest and best cable; that attached to the sheet-anchor.
SHEET-GLASS, a plate of glass, run or cast in a solid frame.
SHEETING, linen or cotton cloth for bed-sheets. Calico is now much substituted for linen sheeting, on account of its cheapness and warmth. It is sold bleached and unbleached.
SHEETS, a name given by railway companies to wagon covers, of oiled canvas, made of different qualities and sizes, from 23 to 42 square yards.
SHEET-ZINC, zinc rolled into plates or sheets.
SHEFFIELD-WARE, fine cutlery, and plated and other metal articles, of which Sheffield is the chief seat of manufacture.

Shekel, an ancient Hebrew weight, equal to 9 dwts. 26 grains; a shekel of gold = £1 16s. 5d.; of silver, = 2s. 3½d.

Shelf, a ledge; a board in a cupboard, or fixed against a wall, to place articles on.

Shell, a rough coffin to be enclosed in another: an engraved copper-roller used in print-works; a hollow cast-iron projectile filled with combustibles; the case of a block; the hard envelope of eggs and of certain seeds and fruits; the crustaceous or testaceous covering of certain animals, as the shell of a tortoise, an oyster, a lobster, &c. Shells are occasionally cut through to show their internal sections or structures; others are simply polished exteriorly in their entire state as specimens of natural history, or for their intrinsic beauty; and some few are cut up in the manufacture of various useful and ornamental works. Porcelainous shells are generally univalve, or single shells, such as chanks, whelks, limpets, and cowries. Nacreous shells are much softer than the porcelainous, and are for the most part bivalves, such as those of the various oysters, mussels, &c. A large trade is carried on in various kinds of shells either locally or generally.

Shellac, crude lac resin melted into plates. *See* Lac.

Shell-bark Hickory, the *Carya alba*, the largest and finest of the American hickories. It is an ornamental tree, and produces, every alternate year, an ample crop of the best of nuts. The wood is unrivalled for fuel.

Shell-button, a hollow button made of two pieces of metal, one for the front and the other for the back: these are mostly covered with silk; a button formed of mother-of-pearl shell.

Shell-cleaner, a person who makes a business of cleansing and scouring shells, by water and strong acids, for dealers or manufacturers.

Shell-comb, a lady's comb for the hair, or a toilet comb, made of tortoiseshell.

Shell-fish, aquatic animals having a testaceous or crustaceous covering; the term is chiefly applied in commerce to crabs, lobsters, and cray-fish, oysters, mussels, periwinkles, and whelks, in which a large trade is carried on.

Shell-flowers, ornaments made with small shells, plain or coloured.

Shelling, a commercial name for groats, the grain of oats when the shudes are removed.

Shell jacket, an undress military jacket.

Shell lime, lime burned from shells. *See* Chunam.

Shell-marl, clay abounding with small shells, which is found valuable as a manure.

Shell-work, flowers, baskets, and various ornamental articles made of shells.

Shelon, a Polish and Prussian coin, worth from 4 to 6 deniers, or about the eighth or tenth of a penny.

Shepherd, a person who has the care and management of a flock of sheep.

Sherbet, a decoction of barley-meal and sugar, perfumed with roses, orange flowers, violets, or citron. What is sold in the lower-class confectioners' and other shops as sherbet, is merely lemon kali or tartaric acid and potash.

Sheriff, the chief executive civil officer of a county or city; the high bailiff of a colony; an inferior local judge in Scotland.

Sheriff's-carriage, the state carriage of the sheriff of the city of London.

Sheriff's-court, a county court; a court of requests for the recovery of debts under £50.

Sheriff's-officer, a sheriff's assistant; one charged with arrests and the service of processes; a catch-pole.

Sheristadar, one having the custody of documents in India.

Sheronta, a Turkish silk kerchief used for a turban piece.

Sherry, a favourite Spanish white wine, the produce of Xeres, of which the average imports, in the three years ending 1856, were about 4,000,000 gallons, the consumption being about 2¾ million gallons.

Sherry-cobler. *See* Cobler.

Sherry-negus, hot water and sherry, sweetened.

Shetland Pony, a small shaggy pony bred in the Shetland islands.

Shield, a buckler or protection for the person; an escutcheon.

Shield-maker, a shield-wright; one who works on gold and silver of which ornamental shields are made.

Shift, a woman's linen or calico undergarment; a miner's spell or turn of work.

Shih, a grain-measure in China, equal to about 160 lbs. weight.

Shikarry, a specially organized hunt in India, to destroy wild animals, which may have become numerous and troublesome.

Shilling, the principal current British silver coin, the 20th part of a pound sterling, and worth 12d.; it weighs 3 dwts. 15·27 grains. The British shilling generally passes on the Continent, for 10 silver groschen in Prussia; 35 kreutzers in Frankfort; 58 cents in Holland; and 1 franc 20 centimes in France. The following figures give the number of shillings coined at the Royal Mint in the last few years:—

1848	104,040	1853	4,250,188
1849	645,480	1854	552,414
1850	685,080	1855	1,368,400
1851	470,071	1856	3,168,000
1852	1,806,574		

The Americans call the eighth of a dollar a shilling.

Shim, a tool for breaking up land.

Shingle, an oblong thin piece of wood, used as a roofing material in the same manner as slates. In the United States they are made of pitch pine, in the East and West Indies of other woods; coarse beach gravel used as ballast for a ship.

Shingle-machine, an American machine for riving, shaving, and jointing shingles, which is capable of making 30,000 per day.

Shingle-mill, a saw-mill for cutting planks or logs into shingles.

Shingling-hammer, a ponderous machine for hammering or shaping the blooms of iron into square or oblong pieces.

Shingling-mill, a forge or large workshop where iron is made malleable.

Shin-plaster, a name given in the United States to coins and notes, which are not current money payments.

Shinty, a kind of exhilarating Scotch game in which bats like golf-clubs are used.

Ship, a three-masted vessel, with tops, yards, and square sails, to each mast.

Ship and Insurance Broker, a person who deals in marine insurances, effecting insurances on vessels, cargo, and passengers' effects.

Ship-biscuit, hard, coarse biscuit, specially prepared for use on shipboard.

Ship-biscuit Baker, a maker of hard biscuit for seamen's use.

Ship-breaker, a person who buys the hulls of worn-out vessels, to break up for the timber and metal they contain.

Ship-broker, a mercantile agent who transacts the business for a ship when in port, and usually combines the business of insurance.

Ship-builder, a shipwright; one who constructs vessels.

Ship-captain, the master and commander of a merchant-vessel.

Ship-carpenter, a workman who fits up cabins, or performs the finishing work in ships. *See* Carpenter.

Ship-carver, one who carves figure-heads, and the work on the stern, or shapes, mouldings, &c., for a ship.

Ship-caulker, one whose business it is to stop, with oakum and pitch, the seams of ships' sides and decks.

Ship-chandler, a tradesman who supplies the small wares and stores required for a ship.

Ship-deliverer, a person who contracts to unload a ship.

Ship-hearth Maker, a manufacturer of the cooking galleys or stoves used on shipboard.

Ship-joiner. *See* Joiner.

Ship-letter, a letter forwarded by a private sailing vessel, and not by the steamer or packet chartered to carry the post-office mail.

Ship-load, as much as a vessel can stow; 424 tons of coals.

Ship of the Line. *See* Line-of-Battle-ship.

Ship-modeller, a designer; one who lays down the proposed lines of a vessel.

Ship-owner, a person who owns one or more ships.

Shipped, transmitted by sea; goods consigned or forwarded to order.

Shipper, an exporter of goods; the person who enters at the Customs, in his name, goods sent by a ship.

Shipping-agent, a licensed broker or agent appointed by owners to transact business for a ship. *See* Ship-broker.

Shipping-bill, an invoice or manifest of goods placed on board a ship.

Shipping-clerk, a merchant's clerk who attends to the shipment of goods.

Shipping Interest, the owners of ships and parties generally interested by business with shipping.

Shipping-note, a delivery-note of particulars of goods forwarded to a wharf or dock for shipment.

Shipping-office, the place of business of a broker, who receives small packages for shipment; a steam-packet office; a wharfinger's or dock-master's office.

Shipping-master, an officer under the Local Marine Board, subject to the control of the Board of Trade.

Shippound, a commercial weight in Russia and Sweden, of 400 pounds avoirdupois; in some of the other northern countries equal to only 300 lbs. In estimating the carriage of goods, the shippound is reckoned at 380 lbs. In Sweden the shippound is 400 skaalpounds of 15 ounces avoirdupois.

Ship-provision Merchant, a dealer in stores for ships, such as salted or preserved provisions, spirits, groceries, flour and meal, ship biscuit, &c.

Shiprigged, square-rigged, as a three-masted ship is with large square sails, and spreading yards.

Ship-rigger. *See* Rigger.

Ship's Articles, the conditions and terms which seamen condition to conform to, and abide by, on taking service on board a merchant ship, and which are binding on master and seamen.

Ship's-block Maker, a manufacturer of large blocks for ship's use.

Ship's-husband, a part owner, or other person appointed as a manager to look after and provide stores, provisions, or assistance for a ship when in port.

Ship's-papers, the certificate of registry, charter-party, manifest, and other official documents, required to be produced on certain occasions.

Ship's-smith, an iron worker who fits the metal work, bolts, &c. in ships.

Ship-surveyor, an examiner of the condition, fittings, and sea-worthiness of ships. *See* Lloyds' Surveyor.

Ship-thimbles, concave iron rings or eyes, used in the sails and rigging of vessels, to prevent the chafing of ropes when attached to hooks, bolts, staples, &c.

Shipwreck, the loss of a vessel at sea; or the stranding of a vessel.

Shipwright, a ship-builder; a carpenter who works on ships.

Shipwrights'-company, one of the minor livery companies of London, which, having no hall, transacts its business at Guildhall.

Ship-yard, a marine building-yard; the works of a ship-builder.

Shiraz, a Persian wine.

Shiraz Tobacco. *See* Persian Tobacco.

Shire, a division of land, less than a county, sometimes only a parish.

Shirr, an insertion of elastic cord between two pieces of cloth.

Shirt, a man's under-garment of linen, cotton, or flannel.

Shirt-button, small buttons of mother-of-pearl shell, porcelain, or other material, for attaching to the wrists, collar, and front of shirts.

SHIRT-FRONT, a dickey, or loose shirt bosom, to be worn over a soiled shirt.
SHIRTING, a kind of calico or long loth, made to imitate and supersede linen.
SHIRT-MAKER, a sempstress; a tradesman who employs females to make shirts.
SHIRT-STUDS, metal or other links, used instead of buttons.
SHIVE, a thin slice; a sheave; a small species of onion. *See* CHIVES.
SHOAD, SHODE, a stone containing ore mixed with rubbish.
SHOCK, a commercial term applied to loose goods in some parts of the Baltic, signifying a lot of 60 pieces, as 60 staves, &c.
SHODDY, worsted yarn from old stockings, tailors' clippings, and old woollen rags, torn up, fibre by fibre, in a "devil" (as it is technically termed), and re-spun into yarn, with the addition of a little fresh wool. Shoddy is made into an inferior cloth, into druggets, padding, and other articles.
SHOE, a miner's name for a trough, in a crushing-mill; a covering for the feet, chiefly made of leather; an iron protection for a horse's foot; a socket or runner; the sled or drag for a wheel.
SHOE-BINDER, a female who attaches the leather or ribbon binding to a shoe.
SHOE-BLACK, a boy in the streets who cleans shoes; a name in Jamaica for the *Hibiscus rosa sinensis*, which furnishes a valuable fibre.
SHOE-BUCKLE, a buckle for the front of shoes, now seldom or never used.
SHOE-BUTTS, stout leather salted for soles.
SHOE-FACTOR, a wholesale dealer in shoes.
SHOEING-SMITH, a blacksmith who shoes horses.
SHOE-LAST MAKER, a shaper of wooden models of the foot to fit shoes by.
SHOEMAKER, a workman who makes shoes; a tradesman who sells shoes and boots.
SHOE-PACK, in North America, a mocassin made of tanned leather, the black side in.
SHOE-PEG MANUFACTURER, a maker of the wooden or metal pegs, sometimes used to fasten on the soles of shoes.
SHOES, coverings or protections for the feet, usually made of strong leather; a currency medium in China, being a mass of pure silver in the shape of a shoe, and weighing about ten taels, or 13½ ounces.
SHOE-SCRAPER. *See* SCRAPER.
SHOE STONES, sharpening or setting-stones, imported from France for the use of shoemakers, book-binders, saddlers, harness-makers, pianoforte-makers, cork-cutters, &c.
SHOE-STRING, a piece of black tape or ribbon for tying shoes.
SHOE-THREAD MAKER, a manufacturer of the thread used by shoemakers to sew leather together.
SHOLA, an Indian name for a cellular substance, obtained from the pith-like stem of *Æschynomene aspera*, used for making hats, bottle and glass covers, life-preservers, and toys.
SHOOKS, SHAKES, the staves and battens of wood used for making sugar-boxes and hogsheads.
SHOOT, a shaft, pit, or trough full of water; a branch from a main stock or trunk.
SHOOTHEE, a name in Bengal for the long zedoary of pharmacy, the roots of *Curcuma Zerumbet*.
SHOOTING-BOX, a sportsman's country-seat or quarters.
SHOOTING-STICK, a tapering piece of wood, generally of box or hawthorn, about nine inches long, used by letter-press printers: it is applied to the quoins, and struck heavily with a mallet, till the types are firmly fastened in an iron frame called a chase.
SHOP, a place where any thing is sold; a working-place; a name in the manufacturing districts for a collection of six or eight looms, occupying the lower flat or story of a building.
SHOP-BILL, a tradesman's hand-bill or business announcement.
SHOP-BLIND. *See* BLIND.
SHOP-BOOK, a tradesman's book of memorandums or accounts; *a day-book*.
SHOP-COUNTER, a shop-board or resting-place, for goods, &c. to be examined, measured, or weighed.
SHOP-FITTINGS, the counters, desks, shelves, gas-burners, and other fixtures of a shop.
SHOP-FRONT, an ornamental window or front to a shop.
SHOPKEEPER, a retail dealer or store-keeper.
SHOPMAN, an assistant who serves or attends in a shop.
SHOP-WALKER, the general superintendant in a linen-draper's shop, who directs the customers to the proper department for the goods they seek, and sees they are attended to.
SHOP-WINDOW, the large display window of a shopkeeper.
SHOP-WOMAN, a female who attends upon customers in a shop.
SHORE, a timber prop; a buttress or support to a wall; a stanchion.
SHORLING, the skin of a sheep that has been lately shorn.
SHORTHAND-WRITER, a reporter who takes notes quickly and accurately in stenography or shorthand; an official engaged to take notes at a public meeting, trial, &c.
SHORTHEADS, a sailor's term for sucking whales under one year old, which are very fat, and yield above thirty barrels of blubber.
SHORTS, coarse flour; bran.
SHORT-SHIPPED, a deficient quantity; goods shut out from a ship, accidentally or for want of room, although passed and cleared at the Customs.
SHOT, an alloy of lead and arsenic run into very small globules, by dropping through a cullender, at the top of a shot-tower, into a tub of water at the bottom. It is afterwards sorted through sieves into the different sizes, No. 0 to 4.
SHOT-BELT, a leather sling pouch carried by sportsmen, to hold shot.
SHOT-MANUFACTURER, a melter and maker of shot.
SHOT-TOWER, an elevated tower from which shot is dropped into water.

SHOULDER OF MUTTON, the fore-leg of a sheep.
SHOULDERS, a name in the leather trade for tanned or curried hides and kips, as well as for English and foreign offal.
SHOVEL, a wooden or iron scoop with a long handle; a kind of spade.
SHOVEL MAKER, a manufacturer of iron or wooden shovels and spades.
SHOW, an exhibition on a large or small scale; a booth at a fair. There are poultry shows, cattle shows, horticultural and floricultural shows, &c.
SHOW-BILL, SHOW-BOARD, a placard or display-board with large letters or devices.
SHOW-BOX MANUFACTURER, a maker of glass cases for shops, &c.
SHOW-CARD, a tradesman's placard or announcement; a pattern card for displaying in a shop.
SHOWMAN, one who keeps a small exhibition.
SHOW-ROOM, a shopkeeper's or workman's display room.
SHRAPNELL, a kind of bombshell filled with bullets, named after the inventor.
SHREETALY, an Indian name for the tailpot palm, *Corypha umbraculifera*, from which a kind of flour is obtained. The seeds are a species of vegetable ivory, which are turned into marbles, beads for necklaces, chessmen, button-moulds, &c. They may be obtained in large quantities in India.
SHRIMPER, a fisherman who catches shrimps on the sea shore.
SHRIMP-NET, a dredge-net fixed on a pole, or a sweep net dragged over the fishing ground.
SHRIMPS, small crustacea, the *Crangon vulgaris*, caught in large numbers, and sold in towns.
SHRINK, to warp or contract.
SHROFF, the native name for an Indian banker or money-changer.
SHROFFAGE, the examination of coins, and separation of the good from the debased.
SHROUD, grave-clothes for a corpse.
SHROUDS, sets of ropes reaching from the lower mast-heads to the vessel's sides, to steady and secure the masts.
SHUBE, a sledge wrapper of fur.
SHUBIT, an Arabic name for the aromatic and carminative fruit of *Anetham Sowa*.
SHUDE, a name given to the husks of rice, and other refuse of rice-mills, largely supplied to oil-crushers, as an adulterating ingredient for linseed cake.
SHUMA, an Arabic name for bees'-wax.
SHUMAC. *See* SUMACH.
SHUPRAK. *See* PELIJURREE.
SHURIFA, the Persian name for the custard-apple.
SHUTTERS, safeguards to windows, of wood or iron, closing horizontally or perpendicularly.
SHUTTLE, in weaving, the instrument for passing the weft between the opened warps: in foundry operations, a gate or stop in the sow or trough by which the melted metal is let out into the mould.
SHUTTLE-MOUNTING MAKER, a constructor of the frame-work or fittings for shuttles and looms.
SHUTTLE-RACE, a sort of shelf in the weaver's loom.
SHUTURKHAR, an Indian name for the camel's-thorn, *Alhagi Maurorum*, which yields the manna of the desert.
SIAMOISE (French), a coarse cotton cloth.
SIBERIAN OIL-SEED, a local name in Canada for the *Camelina sativa*, or Gold of pleasure.
SICCA, a term formerly very generally applied to the rupee as a money and a weight. The rupee was called a sicca only during the year after its coinage, and subsequently a sonaut or sanat rupee. The various siccas or sonauts are now estimated by the shroffs or native money-changers, in comparison with the legal current rupee of the East India Company's mint. *See* RUPEE.
SICKLE, a short, curved, reaping-hook.
SICKLE-MANUFACTURER, a maker of sickles.
SIDE-ARMS, weapons carried on the left side, as a bayonet, sword, hanger, or dirk.
SIDEBOARD, a shelf or fixed table in a dining-room.
SIDE-SADDLE, a woman's riding-saddle with a pommel and one stirrup.
SIDESMAN, a churchwarden's deputy or assistant.
SIDE-WALK, a foot-path; a causeway.
SIDHEE, an Indian name for the large dried leaves and young capsules of the Indian hemp-plant, without the stalks; used for making an intoxicating-drink, for smoking, and in the conserve or confection, termed majoon.
SIDING, a passing place or turn out; a resting-place for trains on a railway-line.
SIDINGS, a name in America for long wedge-shaped boards, used for the sides or roofs of houses.
SIEGE-GUN, a heavy gun carrying a large charge of powder and ball, used to batter down or effect a breach in an enemy's wall.
SIESTER, a Bavarian coin. *See* KOPF-STUCK.
SIEVE, a strainer, riddle, or searce, with hair, wire, or zinc bottom; a coarse basket; a bolting-cloth.
SIEVE-BOTTOMS, attachments for the frame of a sieve made of horse-hair or wire, &c. and of various kinds; cylindrical ones for paper-manufactories, as well as other kinds, are made in Illyria in considerable quantities for export, and at very moderate prices.
SIEVE-MAKER, a manufacturer of screening machines and sieves.
SIGNAL, a mark or beacon; a warning given by guns, blue lights, or rockets, &c. *See* FOG-SIGNAL.
SIGNAL-LIEUTENANT, an officer in the Royal Navy having the charge of signals on board a flag-ship.
SIGNAL-MAN, a railway official; also one employed at a flag-staff, semaphore, or on board-ship, &c. to manage signals.
SIGNAL-STAFF, SIGNAL-POST, an elevated pole or spar, erected on some prominent or distinguishable situation, for making signals to shipping, &c. Flagstaffs are often erected in gardens, and on the tops of houses or public buildings, to suspend flags for holidays or festive occasions, &c.

SIGNATURE, a person's name subscribed to a writing, cheque, or other document; in printing, the letter or figure at the lower part of the first page of a sheet, intended to facilitate the arranging and gathering of the sheets for binding them.

SIGN-BOARD, a tradesman's announcement affixed to his shop, store, or dwelling.

SIGNET, an engraved stamp; a seal.

SIGNET-RING, a ring with a stone or metal shield for cutting letters, arms, or devices on.

SIGNET, WRITER TO THE, a law-officer in Scotland so named; abbreviated, "W. S."

SIGN-PAINTER, a painter of publicans' hanging signs, or of fixed signs for shopkeepers.

SIGN-POST, the post on which a sign is suspended.

SIKAT, the Malay name for a harrow.

SIKTHA, a Sanscrit name for bees'-wax.

SILBADANI, a furniture wood of Demerara.

SILBERGROSSCHEN, a Prussian coin of 12 pfennings.

SILESIA, a linen made in Germany.

SILHOUETTE, a profile likeness or picture represented in black, the shadows and prominent features being touched in with gum.

SILK, the fibre enveloping the silk-worm cocoon, which, when simply reeled, is termed raw silk, and after being worked in the mills, thrown silk. Our imports of raw silk in 1856, amounted to 7,383,672 lbs.; of thrown or spun silk, 853,015 lbs.; of waste knubs and husks, 17,994 cwts. Of silk manufactures of Europe we received 905,018 lbs.; and of Indian silk 597,752 pieces. The imports of raw silk were derived from the following quarters:—China, 56,561 bales; Bengal, 18,820 bales; Persia, 7,888 bales; Brutia, 149 bales; Italian, 2,784; total, 78,166.

SILK AND VELVET MANUFACTURER, a weaver and maker of these articles.

SILK-BUYER, a clerk employed to purchase silk at public sales.

SILK, CONDITIONING. *See* CONDITIONING SILK.

SILK-COTTON, a name given to the silky down or fibre obtained from the *Bombax*, *Calotropis*, *Cryptostegia*, and other plants, which is useful for stuffing pillows, paper-making, &c. *See* KAPOK.

SILK-DRESSER, a stiffener and smoother of silk.

SILK-DYER. *See* DYER.

SILK-EMBOSSER, one who ornaments silk by passing the plain stuff between rollers, the surfaces of which contain the desired pattern raised on one cylinder, and depressed or sunk on the other.

SILK-GAUZE MANUFACTURER, a gauze-weaver. *See* GAUZE.

SILK-GOWN, the distinguishing robe of a Queen's Counsel; a dress worn by females.

SILK-GRASS, a name for the fine fibres of the *Agave vivipera*, and of *A. yuccæfolia*.

SILK-HANDKERCHIEF, a pocket or neck kerchief of silk, white, or coloured.

SILK-HAT, a light hat with a silk plush cover; not a felted or beaver hat.

SILK-HOSE, stockings made of silk.

SILK-MANUFACTURE, an important industrial occupation, which gives employment, in its several branches, to about a million persons. The declared value of the exports of British manufactured silks in 1856, was close upon £3,000,000. In 1850, there were 272 silk factories in England, with 1,888,908 spindles, 6092 power-looms, the steam and water power employed equal to 3 571 horse power. In these factories 12,513 male operatives, and 20,190 female operatives were engaged. Ninety-seven of the factories were situated in Cheshire, chiefly in Macclesfield and Congleton. There were only five silk factories in Scotland, employing 841 persons, and no silk factory in Ireland or Wales.

SILK-MERCER, a dealer in articles made of silk, usually combined with the general linendrapery business.

SILK-MERCHANT AND MANUFACTURER, a maker and wholesale dealer in silk goods.

SILK-MILL, the building or factory in which raw silk, as imported, is prepared for the weaver, the stocking-maker, or the sempstress, by spinning or twisting, and other processes. They are sometimes subdivided into silk-throwing mills, and silk-spinning mills, the former being for the manufacture from good and perfect raw silk, and the latter from waste and inferior silk.

SILK-PLUSH, a material used for articles of ladies' dress; also very extensively for covering the stuff bodies of men's hats.

SILK-PRINTER, a stamper of silk.

SILK-PURSE MAKER, a knitter of purses of coloured silk.

SILK-SHAG, a coarse, rough woven silk like plush.

SILK-SPINNING MILL. *See* SILK-MILL.

SILK-THROWER, one who twists or spins and prepares silk.

SILK-THROWERS'-COMPANY, one of the minor livery companies of London, which has no hall.

SILK-THROWING, the process of spinning and preparing hard silk for warp and weft threads for the weaver; for yarn for the silk-stocking maker; for sewing-silk, and other purposes.

SILK-WATERER, one who clouds, waves, or waters silk, by passing two pieces placed lengthways between metallic rollers, where they are subjected to different degrees of pressure.

SILK-WEAVER, a manufacturer of articles of silk in breadths for dress-pieces, &c., or narrow strips for ribbons.

SILK-WEED, an American name for the *Asclepias Syriaca*, the root of which has some medicinal properties. A sugar is made from the odoriferous flowers, which are gathered in the morning when they are covered with dew, and the cotton from the pods is collected to fill beds. On account of the silkiness of this cotton, Parkinson calls it Virginian silk. The plant is sometimes called Milk-weed.

SILK-WEIGHT-AND-MEASURE. The size or substance of a silk thread is usually estimated by deniers, an Italian and French weight, the comparative proportion of which will be understood by the appended remarks. The ounce troy and the ounce "Poids de Marc" of Lyons, by the latter of which silk is tested in France and Italy, are equal in weight, but are differently subdivided. The ounce troy in England is divided into 20 pennyweights × 24 = 480 grains; the ounce of Lyons, "Poids de Marc," into 24 drams × 24 = 576 deniers. The denier is therefore 1-6th less than the English grain, or, as the decimal 0·8333 is to 1·0000.

	Deniers.		Grains.
Therefore	1·000	=	0·8333
"	1·200	"	1·0000
"	6	"	5
"	100	"	83⅓
1 dram, "Poids de Marc"	24	"	20
1 pennyweight, troy, about	28⅘	or	24
1 dram, avoirdupois "	32⅘	or	27⅓
1 oz. avoirdupois (16 drams of 27⅓ grains)	525	or	437½
1 oz. troy (20 pennyweights of 24 grains)	576	=	480
1 oz. "Poids de Marc" (24 drams of 24 deniers)	576	"	480
1 lb. troy (12 oz. of 480 grains, or 576 deniers	6912	"	5760
1 lb. avoirdupois (16 oz. of 437½ grains)	8400	"	7000
1 lb. "Poids de Marc" (16 oz. of 576 deniers)	9216	"	7680

The pound troy is to the pound avoirdupois as 14 to 17, nearly. The pound avoirdupois is to the pound "Poids de Marc" as 10 to 11, nearly. The pound "Poids de Marc" is to the pound troy as 4 to 3. The English silk reel is 818 bouts of 44 inches, = 1000 yards. The French, 400 ells, or 475 metres, of 39·371 inches, = 520 yards. The custom of the trade is to reckon 32 deniers to a dram. This has probably been adopted from ease of subdivision, but when carried out creates much error. The standard of silk measure is about 400 yards; that length of a single filament from China cocoons will weigh 2 deniers, and from French or Italian 2½. A 10-denier silk will thus be the combined thread of four or five cocoons.

Silk-winder, a silk-thrower; a small reel, or machine for winding off silk.

Silk-worm, the caterpillar of the silk-moth, the *Bombyx mori*.

Silk-worm rot, a disease affecting silkworms. *See* Muscardine.

Sill, Cill, the lower beam of a window or door.

Sillabub, a mixture of new milk, wine, sugar, and spices.

Silo, a pit, or subterraneous store for keeping grain.

Silt, the accumulated alluvium washed down by rivers, and forming deposits.

Silver, one of the precious metals. The British silver coinage consists of crowns, half-crowns, florins (first coined in 1849), shillings, sixpences, fourpences, threepences, twopences, and pence. From a pound of standard silver, are coined either 13 1-5th crowns, 26 2-5ths half-crowns, 66 shillings, or 132 sixpences. Silver is not a legal tender in Great Britain and her colonies, for more than 40s. at any one time. The relation of gold to silver, in the legal coinage of the United States, is as 1 to 15·988; in Great Britain, as 1 to 14·288; and in France, as 1 to 15·499. Thus it will be seen, that one ounce of pure gold will, in the United States, be equal to that produced from the coinage of 15·988 ounces of pure silver; in Great Britain it will be equal to that derived from only 14·288 ounces of silver; and in France to 15·499 ounces. Silver is the legal tender in France, and most largely circulated in China and the East. In March, 1853, an act came into operation in the United States, for reducing the quantity of silver in the silver coins, retaining the same denomination, on the principle followed in issuing the silver coins of England. Prior to that period, the coined silver always disappeared from circulation, but not since. The mint value of silver, is 5s. 6d. the ounce. The price of silver bars, standard, was in London, 59½d., in January, 1850; reached 62½d. in January, 1856, and stands at 62d. in January, 1858. The silver coined at the British Mint since 1840, has been as follows:—

Year	£	Year	£
1840	£216,414	1849	£119,592
1841	96,175	1850	129,096
1842	102,852	1851	87 868
1843	230,580	1852	189,597
1844	610,632	1853	701,545
1845	647 658	1854	140 480
1846	559,548	1855	195,511
1847	125,730	1856	462 528
1848	35,442		
		Total	4,750,218

These figures show that our silver coinage is not regulated by the demand necessary to satisfy the hands of the public, but by some other undefined system. It is generally understood that the Bank of England has no control whatever over this coinage. In the last 17 years the British silver coinage has been under 5 millions (and of this £677,550 was worn silver, recoined since 1847), certainly an insufficient amount to supply the loss by wear and tear, export, melting, and the growing demands of commerce for small change. The following is a summary of the silver coinage since 1848.

	Weight, oz	Number of Pieces.
1848	128,880	1,281,570
1849	434,880	2,034,778
1850	469,440	3,232,978
1851	319,520	3,292,608
1852	689,442	5,347,030
1853	2,551,072	12,078,946
1854	510,858	4 525,120
1855	710,979	4,379,309
1856	1,081,920	9,279,703

The value of the imports of silver coin and bullion into the United Kingdom, in the five years ending with 1855, was as follows:—

Year	£	Year	£
1851	5,000,000	1854	5,500,000
1852	6,000,000	1855	6,000,000
1853	7,500,000		
		Total	£30,000,000

The silver bullion received at the Bank of England, in the three years ending with 1855, averaged nearly 20,000,000 ounces per annum; but it was all sent out again, and did not go into circulation as coin in England.

SILVER-BALLI, a wood obtained in Demerara from a species of *Nectandra*. There are two varieties, the yellow and the brown. The wood being light floats. It contains a bitter principle, which protects it from the attacks of worms; hence it is much used for the outside planking of the colony craft; also for booms and masts. It will square sound from 10 to 14 inches from 40 to 50 feet long.

SILVER-BURNISHER, a polisher or brightener of articles of silver.

SILVER-CASTER, a moulder or melter of silver.

SILVER-CHASER, an embosser of silver.

SILVER-FISH. *See* GOLD AND SILVER FISH DEALER.

SILVER-HANDLE MAKER, a manufacturer of the handles for dessert knives, &c.

SILVER-KNIFE MAKER, a manufacturer of knives for paring fruit.

SILVER-LACE, wire coated with silver, and woven into lace.

SILVER-LEAF, thin foil of silver.

SILVER-PAPER, fine tissue paper for wrapping articles, &c.

SILVER-PIERCER, a worker in silver.

SILVER-PLATE-CHEST MAKER. *See* PLATE-CASE MAKER.

SILVER-PLATER, an electrotyper.

SILVER-POLISHER, a burnisher of silver ware, &c.

SILVER-SALVER, a hand-tray of silver.

SILVER-SMITH, a worker or dealer in silver; mostly combined with the business of jeweller, &c.

SILVERSMITH'S LICENCE, a government licence of £2 6s. required under the 43rd. George III. cap. 69, to be taken out by all persons trading in, or vending, gold and silver plate, or wares in which there is more than 2 dwts. of gold, or 5 dwts. of silver, in any one price.

SILVER-SPOON-AND-FORK MAKER, a manufacturer of these silver articles for table use.

SILVER-THIMBLE, a sempstress's protection for the finger in sewing, made of silver.

SILVER-TURNER, one who shapes articles of silver.

SILVERWEED, the popular name of the *Potentilla anserina*, a roadside weed, the roots of which, being extremely astringent, are sometimes used for tanning, and the distilled water is employed as a cosmetic.

SIMARRE, a sort of long gown.

SIMBLOT, the harness of a weaver's draw-loom.

SIMIRI, an Indian name for the locust-tree in Demerara.

SIMMAL, a building-wood of Sierra Leone.

SIMMER, SIMRA, a variable German corn-measure, the fourth part of the malter or schtel, but usually considered equal to 3½ imperial bushels: 100 simmer = 78·91 imperial bushels; 100 imperial bushels = 126·67 simmer.

SIMNEL, a kind of cracknel or sweet-cake.

SIMRA, a building wood of Sierra Leone.

SINAPISMS, compounds of mustard flour and water, used for poultices.

SINDAWA, the Malay name for saltpetre.

SINDHOOKA, SINDUYA, vernacular names in India for the *Vitex Negundo*, the fruit of which is considered vermifuge. The Mahommedans are in the habit of smoking the dried leaves in cases of headache and catarrh.

SINDOO, a vernacular name in India for Culilaban bark.

SINDUVARA, a Sanscrit name for the *Vitex trifolia*.

SINECURE, an office without duties; money paid for work not performed by the recipient, but done by a deputy.

SINEW, a tendon. Sinews are used by many nations as thread for sewing together skin garments, and, when dried, some are eaten. *See* DENDENG.

SINGARA-NUTS, a name for the fruit of *Trapa natans* and *T. bispinosa*, which abounds in fecula. It forms the principal food of the inhabitants of Cashmere, and yields a large revenue to the Government. In China the kernel is roasted or boiled, like the potato.

SINGLES, a name in the silk trade (a collective term), expressing a reeled thread of raw silk, twisted, in order to give it strength and firmness.

SINGLE-STICK, a stout cudgel for fencing or fighting with.

SINGLE-TREE, a cross piece for fastening harness.

SINGLO, a fine kind of tea, with large flat leaves, not much rolled.

SINK, a drain or stone basin used in sculleries, &c. These shaped stones are sold by the superficial foot measurement, and are made either of Yorkshire tooled or Purbeck stone.

SINKER, a lead weight for a net or fishing-line.

SINKING-FUND, an appropriation for gradually paying off the debt of a Company or State.

SINNET, spun-yarn; platted straw for hats.

SIPHOID, a French constructed vase or apparatus for receiving and giving out gaseous waters. [liquids.

SIPHON, a bent pipe or tube for drawing off

SIRCAR, a general division of a province in India; a Hindoo writer or accountant.

SIRDAR, the Hindustani name for a chieftain or head man; a principal palankin bearer.

SIRI-OIL, a name in the Eastern archipelago for the essential oil obtained from lemon grass.

SIRITOH, an Arab name for the sweet oil obtained by expression from the seeds of the *Sesamum orientale*, which is much used as an article of diet, for friction of the body, and for lamps. The oil-cake, mixed with honey and preserved citron, is esteemed an oriental luxury. When well prepared this oil is quite equal to the best olive oil. *See* GINGELIE.

SIRLOIN, the best part of a loin of beef.

SIRRUS, a name in India for country-made glue.

Sirsingle. *See* Surcingle.
Siruba, a tree of great size, found in the interior of British Guiana, and much used in the colony for ship-building.
Sirup. *See* Syrup.
Sisek, a Malay name for tortoiseshell.
Sissoo, a large Indian tree, the *Dalbergia Sissoo*, the wood of which is hard, strong, tenacious, and compact, and of great durability.
Sister-block, a solid piece of wood, with two holes, one above the other, with or without sheaves, to pass a pulley through.
Sitio, a Spanish superficial measure used in Mexico, whose side shall be a league of 5,000 varas, each of 3 geometrical feet. The sitio or league of land is 4,428 English acres. Five sitios make a hacienda, or ordinary sized plantation.
Sitting, the time given to an artist who takes likenesses; a seat in a pew at church.
Sixpence, an English current silver coin, the half of a shilling, weighing 1 dwt. and 19·03 grains. The following gives the coinage of sixpences in the last ten years. None were coined in 1848:—

1847	586,080	1853	3,837,930
1849	205,920	1854	840,116
1850	498,960	1855	1,129,084
1851	2,288,107	1856	2,779,920
1852	904,586	Total	13,070,703

Sixth-rate, a British vessel of war bearing a captain.
Size, a kind of glue, made by boiling down in water the clippings of parchment, glove-leather, fish-skin, and other kinds of skin and membrane. It is used in paper-making, by bookbinders, paper-hangers, whitewashers, and painters in distemper.
Sizel. *See* Scissel.
Size-manufacturer, a boiler down of skins, &c., and maker of size.
Size-roll, a piece of parchment added to a roll.
Sizers, machines used in Ceylon made of perforated sheet zinc or wire gauze, for separating the coffee into three sizes, the round or pea berry, and a larger and smaller berry.
Sizing, pieces of skin and hide used for making glue.
Sjambock, the Dutch name in the Cape colony for a riding-whip made of hide.
Skaalpund, the name for the commercial pound in Sweden.
Skate, an edible flat fish, the *Raia Batis*, which attains a large size, some individuals weighing upwards of 200 lbs. The females are generally called maids; a wooden or gutta-percha shoe or sandal, with a curved iron runner to slide or travel on the ice.
Skate-liver Oil, a fish oil often sold for the same purposes as cod-liver oil.
Skate-maker, a manufacturer of iron sliding shoes.
Skeet, a long scoop.
Skein, a small hank of thread or silk, &c; a quantity of cotton-yarn after it has been taken off the reel. The skein contains 80 threads of 54 inches: 17 skeins make a hank: 18 hanks a spindle.
Skein-silk Dyer, a dyer of raw silk in one of the forms of singles, tram, or organzine.
Skelp, a name for the rolled metal or welding of wrought iron, from which a gun-barrel is made.
Sketch, an outline or first draft; a plan of operations, &c.
Sketch-book, a book for taking drawings from nature.
Skew-back, a bedding stone.
Skew-bridge, a bridge placed obliquely to the road, &c.; not running at right angles.
Skewer, a metal or wooden pin for keeping meat together; metal skewers for kitchen use are sold in sets, of sorted sizes.
Skid, a chain with a shoe to drag a wheel: a log laid crosswise to support other logs in making a fence, &c.
Skieppe, a grain-measure in Sweden and Denmark, of 3·837 gallons.
Skiff, a small light boat.
Skillet, an iron pot or kettle with a handle.
Skilling, a money of account in Sweden, Norway, and Denmark, worth about a halfpenny.
Skim, to remove the scum from the surface of liquors.
Skim-coulter, a plough cutting-knife for paring land.
Skimmer, a cook's utensil for taking up victuals from a pot; a strainer.
Skim-milk, milk from which the cream has been taken off.
Skimmings, waste substances skimmed off; fat from a saucepan in which meat is boiled; thick syrup or scum in sugar-boiling, &c.
Skin, a husk or hide; a wine-bag or water-bottle. *See* Skins.
Skin-dealer, a skinner; a furrier.
Skin-dresser, a currier, or furrier.
Skinner, a leather-dealer, a furrier; a butcher who strips off the pelts from carcases.
Skinners'-company, the sixth in order of the twelve great livery companies of London, who received their charter from Edward III. Their hall is in Dowgate-hill.
Skins, a name generally applied by tanners to the pelts of small animals, as sheep, goats, seals, dogs, &c. The skins of the marine mammalia, as the seal, and whale, and the porpoise, when properly manufactured, are stronger than those of land animals. In 1855, we imported 8,606,780 skins of the lamb, goat, sheep, kid, and seal; and 653,961 cwts. of hides, worth together about £2,500,000. This was exclusive of furs.
Skin-wool, wool pulled from the dead skin, not sheared from the live animal.
Skip, in sugar-making in the West Indies, a charge or strike of syrup from the coppers.
Skipper, a ship-master or captain of a small craft; a popular name for a species of the *Esox* or saury pike, a migratory fish, which is sometimes caught in large shoals in the Forth.

Skipping-rope, a child's short cord for skipping over, often sold mounted with handles.

Skippund. *See* Shippound.

Skirret, a plant, the *Sium Sisarum*, the sweet succulent roots of which, being nutritious and sub-aromatic, are employed in cookery, in the same way as Scorzonera.

Skirt, the flaps and lower part of a man's coat below the waist; the loose flowing breadths of a woman's dress attached to the body.

Skirting-boards, narrow lining-boards round the walls of a room near the floor.

Skittle-ball, a flat ball of hard wood for throwing at skittles, or nine-pins.

Skittle-ground, a yard or enclosed shed, where the game of skittles or nine-pins is played.

Skittle-maker, a turner who shapes wooden skittles.

Skittles, shaped blocks of wood, used as nine-pins, to be aimed at with a skittle-ball.

Skive, the iron lap used by diamond-polishers in finishing the facets of the gem.

Skiver, an inferior kind of leather used for hat-linings, pocket-books, work-boxes, toys, and other cheap purposes. It is made of sheep's-skins, split in two by a machine, when in the state of pelt, tanned by immersion in sumach, and afterwards dyed.

Skow, Scow, a flat-bottomed lighter, used in North America.

Skull, to propel a boat by an oar at the stern. *See* Scull.

Skull-cap, a tight-fitting cap; a Turkish fez.

Skull-fish, the technical name among whalers for an old fish; a whale which is more than two years old, previous to which they are named stunts and short-heads.

Skunk-cabbage, a wild North American plant, the *Symplocarpus fœtidus*, the acrid seeds and rhizomes of which are antispasmodic and expectorant, and administered medicinally as palliatives in paroxysms of asthma.

Skute, a small boat.

Sky-light, a window in the roof of a house, or an apartment; or in the deck of a ship, giving light to the cabin.

Sky-rocket. *See* Rocket.

Sky-sail, a light upper sail of a ship, set above the royal.

Sky-scraper, a name given to the sky-sail when it is of a triangular shape.

Slab, a flat piece of stone; a plane or table of slate, or marble; the outer plank of a log of timber; a small mass of metal run into a mould; about thirty slabs of foreign tin go to the ton.

Slack, a kind of small broken coal, used for smiths' purposes, sometimes mixed with better coal for fuel in engine fire-grates; the loose part of a fixed rope.

Slag, a molten vitreous product of metals or minerals, after fusion in blast-furnaces; the scoria left after smelting metal, which is now applied to various useful purposes. The slag of iron-works is usually called cinder. Silica, alumina, chloride of calcium, and alum are obtained from slag, and it is cast into table-tops, and architectural ornaments, which take a beautiful polish. It may also be used for roofing, like rough glass, and in thin slabs like Dutch tiles, instead of plaster. It was formerly only used for road-making, or for rough walls.

Slaked-lime, lime reduced to a powder.

Slam, a name given to the refuse from alum works.

Slat, Sloat, a piece of wood used as a stretcher, as the bar of a chair, the sloats of a cart.

Slate, argillaceous schist or mountain-rock, of which there are many varieties. The property of splitting readily into plates, and the moderate degree of hardness, render some of its varieties useful for many purposes, as for roofing and writing slates, pencils, whet-stones, &c. Its smooth and perfect surface adapts it for ornamental and useful purposes, as chimney-pieces, table-tops, monuments, cisterns, tablets, bathing-tubs, and the beds of billiard-tables. Small slates for schools, and tradesmen's use, &c. are largely used; and many thousands are made and sold annually in different countries. *See* Slates.

Slate-axe, a mattock for shaping slates for roofing, and making holes in them to fasten them to the roof.

Slate Billiard-table, a billiard-table with a slate-bed.

Slate-book, two or more slabs of framed slate bound together for writing on.

Slate-frame, the narrow wood border for a writing-slate or slate-book.

Slate-merchant, an importer or wholesale dealer in slates.

Slate-pencil, a thin, narrow slip of soft slate, for writing on a slab. About 500 tons of these are made annually.

Slate-quarry, a place in which slate is obtained. There are important slate quarries in the North of England and North Wales, in France, Belgium, and the Rhine districts, &c. In North Wales twenty quarries are now worked, and the production of slates in the kingdom is about 300,000 tons.

Slater, a workman skilled in shaping and working slates, and in roofing buildings with slate or slate laying.

Slates, small shaped plates or large slabs of slate, chiefly used for roofing. For commercial purposes slates are classed into the following principal varieties:—Doubles, measuring 13 inches by 7, and smaller, 11 by 7; ladies, 16 by 10, 16 by 8, 14 by 8, or 12 by 8; countesses, 20 by 10; viscountesses, 18 by 10; marchionesses, 22 by 12; duchesses, 24 by 12; princesses, 24 inches long, various breadths. A thousand slates number 1200, and 60 slates are also allowed over for breakage. There are also rags and queens, measuring 36 by 24; imperials and patent slates 30 by 24; Westmorelands, and some other kinds.

SLATE SLAB, a sheet or plate of slate. Those of first quality are sawn all round, and split as near the thickness required as possible. Sorted slabs are of promiscuous lengths and breadths. Some slabs are sawn to order. Ended slabs are those sawn at the ends only. Second-quality slabs are unplaned.

SLATE-WORKS, a yard, &c. where slate is sawn or shaped.

SLAUGHTER-HOUSE, a place for killing cattle; an abattoir.

SLAVE, a bondsman; a drudge. Slavery is still tolerated in several countries, especially in the United States, Spain, and the Brazils.

SLAVE-MARKET, a place where slaves are sold.

SLAVER, a clipper-built vessel, intended to take on board and run a cargo of slaves.

SLAVE-TRADE, the illegal purchase and sale of negroes for slaves.

SLAY, a weaver's reed.

SLEDGE, a carriage on iron runners to travel over ice and snow.

SLEDGE-HAMMER. *See* HAMMER.

SLEEPERS, beams of wood, as of larch, hackmatack, hemlock, &c. 9 feet long by 9 or 10 inches broad and 4½ to 6 inches thick laid horizontally across a railway, to support the chairs, joists, and rails, &c.

SLEEPING-PARTNER, a dormant partner; one who puts in capital, but does not take any active share in the business.

SLEETCH, the thick mud or slush lying at the bottom of rivers.

SLEEVE, the part of a garment which covers the arm.

SLEIGH, a sledge; a Scottish car without wheels.

SLEIGH-BELLS, small bells attached to a horse drawing a sledge.

SLENDANGS, a textile fabric imported into the Dutch ports in the Eastern archipelago, of which there are woven and printed kinds, imitation Battick and Turkey-red slendangs.

SLICE, a thin piece cut off any thing; a spatula for serving cooked fish.

SLICER, a name for the slitting-mill or circular saw of the lapidary.

SLIDE, a place in a river for timber-logs or rafts to go down; part of a forcing-pump.

SLIDE-REST, part of a lathe.

SLIDE-RULE, SLIDING-SCALE, a mathematical instrument much used in gauging and other kinds of mensuration.

SLIM, to shuffle over work.

SLING, a coin current in Siam, worth about 2s 2d.; a leather loop or cord for throwing stones; a brace or support of any kind.

SLINGS, ropes or iron-bands for securing a yard to the mast; tackle with hooks passed round a cask or package, to hoist or lower it.

SLINK-LAMB, one that has been dropped or born prematurely. The soft skin of such is used for glove-linings and military purposes.

SLINKS, the skins of prematurely born lambs, calves, &c.

SLIP, a narrow dock or place for hauling up a ship, or building a ship on; a leash for holding a dog; a woman's muslin or satin under-skirt or petticoat; a printer's galley-proof of a column of type; a quantity of yarn; the rubbings of grindstones.

SLIPCOAT, new-made cheese; a small and very rich variety of Yorkshire cheese, not unlike butter but white.

SLIP-KNOT, a cord with a noose; a knot easily untied.

SLIPPER, an easy shoe of different materials; a skid for a wheel.

SLIPPER MANUFACTURER, a maker of carpet-shoes, or light thin in-door leather shoes.

SLIT-DEAL, an inch and a quarter plank cut into two boards.

SLITTING MILL, a thin sheet-iron disk used for slicing by the lapidary; a mill for making nail-rods.

SLIVER, a piece torn or split off; a long continuous lap or twist of wool or cotton; in wool, formed by a machine attached to the carding-engine, and used for making the warp of cloth.

SLOE, the fruit of the *Prunus spinosa;* the juice of the fruit is used in France as an astringent substitute for catechu.

SLOKAN, SLOKE, names for the edible seaweed, *Porphyra laciniata*, also called laver; the green sloke is *Ulva latissima*.

SLOOP, a cutter; a one-masted fore-and-aft-rigged vessel, having its main-sail attached to a gaff and lower boom.

SLOOP OF WAR, a naval vessel of any rig, mounting from 18 to 32 guns.

SLOP-BASIN, a crockery-ware basin forming part of a tea-service, for emptying the dregs from tea-cups into.

SLOPE, an inclination or gradient.

SLOP-PAIL, a metal bucket for chamber use.

SLOPS, ready-made clothing; a seaman's name for all kinds of clothing, or fabrics suited for clothing, supplied by the paymaster from the ship's stores.

SLOT, a bolt or bar.

SLOTE, a trap-door in the stage of a theatre.

SLOT-HOUND, a blood-hound.

SLOTTING AND KEY-GROOVING MACHINE, a machine for cutting the key-grooves and bosses of wheels.

SLUB, SLUBBING, a preparatory thread or roll of wool, drawn out and slightly twisted in the first spinning frame, used for the weft in cloth-making.

SLUBBING-BILLY, the first spinning frame or machine for preparing wool in threads, from short lengths of scribbled wool called cardings.

SLUBBING-MACHINE, a machine for drawing the slivers or laps of cotton, and twisting and winding them on bobbins.

SLUGS, small leaden bullets; half-roasted ore; heating-irons for hatters and tailors; naked molluscs, species of *Limax* which are still, in some countries, a popular remedy in consumptive complaints. *See* TRIPANG.

SLUICES, the tide or flood-gates by which water is admitted to locks, docks, &c.

SLUSH, soft mud; a name on ship-board for the grease of pork and beef skimmed from the ship's coppers, usually, like the refuse fat in kitchens, the perquisite of the cook.

SLUSH-TUB, a vessel for holding grease.

SMACK, a small sloop; a cutter or fishing-boat.

SMALL-COAL. *See* BREEZE, BURGEE, and SLACK.

SMALL-CRAFT, decked or half-decked boats and vessels; all under 100 tons. Some of these are limited to a certain distance from the shore, four to twelve leagues sea-ward, and cannot proceed beyond without special licence, or permission obtained from the Customs.

SMALL-DEBTS COURT, a Court of requests; a county court, or sheriff's court.

SMALL-TOOTH COMB, a comb of ivory or bone with small teeth on each side.

SMALLWARE-DEALER, SMALLWARE-MERCHANT, a shop-keeper who keeps small wares: a merchant who supplies them.

SMALLWARES, a trade name in haberdashery for knitting and reel cotton, ribbon, wire, webbing, tape, fringes, braid, buttons, laces, bindings, &c.

SMALTS, a vitreous substance obtained by melting together zaffres, a regulus of cobalt, potash and siliceous matter, and grinding the produce to a fine powder, commercially known as powder-blue. It is employed to give a blue tinge to writing-paper, linen, and starch, and, not being affected by fire, is much employed in painting earthenware. Some is made in this country, but the bulk used, about 60 tons a-year, comes from Holland.

SMART-MONEY, the money paid to a recruit on enlisting for the army, which he wishes to return to be free of his bargain. Unless this is returned within 24 hours, he is mulcted in a heavy sum for his release.

SMEAR, a stain or daub.

SMECTITE (French), a kind of fuller's earth.

SMELLING-BOTTLE, a small fancy glass-bottle carried by a lady, containing pungent salts to sniff at.

SMELLING-BOTTLE-CAP MAKER, a manufacturer of the silver or other metal tops for glass smelling-bottles.

SMELLING-SALTS. *See* AMMONIA and PRESTON-SALTS.

SMELT, a small delicate river-fish, the *Osmerus eperlanus*, abundant in the Thames and Medway, from August to May.

SMELTER, one engaged in running ores into metal.

SMELTING, the operation by which crude ores are reduced to the metallic state.

SMELTING-HOUSE, a place for smelting ores.

SMIDDUM-TAILS, in mining, the sludge or slimy portion deposited in washing ore.

SMIDDY, a smith's shop; a blacksmith's forge.

SMITH, a forger of metals by heat and blows; one who strikes metal with a hammer. There are white-smiths, black-smiths and general smiths.

SMITH AND IRON-FOUNDER, a worker in metals; one who has a foundry.

SMITH, GENERAL, one who works in all kinds of metals.

SMITH'S HAMMER. *See* HAMMER.

SMITHY, the workshop of a blacksmith, or worker in metals.

SMOCK, a farm labourer's blouse; a woman's shift or under-garment.

SMOCK-MILL, a wind-mill with a revolving top; the frame and sails of which can be moved round to the wind.

SMOKE, the vapour of burning vegetables or minerals; to cure and dry animal substances by smoke.

SMOKE-BLACK, a substance prepared by the combustion of different resinous bodies, especially of pitch in large pans under a dome or chimney; within this cloths are suspended to which the soot becomes attached. This species of carbon is employed only in the arts; in the manufacture of printers' ink, of blacking for shoes, &c.

SMOKE-JACK, a roasting machine turned by the smoke of the chimney. *See* JACK.

SMOKING-ROOM, a room in a tavern, coffee-house, or cigar divan, &c. where smoking is permitted.

SMOLT, a salmon of a year or two old, that has acquired its silver scales.

SMOOTHING-IRON, a flat iron to be heated, used by tailors and laundresses.

SMOOTHING-PLANE. *See* PLANE.

SMUGGLER, a contrabandist; one who brings in foreign goods without paying the Customs' duties; a vessel engaged in smuggling.

SMUGGLING, secreting or hiding dutiable goods; bringing them from the Continent in boats, or concealing them about the person.

SMUT, a mildew or blight in corn, caused by a species of *Uredo*, which destroys the interior of the grain; four millions of the small powdery spores may be contained in a grain of wheat.

SNAFFLE, a bridle with a slender or simple mouth bit.

SNAG, a name in North America for a projecting stump or sunken rock in a river.

SNAG-BOAT, a steam-boat fitted with an apparatus for removing snags, or obstructions to navigation in rivers.

SNAILS, species of *Helix*. The great vine snail, *Helix pomatia* is esteemed as a table luxury on the Continent, and in other localities: on the shores of the Mediterranean they are boiled in the shell and eaten with rice. In some countries as in Switzerland and parts of France, snails form a considerable article of commerce. They are fed by thousands in places called *escargatoires*, which are made on purpose for them. They are used, boiled in milk, for diseases of the lungs.

SNAKE-MOSS, a name for the common club moss, *Lycopodium clavatum*, the inflammable spores of which are used in Germany for artificial lightning on the stage, and are sold in the shops. They are also used for rolling up pills; for powdering infants, and in cases of Plica Polonica, and scorbutic affections.

SNAKE-ROOT. *See* SENEKA-ROOT.

SNAKE STONE, a kind of hone slate, or whetstone obtained in Scotland, and also known as Ayr stone; a name given to the fossils termed ammonites.

Snake-wood, a name applied both to the *Cecropia peltata*, and the *Plumeria rubra*, Linnæus.

Snap, a catch, or small fastening to a bracelet, necklace, purse, or book lock.

Snap-dragon, an amusement; a dish with raisins covered with spirits set on fire.

Snapper, a general name in the West Indies for several species of *Mesoprion*, a fish common to the East and West Indian seas, remarkable for the richness of their colours. They attain a large size, and are much esteemed as an article of food.

Snatch-block, an iron-bound wooden single block with a hook at the end, or an opening below the sheaves, to receive a rope.

Sneeze-wort, the *Achillea Ptarmica*, the powdered leaves of which produce sneezing.

Snie, a Canadian name for a water channel.

Snigg, an eel; a kind of sailing vessel.

Snipe, a wild bird, the *Scolopax gallinago*, which is much esteemed as a delicious and well-flavoured dish.

Snook, a common fish, both of the sea and the rivers of the West Indies, the *Centropomus undecimalis*.

Snow, a two-masted vessel with a small supplementary mast for carrying a try-sail.

Snow-plough, a machine for clearing away snow from railway tracks.

Snow-shoes, pieces of wood 2 or more feet long, by 6 or 8 inches wide, bound to the feet and ancles, by deer-skin thongs, for travelling over snow. Other kinds in Nova Scotia, &c. are made of strings of hide or gut, strung in a frame like a racket or battledore.

Snow-sweeping Engine, a plough or other contrivance for removing snow from railways and common roads.

Snuff, powdered tobacco, to be taken through the nose.

Snuff-box, a small box for the pocket to contain snuff, made in endless variety, and of different material, wood, metal, papier-mâché, &c.

Snuffers, pincers or scissors for cutting the wick of a candle, now little used, owing to the introduction of prepared wicks.

Snuffers'-maker, a manufacturer of metal snuffers.

Snuffers-tray, a small stand of metal or papier-mâché, for snuffers.

Snuff-maker, one who pulverizes the stalks and leaves of tobacco for snuff, which is usually flavoured.

Soap, a detergent substance, soft soap being made of fish oil, tallow, and a ley of caustic potash; hard, from almost any fatty matter, in combination with soda; white or mottled soaps contain no resin.

Soap-berries, the seeds of *Mimosa abstergens*, *Sapindus Saponaria*, *S. emarginatus*, and other species. The aril, which surrounds the seeds, is used as soap in South America and India. The seed-vessels are very acrid; they lather freely in water, and will cleanse more linen than thirty times their weight of soap; but in time they corrode or burn the linen. The kernel or seed is used for rosaries, bracelets, and other ornaments.

Soap-boiler, a maker of soap.

Soap-dish, a small porcelain or other vessel, for holding soap for toilet use.

Soap-liniment, a medicinal external application, used as a stimulating lubricant for local pains.

Soap-manufacturer, a soapboiler; a maker of soap.

Soap-nut, a name for the seed of the *Mimosa abstergens*.

Soap-stone, or **Steatite**, a hydrous silicate of magnesia and alumina, which is much used for the lining of stoves and fire-places, for sinks, and for the baths, and sizing rollers used in cotton mills. It is so soft as to be easily wrought, turned, and planed with the ordinary tools of the carpenter, and it may be screwed together as easily and as tightly as wood.

Soap-suds, water impregnated with soap, in which linen has been washed, or for scouring wool, &c. It forms a good liquid manure.

Soap-wort, the root of *Vaccaria vulgaris*, which, like the aril of the soap-berry, contains saponine. The herbage of this European plant is said to increase the milk of cows.

Socage, a tenure of land by certain services or rent.

Socarga, an ancient Arab measure of 0·102 pint.

Sociable, a private carriage for town use, with two seats facing.

Society, an association or partnership. In France a *société en commandite* is one where the manager is liable; a *société anonyme* is one without personal liability.

Sock, a short stocking; an inner warm sole for a shoe.

Socket, a hollow tube or receptacle for any thing; the joint in which a ball turns.

Socket-castor, a metal castor which moves in a socket.

Socket-pipe, a pipe worked in a socket. *See* **Socket**.

Sococonusco, a choice species of cocoa produced in the department of Suchitepequez in Guatemala.

Socque (French), a wooden sandal.

Soda-ash, the alkali obtained from common salt, manufactured to the extent of from 100 000 to 120,000 tons a year. It is used instead of barilla for soap-making, as a substitute for pot and pearl ashes in glass-making, and for bleaching and cleansing cotton.

Soda, Carbonate of, the dissolved soda ash, crystallized, of which 25,000 to 30,000 tons a year are made, and used medicinally, or for domestic purposes.

Soda-water, an incorrect name generally applied to a common effervescing beverage. The effervescent quality is not due to soda, but is produced by carbonic acid gas, which is forced into the water by an apparatus. The gas is produced by pouring sulphuric acid upon marble dust, or upon the super-carbonate of soda. The quantity of this cooling beverage made is very large, and with lemonade has been estimated to amount in value to £1,250,000 a year.

Soda-water-bottle, a strong oval-shaped glass bottle, the cork of which is secured by twine and wire to confine the aërated water.

Soda-water Manufacturer, a maker and bottler of soda-water, who often also makes ginger-beer, lemonade, and other aërated beverages.

Sof, a plain cloth made from goats' hair at Angora.

Sofa, a long stuffed couch or reclining seat.

Soft-soap, a dark potash soap that is nearly liquid. *See* Soap.

Sohaga, a Thibetian name for tincal or unrefined borax.

Sok, Sook, a long-measure of Siam, nearly 19 inches.

Sol, the twentieth part of a florin or of the old livre tournois of France: in Brabant, 12 deniers make 1 sol.

Sola, the *Æschynomene aspera*, the light sponge wood of Bengal. *See* Shola.

Solah, the name for the half of a seer; a grain-measure in Masulipatam, = 1 1-16th pint.

Solamire (French), a sieve cloth.

Solare, a Spanish land-measure of 25 estadales, about 884 square yards.

Solder, a metallic cement used by plumbers and tinmen, consisting of an alloy which has an affinity for both metals to be united.

Soldering-iron, a metal tool for heating and melting solder.

Solder-manufacturer, a maker of cements for metals.

Soldier, one employed in an army, or who fights in defence of his own country; a supernumerary or auxiliary engaged by a foreign state.

Soldo, an Italian money of account, about equal to the English shilling, and divided into 12 denari or pence. There are silver pieces, of 5, 8, and 10 soldi.

Sole, a support or rest for a draining-tile; the bottom part of a shoe or boot made of leather or gutta percha; an esteemed flat fish, the *Solea vulgaris*, of Cuvier, caught off the British coasts in large numbers: one hundred millions, or 12,000 tons in weight of this fish are said to be sold annually in Billingsgate.

Sole-leather, thick ox-hide or shoe butts, suitable for soles of shoes and boots.

Solicitor, an attorney at law.

Solidare, a small coin.

Solidified-milk, concentrated or preserved milk for use at sea.

Sollagay, a grain-measure in Bellary, East Indies, = 8 lbs. 10 oz.

Sollar, the entrance to a mine: a loft.

Soller, a name in Stettin for 80 pieces of whetstones.

Solograph, a name which has been given to some pictures on paper taken by the talbotype or calotype process.

Solota, a former Turkish coin of 2 2-5ths oslica, and worth 11d. or 1s.

Solotnick, a Russian weight, the third part of a loth. *See* Zolotnic.

Soltanee, an Egyptian variety of natron or bicarbonate of soda.

Solvent, able to pay all debts contracted.

Soma, an Italian measure for liquids ranging from 18½ to 36 gallons; but as a dry-measure from 3½ to 6 bushels.

Sombrero (Spanish), a hat.

Sommage (French), manor dues on cattle.

Sommelier, a French butler.

Sommier, an animal carrying a pack-load; a horse-hair mattress.

Sompayr, Sompi, a weight of 60 grains used for the precious metals in Madagascar.

Son, the French name for bran; the husks of ground corn.

Sonali, a name in Bengal for the pods of the *Cathartocarpus Fistula*. *See* Cassia-fistula.

Sonar, a worker in gold, an Indian goldsmith.

Sonat (French), a tawed sheep-skin.

Sonf, a local Indian name for aniseed.

Song-fai, a money of account of Siam, the half of a fuang, and worth about 1½d.

Sonnette (French), a small bell.

Sonometer, an instrument for testing the efficacy of treatment in deafness, consisting of a small bell fixed on a table.

Sonsonate Balsam, a name given to two species of balsam of Peru, a black and a white, obtained in St. Salvador from *Myrospermum Peruiferum*.

Soocey, a mixed striped fabric of silk and cotton in India.

Soocoo, a name in Bencoolen for the fourth part of a real, and valued at 1s. 3d.

Soogree, a name in Canara, India, for boiled coarse rice.

Soojee, Indian wheat, ground but not pulverized; a kind of semolino.

Sooparee, Soopari, a vernacular name in India for the areca palm and betel nut.

Soorma, a preparation of antimony with which Indian women anoint the eyelids.

Soot, condensed smoke, collected by chimney-sweepers, and sold for manure. *See* Smoke-black.

Soovarnuka, an Eastern name for cassia-fistula pods.

Sorbet, a Turkish beverage, lemonade or sherbet. *See* Scherbet.

Sorbine, a saccharine matter obtained from the berries of the mountain-ash (*Sorbus acuparia*).

Sorie, a French name for merino or Spanish wool.

Sorrel, a buck of the third year; a horse of a reddish colour; a name for two plants, one the wood sorrel, *Oxalis acetosella*, the leaves of which, being acid and refrigerant, are used in salads and as an infusion in fevers; the other, the *Rumex acetosa*, possesses similar properties, and is also used as a pot-herb and salad, and in cooling drinks.

Sorted, classed, arranged, put in order.

Sorts, varieties; a mixture of printing-type.

Sota (Spanish), a deputy or aid; hence *Sotacocinero*, an under cook; *Sotacomitre*, a boatswain's mate; *Sotamontero*, an under huntsman; *Sotasacristan*, an under sexton; *Sotacochero*, a postilion, &c.

Sou, a French copper coin, the 20th part of a livre, consisting of five centimes, and equivalent to a half-penny English. In Belgium the sou or sol is divided into 12 deniers. A former weight of France used by moneyers, of 192 grains.

Souari, a most durable timber obtained in Demerara from the *Caryocar tomentosum*, which greatly resembles in its properties the Mora; being excellent for ship-building: mill-timbers and planks may be had from 16 to 20 inches square, and from 20 to 40 feet long.

Soubrette, a French waiting-maid.

Soucar, an Indian banker or merchant; a money-lender.

Souchet, a kind of free-stone; a French name for the pendulous mucilaginous tubers of the *Cyperus esculentus*, which are cultivated in the South of Europe, and eaten like nuts, being nutritive, restorative, and stimulant. They are also employed in the preparation of orgeat. They are sent to Cairo and Alexandria in considerable abundance, and sold in the bazaars, combined with rice, in the form of cakes. The toasted roots have been used as a substitute for coffee, and yield a preparation resembling chocolate. The cultivation of the plant deserves attention for its considerable alimentary value.

Souchteur, an inspector of woodcutters in France; a person who marks or verifies timber that has been felled.

Soufflé, an omelet made of the whites of eggs, cream, and sugar, beaten up.

Soufflons, an Italian name for a very imperfect silk cocoon.

Sough, an adit level for carrying off water, or an entrance to a mine.

Sound, the air-bladder of a fish: many of these are eaten, especially cods' sounds, fresh or salted; others furnish isinglass; a narrow strait of water where vessels lie at anchor; to ascertain the depth of water with a plummet and line.

Sounding-board, a board over a pulpit, to make the speaker's voice heard at a distance; a board for propagating sound in a musical instrument.

Sounding-line, a line attached to a leaden plummet for determining the depth of water.

Sounding-rod, an iron-rod marked with inches and feet, to ascertain the depth of water in a ship's hold.

Soundings, the depth of water when the bottom can be reached.

Soup, rich or thick broth made of different materials.

Soupière (French), a tureen for soup.

Soup-kitchen, a public establishment supported by voluntary contributions for preparing and supplying soup to the poor.

Soup-ladle, a spoon with a large bowl, and long handle for dipping out soup.

Soup-plate, a deep plate for holding soup.

Soup-pot, **Soup-kettle**, a boiler for preparing the stock for soup.

Soup-ticket, an authority for receiving soup at a public kitchen.

Soup-tureen. *See* Tureen.

Sour, sharp, acid; fruit that is not ripe.

Sourbassis, a French name for fine Persian silk.

Sour-krout. *See* Saur-kraut.

Sour-sop, the fruit of the *Anona muricata*, a tropical tree; the sweet sop is the produce of another species, the *Anona squamosa*.

Souscrivant (French), the acceptor of a bill.

Souse, to dip or steep; to pickle fish in vinegar, and bake them.

Souter, a Scottish name for a shoemaker.

Southernwood, the *Artemisia abrotonum*; the fragrant bitter acrid leaves are dried to drive away moths from linen, and are said to form an ingredient in some Continental beer.

Souvenir, a keepsake; a friend's gift of remembrance.

Sou'-wester, a painted canvas hat, with a flap over the neck, for use at sea in rough weather, and also worn by coal-heavers.

Sovereign, the principal English gold coin weighing 5 dwt. and 3·274 grains. It is current by proclamation if it weighs 5 dwts. 2½ grains, and the half sovereign 2 dwts. 13½ grains. There have been double sovereigns coined, but these are seldom met with in circulation. The following is the value of the sovereigns coined in this country, in the last ten years:

Year	Value	Year	Value
1847	£4,667,127	1852	£8,053,435
1848	2,240,702	1853	10,597,993
1849	1,755,399	1854	3,589,611
1850	1,402,039	1855	8,448,482
1851	4,013,624	1856	4,806,160
		Total	49,580,572

The value of the gold coined at the British mint in the years 1855 and 1856, was £15,010,778, which added to the sum mentioned already under the head of Gold Coinage, makes a total of gold coined in the last seventeen years of £86,645,106. *See* Gold and Half Sovereign.

Sow, a large trough in a foundry for holding melted metal; a she pig; an ingot or mass of metal.

Sowans, a porridge or gruel made in Scotland from oatmeal.

Sowar, an Indian trooper; a horse-soldier, belonging to the irregular horse cavalry.

Sowing-machine, a drill; a seed-planter.

Sox, a Scotch mode of spelling socks.

Soy, a sauce or flavouring originally made in the East; and said to be produced from a species of *Dolichos* bean.

Soya. *See* Sherbet.

Sozellie, an Indian name for small fish-maws.

Spa, a mineral spring.

Space, area; room; a small piece of cast metal to divide letters or words in printing.

Space-lines, printers' leads for justifying, or filling up lines or words, made from 4 to 12 in pica.

Space-rule, a thin piece of metal, type-height, of different lengths, used by compositors for making a delicate line in algebraic and other formulæ.

Spade, a digging-tool of iron with a wooden handle; a deer three years old.

Spade and Shovel-maker, a manufacturer of the implements so named.

Spadesman, a name for an agricultural labourer in Tasmania.

Span, a yoke of oxen; a measure of 9 inches; a cord to confine a rope; to shackle the legs of a horse to prevent its wandering; to attach draught cattle to a wagon.

Spandrel, a triangular space between the square head over an arch and the curve of the arch.

Spangle, a small shining piece of metal to attach to theatrical or other dresses; to glitter.

Spangle and Tinsel Maker, a manufacturer of small bright metal scales to sew on to garments.

Spaniel, a valuable species of dog, of which there are many varieties.

Spanish Black, a powder obtained by burning cork in close vessels.

Spanish Chestnut-wood. *See* Chestnut.

Spanish-flies. *See* Cantharides.

Spanish-leather Maker, a manufacturer of Cordovan-leather.

Spanish-liquorice, the inspissated juice of the *Glycirrhiza-root*. *See* Liquorice.

Spanish Mahogany. *See* Mahogany.

Spanker, the after sail of a ship.

Spanner, a tool for turning a nut or bolt-head.

Sparables, small iron shoe-brads.

Spar-deck, the upper deck of a ship, on which loose or spare spars are secured.

Spare-rib, a joint of pork with the fat and other flesh taken off the rib.

Sparger, a copper cylinder, used by brewers for dashing or sprinkling.

Sparrowbills. *See* Sparables.

Spars, a general marine term for all masts, yards, booms, &c.; a name for several kinds of mineral.

Sparterie, mats, ropes, and cordage, made of *Esparto* or Spanish broom.

Spat, the young of oysters.

Spatch-cock, a fowl or bird killed, split open, and broiled or grilled.

Spathic Iron-ore, spar-shaped or lamellar ore.

Spatterdashes, a kind of long gaiter or covering for the legs, to keep off mud.

Spatula, an instrument for spreading plasters.

Spawn, the seed of fish; the matrix of fungi. *See* Mushroom-spawn.

Spawner, a she-fish; a female salmon.

Spay, to extirpate the ovaries of a female beast to prevent breeding, and to increase the fattening powers, as a spayed heifer, a spayed sow, &c.

Speaker, the chairman of a legislative body; a book for school-reading.

Speaking-trumpet, a metal tube for hailing ships at sea, and for making the voice heard at a distance.

Speaking-tube, a gutta-percha or other pipe for communicating orders from one room in a building to another.

Spear, a lance; a name in Riga for a spar suited for a small mast.

Spearman, one armed with a spear.

Spearmint, another name for the *Mentha viridis*. *See* Mint.

Special-constable, a person sworn in temporarily to aid in maintaining the peace.

Special-jury, a superior class of jurors, merchants, or esquires, summoned to try a cause.

Special-pleader, a person whose occupation it is to draw pleadings. The Inns of court have power to license, and they can practise before being called to the Bar. They may also sue for their fees, and be sued for their defaults, and in these [illegible]ters they stand differently from a barri[illegible]

Specie, metallic currency; current coin [illegible] bullion, as opposed to paper money.

Specification, the particulars given [illegible] a patent; a minute detail of quantities, [illegible]terials, and plans, for a work or building.

Specimen, a sample; an illustration.

Speckled-wood, wood marked with small spots or dashes.

Spectacle-case Maker, a person who makes the small pocket cases of leath[illegible] or other material for holding a pair [illegible] spectacles.

Spectacle-makers' Company, one of th[illegible] livery companies of London. It has no hall.

Spectacles, glasses for the eyes, to aid those who have weak sight.

Spectioneer, a whaling name for the first harpooner.

Speculation, a scheme or project; a money venture on the chance of profit.

Speculator, an adventurer; one who enters into a risk, dabbling in the funds, shares, or stocks, or buying or selling goods upon the chance of a rise in price.

Speculum, a reflector of polished metal; a surgeon's instrument for examining inward parts.

Speed-indicator, a gauge for testing the velocity of steam engines or machines.

Speiss, impure nickel.

Spelding, a dried haddock.

Spell, a turn; the portion of time given to any work.

Spelling-book, a book for teaching the young to spell.

Spelt, an inferior kind of wheat gro[illegible] France and Flanders, the *Triticum* [illegible], of which there are two kinds, the [illegible] the white, some being bearded. It [illegible] an excellent provender for horses, [illegible] straw being very strong, it is much [illegible] after for the manufacture of hats.

Spelter, impure zinc. *See* Zinc.

Spencer, a coat without skirts; an [illegible] fashioned ladies' garment; a fore-a[illegible] sail set on a spencer mast in a ship.

Spermaceti, a kind of waxy body [illegible] separates in cold weather from [illegible] oil obtained from the head-matte[illegible] the sperm whale (*Physeter macroceph*[illegible]). It is used for making candles with ab[illegible] 3 per cent. of bees'-wax added to pr[illegible] crystallization.

Spermaceti-candles, fine transparent [illegible]dles, used as wax lights.

Spermaceti-ointment, a pharmaceutic[illegible] preparation consisting of lard, sperm[illegible], and bees'-wax.

Spermaceti-refiner, a person who purifies spermaceti, chiefly by pressure and crystallization.

Speronare, a vessel employed in Ge[illegible]

Spetches, a name for glue pieces; the [illegible] of skin and hides.

Spherometer, an instrument invent[illegible] by Mr. Ross for measuring the curvat[illegible] of lenses.

SPICE, the common name for pleasant or pungent aromatic vegetable substances, used for flavouring food and condiments, such as nutmegs and mace, cinnamon, pimento, ginger, and pepper; a technical name among sugar-refiners for bullocks'-blood.
SPICE-BOX, a kitchen-box with several divisions for holding different spices.
SPICE-BUSH, a name in North America for the *Laurus Benzoin*.
SPICE-NUT, a gingerbread-nut.
SPICERIES, a collective term under which many of the stimulant and aromatic condiments are grouped.
SPIGOT, a peg to stop the vent-hole in a cask or a faucet.
SPIKE, a large nail; to destroy the utility of a cannon, by plugging the vent-hole with a nail.
SPIKENARD, the *Nardostachys Jatamansi*, a dwarf herbaceous plant, with a long hairy tap-root, a native of the Himalayas, possessing stimulant and bitter properties, having a strong and fragrant odour, and it is used as a perfume by Eastern nations, and also against hysteria and epilepsy. The blackish coloured roots are brought down in large quantities from the mountains in the north of India.
SPILE-HOLE, the air-hole or vent of a cask.
SPILL-CASE, a box for holding thin strips of wood, used as matches or lighters.
SPILLET-FISHING, SPILLIARD-FISHING, a name on the west coast of Ireland for a system of fishing by a number of hooks set on snoods, all on one line. In North America it is called bultow-fishing.
SPILLIKINS, pegs of wood, bone, or ivory, for marking the score of cribbage or other games.
SPILLS, small pieces of wood used for lighting pipes, or making matches.
SPIN, to twist or twirl threads.
SPINACH, the *Spinacia oleracea*, the leaves of which are a common nutritious pot-herb. In New Zealand, the leaves of the *Tetragonia expansa* are used instead of spinach.
SPINAL, a kind of unwrought inkle.
SPINDLE, any long pin or bar upon which something revolves; a watch fuzee; the pivot of a capstan; the small shaft of a pinion. In factories the bright iron-pins on which threads are formed and wound. In England there were at work, in 1855, 3,471,108 spindles; in France, 1,886,783. Spindle is also a yarn-measure; in cotton-yarn a spindle of 18 hanks is 15,120 yards; in linen yarn a spindle of 24 heers, is 14,400 yards.
SPINDLE-TREE, a large and ornamental shrub, of which one species, the *Euonymus Europæus*, and its several varieties, is a native of Britain. It obtains its popular name from the hard and fine-grained wood being preferred for spindles and for skewers.
SPINET, an old keyed-instrument, a kind of harpsichord.
SPINNING-JENNY, a machine for spinning cotton.
SPINNING-MACHINES, various machines and contrivances for spinning wool, silk, cordage, &c.
SPIRACLES, the blow-holes, or breathing-holes of a whale.
SPIRE, a steeple; a pinnacle.
SPIRIT, any inflammable liquor. [spirits.
SPIRIT-BOTTLE, a glass bottle for holding
SPIRIT-DEALER, one who has a licence to vend spirituous liquors; a tavern-keeper.
SPIRIT-ENGINE MAKER, a manufacturer of the tavern, or bar, engines for drawing spirits for retail sale.
SPIRIT-JAR, a two-gallon earthenware jar, for sending out spirits.
SPIRIT-LAMP, a lamp for burning spirits to heat anything, as metals; or for an allblaze or small cooking-stove. Spirit lamps produce little flame, but intense heat.
SPIRIT-LEVEL, an instrument for levelling, in which a small horizontal tube, with spirits, fixed on the summit, shows the true level.
SPIRIT-LICENCE, a licence granted by the magistrates in quarter-sessions, to retail spirits.
SPIRIT-MERCHANT, a vender of spirits.
SPIRIT, METHYLATED. *See* METHYLATED SPIRIT.
SPIRIT OF SALT, a name for muriatic-acid.
SPIRIT OF TURPENTINE, the oil of turpentine.
SPIRIT OF WINE. *See* ALCOHOL.
SPIRIT-STORE, a shop where spirits are kept for sale, wholesale and retail.
SPIRIT-VARNISH, a resin dissolved in spirit.
SPIROMETER, an instrument for determining the capacity of the human lungs, bearing a close resemblance to a gas-holder.
SPIT, a long metal spike or bar for sticking viands on to roast.
SPITTOON, a box of metal or other material for a smoker to spit in.
SPLASH-BOARD, the leather or wooden protection in front of a gig.
SPLICING, a sailor's term for uniting the ends of ropes by opening and interlacing the strands.
SPLINT, a thin piece of wood to support a broken bone or fractured limb; thin wood for matches. [splints.
SPLINT-CUTTER, a shaper and maker of
SPLINTER-BAR, a cross-piece supporting the springs of a carriage. [parts.
SPLIT, to burst asunder; to separate in
SPLIT-LIFT, a piece of in-sole leather used in shoe-making.
SPLIT-PEASE, husked peas, split for making pease-soup or pease-puddings.
SPLITS, a term, in the leather trade, for divided skins which have been separated into two sections by the cutting machine; there being tanned splits and salted splits.
SPLITTER, a name in Tasmania for a wood-cutter.
SPOKE-RIVER, a wheelwright, or shaper of spokes or rounds for ladders.
SPOKES, bars of oak radiating from the nave of a wheel to the felly, at equal distances from one another; the rounds of a ladder; a contrivance for skidding the wheels of a vehicle.
SPOKE-SHAVE, a workman's knife or smoothing instrument for shaping spokes.

SPONGE, a marine product, of which there are many varieties. Large quantities of both coarse and fine sponge come into commerce for toilet and surgical use, for common washing purposes, for making into cloth, hats, and for other uses; the soft fermenting dough of which bread is made.

SPONGE-BAG, an oil-skin case for a toilet sponge.

SPONGE-CAKE, a light sweet cake, made with milk and eggs.

SPONGE-MERCHANT, an importer of sponges either from the Bahamas or the Mediterranean, the two chief seats of the sponge fisheries.

SPONGE-TENTS, a surgical appliance for a wound, though the practice is now nearly obsolete. Sponge tents were prepared by dipping sponge in melted wax, and pressing it till the wax is hardened. A tent of this kind, introduced into a wound or cavity enlarges as the wax softens.

SPONGING-HOUSE, the lock-up house of a sheriff's officer, where debtors are lodged before they are conveyed to prison.

SPONGIO-PILINE, a substitute for the ordinary poultice, made of small pieces of sponge and wool or cloth felted together, on an impermeable back, and held by a coating of India-rubber varnish on one side. It is used when softened in hot water for the same purpose as a bread or meal poultice.

SPOOL, a weaver's bobbin of cane or wood to wind yarn on.

SPOOL-STAND, a rest or support for bobbins.

SPOON, a small domestic utensil for taking up food, or for culinary use.

SPORTSMAN, a hunter; one who follows game with a gun, or pursues the sports of the field.

SPOUT, a tube or shoot; a curved mouth or nozzle, as to a tea-pot, watering-pot, &c.; a slang term for pledging goods at a pawnbroker's.

SPOWTS, boxes or shoots down which coals are run from wagons into ships.

SPRAT, a diminutive fish, the *Clupea sprattus*, used as food, and caught as the cold weather approaches in large quantities.

SPRAT-GRIDIRON, a gridiron made specially for broiling sprats.

SPREADER, an attachment; the branch pipe of a fire-engine for scattering the water over a large surface.

SPRIG, a nail without a head; an embroidered branch of a flower.

SPRING, an elastic body or band; in marine language a check on the cable for disconnecting it; to crack or split a mast or spar; "to spring a leak" is to let in water suddenly.

SPRING-BALANCE, an elastic spring counterbalancing a valve or lever.

SPRING-BED, an elastic or air mattress.

SPRING-BLIND MAKER, a maker of window blinds working on springs.

SPRING-BRACES, elastic suspenders for men's trousers.

SPRING-CARRIAGE, a vehicle suspended on springs for travelling easy.

SPRINGE, a gin, noose, or snare to catch birds.

SPRINGER and LINER, a workman who puts in watch springs.

SPRING-FORGERS, workmen in the cutlery trade, who form the spring or piece of steel at the back of clasp and folding pocket-knives.

SPRING-MAKER, a manufacturer of, steel compound springs for carriages, or of metal springs for easy chairs.

SPRING-SEAT, a chair or couch with a spring in it.

SPRING-TIDES, the highest course of tides, occurring every new and full moon.

SPRIT, a small boom or gaff used with a sail in some boats.

SPRIT-SAIL, a sail extended on a sprit-sail yard.

SPROUTS, BRUSSELS, a kind of small cabbage.

SPRUCE, a name for several species of the fir tribe, *Abies communis*, and *A. nigra* being the principal species, and supplying much of the deal timber of commerce. A fermented liquor made of treacle or molasses, and a decoction of the leaves and branches of the *spruce-fir*. It is sometimes called black-beer. *See* MUM.

SPUD, an agricultural tool for cutting up weeds.

SPUNK. *See* AMADOU.

SPUN-YARN, a cord formed by twisting together two or three rope-yarns; old junk, or rope twisted into yarns, used for various purposes on shipboard.

SPUR. *See* SPURS.

SPURGE, a name for several species of *Euphorbia*, used medicinally, but possessing purgative and poisonous properties.

SPURIOUS, adulterated; not genuine.

SPUR-MAKER, a manufacturer of spurs.

SPURRED-RYE. *See* ERGOT.

SPUR-ROWEL, the revolving pricking wheel of a spur.

SPURS, spiked irons for the bottoms of the boots of seamen, who stand on the carcase to strip the blubber from a whale; pricking instruments with rowels fastened on the heels of a horseman's boot.

SPUR-WHEEL, a cog-wheel.

SPY-GLASS, a small telescope.

SQUAB, a soft cushion; a sofa; a name applied to a young, unfledged bird, as, a squab pigeon.

SQUAB-PIE, a Cornish pie containing a mixture of fish, flesh, and vegetables.

SQUADRON, a detachment from a fleet; part of an army; two or more troops of cavalry.

SQUARE, an inner court; an open space or market area; a mechanic's measure for gauging and squaring his work; a workman's tool for measuring angles; also 100 feet superficial of boarding; a term commonly applied to a pane of glass; a rectangle surrounded by houses.

SQUARE-RIGGED, in seamanship, vessels which have the yards and sails across the masts, instead of fore and aft, or in the direction of the length of the vessel.

SQUARE-SAIL, a large four-sided sail extended on a lower yard.

SQUASH, a name for the *Cucurbita Melopepo*. *See* GOURDS.

Squat, a mineral of tin ore and spar; to locate or settle down on waste land without right.

Squatter, a name in the Australian colonies for sheep-farmers and cattle breeders, who occupy large ranges of land, under licence from government, at a small rental.

Squib, a noisy firework or cracker; an election placard or lampoon.

Squid, a fish used as a bait by the Newfoundland fishermen.

Squill, a name for the *Urginea Scilla* of Steinhell, the *Scilla maritima* of Linnæus; a plant inhabiting the sea-coast of the Mediterranean, the acrid bulbs of which being diuretic, expectorant, emetic, and purgative, are used medicinally.

Squirrel, a small rodent, a species of *Sciurus*. The fur of several varieties of squirrel is much used for linings, for tippets, for cuffs, and other articles of ladies' dress. From fifteen to twenty millions are said to be killed in Russia annually. In the trade returns they are sometimes called Calabar-skins. In 1856, about 2,200,000 squirrel-skins were imported, and chiefly used up in this country.

Squirt, a syringe.

Squirting-cucumber, a name for the *Ecbalium agreste* of Richard, the *Momordica Elaterium* of Linnæus; the drastic juice of which is used medicinally in cases of gout, dropsy, apoplexy, constipation, &c.

Srigunda, a local Indian name for sandal-wood.

Stabber, a marling-spike; a sailmaker's [pricker.

Stabbing-press, a press used by bookbinders.

Stablat, a winter cow-house, in which Swiss herdsmen live with their cattle.

Stable, a house or shelter for horses, either public or private.

Stable-boy, Stable-man, an ostler or groom; a person who attends on horses.

Stable-fixture Maker, a person who prepares and fits racks, mangers, and other fittings for stables.

Stack, a pile of any thing, as a stack of wood, hay, corn, &c.; a column of chimneys, or an elevated chimney to a factory; a pile of muskets rested together. A stack of wood is 108 cubic feet.

Stack-yard, an enclosure for ricks or stacks.

Stade, a landing or shipping place: an itinerary measure. *See* Stadio.

Stade-duties, tolls levied on ships in the [Elbe.

Stadio (Italian), a furlong; a measure of length in the Ionian islands, consisting of 22 yards.

Staff, a crutch or support; a flag pole; an ensign of office; a policeman's hand-club or bludgeon; the round of a ladder.

Staff-officer, a military officer assisting a general or commander of an army.

Stag, a male red deer; a stock-exchange term for applicants for letters of allotment for shares in a new company, whose object is to sell immediately at a premium, without any intention of subscribing or holding shares.

Stage, a landing-quay or pier; a platform in a theatre; a scaffold erection for building; a public carriage; an assigned portion of a journey or limit travelled by horses.

Stage-box, a box in a theatre close to the [stage.

Stage-carriage, Stage-coach, a public conveyance plying for hire.

Stage-door, the back or side door; the actors' and workmen's entrance to a theatre.

Stager, a horse running in a stage [carriage.

Stag-horn Cutter, a worker up of deer horn for knife handles, &c.

Stag-hound, a dog for coursing deer.

Stails, handles for mops and brooms.

Stained-glass, painted glass for windows.

Staio, the Tuscan bushel, which is equal to about two-thirds of the English bushel. *See* Stajo.

Stair-baluster Manufacturer, a turner of wooden balusters, or a caster of iron rails for stairs.

Stair-carpet, narrow carpeting of different make and material, usually ¾ of a yard wide, for covering flights of stairs.

Staircase, a series of stone or wooden steps for ascending buildings.

Stair-head, the top of a flight of stairs.

Stair-rods, metal rods, usually of brass, fixed in eyes, to secure and keep a stair-carpet smooth in the bend of each step.

Staithmen, men engaged in weighing and shipping coals at a staith.

Staiths, lines of rails projecting over a river; a drop from which vessels are loaded with coals, &c.

Stajo, an Italian dry-measure: in some districts one bushel or less, in others 2 or 2½. For liquids the stajo varies from 2¼ to 6¾ gallons. 100 staji of corn = 28 two-fifths imperial quarters; but estimated, commonly, at 342 staji to 100 imperial quarters. In some parts 100 staji = 50·2 imperial bushels.

Stalk, to hunt deer.

Stall, a crib or portion of a stable; a stand or booth in a market; a small open or partially closed shop in a street, as a fruit-stall, a book-stall, a cobbler's-stall; a select and reserved front seat in the pit of a theatre or other place of public amusement.

Stall-fed, cattle that have been stabled and fattened in stalls; not permitted to roam at large.

Stallion, an entire or ungelded horse; one kept for serving mares.

Stamp, a die or mark; an instrument for sealing or making impressions; an official tax or mark, as a postage-stamp, a receipt-stamp, a post-office letter-stamp. *See* Postage-stamp and Receipt-stamp.

Stamp-collector, a receiver of stamp duties.

Stamp-cutter, an engraver of dies on wood, stone, or metal.

Stamp-duty, a Government tax on newspapers, deeds, bills, receipts, and postage stamps, &c.

Stamp-distributor, an issuer or vender of Government stamps, who is an official, or holds a licence.

Stamper, a marker of letters in a post-[office.

STAMP-HEADS, the crushing parts of a mill for pounding ores.

STAMPING-PRESS, a press for imprinting, by a sunken die, bills of lading, notes, envelopes, drafts, &c.; a crushing mill for ores.

STAMP-MAKER, a die-sinker; a manufacturer of adhesive receipt or postage stamps.

STAMP-NOTE, a memorandum delivered by a shipper of goods to the searcher, which, when stamped by him, allows the goods to be sent off by lighter to the ship, and is the captain's authority for receiving them on board.

STAMPS, official impressions to be affixed to letters to pre-pay the postage, or on bills and receipts. *See* POSTAGE-STAMP, and RECEIPT-STAMP.

STANCHION, an upright iron pillar or support.

STANCHION-GUN, a pivot gun; a boat-gun for wild-duck shooting.

STAND, a counter in a bazaar; a stall in a market; a station where public vehicles wait to be hired; an erection with seats for spectators on a race-course, review ground, &c.; a desk or rest for music, newspapers, &c.; a weight for pitch of 2½ to 3 cwt.; a support for a barrel, &c.; a set of arms, as a soldier's musket and bayonet.

STANDARD, an upright of iron, *for fencing*; a flag; a test or rule of measure; a solid measure by which hewn timber is estimated, varying in different timber countries. The St. Petersburg standard hundred of deals, and deal ends, contains 120 pieces, 12 feet long, 1½ inch thick, and 11 inches broad, = 165 cubic feet. The Swedish standard hundred contains 121 pieces, 14 feet long, 3 inches thick, and 9 inches broad. The Norwegian standard hundred contains 120 pieces 12 feet long, 3 inches thick, and 9 inches broad. The standard hundred by which battens are commonly sold, contains 120 pieces, 12 feet long, 2½ inches thick, and 7 inches broad. Dantzic and Memel deck deals are sold by a standard of 40 feet long, 3 inches thick, and 12 inches wide. The standard of red deals would weigh about 2¾ tons, and that of white wood 2¼ tons. The term *standard* is used to designate the purity and weight of coins, that is, the fineness of the metal of which they are made, and the quantity of it contained in them. A pound troy, or 12 oz. of the metal of which English silver coins are made, contains 11 oz. 2 dwts. pure silver, and 18 dwts. alloy. This pound is coined into 66 shillings, so that each shilling contains 80·727 grains fine silver, and 87·27 grains standard silver; and the *money pound*, consisting of 20 shillings, contains 1614·545 grains pure silver, and 1745·454 grains standard silver. The fineness of gold is estimated by carats, gold of the highest degree of fineness, or pure, being said to be 24 carats fine, 22 being the purity of our present gold coins. The sovereign, or 20 shilling piece, contains 113·001 grains fine gold, and 123·274 grains standard gold. The pound troy of standard gold, is coined into 46 sovereigns, and 22-120ths of a sovereign, or into £46 : 14 : 6d. The mint, or standard price of gold, therefore, is said to be £46 : 14 : 6d. per pound troy, or £3 : 17 : 10½d. an ounce. The alloy in coins is reckoned of no value; it is allowed in order to save the trouble and expense that would be incurred, in refining the metals to their highest degree of purity; and because, when its quantity is small, it renders the coins harder, and less liable to be worn or rubbed. Were the quantity of alloy considerable, it would lessen the splendour and ductility of the metals, and would add too much to the bulk of the coins.—*M'Culloch's Principles of Commerce.* There are several standards for gold now used, as 22, 18, 15, 12, and 9 carats.

STANDARD-BEARER, an officer who carries a banner or colours in a procession.

STANDARD-MARK, a legal assay mark for gold of 22 carats fine, and for silver of 11 oz. 2 dwts. Articles of all standards, capable of bearing a stamp, are marked also with the initials of the maker's name, the arms or mark of the Assay Office, and a letter for the date of the year. Different kinds of letters are used by the Goldsmiths' Company; the one now employed is the old black letter. The alphabet was begun in 1856, C being the letter for the present year, 1858. It runs on to 20 letters, J being omitted; a fresh alphabet is then again commenced. The standard mark for England is a lion passant: for Edinburgh, a thistle: for Glasgow, a lion rampant: for Ireland, a harp crowned. Gold of 18 carats fine, a crown and the figures 18. Silver of the new standard, which is 11 oz. 10 dwts. fine, bears the figure of Britannia. *See* HALL-MARK.

STANDING, a stall placed in a market, or on the foot pavement in a street; a workman's loom in a lower flat or story.

STANDING-RIGGING, the stationary or fixed ropes and chains, &c. of a ship, attached to the hull; used as stays and hold-fasts to keep the masts, bowsprits, &c. firm and secure.

STANHOPE, a sporting phaeton.

STANHOPE-PRESS, a printing-press, named after the inventor, Earl Stanhope.

STANNARY, a tin-mine or tin-works.

STANNARY-COURT, a court of law and equity, held in Cornwall, of which the Prince of Wales is Lord-Warden, and a Judge the Vice-Warden, held to adjudicate upon, and settle, disputes between parties connected with mines.

STANNATE OF SODA, a salt obtained from tin, largely used by calico-printers.

STAPELSTADER, a privileged weight for metals, in certain towns in Sweden, which is 4-5ths of the common standard, or victuali weight; 100 lbs. stapelstader = 74·93 lbs. avoirdupois; 100 lbs. avoirdupois, = 133·46 stapelstader victuali; 112 lbs. avoirdupois, = 149·47 lbs. stapelstader victuali; 7¾ skippund stapelstader victuali are about equal to the English ton.

STAPLE, in the Newcastle coal district a small pit; an iron loop driven into a wall or door, &c. for holding a padlock.

STAPLE ARTICLES, the chief commodities dealt in; the principal produce of a district or country.

STAPLER. *See* WOOL-STAPLER. [*See* STAJO.

STAR, STARO, an Italian grain-measure.

STAR-ANISE, the *Illicium anisatum*, a native of China and Japan, the aromatic and carminative fruit of which is used in the preparation of liqueurs. The star-shaped capsules and seeds abound in an essential oil, easily procured by distillation with water. *See* ANISEED.

STAR-APPLE, the *Chrysophyllum cainito*, and its varieties, a luscious tropical fruit.

STARBOARD, the right-hand side of a vessel, looking forward.

STARCH, a fecula; an amylaceous matter obtained from various substances, roots, and seeds, and the trunks of trees. It is chiefly made from potatoes, wheat, and rice. In America it is obtained from maize. It is largely used by laundresses for stiffening linen, by calico-printers, bleachers, and others, and the consumption is said to exceed 20,000 tons per annum. *See* ARROW-ROOT, and DEXTRINE.

STARCHER, a laundress; a clear starcher; one who stiffens fabrics.

STARCH-MANUFACTURER, a preparer of starch from roots or grains. The manufacture is carried on in most of the large towns, especially in those which are the seats of some of the principal textile manufactures.

STARELLO, an Italian grain-measure; in Milan 2 gallons, in Rome 4 gallons.

STARIE, the French name for demurrage.

STARO. *See* STAJO.

STARTIN, a measure of capacity used in Styria, nearly 2 quarters.

STATE-BARGE, a royal or corporate barge.

STATE-BED, an elaborately carved or decorated bed.

STATE-CARRIAGE, a highly decorated carriage for officials going in state, or taking part in public processions.

STATEMENT, a declaration; an account rendered; details or explanatory particulars furnished. [senger steamer.

STATE-ROOM, the principal cabin of a passenger steamer.

STATHEL (Scotch), a support or prop for a stack of grain to raise it above the ground.

STATION, a depot; a starting or stopping place on a railway; an assigned post of duty; a garrison for troops; the sea district under the jurisdiction of an admiral; the quarters for police.

STATION-CLERK, a railway clerk.

STATIONER, a dealer in pens, ink, paper, &c. or in small periodicals.

STATIONERS'-COMPANY, one of the livery companies of London whose hall is in Stationers' court, Ludgate hill. [binders.

STATIONERS'-RULE, a measure used by bookbinders.

STATIONERY, writing materials and books; the articles dealt in by a stationer.

STATION-MASTER, an officer in charge of a railway station.

STATION-POINTER, STATION-STAFF, surveying instruments.

STATISTICS, facts and figures relating to the commerce, progress, or social condition of a country; parliamentary returns or private computations.

STATUARY, a carver or sculptor in stone; a maker of statues; a collection of statues.

STATUARY-MARBLE, crystalline, granular, white marble, used for monuments, busts, furniture, &c. [stone or metal.

STATUE, an image or carving of a figure in stone or metal.

STATUETTE, a small statue.

STATUTE, an annual public gathering or fair, for hiring farm servants, in some parts of the country; a legislative enactment.

STATUTE-LABOUR, a definite amount of labour required for the public service in making roads, streets, bridges, &c. in certain colonies; which has to be performed personally or by substitute, but may be commuted by a money payment.

STATUTE OF LIMITATIONS, an assigned period within which an action must be brought, which varies; for debts it is six years.

STAVES, shaped lengths of wood for making casks; chiefly of white or red oak; but also made of ash and other wood. They are sold by the standard mille, or thousand, of 1200, or ten standard hundreds of 120 pieces. Staves vary in length, according to the purpose they are intended for, from 31 inches long to 72 inches, and in breadth from 3 to 7 inches; in thickness from ¾ to 3 inches. Prepared staves are reckoned, in some parts of the Continent by the schock. Thus a long thousand of staves usually consists of 20 schock, each of 60 pipe staves; for hogshead and barrel staves the long thousand consists respectively of 30 and 40 schock, and for pipe, hogshead, and barrel headings, of 40, 60, and 80 schock. The imports of staves in 1855 were 67,747 loads or tons.

STAVESACRE, the acrid, emetic, purgative seeds of *Delphinium Staphisagria*, which are used against worms and itch. The seeds are also employed in the Levant for intoxicating fish.

STAY AND CORSET MAKER, a maker of stiffened waist-supports for females.

STAY-BUSK, a stiff piece of wood, steel, or whalebone for the front support of a woman's stays.

STAY-LACE, a silk or thread cord for fastening a lady's stays.

STAYS, large ropes used to support and secure the masts of ships; corsets for females.

STAY-SAIL, a ship's sail which is hoisted by rings upon a stay or rope.

STEAD, the frame of a bed; a place or locality, as a homestead, a farm-steading.

STEAK, a fleshy slice of meat for broiling, frying, or stewing.

STEAK-BEATER, a roller for beating beefsteaks before cooking, to make them tender.

STEAK-BROILER, a gridiron which catches the gravy from the steak.

STEAK-TONGS, small tongs for turning chops or steaks when broiling on a gridiron.

STEAL, to thieve; to remove clandestinely; to defraud.

STEAM, water converted into an elastic fluid by the application of heat, and largely applied as a motive-power in propelling vessels and carriages, and driving machinery.

STEAM-BOAT BUILDER, a constructor of vessels to be driven by steam, either paddle-wheels or propellers.

STEAM-BOILER, the metal vessel in which steam is generated.

STEAM-CARRIAGE MAKER, a manufacturer of vehicles to be propelled by steam-power.

STEAM-CHEST, a box attached to the cylinder in which steam is admitted by the regulator.

STEAM-CYLINDER, the vessel in which the moveable disk or piston moves.

STEAM-DREDGER, a machine worked by steam, with buckets on a revolving frame, to keep the beds of rivers and harbours clean.

STEAM-ENGINE-BOILER MAKER, a constructor of steam-boilers for locomotive, marine, or stationary engines.

STEAMER, a spare top fitting on a saucepan, with holes at the bottom, for cooking potatoes by steam; a steamboat.

STEAM-GAUGE, a contrivance to show the exact amount of pressure of the steam.

STEAM HAMMER, a heavy hammer worked by steam-power.

STEAM-INDICATOR. *See* STEAM-GAUGE.

STEAM-MILLS, machinery worked by steam for different purposes.

STEAM-PACKET, a steam-vessel running periodically between certain ports.

STEAM-PAN, a vessel heated by steam.

STEAM-PIPE, in locomotive engines the pipes which collect and convey the steam to the steam-chest; hot-water pipes for heating buildings.

STEAM-PRESS, a printing-press worked by steam.

STEAM-PROPELLER. *See* STEAMER and PROPELLER.

STEAM-PUMP, a pump worked by steam.

STEAM-TUG, a small steam-boat employed to tow vessels, barges, dredgers, &c.

STEAM-WHISTLE, an attachment to locomotive-engines; an escape of steam through a pipe which produces a shrill warning whistle, that can be heard several miles.

STEARIN, STEARIC-ACID, the solid constituant of fatty substances.

STEATITE, a soft, unctuous, magnesian mineral, used by the Chinese for making figures, and suitable for statuary and decorative purposes. *See* SOAPSTONE.

STEEKKAN, STECHKANNE, a Dutch liquid-measure, the 12th part of a barrel, and averaging about 4 gallons: 6 stechkannes make a tun of train-oil.

STEEL, a compound of iron and carbon. The principal varieties manufactured are bar or blistered steel, to which shear-steel belongs, cast-steel, Damascus, and German-steel; an instrument for sharpening a knife; a piece of metal for striking a light with a flint. *See* WOOTZ and GERMAN-STEEL, &c.

STEEL-BUSK MAKER, one who makes metal busks or bones for women's stays.

STEEL-CONVERTER AND -REFINER, one who carbonises bar-iron in a converting furnace, prepares it into blister-steel, and afterwards refines it.

STEEL-MANUFACTURER, a maker of shear or cast steel; a hammerer and roller of steel into the sizes required for files, edge-tools, table-knives and forks, coach-springs, &c.

STEEL-MILL MAKER, a manufacturer of forge tilts, or rolling-mills, for hammering steel into bars, or rolling it into sheets.

STEEL-PEN MAKER, a manufacturer of metal pens, which are now largely used for writing.

STEEL-PLATE MAKER, a preparer of plates for the use of engravers.

STEEL-PLATE PRINTER, one who takes impressions by a press from steel-plates.

STEEL-ROLLER, the cylinder of a mill for rolling out steel into sheets.

STEEL-SCRAPER, a bookbinder's tool.

STEEL-WINE, sherry wine in which steel filings have been placed for some time, used medicinally.

STEELYARD, a balance by leverage, having arms of unequal length; the weight being moved along the rod or longer arm, grows heavier in proportion as it is removed further from the fulcrum or support.

STEENING, a term in well-digging, implying enclosing or walling in half a brick thick.

STEEP, a dye; a cleansing wash; a rennet-bag; to dip or soak.

STEEPLE-CHASE, a hunt or race, in which the horseman proceeds, regardless of obstructions, over rivers, hedges, or ditches.

STEER, a young bullock; a castrated bull; in Scotland, to plough land.

STEERAGE, that part of the between-decks of a vessel which is just forward of the cabin; the accommodation afforded to second-class passengers in a passenger-ship.

STEERING-WHEEL MAKER, a manufacturer of the tiller-wheels with handles, used to work the rudders of large ships.

STEERSMAN, the pilot of a boat; a helmsman.

STEIN (German), a stone; a weight of 20 lbs. to 22 lbs., by which flax is weighed in Saxony; this weight varies with the goods weighed.

STEINBERGER, a kind of wine.

STEINBOCK, a species of Cape antelope, the *Antelopa tragulus*.

STENCIL, a piece of metal, oil-cloth, or leather, in which patterns have been cut out, to be placed on some surface, and brushed over with ink or colour, when the pattern, letters, or device is left.

STENCIL-CUTTER, a person who pierces patterns, letters, or ornaments, on thin metal plates, or on oil-cloth, &c. for the use of a stenciller.

STENCILLER, one who works with a stencil.

STENCILLING, a kind of painting on walls with a stencil, to imitate the figures of paper-hangings.

STENCIL-PLATE. *See* STENCIL.

STENOGRAPHER, a reporter; a shorthand-writer.

STENOGRAPHY, abbreviated writing; the art of taking down the words of a speaker in short-hand characters.

STENT-MASTER, an assessor or valuer of property, for taxation in Scotland.

STEP, a stair, or the round of a ladder; a pace; the hole or socket which supports a boat's mast.

STEPPES, vast, untilled, or barren plains.
STEPPING-STONES, stones laid in a brook or in a miry road.
STERE, the unit of French solid-measure employed for measuring fire-wood, stone, &c. It is equal to 35·31741 cubic feet, and is the same as the kilolitre in measures of capacity.
STEREOSCOPE, a frame with a pair of lenses, in which two pictures or representations of an object, taken at slightly different angles, are made to combine, and appear as one statue or figure, &c. standing out in bold relief. Cities, portraits, and scenes are thus brought out vividly before the eye.
STEREOTYPE, a solid page of metal cast from the letter-press, which releases a certain weight of type, and enables a work to be kept in print at a smaller expense.
STEREOTYPE-FOUNDER, a person who casts metal plates from forms of moveable type. A mould is first taken in plaster of Paris, and into this an alloyed metal is poured.
STEREOTYPE-MAKER, a workman employed in making stereotypes.
STEREOTYPE-PLATE, a sheet of metal taking the place of type or wood-cuts, for printing. These plates are usually mounted on blocks of wood to the height of type.
STERLET, the *Acipenser Ruthenus*, a species of sturgeon, the swimming-bladder of which yields the best Russian isinglass. Its flesh is prized, and its roe yields caviar.
STERLING, according to a fixed standard; a term which has long been applied to the genuine and standard money of the United Kingdom.
STERN, the after-end or hindermost part of a vessel.
STERN-FAST, a rope attached to the stern of a vessel, when lying at a wharf, &c.
STERN-POST, the aftermost timber in a ship; that on which the rudder hangs.
STERN-SHEETS, the after-part of a boat, abaft the rowers, where the passengers sit.
STERNUTATORY, a medicine or application to the nose, which causes sneezing.
STETCH, a farming term for a division of land; the ridge or row between the furrows, made by a plough, which may be a 6-feet or a 12-feet stetch.
STETHOMETER, an instrument for measuring the comparative mobility of the chest, in cases of disease of the lungs. It consists of a dial-plate with a moveable index, which is acted on by the pressure of the sides of the chest on a cord which is made to extend around the chest.
STETHOSCOPE, a surgeon's sound instrument; a hollow tube or cylinder of cedar-wood, perforated throughout its length, having an ear-piece at one end, and a funnel-shaped cavity at the other, for ascertaining the action of the lungs and heart.
STETHOSCOPE MAKER, a manufacturer of the wooden sounding tubes used by surgeons.
STEVEDORE, a person who superintends the stowage of a ship's cargo.
STEW, meat hashed or mixed with vegetables; a store-pond for fish. *See* IRISH STEW.
STEWARD, the manager of a landed estate; one who acts for another; a director of a public dinner, ball, or charitable festival; the providore or chief cabin servant in a steamer or passenger ship.
STEW-PAN, a shallow sauce-pan of iron, copper, or block-tin.
STIBIUM, a name for antimony ore.
STICCATO (Italian), a musical instrument, the sounds of which are produced by striking on it with bars of wood.
STICK, the mast or spar for a ship; a walking-cane or straight twig; a compositor's instrument for holding type.
STICK-FLOUR, a Brazilian name for cassava meal; in Portuguese, farinha de pão.
STICKFUL, a printer's term for as much arranged type as his composing-stick will hold, and which has to be transferred to a galley, to enable him to go on composing or setting up type.
STICKING-PLASTER MAKER, a maker of court plaster, or of a more common adhesive plaster, for closing wounds.
STICK-LAC, the crude lac or red colouring resin formed by the *Coccus lacca*, and encrusting small twigs.
STICKLEBACK, the *Gasterosteus aculeatus*, a small fish, not eatable, because it is too fat: its fat might, however, be made useful. On the coasts, it is often spread in cartloads over the land for manure.
STICK-LIQUORICE, Spanish liquorice-paste in the form of sticks. *See* LIQUORICE.
STICK-POMATUM. *See* BANDOLINE.
STIFFENING-ORDER, a permission granted by the Customs' to take on board heavy goods, by way of ballast, to steady the ship.
ST. IGNATIUS' BEANS, another name for the seeds of the *Strychnos nux vomica*, and *ignatia*. *See* KOU-KOU.
STILE, a kind of stepping-gate in a field; a set of steps to pass over a fence.
STILETTO, an instrument for making eyelet-holes in needle-work; a slender dagger or knife.
STILL, a metal apparatus with a boiler, a head, and a condenser or worm-pipe, through which the vapour ascends, in the distillation of liquids.
STILL-HANGER, an engineer or worker, who fixes the stills for making rum in the West Indies.
STILL-HOUSE, a building where distillation is carried on.
STILLIARD, an incorrect mode of spelling steel-yard.
STILL-ROOM, an apartment for keeping liqueurs, preserves, &c.; a room where a still is worked, for making spirits or essences.
STILL-YARD. *See* STEELYARD.
STILTON, a solid, rich, buttery, and white cheese, made in Leicestershire. It is the dearest of English cheeses, and is seldom used till it is two years old.
STILTS, props or poles for walking on.
STIMPART, in Ayrshire, the fourth part of a peck.
STIMULANTS, medicines or strong drinks, which increase the action of the pulse, and excite the energies of the system.

STINGER, in Scotland, a thatcher; one who repairs thatched roofs.

STINK-POT, an offensive projectile, containing stinking combustibles.

STINK-TRAP, a kind of patent sink, to prevent the exhalation of noxious vapours from the sewers.

STINT, a miner's name for a given quantity of work to be performed; a term in the north for cattle and sheep taken in to graze.

STIPEND, an allowance or salary.

STIPENDIARY MAGISTRATE, a resident paid magistrate.

STIPPLE, to engrave with dots.

STIPULATE, to bargain; to covenant.

STIRABOUT, a hasty pudding.

STIRK, STURK, a young ox or heifer.

STIRRUP-IRON, an iron hoop or rest for a horseman's foot.

STIRRUP-LEATHER, the strap or suspending support for a stirrup-iron.

STITCH, to fasten with a needle and thread; to form land into ridges. *See* STETCH.

STIVE, a name given to the floating dust in flour-mills, during the operation of grinding.

STIVER, a small Dutch money, equal to a penny.

STOCK, the cross-piece of an anchor, at right angles with the shank, which is either of iron, or wood firmly bound together with iron hoops; a computation for grain in Hamburgh, 1½ last, about 16½ quarters; a log or trunk of a tree; a kind of stiff neck-band; material for soup; capital; farming animals.

STOCKADE, a fortification or fence of pointed stakes, in New Zealand called a pah; a cattle-pen.

STOCK AND BIT, an instrument for boring wood, used by carpenters; a centre-bit.

STOCK AND SHARE BROKER, a dealer in the public funds and joint-stock companies' shares, who is required in London to hold a licence from the corporation.

STOCK-EXCHANGE, a body of stock-brokers who meet and transact business in their hall in Capel court, under certain recognized forms and regulations.

STOCK-EXCHANGE COMMITTEE, a body elected from among the stock-brokers, to manage the general affairs of the stock-exchange, and decide upon matters brought before them.

STOCK-FISH, a kind of cod-fish which is caught on the coasts of Spain, and, after washing in the sea, is simply sun-dried and not salted.

STOCKING-FRAME, a machine for weaving stockings.

STOCKING-MAKER, a weaver or manufacturer of stockings.

STOCKINGS, hose; coverings for the feet and legs, of cotton, silk, or worsted.

STOCKING-TRIMMER, a decorator or ornamenter of stockings; one who removes loose threads or imperfections.

STOCK-IN-TRADE, the goods kept on sale by a shop-keeper; the fittings and appliances of a workman.

STOCK-JOBBER, an outsider or intermediate agent between the buyer and seller of public securities, who makes a marginal price at which shares, &c. are to be bought or sold in the Stock-exchange.

STOCK-LIST, a list published daily or periodically, enumerating the leading stocks dealt in; the prices current; the actual transactions, &c.

STOCK-MAKER, a manufacturer of stiff neck-bands worn by men.

STOCKMAN, a herdsman; a keeper of cattle.

STOCK-MARKET, the stock-exchange; a place for the sale of cattle.

STOCKS, public funds or securities; the red and grey bricks which are used for the exterior of walls and fronts of buildings; the frame upon which a vessel is built; men's stiff bands or ties for the neck. *See* MARLE-STOCKS.

STOCK-SHAVE, a block-maker's tool.

STOCK-STATION, a district for rearing and herding cattle.

STOCK-TAKING, a periodical examination and inventory of goods, or stock, in a shop or warehouse.

STOF, a liquid-measure used in Germany and Russia, averaging 2¼ pints.

STOKE-HOLE, the mouth of the grate of a furnace.

STOKER, one who pokes or kindles a fire; a man who attends to a fire-grate or furnace and supplies it with fuel: the term is chiefly applied to men so employed on locomotive and marine steam-engines.

STOMACHER, a lady's ornament of net or lace for the breast.

STOMACH-PUMP, an apparatus for emptying the stomach, or injecting liquids, &c.

STOMACH-WARMER, a metal vessel for holding hot water to place on the stomach.

STONE, a commercial weight varying with the article weighed, but legally 14 lbs. The stone of butcher's meat or fish is usually reckoned at 8 lbs.; of cheese 16 lbs.; of hemp 32 lbs.; of glass 5 lbs. In Hamburgh a stone of flax is 20 lbs.; of feathers 10 lbs. The Prussian stone of 22 lbs. is equal to 22¾ lbs. avoirdupois, 5 stone making 1 trade centner, or 110 lbs. = 113 lbs. avoirdupois, nearly.

STONE-BREAKER, one who is employed in preparing metal for road-making.

STONE-CUTTER, an operative employed in a stone quarry, or in working marble and other stone: a lapidary.

STONE-DRESSER, one who tools, smooths, and shapes stone for building purposes.

STONE-HAMMER, a small hammer for breaking stones to mend roads.

STONE-MASON, one who works or builds in stone.

STONE-MERCHANT, an importer of granite from the Channel islands, Scotland, &c.; a dealer in paving or building stones.

STONE-PLANING MACHINE, a machine for facing or smoothing marble and other stone.

STONE-QUARRY, a place where stones are dug or cut.

STONES. Large quantities of different kinds of stone are imported. For instance, in 1855, there were brought in 103,850 solid feet of rough marble; 12,018 cwts. of sawn or manufactured marble; 6765 tons of stone in lumps; 620 tons of hewn stone and slate; 12 tons of limestone; 125 tons of flint; 47 tons of felspar and stones for potters' use; 15 tons of pebble stone; 311 tons of lithographic stone; 12,000 tons of shaped or rough scapled stone; 117 tons of mill-stones, and 2436 tons of burr stones. The whole quantity of stone worked up yearly in the kingdom is estimated at 42,000,000 tons.

Stone-slab, a plate of stone.

Stone squarer, a worker in stone; one who shapes stones.

Stone-ware, a perfect kind of pottery, approaching very nearly to a true porcelain, used for drain pipes, which is composed of clay and silex, partially vitrified by heat, and over which a glaze or kind of glass coating is diffused by throwing salt into the furnace.

Stone-wharf, a landing or reception place for cargoes of stone.

Stone-yard, a contractor's or other yard where paupers are set to break stones.

Stook, a name for 12 sheaves of corn.

Stool, a low wooden seat on legs; a carpenter's bench; the root of a timber tree, which throws up shoots.

Stoop, an old liquid-measure of Germany of 4½ pints.

Stop, a Swedish liquid-measure of 2½ pints.

Stop-cock, a tap with a turning handle. *See* Ball-cock.

Stope, part of the workings of a mine.

Stopello, a grain-measure used in Naples and Messina, about 1½ gallon.

Stoppage, an obstruction; a discontinuance of work; setting machinery at rest; a deduction made from pay or allowances to repay advances.

Stopper, the cork or glass mouth-piece for a bottle; a plug.

Stopping-knife. *See* Knife.

Stopple, a cork for a bottle.

Stop-watch, a watch, one of the hands of which can be stayed, to reckon the time elapsing.

Storage, a charge for warehousing goods.

Storax-tree, the *Styrax officinalis*, a native of the Mediterranean coasts, furnishing the balsamic resin, which is stimulant, expectorant, and detergent.

Store, a general warehouse; a retail shop; to lay up, to stock.

Store-keeper, an officer having charge of stores; the name for a retail dealer or shop-keeper in the Colonies, who keeps a miscellaneous assortment of all kinds of commodities.

Storeman, the keeper of a general store; a shopman, one who serves in a store.

Store-master, the tenant of a store farm, that is, a sheep walk in Scotland.

Store-pigs, swine put up to fatten for sale or slaughter.

Store-room, Store-house, a magazine or deposit-place; the space assigned for securing or stowing stores.

Stores (French), spring-roller blinds; the supplies laid in for a ship.

Store-ship, a ship which accompanies a fleet or expedition with surplus stores; a stationary transport or depot.

Storey, the elevation of a dwelling-house or other building, being the division from floor to floor.

Storm-sail, a strong-bound sail of coarse material, hoisted in gales of wind.

Stot, a provincial name for a steer or young bullock.

Stotz, a Swiss liquid-measure, holding ¾ a pint to ¾ of a pint.

Stove, a cast-iron fire-place, heated by coal or gas, for warming and ventilating shops, warehouses, offices, &c.

Stove-brush, a housemaid's polishing-brush, for blackening or shining a grate.

Stove-maker, a founder and caster of stoves and ranges, for grates and fire-places.

Stove-polish, black-lead.

Stowage, room for packing or placing goods in a ship's hold or warehouse.

Stowce, a miner's name in Derbyshire for a small windlass.

Stower, one who puts away the cargo in a ship's hold.

Stracke, a refuse of silk. *See* Strasse.

Straggling, a mode of dressing the surfaces of grindstones, also called ragging.

Straighten, to level or smooth; to plane.

Strait-jacket, a waistcoat or bandaged garment for confining a lunatic, to prevent his injuring himself or others.

Strake, a narrow board or plank; the tyre of a wheel.

Strand, the sea-shore; a division or twist of a rope; an aggregation of yarns from 15 to 25 twisted together, three strands being spun into a rope, and three ropes making a cable; to drive or force a ship on shore.

Strap, a narrow leather band or long strip of any thing, used as a fastening.

Strasse (French), the waste or refuse of silk in working it up into skeins; wrapping paper; colourless glass.

Straw, the stalks or culms on which corn and other grasses grow, and from which the grain has been thrashed. Straw is cut into chaff for feeding cattle and other purposes and used as a litter. Some straw is plaited into braids for hats and bonnets; and artificial flowers, mats, and baskets, are made of it: it is also twisted into straw ropes, and cigar-cases.

Strawberry, an esteemed and choice fruit; a species of *Fragaria*, largely cultivated as a table-fruit, and for making jam. Upwards of 700 tons are annually disposed of in the London markets.

Straw-cutter, a chaff-engine; a machine with knives for chopping straw for horse-provender.

Straw-hat and Bonnet Maker, a sewer of straw-plat into shape for head coverings.

Straw-hats. In many places these form a considerable item of trade, especially in warm countries, the East and West Indies, United States, South America, the Cape, and Australia. Besides the common English straw-hats, there are the finer qualities of Panama, cabbage-tree, and Manila.

Straw-plat, twisted or plaited straws. A peculiar wheat-straw grown in Bedfordshire, and known as Dunstable, forms one of the chief plats. There are seven principal descriptions of plats in use, besides half-a-dozen varieties in fancy straws. Sometimes as much as 100 tons a-year of straw-plat, chip, and grass, for hats and bonnets, are imported.

Stray, an animal found wandering and unclaimed.

Streak, Strake, a range of planks running 'fore and aft on a vessel's side.

Stream-anchor, a lighter anchor than the bower-anchor, but larger than the kedges.

Streamer, a pennon; a long floating flag or ribbon.

Stream-ice, a continued ridge of pieces of ice, running in a particular direction.

Stream-tin, diluvial ore in tin-mines.

Streep, a petty Dutch measure of length, the line, forming the ·001 part of the Belgian aune, which is 27·386 inches.

Street, a thoroughfare; a public way in a town.

Street-car. *See* Car.

Street-crossing Sweeper, a beggar; one who sweeps a crossing clean, depending upon the charity of passengers for remuneration.

Street-door, the front or entrance door of a dwelling-house or shop.

Street-door Key, a private latch-key, or large entrance door-key.

Street-keeper, a street-ward; a beadle having the charge of a private street or thoroughfare.

Street-orderly, a street-sweeper.

Street-sweeping Machine, a cart fitted with revolving brooms, or a rotatory brush and scraper, for cleansing public thoroughfares.

Street-ward, an officer having the care of the streets.

Strema, a land-measure in Greece, about the third part of an acre.

Stretch, to draw out or lengthen; to extend.

Stretcher, a thin piece of wood placed across the bottom of a boat, for the oarsman or rower to rest his feet against; an instrument for easing boots or gloves; a closing bed-frame.

Stretchers, a building term for bricks or stones placed length-wise along the wall, in contra-distinction to headers, which lie across the wall.

Strickle, an instrument used in moulding pipes; a stick to strike off the surplus from a heaped measure; a scythe whetstone.

Strike, an old English dry-measure, containing 2 bushels; a stoppage of workmen for a higher rate of wages, or for discontent at existing regulations; a hook in a foundry to elevate metal by; a strickle; a rake or stirrer; to lower a boat's sail or a vessel's upper masts; to repeat as a watch.

Strike-block, a plate shorter than a jointer.

Striker, a harpoon; in the hardware districts, one who manages the fire, heats the steel, and assists the forger.

String, small cord; the wires or gut of a musical instrument; a row or thread of beads; a term used in Libau, Courland, for 30 pieces, or the half of the shock.

Stringy-bark, the name given in Australia to a species of *Eucalyptus*; the bark is used by the aborigines to make canvas and cordage.

Strip, a narrow shred.

Strip-leaf, tobacco from which the stalks have been removed before packing in the hogshead.

Stripe, a line, band, or mark of colour.

Strockle, in the glass trade, a shovel with a turned up edge, suited to filling the pots or moulds, from the chests or harbours of materials.

Stroh, a name in Bremen for 125 red-herrings, or the 20th part of a last; at Stettin, 6 wall, or 480 shock.

Stroke, the sweep of an oar; the movement of a piston.

Strokeall, Snatch, a fishing instrument employed in the rivers of Ireland, the use of which is now prohibited under the fishery act.

Strokesman, the rower who pulls the after or leading oar in a boat.

Strolling-player, an itinerant actor of a low class.

Strontia, a mineral which gives a red colour to flame, and is therefore used for fire-works, in theatres, &c.

Strontites, oxide of strontium.

Strontium, a metal, the base of strontia.

Strop, an instrument for sharpening a razor.

Strosse, the second class of wool in the Danubian Provinces, the classification being into 3 sorts, cigais, strosse, and ordinary.

Stroud, an article made from rags, used by the North American Indians.

Struin, a name for silk waste in Italy.

Struntain, the name in Scotland for a kind of coarse worsted braid, less than an inch broad.

Struse, a long burdensome craft, used for transport on the inland waters of Russia.

Strychnia, a powerful alkaline poison, obtained from species of *Strychnos* or the *Nux vomica* bean.

Stub, the stump of a tree; a log.

Stubble, the root-ends of the culms of corn, left standing in the field after the corn has been reaped.

Stubich, a measure for charcoal in Vienna, = 3·384 bushels.

Stub-nail, a short thick nail.

Stubschen, Stubgen, a German liquid-measure, varying from 5¾ to 6¾ pints, in different localities. In Hamburgh, 2 kannes make a stubgen; in Hanover, 40 stubgen = 34·24 gallons; and 25½ stubgen, weighing 300 lbs., make a tonne of honey.

Stub-wood, young wood cut from stools, or small hedgerow timber.

Stucco, a fine plaster used for covering walls, &c. as a preservative from damp; a combination of gypsum, which generally contains carbonate of lime, with gelatine, or strong glue. This composition dries more slowly than that made with water, but is harder and more durable, and is much used for interior decorations.

Stuck, a German name for piece, also applied to several casks for liquids; a German liquid-measure of 8 ohms, the ohm being equivalent to 31 5-16th gallons.

Stud, a link, button, or catch; a furnace casting; the number of racing horses kept by one breeder or trainer; a nail with a large head; a stable of 10 hack-horses for running in omnibuses; a prop; to adorn with knobs.

Studding-sail Boom, an additional or extended yard added to another.
Studding-sail Halliards, the hoist ropes for supporting a studding-sail boom.
Studding-sails, extra sails set outside the regular square sails in fine weather, on booms run out for the purpose.
Student, a scholar; a young artist; one who studies.
Studio, an artist's workshop.
Study, a painter's preliminary sketch for a finished work; a draught copy for improvement.
Stuffing, minced seasoning; savoury ingredients put into meat or poultry.
Stuffing-boxes, a space in a cylinder or parts of a steam-engine, which has to be closed with tow, yarn, or some other substance, to keep in the steam.
Stuff-manufacturer, a maker of thin woollen cloth.
Stuff-shovel, an implement used by the paper-makers.
Stum, grape juice, or wine that has not fermented: this is frequently mixed with vapid wines to renew fermentation.
Stump, a stub or root block; the root of a tree left in the ground; an artist's soft pencil or rubber; a thin post used at cricket, three of which support the wicket bales.
Stun-sail, an abbreviation of "studding-sail."
Stunts, a name for young whales of two years old, which, having been weaned, are lean, and scarcely yield more than 20 to 24 barrels of blubber.
Sturgeon, a large and fine fish, a species of *Acipenser*, which is occasionally imported pickled, from Russia. When caught on our shores, it is considered a royal fish. The flesh is white, delicate, and firm. The varieties of sturgeon furnish the best kinds of commercial isinglass, as well as the delicacy known as caviar. *See* Caviar.
Sty, a pen or house for keeping swine.
Style, a hard bone or metal-pointed pencil, for writing on tracing or copying paper, on waxed tablets, or for graving with.
Stylish, fashionable; elegant.
Stylometer, an instrument for measuring columns.
Styptic, an astringent medicine applied to stanch bleeding, as Ruspini's styptic, &c.
Styrax. *See* Storax-tree, and Benzoin.
Sub (Latin), under; less: a prefix to words expressing a depute agent.
Subadar, a viceroy; the governor of an Indian province; a native military officer, corresponding in rank with a captain.
Subaltern, a cornet, ensign, or lieutenant; a military officer under the rank of a captain.
Sub-contractor, one who takes a portion of a contract for work from the chief or principal contractor.
Sub-deanery, the office of a dean's deputy.
Sub-editor, an assistant editor of a periodical or journal.
Subjee, a name in Hindustan for the leaves or capsules of the Indian hemp used for smoking, &c.
Sub-let, to underlet a tenement.
Sublimate, to refine; to raise volatile substances by heat, and again condense them in a solid form; the product so refined.
Sublimate, Corrosive, the bichloride of mercury.
Submarine Telegraph, a cable laid in the sea enclosing electric wires.
Submerged, put under water.
Subpoena, a writ or legal command, from some authorized court, to appear as a witness, under a penalty for failure.
Subscription, a contribution given; the writing or signature appended to a deed or document.
Subsidence-vat, a dyer's settling-vat.
Subsidy, a pecuniary State assistance or grant; a tax.
Subsoil-plough, a trench or draining plough; one for turning up the substratum, and loosening the soil.
Substitute, a deputy; one acting for another; a person paid to serve in the army or militia, in place of another who had been drawn or chosen.
Suburban, beyond the walls or boundaries of a city.
Suburbs, the outlying or circumjacent parts of a town or city.
Subvention, a government grant or aid; a subsidy.
Subway, an underground way.
Succades, the sweet constituent of certain vegetable products, imported, preserved with sugar, from the East and West Indies, and the Levant, for confectionery.
Succatosh, an American dish made of green Indian corn or maize and beans, boiled together.
Succinic-acid, an acid obtained from amber resin by distillation.
Succory, a general name in the United States for chicory.
Succulent, full of juice.
Sucker, a piston; a piece of wet leather in the box of a pump; the off-shoot of a plant.
Sucking-bottle, an infant's feeding-bottle for holding milk, with a sponge or Indian-rubber cork.
Sucking-pig, a young pig.
Sucking-pump, a pump where the water is raised into the barrel by atmospheric pressure.
Suds, water impregnated with soap, for washing or scouring.
Suedo, the twentieth part of the Catalan libra, a coin which is worth about 2s 4d. sterling.
Sueldo, a money of account in Spain, about 3s. 8d.
Suerie (French), a drying-room for tobacco.
Suerte, a Spanish long-measure of 100 estadales. *See* Estadal.
Suet, the hard-solid fat near the kidneys of oxen and sheep.
Suet-chopper, a mincing knife for cutting up suet.
Suet-pudding, Suet-dumpling, hard-boiled plain puddings, mixed with suet.
Suffed-til, a name in India for the white-seeded variety of *Sesamum orientale*, the black seeded being called *kala-til*.
Sufferance, a permission granted by the Customs, for the shipment of certain goods.

SUFFERANCE-WHARF, a wharf licensed by the Customs, and where Custom-house officers attend.

SUFRIDERA (Spanish), a smith's tool for punching holes on an anvil.

SUGAR, the saccharine constituent of vegetable and animal products. The sugars of commerce are obtained chiefly from the juice of the sugar-cane, the beet-root, the sap of the sugar-maple, and from some of the palms. The following figures show the quantity in cwts. of raw cane sugar consumed in this country within the last four years:—

1853......	7,307,080	1855.......	7,396,697
1854.......	8,100,423	1856.......	7,240,826

Besides the raw sugar, there are about 300,000 cwts. of refined sugar used.

SUGAR-APPLE TREE, a name for the sweet sop, *Anona squamosa*.

SUGAR-BAKER, a refiner of sugar.

SUGAR-BASIN, a glass, silver, or other vessel for holding loaf or moist sugar, for table-use.

SUGAR-BEAN, the *Phaseolus saccharatus*, a sweet and nutritious pulse, cultivated in the West Indies; the scimitar-podded kidney-bean, *P. lunatus*, a native of Eastern India.

SUGAR-BEET. *See* BEET-ROOT-SUGAR.

SUGAR-BOX, a kind of long case in which Havana and some other sugars are imported.

SUGAR-CANDY, crystallized or clarified sugar.

SUGAR-CANE, the *Arundo saccharifera*, and its varieties, largely grown in many tropical countries for the sugar obtained from its sap.

SUGAR-CANISTER, a large tin canister for holding chopped loaf-sugar.

SUGAR-CHOPPER, a small hatchet for breaking up loaf-sugar.

SUGAR-DREDGER. *See* DREDGING-BOX.

SUGAR-KETTLE, an iron pot used for boiling down the sap of the sugar-maple in North America.

SUGAR-LOAF, a conical mass of white sugar, which has been shaped in a pot, and refined and baked.

SUGAR-MACHINERY, the rolling mills necessary for squeezing out the sap of the sugar-cane.

SUGAR-MAPLE, the *Acer saccharinum*, from which a large quantity of sugar is made for home use, in New Brunswick, Canada, New England, and some of the other North American States. A single tree will yield 5 or 6 lbs. of sugar. *A. nigrum*, the black sugar-maple, is found in Ohio and the States further south.

SUGAR-MILL, a crushing-mill for squeezing the juice from the sugar-cane, between sets of three or more rollers, placed either horizontally or vertically, and worked by different power, but usually now by steam.

SUGAR-MILL MAKER, a founder and millwright, who constructs the crushing-mills used on sugar-estates; also a maker of cast-iron mills used by grocers for mixing sugars.

SUGAR-MOULDS, small conical-shaped pots, made of common red pottery-ware, or of sheet-iron, for moulding sugar in the process of refining.

SUGAR-NIPPERS, tools for cutting loaf-sugar into lumps.

SUGAR OF LEAD, the acetate of lead, a compound of acetic acid and oxide of lead. Acetate of lead is much used in calico-printing.

SUGAR-PANS, large, circular-shaped cast-iron or copper boilers, used for boiling down sugar.

SUGAR-PLANTER, a tropical agriculturist engaged in the cultivation of sugar-canes; an overseer or book-keeper on a sugar estate.

SUGAR-PLUM, a comfit; a small sweetmeat.

SUGAR-REFINER, a re-boiler and bleacher of raw or muscovado sugar.

SUGAR-REFINERS' IRON-MOULD MAKER, a founder who casts the iron moulds to pour sugar in to be refined.

SUGAR-TONGS, a pair of metal pliers to take up nubs of sugar.

SUGAR-VINEGAR. In the West Indies and other cane-growing countries, the spoiled and waste saccharine juice and washings, are used to make vinegar.

SUGBEENUJ, an Arab name for gum sagapenum.

SUGEY. *See* SOOJEE.

SUGMOONEA, the Arab name for scammony, implying purgative properties.

SUIT, a set of the same kind of things; a set of wearing apparel; an assortment of playing cards in a pack; a law-process or action; a technical name in the government biscuit manufactories for a batch of biscuits, weighing about 1 cwt., or one charge of the oven.

SUITE, a retinue, or train of followers; a set of apartments opening into each other.

SUITOR, one who proceeds in a court of law.

SUKAT, a measure of capacity used in Sumatra, nearly 1½ gallon.

SUKON, the Malay name for the bread-fruit.

SULEA, a name in Bengal for the *Polynemus Sele*, a fish from which isinglass is obtained.

SULEESHE, an Indian name for the aromatic bark of the *Cinnamomum Culilaban* of Blume. *See* CULILABAN-BARK.

SULKY, an American two-wheeled carriage for a single person.

SULLAGE, a founder's name for metal scoria or slag.

SULPHATE, a salt formed by the union of sulphuric acid with a salifiable base. The sulphates are an important class of salts, most of which are noticed under their popular commercial names.

SULPHUR, a simple inflammable body, of great importance in chemistry and the arts. It is found abundantly in deposits near volcanoes, and is also obtained by the roasting of pyrites. It is used extensively in the manufacture of gunpowder, and of sulphuric acid. We import annually about 75,000 tons.

SULPHURET, a combination of sulphur with a simple base.

Sulphuric-acid, one of the most important chemical agents used in the arts and manufactures, made by conducting the burning fumes of sulphur through a leaden vessel, exposed to the action of an oxide, water, and steam. It is used in the manufacture of soda-ash, in bleaching woollens, straw, &c., and for a variety of chemical productions, to the extent of 300,000 tons per annum. It is also called oil of vitriol.

Sulphur-impressions, casts and medallions composed of wax and sulphur, chiefly made by Italians. Besides those made here, some are imported.

Sultana, a kind of raisin.

Sultanin, a former Turkish money of 120 aspers; also a gold coin worth 10s.; a name for the Venetian gold chequin.

Sumach, Shumac, the dried and chopped leaves and shoots of the *Rhus coriarius*, a shrub growing in Southern Europe. When ground to powder in a mill, sumach is largely used for dyeing and tanning. The colouring matter is yellow. Our imports, in 18[illegible], were 18,658 cwts.

Sumbul, an Eastern name for the root of the *Nardostachys Jatamansi*, a dwarf herbaceous, perennial plant. It has a strong and fragrant musky odour, and is much esteemed by all Eastern nations.

Sumgay, a Canara name for boiled coarse rice.

Summer-house, a small alcove, or garden shelter.

Summons, a writ commanding a person to appear before a justice.

Sump, a mine pit; the bottom of the engine-shaft below the lowest workings; a pond of water for salt works.

Sumpmen, the pitmen's assistants in a mine; men who attend to the machinery in the engine-shaft.

Sumpter, a beast that carries provisions, [illegible], &c.

Sunapang, the Malay name for a musket.

Sun-burner, a kind of large gas-burner for lighting and ventilating public buildings.

S[illegible]oral, a medicinal salt imported from Bombay. *See* Black-salt.

Sunday-school, a free school in connection with some place of worship for instructing the young in moral and religious duties.

Sunday-school Teacher, a person who attends gratuitously at a Sunday-school to instruct.

Sun-dial, an instrument to show the time of the day by the sun's shadow.

Sun-fish, a genus of cartilaginous fish, the *Orthagoriscus*, some of which grow to an immense size, individuals occasionally weighing from 300 to 500 lbs. It is very fat and yields a large quantity of oil, but the flesh is ill-tasted.

Sunflower, a name for species of *Helianthus*, a large garden flower. The seeds form a good food for poultry, and a useful oil is obtained from them; the leaves and stalks furnish a strong fibre, and the refuse or marc from the seeds, after the oil has been extracted, yields a good cake for cattle.

Sunn, an Indian name for the *Crotalaria juncea*, a fibrous plant which has a close resemblance to the Spanish broom. The fibre is exported from Madras under the name of Madras hemp, and from Bombay under that of brown hemp.

Superannuate, to pension off from old age or incapacity.

Supercargo, a merchant's agent on board ship; the superintendant of the cargo.

Superficies, the outside surface; length and breadth without thickness.

Superfine, of superior quality; excellent in manufacture or texture.

Superintendant, an overlooker; a director or overseer of others, as a superintendant of police, of buildings, harbours, railway works, machinery, &c.

Superior, a chief; the head of a convent.

Supernumerary, an extra hand; a name for the persons casually employed to fill the stage, &c. at a theatre.

Super-phosphate, any substance with an excess of phosphoric acid, as the superphosphate of iron, of lime, &c.

Superstructure, any building raised on a foundation.

Supervisor, an inspector, as a supervisor of inland revenue.

Suplicacion, a kind of Spanish pastry or confection.

Supper, an evening or final meal before rest.

Supper-rooms, shell-fish shops and taverns in London, where suppers and refreshments can be had, after public amusements are terminated.

Supple-jacks, pliable vine stems or canes used as walking-sticks in the West Indies, the produce of *Paullinia Jamaicensis*, *Barbadensis*, and *Cururu*.

Supplement, an appendix; an additional sheet to a newspaper.

Surachat (French), money paid on account.

Suradanni, a wood obtained about the Demerary river in South America, which is much used for timbers, rails, and covering boards for colony craft, and for naves and felloes of wheels. It will square from 14 to 18 inches from 30 to 40 feet long.

Surat-candy, a variable Indian heavy weight as applied to different goods. *See* Candy.

Surat-maund, an Indian weight varying with different commodities: for tin and tortoise-shell, 37·33 lbs.; for light goods, 39·30; for ores and heavy substances, 41·6. *See* Maund.

Surcharge, an extortion or over-charge.

Surcingle, a band over a packhorse's load; the girdle with which clergymen bind their cassocks.

Surety, a bondsman; bail or security.

Surge, a French name for raw wool.

Surgeon, a medical practitioner; one skilled in the cure of diseases, and in surgical operations.

Surgeon-dentist. *See* Dentist.

Surgery, a private shop for dispensing attached to the house of a surgeon.

Surgical Instrument-case Maker, a manufacturer of such articles, usually for the pocket.

Surgical-Instrument Maker, a skilful cutler who forges and makes the various instruments required in surgical operations.

Surinam-bark, a cinchona bark of indifferent quality, the produce of *Cinchona magnifolia*.

Surisha, Sursah. *See* Sursee.

Surloin. *See* Sirloin.

Surplice, a clergyman's or chorister's white robe or vestment.

Surplusage, overweight; a remainder after work has been done, &c.

Surrogate, an ecclesiastical deputy, a judge of probates; an officer authorized to issue marriage licences.

Sursee, Surson, Indian names for varieties of mustard seed, as *Sinapis nigra* and *S. dichotoma*.

Surtout, a walking-coat; a great coat.

Survey, an examination into the condition of a ship or stores, &c.; a plan of lands or an estate; to measure and plot out lands.

Surveyor, a land-measurer; an engineer's assistant; an inspector of shipping, tonnage, &c. for Lloyds; an examiner of buildings for a fire-insurance office; an overseer.

Surveyor General, a chief land-officer in the Colonies, a head officer of customs, &c.

Susamiel (Spanish), a paste made of almonds, sugar, and spice.

Susin, the French name for the quarter-deck of a ship.

Suspended, temporarily removed from employment pending inquiry, &c.; work that is stopped; a trader or company that cannot meet his or their engagements.

Suspension-bridge, a bridge resting on chains or ropes, thrown over fixed supports. Suspension-bridges are of two kinds:—1st, those in which the weight of the roadway is suspended by vertical rods, wire ropes, &c. to chains or cables, which, passing over high piers, hang in catenary curves between them, and are firmly fastened to abutments: 2nd, those in which the roadway is suspended from rigid abutting arches of wood or iron, or both combined.

Susu, the Malay name for milk.

Sutiera, a necklace of pearls, and other rich jewels, worn in India.

Sutler, a vender of provisions, liquors, &c. to soldiers.

Sutrunjee, an Indian cotton carpet.

Suttle, goods after tare has been deducted, and before tret.

Suwasa, the Malay name for pinchbeck.

Swab, a rough kind of mop, without a fixed handle, made of long rope yarns, used in ships for washing and drying the decks.

Swabber, one who cleans the decks.

Swak, a kind of wood like the chewstick, used by the Moorish women for whitening their teeth.

Swallow-tail Coat, a body coat with pointed skirts.

Swamp, to upset a boat in the water or surf on the beach.

Swan, a well-known genus of web-footed birds, the *Cygnus*, some of which are esteemed for their flesh, while their skins enter into commerce for swans'-down trimmings, and the feathers are imported for quill-making. Swan-quills are combined in the trade returns with goose-quills.

Swan-pan, a Chinese instrument for reckoning.

Swans'-down, the small short feathers on the skin of the swan, used for ladies' dress trimmings, powder-puffs, &c.

Swan-skin, a soft flannel; a kind of woollen blanketing used by letter-press and copper-plate printers; the skin of the wild swan, *Cygnus ferus*, with the feathers on, imported from North America, and the Continent of Europe, to the extent of about 2500 a-year.

Swap, to barter; to exchange.

Sward-cutter, a machine for bringing old grass-lands into tillage.

Swarf, iron filings.

Swarm, a cluster or throng of bees leaving a hive, or taking up new quarters.

Sweating, a kind of fermentation promoted in the manufacture of tobacco; a term applied to a rough process of debasing the current gold coin, by shaking it in bags: by the friction a portion of the metal is worn off. Also a term for employing working tailors at low wages.

Sweating bath, a sudatory; a bath for producing sensible sweat.

Sweep, a very long oar used in low vessels, to force them a-head during calms; a man who cleanses chimneys of the accumulated soot; a crossing-sweeper.

Sweeping-machine. *See* Street-sweeping Machine.

Sweep-net, a large draw-net used in sea-fishing.

Sweep-washer, one who extracts gold, &c. from refiners' sweeps.

Sweetbread, the pancreas of a calf.

Sweet-corn, a name in the United States for certain varieties of maize.

Sweet-flag, the *Acorus Calamus*, the rhizomes of which are aromatic, stimulant, and used as an adjunct to other tonics. It is also employed to scent aromatic baths, perfumery, and hair-powder.

Sweetmeats, a general name for succades; fruits preserved in sugar, and confectionery articles made of sugar.

Sweet-milk Cheese, cheese made of milk without the cream being skimmed off; Dunlop-cheese.

Sweet-oil, olive oil used for salads; Lucca or Provence oil.

Sweet-potato, the *Batatas edulis* of Choisy, the *Convolvulus Batatas* of Linnæus. *See* Batatas.

Sweets, any saccharine substance, as honey, manna, or treacle, but most commonly applied to home-made or British wines, and cordials, or sweetened spirituous compounds.

Sweet-stuff, a popular name for sweetmeats of all kinds.

Sweet-water, a variety of white grape.

Swift, part of a silk-winding machine, on which the skeins of raw silk are stretched or held.

SWILL, a fish-basket or measure, which will contain about 5 long hundreds (600) of herrings, 20 of these baskets making a last; hog-wash.

SWIMMING-BELT, an air-inflated belt worn round the person, as a support in the water.

SWIMMING-BLADDERS, inflated bladders; buoyant supports sometimes used in the water by those who cannot swim; the air-bladders of fishes, many of which yield isinglass.

SWINE, a collective name for animals of the pig tribe.

SWINE-HERD, a driver and care-taker of swine, when feeding in forests, or on the way to markets.

SWING, a rocking-seat, or rope attached to poles, or the boughs of a tree; a name in country districts for incendiarism.

SWING-BRIDGE, a moveable or swivel dividing bridge employed in docks.

SWINGLE, an instrument for beating flax; the end of a flail. *See* SWIPLE.

SWINGLE-TREE, a bar to keep the horses' traces open; part of a plough; in Scotland the striking end of a flail.

SWING-PLOUGH, a turn-rest plough.

SWING TEA-KETTLE, a kettle on a stand for table use, moving on pivots.

SWIPLE, the beating end of a flail, connected to the part held in the hands by a thong of leather or fish-skin.

SWITCH, a small twig or cane; a thin riding-whip.

SWITCHEL, a drink of molasses and water.

SWITCHES, moveable rails forming the junction of a siding with the main line.

SWITCHMAN, a railway servant who has charge of the switches.

SWIVEL, a chain or link for twisting round; a link of iron in chain cables.

SWIVEL-BRIDGE, a bridge that turns and opens in the middle.

SWIVEL-GUN, a small piece of cannon moving on a pivot, which may be freely pointed in any direction.

SWIVEL-HOOK, a hook turning in the end of an iron strop-block.

SWORD, a cut and thrust weapon.

SWORD-BEARER, a corporate officer in London, who carries the sword of state of the Lord mayor.

SWORD-BELT, a waist-belt of leather, to support or carry a sword by.

SWORD-BLADE, the sharpened steel part of a sword.

SWORD-CUTLER, a worker in metal who makes swords.

SWORD-HILT, the handle or grasping part of a sword.

SWORD-SHEATH, the scabbard or case for a sword.

SWORD-STICK, a walking-cane concealing a sharp, rapier-like weapon.

SYCAMORE, a large handsome tree of quick growth, the *Acer Pseudo-Platanus*. The wood is white and soft, useful for many purposes, such as making musical instruments, Tunbridge-ware, cheese and cider presses, mangles, and some parts of machinery; but is chiefly employed by coopers.

SYCE, an Indian groom or horse-keeper.

SYCEE-SILVER, a species of Chinese currency in the form of ingots, called "shoes," which are of various weights, but mostly of 10 taels each. The purest quality has 97 to 99 per cent. of pure silver.

SYDEROLITE, a description of Bohemian earthenware resembling the pottery called Wedgewood-ware.

SYOWAM, an Indian name for teak-wood.

SYLLABUB. *See* SILLABUB.

SYLLABUS, an abstract, compendium, or programme, containing the heads of a lecture.

SYMPIESOMETER, a very simple and beautiful instrument, which indicates with great precision the changes in the pressure of the atmosphere.

SYNAGOGUE, a Hebrew chapel, a place of worship attended by Jews.

SYNDIC, a German magistrate or municipal officer; the French name for an assignee.

SYNOPSIS, an abridgment.

SYPHON, a bent tube; a large receiving vessel for holding cane-juice from the mill in a sugar-boiling house in the West Indies. *See* SIPHON.

SYPHON-CUP, a receptacle in a steam-engine for supplying oil to the working parts of the machinery.

SYRACUSE, a luscious, red, muscadine wine made in Italy; the name is also given to a white *vin de liqueur*.

SYRIAN TOBACCO, the *Nicotiana rustica*, a milder flavoured leaf than that raised in America, and which furnishes the Turkish, Latakia, and some of the Asiatic tobaccos.

SYRINGE, a squirt; an injecting instrument; also a small hand-pump for throwing water over plants, &c.

SYRUP, sugar boiled with vegetable infusions.

SYTHE. *See* SCYTHE.

SZE, in China the hundredth part of a dollar.

SZOSTACK, a Polish coin worth about 2½d.

T.

TA, a Burmese measure of length, 3½ yards, also called a bamboo: 20 tas make one okthaba of 70 feet.

TAAG, a name for the Bengal hemp, or sunn hemp of India, obtained from the *Crotalaria juncea*.

TAB, a woman's bonnet-cap or border; a tag or shoe-lace.

TABAGIE (French), a tap-room; a cigar divan, or smoking-house.

TABAQUE (Spanish), a small work-basket; a kind of nail.

TABAQUERO, a Spanish tobacconist.
TABARD, a herald's coat.
TABARET, a stout satin-striped silk.
TABASHIR, a white secreted silicious matter, found in the joints of the female bamboo, also called bamboo-salt, which has some medicinal repute in the East, being deemed tonic and astringent. At a red heat it fuses into a transparent glass.
TABBY, a rich watered silk, a variety of taffety, *also* called tabinet; a brindled cat; a mixture of lime with shell, gravel, and stones.
TABELLION (French), a notary or scrivener.
TABERNACLE, a place of public worship; a Dissenters' meeting-house.
TABLE, any flat or level surface; a certain piece of furniture on a pedestal or legs; a sheet of crown-glass; a catalogue or index; a collection of numbers or statistical details methodically arranged.
TABLE-ALE, TABLE-BEER, weak dinner-ale.
TABLE-BELL, a small hand-bell for summoning domestics or office attendants.
TABLE-CLOTH, a damask or diaper cover for a dinner-table. Table-covers for ornament are also made of other materials, as printed, embossed, or plain cloth, velvet pile, French silk damask, cotton, or worsted damask, Turkey-red checks, &c.
TABLE-COVER, a woollen ornamental cover for a drawing-room or other table.
TABLE-D'HOTE, an ordinary where meals are served at fixed hours and prices.
TABLE-DIAMOND, a gem cut with a flat surface.
TABLE-FLAP, the leaf of a folding-table; a spare piece to lengthen a sliding dining-table.
TABLE-FORK, a fork for using at meals, usually now of silver or plated metal.
TABLE-KNIFE MAKER, a cutler; a manufacturer of the blades for knives to be used at meals.
TABLE-LINEN, a collective name for the dinner napkins and cloths spread on a table for serving meals.
TABLE-NAPKIN, a small linen napkin used at meals.
TABLE-SPOON, a large spoon for eating soup, or for serving vegetables, &c. at meals.
TABLET, a small hard writing plate; a little square; a monumental slab, a table for drawing or painting on; a thin sheet of ivory.
TABLETS, a pocket-memorandum-book.
TABLETTERIE, a French commercial name for small works in shell, ivory, bone, &c. and other turned articles, which are not classed under the head of Mercerie.
TABLE-URN, a metal vessel bronzed, for holding hot water, *See* URN.
TABLE-WORK, a printer's term for any work set between column rules, which, from the labour and time bestowed on it, is usually charged double the ordinary composition of letter-press.
TABLON (Spanish), a plank.
TABOR, a small shallow drum used to accompany the pipe in rustic dances.
TABOURET, a stool or seat without arms or back; an embroidery frame.
TACAMAHACA, a fragrant resin obtained from several species of *Icica*.

TACAPOW, in the Pacific, mats made from the fronds or leaves of the cocoa-nut palm, used for covering floors.
TACETA (Spanish), a copper basin or bowl.
TACHE, TRACHE, the name of a large sugar boiler in the West Indies, varying in size from 70 to 150 gallons.
TACHOMETER, a measurer of minute variations of speed.
TACK, a small nail with a large head; a shelf for cheese; the weather clew of a sail: to put a ship about, so as to bring the wind on the opposite side; to fasten together loosely by long stitches.
TACKEDA, a name in Hindustan for the visa, a weight of 3¾ lbs; 5 sirus.
TACKLE, a purchase formed by a rope rove through one or more blocks; a general collective name for all fittings, harness, and appurtenances required for working, as fishing-tackle, running rigging, &c.; in Scotland, an arrow.
TACK-LIFTER, a tool for taking up tacks from carpets on a floor.
TACKS, small short iron nails tinned, for holding down carpets and other purposes.
TACKSMAN, a tenant of the higher class in Scotland; one who holds a lease.
TAEL, a Chinese weight of 1 1-5th oz. or 579·84 grains; a variable money.
TAFETA. *See* TAFFETY.
TAFEU, an artificial fertilizer, made in New York by a Manure Company: it is composed of three-fourths night-soil chemically disinfected, dried, and screened, and one-fourth Peruvian guano.
TAFFETY, a thin glossy silk fabric, of a wavy lustre, imparted by pressure and heat, with the application of an acidulous liquor, which produces the effect called "watering."
TAFFOO, a Chinese name for dried cakes of night-soil and clay, extensively used for manure.
TAFFRAIL, the carved-work or rail round a ship's stern.
TAFIA, a kind of rum.
TAFILETE, the Spanish name for morocco leather; marroquim, Portuguese; marrocchino, Italian; saffian, German.
TAFUREA (Spanish), a kind of flat-bottomed boat.
TAG, a piece of brass or other metal fixed to the end of a boot or stay lace, or string, to give rigidity, and facilitate threading; the end or catch-word of an actor's speech. *See* TEG.
TAGGERS, a very thin kind of tin-plates used for coffin-plate inscriptions and tops of umbrellas. They measure 14 inches by 10, and are packed in boxes of 450 sheets.
TAHONA (Spanish), a horse-mill; a bake-house.
TAHULLA (Spanish), a piece of ground of about 40 square yards.
TAHUN, the Malay term for year.
TAI. *See* TAEL.
TAIL, the hinder feathers of a bird; the obverse of a coin; the skirt of a coat; a horse's tail as a standard. *See* TAILS.
TAIL-BLOCK, a block strapped with an eye-splice, having a long end left, by which to fasten the block temporarily to the rigging.

TAIL-BOARD, the hinder side or flap of a cart which lets down on hinges.

TAIL-COAT, a dress or body-coat; not a walking or frock coat.

TAILINGS, the chaff or lighter parts of winnowed grain.

TAILLANDERIE (French), edge-tools; hardware.

TAILLE-DOUCIER, a French copperplate engraver or printer.

TAILLETTE (French), a kind of slate.

TAILLEUSE, a French mantua-maker or dress-maker; a sempstress.

TAILOR, a cutter out and maker of garments in cloth, &c. for male attire.

TAILORS AND CLOTHIERS, shopkeepers who make men's garments to measure, or keep ready-made articles.

TAIL-PIECE, the piece of wood to which the strings of bow instruments are fastened. See TAIL-BOARD.

TAIL-PIN, part of a lathe.

TAIL-RACE, the stream running from a water-mill.

TAILS. The tails of several animals are used for different purposes. Fox-tails or brushes are mounted as ornaments, &c. The tails of the squirrel (or Calabar, as they are termed,) are valued for trimmings. Those of the ermine, or martin (sable tips), are used for the same purpose. Elephants' tails are used as fly-flappers in Africa. Horses' tails furnish the longest and best horse hair.

TAILS-COMMON, a mining name for washed lead ore.

TAIM, a cubit-measure in Rangoon of 18 inches.

TAIN, a thin tinplate; tin-foil for mirrors.

TAING, a Burmese itinerary measure, containing 7000 cubits, and = 2 miles 1 furlong, nearly.

TAKLI, a kind of spindle used by the natives of India, which is turned upon the thigh or the sole of the foot.

TALANTI, a local name in Corfu and the Ionian islands for 100 lbs. avoirdupois.

TALAXAX, a solid-measure for firewood in Manila, equal to 72 cubic feet.

TALBOTYPE, a photograph taken on paper.

TALC, a beautiful and useful mineral found in India, which readily splits into transparent elastic flakes. It consists of silica and magnesia and a small proportion of lime; combined with alkaline salt it is fusible, and forms a greenish-yellow glass. The Chinese make splendid lanterns, shades, and ornaments of it; they also use it, when calcined, in medicine. Powdered it makes a silver sand for writing.

TALE, a number reckoned; a Chinese money and weight of 10 mace. See TAEL.

TALEGA (Spanish), a bag containing a thousand dollars.

TALENT, an ancient Scripture weight, equal to 113 lbs. 10 oz. 1 dwt. 10⅔ grains. The talent of silver, containing 50 manehs, was worth £341 : 10 : 4½d. The talent of gold, worth 16 talents of silver, was equal to £[illegible] : 5 : 8½d.

TAL[illegible], a silver coin of Venice, worth about 4s. 4d.

TAL[illegible], an Indian name for the highly fragrant stimulating leaves of *Rhododendron aromaticum*, used as a medicinal snuff in India.

TALE, TALESMAN, a person called upon to serve on a jury, in the absence of a summoned juryman.

TALI, a name in the Eastern archipelago, for the treble fanam, formerly coined at Madras, the 24th part of the Spanish dollar.

TALISMAN, an amulet; a magical stone, figure, or charm, worn to ward off evil.

TALISPATHREE, TALISPUTRIE, names in the Indian prices-current for the *Flacourtia cataphracta*, the leaves, shoots, and bark of which, are all found in the Indian *Materia medica*. The leaves resemble rhubarb in flavour, and are used as gentle astringents.

TALLAROLA (Spanish), sheet-iron.

TALLEH, an Arabic name for the Abyssinian myrrh, produced by the *Acacia Sassa*.

TALLIAGE, an excise or tax levied.

TALLOW, the most important animal fat of commerce, obtained chiefly from oxen and sheep. Our home production is estimated at 120,000 tons a-year, besides which, we import large quantities from abroad. Our foreign imports, in 1856, exceeded 50,000 tons. In former years it was larger.

TALLOW-CANDLE, a mould or dip made of tallow.

TALLOW-CHANDLER, a dealer in candles.

TALLOW-CHANDLERS' COMPANY, one of the livery companies of London, whose hall is in Dowgate-hill.

TALLOW-MELTER, a maker of candles, a purifier of grease and suet, &c.

TALLOW-TREE, the *Stillingia sebifera*, the *Croton sebiferum* of some authors. Its seeds are covered with a waxy substance, used in China for making candles.

TALLY, a piece of wood on which notches are marked to reckon by, now seldom used.

TALLYMAN, a retail dealer who supplies persons with goods, to be paid for by weekly or monthly instalments.

TALOOKAH, a district or dependency, in India, the revenues of which are under the management of a talookdar.

TALOOKDAR, a native filling the head of a revenue department, but acting under a superior.

TAMARIND, a pleasant acid fruit, the produce of the *Tamarindus Indica*. The pulp of the fruit is nutritive, refrigerant, and laxative, and an infusion forms a cooling drink. The pods are picked before being fully ripe, and preserved between layers of sugar, or boiling syrup is poured over them.

TAMARIND-FISH, a preparation of white pomplets, a famous Indian fish, which is much esteemed as a breakfast relish. The fish are cut in transverse slices, and preserved in kegs with the acid pulp of the tamarind fruit.

TAMARIX, a well-known genus of trees, the bark of all of which is slightly bitter, astringent, and tonic. In Denmark, it is used instead of hops for making beer. Galls are formed on *T. Furas*. The Arabian manna, consisting of pure mucilaginous sugar, is formed on *T. gallica*.

TAMBAC, TOMBAC, the white alloy of copper of the Chinese.

TAMBIS, a hair bolter or strainer, made on the Continent.

TAMBOOKIE-WOOD, a hard handsome furniture-wood: when powdered it is used by the Zulus of Africa as an emetic.

TAMBOUR, an embroidered muslin or lace, the tambouring being performed by a small hook instead of a needle; a species of fancy-work in threads, sometimes of gold and silver; a round course of stone; a large French military drum.

TAMBOURINE, a musical instrument something like the head of a drum, with metal clappers placed round it to increase the noise.

TAMBOUR-WORK, raised flowers, figures, &c. worked on muslins, silks, woollens, &c.

TAMBULI, an Indian name for the leaf of the betel pepper.

TAMBURONE (Italian), the great drum.

TAMINY, a thin woollen stuff highly glazed.

TAMISE, a searce, bolter, or strainer.

TAMKAI, a vernacular Indian name for the Belleric myrobalan, the kernels of which are eaten, and deemed intoxicating.

TAMLUNI, a name for the Siam tael; a money of account of 4 silver ticals, or 2 Spanish dollars.

TAMMIES, a commercial name formerly given to Scotch camlets; a worsted fabric resembling *bunting*, but closer and finer, made of various colours.

TAMPANG a weight used in Malacca for tin, about $1\frac{1}{4}$ lb.

TAMPING, the Malay name for a package; thus in the Singapore imports "sago tamping" is baled sago, wrapped in the leaves of the Pandanus-tree; a kind of oil-cake extensively imported into Shanghae, China, made from a large white pea; a soft stone, or some other earthy substance, placed on the charge of gunpowder by miners in blasting.

TAMTAM, an Indian drum or gong, very sonorous, made of an alloy of copper and tin.

TAN, TANNERS'-OOZE, spent or waste oak or other bark, exhausted of the tanning principle, by being steeped in water. When dry it is sold to gardeners for producing artificial heat, by fermentation, in pits or beds, and in bark stoves.

TANDEM, a gig or dog-cart, with horses driven one before the other, and not harnessed abreast.

TANDOK, a Malay name for horn.

TANG, the metal point of a knife or fork which is inserted in the handle.

TANGA, TANJA, a money of Goa on the Malabar coast, worth about $7\frac{1}{2}$d.

TANG-FISH, a name in Shetland for the seal.

TANGLE, a knot or twisted thread; a name on the Scotch coasts for an edible seaweed, the *Laminaria digitata*.

TANGOURS (French), small levers for carriages.

TAN-HOUSE, a deposit place for tanners' bark.

TANIERS, one of the names given to the blue eddas, or nut eddas, *Caladium sagittæfolium*, Ventenat.

TANJIB, a cotton fabric made for India.

TANK, a square cistern or receptacle for liquids; an iron vessel for holding oil, water, &c. carried in ships' holds; a small Indian dry-measure, averaging 240 grains in weight; a Bombay weight for pearls, of 72 grains; the end of a file, &c. inserted in a socket.

TANKARD, a large metal jug with a lid.

TANKARD-TURNIP, a name applied to such common field turnips as are of an oblong shape, and the roots of which in general grow a good deal above the surface of the ground. There are several varieties.

TANK-ENGINE, a combined engine and tender for supplying water for a locomotive, and which is made to contain from 800 to 1000 gallons.

TANK-MAKER, a manufacturer of iron cisterns for ships, or of slate, or well-secured plank cisterns on shore.

TANNAH, an Indian police-station.

TANNER, one who converts skins into leather.

TANNERS'-BARK, oak and other barks containing tannin, used for forming a steep for the conversion of skins into leather. The foreign barks imported for the use of tanners and dyers, averaged in the three years ending with 1856, 19,500 tons a-year. The spent bark is sold to lead manufacturers, to be used in the process of making white lead.

TANNERS'-WASTE, the hair, fleshings, and other refuse from a tan-yard, sold for mixing with mortar, making glue, &c.

TANNIN, an astringent vegetable principle met with in several barks and other parts of plants, but especially concentrated in nut-galls.

TANNING-SUBSTANCES, oak and larch bark, valonia, sumach, divi-divi, gambier, catch, and other astringent matters containing tannin.

TAN-PIT, a pit in which tanning substances are infused to steep skins for making leather.

TANSY, a garden-flower; also the *Tanacetum vulgare*, a roadside plant, which has a very strong and fragrant odour, and aromatic, bitter, and tonic properties, which cause it to be administered in dyspepsia, intermittents, and gout; as an anthelmintic it is also used in cases of worms. The leaves are employed as a seasoning ingredient in puddings and cakes.

TAP, a subordinate bar attached to an inn or tavern, where beer and tobacco are served; a spile or pipe for drawing liquor from a cask; a square-headed screw; to new sole or heel boots and shoes.

TAPE, a narrow band of cotton, made either red, white, or black; the former is chiefly used for tying up office-papers. White and black tapes are used for dress and binding purposes.

TAPE-LINE, a workman's measure of about 50 feet; a surveying line; a yard-measure rolled in a small case.

TAPE-MANUFACTURER, a weaver of tape.

TAPER, a small wax candle, or roll of wax for office use.

TAPER-STAND, a holder for tapers.

Tapestry, woven or ornamented figured cloth of worsted or silk for covering walls, making bed-hangings, &c.

Tapestry-carpets, the name generally given to a very elegant and cheap two-ply or ingrain carpet, the warp or weft being *printed* before weaving, so as to produce the figure in the cloth.

Tapete (Spanish), a small floor-carpet; worked or figured stuff.

Tapia, the garlic-pear (*Cratæra tapia*), a native of Ceylon. The juice of the astringent bark is used as a tonic and a febrifuge.

Tapioca, a starch prepared from the cassava root (*Janipha Manihot*). The juice of the root deposits a white fecula, which, after being well washed and dried, constitutes what is called "moussache." When the moussache is dried on hot plates, the grains partly burst, and the fecula agglomerates in irregular, semi-opaque, gum-like masses, and is then called tapioca.

Tapis (French), a table-cover.

Tapissier, an upholsterer; a tapestry or carpet-maker in France.

Tapnet, a frail or basket made of rushes, &c. in which figs are imported.

Tappal, an Indian post-office.

Tappet, a lever connected with the cylinder valve of an engine.

Tap-room, a sitting-room common to the frequenters of a tap-house, for drinking and smoking in.

Tapsman, in Scotland, a servant who has the principal charge.

Taqua-nut, a name for the fruit of the *Phytelephas macrocarpa*, which furnishes vegetable ivory.

Taquigrafo (Spanish), a short-hand writer.

Tar, a thick, viscid oleo-resin, obtained by combustion from pine-trees, and used for coating the planks and cordage of shipping, making pitch, sheathing vessels, &c. Coal tar is also made in this country at gas-works, to the extent of 300,000 or 400,000 tons a-year. We import about 10,000 lasts or tons of tar a-year from abroad; a seaman; also a name in Calicut, on the Malabar coast, for the vis, a petty silver money, the 16th part of the fanam, and worth rather more than the third of a penny, the fanam being valued at 6d.

Tara, a name in Bengal for the *Corypha Taliera*, or talipot-palm, much employed for making leaf-hats and leaf umbrellas.

Taracea (Spanish), marquetry, or inlaid work.

Tar-asun, a kind of Chinese beer, made from barley or wheat, a prepared hop being added to the wort in brewing.

Tar, Barbados. *See* Barbados-tar. Our imports, in 1855, were 122 cwts.

Tar-barrel, a cask that has held tar.

Tarbouches, a name for the red Fez-caps worn in Turkey.

Tar-brush, a long-handled strong brush for spreading tar on wood.

Tare, an allowance by the Customs, and merchants, for the weight of a bag, cask, or other package, in which goods are imported, or for the papers, string, wrappers, and bandages, &c. that inclose merchandise.

Tares, a name for the common vetch, *Vicia sativa*, a generally cultivated fodder plant; the seed is also used for feeding poultry. Of this seed the average annual imports from abroad, in the three years ending with 1856, were about 20,000 quarters.

Target, a butt in archery; a mark to aim at in rifle shooting.

Tari, the sap or juice of the *Phœnix sylvestris*, which is drunk in India, fresh from the tree, or fermented for distillation. It also furnishes date-sugar. Each tree, on an average, yields 180 pints of juice. A nominal Italian coin, worth in Malta only 1½d., but in Naples about 8d., the fifth of the ducat; 2 carlins, or 20 grains.

Tariff, a table of Customs duties chargeable on goods imported or exported; a book of rates or sale prices of goods.

Tarin, a money of account in Sicily, the thirtieth part of the gold once, and worth about 4d., a Spanish silver real of 8½ cuartos.

Tarja, an ancient Spanish copper coin.

Tar-kettle, a pot for heating tar in.

Tarlatan, a kind of book-muslin principally made in Scotland. *See* Muslin.

Tarnish, to stain, to lose colour, as the brilliancy of silver and other metals becomes dull. The tarnish of silver is occasioned by sulphureous vapours.

Tarnishing, a process of giving gold or silver a pale or dim cast, without either polish or burnish.

Tarpaulin, breadths of canvas sewn together, oiled and coated with tar, used to cover the hatchways of vessels, barges, wagons, &c. Railway companies term them sheets, carriers call them cloths, and carters, covers; a sailor's hat or garments made or covered with tarred or painted cloth.

Tarpaulin-manufacturer, one who oils or tars canvas for covers.

Taro, the tuberous roots of a species of [Arum.

Tarragon, a common garden herb, the *Absinthia Dracunculus*, which has warm, aromatic qualities, and is employed as a pickle, and to flavour vinegar.

Tarraja (Spanish), an instrument for cutting ornamental mouldings.

Tarrass, a volcanic product used with quick-lime, to make a coarse kind of water cement, for lining cisterns and other reservoirs of water, being highly durable. It is also called trass and terrass.

Tarrie, Terrie, a dry-measure of Algiers; the 16th part of a caffiso, equal to 8·493 gallons.

Tarro (Spanish), a glazed earthenware pan.

Tart, a pie or pastry of fruit or preserves; a sour or sharp flavour.

Tartan, a Highland plaid, of which each clan has a particular pattern. The material is either silk, cotton, or worsted, or a mixture of two of these. Fancy plaids are, however, made for the general public, for tartans, hose, caps, &c.; a small Spanish coasting sloop; a long covered carriage.

TARTAR, CREAM OF, pure bitartrate of potash; purified argol, the concretion which forms on the inside of wine casks.

TARTAR-EMETIC, the tartrate of potash and antimony, a valuable medicine in catarrh and lung diseases, &c.

TARTARIC-ACID, the acid obtained from the acidulous salt of tartar or argol, occurring in powder or crystals. It is commonly vended for the same purposes as citric acid, and is largely used for making effervescing powders, and as a discharge in calico-printing.

TARTLET, a small flat open fruit tart, baked on a tin or dish.

TARTLET-CUTTER, a confectioner's shaping utensil for dough.

TARTLET-PAN, a small metal shape for baking tarts in.

TAR-WATER, the ammoniacal water of gasworks; water impregnated with tar, formerly considered a remedy for diseases of the lungs, &c. See GAS-WATER.

TASAJO (Spanish), a name in New Granada for dried meat; hung beef.

TASCO (Spanish), the refuse of flax; the toppings of hemp.

TASKER, a labourer in Scotland who receives his wages in kind.

TASKMASTER, an overseer or superintendant; one who sets work.

TASK-WORK, piece-work; work done by the job.

TASSEL, a hanging ornament, as a bunch of silk, or gold fringe, &c.; a piece of board under the mantel shelf.

TASTAG (Spanish), polishing powder.

TASTER, one who judges wine or tea; a scoop for tasting cheese; a skewer for trying hams; a dram cup.

TAT, a name in India for cloth made from the fibre of the *Corchorus olitorius*.

TATABA, a tree of large size in Guiana, yielding a hard and tough wood, well adapted for mill timbers and planks, and also for ship-building, gun-carriages, coffee-stamps, &c.

TATACUA, an enclosed space of ground, with a hard foundation, in which Paraguay tea is prepared.

TATAR, a Turkish courier.

TATHAM'S CLUMPS, a contrivance or apparatus used in excavating, &c.

TATTA, a split bamboo matting-frame, at a door or window, over which water is poured in India, to cool the air of the apartment. See JOWASSA.

TATTANNY, a Japanese measure of length, equivalent to 6 feet 4 inches. It is also called an ink.

TATTINGS AND PEARLS, narrow lace used for edging nets; tattings vary in width, from a quarter to the sixteenth of an inch, while pearls are still narrower.

TATTOO, an Indian name for a pony; a beat of the drum to call soldiers to quarters.

TAUNT, a marine term for too high or tall, as applied to the masts of a ship.

TAURESCITE, a new iron vitriol, formed along with melantirite, from the decomposition of pyrites.

TAUT, a sea phrase for tight, as applied to a rope drawn up.

TAUX, a land-measure of Switzerland, equal to 7,855 square yards.

TAVADU, a dry-measure in Mysore, of 1 lb.; 2 solis of 8 oz.

TAVERN, an inn or resting-place; a house licensed to sell wines and spirits.

TAVERN-KEEPERS AND VINTNERS, innkeepers and wine-dealers.

TAW, a large ornamented marble for boys.

TAWAS, the Malay name for alum.

TAWING, a process of preparing kid, sheep, and goats' skins, by alum, some being left white or undyed, to make gloves, lineshoes, and other inferior purposes; while others are dyed.

TAWNY, a pale, dirty orange colour.

TAX, a tribute or impost levied by government for national purposes.

TAX-CART, a spring-cart paying a low rate of duty.

TAX-COLLECTOR, TAX-GATHERER, a receiver of taxes.

TAXED-COSTS, the allowed charges of a solicitor, which have been legally examined and assessed before a taxing-master.

TAXIDERMIST, a stuffer of animals, and preserver of specimens of natural history.

TAXING MASTER, a law officer appointed to investigate the charges made in a solicitor's bill, when disputed by the client, striking off overcharges, or unwarranted items.

TAYNDAUNG, a name for the basket-measure, by which rice is sold in Rangoon, equal to 56 lbs. nominally, but in reality often but 53½ lbs.

TAYOVA, a Brazilian name for the roasting cocos, or white eddas, *Arum macrorhizon*.

TAYSAAM, a species of Chinese raw silk, obtained from the district of Nanking, the Tat-san of the Chinese, inferior in quality to Tsat-lie, but superior to Canton silk.

TAZZA, an ornamental cup or vase, with a large flat top.

TCHETWERT, CHETWERT, a Russian dry-measure of 8 chetweriks or 5 bushels, 6·170 gallons.

TEA, a general name for an infusion of herbs used as a beverage, but specially applied in commerce to the dried leaves of the *Thea Bohea* and *T. viridis*. Black tea is the leaf more fermented than green-tea. Our imports of tea in 1856 were, 86,139,517 lbs. of which 63,295,727 lbs. were taken for home consumption.

TEA, ARABIAN, the leaves of the *Catha edulis*, which, being stimulant, anti-soporific, and anti-narcotic, are employed by the Arabs instead of green tea to produce watchfulness.

TEA-BELL, a small hand-bell for a tea-table; a bell rung to summon school children or boarders to tea.

TEA-BOARD, a metal or papier-mâché tray for holding a tea service.

TEA-CADDY, a small ornamental box for holding tea to supply a teapot.

TEA-CAKE, a light dough-cake or kind of bread toasted and buttered for tea.

TEA-CANISTER, a small tin for holding tea for domestic use; a grocer's shelf canister containing tea to supply customers.

Tea-canister Maker, a manufacturer of painted or japanned metal canisters for grocers' shops, &c.

Teache, the last copper or receptacle for boiling sugar in a sugar-house.

Teacher, an usher; a monitor; a schoolmaster or instructor.

Tea-chest, a small square wooden case, in which tea is imported from China, holding about ¾ cwt., the half-chest, ½ cwt.

Tea-cup, a small china or earthenware bowl, with a handle, standing in a saucer, for drinking tea from.

Tea-dealer, a retailer of tea, who most generally sells coffee and groceries. There are about 120,000 licensed tea dealers in the kingdom.

Tea-garden, a public-house garden where refreshments are served.

Teak, a hard, heavy, and durable timber obtained from the *Tectona grandis*, used for ship, wagon, carriage and other building purposes. Our imports, in 1855, were 22,830 loads, about two-thirds from the East Indies and one-third from Sierra Leone. African teak does not however belong to the same family; it is the *Oldfieldia Africana*.

Tea-kettle, a metal boiler for water, with a pouring spout, made of iron, copper, or tin.

Teal, a small well-known species of wild duck, the *Querquedula crecca*, common over Europe in the winter, and in request for the table.

Team, a set of oxen or horses working together. In Australia and the Cape, owing to the bad nature of the roads, many spans of oxen are yoked to the wagons.

Team-driver, **Teamster**, a waggoner; one who drives a team.

Tea-meeting, a religious or missionary meeting provided with tea; a school gathering, &c.

Tea, Paraguay. *See* Paraguay Tea.

Tea-plant. *See* Tea.

Tea-pot, a vessel, usually of metal, with a handle and spout, for making and pouring out tea.

Tea-pot Handle-maker, a manufacturer of horn and other handles of non-conducting materials to fit to metal tea-pots.

Tea-poy, an ornamental pedestal table, with lifting top, enclosing caddies for holding tea.

Tear, a rent or slit in a garment.

Tea-saucer, an earthenware stand for a tea-cup.

Tease, to comb or clean wool; to card or raise a nap on woollen cloth.

Teasel, **Teazle**, the *Dipsacus fullonum*, a plant cultivated to a considerable extent in the woollen cloth manufacturing districts, for its use in raising the nap upon those stuffs, which it does by means of the rigid hooked awns or chaff of the heads. Upwards of twenty millions of these teasel heads are also imported annually from France.

Teasel-frame, a set of iron bars or a frame to fix teasel heads in for carding woollen cloth.

Tea-service, **Tea-things**, the whole appurtenances or utensils required for a tea-table; sometimes applied only to the tea-pot, milk jug, and sugar basin, when of silver.

Tea-spoon, a small metal spoon for stirring [tea.

Tea-table, a small round or other table for serving tea on.

Tea-taster, a person who tests the qualities of teas in the Chinese ports, or in the London brokers' offices.

Tea-things. *See* Tea-service.

Tea-tray Maker, a manufacturer of tea-boards, for holding cups and saucers, &c.

Tea-urn Maker, a manufacturer of ornamental metal vases, containing a heater, for keeping water boiling on a tea-table.

Teaze-hole, the opening in the furnace of a glass-work, through which coals are put in.

Teazer, the stoker or fireman in a glass-work who attends the furnace and leer or arched building. [or manufacture.

Technical, relating to any particular art

Technologist, a writer or lecturer on the useful arts and manufactures.

Tecum-fibre, the produce of a palm leaf resembling green wool, imported into Liverpool from Brazil. *See* Tucum.

Tedge. *See* Ingate.

Teea, a Bornean weight, the 6th part of the pince; about 6¼ grains.

Teel-seed, **Til**, Indian names for the seed of the *Sesamum orientale*, the *S. Indicum* of Linnæus. *See* Gingelie and Sesame.

Teenage, fence-wood.

Terso-flowers, **Kerso-flowers**, the large flowers of *Butea frondosa*, which yield a beautiful dye.

Teeth, the incisors of animals, many of which enter into commerce for economic purposes. The tusks of the elephant are misnamed teeth; but the grinders or teeth proper are also used for knife handles and other purposes. The canines of the walrus or sea-horse, and the teeth of the hippopotamus are in demand by the dentist for artificial teeth; while the teeth of many carnivorous animals are used in the East for necklaces and other ornaments. The term teeth is also applied to the tines of a prong or pitch-fork, the spikes of a harrow, the divided points or dents of a comb, the sharp wires of a carding instrument, the projecting nobs on the edge of a machine or horological wheel, &c.

Tee-totaller, a person who refrains from spirituous and malt liquors.

Teetotum, a child's small toy or top of bone or ivory, spun with the fingers.

Teffe, **Taffee**, a Turkish silk weight of 4·32 lbs.; a variable weight in the Levant, for silk, consisting of 800 drachmas, each 49 3-5ths grains troy, and for opium 250 drachmas.

Teg, a young sheep.

Teinturier (French), a dyer.

Tejamanil (Spanish), shingles for roofing.

Tejbul, a native name for the warm, spicy pepper-like capsules and seeds of *Xanthoxylum hostile*, employed in Northern India for intoxicating fish, and chewed as a remedy in toothache.

Tejo (Spanish), a cake of metal.

Tej-pat, the leaves of the *Cinnamomum Tamala* or *C. Malabatrum*, the "Folia Malabathri" of Indian shops. Their odour resembles that of cloves; the flavour is aromatic and hot.

Telakal. *See* Sindoc.

Telegram, a recently coined word for a despatch or message received by telegraph.

Telegraph, electrical wires on land, or in the bed of the sea, or some other contrivance or apparatus, for signalizing between distant points.

Telegraph-cable, a submarine cable of strands of wire, coated with gutta-percha, for transmitting messages by electricity.

Telegraph-clerk, a subordinate officer in a telegraph-office.

Telegraph-line, the suspended or buried wire over which messages are forwarded.

Telegraph-messengers, lads in the employ of a telegraph company, who deliver despatches when received.

Telegraph-office, **Telegraph-station**, a business-place for receiving and forwarding messages.

Telegraph-post, a prop or support for lines of wire.

Telegraphic-despatch, a telegram or message received by telegraph.

Telescope, a spy-glass; a connection of optical tubes for making distant objects visible to the eyes.

Telescope-maker, an optician.

Telescope-stand, a tripod or moveable support for a telescope.

Teleton (Spanish), a strong silk fabric.

Telini, a vernacular name in India for the *Mylabris cichorei*, a blistering fly, which has been used for ages by the native physicians of India and China.

Teller, derived from tallier, one who reckons or counts; an officer in a bank, &c. who receives or pays money.

Tellière (French), foolscap-paper.

Tellinga, a dhoney or native coasting-vessel on the coast of Coromandel.

Tell-tale, a cabin compass suspended from the beams; an instrument connected with the rudder wheel for showing the position of the tiller; an indicator or gauge of numbers entering or leaving by a turnstile, &c.

Tellurine, a kind of French tripoli, for polishing metal, and cleaning marbles, &c.

Tellurium, a tin-white metal.

Telotype, the name given to a printing electric telegraph.

Teman, **Tommond**, a dry-measure or weight of Arabia, for rice; weighing 168 lbs.

Temazualis, an oven in Central America, for drying the cochineal insect.

Tembili, a name in Ceylon for a variety of coco-nut, called King coco-nut, of a bright orange colour, and somewhat oval shape.

Temen, a grain-measure of Tripoli, nearly 6 gallons.

Temper, a due mixture of different qualities; the condition of a metal, as temper-steel; a name given in the West Indies to purified lime, used for mixing with cane-juice when boiling, to clarify it, or separate the feculencies, an operation called by sugar-planters "tempering." Wood-ashes also bear this name in Brazil, being used for the same purpose.

Template, **Templet**, a short piece of timber under a girder, like a purlin; a bricklayer's mould; a gauge of thin metal of the form to be followed.

Temple, a building or place of worship in honour of some god; one of the Inns of court in London.

Tempoh, a long-measure of Sumatra, of 4¼ inches.

Temse, a bolting-cloth; a sieve, or searce.

Ten, a Newcastle coal-measure, containing 420, and in other cases 440 bolls, Winchester measure.

Tenaculum, a fine hook used by medical men to get hold of arteries in wounds, for tying.

Tenant, one who occupies or rents houses or lands belonging to another, on lease, or for a shorter term.

Tenant-farmer, an agriculturist who cultivates land not his own freehold.

Tenantero (Spanish), a carrier of ore, in sacks termed tenates, from the workings in mines to the surface, &c.

Tench, a fresh-water fish of the carp tribe, the *Tinca vulgaris*.

Tender, an attendant wagon carrying water and fuel for a locomotive on a railway; a bidding under a contract; an offer made for goods; a proposed compromise, or payment of money considered due. *See* Legal Tender, and Railway Tender.

Tendon, a sinew. Sinews are used by many savage tribes as a sewing material, and also for making cord or string. They serve for making glue, and are occasionally eaten as food. *See* Dendeng.

Tenement, a house or dwelling; land that is held from another.

Teneriffe, a dry Canary wine, resembling Madeira, but inferior; imported from Teneriffe in pipes of 100 gallons. It is also called Vidonia.

Teneriffe-cochineal, a cochineal raised at Teneriffe.

Teng, a Burmese grain-measure, equal to about 2 bushels, and usually termed by foreign merchants a basket.

Tenga, a name in India for the coco-nut.

Tenney, the Tamil name for the Italian millet, *Setaria Italica*.

Tennis-ball, a ball to be driven by a racket or stringed battledore.

Tennis-court, a walled or enclosed building with nets, where the game of tennis is played.

Tennis-racket, an expensive kind of stringed battledore, made of gut, for playing at tennis.

Tenon, the end of a piece of wood cut so as to fit into another piece; the heel of a mast made to fit into the step or socket.

Tenon-saw, a saw for cutting tenons. *See* Saw.

Tenor, a vocalist; a high male voice.

Tent, a shelter or canvas enclosure for field use, of which there are many kinds made, round or oblong shaped, &c. Some are called marquees, and booths, the smaller circular kinds being those chiefly known as tents; a roll of lint put into a wound; a rich red muscadine wine, grown near Cadiz, drunk generally as a stomachic, which is imported in hogsheads of 52 gallons. *See* Sponge Tent.

TENTER, a stretching-machine; a drying-room.

TENTER-HOOK, a sharp hooked nail.

TENTERING, a technical term for stretching woven goods to dry, after being stiffened or dyed.

TENT-MAKER, a manufacturer of canvas tents, suited for different purposes.

TENTURE, paper-hangings or tapestry for a wall.

TEORA, a name in Bengal for the *Lathyrus sativus*: the expressed oil of the seeds is a powerful and dangerous narcotic.

TEPEJILOTE, a name given, in Central America, to the flowers of a species of *Chamaedorea* when still enclosed in the spathes, which are highly esteemed as a culinary vegetable.

TERÇO, TERCIO (Portuguese and Spanish), one-third; the vara is divided into three.

TERCENA, a wholesale tobacco warehouse in Spain.

TERCIADO (Spanish), a cutlass; a kind of ribbon.

TERIN (French), a mule canary.

TERMINATE, to put an end to an engagement, lease, or occupancy.

TERMINO, a weight in Tunis and other African towns, also called a miscal or metical, variable in weight, but about 60½ grains.

TERMINUS, the station at the beginning or end of a railway.

TERNE-PLATES, thin sheet-iron coated with an amalgam of tin and lead.

TERRACE, a raised platform or walk; an open gallery or flat roof.

TERRA-COTTA, a species of vitreous stoneware, the *Terre cuite* of the French; fine clay, hardened by heat.

TERRA-COTTA MANUFACTURER, a maker of earthenware.

TERRAILLE (French), earthenware.

TERRA-JAPONICA, an old trade misnomer, still retained, for gambier, an inspissated vegetable juice, obtained from the *Uncaria Gambir* of Roxburgh. The imports of Terra Japonica, in 18[illegible], were 6647 tons. *See* GAMBIER.

TERRASSIER, a French plasterer.

TERRE-NOIX (French), the ground-nut.

TERRIER, a small dog for ferreting out vermin: a wimble or auger; a register of lands, rents, &c.

TERRY-VELVET, a kind of silk plush or ribbed velvet.

TERTIAN, a liquid-measure for wine, equal to 70 gallons.

TESKARÉ, TESKERE, a Turkish Custom-house certificate; a receipt or release for duties paid.

TESSELLATED PAVEMENT, a mosaic or chequered work; a marble flooring in black and white squares.

TEST, a standard or trial; a chemical examination; a cupel for assaying or refining metals.

TESTAMENT, the new book of the Scripture law; the latter half of the Bible; a written will.

TESTATOR, TESTATRIX, the person who makes a will.

TESTER, one who examines or makes a trial; a taster; the frame-work over a four-post bed: when the bedstead is only partially covered it is called a half-tester.

TESTIF (French), camels' hair.

TESTIMONIAL, a letter of recommendation; a certificate of character.

TESTONE, TESTOON, an Italian coin of 2 lire, worth about 1s. 4d.; a Portuguese coin of two denominations, one, the escudo of 1600 reis, the other, of 100 reis.

TEST-PAPER, litmus, or unsized paper used as a test for acids, when it becomes red; and for alkalies, by which the blue colour is restored.

TETHER, the rope with which a grazing horse is tied to a stake.

TEWING-BEETLE, a spade for beating hemp.

TEXAS MILLET, the *Sorghum cernuum*, a prolific bread-corn cultivated in the tropics.

TEXT, a subject chosen to enlarge or comment on.

TEXT-BOOK, a book explaining the principles of a science, &c.

TEXT-HAND, a large round hand in writing.

TEXTILE, any thing that can be woven.

TEXT-PEN, a metallic pen for engrossing.

TEXTURE, the web of a fabric; the manner of weaving.

TEYNI, a native Indian name for honey.

THAIL, a Japanese coin worth about 5s. 10d.

THALAY-FIBRE, THAULAY-FIBRE, Indian names for the fibre of the *Pandanus odoratissimus*, screw pine.

THALER, a German coin of 30 silver groschen, worth about 3s. sterling. It passes current in Frankfort for 1 guilder and 45 kreutzers; in Holland for 1 guilder and 70 cents; in France for 3 francs 70 cents; in Hamburgh for 2 marks 8 schillings current, or 2 marks banco.

THALASSOMETER, a tide-gauge.

THANGTOUNG, the royal cubit in Burmah, = 19 1-10th inches.

THANNADAR, the chief officer of police in an Indian town, also called a cotwal.

THARM, twisted gut.

THARRAN, a small Burmese violin.

THAS, another name for the bamboo-measure. *See* BAMBOO.

THATCH, dried grass, straw, palm-leaves, or other vegetable materials, used for covering barns or houses.

THATCHER, one who lays straw, &c., on the roof of a house, and binds and secures it there.

THEALEK, an ancient grain-measure of Bellary, East Indies, = 2 lbs. 14 oz., sometimes called a thimmanoo.

THEATRE, a play-house; a lecture-hall.

THEATRICAL-ORNAMENT MAKER, a maker of tinsel ornaments, mock jewels, &c., for play-actors.

THEAVE, the name in Scotland for a ewe of 3 years old.

THEET, in Burmah the eighth part of a hand's-breadth; 12 theets are equal to 1 span.

THEODOLITE, a most important surveying instrument for measuring horizontal angles, or the angular distances between objects projected on the plane of the horizon.

THERMOGRAPHY, the art of copying engravings or any printed characters from paper on metal plates.

THERMOMETER, an instrument for measuring the degrees of heat. There are three different kinds in use:—1. Fahrenheit's, which is chiefly used in Great Britain, Holland, and North America, the freezing point on which is at 32°, and the boiling point 212°: 2. Reaumur's, now generally used in Spain, and in some other Continental States, the freezing point, or zero, of which is 0°, and the boiling point 80°. 3. The Centigrade thermometer, which is now almost universally used throughout France, and in the northern and middle kingdoms of Europe: the zero or freezing point is 0°, and boiling point 100°. As there are 180 degrees between the freezing and boiling points of water, 18 degrees of Fahrenheit correspond to 10 of the Centigrade, or 8 of Reaumur's: 1° Fahrenheit's = 5-9ths Centigrade, = 4-9ths Reaumur's; 1° Reaumur's = 1¼ Centigrade, = 2¼ Fahrenheit's; 1° Centigrade = 4-5ths Reaumur's, = 1 4-5ths Fahrenheit's.

THERMOSCOPE, a very sensitive kind of thermometer.

THERMOSIPHON, an instrument employed for horticultural and other useful processes.

THIRSPE, a varnish obtained from *Melanorrhœa usitata*, in Arracan, and used for lacquering.

THIBAUDE (French), cloth made of cow-hair.

THIBET-CLOTH, a camlet or fabric made of coarse goats'-hair.

THICK-SET, a stout, twilled cotton cloth; a fustian cord or velveteen. *See* FUSTIAN.

THIEVES'-VINEGAR, a kind of aromatic vinegar for a sick-room, consisting of the dried tops of rosemary, sage-leaves, lavender-flowers, and bruised cloves, steeped in acetic acid and boiling water. It derives its name and popularity from a story, that four thieves who plundered the dead bodies during the plague with perfect security, attributed the cause of the impunity to the use of this disinfectant.

THILL, the shaft of a wagon.

THIMBLE, an iron ring with a concave rim for a rope or strap used on shipboard: a metal cap or protection for the finger of a tailor or sempstress.

THIMBLE-MAKER, a shaper of iron ring thimbles; also one who makes finger-caps to be used by those who sew with a needle.

THIMMAPOO, an Indian grain-measure. *See* THEALER.

THIRD-RATE, a ship of war carrying from 70 to 80 guns.

THISTLE, FULLER'S. *See* TEASEL.

THOLES, THOWLS, the pins in the gunwale of a boat between which an oar rests when pulling, instead of on the rowlocks.

THOLLAR, a name in Bellary for the East India Company's old rupee, weighing 176½ troy grains.

THON, the French name for the tunny-fish.

TISORO, a strap of leather.

THONNINE (French), a pickled tunny-fish.

THORN-APPLE, a wild plant, the *Datura Stramonium*, which has qualities like those of henbane and belladonna. The seeds produce maniacal delirium, but are used medicinally to allay pain in tic-douloureux, mania, epilepsy, &c.

THORNBACK, the *Raia clavata*, a fish of the skate family, which is in the best condition for the table about November.

THOROUGHFARE, a passage; a much frequented way; a street.

THOWL. *See* THOLES.

THRASH, THRESH, to beat corn with a flail; to free it from the straw or chaff by a machine.

THRASHING-MACHINE, an apparatus for beating out grain by horse or steam power.

THRAVE, THREAVE, in Scotland 24 sheaves of corn; two shocks, or stooks as there styled.

THREAD, fine line or yarn, in skeins or reeled, for sewing; the spiral part of a screw; a yarn-measure, containing in cotton-yarn 54 inches; in linen yarn 90 inches; in worsted yarn 35 inches. On the Continent 85½ England inches make one thread: to string beads, &c.; to pass cotton or silk through a needle's eye.

THREADBARE, articles of cloth that have become shabby or worn-out.

THREAD-LACE, lace made of linen-thread; not silk or blonde-lace.

THREAD-PAPER, thin strips of paper for wrapping skeins of thread in.

THREE-DECKER, a vessel of war which carries guns on three decks.

THREEPENNY-PIECE, a British silver coin, the fourth part of a shilling, of which the following numbers have been issued since 1847:—

Year	Number	Year	Number
1847	4,488	1852	4,488
1848	4,488	1853	[illegible]
1849	131,208	1854	1,47[illegible]
1850	954,888	1855	287,[illegible]
1851	483,555	1856	1,018,[illegible]

THRIFT, the *Armeria vulgaris*, a border-plant or edging in gardens, the flowers of which are useful as diuretics.

THRONE, a seat of honour.

THROSTLE, a spindle for wool.

THROUGH-TICKET, a passenger's paid ticket for the whole journey intended to be travelled.

THROUGH-TRAIN, one that proceeds over the whole line of railway between certain main termini.

THROWN-SINGLES, a name in the silk-trade for silk wound, cleaned, and thrown, fit to be used in the weaving of ribbons and common silks.

THROWSTER, a maker of organzine; one who twists singles of silk into a contrary direction to that in which they had previously been wound.

THRUM, coarse rope-yarn; the ends of weavers' threads; to insert yarn, &c. into a piece of canvas, as in making a rope-mat.

THRUSH LICHEN, the *Peltidea aphthosa*, a lichen, found growing on moist alpine rocks, which has purgative and anthelmintic

tic properties. When boiled in milk it is given by the Swedes as a cure for aphthæ.

THRUST-SCREW, a lever for pressing curd.

THSAN, an itinerary measure of China. = 28 033 miles. [1¼ inch.

THSUN, TSUN, a Chinese long-measure nearly

THUMB-BLUE, a name for small knobs of indigo used by washerwomen to give a slight tinge of blue to linen.

THUMB-STALL, a cover or protection for the thumb used by workmen.

THUOC, the Chinese "chih," cubit, or foot, and the generic name for the measure of length in Cochin-China, which varies according to circumstances. Those more commonly employed are:—

	Metre.	Eng. inches.
1 That used for measuring ships for the service of ports	0·405	= 15·943255
2 That used for wood at Turon	0·425	= 16·732675
3 That mentioned by Taberd in his valuable Anamitic dictionary	0·48726	= 19·18391346
4 That used by the king for measuring silks and other cloths in his transactions with foreigners	0·594	= 23·386374
5 That used by natives in the Turon market	0·61	= 24·01631
6 That used according to Morrison	0·64968	= 25·57855128

THWARTS, the cross planks of a boat on which the rowers sit.

THYME, dwarf shrubs, the *Thymus vulgaris*, and *T. Serpyllum*, of agreeable, strong, and penetrating odour, yielding a volatile oil, and much used in Europe as an ingredient in culinary seasoning.

TIARA, a diadem; a high head-dress.

TIAYANG. *See* COYAN.

TIBIR (Spanish), African gold-dust.

TIAIAHI, a native name in Berbice for the fibre of the Ita palm (*Mauritia flexuosa*) used by the Indians for making hammocks, cordage, &c.

TICAL, a Chinese weight and money of account; as a weight about 4½ oz. or the 16th of the catty; as a money reckoned at the third of a pound sterling. It is also called a tyank: another name in Burmah for the kyat, a weight which consists of 252 grains. In Siam the tical coin and weight is 236 troy grains. Its value in this currency is about 2s. 6d. sterling.

TICK, a fabric made of flax; a bed-case for holding flocks or feathers, &c.; a credit score; trust.

TICK-BEAN, a small horse-bean.

TICKET, a marked slip of paper or card-board; a pawnbroker's duplicate; the acknowledgment of goods pledged; an admission card which has been issued for giving the right of entry to a place of public amusement, to travel on a railway, or in a steam boat, &c.; to docket or label with a price.

TICKET-DAY, the day before the settling or pay-day on the stock-exchange, when the names of bona-fide purchasers are rendered in by one stockbroker to another.

TICKETING, a periodical sale of ore in the English mining districts.

TICKET OF LEAVE, a licence or permit given to a convict or prisoner of the Crown to be at large and to labour for himself

TICKET-PORTER, a licensed porter of the city of London, who wears a silver badge.

TICKET, SEAMAN'S, a register ticket given to seamen from the General Register and Record office of Seamen.

TICKET-WRITER, one who writes or paints showy placards and legible tickets for goods in shop windows, &c.

TICKLENBURGHS, a coarse, mixed linen fabric made for the West India market.

TIDAL BASIN, a dock that is filled upon the rising of the tide. [every 12 hours.

TIDE, the alternate ebb and flow of the sea

TIDE-GATE, the entrance gate of a dock.

TIDE-GAUGE, an instrument, sometimes self-registering, used on coasts and harbours for ascertaining the rise and fall of the tide, thus indicating the depth of water, and enabling vessels to enter tidal harbours at the proper times.

TIDE-TABLE, an almanac which records the time of high water, &c. for each day.

TIDE-WAITER, an officer of the Customs, whose duty it is to remain on board ships, lighters, &c. until the cargo is discharged.

TIDIES, crochet covers; cases for furniture.

TIE, a fastening; the knot of a cravat; an equal number of votes, &c. on two opposing sides. [principal rafters.

TIE-BEAM, a connecting beam for a pair of

TIER, a row or rank; a range of any thing, as of casks; the coils or fakes of a cable, &c.

TIERCE, a cask containing about 42 gallons, or the third part of a pipe. The tierce is used for oil, and more especially for the packing of salted provisions for ships' stores. The tierce for salt provisions to contain 336 lbs. should be 21½ inches head, 24½ inches bilge, and 33½ inches length; to contain 304 lbs. 19½ inches head, 22½ inches bilge, 31½ inches length.

TIFFANY, a species of gauze or thin silk.

TIFFIN, a luncheon or midday meal in India.

TIFTIK, a Persian and Turkish word for goats' hair.

TIGER, a boy in livery; a page.

TIGERS'-SKINS, the skins of this beast of prey, are used for hearth and carriage rugs; but the annual imports are small.

TIGER-WOOD, a valuable wood for cabinet making, the heart of the Itikiribourabulli, obtained in Guiana.

TIGO-GIN, a silver coin of Japan of 40 mas, worth about 13 shillings.

TIGHTS, close-fitting pantaloons.

TIKOOR, TIKUL, a name in India for the *Garcinia pedunculata*, a lofty tree. The fleshy part of the fruit and arillus which are large, firm, very sharp and acid, are used in curries and for acidulating water; cut and sliced it retains its qualities, and is recommended as a succedaneum for limes and lemons during long voyages.

TIKOR, a vernacular name in India for the long and straight pale yellow tubers of the *Curcuma leucorrhiza*, which yield an abundance of fine nutritious fecula.

TIKUL. *See* TIKOOR.

TILBURY, an open carriage on two wheels.

TILE-ORE, a native oxide of copper.

TILES, earthenware squares or plates, &c., for roofing, paving, draining, &c. There are encaustic and inlaid, as well as common tiles.

TILE-TEA, a kind of flat brick tea, of much solidity, made in China, and taken to Kiachta, where it is sold to the Armenians and Tartars, who distribute it to the Caucasian provinces and Eastern Siberia. The Kalmucks, Kirgheses, and Burats consume the greater part of it. It is prepared in a different manner from common tea, being stewed with milk, butter, salt, and herbs, constituting rather an article of food than a dietetic beverage.

TILL, a counter-drawer or desk receptacle for money received.

TILLA, a gold coin of Bokhara, worth [13s. 4d.

TILLAC (French), the deck of a ship.

TILLAGE, husbandry; agriculture; land under cultivation.

TILLER, a bar of wood or iron placed in the rudder to move it for steering the vessel.

TILLER-ROPES, the connected ropes or chains running from the tiller of the rudder to the steering-wheel.

TILLY-SEED, a small tree, the *Croton Pavana* of Hamilton, common in the Eastern archipelago, the seeds of which have the same properties as those of the *Croton Tiglium.*

TILT, an awning or cover for a boat or cart; the leaning forward of a cask.

TILTED-STEEL, blistered steel drawn down into smaller bars and beaten, for the purpose of forming (after further heating, welding, and drawing) shear steel.

TILTERS AND FORGERS, workers on steel.

TILT-HAMMER, a very heavy mass of iron with a steel face, moved by machinery, used in iron-works for manufacturing steel, forging anchors, axles, &c.

TILT-MANUFACTURER, a maker of the heavy helves and tilt-hammers used by metal workers; also another tradesman who makes awnings or covers for boats and carts.

TILTS, the local name for certain steel works in Sheffield, where the crude steel is further prepared or developed.

TIMBALES, a French name for kettle-drums; parchment battledores.

TIMBANG, a Chinese weight for rice used in Batavia, of 5 piculs or 10 sacks, = 678·21 lbs.

TIMBER, a general term for all large pieces of wood; the trunks of trees. *See* TIMBRE.

TIMBER-BRIDGE, a wooden bridge.

TIMBER-MEASURE. All large timber is bought and sold by the load, and a load is estimated at 40 feet of unhewn or rough timber, and 50 feet of hewn timber, which is supposed to weigh one ton.

TIMBER-MERCHANT, a wholesale dealer in timber; one who keeps a timber yard or wharf.

TIMBER-SCRIBE, a metal tool or pointed instrument for marking logs and casks.

TIMBER-SHIP, a vessel constructed for carrying timber from the Baltic or the St. Lawrence.

TIMBRE, TIMMER, a legal quantity of 40 or 50 small skins, packed between two boards; in some skins, however, the timbre counts to 120.

TIME-BALL, a ball moved by electricity, which is dropped from the summit of a pole to indicate the true meridional or mid-day time.

TIME-BARGAIN, a contract for the sale or purchase of merchandise, or of stock in the public funds at a certain time. Sometimes these bargains are mere gambling transactions, carried on from time to time, by the mere payment of the difference between the stipulated price and the actual price of the day fixed for its pretended delivery.

TIME-BILL, a time-table of the arrivals and departures of railway trains, omnibuses, steamers, &c.

TIME-KEEPER, a person appointed to watch the departure of vehicles; also a chronometer; a watch, &c.

TIMES, the leading London morning paper; a journal which has obtained a world-wide celebrity for the priority, fulness, and authenticity of its intelligence, and which, as a commercial speculation, is most remunerative in its returns.

TIME-TABLE, a register of the time of high-water, and of the departure of steam boats, railway trains, &c.; a check upon the period of labour of workmen.

TIMONERO (Spanish), a helmsman; one who steers.

TIMOTHY-GRASS, a pasture grass, the *Phleum pratense*. Quantities of this small grass seed are imported from North America. There are several varieties of Timothy, which are extensively cultivated as spring grass for fodder, and are considered very valuable herbage.

TIMPANI (Italian), kettle-drums.

TIMWHISKEY, a heavy lumbering low-wheeled carriage.

TIN, a scarce but very useful metal, so named; a shape for baking bread or cakes. *See* TIN-ORES.

TINAJA (Spanish), immense earthen jars made in Spain, for holding wine, oil, or grain; a liquid-measure in the Philippines, which, for coco-nut oil, weighs from 8 to 21 lbs.

TIN-BOX, TIN-CASE, a strong iron box tinned and japanned, for holding papers, dress articles, &c.

TINGAL, crude borax; borate of soda, imported from India in an impure state, and covered by a soapy matter. When purified, it forms the refined borax of commerce, and is used as a flux in glass-making, and in soldering.

TIN-CAN, a metal vessel for holding liquids.

TIN-CANISTER, a case for holding sugar, coffee, spices, or dry goods.

TINCTURE, in pharmacy, an infusion of the various drugs of the materia medica in spirit of wine or proof spirit, for the sake of extracting their more active principles.

TINDAL, a boatswain's mate in the Indian seas; an attendant on an Indian army.

TINDER, an inflammable substance; charred lint or rags, &c. German tinder is the soft amadou. *See* AMADOU and GERMAN-TINDER.

TINDER-BOX, a box containing charred old linen, to be ignited by sparks from a flint and steel.
TINES, the iron spikes or teeth of scarifiers, harrows, forks, and other agricultural implements and machines.
TIN-FOIL, thin sheets of metal used for lining tea-chests, boxes, &c. to prevent contact with wet.
TIN-FOIL MAKER, a manufacturer of thin leaf-metal.
TIN-GLASS. *See* BISMUTH.
TINKER, a solderer and mender of old pots, kettles, &c.
TIN-KETTLE, a boiler of iron tinned, with a spout.
TIN-LIQUOR, a solution used by dyers, prepared by digesting tin filings in hydrochloric and nitric acids, to each pound of which about two ounces of common salt are added.
TINMEN AND BRAZIERS, workers in metal, and solder.
TIN-MUG, a pannican; a metal drinking vessel.
TINNING, the process of coating iron with tin.
TIN-ORES, the native peroxide or tin-stone, and the double sulphuret of tin and copper. The latter, sometimes called bell-metal ore, is extremely scarce.
TIN-PAIL, a metal bucket for holding water; a slop pail.
TIN-PAN, a tout pan of metal; a shallow vessel for domestic use.
TINPLATE LACQUERER, a japanner.
TIN-PLATES, sheets of iron of different dimensions and strength, scaled, cold-rolled, immersed in an acidulous ley, and, after undergoing other preparations, coated with molten tin. They are used for lining packing-cases, making domestic utensils, and, in America, are extensively employed for roofing churches and dwelling-houses.
TINPLATE-WORKER, a roller of iron plates, who passes them through various processes, and then dips them into molten tin.
TINPLATE-WORKERS' COMPANY; also known as the Wire-workers' Company, one of the minor livery companies of London, which, having no hall, transacts its business at Guildhall.
TIN-PLATTER, a trencher or plate of tin.
TINSE, a Polish coin. *See* TYMPSE.
TINSEL, a kind of shining metallic plate or cloth, either of gold or silver.
TINSEL LACE-MAKER, a maker of imitation gold or silver lace.
TIN-SMELTER, one who roasts tin ore and prepares the pure metal.
TIN-SMITH, a worker in tin.
TIN-STONE, an ore of tin occurring in veins, usually blended with the oxides of iron and manganese. *See* TIN-ORES.
TINT, a shade; a hue of colour.
TIN-TACK, a very small iron nail coated with tin.
TINTEREE, a vernacular name in India for the tamarind.
TINTO, a red Madeira wine, wanting the high aroma of the white sorts; and, when old, resembling tawny port.
TIN-WARE, iron articles coated with tin.

TIP, the point or top of any thing, as a horn tip, a shoe tip.
TIPILEE, a vernacular Indian name for long pepper.
TIPPET, in Scotland, one length of twisted hair or gut in a fishing-line; a handful of straw bound together at one end, used in thatching.
TIPPINGS, tops for glass ornaments, &c.
TIPREE, a small dry-measure of India, = 1½ pint English; also a weight in Bombay, the half of the seer, and weighing 2450 grains.
TIPSTAFF, a constable; an officer of a law court having a wand or staff of office.
TIRAILLEUR, a French sharp-shooter; a rifleman.
TIRE, a Singhalese name for curd; milk coagulated by the addition of a small quantity of sour milk, or of a little tire of the day preceding; the iron hoop or band which binds all the felloes of a wheel closely together.
TIRETAINE, the French name for linsey-woolsey.
TIRE-WOMAN, a milliner; a dresser in a [theatre.
TIRING-ROOM, the dressing-room in a theatre.
TISI, a vernacular Indian name for linseed.
TISSANTIER, a silk weaver.
TISSERAND, a French weaver.
TISSUE, a texture or fabric; cloth interwoven with gold.
TISSUE-PAPER, a very thin unsized paper for wrapping and packing fine articles.
TITHE, the tenth part of landed produce, levied by a rector.
TITHE-COLLECTOR, a receiver of tithes.
TITHE-COMMISSIONER, a government officer; one of a board authorized to arrange propositions for commuting or compounding for tithes.
TITLE, a general head; a name or prefix to a work, &c.; the claim of right to a territory or estate.
TITLE-DEEDS, the legal documents of an estate conferring a title.
TITLE-PAGE, one of the early or commencing pages of a book, which contains the name, and some details respecting the work of the Author.
TITLERS, a description of refined sugar.
TITLING, an old Customs name for stockfish.
TIVAKSHERA, another Eastern name for [tabashir.
TIWAJ, a vernacular Indian name for the *Wrightia antidysenterica.*
T-JOINT, the union of three joints in a pipe, resembling the letter T.
TOAD-FLAX, a wild plant, the *Linaria vulgaris,* which has purgative, diuretic, and bitter qualities. It is administered in chronic diseases of the skin, and a decoction of it forms a poison for flies.
TOAST, bread browned before the fire.
TOASTED-CHEESE, cheese warmed before a fire, to make a Welsh-rabbit, &c.
TOASTER, a metal pan with hooks, for cooking bread, bacon, cheese, &c. before the fire.
TOASTING-FORK, an implement for holding bread, &c. before a fire, to bake; either a twisted metal prong, or one with a telescope or sliding handle.

TOAST-MASTER, an attendant on a chairman at public dinners, who announces the toasts to the company, and leads the cheering.

TOAST-RACK, a stand for a table, of metal or earthenware, with partitions for placing slices of dry toast in.

TOB, a piece of Dammour cotton cloth, sufficient to make a shirt, which passes as a currency money in Nubia.

TOBACCO, species of *Nicotiana*, in which a large trade is carried on in most parts of the world; the leaf being used for smoking, chewing, and, when powdered, inhaled through the nose. The quantity of tobacco imported into the United Kingdom, in 1856, was, 44,788,180 lbs., besides two million lbs. of manufactured, and snuff: of this quantity there were entered for home consumption, 32,578,937 lbs. *See* SHIRAZ TOBACCO, and SYRIAN TOBACCO.

TOBACCO-BOX, a small metal case for holding tobacco to fill pipes from.

TOBACCO, INDIAN, the *Lobelia inflata*, a wild American plant, which has been used instead of tobacco in asthma, and, in the form of enema, in strangulated hernia. *See* LOBELIA.

TOBACCO-JAR, a retail tobacconist's shop-jar.

TOBACCO-MANUFACTURER, a stemmer of tobacco; one who prepares and works up the leaves for smokers, into the various trade kinds sold.

TOBACCO, MOUNTAIN, a wild plant, the *Arnica montana*, which has acrid and emetic properties, and causes constipation. It is used medicinally in typhoid fevers, dysentery, and other cases.

TOBACCONIST, a wholesale or retail licensed dealer in tobacco.

TOBACCO-PIPE MAKER, a maker of clay or meerschaum pipes for smokers.

TOBACCO-PIPE MAKERS' COMPANY, one of the minor incorporated companies of London, not on the livery, and which, having no hall, transacts its business at Guildhall.

TOBACCO-PIPE MOULD MANUFACTURER, a maker of the folding brass or iron moulds in which plastic white clay pipes are shaped.

TOBACCO-PLANTER, a grower of tobacco in the United States or Cuba, from whence our chief supplies are derived.

TOBACCO-POUCH, a pocket-case of skin, India-rubber, or leather, for holding tobacco for the use of a smoker.

TOBACCO-STOPPER, a small instrument used by smokers for pushing down the tobacco in the bowl of a pipe.

TOBAGO CANES, a name under which the trunks of *Bactris minor*, Jacquin, a native of New Granada and the West Indies, are sometimes imported into Europe, to be made into walking-sticks.

TOBINE, a stout twilled silk.

TOD, an English measure of weight, used by dealers in wool, equal to 2 stones of 14lbs. each: 6½ tods make one wey, and 2 weys one sack.

TODDY, palm wine obtained from the sap of the *Arenga saccharifera*; a name for whisky-punch in Scotland.

TODDY-KETTLE, a small hot-water kettle used in Scotland for making toddy.

TODDY-LADLE, a small deep spoon or ladle, used in Scotland for conveying whisky-toddy from a rummer or punch-bowl to a wine glass.

TOENDE, the Danish name for the ton, a grain-measure of 8 scheffels; 21 tons being equal to 10 quarters. Some calculate 208 tons = 100 quarters for wheat, and 210 tons = 100 quarters for oats.

TOFFY, a kind of hard-baked candy or sweetmeat, made of treacle or sugar, and butter.

TOGGLE, a pin placed through a rope, strap, or bolt; a button.

TOGGLE-JOINT, an elbow or knee joint.

TOGGRYI, a name in Canara for the *Cytisus Cadjan*, a common pulse.

TOI, TOWYAH, an undefined Indian grain-measure, the 4th of the cossa.

TOILE (French), linen cloth.

TOILET, a bag or case for night-clothes; a cotton cover for a dressing-table.

TOILET-CAN, a tin can for water for a dressing-room.

TOILET-COVER. *See* TOILET.

TOILET-GLASS, a looking-glass for a toilet-table.

TOILET-PAIL, a tin pail for holding slops in a bedroom.

TOILET-QUILT, a bed-cover or cover for the dressing-table.

TOILET-SET, TOILET-SERVICE, earthenware and glass utensils for a dressing-room.

TOILETTE (French), a dressing-table; an ante-room for dressing; the personal attire of a female.

TOILIER, a French linen-draper.

TOILINET, a kind of German quilting; silk and cotton warp with woollen weft.

TOISE, the French name for the fathom; a measure of length about 2 metres, and = 76 English inches, or ·3838 of a perch; 2000 toises make up the French legal or posting league.

TOISON (French), a fleece.

TOKAY, a rich luscious Hungarian wine of a peculiar aromatic flavour, seldom met with in the United Kingdom.

TOKENS, certain tradesmen's coins which were formerly current, but called in about 40 years ago. A token is a coin ordinarily of less value than its current price, or not of public mint coinage. Gold tokens were issued in California previous to the establishment of a branch United States' mint. The gold coins minted in Australia are only tokens of purely local currency. One pound gold tokens were issued by the South Australian Assay Office in 1852. They are very neatly executed coins, about the sixteenth of an inch more in diameter than a sovereign, and have milled edges. On the one side is a crown with the date, and the words "Government Assay Office, Adelaide;" on the reverse is "Value One Pound" in the centre, and on the margin, "Weight 5 dwts., 15 grs., 22 carats." They are fully 5 per cent. better than their nominal value. There are tokens at Mauritius worth about 8d. A token is also 10½ quires of paper; a name in the Newcastle coal districts for a piece of leather, bearing a distinctive mark for each hewer, one of which he sends up the shaft with each corf or box of coal.

TOLA, an Indian weight equal to 180 grains troy.

TOLAM, an Indian weight used in Malabar of 40 seers, = 27 lbs. 8 oz.

TOLDERO, a retailer of salt in Spain.

TOLE, a weight of Manilla, for silk 4504 grains, for gold, 4176¼ grains; the French name for sheet-iron.

TOLEDO-BLADE, a fine sword made in Toledo.

TOLL, a charge made on foot-passengers, vehicles, or goods passing over a bridge or turnpike-road; a miller's proportion or allowance for grinding corn; the slow ringing of a church-bell.

TOLL-BAR, a turnpike-gate or side-bar on a road, where a toll-collector is stationed to receive toll for foot-passengers or vehicles.

TOLMEN, a large stone with holes drilled through it.

TOLOOM, an agrarian measure in Asia Minor, being a hide of land, about 1600 square yards.

TOLU, BALSAM OF, a thick tenacious balsam obtained from the *Myrospermum toluiferum*, in South America. It has a pleasant odour, and a sweet and agreeable taste, and is much employed in European pharmacy, and for making pulmonic lozenges by confectioners.

TOLVA (Spanish), a hopper into which corn is put to be ground.

TOMAHAWK, an Indian hatchet, an offensive weapon.

TOMAN, a conventional money of Persia of a very variable character, although nominally divided into 100 mahmoodies: it may be valued at about 12s. 6d.

TOMAND, an Arabian dry-measure containing 40 killas, used for rice, of which 168 lbs. go to the tomand.

TOMATO, a well-known vegetable, the *Lycopersicum esculentum*, the fruit of which is used for ketchups and seasonings.

TOMATO SAUCE, a ketchup or condiment, made from the love-apple or tomato.

TOMB, a vault or sarcophagus, in which dead bodies are laid.

TOMBAC, red brass; the white tombac is an alloy of copper and zinc, containing not more than 20 per cent. of the latter.

TOMBAK, the Malay name for a spear.

TOMBEKI, the narcotic leaf of a species of *Lobelia*, which, in Eastern countries, is steeped in water for a few hours, and smoked, with a preparation of Indian hemp, in a narghile or water pipe.

TOMBELIER, a French carman.

TOMBEREAU, a dung-cart in France.

TOMB-STONE, a shaped stone laid over a grave.

TOM-COD, a small variety of the cod found in the North American seas.

TOME, a volume.

TOMIENTO (Spanish), coarse tow.

TOMIN, a Spanish weight for gold and silver, the sixth part of the ochava: for gold 8·875 grains; for silver, 9·245 grains.

TOMJOHN, the name for a kind of sedan chair in Ceylon, open in front, and on each side, carried by a single pole on men's shoulders.

TOMME, a Danish name for the inch.

TOMOLO, TUMOLO, an Italian and Sicilian grain-measure. In Naples 5 2-5ths tomoli = 1 quarter. In Palermo, 80 tomoli, 5 quarters old measure.

TOMPION, a bung or plug for the mouth of a cannon.

TOMPONG, a weight of Sumatra, ranging from 70 to 80 lbs., according to the nature of the goods weighed.

TOM-TOM, a native Indian drum, of which there are several kinds, generally made of jack-wood, and covered with deer-skin, from which the hair has been removed. The skin is laid on in a wet state, and dried in the sun.

TON, the principal ponderous commercial weight, which varies considerably in different localities for weight or measurement goods. In Great Britain, the legal ton by weight is usually 20 cwt., or 2240 lbs., but in long weight it is 2400 lbs. A ton of flour, in commerce, is 8 sacks or 10 barrels; a ton of potatoes, 10 bushels. In Cornwall, the miner's ton is 21 cwt., or 2352 lbs. In Philadelphia, by agreement, the ton of coal is only 2000 lbs. The French legal ton for heavy weights contains 1000 kilogrammes; in Germany, Spain, &c. it is 2000 lbs. The ton of freight or merchandise, varies with the article and the locality from whence shipped, different rules being laid down by different Chambers of commerce. The Russian measurement ton for goods, is 5 chetwerts, or about 28 bushels, equal in English weight to about 17¼ cwt. In timber, the ton is 40 feet for rough timber, and 50 feet for hewn timber. In the measurement of a ship, the ton is reckoned at 40 cubic feet.

TONALCHILE (French), Guinea-pepper.

TONDEUR, a French sheep-shearer.

TONDINO (Spanish), a moulding on the astragal of a column.

TONELADA, a Portuguese liquid-measure, equal to 227½ English wine-gallons, and containing 52 almudes; (Spanish), a tun; tonnage dues.

TONELERIA (Spanish), the trade of a cooper; a quantity of water-casks for ships.

TONGA, a silver coin of Bokhara, worth about 7½d.

TONGKANG, a kind of boat or junk used in the seas of the Eastern archipelago.

TONGO, a name for the mangrove in the Pacific.

TONGS, dividing instruments to lay hold of any thing, as a fire-tongs, tongs for holding hot metal, &c.

TONGUE, the clapper of a bell; a projection, as of a buckle or stock; an organ in the mouth of a quadruped, many of which are used for food, fresh, salted, or dried and smoked; as pigs'-tongues, sheep's-tongues, calves'-tongues, ox and reindeer-tongues, &c.

TONGUE-SCRAPER, a thin wire or horn scraper for cleansing the tongue.

TONICS, strengthening medicines.

TONINA, the Spanish name for fresh tunny-fish.

TONKA-BEAN. *See* TONQUIN-BEAN.

TONLIEU, a market toll or tax in France.

TONNAGE, the internal measurement of a ship, representing the number of tons of cargo she will carry. Tonnage is estimated sometimes by bulk, but more generally by weight; a ton by bulk being equal to 40 cubic feet: and a ton by weight equalling 20 cwt. There are certain formulæ employed by ship-builders, whereby the tonnage is calculated, from the length, breadth, and depth of the vessel; but these formulæ seldom give the real tonnage, or the true amount of cargo which the vessel will carry; because two vessels exactly equal in length, breadth, and depth, measured as those dimensions usually are, may have very different internal capacity, owing to different curvatures of the hull. A ship will sometimes carry more than her registered tonnage indicates, sometimes less; and therefore the word "tonnage" is to be regarded only as a rough approximation to the burden which the vessel will carry.

TONNELIER, a French cooper; a seaman who fills a water cask.

TON OF WATER. Taking water to weigh 10 lbs. per gallon, there ought to be 224 gallons in the ton. The French cubic mètre or ton is equal to 220 English imperial gallons. The London Water Companies use in their computations a ton of 216 gallons, namely, 6 barrels of 36 gallons each.

TONQUIN-BEAN, the fruit or seed contained in the capsules of *Dypteryx odorata*, principally used to impart fragrance to snuff. *See* CAMARA.

TONSON, a barber.

TONTINE, a life annuity association, founded upon the principle that, when a person belonging to it has subscribed his stipulated share or sum, he is at liberty to name any life he pleases, during the existence of which he draws a certain annuity; and as the shares of the dead nominees are distributed among the living ones, that annuity continually increases, until the last survivor gets the whole. Tontines have been frequently resorted to by Government, for the purpose of raising loans for the service of the State.

TONTISSE (French), flock paper; paper-hangings ornamented with flock or powdered wool coloured.

TOODA, an Eastern timber measure, = 1·184 cubic foot English.

TOODOOVALAH, a weight in Travancore of 18 lbs. *See* TOOLAM.

TOOKOO, an African money denomination, applied to 5 strings of cowries, about 200 shells, worth 8d. nominally.

TOOL, a mechanical instrument of any kind for working with.

TOOLAM, an Eastern weight: in Malabar = 15 lbs. 0 oz. 11 drs.; in Travancore it is rather more, viz., 15 lbs. 9 oz. 7¾ drs; the Tricoor toolam is 16 lbs.; the Toodoovalah toolam, 18 lbs.; the toolam for dummar, wax, and other light goods, 28 lbs.

TOOL-BASKET, a carpenter's or other workman's basket, for holding tools: these baskets are made of different sizes.

TOOL-CHEST MAKER, a manufacturer of small boxes for holding tools for amateurs, or larger chests for ship-carpenters' and other workmen's tools.

TOOL-FUND, an insurance fund for the reimbursement of workmen for the loss of their tools by fire.

TOOL-HOUSE, a shed or shelter for garden tools.

TOOL-MAKER, a manufacturer of different working hand instruments, of which there are various kinds.

TOOLSI, TULASI, the name in India for species of basil. The dried aromatic leaves of *Ocymum album*, are used there as a substitute for tea. The juice is given to children in colds, to the extent of a tea-spoonful twice daily. The root of *O. sanctum* is given in decoction in fevers. The Brahmins regard this plant as sacred to Vishnu, and use it in their funeral ceremonies. The Malays also strew it over the graves of their dead.

TOOMBIKAI, another name for gaub. *See* GAUB.

TOONA, the Hindustani name for the *Cedrela Toona*, a valuable tree, of large size, abundant in Travancore, and other parts of India. The reddish-coloured wood, used all over India in cabinet-making, is scarcely inferior to mahogany, but lighter, and not so close in the grain. It is often sold under the general name of Chittagong wood.

TOOROO, a species of palm of South America, which grows to the height of from 30 to 50 feet. Its woody outside is used by cabinet-makers for inlaid work, walking-sticks, billiard-cues, &c.

TOOSEH, a native land-measure in India, of about 4½ beegahs, or about 2 acres.

TOOTH. *See* TEETH.

TOOTH-BRUSH, a small hair-brush for washing and scrubbing the teeth.

TOOTH-FORCEPS, dental instruments used for extracting teeth.

TOOTH-GLASS, a toilet water-glass for washing the mouth.

TOOTHING, irregular projecting bricks left standing at the end of a wall or building to form a union.

TOOTHING-PLANE, a tool for working on veneers.

TOOTH-PICK, a sharpened piece of wood, a shaped piece of bone, quill, or tortoise-shell, used to remove obstructions between the teeth.

TOOTH-POWDER, a dentifrice, of which various kinds are made.

TOOTH-POWDER-BOX MAKER, a maker of wooden or China jars for holding tooth-powder on a toilet-table.

TOOTH-POWDER MANUFACTURER, a wholesale maker and vender of dentifrices.

TOOT-NET, in Scotland, a large fishing-net anchored.

TOP, a name among cloth-manufacturers, &c., for the combed wool ready for the spinner, from which the "noil" for shorts and dust, have been taken out: a platform at the head of the lower masts of a ship, for the convenience of seamen working aloft; a child's spinning-toy.

TOPAZ, a gem of which there are two kinds, the Brazilian and the Oriental; the latter is nearly all alumina, while the former contains but 50 per cent of alumina. The yellow Brazilian is the best known.

TOP-BLOCK, a large block fixed under the cap of a lower mast to aid in sending down the top-masts.

TOP-BOOTS, riding-boots which have light tops to them.

TOP-CHAIN, a chain to sling a lower yard.

TOPCHAN, pieces of cotton cloth, 20 or 30 ells long, and one yard and a half broad, used in barter in parts of Africa, near Abyssinia.

TOP-CLOTH, tarred canvas to cover hammocks when stowed away.

TOP-COAT, a great-coat for walking or driving in.

TOP-DRESSING, manure laid on the surface of land, instead of being ploughed in.

TOP-GALLANT MAST, the third mast above the deck of a ship.

TOP-GALLANT SAIL, the third elevated square sail of a ship from the deck.

TOPIES, grass and other hats used in India.

TOPINAMBAR, a name for the Jerusalem artichoke.

TOP-LIGHT, a signal lantern carried in the top or mast platform of a ship.

TOP MAST, the second mast in a ship above the deck.

TOPO, a measure of a league and a half among the Indians of South America.

TOPPING-LIFT, a hoisting rope used for raising up the end of a boom in a ship.

TOP-SAIL, the second large square sail of a ship from the deck.

TOPS AND BOTTOMS, small rolls of dough baked, cut in halves, and then browned in an oven, used as food for infants.

TOPSMAN, the uppermost sawyer in a saw-pit.

TOQUE, literally touch; a small nominal money of account used in trading, on some parts of the West Coast of Africa: 40 cowries make one toque, and 5 toques 1 hen or gallinha. The French name for a cap or bonnet, a head-dress for females.

TOQUERO (Spanish), a veil maker.

TOQUILLO (Spanish), a small head-dress.

TORADA, a drove of bulls.

TORAL, cakes of unbleached yellow wax.

TORCAS (Spanish), a certain quantity of fish wrapped in straw.

TORCEDERO, (Spanish), a twisting mill.

TORCHDURA, a light Spanish wine.

TORCH, a large taper, a flambeau or blazing brand.

TORCH-BEARER, a link-boy.

TORCIDA, a daily allowance of meat given to labourers in oil-mills.

TORCIDO, a kind of sweetmeat; a light, bad wine.

TORDIGA (Spanish), neats' leather for coarse shoes.

TORRADOR, a Spanish bull-fighter.

TORGA, a yoke put on the necks of swine in Spain to keep them from breaking through fences.

TORIA, an Eastern name for the *Sinapis glauca*, extensively cultivated in India for the oil obtained from the seed.

TORMENTIN (Spanish), a small mast on the bowsprit.

TORNATURA, an Italian land-measure, of 2 acres 1 rood 35 perches.

TORON (French), the strand of a rope.

TORONJA, a Spanish name for the citron.

TORQUE (*French*), a ring of brass wire; a bandage or crown for the head.

TORQUETTE (French), fish wrapped up in straw; tobacco leaves rolled and pounded in a particular manner.

TORREFY, to roast ores or drugs; to dry by a fire.

TORRONTES, a kind of white grapes grown in Spain.

TORROO, a palm growing in Berbice to the height of 60 or 70 feet. Its woody outside is used for inlaid work, billiard-cues, walking-sticks, &c. Of the fruit a drink resembling chocolate is made.

TORSION-BALANCE, an instrument for estimating very minute forces.

TORSION-ELECTROMETER, an apparatus for measuring the intensity of electricity.

TORSK, a fish of the Northern seas, the *Brosmus vulgaris*, allied to the cod.

TORTA (Spanish), a round cake made up of various ingredients; a cake of wax.

TORTERA (Spanish), a pan for baking tarts or pies.

TORTILLA, a small cake; an omelet.

TORTILLA-BAKER, a pastry-cook, a baker of small cakes.

TORTILLON, a cushion for the head, used by persons who carry loads in France.

TORTOISES, shielded reptiles, species of *Testudo*, and *Emys*. Some are edible, as the large *Testudo Indicus*, which is eaten both fresh and salted, and a beautifully clear oil is prepared from the fat. The *Emys trijuga* and the *Emyda punctata* are kept as scavengers in wells. The horny shield plates of some are occasionally applied to manufacturing purposes. See TURTLE.

TORTOISE-SHELL, the imbricated plates covering the back of the sea-turtle, *Chelone imbricata* and *caretta*, used for making combs, and veneering on fancy cabinet-work. Five large plates are obtained from the middle of the carapace or upper buckler, and four large ones from the sides, called "blades," and twenty-five smaller plates from the edges called "feet or noses." In an animal of the ordinary size, about three feet long and 2½ wide, the largest plates will weigh about 9 oz., and measure about 13 by 8 inches, and one-fourth of an inch thick in the middle. The belly shells are of a yellow colour, and are used for the purposes of horn.

TORTOISE-SHELL COMB, a toilet or female's hair comb made of tortoise-shell.

TORTOISE-SHELL DEALER, an importer and retailer of tortoise-shell.

TORTOISE-WOOD, a variety of zebra-wood.

TORTOZON, a kind of large Spanish grape.

TORUS, a convex moulding in a column base, the section of which is nearly a semicircle, projecting from a flat circle.

Tozzal (Spanish), a cord or twist.
Toty, a name in some parts of the Pacific for a sailor or fisherman.
Touansé, a kind of Chinese silk fabric.
Touch-hole, the vent of a gun; the aperture through which the charge of powder is ignited.
Touch-paper, paper steeped in saltpetre, that ignites slowly, and burns in sparks.
Touch-stone, a compact black basalt, used as a test to determine readily the value of gold or silver by the touch.
Touch-wood, dry, decayed wood that serves as a kind of tinder, igniting readily when a spark is applied; a name for the *Polyporus igniarius*.
Toumbeki, a Turkish name for Schiraz tobacco.
Toung, the Burmese name for the cubit, = 1 foot 6 inches.
Toupee, Toupet (French), an artificial curl or tuft of hair.
Tour, a business circuit; the journey of a commercial traveller.
Tourmaline, some of the transparent crystals are used as gems, the yellow variety being quite as valuable as the topaz.
Tourmentin (French), a fore stay-sail.
Tournament, a sham fight by mounted horsemen with lances.
Tournay, a printed worsted material used for furniture.
Tournée (French), a kind of garden mattock.
Tournette (French), an instrument used by potters in shaping and painting delft and porcelain ware; an instrument for spinning.
Tournevent (French), a cowl or chimney-pot.
Tourniquet, a tight bandage round a limb to stop bleeding.
Tournois, a word which, in the old monetary system of France, had the same meaning as "sterling" in English, implying standard or genuine.
Tourons, a kind of French confectionery.
Tourte (French), a tart. [France.
Tourteau, a small crusty loaf made in
Tourtière (French), a baking pan for tarts.
Tous-les-mois, a name given to the starch obtained from the tubers of some species of South American *Canna*, *C. glauca*, and *C. edulis*; the latter, a native of Peru, is believed to furnish the chief quantity of this fecula sold in the shops.
Touter, one who canvasses for custom; a runner employed by minor hotel-keepers, ship-agents, and others, to secure patronage from strangers arriving in a port; a pressing shopkeeper who stands at his door inviting customers to purchase his wares.
Touzee, Towzee, a government rent-roll in India.
Tow, the waste fibres or refuse after carding flax and hemp which is made into bags, sheeting, and yarn, and used for various other purposes; some kinds are called codilla; we imported, in 1856, about 11,000 tons; to draw a vessel along by means of a rope.

Towah, in Aberdeen, a rope-maker.
Towboat, a row-boat employed in calm weather to draw a ship along; a steam-tug.
Towel, a cloth to dry the hands and face after washing; a cleaning cloth used by servants.
Towel-gourds, the fruit of a trailing-plant, the *Luffa Egyptiaca*, common throughout the tropics, used for sponges, drying rubbers, gun-wadding, the manufacture of baskets, hats, &c.
Towel-horse, a wooden frame or stand for a dressing-room, to hang towels on.
Towelling, a coarse fabric made of flax, diaper, huckaback, &c.
Towel-roller, a revolving wooden pin affixed to a door, for hanging a circular towel on.
Towing-path, a path on the bank of a river or canal, where, in towing barges, horses travel.
Tow-line, a rope or cable affixed to a barge on a river or canal, or to a ship drawn along by a steam-tug.
Towmondall, Towmontell, a name in some parts of Scotland for a yearling animal.
Town, a collection of houses on a larger scale than a village, and having usually many public buildings and streets; a seat of commerce; a place where a market is held.
Town-clerk, a civic officer who keeps the public records, and attends to the public legal duties of the town.
Town-council, a body of cou[illegible] representatives, elected by the [illegible] burgesses in order to manage t[illegible] pal affairs of a borough or town[illegible]
Town-crier, a public officer w[illegible] outcry or proclamation in the [illegible]
Townet, in Shetland, the work[illegible] wool.
Town-hall, a chief public build[illegible] business is transacted, and m[illegible] assizes, &c. held.
Town-house, a residence in a tow[illegible]
Township, a community, or the p[illegible] of a district situate around a [illegible] village, having the power of s[illegible] ment; in Scotland, a farm o[illegible] two or more farmers in common, [illegible] separate lots, who reside in a [illegible] hamlet or village.
Towranero, Turanira, a na[illegible] bastard bully-tree of Guia[illegible] grows to a large size, and wil[illegible] inches, and from 40 to 50 feet [illegible] It is a hard, even-grained wood [illegible] brown colour, and is used fo[illegible] timber, spokes, &c. The fruit i[illegible]
Tow-spinner, a manufacturer who [illegible] up tow into yarn.
Towyah, Twier, a grain-measure [illegible] ranging for different grains, fr[illegible] to nearly 7½ lbs.
Tow-yarn-maker, a tow-spinner.
Toxophilite, a lover of archery.
Toy-dealer, the keeper of a baz[illegible] shop; a vender of children's pl[illegible]
Toy-maker, a manufacturer o[illegible] horses and other children's toys.

TOYO, a fragrant, undefined plant of British Guiana, of which an infusion and syrup of the leaves and stems have been strongly recommended in chronic coughs.

TOYS, playthings, marbles, trifles, and small articles of various kinds, largely imported from the Continent. The value of those imported in 1855 exceeded £52,000.

T-PIPE, a pipe shaped like the letter T.

TRACE, a chain or harness strap by which horses draw; to outline or copy; to mark out or draw; to follow by the spoor or trail.

TRACES, hide or rope harness bands.

TRACING-PAPER, a kind of thin oiled paper for taking impressions. Tracing-paper may be made by dipping a sheet into a thick solution of gum arabic, and pressing between two dry sheets, thus rendering all three transparent.

TRACING-PAPER MAKER, a manufacturer of thin transparent paper for copying purposes.

TRACK-WAY, a tram-road; a foot-path.

TRACT, a brief treatise; a small religious hand-bill or pamphlet.

TRADE, the commerce of a country; commercial or mechanical employment; traffic; a body of persons engaged in some particular employment; a Derbyshire mining term for refuse or rubbish from a mine.

TRADE-ALLOWANCE, TRADE-PRICE, a wholesale discount, allowed to dealers or retailers on articles to be sold again.

TRADE-HALL, a meeting-hall, or sale-room in a town, for manufacturers or traders.

TRADER, a merchant; a shopkeeper.

TRADE-SALE, a special auction or sale of articles suited to a particular class of dealers.

TRADESMAN, in England, a common name for a shopkeeper, but in Scotland a handicraftsman; all who keep shops being, according to the constitution of boroughs, called merchants.

TRADESMAN'S-ASSISTANT, a shopman; an apprentice.

TRADES-UNION, a combination of workmen, to maintain their rights and privileges, as to wages, hours of labour, customs, &c.

TRADING-POST, a fort or station of the Hudson's Bay Company, for bartering with the Indians.

TRAEDOR (Spanish), a carrier.

TRAFFIC-RETURN, a periodical statement of the receipts for goods and passengers on a railway line.

TRAFFIC-TAKER, a computer of the returns of traffic on a particular line of road.

TRAFICANTE (Spanish), a merchant or trader.

TRAGACANTH, a partially soluble gum obtained from the *Astragalus Tragacantha*, and less valuable than the true gums.

TRAGEDY, a melancholy drama.

TRAGILLA (Spanish), a kind of harrow without teeth, for levelling the ground.

T-RAIL, a railway bar shaped like a T.

TRAIN, something drawn along; a connection of carriages and wagons, &c. drawn by a locomotive forming a railway-train; a line of artillery carriages and equipments; a file of carts; a line of gunpowder to fire a mine; a body of servants or retinue; in the Orkneys a rope used for drawing; in Scotland, the shafts of a cart or carriage; the hanging part or finish of a lady's court dress; to exercise; to educate; to drill, to spread out fruit-trees or climbers in a particular manner.

TRAIN-BAND, a local or city militia.

TRAIN-BEARER, a page; a supporter of the long, state robes of a lady, or public officer.

TRAINER, a person who exercises and prepares race-horses for a trial of speed; a wire or wooden frame for fastening flowers or shrubs to.

TRAIN-OIL, oil obtained from the blubber of the whale by boiling.

TRAIN-TACKLE, the pulleys used for running guns in and out of ports, &c.

TRAITEUR, a French eating-house keeper.

TRAITOIRE (French), a cooper's tool.

TRAM, in the north, a local name for a small coal wagon, whence the word tramway; a doubled kind of silk, in which two or more thicknesses have been twisted together, used for the weft or cross threads of gros-de-Naples velvets, flowered silks, and the best varieties of silk goods.

TRAMA (Spanish), the weft or woof; a kind of weaving silk.

TRAMADOR, a Spanish weaver.

TRAMAIL (French), a drag-net.

TRAMEUR, a French weaver.

TRAMMEL, a joiner's instrument to draw ovals; an iron hook to hang a kettle on.

TRAMMEL-NET, a draught-net for catching pollen, or fresh-water herring.

TRAMON (Spanish), the shortest wool, that which remains on the comb during the process of combing.

TRAMP, a foot traveller; a vagrant; also a workman who wanders from town to town in search of employment; an instrument for trimming hedges; a plate of iron worn by ditchers in Scotland, below the centre of the foot, for working on their spades; to cleanse clothes by treading on them in water.

TRAM-PLATE, a flat piece of iron laid as a rail.

TRAM-ROAD, short lines of iron rails laid down, usually to facilitate traction by horses.

TRAM-WAY, a kind of laid granite lines, in streets or roads, to facilitate the passage of loaded carts.

TRANCE, TRANSE, a passage.

TRANCHET (French), a shoemaker's heel knife.

TRANGRUM, a name in Sweden for the mass remaining in the boiling pans, after subjecting herrings to heat for the extraction of the oil. This trangrum is used as a manure, either mixed with clay, or with charred sea-weed.

TRANSCRIBE, to write out a copy.

TRANSCRIPT, a written copy.

TRANSEPT, the north and south aisles of a church, when built in the form of a cross, the position of the main building being east and west.

TRANSFER, a change of property, government funds, or joint-stock shares, &c., from one person to another; a delivery or removal of warehoused goods; to mark or impress on a lithographer's stone

TRANSFER-BOOK, a register of transfers of shares or stock.

TRANSFER-DAYS, certain regular fixed days at the Bank of England, for registering transfers of Bank-stock and Government funds, in the books of the Corporation. The transfer-books of the various Government securities are shut about a month previous to the day on which the dividend on any stock becomes due, and a fortnight or three weeks after, when no transfer is permitted to be made, except in the former case, under special circumstances, and by express sanction of the Governor of the Bank, and in the latter by what is termed a "Private Transfer," upon which an extra 2s. 6d. is charged. Powers of Attorney must be deposited before two o'clock, the day prior to sale or transfer. There is no expense for the transfer of Government securities. Bank-stock, above £25, 12s.; India-stock, 30s.; Brokerage, 2s. 6d. per cent.

TRANSFER-PAPER, prepared paper used by lithographers; thin, unsized paper for taking copies of letters with a copying-press.

TRANSHIPMENT, the act of removing from one ship to another.

TRANSIRE, a custom-house clearance for a coasting-vessel.

TRANSIT-CIRCLE. *See* TRANSIT-INSTRUMENT.

TRANSIT-DUTY, a Government toll levied on the passage of goods through a State.

TRANSIT-INSTRUMENT, an instrument for determining the place of the heavenly bodies, or the passage of a star across the meridian of any place on the sun's disk.

TRANSLATOR, a linguist; one who explains or translates from one language into another. There are sworn translators for public courts, and private individuals who make a business of translating documents, writing letters, &c. in foreign languages.

TRANSOM, a cross bar of any kind, as across a railway, a double window, or door-post, the stern-post of a ship, &c.

TRANSPARENCY, a painting illuminated at the back.

TRANSPARENT-BLIND MAKER, a manufacturer of thin or gauze wire window-blinds to be seen through.

TRANSPORT, a felon sentenced to penal servitude in a colony; a ship for conveying stores and troops; an escort of gold.

TRANSPORTATION, penal servitude abroad, undergone by convicted felons.

TRANSPORTIN (Spanish), a thin and small mattress.

TRAP, a drain-pipe for gullies, sinks, or syphons, of different bore; a sort of moveable ladder or steps; a gin or snare for vermin and wild animals; a small wooden shoe for holding a ball to strike at; a rock of felspar, hornblende, and augite.

TRAPACETE, the Spanish name for a waste-book.

TRAP-DOOR, a lifting or sliding door in a loft, a roof, or on the stage of a theatre.

TRAPE, the Spanish name for buckram.

TRAPEAR (Spanish), to make cloth.

TRAPERIA, a woollen-draper's shop in Spain.

TRAPESO, an Italian weight for gold and silver; in Malta it is reckoned at 12·725 grains; in Naples and Sicily, 13½ grains; the twentieth part of an ounce.

TRAPICHE (Spanish), a small sugar-mill.

TRAPO (Spanish), cloth of any kind; the sails of a ship.

TRAPONG-FRY, the West Indian name for a small species of anchovy.

TRAPPER, one who hunts wild animals for their skins or fur.

TRAPPINGS, ornaments or dress for a soldier, a horse, &c.; luggage.

TRAP-TREE, a name for a species of *Artocarpus*, which furnishes a gutta or glutinous gum, used as bird-lime. The fibre of the bark is used for fishing-lines, cordage, and nets, in Singapore.

TRASCA (Spanish), a leather thong.

TRASH, a planting name in the West Indies for the waste leaves and stalk of the sugar-cane after the juice has been expressed; bruised straw; the loppings of trees; waste or rubbish.

TRASH-HOUSE, the building on a sugar-plantation where the expressed stalk of the sugar-cane is stored for fuel.

TRASQUERO (Spanish), a leather-cutter.

TRASQUILADOR, a Spanish sheep-shearer.

TRASS, TARRASS, a name given to the calcareous tufa, a volcanic earth, when ground for making hydraulic cement; a kind of artificial stone. *See* TARRASS.

TRASTEJADOR (Spanish), a tiler.

TRASTRIGO (Spanish), wheat of the best quality.

TRAVELLER, an iron ring fitted so as to slip up and down a rope or mast.

TRAVELLER, COMMERCIAL, an agent who visits towns to obtain orders for merchants and manufacturers, or to sell goods on commission. A town traveller is one who makes the circuit of a city or town, and does not make country journeys.

TRAVELLERS'-JOY, the *Clematis Vitalba*, a wild plant, the leaves of which are used as a rubefacient in rheumatism.

TRAVELLING-CASE MAKER, a manufacturer of portable fitted boxes of different kinds suited for journeys.

TRAVELLING-COMPANION, a pocket or portable case or bottle.

TRAVELLING-CRANE, a crane working on a tramway upon scaffolding, for lifting stones or heavy materials.

TRAVERTINE, a name in Italy for the calcareous tufa, a species of limestone much used for making hydraulic cements, and as a building stone; part of St. Peter's, the Colosseum, and many ancient Roman works, were built of travertine. *See* TARRASS.

TRAVESERO (Spanish), a bolster.

TRAVIS, a wooden frame for confining unruly horses to be shod.

TRAWL-NET, a sea drag-net for fishing.

TRAY, a flat shallow board, trough, or stand, for holding, lifting, or carrying articles upon, of which there are many kinds, as a butler's-tray, tea-tray, glass-tray, snuffers'-tray, butcher's-tray, &c. Trays of sheet-iron, silver, and other metals, and of papier-mâché, are largely made at Birmingham.

TREACLE, refuse sugar; the uncrystallizable substances generated out of sugar by the application of heat in the process of refining. *See* MOLASSES.

TREACLE-MAKER, a refiner of molasses.

TREACLE-POSSET, boiled milk curdled by a mixture of treacle, considered a useful drink for colds.

TREADLE, the part of a loom, turning-lathe, or grinding-wheel, worked by the foot.

TREAD-MILL, a wheel with steps propelled by the feet of persons in a gaol, by which motion is given to machinery.

TREASURER, an officer who has the charge of money belonging to a society or State.

TREASURY, a State office or department for managing public finances, under the superintendence of a board, termed Lords of the Treasury; a Turkish sum of money, made up of 1000 purses, and equal to £5000 sterling.

TREASURY-BOND, a species of exchequer-bill.

TREASURY-WARRANT, an official decree or notice, issued by the Lords of the Treasury for the information of the public.

TRECHOMETER, a French machine for reckoning distances, specially adapted for vehicles.

TREENAIL, TRUNNEL, a wooden pin or plug, employed where metal bolts would be injurious, as in ship-building, for nailing planks to the timbers.

TREFOIL, a name for species of *Trifolium*, or clover, many of which are highly important as food for cattle, either fresh or in the state of hay.

TREILLIS, a kind of coarse quilted linen, imported into France.

TREKKING, a colonial term in the Cape colony, for departing or leaving to settle in another locality.

TREK-TOW, a Dutch name, in Southern Africa, for strips of hide twisted into rope traces, for oxen to draw waggons by.

TRELLIS, a cross-barred frame of wood; lattice-work.

TRENCH, a ditch, drain, or pit.

TRENCHER, a wooden platter for bread, &c.

TRENCH-PLOUGH, a plough for making deep furrows.

TREND, clean wool.

TRENT-SAND, a fine sharp kind of silex, obtained from the banks of the Trent, which is a cheap substitute for polishing powders.

TRE'OU (French), a square or lug sail.

TREPANG, a name in the East for species of sea slug (*Holothuria*), in the fishing for which, and after preparation, a large trade is carried on.

TREPANNING-INSTRUMENT, a cylindrical saw for removing pieces of the skull.

TRESSEL, TRESTLE, a frame or moveable crossed legs for supporting a table, coffin, &c.

TRESSEL-TREES, supports for the top or platform on a mast, to which the stays and standing rigging of the upper masts are secured.

TRESSOIR (French), an instrument to plait hair with.

TRET, an old allowance like the tare, or deduction on packages of goods, now nearly obsolete.

TREVAT, a weaver's cutting instrument for severing the pile threads of velvet.

TRE'VIER (French), a sail-maker.

TRIAGE (French), sorting, picking; any thing calculated to injure the appearance of coffee or other staples, and which have to be separated.

TRIAL, a judicial process; a lawsuit.

TRIAL-TRIP, an experimental trip.

TRIANGLE, a metal instrument for jingling.

TRIANGULATE, to divide into plots or triangles for surveying.

TRIBLET, a goldsmith's tool for ring-making.

TRIBOMETER, an instrument for estimating the friction of metals.

TRIBUNAL, a court of justice.

TRIBUNAL OF COMMERCE, a chamber of commerce, or court of traders for settling mercantile disputes.

TRIBUTE, a tax or contribution; a miner who works for an agreed share of the ore obtained.

TRICOLOR, the French national standard, red, white, and blue.

TRICOOR, a prefix of the toolam, an Eastern weight.

TRICOT, a kind of German silk netting, or weaving, for purses or fancy articles; a cotton fabric.

TRIDENT, a harpoon; a spear with three prongs.

TRIFLE, a confectionery of whipped cream, with aromatics and spirituous flavourings.

TRIG, a wedge or block to prop up a cask, or to stop a wheel.

TRIGGER, the catch or movement by which a gun is fired.

TRIM, to arrange, to ornament; the condition of a vessel with regard to her cargo and ballast.

TRIMMER, a piece of wood in a wall to support the ends of a joist or rafter; one who fits, ornaments, or arranges; a coal-trimmer is a hand employed to spread or arrange the coals in the hold of a collier.

TRIMMING-CAN, a small tin vessel with a spout, for pouring oil into a table-lamp.

TRIMMING-MANUFACTURER, a maker of braids, tassels, gimps, fringes, silk buttons, and such like ornaments and appendages for ladies' dresses.

TRINGLE, a lath extended between the posts of a bedstead; a curtain-rod.

TRINITY-HOUSE, the office of a board of commissioners having the charge of the light-houses, buoys, pilots, &c., in England, who are termed the Honourable Corporation of the Trinity-house.

TRINITY-MASTER, one of the corporation of the Trinity-house or Town-hall.

TRINITY-TERM, the sitting of the law-courts between May 22 and June 12.

TRINK, a kind of fishing-net.

TRINKET, a small ornament for the person; a toy or jewel.

TRINKET-BOX, a small case for holding jewellery.

TRINRAGAN, one of the Eastern names for the palmyrah palm.

TRIP, a flock of sheep or goats; a journey; to raise an anchor clear of the bottom.

TRIPE, the stomach of a cow, &c. cleaned and cooked for food.

TRIPE-DE-ROCHE, a lichen of the arctic regions, the *Gyrophora cylindrica*, which has occasionally supported life among famishing travellers in the desolate northern wastes of arctic America.

TRIPE-DRESSER, a person who cleanses the maws of animals, and parboils them for sale as food.

TRIPE-SHOP, a place where tripe and neats'-feet, and frequently cats'-meat are vended.

TRIPOD, a stand or support; a three-legged stool or table.

TRIPOLI, rotten-stone; a greyish-yellow or red earth, chiefly composed of silex, used in polishing gold and silver; also made from clunch or from septaria.

TRISE, a nautical term, to haul up by means of a rope.

TRIST, TRYST, a fair for the sale of cattle.

TRITURATE, to grind to powder or dust.

TRIVET, an iron frame or stand to support a boiler on a grate, and keep it from pressing on the coals.

TROCHOMETER, TRECHOMETER, a measurer of the revolutions of a carriage-wheel.

TROJAC, a Polish coin of 6 grains or 3 gros, worth rather more than 1d.

TROJERO, a store-keeper in Spain.

TROLL, to angle with a fishing-rod, which has the line on a running wheel or pulley.

TROLLEY, a kind of railway vehicle.

TROMBA (Italian), a trumpet.

TROMBONE, a large and powerful trumpet, composed of sliding-tubes, by which every sound in the diatonic and chromatic scales, within its compass, can be perfectly obtained.

TROMPE (French), a water-blowing engine; a blowing machine for furnaces.

TRON, a steel-yard balance.

TRONG, the Malay name for the egg-plant.

TROOPER, a mounted soldier.

TROQUIL, a Spanish dye.

TROTTERS, sheep's feet cooked.

TROUGH, a long deep tray; a spout.

TROUSERING, broadcloth, tartans, drills, and other materials for men's trousers.

TROUSER-MAKER, a tailor who makes pantaloons, or men's garments for the legs and lower part of the person.

TROUSSEAU (French), a bride's general outfit; clothes or presents.

TROUT, a small fresh-water fish, the *Salmo fario*, the flesh of which is of the finest quality.

TROVER, an action on a disputed question of property. [kind of boat.

TROW, a wooden air spout in a mine; a

TROWEL, a small flat, triangular metal moulder's tool used by bricklayers and plasterers for spreading mortar, or for gardening.

TROYKEN, TROISKEN, a small weight formerly used in Holland, for gold and silver, nearly 3 grains.

TROY-WEIGHT, a term applied to the English weight for the precious metals. The troy pound contains 12 ounces, or 5760 grains; 3 1-6th grs. make 1 carat of diamonds; 24 grs. 1 dwt.; 20 dwts. 1 oz.; 12 oz. 1 lb; 25 lbs. 1 qr.; 100 lbs. 1 cwt. The moneyers have a peculiar subdivision of the troy grain, dividing the grain into 20 mites, the mite into 24 doits, the doit into 20 periots, the periot into 24 blanks.

TRUCK, barter or exchange dealing; paying wages in goods at overcharged prices; a hand barrow; a two-wheeled carriage; the low solid wheel of a gun-carriage; a circular cap or block of wood at the head of a flag staff, or on the highest mast of a ship; a low-sided railway vehicle.

TRUCKLE, a small wheel or castor.

TRUCKLE-BED, a low sliding bed on rollers or castors.

TRUCKLE-CHEESE, a small thick solid cheese, that can be rolled on its edge.

TRUCKMAN, a carman; one who moves goods by hand in a truck.

TRUFFLES, the *Tuber cibarium*, a fungus found in the earth beneath trees, especially oaks, beeches, and hawthorns. Being nutritious, fragrant, and stimulating in its properties, the truffle is a common ingredient in sauces and made dishes.

TRUMEAU (French), a shin of beef; a pier looking-glass.

TRUMPET, a metal wind instrument used in bands, or for signalizing in war; a tube for conveying sound, or for speaking through.

TRUMPETER, an officer of a cavalry regiment; a soldier in an infantry regiment, who blows a trumpet.

TRUMPET-FISH, a name given to the *Centriscus scolopax*, a fish found in the Mediterranean, the flesh of which is reckoned good.

TRUMPET-MAKER, a manufacturer of the shrill brass wind instruments, or of speaking trumpets.

TRUMPET-SHELL, a species of *Buccinum*, used as a sounding instrument in the East and in the Pacific.

TRUNDLE, to roll any thing along.

TRUNK, the main stock of a tree; a chest for clothes.

TRUNK-FISH, the name given to several species of *Ostracion*, natives of the Indian and American seas, some of which are considered excellent fish for the table.

TRUNK-LINE, the main line of a railway, separate from the branch lines or feeders.

TRUNK-MAKER, a manufacturer of chests, and of leather portmanteaus, &c.

TRUNNIONS, the arms or side supports of a cannon, by which it rests upon the carriage.

TRUSE, an old Prussian coin of 3 coustics, worth about 7d.

TRUSI, the Malay name for copperas.

TRUSS, a small hand-packed bundle of dry goods, not bound with iron hoops or cordage, in size a yard square or less, and in weight not exceeding 3 cwt., the outer covering being frequently of canvas. If press-packed, it is denominated a bale: a truss of hay is 56 lbs. of old, and 60 of new; a truss of straw is 36 lbs.; a triangular frame of wood; an abdominal support in cases of hernia; to bind or secure; to prepare poultry for cooking.

TRUSS-MAKER, a maker of support bandages for rupture or hernia.
TRUST, a turnpike road or district managed by commissioners; property or estate managed for the benefit of others.
TRUSTEE, one appointed to act for another, as in the case of an agent for infants' property, or one deputed to act for the general benefit of creditors, &c.
TRUSTWORTHY, faithful; honest; worthy of being confided in. [or fat.
TRYING-DOWN, refining, or boiling blubber
TRYING PLANE. See PLANE.
TRYSAIL, a storm stay-sail; a fore and aft sail set with a boom and gaff, upon a try-sail mast, abaft the lower main-mast.
TRYSSIL, TRYSLE, a native bark used in Demerara for tanning, and also as an emetic and fish poison by the Indians.
TRYSTER, in Scotland, a convener; one who summons a meeting.
TSALAYS, a Burmese measure of capacity, equivalent to an English pint.
TSAMBA, a Tartar name for the meal of barley.
TSAROOT, a Burmese measure of capacity, equal to an English gallon.
TSAT-LIE, TSEU-LI, a species of China silk obtained in Nankin and the Northern parts of the empire, superior to the Canton kinds.
TSAVILA, a weight in Hindustan, of 20 grains; 2¼ chinams.
TSCHVERIC, a Russian dry-measure, 60 of which are equal to about 14 English Winchester bushels, = 13·5722 imperial.
TSEEN, another name for the mas or mace, a Chinese weight and measure, and which contains from 100 to 140 copper cash.
TSEIT, a Burmese measure of capacity, equal to 2 gallons. [breadth.
TSHAKYU, the Burmese name for a hair-
TSHELLIK, TJETLIK, an Eastern name for the *Strychnos Tieute*, a large climbing shrub, native of Java. An exceedingly violent poison, which acts in the same manner as strychnine, is prepared from the bark of the root.
T-SQUARE, an instrument for drawing.
TUALIKA, a native Indian name for the *Schmidelia serrata*, the ripe berries of which are eaten, and the astringent root is employed to check diarrhoea.
TUB, a cask without a head. Nests of wooden tubs are frequently exported. The tub of butter must contain at least 84 lbs.; the tub of camphor is 130 Dutch lbs. or about 1 cwt.; the tub, a measure of Sumatra, is equal to 1·816 bushel; a wooden vessel for a shrub or plant; a miner's name for the boxes in which coal is sent up the shaft.
TUBE, a long narrow hollow rod, pipe, or syphon, made of tin, lead, zinc, iron, brass, or copper.
TUBE-DRAWER, a maker of metal piping.
TUBER, a kind of root.
TUBEROSE, an odoriferous plant, yielding a pleasant essential oil.
TUBING, materials for pipes. See TUBE.
TEBU, the Malay name for the sugar-cane.
TUBULAR-BOILER, a boiler consisting of tubes.
TUBULAR-BRIDGE, a bridge consisting of a hollow trunk or tube, as the Britannia bridge across the Menai Straits.
TUB-WHEEL, a peculiar kind of wheel to a water-mill.
TUCK, a horizontal pleat or fold in a female's gown or petticoat.
TUCKA, a weight used for pearls in Bombay, equal to 0·2182 grain.
TUCKER, a piece of lace or net worn by females on the bosom or round the neck of a low dress.
TUCK-NET, a small net employed to take out pilchards from the large seine nets.
TUCUM, a name given by the Indians of Brazil to the fibre they obtain from the *Astrocaryum vulgare*, of Martius. From the unexpanded leaves they manufacture cordage, bow-strings, fishing-nets, hats, fans, beautifully fine hammocks, and other articles, where fineness, combined with strength, is required.
TUCUWARI, an Indian name in Guiana for porous water vessels or goglets.
TUDEL (Spanish), a metal pipe.
TUDESCO, a kind of wide cloak worn in Spain.
TUE-IRONS, blacksmiths' tongs.
TUERO, dry wood cut for fuel in Spain.
TUF, a fat loam, an unctuous marl.
TUFA, a porous variety of limestone deposited by calcareous springs, 30 or 40 quarries of which are worked in Prussia. Tufa possesses the valuable property of hardening on exposure to the air. See TRAVERTINE and TARRASS.
TUG, a tow-boat; a four-wheeled timber-frame: a hoop of iron to hold a tackle; to draw along.
TUGUE (French), the poop of a frigate or sloop. [in India.
TUHSEELDAR, a chief native revenue-officer
TUILES (French), tiles.
TUILIER, a French tile-maker.
TULAM, TOLA, a weight in Hindustan of 4 drachms; 3 madas.
TULIP, a beautiful liliaceous flower.
TULIP-TREE, the *Liriodendron tulipifera*, a North American forest tree. The bark is very bitter, and strongly fragrant, and is used for its stimulant, tonic, and aromatic qualities, in fevers, agues, and rheumatism, with the best results. The wood is smooth and fine-grained, very easily wrought, and not liable to split. It is used in carving and ornamental work, and to make the panels of coach and chaise bodies.
TULK, the Persian name for talc.
TULLE, a plain silk lace blonde or net.
TULOH, the Malay name for an egg.
TUM, a species of mastic resin obtained in Africa from the *Pistacia Atalantica*; a weight in Mysore of 32 lbs.; 2 irasas.
TUMBLER, a kind of latch in a lock, which, by means of a spring, detains the shot-bolt in its place, until a key lifts it, and leaves the bolt at liberty; a drinking-glass without a foot; an acrobat; a juggler; a posture-master; a species of pigeon. [holding hay.
TUMBREL, a dung-cart; a wicker crib for
TUMTUM, an Arab name for sumach.

Tun, a large cask, of an undefined and variable measurement, but in wine-measure assumed to contain 252 gallons, 2 butts of 126 gallons, or 4 hhds. of 63 gallons; a Finnish dry-measure of 4 English bushels; a grain-measure of Sweden containing 2 spann: 18 tuns = 10 quarters. Some reckon 176½ tuns or barrels = 100 quarters. The tun of whale oil (252 galls), according to Scoresby, weighs 17 cwt. 29 lbs. 12 oz. 14 drs.

Tunbridge-ware, inlaid or mosaic work in wood; which obtains its name from the place of manufacture, Tunbridge Wells, in Kent. They consist of fancy articles, work-boxes, caddies, desks, reels, &c.

Tuner, one who tunes a piano-forte.

Tung, a long-measure of Sumatra corresponding to the English foot.

Tung-oil, a valuable wood oil expressed in China from the seeds of *Elæococca oleifera*, which is much used for painting boats, furniture, &c.

Tun-hoof, another name for ale-hoof, the *Nepeta Glechoma* of Bentham, the *Glechoma hederacea* of Linnæus. A tea is prepared from the leaves, in great repute among the poor. *See* Ale-hoof.

Tunic, a short frock coat; a young boy's dress.

Tuning-fork, Tuning-hammer, instruments used in tuning.

Tunna, a name in Bengal for the toon tree. The bark is powerfully astringent, but not bitter. The natives use it in conjunction with the powdered nut of the *Cæsalpinia bonducella*, an intense bitter. *See* Toona.

Tunnel, a subterraneous passage for a railroad or canal; a chimney-shaft.

Tunneland, a land-measure of Sweden, 5000 square yards.

Tunnel-shaft, a pit or shaft sunk to give air to workmen or light to a tunnel, or to facilitate the raising of earth and stones to the surface.

Tunny, a fish caught in large quantities in the Mediterranean, the *Thynnus vulgaris*. The firm flesh is considered delicious. It is dressed in a variety of ways, plain-boiled, or fried, made into a ragout or soup, into pies, or pickled and eaten cold like pickled salmon.

Tup, a name in Scotland and the north of England for a ram or male sheep: after weaning he is called a tup hog.

Tupong, the Malay name for flour.

Tupoz, a name in Manila for the intermediate layers of the stem of the wild plantain, *Musa textilis*, of which are made web cloths and gauzes four yards long, of different degrees of fineness.

Tupsee, Tupsey, a name in India for the mango-fish. *See* Mango-fish.

Turanira-wood. *See* Towranero.

Turban, a linen or shawl wrapper worn round the head by males in Eastern countries; a lady's old-fashioned head-dress.

Turbine, a horizontal water-wheel used on the Continent, the water entering in the centre and filling all the buckets at once.

Turbot, the *Pleuronectes maximus*, one of the best and largest of our flat fishes: 500 or 600 tons of turbot are imported yearly into London. In Scotland this name is often given to the halibut.

Turbot-kettle, a fish boiler, of a suitable shape to hold a turbot flat.

Tureen, an earthenware or metal deep vessel for holding soup at a dinner table.

Tureen-ladle. *See* Soup-ladle.

Turf, a racecourse; the green surface or sward of grass lands; a name given to peat when cut and dried for fuel. Several chemical and economical products are now obtained from turf.

Turf-cutter, a digger of turf.

Turf-house, a shed of turf.

Turf-spade, an implement for cutting turf.

Turkey, a large domesticated fowl, the *Meleagris gallipavo*, which is bred in large numbers, in the home counties and Ireland, for the London markets, about 130,000 being annually sold in the metropolis.

Turkey-carpets, floor-coverings made entirely of wool, the loops being larger than those of Brussels carpeting, and always cut: the cutting of the yarn gives it the appearance of velvet.

Turkey-feathers, the feathers of the domestic turkey. Besides their use for bedding, these are now made into very elegant muffs, tippets, and other dress articles for ladies.

Turkey-red, a valuable dye prepared from madder.

Turkish-millet. *See* Dhurra.

Turkish-watches, watches made in pieces or sets, for the Turkish market, with several cases and Turkish figures engraved thereon.

Turk's-cap, a species of lily, a garden flower.

Turks-head, a name for the large globular *Melocactus communis*, a plant which is often imported in large quantities from the Leeward islands for cultivation in this country.

Turmeric, a name for the tubers of the *Curcuma longa*, which are bitter and aromatic, and largely used in the East as an ingredient in curries. Turmeric is imported into this country as a dye-stuff, and used to colour butter. The colouring matter of the dried root is bright yellow. White paper, dyed by an alcoholic turmeric, is a very sensitive test for alkalies.

Turn, the twist of a rope round a cleat or belaying pin; a rota or spell of duty; a pit sunk in some part of a drift.

Turn-bench, a simple and portable lathe used by clock and watch makers.

Turn-cock, the servant of a Water-company, who regulates the fire-plugs, and turns on the water from the mains to the supply pipes at stated intervals.

Turner, one who shapes articles in a lathe, a worker in ivory, hard woods, pottery-ware, &c.

Turner's-cerate, an excellent application for ulcerous wounds.

Turners'-company, one of the minor livery companies of London, which, having no hall of its own, transacts its business at Guildhall.

TURNERY-WARE, wooden articles made by a turner; wooden bowls, butter prints, blocks, &c.; goods shaped with a lathe.

TURNING-BRIDGE, a swing-bridge.

TURNING-LATHE, a lathe used by amateurs or working turners. The common lathe of the turner in wood is called a pole-lathe.

TURNIP-CUTTER, a revolving machine with knives for slicing roots for cattle and sheep.

TURNIPS, important succulent roots, forming a field or garden crop culture.

TURNIP-TOPS, the young green leaves and stems of field-turnips, sold as a potherb in spring.

TURNKEY, an assistant gaoler.

TURN-OUT, a railway siding; a short loop-line of railway; a strike of workmen, or muster of them; the net quantity of produce yielded; an equipage.

TURN-OVER, a small pastry puff: a turn-over at case, is an apprentice or compositor who is handed over from one master to another to complete his time.

TURNPIKE-MAN, a toll collector at a turnpike gate.

TURNPIKE-ROAD, a public road governed by a board or commission, having the power to levy tolls on the traffic for its proper maintenance and repairs.

TURN-PLATE. *See* TURN-TABLE.

TURN-REST PLOUGH, a swing plough.

TURN-SCREW, a blunt chisel-shaped tool for inserting or removing screws from wood-work.

TURN-SCREW MANUFACTURER, a tool maker.

TURN-SPIT, a clock-work machine for cooking, also the person who attends to the same.

TURN-STILE, a revolving frame in a foot-path to pass passengers, but to keep out animals.

TURN-TABLE, an iron revolving platform for removing carriages from one line of rails to another.

TURN-UP BEDSTEAD, a bedstead that shuts up in the middle, or packs away.

TURPENTINE, a resinous substance which flows from incisions made in the stems of trees of the pine species, of which there are several varieties, as common, Venice, French, Strasbourg, Carpathian, and other turpentines. The imports of common turpentine are from 250,000 to 350,000 cwts. annually, chiefly from the United States.

TURPENTINE AND TAR DISTILLER, a refiner of these substances for the use of those who employ them in the arts and manufactures.

TURPENTINE, OIL OF, the spirit or essence of turpentine obtained from the crude article by distillation. About one-fourth part of oil is obtained from the turpentine, the colophony being left behind in the retort.

TURPENTINE-TREE, a name for the birch gum-tree (*Bursera gummifera*).

TURPIN, a name for the land-tortoise.

TURQUOISE, a valued blue gem for ornamental purposes. It is very common in Persia.

TURREL, a cooper's tool.

TURRET, a small slender tower.

TURRET-CLOCK, a large clock fixed in a small tower or in the steeple tower of a church. The face is sometimes illuminated.

TURSKIL, TUSKAR, the flaughter-spade, an instrument used in Scotland for cutting peats.

TURTLE, a name for the marine tortoise. *See* GREEN TURTLE.

TURTLE-SHELL, a common name for the shield plate or armour of all tortoises. *See* TORTOISE-SHELL.

TURTLE-SOUP, the most expensive and esteemed soup made; the flesh of the edible or green turtle added to an ordinary soup stock.

TURUNJABIN, an Indian name for the manna of the desert, obtained from the camel's thorn.

TUSBIE, the rosary or string of beads used by the Hindoos.

TUSCAN-HAT, a Leghorn hat; a bonnet of straw-plat.

TUSCAN-PLAIT. *See* LEGHORN.

TUSK, a long fang or tooth. The tusks of the elephant form an important article of commerce.

TUSSAC-GRASS, a large hardy coarse grass, the *Dactylis cæspitosa*, native of the Falkland Islands, which has been introduced and cultivated in Scotland.

TUSSAH-SILK, TUSSEH-SILK, the produce of a wild silk-worm found in the forests of Bengal, from the cocoon of which a coarse dark strong silk is obtained, and woven into the dooties or cloths worn by the Brahmins and other sects of Hindoos. This silk-moth cannot, however, be domesticated.

TUSSOO, an Indian measure of length, 16 of which equal 1 hath or 18 inches.

TUTENAG, an alloyed metal made by the Chinese in the proportion of 8 parts of copper, 3 of nickel, and 6½ of zinc; which is fusible, very hard, and not easily rolled, but well adapted for casting.

TUTOR, a private teacher; the guardian of a scholar or learner.

TUTSAN, the *Androsæmum officinale*, a wild astringent subarid plant, the bruised leaves of which are an ancient and powerful vulnerary.

TUTTAL, a name in some parts of the East for six pice, or about 2d.

TUTWORK, a miner's name for piece-work or task-work.

TUWAK, a Malay name for the spirituous liquor or toddy obtained from the *Arenga saccharifera*.

TUYERE, TWEER, a round aperture made in one of the sides of a crucible to admit the extremity of the blast pipe, through which the air, in a high state of compression, is forced into the furnace.

TWA, the Burmese name for a span.

TWANKAY, a superior kind of green tea, of which there are several sorts: the best is sometimes sold for hyson of an inferior growth.

TWEED, a light woollen stuff; a milled Scotch trousering or wrapper worn by shepherds and others.

TWEER, TWEERE, the point of a blast pipe, a tube analogous to the nose of a bellows, by which compressed air is forced into a blast furnace. The term is also applied to the hole or aperture in the crucible. *See* TUYERE.

TWEEZERS, a small kind of pincers or holders; nippers to pluck out hair from the face.

TWELFTH-CAKE, an ornamented cake distributed among friends or visitors on the festival of Twelfth-night, the 6th January.

TWELFTH-NIGHT CHARACTERS, a sheet of printed fancy figures coloured, to be cut up and distributed by lottery among young persons.

TWIBILL, a tool of different kinds for mortising, paving, &c.; a mattock; a reaping-hook.

TWILL, a woven, ribbed cloth.

TWILLY, a common name for the willying machine.

TWINE, thread or string; small yarn or cordage that has been twice twisted.

TWINE-REEL, a shop reel or box for holding string.

TWINE-REELER, a mule doubler; a string-twister.

TWIST, silk in hanks, balls, and reels, &c. for sewing, used by tailors and milliners, saddlers, book-binders, stay-makers, &c.; a roll of tobacco; a small roll of twisted dough baked; a kind of cotton yarn, of which there are mule, *water, and* green twists: the *Nos. run from 20 to 100.*

TWISTER, an American drink.

TWO-DECKER, a vessel of war, carrying guns on two decks.

TWO-FOOT RULE, a carpenter's measure; a folding pocket-rule.

TWOPENCES, small silver coins, specially minted to a fixed amount, being 4752 in number annually, for alms-giving by the sovereign, on Maunday-Thursday. In 1848, however, a larger quantity was issued, of the value of £2217, and numbering 266,112 pieces; 7920 silver pennies are also annually coined for the same special purpose.

TWOPENNY, a weak kind of beer sold at twopence the Scots pint, or 1½ quart English.

TWO-SHILLING-PIECE. *See* FLORIN.

TWYER, an Indian grain-measure. *See* TOL.

TWYERE. *See* TWEER.

TYE, a rope connected with a yard, to which a hoisting tackle is attached.

TYLERS' AND BRICKLAYERS' COMPANY, one of the minor livery companies of London, which has no hall.

TYLT, the Danish name for a dozen.

TYMPAN, the parchment frame or panel of a hand printing-press, on which the blank sheets are put in order to be impressed when laid on the form.

TYMPSE, a Polish coin of 18 gros, or half a florin, worth about 9d. or 10d.

TYPE, a model or pattern; metallic letters, spaces, figures, &c. used for printing.

TYPE-FOUNDER, one who casts printing or music type.

TYPE-FOUNDRY, a place with furnaces, &c., for casting type in moulds and matrices.

TYPE-METAL, an alloy of about one part of antimony to three of lead, used in casting printing-type; other metals are sometimes added.

TYPE-MOULD, a die, steel-punch, or matrix of brass or copper for casting types.

TYPE-MOULD MAKER, a maker of casting moulds, which consist of two parts, the outer of wood and the inner of steel: there is a hopper mouth into which the fused type-metal is poured.

TYRE, an Indian name for curdled milk.

TYRIAN-PURPLE, a beautiful animal dye, formerly obtained from certain molluscs, species of *Murex* and *Purpura*.

U.

UBI, the Malay name for yams; ubi bungala being potatoes.

UBRUK, the Hindustani name for talc.

UBUDI, a name in Guiana for the bark of the wild cashew-tree, a powerful astringent. Surprising effects are ascribed to warm applications of the decoction in the cure of sores.

UCHAUX, a liquid-measure, in use in some of the departments of France, being the half pint, or fourth of a pot, of the ancient measures of Paris.

UDOMETER, a rain-gauge.

UEBA, an African dry-measure, about 8 bushels, used in Barbary and Tripoli; for flour it weighs 230 2-5th lbs.

UFYOON, an Arabic name for opium.

UGOORO, a vernacular name in India for eagle-wood, and aloes wood, obtained from species of *Aloexylon, Aquilaria*, and *Excœcaria*.

UKASE, a Russian imperial decree.

UKKAH, the Eastern name for the oke, about 2¾ lbs English.

ULAN, a Tartar horse-soldier.

ULEMA, a Turkish magistrate.

ULLAGE, what remains in a cask, after a portion is gone; a cask only *part full*.

ULSEE, a Hindustani name for flax.

ULTRAMARINE, a beautiful blue pigment, formerly very expensive, and obtained from the variegated blue mineral called lazulite, but now artificially compounded, and greatly reduced in price.

UMBAREE, a vernacular name in India for the fibre of the *Hibiscus cannabinus*, also for inferior hemp.

UMBER, a massive mineral pigment, used by painters as a brown colour, and to make varnish dry quickly. It is used either in its natural state, or burnt.

UMBLES, HUMBLES, the entrails of a deer.

UMBRELLA, a portable folding shade, or protection against heat and rain; a screen of linen, silk, or paper, on a frame of cane, wire, or whalebone ribs or stretchers. *See* KITTYSOLS, and PARASOL.

UMBRELLA-CASE, a narrow oilskin bag or cotton case for covering an umbrella when folded and closed.

UMBRELLA-FURNITURE MAKER, a manufacturer of alpaca, cotton, &c. for covering umbrellas.

UMBRELLA-GINGHAM, a kind of fine material for covering the frame of umbrellas.

UMBRELLA-HOOK MAKER, a manufacturer of the handle-ends for umbrellas, consisting of horn, bone, ivory, &c.

UMBRELLA-MAKER, a manufacturer of umbrellas.

UMBRELLA-STAND, a frame or support for resting or draining umbrellas.

UMBRELLA-STAND MAKER, a maker of wooden, wire, or cast-iron stands for umbrellas.

UMBRELLA-STICK, the centre support for carrying and extending the frame of an umbrella.

UMBRELLA-TREE, a name in India for a species of screw-pine, the *Pandanus odoratissimus.*

UMLI, a name in Hindustan for the tamarind.

UMPIRE, an arbitrator chosen to decide a disputed question.

UMRITI, USEEKKEE, vernacular names for the myrobalon of the *Emblica officinalis* used for tanning leather, and as a remedy in diarrhœa.

UNBEND, to cast off the tie of a rope; to relax.

UNCIA, an ounce troy, or in liquids the twentieth part of a pint. It is thus abbreviated in prescriptions ℥.

UNCIR (Spanish), to yoke oxen or mules for labour.

UNCOCK, to let down the hammer of a gun or pistol.

UNCOOKED, raw; not dressed by heat.

UNCTUOUS, fat, oily, having a resemblance to grease.

UNDER-COAT, a coat worn under a paletot or great-coat.

UNDERFOOT, a kind of granite paving.

UNDER-GROUND, below the surface of the earth.

UNDERLEAF, an apple for making cider [from.

UNDERLET, to sub-let.

UNDER-SECRETARY, an assistant secretary.

UNDER-SHERIFF, a sheriff's deputy.

UNDERSHOT-WHEEL, the wheel of a water-mill, where the water is received into the buckets on a low level.

UNDERTAKER, a contractor or manager of funerals; a coffin-maker.

UNDERWRITER, one who takes a risk or share in marine insurance, writing his name on the policy of insurance as answerable for a certain amount in case of loss, upon receipt of an agreed rate of premium.

UNDERWRITERS' ASSOCIATION, a union of merchants interested in marine assurance or underwriting, of which there are many at different ports, as at Glasgow, Lubeck, Liverpool, &c.

UNDOCK, to remove a vessel from a wet dock or basin.

UNFASHIONABLE, garments, furniture, &c. not in the present mode.

UNFLAVOURED GIN, pure, distilled gin; not sweetened or doctored.

UNGEROOT, an Arabic name for gum sarcocolla.

UNGLEE, a cloth-measure in the Nizam territory: 8 unglees = 1 gerah of 2 1-10th inches.

UNGOOR, a Persian name for the kind of grape grown for wine-making in that country, the *vitis vinifera.*

UNGOOZEH, a Persian name for asafœtida.

UNHAIR, to scrape the skins of pigs; to remove the hair from seal-skins, sheep-skins, calf-skins, or horse-hides, &c., by steeping in lime and water. [hinges.

UNHANG, to take a door or gate off its

UNHOOK, to undo a hook and eye.

UNIBIE, a coin formerly current in the dominion of the Grand Mogul, = to one French crown and 3 livres.

UNIDURA (Spanish), the act of yoking oxen or mules for labour.

UNIFORM, an official or state dress or equipment for court, naval, military, company, and other officers; a livery for police, gaolers, &c.; articles made of the same shape or pattern.

UNIFORM SWORD, an officer's sword of the regulation pattern prescribed for the army or navy.

UNION, a fabric made of flax and cotton; a confederation of States; a workhouse or poor-law district of several townships; a joint or connection; the upper inner corner of an ensign.

UNION-JACK, the national flag of the Royal navy of England; a small square containing only the union of the three crosses without the fly of the ensign.

UNION-JOINT, a band or T cross-piece; a T joint for uniting iron and other metal pipes.

UNION-TICK. *See* COTTON-TICKS.

UNIVERSITY, a corporation or community; an assemblage of colleges, with an examining body, where the arts and sciences are taught, and educational degrees granted.

UNLADE, to remove the cargo; to take merchandise or stores out of a vessel.

UNLAY, to untwist the strands of a rope.

UNLICENSED, acting without a legal authority or permit.

UNMOOR, to heave up one anchor, so that a vessel may ride at single anchor; to cast off from moorings.

UNOFFICIAL, in a private capacity, not emanating from an office, or state bureau.

UNPACK, to take goods from their wrappings or cases; to unbale.

UNPAID, sent or received without the carriage, freight, or postage being paid; an honorary officer, one who gives his services or opinions gratuitously.

UNQUOTED, goods not in the sale lists, or prices current; shares or stocks not dealt in or recognized in the official lists of the Stock Exchange.

UNREAD, a proof not examined by the Reader or Corrector of a printing-office.

UNREEVE, to remove ropes or pulleys from a block or tackle.

UNRIG, to take down the standing and running rigging, or ropes of a ship, leaving the bare masts, with only the stays, &c., as supports.

UNRIP, to open seams; to separate, or tear cloths or sails asunder.

UNSEAL, to open; to take off or remove the seal which closes a letter or package.
UNSEAWORTHY, a ship not safe, or properly found and fitted for navigation, or for carrying cargo. [any thing.
UNSHIP, to take out of its place, to remove
UNTAMOL, a name in Hindustan for the Indian Ipecacuanha, the dried roots of *Tylophora asthmatica*.
[U]NTIE, to loosen a bandage; to unbind.
UNUNTAMUL, a name in India for the roots of *Hemidesmus Indicus*, which have long been employed on the Madras coast as a substitute for sarsaparilla.
UPER, the Belgian half-pint measure, equal to 0·605 English pint.
UPHOLDER, an old name for an upholsterer.
UPHOLDERS' COMPANY, one of the minor livery companies of London, which has no hall.
UPHOLSTERER, one who supplies the furniture and fittings for dwelling-houses.
UPHOLSTERY, the beds, curtains, furniture, tables, chairs, and general household articles sold by an upholsterer.
UPPER-LEATHER, the vamps and quarters of boots and shoes.
UPPER NURSE, a head nurse having the care of children in a private family.
UPPER SERVANT, a superior female domestic in a private family.
UPRIGHT, a timber supporting a rafter; an iron stanchion or pillar.
URADO, a peculiar kind of rock-salt met with in Colombia.
URCHILLA (Spanish), orchilla-weed; archil.
URINAL, an erection in a street for public convenience; also a portable water-proof case for travellers and others.
URJOON, a name in Hindustan for the *Terminalia alata*, the fruit and bark of which are used medicinally.
URKAN, the Arab name for the *Lawsonia inermis*, an important dye-stuff. *See* HENNA.
URLINGS' LACE, a quilling net, figured; a raised lace, a showy, low-priced substitute for pillow or thread lace.
URN, a metal hot water receiver for the tea-table, formerly more extensively used; a vase bending outwards at the top; a measure of 3½ gallons; a ballot-box.
URN-POWDER, a bronzing powder for renovating the varnish or coating on metal urns.
URN-RUG, a table mat or stand made of various materials, for resting an urn on.
UROOS, UTARASHA, Indian names for the *Adhatoda Vasica*, Nees. All parts of the plant are bitterish, and slightly aromatic, and supposed to be antispasmodic: the wood is soft, and much esteemed for making charcoal for gunpowder.
USAGE, custom; the ordinary course of business.
USANCE, the customary period or space of time allowed for the payment of foreign bills of exchange; days of grace.
USEREKRE. *See* UMUITL.
USHER, an under-teacher; an attendant upon strangers or guests; the doorkeeper of a court of justice.
USINE, a glass-house; an iron-work.
USQUEBAUGH, a kind of whisky.
USTORUK, a vernacular name in India for storax.
USULSOOS, an Arabic name for liquorice-root.
USURY, the taking an excessive or exorbitant rate of interest for money loaned. Usury-laws, or those fixing a legal rate of interest, are now abolished in most trading countries, leaving floating capital to find its proper market value.
USWUKUNIDA, a vernacular name for the saul or sal tree, the *Shorea robusta*, Roxburgh, which yields the dammar resin.
UTCHLIK, a small silver money of Turkey, of the value of 5d. or 6d. English.
UTR, an Eastern name for the essential oil or attar of roses.
UTRECHT-VELVET, a kind of velvet, used for decorations, furniture, upholstery, and carriage linings.
UTRERO (Spanish), a bull or heifer between two and three years old.
UVATE, a conserve made of grapes.
UVERO, a retailer of grapes in Spain.
UZALTUN, the half of an abassi in Georgian money.

V.

VAAG, WAGE, a German name for a balance or weight.
VAAM, VAEM, VADEM, Dutch and Belgian names for the fathom; in Holland 6·178 feet, in Belgium, as in England, 2 yards.
VAARSILD (Danish), spring herrings.
VAATJE, the Dutch name for a barrel.
VAGA, a name in some of the Pacific islands for a vessel or canoe.
VACH, the Sanscrit name for the sweet flag, *Acorus Calamus*.
VACOA, a name for a species of screw pine, the *Pandanus utilis*, which abounds in the Mauritius and Bourbon, where, from the tough longitudinal fibres of the leaves, sacks for colonial produce are made. (The leaves are cut every second year, and each plant yields enough for two large bags. [in the colonies.
VACUUM-PAN, a pan used for making sugar
VACUUM-PUMP, a pump attached to a marine steam-engine.
VADARI, a vernacular name in India for the jujube-tree, *Zizyphus Jujuba*, which affords a large and very pleasant fruit, called ber and berree. *See* JUJUBE.
VADE-MECUM, a book of ready general reference; a manual of instruction, or recipes.
VAGABOND, VAGRANT, an idler; a man with a bad character.
VAGOLE, a name in the Shetlands for a place where meat is hung to be smoked.

Vail, a gratuity or fee given to domestics; a perquisite, customary or stipulated, such as bones, and grease, and broken meat to a cook; left-off garments to a personal servant.

Vainero (Spanish), a scabbard-maker.

Vainga, Vengay, an Indian name for the dark-red astringent, brittle, gum-resin or kino, obtained from the juice of the *Pterocarpus Marsupium*.

Vakeel, a native attorney in India; an ambassador or agent.

Vakia, an Eastern weight used chiefly in Arabia for spices, &c., consisting of 10 coffolks and nearly 1¼ oz. English: in Bassora the heavy vakia is 4·833 pounds, and the light weight for spices, &c., 1·166 pound.

Val, Wall, a variable Indian weight for gold and silver; in Bombay = 4·475 grs.; in Ahmedabad, 6·045 grs.; in Anjar, 5·6 grs.; in Delhi, 5·63 grs.; in Poonah, 8·90 grs.; and in Surat, 5·850 grs.

Valance, drapery or hangings for a window, bedstead, &c.

Valbriok (Danish), maple.

Valenciennes-lace, a rich lace which has a six-sided mesh formed of two threads partly twisted and plaited, the pattern being worked in the net.

Valendar-clay, a kind of potters'-clay exported, in a raw state, from the Duchy of Nassau.

Valentine, an ornamented billet-doux, or printed love-letter with verses and devices, sent out extensively on the 14th February, St. Valentine's day.

Valerian, the common name for a genus of plants which have stimulant and aromatic qualities. The true valerian (*Valeriana officinalis*), is a remarkable feline stimulant. All the species have some medicinal properties. *V. celtica* is largely employed as a substitute for spikenard (*Nardostachys Jatamansi*) by Eastern nations.

Valet, a man-servant; a personal attendant on a gentleman when dressing.

Valisalou Oil, an oil expressed in India from the seeds of the *Guizotia oleifera*.

Valise, a small leather portmanteau or carpet-bag.

Valle-cypre, a name formerly given to a silk mourning crape, also known as Bologna-crape.

Vallum, an Indian measure of capacity in the Carnatic, = 8⅜ quarts.

Valonea, Valonia, a commercial name for the large capsules or acorn cups of the *Quercus ægilops*, which are imported in considerable quantities for the use of tanners, being much more portable and concentrated in its tanning properties than bark. In 1850, we imported 22,783 tons of valonea.

Valve, a close lid affixed to a tube or hollow piston, or the opening in a vessel, by means of a hinge or other moveable joint. There are various kinds, as the clack-valve, steam-valve, safety-valve, &c.

Vamp, the upper leather or covering of a shoe above the sole. In Russia, there are velvet, satin, silk, chamois, and morocco leather vamps, embroidered in silver and gold.

Van, the front of an army or fleet; a large, covered wagon for pleasure excursions, &c.; a provincial term for sifting ore or cleansing it by a shovel.

Vandola, a musical instrument used by the Arawack Indians, Guiana.

Vandyke, an indent or scollop to a flounce or border, &c.

Vandyke-brown, a colour so named.

Vane, a flag or weather-cock at the mast-head of a ship, or the top of a flag-staff, or on a steeple, &c. to indicate the direction of the wind.

Vaneza, a superficial measure of Verona, = 0·0314 acre.

Vang, a seaman's term for a rope for steadying the peak end of a gaff.

Vanglo, a West Indian name for the teel seeds of the East (*Sesamum orientale*).

Vanilla, an exquisite perfume and aromatic, the thin pod-like capsule of the *Vanilla planifolia*, a native of South America. Vanilla is one of the most esteemed of all aromatics, and very expensive, costing five or six guineas the pound. It is used to flavour chocolate and confectioneries, and is much esteemed on the Continent as an ingredient in some stimulating and tonic remedies.

Vannerie (French), basket-work.

Vanning, a rocking motion given to a shovel with ore by miners.

Vapour-bath, an application of steam and friction, to produce copious perspiration.

Vaquero, a Spanish cow-herd; a jacket worn by women and children.

Vara (Spanish), a rod or pole; a yard; a herd of 40 or 50 swine; a Spanish measure of length, the Castile ell, ordinarily = 0·925 English yard. The Havana vara = 0·927 English yard, and 1 English yard = 1·078 Havana vara. Usually 100 varas are considered equal to 90 English yards, but in Chili 108 varas make 100 imperial yards, and 5000 varas make one Mexican league: the Mexican vara is 3 geometrical feet. In Teneriffe the vara is 34½ English inches; in Alicant 29⅞ inches; in Buenos Ayres and Mexico 0·92741 yard; in Valparaiso and Lima, 0·92687 yard; in Brazil, 1·18878. The standard vara of Burgos is 0·91319 yard, and the miners' vara of Gallicia 1·19715 yard. The solid vara of Spain is 20·561 cubic feet. In Chili the vara is about 33 English inches. *See* Sitio.

Varagoo, the Tamil name for the millet seed. *Panicum miliaceum*.

Varahun, a name in the Madras presidency for the commercial pagoda, the 10th of the pollam and the 8th of the seer, weighing 54·68 grains; and for the native pagoda which is 52⅝ grains.

Varana, a vernacular name in India for the garlic pear *Cratæva tapia*. *See* Tapia.

Varchilla, a Spanish grain-measure, the third part of a fanega.

Varbage (Spanish), retail trade.

Vareo (Spanish), measurement.

Vari, a weight used for the precious metals, in Madagascar 80 grains.

Varicose-stockings, elastic or bandaged stockings for giving pressure and support to swelled veins in the legs.
Variegated, mottled; stained with different colours.
Varina's-roll, a kind of tobacco generally plaited round a thick stick, very much like Canaster.
Varnish, a thin resinous coating for wood, paper, metal, &c. impervious to air and moisture. Turpentine and all the principal resins are used to form different varnishes, of which there are numerous varieties; these may, however, be broadly classified into two kinds, spirit and oil varnishes.
Varnish-maker, a manufacturer of spirit and oil varnishes, who dissolves the commercial resins in rectified alcohol or fixed and volatile oils.
Varsar, a Sanscrit name for the aromatic seeds of *Cleome pentaphylla*. See Caraila.
Vase, a large cup with handles; a kind of urn.
Vassa, an Indian weight for pearls and the precious metals, used at Surat, = 0·1423 grain.
Vassal, a dependant or retainer.
Vasseau, Vaisseau, French names for the Flemish vat.
Vat, a large wooden or metal cistern or tub; the legal liquid-measure of Belgium and Holland, containing 100 kannen or litres corresponding to the French hectolitre, = 22·01 imperial gallons. The old Dutch grain vat averaged 0·76215 Winchester bushel. The shipping vat weighs 2204·74 lbs. The old London coal vat contained 9 bushels. The solid measurement vat of Amsterdam contains 40 cubic feet; the wine vat 241·57 gallons, and the vat for olive oil 225·45 gallons.
Vaudkikeat, a water telescope invented in Norway, for discovering objects below water.
Vault, an arched roof; an underground apartment, generally used as a store for wine, and other articles not injured by damp; a tomb or crypt; a repository for the dead.
Veal, the flesh of the calf.
Veal-cutlet, a steak from the thick part of the leg of a calf.
Veal-pie, a pastry of veal.
Veal-skins, an Irish trade-name for hides of the calf, which are dearer than other leather. See Calf-skins.
Veal-tea, a thick gelatinous soup or broth made of the fleshy part of the fillet or knuckle of veal, and given to sick persons.
Veata, a Singhalese long-measure equal to an English foot.
Vedette, Vidette, a mounted sentinel; an out-post; one sent out to reconnoitre.
Vedro, the principal Russian measure for liquids = 2·7051 imperial gallons, and containing 100 charkeys. This measure was definitively determined at 750 cubical English inches for its contents: 100 vedro are equal to 270·51 imperial gallons, and 100 imperial gallons = 36·97 vedro.
Veer, to let out, as slacking a cable or hawser; to change, to shift suddenly.
Veerker, a dry-measure of Oldenburg = 1·6436 bushel, and corresponding to the werp, a measure used in the kingdom of Hanover.
Veete, the smallest Singhalese long-measure, equal to a grain of rice.
Vega (Spanish), an open plain.
Vegetables, a common name for all plants and roots raised for food.
Vegetable ivory, a name given to the osseous albumen in the nut of a dwarf South American palm, the *Phytelephas macrocarpa*. These nuts (called corossos) are much used by turners, for many ornamental purposes, in imitation of elephant ivory. See Corozo.
Vegetable-ornament-cutter, a person who cuts out with a shape, vegetables for supper tables, déjeûners, &c. as ornaments or garnishes for dishes.
Vegetable-marrow, an important gourd, the *Cucurbita ovifera*, used as a pot-herb in its intermediate or half grown state.
Vegetable-soups, soups made with green pease, turnips, and carrots cut small, cabbages, &c.; pease-soup; julienne; soup maigre, and other thin pottages.
Vegetable-wax, a kind of wax obtained from the candleberry myrtle and other sources. See Candleberry Myrtle and Wax-palm.
Veguer, in Arragon, the magistrate of a district.
Vehicle, a conveyance of any kind; the means of carrying out any operation.
Vehrte, a dry-measure used in Stralsund = 0·27640 Winchester bushel.
Veil, a lady's bonnet-fall; a thin gauze or lace screen for the face.
Vein, a stratum of ore or mineral; to stripe or mottle, to marble, &c.
Velarte, a kind of fine Spanish broad-cloth.
Velenge, a Ceylon wood used for making betel trays, &c.
Veleria, a tallow-chandler's shop in Spain.
Velete (Spanish), a light thin veil.
Velfalla, a kind of Spanish linen.
Vellanga, Yelanga, vernacular Indian names for the wood-apple, *Feronia Elephantum*, from which a large quantity of good gum is obtained. The young leaves are used by native practitioners as a gentle stomachic stimulant in the bowel-complaints of children.
Vellon, a money in which accounts are kept in many parts of Spain. The Spanish term strictly means copper coin.
Vells, a provincial name for the maws or stomachs of young calves used for rennet.
Vellum, a fine kind of parchment made from the skins of very young calves; a name for crystallized jaggery or palm sugar in Ceylon.
Vellum-binder, a bookbinder who covers books with vellum.
Vellum-post, a smooth kind of writing paper.
Velocimeter, an apparatus for measuring the rate of speed of machinery.
Velocipede, a propelling machine, a light seat or road carriage, worked through the agency of a lever, connecting rod, and crank, by the pressure of the feet on pedals attached to the wheels.
Velon (Spanish), an oil-lamp.

VELOURS, a kind of velvet or plush for furniture, carpets, &c. manufactured in Prussia; partly of linen and partly of double cotton warps with mohair yarn weft.
VELOURS-D'UTRECHT, a woollen velvet for tapestry and furniture coverings made in the Netherlands.
VELOUTE (French), velvet lace.
VELOUTIER (French), a velvet-maker.
VELTE, a small cask used in France for brandy, measuring about 6 quarts (1·640 gallons). In Germany and Holland this measure is called a viertel.
VELVERET. *See* FUSTIAN.
VELVET, a soft dress material woven wholly from silk, or of silk and cotton mixed, having a loose pile or short shag of threads on the surface.
VELVET-BRUSH, a brush used by ladies to remove dust, &c. from garments made of velvet.
VELVET-DRESSER, a cleaner and dyer of [velvet.
VELVETEEN, a kind of fustian. *See* FUSTIAN.
VELVET-MANUFACTURER, a weaver of velvet.
VELVET-MOSS, a name for the *Gyrophora murina*, a lichen used in dyeing, obtained in the Dovrefeldt mountains of Norway.
VELVET-PILE, a kind of carpet with a long soft nap.
VELVET-WEAVER, a maker of velvets.
VEND, a sale; the whole quantity of coal sent from a colliery in the year.
VENDOR, one who disposes of any thing: a usual condition in a public sale of landed property, is, that the vendor shall be entitled to bid only once for an estate.
VENDUE-MASTER, a licensed auctioneer in the Colonies.
VENEER-CUTTER, one who saws furniture wood into thin lengths, by steam-power machinery.
VENEERS, thin sections or sheets of choice fancy woods, for overlaying furniture. By the aid of beautifully adapted circular saws, worked by machinery, veneers are often cut of the thickness of one-fortieth of an inch, a little thicker than a sheet of writing-paper. *See* SCALE-BOARDS.
VENETIAN-BLIND, laths of wood strung together serving for a window-blind, and which can be raised or lowered by a string.
VENETIAN-DOOR, a door lighted by panes of glass on each side.
VENETIAN-RED, a scarlet ore when pure, but the colours usually sold under this name are prepared from sulphate of iron. Venetian red is sold either in lumps or in powder.
VENETIAN-WINDOW, a window with three separate lights.
VENGAY-GUM. *See* VAINGA.
VENICE-SOAP, a mottled soap made with olive-oil and soda, with a little sulphate of iron in solution, or sulphate of zinc.
VENICE-TURPENTINE, an oleo-resin obtained from a variety of the larch, *Larix Europœa*; it is used in the manufacture of sealing-wax.
VENISON, the flesh of the *Cervus dama*. *See* FALLOW-DEER.
VENISON-DISH, a metal dish to keep venison hot at table.
VENISON-PASTY, flesh of the fallow-deer made into a pastry baked, &c.
VENISON-PLATE, a hot plate for eating venison on.
VENTAPOLLAM, a kind of Indian handkerchief.
VENTIER (French), a wholesale dealer in standing wood; a woodmonger.
VENTILATOR, a windsail or canvas funnel or machine for conveying air into a ship, mine, or building; a pane of perforated plate-glass, or revolving sheet of metal in a window or door; an apparatus in the chimney of a room to carry off heat, &c.
VENTOUSE, a cupping-glass.
VENTOY, a fan.
VENT-PEG, a spile or peg to stop a vent-hole.
VENT-PIPE, an air-pipe; an escape pipe for steam.
VENTS, a Scotch name for chimneys, as kitchen and room vents.
VENTURE, a risk or stake; a speculation.
VENTURINA (Spanish), a precious stone, of a yellowish-brown colour.
VENUE, the county, district, or locality in which an action is to be tried.
VENUS'-HAIR, the *Adiantum capillus-Veneris*, given as an expectorant, and forming the basis of the celebrated syrop of capillaire. *See* CAPILLAIRE.
VERANDAH, an open portico attached to a house; trellis-work round a colonnade or covered walk facing the lower windows, opening to a lawn or garden.
VERANDAH-BUILDER, a maker of wire or wood lattice-work.
VERBAL-AGREEMENT, a contract or agreement made by word of mouth.
VERBENA, an otto, one of the finest perfumes, obtained by distillation from the citron-scented leaves of *Aloysia citriodora*. Owing to its high price it is successfully imitated for ordinary purposes, by mixing the otto of lemon grass with rectified spirits, and this passes as oil of verbena.
VERCHOKE, a Russian linear measure, the sixth of an archine, = 1¾ English inches.
VERD-ANTIQUE, a species of green mottled serpentine marble, much valued for its beautiful markings.
VERDE, VERDEA, a white Tunisian wine.
VERDEE, a white Florentine wine.
VERDELHA, a variety of white grape producing a Madeira wine.
VERDERER, a forest officer.
VERDICT, the judgment or award of a jury.
VERDIGRIS, the acetate of copper, obtained by exposing thin plates of copper, for some time, to the action of the cake or marc of the wine-presses in the South of France. Besides the French verdigris, there are green distilled, common, and crystallized verdigris.
VERDITER, a name for varieties of a blue pigment; a hydrated percarbonate of copper. It is generally prepared by decomposing the solution of nitrate of copper by the addition of chalk. There are refined blue, and green verditers.
VERDULERO, a green-grocer in Spain.

VERGE, the spindle of a watch balance; a rod, wand, or mace; a jurisdiction; a measure of length in France or Belgium, the mean of which, in the former country, is 6·70645 yards, and in the latter 5·50404 yards. It is also a superficial measure, the mean being 0·00026 acre in Belgium; 0·00654 in Holland; and 0·00029 acre in France. A French name for the English yard-measure.

VERGEE, an ancient land-measure in Normandy and the Channel islands, = ·5046 acres, 2 ⅔ vergees making a statute English acre; a French measure of 538 square yards.

VERGE-MAKER, a maker of pallets; a branch of the watch-movement trade.

VERGER, the beadle of a cathedral church.

VERGUILLA (Spanish), gold or silver wire without silk.

VERIFICATEUR (French), a custom-house landing-waiter; an auditor.

VERINO, a fine kind of Spanish tobacco, named from the place of its growth. *See* VARINAS-ROLL.

VERITAS, the name of the French shipping establishment, similar to the English "Lloyds."

VERJUICE, the sour juice of fruit not ripe.

VERLE, VERGE, other names for the velte, a German liquid-measure. *See* VELTE.

VERMEIL (French), silver gilt, or gilt bronze.

VERMICELLI, the flour of a hard small-grained wheat, made into dough, and formed into smaller pipes or threads than maccaroni, and then dried until hard. It is drawn out into slender cylinders, more or less tortuous, like worms, whence the Italian name. Maccaroni is made of a less compact dough than vermicelli.

VERMIFUGE, an anthelmintic; a medicine that expels worms.

VERMILION, the bisulphuret of mercury in powder, a delicate bright red colour, which is pale or deep. The Chinese vermilion is sold in packets.

VERMIN, a collective name for all kinds of predatory animals and insects, as foxes, moles, rats, beetles, &c.

VERMUTH, a kind of wine.

VERNIER, a moveable index, used for measuring minutely the parts of the space between the equidistant divisions of a graduated scale, affixed to barometers, theodolites, and most optical instruments used in surveying.

VERNIMBOK (French), a name for the Pernambuco dye-wood.

VERNIX, a name for sandarac.

VERRE (French), glass; a liquid-measure, the tenth part of the new pint of France. *See* DECILITRE.

VERONA-SERGE, a thin worsted and cotton fabric. It is also made of mohair and cotton, and of various colours.

VERSARA, an Italian land-measure, equal to 3 English acres.

VERST, WERST, a Russian itinerary measure of 3501 feet; 1 verst = 0·663 British statute mile; 1 British statute mile = 1·508 Russian verst.

VERVEUX; LOUVRE (French), a sweep-net; [a fruit basket.

VESA, a name in the Pacific islands for an armlet or bracelet.

VESNO, a weight used in Syria, equal to 25·3274 lbs. Some authorities make it rather less, 25·136 lbs.

VESSEL, a ship or boat; a cask or utensil for holding liquids.

VESSETS, a kind of cloth.

VESSIES (French), bladders; blisters.

VEST, a man's waistcoat.

VESTA, a kind of wax match.

VESTIBULE, a porch or entrance hall; an ante-chamber or lobby. [coats.

VESTING, cloth or silk material for waist-

VESTRY, an ante-room in a church for priests to robe in, for keeping documents, or transacting parish affairs in; a body of assembled parishioners.

VESTRYMAN, a delegate from parishioners.

VETCH, a leguminous plant, the *Vicia sativa.* *See* TARES.

VETCHLING, the *Lathyrus Aphaca*, the seeds of which produce intense headache, if eaten in any quantity.

VETERINARY-SURGEON, one who attends to the diseases of horses and cattle.

VETIVEYR, a name for the Khuskus grass; a scent or perfume so named. *See* CUSCUS-ROOT.

VETTILEI, an East Indian name for the *Piper Betle.* *See* BETEL-LEAF.

VETTURA (Italian), a travelling-carriage.

VIADRA, WIADER, a liquid-measure of Wallachia, = 3·144 gallons.

VIADUCT, an elevated erection, resting on a series of arches, for the conveyance of a road or railway across a valley.

VIAL, a small long bottle.

VIANDS, dressed meat; food.

VICAR, the clergyman of a parish receiving the small tithes; a deputy or substitute.

VICARAGE, the residence or dwelling-house of a parish priest.

VICAR-GENERAL, the deputy of a bishop; an officer of a clerical convocation.

VICE, an iron screw-tool or holdfast, used by smiths, of which there are many kinds, as hand, bench, and parallel vices, fishing-vices, &c.; a machine used by glaziers for drawing lead into flat rods for case windows; a deputy; an acting chairman.

VICE-ADMIRAL, a superior officer of the Royal navy; a junior admiral, ranking with a Lieut.-general of the army. There are vice-admirals of three grades, who hoist respectively a red, white, or blue flag.

VICE-ADMIRALTY COURT, a court in a district having Admiralty powers.

VICE-BENCH, a workman's bench to fasten a vice to.

VICE-CHAIRMAN, a person who presides at the lower end of a table, supporting and aiding the chairman or president; the deputy-chairman of a board of officers.

VICE-CHANCELLOR, a lower judge of chancery; the acting president of a university.

VICE-COMMODORE, a deputy commander of a naval squadron. [consul.

VICE-CONSUL, an assistant or deputy-

VICE-MAKER, a manufacturer of iron vices.

VICE-MEN, coach-smiths whose work is at the vice instead of the anvil.

Vice-president, a deputy-chairman.

Viceroy, a governor or officer administering the powers of a Kingdom or State.

Vicessis, an ancient Roman weight of 20 lbs., equal to 14·937 pounds avoirdupois.

Vice-warden, the acting or depute officer of a warden, as of the Lord-Warden of the Stannaries court.

Vichy-water, a mineral water.

Vicissy-duck, a West Indian water fowl, smaller than the European duck, and very excellent eating.

Victimize, *to rob* or cheat; to impose upon a person.

Victorine, a small tippet or short tie of fur for a lady's neck.

Victual, a general name for food, provisions.

Victualler, in Scotland a corn factor; in England a publican or innkeeper. There are about 70,000 victuallers in England: in 1855 there were 155,144 licensed retailers of beer, either classed as victuallers, or merely licensed to sell beer to be drunk or not drunk on their premises.

Victualling, laying in stores; taking in provisions.

Victualling-bill, a certified account of a ship's stores or provisions.

Victualling-note, an order given to a seaman in the Royal navy by the paymaster, when he joins a ship, which is handed to the ship's steward as his authority for victualling the man.

Victualling-society, a union or association of operatives, &c. to supply themselves with meat and bread, &c. at the lowest prices.

Victualling-yard, a government storeyard for supplying provisions to vessels of war.

Vicuna, a species of the alpaca tribe furnishing a long reddish wool used for fabrics and for felting to cover hats.

Vidange (French), ullage.

Vidette. *See* **Vedette**.

Vidimaram, a vernacular Indian name for the *Cordia Myxa*. The wood is soft, and one of the best for affording fire by friction. The bark is deemed a mild tonic. The dried fruits of this and of *C. latifolia* have long been used as a medicine in India under the name of Sebistans or lobestens. They are slightly laxative, and are much esteemed as a pectoral. The seeds are deemed an infallible remedy in ringworm. The pulp is equally as aperient as that of the Cassia fistula.

Vidonia, a Spanish wine imported in pipes of [illegible] gallons. *See* **Teneriffe**.

Vidrecome (French), a tumbler or large drinking glass.

Vidriero (Spanish), a glazier.

Vierdevat, an old grain-measure of Amsterdam, equal to 1½ gallon.

Vierding, an Austrian weight, the quarteron or fourth of the Vienna pound, equal to [illegible] lb.

Vierdupt, a Dutch word for quarteron or fourth, an old weight of Amsterdam equal to [illegible] lb.

Vierfass, **Viermass**, a dry-measure of Germany, ranging from 1·455 gallon to 1·711 gallon.

Vierkante, the Dutch term for square, thus the vierkante elle is the square ell of Amsterdam. The unit of superficial measure, answering to the centiare or mètre carrée of France.

Vierkante-bunder, the square bunder or bonnier, a Belgian superficial measure of 0·0247 acre.

Vierling, an Amsterdam weight of 5·933 grains; a liquid-measure of Bremen, = 0·21276 wine gallon; a dry-measure used in Germany and Switzerland, varying from 0·14669 Winchester bushel to 1·04028 ditto. It is also a superficial measure equal to 0·3236 acre in Hanover, and varying in dimensions in Zurich according as it is applied to woodland, tillage, or vineyard.

Viermass, a dry-measure of Brunswick equal to 0·22112 Winchester bushel. *See* **Vierfass**.

Viersel, a dry-measure of Germany of 5½ to 6 gallons.

Viertel, a German word for fourth, applied to liquid and dry measures, of very variable capacity in different towns and States; also a solid and superficial measure. For beer and spirits it is ordinarily about 2 English gallons, though occasionally much more. The Hessian viertel, as a grain-measure, is equal to 53-100th parts of an English quarter. In Vienna the metzen, of 4 viertels or 8 achtels is equal to 1·69 imperial bushel. The last of 37½ viertels in Belgium is equal to 10½ imperial quarters. As a liquid-measure the Cologne viertel = 1·171 gallon; in Vienna it is 3·102 gallons.

Viertelein, a grain-measure used in Wurtemberg, = 0·3047 pint. This name is also sometimes applied to the Swiss chopine.

Viertell, a liquid-measure of Berne in Switzerland, = 0·7257 pint.

Vierzel, a grain-measure of Treves varying from ⅛ to 1 Winchester bushel; in Switzerland it is 7·519 bushels.

View, a sketch or design; a survey or examination.

Viewer, the superintendent of a coal mine; a road surveyor.

Vigessis, a multiple of the as, a Roman weight, and expressing 20 lbs. *See* **Vicessis**.

Vignette, a small woodcut or printed illustration on a page.

Vignoble, a French vineyard.

Villa, a country residence; a detached house; one surrounded by a garden or grounds.

Villivina, a kind of Spanish linen.

Villoria, a farm-house in Spain.

Villorin, coarse Spanish cloth.

Vinaigaret, **Vinaigrette**, a small fancy bottle for ladies to hold aromatic vinegar or smelling salts.

Vinaigrette (*French*), a kind of two-wheeled chair drawn by a man, like a Bath chair.

Vinaza (Spanish), the last wine drawn from the lees.

Vine, a general name for any climbing plant, but applied especially to the *Vitis vinifera*, a shrub or climbing tree cultivated for its fruit for the table or for making wine.

VINE-DRESSER, a cultivator and trimmer of grape vines.

VINEGAR, an acid liquor largely manufactured by fermenting vegetable juices, or from alcohol, sugar, cider, wood, &c. *See* ACETIC-ACID. [gar.

VINEGAR, AROMATIC. *See* AROMATIC-VINE-

VINEGAR-CRUET, a bottle in a set of table-castors for vinegar.

VINEGAR OF CANTHARIDES, a pungent blistering liquor, extracted from the vesicatory beetle: a piece of blotting paper soaked in it makes a ready blister. *See* CANTHARIDES.

VINEGAR-PLANT, the *Mycoderma aceti*, called the mother of vinegar, which acts as a ferment in making vinegar, serving the purpose of yeast.

VINEGAR, THIEVES'. *See* THIEVES'-VINEGAR.

VINEGAR-YARD, a place where vinegar is exposed to season.

VINERO, a Spanish vintager; one who owns and cultivates vineyards.

VINERY, a greenhouse or hothouse where vines are cultivated, and grapes ripened by artificial heat from stoves and flues.

VINE-YARD, an enclosure or garden where grape vines are grown.

VINGERHOED, the legal Dutch and Netherlandish liquid-measure, corresponding to the French centilitre, = 0·0176 pint. 10,000 vingerhoeds make a vat, and 100 vingerhoeds or 10 maatjees, a Netherland kan.

VINTAGE, the season of gathering grapes.

VINTEM, a Brazilian copper coin of the value of 1½d.; a Portuguese coin formerly current at Goa, containing 15 basaracos of 2 reis each. [made and used in France.

VIN-ORDINAIRE, a kind of common claret

VINTNER, a wine-seller; a privileged member of the Vintners' company who can sell wine without licence.

VINTNERS'-COMPANY, the eleventh in rank of the twelve principal livery companies of London, which received its first charter in the 38th year of the reign of Edward III. Its hall is in Upper Thames-street.

VIOL, a stringed instrument larger than the violin.

VIOLET-DYE, a dye produced by a mixture of red and blue colouring matters which are applied in succession.

VIOLET-POWDER, powdered starch or flour scented, used by females to powder the skin.

VIOLETS, SYRUP OF, a pleasant medicine, formerly used, but now considered of little or no value except as a *placebo*.

VIOLET-WOOD, another name for king-wood.

VIOLIN, a musical instrument which has four gut-strings, the last or lowest covered with silver wire. The back, neck, sides, and circles, are generally made of sycamore, the belly, bass-bar, sound-post, and six blocks of deal; the finger-board and tail-piece of ebony.

VIOLIN-BOW, a bow strung with horse-hair, for playing on a violin. [violins.

VIOLIN-MAKER, a maker of fiddles or

VIOLIN-STRING, prepared gut stretched across the bridge of a violin.

VIOLONCELLO, an instrument somewhat similar to the violin but larger, and held between the knees of the player. [illegible] the two lowest strings covered with [illegible] wire.

VIRGINAL, a kind of piano; a stringed [illegible] keyed instrument resembling the sp[illegible] —formerly in great repute.

VIRTUOSO, one skilled in antique or n[illegible] curiosities.

VIS, VISS, an Indian weight which [illegible] times bears the name of the [illegible] The Burmese viss or picktha is 140 [illegible] 100 ticals, 40 pollams or 8 catties, = [illegible] 2 oz.; 8 vis, therefore, make a ma[illegible] 25 lbs. The viss, however, varies [illegible] ferent localities: in Trichinopoly, [illegible] 3 lbs.; in Masulipatam, 3·515 lbs.; [illegible] some other places it is much more.

VISA, an official endorsement on a pa[illegible] &c.

VISARY, a name in the Madras presid[illegible] for the vis, which there weighs 3·14 [illegible]

VIS-A-VIS, a dress carriage for town u[illegible]

VISCOUS, clammy or tenacious.

VISHALA, an Indian name for the colo[illegible] or bitter apple. The seeds are s[illegible] constitute an important article of [illegible] Northern Africa.

VISIT, the attendance of a surge[illegible] physician, inspector, &c.

VISITE, a lady's mantle worn over the [illegible] ders. [illegible]

VISITING-CARD, a name-card; an ad[illegible]

VISSARY, a large kind of fan made [illegible] East, from the leaves of the Palm[illegible] palm, *Borassus flabelliformis*.

VISWAKEE, WISWEESA, an Indian [illegible] measure, of from 4½ to 5 inches; a [illegible] ficial measure of 20 to 24 square inc[illegible]

VITELA (Spanish), calf-skin leather; v[illegible]

VITELLUS (Latin), the yolk of an egg.

VITELOTTE (French), a kind of lo[illegible] potato.

VITRE (French), a pane of glass.

VITREOUS, resembling glass.

VITRIOL, white vitriol is a combina[illegible] sulphuric-acid and oxide of zinc. [illegible] other vitriols. *See* BLUE-VITRIOL, G[illegible] VITRIOL, and RED-VITRIOL.

VITTIE-VAYR, another Indian name [illegible] cuscus grass, *Andropogon muricat[illegible]*

VIVANDERO (Spanish), a sutler.

VIVARIUM, a pond or tank, &c. for k[illegible] fish in.

VIVDA, VIFDA, a name in Orkney [illegible] Shetlands for beef or mutton hu[illegible] dried, without being salted.

VIVIANITE, a blue phosphate of iro[illegible] sionally used as a pigment. [fo[illegible]

VIVRIER (French), an agent or vict[illegible]

VOKBOKETZ, a kind of German w[illegible] goods, sold in the Cape colony [illegible] Dutch.

VOET, a Dutch long-measure, vary[illegible] different towns from 0·30016 ya[illegible] 0·31194 yard. [open [illegible]

VOIDER, a tray for table leavings; a [illegible]

VOIE, an old dry and solid measure [illegible] France, of very variable quantity.

VOILE (French), a sail. [illegible]

VOITURE (French), a carriage or [illegible]

VOLA, a Sanscrit name for myrrh.

VOLIGE (French), a thin plank of w[illegible] wood.

Voltigeur, a light horseman.
Volume, a chemical expression for a portion or part; a roll or book; a body of gas.
Volunteer, one who serves in any capacity as a soldier, and of his own accord, and at his own charge.
Vomit-nut. *See* Nux-vomica.
Vording, a Riga coin, = 1½ grosschen or 4½ whittens, and about nine-tenths of a penny in value.
Vorling, a Hanoverian superficial measure, = 0·3234 acre.
Vortanqui, the Spanish name for sapan-wood.
Vote, a suffrage; a decision given by division, by word of mouth, or by ballot.
Voting-paper, a balloting paper; a proxy.
Vouah, a measure of length in Siam, = 2·10193 yards.
Voucher, an instrument or document of any kind produced to substantiate a statement of account or disbursements, &c.
Voussoirs, a name for the ring-stones or those forming an arch.
Voyage, a passage taken by sea.
Voyageur, a Canadian river boatman.
Voyol, a large rope for weighing an anchor.
Vuccah, a thick rope for dragging timber, made in Travancore.
Vuccoonar, a kind of yarn, of which canvas is made in Travancore.
Vugh, a mining term for a large cavity.
Vulcanized India-rubber, a mixture of 23 parts of caoutchouc with 5 of sulphur and 7 of white lead, largely used for tubing.
Vulnerary, any application useful in the cure of wounds.
Vulture-feathers, feathers of species of *Accipitres*, imported from Bombay, and sold for stuffing beds, &c., the larger ones for making artificial flowers, &c.
Vushira, a vernacular name in India for the *Pothos officinalis*, a large creeper. The fruit cut in thin transverse slices is the "guj-pipul" of the Bengal bazaars, and highly esteemed as a stimulant tonic.

W.

Waag, a Danish and Norwegian weight, = 39·631 lbs. The waag for tin in Sweden is 123·2608 lbs.
Wad, old rope or rounding for covering the charge and shot in a cannon; paper, card-board, &c. used to ram down the charge of a fowling-piece, &c.
Wadaduri, a native name in British Guiana, for the monkey-pot tree, *Lecythis grandiflora*, Aublet. It grows to a large size. The wood is hard, close grained, and handsome; it is used for furniture, and makes good staves for hogsheads. The very singular pericarps contain a great number of oleaginous seeds, larger than almonds, which are much esteemed by the Indians, although they leave a bitter taste in the mouth.
Wadaler-gum, an Indian name for the inspissated juice of *Acacia catechu*.
Wadd, Wad, provincial names for plumbago, and for manganese ore.
Wadding, a soft loosely woven stuff used by tailors; a spongy cotton web for quilting or lining clothes; loose tow for a cannon. *See* Wad.
Wadding-manufacturer, a maker of sheets of cotton wool for padding or stuffing, and for packing jewellery and other delicate articles in boxes.
Wadmal, a coarse, hairy, woollen fabric.
Wadset, a mortgage of goods.
Waduhanea, a Cingalese carpenter's measure, composed of 24 angulas, which is divided into four parts. The angula is equal in length to a grain of rice.
Wafer, a thin, round leaf of baked paste for sealing letters, or for making official impressions on, at the foot of documents. Wafers are made of flour, isinglass, yeast, and white of eggs, dried in thin layers upon tin-plates, and cut out by a circular instrument; they are coloured by red lead, &c.; a thin, crisp sweet cake.
Wafer-stamp, a metal or other seal with a handle, engraved with some device to impress wafers.
Waffle, a thin cake baked hard on an iron.
Waffle-iron, a griddle for baking cakes.
Wage, Waag, a Prussian and Belgian weight. In Belgium [illegible] lbs.; in Antwerp the waag for [illegible] is [illegible] lbs.; in Bremen for [illegible] lbs.; in Denmark and Norway it is only [illegible] lbs.
Wages, hire; the price paid for labour or services.
Waggonette, a carriage to carry six or eight persons.
Waggonette-phaeton, a convenient, roomy carriage.
Wagon, Waggon, a long, four-wheeled, strong-built luggage cart; a railway goods van; a travelling-cart drawn by bullocks in the Colonies.
Wagon-boiler, a low-pressure boiler for an engine, with an arched top.
Wagoner, the driver of a wagon.
Wagon-master, the officer in charge of a baggage train. [wagons.
Wagon-shed, a shelter for carts and
Wagon-wright, a maker and mender of wagons.
Waif, a stray; an article picked up at sea; any thing left without an owner.
Wai-fa, the unexpanded flower-buds of *Sophora Japonica*.
Wain, another name for a wagon.
Wainscoting, the timber lining of a room.
Wainscot-oak, logs of oak imported from the Baltic, for cutting into planks or slabs for furniture, or for panelling rooms.
Wair, a plank 6 feet long by 1 foot broad.
Waist, the part of the upper deck of a ship, between the quarter-deck and forecastle.

WAISTBAND, a lady's sash; the band of the trousers above the waist.

WAIST-BELT, a child's or man's leather belt.

WAIST-CLOTH, a long cotton wrapper worn round the waist by natives of India. *See* DHOTEE.

WAISTCOAT, a man's sleeveless vest; an under-garment worn within the coat. Grooms and other servants sometimes wear outer waistcoats with sleeves.

WAISTCOATINGS, a kind of fancy fabric made of worsted, worsted and cotton, or worsted and silk, in which there is a pattern of some kind or other, worked by the loom; different-coloured yarns being employed. These fancy goods are chiefly made at Huddersfield.

WAITER, a table attendant at an inn or eating-house; a salver or tray.

WAITING-MAID, a lady's toilet assistant.

WAITRESS, a female attendant at table in an eating-house, or refreshment-room.

WAITS, night-musicians at Christmas-time.

WAKEA, a weight of Northern Africa, = in Algiers to 0·752470 pound; in Abyssinia to 0·057823 lb. It is also used commercially, and for gold and silver in Mocha, and the Red Sea coasts. *See* VARIA.

WAKSA (Russian), shoe-blacking.

WALES, the strong side-planks of the body of a ship, running fore and aft.

WALK, the district served by a milk-man; any portion of the ambulatory of the Royal Exchange, London, which is specially frequented by merchants or traders to some particular country. *See* MILK-WALK.

WALKING-STICK, a staff or cane to walk with; of these there are numerous kinds, as Malacca-canes, Penang-lawyers, Whanghees, Supple-jacks, and other fancy varieties.

WALKING-STICK MAKER, a preparer of sticks and canes, who barks, varnishes, mounts, and ornaments them, and often also makes handles for umbrellas and parasols. The walking-stick trade is a very extensive and profitable one.

WALL, a brick or stone erection for a fence; the side of a building or room; a sailor's term for a large knot put at the end of a rope; a German name for four-score, or eighty pieces; an Indian weight for gold and silver. *See* VALL.

WALLABA, the *Eperua falcata* of Aublet, a tree abundant in British Guiana, the wood of which is of a deep red colour; it is hard and heavy, but splits freely and smoothly, and is much used for shingles, staves, palings, posts, house-frames, &c. The wood may be cut 30 or 40 feet long, and 15 to 20 inches square. It will not bear any lateral strain, and therefore should not be used for beams longer than 12 feet. The bark may be used for tanning, and a resin, that exudes from the tree is applied to fresh-cuts or wounds.

WALLAMBA, WARRAMBI, a kind of sieve made by the Indians of Guiana.

WALLER, a mason; a term applied to men loading flats, a description of river-boat or barge.

WALLET, a travelling-bag; a pedlar's bundle.

WALL-FRUIT, grapes, stone-fruit, &c. grown on trees trained along walls.

WALL-PAPER. *See* PAPER-HANGINGS.

WALL-PLATES, timber resting on side-walls to support girders, &c.

WALL-ROCK, an American name for granular limestone.

WALL-STREET, the thoroughfare in New York, occupied by bankers and brokers, corresponding to Lombard street in London.

WALNUT, a well-known tree and its fruit; a common name for several species of *Juglans*, forming tall, stately trees, and esteemed for their seeds or fruit. The wood, from its handsome marking, is extensively used by cabinet-makers and turners, solid and veneered; it is also considered superior to any other for gun-stocks. Large quantities of walnuts are imported from the Continent.

WALNUT-OIL, a bland and useful oil obtained by expression from the walnut, which is made to some extent in Europe and in Cashmere.

WALNUT-PICKLES, young walnuts with the outer rind on, salted and pickled in vinegar.

WALRUS, a name for the morse or sea-horse, the *Trichechus rosmarus*, sought after in northern latitudes for the oil obtained from its blubber, and for its teeth, which furnish the most dense ivory for dental purposes.

WAMARA, a native name for the brown-ebony of Demerara, the wood of which is hard and cross-grained; consequently not apt to split; it would therefore answer various purposes in naval architecture. It may be had from six to twelve inches square, and from 20 to 40 feet long. It is one of the handsomest woods of the colony, and would make beautiful furniture.

WAMPUM, a native name given to certain white and black shells, used as money, strung on a belt, by some of the North-American Indians. The shells used are a periwinkle, and the *Venus mercenaria*, a bivalve.

WAND, a thin rod of office; a lecturer's pointing-stick.

WANGALA, WANGLO, a name in British Guiana for the seeds of the *Sesamum orientale*, which, when parched and pounded, make a rich soup. Their use as an oil-seed has been noticed under Gingelie. The fresh leaves of this plant, when broken and slightly bruised in cold water, form a mucilaginous drink, used as a domestic remedy in dysentery.

WANGHEE, WHANGHEE, a name given to some canes imported from the East as walking-sticks, derived from the Chinese *Wang* yellow, and *hee* root, and said to be the root of the narrow-leaved bamboo. They are valuable on account of the sufficiently straight roots being difficult to procure. Many bamboos must consequently be destroyed before those particular roots of the requisite length and straightness can be obtained. The whanghee has a pale, hard bark, and flexible stem, with internodes of about an inch and a half, or two inches, and a number of little holes at the knots.

WANKELU, an inferior kind of paddy used by the poorer classes in Cuddapah and other parts of India.

WANNE, a solid measure for hay used in Wurtemberg, being a cube of 8 feet, or, according to some authorities, 425·187 cubic feet.

WANTY, a leather girdle.

WAPENTAKE, a hundred or district; the term is derived from weapon taking, a review or inspection of arms in olden times.

WARANANA, a large timber-tree of British Guiana, the wild orange, the wood of which is much used in the colony for oars and staves.

WARANDEUR (French), an overseer or inspector of herring-salting; a herring-curer.

WARD, a division or section of a lock; an apartment in a penitentiary, hospital, workhouse, &c.; a division of a city or town.

WARD-BEADLE, a parish or district officer; the summoner of a ward-meeting, &c.

WARD CLERK, an officer of a city ward.

WARDEN, a custodian or guardian; a head officer in some companies, colleges, &c.; a kind of pear.

WARDIAN-CASES, glass enclosures for keeping ferns, &c., or transporting growing plants from a distance; named after the inventor.

WARD-INQUEST, a meeting of the citizens of a ward at a court-leet, or to inspect weights and measures, examine into nuisances, collect alms for the poor, &c.

WARD-MOTE, a ward-meeting or assemblage of citizens of a ward for public business.

WARDROBE, a collection of wearing-apparel; a detached piece of furniture for keeping the same in.

WARD-ROOM, the room in a ship of war, in which the commissioned officers, down to the assistant-surgeon, live and mess.

WARE, any saleable merchandise, as hardware, tinware, earthenware, smallwares, &c.

WAREE, a grain-dealer in India.

WAREHOUSE, a store-room or wharfinger's premises; a shop; a place for depositing goods which have not paid customs-duty.

WAREHOUSEMAN, the owner or keeper of a dock-warehouse or wharf-store; a person who keeps a wholesale shop or store for Manchester or woollen goods.

WAR-HORSE, a charger; a trooper's horse.

WARIALEE, an Indian name for fennel-seed.

WAR-INSURANCE, an extra premium paid for the risk on marine insurance in time of war.

WARMER, a vessel to heat beer, &c.

WARMING-PAN, a brass covered pan holding heated coals to warm the sheets of a bed.

WARP, a small rope or short hempen cable for a ship; a tow-line; the threads which run longitudinally from end to end of a fabric, and are crossed by the weft or woof; a name among the Yarmouth fishermen for 4 herrings; to flood land so as to leave a deposit of rich slime or soil; to tow or draw a ship by a rope made fast to buoys, piers, &c.

WARPER, a woman who forms the woollen yarn or thread into warps or webs for the looms.

WARPING-HOOK, a rope-maker's hook for turning yarn.

WARP'S-LENGTH, a short cable distance.

WARRACOORI, a native name for the wood of the white cedar, obtained in Demerara from the *Icica altissima*. It is light, easily worked, and very aromatic, and is used for oars and paddles, and for boards for the inside work of houses.

WARRANT, an authority or commission of any kind from a magistrate, or superior executive officer or body; a commission from the Admiralty to petty officers of a vessel of war. A dock warrant is a custom-house licence or authority.

WARRANT OF ATTORNEY, a special power of attorney to do some particular act for another, as to receive dividends, execute transfers of stocks, &c., which differs from a general power of attorney.

WARRANT-OFFICER, an executive officer in a ship of war, ranking next to a subordinate commissioned officer; the gunner, boatswain, and carpenter, are warrant-officers.

WARRANTY, a guarantee given of the character or soundness of merchandise or goods sold, or of a horse.

WARREN, a piece of waste ground where rabbits are bred.

WARRI-WARRI, a kind of Indian fan made by the natives of Guiana, of the leaves of the acuyuru palm, the *Astrocaryum aculeatum* of Meyer.

WARRY, a name in India for the sedimentary deposit from carnelian in grinding the stone, which is used for polishing the beads.

WASH, ten strikes of oysters; the wet refuse of cookery, or of distilleries, &c.; a cosmetic or lotion; fermented wort; a mixture of dunder or waste saccharine juices, used for distilling.

WASH-BALL, a ball of soap; a sand-ball for washing the hands with.

WASH-BOARDS, pieces of board placed above the gunwale of a boat; skirting boards.

WASHED, covered with a thin coat of metal; linen cleansed by soap and water, and friction.

WASHER, a circular ring of stamped iron or leather used in connection with a bolt or screw.

WASHERWOMAN, a laundress.

WASHHAND-BASIN, an earthenware basin for a toilet stand; they are also made of gutta-percha or metal, for office, kitchen, or ship use.

WASHIBA, a strong, hard, durable, and elastic wood of Guiana, much esteemed by the Indians for bows.

WASHING-MACHINE, an agitating machine with revolving balls, or beaters, to save manual labour in cleansing linen.

WASHING-TUB, a long deep wooden tray or round hooped tub, for washing clothes in.

WASH-LEATHER, split sheep-skins prepared with oil in imitation of chamois, and used for household purposes, for dusting, cleaning glass, plate, polishing brasses, &c.; alumed or buff leather for regimental belts.

WASHSTAND, a piece of bedroom-furniture for holding ewer and basin and other requisites for washing the person. Sometimes it has a marble top.

WASTE, the refuse of cotton or silk; moorland or untilled ground.

WASTE-BASKET, a small office or library basket, for holding loose waste papers.

WASTE-BOOK, a tradesman's book for making rough entries in.

WASTE-PAPER, spoiled paper; old office writings, newspapers, &c. bought by waste-paper dealers, to sell again to shopkeepers, for wrapping-paper, or to papermakers to work up into fresh paper.

WASTE-PIPE, a discharge-pipe for surplus or used water, &c.

WASTRELS, waste substances.

WATCH, a pocket time-piece, a well-known horological instrument for computing time, convenient for its portability: 14,000 or 15,000 gold watches, and 80,000 or 90,000 silver watches are annually assayed at Goldsmiths' Hall. Besides these, large numbers are imported from the Continent. In 1855, we received 82,706 gold, and 61,922 silver, watches, valued together at £218,410. Some watches are now made with such precision as to vary but a few seconds in the course of a year. Those constructed with the greatest possible accuracy, and intended for astronomical or nautical observations, are called chronometers. A labour spell, or division of time aboard ship, usually of four hours, but there are two watches called dog-watches, of only two hours.

WATCH AND CLOCK DIAL SILVERER, one who silvers the face of time-pieces, a branch of the dial-maker's trade.

WATCH AND CLOCK GLASS MAKER, a branch of the clock trade, a person who employs blowers and makers of glass. *See* WATCH GLASS.

WATCH AND CLOCK TOOL MAKER, a mechanist who prepares the fine class of tools required in watch and clock making.

WATCH BALANCE-WHEEL MAKER, a branch of the movement-maker's trade.

WATCH-BARREL, the brass box which contains the spring, and to which it is attached at one end.

WATCH-BOX, a sentry-box.

WATCH-CAP MAKER, a branch of the watch-making trade; a workman who makes the cover for the works, and employs the springer, &c.

WATCH-CASE GILDER. *See* WATCH-GILDER.

WATCH-CASE MAKER, a branch or division of the watch-making trade; a person who employs a box-maker, outside-case maker, and joint-finishers.

WATCH-CHAIN, a short gold chain, attached to the pendant of a watch, to suspend a key and seals to; a guard-chain or broquet for a watch carried in the waistcoat-pocket.

WATCH CHAIN MAKER, a manufacturer who employs several separate workers, as wire-drawer, link-maker, and rivetter, hook-maker, &c.

WATCH-COCK AND POTENCE MAKER, a branch of the movement-maker's trade.

WATCH-DIAL-PLATE MAKER, a branch of the watch-making trade, a person who makes the face, and employs a copper-maker, an enameller, painter, &c.

WATCH-DOG, a house-dog; one kept to guard premises, or to give notice of trespassers.

WATCH-ENAMELLER, a branch of the watch-making trade. *See* WATCH-DIAL-PLATE MAKER.

WATCH-ENGRAVER, a branch of the watch-trade; a workman who employs a piercer and name cutter.

WATCH-ESCAPEMENT MAKER, a manufacturer of that part of a watch connected with the beats which we hear it give; these beats are the effects of the moving power, carried forward by means of the wheels in the movement to the last one, called the balance-wheel.

WATCH-FINISHER, a workman who puts the parts of a watch together, and employs a wheel and fusee cutter, and other workers in smaller branches.

WATCH-FITTER-IN, a branch of the watch trade; a person who overlooks the whole, fits hands on the dial, &c.

WATCH-FRAME-MOUNTER, a branch of the watch-movement maker's.

WATCH-FUSEE MAKER, a branch of the watch-movement maker's trade.

WATCH-GILDER, a division of the watch trade, which is divided into two branches, the gilder and brusher.

WATCH-GLASS, a small convex glass; a crystal segment of a hollow sphere, used to cover the face of a watch, in order to read the time and protect the hands. Lunette glasses are not segments of spheres, but have their edges abruptly raised, and the interior flattened; an hour-glass.

WATCH-GUARD, a ribbon or chain worn round the neck, attached to a watch pendant.

WATCH-HAND MAKER, a branch of the watch-making trade; a person who makes the metal pointers or indicators for the face of a watch, and employs a die-sinker, finisher, &c.

WATCH-JEWELLER, the person who attends to the diamond-cutting, setting, making ruby holes, &c.

WATCH-JOINT FINISHER, a branch of the watch-making trade.

WATCH-KEY MAKER, a manufacturer of the metal keys of different kinds, made to wind up watches.

WATCH-MAKER, a manufacturer, finisher, vender, examiner, or cleaner of watches; an artificer who arranges and fits together, in due order, the separate parts of a watch, after they have been cast or prepared by special workmen.

WATCHMAN, a night-guardian or policeman.

WATCHMAN'S-RATTLE, a large spring rattle to sound an alarm or to call for assistance.

WATCH-MOTION MAKER, a division of the watch-making trade, which includes other branches, as slide-maker, edge-maker, and bolt-maker.

WATCH-MOVEMENT MAKER, a division of the watch trade, comprising many branches, as pillar maker, stop stud maker, frame mounter, screw-maker, cock and potence maker, verge-maker, pinion-maker, balance-wheel maker, wheel-cutter, fusee-maker, and other small branches.

WATCH-OIL MAKER, a person who prepares and vends the limpid oils required for oiling the movements of a watch.

WATCH-PALLET JEWELLER. *See* WATCH-JEWELLER.

WATCH-PALLET MAKER, a maker of the verge of watches, the pallets of which alternately stop the teeth of the swing or balance wheels.

WATCH-PAPER, an old-fashioned fancy ornament, or thin tissue lining, for the case of a watch.

WATCH-PENDANT MAKER, a person who makes the handle and ring outside of a watch to hold or suspend it: both case and pendant are sent to Goldsmiths' Hall to be marked.

WATCH-PILLAR MAKER, a branch of the watch-movement trade.

WATCH-PINION MAKER, a branch of the movement-maker's trade.

WATCH-POCKET, a small pocket fastened to the head curtains of a bed to place a watch in at night.

WATCH-SCREW MAKER, a branch of the movement-maker's trade.

WATCH-SECRET-SPRINGER, AND SPRING-LINER, a division of the watch-making trade, which is further subdivided into other branches, comprising the spring-maker, button-maker, &c.

WATCH-SPRING, the fine steel main-spring, which, being fastened at one end to the barrel, and at the other end to an arbor or axle, unwinds off the fusee, turning it, and keeping the watch going, while the action accords by its varying size with the varied energy of the spring. By the force thus produced other wheels are put in motion, from which the time is exactly measured by the hands on the dial.

WATCH-SPRING MAKER, a manufacturer of main-springs for watches, who employs a wire-drawer, hammerer, polisher, temperer, &c.

WATCH-STAND, a mantel-piece or toilet rest or support for a watch.

WATCH-STOP-STUD MAKER, a branch of the business of the watch-movement maker.

WATCH-WHEEL CUTTER, a branch of the watch-movement maker's trade.

WATCH-WORK, the steel, brass, and other machinery and parts of a watch.

WATER, the lustre of a diamond; a common well-known fluid. As an article of trade, water is vended from house to house in many towns, where the inhabitants have not easy access to it: it is supplied by itinerant water carts, at so much per bucket. In cities there are water companies, with certain vested rights, that convey the water through streets by large pipes called mains, and supply the cisterns, &c. of the householders at an annual rent charge. Water is often supplied to ships' boats in casks or breakers, or by hose, and taken on board for use on the voyage.

WATER-BAILIFF, an officer having charge of the police of a fish-market, harbour, or river.

WATER BOTTLE, a glass toilet-bottle; a bottle for holding water at table.

WATER-BUTT, a puncheon or large cask without a head, used for collecting rain water.

WATER-CAN, a tin vessel for holding water for a dressing-room.

WATER-CARRIER, a bearer or vender of water.

WATER-CART, a cart with water for sale, or for watering the roads and streets.

WATER-CASKS, breakers or other casks used for holding water for ships' use.

WATER-CEMENT, hydraulic cement. *See* BETON, and CEMENT.

WATER-CLOCK, a contrivance for measuring time by the flow of water; the clepsydra of the ancients.

WATER-CLOSET MAKER, a manufacturer of house privies, supplied with water for cleansing them.

WATER-COCK, a tap for drawing water; a street plug to supply water from the mains in case of fire.

WATER, COLOGNE. *See* COLOGNE-WATER.

WATER-COLOUR-DRAWING, a painting executed and finished with colours worked up with water.

WATER-COLOURS, cakes of pigment for drawing, that can be rubbed down with water.

WATER-COMPANY, a joint-stock company, which collects water for distribution through a town.

WATER-COOLER MAKER, a potter who makes porous jugs, &c.

WATER-COURSE, the bed of a stream; a channel for water through a town or fields.

WATER-CRANE, a machine for supplying water to locomotive engines.

WATER-CRESS, a wholesome vegetable, the *Nasturtium officinale*, of which fully 750 tons are annually sold in the London markets.

WATER-CRESS SELLER, an itinerant vender, usually a female, of bunches of water-cresses.

WATER-DISH, a dish-metal, or tin lined with china.

WATERED-SILK, variegated silk; silk with a shaded or diversified surface. *See* SILK-WATERER.

WATER-ENGINE, a steam-engine to raise water.

WATER-FILTER. *See* FILTER.

WATER-FLASK, a portable bottle for water.

WATER-GAUGE, a tide-gauge; a rain-gauge; any measurer of the depth or fall of water.

WATER-GILDER, a person who gilds with a thin coat of gold amalgam, and volatilizes the mercury.

WATER-GUARD, a river police; Customs officers stationed on the water.

WATER-GUM, a very fine tree of New South Wales, the *Tristania nerifolia*, with lofty cylindrical boll. The timber is close-grained and elastic, and valuable for boat-building. The tree reaches 100 to 120 feet, with a diameter of 30 to 50 inches.

WATERING-CART. *See* WATER-CART.

WATERING-PLACE, a seaside resort; a town frequented for drinking mineral waters or bathing; a cab-stand where water is supplied to horses; an oasis in the desert where caravans obtain water from a well; a pond or water-hole for cattle; a spring or river whence ships are supplied.

WATERING-POT, a metal pot with a rose or perforated spout for watering plants.

WATER-JAR, WATER-JUG, vessels for holding water.

WATER-LEADING, a permitted leat or water channel in the Cape colony, for bringing water for irrigation.

WATER-LILY, a general name for species of *Nymphæa*, beautiful plants which are much cultivated. The stems of *N. alba* are superior to oak galls for dyeing grey. The *Victoria Regia* is one of the most elegant and prized water-lilies.

WATER-LOGGED, a marine term applied to ships which have so much water in the hold as to be unmanageable.

WATERMAN, a boatman or ferryman; an attendant on cab-stands who supplies water to the horses.

WATER-MARK, a letter, device, or impression, wrought in paper during the process of manufacture, by means of wire or brass plates sewn on the hand-mould, or the dandy-rollers of the paper-machine; the tide-level on a shore, indicating the extent of the rise and fall of the tide; the float-line or sinking depth of a ship.

WATER-MEADOWS, low, flat pasture ground, capable of being irrigated from some adjoining river or stream.

WATER-MELON, a variety of the *Cucumis Citrullus*, an esteemed cooling fruit in warm climates.

WATERMEN AND LIGHTERMEN'S COMPANY, one of the livery companies of London, whose hall is at St. Mary-at-hill.

WATER-METER, an instrument for registering the supply of water.

WATER-MILL, a flour-grinding or other mill, the machinery of which is set in motion by the action of water upon a wheel.

WATER-PIPE MAKER, a caster or moulder of pipes for supplying water.

WATER-PITCHER, an earthenware jug for carrying water.

WATER-PLUG. *See* WATER-COCK.

WATERPROOF-CLOTH MAKER, a person who prepares cloth to stand the wet; an India-rubber cloth maker.

WATERPROOFING, rendering cloth, linen, or leather, &c., impervious to water.

WATER-PURIFIER, a filter.

WATER-RATE, a tax levied for the supply of water to householders.

WATER-RETTING, steeping flax in water to soften the stem, and fit the fibre for beating.

WATERS, MINERAL, about 37,000 gallons of these are annually imported from abroad.

WATER-TABLE, a projection or horizontal set-off on a wall, so placed as to throw off the water from the building.

WATER-TANK, a fixed cistern on shore, or a metal receiver on board ship for holding water. *See* TANK.

WATER-TAP, a cock to let out water.

WATER-TRUNK, a deal cistern lined with lead to hold water.

WATER-WAYS, the timbers of a ship connecting the sides to the deck.

WATER-WHEEL, a wheel with buckets for impelling a mill by water-power. The principal varieties are undershot, overshot, breast, and horizontal, turbines, pitch-back, tub, and flutter wheels.

WATER-WORKS, the reservoir or pumping station, for supplying water to a town; hydraulic engines or structures.

WATTLE, an Australian name for species of *Mimosa*, the bark of which is sometimes imported for tanning; a hurdle of twigs; a rod laid on a roof to support the thatch.

WATTSEIDE (German), floss-silk.

WAX, the comb of cells constructed by bees to hold their honey. We import about 530 tons a-year from different quarters, while fully 300 tons are obtained from the hives in Britain. *See* BEES-WAX.

WAX AND TALLOW CHANDLER, a dealer in candles.

WAX-BASKET, a fancy basket made of or coated with wax.

WAX-BLEACHER, a person who extracts the foreign bodies that have insinuated themselves into bees-wax, and obscured its originally pure white colour.

WAX-CHANDLERS' COMPANY, one of the livery companies of London, whose hall is in Gresham-street.

WAX-DOLL, a child's doll with a wax face and arms, or with a wax body.

WAXED-END, thread covered with shoemakers' wax for sewing leather together.

WAX-FIGURE MAKER, a moulder of wax in imitation of real persons.

WAX-FLOWER MAKER, a modeller of flowers, fruit, &c. in wax, coloured to imitate nature.

WAXING, the process of stopping out colours in calico-printing; rubbing thread with wax to strengthen it; polishing tables with bees-wax.

WAX-LIGHT, a candle or taper of wax.

WAX-MANUFACTURER, a melter or bleacher of wax; a maker of candles, or different articles of wax.

WAX-MODELLER, an ornamental worker in [wax.

WAX-MYRTLE. *See* MYRTLE-WAX.

WAX-PALM, a lofty species of South American palm, the *Ceroxylon andicola*, from fissures in the stem of which flows spontaneously a kind of grey, waxy substance, containing two-thirds of resin, and one-third of wax, identical with that formed by the bee. Melted with a little suet, this wax makes excellent tapers.

WAX-WORKS, a collection of figures dressed to represent life, shown to the public.

WAY-BILL, a carrier's invoice; in inland conveyance applied to a coachman's document, showing the list of goods, with the transport or delivery of which he is intrusted.

WAYS, the timbers or slides on which a ship is launched.

WEAPON-HOUSE, an armoury.

WEAPONS, small-arms; offensive or defensive instruments.

WEAR, a dam to shut up and raise water; an enclosure of twigs to catch fish; to turn a vessel round by the stern, tacking being the reverse movement. *See* WEIR.

WEARING-APPAREL, garments for the person; articles of attire.

WEASEL, the *Mustela vulgaris*, a ferret-like animal; a destroyer of vermin. Other species of this family are described under ERMINE, MINK, SABLE, &c.

WEATHER-BOARD, a board to keep off the wet or cold; nailed boards lapping over one another at the side of a house, &c.

WEATHER-COCK, a vane made to show the direction of the wind.

WEATHER-GLASS, a name commonly given to the barometer, but also occasionally applied to the thermometer, hygrometer, and other instruments, for measuring atmospheric changes.

WEAVE, to entwine; to form cloth on a loom by the union or intertexture of threads.

WEAVER, an operative who works at a loom.

WEAVERS'-BEAM, a web beam.

WEAVERS'-COMPANY, one of the livery companies of London, whose hall is in Basinghall-street.

WEAVERS'-ENTERER, a shuttle.

WEAVERS'-HARNESS MAKER, a manufacturer of the loom apparatus used by a weaver.

WEAVER'S-HEDDLE, the healds or harness for guiding the warp-threads in the loom.

WEAVERS'-HOOK, the stay of a beam.

WEAVERS'-LEASH, part of the apparatus of a weaver.

WEAVERS'-LOOM MAKER, a manufacturer of looms for weaving.

WEAVERS'-SHUTTLE, the instrument with which the weaver shoots the cross threads.

WEAVERS'-TURNER, a workman who turns shuttles and other instruments for weavers.

WEAVERS'-UTENSIL MAKER, a workman who makes the leash and other parts of the apparatus and instruments required in weaving.

WEB, linen cloth; any thing woven.

WEBA, WHIBA, a grain-measure of Tunis and Barbary, = 0·0987 bushel.

WEBBER, a weaver.

WEBBING-TAPE, a kind of broad tape.

WEBE, a term in Hamburg, in the linen trade, signifying a roll of 6 dozen, or 72 ells.

WEBERKARDEN (German), teasels.

WEDDER. *See* WETHER.

WEDDING-CAKE, a rich plum-cake, ornamented and frosted with sugar, to decorate a wedding breakfast table, and served to guests and subsequent visitors to the new-married couple.

WEDDING-CAKE-ORNAMENTS, silvered ornaments to decorate a wedding-cake.

WEDDING-CARDS, the name and address cards of a new-married couple, usually printed in silver, or tied with silver-cord, sent to friends to announce the event, and stating when they receive return calls.

WEDDING-DRESS, superior garments for either sex, to be worn in church at the marriage ceremony.

WEDDING-FAVOUR, a bunch of white ribbons or a rosette, &c. worn by males attending a wedding.

WEDDING-RING, a lady's plain hall-marked pure gold ring, given by the bridegroom to his future wife at the altar.

WEDGE, a mass of metal or wood thick at one end, and thin at the other, used for rending wood and other substances; a lever; a mechanical power or tool of various kinds and modifications; a small fastening for a door or window.

WEDGEWOOD-WARE, a fine kind of pottery, named after the late Mr. Wedgewood, who carried out many improvements in the manufacture.

WEDRO, VEDRO, a Russian liquid-measure of about 2¾ gallons, but varying in some districts. *See* VEDRO.

WEEDING-FORK, WEEDING-HOOK, WEEDING-IRON, implements or tools for cutting down or eradicating weeds.

WEEDS, the mourning garments of a widow.

WEEKLY-TENANT, one paying rent by the week, and liable to removal on a week's notice.

WEEPER, a white linen cuff, worn on mourning by widows.

WEFT, the woof of cloth; the yarns or threads which run from selvage to selvage in a web.

WEHR, a superficial measure used by miners in Prussia, = 0·1063 acre; in Saxony to 0·0948 acre.

WEIGH, to poise; to estimate the ponderosity of an article by the steelyard, balance, scales, &c.; to lift an anchor from the ground. *See* WEY.

WEIGH-BRIDGE, a contrivance near a toll-gate, market, &c. for weighing loaded carts subject to toll, &c.

WEIGHER, an officer of customs and assize; one who tests weights, or sees goods weighed.

WEIGH-HOUSE, a public place for weighing.

WEIGHING-MACHINE, any contrivance by which the weight of an object may be ascertained. *See* BALANCE, LETTER-WEIGHER.

WEIGHING-MACHINE MAKER, a balance maker; a person who makes large apparatus for poising.

WEIGHTS, masses of metal, porcelain, &c. accurately adjusted, as a standard of ounces, pounds, cwts., and their subdivisions. *See* APOTHECARIES-WEIGHT, AVOIRDUPOIS, and TROY-WEIGHT.

WEIHRAUCH (German), frankincense.

WEIR, a permanent dam thrown across a river; an enclosure for catching fish. The Scotch weir consists of iron and wooden stakes with nets fastened thereto: a cruive weir is one with hatches.

WELD, an annual herbaceous plant, the *Reseda luteola*, a native of Europe, the stems and leaves of which dye yellow. The whole plant is cropped when in seed, at which time its dyeing power is greatest; and, after being simply dried, it is brought to market.

WELDBORES, a description of woollen goods manufactured in Bradford.

WELDING, the union of two pieces of metal together by heat and pressure.

WELL, a pit sunk to arrive at springs, for obtaining water. Artesian wells are carried to a great depth, to ensure a continuous flow of water. A compartment with holes in a fishing-boat, to keep fish alive; the cavity in a building, in which a flight of winding stairs is fixed.

WELL-BOAT, a fishing-boat with a well to keep fish in, to bring them alive to market.

WELL-BORER, one who digs or bores for water; a constructor of wells.

WELLINGTONS, men's long boots so named.

WELL-ROOM, an apartment or building containing a mineral spring or spa, where the waters are drunk by invalids.

WELL-SINKING, the operation of boring for water.

WELL-STAIRCASE, a winding staircase, which occupies but little room in a building.

WELSH-FLANNEL, the finest kind of flannel, made from the fleeces of the flocks of the Welsh mountains, chiefly manufactured by hand. It is held in high repute for under-vestments and other purposes, but is dearer than that made by machinery in Lancashire and Yorkshire.

WELSH-MUTTON, a choice and delicate meat, obtained from a small breed of sheep in Wales.

WELSH-ONION, a name for the *Allium fistulosum*, a native of Siberia.

WELSH-RABBIT, toasted cheese seasoned with mustard, &c.

WELSH-WIG, a worsted cap.

WELT, a joint or fold; a border or edging; the inner lining reaching to the edge of the sole of a boot or shoe

WELTED BROCADES AND QUILTS, articles with folds, lined and ribbed.

WELT-SHOULDERS, a name in the leather trade for curried leather, fit for the welts of boots and shoes.

WERP, a Hanoverian dry-measure, the mean of several of which may be given at 1·59757 Winchester bushel.

WERST. *See* VERST.

WEST-END, the fashionable part of London, commencing in the East from Charing-cross.

WEST INDIA TEA, a name for the shrubby goat-weed, *Capraria biflora*, the leaves of which are occasionally used for infusing as tea, in the Antilles.

WESTMINSTER HALL, the seat of the principal English law courts.

WETHER, WEDDER, a gelded ram.

WET-NURSE, a female who suckles and nurses the infant of another woman.

WEY, WEIGH, an English measure of weight; for wool, equal to 6½ tods of 28 lbs.; a load or 5 quarters of wheat; 40 bushels of salt, each 56 lbs.; 32 cloves of cheese, each 7 lbs.; 48 bushels of oats and barley; 2 to 3 cwt. of butter.

WEYBEK, an Egyptian corn-measure, the 6th part of an ardeb, not quite a bushel.

WHALE, a large mammiferous marine animal of several species, frequenting high northern and southern latitudes, sought for its commercial products. *See* SPERMACETI, and WHALEBONE.

WHALE-BLUBBER, the thick fat of whales. *See* BLUBBER.

WHALE-BOAT, a long narrow boat, used by whalers, to pursue and harpoon the whale.

WHALEBONE, the commercial name for the baleen plates in the mouth of the whale, of which there are about 300. They are chiefly obtained from the Greenland and Southern whales, *Balæna mysticetus*, and *australis*. It is softened by boiling, and is dyed black. The principal use of whalebone is for the ribs or stretchers for umbrellas, for canes, whips, and as a substitute for bristles in common brushes. In the form of shavings, it is sometimes braided into hats and bonnets. *See* FINNER-WHALE.

WHALEBONE-CUTTER, a workman who slices or draws whalebone into assorted lengths, for different purposes.

WHALE-FINS, a commercial misnomer for whalebone; the imports in 1856 were 281 tons.

WHALE-FISHERY, the pursuit of the whale in vessels specially stored and fitted for the purpose. This fishery is now chiefly carried on by the Americans who had, in 1856, 655 vessels, registering 204,209 tons employed in the South Seas and the North Pacific. There are some few British ships still prosecuting the Greenland fishery. The American vessels in the North Pacific have averaged 1000 barrels of oil to each ship for some years past.

WHALE-LINE, a long coil of small rope fastened to a harpoon, carried in a whale-boat, to secure the whale when struck.

WHALER, a ship employed in the whale fishery; a seaman engaged in the fishery.

WHALE-SHOT, a name among the Dutch and some English whalers for head matter or spermaceti from the whale.

WHANGHEE, a kind of Chinese cane. *See* WANGHEE.

WHARF, a landing-place or mole by the water side, in a harbour or river, for landing or shipping goods.

WHARFAGE, the charge paid on goods to a wharfinger.

WHARFINGER, the owner or occupier of a wharf; an officer or clerk appointed to attend at a wharf.

WHARNCLIFFE-KNIFE, a pocket knife with one large and two small blades.

WHARP, a name for Trent sand. *See* TRENT-SAND.

WHAT-NOT, a fancy side-board or stand for ornaments and knick-knacks in a drawing-room.

WHEAL, a Cornish name for a mine.

WHEAT, a name for species of *Triticum*, one of the most important of the food grains, and that most generally cultivated in Europe; the flour being the most nutritious and palatable of all the cereal grasses. The quantity raised in this country is very large, amounting to about 19,000,000 quarters, and we also import 3,000,000 or 4,000,000 quarters a year. *See* FLOUR.

WHEEL, a revolving disk or frame in machinery, or on which a vehicle is supported and moved. There are many kinds of wheels, as driving-wheels, leading and trailing-wheels, carriage-wheels, cart-wheels, wheelbarrow-wheels, &c. A circular frame with handles, attached by ropes or chains to the tiller, for moving a ship's rudder; a potter's round board turned by a lathe; a disk with floats or paddles for propelling a steam-boat in the water; a machine for spinning thread; a revolving fire-work; in Sheffield, a building fitted up with a number of grindstones, most of which are hired at a weekly or yearly rental, by a grinder, who grinds cutlery for other persons.

WHEEL-BARROW, a small hand-carriage for loads, with handles for supporting it, and moving on one wheel.

WHEEL-CARRIAGE, any vehicle moving on wheels; not a sled or sleigh.

WHEEL-CHAIR, an invalid or Bath-chair.

WHEELSWARF, a clayey cement or putty made from the dust obtained in Sheffield from the abrasion of grindstones, which is used in the steel-converting furnaces for covering the layers of iron and charcoal.

WHEELWRIGHT, a maker and repairer of wheels and wheel carriages.

WHEELWRIGHTS'-COMPANY, one of the minor livery companies of London, which, having no hall, transacts its business at Guildhall.

WHELK, a marine univalve shell, the *Buccinum undatum*, the fish inhabiting which, boiled or pickled, is esteemed by the poorer classes in large towns.

WHELP, the young of a dog; an appliance to a windlass to prevent fleeting and surging.

WHERRY, a waterman's light river boat; a ferry boat in a harbour.

WHERRY-MAN, a river boatman.

WHETSTONE, a smooth flat stone for sharpening edge-tools by friction. Whetstones of every degree in quality are obtained from the older and newer metamorphic formations. The finer varieties of mica schist and talco-micaceous schist afford a great abundance of such stones. *See* HONES, and SCYTHE-STONE.

WHEY, the residual thin liquor, after the butter and caseum or curd are removed from milk; a posset; milk curdled by rennet, which, when good, should be nearly transparent, of a pale yellow colour, and should have a sweetish taste. It is an excellent diluent in febrile affections, as it contains a crystalline substance, termed sugar of milk. Various substances are added, which give characteristic names, such as acid whey, aluminous whey, beer whey, mustard whey, orange whey, tamarind whey, and white wine whey. A cooling whey drink is made with milk, wine, tamarinds, or cream of tartar.

WHIFFING, a mode of hand-line fishing for pollacks, mackerel, &c.

WHIFFLE-TREE. *See* WHIPPLE-TREE.

WHIM, a windlass or large capstan for raising ores, &c. from a mine-shaft, usually worked by horse-power.

WHIN, a name for the furze or gorse bush.

WHIN-BERRY. *See* WHORTLE-BERRY.

WHIN-BRUISER, a machine for cutting and bruising furze or whins to feed cattle on.

WHINSTONE, a kind of basalt.

WHIP, a small lift-purchase made by a rope rove through a single block; a tied-up flag used for signalizing; a lash secured to a stick for driving with. Cart-whips have a very long lash. In the colonies cattle-whips have a thong of twisted bark or hide. Small twisted whalebone whips, &c. are made for ladies.

WHIP AND THONG MAKER, a manufacturer of whips of different kinds which are sold by saddlers and harness makers.

WHIP-CORD, fine double-twisted strong cord, used for whip-lashes and other purposes.

WHIP-LASH, twisted hide, bark, or cord fastened to the thong of a whip.

WHIP-MOUNTER, a person who puts handles, ornaments, &c. on whips.

WHIP-MOUNT MAKER, a person who makes the metal ornaments, ferrules, thongs, &c. for whip-sticks and handles.

WHIPPER, a porter who raises coal with a tackle from a ship's hold.

WHIPPER-IN, the assistant-huntsman of a pack of hounds.

WHIPPLE-TREE, WHIFFLE-TREE, a swing bar to which traces are fastened.

WHIP-TOP, a child's top driven round with a lash.

WHIP-SAW, a saw set in a frame to be worked by two persons.

WHIP-STICK, the stock or handle for a driving-whip;—these are of various woods, according to the purpose intended, as for coachmen's whips, gig whips, stock whips, and carters' whips.

WHIRLABOUT, a round-about for children at fairs, with small carriages or wooden horses.

WHIRLIGIG, a toy spun round by children.

WHISK, a wisp or broom of dried stalks; a cook's wire instrument for beating up the whites of eggs, &c.; a cooper's plane.

WHISKERS, the hair growing on a man's cheeks;—these are made and sold for play actors, masqueraders, and others.

WHISKET, a scuttle or basket.

WHISKY, a spirit distilled from grain, largely made and drunk in Ireland and Scotland; (——EY) a light carriage for quick travelling.

WHISTLE, a child's toy; a boatswain's or sportsman's call; a shrill warning noise made by a locomotive. *See* RAILWAY WHISTLE.

WHIST-MARKERS, small coins or medals used for counting or scoring the points of the game of whist.

WHITE, a painter's negative colour; ceruse; the albumen of an egg; a mark in a target for an arrow.

WHITE-BAIT, a small esteemed river fish. *See* BAIT.

WHITE-BEAR, the large Arctic bear. *See* POLAR-BEAR.

WHITE-BEER, a Flemish beer.

WHITE-CEDAR, the *Cupressus thyoides*, a North American tree. *See also* WARRA-COOMI.

WHITE-COATS, a fisherman's name for the skins of young seals, which weigh but from 60 to 70 pounds the dozen.

WHITE-COPPER, an alloyed metal; German silver.

WHITE-CROPS, grain and seed crops, as distinguished from green crops, or those cultivated for their roots or herbage.

WHITECROSS-STREET, a name for the debtors' prison of the City of London which is situated in that street.

WHITE-FISH, a name given by the Canadians to the *Coregonus albus*, a fish which abounds in the lakes of North America.

WHITE-LEAD, a carbonate of lead; a zinc paint; the painters' principal white colour.

WHITE-LEAF. *See* LEAF-METAL, and BRONZE-POWDER.

WHITE-LEATHER, buff leather; alumed leather. *See* CHAMOIS-LEATHER, and WASH-LEATHER.

WHITE-LIME, whitewash for cleansing or colouring walls, &c.

WHITE-LINE, in printing, a broad division or blank space between the lines of types.

WHITE-MEAT, a term applied to young or delicate flesh food, as veal, poultry, rabbits, pork, &c.

WHITENER, a name in the United States for a colourer or white-washer.

WHITENING. *See* WHITING.

WHITENING-STONE, a sharpening and polishing-stone employed by cutlers; a name in the Sheffield district for a finishing grindstone of a finer texture than the common large ordinary sandstones.

WHITES, a miller's name for the finest flour made from white wheat.

WHITE-SATIN, pure, undyed satin, much used for bridal dresses, and lady's slips or under petticoats.

WHITE-SMITH, a worker in metals.

WHITE-SPRUCE, the *Pinus alba*.

WHITE-TALLOW, a class of Russian tallow, obtained from the fat of sheep and goats.

WHITE-VITRIOL, an old name for sulphate of zinc.

WHITE-WASH, a mixture of whiting, size, and water for whitening ceilings and walls; a slang term for getting rid of importunate creditors by passing through the Insolvent court.

WHITE-WAX, bleached or pure wax.

WHITE-WINE, Sherry, Marsala, Madeira, or any pale-coloured wine.

WHITING, ground chalk washed in alum-water, to cleanse it from sand and other impurities, and dried in lumps; it is used as a polishing material, and for making putty and white-wash. A small delicate sea-fish, the *Merlangus vulgaris*.

WHITING-MERCHANT, one who grinds and levigates chalk, and makes it up into small oblong cakes.

WHITING-POLLACK, the *Merlangus pollachius*, common on the rocky coasts of Britain.

WHITING-POUT, a small seafish, the *Morrhua barbata* of Bloch; the *Morrhua lusca* of Yarrell; the *Gadus luscus* of Linnæus.

WHITLING, a name at Berwick for the salmon-trout.

WHITSTER, a woman who bleaches linen.

WHITTEN, a Swedish coin sometimes called ant ore or schilling: a subdivision of the rixdollar; in Riga, Revel, &c. 64 whittens are equal to 1 rixdollar. The black whitten is only half the value of the whitten, or white schilling.

WHORLER, a potter's wooden wheel by which a rotatory motion is given to plates and other flat vessels.

WHORTLEBERRY, WHURT, a name for the fruit of species of *Vaccinium*, the blue, black, or red berries of which are acid, and eatable. Some are known under the name of bilberries and cow-berries. *See* CRANBERRY.

WICK, a cotton or rush thread for a candle or lamp, which supplies the flame.

WICKER, a small grown twig or osier; a basket-rod.

WICKER-BASKET, a basket formed of osiers. They are sometimes made lined with tin, for knives and plates. *See* KNIFE-BASKET, and PLATE-BASKET.

WICKER-WORK, a texture of osiers; baskets.

WICKET, a small gate; a row of stumps to be bowled at, at cricket.

WIDDELILAM, a vernacular name in India for peppermint.

WIDE-AWAKE, a low-crowned felt-hat.

WIDE-GAUGE, the broadest gauge used on a railway, as in the Great Western, the rails in which are set 7 feet apart.

WIDGEON, a wild duck or water-fowl, the *Mareca Penelope*.

WIDOW'S-WEEDS, the mourning attire for a female who has lost her husband.

WIESSE, a Dutch term for the cubic elle of fire-wood.

WIG, an artificial covering of hair for the head. There are various kinds of wigs made, as horse-hair wigs for judges and barristers; mohair wigs for coachmen; gentlemen's and ladies' wigs of human hair; play-actors' wigs, &c.; a fisherman's term for an old seal.

WIG-BLOCK, a shaped piece of wood for fitting a wig on.

WIG-BOX, a box for holding a wig.

WIG-MAKER, a peruke-maker, a person who makes wigs of human or other hair.

WIGTE, the Dutch name for the French gramme, which is equal to nearly 15½ grains, viz. 15·4330.

WILD-FOWL, a trade-name for wild ducks and other birds obtained in winter, in decoys, or by shooting.

WILL, a testamentary document giving instructions as to the disposal of a person's property and effects after death.

WILL-OFFICE, a prerogative-court; a registry for wills.

WILLOW, a species of *Salix*. *See* OSIER.

WILLOWING, WILLYING, the process of opening the locks of wool by a devil or machine of many rollers with teeth.

WILLOW-RODS, thin twigs grown in marshy lands, used for making hampers, panniers, skips, &c. *See* BASKET-RODS and OSIER.

WILLYING-MACHINE, a revolving cone with rows of iron spikes, for preparing wool. In some districts it is called the shakewilly and the twilly.

WILTON-CARPETS, a name for Brussels carpeting with the yarn cut.

WIMBLE, a carpenter's boring instrument turned by a handle.

WIMPLE, a hood, or veil; the winding of a river.

WINCEY, another name for linsey-woolsey.

WINCH, a purchase to a revolving-wheel; the crank or handle by which motion is given to the axles of lifting machines.

WINCHESTER-BUSHEL, the original British standard measure of capacity, given by King Edgar, and kept in the town-hall, Winchester; an old English grain standard-measure, used until 1826, when the imperial bushel was introduced. The Winchester bushel is 18½ inches wide, and 8 inches deep, and contains 2150·42 cubic inches; while the imperial standard bushel contains 2218·1907 cubic inches.

WINDER, a reel for winding silk or cotton on.

WIND-FALLS, fruits which have dropped from trees.

WINDGAGE, an anemometer.

WINDING-ENGINE, an engine for drawing up buckets, &c. from a well or shaft.

WINDING-MACHINE, a twisting or warping machine.

WINDING-SHEET, a linen wrapper for a dead body formerly used.

WINDING-UP ACT, an official act or judicial course of proceeding, for ascertaining the liabilities, and distributing the assets, of an insolvent company.

WINDLASS, a circular axis or revolving machine, moved by crank handles, by which anchors and other heavy weights are raised on board a merchant-vessel.

WINDLASS-MANUFACTURER, a maker of machines for raising weights.

WIND-MILL, an engine or mill impelled by the wind for grinding corn.

WINDOW, an opening in a wall, &c., for admitting air or light; a lattice-work frame. There are many kinds of windows, as for cabins, green-houses, churches, and houses.

WINDOW-BLIND, a calico or brown holland roller-blind; a perforated zinc or woven wire short blind. *See* VENETIAN-BLIND.

WINDOW-BLIND MAKER, a manufacturer of Venetian-blinds or of wire-blinds for shop-windows or private dwelling-houses.

WINDOW-CLEANER, a frame for placing outside of a window, to sit or stand on when cleaning the window-panes; a person who contracts for cleaning windows.

WINDOW-CURTAIN, a long tapestry or hanging for a window; a short, muslin or gauze blind.

WINDOW-FASTENING, a bolt or catch to secure the sashes of a window.

WINDOW-FRAME, the wood-work or iron frame or partition for enclosing the panes of glass.

WINDOW-GLASS MAKER, a manufacturer of sheet and plate-glass, &c., for windows. *See* GLASS, and PLATE-GLASS.

WINDOW-GLASS MERCHANT, a vender of sheet-glass; one who supplies glaziers, builders, and others.

WINDOW-SASH, the lifting or opening frame of a window.

WINDOW-SHADES, rolling or projecting blinds or sun-shades, sometimes transparent or painted, at other times canvas on spring-rollers.

WINDOW-SHUTTER, a door closing on the inside or the outside, and bolted or barred to secure a window from entry.

WIND-SAIL, a tube of canvas passed down a skylight or hatchway, to ventilate a ship; the canvas sail or vane of a wind-mill.

WINDSOR-CHAIR, a kind of strong, plain, polished wooden chair.

WINDSOR-SOAP, a scented soap, well-known in all countries for its excellence both as a washing and shaving soap. It is made either brown or white.

WINE, the juice of grapes, largely manufactured on the Continent for home use and export; the juice of various fruit prepared with sugar.

WINE-BAG, a skin vessel for holding or carrying wine.

WINE-BIN, a partition in a cellar for keeping bottled wine.

WINE-BISCUIT, a sweet, fancy biscuit served with wine.

WINE-BOTTLE, a black or white glass bottle for holding wine.

WINE-CELLAR, a vault or cool place for keeping wine in.

WINE-COOLER, a wrapper for a wine-bottle, to be wetted, to promote evaporation; a stand or utensil for wine-bottles, holding ice, &c. to cool the wine in them.

WINE-COOLER MAKER, a manufacturer of metal utensils for standing wine in to cool.

WINE-COOPER'S TOOL MAKER, a manufacturer of the various tools used by the cooper.

WINE-DECANTER, a clear glass-bottle for holding wine at table.

WINE-FINING MAKER, a preparer of isinglass &c. for clarifying wine.

WINE-FLASK, a bottle for wine.

WINE-GLASS, a small drinking-glass, of different shapes, for holding wine.

WINE-GROWER, a cultivator of grapes; the proprietor of a vineyard.

WINE MEASURE. In this the imperial gallon is the legal standard, and is used for every liquid; but the larger measures are used very often only for a particular kind, as wine, beer, oil, &c.

IMPERIAL MEASURE.

4 gills or quarterns...	1 pint
2 pints	1 quart
4 quarts	1 gallon
5 gallons	1 pin or keg (brandy)
9 gallons	1 firkin (beer)
10 galls. (8⅓) old meas.	1 anker (brandy)
18 gallons (14⅞) ditto...	1 kilderkin
31½ gallons	1 half hogshead
36 gallons	1 barrel (beer)
42 gallons (34⅞)... o.m.	1 tierce
63 gallons (52⅜)... ditto	1 hogshead
84 gallons (70) ditto	1 puncheon
126 gallons (104⅞) ditto	1 pipe or butt
252 gallons (209⅞) ditto	1 tun (oil)

Thus the old wine measure will be found to be considerably enlarged,—14·99600 imperial gallons being equivalent to 18 gallons of the old. In regard to all vessels of larger capacity, such as hogsheads, puncheons, &c.—they are gauged and charged according to the exact quantity contained therein. Many of the above measures are, however, entirely nominal. Wine is imported into this country in butts or pipes, and hogsheads, the standards of which are usually as follows:—

Pipe of Cider	100 to 118	gallons
" Port	115	"
" Sherry	108	"
" Lisbon	117	"
" Cape or Madeira	92	"
" Teneriffe	100	"
" Malaga	105	"
Butt of Sherry	108	"
Hogshead of Claret	46	"
" Cape	92	"
" Marsala	93	"
" Brandy... 45 to	50	"
" Rum ..... 45 to	50	"
" Tent	52	"
Aum of Hock	30	"

See the various measures and wines.

WINE-MERCHANT, a general dealer in wines.

WINE-MULLER. *See* MULLER.

WINE-PALM, the *Manicaria saccifera*, of Gaertner; also called the troolie palm. The leaves are used as thatch, and caps are made of the spathe in Guiana.

WINE-PRESS, a screw or roller press for expressing the juice from grapes.

WINE-ROOMS, a place where draught or bottled wine can be drunk.

WINE-STONE, a name in the Cape colony for argol, or the deposit in wine-casks.

WINE-STRAINER, a funnel with a sieve or perforated metal holes for straining wine through.

WINE-VAULTS, the bar of a tavern or wine store; a place where wine is served at the bar or at tables.

WINE-VINEGAR, the ordinary vinegar of France and other wine-producing countries.

WINGS, side buildings or appendages; the sides of a stage; small imitation epaulettes or shoulder-knots.

WINNA, an Indian name for layers of the bark of the *Lecythis ollaria*, dried in the sun, and used in Guiana as wrappers for cigars. *See* POT-PLANT.

WINNOW, to fan grain, and separate the chaff.

WINNOWING-MACHINE, a fanner or blower, which drives off chaff, dust, &c. by means of wind.

WINSPEL, a dry-measure used in Berlin for lime, = 6 14128 bushels.

WINTER-BARK, an aromatic medicinal bark, resembling Canella alba, obtained from the *Drimys Winteri*, a tree found in the Straits of Magellan.

WINTRALEIN, a German name for the *Linum usitatissimum*.

WINZE, a mining term for a small pit or shaft, sunk from one level to another, for the purpose of ventilation.

WIRE, thread or filament of metal; the electric telegraph.

WIRE-BLIND MAKER, a manufacturer of transparent blinds, or thin gauze wire blinds.

WIRE-CARTRIDGE, a patented cartridge strengthened by wire ligaments.

WIRE-CLOTH, a twisted or woven substance made of copper, brass, or iron wire, used for flour machines, paper-making machines, kiln-floors, meat-safes and larders, window-blinds, sieves, &c. The finest wires are made on the Continent, often of sizes nearly as small as human hair.

WIRE-DRAWER, a person who extends the ductile metals, platinum, copper, silver, and gold into wire, by drawing bars of the metal through holes in a steel draw-plate, each hole being smaller than the preceding one.

WIRE-FENCE, hurdles or fencing of wire to keep out cattle from parks, lawns, or pleasure grounds; and also for shrubberies and vineries, and for training flowers on.

WIRE-GAUZE, a texture of fine wire used for window-blinds, sieves, &c. *See* WIRE-CLOTH.

WIRE-GUARD, a protection for the front of a fire-grate, to prevent the sparks flying out.

WIRE-IRON, black rod iron made in South Staffordshire, and used for drawing out into wire.

WIRE-MAKER, a wire-drawer.

WIRE MEAT-COVER, a hollow shape of gauze wire to place over a dish with meat.

WIRE-PENDULUM MAKER, a manufacturer of the metal pendulums for clocks.

WIRE-RIBBON MAKER, a weaver of bands or lengths of crossed wire.

WIRE-ROPE, iron wire twisted into ropes for cordage, draw ropes, &c.

WIRE-ROPE MAKER, a manufacturer of rope of wire strands for rigging, and for other purposes.

WIRE-SIEVE, a bolter or strainer with a wire bottom.

WIRE-THREAD MAKER, a manufacturer of the flattened gilt wire with which silk thread is covered.

WIRE-WORKER AND WEAVER, a manufacturer of articles from wire.

WIRE-WORKERS' COMPANY. *See* TIN-PLATE-WORKERS' COMPANY.

WISP, a broom; a small bundle of straw, &c. *See* WHISK.

WISPEL, WISP, a German corn-measure used in Bremen, Hanover, &c., containing 10 scheffels. Two wispels in Hanover make one last, equal to 82 imperial bushels. This measure ranges from 29·8810 Winchester bushels in Hamburgh, to 70·7640 ditto in Saxony. The general range is from 35 to 40 bushels in different German and Prussian towns.

WISSE, the Belgian name for the cord, or measure for firewood.

WISWUSA, an Indian measure of length, in Malwa, = 4 4802 inches; in Surat, to 4 8706 inches.

WITNEY-BLANKET, a superior kind of blanket.

WLOKA, a Polish superficial measure of [41 4896 acres.

WOAD, a dye plant, the *Isatis tinctoria*.

[illegible], a name in Nubia for sixteen dollars.

WOLF, the *Canis occidentalis*. Of the skins of this animal we import about 10,000 yearly. They are much used as cloak and coat linings in Russia.

WOLFRAM, the native tungstate of iron and manganese, termed in Cornwall mock lead.

WOLVERINE, another name for the glutton, a wild animal, the *Gulo Arcticus*, of whose skins about 1,000 are annually imported for furriers' use from North America.

WOOD, a general name for timber or fuel; a forest.

WOOD-ACID, an inferior pyroligneous acid, distilled from oak, beech, ash, &c., made to the extent of about 200 tons a-year, and used by calico-printers as a substitute for the higher priced acids. [ASH.

WOOD-ASHES, the ashes of wood. *See* POTASH.

WOOD-CARVER, a shaper and ornamenter of wood; one who cuts figures and designs in wood.

WOODCOCK, a migratory bird of the snipe family, the *Scolopax rusticola*, whose flesh is highly esteemed.

WOODCUT, an engraving on wood; an impression taken therefrom.

WOOD-CUTTER, one who fells timber; a person who saws or chops up wood.

WOOD-ENGRAVER, an artist who cuts pictures or drawings on blocks of box-wood, to take impressions from.

WOODEN-CLOCK, a clock in which much of the movement, the case, &c. are of wood.

WOODEN-LEG, a stump or support made for a person who has lost a leg.

WOODEN-SHOE, a sabot; a shoe shaped out of wood.

WOODEN-SPOON, a spoon made of wood, plain or carved, for culinary use, serving salad or other purposes.

WOODEN-WARE, a general name under which buckets, bowls, and various articles of American manufacture are shipped from the United States' ports.

WOOD-HOUSE, WOOD-LOFT, a shed or storeroom for fuel.

WOODLAND, ground covered or interspersed with timber; forest-land.

WOOD-LOFT. *See* WOOD-HOUSE.

WOODMAN, a timber-cutter; a lumberer; a forest-ranger.

WOOD-MERCHANT, a dealer in timber; a vendor of fire-wood.

WOOD-OIL, a resinous oil obtained in Canara from the *Dipterocarpus lævis*.

WOOD-PAVEMENT, blocks of wood laid down in streets instead of flag-stones or paving-stones.

WOODROW, WOODRUFF, a wild plant, the *Asperula odorata*, found in woods in England. The herb while drying has the scent of new hay, approaching to bitter almonds or heliotrope. This pleasant scent has been used for flavouring wine, perfuming clothes, &c. It is deemed diuretic, and used as a substitute for tea.

WOODSKIN, a large kind of river canoe made in Guiana by the Indians, from the bark of the purpleheart-tree and the [illegible] or locust-tree: some of these canoes are large enough to carry from 20 to 25 persons with perfect safety in smooth water.

WOOD-SORREL, the *Oxalis Acetosella*, a wild plant, which is powerfully and most agreeably acid, making a refreshing and wholesome conserve with sugar.

WOOD-STAMPS, block-prints, and carved work for impressing figures and colours on paper or fabrics.

WOOD-TYPE, large letters for printing with, cut in wood, used for placards and job-work.

WOOD VINEGAR. *See* PYROLIGNEOUS ACID.

WOOF, the weft or cross texture of fabrics.

WOOGINOOS, a name in Abyssinia for the *Brucea antidysenterica*, the bark of which is considered in that country a valuable remedy in dysentery and severe cases of diarrhœa.

WOOL, the soft curly hair or fleecy covering of sheep—one of the most important of animal fibres, in which the trade, home and foreign, reaches nearly 100,000 tons a year. The kinds of wool raised at home, and received from abroad, are very numerous.

WOOL-BROKER, a dealer in wool, on account of importers and merchants.

WOOL-BURLERS, women who remove the little knots or extraneous matters from wool, and from the surface of woollen cloth.

WOOL-BUYER, a person conversant in the properties and qualities of wool, employed to buy for manufacturers.

WOOL-CARDER, a person who prepares wool for yarn by passing it over wire dents or cards, and forms the wool into slivers or short rolls.

WOOL-COMB, a metal-toothed hand instrument for combing wool; also a machine to perform the same operation.

WOOL-COMBER, a person employed to comb the long wool of which stuffs and worsted goods are made. This is done by passing the wool through heated iron combs, which takes away the laminæ or feathery part of the wool, and approximates it to the nature of silk and cotton.

WOOL-DYED, yarn dyed after being scoured and before making up; not piece-dyed.

WOOL-GROWER, a grazier or breeder of sheep for their fleece. [districts.

WOOL-HALL, a trade-market in the woollen

WOOLLEN-CARDING MACHINE, a scribbling-machine or carding-engine for breaking down the fibres, and making them more uniform in length, so as to render the thread, subsequently formed, free from inequalities.

WOOLLEN-CORDS, a manufacture of one part cotton and three parts wool.

WOOLLEN-DRAPER, a dealer in woollen cloths.

WOOLLEN DRIVING-BELT MAKER, a maker of stout straps or bands for connecting machinery.

WOOLLEN-DYER, a person who dyes wool in the piece or in the yarn.

WOOLLEN-PRINTER, an operative who impresses patterns or colours on woollen or mixed fabrics.

Woollen-scribblers, Wool-scribblers, machines for combing or preparing wool into thin downy translucent layers.

Woollens, textile fabrics made of wool, or of wool mixed with cotton, or some other similar material.

Woolly-butt, a local name in New South Wales for a very large and fine timber tree, a species of *Eucalyptus*, which reaches an average height of 100 to 150 feet, and a diameter of 36 to 72 inches. The wood is much prized for felloes of wheels, and other work requiring strength and toughness.

Woolman, a dealer in wool.

Woolman's Company, one of the minor livery companies of London, which has no hall.

Wool-merchant, a wholesale dealer in wool; an importer of foreign and colonial wool.

Wool-moater, a boy employed in picking wool, and cleansing it from lumps of pitch, and other impurities.

Wool-pack, a large bundle or bale of wool [240 lbs.

Wool-sale, a periodical public sale, in London or Liverpool, for the disposal of large quantities of wool.

Wool-sheet, a packing-wrapper for bales of wool.

Wool-sorter, a man employed in sorting the wools of different lengths, qualities, and countries, into the kinds suited for special manufactures.

Wool-stapler, a wool-sorter in the manufacturing districts; a wholesale dealer in wool.

Wool-stocks, heavy wooden hammers for milling cloth, or driving the threads of the web together.

Wool Weight. The following are the subdivisions used in weighing wool:—

7	lbs. avoirdupois	1 clove.
2	cloves, or 14 lbs.	1 stone.
2	stones, or 28 lbs.	1 tod.
6½	tods, or 182 lbs.	1 wey.
2	weys, or 364 lbs.	1 sack.
12	sacks, or 4368 lbs.	1 last.
20	lbs.	1 score.
12	scores	1 pack.

The weight of the bale or pack of wool from different countries varies. *See* Bale.

Woo-pei-tze, the name for the large curious-shaped Chinese galls found, it is believed, on the *Rhus semialata* of Murray, or on the *Distylium racemosum* of Zuccarini. These galls have been lately imported to some extent.

Woorari, Wourali, a virulent poison made by the Indians of Guiana from several plants, of which the *Strychnos toxifera* appears to be the principal.

Wootz, a valuable kind of steel made in India from magnetic iron ore, and celebrated for the toughness and durability of the cutting edges made from it.

Work, labour or employment; occupation of any kind; embroidery, needlework, or sewing; the resulting product of labour; a book; to ferment or froth.

Work-bag, a lady's reticule for holding needlework.

Work-box, a lady's table-companion, with instruments and materials for work.

Work-box-instrument Maker, a manufacturer of scissors, bodkins, reels, and other instruments, fittings, and appliances for a lady's work-box.

Workhouse, a poor-house; a union house, maintained by poor's rates, for the reception and maintenance of paupers.

Working-classes, labourers and operatives; those engaged in manual labour.

Workman, a mechanic or operative; an assistant in any handicraft.

Workshop, a carpenter's shed; a tailor's working-room; any place where work is carried on.

Work-table, a small fancy table for ladies to sit to.

Worlok (Russian), felt.

Worm, a spiral, metal pipe or screw; the tubular coil of a still, lodged in water, through which the spirit is run or condensed.

Worming, a seaman's term for filling up the interstices of a rope, so as to render it even for wrapping over, or serving, as it is termed, with yarn; removing the ligament under a dog's tongue.

Worm-powder, a vermifuge, or medicine for expelling worms.

Worm-seed, a commercial substance composed principally of the flower-buds of some doubtful species of *Artemisia*, largely used in medical practice in Germany, and imported into this country. The American worm-seed, or "Jerusalem oak," *Chenopodium anthelminticum*, is a very common weed: the herb and seeds contain a peculiar essential oil, of very strong vermifuge properties.

Wormwood, a common name for several species of *Artemisia*, bitter aromatic herbs cultivated for medicinal purposes. *See* Southernwood, and Semencine.

Worsted, a thread spun of wool that has been combed, and which, in the spinning, is twisted harder than ordinary. It is chiefly used for knitting or weaving into carpets, stockings, caps, gloves, &c.

Worsted and Yarn Merchant, a dealer in woollen thread and carded wool, yarn for the weaver, merino, lustre, and smallware yarns, &c.

Worsted-dyer, a person who dyes the worsted yarn of different shades of colour.

Worsted-repository, a Berlin warehouse; a shop where fancy knitting-wools are sold.

Worsted-spinner, a twister of wool into yarn, or long filaments.

Worsted-yarn Measure. *See* Yarn-measure.

Wort, a sweet infusion of malt; new beer unfermented.

Worwan (Russian), train-oil.

Wourali-poison. *See* Woorari.

Wove-papers, writing-papers with a uniform surface, and not ribbed like laid papers.

Wrack-grass, the *Zostera marina*, an aquatic plant, collected for manure, and for making kelp.

Wrapper, a railway rug; a stock shawl; a dressing-gown or loose garment.

Wrapping-paper, coarse packing paper.

Wrasse, a name for the *Labrus tinca*, or old wife, a fish with soft flesh, and not much esteemed as food.

Wreath, a garland of artificial leaves and flowers, worn on the head by ladies.

Wreck, the hull or remains of a stranded ship, or a vessel abandoned on the ocean.

Wrecker, one who robs the wrecks of ships or collects the goods cast on the shore by the sea.

Wreck-master, a person who takes charge of the salvage from a wreck, for the interest of the owners.

Wrench, an instrument for screwing or unscrewing.

Wrench-hammer. *See* Hammer.

Wrest, a turning instrument.

Wrestler, an athlete; one who contests with another in a trial of strength.

Wright; a maker; a workman; thus there are cartwrights, ploughwrights, shipwrights, wheelwrights, &c. In Scotland, a joiner or carpenter.

Wringing-machine Maker, a manufacturer of machines for squeezing or twisting wet linen.

Wristband, the narrow band at the end of a shirt sleeve.

Wrist-link, a link, or connected buttons for a shirt sleeve, to hold the sides of the wristband together.

Writ, an official notice or precept from a law-court; the first offensive step or procedure in a lawsuit.

Writer, an author or clerk; a civil officer in the East India Company's service; a Scotch attorney; a sign-painter or letterer.

Writing, an inscription; a book; a deed of conveyance.

Writing-book, a copy-book.

Writing-case, a portable case holding writing materials.

Writing-desk, a sloping school-desk; a lock-up case with stationery, and the appliances for corresponding.

Writing-ink Maker, a manufacturer of fluid inks for writing with. *See* Ink.

Writing-master, a good penman; a teacher; one who gives instruction in writing.

Writing-paper, brief-paper; foolscap, post, and note papers, for writing on.

Writing-table, a table of convenient height for writing at; a table for a library or study.

Wrought-iron, malleable iron; metal which has been beaten; not cast iron.

W.S., abbreviation for "Writer to the Signet."

Wuboika (Russian), calico.

Wudru (Russian), sea-otter skins.

Wukarea, the keeper of an establishment for cleaning cotton in India.

Wundersalz (German), Glauber's salts.

Wuporotki (Russian), slink lamb-skins.

Wurd, an Arab name for the hundred-leaved rose, cultivated for preparing distilled water, and for obtaining the essential oil from.

Wurrus, a brick-red powder somewhat resembling dragon's-blood, collected from the seed-vessels of an euphorbiaceous tree, *Rottlera tinctoria*, and used in Eastern Africa and the East Indies, as a dye for silk, and also medicinally.

Wurst (French), a wagon for the surgery department of an army; a kind of wooden horse, running on wheels, used in the salt mines on the Continent.

Wusa, an Indian long-measure, in Surat, = to 2·7111 yards; in Malwa, to 2·488 yards. For timber measurement the Surat wusa is only 1·3883 inches.

Wych-elm, the *Ulmus montana*.

Wyth, a name for the white hoop, or basket wyth of Jamaica, *Tournefortia bicolor*, Swartz.

X.

X, the Roman numeral for 10; a mark on malt-liquor casks, two X's meaning ale of second quality, three X's of first quality.

Xadrez (Portuguese), a chess-board.

Xanthic-acid, a yellow acid obtained in combination with potassa, by agitating sulphuret of carbon, mixed with solution of pure potassa, in strong alcohol.

Xanhpa, a kind of pancake made in Spain.

Xato (Spanish), a yearling calf.

Xebec, a small lateen-rigged three-masted vessel in the Mediterranean.

Xeraphim, an old money of account in Bombay, equal to three-fifths of a rupee.

Xeres, a name for sherry, from the district of its growth.

Xeriff, a former gold coin, current in Egypt and Turkey, for about 9s. 6d. Another name for the ducat in Morocco.

Xestas, an ancient Greek liquid and dry measure. The former was equal to 0·14252 gallon; the latter to 0·015310 ditto.

Xylon, an ancient Greek measure of length, = 1·31718 yard.

Xylopyrography, a new art of representing objects on wood, by means of fire.

Xyster, a surgeon's instrument for scraping bones.

Y.

Yabba, a name in the West Indies, for a small glazed earthen pot or pipkin.

Yabbolam, a weight in Masulipatam equal to ⅝ lb.

Yacca-wood, an ornamental Jamaica-wood, the produce of a small tree, the *Podocarpus Yacca*, used for cabinet purposes.

YACHT, a fast-sailing decked pleasure vessel which enjoys certain exemptions and privileges from port-charges and other regulations. A first-class yacht is one above 30 tons burthen.

YACHT-CLUB, an assemblage or union of yacht owners, conforming to certain rules and regulations, and acting under a commodore. There are 18 or 20 royal yacht clubs in the United Kingdom, comprising in the aggregate 500 or 600 yachts.

YACHT-SQUADRON, the principal English yacht club, whose club-house and meeting place is at Cowes.

YADUM, a weight in Mysore of 150 lbs.; also called a panckakum.

YAGER, a rifleman.

YAGRE (Spanish), a kind of palm sugar.

YAHO-BARK. *See* MAHOE.

YAK, a species of wild ox, the *Poephagus grunniens*, found in Thibet. The flesh serves for food. The hair is made into tents and ropes, and jackets and caps are formed of the skin. Its bushy white tail is much esteemed in the East, where it is borne as an emblem of authority, and used as a fly-flapper.

YAM, a climbing plant, with large tuberous roots, forming one of the bread-stuffs of the W. Indies, and other tropical regions, of which there are several species. The roots are very rich in nutritive fecula; hence they are much used as articles of diet. The common yam is the *Dioscorea sativa*; the wing-stalked or red-yam (*D. alata*); the prickly-yam (*D. aculeata*); and the bulb-bearing, or Grenada-yam (*D. bulbifera*). There are also other varieties, known under the names of Creole, Portuguese, Barbados and Guinea yam. If sun-dried and packed in ashes yams will keep for about a month or six weeks.

YAN, a Chinese measure of length, equal to 36·45833 yards.

YAOURT, a fermented liquor or milkbeer, similar to koumis, made by the Turks.

YAPAK, YUNK, Turkish names for sheep's wool.

YAPON, YOUPON, the South Sea tea, the *Ilex Cassine* of Carolina, and the Southern States of America.

YARD, a long piece of timber, suspended across a ship's mast, to spread the square sails on; an enclosure with walls at the back or around a house, &c. as a court-yard, or prison-yard; a British standard measure of 3 feet, or 36 inches. As a linear measure, the yard varies considerably in different parts of the kingdom; at Hertford the land-yard is 3 feet; at Saltash, 10½ feet; at Falmouth and Bridgend 18 feet; and at Downpatrick, 21 feet. The Dutch cloth yard measure is equal to 37 17-20ths Rhynland inches. The Hungarian yard, used in measuring cloth, is four-fifths of the Austrian yard, and about 34 English inches.

YARD-ARM, the end or point of a ship's yard, the portion projecting on each side of the mast.

YARD-LAND, a superficial English measure, of variable extent, in some places 15 acres, in others running to 40 acres; but the mean may be taken at 30 acres.

YARD-MAN, a manager or overlooker in a builder's yard.

YARD-MEASURE, a shopkeeper's rod or stick of 3 feet, with subdivisions; a tape 36 inches long.

YARDS, long spars of timber, tapering slightly at the end, suspended upon the masts of vessels for extending the sails, and which are specially named according to their position, and the mast on which they are hung. In a large ship there will be about twenty yards, some of very formidable dimensions. The main-yard of a liner or first-rate will be about 100 feet in length and 2 feet in diameter.

YARD-STICK, a draper's measuring wand of three feet.

YARD-WIDE, carpeting, fabrics, &c. 3 feet in width.

YARE (Scotch), a weir for catching fish. *See* WEIR.

YARI-YARI, a local name in Guiana for the yellow lance wood (*Duguetia quitarensis*), a slender tree. The wood is to be had from 15 to 20 feet in length, and from 4 to 5 inches in diameter. It is very close, tough, and elastic, and is in great repute for gig-shafts.

YARN, a ropemaker's term for a collection of fibres spun together; simple spun thread; wool, cotton, flax, or hemp spun or twisted into lengths. *See* TWIST. Owing to the perfection of our spinning, the export of yarn is now very large. The quantity and estimated value of that exported in 1856, were as follows:—

	Tons.	Value.
Cotton	81,373	£8,065,671
Linen	11,140	1,365,056
Woollen and worsted	11,922	2,745,638
Do. mixed	287	142,764
Silk	268	294,172
	104,890	12,618,921

YARN-MEASURE. The various manufacturers have different measures. The quality of yarn is expressed in England by counts or *numbers*, denoting the number of hanks in a pound, signifying coarseness or fineness; reckoning the length of the hank of cotton yarn at 840 yards, or 7 leas or lays, of 120 yards each. These "counts" range technically, from 2 to 400 hanks in a lb. The hank of worsted yarn is sometimes counted in the same way, but more generally at 560 yards, or 7 leas of 80 yards each. Linen yarn is estimated in England by the number of leas or cuts, each of 3 yards, contained in a pound weight; but in Scotland, by the number of pounds in a spindle, or 48 leas; thus, No. 48 in England, is called 1 lb. yarn in Scotland. The following are the principal subdivisions of each manufacture:—

COTTON-YARN MEASURE.

Inches,
54 = 1 thread.
4320 = 80 " = 1 lea, or rap.
30240 = 560 " = 7 " = 1 hank, or 840 yds.
A spindle of 18 hanks is 15,120 yards.

LINEN-YARN MEASURE.

Inches.				
90 =	1 thread.			
10800 =	120 „ =	1 lea, or rap.		
108000 =	1200 „ =	10 „ =	1 slip.	[dle.
2160000 =	24000 „ =	200 „ =	20 „ =	1 bun-

A heer of 2 cuts, or 240 threads, 600 yards.
A spindle of 24 heer .... 14,400 yards.
A bundle of 4 1-6th spindles...... 60,000 yards.

WORSTED YARN-MEASURE.

Inches.			
35 =	1 thread.		
2830 =	80 „ =	1 lea, or rap.	
20160 =	560 „ =	7 „ =	1 hank, or 560 yds.

Reels.—A cotton or linen reel is 54 inches in circuit. A worsted reel 30 inches in circuit. A hank of worsted yarn is 30 threads.

In the foreign linen-yarn measure

85½ Ermland inches = 1 thread
3120 „ „ = 40 „ = 1 lea.
80 Hamburgh inches = 1 thread.
7200 „ „ = 90 „ = 1 lea.

YARRACOOM, an Indian head-dress, made of wicker-work and parrot feathers, worn by the natives of Guiana.

YARRAWARA, an aboriginal name for the black butt, a tree of New South Wales, one of the largest of the *Eucalypti*, producing excellent durable timber for house carpentry, or any purpose where strength and durability are the chief requisites.

YARURI, a local native name in Demerara for the paddle-wood. *See* PADDLE-WOOD.

YASMAS, a dyed and printed Swiss fabric.

YASTIMADHUKA, a vernacular Indian name for liquorice.

YATAGHAN, a sort of curved knife; a Turkish dagger or scimitar.

YATTRA DHONY, a Ceylon coasting-vessel, with an outrigger.

YAW, a sea term for a temporary deviation from the straight line or course of a boat or ship.

YAWARRIDANI, an undescribed tree of British Guiana, furnishing a very light but even-grained wood.

YAWL, a ship of war's boat, less than the pinnace, but nearly of the same form, and used for similar purposes; it is generally rowed with 6 oars.

YEAR-BOOK, an annual; a book of law cases; a turf register.

YEARLING, a young beast one year old, or in the second year of its age.

YEARNINGS, a name in Scotland for the mawa or stomachs of young calves, used as rennet for curdling milk.

YEAST, the froth of fermenting wort, a substance used for leavening bread. The aggregate quantity produced at the various breweries in the United Kingdom, at 11 lbs. per barrel, is estimated at 75,000 tons in weight, worth £360,000 in value. German yeast is now imported to a considerable extent in a dried form from the Continent; the quantity imported in 1856, was 3,510 tons.

YEGUAS (Spanish), mares.

YELK, the yellow part of an egg. *See* YOLK.

YELLOW, a painter's colour, of which some of the chief varieties are, spruce-ochre, Oxford-stone, common chrome, and G B S T chrome.

YELLOW-ARSENIC, an oxide of arsenic.

YELLOW-BASILICON, a well-known and excellent ointment so called.

YELLOW-BERRIES, the dried unripe berries of the *Rhamnus infectorius*, imported in large quantities from the South of Europe and the Levant, for the use of dyers. They are also known as Persian berries, and Avignon berries.

YELLOW-CANDLE, a description of Russian tallow, obtained from the fat of oxen, of which there are two kinds, the best being known under the mark of P. Y. C., prime yellow candle.

YELLOW-FLAG, a flag hoisted at the masthead of a ship, denoting sickness, or that she is under quarantine regulations.

YELLOWING, a manufacturing term for cleaning pins, a process effected by boiling them for half an hour in sour beer, wine lees, or solution of tartar. After this they are washed and whitened, or tinned.

YELLOW-METAL, a composition metal of two-thirds copper and one-third zinc, for sheathing the bottoms of vessels with: 8,000 to 10,000 tons a year are made at Birmingham.

YELLOW-OCHRE, an argillaceous earth, coloured by an admixture of iron, which, when finely ground, is used as a pigment. It may be rendered red or reddish brown, by calcination in a reverberatory oven, which peroxidizes the iron.

YELLOW-WOOD, a name for the *Xanthoxylum clava Herculis*, a West Indian tree, and for the *Chloroxylon Swietenia*, a lofty timber tree of the East Indies.

YEN, a weight in Annam = 13.7732 lbs.

YEOMAN, a small land-owner or freeholder; a gentleman farmer; a man employed in a vessel of war, under a warrant officer, to take charge of a store-room.

YEOMAN OF THE GUARD, a beef-eater; one of the British sovereign's state body-guard, below the gentleman-at-arms.

YEOMANRY, a volunteer corps of infantry or cavalry, in the English shires, meeting periodically for practice in arms; a kind of militia body, occasionally drafted into the regular army.

YERBAL, a forest or wild grove of the *Ilex Paraguayensis*, the holly from the leaves of which the Paraguay tea is obtained.

YERCUM, a name in the southern parts of India, for the *Calotropis gigantea*, and the *C. Hamiltonii*, the Mudar plant of Northern India, furnishing a useful fibre, and having medicinal properties.

YERGACK, a Russian cloak made of horse hides.

YERGAS, a kind of coarse woollen wrapper, made for horse cloths.

YEROS, a Spanish name for the *Ervum Lens*.

YERVA-MATE. *See* PARAGUAY TEA.

YESO (Spanish), gypsum.

YETTU, a Mysore weight of 7½ lbs.

YEUK-SHI, a Chinese dry-measure, = 0.0010 Winchester bushel.

YEW, a well-known tree. The wood of the European species, *Taxus baccata*, and its varieties, is occasionally used for the construction of bows, handles to furniture and cabinet work.

YIN, a Chinese weight of 2·666 lbs.; also an itinerary measure of 40½ yards.

Y-LEVEL, an instrument for measuring distance and altitude.

YOKE, a bow or curved wooden collar for draught oxen, a piece of timber with straps and hooks, carried on the shoulders to suspend water-buckets or milk pails; a cross-piece fixed at the top of a boat's rudder, with lines to steer by.

YOLK, YELK, a natural oily secretion or greasy substance in wool, intended to nourish the growth and give pliability to the fibre; the yellow part of an egg.

YOODZANA, a Burmese measure of distance, = 12 furlongs 5 yards.

YORKSHIRE-GRIT, a stone used for polishing marble, and copper-plates for engravers.

YORKSHIRE-PUDDING, a batter-pudding baked under meat.

YORKSHIRE-PUDDING PAN, a tin dish for baking batter puddings in.

YOUDOONA, a Singhalese measure of length of four gows, and equal to eighteen thousand feet.

YOWE, an undefined Burmese weight, two small yowes make one large yowe, and four large yowes, one be.

YPADU, a native name for the leaves of the *Erythroxylon Coca*, an herb much valued in Peru. *See* COCA.

YPRES-LACE, the finest and most expensive kind of Valenciennes lace.

YU, a Chinese dry-measure, 24·65 gallons; also an itinerary measure. *See* YIN.

YUCA, a name in the Spanish American States for the cassava. Also for the edible roots of the *Yucca gloriosa*.

YUFTS, a kind of Russia leather, which, when well prepared, is of good red colour, soft and pinguid on the surface, and pleasant to the touch, with an agreeable, peculiar odour.

YUGADA (Spanish), the extent of ground which a pair of oxen can plough in a day; a Spanish superficial-measure, which, in Valencia, is only 0·1506 acres, but in Madrid is 35·0724 acres. Since 1801, the legal yugada, as a land-measure in Spain, has been fixed at 79·3550 acres.

YUGUERO, a Spanish ploughman.

YUREN, a liquid-measure used by the Tyrolese, = 9·78 gallons.

YUSDROM, the ancient Arab pound, equal to 5659·14 grains; a name for the cheque, a Turkish weight of Constantinople, = 0·7015 pound.

YUSERA, the horizontal stone in an oil-mill.

YVOOR (Dutch), ivory.

YZER (Dutch), iron.

Z.

ZABRA, a small Biscayan vessel.

ZACQUES, a small Persian silver coin, the half of a mamoudi, and worth about 4d. or 5d.

ZAFFRES, a regulus of cobalt imported for resmelting to form smalt: 625 cwts. were imported in 1856.

ZAFRAN, the Hindoo name for the *Crocus sativus*, whence our name saffron.

ZAH, a dry-measure of Tunis, another name for the mudde. *See* SAW.

ZAHINA, a kind of tares grown in Spain.

ZAHLER (German), a pay-clerk; a teller or numerator.

ZAHN (German), a tooth or tine; the cog of a wheel.

ZAIMET, a Turkish name for an estate.

ZAIN (German), an ingot or bar; a pig of metal.

ZAINER, a master smith in Germany.

ZAK (Dutch), the sack, a dry-measure of variable capacity. The legal zak in Holland, is 2·8378 Winchester bushels. In Leyden, the zak is 1·88 bushel. In Dordrecht, it ranges from 2·58 to 3·44 bushels. In Amsterdam, the zak (old measure) is 2·30 bushels; 2·907813 zaks = one imperial quarter.

ZALA, a synonyme of borax.

ZAMARRILLA, a short loose coat made of sheep-skins, worn in Spain.

ZAMBARONE, a name in Sicily for the fibre of the agave, generally called aloe, which is used for making cordage and mats. In Spain it is termed pita.

ZAMBRA, a kind of Moorish boat.

ZAMTITE, a hydrous carbonate of nickel from Spain, of a dull emerald green colour.

ZANTE-WOOD, a name for the *Rhus Cotinus* and for the *Chloroxylon Swietenia*.

ZAPA (Spanish), a spade; the skin of the dog-fish or shagreen; a kind of carving on silver.

ZAPATERO, a Spanish shoemaker; in Portugal, sapateiro.

ZAPATO, a shoe; a kind of coloured half-boots worn in Spain.

ZAPFENLEDER (German), shagreen.

ZAPFMASS, SCHENKMASS, German terms applied to the alehouse or retail measure for wine and beer.

ZAPPADA, a superficial-measure of the Ionian islands, the third of the misura, and = 0·9956 acre.

ZAQUE, a bottle or wine-bag made of leather in Spain.

ZARA (Spanish), Indian corn or maize.

ZARANDA, a screen or frame for sifting earth or grain, used in Spain.

ZARCILLOS (Spanish), ear-rings.

ZARDAKHAM, a Turkish dress apron of embroidered silk.

ZARF, a saucer for Oriental coffee-cups.

ZATOU, a dry-measure used in Madagascar, of 100 voules, and weighing about 50 lbs.

ZAVAH, another name for the seer, an Eastern grain-measure of 2½ pints. *See* SEER.

ZAX, a tool for cutting slates.

ZAYAT, a Turkish caravanserai.

ZAKAHAN (Spanish), a kind of flowered silk.

Z-CRANK, the peculiarly-shaped crank of a cylinder, in a newly-invented engine for marine propulsion, so named from its zigzag form.

ZEBEC, a lateen-rigged vessel in the Mediterranean.

ZEBEEB, a refreshing Arab beverage made with dried grapes.

ZEBRA, the *Equus zebra*, a South African animal, nearly allied to the ass. Its hide marked with black and white transverse stripes, is sometimes used for hearth rugs, &c. in this country. This animal, the wild horse of the Cape colonists, has been occasionally tamed, but is little used.

ZEBRAS, a name given to Paisley shawls, which are very generally worn in Turkey, as sashes or other parts of dress.

ZEBRA-WOOD, a beautiful furniture-wood obtained in Demerara from a large tree, the *Omphalobium Lamberti* of Decandolle. *See* HYAWABALLI.

ZEBU, a small humped species of Asiatic ox, the *Bos Indicus*, to which the Brahmin bull belongs.

ZECCHIN, the Venetian ducat; a gold coin passing in Malta for about 7s.; in Egypt for 146 medini or paras.

ZEDOARY, a general name for the roots of several species of *Zingiber* and *Curcuma*. The yellow zedoary is the rhizomes of the *Zingiber Cassumunar*, which have a hot and bitterish taste, but are now very little used; the long zedoary of pharmacy is the palmate and tuberous roots of *Curcuma Zerumbet*, and the round zedoary, *C. Zedoaria*, a native of Bengal and China, which resembles ginger in its qualities.

ZEE-KOE, SEA-COW, a name given by the Dutch colonists, in Southern Africa, to the hippopotamus.

ZEERA, an Indian name for pungent seeds, "zeera secah" being applied to caraway seeds, and "zeera suffed" to cumin-seed.

ZEHENTNER, a tithe-collector in Germany.

ZEICHEN-BUCH (German), a drawing-book.

ZEICHEN-MEISTER (German), a teacher of drawing.

ZEICHNER (German), a draughtsman or designer.

ZEHNLING, a legal weight of Baden, the tenth of the pound, and equal to 771·7 grains.

ZEINE, a soft, malleable substance found in maize, elastic like gluten.

ZEITUNG, ZEITUNGS-BLATT (German), a newspaper or gazette.

ZELT (German), a tent or pavilion.

ZEMINDAR, a landholder; a collector of land-revenue in India.

ZEMINDARY, the office or jurisdiction of a zemindar.

ZEMZEMEEYEH, a large skin water-flask used in Egypt.

ZENITH-SECTOR, an astronomical instrument for ascertaining the zenith distances of the stars.

ZENTNER (German), the quintal or hundred-weight; in Hanover, equal to 103 lbs. avoirdupois. *See* CENTNER.

ZENZERLO, an Egyptian coin containing 107 medini or paras.

ZEPHYR-CLOTH, a kind of kerseymere made in Belgium.

ZEPHYR-SHAWL, a kind of thin light worsted and cotton embroidered shawl.

ZERAPHIM, a former money of account of Goa, of 240 Portuguese reis.

ZERETH, an ancient Hebrew long-measure of 8·6039 inches.

ZERIFF, an old Turkish coin worth about 2¼ dollars.

ZERLA, a wine-measure used in Brescia equal to 13·2036 gallons.

ZER-MAHBOUB, a name for one of the Turkish sequins, a former gold coin worth rather more than 5s.; a coin passing in Egypt for 120 paras, and in some districts for 110 medini.

ZERO, the freezing point of water on the Centigrade and Reaumur scales, and 32 degrees below this freezing point on Fahrenheit's scale. *See* THERMOMETER.

ZETTEL (German), a billet or note; scrip.

ZETTEL-TRAGER, a German ticket-porter.

ZEUG (German), cloth; ordnance.

ZEUG-HOSEN (German), trousers made of woollen stuff.

ZEUG-MEISTER, the keeper of an arsenal in Germany; a master of the ordnance.

ZEUXITE. *See* TOURMALINE.

ZIBEBEN. *See* ZIBIBBI.

ZIBELINE (French), sable.

ZIBET, a species of *Viverra*, native of the East, which furnishes a kind of civet perfume.

ZIBIBBI, (Italian), ZIBEBEN (German), sun-dried raisins; damask-grapes.

ZIEGEL (German), a tile or brick.

ZIEGEN-KASE, cheese made of goats'-milk in Germany.

ZIEGEN-LEDER (German), goats'-leather, kids'-skins.

ZIEGER (German), a kind of whey.

ZIEGER-KASE, cheese made of sour milk in Germany.

ZIEGLER (German), a tiler; a brick-maker.

ZIEH-OCHS (German), a draught-ox.

ZIEH-SCHEIBE (German), a draw-plate for wire.

ZIEH-WAGE, the German name for the steel-yard.

ZIER-GARTEN (German), a pleasure-garden.

ZIG-ZAG, another name for the chevron; an ornament in Gothic architecture.

ZIG-ZAG FENCE, an in-and-out kind of fence, running with short angles or turns.

ZILLAH, a district or local division of a country in India.

ZILLAH-JUDGE, a district magistrate in India; one who presides in a zillah-court.

ZIMMENT, a liquid-measure of Bolzano, equal to 0·09170 gallon.

ZIMMER (German), a room or apartment; timber for building; a term for forty skins.

ZIMMERMANN, ZIMMERER (German), a carpenter.

ZIMMET, ZIMMT, the German name for cinnamon.

ZINC, a bluish-white metal, which may be rolled or hammered out to a certain extent. The ores yielding it are various, and brought from different localities. It comes in chiefly from Germany under the name of spelter, the imports being 18,000 or 19,000 tons annually; in 1856 they were 18,213 tons.

ZINCITE, a name for red zinc ore.

ZINC-MANUFACTURER, a preparer of zinc metal from calamine, blende, and other ores.

ZINCOGRAPHER, an engraver on zinc.

ZINCOGRAPHIC-PRINTER, a printer who takes impressions from zinc plates.

ZINC-PLATE WORKER, a workman who heats the metal to between 220° and 320°, when it becomes malleable and ductile, and may be hammered out and rolled into sheets and leaves.

ZINC-WHITE, the oxide of zinc, a pigment now largely used for the same purposes as white lead. It is more permanent, and not poisonous as lead is.

ZINC WORKER AND DRAWER, a preparer of zinc for making into wire.

ZINDELTAFT (German), sarcenet.

ZINN (German), tin; pewter.

ZINNER, a tinman or pewterer in Germany.

ZINSMANN (German), a tenant or rent-payer.

ZINSMEISTER, a revenue steward; a receiver of rents in Germany.

ZIRBELNUSSE (German), the pignons or seeds of the cones of the Cimbra pine.

ZIRCON, a peculiar and rare gray and brown earth, found in the true rough and opaque varieties of hyacinth stone, which are met with in Ceylon, Norway, Carinthia, and the Ural. The term hyacinth is applied to the transparent and bright-coloured varieties of zircon, and jargoon to crystals devoid of colour, and of a smoky tinge, occasionally sold as inferior diamonds.

ZITHER, an Austrian stringed instrument.

ZITWERSAMEN (German), worm-seed.

ZITZ (German), chintz; printed calico.

ZLOT, a Russian silver coin, worth 5d. to 6d.; there are also pieces of two, five, and ten zlot. This coin is also in circulation in Poland. The five-zlot piece of 1838 weighs 9 dwts., 20 grains, of which 8 dwts. 13·5 grs. are pure silver.

ZOBEL-JAGER (German), a sable hunter.

ZOBEL-PELZ (German), a robe trimmed or lined with sable.

ZOBER, a German liquid and dry measure. As a legal dry-measure in Baden, the zober is equal to 42·56734 Winchester bushels. In Wurtemberg, for charcoal and lime, it is only 2·48523 bushels. As a liquid-measure for brine, its capacity in Halle is 145·17104 gallons.

ZOETELIMOENEN (Dutch), oranges.

ZOFCHEN, ZOFE, a chamber-maid or waiting-woman in Germany.

ZOFRA, a kind of Moorish floor-cloth or carpet.

ZOLL (German), a toll or Customs-duty; the German inch of 12 lines; but as a measure of length, of variable proportion in different towns and States, being 0·86433 inches in Hesse Darmstadt, and 1·1811 in Baden. It is chiefly used by builders and surveyors, and the following are its principal measurements: Aix-la-Chapelle, 0·9251 inches; Berlin, 1·4828; Bremen, 1·1386; Frankfort, 1·4010; Hamburgh, 1·0297; Hesse Cassel, 1·1617; Leipsic, 1·1111; Weimar, 1·7763; Zurich, 1·1812. The ordinary zoll is not so long as the builder's zoll. For general purposes of calculation, 12 Hanoverian zollin may be considered equal to 11½ English inches.

ZOLLHAUS, a German Custom-house.

ZOLLNER, a German toll-gatherer; a publican.

ZOLLVEREIN, a union of States under one Customs-tariff.

ZOLOTNIK, the Russian pound weight for gold, which is subdivided into 96 parts. It is equal to 0·009393 lb.

ZOMA (Spanish), a coarse kind of flour.

ZOOLLEDER (Dutch), sole leather.

ZOOLOGICAL-GARDEN, a collection of foreign animals, &c. in ornamental pleasure-grounds, shown to the public.

ZOOMARA, an Arab double clarionet.

ZOPISSA, a mixture of pitch and tar impregnated by salt water, scraped from ships' sides, formerly used in external applications as resolutive and desiccative.

ZOROCHE, a name in South America for a rough kind of silver ore.

ZORROCLOCO (Spanish), a thin paste rolled up in a cylindrical shape.

ZOURZOLINA (Italian), the oily grain or sesame-seed.

ZOUT (Dutch), salt.

ZUCCA, a liquid-measure of Corsica, equal to 3·08206 gallons; by some authorities stated at 2·568 gallons.

ZUGEL (German), a rein or bridle.

ZUNGEN (German), tongues.

ZUNU, a singular kind of sheep found in Angola, with a slender and almost naked tail, reaching nearly to the ground.

ZUOJA, a superficial measure of Udina, in Austrian Italy, of which there are two kinds, viz., the "grande" zuoja = 1·2892 English acre, and the "piccola zuoja" = 0·8063 acre.

ZUP (Dutch), soap.

ZURRADOR, a Spanish currier or leather-dresser.

ZURRON (Spanish), a sack made of leather. *See* SERON.

ZUURLEMOENZAP (Dutch), lemon-juice.

ZUZAH, an ancient Hebrew silver coin, worth about 6d.

ZWANZIGER, an Austrian silver coin of 20 kreutzers, worth 85 cents. or 8½d. In Italy it is called a lira and passes for 24 kreutzers, and in some places for 26.

ZWARTZEL (Dutch), blacking.

ZWEILING (German), a two-inch board or plank.

ZWEYDRITTEL, a silver coin of Hanover, worth about 2s. 3d.

ZWOLFER, a German coin of twelve kreutzers.

ZYMOMETER, a measurer of the degree of fermentation.

ZYTHEM, a beverage made from malt and wheat.

THE END.

M'CORQUODALE AND CO., PRINTERS, LONDON—WORKS, NEWTON.

CPSIA information can be obtained
at www.ICGtesting.com
Printed in the USA
LVHW101942050123
736480LV00003B/80

9 783375 126797